GW00689509

THE
COMPLETE
TIMURAS

THE COMPLETE TIMURAS

Wizard of the Winds

Wolves of the Gods

The Gods Awaken

ALLAN COLE

WILDSIDE PRESS

Published by Wildside Press
www.wildsidepress.com

WIZARD OF THE WINDS

For Kathryn

Think, in this battered caravansari
Whose doorways are alternate night and day
How sultan after sultan with his pomp
Abode his destined hour and went his way

The Rubaiyat of Omar Khayyam
Edward Fitzgerald Translation

Part One
When The Gods Slept

PROLOGUE
STRANGER ON A HILL

The villagers fear him.

They draw lots each day to see who must fill his beggar's bowl.

The loser creeps up the hill trembling and clutching a talisman. The stranger knows they fear the evil eye so he doesn't look when the approach is made. He makes no sound or movement until the deed is done and the villager flees as if there were a dervish at his heels.

The villagers think the stranger is a mad priest and curse the day he came to hide in these hills.

He's not mad and he is no priest. But he lets them believe what they like. If his true identity were revealed the village treasury would soon be bursting with gold. For the stranger is a fugitive from the King. Safar Timura, who was once Grand Wazier to King Protarus, is hunted by him now.

They were blood oath brothers. Safar sat by his friend's throne and gave him counsel and exorcised the devils troubling his sleep. Several times he saved the King's life. He was rewarded with lands and palaces and jewels and more honors than most men have ever dreamed.

When the history of King Protarus is written they'll say it was Lord Timura who betrayed him. They'll say Safar gambled and lost all for love.

To the first he pleads innocent. It's Safar's view it was the King who betrayed him. As for the second he admits guilt. And it is for that crime Protarus wants his head. But for the *King's* offense Safar demands more.

And he *will* have his payment—if the king doesn't catch him first.

Safar can see his enemy's city from his lonely post. At night, under the swirling Demon Moon, he can see the lights of Zanzair blur the stars. See the smoke from the foundries and kitchens rise up each morning to haze the day. And he can see the King's Grand Palace quite clearly, its windows a rosy glow in the dawn.

He models the palace in clay of the purest white—skillfully forming the towers between wet palms, etching the designs on the parapets with his silver witch's knife. He whispers potter's spells as he shapes the domes and pillars. Breathing his hate into the clay.

At night he wraps the model in wet leaves and sets it aside to await the new day. He empties the beggar's bowl, then wraps himself against the chill in a black mourning cloak. At dawn he begins anew.

When the palace is done and the great spell is cast Safar Timura's revenge will be complete.

Then he'll depart that lonely hill. He'll flee across deserts and grasslands and wide rocky plains to the mountains of his birth.

Where the snowy passes carry the high caravans to clear horizons.

The place he should never have left.

The place where this tale begins.

CHAPTER ONE
VALLEY OF THE CLOUDS

It was a time when the world was large and dreams were small. Few ships strayed from the four great turtles who bore the mountains and plains across the seas. Humankind and demonkind alike brooded under the faded banners of kings who'd ruled too long. Borders were no more distant than a fast march could secure. All who dwelt beyond huddled in armed settlements to keep thieves and beasts at bay.

It was an uneasy time, a time crying out for change. Royal wizards studied the stars for signs to reassure their masters. Subjects gathered in secret to implore the gods to rid them of those same masters.

But the gods gave no clue of their intentions. The starry wheel where the gods slept in their ten holy realms churned onward year after year, heedless to all pleas.

Then the portent came. It was not from the slumbering gods but from the molten depths of the world itself. And it was a boy, not a master wizard, who first marked the sign.

That boy was Safar Timura.

He lived in the land known as Esmir, the Turtle of The Middle Seas. It was a land where demons faced humans across the Forbidden Desert. Only an ancient curse and constant internal warfare kept those ancestral enemies from overrunning and slaughtering the other.

In the demon city of Zanzair, however, King Manacia and his sorcerers plotted and waited for the right moment. Although humans were greater in number, Manacia knew their magic was weak and their leaders cowardly. And he yearned for the day when he'd make their corpses a staircase to a grander throne.

To achieve his dreams he pored over ancient maps and tomes and consulted many oracles. Then he created the greatest oracle of all, sacrificing five thousand human slaves in the process.

*   *   *

The human head was mounted on a metal post in the center of Manacia's courtroom. The eyes were closed. The mouth slack. The skin ghastly.

Manacia cast his most powerful spell and then commanded: "Speak, O Brother of the Shades. What is the key to my heart's desire? What road do I take, what passage do I seek, to win the throne of the King of Kings?"

The head's eyes came open, blazing in hate and agony. Stiff lips formed a word:

"Kyrania," the head croaked, sounding like an old raven with its mouth full of gore.

"What place is that?" the king demanded.

"Kyrania," the head croaked again.

The whole court looked on, demon jaws parting in anticipation, as the king jabbed a long sharp talon at an ancient wall map of the human lands.

"Where do I find this . . . Kyrania?" he asked.

"The Valley of the Clouds," the head answered. And then its eyes dulled and its mouth sagged back into death.

"Speak!" the king ordered, casting another mighty spell. But it was no use. The oracle was emptied of its power.

The Demon King turned to his assembled wizards and advisors. "Find me this place," he thundered. "Find me this Kyrania! . . .

". . . This Valley of the Clouds!"

*   *   *

A thousand miles distant Safar Timura and his people toiled the land and tended their flocks in relative peace. They lived high above the troubles of the world and had grown to think they were of small concern.

Their valley was so remote it appeared on few maps. And those were jealously held by the merchant princes who transported their goods across the Gods' Divide, which separated the ancient human kingdoms of Walaria and Caspan.

The valley was known as Kyrania—meaning, in the language of Safar's people, "Valley of the Clouds."

It was a bountiful place and each spring and summer the valley became a bowl of blossoms and fruit cradled high in the craggy range they called The Bride And Six Maids. The name came from seven graceful peaks shaped like slender young women. From the south they appeared to march in an eternal procession. The tallest and most graceful promontory was in the lead and to all Kyranians this peak was The Bride because she was always covered with snow and veiled in lacy clouds. Although the valley was so high strangers sometimes found it difficult to draw enough breath, it was sheltered by the maidenly peaks and the weather was nearly always mild.

Filling half the valley was the holy lake of Our Lady Felakia and sometimes pilgrims traveled with the caravans to pay homage to that goddess of purity and health and to drink from the curative waters. They gathered to be blessed at the ancient temple, set on the eastern shore and so small and unimportant it was attended by only one old priest. Twice a year flocks of birds stopped at the lake to rest on their seasonal journeys. No one knew where they came from or where they went but they were always welcome visitors—filling the air with their song and the cooking hearths with their roasted flesh.

The people of Kyrania grew barley and corn and beans, irrigating the fields with water from the lake. Olive and fruit orchards also abounded, but the growing season was short so the Kyranians placed great value on their goat herds. In the spring and summer Safar and the boys would lead them into the mountains to graze on tender shoots. When winter came the goats huddled in stables beneath the people's homes, eating stored grain and keeping the families warm with the heat of their bodies.

All those things, which might seem trivial and even dull to city dwellers, were of prime importance to Safar and his people. They made up their talk, their dreams and all the rhythms of life.

In his own way—the way of Kyrania—Safar was royally born. He was the son of a potter and in Kyrania such men as his father were second only to the village priest in importance. His father's father had been a potter as well, and *his* father before him. It had always been so for the Timura clan and many generations of Kyranian women had balanced Timura water jugs on their heads as they made the hip-swaying journey to the lake and back. All food in the village was cooked in Timura pots or stored in Timura jars, which were sealed with clay and buried in the ground for winter. Spirits were fermented in Timura jugs, bottled in Timura vessels and it was said all drink tasted best when sipped from Timura cups and bowls. When the caravans arrived Timura pottery was more sought after than even the few fresh camels and llamas the villagers kept to resupply the merchant masters.

When the troubles came Safar was being trained to succeed his father as a practitioner of that once most sacred of all the arts. To accomplish this was Safar's sole ambition. But as a wise one once said—"If you want the make the gods laugh . . . tell them your plans."

The day that marked the end of those youthful ambitions began well before first light, as did all days in Kyrania. It was early spring and the mornings were still cold and one of his sisters had to bang on his sleeping platform with a broom handle to rouse him from his warm feather mattress.

He grumbled as he broke away from a dream of swimming in warm lake waters with nubile maidens. He was just seventeen summers—an age when such dreams are remarkably vivid and nearly as frequent as the grumblings at the unfairness of life.

Then he heard Naya, the family's best milking goat, complaining in the stable below. She was the sweetest of animals and he hated to think of her suffering. Safar leaped from the platform onto the polished planks that made the floor of the main living area. He dragged out the trunk where he kept his belongings and hastily pulled on clothes—baggy leather trousers, pullover shirt and heavy work boots. His mother was already at the hearth stirring handfuls of dried apple into the savory barley porridge that would make his breakfast.

She clucked her tongue to chide him for being tardy, but then smiled and gave him a hunk of bread spread with pear jam to tide him over until the milking was done. Safar was the middle child but the only boy of his parents' six children, so he was lovingly and deliberately spoiled by his mother and sisters.

"You'd better hurry, Safar," his mother warned. "Your father will be back for his breakfast soon."

Safar knew his father would be in the adjoining shop inspecting the results of the previous day's firing. The elder Timura, whose name was Khadji, preferred to have the family together at mealtimes. It would be especially important to him this morning. There had been a late-night meeting of the Council of Elders and Khadji would be anxious to report the news.

Mind buzzing with curiosity, mouth full of bread and jam, Safar thundered down the ladder and lit the fat lamps. He got out several pots made of his father's purest clay and glazed a dazzling white. As usual he tended Naya first. Her milk was delicious and his mother frequently accused him of squirting more into his mouth than in the pot.

"Why am I always to blame when something goes wrong around here?" he'd protest.

"Because you've got some on your chin, my little thief," she'd say.

Safar was always taken in, giving his chin a reflexive wipe and making the whole family howl at his embarrassment.

"Don't ever decide to become a bandit, Safar," his father would joke. "The master of the first caravan you rob is certain to catch you. Then the only thing we'd have left of our son would be his head on a post."

Naya seemed more anxious that morning than an overly full udder should warrant. When Safar removed the canvas bag kept tied about her teats for cleanliness' sake he saw several angry sores. He checked the bag and saw it was frayed on one side. The rough area had rubbed against her udder all night. The sores would fester quickly in the damp spring.

"Don't fret, little mother," he murmured. "Safar will fix you up."

He looked about to make certain there were no witnesses. His sisters had gone to fetch water from the lake so besides the goats and other animals the stable area was empty. Safar scratched his head, thinking.

His eyes fell on the lamp beside the stool. He dipped up thick, warm fat with his fingers and rubbed it gently on Naya's udder. Then he made up a little spell and whispered it as he dipped up more oil and coaxed it gently over the sores.

Rest easy,
Little mother;
Safar is here.
There is no pain,
No wound to trouble you.
Rest easy
Little mother;
Safar is here.

He looked down and the sores were gone. There was only a little pink area on her udder and that was quickly fading.

Then he heard his mother say, "Who are you talking to, Safar?"

He flushed, then answered: "I wasn't talking to anyone, mother. I was just . . . singing a song." In those days Safar felt compelled to hide his magical talents from others.

Satisfied, his mother said nothing more. Safar quickly finished the milking and his other chores and by the time he was done his father and sisters were sitting down to breakfast. There was one absent place at the table—the spot where Safar's oldest sister, Quetera had held forth all his life. Safar saw his mother give the seat a sad glance. His sister lived with her husband now and was pregnant with their first child. It had been a difficult pregnancy and the family was worried.

His mother swiped at her eye, forced a smile, and began to pass the food around. There was porridge and bread toasted over the fire, with big slabs of cheese from the crusted round Safar's mother always kept sitting near the embers. They washed their breakfast down with milk still warm from the goats.

"You were late coming home last night, Khadji," his mother said as she gave his father another slice of buttered toast. "There must've been much business for the council to discuss. Not bad news, I hope."

Khadji frowned. "It wasn't exactly *bad* news, Myrna," he said. "But it certainly was troublesome."

Myrna was alarmed. "Nothing to do with the caravan, I hope?" she said.

Caravan season was just beginning and the village had received word the first group of traders was making its way to Kyrania. It had been a long winter and the money and goods the caravan would bring were sorely needed.

"No, nothing to do with the caravan," Safar's father said. "It's not expected for a few weeks, yet."

Myrna snorted, impatient. "If you don't want a second bowl of porridge served on your head, Khadji Timura," she said, "you'll tell us right now what this is all about!"

Usually, Khadji would have laughed, but instead Safar saw his frown deepen.

"We agreed to accept a boy into the village," Khadji said. "He was presented to us by an elder of the Babor clan, who begged us to give him sanctuary."

The Babors were the leading family of a large and fierce clan of people who lived on the distant plains.

Myrna dropped a serving spoon, shocked. "I don't like *that*!" she said. "Why, they're practically barbarians. I'm not sure I like having one of their young ruffians among us."

Khadji shrugged. "What could we do? Barbarians or not, the Babors have kinship claims on us. It wouldn't be right to say no to our cousins."

Myrna sniffed. "Pretty *distant* cousins, for all that."

"He seems a likely enough lad," Khadji said in the stranger's defense. "His family is related to the Babor headman's wife. They live somewhere in the south. People of influence, from the cut of the boy. He's a handsome fellow about your age, Safar. And tall—about your size, as well. Very mannered. Good clothing. And well spoken. Seems the sort who's used to having servants to order about."

"He'll soon learn there are no servants in Kyrania," Myrna said sharply. Then, "Why is he being sent to us?"

"He's an orphan," Safar's father said.

Myrna was scandalized. "An orphan? What kind of orphan is he? No, I take that back. The Gods make orphans. It's no fault of a child's. It's the boy's kin I wonder about. What manner of people are they to push an orphan on strangers? Have they no feelings?"

Safar saw his father shift, uneasy. "It seems there's some sort of difficulty in his clan," Khadji said. "A quarrel of some kind."

Myrna's eyebrows rose. "With those sort of people," she said, "quarrel usually means violence and bloodshed. It's the only way they know how to settle an argument."

Khadji nodded, unhappy. "I suspect you're right, Myrna," he said. "The boy's uncle said as much. I think he fears for the boy's life. He's asked us to let the lad stay at the temple until the danger has passed."

Safar could have told his father he'd used the wrong words.

"Danger?" his mother exclaimed. "What danger, Khadji?"

"Only to the boy, Myrna," his father soothed. "Only to the boy."

"But what if *they* come here? What if *they* cause trouble?"

"Only his uncle will come," his father said. "And only when it is safe for the lad to return to his family. Be reasonable, Myrna. We have to explain this to the others and if you're opposed to it, why, we'll have to go back on our agreement.

"Besides, who would travel so far to Kyrania just to cause us grief? We have nothing they want. At least nothing that's worth so much trouble.

"And, as I said, how could we refuse?"

"Next time ask me!" Myrna said. "I'll show you all you need to know about refusal."

Then she relented as her natural Kyranian hospitality came to the fore. "We'll make the best of it," she declared. "Can't blame a boy for the troubles caused by his family."

"What's his name?" Safar asked.

"Iraj Protarus," his father said.

The name struck Safar like a thunderbolt.

He heard his mother say, "Protarus? Protarus? I don't know that family name."

But Safar knew the name quite well—much to his sudden discomfort.

He'd experienced a vision some days before while working in his father's shop. Whether it meant good or ill, he couldn't say. Still, it had disturbed him deeply.

The vision had seized him while he was cleaning pebbles and roots from a new batch of clay his father had dug up from the lake.

Besides the lake, there were many fine clay beds in Kyrania. The lake clay was pure and therefore gray. But as any potter knows pure clay needs to be mixed with other kinds or it will not fire properly. Within a week's stroll in any direction the Timuras could find clay of every color imaginable—red, black, white, a yellow ochre, and even a deep emerald green. Clay was long considered a holy substance and the clay from Kyrania was considered the holiest of all because it was said that Rybian, the god who made people, once spent much time in the Valley of the Clouds wooing the beautiful goddess, Felakia. The tale was that she spurned the god's advances and during the long lovers' siege Rybian became bored and pinched out all the races that make up humankind and demonkind. He used the green clay, it was claimed, to make the demons.

As Safar worked his thoughts were far from heavenly speculation. Instead, his imagination was fixed on the hiding spot he'd discovered overlooking the pool where the village maids liked to bathe.

Then he found an unusual stone in the clay debris. It was a broad pebble—smooth and blood red. Examining it, he turned the pebble this way and that. There was a clear, thumbnail-size blemish on one side. The blemish was like a minuscule window and he was oddly drawn to look into it.

Safar jumped back, thinking he'd seen something move . . . as if trapped in the stone. He looked again, blinking. The image blinked back and he realized he was looking at a reflection of his own eye. He peered closer, wondering the idle things people contemplate when they are alone and staring at a mirrored surface.

Suddenly Safar found himself falling. But it was unlike any sensation of falling he'd experienced before. His body seemed to remain kneeling by the clay bucket while his spirit plunged through the window.

His spirit self plummeted through thick clouds, then broke through. Safar felt oddly calm, looking about with his spirit eyes. Then it came to him he was floating rather than falling. Above was a bright sky, with clouds that were quickly retreating. Floating up at him was a wide vista of fertile lands with a broad highway cutting through.

At the end of that highway was a grand city with golden spires.

The last of the clouds whisked away, revealing a mighty army marching along the highway to the city, banners fluttering in a gentle wind. It was a dazzling array of troops and mailed cavalry—both horse and camel. Two graceful wings of chariots spread out on either side. In the lead was a phalanx of elephants Safar recognized only because of the illustrated books at school. The elephant heading the column was the largest by far. It was white and carried an armored howdah on its back. A large silk banner flew over the howdah, displaying a comet moving across a full moon.

The comet was silver, the moon harvest red.

Then he saw the city gates thrown wide and a crowd poured out to greet the army. Safar spread his spirit arms and flew toward the crowd. No one saw him as he sailed over a forest of spears and lances and he took a boy's immense pleasure in doing what he liked amongst so many adults and yet remaining unobserved. Then he overshot his mark and nearly flew through the city gates. Correcting his course, he hovered over the crowd and looked down.

Milling beneath him were hundreds of screeching monsters. He knew instantly they were demons. He should have been frightened. Demons were humankind's most ancient and deadly enemies. But there was an opiate blur to his trance that allowed him to feel nothing more than amazement.

The demons had yellow eyes and were fiercely taloned; horns jutted from their snouted faces. Sharp fangs gleamed when they opened their mouths and their skin was scaly green. All were costumed in the finest of cloth and jewelry, especially the tall slender demons in front, whom Safar took to be the city's leaders.

The tallest of them held a pike. And stuck to the top of that pike was a head. Safar had never seen such a grisly sight and it disturbed him far more than monsters boiling about beneath him. Still, he couldn't help but move closer. It was a demon's head on that pike. Huge—twice that of a human's. Its snout was fixed into a wide grimace, exposing two pairs of opposing fangs the size of a desert lion's. It had a jutting armored brow and long bloody hair. Perched on the brow, as if in mockery, was a golden crown.

The demon king's dead eyes were open and staring. But Safar imagined he saw a small spark of life in their yellow depths. This unsettled him even more than the gory display of death. He stretched his arms and flew away.

Seeing the great white elephant approaching, he flew toward it to investigate. Sitting in the howdah was a large man with long gold hair, flowing mustaches and a thick military beard. His features were so fair he appeared strange to Safar, although not as strange as the demons.

18

Below dark, moody eyes was a strong beaked nose, which added to his fierce looks. His armor was rich and burnished; the hilt of his sheathed sword was finely worked ivory bound with silver wire. Encircling his head was a thin band of gold embedded with rare stones.

Safar knew he was looking at the new king—come to replace the one who had his head mounted on a pike. The demon crowd was shouting to their new king and he waved his mailed hand in return.

They grew wilder still, chanting: "Protarus! Protarus! Protarus!"

The king looked up and saw Safar. Why this man alone could see him, Safar didn't know. Protarus smiled. He stretched out a hand, beckoning the hovering spirit closer.

"Safar," he said. "I owe all this to you. Come sit with me. Let them praise your name as well."

Safar was confused. Who was this great king? How did he know him? What service could Safar have possibly performed to win his favor? Again Protarus beckoned. Safar floated forward and the king reached out to take his hand.

Just before their fingers touched Safar again felt the sensation of falling. But this time he was falling *up!* The movement was so swift he started to feel sick. Then city, army and finally even the green fields vanished and he was enveloped by thick clouds.

The next he knew he was crouched over the bucket, turning away as quickly as he could to avoid fouling the clay with the contents of his belly.

Luckily his father was absent. Safar hastily cleaned up the mess, finished his other chores and crept up to his bed. The experience had exhausted him, unnerved him, so he pleaded ill when the dinner hour arrived and spent a troubled night contemplating the mysterious vision.

That uneasiness returned as Safar sat listening to his family chat about the young stranger who had come to stay in Kyrania—a stranger whose name was also Protarus. He fretted until it was time for school. Then he dismissed it as a coincidence.

In his youth Safar Timura believed in such things.

*   *   *

It was a clear spring day when he set out for the temple school with his sisters. Men and women were in the fields readying the muddy land for planting. The boys whose turn it was to tend the goats were driving their herds into the hills. They would stay there for several weeks while Safar and the others studied with the priest. Then it would be his turn to enjoy the lazy freedom of the high ranges.

The small village marketplace was already closing for the day, with a few late risers arguing with the stall keepers to stay open a little longer so they could make necessary purchases.

The Timura children walked along the lake's curve, passing the ruins of the stone barracks which legend claimed were built by Alisarrian The Conqueror who crossed the Gods' Divide in his campaign to win a kingdom. That kingdom, the Kyranian children were taught, had once included all Esmir and demons as well as humans bowed to Alisarrian's will. But the empire had broken up after his death, disintegrating into warring tribes and fiefdoms. It was during that chaos humans and demons had sworn to the agreement making the Forbidden Desert the dividing point between their species—a "Nodemon's" as well as a "Noman's" land.

Outsiders claimed it would've been impossible for the Conqueror to have driven his great army over the Gods' Divide. But Kyranian tradition had it that Alisarrian settled some of his troops in the valley and they married local women. Kyranians were mostly a short, dark skinned people while Alisarrian and his soldiers were tall and fair. Occasionally a fair skinned child was born in Kyrania, bolstering the claims.

Safar saw his own appearance as evidence that the local tales were true. Although he was dark, his eyes were quite blue and like the ancient Alisarrians he was taller than most. Also, his people tended to be slender, but even at seventeen Safar's chest and shoulders were broadening beyond the size of others and his arms were becoming heavily muscled. Any difference, however, is an embarrassment at that age and so Safar saw his size and blue eyes as a humiliating reminder that he was different from others.

As the Timuras passed the stony inlet where the women did the wash one fat old crone happened to glance up. Her eyes chanced to meet Safar's and she suddenly gobbled in fear and made a sign to ward off evil. Then she cursed and spat on the ground three times.

"It's the devil," she shrieked to the other women. "The blue-eyed devil from the Hells."

"Hush, grandmother," one of the women said. "It's only Safar with his sisters going to school at the temple."

The old woman paid no heed. "Get thee gone!" she shrieked at Safar. "Get thee gone, devil!"

He hurried away, barely listening to the comforting words of his sisters who said she was just a crazy old woman and to pay her no mind. But there was no solace in their words. In his heart he believed the woman spoke true. He didn't know if he actually was a devil. But he feared he'd become one if he didn't abandon the practice of sorcery. Each time he performed a magical feat or had a vision he swore to the gods he'd never do it again.

The older he became, however, the harder it was to resist.

Safar had possessed the talent even when he was a toddler. If a glittering object caught his eye he could summon it at will. He'd pop it into his mouth and start chewing to soothe his tender gums. His mother and aunts would squawk in alarm and drag the object out, fearing he'd swallow it and choke. Safar drove them to distraction with such antics, for no matter how well they hid the things he'd sniff them out and summon them again.

When he grew older he turned that talent into finding things others had lost. If a tool went missing, or an animal went astray, he could always hunt them down. He was so successful that if anything was lost the family would instantly call him to retrieve it. Safar didn't know how he was able to do such things but it all seemed so natural his only surprise was that others lacked the facility.

That innocence ended in his tenth year.

He was in his father's workshop one day, pinching out little pots he'd been taught to make as part of his apprenticeship. Safar's father was engaged in an errand, so the boy quickly became bored. One of the pots had a malformed spout which he suddenly thought looked like the village priest's knobby nose. The boy giggled and mashed the pot between his hands, rolling it into a ball. Then his hands seemed to take on an intelligence of their own and in a few minutes he'd formed the ball into a tiny man.

He was delighted at first, then thought something was missing. In a moment it came to him that the clay man lacked a penis, so he pinched one out where the legs met. He put the man down, wondering what he could do with him. The man needs a friend, Safar thought. No, a wife. So he rolled up another ball and made a woman with pert breasts like his oldest sister's and a little crease where such things should go. Once again he wondered what he could do with his new toys. Then it came to him that if they were man and wife they should have children. The sexual act is no secret to children who live close to nature, much less in homes such as Kyrania's where there is little privacy. So Safar put the two figures together in the proper position.

"Make babies," Safar said to them. But nothing happened.

A childish spell popped into his head, although at the time he didn't know that was what it was. He picked up the figures and held them close together while he chanted:

Skin and bone
was all clay once
until Rybian made people.
Now Safar makes people,
so clay be skin,
clay be bone.

The clay dolls grew warm, then they began to move and the child laughed in glee as they twined together like the young lovers he'd once spied in the meadow.

Then Khadji came in and Safar cried, "Look what I made, father!"

When Khadji saw the figures he thought his son was making the sexual motions and he stormed over and cuffed the boy.

"What filth is this?" he shouted.

He snatched the dolls from Safar's hands and they became lifeless again. He shook them at the boy.

"How could you do something so disrespectful?" he snarled. "The gods blessed us with these pleasures. They are not to be mocked."

"But I wasn't mocking anything, father," Safar protested.

His father cuffed him again just as his mother came in to see what was happening.

"What is it, Khadji?" she asked. "What has our Safar done?"

Angrily he showed her the dolls. "This dirty little boy has been making these obscene things," he snarled. "Behaving like one of those depraved potters in the city instead of a gods-fearing Timura."

Safar's mother eyed the dolls, her expression mild. His father became embarrassed, threw them into a bucket and reared back to give the boy another cuff.

"That's enough, Khadji," Safar's mother warned. "You've made your point. He won't do it again . . . will you, Safar?"

The boy was crying, more in humiliation than pain. His father hadn't hit him that hard. It was the act of being struck by someone Safar thought a hero that hurt worse.

"No, mother," he blubbered. "I won't do it again." He turned to his father. "I'm sorry, father," he said. "I promise I won't be a dirty little boy anymore."

The elder Timura grumbled, but Safar saw him nod. The boy prayed to all that was holy his father was satisfied. He swore to himself he'd never again give him cause to be scornful of his son. Then Myrna led Safar away. She took him up to the kitchen where she put him to work scrubbing the hearth.

Safar bent to the task with a will, sobbing as he scoured the stone with all his little boy's strength. Eventually the sobbing stopped. He chanced a look at his mother and saw she was eyeing him. But she didn't look angry, or ashamed.

"They were very pretty, Safar," she murmured.

The boy said nothing.

"So pretty, I doubt you meant anything wrong. Is that true?"

Safar nodded. Another great sob threatened, but he fought and won control.

"Well, then," she said, "if you meant nothing wrong, don't let it bother you. Just be careful from now on. Would you do that for me?"

She held out her arms and Safar ran into that warm harbor, escaping the emotional storm. But from that day on he associated magic with something shameful—an act performed by dirty little boys. And that shame grew along with his powers and his inability to stop committing such sins. He felt apart from others, the good people of Kyrania who had almond eyes and were properly small.

So when the crone cursed Safar as a blue-eyed devil, she'd unwittingly found a gaping wound for a target.

When Safar and his sisters reached the temple their priest, Gubadan, was already lining the children up for their exercises. He was a cheery little man—with that great knobby nose which had inspired Safar's earlier shame. The priest's ample belly stretched the material of his yellow robes and he had a habit of gripping the sides when he was talking and thumping it with his thumbs. He also had a shaven head and a long white beard he kept in immaculate condition.

As Safar joined the others in the slow, sacred motions and deep breathing Gubadan had taught them to rid their minds of trifles that hinder learning, he looked about for the new boy. He was disappointed when he didn't see him.

Gubadan noted his inattention and snarled: "Put your spirit into it, Safar, or I'll take a switch to you."

The others laughed, which drew more threats of switchings. But that only made them giggle more for Gubadan was a gentle soul who'd no more beat them than he'd defile the altar of Felakia with an unclean offering. Although the exercises were the motions of warriors taught from the time of Alisarrian, Gubadan meant them to be soul cleansers—a means to examine the inner self. Once a week all the boys would use those same exercises on the drilling field. There they were overseen by a fierce old soldier whose duty it was to train them to defend Kyrania in case of attack.

The laughter soon stopped and they all fell into the dreamy motions of the exercise.

When Gubadan was satisfied, he led them through the ancient portals, graced by etchings of Felakia in all her forms—from graceful swan to gentle mother to the beautiful armored maid who protected Kyrania. The temple was a crumbling place that kept the village busy repairing it when the stormy season passed. The classroom was a small room next to the chamber where the incense was stored so it was always filled with godly odors that made even the most unruly child feel serious about his work.

Although Kyrania was remote and the people made their living by hard toil, they were not ignorant. They held learning to be a sacred duty and took pride in their ability to read weighty texts, figure complex sums and write a hand as fair as any taught at the best schools in Walaria. Kyranians were particularly proud of their ability with languages and all could speak half-a-dozen or more. The tradition of scholarship dated back to the legends of Alisarrian, who was reputed to be a learned man as well as a mighty warrior king. Legend had it that the first Kyranian school was founded by the Conqueror for the men he left behind. True or not, all those skills learned in at the temple school were not put to idle use. Kyranians required agile minds and an understanding of foreign tongues to deal with all the caravans that came through. Otherwise the shrewd traders would have skinned them of all their goods long before. Instead, the Kyranians were the ones who profited most from the hard bargaining sessions that always followed the llama trains into the valley.

That day, however, Safar couldn't keep his mind on scholarship. He earned several stern warnings from Gubadan and stumbled when he was called on to name the brightest constellation in the spring heavens. He knew it was the Tiger but when asked the answer fled his mind.

"Is this a game you are playing with old Gubadan, boy?" the priest scolded. "You are my best student. All know this. Your family pays me dearly to spend extra hours with you so you can learn even more. And yet you mock me, boy. And by mocking me, you mock the gods who gifted you. Do you think you are better than others, Safar Timura?"

"No, master," Safar said, ducking his head in embarrassment.

"Then why do you pretend ignorance of the obvious?" the priest roared. "Tell me that!"

"I honestly couldn't think of the answer, master," Safar said.

"Then you are lazy!" the priest shouted. "Which is a worse sin than mocking. Mocking I could excuse to high spirits. But laziness! Inattention! Unforgivable, boy. You should be setting an example to the others."

Safar wanted to say he couldn't help it, that his mind was fixed on the absent boy whose name was Protarus—the name of the king in his vision.

Instead he said, "I'm sorry, master. I'll try to do better."

He did try, but the day progressed slowly and not well. Finally he was free and he dashed out, trying to ignore Gubadan's fierce looks in his direction.

Safar was relieved he had a task to perform for his father and didn't have to walk with his sisters and listen to them tease him about his performance in school. He headed immediately for the clay beds where his father had left buckets for him to fetch home a fresh load. His path took him beyond the temple through a fragrant wood, where he dawdled in the clean air and sighing breezes.

He was just emerging from the wood and turning toward the clay beds on the lake's edge when he heard angry voices. The voices had a familiar ring to them and he wasn't surprised when the angry words became shouts and then sounds of fighting erupted. He hurried up the hill to investigate.

When he reached the summit he looked down and saw a tangle of flailing and arms and legs.

Four brawny youths had another pinned to the ground and they were pummeling him unmercifully.

The attackers were the Ubekian brothers, considered the greatest bullies in Kyrania. They came from a rough, unclean family that'd wandered starving and half-frozen into the valley one winter and begged charity. The Ubekians had claims of kinship, which although distant were strong enough to make their appeal undeniable under Kyranian tradition and law. To everyone's dismay the family settled into a cave near the main village and set up permanent housekeeping. They also got busy making general nuisances of themselves.

Safar had more reason than most to dislike the Ubekian brothers. They'd fixed instantly on his odd, blue-eyed appearance and had mocked him unmercifully. In fact, until the arrival of the family no one had commented on his looks at all. But now others, such as the old woman at the lake, had become bold enough to torment him.

One by one, Safar had caught the brothers alone and thrashed them. Now they no longer mocked him—at least not in his hearing.

Safar had no doubt the brothers were to blame in the fight he saw below. His dislike of the brothers plus the unpleasant events of the day made his blood sing in furious joy as he ran down the hill and threw himself into the fray.

Cries of pain and surprise greeted his attack. But the brothers quickly recovered and turned on him. Safar was hard-pressed for a moment, catching a blow to his nose that made stars brighter than those that formed the Tiger.

Then the brothers' victim jumped up and barreled in. Everything became a fury of fists, knees, elbows and butting heads.

Suddenly the fight ended and the brothers scampered away, pausing at the top of the hill to hurl empty threats to salve their pride. But when Safar and his companion moved forward the brothers dashed off, shouting obscenities over their shoulders.

Safar turned to see who he'd rescued. The youth was about his height and weight. But then shock hit when he saw that the boy was fair skinned with blonde hair, moody eyes and a strong beaked nose.

The features were disturbingly familiar.

The strange boy grinned through bruised lips, showing bloody teeth. "You arrived just in time," he said. "In a moment I would have lost my temper and risen up to break their heads."

Safar recovered his wits. "From where I stood," he said, dryly, "you didn't look like you'd be getting up soon."

The strange boy laughed. "That's because I have such a peaceful nature," he said.

The comment broke the ice and Safar laughed with him. "Next time you meet the Ubekian brothers," he said, "lose your temper as quick as you can. Or it'll be *your* head that's broken."

The strange boy stuck out his hand. "I'm Iraj Protarus," he said.

Safar hesitated, remembering his vision. But the young man's face was so friendly he couldn't see any harm.

He clasped the offered hand. "I'm Safar Timura."

Iraj looked at him oddly. "Safar, eh? I had a dream about a fellow named Safar."

Safar didn't reply. The coincidence froze his tongue.

Iraj noticed, thinking, perhaps, that Safar was only being shy. He shifted his grip into the handshake favored by brothers. "I think we're going to be very good friends, Safar," he said. "Very good friends, indeed."

CHAPTER TWO

THE DEMON RIDERS

Badawi shifted in the saddle, seeking a more comfortable position for his haunches. His gray mare chuffed in complaint, stumbling as she moved to accommodate his bulk. The fat man nearly fell, grabbing wildly at the saddle to save himself.

He lashed the mare, growling, "Watch how you go, you fly-blown daughter of a dung beetle."

The animal was used to such treatment and, other than a painful grunt, showed no reaction as she picked her way across the rocky ground. It was not yet midday and although the worst hours were still ahead the high plains sun was hot enough to make the overburdened gray miserable. The ground was hard on her feet, the brush dry—offering little relief for her growing hunger and thirst. But Badawi had no pity and raked her with his spurs and cursed her again to prod her on.

The mare's breathing quickly became labored, nostrils foaming, coat darkening with sweat. Badawi ignored her plight. He wasn't worried about grinding the beast down and leaving himself afoot. His final destination was in the rolling foothills to the south, no more than five or six miles away. Towering above those foothills were the snow-capped peaks of the mountain range he knew as the Gods' Divide. To his east was the dusty wasteland that marked the border of the Forbidden Desert.

Badawi rode the gray hard a few score paces then suddenly remembered—sawing hard on the reins to slow the mare. "You are a fool, Badawi," he chastised himself. "An unfeeling fool."

He turned, chins descending in a cascade of sorrow, to look at the animal trailing behind. It was a graceful young camel, padding easily across the rocky ground. A rope lead looped from its neck to Badawi's wood-framed saddle.

"Forgive me, little one," he called. "For a moment I forgot you were with me." He lashed the mare. "Blame the foul temper of this ugly daughter of a bonegatherer's ass. She tested my kind nature and I had to teach her a lesson."

Badawi gave the rope a gentle tug and the camel obediently quickened its pace to come to his side. His greedy little heart warmed and he smiled fondly at the animal, who presented him with dark pleading eyes framed by long, upswept lashes. The camel was pure white—white as the snows, Badawi thought in a rare moment of romantic reflection, powdering the peaks of the Gods' Divide.

He pulled honeyed figs from a pouch and the camel's head swept out for the treats. "I can deny you nothing, Sava," he said, shivering as the camel's tender lips nibbled at his fat palm. "Not even the food from my very mouth." He sighed. "What a lucky man I am. The gods must truly love one such as I. To have a thing of such beauty."

Badawi was a man much pleased with himself. Any who knew him would've instantly realized his enjoyment came at the expense of another. They would have guessed, correctly, that he'd ground another man into the dust to win the pretty white camel. He was a man of low cunning who'd made his fortune farming and breeding fine horses and camels in a region no one else would approach. The land he owned was rich, but cost him nothing because of its proximity to the Forbidden Desert.

Years ago his first wife had reacted first in fear, then in rage when he'd announced the news of the place he'd found for their new home. After he'd beaten her into submission he'd given her a good husbandly talking to.

"Don't be such a stupid cow," he'd advised. "The only reason people are frightened of that place is because it's close to the Forbidden Desert. I say, bah to that! Pure foolishness. So what if the demon lands are on the other side of that desert. I mean, it *is* called Forbidden, after all. The demons can't cross it any more than humans can. Besides, there hasn't been a demon seen for hundreds of years. And the only reason there's land for the taking is because people are not only stupid but have no vision.

"I, on the other hand, am not stupid. I see fortune where other see fear. And wife of mine, if you don't have the household packed and ready to move before the week is out I'll whip you within an inch of your life. Then I'll send you back to your father. Let him see if he can knock some sense into such a silly cow."

Badawi's lips curled into a sneer as remembered that conversation of long ago. He'd prospered mightily since then, raising his herds on the lush grass of the foothills and selling them for fat profits to the settlements and nomad encampments in the so-called safer regions. He'd worn out the first wife and three others in the process, as well as many children, all of whom labored on his land like slaves.

Then his grin suddenly became a growl as his mare snorted in alarm, head jerking back and almost striking him in the nose.

"What's this?" he shouted, slashing its flanks with his whip.

This time the gray reacted. It shrilled fear, rearing onto its two hind legs. Badawi plunged to the ground. He struck hard, breath whooshing out, but was remarkably unscathed. He was just coming to the realization the mare had been frightened by something other than himself when he heard his beloved Sava bawl in fear.

The camel attempted to bolt away but became tangled with the rope and the plunging mare. The two animals screamed and fought the rope, trying to escape.

Badawi, who could be agile when called upon, rolled about beneath them, shouting for his maddened animals to stop. Then the rope parted and the mare and camel raced off toward the familiar foothills and the safety of home.

Badawi leaped to his feet crying, "Come back my Sava! Come back, my sweet!"

But his pleas went unheeded and soon both the camel and the mare vanished over a hill.

Badawi cursed the fates. Then he sighed, resigned to the long walk home. It was the gray's fault, he reassured himself. He swore that low creature would suffer miserably for causing him such trouble.

Then a sudden chill gripped him. Danger wormed about in his belly and his hackles rose, stiff and bristly as a desert hedgehog's spines. Instinct made him turn to look out across the Forbidden Desert.

He shaded his eyes but nothing was immediately apparent. Then he saw a dust cloud churning up and wondered if it might be an approaching storm. His wonder turned to dismay as the dusty veil parted and a long column of dark figures emerged.

They were coming toward him fast and he tried to turn and run. But fear turned his feet to stone and he found himself standing there gaping at the approaching figures, trying to make out who they might be.

Then the figures took form so swiftly and with such startling clarity Badawi's bowels broke.

Demons!

Monsters in battle harness, with broad snouts and mottled green skin. The steeds they rode were more horrible than their masters—not horses, but creatures vaguely looking like horses—with long curved fangs to tear flesh and great cat's claws instead of hooves.

Badawi came unstuck and whirled, stubby legs carrying him forward. He'd taken no more than a few steps when his spurs tangled and he pitched face forward to the ground.

Then the monsters were all around him, howling spine-chilling cries. Weeping and crying to the gods, Badawi curled into a ball, trying to avoid the snapping fangs and slashing claws of the demons' mounts. Spear points jabbed at him and he screamed like a pig and jumped each time they pierced his skin.

He thought he heard shouted orders and suddenly there was silence and the torment stopped.

A voice said, "Get up, human. I wish to look upon you." The voice was cold and harsh and quite alien.

Badawi remained curled, but whined, "Please, master. Don't hurt me. I am only a poor horse merchant who means no harm to anyone."

Then he heard another inhuman voice say, "Let's just kill him and cook him, Sarn. I'm hungry! We're *all* hungry!"

The remark brought growls of agreement from the other demons and chants of, "Eat, Eat, Eat!"

Fear sparked inspiration. Badawi uncurled, scrambling to his knees, arms raised to plead for his life.

Sarn, the demon who'd spoken first, and another smaller monster stared down at him from their steeds, drooling amusement.

"Please, master," Badawi wailed. "Spare the life of this undeserving insect. I have daughters, master. I have sons. I have a wife. Take pity, master! Spare old Badawi!"

His pleas brought howls of laughter from all but Sarn. He peered at Badawi with immense yellow eyes. Then he raised a taloned claw for silence, which he got.

"You ask pity of *me?*" Sarn said, scornful. "Sarn pities no one. Much less a human."

"You misunderstand, master," Badawi babbled. "I don't want you to spare me for my own sake. But yours."

"My sake?" Sarn said. "What can you possibly do for Sarn, human?"

"Why, ease your hunger, master," Badawi answered. "If that is what pleases you. However, if I may be so bold as to point out . . . there's only one of me. And many of you. It grieves me to say that ample as I am some will still suffer the pangs of hunger when there's no more of me left. However, master, at my home—which isn't far away—there's more than enough to satisfy every single one of you."

"The daughters and sons you mentioned?" Sarn asked, scaly lips curling back.

"Yes, master," Badawi replied. "And my wife as well. A tender morsel, if I do say so myself. Fed her only the best since she's come to live under my roof."

Giff, the other demon, snarled disgust. "You're offering your family, human? To save your own life? What manner of creature are you?"

Sarn made an ugly noise—a chuckle to demon ears; a horror to humans. "He said he was a horse merchant, Giff," he said. "That should explain everything."

Badawi ignored this, saying to Sarn, "Let me lead you to my home, master. You'll see that all I claim is true."

Sarn stared long at the ugly mound of flesh that was Badawi.

Any other time he'd have quickly dispatched this cowardly human to the cooking pot. They could find Badawi's household on their own. Sarn and his band were one of many bandit clans who stalked the lawless regions in the demon lands. Until recently he had no more ambition than to raid and kill at will. Then King Manacia had sent an emissary to offer a bargain. Sarn would be granted royal permission to strike across the Forbidden Desert, seeking human riches and prey. The King wanted nothing in return but information. Sarn was to sweep west along the Gods' Divide, mapping all major byways. Manacia was particularly interested in a particular place—a route that legend said would lead over the mountain range. Sarn didn't ask why King Manacia wanted such information. Whatever the reason, Sarn was certain it'd be soldier's work—dangerous, with little hope of booty—and therefore of no concern to Sarn and the other bandits. When he was done Sarn would return across the desert, saddlebags and pack animals laden with treasure.

As he weighed Badawi's fate it occurred to him his foray might be made easier if he had a willing human guide. And Badawi certainly appeared willing.

"Tell me, human," he said, "Do you know of a place called Kyrania?"

"Kyrania?" Badawi cried. "Kyrania? Why, Master, there isn't another man within a hundred leagues who knows the way to Kyrania better than this, your most desolate slave."

Sarn nodded in satisfaction. He turned to Giff. "Let him live for now," he said. "It seems this human swine may be of use to us."

Badawi wept in relief. He came to his feet, bowing and blubbering. "Oh, thank you, kind master," he wailed. "May the gods smile on all your efforts."

But even then—life still hanging in the balance—Badawi's greed reared up.

He dried his eyes, saying, "I'm, uh, reluctant to bring up a small matter, master. A boon, if you please, for serving you. When we arrive at my farm do what you like." He waved his arms. "All that's mine is yours, master," he said. "Except . . . well, there's this white camel, you see. It isn't much, master. No breeding at all. Worthless to anyone. But I've grown fond of her, master. And if you'd only—"

Sarn's claw shot forward and Badawi's jaws snapped shut, cutting off the rest. The demon beckoned and Badawi's mouth became a parched desert when he saw the length of the demon's razor talons. He took an obedient step forward, then was rocked as a great smothering force enveloped him. It fell over him like a fisherman's net, dragging him toward the demon chieftain. His throat clogged in fear and he couldn't speak, much less breathe. He staggered forward, drawn by the demon's spell.

Badawi trembled as his chest touched the longest talon, jutting like a curved blade. And still he couldn't stop. The spell made him press forward until the talon pierced first his robe, then his flesh. Blood flowed, staining his robes. The pain was unbearable but no matter how hard his mind struggled he couldn't regain his will. He felt the talon cutting deeper. Then he heard Sarn laugh and suddenly the spell was gone and he was free.

Badawi fell to the ground clutching his wound, too frightened to do more than groan.

"If you want to live, human," Sarn said, "you will do *all* I command. Without question. And you will never ask anything in return."

"Yes, master, yes," Badawi wailed, knocking his forehead against the ground in obeisance. "I was a fool! Please forgive such a stupid one."

"Rise, human," Sarn said.

Badawi did as he was told, standing before the demon trembling and wondering what would happen next.

"Here is my first command to you, human," Sarn said. "You will immediately lead us to your home. And when we arrive . . ."

"Yes, master?"

Sarn grinned, exposing a double row of stained fangs. "You will lead us to the camel first."

Badawi wisely buried his dismay, nodding eagerly in case the demons couldn't read his expression of wild agreement.

"And then, human," Sarn said, "when we are done . . ."

"Yes, Master! Anything Master!"

" . . . When we are done with your family you will lead us to Kyrania!"

* * *

After the demons finished with Badawi's homestead, they raided along the Gods' Divide for nearly six hundred miles. Scores of homes and settlements were overrun and many humans were killed. Some were granted a honorable death as worthy enemies. But many were killed for the pot, or jerked for flesh to feed them on the road.

Badawi led the way, picking out the fattest settlements, betraying the human leaders, and generally making himself useful. And whenever the subject of Kyrania came up, the horse merchant would say, "Just a little further, Master. Just a little further."

In truth, Badawi hadn't faintest idea where Kyrania might be. He knew the legendary caravan route over the Gods' Divide was in the general direction he was leading the demon bandits. But he didn't have the faintest idea where the passage was. Only a few merchant princes knew the route and Badawi, despite his success, was a treasury or two short of actual wealth. So he did what any decent horse merchant would do.

He lied. "This way, Master. Only a little further along . . ."

At first the bandits had been satisfied, gathering up pack animals to carry off their growing booty. In the beginning they'd also taken many young men and women captive for later sale in the demon slave markets. They chained them together, fixing them to long posts which the slaves carried on their shoulders—and made them march along with the baggage animals. But the number of slaves and baggage weight became unwieldy, slowing the demons' progress to a crawl.

Then the day came when the demons had enough and once again Badawi faced the roasting spit.

They'd hit another settlement typical of the human villages scatted through the remote foothills regions. It was rich in bountiful fields and bursting storehouses, but, as Sarn's chief lieutenant complained, there was barely a copper or two for a decent bandit to rub together.

Sarn and Giff took their dinner that night in a wide pavilion pitched above the main encampment. Below them they could see the main roasting pit where their brother demons were gathered about a shrieking victim, slowly turning over a slow fire.

Crouched among them was Badawi, daring many talons to snatch a piece for himself.

Giff sneered at the sight and turned to his leader, saying, "That is the most disgusting mortal to have ever fouled the land. He even eats his own."

Sarn laughed. "It wasn't as if we gave the human a choice," he said. "He's been allowed to eat nothing else."

"Still!" Giff said. "Still. You'd think he'd have more pride."

At that moment Badawi made the mistake of looking up from the fire and staring at the pavilion. Giff growled as their eyes met and the horse dealer quickly ducked to avoid the demon's glowing yellow eyes. He muttered a prayer to himself, beseeching the gods to not let Giff take offense. That prayer went unanswered as in the pavilion Giff gnashed his teeth in anger and turned to Sarn.

"The human was looking at us," he said.

Sarn shrugged. "What does it matter where the human looks?" he asked.

"It matters to me," Giff said. "I hate that lowly creature. I feel filthy in his presence. His very gaze makes me want to scour myself with dust."

Sarn laughed. "That would indeed be a sight, my good but unclean fiend," he said. "Considering that nearly four seasons have passed since you last bothered to bathe."

Giff saw no humor in this. "That's not my point," he said. "This human offends me. His presence disturbs my demonly serenity. Let me kill him so I can have some peace."

"Be a good fiend and try to learn patience," Sarn said. "Peace comes with patience, or so say our priests. This human offends me as well. They *all* offend me. Their odor is worse than the shit of any beast I've ever encountered. And their looks are as bad as their odor. So soft and wriggly they remind me of worms. But worms with hairy heads and bodies. And their small mouths and flat teeth with only four puny fangs make me think of blood suckers." Sarn shuddered. "Two headed demon children have been known to be born to mothers who have looked upon things half so frightening."

"Then why must I be patient, Sarn?" Giff asked. "Let's make the gods happy and kill that fat slug."

"We still have need of the human," Sarn said. "That's why you can't kill him now."

Giff snorted in disgust. "Oh, I forgot what a valuable slave he's been to us," he said, voice dripping with sarcasm. "Why, tomorrow he may lead us to a village rich as this. Once again we'll seize stores of useless grain, poor quality cloth, tools we can't carry, old rusted weapons, and maybe, just maybe—the gods willing—two silver coins for a lucky thief to jangle in his purse."

"I admit the take hasn't been enough to make our enemies gnash their teeth with envy," Sarn said. "We've found only small villages and farming settlements to raid. Most of their wealth has been in their crops and animals. Some also might bring a pretty price at the slave market. But we're too far from home to make that sort of thieving very profitable."

Giff gnashed his teeth. "*Very* profitable!" he said. "You don't see any of us doing a demon dance for joy over the weight of our purses, do you? Why, even if you count the little gold and few paltry gems we've taken, I doubt we'll make any profit at all. And we've missed nearly a whole season of raiding at home."

"It's not the human's fault," Sarn said, circling back to the discussion of Badawi's fate. "The terms of the warrant we hold from King Manacia bade us to stay close to the mountains where the population is small. We can steal what we want, do what we like with anyone we find. But we must leave no witnesses. We must not allow any human to live who might carry the news that we've strayed across the border.

"And, most important of all to our king—and the only reason he even gave us this warrant—was that we were to seek a passage over these mountains. To a place called Kyrania."

Giff snorted, gesturing with his talons at the distant figure of Badawi. "And that human was supposed to lead us to the bedamned place. Well, he's been leading, and leading and so far we've nothing of it. Bah! He's a horse trader! Therefore he's lying."

Sarn gazed out at Badawi, scratching his horny chin with needle-sharp talons. "Perhaps he is," Sarn mused. "Frankly, I was a little too overcome with raidmust to think about it."

He shrugged. "If he is we'll have to find another. It shouldn't be too much of a bother. Humans are such a traitorous lot."

"Why do need to find another?" Giff argued. "To the Hells with Kyrania." He snorted. "Valley of the Clouds, indeed. I think Manacia is suffering from a royally cloudy mind."

"Without Kyrania," Sarn reminded his henchdemon, "we have no warrant. We must at least make an attempt."

"Your precious warrant from the king will be our ruin," Giff said. "What use is it to dare the curse of the Forbidden Desert when we get so little in return? The others feel the same way, Sarn. They were frightened to make this journey to begin with. All know a black spell was cast on that desert long ago. Any demon or human who crosses is becursed."

"King Manacia is a most powerful wizard," Sarn pointed out. "The warrant he gave us will protect us from any curse."

"How do you know?" Giff pressed.

Sarn gave him a blank look. "What do you mean?"

"You told us all about Manacia's curse-defying warrant," Giff said. "That's what convinced us. But now I'm beginning to wonder. How do we know Manacia didn't lie? And he has no power to shield us from such a curse?"

"What reason would he have to lie?" Sarn responded. "The king seeks information from us. Information I suspect his armies will one day follow up on. Why else would he want us to find a way over this mountain range? Why else would he be so particular to even name a place he suspects might be the key?"

Giff scoffed at this. "What's a damned name?" he said. "Kyrania? Humania? Dismania? Hells, he could have picked any name he liked and we'd never be the wiser!"

"Might I remind you, my faithful fiend," Sarn said, "that the king has promised us much gold for these efforts. Over and above any loot we seize. And there will be a particularly handsome bonus if we find a pass that leads through the mountains."

"Let him keep his bonus, Sarn," Giff pleaded. "Listen to me. We've been good fiends together since our youth. You lead. I advise. That's why we've been so successful. You know you can trust my advice. So hear what I'm saying. I speak from my heart like a brother.

"Let us leave this hellish land. Let us return home and breathe good demon air. If we make haste there's just enough raiding time remaining in the season to make all our purses heavy. We've searched every gully, every trail for nearly six hundred miles, Sarn. I don't believe there *is* such a place as Kyrania. Or any way at all over the Gods' Divide. And if there is, it's so well-hidden we'll never find it in a hundred years. We'll wander these hills the rest of our days. It'll be our ghosts who earn the king's bonus. And gold is no good to a ghost."

Sarn thought a moment, then nodded. "If that's what you and the others want," he said, "I won't stand in your way. I'll tell you what. We'll cast lots in the morning. If the majority wants to return home, that's what we'll do. You'll hear no argument from me. I'll add one more thing. No matter what the vote, at least ten of our fiends should return home with the goods and slaves we've already gathered. That's all I can spare, although it ought to be enough. The slaves are quite docile with the spell I cast over them. Then the rest of us shall proceed as quickly as we can, taking no more slaves and carrying away only gold and silver and other easily-transportable goods."

Sarn stretched out a paw. "Agreed?" he asked.

Giff nodded, rasping talons against his leader's claws. "Agreed," he said. "With one provision. If the vote is for our return I want the pleasure of killing the human."

Sarn laughed. "Do what you want with him," he said. "But do it in public. It's been a long time since we've enjoyed a really good entertainment."

Sarn was an artful chief. Giff's protestations of brotherhood didn't fool him. Giff always had his eye on the main chance. But Sarn knew his lieutenant represented a point of view among his band that must be dealt with. For a bandit chief Sarn had a unique ability to appear to shift with the prevailing winds and still get his way in the end. More importantly, he had magical powers much greater than the normal talent for sorcery all demons possessed.

In the morning he gathered his band together and carefully spelled out the two choices. He weighted no side heavier than the other. But he'd prepared well for the vote, casting a mild spell none of his demons would notice that would temporarily make the dangers and unpleasantness ahead seem of no consequence.

Badawi watched the proceedings from a distance, knowing his fate hung in the balance. For the whole time Sarn spoke Giff stared at Badawi, hate and hungry longing in his demon eyes. The night before Badawi had suspected something was up because of the intensity of the conversation between Sarn and Giff. The horse dealer had gone on a frantic, all night search for something, anything, to assure his survival.

Now he held what he prayed was that item in his hand and after the demons had cast their lots—voting to continue on King Manacia's mission—he was waiting with it at the pavilion when Sarn returned.

"What do you want, human?" Sarn demanded.

Badawi stilled his trembling limbs, doing his best to ignore Giff's stares of unrequited hate.

He held out an old firepit-encrusted bowl for Sarn's inspection. "I found this, master," he said.

Sarn struck it away. "Rubbish!" he said. "You present me with rubbish!"

Badawi grabbed the bowl up again, which had remarkably had not shattered. "Please, master," he said. "This isn't rubbish at all. Look at this bowl. See the rich glaze beneath all the filth? Touch the clay, Master. Feel the quality. And old as this bit of pottery is, notice the artfulness of the design. Why, if this were new and we had its twin, we could get a pretty bit of silver indeed at any marketplace."

"Don't insult me with silver, pretty or not," Sarn said. "I'm through with pots and jars and bolts of cloth. That's no way for a decent bandit to make a living."

"Ah, but master," Badawi said, "I'm not suggesting we look for more of this. But I am suggesting we find out where it came from. I've seen this type of pottery but once in my life, master. It's very rare. And therefore highly prized in human markets. The place this pottery comes from is secret to all but the richest caravan masters.

"The story is told in the marketplaces that there is a family of master potters who live in a valley high in the mountains. And in those mountains is a holy lake surrounded by beds of the purest clay. Clay that is used to form pots and dishes and brewing jars fit only for kings and their most royal kin.

"That family of potters, Master, is know as the Timuras. And this is a Timura pot, Merciful One. It could be no other!"

"My ears are growing heavy just listening to you, human," Sarn said. "Say what you came to say and be done with it. What do I care about this tale of lakes and beds of clay and grimy potters who grub in the earth?"

"Yes, master, I'll hurry, master," Badawi babbled, but frightened as he was, he stuck to his point.

"That valley I spoke of, master," he said, "sits on a caravan route that leads over these mountains. At least that's what the stories say. And those same stories also claim the caravan route is the same ancient trail Alisarrian took when he invaded Walaria. It was said that to his enemies it seemed Alisarrian and his entire army suddenly appeared, pouring out of the mountains. They said it was magic, master. Sorcery. However, it wasn't magic that was their undoing, but a secret passage across the Gods' Divide."

Badawi waved the bowl in front of the demon. "The same place this bit of pottery was made."

Sarn used a talon to pick a bit of food from between his fangs. "If you aren't speaking of Kyrania, human, find a good dull knife and slit your throat for me. I grow wearier by the minute."

"Yes, Master, immediately, Master," Badawi said, scrapping and bowing. "I am indeed speaking of Kyrania. This bowl is proof that Kyrania is near."

"You've said that more than once, human!" Giff snarled.

Badawi shivered, but held his ground. "Forgive me, master," he said to Sarn. "This low worm you call your slave admits he stretched the truth a bit when he had the immense honor of first meeting you. I don't know *exactly* where Kyrania is. But I do know how to find it."

He saw the two immense demons exchange a look that did not bode well for him. So he hurried through his logic.

"Listen to me, please," he said. "I'm a merchant. I know things. I know you can't hide something as large as a caravan route. So we must assume it is still to our west. How far I can't say with certainty. However, I can *guess*, master. The route would by necessity go from Caspan, the largest city on this side of the mountains, to Walaria. Which, as you know, is the most important kingdom on the southern side."

Badawi crouched down and scratched a map in the dust. "Caravan masters are secretive, but they wouldn't waste time covering their trail. Time is money and money is time and the length of the shadow between is feared by all men of business. So I think we can assume the route is fairly direct."

Badawi kept scratching until he had the mountains sketched in and the two cities of Walaria and Caspan. Then he drew a circle. "It's only reasonable to assume, master," he said, "that the place you seek is within this circle. Perhaps two or three hundred miles distant at the most."

Sarn turned to his lieutenant, snout stretched in what demons considered a smile. "You see, Giff," the bandit chief said, "this human has been some use to us after all."

Giff peered at the greasy little human, measuring... "A vote is a vote," he said with some reluctance. "I'll let him be for now. But remember your promise."

Badawi was alarmed. "Promise? What promise, O Merciful Masters?"

"Just find us Kyrania, human," Sarn commanded. "And know that your miserable swinish life depends on it."

CHAPTER THREE

THE VISION AT WORLD'S END

Despite Iraj's prediction Safar didn't immediately embrace him and call him milk brother.

They had little in common. One was the son of a potter, the other that of a warrior chieftain. Safar's people were peaceful and generous to strangers. Iraj's were fierce plainsmen who trusted no one. Safar was contemplative by nature. Even as a child he had tended to think before he acted. Iraj, on the other hand, tended to be ruled by the heat of the moment. He was as intelligent as Safar, but impatient with learning. If he couldn't grasp a thing immediately he became bored and disdainful. Safar was willing, on the other hand, to labor long hours until he could command knowledge as easily as Iraj later commanded men.

There was one great similarity which formed the glue that eventually bound them. Both young men thought of themselves as outsiders—apart from the others in the village.

Safar's reason was magic.

Iraj's was a blood feud.

Much time passed, however, before either boy learned the nature of the other's mystery.

It was an idyllic spring. The sun was warm, the first crops bountiful and the herds were blessed with many offspring. During those lazy days Gubadan was hard pressed to hammer learning into the thick skulls of his charges. The young people of Kyrania drove their teacher and their families to distraction as mischief and youthful high spirits lured them from their duties.

Safar soon forgot about the troubling vision and Iraj seemed to have forgotten his dream as well, for he did not mention it again. Although Safar didn't consider him the "best of friends," Iraj *was* his constant companion.

As a stranger, and an object of worry for the trouble he might bring from the outside, Iraj was shunned by all but old Gubadan. On the other hand as an obvious prince everyone was warm and sweet as one of Mother Timura's peach pies when in his presence. Royalty rubs off, as the old grannies said, and sometimes in rewarding ways. So no one was willing to say "begone" to his face. And a few were so bold as to wonder if they could make a good marriage with one of their daughters.

Fleeing these pressures, Iraj went everywhere with Safar. He accompanied him to the clay beds when Safar went to fetch new supplies for his father. Out of boredom he even helped Safar with his most common chores, suffering dirt on his hands and clothing, for instance, while cleaning up after the goats. In repayment, Safar was moved to show Iraj the place near the lake where they could spy on the girls bathing naked in a hidden cove.

The two boys became such a pair they eventually combined their wits at school to bedevil poor Gubadan and divert him from the lesson at hand.

One day that game took a turn Safar found to be most revealing.

Gubadan's subject of the day was once again the starry constellations. It was just after the midday meal and it was all the students could do to keep their eyes open in the overly warm little chamber.

"We can all see how the Lion Cub suckles at his mother's breast during the spring," Gubadan was saying. "But in the winter the Cub must hide while the Hunter is lured away by the Lioness. So it follows that if you are born under the sign of the Cub you are affectionate by nature, but in the winter months you are timorous and hesitate to make decisions. Those of us with the Hunter as our major sign tend to be aggressive, fearless, but easily fooled by stealth when we encounter the Lioness."

Bored, Safar raised his stylus for attention.

"Pardon, Master," he said after he was acknowledged. "I'm having difficulty understanding."

Gubadan's heavy brows furrowed about his odd-shaped nose. "What is it, Safar?" he asked suspiciously.

"Why do we call the Wolf Cub timorous when he hides?" Safar said. "Isn't this actually a sign of wisdom? The Cub has no defense if the Hunter finds him."

Iraj broke in. "Safar has a good question, Master," he said. "I was also wondering about the Hunter. Why is he a fool to pursue the Lioness? She's in plain sight. I'd chase her myself and ignore the Cub. She'd make a much better skin to drape about my shoulders and stave off the cold."

Gubadan thumped a fat volume on his lectern. The leather cover was etched with stars and planets.

"The answer to both of you," he said, "is in this book. It was written by wise men many centuries ago. Stargazers have followed those laws for many years, predicting grand events as well as the future of great men."

"These Stargazers," Safar asked. "Are they never wrong?"

Gubadan harumphed. A sure sign Safar had found a weak spot. "Well," he said, "I can't honestly say there have never been errors. But they were due to faulty interpretation. Not by the laws themselves. All Stargazers are not equally blessed by the gods."

"I suppose, Master," Iraj said, "that some might even purposely make mistakes."

Gubadan flushed in anger, gripping his beard. "That would be sinful," he growled. "Why would a Stargazer commit such a godless act?"

Safar quickly saw Iraj's course. "For gold," he said. "Men *have* been known to sin to possess it."

"Not Stargazers," Gubadan said, horrified. "They are holy men. Why, one might as well doubt the honesty of Dreamcatchers."

"One might indeed, Master," Iraj said. "If enough gold were offered, or bloody threats."

"Master," Safar said, "was not Alisarrian's grandson—King Ogden—betrayed by a Dreamcatcher?"

Gubadan brightened. The Conqueror Alisarrian was his favorite subject.

"You've made my point exactly, Safar," he said. "King Ogden was born under the sign of the Hunter. And the Jester was his lesser sign as well so he was easily taken in by the rogues and charlatans of Zanzair. The demons were at the heart of the conspiracy, of course. Alisarrian, on the other hand, had the Demon Moon for his sign with the Comet ascending. So he was fierce and wise at the same time."

He began pacing, excited by the diversion the boys had caused. Safar wasn't fool enough to mention Gubadan really hadn't made his point at all. There was no disputing a Dreamcatcher had played Ogden the fool. History said so. Which had been *Safar's* point.

"Who was this man, Alisarrian?" Gubadan said. "Was he a monster as his enemies claimed? A monster who bent us to his will with his mailed fists, or was Alisarrian a blessing from the gods who cut the curtain of ignorance with his sword? We were dim-witted savages when he blew over these mountains like the last storm of winter. But when the spring of his enlightenment came, what a lovely field of learning bloomed. What a mighty . . ."

Safar settled back to doze as Gubadan waxed eloquent on the Conqueror. He noticed, however, that Iraj hadn't follow suit. Instead he was intent on Gubadan's every word. Safar examined Iraj, then suddenly remembered the banner with the red moon and silver comet he'd seen in the vision—the Demon Moon with the Comet in ascension! As Gubadan had just reminded him, it was the sign of Alisarrian.

Then Safar heard his friend interrupt Gubadan with a question. "Tell me, master," Iraj said, "do you think a man as great as Alisarrian will ever rise again?"

The priest shook his head. "Impossible," he said. "The gods blessed him with more qualities than is ever likely to be repeated." Gubadan shrugged. "There will be other conquerors, of course. Esmir has always been a divided house and it cries out for unification under one throne. There were conquerors before Alisarrian and others will follow. But they'll always rule under his great shadow."

Safar noted Iraj seemed upset at this answer. But the youth shook it off and pressed on. "May I ask you this, master?" he said. "Do you think any of those future conquerors will rule the demon lands as well? They were once part of Alisarrian's kingdom."

"Empire, not kingdom, lad," Gubadan corrected. "But to your question . . . once again I must answer with a negative. Only a human such as Alisarrian could rule the demons. To begin with, besides being a mighty warrior and leader, Alisarrian was a powerful wizard. Powerful as any demon sorcerer. As you know, few humans possess magical ability."

Safar shifted uncomfortably in his seat.

"And this ability tends to be weak compared to that of the demons," Gubadan continued. "The greatest human wizard I know of is Lord Umurhan who heads the university in Walaria. And powerful as he is, even Umurhan would admit he'd be hard pressed in a match with a demon wizard. Humans have always used superior numbers to defend themselves against the demons. Just as the demons have used their great magic to stave off humans.

"But Alisarrian was strong enough to break that stalemate and conqueror the demons. Why he didn't slay them all is in my opinion one of his great mysteries. He could have rid all Esmir of their foul presence, but he chose not to. For what reason, no one knows. His empire might have lasted to this day if he had done otherwise. It is the one area of his character that has disappointed me."

For Gubadan to admit his hero had a flaw of any kind was a remarkable event. It so disturbed the old priest he quickly ended the diversion and to the groans of all the students, he returned to the boring lecture on the distant constellations.

A few days later Safar and Iraj were strolling by the ruins of the old fort, stopping to watch younger boys playing soldier on its last remaining wall.

Remembering the interest his friend had shown, Safar pointed to the fort, saying, "Supposedly Alisarrian himself ordered this built when he came into our valley."

Iraj shook his head. "I don't think so," he said. "Look at how poorly it's placed." He pointed at a hill a short distance away. "If an enemy took that hill the fort would be within even a poor archer's bowshot. Alisarrian would never build such a thing. He was too good a general."

Safar looked at the rising ground stretching out from the ruins with new eyes and saw how vulnerable any force gathered inside would be.

"It's more likely," Iraj continued, "some fool tried to oppose Alisarrian from that fort. And was easily overwhelmed."

"There are tales that say you're right," Safar admitted. "Those same tales claim he made the whole valley his fortress, with strong guard posts in the passes and hidden caves where supplies and additional weapons were stored."

Iraj looked at Safar, eyes glittering. "Have you ever seen such things?"

Safar nodded, saying, "Many times. While grazing my father's goats in the mountains. There's one place in particular—very high up where you can see a great distance." The boy shrugged. "The grass is poor, but I like to go there and think."

"Take me!" Iraj urged. "I must see this for myself."

Safar was sorry he'd spoken. The place he had in mind was a private retreat where he went to nurse the wounds of youth. Many a tear had been shed there in solitude and many a dream conjured.

"Maybe later," he said. "The snow is still too deep just now."

He hoped his friend would forget, but each day the sun shone warmer, the streams swelled with the melting snow and Iraj pestered Safar to take him to his secret place. Finally, the next time it was Safar's turn to watch the herds he agreed to take Iraj with him.

At first Gubadan fussed about letting his charge out of sight for the weeks the boys would be gone.

"What will Iraj's family say, Khadji," he protested to Safar's father, "if something should happen to him?"

"They'll be just as angry with you if he drowns while swimming in our lake," Safar's mother broke in. Despite her first suspicions—natural to the cloistered people of Kyrania— she'd warmed to Iraj and now even defended the orphan prince to the others.

"The mountains are as natural to Kyrania as that lake," she said. "Let the boy go, Gubadan. Herding goats is not so dangerous an adventure."

"It's knowledge, not danger I'm after, Master," Iraj put in. "I want to see for myself where the great Alisarrian crossed these mountains."

This argument won the day and soon the two young men set out for the high pastures. They were overly laden with supplies, thanks to Gubadan's concerns, and they had to take a llama to carry all the clothing, blankets and food stuff pressed on them. Stirred, no doubt, by romantic dreams, Iraj took along the scimitar his uncle had given him when he left home. He was also laden with a short bow, an ample supply of arrows and an ornate dagger he said his father had bequeathed to him.

Safar carried his sling, a small shot bag of clay missiles made in his father's kiln and a sturdy staff—all he'd need to stave off the occasional pack of hungry wolves intent on goat flesh. He laughed when he saw Iraj struggling under the burden of so many weapons. "There's only trees and rocks up there," he said. "But if they should attack we'll be ready."

Iraj grinned, but his eyes were serious. "You can never tell," was all he said.

The skies were sparkling when they set out, the lower ranges green with new life. Safar picked up handfuls of fallen cherry blossoms to brighten their tea when they camped that night. The boys tarried for awhile at some of the higher huts, clustered among a grove of arrow trees, exchanging gossip for almonds and fat pheasants. The people were glad to see them and it was apparent to Safar that from the way they stared at Iraj they were more interested in this strange youth than in news from below.

One of the girls walked with them for a time, eyes shimmering in admiration of Iraj's tall sturdy figure and handsome looks. She turned back when they reached the trail leading to the pasture where the goats were grazing. She called after them to stop by her home when they returned, promising her mother would feed them well.

"I think she loves you," Safar teased. "If you had asked she'd have crept into the bushes with you and let you pull up her dress."

"I was tempted," Iraj admitted. "It's been too long since I hip-danced with a woman."

Safar was surprised. The other village boys boasted frequently of their conquests but he knew their claims to be lies. He'd heard his sisters and mother joke about young men who were foolish enough to think any well-raised Kyranian girl would lessen her bridal price by dallying with them—unless marriage was the intended result. Sometimes a caravan would be accompanied by prostitutes bound for distant pleasure halls. But their carnal interest was stirred by fat men with fatter purses, not poor, skinny-legged boys.

But when Iraj spoke Safar knew it was no empty boast.

"Are your unmarried women in the habit of bedding anyone who asks them?" he asked. "No offense intended. It's just that such things are frowned upon in Kyrania. The only reason that girl would have gone with you is she thinks you're rich, as does her father. And if you'd opened her legs her father would soon be talking to Gubadan about a wedding date."

"I suspected as much," he said. "That's why I kept my sword in its sheath. And no, our women are not of easy virtue. It's just that I've always had serving maids around to tend my needs. My mother saw to it there were always a few comely slaves about. Among my people it's considered unhealthy for a young man to be denied such pleasures."

"I wish my mother were so concerned for *my* health," Safar said. "But what if there are children? What do you do then?"

Iraj shrugged. "After they're weaned we usually sell them," he said. "It's cheaper to buy new slaves than to raise one to a useful age."

Safar was shocked. "How could you sell your own child?" he asked.

Iraj looked at his friend as if he'd gone crazy. "I've never thought of them as my own," he said. "I might as well claim the blanket lint in my bed as children every time I make love to my fist. Besides, even free women have no more of a soul than say, a camel or a horse. They were put here by the gods for our pleasure and to birth more of us. I'm only making the use of them that the fates decreed."

Safar bit back a heated reply. To hear someone say his mother and sisters were nothing more than brood mares and whores angered him. But he said nothing, thinking Iraj couldn't help how he was raised.

The two continued climbing and soon came to the vale where the herds were grazing. Safar relieved the boys tending them, gathered the goats and drove them higher into the mountains.

The hills were in full springtime bloom, flowers and tempting grasses rising from every flat spot and crevice so he set a slow pace, letting the goats and the llama stop and nibble whenever they liked. The young men made camp early, setting the herd loose in a small meadow and bedding down in a grotto shielded from the night winds. They roasted the pheasants and filled the left over hollows in their bellies with toasted almonds, cheese and hard bread—washed down with milk from the goats. The sunset was brief but spectacular, turning the meadow and grotto into a dreamy, golden landscape. Then the moon and the stars winked into life. Safar and Iraj gazed at them for a long time, silent as acolytes at a temple ceremony.

Then Iraj said, "Did you know my star sign was the same as Alisarrian's?"

Safar shook his head, although it suddenly came to him that he'd known all along. He tried to make a joke of it, saying, "Does that mean you have sudden urges to go a' conquering?"

Iraj didn't laugh. His eyes glittered as if the remark had struck an unintended target.

"I'm sorry if I offended you," Safar said. "It was a silly thing to say."

Iraj nodded. After a moment he asked, "Don't you sometimes imagine you have a destiny to fulfill?"

"Only as a potter," Safar said.

Iraj pierced him with his gaze. "Is that what you truly think, Safar?"

"What else would I be? I'm a Timura. Timuras make pots."

Iraj shrugged as if to say, claim what you like but I know better. Then he said, "I told you I dreamed of a fellow named Safar, did I not?"

"When we first met," Safar answered.

"I was surprised you never asked me more about it. Most people would."

Safar didn't reply, remembering the vision of the king on the white elephant.

Iraj stared at him for a long moment. "If I tell you a secret, will you promise not to reveal it?"

Safar promised, relieved that the conversation seemed to have taken a less dangerous turn.

"If you break the vow," Iraj warned, "I will most certainly be killed."

Safar was taken aback. At that point in his young life he'd never encountered a secret with such a penalty attached.

"It's the reason I'm living here with you," Iraj continued. "My father, you see, was lord of our tribe and I was to succeed him."

"Did your father die recently?" Safar guessed.

"He caught a fever a little more than year ago," Iraj said. "It took six months for it to suck out his life. During that time my family quarreled and became divided—with some favoring me as a successor, while others backed my uncle, Fulain. When my father died the break became permanent."

Iraj went on to explain that at first the tide was in his favor because more family members supported him. One of his cousins—a much respected older man who was rich in land and horses—was to be appointed regent until Iraj came of age and could take up the ruler's staff.

"But Fulain made a bargain with my father's most hated enemy," Iraj said. "An evil man named Koralia Kan who slew my grandfather when my father was a boy. And my father revenged the family by killing Kan's first born. So there is much spilled blood between us."

Iraj said one dark night Fulain gave Kan and his horse soldiers free passage through his land, joining him in a series of surprise attacks. Many died, including the cousin who would have been regent. When Fulain had the rest of the family under his heel he demanded Iraj's head so there would be no one to dispute his claim as clan lord.

"My mother begged one of my uncles—her sister's husband—to help," Iraj said. "I was forced to flee my own home and hide out with his people—the Babor clan. But there were so many spies about it wasn't safe to remain long. My uncle was ashamed to send me away. But he has his own wives and children to look after so he sent me here to hide from Fulain and Kan."

To Safar the tale had the ring of legend about it. He felt like a child listening to his father tell stories of old days and wild ways.

"Will you never be able to return?" he asked.

Iraj jammed a stick into the fire and flames leaped up to carve deep shadows on his face. He looked older in that light. And quite determined.

"The war in my family continues," he said. "But it is a silent war of spies and night raids. When it's safe my uncle will send for me. And then I will be tribal lord."

"How can you be sure?" Safar asked. "What if Fulain and Kan keep the upper hand?"

Iraj went silent. He stabbed moodily at the fire. Then he said, "I must believe it, don't you see? Otherwise I might as well take my own life now."

Safar didn't see. Why should Iraj die because he couldn't be lord of his tribe? Why not stay in Kyrania where no danger could touch him? He could live a long peaceful life. Marry one of the village women and be happy with all the beauty and bounty of Kyrania. But he said none of those things because he could see from Iraj's agitation it would only upset him more—although Safar didn't understand why. Instead, he asked him about the customs of his own people.

"It's nothing like here," Iraj said with unconscious disdain. "We don't farm. We aren't slaves to the land. We fight for what we want. And we fight more to keep it. For I tell you, Safar, I learned at my father's knee that men will either love you or fear you. There is no in-between."

He said his family had roamed the broad Plains of Jaspar for centuries. They were the fiercest of the tribes that remained after Alisarrian's kingdom broke up. They lived by raiding weaker tribes and looting villages and cities in distant lands. In recent years—even before his father became ill—things had not gone well.

"Our horse herds are not so numerous as before," he said. "And a plague took many of our camels. Other tribes have made bargains with the kings of the cities who once paid us tribute. We became surrounded by powerful enemies who are envious of our lands.

"My Uncle Neechan—the one who supports me—blames my father for what's happened." Iraj sighed. "I suppose he's right although I hate to admit it. I loved my father. But I think he was born too rich. His father was a great war lord and perhaps this weakened him. We used to live in yurts, tarrying until the grazing grew sparse, then packing up and moving on. Sometimes we took to the plains just because the notion sparked us and we traveled whichever way the winds blew. Now we live in a grand fortress my grandfather built."

Iraj said life was luxurious in that fortress. There was gold to buy whatever the family cared to purchase—tapestries and carpets and slaves to tend every need. They supped on food made lively with rare spices, some so deliciously hot that the meal was followed by iced sherbets made from exotic fruit gown in distant lands. There was a garden with an ornate fountain in the courtyard of Iraj's home and his father had liked to take his ease there, musing on the antics of the fish, munching on honeyed figs while sniffing at gentle breezes carrying the scent of oranges and roses.

"I think such rich living lessened my father's will to fight," Iraj said. "When he'd drunk too much wine—which was often in his later days—he'd curse those riches and swear that on the morrow he'd pack up our household and take to the Plains of Jaspar again. Living in yurts and going a-raiding like his father had as a young man. But in the morning life would continue as usual.

"I know he felt guilty about it. He even admitted it several times, warning me about the hidden dangers of so many riches. I think this is why he made me take the sword vow. So I might accomplish what he could not. Now the honor of my family is on *my* head."

"I'm sorry," Safar said, thinking this was a burden *he* wouldn't want to carry.

"Don't be, Safar," Iraj said. "This is what I want. The gods willing, one day I shall restore my family to its former greatness." His voice fell until Safar could barely make out his next words. "And more," he murmured.

Just then a flaming object shot through the heavens and the boys' heads jerked up in awe. It hung above them, a vast swirling ball that chased the night from the hills. Then the ball exploded, bursting into a fiery shower.

Safar gaped as the glowing particles floated down until they filled his whole vision with dancing light. There were so many it was like snow from a rainbow and then they were drifting over him and he instinctively stuck out his tongue to catch one like a child marveling at snowflakes. To his surprise one floated into his mouth, which was immediately filled with a taste like warm, honeyed wine. Safar's whole body tingled with pleasurable energy and he suddenly felt above all mortal things.

He heard laughter and looked at Iraj. A glowing blanket of particles swirled around him and his features seemed comically twisted like a pot collapsing in a kiln. He was pointing at Safar, laughing, and the young man knew he must look the same. Then the particles vanished and all was normal again. For some reason Safar was left feeling somber, moody, while Iraj was still chortling.

"You *are* lucky for me, Safar," he said. "I tell you my deepest secrets and immediately we are blessed by a sign from the heavens."

"But a sign of what, Iraj?" Safar asked. "How do we know it has to do with us?"

"It was too wonderful to be anything but a blessing," Iraj replied.

That night, while Iraj slept peacefully, Safar remained awake, wondering what the heavenly display had meant. Was it a sign? If so, what did it portend? His senses were acute and every sound stood out clearly from the usual night muddle of chirps and frantic scurrying. He heard a cricket sing and at first he thought it was a spring song to its mate.

Then he heard, "It's coming! It's coming!"

Another cricket said, "What's coming? What's coming?"

And the first answered, "Better hide! Better hide!"

Then a soft wind blew up and the crickets fell silent. The silence came so abruptly it seemed to have substance, an object Safar could feel and turn about and examine if only he could touch it. In his mind he made a bucket of fresh clay. The silence, he thought, was in that bucket and he began to clean the clay, washing out twigs and pebbles. And then he found it. He fumbled it up—a broad, unusually shaped pebble. Blood red.

His spirit self looked into the stone's polished surface, saw his eye reflected back, and then he was falling . . . falling . . .

He stretched his arms and let the spirit winds carry him. At first he thought he was returning to the conquered city he'd seen before. But the winds bore him up and he was speeding across plains and deserts and then seas. He flew for what seemed an eternity, shooting from dark horizon to dark horizon until those horizons became gray and then startling blue as night turned to day and emerald seas churned beneath him.

Surely, he thought, I must have flown far enough to be on the other side of the world. The place Gubadan's books called "World's End." Just as he wondered when he'd stop he came to a mountainous isle in the middle of a vast ocean.

He heard chanting and drums and strange horns bellowing mournful notes that drew at him like a great tide washing to shore. Safar let the tide of notes carry him to a great grove of towering trees all heavy with ripe fruit.

Among those trees handsome people danced to the beat of big drums with skins made of thin bark. Several men blew through huge shell horns, making the mournful sound that had drawn him here. The people were naked and their sun bronzed bodies were painted in glorious colors. A tall woman danced in the center, high breasts bobbing to the wild, joyous rhythm. Her shapely hips churned and thrust in the ancient act of mating. Safar's young body reacted and he became powerfully aroused.

Suddenly she stopped, eyes widening in such terror that Safar's lust vanished, to be replaced by a feeling of immense dread.

The woman shouted in a language Safar didn't understand—pointing fearfully into the distance. The other dancers froze, their eyes seeking out whatever it was that had frightened her.

Safar looked with them and saw smoke puffing out of a coned mountain top. The people began to shriek and run about in mad confusion, like ants caught in a sudden thunder shower. Safar felt their terror as if it were his own. His heart pounded and his limbs twitching with an hysterical desire to take flight.

There was a blinding flash, followed by an explosion that hammered at his ears. Huge rocks and trees were ripped from the ground by the force of the blast and he instinctively ducked, although he knew he couldn't be harmed. Boiling smoke obscured his view.

Then his vision cleared and he saw a pile of dead, including the dancing woman, crumpled among the uprooted fruit trees. He saw the survivors stagger up and run toward the shore where a line of canoes waited.

There was another explosion, more forceful than the first. Fiery debris crushed the runners and Safar saw the canoes burst into flames from the intensity of the heat.

Molten rock poured out of the mountain, which was split nearly in two. It reached the sea and the waters began to boil. Thousands of dead fish bobbed on the surface, mingled with the blackened corpses of the few people who had made it that far. A yellow acrid smoke streamed from the mountain, filling the sky until the sun was obscured.

And there was a taste of ashes in his mouth.

The vision ended and Safar jolted up and found that he was weeping. He wiped his eyes, then glanced over at Iraj and saw he was still asleep.

Safar wished his friend would awaken. He felt lonely and a tremendous sense of loss had wormed a hole in his gut. There was also dread crouched there. Dread for the future, although he couldn't make out what he ought to fear. He tried to imagine himself ten years from now, a mature potter crouched at the wheel, hands forming wet clay into a perfect vessel. But each time a vague image formed he couldn't hold on to it and it would vanish. Safar struggled to imagine any sort of future at all. Not for himself, but the world. What would it be like if he lived a full span? But his mind seemed to become clouded with a yellow, biting mist.

Miserable, he gave up. He was cold and pulled his blankets close and stretched out on his leafy bower. As he waited for sleep to come he saw the first rays of the rising sun spilling over the ridges. They were the color of blood and so powerful that a distant promontory pushed out from that portion of the range as if it were alive.

Safar closed his eyes, whispering prayers for the souls of all the people who had died in his vision—the handsome people who'd once danced under fruited trees on an island at world's end.

And then he slept a dreamless sleep.

CHAPTER FOUR

ALISARRIAN'S CAVE

When Safar opened his eyes again the sun was higher, casting a peaceful glow on the morning scene. Iraj was bustling about, poking the fire into life and getting things out for breakfast. But when he saw Safar's face he spotted the misery there and asked what was wrong. Still shaken by the vision, Safar blurted out the whole tale.

Iraj made no sign of surprise the whole time Safar spoke and when the story was done he said, "Don't trouble yourself, Safar. It was only a bad dream. Some of those almonds we ate were probably green."

"It was no dream," Safar protested. "But a vision of something that actually happened. It was the cause of the fiery shower we saw last night."

Iraj gave his friend an odd look. "Why do you think that? Have you had visions before?"

"Yes," Safar said in a low voice. "Sometimes about things that are going to happen. Sometimes about things that are happening."

"Do they always come true?"

Safar shrugged, miserable. "Mostly."

Iraj squatted down beside Safar. "I've thought since we met you were keeping something from me," he said. "Is that all of it?"

Safar shook his head. "No."

"Do you want to tell me the rest?"

"Not yet."

Iraj nodded. "We have time."

Safar sat numbly as Iraj did all the necessary work, packing their things, gathering up the animals, and loading the llama. When it was time to go Safar's mood had improved. Everything seemed so normal in the light of day. Visions and sorcery had no place amid such brightness. The morning air was cool and soul cleansing. The birds were out, pecking among the dewdrops for breakfast. Butterflies perched on broad leaves, drying their wings in the warming sun. Fat sleepy bumblebees peeped from the blossoms.

Iraj whistled a merry tune as they set out and he kept it up for most of the morning, although Safar saw him glance in his direction every now and then, eyes hooded, as if measuring. After a time Safar pushed the vision away and made it into the mere nightmare that Iraj had suggested. He began to feel foolish for even mentioning it. He remembered his father's caution that the mountains could create a melancholy, distrustful mood, and finally he decided that what he'd seen was no vision, but the result of a fevered imagination brought on by melancholy's chill.

In a short time his own youthful spirits rose naturally to the fore and he joined in Iraj's tune. As they whistled their eyes met and their lips twisted into grins that turned the notes into airy bleats and they both exploded with laughter. The laughter was followed by much giggling over silly boys' jokes. They staged mock fights and wrestled, behaving like the striplings they were.

The day was half gone by the time the two friends reached their goal. The ground was covered with hard-packed snow, marked here and there by green shoots struggling out to greet the spring sun. The day was warm and windless and as the trail steepened they began to perspire from the effort of their climb, forcing them to shed their coats. The narrow path curved and swooped over the snowy rocks, carrying them to the summit. Progress was impossible to mark. In many places broad overhangs and outcroppings blocked their view of everything but the rocks around them and the path under their feet. The goats and llama scrambled ahead, disappearing around a sharp bend.

Even though Safar knew what to expect when he rounded that bend, the view leaped on him as suddenly and delightfully as the first time he'd come this way.

They emerged into bright light, finding themselves on a broad ledge looking out across the northern side of the mountain range. Just below was a small, grassy hollow where mountain berries abounded. A spring burst from the rock beneath their feet, plummeting down to gather in a crystal pool in the center of the hollow. The goats were gamboling among the berries, bleating with joy. The llama ignored his less-than dignified cousins of the wool, his snout already buried deep in one of the berry bushes.

Falling away from the green hollow was a wonderland of white-capped crags that tumbled down to the great desert wastelands of the north. Fat columns of towering clouds drifted across the blue skies, islands of layered browns and grays and cottony whites. The desert sands caught the sunlight, casting it back at the skies and the whole appeared to be formed of glittering, multi-colored gems.

Beyond the desert there was nothing to stop the eye. Safar's vision sailed swiftly for the horizon's rim, a dark blue line where the vault of the sky mated with the earth. He heard Iraj gasp and knew that even he—born to the vast southern plains—had never looked such a great distance. The view was overwhelming but everything also seemed enlarged in the thin air so the horizon somehow appeared close—although Safar knew from the caravan masters that it would take much time to travel so far.

He glanced at his friend, who had a foolish grin on his face. Iraj reached out—hesitantly—as if trying to touch the horizon. Safar laughed for he'd done the same thing the first time he found the place.

"Follow me," he said. "There's more."

Safar shed his light pack and clambered down the rocks running along the rushing spring. About half way the water sheeted over a cave mouth. Safar pointed it out to Iraj, then showed him how to edge his way between the falling water and the rock face and duck into the cave.

He'd left materials for torches there on his last visit and he quickly assembled several, then struck sparks with his flint tool to fire one. Instantly the cave was flooded with an eerie light. The walls and floors and ceiling were carved from smooth, green stone that captured all light and flung back a ghostly glow.

When Iraj had recovered from his initial amazement he fired a torch of his own and peered about, noting the place where Safar sometimes made a fire when the weather was cold. Then he saw a mass of pentagrams and magical symbols and star signs—some old, some newer—inscribed on one wall and the floor.

"A wizard's den," he said.

Safar nodded, not mentioning that the clumsier and newer symbols were his attempts to copy and learn from ancient masters. He'd yet to make magic with them, hampered as he was by youthful doubts. But in the back of his mind he knew it was only a matter of time before he succumbed to the temptation to cast a real wizard's spell.

Safar pointed to a series of faded red symbols etched on the floor. They led deeper into the cave, as if indicating a path. Iraj gaped as he recognized the symbols—the demon moon and comet of The Conqueror.

"Alisarrian came here?" he gasped.

"I don't know," Safar said. "But I think some of those who knew him used this place."

He motioned Iraj forward and they followed the path through the several chambers that made up the cavern. One room had a stone shelf with ancient jars still sitting on it. Although some of the magical symbols identifying them were still plain, the contents of the jars had dried up long ago. Another room featured a small pile of weapons and armor so rusted they'd bonded together. Iraj examined them with much interest, commenting with authority on their purpose and former quality.

The final room was empty, save for brackets mounted on either side of the far wall. Safar lit two more torches and placed them in the brackets.

"This is what I brought you to see," he said, pointing to the broad space between the two torches.

Iraj peered where he pointed but at first saw nothing remarkable.

"Look closer," Safar said. "It takes a minute to see the first time you try. After that it's easy because you know what you're looking for."

Iraj's eyes narrowed with effort and he turned his head this way and that, trying to make out what Safar was pointing at. Then the young potter smiled when he saw the stare turn into a look of wonder as the image between the mounted torch brackets leaped out.

A large painting had somehow been created just beneath the translucent surface of the stone. It was barely visible until the torches were lit—and only then if it were looked at a certain way.

The picture was of a tall, handsome warrior dressed in the archaic armor of a prince. He was fair skinned and had long light hair and fierce eyes as blue as the waters of Kyrania's holy lake. The warrior carried a helmet under his right arm and about his brow was a simple gold band of kingly authority. He had a sword in his left hand, held high as if greeting or challenging another warrior. Safar had never decided which.

Above the warrior king was the symbol of the Demon Moon and ascending comet.

"Alisarrian," Iraj hissed.

"None other," Safar said.

Iraj laughed in loud delight and clapped the young potter on the back, thanking him profusely.

"A secret for a secret," he said. "Although I got the better bargain, my friend."

At that moment Safar realized that sometime between the moment they'd set out on the journey and their arrival, they *had* become friends. The knowledge made him feel somehow more adult. He'd never had a real friend before.

Iraj gazed at the portrait again. "I've studied everything about Alisarrian," he said, "but I've never seen such a likeness before. He looks every inch a conqueror. A man fated by the gods to rule a great empire."

He drew his sword, flourished it, then struck a pose like that in the painting—sword held high, head lifted and eyes far-seeing.

With a jolt, Safar noticed something for the first time. "You're left-handed," he said, "just like Alisarrian."

Iraj nodded, face sober. "And tall and fair as well," he said. "But my eyes are dark. His eyes are blue . . . like yours."

Safar blushed. One of the many reasons he treasured this secret place was that here was another blue-eyed person like himself. It made him feel not only less strange, but superior—if only for a little while.

Iraj turned, holding his pose. "Tell me, Safar," he said quite seriously. "Do I look like a king?"

Safar studied him carefully. No vision followed, no great bolt from the skies, but realization boiled up from within. And he just suddenly . . . *knew.*

His mouth was dry and his voice came in a croak. "You *will* be king, Iraj," he said.

"What?" Iraj said, startled. "I was only—" he broke off. Then his voice became fierce, harsh.

"What are you telling me?"

"You will be as great a king as Alisarrian," Safar answered. "I see it . . ." he tapped his chest ". . . here."

Iraj's sword hand fell, the blade scraping against the stone. "Don't mock me," he warned.

"I'm not."

"You're speaking of my greatest dream," he said. "To create a kingdom as grand as Alisarrian's."

"I know this," Safar said.

"You don't think I'm crazy?"

"Perhaps." The young potter shrugged. "You'll probably have to be."

"You've seen this in one of your visions?" Iraj asked.

"Just before you came," Safar said. "I saw you . . . wearing a crown."

"Was I sitting on a white elephant?" Iraj asked, chin jutting forward in surprise.

"Yes," Safar said. "You were leading a great army. In my vision you beckoned me."

Iraj came closer, as if drawn by a magnet. "And I told you to sit beside me," he said. "And that you—Safar—were responsible for what I'd won."

"It seems we had the same vision," Safar said, numb.

"I'd believed it was just a dream," Iraj said. "I only thought it might be more than that when I met you and heard your name."

"Somehow," Safar said, "we got into each other's minds."

Iraj shook his head. "It was *your* vision," he said. "Such things never happen to me."

"Well they do to me," Safar sighed.

"You act like it's a curse."

"You don't know how much of one," Safar answered.

"But . . . if what you say is true—"

"It is," Safar broke in. "I'm not often wrong."

Iraj put his arm around Safar's shoulders, pulling him closer. "Then, when I am king," he said, "you will be my most trusted advisor. You will be Lord Timura from the moment I take my rightful place on the throne."

Then he withdrew his arm and stepped away, raising his sword with much ceremony. He gently tapped Safar on the head with the blade, saying, "I, King Iraj Protarus, do so decree."

His face shone with youthful zeal. Emotion made his voice waver and crack and his eyes welled with tears. There was a smear of dirt on one cheek and standing there in his rough boyish clothes attempting to strike an heroic figure, he might have even looked a bit ridiculous.

But Safar didn't laugh.

∗   ∗   ∗

After the impromptu ceremony Iraj investigated the chamber further, taking special note of all the magical symbols and jars.

"What do you suppose was the purpose of the cave?" he asked.

"My guess," Safar replied, "is that it was used by a Dreamcatcher to cast Alisarrian's future."

Iraj grinned hugely, saying, "How fitting for me to have my own future told in this place. And by my own Dreamcatcher as well."

"I'm no Dreamcatcher," Safar protested. "I'm just an apprentice potter."

"A potter who has visions," Iraj laughed.

Oddly, Safar was stung by his comment. "Being a potter may not be as great as becoming a king," he said. "But it is an honorable craft. Some even say it's an art—an art blessed by gods."

"I'm sorry if I said anything to upset you," Iraj said. "The only craftsmen I've ever known were sword and armor makers. But as you say, it's well known that potters are blessed because they work with the same stuff the gods made us from. Did you ever think that could be why you have visions? Maybe you got a double portion of blessings when you were born."

45

"It could be," Safar said. "Although my father has never had anything like that happen to him."

"How do you know?" Iraj asked.

"From the way he acted when—" Safar stopped.

"What happened?" Iraj pressed. "What did he do?"

Safar shook my head, refusing to answer. "I'd rather not say."

"We shouldn't have secrets between us," Iraj said. "Especially after what's happened."

He's right, Safar thought. But instead of confessing all, he became angry. "Nothing's happened!" he snapped. "Just one stupid boy told another stupid boy a silly tale. That's all."

Safar stormed away, ducking between the watery curtain at the cave's mouth and clambering over the rocks until he reached the meadow where the goats were grazing.

Wisely, Iraj took his time in following. Safar raged about the meadow, kicking innocent rocks, tearing up offending plants by the roots and slapping at the llama when he approached and nuzzled him to see what was wrong. When he struck out at the animal it sprang back in shock. Safar had always treated him gently. It stared at him with accusing eyes, then turned and ambled off in that overly casual way llamas have when they don't want to show they've been offended.

A goat got in its way and it charged the animal as if it were the greatest nuisance that had ever crossed its path. The goat dashed off, then revenged its humiliation by butting a smaller animal, which did the same and before Safar knew it the whole field was full of angry animals, butting each other and hopping about like fakir's apprentices attempting their first walks across a bed of hot coals.

By the time Iraj showed up Safar was laughing so hard he'd forgotten the argument. Iraj didn't bring the subject up and the two were soon engaged in the rough play and adventuring of boy goat herders alone in the mountains.

But it hung there between them, an uncomfortable presence.

* * *

When Badawi saw the wide caravan track leading into the mountains he fell from his donkey and dropped to his knees. He thumped his breast and shouted huzzahs to the heavens for saving his life.

That morning when Sarn sent him out to scout the way the horse dealer knew this day would be his last—unless he came up with a miracle. Badawi's luck had seemed to desert him after he'd discovered the old Timura pot from Kyrania. They'd traveled over four hundred miles since then and hadn't even found a goat path, much less a full blown caravan track leading over the Gods' Divide.

As he sang praises to all the holy presences he could think of, Badawi suddenly spotted a mound of camel dung a few feet away. His heart leaped with greater joy and—still on his knees—he scrabbled over and broke the sun-crusted mound open, revealing a still-moist center.

Just then Sarn came riding up, his column of demon bandits not far behind. When Badawi saw him he scrambled to his feet. "Look, Master!" he shouted, displaying two big handfuls of dung as if they were a great treasure.

"What's that in your hands, you filthy human?" Sarn growled.

"Camel dung, O Master," Badawi said, doing a little dance of joy, spilling the stuff on the ground. "The gods have guided your unworthy slave across a thousand miles of wilderness to find the very thing you have been commanded to seek."

46

"Have you gone mad, human?" Sarn said. "What do I want with camel dung?"

Badawi didn't seem to hear. He'd seen still more of the droppings and he raced over to them, leaping from mound to mound like a fat toad, scooping up dung and throwing it into the air, crying, "Praise the gods!"

At that moment Giff came up. "What's wrong with the human?" he asked.

"I think I've pushed him too hard," Sarn said. "He's seems to have lost his senses from the strain." He sighed. "I suppose he's of no use to us anymore. You can kill him if you like, Giff. Just be a good demon and don't say 'I told you so.'"

Giff grinned and started to draw his sword. But Badawi had overhead them. He hurtled over to the two demons, anger momentarily overcoming his fear.

He shouted, "Kill me? Why would you do such a stupid thing? I've found your route over the mountains, haven't I?" Badawi pointed to a wide track winding up into the hills. "There lies Kyrania!" he shouted. "There lies the Valley of the Clouds!"

Badawi became overly excited from his discovery. Excitement bordering on dangerous hysteria. "You'd never have discovered this on your own!" he cried. "Only I, Badawi, could manage such a thing.

"Furthermore, haven't I also just shown you evidence that a caravan passed this way not more than three or four days ago?" He indicated the dung-strewn trail with a stained hand. "Or do you suppose all these animals were out wandering in the middle of nowhere looking for a comfortable place to shit?"

As soon as his outburst ended Badawi realized what he'd done. His nerve collapse and he fell to the ground. "Forgive me, Master," he begged. He beat his head against the ground and threw dust over his head. "This insignificant beetle of a slave has offended you, Master. Cut off a hand, if it pleases you. Pluck out this miserable tongue that wagged without thought when the brain became overly excited by discovery. Only spare me, Master. Spare me. And I shall serve you faithfully, content with crumbs for food and lashes for praise for so long as I live."

While Badawi begged, Giff kicked his mount forward to examine the signs.

"I hate to admit this," he said when the horse dealer was done and reduced to a weeping wreck, "but the human is right. A caravan did pass this way not long ago."

Badawi wiped his eyes and blew his nose on his sleeve. "You see, Master," he said, "I spoke the truth. Even Giff says so. And we both know how much he hates me. I deserve it, of course, although—"

"Shut up, human!" Giff said. "If you dare foul my name again by speaking it aloud I'll cut off your head to make a pisspot!"

Badawi bowed, trembling. "Please, sir," he said. "I meant no harm."

Sarn ignored the exchange. He was noting the width and depth of the trail—more of a wide road, now that he really looked at it. A road worn into the very rock from centuries of use. He stared up at the snow-capped mountains, wondering how rich a prize the caravan would make.

As if reading his thoughts, Badawi said, "My guess is that it's out of Caspan, Master." He pointed northwest, roughly indicating where Caspan would be. "The caravan master is no doubt heading across the Gods' Divide to Walaria." He pointed south across the mountains. "It's a journey of several thousand miles—going there and back, of course. As you no doubt have already supposed, Master, no merchant would travel so far if he weren't expecting to make a handsome profit for his efforts. Seize that caravan, Master, and you will possess a fortune."

Giff had been listening closely, realizing all the horse dealer had said was true. Added to these glad tidings was another fact that delighted him even more.

He clacked his talons to catch Sarn's attention and when he had it he said, quite simply, "Are we done with him now?"

Badawi gawped. "What do you mean, 'are we done with him now?'"

The two demons ignored him. "Actually, I really don't see any further use for him," Sarn said. "We've found what King Manacia wanted, plus what *we* wanted. And soon as we take the caravan we can return home."

"Done with who?" Badawi pressed. "Who do you mean, lords?"

"You promised I could kill him," Giff pointed out.

"Do you mean me?" Badawi said. Then he began to weep again. "Not me," he sobbed. "You *can't* mean me!"

Sarn pulled a huge, gem encrusted ring from a taloned hand. He tossed it to Giff, who plucked it out of the air.

"I'm buying my promise back," Sarn said. "I've had to put up with him more than you. I had to pretend I didn't completely loathe him." He gnashed his fangs. "It's not good for a demon's health to keep things inside that way."

"I'll do anything, Master," Badawi sobbed. "Anything."

Giff growled laughter and jammed the ring on his finger. "Consider the promise retrieved," he said.

Sarn kicked his mount closer to the sobbing Badawi. His steed's snout curled back in disgust at the human's smell. The beast snarled in fear, but Sarn steadied him by digging a heavy heel into his ribs.

"Look at me, human," the demon said.

"No, no, I won't look!" Badawi cried, trying to scrabble away.

"I said look!" Sarn roared.

Badawi sagged to the ground as if the demon's shout had been a blow. They he slowly looked up. Huge yellow eyes stared down at him. Sarn gestured and the horse dealer's body suddenly stiffened. Badawi had no will of his own, but he still had thoughts and he still had fear.

"Don't hurt me, Master," he shrieked.

"I don't intend to, human," Sarn answered. "I wouldn't foul my hands with your cowardly blood. No, you shall have the death you deserve, human. The death the gods must have decreed, or the idea would not have come so quickly into my head."

"Please, Master!" Badawi begged.

"Silence!" Sarn shouted.

Badawi was struck dumb.

"Take this knife," Sarn said, handing over an ornate dagger. Badawi's fingers, acting against his will, stretched out and took the knife.

Sarn pointed to the ground. "Dig your grave there. Make it deep, so no unsuspecting jackal will poison itself with your rotted corpse. And make it wide to contain your bloat."

Like a clockwork machine Badawi came to a crouch and started digging.

"When you're done, human," Sarn said, "climb into the grave and cut your guts out. I want you to do it slowly. To cause yourself as much pain as if I were doing the cutting."

He rode off laughing.

Badawi's mind screamed, "No, no, I won't do it!"

But he kept digging, gouging the hard ground with the knife, scooping up dirt and rock with bleeding fingers. He couldn't slow down, much less stop. And he knew once he did stop he'd have no choice but to carry out the rest of Sarn's sentence. As commanded, he'd take his own life—as slowly and painfully as a spirit possessed could manage.

A mad thought came to him. It was all because of a camel. That's when his luck first left him. When he fell in love with a camel and stole her for his own.

And he thought, but she was such a pretty animal, my Sava. And white, so white . . .
As white as the snows on the Gods' Divide.

*   *   *

Iraj returned to the cave several times over the next few days. He went alone, never announcing his intentions when he left or speaking about it when he returned. Although he never said what he did there, each time he emerged he seemed to stand taller, his bearing more confident and his eyes more commanding.

Safar only returned once and he also went alone. Late one night he relived the nightmare of the dancers who died in the volcanic eruption. After he calmed himself and his mind became clear he remembered something he'd found in the cave several visits ago. After checking that Iraj was asleep he went into the cave to the room with the stone shelf and old jars. In one corner was a shattered pot that had caught his interest because of all the ancient magical symbols painted on it. He'd laid out the shards on the floor in a vague attempt at reconstruction.

Safar held the torch high to get a closer look at the nearly completed puzzle. This time his interest wasn't drawn so much to the symbols, but to what the pot once represented. Which was a round jar shaped like the world with a small opening that had once held a stopper. The major features of the world had been displayed on the jar, consisting mostly of the oceans and the four turtle gods that bore the lands. Here, in the Middle Sea, was Esmir—which in the ancient tongues meant simply the land, or the earth. To the north was Aroborus, the place of the forests. To the south was Raptor, the land of the birds. Last of all was Hadin, land of the fires. Safar studied this arrangement in greater detail, remaking the pot in his mind. On the globe Hadin was on the other side of the world—directly opposite Esmir.

He bent to get a closer look at the large piece of shard that contained Hadin, actually a huge chain of islands rather than a single land mass. The largest island had a picture of a cone-shaped mountain with a monster's face. The monster was breathing fire. The memory of this piece of painted pottery was what had drawn Safar into the cave. He wondered now if the large island in Hadin was the place he'd seen in his vision. If vision it was.

He felt ignorant. He'd always prided himself on his mind, but now all his knowledge of the world and what made it seemed so insignificant he might as well have been an insect contemplating the heavens. He hungered to know more, which made him sad because he realized he'd reached the end of what Gubadan could teach him. And as Safar looked at the shattered glove it occurred to him that much of what he'd learned might be in error, or based on Gubadan's stirring myths. Even the old priest admitted, for instance, that there were no turtle gods carrying the continents. The lands floated on the oceans without assistance, he said. The turtle gods were symbols, not science, he said. Although he cautioned symbols sometimes hid inner meanings that might make science.

Safar determined the next time he traveled Walaria with his father he'd find books to broaden his knowledge—although he didn't have the faintest idea what types of books those might be. To start with, however, he could look for something that could tell him about the four continents. Particularly Hadin.

He reached for the shard containing Hadin and as soon as his fingers touched it his body tingled all over with that warm, honeyed sensation he'd felt the night when the fiery particles had rained from the sky. The feeling quickly vanished and all was normal again. He shook himself, wondering what had happened. He stared hard at the pot shard with its fiery mountain. No answer came. After a time he gave up and tucked the shard away into his shot pouch to be examined later.

He returned to the campsite and his blankets. He slept and this time he didn't dream.

Over the next few days he became uncomfortable in the grotto. Although he didn't show it, there was a buzz of magic and danger in the air that disturbed him. Finally he made an excuse for the two of them to get away for awhile. He told Iraj they needed to find meat for their cooking pot. Always eager for a hunt, Iraj agreed.

Leaving the goats and llama to graze, they wandered along snow-patched trails for hours. Safar felled a few mountain grouse with his sling and Iraj shot a hare with his bow. Safar teased him because he'd brought heavy arrows better suited for bear than rabbits and the creature was so torn up by the missile it was useless.

Iraj pretended to be hurt. "I just saved our lives, you ingrate. Didn't you see that mean look in its eyes? A man-eater if I ever saw one!"

"Eeek!" Safar shrieked. "A man-eating hare! Run! Run!"

And they both bounded down the path as if a tiger were after them.

An hour or so later they came to a promontory that overlooked the main caravan route. Passage through the Bride and Six Maids wasn't easy. It consisted of a complicated series of trails and switchbacks winding up from the desert to the first pass. The pass led to a rickety bridge—built, some claimed, by Alisarrian's engineers—that crossed to the next mountain. More passes and bridges joined into the final route, which traveled over the broad summit of the Sixth Maid, then dipped to catch the trail across the Bride herself and then down into Kyrania and beyond.

Safar had spent many an hour perched on that promontory watching the caravans. At the height of the season, when as many a dozen might be traveling, it was a wondrous sight. He'd once spotted four caravans moving along four different peaks at the same time. He'd never seen an ocean, but to Safar the caravans looked like a small fleet of ships sailing over a sea of clouds and snowdrifts. The Kyranians called the region the High Caravans, for it was said that in all the world there were no higher mountains that traders crossed.

As the two young men stood there that day gazing out at the snow-covered peaks, Safar felt sudden joy when he spotted a caravan, the first of the spring, moving down toward the Bride's Pass. He pointed it out to Iraj, who hadn't been in the mountains long enough to distinguish distant objects easily. As he marveled at it they could both hear the sound of jangling bells echoing strangely in the cold, dry air. Soon they could make out the small figures of people, some on foot, some mounted on horseback—following the heavily-laden llamas and camels that padded over the snow. A few large ox-drawn wagons completed the caravan.

"All the places they must have been," Iraj said dreamily, "and all the places they've yet to see. The very sound of those bells makes you want to join them, doesn't it Safar?"

"Why should it?" Safar said, a little sharply. "I'm happy here. Why would I want to live among strangers?"

Iraj gave him an odd look. "You have visions," he said, "but you don't dream?"

"Not of things like that," Safar answered. "I'm perfectly happy where I am. Oh, I've visited the city once or twice. My father sometimes goes to Walaria to sell his best pots. But whenever I went with him I was always anxious to get back as quickly as I could."

Iraj waved his hand at the caravan and the vista beyond. "But that's the *real* world out there, Safar, " he said. "Where great men determine events. And there are all sorts of mysterious people and things to see. Your valley is beautiful, I admit. But nothing happens here, or will ever happen. Don't you feel left out?"

"Never," Safar declared. "I have all I want here. And all I shall ever want."

Iraj shrugged, then said, "Let's go down to meet them. I've never talked to a caravan master before."

There was plenty of time left in the day so Safar had no reason to deny him. Also, as every Kyranian child knew, the first to meet a caravan were always rewarded with treats and small gifts. Safar's eyes swept the terrain, picking out a route that would intersect with the travelers at the edge of the Bride's Pass. He pointed the way and the two young men charged down to meet the caravan.

They were skirting a jumble of rock when motion caught Safar's eye. He grabbed Iraj's arm to stop him and looked closer.

A line of figures moved swiftly out of a ravine toward the caravan. They were traveling in a wide loop that kept cover between them and the caravan and Safar knew they were doing this purposely so they wouldn't be seen.

At first he thought they were bandits. He cupped his eyes so he could see better and the lead group jumped into view so clearly and so frighteningly that he cried out.

"What is it?" Iraj asked. He was peering at the figures, still not able to make them out.

"Demons!" Safar shouted. "They're going to attack the caravan!"

CHAPTER FIVE

A WIZARD IS BORN

As Giff watched the caravan crawl along the snowy pass, camel bells chiming, oxen grunting, horses blowing steamy blasts into the chill air, a sudden feeling of foreboding descended on him. He glanced at the other nine mounted demons waiting with him in ambush. They were tense, but professionally so, as they made last-minute inspections and adjustments to their weapons and gear. They were the best of Sarn's fiends with scores of successful raids to their credit.

Giff was not reassured.

He couldn't put a talon on it but it seemed to him that something wasn't quite right. He thought, I should have killed the human myself. It had been bad luck to let Sarn do it. He should have insisted on his rights. But then he thought, don't be so superstitious. You've always made your own luck. Besides, what could go wrong?

He studied the mounted soldiers guarding the pack animals and covered wagons that made up the caravan. The humans were well-armed and seemed skilled enough to cause alarm but this wasn't the source of Giff's worry. Sarn had sent their best scout into the caravan's encampment the night before to steal small items from each of the sleeping human soldiers. Sarn had used those items to make a spell that would confuse the soldiers and turn them into cowards when attacked.

The only defender who wouldn't be affected was the caravan master, a big brawny human Giff would dislike to meet in anything but an unequal fight. He slept apart from his men in a pavilion the scout couldn't approach without being discovered. Even so, Giff thought, when the attack came the caravan master would be quickly overwhelmed without his soldiers to support him.

The plan was simple enough: a double ambush. Giff and a small force would attack the caravan first. It would be a fierce, no mercy attack, designed to frighten the humans as much as to harm them. "Be as bloody and horrific as you can," Sarn had said. "Soften them well for me."

At that point Sarn, striking from another vantage point, would hit full force. The entire action shouldn't take more than a few minutes, Giff thought. Yes, it was a good plan. An artful plan that seemed to guarantee success. But why was it he still felt so uneasy?

As if he were being watched himself.

*　　　*　　　*

"They can't be demons," Iraj said. "You must be mistaken. It's forbidden for them to be here."

"Well, I guess nobody told them!" Safar snapped. "Look for yourself." He pointed at the monstrous figures hiding in ambush below. "What else could they be?"

Dazed, Iraj aped Safar, funneling his hands so he could see more clearly. His head jolted back as the full realization sunk in. Then he swiveled, taking in more of the scene.

"Hells!" he said. "You're right. And look! There's more! A second group—moving through that ravine."

Safar spotted them immediately. It was a much larger group than the first—possibly thirty demons or more. He watched them snake through a ravine with high, snow-packed walls. The ravine narrowed at the mouth and Safar saw the leader pull in his mount and signal the others to stop. The group paused there to reform its lines.

"I think I see what they're going to do," Iraj said. His tone was oddly casual as if he were commenting on an interesting tactic in a military text. "The first bunch will jump the caravan, while the others hold back. Then when the caravan soldiers are fully committed the rest will charge out of the ravine and roll them up."

Iraj dropped his hands. "It's a good trick," he said. "I'll have to remember it."

*　　　*　　　*

Sarn made certain his demons were ready, deploying them in short-winged cavalry ranks so the ravine's narrow mouth wouldn't diminish the force of his attack. Giff's position was opposite the ravine in a clump of frozen boulders. When the caravan moved between them Giff would strike first and then, when the panicked soldiers turned their backs to confront him, Sarn would leap out and close the pincer's jaws.

The bandit chief unlimbered his sword and made a few practice passes in the air. His blood sang as his demon heart pumped battle lust into his veins. In a few moments all the riches his scouts had told him were on the caravan would be his. Then he'd speed up the mountain, following the pass to Kyrania. He doubted it would difficult to eliminate everyone in such a remote village. Sarn surmised that the humans in Kyrania might be expecting the caravan. Some could even be on their way now to meet it, which meant he might not have enough time to wipe all traces of his demonly presence from the snows. King Manacia had commanded that no witnesses be left behind. So Sarn had to make it appear that bandits—human bandits—had hit the caravan. He'd do the same with Kyrania, perhaps even picking up a bit more booty in the process. Then he and his fiends could make their way home with nothing at their backs to worry them.

Sarn was already imagining the greeting awaiting him on his return. A hero ladened with so much loot that other bandit clans would clamor to join him. Better still, the king himself would be in his debt. Sarn was by now convinced King Manacia was planning an invasion of the human lands. An invasion this mission had just proved was possible.

He was wondering if he ought to press the king for some sort of noble-sounding title when a sudden uncomfortable thought occurred to him. Wasn't it Giff who'd asked if perhaps Manacia had lied about the shield he'd conjured to protect them from the curse of the Forbidden Desert? What if Sarn had been too quick to dismiss Giff's supposition? After this mission Sarn would be a much more important demon than before. For daring the Forbidden Desert and striking out at the hated humans he'd be a fiend to be reckoned with. And the king hadn't held his throne so long by being stupid, or by allowing potential rivals to live. He might consider Sarn as one of those rivals. In fact, King Manacia, who was a mighty wizard, might have foreseen such a possibility in his castings. In which case he'd want Sarn to be weakened from the start. One way to accomplish that would be to lie about the potency of his shield. Sarn might have done the same himself if he were in Manacia's place.

Another thing: what if the curse didn't kill right away? What if it allowed him to live long enough to return home with the information the king wanted? And afterwards he'd die a horrible, lingering death, made worse by the knowledge Manacia had never intended to reward him for his faithful service. It was not unlike the way Sarn had treated the human, Badawi. For the first time he felt a touch of empathy for the horse dealer.

Then he thought, you're being a fool, Sarn. Pre-battle jitters, that's all. If royal betrayal had been in the wind he would have sniffed it out at the start. The bandit chief considered himself a most devious demon who could show even a king a trick or two about the art of treachery.

Nerves steadied, all self-doubt conquered, Sarn peered out and saw the caravan nearing the mouth of the ravine.

The attack was about to begin.

His yellow eyes glowed in anticipation.

*　　　*　　　*

Safar watched the smaller group of demons brace for the charge. His mind was numb, his limbs oddly heavy and when he spoke his voice came in a croak.

"What will we do?"

There was nothing numb about Iraj. The tragedy about to unfold below seemed to have the opposite effect, charging him with an inner fire.

"Warn the caravan," Iraj said, eyes dancing, "What else?"

Before Safar could fully register the answer, Iraj burst out of their hiding place and bounded down the hill. His action swept away all of Safar's caution. Hot blood boiled over and without a second's hesitation he leaped forward to follow.

But as he scrambled down the steep hillside in Iraj's wake he thought, "My father's going to kill me."

It was a small caravan, spread out and weary from hard travel. As Safar drew closer he heard the harsh voice of the caravan master urging his men on.

"Your fathers were brainless curs," he was shouting. "Your mothers were lazy mongrel bitches. Come on, you dogs! Listen to Coralean! Only one more day's travel to Kyrania, I tell you. Then you can bite your fleas and lick your hairless balls all you like."

Safar heard a camel bawl and a driver curse its devil's nature. He also thought he heard the high-pitched voices of angry women. That was impossible, he thought. Women rarely traveled with the caravans.

He strained his aching lungs for air and in a burst of speed caught up to Iraj. They reached the caravan just as it crossed the mouth of the ravine. Three outriders spotted them first. Safar and Iraj raced toward the soldiers.

"Ambush!" Iraj shouted. "Ambush!"

The soldiers were slow to react. Their eyes were dull, their mouths gaping holes in frosted beards. But when Safar and Iraj ran up they suddenly came to life, drawing their horses back in fear. Safar realized with a shock they thought he and Iraj were the threat.

Safar desperately grasped the reins of the nearest horse. "Demons!" he screamed into the face of a dull-faced soldier. "Over there!"

He turned to point and saw monstrous figures storm out of the mist, sweeping in to crowd the caravan defenders closer to the ravine where the main force waited. Safar heard a demon war cry for the first time—a piercing, marrow-freezing ululation.

A series of images jumped out at him. He saw swords and axes raised high in taloned paws. Crossbows lifting to aim. Black bolts taking flight.

The soldier kicked at him—reining back sharply at the same time. The horse reared and Safar leaped aside to avoid its lashing front hooves. A heavy crossbow bolt caught the animal in the throat. It toppled over and Safar heard the soldier scream as the horse's weight crushed him. He'd never witnessed such agony before.

The other two soldiers turned their horses and raced away.

"Stand and fight!" Iraj cried after them. "Stand and fight!"

But his shouts only seemed to add to their panic.

"Ambush!" Safar heard them scream. "Ambush!"

The soldiers piled into the main caravan, knocking over men and animals alike. Then the air was shattered by the shrieks of what Safar realized *had* to be women. Their screams mingled with the bawling of beasts and the desperate cries of men fleeing death.

Safar and Iraj ran into the center of the chaos. Pack animals charged about dragging their drivers and strewing their loads into the snow. Camels careened into wagons, tumbling them over. Oxen tangled their traces. A half dozen soldiers milled around, striking hysterically at anything that came near, as if llamas and camels were the enemy.

A huge man—the caravan master—thundered up on his horse, waving his sword and shouting orders. Then, from behind, Safar heard the demons howl closer and then the distinct meaty thunk of steel cutting into flesh. Followed by the screams of wounded men.

It was his first battle and an odd calm descended on him. Everything seemed to move slowly and yet quickly at the same time.

He saw gore stain the snow.

He smelled fear's foul musk mixed with the powerful odor of demons gone berserk.

He heard men choke and die.

Then a demon loomed over him, rising high in the saddle to strike with his sword. The image seemed more dream than real and Safar became intensely curious, noting the pale green of the demon's skin, the studs on his leather armor, the short snout and sharp fangs and the small, pointed ears. As Safar studied him Gubadan's training took hold. His mind became clear, his breathing slow.

He slipped to the side as the sword sliced down. He heard the demon grunt in surprise as he missed.

Safar jabbed at him with his staff, but the demon's blade swept in and back and Safar found himself holding nothing but a mass of splinters. He gaped at his now useless weapon, dumbfounded. The only reason he didn't die then was that the demon kicked his mount forward to meet a charging caravan guard. He cut the man down, whirled to find another and plunged out of Safar's view.

Safar heard shrill human cries and turned to see two demons attacking an ox-drawn wagon. They reared their mounts and the beasts' claws ripped away the canvas, revealing a writhing tangle of frightened women. They screamed and tried to fend the demons off.

One creature grabbed a girl by the hair and charged away, howling gleefully as he dragged her through the snow by long black tresses. Frozen rocks shredded her garments and for the first time Safar saw the naked limbs of a young woman who was not of his village. She cried out as a rock tore her leg and Safar found himself running forward to face the demon with nothing more than a shattered wooden staff.

Safar was not a killer by nature. He was raised to believe all life was precious, including that of the animals killed for the table. But at that moment he was stricken with a murderous fury—triggered as much by the young woman's humiliation as the threat to her life.

As he charged forward words came to him—the words of a spell. And he chanted:

> *I am strong.*
> *You are weak.*
> *Hate is my spear.*
> *May it pierce*
> *Your coward's heart.*

In his mind the ruined staff became that spear. It was perfectly formed—heavy, but balancing easily in his hand. He reached back, then hurled the staff with all his strength. Before his eyes he saw the splintered wood reform itself in mid-flight.

And he had caused it to happen. Somehow he caused the splintered wood to become hard black metal. He caused the tip to broaden and become killing sharp. He caused the weapon he'd made to fly straight and true. And he caused the spear to pierce the leather armor and thick demon skin and then burst that demon's heart.

The demon fell, releasing the girl. His mount veered wide but the force of the charge carried her body forward and she slammed into Safar. His breath whooshed out. As the two tumbled into the snow together the girl flung her arms around him, fastening him in a grip made strong by fear.

Safar's breath returned and he tore away from her grasp and leaped up. The scene was madness. Demons were hewing left and right, killing men and animals without discrimination. But in that madness Safar saw the caravan master had managed to rally a small group that was beginning to fight back. His immense body weaved this way and that as he dodged blows and kicked his horse toward one of the demons. Safar gasped as another demon charged in from the side, bearing down on the caravan master with a battle ax. Before the demon could strike Safar saw a tall figure leap from a felled wagon.

It was Iraj!

His legs scissored open as he vaulted onto the saddle behind the demon, then closed to grip the mount's flanks with the ease of a practiced plains rider.

Iraj flung one arm around the demon's head, heaving to draw it back—and he plunged a dagger into the exposed throat.

It was then Safar learned that demons die hard.

The creature gouted bright red blood, but reached for Iraj, talons scything out. Iraj somersaulted off the saddle just in time, landing on his feet and drawing his scimitar as he came up. The wounded demon rolled off and rushed at Iraj, fouling the snow with his bloodspray.

Iraj stepped forward to meet him but his foot slipped and he fell face forward. The demon was on him, raising his ax to kill his fallen enemy before his own life drained away.

Once again all time slowed for Safar. This time it wasn't only magic that came to his aid. His sling was suddenly in one hand. With the other he was withdrawing a heavy clay ball from his shot pouch.

Then time jumped and the demon's ax was descending.

Time froze again as Safar loaded his sling and swung it about his head.

He let loose just before the demon's blade struck. The ball caught the beast full in the mouth and Safar cursed, for he'd aimed at the killing spot between the demon's eyes. His fingers suddenly turned numb, betraying him as he fumbled for another clay ball. But it wasn't necessary.

The monster sagged back . . . slowly, so slowly . . . then toppled over into the snow.

The demon tried to struggle up on one elbow. Safar drew his knife and raced over to finish him off.

But then the demon looked at him, freezing him with his strange yellow eyes.

"I should have killed the human myself," the demon said. "Bad luck all around."

Then blood burst from his mouth and he fell back, dead.

Too fired by the battle to wonder what the creature meant, Safar rushed over to Iraj to help him to his feet. As he bent down, back unprotected, a huge shadow fell over him. He looked up, thinking he'd see the face of death. Relief flooded in when he saw a bearded human face peering at him instead of a demon's. And it was an ordinary horse the man sat upon, not a monster with fangs and claws.

The caravan master's gaze went from Safar to Iraj.

"Thank you for my life, young fellow," he said to Iraj. "If the gods are kind and Coralean survives this day you will learn just how much I value my skin."

Then he spurred his mount back into the action. But now the winds of fortune had shifted and it was the demons who were being routed and slain.

Safar's relief lasted only the length of time it took for Iraj to leap to his feet.

"There's more, Safar!" he cried. "It's not over yet!"

And Safar remembered the other—much larger—force waiting in the ravine.

No sooner had memory wormed its cold way through the mud of his confusion then he heard the shrill ululation announcing the second attack. His head shot up and he saw the demons beginning to pour out of the mouth of the ravine.

"Stop them!" Iraj shouted.

Safar gaped. Had his friend gone mad? How was he supposed to accomplish that?

"You can do it!" Iraj said. "I *know* you can!"

Then all questions and fear dissolved and he saw quite clearly that Iraj was right. He could stop them.

Once again he gripped his sling. Once again he reached into his pouch. But instead of a heavy ball his fingers touched the pot shard he'd taken from the cave. The shard that bore the picture of Hadin, the land of fire. A shock of magic clamped his fingers closed.

Instinctively letting the moment rule, Safar didn't fight the magic. He drew the shard out and carefully inserted it into his sling. He swung the weapon about his head, eyes searching for a target. He saw an immense demon leading the charge out of the ravine. But it wasn't that demon he wanted. One death would accomplish nothing. He had to kill them all.

His eyes were drawn up and once again he noted the heavy snow clinging to the sides of the ravine. In his mind he also saw the rotten slate beneath that snow. And then the mass of boulders hanging above the frozen incline the ravine bisected. He knew what to do.

Whirling the sling, Safar pictured the pottery shard in his mind, chanting:

You were made in fire
And within you fire
Yet remains.
It grows from spark
To finger flame
To kiln fire.
And now I release you . . .
Fly free!
Fly free!

And he let loose the missile.

*   *   *

When Sarn led his demons out to fight he knew he'd already failed.

Moments after Giff had attacked a sudden blast of sorcery had seared the air. It wasn't directed toward him, but it was so strong it rasped his senses. Fear iced his heart and he thought, there must be a wizard with the caravan. How could I have missed him?

Then he'd seen Giff go down and a human—a mere stripling at that—standing over him. Sarn goggled. This was the wizard?

But there was no mistaking the aura of raw power radiating from the stripling. It was so strong it had swept away Sarn's spell of cowardice and the human soldiers were already rallying. One part of him insisted this was impossible. No human was capable of such magic. The other part took stock, recognized that impossible or not there the boy stood with all the magic he needed at his command.

Sarn saw instantly his only hope was to strike while an element of surprise still remained. Any moment now the caravan master and his soldiers would realize a threat still remained in the ravine. With the young wizard's help Sarn and his demons would be trapped in this all-too-perfect ambush.

If he were lucky he'd merely be killed. If not, he'd be captured. And he'd be damned if let himself fall into the foul hands of a human.

So he made the signal. Heard his fiends shrill their battle song. And he booted his mount forward into the attack.

As he charged from the ravine Sarn saw that the stripling wizard was already in action, whirling a loaded sling about his head and searching for a target. Just then the boy looked directly at Sarn. A chill scuttled up the demon's spine. It was as if he were being measured for the grave.

Then the human let lose and Sarn laughed because he saw immediately that the human was off his mark. The missile was arcing high into the air instead of towards him. Wizard or not, he thought, the boy was a coward. Fear had spoiled his aim.

Then the missile sailed over his head, a strong current of sorcery rippling the air, and his laughter was choked off.

The boy was no coward. His aim had been true.

Sarn's last thought was that Giff had been right. The king *had* lied.

Now that lie was about to cost Sarn his life.

*   *   *

Safar smiled as the shard sailed over the lead demon's head.

Then, in midflight it exploded into a ball of flame. The back-blasting heat was so

57

intense it scorched his face. But he didn't shrink away. Instead he watched the fiery ball loft upward toward the big snowy brow that frowned over the mouth of the ravine. It sailed farther than he normally had strength to fling any object. He noted this with casual interest, not amazement.

Safar felt as if he were standing several feet away from his own body, calmly studying his own reactions as well as the course of the flaming missile. His separate self found it oddly amusing to see the ball of magical fire slam into the frozen ridge. It was even more amusing to note the wild joy in the boy's eyes who had made it.

A explosion shook the ridge and with calculated interest Safar pondered whether the force of the blast would be enough.

As the frozen mass began peel off, he thought, Hmm. Yes, it was. . . . But will it have the effect I desire?

The mass crashed down onto still another ridge below.

And Safar thought, The snow and ice will shatter. But what of the shale? And if so, will the weight of the whole create a still larger force?

An avalanche was his answer.

Shale and ice and snow thundered down on the demons, moving so fast it overtook them in midcharge.

The boiling wave of snow and ice and rock swallowed them from behind, gobbling them up with an awful hunger. Then all was obscured by an immense white cloud.

Safar stood there, waiting. Then the avalanche ended and a silence as thick as the cold blinding cloud settled over him.

The mist cleared and the only thing Safar could see in the sun's sudden bright light was a broad white expanse running to the edge of a blank-faced cliff that had once been cut by a deep ravine.

Safar nodded, satisfied. The experiment had gone quite well, he thought. Then, still in his mode of the cold observer, he began to wonder about himself. The boy who'd just killed all those living beings. They were demons, of course, and deserved to die. Still.

Still.

Then someone was pounding his back and he turned to find Iraj, pounding, and was babbling congratulations of some sort. The first emotion that thawed Safar's numb interior was annoyance.

He pushed at Iraj's arm. "Quit that," he said. "It hurts."

Iraj stopped. Safar was surprised to see awe as well as joy on his friend's face.

"You did it, Safar!" Iraj shouted. "You killed them all!"

The numbness thawed more and Safar was suddenly frightened. "Quiet," he said. "Someone will hear."

"Who cares?" Iraj said. "Everyone should hear!"

Safar clutched Iraj's arm. "Promise you will say nothing," he pleaded.

Iraj shook his head, bewildered by the request.

"Promise me," Safar insisted. "Please!"

After a long moment Iraj nodded. "I promise," he said. "You're insane to ask it, but I promise just the same."

Then Safar was struck by a wall of weariness that seemed as great as the avalanche. Iraj caught him as he collapsed and then darkness sucked him down and he knew nothing more.

*　　　*　　　*

Terrible nightmares inhabited that darkness.

Safar dreamed he was pursued by demon riders across a rocky plain. He ran as fast as he could, leaping ravines and even canyons, dodging falling boulders, bounding over thundering avalanches. The sky was aboil with storm clouds and the sun dripped on the landscape, turning it blood red. And no matter how fast he ran the demon riders were faster.

Suddenly he was naked. He was still running, but now shame mingled with his fright. The demon riders converged on him, cutting in from the sides. Their shrill ululations drove every thought from his head until only fear remained. The demons hurled their spears and Safar saw they were spears of crackling lightning. They struck, burning and jolting his body with awful, painful shocks.

Then the demons were gone and Safar was running on soft grass and the sun was a cheery yellow, the breeze gentle on his naked flesh. He came to a hollow where Naya and the other goats gamboled and drank from the sweet waters of a spring. His mouth was suddenly dry and he knelt among the goats to quench a burning thirst.

And Naya said to him, "What have you done, boy?"

"Nothing Little Mother," Safar answered.

But she stuck a lightning bolt in his heart and the lie hurt almost more than he could bear.

The other goats gathered around, baying accusations.

"He's been out killing," one said.

"Our Safar?" another asked.

"Yes," said another. "*Our* Safar has been killing."

"Is this true, boy?" Naya asked, disgust in her tones.

"They were only demons, Little Mother," he answered.

"Shocking," the other goats said.

"But they were attacking the caravan," he protested.

"Oh, Safar," Naya said. "I'm so ashamed of you." She butted him, knocking him down. Sharp stones jabbed into his buttocks. "I suppose you used magic," Naya said.

"I couldn't help it, Little Mother," he confessed. "Honestly I couldn't."

Then Naya rose on her hind legs and became Quetera, his pregnant sister. She was wearing a long white gown, swollen at the belly with new life.

"Naya says you've been out killing," his sister said. "And using magic to do it."

He didn't answer.

"Look at me, Safar," his sister said.

"I can't," he said. "I'm ashamed."

He pointed down. There was a demon's body at her feet.

"Did you do this, Safar?" she asked.

"I had no choice, Quetera!" he cried. "They were killing people." He pointed at the demon. "He was going to kill the girl."

Quetera's face suddenly turned kindly. "Poor Safar," she said. "Such a gentle lad. But now violence and death have found you. And they may never let you go."

Safar groaned and collapsed on the ground. He heard his sister come closer.

He smelled her perfume as she knelt down to comfort him. "Let me take you home, Safar," she said.

He tried to get up but he couldn't rise. His limbs were numb and all he could do was groan.

Then cool water touched his temples. A soft wet cloth wiped his face and he felt as if all his sins were being sponged away.

And he was thirsty. By the gods he was thirsty! He opened his mouth. Not water, but cool milk dribbled in and he lapped it like a hungry kitten.

"Safar," a voice said. It was gentle and as soothing as that milk. "Safar," it said again.

He floated out of the blackness to find a lovely face peering down at him. Dark, almond-shaped eyes full of sweet concern. Long black hair tumbling down like a silken scarf. Lips red and ripe, smoothed into a smile displaying teeth as white as the Snow Moon.

"Who are you?" he mumbled, weak.

The smile became sweeter still. "I'm Astarias," she said.

"Do I know you?" he asked.

She laughed. It sounded like distant music. "You do, now," she said. "I'm the girl whose life you saved."

"Then you're not my sister," he said.

More laugher. Puzzled laughter. "No, I'm not your sister. I'm Astarias."

"Well, thank the gods for that," he said.

And he slipped into a deep, peaceful sleep.

CHAPTER SIX

THE COVENANT

When the caravan rolled into Kyrania Safar learned what it was like to be a hero.

He and Iraj rode in the lead with Coralean, mounted on the caravan master's finest horses. They were high-stepping steeds with painted shells and beads woven into their manes and tails. Behind them, guarded by the surviving soldiers was the caravan itself, bells jouncing, colorful banners waving. The air was pungent with the odor of precious goods from far away places. A boy ran in front carrying a demon's head mounted on a stake. The creature's yellow eyes were open and staring, snout gaping to display many rows of bloody teeth.

Safar felt like a participant in a strange, barbaric dream. The battle seemed distant, unreal. Yet there was the gory head bobbing in his view. His memories of the fight were vague, adding to the dreamlike quality. He felt as if it were not him but another who had cast the great spell that brought the avalanche down. There was no sign of the power he recalled coursing through his body. That morning, before the caravan set out, Safar had quietly attempted to tap some of that power. But it was either denied him, or, he'd thought, perhaps it had never existed at all. Maybe the avalanche had been a coincidence. Perhaps it was an accident of nature that killed the demons and not Safar Timura.

They rounded the last bend and excitement rushed in and all introspection vanished. Safar saw one of the Ubekian brothers posted at the old stone arch marking the village entrance. With much satisfaction he saw the bully's eyes widen in fear when he spotted the demon's head. Then he whirled and sprinted out of sight, crying the news of the caravan's arrival.

Iraj cantered close to Safar, face beaming with pride and he pointed to the gay ribbons festooning all the trees that lined the road. He started to speak but then the sound of glad music caterwauled from up ahead.

Coralean's smile was a bow of pleasure in his beard. "It is good," he boomed, "that your friends and family are giving you a proper reception. A true welcome for young heroes."

In the two days since the battle the people in the caravan had tended their wounded, repaired the damage and had bathed and wrapped their dead in white linen sheets. The bodies were loaded into a wagon for later funeral ceremonies. While Safar slept off the effects of the battle, Coralean had sent word to Kyrania, assuring everyone their young men were safe and unharmed. Iraj had been clear-headed enough to tell Coralean of the herd left in the mountain meadow and the messenger had carried that news with him as well so a boy could be sent to fetch the goats and llama.

When Safar had finally awakened there was no sign of Astarias. Iraj reported she'd been returned to the wagon with the other women. Safar had pined for her, although he'd been shocked when Coralean had informed him the women were being taken to the brothels of Walaria where they'd be sold.

"If it were not for you and your brave friend," he'd told Safar, "Coralean's wives would not only have lost their loving husband, but would have been impoverished as well—without even the price of a bowl of barley and rice to stave off starvation. As for the fair Astarias, she and her sisters in seduction squabbled so heatedly over who would care for you they gave poor Coralean a headache that could only be treated with a large jar of brandy."

He'd rubbed sore temples, groaning. "But the cure, as always, has afflicted your humble servant anew. I fear Coralean must apply yet more brandy to treat this malady." Then he'd winked at Safar. "Astarias surprised us all with her fire," he said. "She may be small, my boy, but she's as fierce as a desert lynx."

Then he'd leaned closer to confide: "Coralean was worried that after they'd survived the demon attack with little harm, the gods would mock me. And the women would then be damaged in a silly harem fight. I have a large investment in those women, you know. Not only their purchase price, mind you, but I spent much Coralean silver assuring they were fresh and free of all diseases. And I gave a witch a fat purse to cast spells that will make them inventive and full of passion for any man who pays to be taken into their embrace."

Safar had flushed, angry at such treatment of Astarias and her sisters. Coralean mistook his angry coloring for a village boy's blush from hearing of such worldliness.

"You'll learn of these things soon enough, my boy," he'd said. "As a matter of fact we should consider furthering your education soon. I'll make your schooling in such matters my personal responsibility. I, Coralean, do so swear. And there is not a man who knows me who will dispute that the word of Coralean is sounder than any coin a king has minted."

His promise echoed in Safar's thoughts as they approached Kyrania. What the caravan master intended, he didn't know. He had several guesses, however, that had him squirming like a fly in a honeyed dilemma. If Safar was right, one part of his nature was insulted that Coralean thought so little of him. The shameful human side of him was powerfully intrigued.

Then all thoughts were swept away when Safar saw the huge gathering at the outskirts of the village. All of Kyrania had turned out. The musicians played horns and bagpipes and drums and the whole village cheered when they saw the caravan. Safar's family was in front with Gubadan and the village headman and elders. Everyone was dressed in their best costumes. Boys stood tall, chests puffed out, trying to look like men. The girls wore flowers in their hair and blew kisses as Safar and Iraj came near.

All goggled and pointed excitedly when they saw the gory head. "It's true, then," a man said, "that the demons got out!"

"Too bad for them they met our lads, eh?" said another. "This'll teach them to stay where they belong."

Coralean called a halt. He raised his hand for silence and the crowd hushed. He rose up in his stirrups so all could hear.

"Greetings, O gentle people of Kyrania," he said. "I am Coralean of Caspan. We meet in circumstances filled with both joy and fear." He pointed at the head. "There is the fear. But you will notice, no doubt, that this particular demon is taking a long rest on a stake made of good Kyranian wood." There were chortles in the crowd. "This one and his companions," Coralean continued, "defied the curse of the Forbidden Desert. Now they have their reward. To dance in the Hells for all eternity."

Laughter and nods followed that statement.

"And now I will speak of joy. And it is joy, not fear, that fills Coralean's heart. For more years than it is comfortable to consider Coralean has heard other caravan masters speak of the warmth and hospitality of the people of Kyrania. My brothers of the road are notorious liars, as I'm sure you all know. But the tales were so frequent and seemed so little exaggerated that Coralean came to believe they were true. So it was with much anticipation of meeting you all that I undertook this trading journey. The Coralean business has never taken him to this side of the Bride and her Maids before.

"During the long, hard months of travel Coralean thought of your peaceful valley many times. When we were thirsty, Coralean dreamed of the sweet waters of your lake. When we were hungry, Coralean took comfort in visions of your fat lamb kabobs and beds of barley spiced with oil from your olive trees and garlic from your gardens. When my men despaired, Coralean cheered them with tales of your charming village. 'All will be well,' I told them, 'when we reach Kyrania.' Yet how was Coralean to know that not only were the tales true, but Kyrania had more than mere hospitality to offer?"

He indicated Iraj and Safar. "She also has brave young men of whom she can rightly boast. Young men whose like I've never had the thrill to see. And Coralean, you should know, has seen much in his long life. Others I've met are more full of bluster than true courage. Such men would most certainly have kept their silence and slipped away when they saw the demons creeping up on a party of strangers. And Coralean and his companions would have been doomed.

"But these two gave not a thought for their own safety. They risked their lives when they charged out to give warning. Then they turned to fight the demons as they rode down on us. Why, none of us would be alive today if they had not taken such a brave course.

"This one—" he pointed to Iraj—"saved Coralean's life with an act of bravery and skill rarely witnessed. While this one—" he pointed to Safar—"joined in the fray as if he were warrior born, instead of a gentle village lad. And then, wonder of all wonders, the gods of Kyrania personally intervened. They caused a great hill of snow and ice to fall on our attackers. Proving that these mountains and this valley are the most blessed in all the world. For it is here that the curse brought these demon interlopers down.

"After we have honored our dead, sending their souls back to the gods who made them, it is Coralean's fondest wish to reward these young men. And to reward Kyrania, as well. The gods willing, we will have a feast tomorrow night. A feast like no other Kyrania has ever seen. And all that is eaten and drunk shall be my gift to you. I, Coralean, do so swear!"

The crowd roared approval and crowded close to praise him and wish him well. In the confusion Safar slid off his horse and into his family's arms. His mother cried, patting him all over to make certain he was uninjured. His father clasped his shoulder in the strong grip men of Kyrania reserve for those they honor. His sisters wept and crowded around him.

Quetera slipped in to hug Safar when his mother stepped away. As he leaned over her child-swollen belly to kiss her she laughed at the awkward embrace.

"I'm so proud of you, Safar," she said.

Safar was surprised at her reaction. His dream had been so real he'd been braced for a scolding. Instead of thanking her, he blurted out that he was sorry.

"Why should be you be, Safar?" she asked. "Why should you be sorry for bringing such honor to our family?"

Iraj heard the exchange and pressed through to join them. "He's just tired." He chuckled. "Spearing demons is weary work."

Everyone laughed as if this were the greatest jest they'd ever heard. His words were passed along through the crowd of well-wishers and soon everyone was roaring.

That was another lesson Safar learned that day: that success could turn a man's every word into the purest gold. Which was something no wizard, living or dead, could accomplish.

*   *   *

The next day everyone gathered at the temple for the funeral ceremonies. Gubadan wore yellow robes of mourning, while the villagers tied yellow sashes around their waists and streaked their cheeks with hearth dust tears. The bodies of the seven dead caravan soldiers were laid out on a raft decorated with the red streamers favored by Tristos, the god who oversees the Kingdom of the Dead.

While a drum hammered a slow beat, Gubadan prayed over the poor strangers who had come among them and sprinkled their white-wrapped bodies with holy oil. When the sun reached its highest point, Coralean—dressed in the flowing golden robes with the scarlet fringe of his kinsmen—stepped forward to light the oil-soaked kindling piled around the corpses. Then Iraj and Safar used long ribbon festooned poles to push the raft out into the lake. The current caught it, carrying it into the middle. Everyone prayed as thick smoke made a dark pathway in the sky. There was no wind that day and the smoke was carried high, curling under a bank of glowing white clouds, then streaming away in pale gray ribbons. Later, all said that this was a lucky sign.

As Safar bowed his head in prayer he chanced a look and saw the women from the caravan gathered in a quiet group. They wore heavy robes and their faces were veiled, so at first he couldn't make out Astarias. Then he saw a small figure slip her veil aside and a single eye peeped out. The eye found him. It was dark, with long flowing lashes. Safar smiled. A slender white hand fluttered at him. Then the veil was drawn back. Safar turned away, heart hammering, loins burning from the promise he thought he'd seen in that eye and fluttering hand.

Gubadan nudged him. It was time to lead the others in the funeral song.

The musette player set a slow tempo and one by one each instrument joined in. Safar lifted his head and let the clear, sad notes pour forth:

> *Where are our dream brothers?*
> *Gone to sweet-blossomed fields.*
> *Where are our dream brothers?*
> *Asleep in the Gods' high meadow.*
> *Our mortal hearts*
> *Yearn to follow their souls.*

The words carried far on the balmy air. And when the last notes fell, all were weeping.

Later, Coralean and the village leaders met to discuss the mysterious appearance of the demons. Safar and Iraj were allowed to attend the gathering in the large, colorful tent the caravan master had erected in the caravanserai.

Safar had never seen such luxury. The floor was covered with many layers of thick, expensive carpets. Pillows and cushions were spread around a central fire, where a servant tended a pot of steaming brandy. All manner of fruit bobbed on top and as the servant stirred the pot it gave off an odor so heavy Safar felt a little drunk from breathing the air. Curtains divided the tent into rooms and on one side Safar saw the shadows of the courtesans moving behind the thin veil, coming close so they could listen in.

"Here is Coralean's view of the situation," the caravan master said. "The demons who attacked us were outlaws of the worst and most foolish kind. Their actions may even end up being a favor to us, for when they fail to return all demons will know the price that must be paid for defying the laws of the Gods."

There were murmurs of agreement from the elders.

"Then what shall we do about it?" Coralean said. "What is our next step? Coralean asks this, believing it would be best if we acted in concert."

"Alert the authorities, of course," Gubadan said.

Coralean's bushy brows lofted. "Do you really think so, holy one?" he asked. He looked around at the others. "And who, after all, are these authorities? Coralean owes no king his allegiance. He is his own man."

Buzal, the headman, who at eighty was the oldest of the group, said, "Kyrania makes its own laws. No one rules us." He indicated Gubadan. "Our priest has superiors, which is only natural." Buzal grinned, displaying dark, rock-hard gums. "But I don't think they talk together much. I'd guess that they barely remember if he exists."

Gubadan stroked his beard, then nodded in unembarrassed agreement. "We're far away," he said. "And the temple isn't considered important. Still, don't we have a duty to warn others?"

"That's a load of goat droppings," Foron, the village smithy, broke in. "Meaning no offense, of course. What's to warn? The demons are dead and stinking. No more are likely to come. And that's that. The tale is told."

"But why shouldn't we tell others?" Gubadan asked. "What would be the harm?"

Coralean harrumphed and all turned to see what he had to offer. "I do not know these parts," the caravan master said. "This is the first time the Coralean business has carried me over these mountains to the markets of Walaria and beyond. It cost me much to buy the necessary maps from my brother merchants. Even if this first journey proves profitable beyond my wildest estimates, it will take many such journeys before Coralean's initial investment is repaid."

He shook his great, shaggy head. "Even so," he said, "if Coralean were a lesser man this incident might give me pause. I might never dare such an undertaking again. And I know my brother caravan masters well enough to say with some confidence that they would feel the same if they suddenly thought these mountains had become unsafe."

There were murmurs among the men. It would be disastrous if Coralean reported such a thing. All trade over the Gods' Divide would cease. And more than just Kyrania would suffer. Life could become very bleak.

"Not only would there be no more caravans crossing," Safar's father said to Gubadan, "but there'd be no more pilgrims."

The old priest winced. Everyone knew how much he depended on the donations of the faithful who visited the Goddess Felakia's temple and holy lake.

"Yes," he said, "I can see the wisdom in your words, Khadji. However, what if we are mistaken and these demons are not the only ones? We are cut off here from the rest of the world. News travels slowly. What if others have been plagued by demons? Our silence could end up being an unnecessary and dangerous decision."

Iraj cleared his throat. All looked at him. He flushed at the attention, then emboldened himself to speak before the elders.

"Forgive me, sirs," he said. "As you know, I made a long journey not many months ago, passing through Walaria on the way. And I heard nothing in the market place of demons . . . or any other dangers, for that matter, other than the usual tales of marauding bandits."

The men listened to Iraj quite carefully and with deep respect. Safar thought it ironic that only a few days before many villagers had gone out of their way to avoid Iraj, fearing the trouble he might bring from the outside world. Now he was a hero because he'd turned back a threat from the outside.

Gubadan gently broke in to explain Iraj's background—carefully skirting the issue that he was hiding out from some of his own tribe. However, Coralean immediately caught on that although demons might not be riding about at will, there were other troubles to be considered.

"May the name of Coralean be bandied about in the company of swine, if I'm wrong," the caravan master said, "But from what your wise priest just said, it sounds to me like the south is about to become a permanent battle ground for warring clans. This would almost be as bad for trade as the demons."

"Not if *I* have anything to say about it," Iraj blurted. Then he turned as red as a ripe apple for making such a seemingly foolish statement.

Coralean studied him for a long moment. Then he smiled. "After hearing of your background I now fully understand where you got your fire," he said. "You didn't learn it here, that's for certain."

He made a soothing gesture to the rest of gathering. "I cast no doubts on the courage of the men Kyrania," he said. "Your own Safar has proven there is steel in your spines. But I know you do not claim to be warriors. Which this young man—" he indicated Iraj—"was surely bred to be." There were mutters of agreement from the men. "It's also my guess," the caravan master said, "that you are the son of a chieftain."

Iraj bowed his head, not saying anything, while Gubadan tried to leap in to save his secret. But Coralean only laughed and shrugged his shoulders. "You needn't reveal more," he said. "Something is going on, or you may call Coralean the son of an ass who mated with a dog who doesn't know from one minute to the next whether he will bray or bark."

He leaned closer to Iraj. "I'll tell you this, my brave young warrior. If you should ever need the help of Coralean, you have only to ask."

When he said that Safar learned it doesn't necessarily take a magical vision to see through the disguise of a future king. A canny merchant can do just as well—and without disturbing the serenity of his dreams.

Iraj lifted his head to return Coralean's curious stare. His lips lifted slightly for a brief smile and then he nodded. This was a promise he would long remember. A silent understanding passed between the two. When the time came—and there was no doubt it would—not only would Iraj ask, but he would repay the caravan master many times over for any assistance he gave.

Coralean turned to others. "Is it agreed, then?" he asked. "We say nothing of this incident. Correct?"

There was a whispered discussion among the elders. Then Buzal said, "What of your men?" He pointed at the curtain that divided the room from the harem. "And the women?

Can you assure us of their silence?"

"My men obey me in all things," Coralean said. "There's no need for worry in that quarter. As for the women, well, Coralean will tell you a little secret of the courtesan trade. Before I deliver these girls to their new masters each will drink a Cup of Forgetfulness. They will have no memory of their past. No reason to pine for home and family and friends. This makes for a most pliable and happy bed slave. No weeping to dampen the ardor of their masters. And in this case, no tales of demons to disturb their dreams."

The men snickered and then relaxed. Carnal jests were exchanged and there was much manly guffawing and knee-slapping. Only Safar was horrified at this casual dismissal of Astarias and her sisters. He glanced over at his father and saw that Khadji had the same knowing look in his eyes as the others. The same flushed and swollen features.

Then Coralean had his servant dip out hot bowls of brandy punch to be passed around. They were quickly emptied and refilled several times. Soon the talk became louder, the men's voices deepening as they recounted the bold adventures of their youth. Coralean held forth for more than an hour, telling every detail of the fight that he'd witnessed. The men murmured in appreciation when he told of how Safar had fought the demons—slaying the beast who took Astarias with a splintered staff that he'd wielded like a war spear. But there were loud gasps at Iraj's courage when he'd rescued Coralean, leaping on the demon's steed like the greatest of plains warriors, testing his strength against a more powerful enemy and finally cutting a path in his throat so the demon's soul could flee.

Safar looked over at Iraj and smiled, grateful he'd kept his promise. But Iraj frowned and made a motion, asking if it were finally time to tell the tale as it had really happened. Safar shook his head—a firm no. Iraj's eyes flickered, wondering why Safar was happy to allow him the greatest praise when Safar deserved much more.

Iraj leaned close, whispering, "Are you certain?"

Safar's answer was a lifted brandy bowl and a loud call for a toast to honor the deeds of his brave friend. It was the first toast he'd ever made in adult company. And all hailed Iraj Protarus, the young man Safar knew would someday be king.

After that everyone became a little drunk. It was another first for Safar. Relief mixed with fuddlement and he was suddenly very happy. He became happier still when Coralean began handing out the gifts.

First he told the elders that he would pay double for any goods, services or animals he purchased during his stay in Kyrania. Then he had his servants bring out heaping baskets of gifts. He asked the men if they would be so kind as to distribute them to the villagers. For each of the elders he had a purse of silver. For every man in the village there were small sacks of tobacco and a single silver coin. For every woman there were vials of perfume and little baubles to string as jewelry or to sew on their clothing. For every child there were ginger sweets as well as a copper coin.

Finally he came to Safar and Iraj.

"Coralean has thought long on this, my young friends," he said. "I have other presents I will give you both a bit later." He snorted. "Money, of course. But what is money, lads? Coins have value only because we all agree to give them such. I have a few pleasures in mind—yet you will have pleasures aplenty in the long lives before you. But I wanted to give each of you something special. A gift you will always remember Coralean by.

"First, my friend Iraj . . ." He took out a black velvet pouch. Iraj's eyes sparkled as Coralean withdrew a small golden amulet. It was a horse—a wondrously formed steed dangling from a glittering chain. "Some day," Coralean said, "you will see the perfect horse. It will be a steed above all steeds. A true warrior's dream, worth more than a kingdom to men who appreciate such things. The beast will be faster and braver than any animal you could imagine. Never tiring. Always sweet-tempered and so loyal that if you fall it will charge back into battle so you might mount it again.

"But, alas, no one who owns such a creature would ever agree to part with it. Even if it is a colt its lines will be so pure, its spirit so fierce, that the man it belongs to would be blind not to see what a fine animal it will become." He handed the horse amulet to Iraj. "If you give this magical ornament to that man he will not be able to refuse you the trade. But do not fear that you will be cheating him. For he only has to find another dream horse and the man who owns *it* will be compelled to make the same bargain when he gives him the amulet."

Tears welled in Iraj's eyes and they spilled unashamedly down his face as he husked his thanks and embraced the caravan master. "When I find that horse," Iraj said, "I promise that I will ride without delay to your side so you can see for yourself what a grand gift you gave me."

Coralean, whose emotions were as large as his frame, harumphed to cover the sob in his throat.

Then he turned to Safar. The first thought the young Timura had was that he hoped Coralean wasn't going to give him a horse as well. What use would such a rare creature be to a potter? It was a foolish thought and he was immediately ashamed of himself for thinking it. He vowed to accept whatever gift he received with loud—although pretended—delight, so as not to spoil the pleasure of such a generous man.

"They tell me, young Safar," Coralean said, "that you are very wise. Some say you are the wisest child ever to have been born in Kyrania." Safar started to protest but the caravan master raised a hand to stop any foolishly modest statements that might burst forth. "For you Coralean has two small gifts. Together they may more than equal the gift I made to Iraj. That depends on whether you are as wise as they say and make good use of them."

He took a scroll from his robes. "This is a letter to a friend in Walaria. He is a rich man, an educated man. A patron to the all the artists and thinkers in Walaria. It asks him to present this to the chief priest at the temple school. He will entreat them to grant you entrance and once you join the great scholars there Coralean will pay all your expenses until you are the wisest man in all the land."

Safar's fingers shook as he took the rolled up scroll. It was heavier than he expected and he nearly dropped it. Then a small silver dagger slipped onto his lap.

Coralean stroked his beard. "That is my second present to you," he said. Safar lifted the knife, knowing it had some hidden purpose and wondering what that purpose might be. "Since you will be among so many wise men," Coralean said, "that knife may prove even more valuable than the education you will receive. Listen to an old merchant. When a thought is too weighty it's probably not to be trusted. When a man's words are thick with the fat of hidden meaning it's doubtful they have as much value as the speaker implies. That knife will cut through those weighty thoughts and fatty words. And you will come to the true answer with little struggle."

He looked at the other men, heavy eyebrows lifting high with humor. "At least that's what the witch Coralean bought it from promised."

Everyone chortled. Safar was stunned, not knowing what to make of either gift, especially the mysterious properties the knife supposedly held. He picked it up, felt a trickle of power and knew it to be as magical as the witch had warranted.

His father's voice came to him from far away, as if in a dream. "Aren't you going to thank Coralean, my son?" Khadji asked. "Otherwise he'll think you were raised without manners."

Safar fumbled thanks, as graceless as any youth of seventeen years, but Coralean seemed to understand the shyness. He embraced the young man, nearly smothering him with his great strength. Safar hugged him back.

"Come, now," the caravan master roared as he pulled away. "Coralean promised the people of Kyrania a feast! Drink up, my friends, so we may all stumble out with a good cargo of spirits in our bellies to begin the celebration."

The men shouted, bowls were emptied in mighty swallows, then refilled to the overflowing.

And there were few in the village who were not of tender years who did not spend the following days in a stupor so blissful that it was spoken of for much time to come.

* * *

That first night the sky was filled with fiery smoke balloons and kites with long flaming tails. There was drunken song and music everywhere and lovers slipped off into the darkness. Many a betrothal was sealed that night and many a child conceived in sighing embraces and barely-stifled cries of pleasure.

Coralean drew Safar and Iraj aside before they'd imbibed too much. He took the brandy bowls from their hands, saying: "You'll have need of *all* your senses tonight, my young friends." He chuckled. "Besides, you're both certain to end up in the arms of a village lass if you become too befuddled."

He wagged a finger. "No sense spoiling your futures with a too early marriage. Coralean is blessed with a passionate nature himself. Ask any of his wives and serving girls." He winked. "They call me their beloved bull. I have swarms of children to prove it. I tell you, if Coralean had been born into a poorer family my father wouldn't have been able to afford to save me from my youthful indiscretions."

Then he threw his arms about their shoulders and led them through a series of curtained rooms to the women's quarters. The main area was filled with pillows piled as high as their knees. Coralean plumped down and patted the pillows for the young men to sit on either side of him.

"I promised to show you a thing or two about pleasure, my boys," he said. "And I, Coralean the Bull, know more of such things than most men. It isn't a boast but a simple statement of fact concerning the Coralean nature."

He clapped his hands and a wide curtain parted. Safar heard high, pleasing voices and the courtesans filed through, parading before the men in a silky, perfumed line.

Safar never seen so much beauty—and certainly not so seductively displayed. He was no stranger to the feminine shape. He was raised with sisters, after all. And he'd spied on the village girls when they went to bathe in the lake. But the women he saw that night were so . . . available. His for the taking. What little they wore was sheer and artfully draped to entice, not conceal. Some were tall, some were small, some were dark, some were light, some were slender, some were plump. And they all displayed practiced smiles and movements. But more than just professional skills were on display. The courtesans were enchanted by the two handsome young rescuers. And eager to show their thanks.

"Pick one," Coralean said. "Or even two or three if you like."

Safar hesitated, but not from indecision. What he was being offered, some might think, was the answer to every young man's greatest dream. All those hot, uncomfortable nights filled with perfumed sirens were about to be exorcised. Such fiery imaginings and desires are as much a part of a youth's nature as the downy beard beginning on his face. Safar knew from listening to his sisters that young women are afflicted with similar feelings. And here was his chance to realize his most lurid fantasies. But a different although related emotion boiled up from that youthful cauldron. And that was sudden blind, unreasoning love. Which at that age is the same as lust, only most mistake it as having a more noble purpose.

So as Safar's eyes swept the line of courtesans, they ignored all that jiggling pulchritude. He was searching for one woman and one woman only. Astarias.

He didn't see her among the group. He glanced around, heart thundering, mind swirling. And his thoughts became . . . pure? At least in his imagination, they were pure. And he determined at that moment that he wouldn't shame Astarias with his embrace. Foolish youth that he was, he thought this would be his gift to her. Furthermore, he'd somehow release Astarias from what he believed was her enslavement. She'd live with his sister Quetera and be as chaste as any maiden in the village. And she'd be free to choose any youth she wanted for a husband. But somehow her love for him—and her admiration for his kind gesture—would overcome any feelings she might have for any other. They would be wed and have many children and live happily forever in each other's arms. All these things were running through his drugged mind. And he heard:

"You should choose first," Coralean said to Iraj. "After all, you saved my life."

Safar looked at Iraj. His friend's face was red with lust. Then he saw Safar and smiled. The redness vanished to be replaced with feigned bored interest. Iraj's eyes returned to the courtesans. He looked each one over slowly, shook his head, then passed on to another. Sudden realization clotted in Safar's belly then rose to become a lump in his throat. He *knew* what Iraj was up to. And then he became angry, certain that for some reason Iraj was about to cheat him of what he desired above all things.

"There seems to be one missing," Iraj said to Coralean. "A dark-haired wench."

Those last four words fell like weighty stones into Safar's well of despair.

Coralean frowned. "You mean Astarias?" he said.

Iraj covered his mouth, hiding an elaborate yawn. "Is that her name?" he said. "Very pretty."

Coralean shifted in his pillows, disturbed—and a bit embarrassed. "I held her back," he said, "because she is still a virgin. I have a dear friend—a very rich dear friend—I was keeping her for."

Iraj raised his eyebrows as if surprised. Then he shrugged. "Well, I suppose that's too much to ask," he said. "I wouldn't want to lessen your profit." He gazed at Coralean, his face mild. "However it was she—Astarias, you say?—I really wanted. But . . . if it's too much *trouble* for you . . ." He rose as if to go.

Coralean grabbed Iraj by the arm and drew him back down. "Is it not known to all that Coralean is the most generous of men?" he said. "Especially to one who preserved his most precious possession, his very life? If it is Astarias you desire most, my good friend, then Astarias you shall have." And he clapped his hands and called her name, commanding her presence.

Astarias came into the room, seeming to float through the curtain. Her dark hair was tied back with a white silk band. Unlike the others she wore a robe that covered her from slender neck to ankle. It was also made of white silk and as she walked it flowed over her body—chaste, but still highlighting all the delicate parts of her. She looked at Safar and the most delightful smile graced her features. She took a step forward, thinking she was meant for him.

"No, no," Coralean barked. "Not Safar! It's Iraj I promised you to."

Her face fell for an instant and in that moment Safar hated Iraj so much he would have gladly killed him. Then her smile returned, although Safar didn't think it was as bright as before . . . and she went to Iraj. He laughed and clasped her around the waist, roughly pulling her down.

The caravan master got up. He grinned hugely at the young men. "Coralean must attend to his duties as host," he said. "Take who you like, Safar. And if you can't make up your mind, let me suggest these two." He pointed at a pair of dark-skinned twins. "They've given me more pleasure, I'll warrant, then any other woman here." He clapped Safar on the back and exited.

The twins moved toward the young potter, expectantly. Safar started to turn away, so full of hateful thoughts that he wanted nothing more than to escape.

"Wait," Iraj said.

Safar swiveled, anger plain on his face. Iraj ignored it, pulling away from Astarias' shy embrace.

"Go to him," he ordered.

Safar was bewildered. "But, I thought . . ."

Iraj laughed. "I know *what* you thought," he said. "I was testing you, don't you see?" He grinned at Safar. "You didn't do too well with that test, my friend," he said. "But maybe it was unfair. So I forgive you for it."

He gave Astarias a gentle push. "Go, on," he said. "If you stay much longer I'll be helpless to let you leave."

Astarias pealed glad laughter and scurried over to leap into Safar's arms. All his noble intentions vanished as he crushed her to him. Then Safar heard Iraj call his name and broke away, gasping. His friend was standing at the curtain opening, arms around the dark twins.

"Thank you," Safar husked. "Coralean might not have agreed if *I* had asked."

Iraj shrugged. "No thanks needed," he said. "After all, we both know who the true hero of this night is." He started to exit, pulling the twins with him. Then he stopped. "Know this, Safar," he said. "From this day forward, all I have is yours."

Safar grinned. "And all that is mine, and all that shall be mine," he said, "will be yours for the asking."

Iraj grew quite solemn. "Do you mean that?"

"I swear it," Safar answered.

Iraj nodded. "Remember this night well, Safar," he said. "For someday I may come to ask an equal favor."

"And you shall have it," Safar vowed.

"No matter what it is?" Iraj asked, his eyes suddenly hard and probing.

"Yes," Safar said. "No matter what. And if you should ever test me again, I will not fail you."

And with that covenant he sealed his fate.

CHAPTER SEVEN

DREAMS OF KINGS

Sarn was wrong—King Manacia hadn't lied. If the gods had still been watching they'd have been highly entertained by his error. Sarn's final torment, when he believed himself undone by royal betrayal, was a heady-enough brew of misery to satisfy any god's tastes.

In truth, King Manacia waited many anxious months for news of the bandit chief's return. As time dragged on the king became increasingly impatient, paying little attention to the business of state. He even ignored his harem and his wives and courtesans became fearful their master had wearied of them. To combat this they sought out the most beautiful and seductive demon maids to stir his lust. It was to no avail, for the king remained in his throne room until late every night wondering what had become of Sarn and drinking himself into a stupor.

It was difficult for King Manacia to admit failure—a condition he'd rarely experienced in his long reign. From the beginning he'd worked patiently, gradually extending his borders until all but a few of the wildest regions had been subjugated. The others had been forced into alliances weighted so heavily on Manacia's side it meant the same thing. Soon all would recognize him as supreme monarch of the demon lands. But this was not enough. The king wanted more.

"It's not as if I do these things for myself, Fari," the king liked to say to his Grand Wazier. "The future of all demonkind rests upon my shoulders."

And Lord Fari, who never reminded the king he'd heard these words before, always answered, "I thank the gods each eventide, Majesty, they made your shoulders wide and strong enough to bear that holy burden."

The Grand Wazier was a wise old demon of nearly two hundred feastings. Skillful flattery and ruthless intrigue had allowed him to keep his head through four bloody successions to the Zanzair throne.

The king took heart from Fari's reassuring display of fealty, greeting the oft-repeated praise as if it were freshly coined. Then he'd frown, as if overtaken by yet another bleak thought. And he'd sigh, saying, "Still, Fari, I'm sure there are *some* misguided ones in my kingdom who disagree. A few might even think me insane."

He'd sigh again, stroking his long curved horn. And shake his mighty head in sorrow.

"Only speak the names of these heretics, Majesty," was Fari's routine answer, "and I shall have their lying tongues plucked from their mouths and their throats filled with hot sand."

"If only they understood as well as you, my dear fiend," was the king's formulaic response. "Peace and plenty will always be denied us so long as more than one king commands the demon lands. It's only natural that there should be a single ruler for all."

And Fari would agree, saying, "How else, O Great One, can we ever rid ourselves of chaos? Or end the years of war and banditry? One demon must rule. And that one, the dreamcatchers portend, is you, My Lord."

"But that isn't enough, Fari," the king would remind him. "The humans must recognize me as well. I must be King of Kings. Ruler of all Esmir."

"I have dedicated the remainder of my humble life to that end, Majesty," Fari would answer. "Demon history has long been awaiting one such as you. What other fiend has had your wisdom? Your strength? Your benevolence? Your sorcerous power? The gods have gifted us with your august presence, Majesty. There's no denying it. It's as plain as the mighty horn on your royal brow."

With that, Fari would knock his old head against the stone floor, then rise with some difficulty, gripping his great dragon bone cane and heaving himself up with much cracking of aging joints and tendons. Then he'd withdraw, his bone cane tap tap tapping against the stone, fainter, ever fainter, until he reached the distant doors to the vast throne room and disappeared beyond. He always left a contented king in his wake, a king with renewed vigor to dream his dreams and plot his plots.

There had only been one King of Kings of Esmir—the human, Alisarrian. It was Manacia's deeply held belief the time was ripe for another such historic occurrence. He was determined this time a demon would hold that scepter. There was no question that demon should be him. Manacia's entire reign had been dedicated to that goal. Yet as the years passed he began to fear he wouldn't be ready in time. That somewhere in the human lands another Alisarrian may have been bred. A conqueror with an army at his back who'd soon come knocking on his palace doors.

One night, as he prowled his Necromancium wondering if the answer to his troubles was hidden in the blackest of magical arts, there came the tap tap tap of Lord Fari's cane, the ghostly herald of the Grand Wazier's approach. When he heard the tapping Manacia turned away from a large jar containing a human head floating in brine. As he looked up Fari came through the portal, the air shimmering like the surface of a vertical pool.

"What news, Lord Fari?" the king asked with exaggerated cheer. "Has our wayward bandit finally returned?"

Fari, whose mind was deeply engaged in another matter, jolted up, scaly jowls rolling in a wave of surprise. "What, Majesty?" he asked. Then, "Oh. You mean, *Lord Sarn*, Excellency. No, Majesty. There's still no word. I'm here on another matter, Excellency. One that requires your urgent attention."

But Manacia abruptly turned away, plunged into as foul a mood as he'd ever experienced. "I've reviewed it from every side, Fari," he said. "And I still don't see where I went wrong."

"Wrong, Majesty?" Fari said. "How can you think that? Give it more time. He'll appear any day now, loaded with spoils, bearing the maps you sought and demanding an enormous reward in that swaggering manner of his." Fari snorted. "As if he were the only *real* fiend in the land."

"It's been nearly a year, Fari," Manacia said.

"So long, Majesty? I hadn't realized . . ."

"I might as well face it," the king said. "I've wasted enough time and energy that could be put to a more positive use. Despite all our efforts, all our experiments and labors, the shield we built to protect Sarn from the curse wasn't good enough. And somewhere in the Forbidden Desert, perhaps just out of sight, his bones and his fiends' bones are bleaching in the sun."

Fari thought, quite correctly, that perhaps the shield hadn't failed at all. Some natural misfortune might have befallen the bandit chief. But he hadn't lived so long by telling his monarchs what he truly thought. So when he saw which path the king was taking he quickly stepped in that direction.

He made a mournful face. "I fear you are right, Excellency," he said. "The shield *has* failed. I'll find out at once who is responsible for this appalling state of affairs and have them suitably tortured and put to death."

The king bared his fangs in what was meant to be a kindly smile. "Spare them," he said. "I too share the blame. And you as well, my dear friend."

Fari gaped, revealing whiter and sharper teeth than he had a right to own at his advanced age. "Me, Majesty? What did I—" He wisely clipped that off. He rapped his bone cane and bowed. "My name should top that list of failures, Excellency," he said. "Tonight my wives will sing your praises when I tell them how you so generously spared this noble fool. Of course it was my fault! I take the whole blame, Majesty. A blame you should never dream of sharing."

Manacia waved a claw, silencing him. "You know who this is, Fari?" he asked, pointing at the human head floating in the jar.

The Grand Wazier stared at it. The human was a young adult. Possibly handsome once—by human standards. "No, Excellency, I don't know him."

"This is the first creature I used to test the shield." Manacia chuckled. "We tied a rope to his waist and used whips to drive him out into the Forbidden Desert. He'd taken not more than a dozen steps when he suddenly screamed, clutched his breast and fell to the ground. When we dragged him back he was dead, although there wasn't a mark on him to hint of the cause. He was a healthy creature straight from the royal slave pens. Clean. Well fed. I examined him myself. There was no reason for his death, other than the curse."

"I recall the incident, Majesty," Fari said, "but not the human."

"How could you?" Manacia said. "There were so many. Demons as well. They were the worst kind of felons, of course."

"Of course, Majesty."

Manacia stared at the head, remembering the four years of experiments. He'd labored hard, delved into every nook and cranny of the magical sciences, casting spell after spell to create a shield strong enough to defy the ancient curse. The curse had been created hundreds of years before by a Treaty Council composed of both demon *and* human wizards. Its purpose was to permanently sever all contact between the two species, permanently ending the years of bloody strife and war-ravaged harvests that followed the fall of Alisarrian's empire. It was believed by all the curse would be impossible for even the greatest sorcerer to render harmless.

Manacia believed otherwise. He was not only a powerful wizard—stronger than any other in the demon lands—but he had a mind for such puzzles and had attacked the curse full force with all the sorcerous resources at his command. Hundreds had died in those experiments. Body after body was dragged back at the end of a rope. But Manacia had hope because each time the victims crept a little further into the desert. The last group made it so far the king's archers had to fire arrows at them to force them to go deeper. Finally, all who were sent out returned unharmed. The shield appeared to work so well Manacia had to have the survivors killed so they couldn't use his spell to escape across the desert.

It was then he made his bargain with Sarn. The king had personally attended the bandit's departure. He'd praised the thief greatly, cast a special spell of blessings and watched Sarn and his friends thunder off into the desert for the human lands to seek Kyrania—the passage through the "Valley of the Clouds" that the Oracle had spoken of. The passage that was the key to forging the two great human regions into a great kingdom.

Manacia's hopes had been high that day. He was already dreaming of the time when his armies could follow. He had visions of swift and easy victories over the humans. Once he had a dream of a grand court ceremony, with human ambassadors bowing before his throne, bearing treaties that declared him King of Kings. Ruler of all Esmir.

Manacia peered into the human's dead eyes. He was certain it was the human side of the sorcerous equation that had foiled him. A side he somehow had not been able to penetrate. It was for this reason, not sentimentality, that Manacia had the head of his first victim displayed in his Necromancium. It was here in this vaulted chamber of watery light that his collection of black arts and books and materials were kept. There were jars and vials of the most evil liquids and powders and unguents. There were scrolls detailing horrid practices and spells. There were strange objects and idols with shapes so menacing they'd haunt the dreams of the most callous and uncaring demon.

Manacia rapped his talons against the jar. The liquid stirred and the head bobbed about. "We'll begin again, my friend," he said to the skull. "And once more you shall have the honor of being first."

He turned to the Grand Wazier. "We'll start in the morning," he said. "Have my wizards meet me here at first light. I'll solve this riddle no matter how long it takes."

"That's the spirit, Majesty," Fari said. "Never admit defeat. Consider it an unpleasant setback, nothing more. I'll send word to the royal wizards at once!"

He turned as if to go, hesitated, then turned back, saying, "There's still that other matter, Excellency. The matter that forced me to come here and disturb your thinking."

The king's mood had brightened now that he'd formed a course of action. He said, "Yes, yes. I'd almost forgotten. What is it?"

"Many months ago, Majesty," Fari said, "not long after Sarn and his friends left for the human lands, a strange event occurred which has only just come to my attention. A celestial disturbance, Majesty, that went unnoticed by our stargazers because Zanzair was heavily overcast that night. But a shepherd, far to the north where the skies were clear, reported seeing an immense shower of fiery particles. Other reports have trickled in since then, confirming the shepherd's sighting. As near as we can determine the display was in the human lands, over the Gods' Divide."

Manacia shrugged. "What of it?" he said. "There's nothing unusual about fiery particles falling out of the sky. Rarely do such occurrences have anything to do with our affairs. If it were a comet perhaps there'd be cause for concern. Or deeper study."

"Quite true, Majesty," Fari said. "And if that were all there was to it I would not be here troubling you with news of such a minor event."

The king rapped his claws against the glass jar, impatient. Fari hurried on. "Once the event was dated with some certainty," he said, "your wizards recalled other signs that occurred at, or near, the same time. The water from our wells suddenly tasted foul and bitter, a condition that lasted for some weeks."

Manacia nodded, remembering that trouble.

"The day after the sighting," Fari continued, "it was noticed that the liquid in the water clocks turned in the opposite direction. And one of the temple acolytes claimed when he rose that morning his reflection in the mirror was backwards, or, that is to say, he looked just like one demon sees another, left claw on the true left, right to right. Neither anomaly lasted long, Majesty, but there *was* concern at the time. Since then it has been observed that the ground has settled dangerously under some of our older buildings, causing them to sag. Moreover, bees have been swarming out of season, birds have appeared of a kind never seen before. And there has been an unusual number of birth oddities, two-headed swine, limbless dogs, fish with no eyes."

"This is indeed disturbing news, Fari," the king said. "You were right to report it to me. Does anyone know what these things mean? Could it have anything to do with our attempt to defy the curse?"

Fari jolted in surprise. He thought a moment, tapping his bone cane against the floor. Then he said, "I don't know, Excellency. It's a thought that hadn't occurred to me."

"But it *is* possible," the king said.

"Yes, Majesty. I suppose it is."

"What would you advise?" the king asked.

Fari saw the danger at once and sadly shook his head. "I'm ashamed to admit, Excellency," Fari said, "that I am at loss. Not enough is known to form an opinion."

"We must find out," the king said. "It might be dangerous to begin my experiments until we do."

Fari nodded. "I can see how that could be so, Majesty," he said. "This is a most unfortunate situation. Your Excellency's plans for invading the human lands will most certainly suffer a delay."

"It can't be helped, Fari," the king said. "Curses have a way of spreading beyond their original intent. There are so many links, some not even known to the original spell casters, that it's impossible to account for all the effects a curse might trigger. That's why I first sent bandits instead of our own soldiers across the Forbidden Desert.

"As much as it grieves me to say this, Fari, it would be wise for us to proceed cautiously. But I want you to spare no expense. I want all my stargazers working on this. All my dreamcatchers. And I want daily sacrifices to the gods at the main temple, with weekly ones for the lesser houses of worship."

"Yes, Excellency," Fari said, bobbing his head and rapping his cane. "Without delay." He hurried off, relieved that he'd once again shifted all possible blame and responsibility onto the backs of others, while still being assured of winning praise and honors for any successes.

For a change, however, he did not leave a happy king in his wake. Manacia was deeply troubled as he turned back to examine the head. The old fear of a rival oozed up to torment him. A shiver ran up his long bony spine.

Manacia suddenly wondered if even now his enemy was thinking of him.

If so, did that enemy have a human face?

And if he did, was it possible he had already discovered the way through the Gods' Divide.

Had he found Kyrania?

*   *   *

Not long after Manacia's eve of disappointment, Safar and Iraj said farewell. They made a ceremony of it, returning to Alisarrian's Cave and the snowy pass where they'd battled the demons. Storms had further buried the evidence of the carnage and as they pushed across the snows on rough wooden skis there was nothing to hint of the events that had occurred there.

"Maybe it was just a dream," Safar said. "Maybe it never happened at all and any moment now we'll wake up to an ordinary day in ordinary two ordinary lives."

Iraj barked laughter. "I've never been ordinary, Safar," he said. "And, admit it or not, neither have you. You'd save yourself a lot of bother if you just accepted it." He grinned. "If you dreamed Astarias," he said, "then you have the greatest imagination of any man in Esmir—a courtesan, young, beautiful, virginal and trained in all the arts to please a man. That was no dream, my friend. To make her one would be the greatest sin any god could imagine. When you're an old man it'll be memories of women like Astarias that will make your life seem well spent."

Safar made a sour face. "I'd just as soon forget about it," he said. "I'm afraid I embarrassed myself with Astarias."

Iraj clapped him on the back. "Don't be ridiculous," he said. "So you fell in love with a courtesan. You're not the first man. Nor will you be the last. So you professed undying love. So you promised her the moon and the stars and all the heavens contain, if only she'd remain in your arms. I said that to both of my twins. Separately. And together."

"You didn't mean it," Safar said. "I did, I'm ashamed to say."

"Of course I meant it," Iraj replied. "At the time, anyway. Especially when I had one curled up in my left arm, the other my right."

"That was lust talking," Safar said.

Iraj snickered, then wrapped his arms around himself in a comic embrace. "And yours was undying Love, right? A Love that *could not* be denied. Come, my friend!"

"She laughed at me," Safar confessed, blushing.

"What of it?" Iraj answered. "You rode her all night and half the next morning. And then, in a moment of weakness, you asked her to be your wife. She tells you, charmingly, I imagine, and with a few tricks to arouse you some more, that she has no intention of making bread and babies for a village boy the rest of her life. She's a courtesan with as much beauty as ambition. You persist. Climbing between those lovely thighs once again, I expect." Another blush from Safar told Iraj he'd guessed right. "And then she laughed. You should be the one laughing. You got what you wanted. *I* saw to that. And now you're done with her and she's the loser for spurning you. You are Safar Timura! A man meant for great things. The very sort of man she prays every day is in her future."

"I can't look at things as coldly as you," Safar said.

"Don't then," Iraj said, shrugging. "But I suspect you'll come around to my view soon enough. Bed your women when you can, whenever you can. A courtesan's scornful laugh—*after* the deed is done—is no price at all. The truth is the next man who rides Astarias will be old and fat and it'll be your memory she'll cleave to when she's forced to pretend her fat old master is a handsome god."

Iraj's callous words of comfort, although spoken in friendship, did little to soothe Safar's wounded spirit. So he was grateful when Iraj gave a sudden shout of discovery.

"Look at this!" he cried, dropping to his knees and digging in the snow.

Safar crowded close to see. A demon's face emerged beneath Iraj's scraping fingers. The corpse's features were a pale, bluish green. Dagger-size fangs hooked out from the grimacing mouth. Although Safar and Iraj had no way of knowing it, the demon was Giff and the look on his face was as surprised in death as it had been when Iraj had drawn his blade across his throat. Safar turned away.

"This is the demon I killed!" Iraj said. "I can tell from the wounds." With a finger he traced the gaping red gash beneath Giff's pointed chin.

"Cover him up," Safar urged.

"I will," Iraj said, but first he unsheathed his knife.

Safar glanced over and was horrified when he saw his friend digging out the fangs with the blade point. "What are you doing?"

"Taking his teeth," Iraj said. "I want to make a necklace of them."

Safar, who had never become used to his friend's plains' savage ways, kept his eyes averted. "I thought we'd agreed to keep the whole thing a secret," he said. "So people don't become unnecessarily alarmed."

Iraj snorted. "I'll keep my promise to Coralean," he said. "But in my own way."

He held up the bloody fangs and Safar couldn't help but look. "I'll make a chain of these to wear around my neck when I greet my enemies. They'll won't know what they are, exactly. But they'll be dripping green slime from their arses wondering what kind of a beast it was I killed."

Despite his revulsion, Safar understood. Iraj's kinsman had just arrived in Kyrania to inform the young prince it was safe to return home. Apparently Iraj's turncoat uncle—Lord Fulain—had fallen ill. His soldiers had become dispirited and his ally, Koralia Kan, had been forced to sue for peace. As part of that peace Iraj was permitted to return and take his place as hereditary leader of the clan. There were provisos, of course, intended to keep him weak—leader in name only. But Iraj was already planning how to get around them.

Iraj put the teeth in a leather pouch and tucked it into his belt. Then he covered up Giff's corpse, smoothing the snow until all looked as before.

"I wish I could convince you to stay in Kyrania," Safar said. "This could all be a lie to entice you out of the mountains."

"At least part of it *is* a lie," Iraj said, rising to his feet and brushing snow from his knees. "But they'll pretend otherwise for awhile. When Fulain becomes well the blood feud will start again. But I intend to be ready when that happens." He touched the leather pouch containing the demon fangs. "I'm young, they'll claim. Untested in battle. These teeth will say otherwise. I'll keep where I got them a mystery, which will only add to their power."

Safar, wanting to avoid further discussion of the matter, said, "I'm getting cold. Let's go back to the cave."

A half hour later they were crouched in the cavern, warming their hands over a small fire. The painting of Alisarrian hung over them, glowing eerily.

"You haven't mentioned your own plans," Iraj said, digging out some dried goat's flesh. "What will you do after I leave? I still can't imagine you being content as Safar Timura the potter."

"I don't know why," Safar said. "It's easy enough for me to envision."

"You know as well as I do," Iraj said, "that you're dodging the truth. You're a wizard, Safar. The teeth I collected are nothing compared to what you have a right to. How can you possibly refuse Coralean's gift of an education at the finest university in Esmir?"

Safar sighed. "I wish I could," he said, "but I don't think my family is going to let me."

"Or Gubadan," Iraj pointed out.

Safar nodded. "He's worse than they are," he said. "He claims I'll be shaming all Kyrania if I refuse the chance. That there's much good I'll be able to do when I return home with all that learning."

"He's right about the first," Iraj said. "It *would* shame your people. In the whole history of Kyrania it's unlikely any of its sons had such an opportunity. But Gubadan's wrong about the second part. You won't return, Safar. I'm no Dreamcatcher like you, but I know once you leave Kyrania you'll never return. Because you'll be with me, remember?"

"That was a false vision," Safar said.

"Are you sure?" Iraj asked, smiling.

"Absolutely," Safar answered. "You're the ambitious one. Not me."

"What of your other vision?" Iraj said. "The dancing people and the volcano? Do you think that's wrong as well?"

Safar hesitated, then, "No, I don't. And that's the main reason I'll probably end up giving in to my family and Gubadan. The only place I can find out what the vision meant is Walaria."

"Whatever your reason, Safar," Iraj said. "I beg you to make up your mind as soon as possible. Learn as much as you can. As fast as you can. For I promise that someday, when you least expect it, I'll show up to plead with you to join me."

"And I'll refuse," Safar said. "You are my friend. But I'll still say no."

"Why don't we test it?" Iraj asked. He hauled out the leather pouch and shook Giff's bloody teeth into a palm. Then, in a mock intonation, he said, "Cast these bones, O Master Wizard, and pray tell us what the future holds."

"Don't be silly," Safar said. "I'm no bone caster."

"Then there's no reason to be afraid," Iraj said. "Here, I'll even clean them up for you."

He rubbed some of the blood off on the leather pouch and held them out. Safar didn't move, so Iraj grabbed his right hand, pulled it forward and dropped the four fangs into Safar's outstretched palm. Safar didn't resist, automatically closing his fist over them.

"What do we do now?" Iraj said. "Make some kind of chant and toss them, I suppose?"

"I don't want to do this," Safar said.

"I'll tell you what," Iraj said, "to make it easier, I'll chant and you toss. Okay?" Without waiting for an answer Iraj drew a breath and then intoned:

"Bones, bones, demon's though you be,
Tell us what the future holds,
What roads shall we see?"

As Iraj chanted the demon's teeth suddenly grew warm in Safar's hand. Instinctively he loosened his hand and shook the fangs like dice.

"Chanting was never one of my best subjects," Iraj said. He laughed. "But if I can chance making a complete fool of myself, so can . . ." and his voice trailed off as he saw Safar rattle the bones, blue eyes glowing in concentration.

Safar cast them on the cave floor and instead of a dull clatter, the sound was like the ring of steel against steel.

Red smoke hissed up, rising like a snake and the two lads drew back in alarm. The smoke was thick, smelling of old blood, and it swirled in front of them like a miniature desert dervish—a slender funnel at the bottom, billowing into a fist-size head on top. Then a mouth seemed to form, curving into a seductive smile.

The lips parted and they heard a woman speak—*"Two will take the road that two traveled before. Brothers of the spirit, but not the womb. Separate in body and mind, but twins in destiny. But beware what you seek, O brothers. Beware the path you choose. For this tale cannot end until you reach the Land of Fires."*

The smoke suddenly vanished, leaving the two young men gaping at the four small gray piles of ash where the demon fangs had been. It was as if they'd been consumed by a hot flame.

Iraj recovered first. "You see?" he chortled. "We heard it from the mouth of the Oracle herself." He threw an arm around Safar's shoulders. "'Brothers of the spirit, but not the womb,'" he quoted. "What a pair we shall make! The King of Kings and his Grand Wazier!"

"That's not exactly what the Oracle said," Safar replied. "Hells, whoever she was, we don't even know if she was speaking about us."

Iraj made a rude noise. "I don't see anyone else here in this cave with us," he said. "Who else could she mean?"

"There was also a warning," Safar said. "Don't forget the warning."

"Sure, sure," Iraj said, impatient. "I heard. And I'm forewarned. It's settled then. I'll return home with my uncle and start building my forces. And you'll go to Walaria and learn as much as you can until it's time for us to be rejoined."

"I'm not convinced that was what the Oracle was predicting," Safar said.

"Of course she was," Iraj replied. "But it doesn't matter what either of us think. We'll find out for ourselves in the days to come. Just think of me sometimes. When you're in Walaria up to your elbows in dusty books and scrolls, think of me riding free across the southern plains, an army of horsemen at my back carrying my standard. It will be the banner of Alisarrian that I fly as I charge from victory to victory."

He tapped Safar's chest. "And it will be the banner of Alisarrian you will be carrying in your heart," he said. "We'll make a better world before we're done, Safar. A better Esmir for all."

It was then that Safar finally made up his mind. He'd leave his beloved Kyrania and go to Walaria. He'd enter the university at the Grand Temple, pore over every tome, soaking up all the knowledge he could hold.

The decision had nothing to do with Iraj's impassioned speech. Safar was remembering the Oracle's final words about the land of fires. Hadin was known as The Land of Fires! Hadin, where the handsome people of his vision danced and died and a mighty volcano raged, spewing flames and poisonous clouds into a darkening sky.

"You *have* decided to go, haven't you?" he heard Iraj say.

Safar looked up and saw his friend's eyes ablaze with joy as he read Safar's intentions on his face. "Yes," he answered. "I've decided."

"Then let us say farewell now, brother mine," Iraj said. "A great dream awaits us. The sooner we get started, the sooner that dream will come true."

And so the two young men embraced and swore eternal brotherhood and friendship.

Iraj took one road. Safar another. But neither doubted—for entirely different reasons—the roads would someday converge.

And that they'd meet again.

Part Two
WALARIA

CHAPTER EIGHT
THE THIEF OF WALARIA

Nerisa watched the executioner sharpen his blade. It was long and broad and curving and he stroked the edge with such tenderness one might have thought his sword was a lover.

And maybe it was, Nerisa thought. She'd heard of stranger things.

The executioner was a big man, naked torso swelling out of baggy silk pantaloons of the purest white. He had thick arms, a neck squat and strong as an oak stump. His features were hidden by a white silk hood with two holes for his dark gloomy eyes to contemplate his victims' sins. Masked or not, everyone knew who he was—Tulaz, the most famous executioner in all Walaria. Five thousand hands had been severed by his legendary sword. One thousand heads separated from their shoulders. And he'd never needed more than one cut to accomplish his task.

There were seven condemned to test his record that morning. The plaza, set just inside the main gate, was packed with gawkers, hawkers, purse snatchers and pimps. Gamblers were betting heavily on the outcome for Tulaz had never attempted so many heads before. The odds were in his favor for the first six—a mean lot who hadn't learned their lesson from previous mutilations. The seventh, however, was a woman charged with adultery. She was said to be beautiful and there were many among the crowd who wondered if Tulaz might falter when confronted with such a tender and record-breaking neck.

Nerisa had an excellent vantage point to view the proceedings. She was crouched atop a high freight wagon just returning from market and had a clear view of the six felons chained to the dungeon cart. But the adulteress was hidden by a tent pitched on the cart. It wasn't out of humanity her jailers had provided such privacy. They knew a featured attraction when they saw one and were among the heaviest bettors. They were also, Nerisa noted, selling quick glimpses of the woman to all who'd grease their palms.

Nerisa didn't have slightest interest in the executions. In her twelve summers of life she'd witnessed many such things. For as long as she could remember she'd been a child of the streets. She'd awakened in alleys next to fresh corpses—corpses not so cleanly slain as Tulaz was wont to do. There were worse things, she'd learned, than being executed. She'd spent her whole young life dodging those things with a skill matched by few young denizens of Walaria. Her only fear of Tulaz was she might someday make an error that would cost her a hand—the traditional penalty a thief paid for a first offense. Nerisa was a thief intent on keeping all her parts.

It was professional purpose, not entertainment, that had drawn her to the plaza; although she'd experienced an added thrill when she realized she'd be breaking the law under the executioner's nose. She peeped out of her hiding place to check on the stall keeper - her intended victim. She buried a giggle as she watched him step up on a box so he could see over the crowd. He was a fat old turd, she thought. The crate would never hold such a skin load of grease.

True to her estimate the crate collapsed, sending the stallkeep sprawling. Nerisa hugged herself to keep from laughing. The joke was especially delicious because the crowd was so intent on the executions that she was the only one to see his humiliation. There was nothing that Nerisa—by circumstance and nature a solitary person—enjoyed more than a private joke. The merchant grumbled up, found a heavy barrel and rolled it over to the edge of his stall. He leaned on the trays bearing his wares and clambered gingerly onto the barrel. It held and he looked around, a yellow-toothed smile of victory dissolving when he realized no one was watching. With a belch, he turned to see Tulaz prepare for his legendary work.

Nerisa examined the trays set up under the tented stall. They were overflowing with all manner of poor quality merchandise; old lamp parts, broken toys, tawdry jewelry, spoiled cosmetics, healing powders and love potions of doubtful quality. The wares were typical of the stalls lining the old gray stone city walls inside the gates. Amid all that trash was an object that had great value to Nerisa. She'd spotted it while foraging the day before. But when she'd tried to examine the object closer the stallkeep had leapt from his wide chair and rushed her, driving her away with a thick stick, shouting, "Begone boy!"

Nerisa, who was tall for a girl and slender, was frequently mistaken for a boy. It was a mistake she'd made a habit of not correcting. She'd even adopted a male urchin's raggedy costume of breeches and baggy shirt. Until recently she'd worried that the bumps and curves of womanhood would soon appear, making it more difficult than ever to avoid the evil-eyed men who preyed on young women with no home but the streets. If they ever did catch her there was no one to care about her fate, except the old bookseller who let her sleep in his shop. It was there she'd met the handsome youth who'd turned her thinking upside down. Now she worried that she wouldn't grow up soon enough.

A vision of the young man who'd awakened this interest floated into her mind and her heart knocked hard against her ribs. She pushed the image away. Don't be such a stupid cow, Nerisa thought. Keep your mind on that fat dog turd of a stallkeep. He'll get you if he can.

The crowd roared and Nerisa swiveled to see the jailers unchain the first felon and lead him to Tulaz's stone platform. Indentations in the stone marked the place where many a poor soul had been forced to kneel on hands and knees and the stone surface was stained black from all the centuries of spilled blood. The sudden realization that the gory platform would be the condemned's last view of the world sent a shiver down Nerisa's spine.

The crowd laughed when the first felon mounted the platform, heavy chains rattling. The man was a thief, a poor thief at that—he was already missing his ears and nose, as well as both his hands.

"Not much left to aim for, Tulaz," some wag shouted above the din. "Already cut most of him off!"

The crowd roared laughter.

"What'd he use to steal with?" someone else cried. "His toes?"

Immediately an crone piped up, "Not his toes, you blind shit. His prick! Can't you see it peepin' out at us?"

Nerisa couldn't help but look. Sure enough she saw a long, very male part of the thief, dangling from his dungeon-rotted costume. The thief was a good natured fool and went along with the game. To the immense pleasure of the crowd he held up the two stumpy things that were arms and jerked his hips back and forth, humping the air. The crowd howled delight and rained coins onto the platform to bribe Tulaz to make the thief's agony short for rewarding them with such fine entertainment. Tulaz saw the copper mount up and dispensed with his usual ceremony, which consisted of ominous cuts in the air and much stance and grip shifting.

"Get him down," he shouted to the jailers.

Instantly the thief's guards threw him to the ground and jumped out of the way. Tulaz took one mighty pace forward and swung just as the thief's head bobbed up.

It was so swift there wasn't a cry or a gasped breath. Just a snick of resistance then blood fountained from a suddenly empty neck. The thief's head, broken-toothed grin still fixed to his face, sailed into the crowd where pigs, dogs and children quarreled over it.

"Oh, well done, Tulaz! Well done!" Nerisa heard the stallkeep cry. He'd obviously had a wager on the first cut of the day.

Nerisa thought she saw her chance when they led out the second victim. The stallkeep was highly interested, raising himself on his toes to get a better look. Nerisa started to slip off the wagon. All she needed was a single moment of inattention and she'd snatch her prize and disappear into the crowd before anyone was the wiser. A barrel shifted under her and she had to grab to steady herself. Although there was little noise, the stallkeep sensed something was amiss and jolted around. Nerisa swore and ducked back into her hiding place just in time.

The girl settled down to wait. She'd have to be patient to get the better of this sow's breath of a stallkeep. Nerisa prided herself on patience and stubborn intent. Put a goal in her head and she'd achieve it no matter how long it took. The best time, she thought, would be when they brought the adulteress out. The jailers most certainly had been paid to strip the woman before she was killed. The stallkeep, along with the rest of the viewers, would be so fixed on all that doomed nakedness he'd never notice Nerisa's bit of business.

As she crouched there waiting for the moment to come, Nerisa thought of the poor woman waiting in the tent. The terror she had to be feeling made Nerisa's heart pang in empathy. What a price to pay for something so natural as being in your lover's arms. The unfairness of it clawed at her. For a moment it was painful to breathe.

Stop it, Nerisa, she commanded herself, fighting for control. It's not like you haven't seen it before.

*   *   *

Safar sat in a small outdoor cafe, shaded by an ancient broad-leaf fig tree, counting coins piled in a sticky puddle of wine. A pesky wasp made him lose count and he had to tot it all up again. A little drunk, he rubbed bleary eyes and decided that he had enough for another jug of the *Foolsmire's* best. Which is to say it was the worst and therefore cheapest wine in all Walaria.

It was late afternoon and the summer heat lay thick over the city, stifling thought and movement. The streets were empty, the homes and shops shuttered for the hours between the midday meal and evening call to prayer. It was so quiet that in the distant stockpens the bawl of a young camel, lonely for its mother, echoed across the city. The people of Walaria dozed fitfully in shuttered darkness, gathering their energies to face the day anew. It was a time for sleep, for lovers' trysts. A time for self reflection.

Safar rapped politely on the rough wood of the table. "Katal," he cried. "My strength is fading. Fetch me another jug from the well, if you please."

There was a muttering from the shadowy depths of the bookshop abutting the cafe and in a moment an old man emerged, carelessly dressed in worn scholar's robes. It was Katal, proprietor of the *Foolsmire*, an open air cafe and bookshop tucked into the end of a long dead-end alley in the Students' Quarter. Katal had a book in his hand, index finger pushed between the pages to keep his place.

"You should be resting, Safar," he said, "or tending to your studies. You know as well as I that the second level acolyte exams are less than a week away."

Safar groaned. "Don't spoil a perfectly good drunk, Katal. I've invested a week's room and board to reach my present condition of amiable insobriety. It's drink I need, sir. So dig into your holy well for the precious stuff, my dear purveyor of bliss. And dig deep. Find me as cold a jug as these coins will buy."

Katal clucked disapproval, but he set his book on the table and hobbled to the old stone well. A dozen ropes were strung around the rim, tied to heavy eyebolts imbedded in the stone and disappearing into the cool black depths. He hauled on one of the ropes until a large bucket appeared. It was full of jugs made of red clay, all the width of a broad palm and standing a uniform eight inches high. Katal took one out and fetched it to Safar.

The young man pushed coins forward, but Katal shook his head, pushing them back. "I'll buy this one," he said. "My price for you today is talk, not copper. A *Foolsmire* special, if you will."

"Done," Safar said. "I'll listen to your advice hour after hour, my friend, if you'll keep my cup full."

He sloshed wine into a wide, cracked tumbler. He stoppered the jug then held it up, studying it. "Three years ago," he said, "I helped my father make jugs like these. They were much better, of course. Glazed and decorated for a fine table. Not turned out in factories by the scores."

Katal eased his old body into the bench seat across from Safar. "I could never afford such a luxury," he said. "If I had bucketsful of Timura jugs in my well I'd pour out the wine and sell the jugs. Think of all the books I could buy with the price I'd get!"

"I'll tell you a secret, Katal," Safar said. "If you had Timura jugs you could make your own wine, or brandy or beer, if you prefer. My father makes a special blessing over each jug he produces. All you need then is some water, the proper makings for whatever brew it is you desire and you'll have an endless supply of your favorite drink."

"More pottery magic!" Katal scoffed. "And this time water into wine. No wonder your teachers despair."

"Actually," Safar said, "there's no magic to it at all. My father would dispute that. But it's true. Part of the spell, you see, is that we pour spirits from an old tried and true brewing bowl into the new jug. We shake it up and pour it back. And the little animals left in the clay will produce spirits until the end of time—as long you don't wash the jug."

"Little animals?" Katal said, bushy gray eyebrows beetling in disbelief.

Safar nodded. "Too small for the eye to see."

Katal snorted. "How do you know that?"

"What else could it be?" Safar said. "As an experiment I've made several such jugs. Some I chanted the spell over, but failed to use the brewing bowl liquid. Others got the liquid, but not the chant. The latter produced a good wine. The former nothing but a watery mess."

"That still doesn't explain the small spirit making animals," Katal pointed out. "Did you see them?"

"I told you," Safar answered, "they're too small for the unaided eye to behold. I theorized their existence. What other explanation could there be?"

Katal snorted. "Be damned to theory," he said. "When will you learn that supposing doesn't make it so."

Safar laughed and drained off his cup. "Then you don't know anything about magic, Katal," he said, wiping his chin. "Supposing is what sorcery is all about." He belched and refilled his cup. "But that answer is a cheat. I admit it. It's scientific observation you were speaking of. And you were right to chastise me. I've never seen the little animals. But I suspect their presence. And if someone gave me money I could grind a glass lens so powerful I might be able to see them and prove their existence."

"Who would give you money for such a thing?" Katal said. "And even if your proved your point, who would care?"

Safar was suddenly serious. He jabbed a finger into his chest. "I would," he said.

"And so should everyone else. If we are ignorant of the smallest things, how can we know the larger world? How can we guide our fate?"

"We've had this argument before," Katal said. "I say the fate of mortals is the business of the gods."

"Bah!" was Safar's retort. "The gods have no business but their own. Our troubles are no concern of theirs."

Katal glanced about nervously and saw no one in earshot, except his grandson, Zeman, who'd come out while they were talking and was brushing fig leaves off the tables on the other side of the patio.

"Be careful what you say, my young friend," Katal warned. "You never know when one of the king's spies will be about. In Walaria the penalty for heresy is most unpleasant."

Safar ducked his head, chastened. "I know, I know," he said. "And I'm sorry to be so outspoken in your presence. I don't want to get you in trouble because of my views. Sometimes it's difficult to remember that I must guard my tongue here. In Kyrania a man of twenty may speak his mind about any subject he chooses."

Katal leaned close, a fond smile peeping out from his untidy beard. "Speak to me all you like, Safar," he said. "But discreetly, sir. Discreetly. And in well modulated tones."

The old man had been a kindly uncle to Safar since he'd arrived in Walaria some two years before. In that spirit Katal dipped into his robe and fished out a small cup. He cleaned it with a sleeve, then filled it with wine.

He drank, then said, "Tell me what this is all about, Safar. If your family were here they'd be worried. So let me worry for them. I'll tell you what your own father would say. Which is that you've been drinking heavily for nearly a month. Your studies must be suffering as much as your finances. You've had no money for food, much less books. I'm not complaining, but I've been feeding you for free. I'd even be willing to forgo my usual rental fee for any books you required, if only I thought you'd make some use of them. There's an exam coming up. The most important in your career as a student. All the other second level candidates, except the sons of the rich whose success is assured by the fact of their wealth, are studying hard. They don't want to bring shame to their family."

"What's the use?" Safar said. "No matter how well I do Umurhan will fail me anyway."

Katal's eyebrows shot up. "How can that be?" he said. "You're the best student Umurhan's had in years." Umurhan was Walaria's Chief Sorcerer. As such he supervised the temple and attached university where scholars, priests, healers and wizards were trained. He answered to no one but King Didima, ruler of the city and its environs.

"He's going to fail me just the same," Safar said.

"There must be some reason," Katal said. "What did you do to earn his wrath?"

Safar made a sour face. "He caught me in his library," he said, "making notes on a forbidden book."

Katal was aghast. "How could you take such a chance?"

Safar hung his head. "I thought it was safe," he said. "I've slipped into his study before without being caught. I knew the risk I was taking. But I'm on the trail of something important, dammit! And I thought one more trip might turn up what I needed. I slipped in well before first light. Everyone knows old Umurhan likes his sleep, so there shouldn't have been any danger. But this time I'd barely entered the room and lit a candle when he suddenly appeared from the shadows. As if he'd been waiting there for me."

"Did someone alert him?" Katal asked.

"I don't see how they could," Safar said. "It was a last minute decision. No one knew. My only guess is I left some clue on my last visit. And he's been waiting all this time to pounce."

"You were fortunate he didn't expel you at once," Katal said. "Or, worse, report you to Kalasariz as a dangerous heretic." Lord Kalasariz was Didima's chief spy. There were so many in his employ the joke was that in Walaria even the watchers were watched.

"Umurhan said the same thing," Safar replied. "He said he could have me thrown into one of Kalasariz' cells where I could rot for all eternity for all he cared. And the only reason he didn't call one of Kalasariz' minions right then was because I was such a good student."

"You see?" Katal said. "There *is* hope. You've completed four years of work in two. No one else your age has ever qualified to take the second level acolyte exams in so short a time." He indicated the wine jug. "Now you're destroying the chance he's giving you to make amends."

Safar grimaced, remembering Umurhan's wrath. "I don't think that's possible," he said. "The only reason I wasn't thrown out immediately is because my sponsor is Lord Muzine, the richest merchant in the city." Muzine was Coralean's friend, the man he'd said he'd call on to help get Safar admitted to the university. "Umurhan doesn't want a scandal and he certainly doesn't want to offend Muzine. He'll fail me, then report the sad news to Muzine. It's the cleanest way to be rid of me."

"Well I for one won't be sorry," came a voice. The two turned and saw that Zeman had worked his way across the patio and was now cleaning the table next to them. Zeman was about Safar's age and height. But he was so thin he was nearly skeletal. His complexion was bad, his face long and horse-like, with wall eyes and overly large teeth.

"It's leeches like you who keep my grandfather poor," Zeman said. "You all eat and drink on credit, or for nothing at all. You rent books and scrolls and keep them as long you like without paying for the extra time. And it isn't only the students. What of that bitch Nerisa he's taken under his wing? A thief, of all things. No, I fear my grandfather is too charitable for his own good. And for mine. I go without as well because of your sort."

He indicted his costume—tight brown leggings, green thigh-length smock, slippers with curled toes—a cheap imitation of what the fashionable lads wore. "I'm forced to clothe myself in the alley markets. It's an insult to a young man of my class and prospects."

Katal was angry. "Don't speak to my friend like that! Safar only receives what I beg him to take. He is a friend and he possesses one of the finest young minds I've met in many a day."

Safar intervened. "He's right, Katal. You are too generous. I'll wager you haven't raised the prices since you opened the *Foolsmire* forty years ago. That's why we all come here. You have a right to a decent profit, my friend. And at your age you deserve to live a life of ease."

Zeman pushed in. "I'll thank you to let me defend myself to my own grandfather," he said to Safar. "As if I need defending. I'm only being sensible, not mean."

"Both of you speak with the arrogance of youth," Katal said. "Neither has the faintest notion of why I live my life as I do."

He pointed at the faded sign hanging from a rusty iron post over the door of bookshop. "The name speaks it for all to see—'*Foolsmire*.' I was a young man when I hung that sign. I planted that tree at the same time. It was just a stick with a few leaves then. Now it shades us with its mighty boughs." His old eyes gleamed in memory. "I was a bright young fellow," he said. "Although probably not as bright as I thought. Still, I had a mind agile enough to compete at the university. But I had no money or influence to gain entrance. Yet I loved books and knowledge above all else. And so I sought a fool's paradise and became a seller of books. I wanted the company of the most intelligent students to discuss the ideas the books contained. I created a place to attract such people, offering my wares at the lowest prices possible. You see before you a poor man, a foolish man, but a happy man. For I have achieved my dreams at the *Foolsmire*."

Safar laughed and nodded in understanding. Zeman frowned, more unhappy than before. "What of me, Grandfather?" he protested. "I didn't ask for this life. I didn't ask for the plague that killed my parents. My mother—your daughter—was comely enough to attract a man with prospects for a husband. But he died before he could prosper and see that I had a chance to prosper as well."

"I gave you a home," Katal said. "What more could I do? Your grandmother died in the same plague, so I lost my whole family, except for you."

"I know that, Grandfather," Zeman said. "And I appreciate the sacrifices you've made. I'm only asking that you try a little harder. Don't give so much away. And when I inherit this place someday you can go to your grave in peace, knowing I've been cared for." Zeman glanced about, noting the shabbiness of his inheritance. "It *does* have a good location, after all. Right in the heart of the student quarter. It should fetch me a decent sum."

Safar had to fight his temper. In Kyrania it was unheard of for a lad to speak so coldly and rudely to his grandfather. But to leave Zeman's comments completely unanswered would bedevil his dreams.

"If it were me," he said, "I could never sell all these books. To misquote the poet—What could you possibly buy that was half so precious as what you sell."

"A brothel, for one," Zeman said. "With a well-planned gaming parlor attached." He gave the table an angry swipe and stalked off.

"You shouldn't let him get away with that," Safar said, hotly. "He shows no respect."

"Never mind him," Katal said. "Zeman is what he is. There's nothing to be done about it. It's Safar Timura I'm worried about just now."

"There's nothing to be done about that either," Safar said.

"What possessed you to take such a chance with Umurhan?" Katal asked, giving his beard a tug of frustration.

Safar lowered his eyes. "You know," he said.

Katal's eyes narrowed. "Hadin, again?"

"Yes."

"Why are you so obsessed with a place on the other side of the world?" Katal said. "A place we're not even certain exists. 'The Land of the Fires,' it's called. For all we know it might really be 'The Frozen Lands.' Or 'The Lands of the Swamps.'"

"I know what I saw in the vision," Safar said. "And I know deep in my bones it's vital that someone find out what happened."

"I gather you think the trail leads into Umurhan's private library," Katal said, dryly. "Among his forbidden books."

Safar nodded, then leaned closer. "I've run across a name," he said, low. He gestured in the direction of the book shop. "It's repeated many times in some of your oldest scrolls. Scholars refer to an ancient they call Lord Asper. A great magician and philosopher. He measured the world and also the distance from Esmir to the moon. He made many predictions that came true, including the rise of Alisarrian and the collapse of his empire."

Katal looked interested. "I've never heard of such a man," he said.

"I don't think Asper was a man," Safar answered.

"What else could he be?"

"A demon," Safar answered.

Katal was so startled he nearly came to his feet. "A demon?" he cried. "What madness is this? The demons have nothing to teach us but evil! I don't care how wise this Asper was, he was most certainly wicked. All demons are. That's why there's a barrier between our species. The curse of the Forbidden Desert."

"Oh, *that*," Safar said. "It's nothing."

"How can you call the greatest spell ever cast in history nothing?" Katal said, aghast. "The finest minds—and, yes, some were demon minds,—composed that spell. It's unbreakable."

Safar shrugged. "Actually, I suspect it can be broken quite easily," he said. "I really wasn't looking for the details, but I do know the curse is based on Asper's work. He had many enemies, many rivals, and to protect his most powerful magic it's said he created a spell of complexity. It made the most simple bit of sorcery appear so tangled and difficult that it would confound even the greatest wizard. If I wanted to break the curse I'd attack the spell of complexity, not the curse itself. I don't think that would take much effort to solve. I'm sure I'd find the key if I could lay my hands on one of his books. Which is exactly what I was looking for when Umurhan surprised me."

"Would you really do such a thing, Safar?" Katal asked, shocked. "Would you really try to lift the curse?"

"Of course not," Safar said, to Katal's vast relief. "What purpose would that serve, except to endanger us all? I have no greater opinion of demons than you."

As he'd promised Coralean, Safar had never mentioned his own experience with demons to anyone, even Katal. So he didn't add he had even more reason to fear the creatures than the old book seller could imagine. And it had occurred to him more than once that despite Coralean's rationalizations, the demon raiders might have found a way to cross the Forbidden Desert. If so, it was his frequent prayer the knowledge had died with them in the avalanche.

He said nothing of this to Katal. Instead, he said, "I'm only interested in what Asper had to say about Hadin. I think it goes to the origins of our world. And all of us. Humans and demons alike."

"This is all very intriguing, Safar," Katal said. "But merely for intellectual discussion among, I might add, the most select few. For it's dangerous talk. Please, for your sake and your family's sake, let it go. Forget Asper. Forget Hadin. Study hard and pass the exam. Umurhan will relent, I'm sure of it. You are capable of great things, my young friend. Don't stumble now. Look ahead to the future."

"I *am*, Katal," Safar said passionately. "Can't you see it? In my vision . . ." he let the rest trail off. He'd been over this ground with Katal many times. "I never wanted to come to Walaria in the first place," he said. "My family insisted I take advantage of Coralean's generous offer." Safar had told various vague tales of why the caravan master felt beholden to him. Katal, realizing it was a sensitive area, had always avoided pressing him for the details. "Old Gubadan wept when I first refused. It was as if I were robbing him of his pride."

"I can see that," Katal said. "You were his prize student, after all. Not many young people like yourself come before a teacher, Safar. It's an experience to be treasured."

"Still, that's not what shook me from my resolve," Safar said. "I love Kyrania. I never wanted to leave it. I loved my father's work. And yet I haven't touched a bit of wet clay in nearly three years. But I was haunted by the vision of Hadin. I couldn't sleep. I could barely eat. The more I thought about it, the more ignorant I felt. And the only way to relieve that was to go to the university and study. So it was Hadin that drove me from my valley, Katal. And Hadin that drives me now."

Safar's blue eyes were alight with the holy zeal of the very young. Katal sighed to himself, only dimly remembering his own days of such single-mindedness. It seemed likely to him, however, that Safar's tale was much more complex than the one he told. There were other forces at work, here. A bitter experience. Perhaps even a tragedy. Could it be a woman? Unlikely. Safar was much too young.

He was forming the words for a new plea of caution when loud voices and the sound of running feet interrupted.

The both looked up to see a small figure in bare feet and raggedy clothes sprinting down the alley towards them.

"What's wrong, Nerisa?" Safar cried as she approached.

Then he heard voices just beyond the alley mouth shouting, "Stop thief! Stop thief!"

Nerisa ran past him and shot up the fig tree like a bolt fired from a bow, disappearing into the thick foliage.

A moment later the fat stallkeep, trailed by several hard-looking men, lumbered into view. They slowed, panting heavily.

"Where is he?" the stallkeep demanded when he'd reached them. "Where'd he go?"

"Where did who go, sir?" Katal asked, face a mask of surprised innocence.

"The thief," one of the rough men said.

"He's a big brute of a lad," the stallkeep broke in. "A real animal, I tell you. I don't mind saying I was in fear for my life when I caught him stealing from me."

"We've seen no one matching that description," Safar said. "Have we, Katal?"

Katal made a face of grave concern. "We certainly haven't. And we've been sitting here for hours."

"Let's check around," one of the rough men said. "Maybe these two good citizens were dipping in the wine too deeply to notice."

"I assure you no one looking like the one you described has come this way," Katal said. "But feel free to look all you like."

Nerisa gently parted a branch to peer at the scene below. While the rough men searched, Safar and Katal engaged the stallkeep in casual conversation to soothe suspicion.

The young thief was not pleased with herself. She'd let her emotions spoil her timing and then she'd reacted in a panic when things went wrong. The execution, to the dismay of many of the heaviest gamblers, had gone off without a hitch. Tulaz's reputation was intact. The adulteresses' head was not. And the plaza crowd had gotten a good show. The victim had been as beautiful as advertised. And she'd wailed most entertainingly when the jailers stripped her, trying pitifully to hide her nakedness with chained hands. Tulaz had played the showman to the hilt, pretending to hesitate several times over the lovely curls bent beneath his blade. Then he'd whacked off her head with such ease that not even a blind fool could doubt the minuscule size of his stony executioner's heart.

But just before he'd struck, the woman had let out a mournful groan that had echoed across the hushed plaza. It was a groan of such anguish, hauled up from the darkest well of human misery, that Nerisa had been wrenched from her emotional moorings. For the first time in her life she'd burst into tears. An uncontrollable urge to leave that place of horrors, and leave it quickly, had overwhelmed her.

Then Tulaz's blade severed the woman's head. The crowd thundered its approval. Nerisa leaped off the wagon, landing with her face to the stall. The object she'd come for gleamed at her from the trays and instinct took over. She scooped it up, heard the stallkeep's alarmed howl of discovery, and dived blindly into the crowd.

"Thief!" the stallkeep had cried.

Despite the after-execution chaos the plaza guards had heard the stallkeep's cry and had come running. The blackest of fates must have made the crowd part before them. One of the men had even managed to get a grip on her arm, but she'd clawed him and he'd yelped and let go. Nerisa ran as hard as she'd ever run in her life. But the plaza guards were street-smart pursuers and so they knew all her tricks, blocked all her avenues of escape. And Nerisa, to her present immense shame, had taken the panicked route of least resistance and had led her pursuers directly to the *Foolsmire*—her only place of refuge where anyone at all cared about a skinny little girl thief who had no memory of mother, father, or even the slightest touch of warmth.

She patted the small object hidden under her shirt. It was a gift for Safar. She peeped through the broad leaves of the fig tree and saw him shove coins forward to buy the stallkeep a jug of wine. She hoped Safar would like his present. Stolen or not, it had been purchased at a greater price than he could ever know. Nerisa saw the rough men return, shaking their heads and saying their quarry had escaped. Safar called for more wine. Katal obliged. And while the tumblers were poured and the first toasts drunk, Nerisa slipped off the branch onto the alley wall.

Then she shinnied up a drain pipe to the roof and then to an adjoining building and was gone.

CHAPTER NINE
GOOD MEN AND PIOUS

The Student Quarter was the oldest section of Walaria, an untidy sprawl between the rear of the many-domed temple and the western most wall. The western gate had been built many centuries before. It was so little used it had fallen into disrepair and the king had it permanently sealed to avoid the expense of fixing it. The Quarter itself was a warren of broken cobbled streets so narrow that front doors opened directly into traffic. The residences and shops were among the poorest in the city and were stacked atop one another with no particular plan, leaning crazily over the streets.

Safar lived in the near ruins of the one remaining gate tower on the western wall. He'd rented it from an old warder who considered himself the owner because in his view the king no longer had any use for it. He also offered board—one meal a day cooked by his wife. The gate tower consisted of two rooms, one without a roof, and strolling rights along the wall. It wasn't just the cheap price that had attracted Safar to his accommodations. He was a child of the mountains, the gate tower gave him an unimpeded view of the entire city on one side and the broad empty plains on the other. At night the tower also made a marvelous observatory where he could study the heavens and check them against his Dreamcatcher books.

It was also good for sunsets and on this particular day, some hours after he'd left the *Foolsmire*, Safar was sprawled across the broad stone windowsill, toasting the departing sun with the last of his wine. From the other side of the Quarter he was serenaded by a priest singing the last prayer of the day from the Temple's chanting tower. It was magically amplified so it resounded across the city. The song was a daily plea to the gods who guard the night:

> *We are men of Walaria, good men and pious.*
> *Blessed be, blessed be.*
> *Our women are chaste, our children respectful.*

Blessed be, blessed be.
Devils and felons beware of our city.
Blessed be, blessed be.
You will find only the faithful here.
Blessed be, blessed be . . .

When the song ended Safar laughed aloud. He was still a little drunk and found the song's sanctimonious lies amusing. The prayer was a creation of Umurhan's, coined in his youth when he was second in command of the temple. It was considered by many—meaning Umurhan's most fervent political supporters—to be the mightiest spell against evil in the city's history. Umurhan had used the acclaim to help topple his wizardly superior. Once that had been accomplished he'd joined with Didima and Kalasariz, both ambitious young lords at the time, to make Didima king and Kalasariz the chief wazier. The three ruled Walaria to this day with brutal zeal.

To Safar the nightly spellsong had become an ugly jest, a riddle that would be a worthy creation of Harle, himself, that dark jester of the gods. Was the evil outside the walls of Walaria? Or within?

He'd heard the song the first time only a short two years before. The setting sun had been in his view that day, just as it was now . . .

*   *   *

It was a small caravan, a poor caravan, carrying castoffs from the stalls of distant markets. The finest animal was the camel Safar sat upon, a fly-blown, bad-tempered male he'd hired for the journey. He'd made the jump from Kyrania—more a wobble, actually—in three stages. The first was a traveling party to the river towns at the foot of the Gods' Divide. The second was with a group of drovers herding their cattle across the dry plains to new grazing grounds. He'd come across the caravan during that leg of the trip. It was heading directly for Walaria and so he'd joined it, saving many days and miles.

The sun was falling fast as he approached the city, rolling in his camel saddle like a fisherman in troubled waters. Walaria was backlit by a rosy hue casting the city's immense walls into shadow so they looked like a forbidding range of black mountains. Palace domes and towers of worship glittered above those walls, with high peaked buildings steepling the gaps in between. The night breeze brought the exotic sounds and scents of Walaria: the heavy buzz of crowded humanity, the crash and clang of busy workshops, the smell of smoke from cooking fires and garbage heaps—good garlic and bad meat. The atmosphere was sensuous and dangerous at the same time—as much was promised as was threatened.

Guarding the main gate was a squad of soldiers bearing Didima's royal standard—gilded fig leaves, harking back hundreds of years to when Walaria was nothing more than a small oasis for nomads. The gate was menacing—looking like the cavernous opening of a giant's mouth. The gate's black teeth were raised iron bars thick as a man's waist and tapering to rough spear points. The caravan master, a vaporous little man with shifty eyes, bargained with the soldiers for entrance. But he couldn't, or wouldn't meet the bribe price and so the caravan was ordered to camp overnight outside the walls—just beyond the enormous ditch encircling the city. The ditch was as much for waste disposal as it was a defense and it was filled with garbage and offal and the cast-off corpses of citizens too poor for a proper funeral. Smoke-blackened figures scurried along the ditch, tending the many fires kept burning to dispose of the waste. These were the city's licensed scavengers, so low in station it was considered a curse to stare at them overlong, much less suffer their touch.

Safar, hoping to avoid an unpleasant night, shyly approached the sergeant in charge of the squad and presented him with Coralean's letter of introduction. It was written on fine linen and bound by thick gold thread and so impressed the sergeant that he waved Safar through the gate. Safar hesitated, peering into the huge tunnel bored through the walls. It was long and dark with a small circle of dim light—looking like the size of a plate—announcing the exit on the other side.

It was then he first heard the spellsong, a wailing voice from far away, and seeming so close . . .

"We are men of Walaria, good men and pious.
Blessed be, blessed be . . ."

It filled him with such dread he tried to turn back. But the sergeant shoved him forward. "Get your stumps movin' lad," the sergeant said with rough humor. "I've had a long day and there's a flagon of Walaria's best missin' me down at the tavern."

Safar did as he was told, treading through the darkness to the gradually widening circle of light, the spellsong wailing in his ears:

". . . You will find only the faithful here.
Blessed be, blessed be . . ."

It was with immense relief that he exited the other side. The spellsong had faded, boosting his spirits. He looked about to see which way he should go, but the night had closed in and he was confronted with dark streets glooming in every direction. Here and there light leaked through heavily-shuttered windows. Only the hard cobbles beneath his feet hinted there was a path through that darkness.

Then torches flared and he saw the sign of a nearby inn. Beneath it the inn's crier extolled its virtues for all to hear: "Soup and a sleep for six coppers. Soup and a sleep for six coppers . . ."

Safar hurried toward the crier, a wary hand on his knife hilt. Cheap as it was, the inn proved to be a cheery stopping place for travelers and he spent the night in comfort. The following day he presented himself at the house of Lord Muzine, letter of introduction clutched in his hand.

The Lord's major domo was not so impressed by the fine linen and gold thread as the sergeant. His face was stone as he took the letter, glanced boredly at Coralean's wax seal.

"Wait here," he said in imperious tones.

Safar waited and he waited long—pacing a deep path in the dusty street outside Muzine's gated mansion. For a time he marveled at the passing crowds and traffic. Although he'd been to Walaria before, he'd been in his father's company and seen things through a child's eyes. Now he was an adult on his own for the first time. He eagerly searched the crowds for signs of the decadence Gubadan had warned him against. He wondered what he'd missed during the previous visits besides the evening spellsong. But if there was anything to tempt a young man in that neighborhood it was kept hidden behind the walls of the mansions lining the avenue. He became bored and hungry but he didn't dare leave his post and miss the major domo's return.

Finally, when the day was nearly done and the time approached for the nightly spellsong, the man emerged. He sniffed at Safar as if he smelled something bad.

"Here," he said, limply handing Safar a rolled up tube of paper bearing Muzine's seal, so recently dripped it was still soft to the touch. The linen was of poorer quality than Coralean's letter of introduction and there was only a black ribbon binding it instead of gold thread.

"The Master directs you to present yourself at the Grand Temple tomorrow. You will give this to one of Lord Umurhan's assistants."

The major domo brushed empty fingers together as if they'd previously held something offensive, then turned as if to go.

Safar was confused. "Excuse me, friend," he said. The major domo froze in his tracks. He looked Safar up and down, wrinkling his nose in disgust. Safar ignored this, saying, "I was hoping for an appointment with your master. I have gifts to give him from my father and mother who also send their wishes and prayers for his good health."

The major domo sneered. "My Master has no need of such gifts. And as for an appointment . . . I will not insult my lord with such a request from someone of your station."

Safar felt his temper rise and quickly doused it. "But he *has* agreed to sponsor me at the university, hasn't he?" he asked, indicating the letter.

"My Master said that was his intent," the major domo answered. "Funds will be deposited for your care. He has the Lord Coralean's promise of repayment for any necessary expenses." The major domo paused for emphasis, then said, "But he said to warn you not to take advantage of his good nature and friendship with Lord Coralean. My Master's charity will only extend so far. So do not return here for more. Do I make myself clear?"

Safar wanted to throw the letter into the man's sneering face. But he'd made promises he couldn't break and so he swallowed his pride and turned away without comment. The next day, after a night of angry teeth-grinding, he made his way to the Grand Temple of Walaria.

The route took him through the heart of the great crossroads city and the sights and scents and sounds were enthralling. The crowds were thick, barely making room for cursing wagon drovers ladened with market goods. Except for irritated grunts when he bumped into them, the people ignored him—keeping their heads low so as not to meet another's eyes. The traffic flow carried him past beggars crying "alms, alms for the sake of the gods," and open windows framing scantily clad women who called for the "blushing boy" to come tarry in their arms. There were shops with luxurious carpets and rich jewelry mixed with coffee houses and opium stalls. Thieves of all ages and sexes darted in and out of the crowd, snatching at opportunity.

And all the while cart pushers sang out their wares and with the drums and bells and whistles of the street entertainers it made a thrilling song: "Pea-Nuts! Pea-Nuts, Salted And Hot! " Or, "Rose Pud-Ding! Rose Pud-Ding. Sweet As The Bud!" And, "Sher-Bet Iced So Nice! Sher-Bet Iced So Nice!"

The Grand Temple and University was so vast it made a walled city of its own. It had a wide gateless archway for an entrance with fearsome monsters carved in the stone. There were no guards and men dressed in priestly togas or rough student robes poured in and out with the single-minded purpose of bees tending a forest hive. Safar asked directions and soon was making his way through the confusion of temple buildings to the busy office of the High Clerk. There he presented his sponsor's letter and was again commanded to wait.

This time he was ready. He'd brought food and drink and an old stargazer's book to while away the hours. His supplies as well as the day were gone and he'd memorized the book by the time a skinny priest with prunish lips and a rushed manner returned with an answer.

"Come with me, come with me," he said. And he turned and raced away without waiting to see if Safar was following.

Safar had to hurry to catch him. "Have I been accepted, Master?" he asked.

"Don't call me master. Don't call me master," the priest chided. "Holy one will do. Holy one will . . ."

"Pardon my ignorance, Holy One," Safar broke in. "Have I been accepted to the school?"

"Yes, yes. This way, now. This way now."

Safar was led to a large empty dining hall with stone, food-encrusted floors.

The priest said, "Scrub it down. Scrub it down." He pointed at a wooden bucket of greasy water with a brush floating on top.

Safar looked and by the time he raised his head the priest had darted off. "Wait, Holy One!" he shouted after him. But the little priest had already gone out the door, slamming it behind him.

Safar fetched the bucket and brush and got on his knees and scrubbed. As a village lad he saw no shame in necessary labor, no matter how mean the task. He scrubbed for hours, making little headway because the water was as filthy as the floor. At spellsong an older acolyte came to take him to a huge dormitory, crammed with first-year students. He was given a blanket, a place to stretch out on the bare floor and a rusty metal pail containing a cold baked potato, a hard wheat roll and a boiled egg.

While he wolfed the food down the acolyte gave him a quick summery of his duties, most of which seemed to involve scrubbing dirty floors.

"When do my studies begin?" Safar asked.

The acolyte laughed. "They've already started," he said. And he left without further explanation.

Safar had learned long ago from Gubadan that teachers liked to make obscure points. Very well, he thought, if floor scrubbing is my first lesson, so be it. He scrubbed for a month, lingering as he toted buckets of water past foul-smelling workshops and lecture halls that echoed with the wise orations of master priests.

Then Umurhan summoned him and he never had to scrub another floor again.

*   *   *

Safar drifted out of his reverie. He rubbed his eyes, noting the view through the window had been replaced by glistening stars. He saw a comet tail just near the House of the Jester and became absorbed in the astral meaning of the occurrence. Then he heard a sound—a scratching at his door. Through a fog of concentration it came to him that he'd heard this sound only a moment before. And he thought, Oh, yes . . . I was thinking about Umurhan and something interrupted me. And that something was a noise at my door.

He heard a voice call, "Safar? Are you awake?"

It was a young voice. Safar puzzled, then smiled as he realized who it was. "Come in," he said.

CHAPTER TEN

NERISA

On the other side of the rough plank door Nerisa hastily combed fingers through her hair and straightened her clothes. She wore a short loose tunic that showed off her long legs, belted tightly about her small waist to draw attention away from her boyish figure. The gray tunic and pale leggings were castoffs, but the cloth was of such good quality that the patches barely showed.

"That *is* Nerisa, isn't it?" came Safar's voice. She heard him laugh. "If it's some rogue instead, you're wasting your energies, O friend of the night. For I've spent all my money on drink and other low pursuits."

Nerisa giggled and pushed the door open. Safar was grinning at her from the other side of the room, lolling on the windowsill, white student robes hiked up over his strong mountaineer's legs. Nerisa thought she'd never seen such a handsome young man. He was tall and slender, with wide shoulders and a narrow waist, accented by his red acolyte's belt. His skin was olive; his nose curved gracefully over full lips. His dark hair was cut close, with a stray curl dangling over eyes so blue they had melted her heart when she first looked into them.

He beckoned her to the window. "I've just sighted a comet," he said pointing out at the star-embedded heavens.

She came to him, leaning over his sprawled out legs so she could see.

"Right there," he said, directing her. "In Harle—the House of the Jester."

She saw the long, narrow constellation of Harle, with its distinctive peaked hat and beaky-nosed face. Crossing at about chin level was the wide pale streak of a comet's tail.

"I see it," she said, voice trembling from being so close to Safar. Troubled, she drew away, turning her head so he wouldn't see her blush. "I hope I wasn't bothering you," she said.

"Nonsense," Safar replied. "I'm lonely for my sisters. If you ever meet them don't you dare say I told you that. They'd never let me forget it." He chuckled. "But I do miss them. There, I've said it. I grew up surrounded by my sisters and now I pine for them. I hope you don't mind being a substitute."

Nerisa *minded* very much! She wasn't quite sure exactly what reactions she wanted from Safar but she could say most definitely brotherly feelings were not among them.

She put a hand on her hip, trying to look as adult female as possible. "If you miss women so much, Safar Timura," she said, bold as she dared, "why don't I ever see you with one? Except *me*, of course." She unconsciously touched her hair. "The other students spend all the time they can chasing women at the brothels."

To Nerisa's enormous delight Safar blushed and attempted a stumbled answer—"I . . . uh . . . don't go in for . . . that sort of thing." He recovered, saying, "I made a fool of myself once. I hope I know better now."

Nerisa nodded, thinking, I *knew* it was a woman! A bad experience, obviously. She hated the woman who'd made Safar suffer. But she was also delighted that her rival, although probably beautiful and certainly more mature, had made a bad job of things.

"What happened to her?" she asked.

"Who?"

"The woman in the bad experience."

Safar made a wry face. "I didn't know I was being that obvious," he said. Then he shrugged, saying, "Her name was Astarias. A courtesan I was fool enough to fall in love with. But she made it plain she had no intention of making a life with a potter's son. It seems she had grander plans which didn't include me."

As Nerisa was mulling this over Safar motioned for her to sit on the pile of old pillows and rugs that were the room's sole furnishings. She sank down and he joined her. She made herself look away as he sat, robes carelessly riding up over his long limbs.

"I suppose Katal gave you a bad time," Safar said, sliding away from the previous subject.

"What?" said Nerisa, in a bit in a daze.

Safar smiled saying, "After the, ah, large gentleman and his . . . friends left I believe you called the entire thing a, ah . . . 'misunderstanding?'"

"Well it was!" Nerisa said. She saw with relief—and some disappointment—that his robes had been properly tucked over his lap. "I was *trying* to pay for it. But he thought I was a thief. Guess he didn't see the money in my hand."

"You must admit, Nerisa," Safar said, "you have been known to engage in, shall we say, long term *borrowing?*"

Nerisa shrugged. "It's how I live," she said. "I know old Katal can't understand it. Maybe he thinks I've got a family someplace. And any day they'll come back and I can stop sleeping at the *Foolsmire* and be with my family again. But that isn't *ever* going to happen. So I steal. I'll stop when I don't have to anymore."

"I understand that," Safar said. "It wasn't how I was raised, but I can see how things can be different in Walaria. I wish I could do something to help you. But I have a hard enough time helping myself."

"Oh, but *you have* helped me," Nerisa said with unintended passion. She calmed herself, took a breath, then, "I mean, you show me your books. And teach me things out of them. It's almost like I'm a student myself. The only gir—I mean, woman student at the university."

Katal had given her reading and writing lessons, but her interest hadn't really been sparked until Safar had taken her under his intellectual wing. Nerisa was so bright and eager to please that she quickly caught on to everything he introduced her to.

Safar sighed. "I've also tried to teach you logic," he said. "Let's go back to your basic defense. Which was that as a poor orphan child you're forced to steal in order to live."

"That's true," she replied firmly.

"Very well," he said. "I'll accept that. But pray tell me what did you find at that fat old knave's stall that was so important?"

"This," Nerisa said, softly, shyly pushing forward a small paper wrapped package. "It's for you. It's a . . . present."

Safar's eyebrows shot up. "A gift? You *stole* a gift?" There was an edge to his tone, indicating that such an act was anathema to someone of honest rearing. But he was unwrapping the package just the same, saying, "This isn't right, Nerisa. You shouldn't steal a gift. Hells, you shouldn't steal at all. But to think that I was responsible for . . ."

His voice trailed off as the wrapping fell back and the object was revealed.

It was a small stone turtle, black with age, stumpy legs arching from its shell. Its head stretched to the end of a long wrinkled neck, beaked jaws open as if the turtle were chasing a fish. All in all a charming toy for a child in some long ago day.

Safar's first jolt came as he realized the little object was no toy, but an ancient idol representing one of the turtle gods. Great care had been exercised in carving it—the detail so intricate the turtle seemed alive, as if it were in motion instead of a piece of stone at permanent rest. His second and decidedly greater jolt came when he saw the painting on the turtle's back. It was of a large green island, a jagged line of blue surrounding it to mark the seas that washed its shores. On that island was a huge red mountain, with a monster's face spewing painted flames from its mouth.

"Hadin," Safar breathed.

"You're always going on about it," Nerisa said, pleased at the awe she saw in his face. "And you've shown me pictures in your books. When I spotted it I knew right away it was something you'd want." She shrugged. "So I got it."

Safar was smiling and nodding, but from the absent stare in his eyes she doubted he'd heard a word. She fell silent, watching in fascination as his hand seemed to be drawn to the turtle as if it were a powerful lodestone. He twitched when his fingers met the stone, and his eyes widened in surprise.

"It's magical," he whispered.

He lifted the idol up, turning it about to study it from every angle. "I wonder where it came from," he mused "And how it got here."

Nerisa said nothing, realizing that Safar was only speaking his thoughts aloud. He was so absorbed in the turtle god she felt as if she were peeping through a window at a private moment.

His face cleared and he lit up the room with his smile. "Thank you, Nerisa," he said, quite simply. "I can never repay you for such a gift."

Then to her enormous, heart-stopping thrill he leaned over, put an arm about her shoulders and pulled her close. He kissed her lightly on the lips and she shuddered, excited and frightened at the same time. Then the moment ended and he drew away and she hated the tender brotherly look in his eyes.

To revenge herself she pointed at the turtle, saying, "I stole it, remember? Are you sure you want to dirty your hands with it?"

"It doesn't matter," was all he said, voice so loving she forgave him.

And so she asked, "What's it for?"

Safar shook his head. "I don't know," he said. "Whatever its purpose, it's definitely magical. I can feel it!" He hesitated, thinking, then went on, "I think it must be like a harp feels when a musician plucks a string. A sound resonates all through me."

"How do we find out what it does?" she asked, casually including herself.

Safar frowned. "I have to cast a spell to find out," he said, "and I really shouldn't do anything with you here. Lord Umurhan doesn't approve of his acolytes performing magic in public." Actually, the penalty for discovery was immediate dismissal, but Safar didn't mention that.

"Oh, please! Please!" Nerisa said. "I've never seen magic done before."

Safar hesitated and she leaped into the gap. "If you *really* want to thank me," she said, "let me watch what you do. Please, it's important to me. I see the spells and stuff in the books you show me. And sometimes you explain it to me. But if I could see it for myself I'd understand it better."

Her lips curled into a twisted little grin. "And you *know* I won't tell anybody. There's probably nobody in the world better at keeping their snapper snapped than me."

Safar was watching her closely the whole time she spoke. He'd liked her the first time they'd met at the *Foolsmire* nearly two years before. She'd have been ten summers old then, he thought. He'd been shocked to see a little girl living alone on the streets. Nothing like that would ever happen to any child in Kyrania. She was also amazingly bright. She had only to look at a page and she could turn away and recite every word exactly. Katal had told him she'd learned to read and write in less than two weeks. And whenever he corrected her speech she never made the same mistake again. Safar had not only found her easy to converse with but sometimes used her to test news ideas. No matter how complex the subject, he'd soon learned, if Nerisa didn't understand the fault was either because he didn't truly understand it himself or because he was putting the matter poorly.

To the Hells with Umurhan, he thought. He's going to throw me out anyway. What do I have to lose?

So he said, quite formally, "Your wish, Ladyship," he said, "is my command."

Nerisa clapped her hands and cried, "Thank you, Safar! You won't be sorry. I promise."

Overcome with her delight she threw caution to the winds and hugged him and dared to kiss him on the lips. Then she pulled back, blushing furiously. She ducked her head and concentrated on a stray thread as if the task were one that required immense concentration. For the first time Safar noticed she wasn't wearing her usual urchin rags. There was no sign of boyish pretense in the Nerisa sitting beside him. She was feminine through and through, from the tilt of her chin to the graceful arc of her wrist as she plucked at the thread. He saw she'd also dressed with care in a costume that set off her best womanly features—long legs beginning to find shape despite their slenderness. Soft slippers defining her small, well-formed feet. A narrow waist with a broad belt pulled tight over budding hips. From the experience of a large but close family he guessed her bosom—hidden under the loose material of her tunic—was just beginning to develop. He remembered his sisters' embarrassment at Nerisa's age. And how that embarrassment had quickly become something else entirely when they started looking at the village lads differently and the age of long romantic sighs began.

Nerisa recovered and raised her head to look at him. She was smiling, but her lower lip was trembling. Her eyes were unguarded and he could see emotion boiling just beneath their dark surfaces. He realized that if he said the wrong thing just now she'd burst into tears—and suddenly he knew the reason for those welling tears. Nerisa was in love with him. He'd seen his sisters fall in love with much older lads and suffer the same torment. It was a quickly passing illness, he knew. A malady of the very young—although just as painful as anything an adult endured. It would be even harder on Nerisa, he thought, because she was so alone—so unloved. Safar, who still wore scars from his encounter with Astarias, knew that anything he did to hurt Nerisa would wound her deeply. He wondered what he ought to do about the situation. Then he thought, why do anything at all? Give her a chance to grow out of the crush, like his sisters had. He'd just have to tread carefully from now on.

Safar cleared his throat and picked up the turtle. Nerisa tensed for words of scornful dismissal.

"This spell will be much easier if you help me," he said calmly.

Nerisa's reprieved heart soared. She leaped to her feet. "What do you want me to do?" she asked eagerly.

He pointed to a battered trunk across the room. "You'll find a wooden case in there," he said, "with most of the things I need. Then, if it's no trouble, you might start a fire under the brazier."

"No trouble at all," she said, adopting Safar's casual tones.

She fetched him the case, and while she got the fire going he poured different colors of scented oils into a wide-mouthed jar. Then he sprinkled packets of mysterious powders and strong-smelling herbs into the oil, mixing it all together with a stone mortar. Nerisa heard him chanting as he worked, but his voice was so low she couldn't make out the words. When he judged the fire hot enough, he carried the large jar and turtle to the brazier. He set the jar on the grate and while it heated he drew colored chalk marks on the floor, making an elaborate, many-sided design that enclosed the fire.

When he was done he said, "Now, if you'll sit right there . . ." He motioned to a spot well inside the design.

She did as he directed, scooting in as close as she could to the brazier. Safar sat across from her. His image appeared watery through the heated fumes rising from the jar.

"Are you comfortable?" he asked.

She nodded.

"We'll get started then," he said. "But you have to promise me you won't laugh if I make a mistake. I'm just a student, you know."

Nerisa giggled. She was sure that, student or not, Safar just had to be the best wizard in all Esmir. Then she realized how relaxed she'd become since he'd asked her to help. She wondered if his request had been a ploy to put her at ease. If so, she loved him even more for it.

Safar sniffed the fumes. "It's ready now," he said.

"What do I do?" she asked.

Safar handed her a long-handled brush with a narrow blade made of boar's bristles. "Dip this into the jar," he told her. "Stir it around and get a good load on the bristles."

She stirred the brush through the thick, bubbling mixture. She wrinkled her nose at the fumes, although later she couldn't have said if the scent was foul or fair, sweet or sour. Safar signaled with a nod and she withdrew it. He picked up the stone turtle, centered it in his flattened right palm, then extended it over the fumes.

"Now paint the turtle's back," he said.

Nerisa gently stroked the brush across the green image of the island. Although the mixture from the jar was tarry black, it left only gray streaks on the green.

"Lay it on thick," Safar said. "This isn't a job for a timid hand."

Nerisa furrowed her brow and daubed with a will until the goo spread all over the stone and spilled into Safar's hand.

"That's exactly right," he said. "Now dip up some more and do another coat. Thicker than the last, if you can. But this time we need a chant to help things along. So listen closely to what I say and repeat it exactly."

Nerisa nodded understanding, loaded the brush again, and as she laid the mixture across the idol's back they chanted together:

> "Light dawning through the night,
> What pearls hide beneath the stone?
> All that is dark emerge into bright,
> Give flesh to rock and marrow to bone."

Nerisa's pulse quickened as she saw a faint light emanating from the stone idol. She swore she saw the turtle's legs move and then she gasped as the idol twitched into life and scuttled across Safar's palm. He whispered for her to be still and laid the turtle on the floor. Instantly the light died and the idol sank down, freezing into its former lifeless pose. Safar swore, then looked up to give Nerisa an abashed grin.

"This is going to be harder than I thought," he said. "We could chant all night and still not come up with the right spell.

From his sleeve he withdrew a small silver knife, double-edged and etched with elaborate and mysterious designs. It was the witch's knife Coralean had given him to unravel difficult problems.

"Fortunately," he said, indicating the knife, "I have a way to cheat."

Again he signaled for Nerisa to be silent and he laid the knife against the idol's stone shell—point touching the red painted mountain with the monster's face. He chanted:

> "Conjure the key
> That fits the lock.
> Untangle the traces,
> And cut the knot . . ."

Safar's voice dipped lower and the rest of the chant was lost to Nerisa. But she was so struck by his intensity that she probably wouldn't have heard the words even if they'd been shouted. She'd never seen such concentration. Safar's eyes seemed to be turned inward, smoldering with smoky blue fire. A soft light formed about his whole body, a rosy band shot with pinpricks of color. His long face shone with perspiration, making the hollows seem deeper and the edges sharper. Nerisa smelled the faint musk rising from his body and felt a great calm settle around her like the softest of blankets. Her eyes, as if they had a will of their own, fixed on the monster's painted face and became riveted there.

Safar gave the stone a final sharp rap with his knife and suddenly the monster's face broke free from the stone, floating up and up, and then the painted eyes blinked into life and its mouth moved, forming words:

"Shut up! Shut up! Shut up!" Nerisa heard it say.

A body formed beneath the face, and Nerisa pulled back in surprise as a little creature, perhaps three hands high, hopped off the turtle's back and stood on the floor. It had the visage of a toad, with huge eyes and a mouth stretched wide to reveal four needle-sharp fangs. But the rest of its body was that of an elegant little man, richly clothed in a form-fitting costume covering it from toe to neck. The creature seemed angry, hands perched on narrow hips, ugly toad head turned toward the stone turtle.

"If you don't shut up," it said to the idol, "I'll make you! Just wait and see if I don't!" Then the creature looked up at Safar, complaining, "He gives me a headache! Always talking. Never listening. Sometimes I can't even hear myself think!"

"I'm sorry you're forced to live with such noisy company," Safar said, as natural as could be. "But in case you haven't noticed you've just been summoned. And if you'll pardon my rudeness, whatever quarrel you have with your companion is of no interest to us."

The creature glared at Safar, then at Nerisa. "That's the trouble with humans," he said. "No concern for others." He cocked his head at the idol as if listening, then nodded. "I couldn't agree more, Gundaree, " he said to the idol. "For a change you speak wisely." Then, to Safar, he said, "Gundaree says all humans are selfish. And you've certainly done nothing since we met to disprove it."

"Who is Gundaree?" Safar asked.

The creature snorted, tiny flames shooting from its nostrils. "My twin! Who else?" He spoke as if Safar were the most ignorant mortal in existence.

"And you are?"

Another fiery snort. "Gundara, that's who!"

"Why hasn't your twin also appeared?" Safar asked. "Tell him to come out so we can see him."

Gundara shrugged, the gesture as graceful as a dancer's. "He never appears to humans," he said. "It's not in the rules. I take care of your sort. He does the demons."

"Then you *do* understand you've been summoned," Safar said. "And that you must do my bidding."

Gundara hopped up on a three-legged stool, perching there so he was eye-level with Safar. "Sure, sure. I understand. Bid away, O Master of Rudeness. But would you mind getting to it? I haven't eaten my dinner yet." He gestured at the idol. "That damned greedy twin of mine will get it all if I don't get back soon."

He turned to Nerisa, perhaps hoping to find more sympathy there. "You won't believe how hard it is to come by a decent meal when you live in a stone idol."

"I can see how it might be," Nerisa said. She rummaged in a pocket and came up with a sweet.

Gundara's eyes lit up. "Haven't had a taste of sugar in a thousand years," he said. He held out a tiny hand for the treat.

Nerisa hesitated, looking at Safar. He nodded for her to go ahead and she extended the sweet, which was immediately grabbed by Gundara and popped into his mouth. He chewed, closing his eyes as if he were in paradise. Then he gave a delicate flick of his long red tongue, picking off any stray sugar crumbs from his lips.

When he was done he turned Safar. "What do you want, human? And don't make it too difficult. You don't get the world for a sweet, you know."

"First I want to know something about you," Safar said. "Where are you from? And what is your purpose?"

Gundara sighed. "Why do I get all the stupid ones?" he complained. "Three times out in five hundred years and each one dumber than the other."

Safar proffered the silver knife and the creature shrank back, petulant look turning to one of fear. "I've had just about enough of your smart talk," Safar said. "I'm the one in command here."

"There's no reason to get so excited," Gundara replied.

"Answer my questions," Safar demanded.

"I'm from Hadin, where else?" Gundara said. "My twin and I were made there long ago. How long, I can't really say. A few thousand years, at least. We were a gift to a witch on her coronation as queen."

"And your purpose?" Safar asked.

"We're Favorites," Gundara said, rolling his eyes at such a stupid question. "We help wizards and witches with their spells."

"You said you and your twin's duties were divided between humans and demons," Safar said. "Why is this?"

"How do I know?" Gundara said with barely disguised disgust. "That's how we were made, is all. Those are the rules. I do humans. Gundaree does demons. Simple as that."

"Is your twin exactly like you?" Safar asked.

Gundara laughed, and the sound was like glass breaking. "Not in the slightest," he said. "I'm beautiful, as you can see. Gundaree, on the other hand, has a human face." The creature shuddered. "What could be uglier than that, no offense intended, I'm sure."

"How did you come to be in Esmir?" Safar asked.

"Now that," Gundara said, "is the saddest tale in the whole history of tragic stories. We were being transported in the Queen's treasure chest and pirates attacked our ship. From that time on we have been the property of the foulest creatures you can imagine. Traded from one filthy hand to another. Then we got mixed in with worthless goods about fifty years ago and were lost. We've been living in market stalls ever since. Ignored by everyone."

He gave Nerisa a fond look. "That was quite a trick you pulled at the market place," he said. "I've always thought females made the smartest humans." Nerisa blushed, but said nothing.

Gundara turned to Safar. "I suppose my twin and I are stuck with you for awhile," he said. "Until somebody kills you, or you trade us to someone else, that is."

"If you don't show some manners soon," Safar replied, "I'll make you and your brother a gift to the oldest, dirtiest, wartiest witch in all Esmir."

"Okay, okay," Gundara said. "Don't get so upset. I was only making conversation."

"What can you do," Safar asked, "besides act as my Favorite?"

"As if that wasn't enough," Gundara grumbled. "I guess no one's satisfied with good, sound sorcerous enhancement these days. Why, in the old—" he broke off when he saw Safar's warning look. "Never mind. Forget I said anything. Apparently a poor Favorite doesn't even have the gods-given right to grumble around here. If you want more, more you shall get. I can fetch and carry things that would be fatal for a mortal to touch. I can also spy on your enemies, if you like. Although that's kind of limited since I can't get more than about twenty feet from the turtle. So you'd have to hide me in your enemy's quarters, or whatever else your feeble human imagination can come up with. I'm also pretty good at giving warning if evil-doers are about."

Gundara snickered at some private joke. "As a matter of fact," he said, "if I were you I'd command me to get busy with that job right now."

"What do you mean?" Safar demanded.

Another snicker. "Never mind," Gundara said. "My loyalty can only be tested so far, you know. If you can't take a hint, O Wise Master, sod off!"

"Favorite!" Safar barked. "Post guard! Immediately!"

The creature laughed and hopped to his feet. "Right away, Master!" he said. "Never fear, Gundara is near!"

Then, to Nerisa, "The only reason I said anything at all, my dear, is that you were nice to me. Gave poor Gundara a sugar treat to snack on, you did. If those men outside were coming for my sour-humored Master, I wouldn't have said anything at all.

"But they're coming for you, Nerisa. And if you're the cunning little dear I think you are, you'll get out of here quick!"

With that there was a sharp *pop!* and Gundara vanished.

Instinct jolted Nerisa to her feet and without a word she threw herself at the window. She disappeared through it just as the door slammed open and four very large, very pale men rushed inside. Safar scooped up the idol, hiding it in his robes as he scrambled to his feet to confront the invaders.

"What's the meaning of this?" he demanded.

The tallest and palest of the men answered, "Any meaning I like, Acolyte Timura! Now, tell me where the thief Nerisa is! And tell me quick if you value your hide!"

Safar's heart climbed into his throat.

The man confronting him was Lord Kalasariz—Walaria's notorious spymaster.

CHAPTER ELEVEN
KALASARIZ

Tall as Safar was, the spy master was taller and so thin and pale in his black robes and skull cap that he looked like a specter.

Safar should have abased himself—should have fallen to his knees and knocked his head against the floor, begging his Lord's forbearance. But he had to give Nerisa time to escape so instead he brazened it out, rudely yawning and stretching his arms as if he'd been awakened from a deep sleep.

"Forgive me, my friend," he said, "but I've been studying late. Exams coming up, you know."

"How dare you call me Friend!" Kalasariz roared.

Safar peered at him in mock surprise, then shrugged. "My mistake," he said. "I can see from your attitude that few, if any, would care to make that claim."

"Don't you know who I am?" Kalasariz thundered.

"Apparently not," Safar lied. "Or I'd know how to properly beg you to please lower your voice. I'm of nervous disposition. Loud sounds make me ill and I find it difficult to concentrate."

"I am Lord Kalasariz," the spy master hissed. "Do you know that name, bumpkin?"

Safar scratched his head, then pretended to jolt and gape. "Forgive me, Lord," he said, bobbing his head. "I had no idea that—"

"Silence!" Kalasariz commanded. "I asked you a question when I entered. Answer it now—where is the thief, Nerisa?"

Safar put on his best look of puzzlement. "Nerisa? Now, where do I know that name? Nerisa? Is she the wife of the baker on Didima Street? No, that can't be . . ." He snapped his fingers. "I've got it! You mean that child that hangs around the *Foolsmire*? Is that who you seek?"

"You know very well who I mean, Acolyte Timura," Kalasariz said.

Safar nodded. "I do now, Lord," he said. "But I don't know where she is. Except . . . have you checked at the *Foolsmire*? She sleeps there sometimes."

"I *know* that," Kalasariz gritted out.

"I suppose you would," Safar said. "Being chief sp—I mean Guardian of Walaria and all."

"Do you deny you were in her company today?" Kalasariz demanded.

"No, I . . . uh . . . suppose I don't deny it," Safar said. "But I can't confirm it either." He gave a sheepish grin. "I was taken drunk most of the day, you see. I don't remember much about it. Maybe I saw Nerisa. Maybe I didn't. Sorry I can't be of more help."

"I dislike your manner, Safar Timura," Kalasariz said. "Perhaps you think you're safe from me because you are under the protection of Lord Umurhan. That I have no sway over University affairs."

"Forgive my rough mountain manners, Lord," Safar said. "Sometimes I unintentionally give city people offense. I know quite well that you are charged with seeing the law is kept in Walaria. Quite naturally those duties would include the temple and university."

Kalasariz ignored him, peering about Safar's room, long nose twitching like a hunting ferret's.

To draw away suspicion, Safar plunged onward. "Pardon my foolishness, Lord," he said, "but why would someone of your eminence be looking for a common thief? And a child thief, at that?"

Kalasariz' eyes swept and Safar suddenly felt very cold as he was confronted by the spymaster's glittering eyes. "I was told you were the brightest student at the university," the spymaster said. "Too bright for your own good, perhaps. And disdainful of rules and authority."

He paused, waiting to see if Safar would be foolish enough to answer. At last he nodded in satisfaction. "At least you're bright enough to know when to keep your tongue still," he said. "I'll answer your question two ways, Acolyte Timura. If you're so intelligent you'll know which one to choose for a correct answer.

"The first is this: I'm looking for the girl because an informant has reported that she is a vital messenger for a group of traitorous students."

Safar needed no acting help to make his eyes widen. "*Nerisa?*" he said, amazed.

Kalasariz' eyes gleamed with renewed suspicion. "Are you claiming you know nothing of these students?"

Safar knew better than to lie about something that was common knowledge in Walaria. "I've heard, Lord," he said, "that there are certain students at the University who are misguided enough to question the policies of the good King Didima." Then seeing that this bit of truth had been swallowed without difficulty he chanced a lie. "I have no personal experience or knowledge about those foolish ones," he said. "Just as I had no idea who you were when you came into my room. I have no interest in politics, My Lord. Nor have I ever displayed any."

Kalasariz looked Safar up and down, studying every crease in his costume, every twitch in his face. Then he said, "The second answer is that the girl, Nerisa, is only an excuse. And that I'm here for an entirely different reason."

Kalasariz paused, fixing Safar with a stare. Then he said, "I understand you are a close friend of Iraj Protarus."

Safar was too startled to hide his surprise. "Why, yes, I am," he said. "Or I was some time ago. I haven't seen him or heard from him in years."

"What if I told you I had different reports, Acolyte Timura?" Kalasariz said. "What if I told you that I have a reliable informant will to testify that you are communication with Protarus regularly?"

"I'd say your informant was a liar, My Lord, " Safar replied, quite firmly. "And I'd also say, who cares? Iraj Protarus has nothing to do with Walaria."

Kalasariz curled a lip. "Are you claiming ignorance of Protarus' activities?" he asked. "Are you saying you know nothing of his many conquests?"

Safar shrugged. "I've heard the market gossip, Lord," he said. "Some of it might even be true. When I knew Iraj he was determined to become leader of his clan. And I understand he's achieved this. That he's undisputed ruler of the Southern Plains."

"Oh, his claims are disputed, all right," Kalasariz said.

"You mean by his uncle, Lord Fulain," Safar said. "And his uncle's ally—Koralia Kan. Iraj told me about them years ago. He hated them with good reason, it seemed to me. The last bit of market gossip I heard was that Fulain and Kan were routed and have fled to Lord Kan's kingdom. "

"You know much," Kalasariz said, "for one who pretends no interest in politics."

"Iraj was my friend, Lord," Safar said. "It's only natural I'd take an interest in any news I heard."

"Then how did you miss the news, Acolyte Timura," Kalasariz said with a sneer, "that Iraj Protarus has been proclaimed an enemy of Walaria?"

Safar reacted, shocked. "When?" he said. "I've heard nothing of this."

Kalasariz smiled. "Actually," he said, "it hasn't been announced yet. The king has entered into an alliance with the Lords Fulain and Kan. He suspects Iraj will not be satisfied with his southern holdings and will soon seek to extend his borders. This alliance will be announced tomorrow."

Safar had every reason believe everything Kalasariz said was true. He remembered quite clearly Iraj's dreams of grand conquest—as clearly as he recalled his own vision of Iraj leading a great army.

Kalasariz' harsh voice broke through his thoughts. "Do you still claim, Acolyte Timura, that you have had no communication with the barbarian who now claims a royal title?" He spit on the floor. "King Protarus," he sneered. "Such savage pretensions."

Safar took a deep breath. "I have not spoken with him, or corresponded with him, My Lord," he said, quite truthfully, "since I left my home in the mountains. I doubt if Iraj even remembers me. Why should he? I'm no one of importance. We were just boys thrown together by circumstance."

Kalasariz gave him another long, probing look. Then he nodded, as if satisfied. "You will send word to me, Acolyte," he said, "if you hear from your old friend."

Safar bobbed his head, relieved. "Certainly, Lord," he said. "Without fail."

It was a lie, but one Safar thought was unlikely to be tested. What reason would Iraj have to seek him out after all this time? Like he told Kalasariz, it had been a boyhood friendship—long forgotten.

Then the spy master suddenly turned on his heel, signaling his men he was ready to depart. Safar sagged as Kalasariz stepped through the door. But any relief he felt was short-lived. Just as Kalasariz reached the door he swung back.

"You may or may not be the fool you claim, Acolyte Timura," he said. "Be advised that I will make it my personal business to find out."

And he was gone.

Safar heard a dry chuckle coming from the inside pocket of his robe. It was Gundara.

He heard him say: "Nice friends you have, Master. And good fortune for me. When they kill you I'll be in much better company."

Then, to his twin, "Shut up, brother! Save it for the demons. You'll have your turn soon enough."

Safar swatted the bulge in his pocket and heard Gundara give a satisfying "Ouch!"

"Don't trifle with me," Safar warned. "I may only be a student, but the handling of Favorites is a first year course. And the number one rule, according to my master, the Lord Umurhan, is never to trust a Favorite. The second is to use a heavy hand. I don't agree with Umurhan about a lot of things, but from your behavior so far I intend to take his teaching to heart."

He swatted the bulge again. "Do I make myself clear?"

"Okay, okay," Gundara said from his pocket. "What ever you say, Master."

Then to his twin: "Shut up, Gundaree! Shut up! Shut up! Shut up!"

✻   ✻   ✻

The letter, although written on expensive paper, was smudged from camp smoke and battered from being passed through many hands.

Kalasariz smoothed it out on the table and moved an oil lamp closer so the two other men could see.

This is what the letter said:

My Dear Safar

All you predicted has been coming true and at a faster pace than even I expected. Even as I write my whole camp is drunk with wine and joy at yet another grand victory. Once again our losses were few, while our enemy suffered greatly. My army grows larger and more able each day. But I'll tell you this, my friend. I've learned that success can be more dangerous than failure. Every city I capture, every border I cross, increases the pressure to achieve more. For if I stop my enemies will have time to join forces against me. The greatest problem I face, however, is that I'm surrounded by self-serving advisors whose words and loyalty I'd be a fool to trust.

But you, my friend, I know I can trust. We proved our mettle together in that fight against the fiends. You know my mind, my private thoughts, more than any other. Just as I know yours.

I beg you, Safar—come to me at once. To help speed you to my side I have deposited ample funds in your name with the Merchants' Guild in Walaria.

I have great need of you, friend and oath brother.

May the gods look with favor on you and your dear family in Kyrania.

When the men had finished reading the letter Kalasariz said, "I have verified the signature. Without question it's that of Iraj Protarus."

"This is most disturbing news, gentlemen," King Didima replied. "Most disturbing indeed."

"Damned embarrassing for me," Umurhan said. "Can you imagine how *I* feel? To think I've been nursing a viper at my bosom all this time."

"There, there, Umurhan," Didima said. "No one's blaming you. How were you supposed to know? After all, the young man came so highly recommended."

The three men were gathered in the king's private study. They'd ruled together for so long—equally dividing power and wealth—that they were at ease in each other's company. They were accustomed to compromise and once a goal was set they worked smoothly towards its end. Didima was a stumpy man, with thick limbs and a barrel-like trunk. His face was round like a melon and shadowed by a dark thick beard streaked with gray. Umurhan was every inch a wizard, silver eyes glowing under a sorcerer's peaked hat. He had heavy, bat-winged brows and a beard of flowing white. And Kalasariz was the dark presence who made this unholy trinity complete.

"Thank you for your confidence in me, Majesty," Umurhan said. "Although I must say I *have* become suspicious of young Timura lately. I wanted to dismiss him from the school, but I didn't want to offend his sponsor, Lord Muzine. Instead I was going to make sure Timura failed the upcoming exams. Then I'd be rid of him without controversy."

"I'll speak to Muzine," Didima offered. "He'll be grateful we gave him a chance to distance himself from the little traitor."

"Let's not mention this to anyone just yet," Kalasariz cautioned. "I want to see where this leads us."

"That's good advice," Didima said. "Why seize one troublemaker when we might have a chance to sweep them all in." He absently combed his beard with thick, blunt fingers. "These are dangerous times, gentlemen, as I've said many times before. Two years of poor harvests. Plague outbreaks among our cattle and sheep. More bandits stalking the caravans than we've seen in years. Which has done nothing to help trade. And this increasing reluctance, which I lay to poor upbringing, of our citizens to pay the increased taxes we require just to keep the kingdom whole and on the right course.

"Now this upstart, Iraj Protarus, comes along with his army of barbarians invading the realms of innocent, peace-loving kings. Why just last month my old friend, King Leeman of Shareed, had his head cut off by this Protarus fellow. After he'd sacked the city, of course, and burned it to the ground."

Didima touched his throat and shivered. "It isn't right," he said, "cutting off royal heads. It injures the dignity of thrones everywhere."

"I couldn't agree more, Majesty," Umurhan said. "And I think we made a wise decision to ally ourselves with Protarus' enemies, Koralia Kan and Lord Fulain."

"We'll have to raise taxes again," Didima warned, "to pay for the mercenaries and arms we promised our new friends."

"It will be worth every copper," Umurhan said, "if it stops Protarus once and for all. Someday our citizens will thank for saving them from that madman."

"Thank us, or curse us," Kalasariz said, "they'll pay just the same. But that's old business and as much I'd like to talk politics with you two all night I want to set a proper course concerning Safar Timura. How shall we proceed?"

Umurhan indicated the intercepted letter. "How did this fall into your hands?"

"I have an informant at the *Foolsmire*," Kalasariz said, "which as you all know is a favorite meeting spot for the students. Safar is a close friend of the owner and has all his messages and post directed there."

"I know of this place," Umurhan said. "The owner is a cranky but harmless old fellow who distrusts authority. Katal, I think his name is. I can't imagine him having a sudden change of heart and turning informer for the crown."

Kalasariz smiled thinly, making him look even more like a skeleton. "It's the owner's grandson who is in my pay," he said. "Zeman's his name. He's as dim-witted as he is ambitious. Full of cunning and all of it low. Zeman is anxious to inherit, but unfortunately for him his grandfather gives every sign of living on for many years. My emissaries have led young Zeman to believe that if he helps us we might hasten his grandfather's journey to the grave."

"Excellent, excellent," King Didima said. "The blacker the soul the more willing the flesh."

Kalasariz chuckled. The sound was like a broken bone grating against itself. "That's certainly true in Zeman's case," he said. "He seems to particularly hate Safar Timura. I don't know why—to my knowledge Timura has never done anything against him. I think he's jealous because his grandfather holds Timura in such high affection. There's also a child at the *Foolsmire*, a thief named Nerisa, whom he appears to hate nearly as much as Timura. Once again, I can't say why. Nor do I care. Suffice it to say Zeman has been looking on his own for evidence against Timura for some time. We had no reason to suspect him, the gods know. And then this letter came along and Zeman contacted us immediately."

Kalasariz made another death mask smile. "He managed to construct the accusations so they involved the child as well."

"My, my," Didima said. "Two enemies at one blow. Zeman must be a very happy fellow."

"Not as happy as he's going to be if this works out right," Kalasariz said. "I believe in keeping my best informants rich enough to dream large, but poor enough to keep those dreams just beyond their reach."

"What did Timura say when you confronted him with the letter?" Didima asked.

"I didn't mention it," Kalasariz said. "I let him lie. He claimed he'd heard nothing from Protarus since they were boys. He also said he doubted his old friend even remembered him."

Umurhan snorted. "A likely story," he said. "That letter is clearly one of several urging Timura to join Protarus in his evil adventure. And look here . . ." he jabbed his finger at one phrase in the letter . . . "Protarus says he's deposited funds for Timura at the Merchants' Guild."

Kalasariz snorted. "I've seized them, of course," he said. "One hundred gold coins."

Umurhan's bat-winged brows flared up in surprise. "So much?" he said. Then, "That's more proof, as if we needed it. No one would give away such an amount casually."

Didima leaned forward. "Why do you think Timura has resisted Protarus' pleas?"

"That's simple enough, Majesty," Kalasariz said. "He's holding out for a greater share of the spoils."

Umurhan looked thoughtful. Then he said, "I'm sure that's part of his game. However, I'm also certain he wants to steal my most important magical secrets to take along with him. I caught him in my private library the other day. That is why I nearly dismissed him. The books and scrolls there are forbidden to anyone but a few of my most trusted priests and scholars."

A long silence greeted this revelation. Then, from Didima, "What of this battle Protarus refers to? The bit about the fiends? What do you make of that?"

"Some boyhood adventure, I suspect," Kalasariz answered. "Exaggerated, of course."

Didima nodded. "Yes, yes. What else could it be?"

He thought a moment, then asked, "What shall we do about Acolyte Timura?"

"Nothing just now," Kalasariz said. "Let him have his head. At the right time we'll make certain he pays a very public visit to our executioner to have it removed." He slipped a scroll from his sleeve and rolled out it out on Didima's desk, saying, "And to that end, Majesty, I'll need your signature authorizing his execution and the execution of his fellow conspirators when the time comes to sweep them up. We don't want any messy trials or other delays that might give their supporters time to whip up public support."

The king chuckled, picking up his quill pen and charging it with ink. "I see you have only Timura's name listed now," he said.

"Oh, there'll be more, Majesty," Kalasariz said. "You'll notice I left a great deal of room on the page."

The king nodded approvingly. "Tulaz *is* anxious to improve his record," he said. "We'll make a day of it, eh? A public holiday. Free food and drink. A bit of carnival to mark the moment." He scratched his name on the document, saying, "There's nothing like a mass execution to calm the citizenry."

Kalasariz smiled thinly, blew on the wet signature and passed the document to Umurhan. "I'll need you to witness this," he said. "Just a formality."

Without hesitation, Umurhan signed. "It's a pity," he said, "I had such hopes for the lad."

*   *   *

Some hours later Kalasariz made himself ready for sleep. While his pretty maids drew the blankets and plumped up the bed he drank his favorite hot sweet potion, laced with brandy and mild sleeping powders.

He was a not a man who slept well. It wasn't all the blood he'd spilled that disturbed his dark hours, but the constant worry that he'd overlooked something. His tricks and betrayals were legion and he had so many enemies he didn't dare let down his guard. He was a master of the great lie and was therefor continually occupied with keeping track of his untruths and half-truths. During the day he never had a weak moment, but at night his dreams were bedeviled with plans that went awry because of a stupid mistake or over-sight. Without his nightly ritual he'd awaken so exhausted from nightmares that he'd be stricken with doubts. And so, despite the lateness of the hour, he let his maids pleasure him after he'd had his potion. Then they'd bathed him and dressed him in a nightshirt of black silk.

He dismissed them, reaching for the black silk mask he wore to shut out any stray light. Just before he put it on he remembered the document of execution, still sitting on his dressing table. Despite the sleeping potion and the attention of his maids he knew he wouldn't sleep well as long as it sat there unattended. Never mind that no one would dare creep into the home of Walaria's spymaster, much less rob his sleeping chamber. His unguarded mind was so active that as he tossed and turned through the night he would come up with countless scenarios in which such an unlikely deed would suddenly become real.

Close as he was to sleep, he got up to attend to it. He'd taken much care to collect the signatures of his brother rulers on Safar's death warrant. His name did not go on it—a remarkable absence in its own right. Kalasariz rolled it up with another document which *did* bear his name. It was an official protest of the decision, praising Timura as a young man of many notable qualities and virtues. He locked them away in his special hiding place behind the third panel from the entrance of the bedchamber.

Kalasariz had no ambitions besides survival in his current position as co-ruler of Walaria. He certainly had no more desire to see Didima dethroned than he did to see himself king. But as Didima had said, these were dangerous times. If by some distant chance the young upstart, Iraj Protarus, should someday be in the position to seek revenge for the death of his friend, Kalasariz preferred to be viewed as one of Timura's champions. The spymaster had little doubt he was right to support the decision for Walaria to ally itself against Protarus. But there was a slight chance the alliance would fail and

Protarus and his army might someday show up at the gates. Didima and Umurhan would pay for their crime with their heads. Tulaz would most likely perform the honors, since good executioners are difficult to find and he'd be instantly welcomed into the new king's service. Armed with the documents proving his innocence, Kalasariz would also be welcomed. Protarus would need a spymaster, and who could be a better man for the job than Kalasariz himself?

Timura had presented Kalasariz with a unique opportunity. One the one hand, as a friend of Iraj Protarus it was necessary to remove whatever danger he might represent. On the other, as an outsider great blame could be heaped upon him. He would be declared the ringleader of all the young hotheads who opposed Walaria's rulers. A dozen or more of his "lieutenants"—in reality the real leaders of the opposition—would also earn the ultimate punishment. This would not only quell their followers and sympathizers, but outside and unnamed influences would get the ultimate blame.

There was a saying about "getting your sweet and eating it too."

Kalasariz wasn't fond of sweets. But he did enjoy the sentiment.

The spymaster slept well that night. But just before First Prayer he had a dream about a strange little creature with a man's body and a demon's face. It was gobbling up a sweet roll, scattering crumbs, left and right.

When it was done it brushed itself off and looked him square in the eye.

"Shut up!" it said. "Shut up, shut up, shut up!"

He didn't know what to make of the creature or its antics. But for some reason it frightened him.

CHAPTER TWELVE
THE GRAND TEMPLE OF WALARIA

Unlike Kalasariz, Safar slept little that night. Every straw in his mattress and lump in his pillow made itself known. A few days before the only major worry he'd had was a vague and somewhat academic fear that the world faced some great threat. At the age of twenty summers he was incapable of taking it personally. The spy master's visit, coupled with his recent difficulties with Umurhan, made him feel less immortal. He was in trouble and that trouble had grown from the granite hills of Umurhan's displeasure to the bleak peaks of Kalasariz' suspicions.

In short, he was besieged from all sides and was in a confusion about what he ought to do. Adding to that morass was the confusion created by Nerisa's gift plus his fears about Nerisa herself. Someone, for whatever reason, had marked her.

Everyone on the streets knew Nerisa ran personal errands for anyone at the *Foolsmire* with a copper or two to pay. Most certainly some of the young men who hired her held controversial views. That didn't make Nerisa a conspirator. This was also a fact all knew—including any of Kalasariz' minions who made the *Foolsmire* their territory. So why had the informer lied? Why had he singled Nerisa out?

Then it occurred to Safar that he was the target. Someone might be striking at him through Nerisa. But once again came that most important of all questions: Why? Then he realized that answer or not, his fate might be racing toward an unpleasant conclusion.

The only intelligent thing to do was to flee Walaria as quickly as he could. Such an act would certainly turn Kalasariz' suspicions into an outright admission of guilt. Safar thought, however, it would be even more dangerous to remain in Walaria at the mercy of the spymaster.

He decided to run. He'd flee home to Kyrania as fast as he could. But what about Nerisa? He'd have to come up with some plan to protect her from any reprisals his flight might cause.

Safar was relieved as soon as he made the decision. He'd learned much in Walaria, but it had been a mostly unpleasant stay in an unpleasant city. He missed his family and friends. He missed the clean mountain air and blue skies and molten clouds and snowy slopes.

Only one thing stood in his way—a lack of money. To make a successful escape he'd require a hefty sum. He'd need a swift mount and supplies for the long journey home and money for Nerisa as well. Where could he lay hands on it? There was no sense asking his sponsor, Lord Muzine. Not only would the money be denied, Safar thought it likely the request would be immediately reported to Kalasariz.

There was only one person he could think of who could help.

But once that approach was made, there'd be no turning back.

*　　　*　　　*

Safar rose before first light. He washed and dressed and made a quick trip to a nearby bakery and bought a sticky roll filled with plump currants. He rushed home, brewed a pot of strong tea and while he drank it he summoned Gundara.

The little Favorite popped out of a cloud of magical smoke, coughing and rubbing sleepy eyes.

"Don't tell me you get up early *too*!" Gundara whined. "The gods must hate me. Why else would they allow me to fall into the hands of such a cruel master?"

Instead of answering, Safar held up the sticky roll. The Favorite's eyes widened. "Is that for me, O Wise and Kind Master?" .

"None other," Safar said.

He extended the roll and the Favorite grabbed it from his hand and gobbled it up, moaning in pleasure and scattering crumbs and currants all over the floor.

When he was done he sucked each taloned finger clean, smacked his lips, then said, "If you gave me another, I'd *kill* for you, Master." From his tone Safar knew it was no jest.

"You'd kill for a piece of pastry?" Safar asked.

Gundara shrugged. "Money is no good to me. Or jewels or treasures. I live in a stone turtle, remember? But a bit of something sweet . . . mmmm . . . Oh, yes, Master. Lead me to your victims this instant. I can help you conjure a decent poison guaranteed to reduce an entire city to a hamlet."

"I don't kill people," Safar said.

"More's the pity," Gundara answered. "Killing's much easier than most tasks." He stretched his arms, yawning. "If it isn't killing, Master, exactly what is it you want me to do?"

"Make yourself as small you can," Safar said, "and hop up on my shoulder."

"How boring," Gundara complained, but he clicked his talons together and instantly shrunk to the size of a large flea. Safar had to look very hard to see him. Gundara called out, voice just as loud as when he was full size, "You'll have to help me with the shoulder part, Master. It's too far to hop."

Safar held out his hand and the black dot that was Gundara ran up it, scrambling over the rough cloth of his sleeve until he reached his shoulder.

"I have some important business to conduct this morning," Safar said. "I want you to keep a close watch for any danger or suspicious people."

"Do I get another roll when I'm done, Master?" came Gundara's voice.

"If you do a good job," Safar promised.

"And one for Gundaree too?" the Favorite pressed.

Safar sighed. "Yes," he said. "Gundaree can have one too."

"Make it with berries, next time," the little Favorite requested. "Currants give me gas."

* * *

The city was stirring to life when Safar set out. Traffic was light but a few shops were opening and workmen were gathering in the front of others, munching olives and black bread while they waited for their employers' arrival. Safar passed the wheelwrights' shop, which always started early to repair wagons that'd broken down on the way to market. A hard-eyed man leaned against the wall near the entrance. He stared at Safar when he went by.

Safar bent his head closer to shoulder. "Any trouble there?" he asked.

"Just a cutpurse," the flea speck that was Gundara answered. "Don't worry. You're too poor for his taste."

Safar went on, but kept his pace slow so his Favorite could sniff for spies. He was certain Kalasariz would order his informers to trail him. Although Safar was only a mountain lad, unwise in the ways of the city, he had much experience with nature to rely on. Animal or human, hunters always behaved the same way. Wolves on the stalk, for instance, might post a sentry near their intended victim. When the flock moved about the sentry would keep close watch on the sick sheep that had been chosen for dinner. As the flock moved from place to place the wolf would follow only so far, passing on his duties to another sentry so as not to arouse suspicion. And so on throughout the day until the intended victim fell behind the flock, or strayed too far from the rams. Then the sentry would howl the news and the pack would strike.

This is how Safar imagined Kalasariz' informers would work. They'd post a spy on the street near his home, who would alert the others when he emerged. Then he'd be passed along from spy to spy until he returned home for the night.

As he neared the end of his street an old woman with rags for clothes and a torn horse blanket for a shawl rose up from beside her push cart. There were pigeons cooing in a wooden cage on one side push cart, hot meat pies steaming from a basket in the other.

"Fresh pigeon pies?" she called out to Safar. "Two coppers a pie, sir."

"No thank you, Granny," Safar said, moving by.

The old woman gripped his sleeve. "That's my usual price, sir. Two coppers a pie. And fresh and hot they is, sir. Fresh killed this morning. But you're such a handsome lad, sir, if you don't mind me saying so. You make this poor granny's heart sing like she was a maid. For you sir, for bringing back my girlhood, I'll charge only a copper for two."

The spy saw Safar hesitate, then nod and hand over a copper in exchange for two pies which he tucked into his purse. He said thank you to the granny, polite as you please, and passed on—turning the corner and heading down a broad street. The old woman waited until he'd disappeared from sight then quickly opened the door to the pigeon cage. She grabbed the only white bird, which was also much larger and fatter than the others. She petted it, whispered soothing words and threw it high into the air, moving with a surprising agility for someone who appeared so old and bent.

The pigeon flew up and up—circling the street as it oriented itself. Then it shot for the high tower that marked the entrance to the Central Market. The spy smiled, knowing what would happen next. The pigeon was trained to circle the tower three times. This would alert all the informers planted about the city that Safar was on the move. Then the pigeon would return to the pushcart for a nice treat and whispered praise that it was such a smart and pretty bird.

The old woman, who was the spy, was quite fond of the pigeon. She'd raised it from the egg and spoiled it more than any other bird she'd had. She watched proudly as her little darling flew toward the tower. Then she gasped as a deadly black figure winged its way over the rooftops and headed for the pigeon. The hawk hurled itself at her prize bird, talons stretching out. The pigeon sensed its peril and tried to dodge but the hawk was quicker and there was an explosion of blood and feathers. The hunter flew away, the remains of the pigeon clutched in its claws.

The spy groaned in dismay. She'd not only lost her favorite pet, but Safar as well. Quickly she grabbed a passing boy by the ear and gave him a coin to mind her cart, promising more if all was safe when she returned. Then she hurried off to warn her superiors that a hawk had spoiled their plans.

Two streets away Safar cut around a corner at top speed, then slowed to a fast walk. It was a tenement neighborhood with high, crooked buildings. There was no one about except housewives illegally emptying chamber pots into the street, instead of paying the slopwagon men to carry away the filth. Shutters would bang open, slop would stream into the street, then they'd bang shut before anyone in authority could see. And woe betide the passerby who didn't jump in the correct direction when he first heard the shutters open.

Safar slipped smoothly to the side as a murky stream poured down the heavens, avoiding getting even a spatter of filth on his robes. He whistled and the hawk darted down from a roof. It landed on his shoulder, beak and chest feathers clotted with blood. Safar made a face at the mess, then gestured and the hawk transformed into Gundara who became a flea spot on his shoulder.

"Look at me! I'm covered with pigeon blood," the Favorite complained. "The gods know I hate the taste of blood, especially pigeon blood. You don't know where the filthy things have been. They're worse than chickens."

"I'm sorry," Safar said. "Still, you did a good job."

"I have a ninny for a master," Gundara said. "Of course I did a good job. What did you think, that I'd just been spellhatched? I've been doing this for more centuries than I care to mention because it depresses me so much.

"Yech! There's blood in my mouth, too. And feathers. You have no idea what it does to you when you bite down on a feather."

Safar felt sorry for him and soothed him as best he could. A few streets later he bought a dish of pudding, floating in sugared rose water. He ate half the pudding, then pushed the remainder aside with his wooden spoon so Gundara could jump in and bathe.

He continued on, Gundara a fat wet black spot on the shoulder of his robe.

The Favorite burped. "Maybe you're not such a bad master after all," he allowed. "Do you eat rose pudding every day?"

"I will from now on," Safar promised.

"You hear that, Gundaree?" the Favorite said to his invisible twin. "I'm absolutely soaked with sugar water! Existence is wonderful. And I have the best master in all the world. So go sod yourself, see if I care!"

Safar grimaced at the one-way conversation. He was glad he only had to deal with one Favorite at a time. Together they'd drive him mad.

He was moving under a large awning shading the entrance to a rug shop, when he heard someone hiss from overhead—"Safar!"

It was Nerisa. He covered his surprise, looking around to make sure no one was near. Then he chanced a look upward and saw a dark eye gleaming through a hole in the awning.

"Don't look!" the girl commanded.

"I'm sorry," Safar whispered back. He toyed with a pile of rugs near the entrance, pretending to examine them for quality. "Are you all right?" he asked under his breath.

Nerisa snorted. "Scared half to death, is all. What'd I do to get Kalasariz after me?"

"You saw him?"

"I hid outside until he left. I thought I was seeing things at first. Or maybe I was in the middle of a nightmare and couldn't wake up. Then he went by my hiding place and I got a good look and knew it was no nightmare. Who could miss that face of his? Looks like somebody who doesn't see the sun much. Or a ghost."

Safar nodded, fingering another rug. "Listen," he said. "I don't have time to explain what's happening. They're just using you as an excuse to get to me. I don't know why. But I'm going to do something about it now. Just keep low. Stay away from the *Foolsmire*. And meet me tonight."

"Okay, Safar," Nerisa said. "Tonight then. Say three hours after last prayer?"

"Where? My place isn't safe."

"Don't worry," Nerisa said. "No one will see me. Just be there. I'll come to you."

He started to argue, but there was a slight rustling noise above and when he looked up at the rent in the awning the eye was gone.

Safar was troubled as continued on his way. Nerisa took too many chances for his liking. But there was nothing he could do about it now and so he pushed away the worry as best he could to concentrate on his mission. Before long he reached his destination. He smiled to himself as he approached, thinking all the spies who'd been set on his trail would be scurrying all over the city looking for him. But he'd be hiding in plain sight in a place they'd never think to look—the Grand Temple of Walaria.

It was an ugly edifice—a series of massive buildings and onion-domed towers enclosed by high, fortress-like walls. The temple had begun as a simple stone structure. It had been built centuries before by the first high priest in the days when Walaria—which meant the place of the waters—was little more than a few ramshackle buildings encircled by immense corrals to hold the great cattle herds that enriched the original settlers. Legend had it Walaria was founded by a wandering wizard. It had been nothing more than a dry thorny plain then. According to the myth, the wizard had thrust his staff into the ground. The staff instantly grew into a tall tree and a spring had burst out from under its roots. Over time a great market city had been born from that spring, with a king to rule it and a high priest to build and tend that first temple.

Afterwards each high priest constructed another holy structure—more to glorify *his* name then those of the gods. Temples were hurled up willy nilly, with each high priest competing with the bad taste of the man he'd replaced. Most of the buildings were dedicated to the many gods worshipped by the people of Esmir. It was Walaria's boast there were idols to as many gods as there were stars in the heavens.

Safar went through the main gate, passing by scores of shops and stalls catering to the business of worship. There was incense of every variety and price, holy oils, special candles and thousands upon thousands of idols of the different gods—large ones for the household altar, small ones to make talismans to hang from a chain. On both sides of the thoroughfare were hutches and small corrals containing animals and birds that could be purchased for sacrifice. Blessings and magical potions were also on sale and if you were a pilgrim with foreign coin, or letters of credit, there were half-a-dozen money changers eager to service you from first prayer to last.

A crowd was already gathering when Safar arrived and he had to elbow his way through the throngs. He turned right when he reached the end of the main boulevard and here the street was empty except for a few students like himself hurrying to the university—a low-slung building two stories high and three deep.

The top level was where Umurhan and the other priests lived—although Umurhan's quarters took up almost half that space. The ground level was for offices and classrooms—and the great meeting hall where they all gathered for special ceremonies and announcements. Two of the below-ground levels were given over to dormitories for students too poor to come up with the price of a private hovel or garret such as Safar's.

Leering gargoyles decorated the portals leading into the university. Safar shivered as he passed under them.

"There's no danger," Gundara said from his shoulder. "It's only stone."

Safar didn't need the reassurance. He knew quite well the gargoyles were nothing more than lifeless symbols to ward off evil spirits. Still, even after being confronted with those leering stone faces every day for nearly two years, he couldn't help the reaction.

Just beyond the portal was a large courtyard with stone steps leading to an altar. It was here the students practiced making blood sacrifices to the gods. An animal would be driven out from barred cages to the left of the altar. The animals were always drugged so they rarely gave any trouble. A priest would direct a youth in the grisly task of slicing the creature's throat. Others would dash in to catch the flowing blood before the animal fell. Then prayers would be said as the animal was butchered out and the meat and blood burned in sacrificial urns to glorify the gods. Safar had always been uneasy about blood sacrifices and the more he learned the less he thought they were necessary. He'd also noticed that the best cuts of meat were set aside for Umurhan and his priests—hardly an act that would please a deity.

As he went by the altar he saw five acolytes cleaning up after a recent sacrifice. Their shabby robes were hiked up and they were on their hands and knees scrubbing the steps and platform with worn brushes.

Safar remembered a time when that grisly task was his sole and constant duty.

As he passed by the laboring youths he recalled the moment when he'd first met Umurhan.

*　　　*　　　*

It was a dreary winter day and the skies were as ashen as the altar stone. Safar had lost count of the weeks he'd spent on scabby knees washing the steps and platform. It was so cold that every time he plunged his brush into the scrub bucket a film of ice formed moments after he withdrew it.

He'd reported to the repetitious priest each morning, asking when he'd be allowed to attend classes. The answer had always been the same—"You came late in the year. Late in year. Keep working. Working. Soon as there's an opening . . . an opening . . . I'll let you know. Let you know."

And Safar would say, "Yes, Holy One," as contritely as he could—just as Gubadan had instructed him before he'd left Kyrania. As each day blended into miserable day he became more impatient. He'd come Walaria to learn, not to scrub floors. Moreover, Coralean was paying a high price to fund his studies. Safar was supposed to be a student, not a slave.

On that particular day he'd reached the sheerest edge of his patience and was thinking mightily of packing his kit and setting off for home—and to the Hells with

Walaria. He was actually in the act of rising from his knees when there came a sudden hubbub of activity.

The repetitious priest rushed into the courtyard, surrounded by other priests and a great crowd of acolytes from the Walaria school of wizardry. It was an elite group of less than a hundred. These were the students deemed to have talent enough for intense instruction in the magical arts. Safar's own sights were not raised that high. At that time all he wanted was a chance to join the main student body and get a thorough grounding in general knowledge. But when he studied the group, saw their look of immense superiority, noted the weak buzz of their magic, he experienced a momentary flash of jealousy. He brushed it aside and as the excited group crowded into the courtyard he grabbed up his bucket and moved to a far corner where he could watch without being noticed.

From the murmuring of the acolytes he gathered that an important man had approached Umurhan for a great favor. It seemed the man had committed some wrong the group was evenly divided between betrayal of a relative, and the murder of a slave and wanted to make sacrifice to the gods beseeching their forgiveness. But he wanted to do it as privately as possible, so he'd made a large donation to the temple to pay for a non-public ceremony. After the cleansing, Safar heard the acolytes say, rich gifts would be passed out among the students to buy their silence.

When he heard this he made himself even less obtrusive, ducking behind a column overgrown with thick vines.

A moment later cymbals crashed and two men strode into the courtyard, boys scampering before them tossing petals onto the path and waving smoking incense pots to sweeten the air they breathed. There was no mistaking that one of the men dressed in the flowing robes of a master wizard, was Umurhan. Even if he were blind, Safar would have sensed the man's presence, for the air was suddenly heavy with the stink of sorcery. Then Safar was rocked by another surprise. For the richly dressed, heavily bejeweled man striding beside Umurhan was none other than Lord Muzine. Although he'd never been personally introduced to Muzine, the merchant prince had been pointed out to him one day when he passed in his luxurious carriage, drawn by four perfectly matched black horses. Muzine had a face like a double-headed hammer turned handle up. It was long and narrow until it reached the chin which bulged out on both sides.

The courtyard was hushed as the two men mounted the platform and approached the altar of Rybian, the king of the gods and the deity who created all living things from holy clay. Umurhan and two brawny lads in robes of pristine white solicitously helped Muzine kneel before the stone idol of that kindly visaged god.

Umurhan turned to face the acolytes, his eyes fierce under his bat-winged brows.

"Brothers," he said, "we are here today to assist a good man, a kindly man, who by unfortunate circumstance has stumbled off the path of purity he has tenaciously traveled his whole life. We are not here to judge him, for who among us could judge a man known far and wide for his sweet disposition and generous charity? This man has come to me, his heart bared, his soul in torment. He has sinned, but who among us has not? So we will not judge him. Instead we will beseech the great and merciful Rybian, father of us all, to take pity on this poor mortal and forgive him for any transgressions the Fates forced him to commit.

"And so I ask you today, my brothers of the spirit, to join me willingly and wholeheartedly in this mission of mercy. The man you see humbled before you is one who deserves no less and it is an honor for our university and temple to help him in this most delicate of matters."

While Umurhan spoke the lads in white gently removed Muzine's tunic, leaving him bare to the waist, the soft pink flesh of his heavy richman's torso revealed to all. Then they uncoiled small whips, belted about their waists.

"Are there any objections?" Umurhan asked. "Is there anyone present who cannot find it in his heart to help this man? If so, I kindly ask you to withdraw from our company. You will be thought no less of for making such a decision. Your conscience, we all know, must be your guide."

Umurhan swept the crowd with his fierce eyes, but no one stirred.

He nodded and said, "More to your credit, brothers. The gods will bless you for this."

Safar heard someone nearby mutter under his breath, "So will my tavern bill, Master."

There were a few chuckles at this, covered by Umurhan's signal for all to kneel. The acolytes dropped to the ground as one, bowing their heads low and beating their breasts.

Umurhan announced, "Let the blessing ceremony begin."

From somewhere came the sound of lutes and bells and drums. Priests led the acolytes in song after song, begging Rybian's attention.

The first song was Umurhan's famous Last Prayer that everyone heard every evening at the close of day.

> *"We are men of Walaria, good men and pious.*
> *Blessed be, blessed be.*
> *Our women are chaste, our children respectful.*
> *Blessed be, blessed be . . ."*

While the assembly sang, the white-robed lads gently touched their lashes against Muzine's flesh in the motions of whipping. Muzine wailed as if he were being severely tormented, believing, as all did, that the louder his cries, the more painful-sounding his shrieks, the more the God Rybian would be fooled into thinking Muzine was being sorely punished.

Finally, Muzine gave a scream more terrible than the others and collapsed on the floor. His minders quickly anointed his back—which was unmarked—with soothing oils, kissing him and whispering words of sympathy in his ear. When Muzine deemed sufficient time had passed for him to make a recovery, he rose up with much pretended difficulty and pain. Tears streamed down his long face, which was split by the beatific smile of one who has found the Light again. The lads helped him with his tunic and gave him a tumbler of spirits. Muzine drank deeply, wiped his eyes and then joined in the songs.

Safar became bored with the farce and looked about to see if there was a way he could creep off without being noticed. Just then the iron gates of the animal cage clanged open and his head swiveled back to see what poor creature Muzine had chosen to bribe Rybian's forgiveness.

To his surprise, he saw an old lioness being led out on a slender silver chain. Muzine must have done something really awful, Safar thought. He'd been at the temple long enough to know that a lion was the most expensive and therefor rarest single animal to be sacrificed. Safar decided the sin must have been murder, and probably not that of a slave.

He looked closer at the huge lioness—which stood nearly as high as the white-robed boy who led her. Her movements were slow, paws dragging as she took each step toward the altar. Her eyes were so heavy from the drugs she'd been fed that they were mere slits on either side of her broad face. Despite the size of the lioness, Safar's heart gave a wrench, for she reminded him of his family cat in Kyrania who patrolled the goat stalls for greedy rodents. It had sat on his lap for many an hour, cleaning itself and consoling him when he told it his boyhood miseries.

Then he noticed the lionesses' large, swinging pouch and heavy teats and knew she'd recently given birth. Even drugged, he thought, she must be in a torment wondering what had happened to her cubs.

Umurhan signaled and the singing stopped. He turned to the altar, saying, "O Rybian, Merciful Master of us all, take pity on this poor mortal before you. Forgive him his sins. Accept this humble gift he presents you. And let him sleep once again in all innocence."

Umurhan motioned and one of the boys led Muzine to the lioness. He handed the merchant a large sacrificial knife. The other boys crowded close, holding elaborately decorated jars to catch the blood. Muzine gingerly gripped the lioness by her scruff. She made no motion or sign that she understood what was happening. The Muzine drew the knife across her throat. Blood dribbled from the cut, but the flow was so slight that Safar knew Muzine's nerve had failed and he hadn't been able to cut deeply enough to end the lioness' suffering.

Muzine tried again and this time a boy gripped his hand, pushing hard and making sure the deed was properly done. The lioness moaned and blood gushed into the bowls.

She sagged to the floor.

Everyone cheered and jumped up, praising Rybian and welcoming the sinner Muzine's return to the fold. Muzine came forward, Umurhan at his side, to accept the acolytes' congratulations. Behind them the three white-robed lads got busy butchering the lioness out to prepare for the next stage of the ceremony.

Then the din was shattered by a spine-freezing roar and everyone's heart stopped and everyone's head jerked toward the half-skinned corpse.

The air above the dead beast turned an angry red and then all gasped as the lioness' ghost emerged, crouching on the body, tail lashing, lips peeled back over long yellow fangs, screaming her hatred.

The ghost lioness leaped and the frozen tableaux became unstuck. There were screams and the crowd ran for cover, tangling and jamming the exits with their bodies.

Safar stayed in his hiding place and saw that despite the hysteria a dozen priests and acolytes quickly surrounded Umurhan and Muzine and got them to safety through a small door at the edge of the altar.

Meanwhile, the ghost cat sailed into the mass of fleeing figures. She struck out with her translucent claws. Blood sprayed in every direction and there were screams of pain from the wounded. Then she caught someone in her jaws and held him down while the others scrambled away—jamming the exits and hugging the walls.

The ghost lion crouched over her victim, gripping him by the shoulder and shaking him furiously back and forth. The young man she'd caught was still alive and wailed most piteously.

Suddenly what felt like an unseen hand pushed Safar out of hiding. He walked slowly toward the raging lioness, one part of him gibbering in fear, the other intent only on the soul of the poor Ghostmother, alone and agonizing over her newborn cubs the only way she knew how.

The ghost saw him and dropped the screaming acolyte. She snarled and paced toward him, extended claws clicking on the stone. But Safar kept on, his pace slow and measured. He held out his right hand—two fingers and a thumb spreading wide in the universal gesture of a wizard forming a spell.

He spoke, his voice low and soothing. "I'm sorry to see you here, Ghostmother," he said. "This is a terrible place for a ghost. So much blood. So little pity. It will spoil your milk and your cubs will go hungry."

The lioness ghost kept coming, eyes boiling, jaws open and slavering. Safar went on, closing the distance between them, talking all the while.

"Evil men did this to you Ghostmother," he said. "They trapped you and slew your cubs. They brought you to this place to die. But the guilty ones aren't in this courtyard, Ghostmother. There are only human cubs, here. Male cubs, Ghostmother. And it your duty to see that no harm comes to male cubs."

The stalking ghost growled, but her fury seemed lessened. A few more steps and then the two met—and stopped.

Safar steeled his nerves as the lioness, instead of killing him on the spot, sniffed his body, growling all the while. When she was done she looked him in the face, cat's eyes searching deep into his own for any lie that might be hidden there. Then she roared and it was so loud he was nearly lifted out of his sandals. But he held steady, and then the ghostly form of the lioness sat back her heels—face level with his own.

"You see how it is, Ghostmother," he said. "I had nothing to do with your sadness, although I mourn the loss." He gestured at the cowering acolytes. "And these male cubs are as innocent as I. Please don't harm them, Ghostmother."

The lion ghost yawned its anxiety, but sank down at Safar's feet.

"It's time you thought of yourself, Ghostmother," Safar said. "Your cubs are dead and their little ghosts are hungry. You should go to them quickly so they don't suffer. Think of them, Ghostmother. They have no experience in this world, much less the next. Haven't you heard them crying for you?

"Why, listen—they're crying now."

Safar made a gesture and there came the faint sound of mewing from far away. The ghost's ears shot up and she cocked her head, eyes wide with concern. Safar gestured again and the mewing grew louder and more frantic. The lioness whined.

"Go to them, Ghostmother," Safar said. "Leave this place and find peace with your cubs."

The lioness bolted up. Safar forced to himself not to react in alarm. Then she roared a final time and vanished.

For a moment the only sound was the echo of the lioness' roar. Then all became confusion as everyone shouted in relief and ran to Safar to thank him. Then, in the midst of this chaos, the crowd suddenly went silent and parted. Safar, still dazed and weary from his effort, saw Umurhan approach as if in a haze.

"Who is he?" he heard the wizard ask.

"Safar Timura, Master. Safar Timura. A new acolyte. He's new."

Umurhan's eyes swiveled to Safar. They looked him up and down, measuring. Then he asked, "Why didn't tell anyone you had the talent, Acolyte Timura?"

"It's nothing, Master," Safar said. "My talent is very small."

"I'll be the judge of that, acolyte," Umurhan answered. He turned to the repetitious priest. "Begin Acolyte Timura's education tomorrow," he ordered.

Then, without another word or look at Safar, he stalked away.

All became confusion again as Safar's fellow students crowded around to clap his back and congratulate him for being admitted to the ranks of the university's elite.

*   *   *

Safar hurried down the long main corridor of the first floor. There was no one to be seen—most of the students and priests would be gathered in prayer in the main assembly hall at this hour. The classrooms and offices he went by were empty and he could smell the stale stink of old magic from the practice spells his fellow students had cast the day before.

At the end of the corridor he came to the vast stairwell that joined the various levels. One group of stairs led downward, into the bowels of the university. The other climbed to the second floor where Umurhan and the priests lived. Safar hesitated, torn between his original purpose and the sudden thought the knowledge he sought in Umurhan's library would most likely be unguarded. He'd have about half an hour before the daily assembly ended and Umurhan and the other priests returned to the top floor.

"You can go either way," Gundara whispered from his shoulder. "Both are safe."

"Maybe later," Safar muttered, and then he ran down the stairs before the new idea could delay him from his most important task.

*   *   *

Although Safar met with Umurhan many times after the incident with the lioness, the wizard never thanked him or even raised the subject again. As Safar's education progressed and it soon became clear to all that he was a remarkable student of sorcery, Umurhan not only kept his distance but seemed to become colder—and Safar would look up suddenly from his studies and find the wizard watching him. Gubadan had warned Safar about Umurhan before he'd left Kyrania. Although he'd never told the old priest about his abilities, Safar got the impression during that last conversation somehow Gubadan had guessed something was up—and that there was magic behind it.

"Lord Umurhan has the reputation of being a jealous man," Gubadan had told him. "He doesn't like students or priests who show off their intelligence or powers. So beware, my lad. Every teacher doesn't receive his reward from guiding a young man to heights they could never achieve themselves. Go carefully in Lord Umurhan's presence, is my best advice to you. And never, never show him up."

Safar took Gubadan's advice to heart. As he progressed through his classes and spell-casting sessions he was always careful not to outshine Umurhan—although it soon became apparent to him that he could, especially as he learned more and delved on his own into the arcane arts of sorcery. He occasionally made purposeful mistakes when he thought Umurhan was becoming suspicious. Umurhan always took particular pleasure when Safar pretended to bumble, chastising him loudly, calling him a mountain bumpkin and other names intended to humiliate.

Umurhan loved to lord his mastery over the acolytes. He also held back his knowledge. When the classes became more advanced and the students were closing the ground on Umurhan, he protected his self esteem by teaching only so much and no more. When a spell was particularly powerful Umurhan tended to make his explanations so obscure no one could follow them, much less duplicate the spell. He also had a way of excusing himself when a thorny question was asked. He'd nervously plead other business, disappear for a short time, then return and answer the question with a confidence his previous demeanor hadn't shown.

Where he went during that time was no mystery to any of the students. They were at a cynical age, an age when details older people might overlook were easily apparent to them. It was an open secret Umurhan retired to his private library during those moments, cribbing from ancient masters to shore up his own facade. No one but Umurhan was allowed to peruse the books in that library. The excuse given was that there were forbidden books and scrolls on the black arts stored there that were so deadly, so evil, that no one but the High Priest of Walaria should read them—and then only in an emergency and only to ward off black spells cast against the city.

Safar's intense curiosity had led him to investigate the library. The library *did* contain material on black magic. But it was mainly a massive and confused collection of knowledge gathered by Umurhan's predecessors—rare scrolls, books by forgotten masters, volumes in strange languages and hand-written dictionaries of those languages, with magical symbols added by later men as marginalia. Using the books at *Foolsmire*, Safar had gradually deciphered the languages. His late night studies and secret visits put him on the trail of Asper, the ancient master of all master wizards, who also happened—Safar suspected—to have been a demon. One of the bits of marginalia even gave him strong reason to believe Asper's work was hidden somewhere in the chaos that was Umurhan's private library.

He'd been searching for it when he was discovered.

*   *   *

Safar crouched in the darkest of the library, a candle stub his only aid, as he hurriedly combed through cob-webbed scrolls and books with cracked binding—searching for the strange, four-headed snake symbol he knew to be Asper's seal.

Then an oil lamp had flared into life behind him and he whirled to find Umurhan hovering over him—eyes blazing like spear points fresh from the forge.

"What are you doing here, acolyte?" he thundered.

Safar fumbled excuses—"Forgive me, Master. I was worried about the exam and, I, uh . . . uh . . . I thought I, uh . . ."

"Are you claiming to be a cheat, Safar Timura?" Umurhan roared. "Is that your puny reason for violating my privacy?"

"Ye-es, Mas-ttter, ye-ye-yes," Safar stuttered.

"Then why are you among the forbidden books, acolyte?" Umurhan shouted. He pointed down the narrow aisle to the front of the library. "Why didn't I find your filthy, cheating personage up there? Why weren't you stealing your answers from writings that have not been condemned?"

Safar wanted to shout that no knowledge should be forbidden. And that, as a matter of fact, even the supposed innocent works in this library were denied to all but Umurhan. Instead, Safar pretended to panic—with Umurhan looming over him it wasn't hard—babbling that he was only trying to hide from the light and had come here by accident. He streamed forth such a mad babble of half-confessions and false apologies and pleas for mercy that Umurhan's suspicions were quieted.

"Silence," Umurhan shouted, cutting Safar off in mid babble. "You do understand I could have you seized this moment and charged with heresy?"

"Yes, Master," Safar answered, humble as he could.

"The only reason I'm not going to do so is that I believe you are nothing more than a low cheat."

"Yes, Master. Thank you, Master. I'm sorry, Master. It won't happen again, Master."

"Oh, I know you won't do it again, Acolyte Timura. I will see to that. I will withhold my punishment just now. I want you to contemplate your sins while I consider your fate."

"Yes, Master. Thank you, Master."

"The only reason I'm not immediately expelling you . . . or worse, by the gods, because I could do much worse! You understand that, don't you acolyte."

"Yes, Master. I understand."

"The sole reason I don't condemn you on the spot is because of the respect I have for your mentor, Lord Muzine. For some reason I shall never fathom he has a certain regard for your future and well being."

"Yes, Master," Safar mumbled, knocking his head on the ground. But he knew that what Umurhan was really remembering was the lioness and her ghost.

Although Safar had never been called into Muzine's company, his allowance had been increased after the incident. It had been coldly announced by Muzine's major domo, who harshly cautioned him about ever mentioning the ceremony or the event. It was plain to him now Umurhan feared the incident would get out if Safar's crime became a public matter. Questions would be raised about the sin Muzine wanted expunged. And even greater questions would be asked about the quality of Umurhan's magic. How could such a great wizard allow something like that to happen? And worst of all—perhaps Umurhan wasn't as powerful as he claimed.

Safar had been granted a reprieve, but he knew now it was a short reprieve—and getting shorter every moment.

*   *   *

"Hsst!" came Gundara's warning. "Danger ahead!"

Safar stopped. Below him was the final bend in the stairwell. It spilled out into the deepest and least glamorous level of the university. It was a place of boiling kitchen pots, foul garbage bins and huge clay pipes running overhead that carried water in and sewage out. Safar listened closely and after a moment made out the sound of a cleaning brush being rubbed against stone.

He resumed his journey, but at a slower pace. When he rounded the bend he saw a young acolyte kneeling on the steps. There was a bucket of water beside him and a brush in his hands. He was making lazy, half-hearted swipes at the steps with the brush—doing little more than dribbling water on the begrimed stone. But soon as he sensed Safar's presence the lazy swipes were replaced with vigorous scrubbing. The young man looked up, brow furrowed deeply as if the job required great concentration. But when he saw Safar he relaxed. He sat back on his heels, a wide, insolent grin splitting his face.

"Oh, it's only you, Timura. Gave me a start there for a minute. Thought you might be that whoreson, Hunker. Sneaking down here to catch me taking a little break."

Hunker was the priest in charge of punishment details. Any student in trouble learned to hate him on sight. He assigned the filthiest jobs and drove the workers like the spavined ox of the meanest miller.

Safar snorted. "That's me, Hunker, in the flesh. And I'm down here to set all you sinful bastards a good example. That's why I'm going to spend my entire day crouched over a shithole and setting it on fire. Love the smell of that stuff burning. Love to show all you lazy swine how a real wizard works."

The acolyte, whose name was Ersen, had the reputation of being the most indolent troublemaker in the university. Ersen was a constant, unruly presence on the punishment details. It was well know that the only reason he hadn't been expelled was because his father was an elder on King Didima's court. Despite his noble background, Ersen was popular with everyone. He took his punishment in good humor and always presented a sympathetic ear to his fellow miscreants. A sympathy many hoped would translate into protection for that miscreant through his influential father.

Ersen burst into laughter—a loud donkey braying Haw-Haw-Haw that endeared him to every student, but was hated by the priests—since they were usually the object of his uncontrollable laughter.

"I would love to see that, Timura," he said after he'd recovered. "Why, I'd trade my father's fortune—and throw in his flabby old balls as a bonus—to see old Hunker down here burning the shitters."

Safar chortled. "What about your own equipment?" he said. "Would you throw them in, as well?"

Ersen acted shocked. "What, and disappoint all the whores in Walaria? Why, the whole city would be filled with females weeping if their little Ersen was denied them. Besides, my father doesn't have much use for his anymore. He already made me. And there's no way he can improve on that historic feat."

Safar rewarded the reply with more laughter. But the whole time he kept thinking of Gundara's warning. Was Ersen the source of the danger? On the surface it seemed ridiculous. He was the class jester, the instigator of the best practical jokes aimed at authority. It there was mischief, everyone knew instantly that Ersen would be at the bottom of it. How could he be an informer? Then he recalled the comet streaking across the House of the Jester and it dawned on Safar just how good a cover Ersen's behavior would be if he were a spy. Everyone spoke freely in his company because what was there to fear from someone who was always in trouble himself for mocking authority?

Cold realization knotted in Safar's gut. This was exactly the sort of subtle game Kalasariz would play. He looked at Ersen with new eyes and saw the twitch in his cheek, the nervous, preoccupied drumming of his fingers on the steps—small leaks through his genial facade.

Safar sighed and stretched his arms. "Well, it's nice to dream about Hunker taking my place on the punishment detail," he said. "But that's not getting the shitters burned."

"What did you do to deserve that, Timura?" Ersen asked. "Set fire to Umurhan's beard, I hope."

Safar scratched his head. "I don't think so," he said. "The last thing I remember was getting drunk at the *Foolsmire*. Hunker jumped me when I showed up this morning. He screamed a lot, called me the usual names, and ordered me to report for shitter burning. But now that I think of it, he never did say what for."

"It must have been something pretty bad, Timura," Ersen said. "It'll probably be all over the University before the day is over."

Safar grimaced. "Let me know when you find out," he said. "And I pray to the gods that whatever I did was worth it."

With that he strolled away, Ersen's bray echoing after him—"Haw Haw Haw."

When it was safe Safar whispered to Gundara, "Was he the one?"

"How could anyone miss it?" the Favorite replied. "I swear, when the gods made humans they must have run short of intellect to stuff into your skulls."

Safar had no grounds to disagree at the moment, so he continued on in silence, taking a corridor that led away from the kitchens and stank of sewers. The tunnel finally spilled into an immense room pocked with great pits. The sewer pipes emptied into those pits and Safar thought the odor was rich enough to give a starving pig convulsions.

As he entered the room he saw a group of acolytes tending to a pit on the far side. They dumped big jars of oil into it, someone threw in a flaming brand and then they all jumped back as red and yellow flames towered up with a whoosh. Clouds of sewer smoke followed the flames, billowing out over the acolytes who cursed and choked on the filthy air.

The smoke was thinning as Safar came close and one of the acolytes saw him. He shouted something at the others, then ambled forward to meet Safar.

"That's Olari," Safar whispered to Gundara. "The one I have business with."

"I can't say if he's *entirely* safe," Gundara answered. "Only you can judge that. But I can say this—he isn't a spy."

Safar whispered thanks to a few gods for this answer, hedged though it was, and made a hurried prayer to a few others to help him with his plan.

Olari was the second son of the richest man in Walaria. As such he would not inherit command of the family fortunes and so some other worthy occupation had to be found for him. His magical talent was as small as Ersen's—so small that if he had been an ordinary youth he would never have been permitted into the school of wizardry. Everyone knew this, including Olari's father. It was assumed Olari would enter the administrative side of the business of magic, where canniness and family contacts were much more important than sorcerous ability. Safar did not underestimate him because of this. He knew that was the same road Umurhan had taken to power. Olari's reputation was as controversial as Ersen's. Except where Ersen presented himself as a jester and the laziest of all the lazy students, Olari was a rebel.

He was one of the student ringleaders who constantly and loudly challenged the status quo in Walaria. Safar had spent many an evening at the *Foolsmire* listening to Olari and his band of committed brothers debate the great issues of the day, fueled by copious quantities of strong spirits. They deplored the oppression of the *common man*, which Safar thought humorous since the only common men Olari and his rich friends knew were the slaves who waited on them and the tradesmen who catered to their exclusive tastes. Olari and the others roundly denounced the heavy taxes Didima demanded and the corruption of a system where bribery was the rule, not the exception. They condemned the city's leaders as old men, cowardly men, greedy men, who lacked all capacity to understand the new ideas and grand reforms offered by their far-seeing children.

Olari and his companions had tried to recruit Safar into their company. He was popular with all the other acolytes and if he joined them it would do much to strengthen their appeal with the university's intellectuals. Safar had always diplomatically refused, saying he wasn't a citizen of Walaria, nor did he intend to remain here when his studies were completed. He had no stake in Walaria, he said, and it would be wrong of him to take sides. Actually Safar considered the young rebels' ideals empty. Except for Olari, he thought their protests and petty conspiracies nothing more than spoiled children defying their parents. He excepted Olari because he thought it entirely possible the young nobleman was mapping out a shortcut to power. But the main reason he refused was that Olari and the other ringleaders were protected by their noble births. They were coddled by their families, who correctly said they'd soon grow out of this hot-headed stage. So it took no courage at all for them to express their views at the top of their lungs. Someone like Safar, however, would quickly find himself being hauled before Kalasariz as a traitor. In the past that fate had been only a strong probability. But now that Safar had actually met Kalasariz he knew it as a fact.

Another blast of fire and smoke thundered from a sewer pit, adding an odd drum beat of drama to the moment when Safar and Olari took the last few steps that closed the gap between them.

"I won't offer you a glad cry of welcome, Timura," he said, "because you'd curse me for it."

"And no one would blame me if I beat you about the head and shoulders as well," Safar laughed.

"Soon as I saw you," Olari said, "I thought—I'll be poached in shit sauce, if it isn't Safar Timura! The only time he's put on a work detail is when the whole class is being punished."

Safar shrugged. "It's my country upbringing that saves me," he said. "I'm good at ducking for cover and not getting caught."

"And did you?" Ersen asked. "Get caught, I mean. And what in the hells for?"

"Ersen asked the same thing," Safar said. "He seemed as surprised as you to see me here."

"And what did you tell him?" Olari asked.

"I lied," Safar answered, "and said I was here to help you burn the shitters. And that whatever it was I did to deserve it I'd forgotten because I was drunk."

Olari cocked his head, a small smile playing on his lips, considering what Safar's statement meant. Tall and darkly handsome, with deep brooding eyes offset by a dazzling white smile that charmed all who knew him, he was every inch a patrician, even in work robes and daubed with smoke and filth.

After a moment he nodded in satisfaction, smile spreading wider. "Come into my office, and we'll talk."

He gave Safar a follow me gesture and led him to a rubbish heap that hid a small cavelike opening in the wall. Olari dropped to his knees and crawled into it, Safar close behind. After a few feet the hole broadened into a small room. Olari lit a candle, revealing that the room was decorated with old mattresses and blankets. There were makeshift shelves bolted to the wall filled with sealed jars of food.

Olari lit a few more candles and a little smoke pot of incense to cover the sewer smell. Then he sank onto one of the mattresses and laid back, hands behind his head.

"What do you think of my office?" he asked.

"Considering the place it's in," Safar said, "I'm impressed."

"We take turns hiding out here," Olari said. "One group keeps watch while the other sleeps, or eats and even . . ." he reached to a low shelf, grabbed a stoppered jar and tossed it to Safar . . . "drinks."

"This is starting to take on the air of a palace," Safar said as he uncorked the jar. He took a long drink of what turned out to be a fine wine, then passed the jar to Olari.

The youth sat up and raised the jar, saying, "Here's to lies." And he drank.

As he passed the jar back to Safar he said, "I'm guessing that you're here because you've reconsidered my offer."

"That I have," Safar said. "I've decided to take you up on it."

"And why is that, my friend?" Olari asked. "What has suddenly made you see the light and decide to join our cause?"

"To be absolutely honest," Safar said, "I have no intention of joining anyone's cause. Although I'm risking the loss of your good opinion of me, I'll tell you straight out, Olari—I have a sudden need for a large sum of money. Call it a family emergency, if you will."

"There's no shame in that," Olari said. "Although I'd prefer it was your heart that guided you to me, not your purse."

"Oh, my heart's always been with you," Safar said. "You know I agree with most of what you say. I just don't feel involved because this is your home, not mine. If we were in Kyrania you'd feel the same."

"Perhaps I would," Olari said. "Perhaps I would."

"When we last spoke," Safar said, "you asked me to do a bit of creative sorcery for you."

Olari became as excited as his patrician mask would allow. Which meant his brooding eyes lit up and he crossed his legs. "Are you sure you can still do it?" he asked. "There isn't much time, you know. The Founder's Day festival is only two days off."

"There's time," Safar said.

"Are you certain? We need something really big. Something that will knock them out of their boots. Something that will show everyone what kind of fools we are ruled by."

"I think everyone in Walaria already knows that, Olari," Safar said. "They just don't talk about it much. Especially in public."

"Well, they'll talk after Founder's Day," Olari said. "If your magical event is big enough and public enough. The timing is crucial."

"I've thought of that," Safar said. "The spellcast I have in mind would work best if it came off at the Last Prayer ceremony. Right after the bells and the song when Umurhan does his annual magic trick to impress the masses."

"Where would you do it?" Olari asked.

"In the stadium, where else?" Safar answered. "Right in front of altar where Umurhan and Didima and Kalasariz will be holding court."

Olari whistled. "Right under their noses," he said. "I like that. And I can follow it up with spontaneous demonstrations and protest parades all over the city." He slapped his thigh. "That'll make them sit up and take notice."

Absently, Olari took another drink from the jar. "What exactly do you intend to do?" he asked.

"If you don't mind," Safar replied, "I'd really rather not say. It's a very complicated spell and very very delicate. Just speaking about it could disturb one of its parts and have a disastrous effect on the whole." He was lying. He hadn't had time to come up with the kind of magical disturbance Olari wanted. "But I promise you," he continued, "that it will be beyond your wildest wishes." This was only a partial lie. Safar *did* intend to deliver the spellcast, he just didn't know what it would be.

"The word of Safar Timura," Olari said, pricking Safar's conscience, "is good enough for me."

Safar hesitated, then took the plunge. "About the money," he said.

Olari gave a dismissive wave. "Don't worry," he said. "I've not forgotten. I promised you fifty gold coins. But I can see now I was being tight-fisted. Make it a hundred."

Safar's heart jumped—*so much?* "That's very generous of you," he said. "My, uh, family, will be more than thankful. But there's, uh, one other thing I'd like to ask."

"What's that?"

"Can I get it in advance?"

Olari stared at him long and hard.

"Just so you have all the facts you need to make up your mind, I'll tell you this," he said. "I intend to leave Walaria right after I do the casting. I know I'm putting a very large burden of trust on your shoulders, but I assure you I wouldn't ask if it wasn't necessary."

As Safar had hoped, the negative bit of information about his leaving helped sway Olari's decision.

"I think I can manage that load easily enough," the young nobleman said. "I'll do as you asked. Meet me at the *Foolsmire* tonight."

Safar thanked him and they shared a few drinks from the jar.

"I wish I could persuade you to stay," Olari said. "Things really will be different when we get rid of this lot."

"I'm sure it will be," Safar said. "But I worry about you. You've caused them no end of grief of late. Big demonstrations that have nearly turned into riots. Broadsides condemning them spread all over the city. What if they tire of it? Or worse, what if they suddenly think you are a great danger to them?"

"I want them to," Olari said. "That's my intent. How else can we achieve change?"

"I understand that," Safar said. "But you know, times really have been troublesome the past two years. And you can't blame it all on the Unholy Trio, as you call them. The weather has become increasingly unpredictable. As have the harvests. And there's been locust swarms and outbreaks of flux and plague. Not just in Walaria, either. It's happening all over Esmir."

Olari shrugged. "The gods are in charge of those things," he said. "And since it's their responsibility, what can I do? Besides, times will get better. They always do. History tells us that. And things aren't really so bad as you say. Deaths have been few. There's no mass starvation. Actually, many people live in relative plenty. And there's good news in the land as well. What of Iraj Protarus? He's our age. And look at all he's doing to change Esmir for the better."

"I don't call wars and raids on other people's kingdoms change for the better," Safar said.

Olari gave him a puzzled look. "I thought you two were friends?"

"We are," Safar said. "Or were, anyway. But that doesn't mean I agree with him."

Olari chuckled. "It seems Protarus and I have both had the same experience with you," he said. "You give us your friendship but not your company in our cause."

"I suppose you're right," Safar said. "But I've never been enamored of causes. Politics don't interest me. Only the science and history of magic."

"I suppose you'd like to put that interest to real use someday," Olari said. "To help people, for instance. To better their lot, their condition, with your skills."

"I'll admit I've thought of such things," Safar said.

"That's a cause isn't it?" Olari said. "Your cause, of course. But a cause just the same."

"I suppose it is," Safar said.

"So why do you shun my cause, and the cause of your friend Protarus. We're all the same age. We all have similar ideals. It's time for a change, dammit. A massive change. We've lived under the heels of old men for too long."

Safar couldn't say he theorized change might already be occurring. But it was a change on a scale much greater than two young men who wanted to be king.

Instead he said, "Allow me my delusions, Olari. I'm sure you and Iraj will soon prove me to be a blind fool. And I hope you forgive me when that time comes."

"You're forgiven already, my friend," Olari said. "Just make sure that when the time comes you know which way to jump."

"That's wise advice," Safar said. "I'll remember it. But I hope you'll also remember mine. Be careful of Kalasariz. I have a feeling he's becoming anxious."

"What if he does?" Olari said. "What can he do to me? The brutal truth of the matter is that there are two kinds of people in Walaria. Those who have reason to fear Tulaz' blade. And those who do not. And I, my bookish friend, belong in the first category by reason of my birth and my father's fortune."

Just then Gundara whispered in Safar's ear. "The spy approaches!"

Safar held up a hand to silence Olari. A heartbeat later they heard Ersen's sarcastic voice. "Do I hear sounds of merrymaking within?"

Ersen ducked into the room and saw the wine jar in Olari's hand. "What a greedy lot of beggars," he said. "Keeping the wine for yourself when your poor friend Ersen is nearly dying of thirst."

Olari laughed and handed the jar over. Ersen took a long drink, then sat on a mattress. "What are you fellows up to?" he asked. "Plotting the overthrow of the world as we know it, is my guess."

Ersen was not a member of Olari's group. He was too much of a jester to be welcomed. Still, Safar was worried that Olari would say too much. He made a hidden gesture of warning, then said to Ersen:

"You found us out, you canny devil. We've been sitting here for hours planning our revolt. We're thinking of starting with Didima. I've got a recipe we can slip into his food that'll make him limp as a wet rag."

"That's a good start," Ersen said. "What about Kalasariz? I've heard he doesn't have a tool at all."

"Exactly what I've been telling Timura," Olari said. "We have to come up with something different for him."

"Well, I'm just your man," Ersen said. "See if you can find another jar of wine in there, Timura. There's a good fellow. Conspiracy makes thirsty work."

CHAPTER THIRTEEN
ZEMAN'S REVENGE

It was just after Last Prayer and the *Foolsmire* was filling up with thirsty students. Inside the shop Zeman kept an eye on the alley entrance while he handed out books and collected rental fees. The word had come down from Kalasariz that Safar was expected to visit tonight in order to meet with Olari and his group of malcontents. Zeman's orders were to learn the purpose of that meeting and to report back what he found.

Zeman was vastly pleased with himself. His grandfather had been away when the letter from Iraj Protarus had arrived for Safar. Soon as he saw it Zeman thought his fortune was made. As anxious as he'd been to pass it on to the spymaster, he'd first taken time to examine the opportunity from every angle.

He'd been in Kalasariz' employ for over a year. He had a small copper chest under his bed filled with money earned from all the information he'd passed on to the spymaster. The *Foolsmire* was an ideal place to pick up gossip from wine-soaked students and learn of their crimes; past, present, and planned. It was a task Zeman found himself ideally suited for. His awkward ways, bad manners, and sly, short-changing habits had made him an object of derision among the young customers. He'd suffered their mocking remarks for years. Like most insensitive people Zeman's own feelings were extremely delicate and the remarks wounded him deeply. His reaction had been to become more abrasive and to cheat them every chance he had. Once he became a paid informer, however, the jibes no longer injured him. As an informer he was a man of power who secretly repaid every insult with a report that put a black mark next to their names. Also, except for the jibes, no one paid any attention to Zeman when he came near. The students thought so poorly of him they spoke freely in his presence, unaware all they said was being passed on to Kalasariz.

Safar was one of the few regulars who never joined the others in the game of Zeman-baiting. Zeman hated him for it. He saw condescension, not kindness, in Timura. He also strongly believed Safar had designs of his own on the *Foolsmire*. Look at how he toadied up to Katal, pretending he actually liked the old man and cared what he thought. Zeman saw his grandfather as a crazy, irresponsible old man who lived in a dreamworld where food for thought was more important than food for the table. Katal had the audacity to tell him some months ago that when he died he'd made arrangements for two small bequests—one for Timura and the other for that little thiefbitch, Nerisa.

Zeman had been scandalized by the news. The old man was giving away what rightfully belonged to his grandson. He became convinced the bequests had been Timura's goal all along. Safar was stealing Katal's affection and if Zeman didn't put a stop to it soon the old man would end up handing over all his worldly goods to Safar, leaving Zeman with nothing. As for Nerisa, why it was as plain as a full moon on a cold night that she was in league with Timura. Look at how she played on the old man's weaknesses—pretending to be a helpless orphan but all the while cozening up to Katal so she could win a place in his home and at his table. Zeman also believed her relationship with Timura was scandalous. He was certain they were sleeping together, which made Nerisa a child whore and Timura a whoremaster who probably traded her around to other decadent men who savored the flesh of children.

Zeman considered it his holy duty to put a stop to it. He'd plotted long and hard to find the rock that would crush them both. The letter, combined with Nerisa's robbery of the stallmaster, had given him that opportunity. When he'd finally delivered the letter he'd added a report linking the two together as conspirators against Walaria.

Now his plan was about to bear fruit. Other evidence had been found against Timura. At least that's what he surmised when the urgent message came that he was to watch Safar carefully tonight and report back all that he'd found. Zeman sensed a crisis coming—a crisis for Safar and Nerisa, at least. When it arrived the only thing that would make Zeman's world even more perfect would be if he could rid himself of his grandfather as well. He didn't know how he could accomplish that feat just yet. But he was confident if he were especially watchful the idea would come.

A voice broke into his thoughts: "What's the matter with you, Zeman? Got dirt stuffed in your ears?"

He looked up and saw the sarcastic amusement in a young customer's face. "I've told you twice, now," the student said, "that you've given me too much change."

Zeman glanced at the rental book in the student's hand and the coins on the desk. He'd been so lost in thought that he'd forgotten his original intent—which was to shortchange the student. He made a quick count of coins and saw that instead he'd returned too much.

"I don't mind cheating *you*," the student said. "The gods know you've robbed me often enough. But that was for your own pocket. This is for old man Katal."

"No one's forcing you to come here," Zeman snarled as he pulled in the excess change. "If you don't like I how do business, go someplace else. You won't be missed by me."

Instead of getting angry the student laughed at him. "No one cares what you think, Zeman," he said. "You don't own this place. Your grandfather does. We only put up with you because of old man Katal."

He grabbed his change and walked into the patio, laughing and telling the others about the encounter. Zeman was about to shout an insult when he saw Timura coming down the alley. Quickly he put out a coin basket and little sign telling the other bookstore patrons to wait on themselves. It was an honor system Katal had instituted long ago for the busiest hours. Zeman disliked the practice and had argued against it many times. He planned to end it soon as Katal gave up his stubborn hold on life and died. But just now it served his purpose.

As he headed for the patio and the crowded tables of wine drinkers someone tried to stop him and hand him money for a book.

"What are you—blind?" Zeman retorted, pointing at the basket. "Put your money there. I've got other things to do."

He rushed out, not hearing the response. His grandfather was at the well, drawing up buckets of cold wine jugs and stacking them on trays. Zeman saw Timura head for a large table in the far corner where Olari was holding court. Zeman was thrilled—the intelligence he'd received about the predicted meeting was evidently correct.

He snatched a tray from Katal's hands. "Here, let me help you with that, grandfather," he said to the startled old man.

Zeman ignored the pleased expression on his grandfather's face. He balanced the tray above his head and moved slowly through the crowd. People shouted for service as he passed, but he paid them no mind, concentrating instead on Safar and Olari. Timura's arrival was met with shouted welcomes and Olari rose to greet him, slapping him on the back and then leaning close to whisper something in his ear. Safar laughed as if he'd just been told a grand joke, but Zeman saw Olari pass him a small object, which he tucked into his robe.

Instead of going directly to Olari's table Zeman delivered his tray to the one closest to it. Moving at a snail's pace, he put a jug in front of each person; his focus was entirely on the discussion swirling around Timura.

He could pick up only snatches of the excited babble: " . . . history in the making . . . teach them a lesson they'll never forget . . . Umurhan will just shit . . . it's gonna be the best Founder's Day ever!"

When the tray was empty he stepped over to Olari's table; as usual, no one paid him the slightest attention, other than to order a drink or to berate him for being lazy and slow. Zeman smiled blandly at the insults, gradually working his way toward Timura. He was just at Olari's elbow, bending his head close as he could to hear the whispered conversation between the two, when Safar suddenly looked up and saw him. His eyes were wide as if someone had just said something surprising. Then they narrowed in what seemed to be sudden understanding.

Zeman couldn't bring himself to tear his gaze away from Safar's stare.

He *knows*, Zeman thought. Timura knows I'm an informer. But that's not possible! How could he?

Then Timura broke his gaze and touched Olari's hand in warning. The young noble snipped off whatever it was he was saying and leaned closer so Timura could whisper something in his ear. Zeman saw him jolt and start to turn to look in his direction, but another warning touch from Timura stopped him.

Zeman calmed himself. His imagination was running wild, he thought. There was no way Timura could know he was a spy. Safar's behavior was the result of guilt, not knowledge. He and Olari were obviously planning something and Timura was smart enough to make sure that not even someone he held in such contempt as Zeman would overhear. But he still felt uncomfortable, so he hurried away from the table on the pretense of fetching the orders for wine.

✳   ✳   ✳

Safar watched Zeman dodge through the crowd, the empty tray clutched tightly to his side.

"How do you know he's an informer?" Olari asked. "He's so stupid and lazy, it's hard to believe Kalasariz would ever want him."

"Trust me," Safar said. "Or at least, humor me. My information comes from an impeccable source."

Gundara's hissed warning had come just as Olari was discussing the disturbances he intended to stage after Safar's spellcast disrupted the Founder's Day ceremony. Safar had been nearly bowled over when he realized the little Favorite had fingered Zeman. After his initial surprise he had felt pity for poor Katal. His next thought was the realization that it was none other than Zeman who had put Kalasariz on his trail with trumped up charges. Anger boiled over in his belly, rising to sear the back of his throat. It was Zeman's fault that his life and Nerisa's were in danger. Under the circumstances anger was futile, as were any thoughts of revenge that would delay his flight from Walaria.

"You probably think I've suddenly gone mad," Safar said. "Insane or not, you can't be harmed by following my advice and being careful around him."

"I don't think you're mad," Olari said. "But I do wonder how you got your information."

"I can't say," Safar said.

"Anyone else we should be wary of?" Olari asked.

Safar knew if mentioned Ersen, Olari really would think he'd gone crazy. So he said, "Look at it this way—if someone like Zeman can be a spy, then who *can* you trust? The most unlikely person could be a direct pipeline into Kalasariz. Why, even Ersen—jester that he is—could be with the enemy."

"Ersen?" Olari said. "What brought his name into this?"

Safar shook his head. "Please, just be careful. Question everything. Everyone."

"Actually," Olari said, "Ersen makes more sense than Zeman. His father ran into some trouble with Kalasariz a few years ago. He seemed doomed for awhile, but then suddenly everything was fine again. And he's done nothing but rise in the ranks of the Walarian Council since Ersen started at the University."

Safar didn't respond and after a bit Olari realized he wasn't going to say anything more.

"For a man who doesn't like politics," Olari said, "you sure have a talent for wading into it up to your neck."

*   *   *

An hour later Safar lit the oil lamps in his rooms above the old city wall and got out his chest of magical implements. He had an idea for the spellcast he'd promised Olari and he thought he'd work on it while waiting for Nerisa.

The spell links came to him quickly and he jotted them down for reference and then got out a clean casting scroll and his brushes and magical paints. Gundara was busy devouring the sweet rolls he'd been promised and was quiet for a time. As he nibbled on the last of his treats, the little Favorite noticed what Safar was doing and watched with some amusement—picking dried berries and crumbs off his tunic and popping them in his mouth.

Safar used a narrow brush to paint sorcerous symbols on the rough white surface of the scroll, building up the spellcast's foundation.

"You can tell you're a student," Gundara criticized. "Too complicated. And do you really want to put the water sign in the center? Most wizards I know shove it in a corner out of the way."

"I'm not other wizards," Safar said. "And in this particular spell water goes in the center."

"O-kay," Gundara said. "If that's what you *really* want. But I think it's pretty stupid." He'd finished the rolls and with no other tasties in sight he didn't see any reason for continued politeness.

"You'd better pray I'm right," Safar said, "because you're the one who's going to carry it out."

"Oh, that's just wonderful," Gundara complained. "Here I am, the product of history's greatest wizardly minds, reduced to student pranks."

"This happens to be a prank," Safar pointed out, "that may save your master's life."

"Oh, in that case," Gundara said, "leave the water sign in the center. I'll get a new master quicker."

Safar, mind buzzing with the spell cast he was forming, started to get irritated. But when he saw the Favorite licking the sugary remains off his ugly little face he had to laugh.

"You win," he said. He dabbed white magical paint over the blue water sign. "Will the right hand corner do, O Wise One?"

Gundara shrugged. "Put it where you like. Makes no never mind to me. The Master knows best, that's my motto from now on."

"Fine, I'll put it there," Safar said. "Now, what symbol would you suggest for the center?"

Gundara got interested in spite of himself. "How about Fire?" he said. "That's a good symbol."

"Fire it is, then," Safar said, loading his brush with new paint and making red flame-like flares in the center."

"Of course, Lord Asper would've used his serpent symbol," Gundara said. "But I suppose he's out of favor with the younger wizards these days."

The name caught Safar by surprise. "Asper?" he goggled. "You know of Asper?"

Gundara sniffed, superior. "Certainly I do. You don't spend a couple of thousands years knocking around wizards' laboratories and not run into Lord Asper. Of course, his stuff was always more popular with demons. Since he was one. And I don't do demons. That's Gundaree's job. But I've picked up enough about him over the millennia to get by."

Safar pushed the scroll in front of him. "Show me," he said, holding out the brush.

Gundara hopped closer and grabbed the brush. Small as it was, it looked like a large spear in the little Favorite's taloned paws. He washed off the red in a water dish and loaded it with green paint.

Gundara lectured as he drew. "The serpent had four heads so it could see in every direction. Each head had four poison fangs to help guard the center." He daubed in the long body. "And there was a poison stinger on the tail in case the serpent was attacked from overhead. And then up here, right below where the heads join, you need to give the serpent wings so he can escape into the air if he needs to."

When he was done, Gundara stepped back to examine his work. "Not bad," he said, "even if I do say so myself."

His twin must have uttered an insult, for he suddenly turned toward the turtle idol, which was sitting next to the brazier. "Oh, shut up, Gundaree!" he snarled. "Shut up, shut up!" He turned back to Safar. "He's so *rude*," the Favorite said. "You can't believe the things he says to me!"

Safar, who was getting used to the one-way exchange between the twins, paid no attention. He examined the scroll and when he was satisfied he made a magical gesture, stirring the air with a forefinger. A miniature tornado—about the size of Safar's little finger—sprang up over the paper, quickly drying the paint. When it was done Safar blew on it and the tornado vanished.

Then he rolled the scroll into a tight tube and gave it to Gundara.

"Keep it," he commanded. "When you hear me chant the words to the spell you are to activate it. Do you understand?"

"What's to understand?" Gundara said. "You humans make such work out of magic. Demon wizards know it all comes from the gut, not the head. They just do it, while you're still thinking about it."

Despite the retort the Favorite did as he was told, collapsing the paper tube into an object the size of an infant's finger and tucking it into his sleeve for safe keeping. For a change, however, Safar was stung by Gundara's comments.

He'd learned much in Walaria. He had a mental storehouse of spells to confront almost any possibility. And he had the sound intellectual knowledge to create new spells to meet eventualities rote learning didn't cover. Compared to the other students and, yes, even compared to Umurhan, he had much greater power. He could feel it surging forward when he cast a spell—so strong he had to hold back so he didn't betray his true abilities. Still, the force was nothing like he'd experienced when he'd bested the demons in the snowy pass years before. He'd tried in private many times but he'd never been able to equal the river-like surge he'd felt during that life-and-death moment. The failure frustrated him. At first he tried to tell himself it didn't matter. That magic really wasn't his true purpose—which was to find the answer to the puzzle of Hadin. But the more he'd studied, the more he'd realized the solution would only come through sorcery.

"When I have time," Safar said, "which probably won't be until I'm safely on my way home, you and I need to sit down and have a long talk about Hadin."

"Best place in the world," Gundara said. "Smartest mortals around. They made me, which ought to be proof enough. Although, somebody sure made a big mistake when they made Gundaree. Probably a human assistant. You know how there are. Of course, anything I have to say will be pretty old news. The gods were still in swaddling clothes last time we were there."

"Anything will help," Safar said. "Also I want to hear about Asper."

Gundara yawned. "That'll be a pretty short conversation," he said. "All I know is what I've heard from other wizards."

"I understand he wrote a book about his theories," Safar said. "Have you ever seen it?"

"No. And I don't know anyone who has."

"I think there's a copy in Umurhan's library," Safar said. "Among his forbidden books."

"Then why didn't you steal it today?" Gundara asked. "You could have gone upstairs. I told you it was safe. And once you were inside I could have sniffed it out for you easy. You wouldn't have even had to give me another sweet roll."

"There's wasn't time," Safar said. "Now I'm afraid there never will be. I don't dare go back to the University. And after Founder's Day I'll be running as fast as I can. With a lot of angry Walarians chasing me."

Nerisa's voice came from behind them—"I can get it for you."

Safar and Gundara turned to see her perched on the window sill.

"I was starting to worry about you," Safar said.

Gundara snickered. "Stick with worrying about yourself, Master," he said. "She does just fine. I sensed her climbing the watchtower fifteen minutes ago. But you didn't notice a thing until she was inside and announced herself."

Nerisa giggled. She jumped off the sill, dug a sweet out of her pocket and walked over to give it to the Favorite.

"I knew it was my lucky century," Gundara said, "soon as you stole me from that stall." He popped the sweet into his mouth, closing his eyes and chewing with great gusto.

"Why don't you go rest for awhile?" Safar told him. He gestured and the Favorite disappeared in a cloud of smoke. The turtle idol rocked on its legs as the smoke funneled into the stone. Then all was silent.

"His lip smacking gets to you after awhile," he told Nerisa.

"Never mind that, Safar," Nerisa said. "I really meant it. About the book. I can get in and out of Umurhan's place in no time. Especially with Gundara to help me."

"It's too dangerous," Safar said.

Nerisa put a hand on her hip. "Nobody's ever gotten close to me yet," she said. "What could be so hard about an old library? Let me have Gundara and I'll be back before First Prayer."

Safar shook his head. "You don't know what you're saying, Nerisa," he said. "Things are a lot worse since last night."

He made her sit down, brewed her a pot of mint tea, and told her an edited version of what he'd learned. He left out the bargain he'd made with Olari, figuring quite correctly that she'd want to get involved.

Tears welled up when he said he was leaving Walaria.

"It isn't safe for either of us," he said. He dug into the heavy purse Olari had given him and pulled out a handful of gold coins. "Here. This is for you."

Nerisa struck them away. Coins scattered across the floor.

"I don't want money," she said. "I can get money anytime."

Safar gathered them up again. "I'm not abandoning you, Nerisa," he said. "This is *just in case* money. If I'm caught, or . . . there's some other emergency. If all goes well, you can go with me if you want."

Nerisa grinned through her tears. "You'd really take me with you?" she cried.

"It won't be very safe," Safar warned her. "There'll be a lot people after me."

Nerisa threw her arms around him. "I don't care," she said. "Let them come. I know all kinds of tricks. They'll never catch us."

Safar unstuck her, gently pushing her back into her seat amongst the pillows. "You don't have to go all the way to Kyrania," he said. "It's a pretty boring place for someone who grew up in Walaria."

"Well, it won't be boring to *me*," Nerisa said, thinking that for all she cared Kyrania could be the dullest place in all Esmir. It didn't matter as long as she was near Safar.

Safar patted her hand. "We'll see," he said. "Once we're clear of Walaria we can talk about this again."

"Anything you say, Safar," Nerisa said, dreamy.

Then she yawned and stretched. "I'm so tired," she said. "Can I sleep here for awhile? I've been ducking and hiding all day."

Safar hesitated. "They know to look for you here," he said.

Nerisa yawned again. "That's okay," she said. "Gundara will warn us if anybody comes."

Safar started to say it was still too big a chance to take. Then heard her breathing deepen and looked over and saw that she'd fallen asleep. In repose she seemed even younger and more vulnerable. Her lashes were delicate fans on her soft cheeks. He could see the fine bones of her face and thought that someday she'd be a great beauty. If she lived long enough to reach womanhood. He didn't have the heart to awaken her. So he banked the coals in the brazier and pinched out the wicks in the oil lamps. He found an extra blanket and covered her. She sighed, clutching the blanket tight and murmuring his name. Safar found a comfortable place a few feet away. So much had happened he doubted he'd be able to do much more than rest. But he'd barely closed his eyes when sleep rose up to carry him away.

It was a dreamless sleep, although once he thought he heard the rustle of fabric and felt soft lips brush his.

The next thing he knew the door crashed open and four burly men rushed inside.

He rolled out of his blankets but before he could come to his feet the men were on him. They clubbed him down and pinned him to the floor.

Then a heavy boot crashed into his head and stars of pain flared. He lost consciousness for a moment, then he heard steel strike flint and he opened his eyes to see Kalasariz standing over him, an oil lamp in his hand.

"Acolyte Timura," the spymaster intoned, "you are charged with conspiracy against the crown. What do you have to say for yourself?"

Safar was dazed by the beating. He tried to speak, but his tongue was thick and refused to work. Then he remembered Nerisa. His heart jumped and he turned his head to see where she was. But she was nowhere in sight. Relief flooded in—thank the gods, somehow she'd managed to escape. Then another thought pierced the haze. Why hadn't Gundara warned him about Kalasariz' approach?

The spymaster held a heavy purse over Safar's head. It was the purse of gold Olari had given him, minus the coins he'd shared out with Nerisa. Kalasariz shook the purse. "What's this?" he said. Then he opened it and spilled coins into his palm. "This is a great deal of money for a poor student to have in his possession," he gloated.

Safar said nothing.

"Where did you get so much gold, Acolyte?" the spymaster demanded. "And what did you swear to do to earn it?"

Safar still said nothing. What was the point?

Kalasariz kicked him again. "It will do you no good to hide in silence, Acolyte Timura," he said. "Your fellow conspirators have already confessed."

Safar regained enough wit to say, "Then you don't need to hear from me, do you, My Lord?"

The reply won him another kick, this time in the ribs. They hauled him to his feet, gasping for breath.

But he still had presence of mind to look over at the brazier where he'd last seen the stone idol.

It was gone.

The only thing he could think was, Nerisa must have it.

Then Kalasariz roared, "Take him away! The sight of this heretic offends me!"

And they dragged him out the door.

*   *   *

"Hsst! Someone's coming!"

A dim light appeared and Nerisa dropped to the ground. She hugged the stone as a dark figure shuffled out of a corridor and headed her way. She was on the top floor of the University—no more than a hundred feet, Gundara had informed her, from Umurhan's library. The Favorite was a flea speck on her sleeve—he'd told her about Safar's method of carrying him about and she'd adopted it.

The shuffling figure was an old priest. He mumbled to himself, cursing the cold stone on his bare feet and muttering deprecations against the devils who had conspired to hide his sandals. He was carrying a small oil lamp with a nearly burned out wick that gave off just enough light to make her nervous. She flattened herself as he walked right up to her, then veered to the side to fumble at a door. He broke wind loudly and Nerisa guessed the door led to a privy. The priest went inside and shut the door.

Nerisa came up like a cat and ghosted down the corridor until Gundara told her to stop because she'd found the library. It was locked, but that only delayed her for a few seconds. She fished a narrow bar from her pocket, slipped it into the keyhole and forced the big tumbler back. In an instant she was inside, quietly closing the door behind her.

The library was a sealed room and so dark she couldn't make out even the largest objects. But she could smell the dusty odor of old books, just like the ones at the *Foolsmire*, except there was heavy sulfur smell of magic that made her throat feel raw.

"I can't see," she whispered to Gundara.

There was a sudden glow and the Favorite appeared before her full size—which meant he came up to about her knee. His body gave off a dim green light and she could see the hulking shadows of furniture and book shelves.

Gundara made a slow circle, sniffing the air. In her pocket she felt the stone idol become warm as the Favorite drew on its magical power.

Then he said, "This way," and scampered off into the darkness.

Nerisa followed and they moved along the twisting aisles until they came to the far side of the room where tall bookcases lined the blank wall. Gundara hopped from shelf to shelf until he was eye-level with Nerisa.

"There it is," he said, pointing a glowing talon. "Asper in the flesh." Gundara snickered. "The book's bound in leather," he said. "Get it—flesh! Ha ha. I'm pretty funny tonight."

"It must be the sugar," Nerisa said through gritted teeth.

At first she'd thought the Favorite was a cute little thing. She felt sorry for him because he had to live in a hunk of stone. But after several hours in Gundara's company she just wanted to get the job over with and hand him back to Safar. Honestly, he asked such personal questions. Statements, actually. Like accusing her of being in love with Safar. Which was true, but it was none of his fiendish business.

Gundara gripped the edge of a slender book and heaved mightily. It came out so fast he lost his balance. He squealed as he fell, scaring Nerisa half to death. She caught him in midair, but the book slammed to the floor, echoing loudly.

"Be careful," she whispered. "You'll wake them up!"

"Oh, piddle pooh," the Favorite said—although he *did* whisper. "You could shout at the top of your voice and those old gas bags would never wake up."

"Just the same," Nerisa said, "I wish you'd be more quiet. I'm used to working alone and loud sounds bother me."

"You're a pretty good little thief, dearie," Gundara said. "But I bet you wish you had me around *all* the time. You'd be rich! We'd steal everything that wasn't nailed down."

"Riiight," Nerisa said, bending down to pick up the book.

It was thin and seemed to contain so few pages Nerisa feared Safar would be disappointed. The leather was cracked and old, but from the light Gundara gave off she could see the worn image of a four-headed serpent.

"That's Asper's book all right," Gundara said. "There's probably not more than five or six in the whole world." He preened, proud of his work.

She started to fish a treat from her pocket to reward him, when he suddenly said—quite loud—"You shut up, Gundaree. You couldn't of found it if it were on fire. So there. Don't you call me that! Shut up, you hear me? Shut up! Shut up! Shu—"

Nerisa clamped a hand over his mouth, cutting off the rest.

"Stop that," she said. "Or I'll wring your neck. I swear I will."

When she took her hand away Gundara hung his head. He kicked at the floor with his elegant little foot. "I'm sorry," he said. "He just gets me soooo mad, sometimes."

"Just don't do it anymore," Nerisa said. Then she gave him the treat.

Gundara grinned and gobbled it down. "I like you, dearie," he said. "I hope Safar gives you a nice little diddle after he gets the book."

"Don't talk like that," Nerisa said. "It isn't nice."

"But it's what you want, isn't it?" the Favorite teased. "A big old sloppy kiss and then get diddled all night."

Nerisa tucked the book away with the stone idol. "That's enough," she said. "And if you say one word like that to Safar, I'll, I'll . . . never speak to you again. See if I don't."

Apparently this was a greater threat than a neck-wringing, for Gundara instantly apologized and said he'd never, ever do such a thing. Then he led the way back to the library door, shrunk down to flea size again and they slipped out into the corridor. After an hour of creeping about in the dark, Nerisa sprinted through the big main gate and headed down the broad avenue—leap frogging from shadow to shadow as she made her way back to Safar's place.

She arrived just as Kalasariz and his men were dragging Safar down the stairs.

*   *   *

It was a night of terror in Walaria. Kalasariz' men swept through the city, breaking down doors and hauling frightened young men into the streets where they were beaten and questioned under the shuttered windows of their families' homes. Then they were taken to the spymaster's torture rooms where they were questioned further and forced to sign confessions. There were about fifty in all, although less than half were acquainted with Olari. The others were innocent, but had been marked for seizure by Kalasariz' informers who did a record business that night collecting bribes from enemies of the young men and their families.

Justice was swift. There was no trial, nor were any of the condemned present when a High Judge sentenced them to death. The mass execution was set for the following day—which happened to be Founder's Day. Town criers went through the city, shouting the news of the executions and posting notices listing the names of the condemned and their crimes.

At the top of the list was the name of the ringleader—one Safar Timura, foreigner.

At the bottom of the list was the name of one of his dupes—Olari, citizen.

*   *   *

"Apparently I misjudged my family's influence," Olari said.

Safar wrung out the rag, freshened it from the pail of cold water and wiped the blood from Olari's face. He had been beaten so badly his head was swollen to half again its size.

"You always were a master of understatement," Safar said.

Other than the bruises he'd suffered when he was captured, Safar was unscathed. For some reason he hadn't been tortured and his "confession"—an unsigned document with Kalasariz' seal—had been good enough for the High Judge.

"The real pity of it is," Olari said, "I'm not even getting any credit. I'm to go down in Walarian history as a mere minion."

"And I the minion in chief," Safar said. "On the whole I'd rather pass on the honor. But Kalasariz was quite insistent. You know how persuasive he is."

"My father most likely paid a handsome sum to have me listed as a dupe of your devilish tongue," Olari said. "Protecting the family honor and all that. Stupid, I guess, is better than king of the traitors."

The two young men were in the company of six other youths, all suffering from the ghastly work of the torturer. They were slumped in the center of the cell, barely able to chase away inquisitive insects and rats. All eight of them were to be beheaded by Tulaz, the master executioner. The others, crowded in nearby cells, would be parceled out in lots five or less to ten other executioners.

"There is *one* consolation," Olari said.

"What's that?" Safar asked. "I could use a bit of cheering up."

"I'm to go last," Olari said. "Which means whether Tulaz succeeds or fails, I'll be remembered. If he strikes off my head with one blow, I'll be helping him break his record. If not, why I'll go down in the wagering books as the one who ended Tulaz' remarkable streak."

Safar laughed. It was a bitter sound. "I wish I could be there to see how it turns out,"

138

he said. "Unfortunately, I go first."

Olari tried to laugh. A sharp pain in his ribs turned it to a low groan. When he'd recovered, he shook his head, saying, "I always was—"

His words were cut off by a coughing fit. Safar held him until it stopped. Then his companion spit blood into the pail. There was a plop as one of his teeth fell into the water.

He looked up at Safar, grinning a bloody grin.

"What I was trying to get out before nature so rudely interrupted me," Olari said, "was that I've always been a lucky dog.

"And it looks like that luck is going to stick with me until the very end."

CHAPTER FOURTEEN
DEATH SPEAKS

"You're too tense," the trainer complained as he kneaded the massive body stretched out before him. "Can't get the kinks out 'less you relax."

"Slept like shit," Tulaz said. "Don't know what's wrong with me. I al'ays sleep like a babe. 'Specially afore a work day. But it weren't like that last night. Kept dreamin' about this little fiendish thing. Body like a man, face like a toad. Kept on sayin'—'Shut up, shut up, shut up!'"

The trainer's brow knotted in worry. The executions—moved to the main arena to handle the Founder's Day crowds—were less than an hour away. All his savings had been risked on the outcome.

"Bad luck, a dream like that," Tulaz went on. "Got me all out of sorts, it did. Can't figure out what I done to bring it on."

"You purged yourself like I tole you?" the trainer asked, pummeling Tulaz' thick body.

The Master Executioner of Walaria snorted. "'Course. Filled five buckets, didn't I?"

"And you've been stickin' to your diet?"

"Gruel and water'd wine, nothin' more," Tulaz said. "It's this big rush that's botherin' me. I usually get some notice, you know? Couple of days at least to get into shape. 'Sides, I just broke me own record couple a days ago.

"Seven heads takes a lot out of a man, which most people don't appreciate. They just come and see me lop 'em off. Miss all the fine points. Don't know how hard I works to keep a good form. I ain't recovered from the seven, yet. Now I gotta go for eight, afore I'm even ready."

"Don't think about it," the trainer advised. "It's just one more day like any other. Keep that in your noggin' and it'll work out fine."

"Sure," Tulaz said. "That's the trick. Just another day. Nothin' special about it."

The trainer poured scented oil on Tulaz and started working it in. "And each head, too," he said. "Look at 'em the same way. Don't count how many you gots to go. One or eight, what's the difference? They all gotta come off one at a time. Nothin' special about that."

"Yeah," Tulaz said. "That's the only way they go—one at a time. Thanks. I'm feelin' much better already."

The trainer chuckled and said thanks weren't necessary. He finished his task, covered Tulaz with heavy towels and advised him to take a nap.

"I'll call you in plenty of time," he said.

He crept out of the training room, but just before he exited he looked back at Tulaz. The giant executioner was lying face up, a brawny arm shielding his eyes.

And he was muttering to himself: "Shut up, shut up, shut up. Wonder what he meant?"

For the first time in Tulaz' long and illustrious career he was obviously distracted and suffering from a decided lack of confidence. The trainer left the room, wondering where he could get some money quick to lay off his bets.

*   *   *

The crowd roared. Safar was led out first, followed by Olari and six others, all manacled and chained together. Forty two heads had already been severed and the crowd was bored by the spotty performances of the executioners. But this was the main event: Tulaz, the Master Executioner of Walaria, was going for an eighth and record head.

Safar was nearly blinded by the bright morning sun. He tried to shield his face, but his arms were brought up short by a chain linked to a thick iron waist band. A guard cursed and prodded him along with a spear butt.

When his vision cleared Safar could see that he was being taken to a large, hastily erected execution platform in the center of the arena. It had been thrown up next to the dignitaries' stand, where King Didima, Umurhan, and Kalasariz sat in pillowed and canopied comfort.

When Kalasariz announced the results of the roundup, Didima had decided to make the mass executions part of the Founder's Day ceremonies. The king prided himself on making quick, tough decisions, even if others believed them too daring or tradition-breaking. He thought the executions would whet the appetites of his citizens for the festivities that would follow.

"It will bring us all together at a special time," he told Umurhan and Kalasariz. "Heal the discord among our citizens."

Umurhan, a usually cautious man, had agreed without argument. Although he didn't state his reasons, the High Priest of Walaria had been troubled of late that his annual display of sorcery wasn't being greeted with the sort of respectful enthusiasm and awe it deserved. Fifty severed heads would go long way to warming up the crowd.

Kalasariz also thought it was an excellent idea, although he too chose not to mention them to his two comrades. For his purposes it was always better to get political executions out of the way as fast as possible—before families and friends and loved ones had time to work up a good, lasting grievance. Swift executions put the fear of the gods in them, quelling vengeful thoughts.

The crowd gathered to witness the event was the largest in Walaria's history. It spilled out of the stands onto the floor of the arena. Hundreds were packed within twenty feet of the execution platform itself and more were squeezing in every minute, crowing over their good fortune and clutching prized tickets Didima's soldiers were selling at premium prices.

Safar's guards had to push people out of the way as he and his companions in misery shambled toward the platform. People shouted at him, snaking hands past the guards to try to touch him. For luck, he supposed. If so, it was a sorry sort of fortune. Some cursed him. Some cheered him. Some cried "courage, my lad."

Hawkers mingled with the crowd, selling food and souvenirs. One enterprising young man had fistfuls of candied figs mounted on pointed sticks. The figs were painted with food dye to make them look like human heads. Blood-colored food dye streaked sticks to mimic the sharpened stakes Safar and the others would soon have their heads mounted upon.

Safar was too numb to know fear. He concentrated on putting one foot in front of the other. If he had any feeling at all it was to wish it would be over quick.

All eight were led onto the platform, slipping on the bloody planks. Men with buckets and mops were cleaning up the gore from the previous executions. Others sprinkled sand around the cutting block to give Tulaz decent footing. The condemned were lined up at the edge of the platform, where guards doused them with cold water and gave them wine-soaked sponges to suck so they wouldn't faint and spoil the show.

Then Tulaz himself mounted the platform and the crowd thundered its approval. The Master Executioner was dressed in his finest white silk pantaloons. His immense torso glistened with expensive oil allowing the bright sun to pick out the definition of his mighty muscles picked out by the bright sun. His white silk hood was spotless, without a crease or stray thread to spoil its symmetry. Thick bands of gold encircled his wrists and biceps.

Tulaz went right to work, paying no attention to the crowd. First he checked the steps where the condemned would kneel, then the hollowed-out chopping block where each man would stretch his neck to receive the blade. When he was satisfied he shouted for his sword case. While he waited he drew on special gloves created just for him by the best glove-maker in Walaria. The palm surface was pebbled and the fingers were cut out to improve his grip. The crowd was hushed as an assistant presented the open case and Tulaz bowed before it, muttering a short prayer of greeting. The hush turned to a deafening roar when he removed the gleaming scimitar and held it up high for the gods to see.

Tulaz lowered the blade, caressing it and whispering endearments as if it were his child. Then he removed his favorite whetstone from a slot in his wide, leather belt and he began to hone the edge. Each slow practiced movement drew cries of admiration from the crowd, but Tulaz kept his eyes averted, his attention fully on the sword.

After a few moments Tulaz walked over to the condemned, still stropping his blade. He paused in front of Safar, who looked up and found himself peering into the darkest, saddest eyes he'd ever seen.

"It'll be over soon, lad," Tulaz said, his voice remarkably soothing. "There's nothin' personal, you know. Law says what it says and I just do me job. So don't fight it, son. And don't jerk about. I'm your friend. Last friend you'll ever know. And I promise I'll make her nice and clean and send you to your rest quick as I can."

Safar didn't answer—what was there to say? Nonetheless, Tulaz seemed satisfied and he turned away, stone whisk-whisking along the steel edge.

The executioner had mounted the platform still feeling edgy, unsettled. But after talking to Safar he found his nerves steadying. He thought, That's good. Al'ays nice to talk to your first head. Let's the gods know you're serious about your work.

He turned to the soldiers guarding the condemned. "Get those chains off'n my heads," he said. "And rub 'em down good afore the bodies stiffen up."

Safar suddenly felt lighter as the chains fell away. Strong hands massaged him, bringing life back to his numb limbs. Then he was guided forward and he heard Olari call to him, but the words were lost in the crowd noises.

"Steady, lad," he heard Tulaz say as he was pushed into a kneeling position before the block.

Safar raised up to take one last look at the world. He saw a sea of faces screaming for his death. Some snapped out at him with remarkable clarity. There was an old man, howling through toothless gums. There was a matron, babe at breast, watching the proceedings with a look of remarkable serenity. Then, just below him, he saw a young face—a girl's face.

It was Nerisa!

She charged out of the crowd and rushed the platform. Soldiers grabbed at her, but she ducked under their outstretched hands. The nails of those grasping hands raked blood streaks on her arms. Fingers tightened on her tunic, but she pulled away with such force that all they captured was torn cloth.

"Here Safar!" she shouted. "Here!"

She threw something at the platform. It sailed through the air and landed next to the cutting block with a heavy thud. Safar didn't look to see what it was. Instead, he watched in horror as the soldiers reached Nerisa.

A mace crashed down on her head—blood spraying everywhere.

Then she was buried under a dozen soldiers.

The crowd roar diminished to puzzled shouts and then a low buzz as people asked each other what had happened.

Tulaz' voice rose above the buzz—"That's it! I can't work like this. The whole thing's off!"

Safar heard another man speak most urgently—"You can't quit now, Tulaz! Think of all the money riding on this, man! They'll skin you alive!" It was the trainer, who'd evidently found enough coin to copper his bet.

Then a great voice thundered, "Citizens! Friends!"

It was King Didima, who'd come to his feet to address the crowd, his voice magically amplified by Umurhan.

"Today is a great day in Walaria's history," Didima said. "It would be wrong of us and an insult to the gods who favor our fair city to allow a malcontent to spoil these holy ceremonies. We have all had a marvelous time this morning. And we owe a debt of gratitude to Lord Kalasariz for his thoughtful efforts to present us with such marvelous entertainment, while at the same time striking a blow for all law-abiding citizens.

"Now, let us resume our entertainment, my good friends and fellow Walarians. Our great executioner, Tulaz, was about to astound us with a feat never before attempted."

The king turned toward Tulaz, shouting, "Let the executions resume!"

Someone grabbed Safar by the hair and forced his head on the block. Under royal command Tulaz stepped forward, slashing the air with his sword to warm up.

"Hold him steady," he shouted.

The hand tightened its grip in Safar's hair.

Just then a small, familiar voice hissed from beside him, "Shut up, Gundaree! I don't need your help."

Tulaz froze, his nightmare coming back to haunt him. "Who said that? Who said shut up?"

And Gundara said, "Shut up! I'm not listening, Gundaree. Uh, uh. No, no. Don't care what you say. Shut up, shut up, shut up!"

The fingers loosened and Safar jerked free. He glanced down and saw the object Nerisa had thrown—it was the turtle idol. He up and saw Tulaz towering over him, scimitar raised high to strike. But the executioner was motionless, stricken with fear.

"The dream!" he said. "It's coming true!"

"Forget the dream," the trainer cried, pushing at the brawny executioner. "Quick! Cut off his head!"

Safar grabbed up the idol. "Appear, Favorite!" he commanded.

There was a boil of smoke and Gundara leaped out onto the platform.

Tulaz goggled at the little figure. "No!" he shouted. "Get away from me!"

"What's he all excited about?" Gundara asked Safar.

"Never mind that," Safar snapped. "Do something about the sword before he changes his mind."

"Okay. If you insist. But it looks like a pretty nice sword."

"Just do it," Safar said.

Gundara made a lazy gesture, there was a loud *crack!* and the sword shattered like glass.

Tulaz screamed in horror and leaped off the platform.

Gundara brushed his claws together, as if knocking away dirt. "Anything else, Master?"

"The spell," Safar said. "Help me cast it now!"

Gundara plucked a tube of paper from his sleeve and tossed it to Safar. It grew to full size as it sailed the short distance and Safar snatched it out of the air.

As he readied himself chaos erupted all around him. The crowd roared in fury at the interruption. Gamblers attacked odds makers and odds makers shouted for their bully boys' who waded in. The fights spread like a plainsfire and the stands and arena floor became a swarming mass of struggling bodies. Didima thundered orders and soldiers rushed toward Safar and Gundara.

Safar chanted:

> *Here are the hypocrites of Walaria,*
> *Cursed be. Cursed be.*
> *King Didima and Umurhan and Kalasariz,*
> *The unholy three. Unholy three.*
> *Devils and felons are welcome in Walaria,*
> *Say the three. Say the three.*

The scroll burst into flames and Safar flung it into the faces of the charging soldiers. The fiery bits exploded into a white-hot mass flinging the soldiers back, screaming and twisting in pain.

Safar snatched up the stone idol and Gundara hopped onto his shoulder, crying, "Run, Master! Run!"

He leaped off the platform into the madness of the crowd. A soldier slashed with a sword, but Safar dodged the blow and cracked his head with the idol.

Behind him Olari had shouted the other condemned youths into life and they all swarmed off the platform and raced for cover.

Didima's amplified voice thundered, "Seize the traitors! Don't let them escape!"

Safar rushed toward the place where he'd last seen Nerisa. Gundara conjured a flaming brand that shot off spears of magical lightning. Holding tight to his master's collar, he waved the brand about, scattering the crowd. Safar came to the spot where Nerisa had been attacked.

There was nothing there but a drying pool of blood.

"She's dead, Master," Gundara shouted. "I saw her die!"

Rage gripped Safar and he whirled around to face the royal stage. He saw Didima and Umurhan being rushed away to safety by Kalasariz and his men.

He was helpless in his fury. He could feel great pools of power gathering near him. He only had to reach out and take it and then strike. But his enemies disappeared before he could form the killing spell and then a mass of armed men was charging toward him.

He gestured and a white cloud formed overhead. A deadly hailstorm erupted from that cloud, ripping through the soldiers' ranks. Men cried out, falling to the ground, moaning from broken heads and limbs.

Gundara kicked at him with small sharp heels. "Run, you fool!" he shouted. "Quick, before they send more!"

Safar ran.

He bounded up the emptying stands like a mountain goat until he came to the highest wall. On the other side was a broad street leading to the main gate—not more than a hundred yards away. Just beyond was freedom. Safar jumped, tucked and rolled when he hit, and raced for the unguarded gate.

And then he was gone.

*   *   *

Despite the chaos Safar left in his wake, Kalasariz regained order by day's end. He shut down the city at Last Prayer, imposing a dusk-to-dawn curfew. All violators were killed on the spot. Then he sent his men out to seize anyone who might threaten the throne before Didima had a chance to recover the dignity of his office. Only one of Safar's seven companions was recaptured. The rest, including Olari, seemed to have vanished. Kalasariz wasn't concerned about the missing youths. He'd always seen them as more of a symbol to be exploited than a real danger.

He'd once viewed Safar Timura as such a symbol. Now he wasn't so certain. Umurhan certainly viewed Timura as a threat, demanding that men be sent out immediately to capture Safar, and babbling for nearly an hour about the tortures the young man would suffer for his crimes. Kalasariz saw naked fear in the High Priest's ravings—a fear that could only be caused by the magical powers Timura had displayed in the arena. The spy master was no expert on such things, but when he added Umurhan's fear and Timura's friendship with Iraj Protarus, he thought it best to take extra precautions.

The first hedge involved the group of hunters he'd sent after Timura, who were hand-picked for their loyalty. He'd given them secret orders to kill Safar on sight. They were also told if Timura managed to elude them for any length of time they were to give up the chase and return home. By no means was he to be captured and returned to the city as King Didima had demanded.

The incident in the arena prompted Kalasariz to take one other major precaution. Umurhan had unintentionally revealed that as a wizard he was all bluff. Otherwise he would've used his magic to destroy Safar—or least block his spell. It was plain to Kalasariz that if Walaria were ever attacked there'd be little help from the High Priest. This was a huge hole in the city's defenses, a gap that couldn't be filled.

So the spy master penned a careful message to Iraj Protarus. In it, he deplored the actions of Didima and Umurhan. He also subtly hinted if the day ever came when Protarus might wish his assistance, Kalasariz was his humble servant and would be pleased to comply. With the message he included the documents he had hidden away: Safar's death warrant and Kalasariz' letter of protest.

The message was sent the day his hunters returned with the sad news that Safar Timura was nowhere to be found.

*   *   *

Nerisa crouched in the corner of her cell, a blood-crusted bandage wrapped around her forehead. She was weak from hunger and loss of blood. She had no idea how long she'd been in the cell or how long she'd remain before they came to take her.

Despite her weakness, she remained stubbornly unafraid. She held firm to a prisoner's ultimate defiance—they can kill you, but they can't eat you.

She'd rescued Safar. This was satisfaction enough. No one could take that back. If she were to be sacrificed for her love, so be it. Safar would go on living and he'd have the magical idol and Asper's book—which she'd given to Gundara—to remember her by. She was certain he would make a great future for himself and no matter what happened to Nerisa, she would always be a major part of that future.

Nerisa had one real hope. When she'd been captured her unconscious body had been dumped in a holding cell with others caught up in the arena riots. When she'd regained consciousness she'd had the presence of mind to swallow the gold coins Safar had given her. If she ever had the opportunity she intended to use those coins to win her freedom. At the very worst she could bribe the executioner to make her death swift and painless.

It was a slender hope but it was hope just the same.

A rattle of keys and heavy footsteps brought her up. She saw the warder unlocking her cell door. There was another man behind him.

"Oh, it's you, Zeman," she rasped. "What are you doing here? Run out of flies to torture?"

Zeman stretched his lips into a nasty grin. "You should be more polite to me," he said, waving an official looking document at her. "I'm your new owner."

Nerisa spit. "No one owns me," she said.

Zeman stepped into the cell. "They do now," he said. "You have no idea how far-thinking and kind the law is in Walaria when an underage child is involved. I've just paid out a small sum to rescue you from this cell.

"In return for my generosity you have been given to me as a slave."

Nerisa was shocked. The fear she'd fought against since her capture rose up to grip her heart in icy fingers.

She clutched at hope "Your grandfather will never allow it," she said. "Katal doesn't believe in slavery."

Zeman snickered. "Don't look to my grandfather for help," he said. Then he made a mournful face. "Poor old dear. He's dead you know. Something he ate didn't agree with him."

Nerisa became numb. She had no doubt Zeman had poisoned the old man. Tears welled. She shook her injured head violently, using pain to quell the tears. She'd be damned if she'd give Zeman the satisfaction.

"You are looking at the sole proprietor of the *Foolsmire*," he said. "And the sole owner of *you*, as well."

"What do you want with me?" Nerisa snarled. "You know I'll run the first chance I get. Either that, or kill you in your sleep."

"Oh, I don't intend to own you very long," Zeman replied. "I've already approached a buyer who's willing to take you off my hands. I'm making a handsome profit, if you must know. Although not as much as your buyer is going to make. Apparently there are certain men—rich men, I'm told—who have an appetite for little whores like yourself."

Zeman pasted on another of his ugly smiles. "And after you've grown breasts and are no longer any good to your new owner, I'm sure he'll make other arrangements for your future."

Zeman snickered. "He gave me his word on that."

Nerisa screamed in fury and launched herself at Zeman—nails coming out like a cat's to rake his eyes from his head.

The warder stepped in and clubbed her down. She fell to the floor, unconscious. The warder raised his heavy stick to strike again.

Zeman stopped him, saying, "Let's not damage the merchandise."

*   *   *

Safar huddled in the slender shade of a desert succulent. His robe was hitched up over his head to protect himself from the merciless sun. A hot wind blew over the desolate landscape, intent on wringing every drop of moisture from his body. His tongue was a thick raw muscle, his lips cracked and drawn back over his teeth. He scraped at the hard ground with a jagged piece of rock, trying to dig a deep enough hole to expose the moisture held by the succulent's roots. He'd been working at it for hours but was so weak he'd barely managed a slight depression.

The sun had only just reached its zenith. The hottest and longest hours were still ahead. It was unlikely that he'd last until nightfall. But he kept at it, knowing neither hope or despair. He was like an animal with no thought in its head except survival.

A few days before he'd had life enough left to know joy when he saw his pursuers turn back. The hunters from Walaria had tracked him doggedly for a week, forcing him to flee deeper into the desert. With Gundara's help he'd cast spells of confusion to shake them off. Although he'd managed to elude them several times, the hunters kept reappearing on his trail. Gundara said it could only mean they had magic of their own to assist them.

The hunters gave up when they ran out of water. Safar, who didn't have that luxury, had run out long before. Divining spells proved to be useless—he never had a chance to stop and resupply himself. Finally he was even denied Gundara's company and help, the intense desert causing the little Favorite to grow weak and retreat into the stone idol. After that, Safar had paused when he could to kill a lizard or snake and suck out its moisture. It was a losing battle, with the sun and wind draining his life as quickly as he'd drained those poor creatures.

Safar made one more swipe at the dry depression. Then all his strength fled and the rock fell from his grasp. He sagged back on the ground, gasping for breath.

Then even breathing seemed to require too much effort and he thought, Well, I'll just stop. But to his disgust his chest insisted on heaving in and out, drawing in air filled with sharp bits of grit. Then he thought, it has to end sooner or later. I'll lie here until it does. He sighed and shut his eyes.

Then Safar heard music—distant pipes and bells. He thought, this must be what it's like to die.

The sound grew louder and he was overcome with a vague curiosity to look this strange, music-playing Death in the face.

He opened his eyes and wasn't disappointed. A huge low-flying creature swept across the desert towards him. It looked like an immense head, swirling with all sorts of marvelous colors. There were no wings or body attached to the head, but in Safar's daze this seemed quite natural. The creature flew closer and now he could make out its face.

He had strength enough to feel surprise. He thought, I didn't know Death was a woman. And such a beautiful woman—a giantess with sensuous features painted in glorious colors like a savage tattooed queen.

The music seemed to be coming from her lush mouth as if she had a voice composed of wondrous pipes and bells and harp strings.

The woman's head was hovering over him now. Safar smiled, thinking Death was finally going to take him. He closed his eyes and waited.

Then the music stopped and he heard someone speak. It was a woman's voice, but smaller than he thought a giantess would possess.

"Merciful Felakia," the woman said, "spare me this sight. He's only a lad. And a handsome lad at that."

"Handsome or plain, makes no difference to the buzzards," came another voice—a deep baritone—"He's dead, Methydia. Come on! The Deming fair's only two weeks off and we gots a long ways to go."

Safar was disappointed. This wasn't how Death was supposed to behave. Was she going to leave his body here? Abandon his ghost to this wasteland?

He stretched his lips and tried to speak, but only managed a croak.

"Wait!" said the woman. "Sweet, merciful Felakia—he's alive."

No I'm not, Safar tried to say. I'm dead, dammit! Don't leave me here!

Then from above he heard a loud whoosh of escaping air and he felt a huge presence drifting down to him.

Safar smiled. Death was on her way. He ached for her embrace.

Part Three
Wizard of the Winds

CHAPTER FIFTEEN
THE DEMON KING

Do you see anything, Luka?"

"No, Majesty. I see nothing."

King Manacia frowned, his royal brow a deeply plowed field of displeasure.

"Are you certain, Luka?" he asked his oldest son and heir. He jabbed a long talon at a point on the horizon. "Isn't that something, or someone, moving over there?"

Prince Luka shielded his yellow eyes with a claw—peering out over the Forbidden Desert. Manacia and his court were camped on the edge of the blackened wasteland. The King sat on his traveling throne, placed on thick carpets and shaded by a white canopy, billowing in the desert wind. Behind him was the main camp—a city of gaudy tents that housed his court.

After looking long and hard the prince sighed and shook his bony head—a dozen heavy golden chains of office rattling against his armor.

"I don't believe so, Majesty," he said. Then, soothing, "But it's early, yet. Perhaps Your Highness is hungry, or thirsty. Why don't you retire to your tent and I'll send for the stewards. Possibly you'd enjoy a little nap. You look so weary, Sire, that it nearly breaks my heart.

"I'll alert Your Majesty the instant Lord Fari returns."

Manacia exposed his fangs—a wide, multi-rowed smile of fatherly pride. "You're a good and loyal son, Luka," he said. "No king could ask for a better prince. But it wouldn't be seemly. A king must not fear to suffer the same trials and tribulations as his subjects."

Prince Luka laid a claw of sincerity across his mailed heart. "You are an inspiration to us all, Majesty," he said. "I worship and study at your feet, praying I will have half Your Highness' courage and wisdom on that most regretful day when the gods decree that I must succeed you to the throne."

The whole time the Crown Prince spoke he was thinking, I hope you choke on a bone, you horrid old fiend. I hope the sun fries your brains and the hyenas feast on your liver.

Manacia chuckled fondly. "To think I nearly wrung your neck at birth," he said. "I thought you'd grow to be a conspiring little savage like your mother. Instead, you've matured into the most civilized and considerate subject in my kingdom. It's a pity I couldn't let your mother live to see what a fine son you've turned out to be."

Prince Luka bowed low, humbly thanking his father for his kind words. But he thought, You old fool. You wouldn't look so smug if you knew Mother made me swear on her death bed that I'd avenge her.

Manacia gestured and a slave crawled over on his belly with a cup of cold wine. The king sipped, reminiscing.

"Looking at you, my son," he said, "no one would ever guess your mother was a barbarian. You are my strong and serene right claw. And to think when I bedded her the first time she tried to stab me with a knife she'd hidden in her girdle."

He smiled at the memory. "Your mother was understandably overwrought," he said, "because I'd just killed her father and brothers. I had to have her tied to the bed before I could mount her."

"Your Majesty has regaled me many times with the tale of that illustrious moment,"

Prince Luka said. "I never tire of hearing it."

The king laughed and slapped his knee. "Did I ever tell you what your mother said after I'd had my pleasures?"

"Yes, Majesty," the prince said. "But it was such a delicious incident I'd be pleased if you told me again."

"She said I'd raped her!" the king chortled. "Can you imagine that? *Me*, rape *her*?"

"She should have thanked you for honoring her with your royal seed, Majesty," the prince said. "But she was young and of a savage tribe. Mother didn't know what she was saying."

The king was impatient to complete his story. "Yes, yes," he said. "But that's not the point. We already know she was a savage. I said so, didn't I?"

"The point is she accused me of raping her. And do you know what I replied?"

"No, Majesty. What did you say?"

"I replied—'that wasn't rape.' 'That was'—now get this—'assault with a friendly weapon.'"

Manacia howled with laughter at his joke. The prince forced sounds of immense amusement.

Then the prince said, "One thing you've never told me, Sire . . . what was Mother's answer?"

The king's laughter cut off in mid-snort. "What was that?" he growled, green skin mottling with building anger.

"I said, what did Mother reply after you made that marvelous jest about rape being nothing but assault with a friendly weapon?"

"It doesn't matter what she replied," the king snapped. "That wasn't the joke. The joke was the friendly weapon part. Not what she said after. Who cares what that fiendbitch thought? It's what the king has to say that's important. Whole histories are devoted solely to the remarks of kings. In my case, I'm also noted for my sense of humor. The anecdote concerning your mother is only one especially revealing example."

"Absolutely, Sire," the prince said. "How foolish of me not to see it right off."

The king's mood turned from fair to foul. Muttering oaths, he resumed his watch—searching the bleak horizon for some sign of his Grand Wazier.

In the king's opinion—which, as he often said, was the only one that mattered—few truly appreciated how hard he'd labored these past few years. Nothing had come easily and every platter of victory he'd been served up always seemed to hide a nasty little insect under the tastiest morsels.

All of the demon lands had been brought completely under his control. His kingdom now bore the name Ghazban, after the ancient emperor who'd first welded all the demon lands together. Zanzair was now the seat of the mightiest kingdom since the time of Alisarrian, the human conqueror who had cut short Ghazban's long and honorable dynasty.

No sooner had the naming festival ended when trouble began to gnaw at Manacia's accomplishments. First there was the drought, which still held the kingdom in its grip—turning the harvests to ashen husks. Then there were the locust swarms—great clouds that first blackened the sky and then the earth as the insects descended to devour whatever had managed to defy the drought.

Plagues mysteriously erupted across the land, ravaging the populace—turning cities to towns and towns to desolate villages. There were reports of ghastly phantoms rising from graveyards, giants suddenly appearing to threaten distant crossroads, Jinns crouching in ambush to devour unsuspecting travelers.

Manacia and his wizards had worked at a dervish's pace to halt these outbreaks.

Huge spell machines were constructed and hauled out to the troubled regions. Whole forests of cinnamon trees had been felled to make the incense that was burned in those machines. Day and night the furnaces churned out immense clouds of fragrant healing smoke. The expense sometimes made the king nostalgic for simpler times when his realm was smaller and less expensive to maintain.

Despite Manacia's efforts, trouble continued to dog Ghazban. His subjects were becoming increasing restless and unruly. It was whispered that the gods were punishing all demonkind for allowing such a greedy pontiff to rule them. Word leaked out about his experiments with the curse of the Forbidden Desert, fueling further religious fears and discontent.

In the past Manacia had dealt with such things by immediately invading a neighboring kingdom. It not only released domestic pressure but gave him a brother monarch to blame and then bring to task for his sins. This was no longer possible in the brave new world that was Ghazban, where the subjects had only Manacia as a target for their suspicions.

In the beginning Manacia's dream of ruling all Esmir as King of Kings was only that—a private dream. Now it had become a necessity. He needed to challenge his subjects, to fix their minds on a great peril; an historic enemy—godless humans—to bear the blame for their ills.

To achieve this he had to solve the riddle of the curse that kept demonkind and humankind apart. Once he thought he had the answer and sent the bandit chieftain, Sarn, across the Forbidden Desert to spy out an invasion route. But Sarn had never returned. The king falsely blamed the curse and spent every free moment searching for the solution to its riddle. He had ripped apart his original spell and then reformed it many times.

None of his efforts worked. It was as if he had gone back to the original days of failure when hundreds of slaves and felons were forced out into the Forbidden Desert to die horribly before the eyes of the soldiers who had prodded them there. Distracted as he was by domestic toil, it took Manacia a long time to return to the spell he'd used to shield Sarn and his outlaws. He added a few improvements and tried again.

The very first effort met with success. The villain used for the experiment not only survived, but was able to walk to the most distant hill, the soldiers playing out rope and tying on additional lines until he was nearly out of sight and had to be dragged back so he wouldn't escape.

After his experience with Sarn, Manacia was wary of this success. He called for his Grand Wazier, Lord Fari, and asked his advice.

"We require a volunteer, Majesty," Fari said. "Someone loyal, above reproach."

"Exactly my thinking," Manacia said.

The old demon built on this success. "Perhaps Prince Luka," he said. "It would be a mighty accomplishment he could add to his deeds, thus assuring the admiration of your subjects when he assumes the throne some day."

The Grand Wazier hated the Crown Prince and this seemed an excellent time to be rid of him—if the king's spell failed, that is.

Menacia, who kept a firm talon on the pulse of his court, knew what Fari was up to.

"What an excellent thought," he said brightly. Then he frowned, "Unfortunately, that can't be. At this particular time I need him by my side."

He clicked his claws against the arm of his throne, pretending to ponder further. Then he smiled. "I've got it!" he said. "And I have you to thank for the idea, Fari. For it made me focus on who my most loyal subjects were. And the answer was there in an instant. For other than my own son, who could be more loyal than you, my dear fiend?"

The Grand Wazier was aghast. "*Me*, Your Highness? You want *me* to cross Forbidden Desert?" His voice quavered. "As much as I'd love to have the honor to serve in you this, I fear I am too old, Majesty."

"In this case," Menacia said, "advanced age makes you even an even better choice. To begin with you have many years of wizardly experience to draw upon. And if by some distant chance the experiment meets with failure, why you can't be that far away from your natural death.

"It would be tragic, of course. But not as tragic as if a younger wizard were cheated out of a long life."

Fari realized it was hopeless to argue with the king. It was obvious the choice had been made before Menacia summoned him. The advice seeking had only been for appearance's sake.

The Grand Wazier acceded to the king's command with as much grace as he could muster. Preparations were made, detailed instructions were given, and in less than a month Fari and a small expedition set out across the Forbidden Desert. Their orders were much simpler than Sarn's. Once they reached the humanlands they were to turn back immediately and report their success to the king.

Demon scholars estimated the crossing and return journey should take no more than eight weeks. When the time drew near for Fari's return King Manacia became so anxious he ordered his whole court transported from Zanzair to the edge of the Forbidden Desert.

There he sat, day after talon-biting day, waiting for his Grand Wazier. Eight weeks became nine. Nine became ten. The king was so restive he rose before dawn and paced before his traveling throne until late at night.

He'd all but given up hope when Lord Fari finally appeared.

It was at dusk and the sun was just disappearing beneath the horizon. The western-most rim of the desert was a thick red smear that drew the king's eyes like an insect drawn to flame.

His whole being flew out to the rim. He whispered prayers and curses to gods and devils alike. Then his heart bumped hard against his chest. Shadowy figures formed at the horizon. They seemed to be moving, growing larger as they approached. Fearing to spoil his luck the king said nothing, waiting for his lookouts to shout the news.

The cry came and still the king said nothing. He remained motionless, giving no sign of the chaos raging inside.

Then night fell and far out in the desert a score of torches flared into life, bobbing in the darkness like fireflies.

There was no doubt now that it was Fari.

The riddle of the curse of the Forbidden Desert had been solved.

Prince Luka shouted his congratulations, pounding his father on the back—wishing his hand held a knife. Officers and courtiers crowded around the king to praise his wisdom and perseverance.

Manacia was not moved. His excitement had died quickly—he'd waited too long for joy to find a resting place.

When the weary, bedraggled expedition bearing Lord Fari arrived the king was already huddled with his generals in the command tent.

Prince Luka had the great pleasure of seeing the aged demon's shock of disappointment at his poor reception. The journey had taken a heavy toll on Lord Fari.

Slumped in the saddle, every bone aching, he peered first at Luka and then the lights of the tent city.

"Where's the king?" he asked, voice quavering from age and weariness. He despised himself for letting the weakness show in front of Luka, but he couldn't help it.

"My father asked me to relay his apologies," the prince answered. "He said you'd understand that he couldn't actually be present to congratulate you.

"He's busy right now, you see, planning the invasion of the humanlands."

CHAPTER SIXTEEN
THE CLOUDSHIP

For a long time Safar floated on a balmy sea. Below were mysterious depths where nightmares were sea dragons pursuing his dreams.

He dreamed of Kyrania and its fruited fields. He dreamed of clouds melting in the Sun God's forge, dripping colors on the land. He dreamed of clay that leaped into fantastic shapes the moment he touched it. He dreamed of maids bathing in the lake and they were blessed with figures as beguiling as Astarias' and faces with winsome smiles and starry eyes like Nerisa.

But each time a dream popped into being it was devoured by the swift-moving nightmares. He saw the volcano overwhelm the people of Hadin. He saw the demon cavalry charging the caravan. He saw Tulaz lift his sword, saw Kalasariz peeping through a dungeon grate, saw Katal die at Zeman's hands—and Didima's soldiers slay Nerisa.

He dreamed of Alisarrian's cave where he crouched beside Iraj, watching smoke form into a woman's seductive lips and he saw them move and he heard the Omen speak:

"Two will take the road that two traveled before. Brothers of the spirit, but not the womb. Separate in body and mind, but twins in destiny. But beware what you seek, O brothers. Beware the path you choose. For this tale cannot end until you reach the Land of Fires."

Eventually the intensity of this sleeplife lessened and Safar became aware of the world around him. It seemed as mysterious as the ocean of dreams.

He still felt buoyant as if he were floating on that sea, except now he seemed to be lying on a cushioned raft. Instead of hissing surf he heard the flutter-drum of the winds and the whistle and ping of it singing through taut lines. He heard the rhythmic pumping of bellows and the low roar of a furnace.

Strong, gentle hands lifted his head. A spoon touched his lips, which parted and he lapped up a meaty broth. The spoon dipped up more and he ate until he heard the hollow scrape of wood, signaling the bowl was empty and he drifted away again.

The next time he became aware he heard odd voices saying even odder things, like, "Tighten that carabiner." Or, "Work the mouth, dammit! Work the mouth!" And, "Who's minding the burner? It's almost out!"

Once he heard the woman whom he'd thought was Death cast an incomprehensible spell.

"Come to us Mother Wind.
Lift us in hands blessed
By the warm sun.
We have flown high.
We have flown well.
Take us in your arms, Mother Wind.
And when you are done,
Set us gently on the ground."

Safar wondered at the purpose of the spell. While he was puzzling he fell asleep.

Time passed. A time of dreamless drifting. Then a current of cold air washed over him and he opened his eyes.

There was the shock of sudden sunlight and then vision cleared.

He seemed to be lying on a firm surface at the bottom of a fantastic canyon with dazzling walls of many colors. The walls curved inward until they seemed only a few feet apart. Through that hollow he could see skies as blue as the high vaults above the Bride and Six Maids.

Then hazy reason formed and he thought—That's no cliff. It's too smooth. Also—I've never seen slate with all those colors. And so bright! Like they were painted. Then he realized the canyon walls were moving as if they were made of living skin.

Maybe a giant swallowed me, Safar thought, and I'm looking up into his guts. But that conclusion made little sense—it didn't allow for the sky.

I must still be dreaming, he thought. Then a leg muscle threatened to cramp and he stretched the limb until the pain eased.

And he thought—There is pain, which proves I'm awake. But exactly where am I awake? He considered. Then it came to him that he was flying—or, lying upon something that was flying, at any rate. Perhaps he was awake, but in the middle of a vision and in that vision he was perched on a mighty eagle flying to wherever the vision commanded.

No good. Where were the wings? If he were riding an eagle, there'd be wings.

He tried to sit up and reconnoiter his surroundings.

Someone shouted. Weakness overcame him and he fell back. Dizzy, he closed his eyes.

Slippered feet approached.

A whiff of perfume as someone knelt beside him.

He opened his eyes and found a beautiful woman bending over him. She had almond eyes and long silvery hair streaked with black. It was the face of the woman he'd seen floating across the desert; the woman he'd believed was Death herself come to take him away. But this face was of normal size and it wasn't painted with all sorts of savage colors. Her skin was white and smooth as the most expensive parchment, with a fine, barely visible net of age etched on the surface.

"I did this once before," Safar told her. "Awaken from the dead, I mean. With a beautiful woman hovering over me." He was thinking of Astarias.

The woman laughed. It was a rich, earthy laugh. A laugh with appetite.

Instead of answering she turned her head and called to someone, "The lad wakes up pretty as he sleeps, Biner. He has the *loveliest* blue eyes. And you should hear the compliments. First time I've blushed in thirty years."

"That's enough hot air to lift us another thousand feet, Methydia, " Biner replied. His voice was a familiar baritone.

Heavy feet thudded forward. "Last time you blushed," Biner said, "the Goddess Felakia was a virgin."

Safar craned to look. From the deepness of the voice and the obvious weight the feet were carrying, Safar expected to see a huge fellow come into view.

Biner was immense all right. He had the girth of a giant, the mighty arms and hams of a giant, but all that size had been squashed by an enemy giant's hand into a body that stood less than four feet high. He had a huge bearded face with an overly wide mouth filled with broad teeth.

Biner saw Safar staring at him. He displayed his teeth in what was meant to be a comforting smile. "Bet you're glad I wasn't the one to wake you up, lad," he said. "I got a face that'll peel the reflection right off a mirror."

Safar struggled to answer. He didn't want to be rude by appearing to agree with an all-too-obvious truth.

Methydia patted him. "Don't worry about Biner's feelings," she said, guessing what was on his mind. "Ugly as it is, he's proud of that face. People pay good money to see it. Almost as much as they pay to see him lift a wagon of pig iron. Or smash a pile of bricks with his fist."

Biner toed the floor, embarrassed. "Aw, that stuff isn't much," he said. "Just tricks to wow the fair crowds. Besides, Methydia does some of her witchy business first to soften them up."

Methydia gave Safar a look of immense sincerity. "Biner is a fine actor," she said, a dramatic hand going to her flowing bosom. "The best male lead in all Esmir, in my judgment."

Safar's head was swimming. He was very confused. "Excuse me, dear lady," he said. "But would I be wrong in guessing that I've been rescued by, uh . . . *entertainers?*"

Biner and Methydia laughed. Biner stood as tall as he could, shouting: "Come one, come all! Lads and maids of Alllll ag-es! I now to present to you—Methydia's Flying Circus of Miracles!

"The Greatest Show In Esmir!"

Methydia applauded, crying "Bravo! Bravo!"

Safar became alarmed. He propped himself up on an elbow. "Excuse me again," he said. "I know it isn't polite to question one's rescuers too closely, but . . . What was that thing you said about flying?"

Biner seemed surprised. "Of course we're flying, lad," he said. "We're about two miles up, is my estimate."

Safar coughed. "Two miles up? In what?"

"Why, a Cloudship, boy. A Cloudship!"

Fear overcame weakness and Safar stumbled to his feet.

He went to a rail and looked down. Far beneath him was the floor of a wide, fertile valley. He could see a great double-humped shadow moving swiftly across the fields. His veins turned to ice as it came to him that he was probably part of that fast-moving shadow.

He called back to his rescuers, "How far up did you say we were?"

Biner replied, "Two miles, lad . . . Give or take a thousand feet."

First Safar threw up.

Then he passed out.

*   *   *

When he regained awareness a small crowd was gathered around him.

Methydia was beside him, trying to coax brandy between his lips. One look at the crowd and Safar opened his mouth wide and choked down a flood.

Biner was in the center. To his left was a tall, skeletal fellow wearing nothing but a breech cloth and a turban. He had a huge snake draped about his neck—a snake with the face of a man. Just behind him was a stocky man with the hard muscles of an acrobat. He had a too-small head that was detachable, holding it up by the hair to see over the others, a long tube-like neck trailing down to his shoulders. Towering over the group was what had to be a dragon. A white dragon, with a long snout and a spiked tail, which curled up as Safar looked to scratch a place behind its ear. Then someone moved and Safar saw the creature wasn't *entirely* a dragon. The long torso was that of a well-endowed woman, complete with breast plates and a triangular modesty patch tied about the hips with a thong.

There was much to goggle at. But the dragon noticed Safar had fixed upon her.

"I altho' juggle," she lisped. "Thix globth and theven thwords. We thoak them in oil and I thet'm on fire with my breath."

She raised a claw to her snout and burped. Smoke and flames shot around her fist.

"Excuthe me," she said. "Mutht have been thomething I ate."

Safar nodded. What a polite dragon, he thought. Then he passed out again.

The last thing he heard was:

"Really, Arlain!" Methydia said. "Can't you control yourself? You've scared another guest half to death!"

"I'm thorry," the dragon wailed. "Wath'n my fault. The thquath we had for thupper mutht of been thpoiled."

* * *

Several days of dreamless sleep passed, interspersed with half-conscious feedings. Then the sudden moment came when he awoke and felt very strong and very alert. He smelled perfume and immediately he felt very *very* . . .

He opened his eyes. A dim, flickering light illuminated his surroundings. There was a cabin roof above his head, shadows dancing on the dark ceiling. Safar looked down and saw a certain part had made itself embarrassingly apparent beneath the blankets.

Safar heard a familiar, throaty laugh. Methydia's face leaned over him, lips parted in a smile, almond eyes dancing with humor. She glanced down, then back at him again.

"It's good to see you among the living," she said.

Safar flushed. He started to apologize, but Methydia put a finger to his lips, silencing him.

"Don't be embarrassed on my account," she said. "Consider your little upstart welcome. Any friend of yours, and all that."

Safar opened his mouth to speak, but once again a long, slender finger touched his lips.

"You're a young man," Methydia said. "Youth has its advantages and its disadvantages. The advantages are apparent." She glanced at the blanket. To Safar's relief his problem had subsided. "The disadvantages are—what to do with your advantages."

"Oh," was all Safar could say.

"Now, I suppose you have some questions," Methydia said. "Assuming your uninvited guest isn't so consumed with himself that he'll allow you to think."

"First off," Safar said, "I should tell you about myself before I have the right to ask any questions."

"Go on," Methydia said.

"My name is Safar Timura," he said in a rush. "I've just escaped execution in Walaria. I could swear on my mother's soul I didn't deserve such a fate. That I am no criminal. That I am only a student—a seeker of truth who has never done anyone harm. But none of that should matter to you.

"What should matter is that I am wanted by very powerful men who would most certainly do you harm if they learned you had aided me."

Methydia clapped her hands. "What a delicious speech," she said. "And so well spoken. My compliments to your mother and father for raising such an honest lad."

Once again Safar felt the discomfort of a blush. "I was only trying to warn you about what you might be in for," he said, a bit sullen.

Methydia kissed him and patted his cheek. "Don't mind me, dear," she said. "I have an old woman's blathering tongue."

Safar's eyes strayed to her lush figure, swathed in a many-layered, translucent gown. "You're not so old," he mumbled—and tore his eyes away.

"If you keep talking like that, my pretty lad," Methydia said, "we're going to get ourselves in trouble.

"Now. Allow me to compose myself."

Methydia, ever the actress as Safar eventually learned, fanned her cheek with a delicate hand, saying, "You have a way of troubling a woman's concentration, dear."

Safar had learned better than to automatically blurt an apology. He said, "Do you mind if I ask *you* a few questions?"

"Ask away," Methydia replied.

"First I want to ask about the Cloudship," he said. "Then I want to ask about the circus."

*　　　*　　　*

The answers consumed many days and many miles. In fact, during the months Safar spent with Methydia and her troupe, he never did hear the entire tale—although everyone from Biner, the muscular dwarf, to Arlain, the human dragon who preferred vegetables over meat, was more than willing to enlighten him.

The Cloudship had no life of its own and although complicated in design, it was an object and therefore easier to explain.

Essentially, it *was* a ship—a ship with its nose bobbed off and its masts and sails removed. It had a long ship's deck, a high ship's bridge and a ship's galleys and cabins. The timbers it was made of, however, were light as parchment and strong as steel.

Methydia said the rare planks were the gift of a woodsman—a long ago lover—who stole the trees from a sacred grove to prove he'd make a worthy husband. The woodsman's most ardent rival—a magical toy maker of great renown—turned the planks into a marvelous vessel, hoping to upstage his opponent.

"I was very young, then," Methydia said. "But although I was dumb enough to attract men I didn't want, I was bright enough to not only keep my gifts, but to avoid marrying my lovers without giving insult."

The body of the Cloudship dangled beneath two balloons, each ninety feet high and made of a strong, light cloth that was not only moisture proof but offered a marvelous surface for all the colorful paints the troupe used for decoration. Methydia's face graced the front, or forward, balloon. The legend, "Methydia's Flying Circus", the aft.

The quantities of hot air required to lift the vessel were provided by two big furnaces, called "burners," with magically operated bellows to fan the fuel—a mixture of crumbled animal dung, dried herbs and witch's powders that gave off a faint odor of ammonia. Ballast was ordinary sand in ordinary bags that could be spilled out to gain greater heights. To descend, you "worked the mouth"—pulling on ropes that widened the balloons' bottom openings so that gas could escape. One thing needing constant attention were the big clamps—or carabiners—that were attached the cables holding the Cloudship's body to the balloons. They tended to loosen in a rough wind and had to be tightened constantly.

Beyond that, the vessel seemed simple enough to operate. Although sometimes there were periods of intense—and to Safar, bewildering—activity, mostly the Cloudship seemed to run itself. Besides the main members of the troupe, there was a crew of half-a-dozen men and women called "roustabouts." They were usually busy attending to the equipment and props that went into making a circus, leaving the routine operation of the Cloudship to the performers.

Part of that routine was steering. The task was performed on the bridge, where a large ship's wheel was mounted. The spoked wheel was linked to an elaborate system of scoops, sails and rudders that provided steerage.

"How fast does she go?" Safar asked Biner one day. It was Biner's turn at the wheel, while Safar had the task of keeping an eye on the compass.

"Depends on the wind," Biner said, "and the temperature. We've made as much as three hundred miles in a day. Other times we've been becalmed and made less than thirty in a week."

Safar watched Biner work the wheel. Despite the elaborate steering system it seemed to him direction was mainly determined by the wind.

"What happens in a storm?" he asked.

Biner chortled. "We pray a lot. And Methydia casts her spells. But mostly we pray. If there aren't any mountains about it's best just to let the storm be the boss. If there are, we tie up to something and hang on. Worst thing you can do is put her on the ground. That's if the storm doesn't give you any notice and you can't find a barn big enough to hold her. Wind can rip her up before you get the balloons collapsed and stowed away."

Safar could see straight off that, storm or not, the best place to be was sailing high above the earth where no one—king or outlaw—could reach you.

He thought of his recent troubles in Walaria and said, "It's too bad you ever have to come down."

Biner nodded understanding. Safar had told the crew an abbreviated version of his tale of woe.

"Gotta eat," he said. "Food may grow in trees, but not in the air." His massive shoulders rolled in a shrug. "Ground's not all bad. Wait'll you work your first show. Nothing like an audience's applause to restore your good feelings about folks. Especially the tikes, way their eyes light up warms you from the inside out."

It had already been agreed that Safar could travel with the troupe for awhile. To earn his keep he was being trained to handle the hundreds of small details that went into—in circus parlance—"wowing the rubes."

"How did you become a circus performer?" Safar asked. "Or were you born to it?"

Biner shook his massive head. "My parents were actors," he said. "Came from a long line of board trodders, as a matter of fact. Made my first appearance while I was still suckling my mother's breast. Played all kinds of child parts. Kept on playing them way past my time. I'm kind of short, in case you didn't notice. My mother and father were normal-sized and never did figure out what to make of me. Then I started growing out, instead of up. And I couldn't play tikes anymore."

Biner's face darkened at some painful memory. Then he shook it off, displaying his wide teeth in a grin.

"Swept theater floors and other drudge work for a time. Then one day this Cloudship sailed right over the town, music playing, folks way up in the sky waving at us like they were gods and goddesses. They shouted for everybody to follow. So I followed. And I was bitten by the circus bug the very first show. I begged Methydia for a tryout. She gave me one and I've been with her ever since. Going on fifteen years, now. Even gave me a new name after awhile—Biner, from the carabiners that hold us up. She said it's because she depends on me so much."

Although Biner's story was entirely different in its details from the background of the others, Safar soon learned the members of the troupe all had one thing in common—their appearances had made them outcasts from regular society so they'd formed their own. It was Methydia who'd given them that chance, coming along at just the right time, it seemed, to rescue them from unpleasant circumstances.

"Weren't fer Methyida," Kairo said one day, "I'd still be back at me village, gettin' conked wi' rocks." Kairo was the acrobat with the detachable head. "Uster hide in me house," he said, "so's I wouldn't get conked. So th' lads'd stone me house, breakin' windows and stovin' holes in th' roof. So me muvver threw me out. Rather I got conked th'n the house, I s'pose."

Rabix and Elgy—the snake charmer and the snake—had been seasoned circus performers when Methydia found them. But they'd had a disagreement with their employer over unpaid wages and had been left at a roadside in the middle of nowhere.

"We had not even a copper to buy a slender mouse for my weekly dinner," Elgy said in his oddly lilted tones.

Elgy was the snake with a man's face. He was also the "brains in the act." Rabix, he of the turban and breech cloth, was a mindless soul who sat or stood placidly wherever he was put. Elgy alone could communicate with him and cause him to act.

"He plays an excellent tune on the pipes," Elgy said. "As witless as the poor fellow is, he is a much better musician than the last man I had."

Arlain, the dragon woman, was being hunted by a mob set on vengeance when Methydia rescued her.

"I wath hiding in a thed and thort of thet it on fire. And then it thpread and thet fire to the whole thity." Arlain wiped her eyes, overcome by the memory. "It wath an acthident," she said. "I thaid I wath thorry, but they wouldn't lithen."

Arlain had no idea where she came from. "I thuppoth my father dropped me when he wath changing netht," she said. "A farmer'th wife found me and raithed me ath a pet. But then I got older and tharted having acthidenth and her huthband chathed me off the farm. And that'th why I wath hiding in the thed."

Methydia was not so forthcoming as the others. Although she never refused to answer any of Safar's questions, her answers tended just to tease the edges of the central question. Details of her background came only in veiled hints or casually dropped remarks.

Much later, after she took Safar as a lover, he complained about her habit of never revealing anything personal.

Methydia was amused. "I was born to be a woman of mystery, my sweet," she said. "It is a role I have cherished all my life. And with each passing year the mystery deepens, does it not? For then there is more for me *not* to tell."

She shifted in his arms. "Besides," she said, "I fear you would be disappointed if you knew all there was to know. What if I was merely a milk maid who ran away with her first lover? Or a young town wife who fled a fat old husband?"

Safar thought for a moment, then said, "I can't imagine you as either one. You were never ordinary, Methydia. *That* I know for certain."

"Are you, now, my sweet?" she murmured. Then she nibbled her way up his neck. "Are ... you ... really ... really ... *entirely* ... certain ...?" She found his lips, shutting off any reply.

They made love and afterwards Safar thought she was an even greater mystery than before. A delicious mystery, he thought. Then he realized perhaps that was her point.

All he ever really knew about her was that she was a strong-willed woman, a kind-hearted leader others felt comfortable to follow.

She was also a witch.

Safar sensed it the first time he became fully conscious. The atmosphere had been charged with more than her seductive presence. Little whorls of energy swirled about her, making the hair rise on the backs of his hands. And deep in those almond eyes he could see flecks of magic that sparkled when the light struck just so.

He said nothing of his own powers, partly because he didn't know how she'd react. Would she be jealous, like Umurhan? But mainly it was because he was so shaken by his experience in Walaria he was loathe to visit his magical side until he'd had time to recover.

Evidently Gundara felt the same way. The little Favorite was silent for a long time. For awhile Safar worried that the desert ordeal might have been too much for Gundara and his twin. He would take the stone turtle out of his purse from time to time to check. The idol was cold to the touch, but he could still feel a faint shimmer of magic. He thought of summoning Gundara to see if he needed anything, but then he wondered if the spell commanding the Favorite's presence might do more harm than any good he could offer. He thought, Let him rest and heal himself. And so that is what he did.

*　　　*　　　*

Early one morning, a few weeks after his recovery, Safar was awakened by loud music and excited voices. He crept out of the little storage room that was his bachelor's cabin, rubbing his eyes and wondering what was up.

The Cloudship was abuzz with activity. The crew was hauling chests of equipment and props out of the lockers. The members of the troupe were all doing stretching exercises or practicing their specialties.

The music came from Rabix, who was sitting—legs crossed—in the center of the deck, playing his pipes. It was a strange instrument, consisting of bound-together tubes of varying lengths. They were valved and Rabix played by blowing through the tubes while his fingers flowed gracefully over the valves. A marvelous stream of music issued from the instrument, sounding like an entire orchestra of drums and strings and trumpets and flutes. Elgy, anchored by a few coils wrapped loosely about his neck, rose nearly three feet above Rabix' turbaned head, weaving in time to the music.

Kairo practiced his high wire act, strolling along a suspended cable, then pretending to fall. He'd steady himself, then let his head drop from his shoulders. He'd catch it, squeaking in fear, then put it on again.

Arlain, who was so excited she'd forgotten her clothes, bounded naked about the deck, shouting joyfully, "Thowtime folkth! Thowtime folkth!"

There was a roar from Biner, "Here now, Arlain! Put something on! This is a family show!"

Arlain skidded to a stop, tail lashing furiously. She looked down, saw what she'd done, then turned from pale white to the deepest red.

A claw went to her mouth. "Oh, my goodneth grathiouth," she said.

Then she scuttled off, wailing, "I'm thorry. I'm thorry."

As she rushed into the wardrobe room, her tail hooking out to slam the door behind her, Biner shouted, "And watch out for the—"

Fire and smoke blasted out of the wardrobe room's window, cutting Biner off in midbellow. Arlain wailed something incomprehensible and a few crew members came running with buckets of water and sand to douse the fire.

"If only she wouldn't get so excited," Biner said. Then he shrugged. "Oh, well. She's a grand crowd pleaser. So what if she starts a few fires?" He grinned at Safar. "Temperament, my lad," he said. "All the best talent's got it. If you can't take the temperament then you might as well get out of the circus business."

"That's good advice, I'm sure," Safar said. "But would you mind slowing down for a minute, please, and tell me what in the hells is going on?"

"You mean nobody told you?" Biner was aghast.

Safar said, no, he'd not been informed of anything, thank you very much.

"Why, the Deming Fair's only two hours away. First show at dusk, second at eight bells. We'll be there a week. Two performances every night, plus two and a matinee on Godsday."

He clapped Safar on the back, nearly bowling him over.

"So it's just like Arlain said, lad—'It's Showtime, Folks!'"

*   *   *

The town of Deming was the center of a rich farming area, fed by a long snaking river. The fairgrounds sat just outside the town's main gates and it was already packed with people, strolling past tents blazing with color or crowding around exhibits and hucksters of every variety.

Methydia's Flying Circus made a dramatic entrance, swooping low over the town and fairgrounds, Rabix's music blaring through an amplifying trumpet. The troupe had changed into glittering costumes and lined the edges of the Cloudship, waving and shouting invitations to the crowd.

Arlain, wearing spangled breastplates and modesty patch, stood on a rail, breathing long spears of fire and waving her tail. Methydia had donned a red witch's robe, scooped low in front and slit on one side to the hip. She was provocatively posed beside Arlain, the wind whipping the gossamer robe aside to reveal her long shapely legs.

Biner, voice magically enhanced by one of Methydia's spells, bellowed: "See the fire breathing dragon! Gasp at the feats of Kairo, the Headless Marvel. Test the strength of the mightiest man alive! See the Snake Charmer dare the deadly Serpent of Sunyan! Wonder at the Miracles of the Mysterious Methydia.

"Come one! Come all! Lads and maids of all ages. Welcome to Methydia's Flying Circus of Miracles.

"The Greatest Show On Esmir!"

Once a big enough crowd had been gathered the Cloudship sailed slowly and majestically away, leading them to a wide field next to the fairgrounds. Then it descended, stopping about twenty feet above the earth. Biner and a few roustabouts, bags of tools slung over their shoulders, swung down on lines, then quickly hammered iron stakes into the ground and secured the Cloudship to the stakes.

One by one, the members of the troupe slid down the lines. Each pausing midway to show off some acrobatic feat to wild applause from the gathering crowd.

On the other side of the Cloudship Safar and the remaining roustabouts had the more mundane task of lowering chests and crates of equipment. But Safar soon learned even this job had its admirers. Wide-eyed boys were transfixed by the work, oohing and ahhing as each item was swayed to the ground. The roustabouts took immediate advantage of their interest. They handed out free tickets to the biggest lads in return for their help. Soon a score of muscular young men had stripped to the waist and were helping to set up the circus.

Dazed by the excitement of his first circus, Safar was jolted from job to job by barked orders. Before he knew it a huge tent had been erected, stands hurled up, and he was being pushed into a ticket booth at the entrance of the tent. Someone shoved tickets into his hand and he found himself shouting the seller's speech Biner had drummed into him during the journey:

"Five copper's our price, folks. Now that's not much."

He slapped coins down, counting, "One, two, three, four and five!"

Then he swept one away.

"Bring a friend, we'll make it four!"

He palmed a coin.

"If she's pretty, it's only three."

Then another.

"Two for your granny!"

And another.

"One for your babe."

Then he held up the remaining coin for all to see.

"Catch the lucky copper and the ticket's free."

He tossed the coin into the crowd. Children scrambled for it. Safar saw one little girl knocked down in the rush. She sat in the dirt weeping. His heart went out to her and for the first time since he'd joined the troupe he felt the tingle of magic in his veins. He whispered a spell, gestured, and the child suddenly shouted in glee.

She tottered to her feet, crying, "I got it! I got it!" She raised a hand, displaying the lucky copper. "See!"

The other children groaned in disappointment, but the adults were delighted. They lifted the little girl up and passed her over their heads until she was standing in front of Safar.

With a flourish, he presented her with a ticket. She stared at it, eyes huge with wonder.

Safar was really caught up in the spirit now. Words flowed smoothly from brain to tongue.

"We've got ourselves a lucky lady to start the day, folks!" he shouted. "Now, where's her mother and we'll make it two?" A young matron in a patched dress announced her presence and was pushed forward. Safar presented her with a ticket. "Step right in ladies," he cried. "Step right in and we will reveal to you the greatest wonders of Esmir."

As the grateful mother and her child stepped through the entrance the crowd boiled around Safar, practically throwing coins at him in their fever to get their tickets.

He sold out in half an hour. Then he collected the coin box, closed the booth and slipped inside the tent.

The show had already begun. The audience was roaring laughter as Arlain, wearing a gaudy dress, pursued Biner—costumed as a lumpish clown soldier—around the ring. At appropriate moments she'd let loose a blast of fire at Biner's padded rear. He'd jump, hands grabbing his bottom, and let out a falsetto shriek of pretended pain. Then he'd run on, crying for help, Arlain at his heels.

Safar found a seat in a darkened corner and watched the show unfold, intent as any member of the paying audience.

The performance lasted three hours. During the whole time the troupe never stopped and there were so many costume changes it seemed as if there were fifty entertainers with fifty different acts to amaze the crowd.

Rabix and Elgy provided all the music. They were hidden beneath a small bandstand with stuffed dummies for musicians. Besides playing the clown, Biner costumed himself as a dozen different fearsome animals. Each would threaten the audience in some way, only to be foiled by Methydia, who played a mighty huntress dressed in outfits that seemed to get skimpier and gaudier with each change. Biner also displayed many feats of great strength, each more amazing than the last.

Arlain was every bit as good as Biner had said. She not only juggled fiery objects, she proved to be a fantastic acrobat who could swing from her tail wrapped around a trapeze while tossing flaming swords.

Besides his high wire act Kairo played catcher to Arlain, hurling her high into the air to another trapeze. When she swung back he'd pretend to drop his head, fumble getting it back on—then suddenly remember Arlain and catch her just in time.

Talented as everyone was, however, Methydia was clearly the star attraction. She appeared in her role as Methydia The Magnificent four times during the show. Dressed in her filmy red witch's robes, she made each entrance a treat in itself to the growing delight of the crowd. Multi-colored smoke would suddenly erupt, or there'd be a crash of forked-lighting, or a great wall of fire. Then she'd swing through the fire on a flaming rope. Or float above the boiling smoke. Or seem to dive out of the lightning, to be caught in Biner's powerful arms.

She bade objects both large and small to appear and disappear, always accompanied by some kind of dramatic pyrotechnics. She called volunteers from the audience and caused them to float above the ground. With Biner to aid her she put on magical skits, all with romantic themes that didn't leave a dry eye in the house. She sawed Arlain in half, then put her back together again.

To Safar the most amazing thing about Methydia's performance was that although he could feel a faint of buzz of real magic emanating from her, there didn't appear to be any sorcery behind the feats themselves. Some were so difficult he should have been hit by the sear of a powerful spellcast. Instead, he felt nothing but that faint buzz. A few of her feats, like the sawing in half business, were just plain impossible. No wizard could do that! The more Safar watched, the more mystified he became. How did she make magic without using magic?

Then there was a great fanfare announcing the show's end. As the lights came up Safar found himself whistling and cheering along with the rest of the audience.

As the people filed out, chatting excitedly about their experiences and carrying sleeping children over their shoulders, The crew started cleaning the stands and getting ready for the evening performance. Safar went to work with a will, sweeping where he was told to sweep, lifting what he was told to lift.

He was whistling a merry tune when Biner strolled up, wiping the last vestiges of clown makeup from his face.

"So, what did you think, lad?" Biner asked.

"I've never seen anything like it in my life," Safar said. "Especially Methydia. Oh, don't get me wrong. You were grand! Everyone was grand!"

Biner laughed. "But Methydia was just a little grander than the rest of us, right?"

"A *lot* grander," Safar said. "No offense."

"None taken, lad," Biner said. "It isn't just because she owns the circus that she gets top billing. She's the *real* star."

He gave Safar a hand with the heavy trunk, lifting his end with remarkable ease. "Suppose you might elect to stay on awhile, then, lad?" he asked casually. "Pay's not much, but we eat regular."

Safar laughed. "As long as you don't charge me admission," he joked. Then, seriously, "I'd just as soon take a rest from the outside world for awhile. Not much in it is all that worthwhile, from what I've seen."

"That's the spirit, lad!" Biner cried. "To the Hells with them all!"

"And damn everything but the Circus."

✳   ✳   ✳

That night after the final show, the troupe ate and retired to tents set up on the ground. The Cloudship, Safar discovered, couldn't be used for that purpose when a show was going on. He'd been so overwhelmed by all the new experiences he hadn't noticed a good portion of the Cloudship's body was disassembled and turned into parts for the circus, such as the stands the audiences sat in.

He was heading off to sleep in the roustabout's tent when Methydia emerged from a small, gaily-decorated pavilion and beckoned him.

"I think we need to have a little talk, my sweet," she said, gesturing for him to enter.

The pavilion, lit by oil lamps, was spread with thick carpets. Pillows were piled onto trunks to make comfortable chairs. A curtained hammock was strung at the back for a bed.

Methydia bade Safar to sit and poured him a little wine. She raised her glass in a toast, intoning, "May the winds be gentle, the stars be bright. May the crew be skilled, the landing light." And they drank.

After a moment, Methydia said, "I heard about your little trick with the lucky coin. Apparently you made a little girl and her mother very happy."

Safar became uneasy. Although Methydia was smiling and her words were gentle, he could see from the look in her eye the purpose of this visit had nothing to do with compliments. It was time to bare his soul.

"I haven't told you everything about me," Safar confessed.

"If you mean that you left out the small part about being a wizard," Methydia said with exaggerated mildness, "I expect you're right."

"Only a student wizard," Safar hastened to add.

Methydia curled a lip. "I see. *Only* a student. Well, *that* certainly makes me feel much better."

"I'm sorry," Safar said, feeling as socially clumsy as Arlain. "I didn't mean to deceive you."

"Oh, you didn't deceive me," Methydia said. "I sensed you had certain powers right off. And after your little confession about being hunted by powerful men, I just wanted to see how long it would take for you to tell me the rest. But I've never been known for my patience. So I'm asking you to tell me now."

"I was really deceiving myself, more than anything," Safar said. "Magic has brought me nothing but grief. And after what happened in Walaria—I suppose I just wanted a rest. To live normally for a while."

"There was a girl," Methydia said. "Nerisa, I believe?" She saw Safar's look of surprise and explained, "You babbled quite a bit while you were unconscious. Her name was mentioned more than most. A young lover, I presume?"

Safar shook his head. "No, she was just a child. A street urchin who became my friend. She died saving my life."

Methydia drank a little of her wine, eyeing him across the rim. Then, "From the way you railed in your sleep, I *thought* something tragic had happened to her."

"I only wish it could have been Nerisa instead of me you found in the desert," Safar said.

"Some would say you ought to take comfort in the gods," Methydia said. "Pray that they had their reasons for choosing one over the other. Personally, I've never found that sort of thing much help. But *you* might."

Safar shook his head. "No."

Methydia drew a small vial out of her sleeve. "Give me your wine," she said.

Puzzled, he complied. She poured the contents of the vial into his glass and stirred it with a long, graceful finger.

She handed him the glass. "Drink it," she commanded.

"What is it?" Safar asked.

"Oh, just a little potion my old granny taught me how to make," she said. "It will help heal the wounds caused by your friend's death."

Safar hesitated. Methydia pushed the glass to his lips. "It won't make you forget Nerisa, my sweet," she said softly. "It will just make everything seem long ago. And therefore easier to bear."

Safar drank. The potion was tasteless, but when it hit his belly it frothed up into heady fumes that seemed to rise along the back of his spine. He felt his muscles relax, then his tight-strung nerves.

He closed his eyes and saw Nerisa's face with its twisted little grin.

The face filled his mind's eye for a moment, then receded—floating away, deep into darkness, until it was a small image.

Then he put her away in a special chest of memories where the sweet mingled with the bitter.

CHAPTER SEVENTEEN
THE WORM OF KYSHAAT

An unseasonable cold snap ended their stay at Deming and they sailed south to warmer climes, storms and blustery winds at their back.

Safar knew from first-hand experience the storms were from out of the seas beyond Caspan. They came regularly—although usually not this early—racing across the northern lands, bursting over the Gods' Divide, then rolling down the southern slopes of the Bride's gown to sweep across the wide plains to the mountains beyond Jaspar.

Although the Cloudship was untroubled by the storms—always staying just ahead of the frontal winds—it was moving much faster than before, covering as much as two hundred miles in a day.

With every mile Safar was flung farther from Kyrania and soon, like Nerisa's image, all thoughts of home receded into the background. He was overcome by a marvelous feeling of freedom. They sailed across seas of crystal air, over great fluffy fields of clouds, through flocks of bright-feathered birds and under starry skies where the moon was so close it seemed you only had to turn the ship's wheel and you could fly to it.

They sailed on a loose schedule Methydia kept in her head. Day would blend into delightful day, then she'd suddenly issue orders and they'd prepare to land at a town or village where there was always a crowd to fill the ship's larder and the troupe's purses.

After that first night in Deming Methydia evidently came to some sort of decision and began to teach him her own brand of magic. Her training mocked all the forms and conventions of Umurhan's School of Sorcery. In Methydia's view presentation was more important than the spell itself.

"I suppose it's true that magic is a science," she told Safar one day. "There are rules and the scholars tell us there are reasons for those rules."

As she spoke Methydia was sorting through a large wardrobe chest looking for a suitable costume for Safar.

"Personally," she said, "the whys and wherefores never interested me. I'm an artist. I don't care *why* something happens. Only the effect it has on my art."

Methydia held up a dark blue shirt with a plunging neckline and floppy sleeves. It was decorated like a starry night, silvery constellations swirling in the dim light of her cabin's oil lamps.

"This is perfect," she murmured. "It'll bring out the blue of your eyes." Methydia set the shirt aside and continued rummaging.

She said, "I created a circus to display my art. I didn't have the idea until my lovers made the Cloudship possible. I was an actress, then. Billed as a woman of beauty and mystery. I kept my witchery locked in a box, like my makeup. I only used it to cure a blemish, trouble a rival or heighten my performance by wresting a sob from the audience.

"But soon as I saw the Cloudship the idea came to me—'Methydia's Flying Circus of Miracles.' My life as an actress—and hidden witch—suddenly seemed tawdry. Meaningless. Unfulfilling."

Methydia paused, holding up a pair of breeches that were a near match to the shirt. She studied it, then wrinkled her nose. "Too *too* much," she muttered, tossing the breeches back into the chest and continuing her search.

"Where was I?" she asked, then—"Oh, yes. My life as unfulfilled actress." Her face turned serious, gestures dramatic. "I wanted more," she said, "and yes, I admit it, the 'more' was applause. I'm a self-centered bitch, but then what true artist isn't? The circus gave my art purpose. And in that purpose I found my heart. That is the gift I give to my audience now . . ." She laid a light hand on her breast. "My heart."

She held the dramatic moment, then went on. "I like to please people," she said, "to lift away their troubles, to thrill them with danger that is always happening to another, but in the end they know is safe. I like to help them remember how it was to be young, how it was to love, and if they're young—how what *might* be, *may* be."

Suddenly Methydia solemn expression dissolved into one of delight. She clapped her hands, making Safar jump with surprise.

"Here's just the thing!" she cried, hauling a pair of snowy white breeches from the trunk.

Methydia held them up, looking critical and turning them this way and that.

She tugged at the seat. "We'll have take them in here," she said. Then she grinned, "So the ladies can see your assets better."

Safar blushed, mumbling something about it not being seemly.

"Nonsense," Methydia replied. "If Arlain and I can jiggle about for the lads, the least you can do is give the maids a thrill. That's what makes a show. A little sex, a little comedy, a clown chase. All frosting on the cake."

She placed the breeches next to the shirt. "Now all we need is a wide belt and tight boots and you'll have the rubes eating out of your hand."

Then Methydia gave him his first lesson. To his surprise, she started by having him show her the coin spell he'd used on the little girl in Deming.

"That's easy," Safar said, "I did that when I was a babe—moving bright things around to amuse myself."

"Just show me, my sweet," she said, passing him a coin.

Safar threw the coin into the corner. While it was still rolling he gestured, made it vanish, gestured again, and it fell into Methydia's still-open hand.

"What's this?" Methydia said, but in disdain, not amazement. "You call *that* magic?"

She flipped the coin high into the air. Quickly she jabbed a dramatic finger at the deck. Safar's eyes followed. There was the sharp *crack!* of an explosion. A stream of green smoke bloomed up—drawing Safar's eyes with it—and the coin appeared to vanish in the cloud. Methydia leaned forward, her face coming so close Safar thought she was about to kiss him. Her lips grazed his, then she drew back, grinning.

She took his nose between finger and thumb, twisting it gently, once, twice, three times. And each time she twisted a coin dropped to his chest and rolled to the floor. She swept them up, threw them into the air, another crack! a stream of smoke and the three coins became one, which she snatched out of the air.

"Now, *that's* magic!" she said, holding the coin in one hand and rolling it up and down from finger to finger in one continuous, fluid motion.

"But you didn't *use* sorcery at all!" Safar protested. "I would have felt it if you had."

Methydia laughed. "Then how did I do it?"

"I don't know," Safar admitted. "It must be some kind of trick."

"But it's a trick that will get a lot more applause than your magic," Methydia said.

Safar thought he understood. "It's the smoke," he said. "I can make smoke."

He gestured at the cabin deck. A thin stream of smoke boiled out of a spot on the plank. He raised his finger slowly and the smoke became a long stream. Then he snapped his fingers and the smoke vanished. "Like that?" he asked.

"No, no," Methydia said. "It wasn't *what* I did, but *how* I did it. You used magic to make the smoke. I used this—"

She opened her hand, displaying a small green pellet. She made a fleshy fold with her thumb, gripping and hiding the pellet in the fold. Then she rolled her hand over, made a graceful gesture with her forefinger and once again there was crack! and green smoke rose up.

"I used a device," she said, "to cause an effect that looked like magic. You used real magic, but so clumsily it looked more like a device. The audience would have guessed—wrongly, as it may be—that you had something hidden in your hand. The point is, you would have spoiled it for them."

"What about the coin part?" Safar asked.

"Same thing," Methydia said. "You threw it in a corner. People will think you did that to divert their attention away from the real trick. Whereas I threw it up into the air, where it appeared to remain in plain sight while I worked my other diversions."

He remembered the jabbing finger that drew his eyes and the near kiss that clouded his view. "I think I see what you mean," he said. "But you *could* have used real magic, not fakery, to accomplish the same thing."

"Not for two shows a day, I couldn't," Methydia said. "*Plus* two and a matinee on Godsday. You have to pace yourself in this business. You need as much energy for the last act of the last show as you did when you started out. In entertainment, my sweet, that's what separates the green from the ripe."

But Safar was young and stubborn. "It seems to me," he said, "I did well enough with real magic when I conjured the coin into that little girl's hand. The crowd certainly *acted* impressed. And they bought out every seat in the tent to prove it."

"They thought she was a plant," Methydia said. "A part of the show. I overheard some of them talking afterwards."

"Oh."

"It was the spirit of the trick that impressed them," she said. "The poor little waif and her young mother." She smiled at Safar and patted his knee, saying, "Even so, I have to give you credit for the idea. It was a certain crowd pleaser and I think we should make it a permanent part of our act."

Safar was as thrilled as if the praise had come from a master wizard instead of a circus witch.

"You have good instincts, my sweet," she said. "And if you pay close attention to what your Auntie Methydia says, you'll make a marvelous showman."

*   *   *

The days that followed were among the most joyful in Safar's life. His heart was as serene as the skies they sailed through. His troubles seemed far off—like the dark storm clouds edging the horizon behind them.

As a mountain lad he'd spent many a hour perched on high peaks pondering the mysteries of the skies. He'd watched birds wing overhead and dreamed he was flying with them. In Methydia's Cloudship those dreams came true. Although his fellow passengers of the air could be a boisterous lot at time, especially during rehearsals when there was much joking and leg-pulling, at other times they seemed to treasure silence as much as he did. Hours would pass without a sound.

Each member of the troupe and crew had favorite solitary spots where they could watch the world pass by. Only the occasional hiss of the furnace and pumping of bellows intruded. After a time these faint sounds blended into the song of the winds that carried them above the lands where poor earth-bound creatures dwelled.

Safar was exhilarated by his new life. He threw all his efforts into soaking up everything Methydia and her troupe could teach him. He learned about trick boxes and trapdoors, smoke and mirrors, and wires so thin they couldn't be seen against a dark background, yet could hold hundreds of pounds suspended above the arena. Methydia helped him work up a mind reading act and he amazed the crowds during intermissions with details of their lives that seemed to be snatched from their thoughts. He used two sharp-eyed and big-eared roustabouts to gather the information before he staged his act.

Along with the illusions Methydia also added to his store of real magic. He learned subtle spells that enhanced his performance. Some caused a grumpy crowd to feel humor. Others heightened wonder, increased tension or stirred romance in cold hearts. She taught him how to make the magical charms and potions they sold after every performance. Safar added his potter's skills to this job, pinching out marvelous little vials to hold the potions and creating charms made of colorful potsherd necklaces and jewelry.

He learned how to read a fortune in a palm, instead of casting bones. Methydia said this kind of foretelling was more personal and therefore more accurate than "dead bones rattling around and scaring people half to death." Besides palmistry, he was taught how to cast a simple starchart in five minutes, rather than the hours and even days it took Umurhan and his priests.

"Those scholarly castings are so complicated, so ugly with all their mathematical squiggles, only a rich man would want one," Methydia said. "To show he was wealthy enough to hire such a wise dream catcher.

"But ordinary people—real people—want to know now, not days from now. And they want to be able to read the chart for themselves so they can hang it over the mantle and show it off to their friends by pointing out the highlights."

The other members of the troupe also pitched in with his showcraft education. The brawny dwarf, Biner, taught him the delicate art of applying makeup and altering his features so he could play many different kinds of characters. Arlain and Kairo showed him how to do simple acrobatics. They ran him through heart-stopping exercises and plied him with strengthening powders until his muscles vibrated with power. Elgy coached him on timing, getting Rabix to play rhythmic music as Safar performed his acts over and over again until his delivery was as natural as the mental beat Rabix drummed into his head.

To Methydia's amazement—and his own—Safar's magical powers increased with each passing day. It wasn't a gradual strengthening, like his muscles, but leap after leap from one pinnacle to the next. For the first time since he was a boy he actually enjoyed doing magic. The roar of the audiences swept away the shame his father had accidentally instilled in him. He delighted in their amazement. Especially—as Biner had said it would—the wonderment of the children.

As he became stronger and more skilled he even started dispensing with some of Methydia's tricks. His illusions became almost entirely magical, although he still used showmanship to "sell it," as Methydia would say. True, the performances drained him, just as Methydia predicted. Yet never so much he couldn't deliver as many encores as the crowd desired.

For a time Methydia kept herself at a slight distance from him. She still teased him and made suggestive jokes that made him blush. But that was her nature. Mainly she behaved like a kindly teacher or mentor, correcting him when he needed it and praising him when he deserved it. Although Safar was powerfully attracted to her, it never occurred to him that she might feel the same. Why, she was old enough to be his mother. Perhaps even older. He ought to be ashamed of himself for thinking of such disrespectful thoughts.

During that time Safar noticed a small tension building among the troupe and crew, as if they were waiting for something long overdue. Occasionally when he and Methydia were out on the deck together—running through a new twist in the act—he'd noticed people glancing at the two of them. Then there'd be little smiles, whispered asides and shakes of the head.

Once he overheard the roustabouts wondering aloud if "maybe Methydia's lost her sweet tooth." Safar didn't know what that meant. He was doubly mystified when the men saw him and turned away, shamefaced.

*   *   *

The dreamlike days ended when they reached Kyshaat.

It was a regular stop in the troupe's circuit. Over the centuries the people of Kyshaat had turned the vast plains surrounding their walled town into wide fields of fat grain. The circus folk expected a large profit from their visit to the region and were dismayed when they saw the desolation of the usually lush fields. It was as if an enormous ravenous beast had swept through, devouring the grain—stalks and all—nearly to the ground.

Hungry and pitiful eyes stared up at the Cloudship as it sailed overhead. To Safar the usually joyful circus music had an eerie edge to it as they serenaded the crowds and Biner's big booming call of "Come one, Come all," seemed to be flattened and swallowed up by a thick miasma.

"Don't know what's happened here," Biner muttered to Methydia. "But maybe it'd be best if we moved on."

Methydia pressed her lips together and shook her head. "We were eager enough for their company when there was a profit to be made," she said. "I'll not turn away now because fortune no longer favors them."

Biner nodded and turned back to his duties, but Safar could see he was worried. On the ground hundreds of people followed the Cloudship's shadow, but they were so silent Safar could hear the wails of small children carried in their parents' arms.

A few minutes later the Cloudship was tied up over a barren patch and the roustabouts were swaying down the equipment.

When Safar's feet touched ground he turned to face the onrushing crowd. To his amazement they all stopped at the edge of the field. It was as if an invisible barrier had been thrown up. They remained there for two hours while the roustabouts put the circus together. Methydia had them dispense with the tents—the stands were set up in the open.

When she thought all was ready she beckoned to Safar and the two of them advanced on the crowd. About twenty paces away a shout brought them up short:

171

"Beware, Methydia! Come no closer!"

Methydia's pose was unbroken. Her eyes swept the crowd.

"Who spoke?" she demanded.

There were mutters in the crowd, but no one answered.

"Come on," Methydia insisted. "We've traveled many miles to entertain our friends in Kyshaat. What kind of greeting is this? Speak up!"

There were more mutterings, then the crowd parted and an old man, bent nearly double, hobbled out, supported by a heavy cane.

"It was I, Methydia," he said. "I was the one who cried the warning."

Bent over and aged as the old man was, Safar could see the skeletal outline of once broad shoulders. The fingers gripping the cane were thick, the wrists broad-bladed.

"I know you," Methydia said. "You're Neetan. The one with the seven grandchildren I always let in free."

Neetan's wrinkled face drooped like an old beaten dog's. "There's only two, now, Methydia," he said. "All the rest have been called to the realm of the gods."

Methydia's eyes widened. She took a step forward.

The crowd stirred uneasily and once again Neetan shouted, "Come no closer!"

Methydia stopped. "What happened here?" she asked.

"We are becursed, Methydia," Neetan said. "All of Kyshaat is becursed. Flee while you can, or the curse will afflict you."

Safar saw momentary fear register on Methydia's face. Then her chin came up, stubborn. "I'm not leaving," she said, "until I've heard what it is that has brought you to this state."

Neetan stamped his cane. "It wasn't one catastrophe," he said, "but many. First we were visited by King Protarus."

Safar was startled. "Iraj was here?" he asked.

"Beware how you address him, my son," the old man said. "Do not be so familiar with his royal name."

Safar ignored this. He pointed at the barren fields. "Iraj Protarus did that?" he demanded.

"Only some of it," Neetan said. "And it was one of his generals, not the king, who came. The general arrived with a small troop and demanded our fealty to King Protarus and food for his armies."

"And you granted this?" Safar asked, "Without at least asking payment?" It was inconceivable to him that his former friend would not at least offer to pay these people.

"What choice did we have?" Neetan said. "It is well known that King Protarus is not so kind to any who oppose him. Why, several cities have been sacked and burned for defying him. Then the men and old ones were killed and the rest sold into slavery."

Safar was furious. Methydia laid a hand on his arm, steadying him.

"You said this was but the first of many catastrophes," she said to Neetan. "What else has befallen you, my friend?"

"At least King Protarus left us enough to live," Neetan said. "But then we were visited by plague to ravage our homes, birds and locusts to denude our fields and beasts to devour our flocks."

While the old man enumerated the evils that afflicted Kyshaat, Safar caught a glimpse of a shadowy figure at the edge of the crowd. But when he looked directly at the spot the figure was gone. He suddenly caught a whiff of a foul odor. Then the scent vanished.

Meanwhile, Neetan was saying, "We are the most miserable of people, Methydia. The gods have forsaken us. Because we love you, because of all the joy you have brought us over the years, please leave this place. Leave us to our curse. Before you too fall under its thrall."

"Nonsense!" Methydia said. "I fear no curse. The circus will begin in one hour. All who want to come are welcome—free of charge. This is my gift to old friends. So do not insult me by staying away."

Then she turned and marched back to the others, leaving Neetan and the frightened people gaping.

Safar lengthened his stride and caught up to her. "There really *is* something here," he said." "It's . . . some kind of . . ." and then words failed him.

He gestured, wanting to convey the feeling he had of a cold, greasy breath at the back of his neck. "A presence, is the only thing I can think of.

"It's watching us."

Methydia suddenly quickened her pace. "Yes, yes," she whispered. "Now I can feel it too.

"I think I made a mistake coming here. We'd better get away."

Safar heard a sound like boulders grating against one another and then the ground heaved up beneath his feet.

"Run!" he shouted, grabbing Methydia by the hand and sprinting for the Cloudship.

Behind him he heard the screams of the crowd and the long tearing rip of the earth itself. Ahead he saw Biner and the others scrabbling for hammers and axes and anything that would make a weapon. Soon as he reached them, Safar released Methydia and whirled around to confront the threat.

He saw the ground coming up, the roots of bushes and small trees ripping away, gravel and earth and stones showering down a gathering hill. Before his eyes the hill became a towering earthen figure with arms and a head and a torso supported by two mighty legs. A hole opened in the place where a mouth ought to be.

The creature spoke, rocks and gravel tumbling from its lips:

"Mine!" it said, voice grating and grumbling like it was formed in a deep cavern.

It waved a huge arm, showering Safar and others with gravel and clods of earth.

"Mine!" it said again, gesturing at the crowd of people.

Then an immense arm came forward, a gnarly finger as long as a man shooting out—pointing at Safar and his group.

"Now, you mine!" the creature said.

It took a slow step forward and the ground shuddered. Small bushes and trees crashed down. Instantly they took life, brushy limbs and hairy roots clawing up dirt, which formed around their woody skeletons to make bodies.

"Mine!" the earth creature howled and its spawn moved toward Safar and his friends, thorny hands reaching out to grasp.

The creatures fanned out into a half-circle which they tightened around the troupe, their earthen creator urging them on with bellows of "Mine!"

Biner lifted up a huge crate and hurled it at the oncoming horror. The crate crashed into the center of the line, bursting apart three of the monsters. But the others moved on, dragging themselves toward the troupe.

Arlain reared back, drawing in her breath and bracing herself with her tail. Then she jerked forward—long flames shooting from her mouth. There was a series of meaty *pops!* like termites exploding in a forest fire. One whole side of the advancing line burst into flames.

Then the whole circus charged—Biner in the lead—flailing away with axes and hammers and spars.

Safar gripped Methydia's hand, holding her back. He was concentrating on the earthen giant.

"Mine!" it roared, sending off more showers of rock and dirt and brush that quickly formed into new monstrosities to replace the fallen.

"Help me, Methydia!" Safar shouted, squeezing her hand tighter.

He grabbed for her power, felt her resist and shrink back. Then the shield lifted and he had it—a strong, slender fist of energy he added to his own.

Safar turned toward the earthen giant. It was almost on them. He saw it reach out to grab for Biner, black maw gaping to expose the rocky millstones that were its teeth.

"No!" he heard Methydia cry.

Safar drew on a cloak of calmness. Everything became exceptionally slow, like the day he'd fought the demons. Even as the earthen giant's rocky palm was closing over Biner, Safar took his time.

He made a sharp probe of his senses and shot it forward. He felt it slip through the creature's rubble body, find the path of least resistance and drive the probe upward.

Deep inside he found the husk of an insect's body. A locust that had been drained of all its juices. And in that locust he found something small and mean. It wriggled when his probe found it, rising up and bursting out of the locust's corpse.

It was a worm, no more than a finger long. It was maggoty white, with a large black spot on its head that Safar thought was an eye. It was a thing that fed on misery and pain. As Safar probed around, he realized the creature was the infant form of something even more deadly. He could see half-formed legs kicking beneath the worm's skin and an arced tail tipped by a budding stinger.

The little creature blasted him with voracious thoughts. "Mine!" it shrieked. "I want . . . Mine!"

Safar heard Methydia shout, "Hurry, Safar!"

But he took his time. He made the probe into two thick fingers. He reached for the worm, dodging small sharp knives of hunger and hate.

Then he caught it between the two fingers. The worm struggled, fighting back, searing his senses with blasts of sorcery.

He ignored the pain and crushed the worm.

Immediately he was assaulted by the foul stench of death. He staggered back, drawing his spirit self with him.

Safar heard a rumbling sound. Dazed, he looked up and saw the earthen giant crumbling into huge pieces of rock and dirt clods. As it came crashing down Biner leaped away just in time. A thick cloud of dust exploded as it hit, pebbles and debris showering everywhere.

Then the dust settled and there was nothing to be seen but a large mound of rubble.

Safar felt suddenly weak and confused. He turned to Methydia and recognized the look of awe in her eyes. It was the same look Iraj had given him when he'd brought the avalanche down on the demons.

"It was just a worm," he tried to say, but it came out as a mumble. "A stupid little—"

And he pitched forward on the ground.

*　　　*　　　*

The people of Kyshaat got their circus. Many said Methydia and her troupe staged the best performance of their careers. Children would grow old and regale their own disbelieving grandchildren about that fateful day when the creature that had caused so much misery had been defeated. And of the wild celebration that followed.

Safar, the hero of the hour, saw none of it. He lapsed into a coma for nearly a week. When he regained consciousness he was aboard the Cloudship and they were sailing through a storm.

Once again he was lying on a pallet in Methydia's cabin. It was dark and outside he could hear the winds moan through the lines and rain lash the deck.

He was thirsty and fumbled around with a blind hand until he brushed against a tumbler. He drank. It was warm wine and honey.

There was a blast of cold air as the door slammed open. He looked up. Methydia was standing there, a hooded parka covering her from head to ankle. Lightning crash followed lightning crash, illuminating her. She glowed in it, an aura forming around her slender body. Her eyes were glittering wells, drinking him in. A gust of wind hurled the parka aside. She was dressed in a thin white gown, nearly transparent from the rain.

Another gust of wind blasted past her, but the cold seemed to light a fire in him.

"Close the door," he said.

At least he thought he said it. His lips formed the words, but he heard nothing come out.

Just the same, Methydia closed the door.

Then he held out his arms and whispered, "Please!"

Methydia floated across the room into his embrace.

He burrowed into the warm heart of her. Found the storm and let it loose. For a long time all he knew was the sensation of their love making and the sound of her voice calling his name.

CHAPTER EIGHTEEN
THE WINDS OF FATE

King Manacia—Lion of the gods, Future Lord of Esmir, Courageous Protector of Ghazban, Perfect of Zanzair, His Merciful Majesty—suffered from nightmares.

In his dreams he was pursued by naked human devils, with their scale-crawling ghoulish skins, talonless claws and thick red tongues that looked like eels grown fat from eating carrion.

He would no sooner slake his royal lust on a concubine and close his eyes to drift off to sleep, when the human hordes would come charging out, screaming blood-curdling cries and gnashing their flat, flesh-grinding teeth. The king would try to run but his limbs wouldn't obey him. He'd stand frozen as the ugly creatures surged forward, howling their hate.

Two tall humans always led the ravenous crowd. One was fair-skinned, with a golden beard and golden locks encircled by a crown. The other was dark and beardless, with long black hair that streamed behind him. The dark one had huge blue eyes that bored into his soul, ferreting out all Manacia held sacred and secret.

The dreams left him shaken and weak. For a long time he tried to ignore them, telling himself they were caused by nothing more than stress from his royal duties. His plans for invading the humanlands had him overwrought, that's all.

The planning was not going well, which added to his agitation. His generals were driving him mad with their overly cautious counsel. They wanted to gather an army so large, with supply lines so deep, that no human force could stand in their way.

At first King Manacia had nothing against this strategy. Overwhelming force was the common sense answer to any military difficulty. But what the generals considered overwhelming, the king soon learned, was always double whatever figure he proposed.

Manacia understood the careers and very lives of his generals and their staff depended on the outcome. The king made no apologies for his feelings regarding failure. He had no use for the weak or the unlucky, purging any and all who were associated with less than total victory. Yet his generals' caution disappointed him. Where was their patriotism? Where was their sense of duty to king and Ghazban? You had to take a chance in this life, Manacia thought, or nothing great would ever be accomplished.

When the invasion came it was true the king intended to sorely punish any failure. But in his view the rewards he was offering for success should more than overcome his generals' fears.

For some reason they hadn't. The plan was simple enough. Manacia intended to first conquer the regions north of the Gods' Divide. The mountain range was a natural barrier that would allow him to work his will, then gather his strength for the final assault over the mountains. True, the ancient maps gave no hint on what route should be taken to cross the Divide. But Manacia was confident—given time and absolute rule over the northern humanlands—that passage would be found. He would find Kyrania, by the gods! Or there were certain lazy, talon-dragging generals who would experience his royal wrath.

To accomplish the first part of his plan—the subjugation of the north—his forces would cross the Forbidden Desert and set up a base camp just beyond the edge. Supply trains and reinforcement columns would pour into that camp, while the main force leaped forward to wipe out the humans.

It was Manacia's opinion that surprise would carry the day. Yes, he wanted a large force to mount the invasion. But it needn't be as large as his generals said, or attached to such unwieldy supply lines. No one in the humanlands had even a glimmer that their demon enemies were gathering for an assault. Manacia had made certain of this by refusing any request to send vulnerable scouting parties to investigate the humanlands. He'd already taken too great a chance by sending Sarn and didn't intend to dare the fates by repeating that error.

His generals, however, had seized on this secrecy, saying the blade cut both ways. Yes, they said, the wise course was to keep the humans in ignorance. But that meant the demons would know nothing of what transpired in the humanlands. When the king struck, he'd be cutting at the dark. There was no way of knowing who might return the blow and with what force.

The only safe thing, prudent thing, to do, his generals said, was to attack with a well-supplied army of such size that anyone who opposed them would be doomed.

Manacia's generals were a backbiting lot, always maneuvering behind the scenes to attack their brother officers, but on this issue they were united. In a rare alliance, Lord Fari and Prince Luka also joined together to back the generals.

Fari, kept from probing the humanlands with intelligence-gathering spells, had similar concerns as the military. So did the prince, who as heir to the throne was expected to lead the vanguard of the invasion.

"If I am to have the high honor of carrying your banner into glorious battle, Majesty," the prince said, "I want to make certain there is no chance it is sullied or befouled in any way.

"I would fight to the death to prevent that from happening."

"Quite right, too," King Manacia said. "My father expected the same from me when

I was Crown Prince. And I risked my life many a time for his standard."

Prince Luka placed talon to breast and bowed low, honoring his father's youthful bravery. As he did so, he thought, You cunning old fraud. You cut your father's throat in his sleep and seized his standard. And if I only have the chance, I'll do the same to you.

"You are a constant inspiration to me, Majesty," the prince said, smoothly. "And I'll need ten thousand fiends for my vanguard."

The king gave them to him.

After much discussion with his generals, he also agreed that a five hundred thousand demon army would be raised—the largest force in the history of Esmir. Backing them with war magic would be two thousand wizards, led by Lord Fari.

The preparations were massive and seemed to move on as slowly as the Turtle Gods carried the continents across the seas.

Making the task even more difficult were countless emergencies calling for his armies' attentions. Within a single month troops had to be rushed to trouble spots a half-a-dozen times.

Manacia felt as if his whole kingdom was bulging at the seams, ready to erupt.

The feeling was intensified by the nightmares. As troubled night bled into troubled night, the king began to fix on the two human devils who always led the rush—the golden haired one and his blue-eyed companion. They became very real to him and he began to wonder who they might be.

When he could bear it no longer he called on Lord Fari and his wizards for an answer. He tried to make light of the dreams, but he knew he was fooling no one and Fari would mark it down as a weakness.

Starcharts were cast, but proved useless since no chart agreed with the next. With the gods at sleep, the heavens held no answers, although the dreamcatchers were ignorant of the reason for their failure.

Bone cups were rattled, the king had his palm read scores of times. All to no avail.

Finally Lord Fari had a human slave brought forth. He was tortured so his cries would please the gods, then while he was still alive—his belly was slit so the king's wizards could read the entrails.

Manacia watched with much interest as Fari leaned over the moaning victim, sniffing at the gaping wound.

"A healthy odor, Majesty," the old wizard reported. "That's a lucky sign."

He scooped up a coil of entrails with a claw.

"Mercy, have mercy," the victim groaned.

Fari peered closely at the rope of tissue. "Better still, Majesty," he said after a moment. "This is a good strong bowel, symbolizing the soundness of Your Majesty's policies."

The human made a weak cry as Fari pulled up more of his innards. "Please," the man whimpered, "please."

"Aha!" the old demon said. "Here's our trouble, Majesty."

He held out a glistening coil. A thick rope of internal muscle jutted off of it, dividing into two blunt-ended tubes about an inch out.

"It's a cancer, Majesty," Fari said. "Attached to the main branch. You see how it divides into two?"

Manacia nodded, he did indeed. Fari extended a talon and sliced each tube. Black blood gushed out.

"Mother of mercy!" the victim screamed. And then he sagged, unconscious.

Satisfied that he had enough information, Fari let the entrails fall. Two slaves slithered over on their bellies to offer him perfumed water and towels to clean his claws.

Fari paced back and forth, wiping his claws and thinking. While he thought two other slaves approached and dragged the human away.

Fari noticed and his snout came up. "The king will want the heart for his dinner," he ordered the slaves. Then he went back to his pacing.

Finally, when Manacia thought he no longer bear the suspense, Fari began to speak.

"Here is how I read it, Majesty," he said. "The cancer, I fear, does represent a threat. The twin ropes drawing off energy from the main bowel are the two humans who bedevil Your Majesty's dreams. One is a king. The other a wizard."

"So *what* if one's a wizard?" Manacia growled. "Human magic is too weak to be a threat to us."

"Most certainly, Majesty," Fari said. "But perhaps when joined with the king he makes a more imposing adversary. I cannot say. The entrails gave no clue to such things.

"But they did tell me that right now these two forces—king and wizard—are apart. They began together, but then separated for some reason. At the moment each is independent of the other."

"When will they come together?" the king asked.

Fari sighed, wiping the last of the gore from his claws. "That was not revealed to me, Majesty," he said. He let the towel fall and a slave scrabbled over to pick it up.

"But what of my invasion?" the king pressed. "How long dare I wait? It seems to me the longer the delay, the more chance there is these two forces will come together."

"Quite true, Majesty," Fari said.

"Advise me," the king demanded. "When do I invade?"

Fari didn't hesitate. The old demon felt quite sure of himself. The entrails had been that plain.

"In the spring, Majesty," he said. "Soon as the first snow melts."

"And what of this king and this wizard?" Manacia asked. "They won't be together by then?"

"I don't believe so, Majesty," Fari said. "They're too far away from one another. And unless some great wind sweeps one up and delivers him to the feet of the other, we have nothing to fear."

*   *   *

The storm that hastened the Cloudship over the Plains of Jaspar lasted for more than a week. The winds that drove it were as fierce as the love-making in Methydia's cabin.

For Safar it was a wondrous journey to the heart of a woman. In many ways Safar had always preferred the company of women. He'd been raised in a household of generous and intelligent females. As a child he'd sat in their company, so quiet they soon forgot he was about, and he'd listened intently to their troubles and dreams. Safar thought women dreamed better than men. They saw nuances and dimensions where men only saw flat featureless plains. Safar had been unfortunate in his first adult experience with women. Astarias had wounded him. Although he'd been careful not to judge all women by that experience, he couldn't help all the small doubts and fears that remained.

Methydia wiped them away in a stroke.

For Methydia the affair was altogether different. It shook her sensibilities. It rocked her mortality. She'd had many affairs; some for gain, some for lust, perhaps one or two for love—although as she grew older she'd started to think all three were the same and equaled love of self. But with Safar there was something extra—a tantalizing mystery just beyond her grasp.

What Methydia always liked about young men was that they *appreciated* you so much. A woman merely had to be a *woman* and take the upper hand. Young men—well brought up young men—were so accustomed to obeying their mothers they were invariably relieved when responsibility was taken from them. She could beguile them with a look. Arouse them with a touch. Hold them at bay with a frown. Methydia was a consummate actress and could be all things to all men, but with the young it took less effort. There was more time to *enjoy*. As Biner often said, "The boss likes her toys, she does. She likes 'em young with a key to wind 'em up."

Safar could have been such a toy, although she'd plucked him from the desert only out of kindness. When he became well and she'd noted his personality was as pleasing as his appearance, she'd considered him for her bed.

But what truly captivated Methydia was Safar's magical self. It was a beautiful essence, powerful and passionate. It was potent—never in her witchy days had she sensed such strength—but there was good at the heart of it. Safar's spirit self wanted to call you friend before it called you foe. It was young, but graceful rather than clumsy. It had known death—was miserable for being the cause of it—and was reluctant to come out into the light again. For a time Methydia was intimidated by Safar's magical self. She didn't fear it, but she did worry if she wasn't careful she'd injure it so badly all the kindness would vanish. As a villain, a black wizard, a fully mature Safar Timura would be a terrible gift to the world.

Attractive as Safar was, she'd held herself back for a long time. In fact, Methydia had all but decided it'd be best to deny herself an affair.

The incident at Kyshaat had ripped her from that mooring.

In her long life Methydia thought she'd encountered just about everything. She'd visited many realms, entertained many people. She'd dealt with danger and evil aplenty; but in her heart she believed good more than outweighed evil, there were more blessings than ill fortune and she'd made it her life's work to remind people of these qualities.

As a witch she was well aware the sorcerous landscape was riddled with magicians and entities whose sole purpose was to cause harm. She'd always managed to evade such things. To Methydia magic came from the earth itself. She believed she drew her powers directly from nature, which to her was a loving, grandmotherly presence.

The creature she encountered at Kyshaat had badly cracked that image. When it rose out of the ground it was as if the earth itself were attacking her. That nature had suddenly revealed its true self and it had a jackal's face. In that awful moment when the earth beast had towered over her she'd thought she'd lost both her life and her soul.

Safar had saved them both.

She'd fled into his arms for comfort and safety and sheer joy at being alive. For a week she hid there from all the terrors the creature had aroused. Yet they gnawed at the edges. Deep in the night, while the storms howled outside and Safar slept, Methydia let them come out one by one. Examining them in turn. In the end she concluded the beast at Kyshaat was the harbinger of doom. That it was only the first of many evils that lay ahead.

Her instincts told her only Safar could fight the dark tide.

As soon as she thought this she knew she'd lost him. It wasn't possible for Safar to remain with the circus. It would be a much happier life for him, but it was Safar's tragedy that all such happiness would be denied him. And one day it would be Methydia's sad duty to point him down the bleak road of his fate.

She said nothing of this to Safar. When she thought the time was right she gently quizzed him about further details of his past. Everything he said confirmed her view. He told her about the vision of Hadin and its destruction, his fears of future disasters, his search for knowledge in Walaria, his discovery of the demon Asper and how in the end the master wizard's works had been denied him. He showed her the stone turtle Nerisa had given him and she mourned with him the faint pulse of nearly dying life inside.

"I was a fool for even trying to find the answer," Safar said bitterly. "What would it matter if I did? There's nothing a potter's boy from Kyrania could do about it."

Then he swore he'd always love her, always stay with her and he'd never return to the dull, heavy existence of earthbound mortals who stared up at the sky in wonder as the Cloudship sailed overhead.

Methydia kept her silence. It would do him no good to tell him what she thought. But she had to be certain Safar was prepared for whatever was in store for him.

She determined that in the time remaining to them she'd teach him everything she knew about magical guile and peoples' artifice. She'd give him all the love she had in her—emotions she'd kept locked away to better arm herself against the world. She'd bolster his confidence, free him as best she could from his own self-imposed restraints.

And when the time came she'd steel herself and make him confront his destiny.

*   *   *

The storms continued with barely a day between each new blow. The winds drove them onward—across the plains of Jaspar.

They saw much misery in the land the Cloudship passed over. Ruined villages, stripped fields where great armies had passed. Even in the heaviest rains they saw thousands of refugees slogging along the roads, making their way to the gods knew where. They saw the aftermath of fighting; huge muddy fields littered with corpses of men and animals.

The sight made them all moody. Only the most necessary words were exchanged. Safar was moodiest of all, staring out over the bleak landscape before them. Then one day they crossed a low mountain range. And when they broke through the clouds the skies were sunny, the air brisk.

They were floating over a large, peaceful valley. The valley floor was a patchwork of bright green orchards interspersed with blue creeks, gaily-painted villages, bordered by shaded gardens. All looked healthy and prosperous and there was no sign of the troubles they'd encountered before.

A fresh wind pushed the Cloudship forward. At the far edge of the valley was a small city with pearly walls and graceful buildings rising up from behind them.

Safar leaned out over the rails to get a closer look. The sight brought a smile to his face.

"What is this place?" he asked.

"The city of Sampitay," Methydia said. "We've never played there before. But I've heard good things about it. An entertainer's paradise, I'm told."

Safar mused, dimly recalling Gubadan's geography lessons. Then he recognized the orchards—white mulberry trees. Sampitay was well known for its fine silks and the royal yellow dye taken from the roots of the trees.

"Sampitay," Biner said. "That's a lucky place. Now I'm sorry I cursed the gods so harshly for all that bad weather."

Safar turned and looked back at the mountains. Big banks of clouds, driven by a far off storm, were scudding across the sky after them. It was about time, he thought, that the winds of fate took a gentler turn.

CHAPTER NINETEEN
THE RETURN OF PROTARUS

Safar knew there was something wrong before the first performance.

The crowds greeting them were enthusiastic enough, as were the soldiers who directed them to the field outside the city gates. The roustabouts set the circus up in record time and the seats for the first show were sold out before the ticket booth was in place.

The good citizens of Sampitay were so hungry for entertainment they lined up, begging to be relieved of the price of admission, while the Cloudship was still unloading. Methydia's troupe was forced to give a hasty first performance, cutting the encores short so an impatient second audience could be admitted.

No art was required to please them. They roared laughter at the slightest clown antic, gasped in terror at the merest slip of an acrobat, moaned in suspense at Methydia's and Safar's slightest magical gesture.

Oddly enough the troupe was discontented.

"I could fart and get a laugh," Biner complained.

"I could whistle through my fangs and they'd be thrilled," Elgy said.

"They're tho eathy I want to thpit," Arlain said. "And the godth *know* what happenth when I thpit!"

Green as he was, Safar felt a wrongness in the overly-wild applause he received when he cast the first purple-colored smoke pellet that began his performance. He sensed an hysterical edge to the crowd's huzzahs.

During his mind reading act he announced a maid named Syntha was to be wed soon and her love would always be true. The young woman in question shrieked such joy at this news—which Safar had received courtesy of a big-eared roustabout—the entire audience was reduced to tears.

"What's wrong with them?" he asked Methydia between performances.

Methydia smiled thinly. She seemed distracted, applying her makeup with a heavy hand. "Are you so accustomed to applause," she asked, "that you've already begun to question it?"

"Come on," Safar said. "I'm not the only one. Elgy said the last time he played before an audience like this it turned out his troupe had wandered into the middle of a plague."

"The fear of death," Methydia said, "*does* have a way of exciting people's interest in life."

"Do you know something the rest of us don't?" Safar asked, growing irritated.

"Only this," Methydia said, passing him a large ornate card with a distinctive seal of gold wax. "We are to give a command performance tonight for Queen Arma and her royal consort."

Safar looked at the card, an honor at any other time, and said, "Why is this bad news?"

"Because it was accompanied by a chest of silk," Methydia said. "And that silk, according to the messenger who delivered it, is an advance payment on a week's worth of free performances for the queen's subjects."

"A morale booster?" Safar asked.

"I'm talking about a dozen bolts of the *finest* Sampitayan silk," Methydia said.

Safar, who'd spent his life on a caravan route, had a good idea what *that* was worth. "How much morale-boosting do they *need?*" he said. "And why?"

"I don't know," Methydia answered. "The messenger was quite polite, but he worked hard to avoid answering my questions. It was as if he expected us to pack up and leave at the slightest hint of trouble. He went on for an hour about what a wonderful ruler Arma was, the excellent health of her children, the esteem all her subjects hold her in. And the soundness of her kingdom."

Safar winced. In Walaria he'd learned to read fear on the face of royal posture. "Maybe we'd better go," he said.

"I've arrived at the same conclusion," Methydia said. "I told the messenger we had pressing business elsewhere. And we couldn't stay longer than the week purchased by Her Majesty."

Safar, remembering the incident at Kyshaat, said, "What if we slipped off tonight?"

"I've also considered that course," Methydia said. "Much can happen in a week. But I don't think we dare cut our visit too short. We might bring down the wrath of Queen Arma by making a hasty exit. I think it'd be best if we gave the queen the command performance she asked for, then quietly loaded the circus back on the Cloudship. We can do without some of the sets. And make it look like we're unloading things while we're actually putting them aboard. Three nights, no more, and we'll be on our way."

"But the queen paid in advance," Safar pointed out. "What about all that silk?"

"I'll leave it behind," Methydia said. "It's bad money and I don't want any part of it."

*   *   *

As it turned out three days was too long. The circus overshot its luck the night of the command performance.

Knowing she was going to abandon Sampitay as soon as possible, Methydia roused the troupe to put on its best show ever.

Safar, drawing on his years of schooling in Walaria, had created a new kind of magical lighting. The circus tried out his ideas for the first time the night Queen Arma held court in the main tent.

A blazing full moon greeted the royal visitors as they entered the tent. Safar made the moon a spotlight, picking out the grand moment of each performance, then dimmed it with onrushing clouds during costume changes. Flares burst up in the arena during the featured performances, turning all into a mystical herky-jerky of amazing motion.

To close the first half Safar and Arlain debuted a new act they'd been working on for some time.

From the time of its inception—which had merely been to improve on the old "saw the maid in half" gag—the trick had grown into a full-blown tale. Safar cast himself as the villain of the piece—an evil wizard. Arlain and Biner were the odd lovers—the ugly dwarf and the beautiful creature who was part woman, part dragon.

In the story Safar hunts the lovers in bleak otherworlds full of swirling lights, fountaining smoke and spurting flames. Eventually he corners them, appears to slay Biner, then captures Arlain. She fights off his attempts to ravish her but is punished by being put into a deadly trance. In that trance Safar levitates her, then proceeds to slice her in two with his sword. Defiant to the last, Arlain breathes fire. Then the fire is gone. Suddenly Biner is aroused. He heals Arlain. A fight commences. And in the end the two lovers defeat Safar and embrace. Then a lovely note piped by Elgy and Rabix brings the lights down.

Tears and cheers greeted the three performers when they took their bows.

Despite his worries, Safar was feeling mightily pleased with himself as he rushed off to get ready for the second act. The high wail of a herald's horn brought him up short. He turned, alarmed at this sudden interruption of circus routine.

In the royal box Queen Arma was on her feet. In front of her was a boy dressed in the elaborate livery of a court herald. At a signal from the queen he raised his horn and blew again—commanding all present to be silent and attend to the queen.

Arma was a middle-aged woman, running to fat. She had a round pleasant face made to seem rounder still by the tall forepeaked crown she wore. Sitting beside her was her consort, Prince Crol, a handsome, silver-haired man in the glittering dress uniform of a general. The queen drew in her breath to speak and just before the first words issued from her lips Safar saw the soldier gesture and felt the sting of magic. He knew immediately the man was a wizard and the gesture was a magical spell to amplify the queen's words so all could hear.

"Citizens of Sampitay," Queen Arma said, high-pitched voice filling the main tent. "I am sure we are all having a lovely time tonight, are we not?"

The richly dressed crowd answered with loud applause. Arma turned her head, nodding at Methydia who stood near the performers' exit—regal-looking in her own right in a dazzling red gown and slender tiara, decorated with a tasteful spattering of gems.

"We have the good Lady Methydia and her talented troupe of entertainers to thank for bringing a bit a joy to Sampitay during its crisis," the queen said.

Methydia bowed low, but from the stiffness of her bow Safar could see she was as surprised as he at the queen's remarks. And what was that Arma said about a "crisis?"

"As you all well know," Arma continued, "your queen and her representatives have been in almost constant communication with King Protarus and his emissaries for over a month now."

The crowd murmured, troubled—as was Safar at the mention of his old friend's name.

"We have kept you all well informed regarding the nature of those communications," Arma said. "The first message was a demand that this kingdom end its long and historic policy of neutrality. Protarus *commanded* it—and it would be wrong of us to use a weaker word to pretty up his barbaric diplomacy. Our answer to that outrage was a firm although courteous reply that this queen is not his to command!"

A thunderclap of applause greeted this statement. Safar thought of Iraj and knew it would have been unlikely for him to take the queen's refusal well.

"Shortly afterward," Arma went on, "Protarus' emissaries arrived with new demands. He was no longer asking us to ally ourselves with him against his enemies. Instead, he commanded our immediate surrender. He even gave us this . . ." and Safar saw her raise up a familiar banner, bearing the red demon moon and silver comet that was the sign of Alisarrian ". . . to hoist over the palace, marking our subjugation."

The crowd reacted angrily, shouting words of defiance.

Queen Arma waited until the shouts died down, then said loudly, "We refused!"

More shouts and thunderous applause. The queen waited, then at a key moment she signaled for silence.

"It would dishonest of me, my loyal subjects," Arma said, "if we didn't admit our nights were long and sleepless with worry after we made that reply. King Protarus, whose armies now range at will across the Plains of Jaspar, is not known to brook any defiance from any kingdom or monarch whom he deems to stand in his way. Fearing reprisals, we put our own troops in a state of readiness. We were prepared to die to the last defending the sanctity of our realm."

Pandemonium reigned for many long minutes as the crowd roared its approval.

When they had quieted, Arma said, "Tonight it is our supreme pleasure to announce to you the gods have stood firm with the good and righteous people of Sampitay."

She'd dropped the banner and was now holding up a long slender parchment roll.

"This is the latest communication from Protarus," she said. "I received it only this morning.

"Apparently the young King Protarus has seen the error of his ways. He now understands the value and rightness of our neutrality. He has taken back all his demands and now only asks—quite politely, I might add—that we sell his army badly needed supplies at a fair price."

The queen's news charged the crowd into an even greater fever. They shouted joy until they were hoarse, applauded until their fingers were numb.

Then Arma said, "What say you, my loyal subjects? Shall we be magnanimous in our victory? Shall we show King Protarus what civilized people are like?"

Shouts of agreement sealed the bargain. People wept and clutched one another, praising the gods for coming to their aid in this time of need.

In the middle of the chaos, Safar crept over to Methydia. "This isn't good," he said. "I know Iraj. He'd never back down so easily."

Methydia nodded. Safar had told her about his boyhood friendship with Protarus and the vision he'd had of Iraj's conquering army. He'd left out only the fight with the demons.

"We'll finish this show and make ready to leave," she said, not bothering to lower her voice in the din of all those tearful, joyous people. "We'll depart at dawn," she continued. "The whole city will be so sick with from celebrating no one will notice."

They completed the show, although the whole troupe—sensing the wrongness in the air—was much subdued. The queen thanked them when it was over and rewarded Methydia with more bolts of rich Sampitayan silk.

It wasn't easy to make preparations to slip away. There were so many well-wishers and celebrants about the troupe could do little more than pack their things and place them as close to the Cloudship as possible. The roustabouts were given strict orders to rouse everyone an hour before dawn so they could board the Cloudship and flee.

They slept in the tents that night, their most important belongings close at hand so they could make a hasty exit.

"I wish I could send a message to Iraj," Safar said as he and Methydia settled down for a few hours sleep.

"What would you say?" Methydia asked, wiping away the last vestiges of her makeup with a damp sponge. "Spare the city? Or just spare us?" She gave him a cynical look. "I'd like to know the proper way to appeal to a blood-thirsty barbarian."

Safar shook his head. "Iraj is no barbarian," he said.

"You saw the burned cities," Methydia said, "the refugees by the thousands. If that isn't barbaric, I'd like to know what is."

"The whole world is barbaric as far as I'm concerned," Safar said, growing angry. "Iraj is no more a savage than those who confront him. Walaria is supposed to be the civilized center of Esmir. There's nothing but self-serving cutthroats in command there. Look at Sampitay. It's not much better. Queen Arma and her court have their silk trade, their riches. But what of the common folk? They are as poor and put upon as the people of Walaria."

"Perhaps King Protarus is merely ill-advised," Methydia said coolly. "Perhaps he didn't notice all the misery we saw in our journey. Misery caused by his armies."

Safar was silent for a moment, thinking about what she'd said; trying to sort out his boyhood from his adulthood.

"I haven't seen Iraj for a long time," he finally said, "but I don't think he could have changed so much. There was good at the heart of him."

"Maybe *you* were that good," Methydia said. "Maybe your presence brought out whatever finer feelings he had."

"Iraj is his own man," Safar insisted. "The good I saw was his own. It needed nothing from me. He's also a warrior born and although I disagree with his methods, in the end Iraj is seeking a better place than we have now.

"Iraj didn't make the droughts, the plagues or the horrors like the worm at Kyshaat. He didn't make the old kings and nobles who are as great a plague on Esmir as the ones nature sends us."

"Still," Methydia said, "you're as anxious to get out of the way of his wrath as I am."

"Armies have no heart," Safar said. "And it's Iraj's army we'll see first. Queen Arma was fool enough to defy him. His soldiers will have their orders to make an example of Sampitay. And I don't want us to be in their way."

"Are you really so unfeeling about the plight of these people, Safar," Methydia asked. "Am I seeing a side of you I never noticed before because I was so smitten?"

Safar took her hand. She let him, but her manner was wary. "What can I do?" he asked, and there was so much pain in his voice her wariness vanished. "Tell me and I'll do it at once."

"Speak to Iraj," she said. "Reason with him."

Safar thought about her request for a time. He felt he was at the edge of a cliff. At the bottom was a world he wanted to escape. A world of petty kings and wizards. A world where girls like Nerisa died for no good reason. And then he thought of all the maids and lads in Sampitay who would suffer Nerisa's fate, or worse, when Iraj's soldiers came. Methydia squeezed his hand. He took strength from it and made his decision.

"We'll go find Iraj in the morning," he said. He grinned, but it was such a sad grin that Methydia ached for him. "He shouldn't be hard to find. We'll just look for the largest army."

Methydia held back tears and embraced him. They made love, clinging to one another as if they were the last people in the world.

Then they fell asleep.

Safar dreamed of Hadin. He danced with the beautiful people, all cares wiped away by the rhythm of their drums.

Then the volcano exploded with such violence that he was hurled far out to sea. He was suddenly without the ability to swim. He pawed madly at the water, trying to stay afloat—burning embers raining down on him.

And then a familiar voice urged, "Wake up, Master! Wake up!"

Safar's eyes snapped open. Gundara was perched on his chest, sharp little teeth chattering in fear. Safar blinked, thinking he was still dreaming. The last time he'd checked the stone idol—which he always kept near him—it'd seemed like there was barely any magical life inside.

Then he felt the Favorite's weight on his chest and although it was slight, it was very real.

"Where did you come from?" Safar asked.

Gundara ignored the question. "They're coming, Master!" he said, hopping onto the floor. "Hurry! Before it's too late!"

Safar heard sounds of fighting outside and came fully awake. He scrabbled for the knife he kept under his pillow and rolled to his feet. Realizing he was naked, he hastily pulled on clothes. The turtle fell out of his tunic pocket and bounced on the earthen floor. Gundara instantly disappeared into it. Then he heard Methydia cry out from the bed and he shouted for her to stay down. He scooped up the turtle and thrust it into his pocket just as the soldiers burst through the tent opening.

Safar didn't give them a chance to get set, but charged directly into them. He dodged a blow and sank his blade into softness. He heard a gasp, tried to pull his knife free, but it stuck. Behind him Methydia screamed a warning and he let the knife go, ripping the sword out of his victim's dying grasp.

He whirled, striking out blindly. He didn't have time or room to turn the blade so only the flat of it struck his attacker. But the force of his blow was so great it sent the soldier reeling back, exposing his belly. Once again Safar felt soft flesh give under his weapon. He didn't wait to see the man fall, but turned again as other soldiers crowded through the tent opening.

He attacked with such fury they fell over each other to escape his wrath. Then he jumped back, heaved up a chest he'd normally have needed help to lift, and hurled it through the opening. Satisfying yelps of pain told him that he'd hit his target.

Methydia was out of the bed now, hastily drawing on a robe.

"This way," he shouted, slashing at the rear of the tent. The cloth parted and they pushed through the opening.

The night was a mad thing of screams and clashing armor and weapons. Fire raged whichever way they turned.

Methydia clutched him, pointing. Safar turned to see her glorious Cloudship going up in flames.

There was an explosion and the Cloudship became a shatter of burning wood splinters and smoldering cloth. Methydia sagged and he caught her in his arms.

Mailed horsemen charged out of the boiling smoke, flailing about with curved blades that cut anyone down who got in their way.

A banner, carried by the lead horseman, fluttered over them. It bore the ancient symbol of the demon moon and silver comet.

The warriors were shouting, "For Protarus!"

Six horsemen split off from the group and rushed toward Safar. He let Methydia drop to his feet, and grasped his sword in both hands.

He made a spell of strength and power surged through his body until he felt like a giant. He made a spell of sharpness and sliced the air with his blade. It shimmered with the force of his blow.

Then the horsemen were on him. He cut the legs out from under the first steed, slew its rider, then leaped on the horse's body to confront the rest.

A spear floated toward him and he ducked it easily, coming up to deal a death blow to the one who'd hurled it. A huge man with a black beard struck at him with a scimitar. Safar parried and the man's bearded mouth became a wide "O" as Safar's sword pierced his throat. Then there was a horseman behind him and he whirled just as the soldier's mount trampled on Methydia's prone body.

Safar howled in fury and leaped at the man, his weight carrying horse, soldier and himself to the ground. The quarters were too close to swing his blade, so he hammered at the soldier with the haft of his sword, crushing the helmet.

Then he was up again, parrying the next blow, killing the next man.

He fought for what seemed like an eternity. But no matter how many he struck down, there were always others crowding in to take him.

Then there was a sudden respite and he was swinging at empty air. Cutting back and forth, meeting nothing, but still slashing, still fighting, as if there were invisible devils all around him.

He stopped, finally realizing no enemy was within reach.

Safar looked up and all was a haze in his battle-lust view. Then he saw a grizzled old veteran mounted on a warhorse about ten paces away. Safar's head swiveled. He was surrounded, but now instead of swords there were raised bows confronting him, arrows drawn back—waiting for the order to fire.

"You've done yourself proud, lad," the old veteran said. "Now put your sword down and we'll spare you."

Safar grinned. He was covered with the gore of other men and made an awful sight.

Then, instead of tossing his sword down, he pushed it point first into the ground and leaned on it.

"Tell Iraj Protarus," he said loudly, "that a friend awaits him. And begs the pleasure of his company."

The veteran reacted, surprised. "And who might that friend be, lad?"

"Safar Timura of Kyrania," he replied. "The man he once called his blood oath brother.

"The man who once saved his life."

CHAPTER TWENTY

ALL HAIL THE KING

It was well past dawn when Iraj finally came.

The smoke and soot from the burning city was so thick it made the day more like night. The air was filled with the stench of death and the loud weeping of Sampitay's survivors as they were led out to meet their fates.

Safar was pacing within the same circle of bowmen. Although they'd lowered their weapons, he noted they were ready to lift them again and fire if he made a wrong move. They were all fierce plainsmen, small in stature, muscular in build, with misshapen legs from so many years on horseback. They wore flowing robes, cinched by wide leather belts bearing scimitars on one side, long daggers on the other. Their boots were felt, with sharp spurs strapped to them. They had turbans for head coverings, with steel caps beneath and most sported long, drooping mustaches, giving their dark faces a grim, determined look.

A small part of Safar—the child that weeps for its mother even at a great age—quaked at the sight of them. The rest was armed with a cold, tightly-gripped rage he was ready to release at the slightest pretense.

The soldiers didn't know what to make of Safar. He was either the mightiest of liars or truly the king's blood oath brother. The only thing certain was Safar had more than proven himself as a warrior. It was for this reason, almost more than his claim of friendship with the king, that had stayed their hands. Safar had leaned heavily on their respect to rescue most of the members of the troupe and he'd bullied the old sergeant into letting them join him.

He used the circle like a shield, pacing the perimeter to keep it intact, pointing the tip of his sword accusingly at any soldier who dared stray closer. In the center the troupe was silently tending the unconscious Methydia. Safar feared for her—she'd been badly trampled by the warhorse—but he didn't dare show his concern in front of the bowmen.

He knew it would be taken as a sign of weakness.

Then he heard a great horn blare and war drums beat a tattoo. Orders were shouted and the ring of bowmen suddenly parted.

A tall warrior mounted on a fiery black steed cantered down the path they made. He wore the pure white robes of a plains fighter. His head was wrapped in a white turban, with the tail pulled about his face like a mask.

The warrior pulled the horse up a few paces away. He studied Safar for a long moment, taking in the gore stained costume, bloody sword and soot-streaked face. Safar stared back, making as insolent a grin as he could manage. Finally the warrior's gaze came to Safar's eyes and there was a sudden jolt of recognition.

"Safar Timura, you blue-eyed devil," Iraj cried, sweeping away the mask, "it *is* you!"

"In the flesh," Safar said, "although as you can see that flesh is a little worse for wear and definitely in need of a bath."

Safar, remembering the first time he and Iraj had met, pointed at the soldiers and said, "I think I could use a little help here. It seems I'm completely surrounded by the Ubekian brothers."

Iraj roared laughter. "The Ubekian brothers!" he shouted. "What a sorry lot they were!"

Then, to the amazement of his soldiers, the king leaped off his horse and threw his arms around Safar, gore and all.

"By the gods I have missed you, Safar Timura," he shouted, pounding his old friend on the back. "By the gods I have missed you!"

*   *   *

Iraj called for a mount and personally escorted Safar back to his command tent—set on a hill overlooking Sampitay. When Safar indicated the unconscious Methydia and the others members of the troupe Iraj asked no questions about Safar's odd company, or even acted surprised. He immediately issued orders all were to be well cared for and the best healers summoned to tend to Methydia.

"And I want hourly reports on her progress," Iraj demanded. "I don't want my good friend, Lord Timura, to worry unnecessarily."

Lord? Safar thought. How did a potter's son suddenly become a lord? He glanced at Iraj, saw the look of warning in his eyes and realized it wouldn't do for a king to have a blood oath brother who less than noble born.

During the ride back to his command post Iraj kept the conversation light, loudly regaling his aides and guard with exaggerated tales of his youthful adventures with "Lord Timura."

"Why, if it weren't for Safar," he said, "I wouldn't be here today. And you'd all be serving some other king, a weak-kneed, inbred bastard, no doubt. Someday I'll tell you the story of how he saved my life. You've already witnessed how bravely he fought here, so you can all rest assured it is a stirring tale that will take a long winter's evening to give it proper justice.

"But I will tell you this. After the battle the people of Kyrania were so grateful to us for saving them from that gang of bandits that they trotted out fifteen of their prettiest virgins for us to deflower."

He laughed. "I gave up after five."

He turned to Safar. "Or was it six?"

"Actually, it was seven," Safar answered.

Iraj's grin told him that he'd lied correctly.

"Seven it was," Iraj said. "But that was nothing compared to my friend here. He deflowered the remaining eight, then strolled out of his tent, easy as you please, and announced he was still feeling peckish and wouldn't mind a few more."

The aides and guardsmen roared laughter and crowded in close to slap Safar on the back and praise his prowess as a fighter and lover.

"Mind you," Iraj said, "he wasn't playing fair. Even as a boy Lord Timura was a mighty wizard. He confessed to me later that he had a secret potion for such occasions."

Again, Iraj turned to Safar—a frown of mock accusation on his face. "If I recall, my friend," he said, "you promised to supply me with some. A promise you never kept."

Safar held out a hand, palm up. "I was hoping you had forgotten that, Your Highness," he said, adding the royal honorific for the first time and pleasing Iraj immensely. "You see, there were only five virgins left in all Kyrania. And I didn't want us to quarrel over them."

More bawdy laughter—led by the king—greeted his clever reply. The royal party continued on and there were many manly jests and many manly boasts to mark the journey.

They wended their jocular way past scenes of incredible brutality. Sampitay's dead and wounded littered the battlefield. Captives, working under the stern direction of Iraj's fierce soldiers, piled the dead in mounds. Oil was poured on the corpses and they were set on fire; greasy black fumes, smelling like sacrificial sheep, rose to mix with the smoke of the burning city. Other soldiers moved across the field, slitting the throats of the groaning wounded. Thousands of civilians were being separated into groups of young and old, men and women. Construction crews were hammering together execution blocks for the aged and infirm. Sharp-eyed slavers were moving through the rest, drawing up estimates of the price each would bring and whether it would be worth the care and feeding they'd require.

Safar felt as if he were trapped in the worst kind of nightmare—one that required him to wear a mask of light-hearted unconcern amid all that horror. And soaring above that was the dark raven of his fear for Methydia.

Although Iraj had greeted him warmly—as if only a few months rather than years had separated them—Safar didn't let down his guard. His old friend had the same easy, open manner. Other than the beard he looked much the same as before. His manner was casually royal, but it had always been so. He'd also matured. With the beard, which Safar suspected Iraj had grown to look older, he appeared to be in his thirtieth summer, rather than in his early 20's like Safar. He still had that cunning look in his eyes, a cunning he'd had develop at an early age to survive family wars. But Safar could see there was no malice, no cruelty.

Somehow Iraj had drawn on the mantle of a conqueror, had been the cause of much bloodshed, yet seemed untouched by it.

It made Safar, who was wary and secretive at heart, warier still.

Iraj still had the look of a great dreamer. There was an innocence about him—the innocence of all dreamers. That was what confounded Safar the most. How could Iraj appear so innocent, yet move through scenes of such awful cruelty—which he'd ordered—with his innocence intact?

He glanced at Iraj, once again noting his remarkable resemblance to Alisarrian.

For the first time Safar truly understood the enigma Gubadan had unknowingly posed when he'd asked his favorite rhetorical question: "Who was this man, Alisarrian? A monster as his enemies claimed? Or a blessing from the gods?"

Safar wondered if he'd ever learn the answer.

He put confusion aside. His first duty was to Methydia and his friends. After that he'd try his best to keep his promise to Methydia and see what he could do to ease the suffering of the people of Sampitay.

Beyond those two immediate goals was a chasm, deep and wide. Fate seemed to be driving him toward the brink of that chasm.

And there was nothing he could do about it.

*   *   *

After Safar had bathed, changed into fresh clothes and heard a promising first report regarding Methydia's health, he was summoned to Iraj's private quarters.

Other than its size and placement, there was nothing to mark Iraj's tent as the dwelling place of a king. It sat in the center of scores of similar tents, all made of a plain, sturdy material. The hillside encampment was a bustle of uniformed officers and clerks and scribes in drab civilian garb. Safar later learned Iraj conducted all of his business from tents like these—a kind of traveling court, moving from one battlefield to the next. Iraj ruled a vast new kingdom—ranging from The God's Divide to the most distant wilderness—while on the road.

The furnishings in Iraj's tent palace were spare and utilitarian. Chests were used as tables, saddles were mounted on posts to make chairs. A plain portable throne—with Iraj's banner hanging over it—sat on a raised platform against the far wall. When Safar entered the throne was empty. The two aides assigned to him ushered him past officers and sergeants who were bent over maps, or absorbed in reports.

Heavy curtains blocked off one large section of the tent and as Safar approached he caught the scent of perfume. Surprised as he was by this oddity in a place of such military bearing, he was even more amazed when the curtain parted and two young women dressed like soldiers stepped out. Although they were both remarkably beautiful, they had eyes as fierce as the weapons belted about their slender waists.

Without a word they searched him for weapons. It was an odd sensation being handled so intimately by such beauteous, deadly women.

When they were satisfied they escorted him into the room. In the center, wine cup in hand and lolling on soft pillows, was Iraj—surrounded by a dozen other women warriors.

"Safar," he called out, "come join me. It's been a long time since we've had a drink together."

He clapped his hands and women rushed about to fetch food and drink while others plumped up pillows to make Safar comfortable.

It was all very bizarre being waited on by these mailed, perfumed handmaids and Iraj chortled at Safar's bewildered expression.

"What do you think of my royal guard?" he asked.

Safar shook his head. "I'm not sure whether I'm supposed to fight them or make love to them," he joked.

"I've often wondered that myself," Iraj said, smiling. "Sometimes we do both just to keep the nights interesting."

The women laughed at the king's jest and their eyes and actions were so adoring there was no mistaking their pleasure was genuine.

"You of all people know my weakness for women," Iraj said.

Safar grinned. "Very well."

"Then you will admire my military solution to that weakness," Iraj said. "Instead of a baggage train of courtesans and their belongings to slow me down, I've hand-picked a platoon of beautiful women to make up my royal guard. They are all highly-skilled fighters—I saw to their training myself, and let me tell you there is not an assassin in existence who could get by them. And they are marvelous bedmates as well—also due to my personal training."

Safar laughed. "It's a hard job being king," he said. "But I suppose someone has to do it." He toasted Iraj with the goblet that had been thrust into his hand. "Here's to royal sacrifice."

Iraj roared enjoyment at this. He banged his goblet against Safar's—wine sloshing over the brim—then drained what remained in the cup.

He pulled one of the women onto his lap, nuzzling her. "Tell me, Leiria," he said to the woman, "what do you think of my friend, Safar? Isn't he all that I described?"

Leiria gave Safar a sloe-eyed look, guaranteed to light a fire in any man—any man but Safar, that is, whose complete attention was fixed on the situation.

"And more, Majesty," Leiria answered, smoldering gaze still fixed on Safar. "Except you didn't say he was so handsome. And his eyes! I've never seen a man with blue eyes before. It's like looking into the sky."

Iraj slapped her well-rounded haunch. "What?" he shouted, but it was a shout of pleasure, not anger. "You lust for another?"

Leiria tangled her hand in king's golden beard. "Maybe just a little bit, Majesty," she pouted. "But only so I can learn more and return to you with greater pleasures."

Iraj kissed her, long and deep, then pulled away and looked at Safar, eyes filled with amusement.

"You see how it is, my brother?" he said. "It will always be a problem between us. The same women want us. What shall we do about it?"

Safar instantly felt he was walking on dangerous ground. "Thankful as I am at the flattery, Majesty," he said, "Leiria was only being kind, I'm sure."

"Nonsense," Iraj said. "She wants you. Very well, you shall have her."

He untangled himself from Leiria and pushed her into Safar's lap. Leiria went willingly, cooing and snuggling and tracing patterns on his chest with her fingers. Safar shifted his position—her dagger was digging into his side.

"I only ask that you be kind to her," Iraj said. "And send her back in good condition. She's known no man but me." He waved at the others. "None of them have. I am not in the habit of making my women a gift to other men."

He smiled. "In fact, it has only happened one time before. Do you remember when that was, Safar?'

Safar remembered very well indeed. "Astarias," he said. "How could I possibly forget?"

"And what was the oath we swore then?" Iraj asked.

"That all I had was yours," Safar answered, "and all that was yours was mine."

"Freely given and with no ill will, correct?" Iraj pressed.

"Yes, Majesty," Safar said. "Freely given. And with no ill will."

"Good," Iraj said. "I'm glad you remember."

For reasons Safar couldn't determine, what had just occurred had been very important to Iraj.

"Another thing, Safar," Iraj said. "When we're in private, don't call me majesty or your highness or other such silliness."

"That's certainly a relief," Safar laughed. "The first time I said it—when we were with your officers—I kept thinking, this is the same fellow my mother scolded for tromping over her clean floors with muddy boots."

Iraj grinned, remembering. "I thought she'd kill me," he said. "She made me get down on my hands and knees and clean the mess up. A humbling experience for a future king, that's for certain."

He turned suddenly serious, eyes taking on a far-away cast. "But here I am, a king," he said, "just as you predicted in Alisarrian's cave."

Safar nodded, remembering.

"And you predicted other things, greater things," Iraj went on.

"Yes," Safar said.

"Tell me, brother," Iraj went on, "do you still see those things? Do you still see me as King of Kings, monarch of all Esmir?"

The answer leaped up unbidden—a vision of Iraj sitting a golden throne. "I do," Safar said softly.

Iraj was quiet for a moment, toying with his cup. Then suddenly he clapped his hands. "Leave us!" he ordered the women. "I want to be alone with my friend."

Leiria scrambled out of Safar's lap and exited the room with her sister warriors. After they'd gone, Iraj remained silent for a time, thinking.

When he finally spoke, there was an edge to his voice—"Why didn't you come when I sent for you? I practically begged, which is something I'm not in the habit of doing."

Safar was confused. "You sent for me? When?"

"When you were in Walaria," Iraj said. "I sent a letter. And a large purse of gold, as well, to pay for your expenses."

"I received neither," Safar said. "And if I had, I certainly would have come." He grimaced. "Things didn't go well in Walaria."

Iraj searched his face, then relaxed, satisfied Safar had spoken the truth.

"I heard something of your difficulties," he said.

"That's how you came to find me with the circus," Safar said. "There are some very dangerous men in Walaria who want my head."

"You needn't concern yourself with them any longer," Iraj said. "Walaria paid most dearly for troubling you."

Safar's heart trip-hammered against his chest. "What do you mean?" he asked.

"Walaria is no more," Iraj answered. "I turned it back into a cattle station." He casually refilled his goblet with wine, then poured some into Safar's cup. "It wasn't entirely for you," he said. "They were fools. They defied me, like these people here in Sampitay. It was necessary to make an example of them.

"Although in Walaria's case, I took some pleasure in dispensing justice. I thought you were dead and I was avenging you."

Safar was horrified that such a thing had been done in his name.

Iraj noted the expression on his face. His face became mournful. "I'm normally a soft-hearted fellow who doesn't like to cause pain," he said. "It's my father's weakness in me and I have to guard against it. You have to be stern to rule. And much blood must be shed to make a kingdom."

Safar saw moisture well in Iraj's eyes and was surprised at the depth of the emotion.

"But I never knew I'd have to shed so much of it," Iraj said, voice thick.

Then he shook himself and wiped his eyes. He forced a smile on his face.

"You saw that too when we were in the cave, didn't you, Safar?" he said. "When you foretold my future you seemed sad for me."

"Yes," Safar said—almost a whisper.

"But it's my fate, so there's nothing to be done about it," Iraj said. "This is a terrible world we live in. And I am the only one who make it right. If only people could see into my heart and know my true intent they wouldn't resist me. I *will* bring peace to this land. I *will* bring greatness.

"I only wish so many didn't have to suffer first."

Passion burned in Iraj's eyes and for a moment Safar could see his boyhood friend staring out at him through those eyes.

"Will you help me, Safar?" Iraj pleaded. "I'm not sure I can do this on my own."

Safar hesitated, a thousand thoughts crowding into his mind, competing with one another to be heard. Then, in the middle of his mental chaos, there came a scratching at the door.

Iraj looked up, irritated. "In!" he commanded.

Two of his guardswomen entered, an old frightened man in healer's garb between them.

"What is it!" Iraj barked.

"Forgive me O Gracious Majesty," the healer burbled, "this poor worm of a healer trembles in Your Highness' presence. He abases himself for daring to—"

Iraj waved, cutting him off. "Stop driveling, man," he said. "What is it?"

The healer bobbed his head, saying, "I've come about the woman who was placed in my care."

"Methydia!" Safar cried, leaping to his feet. "What's wrong with her?"

"I fear she is dying, my lord," he said to Safar, so frightened his legs were about to give way. "She calls for you, my lord. You must come quickly before it is too late!"

Iraj saw the torment in Safar's face. "Go to her," he said. "We'll talk later."

Safar bolted away like an arrow loosed from its bow, the healer tottering behind him as fast as he could.

*   *   *

When he saw her lying on the camp bed, eyes closed, face pale as bleached parchment, the troupe gathered about her weeping silent tears, he thought he was too late. And she looked old, so old he almost didn't recognize her. But as he approached her eyes came open and she was once again his beautiful Methydia.

"Safar," she said, voice faint as a specter's.

He knelt by her side and took her hand, fighting back tears.

"I must look a sight," she said, voice a bit firmer. "What an awful way for a woman to greet her young swain."

"You're as beautiful as ever, my love," Safar murmured. "Only a little weak from your ordeal."

"You always did lie so sweetly, Safar," Methydia said. "But it isn't the time for sugary words. There's no getting around it—I'm dying."

Safar clutched her hand tighter. "I won't let you!" he cried. But as he said it he could feel her slipping away. "Stay with me, Methydia!" he begged. "I'll send for all the healers. I'll make a spell with them, a spell so strong not even the gods themselves could thwart me."

She smiled and he felt her rally, but faint, so faint.

"Let me tell you a secret, my sweet Safar," she said. "The gods aren't listening. They aren't listening now. And they haven't been listening for a long time. I know this because I'm so close to death I can see into the Otherworlds.

"And do you know what I see?"

"What?" Safar asked, voice quivering.

"The gods are asleep! So deep in their slumber that not even a thousand times a thousand voices lifted at once could raise them."

Safar thought she was raving and he kissed her, murmuring, "Nonsense, Methydia. It's only a fever dream you see, not the Otherworlds."

"I wish it were," Methydia said. "I wish it were."

Suddenly her eyes grew wider and she struggled to sit up. Safar gently pressed her down, begging her to be still.

"Listen to me, Safar!" she cried.

"I'm listening, Methydia," Safar answered.

"Only you can wake the gods, Safar," she said. "Only you!"

"Certainly, my love," Safar said. "I'll do it as soon as you're well again. We'll wake them together."

"I'm not mad," she said, suddenly stern and with such strength it surprised him. "I'm only dying. So don't argue with a dead woman. It isn't polite. Now listen to me! Are you listening?"

"Yes, Methydia," Safar said.

"You mustn't hate Protarus for what was done to me," she said. "It was an accident of war, nothing more. Promise me you won't hate him!"

"I promise," Safar said.

"Good. Now I want another promise from you."

"Anything, my love. Anything at all."

"Go with him. Go with Protarus. Help him. It's the only way!"

"Don't ask that of me, Methydia," Safar begged. "Please! Too many people are suffering."

"Ease their suffering if you can," she said. "But help Protarus get his throne. The throne isn't important. It's only the first step. Protarus isn't important. He's only on the road you must follow. I don't know what's at the end of that road. But you'll know what to do when you get there.

"You'll know, my sweet Safar. You'll know."

"Please, Methydia," Safar said.

"Do you promise me, Safar Timura? Do you promise?"

"I can't," Safar said.

Methydia gripped his hand, squeezing as tight as she could. Putting her all her will and remaining strength in that grip.

"*Promise me!*" she insisted.

"Very well," Safar cried, "I promise! Just don't leave me!"

Her hand went limp. Safar looked at her, tears blurring his vision.

There was a smile on her face.

An awful wailing filled the tent as the shock sank in and the other entertainers shouted their grief.

Methydia was dead.

Safar remembered Biner's words long ago when they'd first met:

"Damn everything but the circus!"

And now that circus was no more.

*   *   *

Safar hurried through the encampment, roughly pushing aside anyone who got in his way. Iraj wasn't at his tent headquarters. Safar snarled at a general for directions and his manner was so fierce the scarred veteran of many wars blurted the answer as if he were green stripling.

Safar found Iraj sitting on his traveling throne, which had been moved to a point about halfway down the hillside overlooking Sampitay. On either side of the throne two tall sharpened stakes had been driven into the ground.

Queen Arma's head was mounted on one stake, Prince Crol's on the other.

At the bottom of the hill long lines of the condemned were being herded to the execution blocks. Posts had been erected just beyond and naked men were tied to those posts, screeching in agony while gleeful soldiers tormented them with spears.

Iraj was surrounded by his royal guard and when some of the women saw Safar's manner they drew their swords and stepped in his way.

"Let him through," Iraj commanded.

Reluctantly they parted but they held their swords at ready.

Iraj was grim, face as pale and bloodless as Methydia's had been. He signaled his women to move farther away.

"Give us some privacy," he barked.

The women pulled back, but they weren't happy about it.

"Why did you come here, Safar?" he asked. "This isn't something that's necessary for you to see."

"I want to ask a favor of you, Iraj," Safar said.

Iraj stirred, irritated. "Can't it wait? This is hardly the time or place."

Then he, too, took note of Safar's expression. "What is it, my friend? What has happened?"

Safar shook his head, too overcome to answer.

Then sad understanding dawned in Iraj's eyes. "Ah, I see. Your woman died, is that it?"

"Yes."

"And you loved her?"

"Yes."

"I'm sorry for that. I hope you don't hate me for it."

"No."

"It was an accident of war."

"Methydia said the same thing before she died."

"A wise woman."

"She was that."

Iraj searched Safar's face, then asked, "What is it you want from me? What can I do to ease your pain?"

Safar pointed at the awful scene below. "Spare them," he said.

Iraj gave him a strange look.

"Let me explain why this would be good for you," Safar said.

Iraj shook his head. "You don't need to explain your reasons to me. You asked a boon. You shall have it. Freely given and without hesitation."

"After all, that is our agreement. Our blood oath pledge to each other."

Iraj shouted for his aides and they came running up to him. "Release these people," he commanded. "Return them to their homes."

"But, Majesty," one of the aides protested. "What of their defiance? We must make an example of people like this."

Iraj glowered at the man, who visibly shrank under the glare. "If you ever dare question me again, sir," the king said, "it'll be your head on one of those blocks. Do as I commanded! At once!"

The aides rushed off to his bidding. A few moments later horns blared, orders were shouted, and the chains were stricken from the limbs of the people of Sampitay. They fell to their knees, weeping and shouting praises to the heavens, thanking the gods and Protarus for sparing them.

Safar watched, thinking it was Methydia they should be thanking, not Protarus.

"To be frank, my friend," Iraj said, "I am relieved to grant you this favor. Viewing mass executions, much less ordering them, is one of my least favorite duties."

"Don't order them, then," Safar said.

Iraj's brow rose in surprise. His cheeks flushed. It was clear he was not used to be spoken to this way. Then he made a rueful smile.

"You speak honestly," he said. "No one in my court dares do that. Which is what I lack most of all. A friend who dares to tell me what he truly believes."

"Not an hour ago," Safar said, "you asked me to join you. Do you still want my service?"

"Indeed I do," Iraj answered. "But I don't want your answer now. I granted you a favor. It wouldn't be right to ask one in return. It would be a stain on our friendship."

"You'll have my answer just the same," Safar said. "And it won't be a favor I'm granting you. I will join you, freely and gladly. All I ask is that you listen to my advice, which I will give you as honestly as I can."

"Done!" Iraj said, face lighting up.

He thrust out his hand. "Take it, my brother," he said. "And I will lift you as high as it is in my powers to do."

Safar clasped his hand.

Iraj said, "Safar Timura, son of a potter, wizard of the High Caravans, I, King Iraj Protarus, proclaim you Grand Wazier. From this moment on you are the highest of the high in my realm.

"And you may command all but myself."

Safar felt the world turn about. It was as if a great circus master had spun the Great Wheel of the Fates. Safar was strapped to it, his head the arrow point, spinning, spinning, spinning. And he heard the circus master's cry, "Around and around he goes . . . and where he stops . . . the gods only know!"

Safar gripped Iraj's hand tighter, partly to steady himself, but mostly to keep himself from snatching his own hand away. He wanted nothing of this. His greatest desire was to climb aboard the Cloudship with Biner and Arlain and the others and flee this place, this fate.

But the Cloudship was no more.

And he had made a promise to Methydia.

Safar steeled his nerve and said as firmly as he could: "I accept."

*   *   *

That night Iraj called his court into session. There was a small ceremony to proclaim Safar Grand Wazier.

The faces of the king's officers and courtiers were all a blur to Safar. He could pick out only a few. Some were friendly. Some were not. Mostly, there were only looks of curiosity and awe.

Who was this man who had been lifted so high, so quickly?

Did his presence bode ill, or fair?

*   *   *

Late in the night Safar dreamed that Methydia came to him.

In his dream he felt soft hands caressing him. He opened his eyes and saw Methydia's face and Methydia's slender body poised over him. He cried out her name and crushed to her to him. They made love, a floaty love like they were aboard the Cloudship once again. Then the Cloudship burst into flames, plunging for the earth and they

196

clasped one another, riding the fire in an endless fall.

When he awoke in the morning Safar found Leiria snuggled in the crook of his arm, smiling in her sleep.

Feeling like a traitor, he gently tried to extract his arm. But Leiria came awake, purring and sloe-eyed and clutching him closer.

He untangled her politely, but firmly. "I have duties to attend to," he said.

At first Leiria pouted, then she giggled and got up, saying, "I mustn't be selfish and take all your strength, my lord."

Safar managed a faint smile for an answer.

She starting pulling on clothes. "You called out another woman's name in the night," she said. Her tones were light, but Safar could sense hurt in them. "Was she the one who died?"

"Yes," Safar answered softly.

Leiria shrugged. "I don't mind," she said. "It's good that your heart is faithful." She had her head down, concentrating hard on buckling on her weapons. "The king has ordered me to comfort you and guard you with my life."

She raised her head and Safar saw tears in her eyes. "The king orders," she said, "but I do it gladly. I will guard you and I will be this other woman for you for as long as you like.

"And perhaps someday it will be my name you speak instead of . . . hers."

Safar didn't know what to say. From the look on her face a word either way might cause a flood of tears. She would despise him for humiliating her.

So all he said was, "You honor me, Leiria."

Weak as that reply was, she seemed to find satisfaction in it. She nodded, finished her dressing, then kissed him—a quick peck on the cheek—and left.

Safar looked after her wondering how much was artifice and how much was truly meant.

And how much would she tell Iraj?

*   *   *

It wasn't long before Safar had a chance to test those questions. He'd barely had time to snatch a quick meal and don his clothes before Iraj summoned him.

Leiria was his guide and guard as he made his hasty way into the king's presence. She gave no hint of the night they'd had together. Her bearing was professional and military, her manner courteous and respectful.

When they came to the king's rooms he didn't have to undergo the usual search for weapons and was instantly swept inside. Iraj was seated in a simple camp chair, maps and charts spread out on a small table in front of him.

When he saw Safar he said, "It seems my little gift to you has caused all sorts of trouble, my friend."

Safar forced himself not to look at Leiria. "What ever do you mean, Iraj?" he asked.

Iraj tapped one of the maps. "I'm planning our next campaign," he said, to Safar's immense relief. "Winter is coming on and there isn't much time."

"What's the problem?" Safar asked. "And how was I the cause of it?"

"Sampitay is the problem," Iraj answered. "Now that I've given it back to its people, as you requested, I'll have those same people at my back when we march again."

"What makes you think they'll be a danger to you?" Safar asked.

"What makes you think they won't?" was Iraj's reply, eyes narrowing.

"Aren't you going to garrison the city," Safar asked "and put one of your own men in charge?"

"Garrisons are trebly expensive," Iraj said. "They cost money, soldiers, and good officers to run them."

"Yesterday," Safar said, "I offered reasons for my request. You kindly chose not to hear. I'd like to offer them again."

Iraj nodded. "Go ahead," he said.

"Sampitay is one of the richest cities in Esmir," Safar pointed out. "The source of its wealth, as you know, is silk. But it takes highly skilled people to produce that silk—skills few others in world possess outside Sampitay.

"So the people are worth more to you alive and free than dead or enslaved. Think of all the gold they'll pay in taxes. Gold you can use to wage your campaign.

"As for the soldiers necessary to garrison the city, why not enlist an equal number of Sampitay soldiers to take their place? You can them train in your ways easily enough.

"Finally, you must have many young officers who ache for more responsibility and promotion. They can replace the senior officers you leave behind to command the garrison to keep the peace and make certain your taxes are collected."

Iraj considered, then said, "I admit I'm in sore need of money. They don't tell you in the histories of warfare how much it costs to wage those wars.

"Thus far I've used plunder and the paltry taxes I'm able to collect from the cities now under my rule. Unfortunately, plunder tends to go more into the pockets of my soldiers than mine. They expect it and it is their right.

"As for the taxes, the rulers who have allied themselves to me are always whining they are hard pressed to pay what I ask. I don't have time to go back and give them a real reason for their moaning and so they've been cheating me without mercy."

"Then garrison them all in the manner I suggested for Sampitay," Safar said.

"What? And use their soldiers as well to replace my own?"

"What's wrong with that?" Safar asked.

"Up until now," Iraj said, "I've only used men from my native plains."

"That was certainly a wise policy when you started out," Safar said. "But if you are to be King of Kings, the true ruler of all Esmir, you must look for loyalty in the hearts of *all* your subjects, not just in the men of the plains.

"And that, my friend, is the best reason of all to end this policy of slaughter. Besides, you told me yourself you disliked all that bloodshed. Perhaps this reluctance really wasn't due to some weakness you inherited from your father. Perhaps it was in the back of your mind that a new way had to be found to rule the kind of kingdom that was once Alisarrian's.

"And all I've done was to put words to ideas that were there all along."

Iraj thought for a time, then said, "I'll do as you suggest," he said. "Starting with Sampitay."

He motioned to the maps. "It'll make this job much easier, that's for certain. Before winter sets in I'll have the whole south under my rule. And in the spring—" he traced a line across the God's Divide—"we'll take on the north, crossing at Kyrania just as Alisarrian did."

He sagged back in his chair, weary. "I'll have to fight my way all the way to the sea," he said. "I wonder how many years it will take? And if I'll live long enough to see it."

"You will," Safar said.

Iraj smiled, remembering. "That's right. We saw each other in that vision, didn't we? The demons under our boots as we marched on the gates of Zanzair."

"I remember," Safar said.

Iraj was silent for a moment, then he asked, "Do you think of the demons often?

When we faced them together in the pass?"

"It's my least favorite nightmare," Safar said.

"Do you think Coralean was right? And they were just a group of bandits who strayed into the humanlands?"

"I've seen no evidence pointing either way," Safar said. "I combed the libraries in Walaria to find some historical precedence." He shook his head. "There wasn't any. However, many strange things have happened since that time. Droughts and plagues and wars."

Iraj made a rueful grin. "Well, we know where the wars came from," he said. He tapped his chest to indicate himself. "As for the other things, they could be naturally caused."

"I don't think so," Safar said. He told him of his investigations into Hadin. And he told him of the sorcerous worm he encountered in Kyshaat.

When he was done, Iraj said, "I've thought of that night on the mountain many times. And of your vision afterwards. I'm no seer like yourself, my friend. But I'll tell you what I think it was all about.

"Perhaps something did happen in far off Hadin. Personally, I think it was a sign from the heavens. A sign that fits perfectly into your other visions about me and Alisarrian.

"I truly believe the world is at a crossroads. In one direction lies disaster, although what that disaster entails I cannot say. In the other, hope and a bright future."

Again he tapped his chest. "And I am that hope and future. Once I succeed, all will be set right again."

"I pray you're right," Safar said. "I plan to do all in my powers to see you have the chance to prove it."

Iraj laughed. "Well said, my brother. Together we will conquer all. Nothing can stand in our way."

Safar's answer was a smile. But he was thinking, there's still the demons, Iraj. There's still the demons.

* * *

The following day Safar made his farewells to the circus. He plumped a bag of gold into Biner's hand. It was so heavy it caught the muscular dwarf by surprise and he nearly dropped it.

"What's this?" Biner asked.

"The price of a century's worth of tickets," Safar said, smiling. "I'm hoping you'll always save a place for me."

"We thirtainly will," Arlain said, dabbing at a tear with a kerchief.

"Won't be much of a circus," Biner said, "without Methydia and the Cloudship."

"I wish I could bring them back," Safar said. "The gold is all I can do."

"We'll make the best damn circus we can," Biner said. "We'll make you proud of us."

"I already am," Safar said. "And for the rest of my life I'll remember the months I was with you."

"You're a rich man, now," Biner said. "A powerful man. But if you should ever need us . . ." Emotion overcame him and he turned to honk his nose into a rag. When he'd recovered, he said, "Hells, you know what I mean!"

"Sure I do," Safar said, wiping at his own tears.

Then he embraced them all one by one.

When he was done he rushed off before he weakened and slipped away with them in the night.

The next time Leiria came to his bed he nearly refused her. In the end it seemed easier to accept her embrace than send her away. She was an ardent lover, a skilled lover. He never again called out Methydia's name, although it was Methydia he thought of. He didn't know what to make of Leiria. Was she truly smitten? Or was she Iraj's spy? She never gave a sign either way. At night she was fire in his arms, by day the cool professional, measuring any man who approached him for signs of ill intent.

Because of his doubts he waited several nights before he delved into a most important task. Then he gave her a difficult errand that would take much time to accomplish.

When she was gone he drew out the stone turtle and summoned Gundara.

The little Favorite was still extremely weak and couldn't take full form. Safar could see the tent walls through his wispy figure.

"I hope you don't have anything hard you want to do, master," Gundara whined. "I'm not feeling very well, you know."

"I have a treat for you," Safar said, offering Gundara a sweet he'd saved from the dinner table.

Listlessly, Gundara took it from his hand. He licked at the sugar, then sighed and let the sweet fall to the ground.

"Doesn't taste as good as it used to," he complained.

"I've never had a chance to thank you for the warning that night," Safar said.

Gundara made another deep sigh. "I almost couldn't get out of the stone," he said. "Gundaree pushed and pushed as hard as he could. It nearly killed us both."

"I'm sorry for that," Safar said. "Still, you saved my life."

Gundara shrugged. "I just hope I don't have to do it again real soon."

"So do I," Safar said. "But what about now? Am I in the presence of enemies?"

"Assuredly, master," Gundara said. "There are enemies all around you. So many I can't single anyone out in particular. Right now they seem afraid to do more than hate you. My advice, master, is to be as careful as you can."

"What about Iraj?" Safar asked. "What about the king? Is he my enemy?"

"No," the Favorite answered. "But he's a danger to you. All kings are. Beware of kings, master, is the best advice I can give you."

"And what of the woman Leiria?" Safar asked. "Does she mean well, or ill?"

"I'm too weak and her thoughts too confusing to say, master," Gundara answered. "When she's with you, she adores you. But when she's near the king, she adores *him*. All I can tell you is don't trust her . . . and keep her close."

Safar hid his disappointment. He'd hoped to get more from the little Favorite.

"Is there anything I can do for you?" he asked. "Anything at all to speed your recovery?"

"Rest, master," Gundara said. "That's all we need and that's all that can be done. We'll be better by and by."

Safar thought, "by and by" could mean a hundred years to a Favorite. He hoped that wasn't the case.

He started to make a motion to send Gundara back into the stone.

"Wait, master," Gundara said. "I almost forgot something."

The Favorite made a gesture and a small object appeared in his hand. He gestured again and the object plopped into Safar's palm, growing before his eyes.

It was a thin, battered old book bound in leather.

"Nerisa and I stole this from Umurhan's library," Gundara said. "She gave it to me to hold for you."

Safar looked closer. He caught his breath. On the cover, in worn gold leaf, was a familiar symbol.

"It's Lord Asper's book," Gundara said. "The one you were looking for." Then he vanished into the stone.

Fingers trembling, Safar opened the book. It took him a few moments to translate the scratchings. Then the words jumped out as if they were alive:

> *"Long, long have I bewailed this world.*
> *Long, long have I mourned our fates.*
> *Swords unsheathed, banners unfurled,*
> *Charge the ramparts fired with hate.*
> *'Slay the humans!' we all cried.*
> *'Drive the devils from our lands!'*
> *I shouted the loudest, but I shouted a lie.*
> *I feared to tell them all were damned!*
> *Demon and human from a single womb,*
> *Bound for Hadin where once I spied*
> *A common death and a common tomb . . ."*

Safar grunted in frustration. Insects had destroyed the rest of the page.

He flipped the leaves. A few were damaged, most were not, but the rest of the book seemed to consist of magical formulas and scribbled notes, with other bits of poetry here and there. It would take much time to decipher the demon wizard's formulas and notes. But at least he'd finally found something—or someone—to point the way.

He thought of Nerisa. Actually, she'd never been far from his mind. Not a day passed when her face, with its huge sad eyes and crooked little grin, didn't rise up to haunt him. He smiled, thinking this book—Asper's book—was her final gift to him.

Outside his room he heard Leiria approach. He put the book away.

Poor Leiria, he thought. Two dead women for rivals, instead of one.

*   *   *

The army marched a week later, Iraj at its head and Safar at his side. Sampitay's citizens turned out for the march, lining the main road and shouting praises and well wishes to the Good King Protarus.

Not long after another city fell, adding to the jewels in his crown. Iraj dealt with this city like Sampitay, following Safar's advice on the treatment of its citizens and the manner of government. A month went by, a month filled with conquests. Some were bloody, some were not.

Then winter came and Iraj's army took up camp. There was plenty of fuel for fire and plenty of food and drink. Messengers came and went, caravans crept over the snow, carrying gold from the tax gatherers to fill Iraj's treasure house.

But the king was moody, pacing the grounds and staring out across the distance at the Gods' Divide, cursing all the cold days that remained until spring.

And he swore to his friend and Grand Wazier, Lord Safar Timura, that he would march for the mountains when the first green buds burst from the ground.

PART FOUR
The Demon Wars

CHAPTER TWENTY ONE
THE INVASION BEGINS

It was the largest military gathering in the history of Esmir.

A demon army—half-a-million strong—formed up along the edges of the Forbidden Desert, armor glowing in the pale spring sun. It looked like an enormous dragon with glittering scales and outstretched wings, poised to take flight to ravage the human lands. Whole forests of spears, pikes and archers formed its body. Huge baggage trains of arms and supplies made its tail. Trumpeting elephants and snarling cavalry mounts, mixed with the rattle of weapons and the shrieks of campfollowers gave it a voice.

Forming its head were ten thousand mounted troops, commanded by Crown Prince Luka.

It was an elite force, composed of the finest young demons in the land. All were of noble blood and all were anxious to shed that blood for Gods and King. They'd been whipped into a fighting frenzy and were impatient for the signal launching them across the desert. They grumbled loudly at any and all delays, gnashing their fangs and casting anxious yellow eyes at their adored Crown Prince, who was at the moment conferring with his father, King Manacia, and his Chief Wazier, Lord Fari.

The prince, pretending to be completely absorbed by his father's final words before the campaign began, heard their grumbling and hated them for it.

He couldn't imagine why they were so anxious to rush off to meet their Makers. The prince didn't care if they all died the most horrible of deaths. What he objected to strongly was he was expected to share their fates. He thought, they're all so inbred you could poke out both eyes with a single talon. They're all balls and no brains. They had thick necks with small heads, whose only purpose—as far as Luka could determine—was to carry a helmet. Why oh why, do the gods hate me so?

"The first part of the campaign rests squarely on you, my son," King Manacia was saying.

"Pardon, Majesty?" Luka said. "I'm sorry, but I'm finding it difficult to concentrate. I confess I was dreaming of the victories my troops and I will lay at your feet once we are in the humanlands."

Manacia exposed his fangs in a proud grin. "What a fighting prince I have for a son, Fari," the king said to his Chief Wazier. "He's so anxious to be off slaying humans he's barely heard a word I said."

Fari bobbed his head, old snout wrinkling into a smile. "Indeed, Your Highness," Fari said, putting claws to chest as he spoke and then adding one his favorite stock phrases: "Prince Luka is an example to us all."

Luka caught the gleam of amusement in the ancient demon's eyes. Fari could read his heart and was delighted at the prince's predicament. You old bastard, Luka thought. I swear I'll live just to spite you. No matter what it takes I'll survive to piss on your grave and shit on my father's.

"It's his mother's hot blood in him," Manacia said. Then, to Luka, "Did I ever tell you about the time your dear lamented mother accused me of raping her?"

"I don't believe you did, Majesty," the prince lied. "I'd be most anxious to hear that tale."

Manacia burst out laughing at the memory. "It was after she tried to stab me and I had to tie her down," he chortled. "She . . . She . . ."

The king broke off, calming himself. He wiped an eye and resettled his crown, which had been shaken over one ear from his laughter.

"Never mind," Manacia said. "We have more important business at claw. I'll save the tale for some night in the future when we're all gathered about a good campfire, sharing a roasted human haunch."

He jabbed at a map, drawing their attention back to the final planning session.

"I want you to cross the desert just as quickly as you can, Luka," the king said. "Ride like the winds. Don't stop for anything. And when you're on the other side I want you to secure a basecamp.

"Give the area a good scrub, mind you. If you see humans, kill them. In fact, it would be best if you scouted out a good fifty miles around the camp. Destroy any settlements you find and make sure no humans escape to spread the news of our invasion. We want to retain the element of surprise as long as we can.

"Once I have my army set and the supply lines secured, we'll roll over them like an eight-beast chariot run amok in the market place. Within six months I predict we'll be at the sea, enjoying a good fish dinner."

Luka bowed. "And it will be my great honor, Majesty," he said, "to cook your meal with my own claws." But he thought, If I have the chance I'll stuff it so full of poison it'll make your scales fall off, you filthy old coward, you.

Manacia rolled up the map and handed it to an obsequious aide, who dropped to his knees and knocked his bony forehead on the rocky ground before withdrawing in a backwards crawl.

"There's only the casting of the bones remaining, Fari," he said. "Then I'll give the signal for the march to begin. Assuming all bodes well, of course."

He glowered at the wizard when he said the last, making it quite obvious what would happen to Fari if the casting did not meet his liking.

"Never fear, Your Highness," Fari said, drawing his casting case from his sleeve. "I ordered special bones made up for this historic moment. That human we used for the last divining session proved so lucky I kept back the knuckles of his dexter hand when we disposed of his corpse."

Fari motioned and two slaves crawled over to unroll a small carpet at his feet. The carpet was night black, with the Star Houses picked out in silver.

He took an ivory cup from his casting case and a small drawstring bag made of silk. He untied the string and upended the sack. The knuckle bones made a dry rattling sound as they fell into the cup. He shook the cup and it was like the buzz of a desert viper as the bones swirled about.

And Fari intoned:

> *"Unloosen thy secrets, let us behold*
> *What tale the Gods will tell of us*
> *When these blessed events unfold."*

He cast the bones on the carpet. King, prince and wizard leaned over to study the result.

"What's this?" Manacia said, delight in his eyes. "They've fallen in a pattern across the Demon Moon." He looked up at the wizard. "I believe the Demon Moon is due to rise soon, isn't it, Fari?"

"Indeed it is, Your Highness," Fari said, bobbing his head. "The Star Gazers tell us it appears but once every thousand years. And they predict that cycle is about to repeat itself.

"This casting brings us good news, Your Highness, as you can see for yourself."

He pointed a talon. "And look here, one knuckle has fallen on a comet. The Demon Moon and the Comet, as Your Highness well knows, is the sign of Alisarrian."

Manacia slapped his thigh in delight. "The Conqueror, himself!" he exclaimed. "Except this time it'll be a demon, not a devil human, who does the conquering!"

Fari gave a mental sigh of relief. He would have lied, if he'd dared, to make this casting come out as the king wanted. But Manacia was the most powerful wizard in the demonlands. He could read a casting as well, if not better, than any of his royal wizards. Such things bored him, however, and he left it up to his magical minions to study bones and entrails for some signpost of the future.

Overcome by emotion, Manacia rose and threw his arms around the Crown Prince. "The gods are with us, my son," he said, embracing Luka. "Let their will guide you on this holy mission."

Luka returned the embrace awkwardly, wishing mightily for a dagger to plunge into his father's back.

"I will do my best, Majesty," he said.

Manacia drew back. "Mount up, my son," he commanded, "and I will give the signal."

Luka bowed low, then strode over to his steed, a huge mailed beast with a long graceful neck, glistening fangs and polished claws. As the prince tried to mount, the beast took a swipe at him with one of those claws. Without breaking stride the prince dodged the claw and vaulted into the saddle, raking the beast with his spurs so hard he drew blood.

The beast shrieked and reared back, pawing the air.

"Good show!" Manacia shouted to his son. "Nothing like a spirited mount to carry one to victory."

Luka was struggling to keep his seat, but he covered this indignity by again raking the beast with his spurs.

"To victory!" he cried, drawing his sword and waving it in the air.

His warriors echoed the cry, roaring in unison. "TO VICTORY!"

Luka pressed the sword against his mount's neck, his next words covered by shouts pouring from ten thousand demon throats. "Get your claws on the ground, you louse-bitten piece of slime," he said, "or I'll cut your throat."

The beast understood and dropped back to earth as agilely as a house cat.

Luka booted his mount to the command point in front of his demon force.

Again he shouted, "To victory!"

"TO VICTORY!" they roared, drawing their own swords and waving them madly in the air.

"The prince is going too far," Manacia complained to Fari under his breath. "This is my moment, not his."

Fari shook his head, hiding his pleasure at this criticism of his enemy. "Just high spirits, I'm sure, Your Highness," he said. "I'm certain it wasn't intended."

"Maybe so, maybe so," Manacia grumbled. "But we'd better hurry it up just the same."

Fari signaled and demon slaves jabbed at the king's great white elephant. It lumbered forward, grand howdah lurching back and forth. More jabs brought it to its knees and the king was hoisted up, panting a little and wondering if perhaps he was letting himself become too fat.

Never mind that, he thought as took his place in the howdah. You'll be slim enough when this campaign is over.

He signaled. Trumpets blared, drums rolled and the whole army came to attention with a great rattling of armor and weapons. A slight pause followed, just a bit longer than good drama warranted.

"For the gods' sake, Fari," Manacia shouted down from the elephant, "cast the damned spell!"

Fari broke out of a delightful reverie in which Manacia and Luka were shrieking and turning on a spit over a slow fire.

"Immediately, Your Highness," he called back.

He threw a glass globe to the ground. It shattered, spilling a thick yellow liquid across the stone. The liquid began to bubble, then to smoke. A sulfurous cloud boiled up, rising high into the sky.

Then the cloud took on the shape of a gigantic King Manacia. Huge lips parted, baring fangs of tremendous length.

"ONWARD, MY FIENDS, ONWARD!" roared the gigantic Manacia. "FOR THE GODS AND THE KING!"

"FOR THE GODS AND THE KING!" a half a million voices shouted in reply.

The whole army lurched forward, shattering the air with war cries.

The elephant handlers had to give the king's animal several sharp jabs to get it moving fast enough so Manacia wasn't overrun. But in a few minutes all clumsiness was gone and the massive army clattered out onto the Forbidden Desert, an immense juggernaut aimed at the humanlands.

Far out in front Luka and his ten thousand elite were speeding over the badlands, battle cries ululating through the thin air. Within moments they'd reached the high dunes that marked the horizon's edge.

Then they vanished from view.

※   ※   ※

Despite his inner feelings, Luka was an able commander. Although he drove his fiends hard, he drove himself even harder and it wasn't long before the ten thousand thundered out of the Forbidden Desert and entered the humanlands.

All were weary from the mad dash, but Luka gave them no time for respite. He quickly found a likely campsite for his father's army. It was nestled among gentle hills and centered at what had once been Badawi's farm. There was nothing remaining of that farm, thanks to Sarn and his bandit horde, except a few charred timbers and a half-a-dozen caved-in roasting pits where Badawi's family and livestock had been cooked and eaten.

Luka sent out patrols to scout the region, but other than a few ragged families huddled in homes made of sun dried mud bricks, there were no human groups of any significance to be found. Partly this was because few dared to settle so close to the Forbidden Desert. Mostly it was because Sarn had gone about his duties enthusiastically, wiping out any of the small settlements he'd found. Luka didn't know this and so he concluded it was superstition alone that had done the work.

Several weeks passed and there was still no sign of Manacia and the main army. Luka pressed a few trusted human slaves into service, sending them deeper into the humanlands to spy out and map the region. Before they'd left he'd promised them rich rewards for success and reminded them he had their families back in Zanzair as hostages if they betrayed him.

"I'll flay every babe you call your own," he warned. "I'll rip off the limbs of your women and stake out their still-living bodies on ant mounds."

They took his words to heart and by the time the first elements of Manacia's gigantic army hove into view, Luka had maps and detailed intelligence covering hundreds of square miles.

"You certainly took a lot on yourself," Manacia grumbled when Luka showed him the fruits of his efforts.

The king was tired and dirty from his long ordeal. The slowness of the pace, the constant bawling of the animals and the absence of certain creature comforts vital to a king's well-being had made his anger swell like a boil. Luka was careful not to prick it.

Luka apologized profusely, saying, "I'm sorry, Majesty. There's no excuse for my behavior. I promise I won't let it happen again."

Manacia was soothed, although he complained the time would have been better spent making the royal camp more comfortable. When he'd grumbled himself out he took a closer look at the maps and reports his son had gathered.

"I suppose these will be of *some* use to us," he allowed. One of the maps he was studying was a rough eagle's view of all the major hamlets and towns from the Forbidden Desert clear to the great human city called Caspan. "I'll have the scribes make copies and pass them out to my generals. I doubt we can rely on them too greatly, but there's no sense wasting effort well-meant."

"Yes, Majesty. You are too kind, Majesty," Luka murmured.

Meanwhile, he was thinking, You misbegotten still-birth of a camel, I've just given you the keys to the whole damned thing. But you won't admit it, you old fraud. Getting praise from you is like pulling fangs. Well, keep your praise. It's your throne I want.

You'd better watch your back, you foul old fiend, because I fully intend to take that crown away from you and mount your head on the gates of Zanzair.

*   *   *

The demon juggernaut swept along the Gods' Divide, ravaging any force that dared stand in its way.

Mostly the humans were stricken with such terror at the sight of the demon hordes they surrendered on the spot. Believing the gods had abandoned them, they gave themselves up meekly, accepting any terms King Manacia demanded.

Some he slew, some he enslaved, but mostly he followed the practices that had won him a demon empire. If the humans threw down their arms without a fight he tended to be merciful. He let the rulers keep their posts and made them swear fealty to him, recognizing him as the one true monarch—the King of Kings—Master of Esmir; lord of all humans and demons alike.

He sealed them to their oath by requiring them to sign documents in their own blood, telling them the documents would always be by his side and if they betrayed him he would cast a spell that would let loose a voracious worm in their guts.

Manacia left only a small garrison force at each place he took, relying on fear and sorcery to keep his human subjects contrite.

First he sent his sniffers out to find and kill any human with magical talent.

Then he had small temples erected at the key cities and hamlets, with a demon wizard in charge of each edifice. Portable spell machines were installed in the temples, spewing out spells by the hour meant to keep the populace fearful and humble and strike terror in the hearts of any outside enemy who might attempt to retake the city.

Once he'd secured the spine of the humanlands—the great mountain range called the Gods' Divide—he struck toward Caspan.

That region proved more difficult. The cities were much larger as were the armies who defended them. He also no longer had the element of surprise. The human monarchs and generals he encountered swallowed their terror and fought grimly to halt the demon invasion.

The enemy generals conscripted everyone of fighting age, hurling the ragged, weeping hordes before Manacia's forces. Most of the humans died, but in dying they slowed Manacia's drive enough so the professionals could attack the weak points. True, ten humans might fall for every demon. But Manacia had no way of replacing his losses.

Manacia began losing fiends at an alarming rate. Of the half-a-million he started with, less than four hundred thousand remained when he approached the gates of Caspan.

Crown Prince Luka's shock troops had suffered the most. When the human hordes charged out to meet him he had only five thousand mounted fiends to meet that charge.

"This is it," Luka thought as he led his fiends into the battle. "This is when I die."

The humans were horrid things, ugly as the devils from the Hells. Flat faces, piggy little eyes and filthy little mouths that screamed hate and fury as they fought.

They had good armor, sturdy weapons and were mounted on huge mailed warhorses that reared up to fight the demon steeds with iron-tipped feet. It was hoof against claw, talon against hand, swords and axes flailing about at close quarters, blood spraying everywhere.

Archers and slingmen sent shower after shower of missiles into the melee, not caring who fell—friend or foe—so long as the demons were kept from the gates.

Two horsemen crowded Luka from either side. A pikeman reared up in front of him. His mount slashed at the pikeman, disemboweling him. But as he died he plunged forward, burying his pike into the beast's shoulder. The animal screamed in pain, but kept its feet. Luka swung left, sword biting through human mail and finding flesh. His opponent toppled from his horse, but before Luka could turn to meet the other he felt a sharp pain in his side.

The human had struck first.

Howling in agony, Luka slashed at the man with sword. In a haze he saw blood gout, feared it was his own, then he saw the human fall and felt relief rush in to dull his pain.

His mount staggered and Luka leaped off moments before it crashed to the ground. Now he was standing in the middle of plunging horses and demon beasts, dodging blows from every side. He saw one of his fiends topple from his mount and Luka vaulted into the saddle and grabbed the reins.

"Victory!" he bellowed. "For the gods and the king!"

His cry rallied his soldiers and they returned his shout—*"Victory! For the gods and the king!"*

They charged the humans with spirits renewed, smashing and slashing them down.

Finally, the humans broke, fleeing through the gates.

Luka and his fiends pursued them, hacking their way through the gates' defenders.

Suddenly there was no one to kill anymore. Luka and his soldiers found themselves in a large square, panting and heaving and bleeding from many wounds.

Behind him he heard trumpets sound.

His father's trumpets.

Then there was a great roar of demon voices and a sea of Manacia's soldiers poured through the gates.

Rising out their midst was his father's royal elephant. The huge animal moved smoothly across the square to Luka.

Manacia grinned down at him from the howdah, fangs displayed in full gleam.

"Thank the gods you are still with us, my son," he shouted. "I saw you fall and feared for the worst."

Luka bowed, fighting not to show pain.

"Caspan is yours, Majesty!" he cried. "It is my gift to you, and demon history!"

And he thought, this was for you, Mother, for you!

And Manacia thought, how dare he make a gift of what is already mine? Then he remembered the day when he'd said something similar to his own father.

The next time Luka falls, he thought, I must make certain he doesn't rise again.

Manacia was a dutiful king, a hard working king, and he had at least twenty other sons to take Luka's place.

I'd best choose the youngest to succeed him as heir to my throne, Manacia thought. Princes grow up so quickly these days.

Why, I was nearly thirty winters old before I slew *my* father.

*   *   *

"Coralean is desolate," the caravan master said. "He is a coin clipped of its worth. A sway-backed camel with more fleas than spirit.

"It seems it is Coralean's fate that each time he greets you, my king, whom I dare call friend, that he drags demons, or news of demons, into your highness' august presence."

"Come now, Coralean," Iraj protested, "I'm not one of those city-bred despots who forgets his friends soon as he wins the throne. And I'm certainly not one to harm the messenger who brings ill tidings.

"Isn't that right, Safar?"

Safar stirred in his seat—a smaller version of Iraj's traveling throne.

"Actually," he deadpanned, "Iraj had his royal torturers put out the eyes and slit the tongue of the last fellow who was in here babbling about demons."

Iraj frowned. "What a thing to say, Safar," he protested, "I gave the man a purse of gold. Don't you re—" he broke off, laughing. "You're joking again," he said.

Then, to the caravan master, "You see how it is, Coralean? My friends are always making jests at my expense!"

"King Protarus speaks the truth," Safar said. "You'll notice I still have both my eyes and a whole tongue, and yet I bring him bad news daily."

He gestured at the empty main room of the command tent. "Why, our king is so grand a monarch he even permits his friends to use his common name in private.

"Isn't that so, Iraj?"

More laughter from the king. "Don't pay any attention to him, Coralean," he advised. "Safar is just punishing me for ignoring his advice."

He leaned out from his throne. "I had to let my men sack the last city we took," he said. "I was short of gold and they hadn't been paid all winter. Safar was opposed to the sacking. He said it was bad business."

Coralean's merchant smile lit the dim room. "An honest dispute among right-thinking men," he said. "One looks at future profits. The other at more immediate concerns. There is no right or wrong in such a disagreement."

He bowed his craggy head in Iraj's direction, saying, "The pity should go to the master, who must torment himself for being forced to ignore his advisors and act according to his best judgment."

The look of pleasure on Iraj's face made Safar fully appreciate why Coralean had been so successful in his long and dangerous career. Despite his common man pretense, Iraj had proven to be a prickly monarch. His dark moods had made the winter long. Then spring had brought the first news of the demon invasion and had plunged him deeper into depression. Iraj had allowed the first city he'd taken to be sacked not to please his men, but to vent his rage.

"What a lucky man I am to have two such loyal friends," Iraj said. "One uses wise and well-put phrases to guide me, the other amusing barbs—which also serve to remind me I am only human."

Don't forget money and magic, Safar thought. We bring you that as well.

Safar had created and cast his first battle spell to help Iraj take the city he later sacked. Coralean, that canny old merchant, had funded Iraj's ambitions from the start. He'd been handsomely rewarded with exclusive trading contracts.

You haven't done so badly either, Safar chided himself. In the short time he'd been at Iraj's side Safar had become a wealthy man by anyone's measurement. As Grand Wazier he had been given vast tracts of land and chests of rare gems and metals.

"So tell us your news, my friend," Iraj said to Coralean. "Don't spare my feelings. I'm braced for the worst."

"Caspan has fallen," Coralean said.

Coming from such a normally loquacious man, his brevity was a shock. Iraj flinched, then tried to cover his concern.

Fingers rapping on the arm of his throne gave him away. "I see. Well, we were expecting that. Weren't we Safar?"

Safar nodded. They'd heard rumors of Manacia's drive toward Caspan and he'd made a castings that did not bode well for the city's defenders.

"Coralean barely escaped with his life," the caravan master said. "I sent my wives into hiding and fled the city just in time."

He went on to describe the series of battles that led to the taking of Caspan. Trying to add a note of cheer he went into some detail on the great losses Manacia had suffered in the campaign.

But Iraj kept rapping his fingers against wood. "So few," he murmured. "I'd hoped he would have suffered more."

He looked up at Coralean. "I suppose it won't be long before he comes over the mountains," he said.

"I fear so," Coralean said. "The last I heard he was preparing his army and searching for the route to Kyrania."

The mention of Kyrania was a heavy spear aimed at Safar's heart. Intentional or not, Safar bent a closer ear to what Coralean had to say.

"A caravan master's life isn't worth a copper on that side of the Gods' Divide," Coralean said. "Many of my brother merchants have been seized and tortured for the information. Luckily the demons know so little of human affairs they keep seizing the wrong men.

"But they only need one success and Manacia's army will be on the march to Kyrania."

Iraj was silent for a time; fingers rap, rap, rapping. Then he said to Coralean, voice so low he could barely be heard, "Leave us for a time, my friend. I must speak with my brother."

The caravan master bowed, murmured a few kind words and departed.

Soon as he was gone Iraj turned to Safar, face full of anguish. "You said I would be king of kings!" he cried.

"And you will," Safar replied.

"Are you certain your talent isn't playing you false?" Iraj demanded. "Am I a fool, bound to a fool's vision?"

"Let me speak plainly," Safar said. "There's no question that you are a fool. Who else but a fool would want to be king of Esmir? But fool or not, that is your destiny."

"Beware!" Iraj snapped. "I'm in no mood for insults, friendly though they may be."

"If you don't want to hear the truth," Safar said, "then command my silence."

"I've given you power," Iraj said.

"Take it back," Safar replied. "It's more of a burden than I care to shoulder."

"I've made you rich," Iraj pointed out.

"In Kyrania," Safar said, "wealth is a bountiful harvest that all share.

Iraj grew angry. "Are you saying that in your view all I've given you is worthless?"

Taking a lesson from Coralean, Safar replied, "Not your friendship. I value that most highly, Iraj Protarus."

Iraj was mollified. His finger rapping ceased. "What should I do, brother?" he asked. "How do I achieve what your vision foretold?"

"Why don't we look at the problem a different way?" Safar said. "Why don't we turn it about and see if luck's barren goat will still give milk?"

"I'm listening," Iraj said.

"When you started out your greatest difficulty was a family feud," Safar said. "An uncle opposed your rightful claim to leadership. A few of your kin were greedy enough to support that uncle. But most—out of long family feelings and tradition—supported you."

"True enough," Iraj said. "Although it was more complicated than that."

"To counter that natural feeling," Safar continued, "your uncle went to an outsider. A man hated by all in your family."

"It gave him a temporary advantage," Iraj said, "but in the end it was a help to me. After a few successes, my family rallied to me."

"So your uncle's alliance with an enemy," Safar said, "was his downfall."

Iraj thought for a moment, then nodded. "Yes. That is so."

"There you have it," Safar said. "The presence of a hated outsider gave you power to rally your clan. Afterwards, you put clan together with clan to take to the road as a conqueror.

"But to those people *you* were the outsider. The barbarian from the Plains of Jaspar.

"They opposed you, fought you, dared to call you a greedy upstart, instead of as the savior of all Esmir. Which is how you see yourself."

"But I am," Iraj said. "You saw it in the vision."

Safar didn't say he'd never seen such a thing. In the vision Iraj had been a conquering king perched on a white elephant, leading his army toward Zanzair. Whether he was a savior or not was another matter.

"Good," Safar said. "I'm glad you believe that. Because that is how you will defeat Manacia."

Iraj's expression was puzzled. He didn't understand.

"The whole human world fears the demons," Safar said. "Use that fear against Manacia. Raise your standard, claim all humankind as your clan . . . and strike him down.

"Before winter set in you faced the prospect of many years of battle to claim Caspan as your realm. Manacia has done your work in less than a season.

"Defeat him and you have the north."

Iraj brightened. "And the demonlands," he pointed out. "I'll have them as well."

"First we have to cross the Forbidden Desert," Safar cautioned.

Iraj gave a cheery wave. "You mean the curse? Hells, I was never worried about that. You'll figure it out when we get there.

"Besides, if Manacia can do it, so can you."

"I'm glad you still have confidence in me," Safar said, again taking a lesson from Coralean and letting a measure of humility leak through.

"As I see it," Safar continued, "our greatest danger will be Manacia's magic. It's well know that demons are much more powerful sorcerers than humans."

"An overblown reputation, as far I'm concerned," Iraj scoffed, gaining confidence by the minute. "I saw you bring down an avalanche on a whole pack of them, remember?"

Safar had few delusions about himself. He'd spent the winter testing his powers and at first had been amazed at the newly possible. But in reading the Book of Asper, the demon wizard, he saw glimmerings of a power that might be beyond him.

"I caught them by surprise," Safar said. "Besides, it was only a score or more we were faced with. Not a whole demon army—with a legion of wizards to support them."

"You just worry about Manacia's wizards, Safar," Iraj replied. "I'll take care of his damned army."

*   *   *

Worry is not such an easy thing to limit. The mind may decree borders, but once erected those borders are immediately beset by fears both large and small. Nights become sleepless landscapes littered with innumerable difficulties and imagined pitfalls threatening the mightiest of beings. Large things may seem insurmountable mountains during those torturous hours when others sleep. Small things may suddenly erupt into fears rivaling those mountains.

In the north, King Manacia consolidated his army and searched for the route over the Gods' Divide. But his nights were haunted by imagined plots involving his son, Prince Luka. Then word filtered through of a mighty human king with flowing hair and beard of gold. This monarch—King Iraj Protarus—bore the standard of Alisarrian and was rousing the populace to oppose Manacia and destroy his long cherished dreams of empire.

Sitting at the right hand of that king, it was said, was a human wizard so powerful he was the equal of any demon lord of sorcery. The wizard, Safar Timura, had eyes as blue as the sunlit heavens.

When Manacia slept at all he was troubled by nightmares in which his son suddenly turned into a human with a golden beard and sky blue eyes. In this nightmare Manacia would be forced to embrace his son and heir before his court, knowing full well a dagger would be thrust into his back.

In the south, King Protarus massed his forces and toured his realm, spreading the news of the demon invasion. He gave thundering speeches, decrying the atrocities committed by the demons—some real, some created. He was a handsome young prince, a compelling speaker who quickly made his subjects forget the atrocities he had committed himself in winning his kingdom. People rushed to support him, swelling his armies, crying for revenge against the demon invaders.

But Iraj's nights were as sleepless as Manacia's.

What if Safar was wrong? What if he were not as great a seer as Iraj believed? And what if his friend was not truly his friend? If he were as powerful a wizard as Iraj believed, might he not seize the throne of Esmir as soon as Iraj had won it? And if not, why not? Which brought him back to the original worry that Safar was so weak Iraj was a fool to rely on him.

Safar was no king, which gave him ample reason to harbor fears equal to both monarchs combined.

If Iraj believed Safar was in the way he'd betray him with barely a thought. Safar wondered about the vision in which he'd seen Iraj's victorious march on Zanzair. What if that part were true, but in reality it was Safar's ghost who'd witnessed it? He'd certainly felt like a spirit during the vision. What if his dreamcatcher self had slipped past the part where Safar was betrayed and slain by his blood brother? It troubled him he'd never been able to see past that moment when Iraj's armies marched on Zanzair. And what of the other vision—the vision of Hadin—in which all was for naught and the world was rushing toward its end?

Then there was the greatest fear of all.

For either king—Manacia or Protarus—the key was Kyrania.

What if the two monarchs met in battle in the High Caravans?

What if Safar's valley and everyone he loved—mother, father, sisters, friends—were destroyed in that confrontation?

After a time this worried Safar even more than the destruction of the world itself.

It was impossible to imagine the last.

But frighteningly easy to see the first.

In the end it was fear for Kyrania that drove Safar. He was willing to dare anything to save it.

CHAPTER TWENTY TWO

THE DEMON FEAST

Safar crouched in the flowered peaks above Kyrania. It was early summer, the rains had been sweet, the heavens kind, and his valley was a misty shimmer beneath the pale morning sun. The fields were emerald green, the lake was a great blue diamond fed by springs flowing down the mountains in a silvery pilgrimage to the Goddess Felakia.

"So this is your home," Leiria said in awe. "I've never seen anything so beautiful. It's like a dream."

Safar motioned for silence. His magical self had arrowed past Leiria's dream and found a nightmare. In his innermost pocket the stone idol blistered warning.

He signaled to the men—fifty of Iraj's finest mounted warriors. They dismounted, positioned feed bags to silence their horses and quickly shifted their gear to ready themselves for battle.

Leiria raised an eyebrow. "What's wrong?"

"Watch," Safar said.

He plucked a glass pellet from his pouch and hurled it to the ground. It shattered and pale green smoke whooshed up, swirling to the height of a knee. First a landscape, then figures toiling in that landscape, took form in the smoke. There were at least two score of them—miniature humans moving through the fields of Kyrania. They seemed agonized, smoke forms twisting and leaping in pain. Larger columns of smoke funneled up, hardening into the givers of that pain. They were creatures of snouted fangs and taloned claws.

Leiria caught her breath. "Demons!"

Safar didn't answer. He gestured and the smoke image vanished. He slumped onto the boulder, so mournful it was all Leiria could do not to console him—branding herself as a weakling in the eyes of her fellow soldiers.

"This changes everything," she said, colder than she'd intended. "We'd best return immediately and tell the king the demons have seized Kyrania."

Safar nodded absently. His thoughts were barely of this world. He was imagining the terrors his family and friends were suffering.

Safar had intended to warn his people of the coming peril, then set up shields to confuse the demons if and when they attacked through the pass. Iraj was even now gathering a force of shock troops to be rushed in to fill the gap until his main army had time to arrive. Safar had convinced Iraj even greater haste must be made—that he should go out in advance of the troops and prepare the way. Now it seemed his mission to Kyrania, which had required much cajolement to win Iraj's approval, was a failure before it started.

"You're right," he replied, mechanical as a clockwork toy. "We must inform the king."

Leiria winced at his pain. But she said nothing. She walked back to the men to order a withdrawal. It would be done quickly, but silently. Weapons and gear were strapped down so they wouldn't rattle. Rags stuffed with brush were tied onto the horses' hooves so all noise would be pillowed.

When all was ready Leiria returned to say it was time to go. She touched him and he suddenly came back to life.

"I must see for myself," he said.

"You can't," Leiria protested. "We might be discovered."

Safar insisted. He made it clear the only way he'd leave now was if he were bound and gagged and tied to the back of a horse.

Everyone was terrified of committing such an indignity to Lord Timura, the Grand Wazier. But they were equally as terrified of his plan.

"The king will have our heads if you're captured," Leiria protested.

"No he won't," Safar said. "Here. I'll make sure of it."

He scrawled a hasty message to Iraj. No one was to be held accountable for his actions. He added a brief report on what he'd seen so far and what should be done if he didn't return. The message was placed in the care of Rapton, the young lieutenant who commanded the warriors. Strict orders were given. If Safar and Leiria—who insisted on accompanying him—did not return by dusk Rapton and the troops were to make all speed to Sampitay—where Iraj and his court were currently ensconced—and deliver the news.

When he was done Safar called for silence. He prepared Leiria and himself, coating their clothes and skin with a smoky herb that would confound sensitive demon noses. He made a spell to shield their human auras from demon wizards. Last of all he hauled out the stone turtle and alerted Gundara to keep watch for danger.

The little Favorite and his twin, Gundaree, were back to normal again. Drawing inspiration from Lord Asper's book, Safar had devised a healing program to hasten their recovery—special powders mixed with warm honey and wine. For two weeks the stone idol had rested in that potion, which Safar refreshed daily. At first nothing had changed. If anything the faint buzz of life had grown fainter.

Then one morning Safar awakened to a familiar—"Shut up, shut up, shuuut upp!" And he knew things were well again in the small world of the Favorites.

Safar turned to Leiria. "I know it's your habit to lead the way," he said.

"It's more than habit, my lord," she said. "It's my duty. I am your bodyguard. I must keep you safe."

"Yes, yes," he said, impatiently. "And you perform your duty well. But this time we have to change the order of things. I was raised here. I was once a boy roaming these hills. I know all the secret places boys know. I know all the secret paths boys favor.

"I want you to follow *me*. Keep close as you can. Walk in my tracks if possible. Do all I do. And nothing that I don't. Do you understand?"

Leiria swore she did and a few moments later they were hurrying down an old deer trail, so faint it might have been made by a population of mice.

They hadn't gone a hundred yards before Safar suddenly veered to the right and was gone.

Leiria nearly panicked, looking madly about for some sign of Safar. Then she saw where the leaves wavered and plunged after him. She heard him hiss before she saw him, jerking back just in time to avoid stepping on his heels. They traveled in silent tandem for a time, jumping onto to trails and jumping off again, veering left and then right and then straight ahead. But from the tension in her calves Leiria could tell the general direction was downward.

Down—to the broad lake and rich fields of Kyrania.

*   *   *

Khadji Timura slipped his trowel into the claybed. He felt the blade grate through sand and gravel and he pushed it in a little deeper. He lifted the load up, hiding his distaste at the poor quality of the clay and all the trash it contained, and dumped it into the waiting bucket.

"Hurry up, old man," the demon said. "I'm weary."

"Forgive me, master," Khadji said. "I am old, as you have repeatedly reminded me this entire day, and my joints give me pain. If I had help, which you have wisely informed me is not possible, I could work more quickly."

The demon, whose name was Trin, scowled at Safar's father, saying, "You think because you are human and demons can't read human expressions that I don't realize you're mocking me."

He swatted Khadji with his club. Khadji grunted and nearly fell. He steadied himself with a hand and blinked away tears that were more from humiliation than pain. Trin was experienced at such things. He knew how to rap a human skull with just enough force to gain their attention, but not so hard they'd be incapacitated.

"You are probably cursing me and your fate right now," Trin said. "This is good. It teaches you how you stand with me. I have better things to do than spend my days here in the damp and cold watching you dig up clay. If I had my way I'd empty your brains from your skull and join my mates in some spirited drinking."

"You're right, exalted one," Khadji said. He'd recovered and was rising, full bucket in hand. "And I thank you for the reminder of what a fortunate person I am."

"Why, what would become of me and family if your superiors weren't so wise? What clever fiends they are. I've often remarked on it to Myrna, my wife."

"Good Timura pottery equals much gold on the marketplace. Gold your king requires to fight his wars."

Trin snorted. "A pot's a pot, as far as I'm concerned," he said. "You put something in it. And you empty it out. I used to pinch them out by the dozen when I was young. Some broke when they were fired. Some didn't. Who cares? The clay costs nothing. And the fire only wants a little fuel."

"Who am I to quarrel with such an expert on pottery?" Khadji said.

"No one," Trin agreed. "I was a potter before I was a soldier. I know good work when I see it."

He looked at the bucket, then dug a tentative claw into its contents. "A little gritty, isn't it?" he said.

"All the beds are nearly worked out, master," the potter lied. The best clay was on the other side of Lake Felakia, snuggled in grit-free beds he had no intention of showing the demons. "This is the best we can do under the circumstances."

Khadji saw two figures steal out of the brush behind the demon. As if sensing their presence, the demon started to turn in that direction.

The potter lifted up the bucket to capture his attention.

"It only needs a little cleaning, exalted one," he said. "And if there are imperfections, why we'll cover them up with the glaze. Like you said, master, a pot's a pot. But when I put my name on it—Timura—there are plenty of fools at the marketplace who think the name is more important than actual quality."

"My father," Trin said, wiping a talon on Khadji's smock, "who was a potter of great renown, used to tell me the same thing."

"He sounds as wise a fiend as his son," Khadji said.

The demon glared at him. "Are you mocking me again, human?" He raised his club. "Are you?"

There was a thunk. The demon's yellow eyes suddenly widened and club fell from his hands. An arrow point protruded through his throat.

Trin pitched forward, quite dead.

Khadji upended the bucket on the corpse and spit.

"A pot's just a pot, is it?" he growled. Then he opened his arms to embrace Safar. "Welcome home, son," he said.

To Safar's immense embarrassment, Khadji started to weep.

"It's all right, father," he murmured, patting him uncomfortably. "It's all right."

*   *   *

"We'd heard about all the troubles in Esmir," his father said, sipping from the mug of trail wine. "Droughts and plagues and wars. But it's always been so in the outside world. And although we worried, especially for you, Safar, we never thought those troubles would arrive to take up residence before our very hearths."

Leiria and the soldiers were gathered about Safar and his father, listening closely to the old potter's tale. Less than an hour had passed since the demon had been killed, his body hidden in the brush. The group was gathered in a safe place high above Kyrania. Guards were posted to give warning if anyone came.

"Not long ago Lord Coralean came this way," Khadji said, "and we heard the news of the demon invasion and capture of Caspan." He looked at Safar, eyes red-streaked, skin sagging from his long ordeal. "We all remembered the demons you and Iraj encountered up in the passes of The Bride And Six Maids."

Khadji sighed. "Lord Coralean was wrong, wasn't he, when he said they were only rogues who'd strayed into the humanlands?"

It was a question that didn't need answering. Safar refilled his father's cup. The old man took another sip of the restorative.

"Anyway, that's when we started worrying," he said. "It seemed only logical the demons would have to come through Kyrania to attack the other side. We've always been blessed by peace in these mountains. But now it seemed that peace would be no more.

"The Elders met. There was much talk of this and that, but it was mostly nonsense, for who among us had ever faced such a situation before? Coralean had promised us he would plead with King Protarus for help, but we didn't know if the help would come at all, much less in time. So we decided to mount our own defenses."

Khadji made a bitter laugh. "The lads drilled and trained and we rebuilt the walls of the old fort. But it was clear that although Kyranians can fight well enough, none of us have the killing instincts of a soldier." He glanced at Leiria and the others. "I hope you don't take offense," he said. "I was only speaking of professional training, not doubting the human kindness I'm sure is natural to you all."

"No offense given, or taken, Father Timura," Leiria said. "We know what you meant."

Khadji looked up a Safar, anguished. "In the end," he said, "there was no time for resistance. They took us in our beds. And then they rounded us up and put us all in that fort we'd labored so hard to rebuild. They killed some of us to set an example. They were humiliating deaths.

"They made us watch."

Khadji brushed away a tear. "I learned what it was to be a weak and selfish mortal," he said. "Much as I mourned the deaths of my friends, I'm ashamed to say I knew joy because I still lived. *And* your mother *and* your sisters."

He drained the cup, covering the mouth when Safar offered more.

"And Gubadan?" Safar asked.

"Gone," his father answered. "He was among the first. The demons have witch sniffers, you know. Gubadan didn't have much magic. But it was enough for them to find him out."

He touched Safar's hand, tentatively, as if amazed his son wasn't a ghost. "It's a good thing you weren't here, son," he said. "We've all heard what a great wizard you've become. They would have found you out immediately."

"I'm surprised they let any of you live, Father Timura," Leiria said. "We have the gods to thank for that."

"Not the gods," Khadji said, "but a human traitor. And it isn't thanks we owe him, but all the curses we can manage."

Safar's eyes narrowed. "There was a human leading them?"

"Not leading, actually," his father answered. "Although they listen to his counsel with much respect. Apparently this human has powerful friends among the demons. Some even say he has the ear of Crown Prince Luka."

"Who is this man?" Safar demanded. "Do I know of him? Would I recognize his name."

"I believe so," Khadji answered. "He certainly knows you."

When he said the name Safar jumped as if he'd been stung.

*   *   *

Kalasariz strolled out of the Temple of Felakia into the warm sunlight. It was late afternoon and the atmosphere in the temple, which he'd turned into his quarters, had suddenly felt too close. So he'd left his scribe to complete the report to Prince Luka and ambled outside to refresh himself.

It was a day of sharp colors and deep shadows. The sun was spun gold, the clouds pure silver, the lake and sky startling blue. He filled his lungs with air, which was heavy with the scent of blossoms. He breathed out, savoring the air's fruity aftertaste. A few birds sang a melody from the small grove down near the lake. Their song made Kalasariz smile.

Another delightful day in Kyrania, he thought. So different from the bustling, smoky squalor of Walaria. Kalasariz, who had spent his entire career eliminating surprise, was amazed at how his life had turned out. Turned upside down, actually, he thought. The only thing unsurprising was that he'd managed to land on his feet when the great emptying had begun. Kalasariz was an agile master of balance. Even his enemies would say that. He grinned—Especially his enemies!

Another bird joined the songfest at the grove. The chorus was quite compelling.

Kalasariz let his feet carry him toward the lake so he could enjoy the concert close up.

He supposed things had gotten rather . . . stressful . . . when King Protarus had shown up at the gates of Walaria. Not surprising, though. Kalasariz refused to accept that description of his feelings those many long months ago when panic raged all about him. He'd kept calm. Kept his footing. Formed his plan. And taken action.

He'd been rather . . . alarmed? No, no. Too strong a word. Disappointed, perhaps. Yes, he'd been disappointed when his carefully laid plan to join Protarus had failed. His secret messages and doctored files claiming friendship with Safar Timura had not found a receptive audience in King Protarus. At first he'd been . . .irritated. Not angry, but irritated. Kalasariz admired suspicion. It was a tool no worthy monarch should be without. But in his view Protarus had taken suspicion beyond reason.

So what if there were a few lies in Kalasariz' messages? He'd honestly intended to fulfill his side of the bargain. Hadn't he seen to it that a certain gate was left unguarded at the appropriate time? Hadn't he delivered Didima and Umurhan just as he'd agreed? And hadn't he promised long and faithful service to his new king?

Kalasariz was sorely wounded Protarus hadn't seen what a valuable ally he would have been. Good spies are difficult to find. And Kalasariz, who wasted no time on things like false modesty, knew he was the best of all.

The best proof of that were the spies he had in Protarus' court. They'd warned him just in time the king meant to betray him and he'd barely escaped with his life.

Kalasariz found it amusing the king's betrayal had ended up being a blessing. Why, if he had joined the king he wouldn't be here in Kyrania so well placed on the winning side. So what if they were demons? They had what Kalasariz considered an enlightened attitude toward human abilities. Luka had immediately seen Kalasariz' potential. As had Lord Fari. Of course, the two would probably appreciate him less, but admire him more, if they knew he'd made separate arrangements with them both.

He stopped at the edge of the grove. The birds broke off their concert and flew deeper into the shadows. There they perched on an old nut tree, branches bursting with bounty, and took up their song again. The music was sweet, very sweet. I must see what sort of birds these are, Kalasariz thought. Then a sudden vision came to him of one of the birds leaping down on his finger. In the vision he carried the creature away and put it in a cage where it serenaded him all the night long.

Teased by the vision, he followed the birds into the woods.

Kalasariz hadn't deluded himself about his safety from Protarus anywhere on the Walarian side of the Gods' Divide. Even if he could have found a suitable place, he had no intention of spending his days as a man without influence, without power, ducking and dodging through alleyways. So he'd decided to cross the mountains and see what kind of life he could make in Caspan. He had well-placed spies in that city, which was an even better start than the fat pouch of gems he'd carried away with him when he'd escaped.

Those were exciting days, he thought with the fondness that distance and success give to anxious times. Disguised as a merchant, he'd hired a place in a caravan traveling to Caspan. He'd crossed the mountains at Kyrania with that caravan, noting with much interest the richness of the valley. He'd even purchased a fine set of wine cups from Khadji Timura, enjoying much private amusement as the old man and his wife smiled and chatted while they wrapped the cups in felt and packed them carefully away in a carved box for his journey. He'd nearly laughed aloud when the dear old couple had boasted of their son, Safar Timura, who was a great scholar and boyhood friend of Iraj Protarus.

He remembered the conversation as if it were yesterday.

"Perhaps you've heard of him?" Khadji asked.

"Safar Timura?" Kalasariz replied. "No, I'm sorry I haven't had that honor."

"No, Iraj Protarus, I mean," Khadji said.

"Certainly I have," Kalasariz said. "Who hasn't heard of the great King Protarus and his famous victories?"

Then Myrna shyly asked, "Some say he's cruel. Is this true?"

"Not at all, good mother," Kalasariz said. "Why, he's the kindest of kings. Oh, there have been deaths, of course. But when isn't there in a war? No, he's a grand king, this Protarus. And good for business as well."

Myrna acted much relieved. "I'm pleased to hear that," she said. "He lived here for a time, you know. He was a *good* lad. A little wild and strong-willed, of course. But a *good* lad. His mother would have been proud, may the gods bless her dear departed soul."

Kalasariz chuckled at the memory. He looked up and saw the birds had moved, but only to a lower branch. He wondered what kind of nut tree it was. Cinnamon, perhaps?

He'd barely settled in Caspan—reacquainting his spies with the solidness of good Kalasariz gold—when the demons struck.

Once again he found himself in a city under siege, hysteria raging all about him. But he'd kept his head low, ordered his spies to do the same, and once the demons had taken the city he'd poked it up again. The demons had engaged in the usual slaughter. But when they thought the lesson had been taught—and taught well—they set up an administration to run the city. Some of those administrators were from the previous government. They were all low level bureaucrats—the kind who do most of the real work and take little notice of who or what might be the current resident of the throne. Among them were Kalasariz' spies.

Once he knew the lay of the land, Kalasariz had approached Luka and Fari—separately, of course. He had many things to offer. The most valuable of all was Kyrania. The key that would unlock the gate to Protarus' kingdom.

He paused under the tree, the birds just above him, but silent now.

So here I am, he thought, enjoying my reward. The first of many and greater rewards to come.

The birds fluttered, catching his attention. He noticed one bird in particular. It was bright green, while the others were drab brown, and seemed to have a large red spot on its breast. It was a plump little fellow. Deliciously so.

Kalasariz recalled that song birds were supposed to be the best meat of all. The sweeter the song, it was said, the sweeter the flesh.

He looked closer at the tree. He was certain now it was a cinnamon. Ah, he thought, a song bird fed on cinnamon. What a meal I could make!

Kalasariz held out his finger. "Fly down, fly down my pretty little bird," he called. "Light upon me. I have nice things for you."

He was mildly surprised when the bird hopped from the branch and perched on his outstretched finger. He'd only been amusing himself—thinking of the vision. But now it seemed that vision was about to turn into dinner.

"Sing to me little bird," he cooed. "Sing to Kalasariz. Sing as sweetly as you can, my pretty. And then I'll wring your little neck and have you for supper."

To his delight the bird opened its beak as if to sing.

"Shut up, shut up, shuutt uuuup!" it said.

Kalasariz' jaw dropped. "What? What did you say?"

"I said shut up, Gundaree," the bird went on. "I saw him first. I don't care if he smells like a demon. He's a people. Look for yourself, you stupid thing!"

I'm dreaming, Kalasariz thought. I fell asleep in the temple and I dreamed I took a walk. And now I'm dreaming this bird is talking to me. He lifted his hand, examining the red spot on the bird's breast. How odd, he thought. It's in the shape of a turtle.

Suddenly the bird sank sharp claws into his finger.

Kalasariz shrieked and tried to fling the creature off.

"Get away, get away!" he cried.

But the bird only sank its claws deeper, grating against the bone.

Screaming, Kalasariz flung himself about, trying to shake the bird from his wounded hand.

"Stop that you stupid human!" the bird shouted at Kalasariz. "You're hurting me."

Then the bird transformed into a snarling little fiend with long sharp teeth. It leaped onto Kalasariz' face, clutching his cheeks with its talons. Then it bit him on the nose.

Kalasariz froze. He felt pain, felt the creature clinging to his face, felt blood flow into his mouth, but he couldn't move. Couldn't even twitch, much less make a sound.

He heard footsteps and saw a figure step from the tree.

And Kalasariz, a man who refused to recognize even mild surprise, much less stark terror, knew both.

"You'd better let go of him," Safar said. "You're getting blood all over your clothes. And you know how you hate that."

Gundara released Kalasariz, then hopped to the ground. The little Favorite examined his gore-stained costume.

"Now, look what you've done," he accused Kalasariz. "If you'd have stayed still like you were supposed to there'd have only been a little pinch. And almost no blood."

Kalasariz, stricken dumb as well as spellbound, could only manage a strangled gag. He saw Safar haul out a stone idol, shaped like a turtle.

"Why don't you go clean yourself up?" Safar said to Gundara. "You can have your treats later."

"What a good master," Gundara said. "What a kind master."

He hopped up on the stone, shrinking in size so he'd fit. He hesitated, clearly torn. "You won't forget, will you?" he said to Safar. "The sweets I mean."

"I won't forget," Safar reassured him.

"Promise?"

Safar sighed. "I promise," he said, as patiently as he could.

Gundara squealed delight. Then—"Look out, Gundaree! Here I come!"

And he vanished into the stone.

Safar put the idol away and approached Kalasariz. He looked him up and down. The spymaster felt another shock when he saw how blue Safar's eyes were—blue as that sky, blue as that cold lake he'd admired only minutes before.

"I suppose you're wondering why you are still alive?" Safar said, so mild it was frightening.

Kalasariz hadn't reached that point yet, but as soon as Safar mentioned it his mind made the leap. His reaction was so violent that a faint tremble of fear made its way through the numbness.

"Good," Safar said. "I can see it in your eyes. Now that you traveled that far you're a bright enough fellow to know the answer. Am I right?"

Kalasariz made a gagging sound.

Safar looked disgusted. He snapped his fingers and Kalasariz suddenly had the ability to speak. Although he was still as immobile as a statue.

"Thank the gods you've come, Safar!" Kalasariz blurted. "You're just in time to—"

Safar snapped his fingers again, returning him to dumbness.

"Don't bother with your lies," Safar said. "I've spoken to my father. I know what's going on here. And I know you're responsible."

He leaned closer, face inches away from Kalasariz. "For your sake, I hope I've made myself clear."

Kalasariz choked on an answer rising up in his frozen throat. Another snap of the fingers and it burst out.

"Yes! Very clear!"

"I'll decide whether to continue to let you live *after* you've helped us with the demons," Safar said. "How many pieces of you remain to enjoy that life is entirely up to you."

Some of Kalasariz' craft returned to him and with it, boldness.

Still, he stumbled on his first attempt. "I can do more than rid Kyrania of the demons, Aco—I mean, my friend."

Safar seemed amused. "You almost called me acolyte, didn't you?" he said. "Odd, isn't it, how things change? The grand become small." He gestured at Kalasariz. "The small become grand." He touched his breast.

Kalasariz recovered from his mistake. He smiled that old thin smile.

"Yes, it is odd, Lord Timura," he said. "But you see how easily I can change with the events? Your new title comes flows smoothly to my lips, sir. And I must say it fits very you very well."

Safar chuckled. "You're good, Kalasariz. I have to admit that."

The spymaster moved for that gap. "Good enough, Lord Timura, to be of immense value to your king. I know the demon court well. I know King Manacia, Prince Luka and their Grand Wazier, Lord Fari. I know their weaknesses, which are legion, and other important things as well.

"King Protarus might be very angry with you if something happened to me and he missed such a great opportunity."

"Oh, it's an absolute certainty that Protarus would want to hear all these things," Safar said. "Preferably from your living lips, rather than a dry report I made after I tortured the information from you.

"But understand this, Kalasariz. The king and I are friends. Close friends. If I killed you I would go to him and confess my error. Then I'd excuse myself, saying, 'But I couldn't help it, Iraj!'"

He paused, chilling Kalasariz with his easy grin. "I call him Iraj in private, you know. And he calls me Safar. Just like when we were boys playing together."

Then he went on, "Anyway, I'd say, 'I couldn't help it, Iraj! I had this sudden hate for him. I wanted his blood to answer for his crimes against me and my family.' Then I'd hang my head in shame and wonder aloud if my mistake was so grave that it might cost us many more lives to win the war.

"And you know what he'd say? He'd say," and Safar deepened his voice to sound like Protarus, "'Well it couldn't be helped, Safar. I'd have done the same thing in your place. When blood cries, it must be answered. Come, my friend. Let us send for the women and strong drink. We'll mourn your failings like men should. We'll get drunk together and pleasure ourselves until dawn!'"

Kalasariz' stomach burned as if lava had flowed into it.

Safar laughed at his discomfort.

"You see how it is for you?" he said to Kalasariz. "You understand your position."

"Yes, Lord Timura," Kalasariz said, barely controlling the quiver in his voice. "I understand quite well."

He heard a rustle in the woods and saw several soldiers step out behind Safar. They wore the uniforms of Protarus' men.

Then he noticed the soldier leading the group was remarkably handsome.

No . . . beautiful! And it was a woman, not a man.

She came up to Safar. "That was magnificently done, Lord Timura," she said.

But her voice was low and the way she spoke revealed that she called him by more loving names in private.

She gave Safar such a look of adoration it crept past Kalasariz' numbness and lit his cunning.

Adoring women, he thought, can be very dangerous.

Both to the enemy of the man who'd earned that devotion.

And to the man himself.

*   *   *

Kalasariz raised his cup in a toast. "My friends," he said, "this night is just one more proof—no matter how small—of King Manacia's grand vision of a united Esmir."

He glanced around the open air banquet area. Rough board tables were spread across a freshly mowed lawn. Immense mounds of food were heaped on the tables, with jugs of heady Kyranian wine running down the center. Demons, scores of demons, sat before the tables, fixing him with their yellow eyes. Cups lifted expectantly, waiting for him to end his toast.

"Even here in far Kyrania," he continued, "a human sits among his demon brethren, supping and drinking. An equal among equals. A mortal—"

"Oh, finish the damned toast, Kalasariz!" the big demon sitting beside him growled. "I'm thirsty!"

"Yes, well, uh," Kalasariz faltered, "Uh—Here's to King Manacia! Long may he reign."

The demons shouted approval, downed their drinks and turned back to their tables, refilling goblets and stuffing their maws with steaming food.

Nervously, Kalasariz slopped wine in his cup and downed it in one quick gulp. Hidden under his clothing—next to his skin—was the stone idol, so warm with anticipation it was almost hot. Once in awhile he even heard—quite faintly—Gundara's excited hiss of "Shut up, shut up," to his twin. Kalasariz had been warned that any suspicious action would bring the little Favorite boiling out to punish him.

Moving through the tables were human slaves, heads low, platters high, going from demon to demon to offer more delicacies. The demons ate greedily, as if all the free food supplied by Kalasariz in this spontaneous banquet had made them more ravenous than normal.

"Would the master wish more wine?" murmured a voice at his elbow. It was Safar, dressed as a slave and bearing a jug. The other humans in the banquet area were his soldiers posing as slaves, all waiting for the signal to strike.

"Yes, please," Kalasariz said, offering his cup. It was refilled and Safar bowed humbly and stepped back.

"Why are you so polite to him?" the demon—whose name was Quan—asked. "Are you drunk?"

"No, no, I'm not drunk," Kalasariz said.

"That's your problem, then," Quan said. "You're distracted by a low level of spirited fluids. That's why you're spoiling our slaves, instead of giving them good solid blows for asking, instead of anticipating.

"Your cup was empty. He should have filled it!"

Quan turned to Safar. "Do the same to me, you little human worm," he said, "and I'll bite off your head."

"Yes, exalted one," Safar said, bobbing his head. "Thank you, exalted one."

Quan turned back to Kalasariz. "You see? That's how it's done!"

"I'll remember that, Quan," Kalasariz said. "It's good advice."

A beautiful slave girl—Leiria in disguise—moved along his table, bearing a tray of roasted kabobs. They smelled so delicious Kalasariz almost forgot the danger he was in. As she approached, hot kabob grease sputtering and splattering, his mouth filled with water.

He reached out a hand to grab a spear as she went by. Safar stepped between them, raising the jug and then leaning over, pretending to top up the wine cup.

"Don't eat the kabobs," he whispered, then withdrew.

Kalasariz suddenly found his mouth had gone dry thinking about what he'd almost done.

Beside him Quan munched with much gusto. "This is delicious, Kalasariz," he said. "You should try it!"

He waved the spear of savory meat beneath Kalasariz' nose. The delicious odor, magically enhanced, was so powerful he nearly forgot himself again. He snatched his hand back just in time.

"I wish I could," he said, making a mournful face. "It does smell wonderful. But I'm forbidden to eat lamb this month. My religion, you know."

All over the banquet area the other demons were gobbling down the kabobs, smacking their lips, wiping their chins and shouting for the slaves to bring more.

"That's the trouble with religion," Quan said with some sympathy. "Always forbidding this and forbidding that. There's so many forbiddens that a poor fiend barely knows what to do."

He stripped the rest of the meat off the spear and popped it into his maw. He chewed mightily, then swallowed, a look of pure bliss on his face.

"You know the first thing I'd do," he said, "if I were king?"

"What's that?" Kalasariz asked.

"I'd banish religion. Toss it right out. Start my own religion. And the first thing I'd do after that is turn the forbiddens on their head. All that was forbidden would become compulsory. And everything that was compulsory would go the king's committee for a good long study."

He gave Kalasariz a friendly jab with his claw.

"I'll bet I'd be damned popular," he said. "The most popular king in his—"

And Quan broke off as his eyes suddenly glazed over and he pitched forward.

Kalasariz yanked his arm away and Quan's head struck the table with much force.

The banquet area was suddenly filled with similar sounds of demon heads slamming into wood. Then there was silence.

Kalasariz looked about and saw the demon guards had noticed something was amiss and were running forward.

Leiria shouted a war cry, ripping off her robe to show the mail beneath. She drew her sword and rushed the guards. Other cries rang out as Safar's soldiers revealed themselves and leaped into the fray.

It was quick, bloody work. Before Kalasariz knew it all the demons but three were dead. And Leiria, along with half a dozen human soldiers, was pressing in to end that annoyance.

Safar dumped Quan's corpse out of the chair and slid into it. He cleaned a winecup with his sleeve and filled it up.

"I won't ask you for a toast," he said to Kalasariz. "Your friend was right." He indicated the dead demon slumped on the ground. "You're much too long winded."

And Safar drank the wine down.

CHAPTER TWENTY THREE
PRELUDE TO BATTLE

Safar slipped the stone idol from his pouch. He patted it, long soothing strokes like a child caressing a cat.

He leaned close, whispering, "Behave yourself, now. We're in the company of the king."

Still stroking the idol, he walked over to Iraj, who was staring up at a painting, deep in thought.

They were in Alisarrian's cave, torch light reflecting off the luminous walls. The picture Iraj was musing over was the magical painting of the Conqueror in his heroic pose.

"I still feel like a boy," Iraj murmured to Safar.

Then he turned, a wry smile on his face. "When we were here before," he said, "I was hiding from my uncle and his friend. As it turned out, neither were more than petty chieftains. But at the time what I had to overcome seemed like the greatest problem in the world."

He gestured at the heroic figure of Alisarrian, who had Iraj's golden beard, but Safar's blue eyes. "When I saw that—somehow, for reasons I can't explain—it made my dream of ruling all Esmir seem not so difficult." He shrugged. "I mean, all I had to do is defeat my uncle, then Esmir would crack like an egg. It felt that easy.

"Now I see the picture differently. I see a man whose accomplishments I truly admire. I've stood in lesser boots and fought in lesser battles. It's difficult enough to hold on to what I've won, much less win more."

"I'm sure Alisarrian had similar doubts about himself," Safar said. "Maybe even more so. He didn't have a great Conqueror to emulate, after all. You *know* it's possible because it's been done before. He didn't have that advantage."

"And the demons," Iraj said, brightening a bit. "He also had to face the demons."

"Exactly," Safar said. "Not only that, but no human king had *ever* defeated a demon army. You know that can be done as well, thanks to Alisarrian."

Iraj frowned again. "Except Alisarrian was not only a great general, but a great wizard as well. I'm only good at war. I know nothing of magic."

"You've got me," Safar said.

"Sometimes that worries me," Iraj said. "What if I didn't have you?"

"That's nonsense," Safar said. "The Fates have apparently decided to put us together. Why worry yourself over something that couldn't have happened?"

"Yes," Iraj said, eyes gleaming, "but what if you decided to leave me?"

Safar snorted. "That's ridiculous," he said. "Why would I do that? For money? You've made me rich. To be richer? Money doesn't mean anything to me anyway. What's next?

"Power? As in power over others? You know I have no such desires."

Iraj's mood lightened. The dangerous gleam in his eyes vanished. "That's true," he said. "You don't even have any *respect* for power. As I am always reminding you, my friend, when you give a kingly fellow like myself such a difficult time."

Safar grinned. "I *know* you're human," he said. "I saw the Ubekian brothers beating on you like a temple drum."

Iraj made a face. "At the time I thought, 'wait'll I get to be king. I'll chop off your tiny heads.' Now that I am king it doesn't seem so important."

Safar guffawed. "Can you imagine their faces," he howled, "if you came walking up to them right now and . . ." the rest was lost in laughter.

Iraj joined him and the cave rang with the sound of the amusement of two old friends. But there was an edge to it and it went on too long. It was the kind of barely controlled laughter that grips people when they are facing a fearful task.

When it stopped, it ended abruptly. The two young men avoided each other's eyes, embarrassed.

"We'd better get started," Safar said, voice a little thin.

Iraj nodded. "Yes, we'd best."

"Sit over there," Safar ordered, pointing to a place at the edge of faded pentagram inscribed on the cave floor.

Iraj did as he was told and Safar sat across from him. Within the pentagram were a host of ancient magical symbols, the ones that had once so mystified him. Some still did, but he was learning more daily from the Book of Asper.

Safar placed the turtle on one of the symbols. The stone began to glow, but very faintly.

"That's the comet," he said.

Then he slid the idol onto another symbol. The idol glowed a little brighter.

"That's the demon moon."

He moved the turtle to a point between them.

"That's us," he said. "Approximately, that is. The real heavenly bodies are moving together right now. In fact, we should see the demon moon very soon."

Iraj shook his head in admiration. "That's something, Safar," he said, sounding like a boy watching a circus performance. "*Really* something."

Safar kept his features immobile. He couldn't help but play the stony-faced master performer. Besides, he'd noticed it didn't hurt to keep Iraj's awe of his magical abilities stoked to the fullest.

"When I cast the spell," he said, "you must sit absolutely still. Do or say nothing. You'll see me here beside you. But I won't be in my body."

He gestured toward the cave mouth. "My spirit will be out there someplace." He pointed at the stone idol. "Keep your eyes on that," he said, "and you'll see everything my spirit sees."

Iraj squirmed. "Remarkable," he breathed.

"Are you ready?" Safar asked.

Iraj licked his lips and nodded. Safar tossed a handful of glass pellets on the floor. Iraj gasped. Curling up were columns of thick smoke, all of a different color, all filled with glittering bits that floated up and down the columns.

This wasn't something that was really necessary, but Safar had learned from Methydia to put on a good show.

He drew in his breath. Deeper and deeper, drawing as if his lungs were a giant's. The columns of smoke, coiling around each other like ribbons, wreathed into his mouth, following the inrushing air.

Then he exhaled. It made a sound like a hard wind whistling through a narrow opening. The ribbon smoke, now tightly coiled into a hazy rope, shot out, bursting over the stone idol like a waterfall.

Safar's vision hazed and he saw things as if in a dream. He saw Iraj look startled, mouth gaping open. He saw Gundara, the object of the king's amazement, leap out of the stone and crouch there, chittering. He heard Gundara squeak one, "Shut up!" Then gleap and snap his jaws shut when he saw Iraj.

Suddenly wings burst from the little Favorite's back—large gossamer wings, pearly like the snow butterflies that come in early spring. Gundara reached out a claw. It stretched, then stretched more, reaching beyond belief—longer and longer, closing the distance between Favorite and master.

Safar raised his own hand. A spectral image of that hand emerged from his body.

His spirit self gripped Gundara's claw.

Then he was flying, flying through mountain stone, then erupting out of the mountain itself and taking to the air. He had no sense of Gundara's presence. It was as if Safar were doing the flying, soaring with the wind, moving his arms to correct his flight.

He flew north, over the topmost peaks of the Bride and Six Maids. Far below he saw a boy leading a flock of goats to pasture. He cleared the last peak, so close he was tempted to see if his spectral hand could disturb the snow.

He soared down the mountain slopes, caught a warm wind, then sailed out over the great northern desert.

Above him thick clouds skated under a blue sky. Below, the white desert sands glittered in the sunlight. Beyond, a limitless horizon.

Safar shifted his arms and flew up to the clouds. He caught a wind and skimmed beneath them, heading for the thin blue line marking the spot where sky and earth met.

He flew on for a time until he came to a place where two enormous rocks speared out of the stony ground. They were sheer on all sides and each seemed to be formed from a single piece a hundred feet high. They were so large they seemed close together, but when Safar came upon them he could see they were a less than half a mile apart.

He flew on toward the still empty horizon.

When he first saw the army he didn't know what he was looking at. It emerged as a long dirty line rising from the horizon's rim. Beneath the line he saw a streak of solid black. The closer he went the broader that streak became, but fading grayer, like charcoal on a sketch. Slowly the streak separated into figures. And then the figures became soldiers.

Demon soldiers.

Safar shot over them, spectral heart fluttering against spectral ribs.

The whole desert plain swarmed with demons, a colossal colony of monstrous ants streaming south toward the Gods' Divide. They flowed beneath him, wide columns of demon soldiers, led by thick spears of mounted cavalry. Hundreds of great baggage trains followed in their wake, winged by immense herds of animals to supply fresh food and mounts.

It took a frighteningly long time to come to the end of the demon army. When he did, he swung around and flew toward the front—looking for the heart of this great creature.

He found Manacia and his court just behind the main cavalry units. The demon king lolled in a rolling howdah perched on a glorious white elephant. Safar recognized the elephant immediately. It was the same one he'd seen Iraj ride in that long ago vision.

Steeling himself, he flew nearer. Manacia's huge head and massive jaws were just becoming clear when Safar felt the sting of magic. It was like running naked through a swarm of bees.

Safar shot upward, rising as fast as he could, then the stinging sensation was gone and he knew he was beyond Manacia's reach. When he'd recovered he realized it was some kind of shield, or warning net, or both. Safar tested for danger and was relieved when he became certain Manacia hadn't noticed his presence. Then, gathering his nerve, he flew around the shield, testing its width and breadth. Soon not the only size became apparent, but also that he was safe as long he kept to the edges.

From far off he heard someone call his name. "Safar . . . Safar . . ."

A hole opened up and he fell into it, plunging down and down, through smoke and heat and then boom! he was back in the cave, crouched on his knees and spewing his guts onto the floor.

When he was done Iraj wet the edge of his cloak and gave it to him to wipe his face, then he handed him a cup brimming with strong brandy. Safar drank it down like water. One more and his nerves steadied.

"I thought I told you to keep silent," he said. "You could have killed me."

Iraj looked surprised, then sorrowful. "I'm sorry," he said. "I thought it was seeing all those demons that made you sick. I was almost ill myself."

"Sure, it scared the Hells out of me," Safar said. "But it was being snatched back so quickly that made me sick! I know you're my lord and master and all, but have a pity, Iraj! Go easy, next time."

While Iraj hung his head and muttered apologies, Safar braced himself with another cup of false courage. Then he picked up the stone idol, whispered a promise of rewards to come for good little Favorites and returned it to his pouch.

"When I saw Manacia's army," Iraj said, "I thought, this is hopeless! Unstoppable! I might as well go dig myself a deep hole and pull the dirt in after me."

"I had similar thoughts," Safar said, "but I couldn't see how I could dig a hole deep enough."

"In the entire history of Esmir," Iraj said, "there is no precedent for what we're facing. No army that size has ever been fielded. And if we closed with him, there's no comparison to any battle ever fought."

"Let's not close with him," Safar said. "That's my strong advice to you."

"Actually," Iraj said, "that's advice I'll immediately reject. The only way we can win is to meet him head-to-head on the field of battle."

"Come, Iraj!" Safar objected. "Put a little more brandy in your blood. And quickly. Senses must be regained."

"I'm not joking," Iraj answered.

"I know you're not," Safar said. "That's why *I* am! Otherwise I'd be frightened to death. You wouldn't say such a thing if you didn't mean it."

"Sometimes I wonder about your sanity, my friend, but never your ability."

"After I was done quaking," Iraj said, "it came to me that if an army that size had never been fielded before, it was also true no army that size has ever been *commanded* before."

Safar nodded. "I see what you mean. Manacia would be have to be not only the greatest general ever, but so far above all the others he'd be a giant among generals."

"He's able enough," Iraj said. "I'll give him that. I've gathered some very reliable intelligence on his battles. He's no fool. And he has that son of his, Luka, leading every attack. There's no fear in them—at least that they show—which is fairly impressive in itself.

"Luka's demons attack so fiercely, so professionally, it takes the heart right out of the enemy. Several times Manacia hasn't had to do much more than mop up."

"Then you have to eliminate Luka," Safar said.

"Perhaps," Iraj said. "I don't know. I'm thinking about the big army, right now.

That's what I have to beat."

"Assuming we survive Luka," Safar said.

"I'm not saying it'll be easy with Luka," Iraj said. "But I have to jump past that. Return to it later. Otherwise I can't think of a way to solve the big problem."

"Do you have any ideas?" Safar asked.

"A few," Iraj said. "But very vague. Number one, I have to use his size against him. Number two, I have to make him smaller."

"Don't forget," Safar said, "it won't be just demon soldiers we'll encounter, but demon magic as well."

Iraj's contemplative look turned to concern. "What of it?" he asked. "What did you see . . . if that's the word for a wizard looking at another wizard."

"Close enough," Safar said. "As close as your problem as a general is to my problem as your Grand Wazier.

"Manacia is very strong. Stronger than me, perhaps. I can't say because I have no experience in such things. I've never fought a battle. Hells, I had more two-fisted fights as a boy than I've ever had magic against magic."

"I was there for your first sorcerous fight," Iraj reminded him. "And it so happens it was against demons."

Safar started to protest, but Iraj waved him down. "Don't tell me you were lucky," he said. "Of course, you were. I'm lucky. Not just good, but lucky. So are you. And lucky wins."

"I won't argue," Safar said. "We'll find out if you're right soon enough."

"But you do have some ideas about Manacia?" Iraj asked.

"Only one just now," Safar said. "And that's this—Manacia may be the wizard of all wizards, but he's no magician."

Iraj looked at him, puzzled. "What are you talking about?"

"Something I learned in the circus," Safar said. "Smoke and mirrors. The art of the Grand Illusion."

*   *   *

While the demon army marched, the humans prepared to meet them.

Manacia's progress was slow. The sheer size of his forces, as Iraj had predicted, made him unwieldy and kept the pace to that of a desert tortoise. He also had to maintain huge supply lines stretching all the way to Caspan.

The humans used that time well. Gear was repaired, horses shod, weapons honed. New training instituted in which speed and quick thinking were emphasized. Iraj wanted no brave death charges. Against Manacia's might, he couldn't afford the losses. Loads were lightened; they'd take only what they needed into the desert. Supplies would also be the minimum required to reach Manacia.

If they lost there'd be no return. If they won they could take what they wanted from Manacia.

As they prepared, Iraj's musings became full blown ideas. He introduced new tactics and had special equipment made.

Safar was similarly occupied. He had only a few wizards, but although their powers were weak they had battle experience. They told him what he could expect and he prepared remedies.

Safar made everything as simple as possible. He created small amulets and used some of the tricks he'd learned from the Book of Asper to make them very strong. The wizards mass produced these amulets and passed them out to the men.

He dispensed with the need for large quantities of magical supplies—instead he commandeered several heavy chariots, drawn by triple teams. In each he put several kegs of certain oils and powders he'd mixed—another idea he'd borrowed from Asper.

The most important thing Safar did, however, was meet with his father.

It was like old times in his father's shop, the kiln glowing merrily, his sister, Quetera, at the wheel, his mother mixing glaze.

Apparently Myrna thought the same thing, for she said, "This is like the old caravan season days, Khadji. I used to love those times. All of us together making pots and plates as fast we could to sell to the caravan masters."

Quetera groaned. "The last time we did that," she said, "I was pregnant." She held her hands out from her sides. "I was *this* big. I could barely get close to the spoke, and when I did it reminded me of that devil husband of mine who'd put me in that condition."

"As if you had no part in it," Myrna sniffed.

Quetera laughed. "Oh, I got my pleasure, true enough," she said. "But so did he. At the time it didn't seem fair I had to do the rest by myself. It still doesn't."

Leiria, who stayed close to Safar even when he visited his family, stirred in the corner.

"I'm glad I chose my path instead of yours, Quetera," she said. "Fighting always seemed like it was less painful than birthing."

"It is," Quetera said. "But it got me Dmitri."

She smiled at the little boy in the corner, making a messy business with his child's potting wheel.

"I was happy in the end."

Quetera suddenly laughed and covered her mouth. "What am I saying? My *end* was definitely not happy."

Everyone laughed, even Khadji who was embarrassed by discussions of that nature. But since it was Quetera who said it, and he loved her humorous nature, he allowed himself enjoyment.

Over in the corner little Dmitri had tired of the clay and was playing in his washing up bucket. He put a straw in the soapy water then held it up and puffed.

A bubble formed on the end of the straw. Delighted, Dmitri puffed more. The bubble became huge, then broke off and floated across the room.

"Look mother," he cried. "A balloon! I made a balloon!"

They all turned to look. The bubble, kiln light wobbling on its surface, sailed slowly into the other corner. It hovered over the glass-making equipment, then burst.

Everyone made automatic noises of sympathy.

"Don't worry, everybody," Dmitri crowed. "I can make more. Lots more!"

He happily dipped his straw in the bucket and started blowing streams of bubbles.

Safar's smile died. He turned to his father.

"I want you make something for me, father," he said.

Khadji frowned, wondering what was in his son's mind.

Safar pulled over some sheets of sketching paper and drew. "Make it like this," he said as he drew. "But make it thin. As light as you can. Don't worry about it being too fragile."

Khadji held up the sketch. "I'll do it, son," he said, "but whatever on Esmir for? What do you want with one of these?"

"Not one, father," Safar said. "It'll take a least a score."

* * *

"You're returning me to Manacia?" Kalasariz quavered. "But whatever for? What have I done, Your Majesty, to deserve such a fate?"

Kalasariz was standing before Protarus and Safar. He was blindfolded. He'd been blindfolded and kept out of the sight of the military preparations, since Iraj's arrival in Kyrania.

"Don't remind us about what you may or may not deserve," Safar said. "We probably have strong differences on that small matter."

"Don't worry, my friend," Iraj said. "Manacia won't kill you. We'll make it look good. You can claim you escaped. You have an agile mind. And I'm sure you can make it a very brave escape. What really happened will be our little secret.

"Make of it what you will. Gamble that I'll lose and join them. Gamble that I'll win and keep your faith with me. You can do either, or both at the same time. Just choose well. Act well. And if you see me again in person you'll know what to expect."

"I have every faith in your eventual victory, Majesty," Kalasariz said. "I'll do anything you instruct me to."

"I have only one instruction," Iraj said. "I want you to deliver a message. And this is what I want you to say . . ."

* * *

The Demon Moon was rising when Kalasariz put spurs to horse and thundered across the desert.

It hovered just above the night plain, red as new death. The landscape had an orange tint to it and was pocked with inky shadows. Kalasariz steered his horse around the shadows, praying to the gods he was correct each time he changed course, digging in his heels to make the horse run faster still.

Low as it was, the Demon Moon captured the whole northern sky, wiping out any sign of the star houses that reigned there. Just above the Demon Moon was a comet so bright it was the only other light that bleared through.

It's the Sign of Alisarrian, Kalasariz thought.

Manacia claimed it was meant for him. Protarus believed the same. Kalasariz had no idea which way to jump.

In his madness he cursed the gods for not allowing him spies on the court of the Demon Moon.

* * *

Luka stared at Kalasariz in amazement.

"This is insane," the demon prince said. "How dare you approach me in such secrecy? If my father hears about it he'll have us killed!"

"If you'll forgive me for pointing this out, Highness," Fari said, "I think this human expected us to understand that . . . and therefore say nothing."

He looked at Kalasariz, yellow eyes glowing. His tones, however, were mild when he said, "Either by foolish design, or cleverness, it seems you have made us *all* conspirators."

Kalasariz kept his features blank. This was no time for arrogance to creep through. "I'm hoping it was by clever design, Exalted One," he said. "Clever for all of us, that is."

The Crown Prince was *not* mollified. "What angers me most," he said, "is for some reason this Protarus, this upstart king, believes I am such a traitorous son that I'd not immediately speak out."

"And me as well, Highness," Fari murmured. "I'm here beside you."

232

Again he glared at Kalasariz. But again his tones were mild. "I suppose you told him about the habits of our court," he said. "Filled him in on our personalities."

"I said as little as I could . . . under the circumstances," Kalasariz replied.

Fari's talon shot out. A burning light speared into Kalasariz who shrieked in pain.

"You really should learn to scream with less vigor," Fari said, letting the talon drop. "Someone might hear us and the conspiracy would be exposed."

"I told them everything," Kalasariz gritted. "Anything they asked."

Fari turned to Luka. "I think from here on he'll be more careful with the truth, Highness," he said.

Luka nodded. He'd become calm. More measuring. "I suppose Protarus knows that you and I are not the fondest of friends," he said to Fari.

"I expect so, Highness," Fari answered.

Luka looked at Kalasariz. "Why does Protarus believe we'd choose each other to help hatch a plot?" he asked.

"I don't know, Your Highness," Kalasariz said. "He simply gave me the message and ordered me to deliver it. In private."

"And that message is?"

Kalasariz took a deep breath, then plunged into it. "King Protarus sends his greetings, warm wishes for your health and said he hopes all will go well with you in the coming battle."

"He *does* intend to fight, then," Fari said.

"Never doubt that, Exalted One," Kalasariz said. "Protarus *will* fight."

"But the odds against him are impossible," Luka said.

"King Protarus guessed you would say that, Your Highness," Kalasariz said. "And he told me in reply that it was not unknown for the impossible to become possible during the Demon Moon."

Fari chuckled. "A lovely myth," he said. "I've heard it before, although it is very old."

"When the battle comes, Your Highness," Kalasariz continued, "he asked that you watch carefully. And if something should happen which gives you pause, to think on his offer.

"If you give him Manacia, he will give you his throne. He said he believed you would be an able administrator of the demonlands—under his direction, of course."

"I think we should just kill this worm," Luka said to Fari. "Kill him quick. And go about our business as if nothing happened."

"Don't be so hasty, Highness," Fari advised. "You will note the message is addressed to both of us. He requires agreement from two traitors, it seems, or his plan won't work. Curious, isn't it, that he also believes we both hate your father more than we dislike one another."

There was an uncomfortable silence.

"That's it?" Luka said to Kalasariz. "He only asks that we watch, and if the course of the battle goes badly—from our point of view—that we consider changing our alliance?"

"Yes, Highness," Kalasariz said.

Another long silence. Broken by a dry chuckle from Luka.

"Ridiculous," he laughed.

Fari also laughed. "Ridiculous in the extreme."

"One other thing, O Great Ones," Kalasariz said. "Safar Timura—his Grand Wazier— commanded me to give you this."

He handed Lord Fari a scroll. The old demon unrolled it and examined the contents. After a time he lifted his head, troubled.

"It's a formula for a spell, Highness," he said to Luka. "A formula that breaks the curse of the Forbidden Desert."

"Meaning the humans can cross as easily as we can," Luka said. "What of it?"

"It pains me to admit this, Highness," Fari said, "but I've never seen a spell so grand—a spell we worked years to perfect—done so simply. It's really quite elegant. And it has the feel of something that came through inspiration, rather than from years of tedious experiment."

"Quick or labored," Luka said. "Why should it matter?"

"Oh, it probably doesn't matter at all, Highness," Fari said. "Although I'd be derelict in my duties if I didn't point out that only a master wizard could have done such a thing. A master wizard as great, or greater than your father."

Luka peered into the old demon's eyes. Then he turned away. There was another long and uncomfortable pause.

"We probably shouldn't bother the king with this," Luka said at last.

"I absolutely agree, Highness," Fari replied with barely disguised relief. "There's no need to burden him with such foolishness."

"What about me?" Kalasariz blurted, not certain which way things were going.

"Oh, I'd sugg est you watch the battle," Fari said. He turned to Luka, "Isn't that right, Highness?"

"Yes, yes, that's what I'd do," the demon prince said. "Watch the battle. And see."

CHAPTER TWENTY FOUR
BATTLE AND FLIGHT

King Protarus quick marched his army to the place of the Two Stones.

His scouts told him King Manacia's main force was two days away. Protarus had perhaps fifty thousand fighting men, nearly all mounted. With these he would oppose about three hundred thousand demons, some mounted, most afoot.

On the surface these odds seemed insurmountable. Protarus' generals told him so in daily meetings. They pointed out he had another seventy-five thousand men spread over his realm, keeping the peace. To this he could add two hundred thousand men who had recently volunteered to fight the hated demon enemy. If Protarus waited a month that number would easily reach five hundred thousand. So many hot-blooded young men were pouring in, begging to fight, Protarus' recruiters were nearly overwhelmed.

"I mean to fight now," Protarus told them. "Not a month from now. A month is too late. A month is certain defeat.

"And we don't have two days to prepare for Manacia, but a day and a half. I want him here faster. I want him here in time to settle into a comfortable camp. He'll want to feed his men, rest them and then surprise us with a dawn attack."

"How can get we get him here more quickly, Your Majesty?" one his aides asked. "We can't command Manacia to speed up."

"True, but we can entice him," Safar said.

Then king and grand wazier explained how this thing could be done.

* * *

The desert heat formed twin devils that attacked Manacia from above and below. The appalling discomfort made him angry and his slaves kept well out of kicking range. Manacia thought the gods were being unreasonable to the extreme. They'd determined his fate, hadn't they? They'd decreed he would be King of Kings. If this were the case—and Manacia had no reason to doubt it—it seemed unfair and undignified to make him suffer so.

Angry as Manacia was at the gods, his wrath knew no end when he considered the pretender, Iraj Protarus. Manacia had heard reports that Protarus shared his ambitions to rule Esmir. How dare he? Why, he was nothing more than a dirty plains savage.

Manacia's belly lurched uncomfortably with each roll of the elephant. The smells around him—beast smells, unwashed demon smells—were so thick it was difficult to breath without gagging. The sounds were so chaotic it was impossible to think—groaning life on the hard march, shrieking wheels in the heat, distant cries of demon kits and the babble of their complaining mothers.

And Manacia thought, Children? How did we end up carrying children with us?

He twisted around and although he couldn't see them, he knew there were thousands upon thousands of demon harlots straggling behind his army. He snorted, disgusted. Apparently he'd been in the field long enough for the harlots to breed.

Looking back, Manacia could see the Demon Moon, red glow smearing the northern horizon. Hovering above it was the lightspear of the comet. When the Demon Moon and comet had first appeared, the king had taken heart. He claimed it as his sign, the Sign of Manacia. A demon king for the Demon Moon.

But in the weariness of the long march to meet Protarus, King Manacia had begun to curse that moon. It was always present, day or night. He felt haunted by it, as if it were a heavenly force driving him on to who knows where?

Manacia felt a stony clatter against his magical shield. He jolted around to face the south—his enemy's lair.

His big demon head came up, yellow eyes drilling the far horizon.

*   *   *

The first thing Luka saw were his scouts racing back to his lines.

Next he spotted watery figures charging across the desert after the scouts. The figures firmed and became mailed horsemen—humans!

His first thought was, It's so hot! How can they keep up such a pace?

His second thought was, By the gods, he's coming! Protarus is coming!

Trumpets sounded the alarm all around him. Action only needed his signal.

He gave it.

His demon brothers howled their war cries and charged, carrying him along at their head.

*   *   *

Fari saw the twister snaking towards him. It was six feet high, which became twelve, and then double that and then it became a towering, screeching force of nature.

All about him he could hear the fearful cries of his colleagues as they leaped from their wagons to abandon Manacia's wizard caravan.

Fari ached to run with them, but he was too old to run and had to use his wits.

The twister struck the first wagons, lifting them up and hurling them in all directions. Fari calmed himself enough to see a human face staring out of that twister. It was many faces, actually, but the same face—a blur of sameness whirling with the twister. It was beardless, hawked nosed and Fari could swear he could see blue skies through eyeholes in the dust-and-debris-choked tornado.

And now it was coming for him, roaring his name, "Fa-ri! Fa-ri!"

*　　　　*　　　　*

Safar saw the old demon wizard and knew who he was. He called his name again, "Fa-ri! Fa-ri!"

He pointed his finger and Gundara hopped over to the twister and "pushed" it toward the demon wizard.

Tornado and demon were among many miniature ghostly figures spread out on the campaign table in Iraj's headquarters tent. At Safar's command, Gundara moved among them, towering over the living map like a giant.

Safar concentrated, barely noticing Iraj's presence next to him, much less the generals and aides crowding close to the table. His gaze swept over the field, taking note of the key figures.

Not far above the destroyed wizard caravan was Manacia, clinging to the howdah as his elephant mount stamped its feet and trumpeted in panic. Demon soldiers rushed all around him, adding to the confusion.

Some distance from Manacia he could see the diminutive figures of Prince Luka and his cavalry of monsters charging across the desert.

Safar turned his attention back to Fari and the twister. He nodded at Gundara, who gave the whirlwind another "push" and it leaped forward to close the distance.

*　　　　*　　　　*

Fari saw the trick just in time.

He felt the twister suck at him, saw the whirling faces, heard them shouting, "Fa-ri," and looked down the whirlwind's column until he saw its tail. It was a small, leaping serpent, no bigger than a demon kit's wrist.

Fari saw in an instant this was where its power resided. He marveled at how such a large force could come from so little energy. Then he made a slicing motion with his talon, cutting it in two.

The twister shattered, showering rocks and bits of debris everywhere. Fari suffered only a small cut on his left claw. But he was badly shaken.

He looked at the chaos raging around him and heaved a long sigh of relief.

*　　　　*　　　　*

Luka took his fear and made it his courage. His battle cry was drowned out by his brother warriors, but it took life from them at same time, wailing out in a long single ululation that resounded across the desert.

They were almost on the human cavalry, which was charging toward them unfazed by the sight and sound of so many demon killers.

Luka saw a tall horseman with a blonde beard and long golden locks flowing from under his helmet. Riding beside him was a dark-featured man, just as tall but beardless. Despite the blur of the charge Luka could see the man's burning blue eyes.

Those eyes were looking at him now.

The bearded man turned his head and caught sight of Luka.

Both humans changed course and charged toward the demon prince.

Luka waved his sword wildly and braced for the shock.

But no clash came.

Instead, he found himself shouting and slashing and jabbing at . . . nothingness. He whirled his beast about and saw his warriors fighting empty air.

The humans had vanished.

Luka blinked. But as it was fully sinking in that he'd faced and fought only his imagination, he saw a human—a real human, not a ghost—leap up from the sand.

The man cried out when he saw the prince. Luka heard similar cries all around. Then the human lifted up a long tube. Luka noted with dazed interest that the tube had probably allowed the man to breathe while he lay in wait buried in the said.

Then he saw the men load the tube with a dart, lift it to his lips . . . and blow.

The dart took Luka's mount in the eye. The beast howled in pain, then collapsed under him. Luka rolled off, taking shelter behind his mount's body. It had died so quickly that he knew the dart was poisoned.

He lifted his head and was amazed to see his human attacker running away. He jumped up to follow, but had taken no more than a few steps when he stumbled over a mailed body. It was the corpse of one of his brother warriors.

Luka came to his feet. The ground was littered by many other demon corpses.

Then he came out of his shock and realized most were still mounted and uninjured. They were only confused, milling about wondering where their enemy had gone.

Luka saw the fleeing humans racing south toward a group of low dunes. They'd thrown down their dart tubes in their haste to escape an overwhelming demon force. From the dunes he saw a long line of horsemen dash out, each leading another animal.

The prince shouted for his fiends. He did not mean to let the humans escape.

Someone brought him a mount and Luka bounded into the saddle and led his warriors on yet another charge. But this time he had the enemy's back to him.

Snarling as wildly as his clawed-mount, Luka closed on the humans. He was so close he could hear their laboring breath.

He dropped his sword point low to take the first man in front of him.

*   *   *

"Now, Master?" Gundara asked.

"Yes, now!" Safar answered.

The little Favorite stomped on the table.

*   *   *

There was a deafening explosion and Luka's mount reared, shrieking in fear, claws pawing the air.

A cloud black as night and stinking of sulfur burst up between him and the fleeing humans.

Monstrous forms, all frighteningly ugly, all human, swirled out of the cloud, gnashing and grinding their flat teeth.

Luka heard his warriors howl in terror and knew they were experiencing the same thing. He tried to call out to them not to panic, to keep going until they reached the other side of the smoke curtain. But no one could make out his commands from the cries of hysteria.

Then it came to him that he was alone.

All his warriors had retreated and he was alone in the sulfurous darkness, filled with nightmare forms.

Luka wheeled his mount and retreated as calmly as he could.

When he'd cleared the smoky curtain he saw his father bearing down on him on his big white elephant.

"Why did you stop?" his father shouted. "Why didn't you go on?"

There was a thinly failed accusation of cowardice in his father's questions and Luka hated him for it.

"The humans caught us by surprise, Majesty," he said. "It seemed best to regroup. Besides, it was only a small force, and most of that was illusion."

Manacia jabbed a talon at the ebbing curtain of smoke. "Are you telling me Protarus isn't waiting out there?"

"I don't believe so, Majesty," Luka answered. "I think he waits where our scouts say he waits. Near the place of the Two Rocks. This was only a diversion. He was testing us."

"Well, you're a fool to think that!" Manacia snarled. "He's out there, all right. I can feel it." He rapped his golden mail. "In here I can feel it." He tapped his demon nose. "And I can smell him. I can smell the human wizard, too."

Lord Fari had come up in time to hear the last. "Are you certain, Your Majesty?" he asked. "I too sense a presence out there. But perhaps it is only another illusion."

Manacia snorted. "Bah! I'm surrounded by fools and cowards."

He shouted for an aide. "Sound the attack," he commanded.

A moment later the air was filled with the cacophony of trumpets and drums and booted feet and clanking mail as Manacia's vast army poured across the empty plain, seeking humans to kill.

To support them, Manacia gathered his best wizards together, including Fari, and they made a mighty spell.

Boiling clouds filled the skies. Lighting cracked Thunder rolled. Horrible beasts, dragons and winged lions, raged across the heavens.

Manacia worked himself to exhaustion, forming and casting war spell after war spell.

Several hours passed and the first scouts returned from the main force to report there were no signs of even a small band of humans to be found, much less a whole army.

By now Manacia had collapsed on his traveling bed, surrounded by his wizards. He'd just heard Fari report that the huge magical hammer they'd created had been for naught.

After Fari heard what the scouts had to say, he dared to approach his king. "I think it is clear, Your Majesty," he said, "that all our efforts are being wasted. There's no one out there."

"So I'm the fool, am I?" Manacia raged.

"Not at all, Majesty," Luka broke in. "Lord Fari meant nothing of the kind."

The old demon was surprised to see this unprecedented show of support from the Crown Prince.

"It is Protarus who is the fool, Majesty," Luka said. "How dare he toy with you? And such empty gestures. A few were hurt, even killed. But it's like a flea bite on a camel's ass. Nothing more."

Manacia was roused from his weariness. He slammed one taloned fist into the other. "I'll teach him to trifle with me," he said.

Again, the demon king shouted for his aides. "We march for the Two Rocks at dawn," he commanded. "We've seen Timura's magic. And it's nothing. Now let's see if Protarus can fight!"

*   *   *

Safar waved and the battlefield vanished. Gundara hopped onto his shoulder and quietly accepted his sugary reward. Safar turned to Iraj.

"Manacia should be good and angry now," he said.

"Good," Iraj said. He gave a hard jerk of his head. "Now, he'll get here quicker."

*   *   *

The night before the battle Safar and Leiria made love for the first time in a long time.

In the beginning Leiria was fierce, but later she wept.

Safar held her, letting her weep. Suddenly she raised her head, tears streaming down her cheeks.

"I would never betray you, Safar," she said, hoarse. "*Never!*"

Safar was surprised at this announcement. He wondered what could be its cause. But all he did was hold her closer.

And all he said, was, "Of course not." Murmuring it over and over again. "Of course not."

Until she fell asleep.

*   *   *

On the second day—just as the sun reached its highest point—Manacia's scouts came to the place of the Two Stones. There they found Protarus waiting.

His forces were arranged strangely. The main group was focused in the center—but pulled well back from the rock columns as if they offered some sort of shield, rather than just two incredibly tall pillars springing out of an otherwise empty wasteland.

Out to the side were cavalry wings, all bristling with the small bows of the plains warriors. Behind them were ranks of slingmen, all on foot. The slingmen were thinly guarded by small cavalry detachments and a few well-armed foot-soldiers—muscular men with short heavy spears in each hand and axes in their belts.

The scouts roamed the edges, letting their witch sniffers loose to find the magical center. The creatures looked like squat dogs with hyena faces. They dashed about, scratching at the ground and sniffing the air.

In the end they returned to their demon masters, tails between their spavined legs to show failure.

*   *   *

Safar watched the scouts ride off—heading north toward the Demon Moon where Manacia's forces were slowly moving forward.

He was perched on the crown of the westernmost rock column and had an excellent view. With him were Leiria, and four wizard helpers. There was a similar number posted on the opposite column, commanded by Horvan, his most able mage.

The spells he'd cast to shield the rock columns from the witch sniffers had been child's play. What had not been child's play was getting on top of those rocks. The task had been so difficult—the rocks so sheer—Safar's plan had nearly been wrecked before he started.

Iraj's soldiers were all men of the plains. Mountains were unknown to them. The

239

highest any had ever climbed was to the backs of their horses.

Safar had watched in awful suspense as the team Iraj had selected attacked the first rock column and failed time and again. They would get no higher than ten feet—fifteen at the most—then come off the smooth rock all flailing arms and shrill cries, like clumsy chicks falling from their nest.

The only fortunate thing was no one got hurt, beyond skinned fingers, knees and pride.

Finally, there was nothing to be done but have Safar attempt it himself. Everyone protested, Iraj the loudest.

"I'll not have my Grand Wazier killed before the battle even starts," he said.

"I'm a child of the mountains," Safar pointed out. "And the only one with climbing experience. Besides, I'm eventually going to have make the climb anyway. The team was just supposed to set up ropes so they could hoist me and my mages into place."

He shrugged. "It seems silly to risk all our plans over something so easily solved."

Finally, Iraj assented and Safar found himself next to the western column, peering up at the crown. He made a few cautious experimental attempts, fingers and bare toes skittering on the smooth rock, searching for hairline cracks just deep enough to give purchase.

The whole army was watching—an army that feared heights—and each time he fumbled and slid gently to the ground they gasped in unison as if he were plummeting to his death.

It reminded Safar of the nail-biting crowds at Methydia's Circus when great acrobatic feats were being performed. The thought brought back the skills he'd learned from Arlain and Kairo, and so on his first true attempt he scampered up thirty feet without pause.

The fifty-thousand man army cheered and applauded like the greatest audience ever gathered under one tent. Safar became carried away with the moment. Although he had good purchase, he pretended otherwise and made as if he'd lost his grip and was falling.

The army moaned in horror. It was an awful sound, a frightening sound. Nothing like a circus audience, which know deep in their hearts the performer will ultimately prevail.

It came to Safar the warriors were putting all their hopes in him. Yes, they knew Protarus was a great king and a mighty general who had carried them through the worst circumstances. Iraj was not a monarch who believed in wasting his soldiers' lives. But they feared the demons, especially demon magic and they were looking to Lord Timura, the Grand Wazier, wizard above all wizards, to save them. Hadn't King Protarus himself attested to Lord Timura's abilities? And hadn't they already seen his early successes with the demons who'd held Kyrania, and in the shadow fight with Manacia?

To them, if Safar fell to his death it might very well portend their own. Safar took pity and ended his antics.

But he was showman enough to free a hand so he could wave while he nodded his head to show it was all in good fun.

A huge explosion of nervous laughter carried him the next ten feet.

He resumed the climb, but cautiously, soberly. It turned out to be much more difficult that way. Without the crowd-stirred energy of a performer to aid him he quickly became tired, his fingers and toes numb and a few times he really almost did lose his grip and come off the wall. When it happened he was at a height that would have crippled him, or spelled his doom.

He was exhausted when he finally reached the top. Although the cheers were thunderous, he felt nothing when he sent down the ropes to let the others up.

All he could think of was the other stone column. There was no getting around the fact it too had to be climbed—and by him and him alone.

The only true blessing the Old Gods granted living things, and this grudgingly, was that all ordeals, all pain, must eventually end—one way or the other. It was Safar's good fortune his ended well. And now he was perched on the first column he'd climbed, a little tired, but certainly ready for Manacia.

After awhile he saw the dust ridge rise up under the Demon Moon and knew the enemy was approaching. He flashed a palm mirror to signal Iraj. Orders were shouted from below, trumpets blared, and there was a shifting sea of warriors coming to life and moving into position.

The dust ridge grew larger by the hour, soon walling the entire horizon. Still it approached, until there came a point when Safar could almost make out the dark outlines of mounted demons. Then all forward motion halted and the ridge became a huge dusty boil. It was like an old, weary dog who'd found a suitable place to rest and was turning round and round, to finally settle nose to tail.

Safar signaled again—Manacia was making camp.

⁎ ⁎ ⁎

The demon king scoffed at the battle map. It was clear to him what Protarus meant to do.

"He wants to use the stone columns to make us come to his center," he said to Luka. "That's where his main force is gathered."

He gestured at the wooden markers to the left and right of the main forces. "And he'll try to use his cavalry to pinch us in from the sides to make certain we stay on the course he prefers."

Manacia slammed his taloned fist onto the table, toppling the markers.

"Well, I don't intend to meekly follow this king's commands," he said. "I've fought this battle before. Hells, I've fought it four or five times at least."

He tapped his horned head. "It's all here," he said to his son. "A game of minds. I almost feel sorry for Protarus. It's clear he doesn't know who or what he is up against."

Fari cleared his throat for attention. "What of the wizard, Timura?" he asked. "He'll most certainly figure into Protarus' plans."

Manacia scowled. "It's true we haven't located him," he said. "Or any source of human magic for that matter. I suppose he's shielded himself. It's not an easy thing to do, so I mustn't underestimate him. Still, I've got similar shields in place, protecting a much larger wizardly force.

"We'll wait until he strikes and reveals himself. He won't stand a chance when we reply."

Luka and Fari exchanged quick looks. Each could tell the other was impressed with Manacia's reading of the situation.

The Crown Prince bitterly accepted his father's military expertise. He had no doubt when the battle commenced Manacia would prevail.

"We'll attack at dawn," Manacia said. "Just as the humans are stirring at the camp fires."

He gestured at the Demon Moon hanging over the northern horizon. "We'll have that at our backs to confound them," he said.

Manacia slapped his thigh in delight. "There's nothing I enjoy more than attacking an enemy with the light in his eyes."

Iraj surveyed his assembled troops. He let a broad grin play through his beard. "Here we are again, lads," he said. "Up to our callused behinds in hyenas and no way out!"

His voice, magically amplified by an amulet Safar had given him, rang with manly good cheer. The warriors roared laughter at their king's humor.

Iraj pointed a dramatic finger through the stone pillars, which perfectly framed the Demon Moon.

"Once again," he said, "we're facing a fellow who doesn't think we're fit to empty his piss pot."

The warriors rumbled their disapproval.

"But we've taught royal prigs like that a thing or two in the past, haven't we lads?"

The warriors shouted agreement.

Iraj waved them to silence. "It so happens that this time the prig we're facing is a demon."

There were low mutters, manly mutters, but forced.

Iraj thumped his chest. "I've fought demons before, lads," he said. "I fought them as a boy. And it was the demons who fell, not your king, boy though he was.

"You've never heard this story. It's a secret Lord Timura and I have kept for many years. But now I think it's time for all Esmir to know."

Iraj commenced to deliver an abbreviated, but highly dramatic account of the event.

"So you see, my lads," Iraj said when he was done, "demons bleed the same as all of us. They have magic, but so do we in Lord Timura. They have us outnumbered, but I've just told you a story of outnumbered boys so you know that's no problem to men like yourselves.

"But I won't lie to you. The demons are formidable foes. Yet, what would be the pleasure of fighting if all our foes were weak?"

This struck the men of Plains of Jaspar particularly well and they all thundered their approval.

"What do you say, lads?" Iraj shouted. "Shall we wait until Manacia brings the fight to us?"

This was met with a resounding "NO!"

"Shall we carry to the fight to him?"

This drew an overwhelming "YES!"

"Then let's go to him, lads!" Iraj thundered. "Let's catch him with his breeches down and buried to the hilt in some demon whore."

The skies shook with their roared approval.

* * *

As it so happened, Manacia *was* pleasuring himself with an enthusiastic demon maid when the news of the attack came. He wasn't "buried to the hilt," but he was definitely considering such an action when someone scratched at the entrance to gain his attention.

Manacia tumbled out of his harem tent, buttoning up his breeches. "Why do you disturb me?" he roared.

His aide gibbered, then pointed south. "Forgive mmm-mmm-me, Mmm-ajesty! But Pppp-protarus is attacking!"

Manacia's eyes shot south. It was dusk, but it was the eerie dusk of the Demon Moon, and the figures he saw—human warriors—were cast large and bloody red.

The demon king was no hysteric. He'd dealt with surprise attacks before. He calmed his fears and shouted for his generals to counter.

*   *   *

It was a Jaspar blood charge. No quarter given, none asked.

It was a screaming mass of horsemen, but not a man among them offered himself as a target. Each rode bareback, a thick leather harness girdling the horse's body, a slender rope lead to its mouth.

They whirled about the harness strap, sometimes to the left, sometimes to the right, sometimes hanging beneath the horse's belly. As they circled their mounts, they fired a constant stream of arrows from their small bows, so many that the sound was like a plague of biting flies descending in a black cloud on a cattle herd.

It was a mad charge, a charge where death was no consideration.

Arrow swarms disturbed the dusk with their black flight.

The screams of the demon wounded defied the desert calm.

And then they were among the demons, dropping their bows and drawing scimitars. Slashing this way and that.

They drove straight up the middle, nearly reaching Manacia himself, who was clambering aboard his elephant.

Iraj led that charge. He was a monster soldier, a soldier who could not be hit when the demon arrows swarmed back. His sword was a monster sword no blade could counter, no pike could match, no battle ax could confront.

He swept through the demon ranks. He was the arrow point, his men were its wounding flare, and the Demon Moon was his target.

He drove through the massed soldiers, aiming for the moon's blood spot, then he whirled and attacked the other way.

Iraj saw Manacia clambering on his elephant. A king-against-king fury took him and he struck toward his ultimate enemy.

But then Manacia's guard swarmed around him, spears tipped with deadly magic were hurled at him—countered by Safar's amulet which he wore about his neck—and Iraj wisely turned aside.

He led his warriors out of the demon horde, doing even more damage in his retreat than in the initial assault.

*   *   *

Gundara shouted, "Shut up, shut up, shuuuttt up!"

Safar broke in. "Quit arguing with your brother. I'm trying to concentrate."

"It's not my fault, Master," the little Favorite whined. "Gundaree won't stop bothering me."

Safar fought for calm. He'd learned from Methydia that Art and Temperament came in the same package. If you couldn't deal with the Temperament you had no business telling Art what to do.

He offered some treats.

"Here's two for you," he said, "and two for Gundaree. And if you behave yourselves, and aren't greedy little Favorites, there'll be two more for each of you when the job is done."

Leiria nudged him. "They're coming," she said.

Safar looked north. Night had fallen, but the Demon Moon was so bright all was clear. He saw Iraj and his men—about two hundred—streaming toward him. Behind them came Manacia's army. It was huge thing, a black plains' gobbling beast, gathering momentum as it came.

As Manacia had guessed, Iraj wanted the his enemy to come at him through the pillars where the main human force waited. If Iraj could squeeze the demons in from the sides, packing them so densely when they came through the pillars that they could barely move, the odds against the humans would be vastly reduced.

Although Manacia had fallen for Protarus' trap, the surprise attack and false retreat, he was no fool. The pursuit was orderly. Only one large group of demons, led by Crown Prince Luka, Safar guessed, was directly involved in chasing Iraj. The rest of the army was spread out across the plain, sweeping toward the humans in a broad wave so deep and strong they'd almost certainly be overwhelmed.

Safar motioned to his wizards. They touched brands to a heap of desert brush and dried dung. It burst into flames, flaring out so quickly the wizards had to jump back. Then it became steady, returning to a more comfortable size, and the wizards started tossing special powders on the fire. It hissed and boiled, sending up a shower of multi-colored sparks. Safar saw a similar glow on the eastern pillar and knew Horvan had joined him in the spell.

He let his mind slip down and down and then he was in a cold gray place with no top or bottom or sides. He called out, "Where are you, Ghostmother? It is I, your friend Safar Timura, come to find you."

There was no answer. Safar called again, "Come to me Ghostmother. Come to me please. I am in difficulty and have need of you."

Safar suddenly felt a presence. It was heavy and animal-like and smelled powerfully of cat. Then the grayness wavered and he could make out the faint of image of the old lioness.

"I am Safar Timura, Ghostmother," he said. "Do you remember how I helped you with your cubs?"

The lioness whined, the sound coming close to his ear.

"Will you help me, Ghostmother?" Safar asked. "As I helped you."

Another whine. And it came to him the old lioness had agreed.

"Thank you, Ghostmother," Safar said. "Wait here until I call, please."

Safar's head came up and he was suddenly back on the rock pillar again, the flames of the magical fire dancing and showering sparks only a few feet away.

He saw Iraj and his troops had almost reached the gap between the pillars.

"Get ready," he said to the wizards.

*   *   *

Manacia felt a warning buzz of enemy magic bloom into life. At the same time he saw the magical fires burning at the tops of the rock pillars.

The demon king gnashed his fangs in delight. "There you are, Timura!" he growled. "I've got you!"

He pulled back his claw, readying a soul-blasting spell.

*   *   *

Iraj and his cavalry swept through the gap.

"Go!" Safar shouted.

Four glass globes were hurled into the fire.

Out on the red-lit plain four white hot explosions erupted along the western edge of Manacia's oncoming army.

Then four more shattered the sky on the east as Horvan's wizards hurled their globes.

"Again!" Safar shouted.

*   *   *

Manacia was nearly hurled from the howdah by the force of the explosions. He was momentarily blinded, but when his vision cleared his first thought was that it'd returned too soon.

The explosions had punched big holes in his army's outermost wings. Other blasts followed and he heard screams of terror and pain. Then the wings started folding in on themselves as the soldiers on the edges scrambled toward the center to escape the blasts.

Manacia shouted orders to make them return to their positions, but in the chaos no one heard.

Furious, the Demon King's eyes swept up to westernmost tower of rock. He felt the presence of a powerful enemy wizard—Timura!

Manacia shrieked in fury and hurled his spell.

*   *   *

Safar was ready.

He sensed the pressure of the oncoming attack, and cried out, "Come, Ghostmother! Come!"

*   *   *

Manacia screamed an oath as he felt his spell blocked.

His attacking spell backblasted and he struggled for a shield and got it up just in time. A hot wave burst over his magical shield, spattering his spirit with hot drops of sorcery.

Before he could recover and strike again, he heard a mighty spine-cracking roar and a huge lion leaped out of nothingness and was on him.

Manacia grappled with it, and the lion's body was so cold it was like fighting death itself. He flung it away, and the lion tuck rolled and came to its feet.

It was then Manacia realized he was fighting a ghost. He could see right through the creature and when it opened its mouth and roared defiance, the sound had the ring of the unreal, the distant.

The lioness came for him again and Manacia dug as deep as he could into his bag of magical tricks.

Just before the massive jaws closed him he cast the spell.

The lioness vanished—returned to its ghost world.

Manacia sagged back, exhausted of all his powers.

*   *   *

Iraj whirled his horse about and prepared to meet the demon onslaught pouring toward the gap, Demon Moon at their backs.

They were packed tightly into a black river of warriors, but not as tightly as Iraj wanted. He signaled his flanks and the slingmen let loose, aiming at the edges of the demon column. At the same time the cavalry units charged in, backed by fast running ground troops.

A heavy swarm of missiles fell on the demons, killing and maiming many. Another swarm struck, dealing out more pain and death.

The human cavalry units slashed in, one from the east, the other from the west. They played a dancing game, darting in to savage the edges and darting out again before the demons could close on them. The ground troops struck immediately afterward, hurling their heavy spears, then grabbing axes from their belts and wading into the fight.

Gradually, the demon column narrowed more and when it finally struck through the portal between the two rock pillars the warriors were so densely packed they were easy pickings for the humans.

Iraj killed so many his sword arm grew tired, then his sword broke and he fought with a hand ax grabbed up from one of the fallen.

He saw Luka, separated from his guard, desperately fighting off three horsemen.

Iraj saw his three soldiers fall and Luka dash back into the demon ranks, a feat which drew Protarus' cold admiration.

Iraj fought on, raging against the demon tide.

Then slowly the battle changed. The sheer size of the demon army finally overcame all its flaws.

Iraj and his men found themselves being driven back as hammer blow followed hammer blow.

It wouldn't be long, he realized, before his lines cracked. And that would be the end of his army, his dreams and most certainly his life.

He chanced a look up at the western rock column.

And he thought, come on, Safar! Come on!

*   *   *

Safar readied his Grand Illusion.

It was the last weapon in his magical quiver.

He had no time to admire his father's artistry as he cast the spell that sent the fleet aloft.

*   *   *

Luka's fighting hopes were at their highest.

They were through the gap now and his army was spreading out, leaving themselves more room to use their weapons against the humans.

Luka could feel the enemy crumbling before him. One more hard effort, no more than two, and victory would be his.

Then, even above the noise of battle, he heard a murmur running through his troops, followed by collective gasps and cries of alarm. He saw several fiends pointing talons in wonder at the red-lit sky.

He looked up and it was all he could do not to gasp himself.

Sky borne warships were hurtling across the heavens to join the battle. They were the strangest vessels Luka had ever seen—fighting ships, suspended under big balloons, all crammed with warriors bearing spears with glowing tips. He couldn't tell what size they were. The ships seemed small and so he assumed they were at a great height. But certainly they were large enough to hold hundreds of warriors.

Then the ships were overhead and those warriors were hurling their spears into the demon masses. The spears grew before his eyes as they fell, each becoming easily as large as a tall demon.

They struck like lightning, glowing tips exploding, sending out great sheets of flame.

Another wave of spears hit. Then another. Blasting holes into the demon ranks. Filling the air with thunder and the smell of sulfur.

Then the demon army lost its nerve.

Luka could feel it, feel the fire go out of his warriors, smell the acrid stench of their fear.

They turned and ran. First a trickle, then a stream, then a full-sized river of shrieking demons, throwing down their weapons, shedding their armor and running over their own comrades to escape the horror from the skies.

Luka ran with them, spurring his mount to keep up. He wasn't running out of fear, although he was certainly frightened enough. He was racing to keep up, shouting for calm and order, doing his best to contain the rout.

Behind him he could hear the crack and thunder of the flying ships.

And the howls of Protarus' pursuing army.

＊　　　＊　　　＊

Hours passed before Manacia restored order. But when he did the best he could manage was to wheel his forces about and set up a fortified camp.

In the distance Protarus paused and set up a camp of his own.

"The fight isn't over yet," Manacia railed, striding about his command tent, kicking and clubbing any slave who got in his way. "He can't stand up to me again. I'll hammer him into dust!"

＊　　　＊　　　＊

Iraj paced his command tent, but his pace was measured, his manner calm.

"I hope we don't have to fight him again," he said to Safar. "If we do, it'll be out in the open on ground of his choosing. He won't fall for our tricks again."

"I suppose this where luck comes in," Safar said.

Iraj paused, considering, then nodded. "Yes," he said. "Now we get to see how lucky we really are."

＊　　　＊　　　＊

"He's lucky, that's all," Manacia said, voice still shaking with fury. "Moreover, he was aided and abetted by cowards in my own court."

Luka, who'd been listening as patiently as possible, turned cold.

"What is it you are suggesting, Majesty?" he asked, not bothering to hide his anger.

Manacia turned on him. "I'm not suggesting anything," he said. "It's clear enough my son is a coward, who leads a band of cowardly fiends."

"Ah!" Luka said as if he'd suddenly made a great discovery. "You intend to blame me, is that it?"

"You've shamed me," Manacia said. "But I'll not hide that shame. Fault will be directed at its source, no matter if that source is my son and heir."

Luka came closer, as if to appeal for reason.

Instead he said, "Father, tell me about the time my mother accused you of rape. It's such a humorous incident it will give us all good cheer."

Manacia frowned. "What's wrong with you?" he snapped. "This is no time for humor."

"Oh, but it *is*, father," Luka insisted. "This is the very *kind* of situation that *does* call for humor."

Manacia drew himself up for another angry bellow.

But Luka quickly drew his sword and cut the bellow off at its source.

He watched his father's headless body flop to the floor.

Luka turned to the others, calmly wiping his blade.

"Any objections?" he demanded.

The generals and aides were frozen, gaping at this turn of events.

Fari was the first to speak. "Not at all, Your Majesty," he said.

Stiffly and with much joint cracking he lowered his aged bulk to its knees.

"Long live King Luka!" he cried.

The generals followed his lead, dropping to the ground and abasing themselves and shouting, "Long Live King Luka!"

Luka peered at his father's head, eyes open and staring.

"What's wrong, father?" he asked. "You're not laughing!"

*   *   *

Some weeks later Iraj crossed the Forbidden Desert, leading a grand victory procession down the road to Zanzair.

Kalasariz had carried Luka's surrender terms to Protarus and acted as a go-between in the ensuing discussions. The demon army was broken up into small groups and sent home. Luka offered himself as hostage, sending Fari back to Zanzair—Manacia's head stored in ice—to arrange for Iraj's arrival.

To Safar's displeasure Kalasariz was rewarded with much gold and a high position on Iraj's staff. Safar advised his king against it, but Iraj had brushed off his advice, saying there was always a desperate need for good spies.

At last the day arrived when the gates of Zanzair came into view.

They were marching along a misty highway, banners fluttering, drums rapping time.

Iraj rode Manacia's great war elephant, Safar at his side. A large flag made of fine Sampitay silk hung from the howdah. On it was the Crest of The Conqueror, the red Demon Moon and silver comet.

But it was no longer Alisarrian's flag. Iraj had claimed it as his own.

In a week an elaborate ceremony would be staged in Manacia's former palace. Dignitaries, both human and demon, would crowd the grand throneroom and humble themselves before Protarus.

There he would be declared King of Kings, supreme monarch of all Esmir.

The breeze stiffened and Safar saw the mist lift. Directly ahead were the gates of Zanzair.

"Look!" Iraj said, excited as a child. "We're almost there."

Hanging from a post above the gates was Manacia's gory head.

The gates swung open and an enormous crowd of demons poured out to hail their new king. Iraj waved a mailed hand in return.

The demon cries became wilder, chanting: "Protarus! Protarus! Protarus!"

Iraj turned to Safar, a broad smile on his face.

"My friend," he said. "I owe all this to you."

Then the smile became a loud laugh of surprise.

"I said that in the vision, didn't I?" he reminded Safar.

"Or something close enough to it," Safar answered.

Iraj clapped him on the back. "And it's all come true," he said. "Everything you predicted."

Safar smiled. "I suppose it has," he said.

But the smile hid gnawing worry. His vision had carried him to the gates of Zanzair, but no farther.

And now all he could think was . . . What happens next?

PART FIVE
ZANZAIR

CHAPTER TWENTY FIVE
THIEF OF HEARTS

She was a rare woman. She had beauty, she had wealth, she had power.

She was also a woman of mystery, which in the time of the Demon Moon made her the rarest of women among men.

Her crest—the sign of the House of Fatinah—was a silver dagger and there was much talk of how it had come to be.

Some said it had been the crest of her late, unlamented husband, Lord Fatinah, a merchant among merchants so smitten by his young wife he'd left her his fortune. The Lady Fatinah, it was said, hastened her husband's departure from this world with his own dagger, which was made of silver. That the woman wore rich gowns all of mourning black and bearing the silver dagger crest added credence to this story.

Others speculated she'd once been the favorite courtesan of a king, perhaps even Protarus himself. In this version she'd come up the loser in a harem war and was driven out, but with many chests of gold and rare stones to speed her departure. Some said she'd slain her rival with a silver dagger, but the death caused such a scandal she was banished from the harem. Once again the tale of the aging Lord Fatinah came into play. Rumor mongers said the marriage was arranged to sidestep the scandal. They also said Lord Fatinah died before the marriage was consummated. Again, the dying nobleman had been so enamored of his beauteous wife that he'd bequeathed her all his worldly goods.

The curious throngs of Zanzair, with nearly as many humans as demons among them, babbled those tales and others when she passed by in her carriage, with the silver daggers emblazoned on each door.

The Lady Fatinah had demon outriders to push the throngs back and a human driver to hurry the matched black team of horses along. A burly demon guard sat next to the driver, sweeping the crowd with his ever watchful eyes.

Inside, Lady Fatinah's representative to Zanzair gushed on about all the arrangements he'd made in anticipation of her visit.

"You will see with your own eyes, My Lady," the man said, "that you chose wisely when you picked Abubensu to tend to your business in Zanzair."

He gestured out the window. They were traveling through the bazaar, an exotic scene of demons and humans haggling with stall keepers, or munching strange delights from the food carts; of families strolling along, purchases in hand, trailing human children and demon kits in their wake.

"Zanzair is surely the most marvelous city in the whole history of Esmir," Abubensu said. "Since our beloved king, Iraj Protarus, made it the center of his empire seven years ago, beings of every variety have flocked here, hoping against hope they can clutch the king's cloak and fly away with him to prosperity."

He raised a cautioning finger. "But Zanzair is also a most dangerous place, My Lady," he said. "Some who came were honest business folk, like myself. But many were thieves, both of the common and noble-born variety.

"And the intrigue!" He shuddered. "I can tell you stories about the intrigue and disgraceful goings on at the Royal Court that would set your teeth on edge."

"I'm sure you can," Lady Fatinah said smoothly. "And I'd be delighted to listen to your delicious tales at another time. But I hope you understand I have other things on my mind just now. Such as the living arrangements."

Abubensu beamed. What a genteel and soft-worded employer he had. Quite unlike a woman who'd supposedly killed her husband. And so beautiful! Abubensu had never been this close to such a woman. She filled her expensive black gown quite pleasingly. Her lips were full, dark eyes sparkling with what he dared dream was promise.

"You'll love the house I've found for you, My Lady," he said. "It sits on a hill, quite by itself. The night view of Zanzair is simply overwhelming. Especially the view of Protarus' palace. It's solid gold, you know, and when all the lights are turned on and the fountains are at play, why you would think it was the heavenly palace of a god."

"The view sounds most pleasant," Lady Fatinah said, wiping the chin of her child—a boy whose age was just past suckling and just short of speech. His name was Palimak, the Walarian word for promise.

"But to be frank," she continued, "it's more important to me that it have a good nursery."

"Remodeled to your exact specifications, My Lady," Abubensu said. "The grandest nursery ever created. No expense was spared."

"I hope it isn't too grand, Lady," the nurse broke in. She was a small woman, round and with a deep grandmotherly bosom. "Large spaces can be frightening to a child."

"There's a separate room for you right next to the young master's, Scani," Abubensu hastened to tell the nurse. "It's quite comfortable and you'll have no trouble keeping your eye on him."

Scani looked doubtful and started to speak, but Lady Fatinah silenced her with a warning look. The nurse took Palimak from Lady Fatinah's arms and fussed and cooed over him, making furiously whispered promises that no matter where he slept, Scani would always be nearby.

Abubensu went on. "Your neighbors," he said, "are all of wealth and breeding like yourself, My Lady. Their homes are close enough to give comfort, but distant enough to ensure privacy."

"I mentioned in my letter," Lady Fatinah said, "that I'd like to host a banquet as soon as possible to introduce myself to Zanzarian society."

"It has been done, My Lady!" Abubensu said with a pleased smile. "As a matter of fact I've taken the liberty of arranging an affair two nights from now. Invitations have been sent to a favored few—all beings of quality, mind you. And your staff, which I picked myself, is at this moment readying the banquet."

"There was one person in particular I asked you to invite," Lady Fatinah said. "Was that done?"

Abubensu bobbed his head. "Yes, My Lady. Lord Timura has been invited."

"And has he accepted?"

He hesitated. "Alas, My Lady, not as yet."

"But you expect him to?" Lady Fatinah pressed.

The little man shrugged. "I can't promise, My Lady," he said. "After all, he *is* the Grand Wazier, second only to King Protarus in importance."

Abubensu attempted a bit of gossip to steer conversation away from disappointment. "They were childhood friends, you know," he said. "They even call each other by their first names—Safar and Iraj—when in private."

He leaned closer, voice conspiratorial. "Although it is said that Lord Timura is not in such good grace with His Majesty these days. He has enemies who whisper ill things in the king's ear."

A dramatic shrug. "Who knows if these things are true, My Lady," he said. "Perhaps it is best after all if Lord Timura fails to attend. Why bring his political troubles to your esteemed doorstep?"

Lady Fatinah's eyes narrowed. "I *want* him at the banquet," she said, and there was no mistaking her firmness in the matter.

Abubensu struggled with his answer, clearly at a loss. "I will try, My Lady," he said, "but I can't swear that it's possible."

Lady Fatinah smiled, saying, "I have every faith in you, Abubensu."

She handed him a silk purse filled with coin. "Favor who you want with those," she said. Abubensu hefted the purse, brows rising as he noted the weight. "And you may keep whatever is left over for yourself.

"But make certain Lord Timura is there."

She turned to look out the window.

They'd come to a wide square and when she looked north she could see the blossoming trees that edged the Royal Gardens.

Beyond were the spires of the Grand Palace, glittering eerily under the ever-present Demon Moon.

Nerisa wondered if Safar would remember her after all these years.

✳ ✳ ✳

"In the end," King Protarus said, "it all reduces itself to money."

He snorted in disgust, an action much noted by the members of the assembled Royal Court. His snort would frame their discussions, dreams and nightmares for many days to come. Policy would be set because of that snort. Alliances threatened, reformed, or shattered. Thousands of miles away, men both small and large would tremble when news arrived of the king's sharply expelled breath.

"Every time I need to do something," Protarus said, "I'm told the cost is too dear. And when I—simple plainsman that I am—suggest the solution is to get more money, why I'm told there's no more to be had!"

The king's glare flowed down the several-leveled courtroom. First it took in Safar, his Grand Wazier and second in command, next the platform where King Luka—whose formal title was Prince of Zanzair—sat with Lord Fari and other important demons. Below were the Protarus' generals and top aides, a mixed lot that included demons and a few of his remaining rough plainsmen. Keeping himself slightly apart from this group was Kalasariz, who daily measured the distance and height between him and Safar. Beyond was the main floor of the courtroom, a vast area of hierarchical flatness where some courtiers were known to wear boosted up bootheels so they could stand taller and imagine they held greater favor with the king.

"Someone explain to me how this can be," Protarus demanded. "I am monarch of all Esmir. I number my subjects by the millions. All of whom seem to be going about making money and prospering, while their king lacks the basic means of running the kind of kingdom where they *can* prosper."

Protarus shook his head. "My problem is that I'm too generous," he said. "I made all my friends wealthy. Palaces, lands, money . . . Money! There's that word again!"

He looked at Safar. "You have money, Lord Timura," he said. "Why don't I?"

"You have only to ask, Majesty," Safar said, "and I will give it all back to you."

Frustrated, Protarus rapped the edge of his throne with bejeweled knuckles. "That's not the point, Lord Timura," he said. "I'm not that sort of monarch. Once I give a gift, I never ask for its return."

Leiria, Safar's guard and bedmate, stirred uncomfortably. She'd once been such a gift.

"The point is this," Protarus continued, "you have money and I don't because you have only your own household to keep up."

Protarus' hand swept across the courtroom, taking it all in. "I've got a kingdom to maintain. That's *my* household! And where does my household money go? Not for luxuries, that's for certain.

"The gods know I'm a man of simple tastes."

No one dared mention this was a great exaggeration. Protarus had long since shed his soldierly past and reveled in the comforts and pleasures of being King of Kings. He had many palaces, all fully staffed, vast stables of fine mounts of every variety and purpose, huge rooms packed with decorative weapons and armor, bulging storehouses and wine cellars, and immense harems stocked with a continuously refreshed supply of women.

The king sighed and sagged back in his throne, weary. The seven year reign had been difficult and it showed. Although he was still a man of less then thirty summers, he looked ten years older. His pride, his long golden locks, had thinned and he'd taken to wearing a jeweled skull cap beneath his crown. His beard was streaked with gray strands and his brow was plowed with worry lines.

"Tell us the problem again, Lord Timura," he said. "Lay it out fully so all can see."

Safar murmured respectful assent and rose. He strode up to Protarus' level and motioned to some men-in-waiting to pull aside the immense curtain behind the king's throne.

The wall was covered with a tremendous bas relief of Esmir. The largest features were the Gods' Divide, splitting much of the land from east to west, and the great desert, no longer forbidden, which had once separated human and demons.

Safar palmed a few pellets, hurled his hand downward in a dramatic gesture and there were several sharp retorts, drawing gasps from the court—including Iraj—and a thin haze of smoke curtained up from floor to ceiling. Behind the haze the bas relief suddenly glowed into being, causing a low chorus of amazement. They were looking at a living map of Esmir, complete with small moving figures, forests waving in the winds and waves beating distant shores.

Safar made a low bow to Iraj, with a sweeping showman's flourish.

"Behold your kingdom, Majesty," he announced.

Fari thought, I wonder how Timura does it? Not the living map . . . I understand that. Possibly even reproduce it, given a look at his notes. But the explosions and haze are another matter. Where was the magic? I sensed nothing!

This mystery was only one of several reasons Fari believed Safar must go.

Iraj's mood lightened. He clapped, saying, "Oh, very good, Safar. Very good!"

This was followed by a small patter of applause from the court. Luka grimly rattled his talons in false appreciation.

He thought, why all the flourishes and dramatic gestures? You would think this was entertainment instead of the serious business of administration. He's playing up to us, especially to Protarus.

Luka bitterly resented Safar's influence over Protarus. As Prince of Zanzair, Luka considered himself the second most important potentate in Esmir. He should be advising Protarus, not that commoner Safar Timura.

"Here are the locations of our most troubled regions, Majesty," Safar said.

He made another gesture and small flames flickered through the haze. There were at least two score spread out all over the kingdom. The flames were of different sizes, some minor glows where trouble was only starting, to larger spears of fire where things were nearly out of control.

"So many," Protarus murmured.

He shot a sharp glare at Kalasariz, saying, "You never told me there were so many!"

"Ah, yes, ah, I can explain, Your Majesty," Kalasariz fumbled. "Delayed reports . . . because of the . . . ah . . . difficulties."

Iraj gave him a cold nod and turned back to the map.

"This is the very latest information I have from our temples," Safar said. "And for the first time I think we can see just how widespread our problems are."

Kalasariz seethed anger for being upstaged by the Grand Wazier. The spy master preferred to show the king what he wanted him to know so he could control events. That damnable Timura, with his damnable network of priests, was stabbing him in the back.

Not for the first time, Kalasariz swore that some day he'd rid himself of Timura.

"The greatest problem seems to be in Caspan, Majesty," Safar said, pointing at the leaping flames near the edge of the western sea.

"Yes, yes," Protarus said. "That's why the subject of money came up. We need to send troops there and put down the rebellion. But I was informed by my treasurer I didn't have the money to pay for it. The coffers, it seems, are empty."

His gaze flickered over the map, once again noting the number. Finally he eyes came to rest on Caspan, nearly ringed with fire.

"Money *must* be found for Caspan," he said. "The question is where to get it."

"Taxes, Your Majesty," Luka broke in. "That's the answer. More taxes must be gathered. As you said, your subjects are enjoying prosperity because of your efforts. They should be willing to pay a fair price for that prosperity."

"I must disagree, Majesty," Safar said. "There is no general prosperity. A few areas, perhaps, but only those untouched by drought and plague. And, I might remind my noble friend, King Luka, these conditions have not only prevailed, but become worse over the past ten years."

Fari snorted. "Hadin, again!" he muttered.

Safar whirled on the old demon. "I've shown you the evidence," he said. "How can you deny the truth?"

"I'm not denying anything," Fari said. "Certainly there are problems. And possibly they were caused by some magical calamity in Hadin.

"What I disagree with most strongly is that these problems are necessarily long lasting. There have been calamities before. Droughts come. Droughts go. Plagues come. Plagues go. It's the gods' natural cycle. So only the best and most devout will live on to enjoy their well-deserved rewards."

"I won't quarrel with my esteemed colleague, Majesty," Safar said. "You want to hear solutions, not debate.

"I have one such solution to propose."

Protarus stirred. "Do you now?"

"I find myself agreeing with King Luka, Majesty," Safar said.

Luka frowned. Where was this going?

"Taxes are the answer, Majesty," Safar said. "Only, don't tax those who already pay. Tax those who don't."

Kalasariz' eyes narrowed. So that's his game, he thought.

"Tax *me*, Majesty," Safar said. "I not only benefited from your gifts, but I pay no taxes on them."

Safar pointed to Luka, then Fari, then Kalasariz, and all around the room, pointing at each nobleman in turn.

"We have *all* prospered, Majesty," he said. "But we pay nothing for it."

Protarus was interested. "I've often commented that generosity is my greatest virtue and flaw," he said. "Apparently I've forgiven more taxes than is good for me."

"Exactly, Majesty," Safar said. "I'm sure all of my colleagues would be delighted to share your heavy burden during this emergency."

"Ah, an emergency tax," Protarus said. "Maybe calling it that would wipe off some of the sour looks in this group." He smiled at Luka and Fari. Both forced smiles in return. He went back to Safar—"A temporary tax, lasting only through the emergency. That might go down better, politically speaking."

"I for one do not fear sacrifice," Luka said. "But I must point out that the money wouldn't be enough. It would pay for Caspan, perhaps." He pointed at the array of trouble spots on the bas relief. "But what of the rest?"

"King Luka is quite right, Your Majesty," Kalasariz said. "And I also join him in my willingness to sacrifice and share your burden.

"I also question the nature of the emergency."

He pointed at the bas relief. "This is very kind of negativism that is at the root of our problems, Your Majesty!"

Protarus lifted his head, interested.

"We are terrorizing your subjects, Majesty," Kalasariz continued, "with all this bad news. It feeds rumor that things are worse. It makes rebels out of weak men. It makes good honest subjects lie to your tax gatherers when they come to collect. And hold back vast amounts of money that rightfully belong to you.

"Vast amounts, Your Majesty. Vast."

"That's theft!" Protarus said, angered by the sudden vision of mean-spirited citizens burying huge chests of gold in their cellars.

"Exactly, Your Majesty," Kalasariz said. "Theft. "No kinder word to put on it. And I propose we end it at once!"

"How would you do this?" Protarus asked.

Kalasariz looked around at the huge assembly, then back at the king.

"I think it would be best discussed in private, Majesty," he said.

*   *   *

"I won't do it, Iraj," Safar said. "It may be in Kalasariz' nature to make such a great lie, but it's not in mine."

"How do you *know* it will be a lie?" Protarus said.

The two men were alone in the king's quarters. Less than an hour before Kalasariz, vigorously supported by Luka and Fari, had outlined his plan. Safar's opposition had been so heated Iraj had sent the three away so he could reason with him in private.

"Kalasariz had a good point about the effect all the negative news is having on the stability of the kingdom," Iraj continued.

"Lies won't make things better," Safar said.

"Again," Iraj said, "I don't see where anyone was proposing to lie. Kalasariz merely *suggested* we declare a national feastday. A feastday that would point up the positive, rather than the negative."

"And what of the casting?" Safar asked. "The casting that I, as your Grand Wazier, am supposed to oversee?"

"What's wrong with asking the gods when this long crisis will end?" Iraj said.

"A great deal," Safar replied, "considering that Kalasariz already had the answer he wanted me to report to all Esmir."

He held up a single finger. "One year!" He shook his head, disgusted. "One year . . . and the world will be well again."

"That's a good number," Iraj said, "If people believe things will be better in a year, they won't be so tight-fisted with tax money. Hells, I can even raise the taxes. An emergency measure, like you suggested."

"But on the poor," Safar said, "not the rich."

Protarus sighed. "It was a good idea, Safar. Not enough money to be gained, but a sound idea just the same.

"Unfortunately it wasn't something I could ever do."

"Why not?"

Another sigh. "These are the beings I eat dinner with, Safar. When I entertain, they are my guests. When I hunt, I hunt with them. They're my friends, after all. I don't want to sit around the table with everyone mad at me because I slapped a fat tax on them."

Safar didn't answer.

Protarus looked at him, then nodded, saying, "I suppose you're thinking if there are some things I won't do, then I should understand when you have similar reservations."

"Something like that," Safar said.

Actually he'd been thinking how revealing Protarus' statement had been. He'd rather starve the starving because he didn't want his wealthy friends mad at him.

"And if we *did* have a big public casting ceremony," Iraj said, "and you saw many difficult years ahead—rather than only one—you'd feel honor bound to report it. Is that right?"

Safar tried to lighten the situation with a smile. "Only some of it would be due to honor, Iraj," he said.

"After all, I've got my wizardly reputation at stake. When a year passed and the troubles continued no one would trust me again."

Protarus studied him for a long moment. Then he returned the smile, but his eyes were shielded.

"I can see how you might consider it too great a sacrifice to make," he said.

The meeting ended on that dissatisfying note.

Just before Safar left, the king said, "Oh, I almost forgot."

Safar was at the door. "What was that?"

"The captain of my guard says it's time for Leiria to drop by the palace for a little brush up on her training."

"I'll be sure to tell her," Safar said.

As soon as the door closed behind him Kalasariz came out of a side room. Behind him were Luka and Fari.

"I'm glad you signaled for us to linger within hearing, Majesty," Kalasariz said. "That was a most revealing conversation.

"And I must say you handled him quite smoothly, Majesty. Quite."

*   *   *

It was night when Safar's carriage made the approach to the grand mansion. It was raining so heavily even the Demon Moon was obscured from view.

"Who is this Lady Fatinah, Safar?" Leiria asked.

"I'm not quite sure," he answered. "Other than she may or may not be a notorious woman."

"She must be more than that," Leiria said, "to get the Grand Wazier himself to show up at her welcoming banquet."

Safar peered through the curtains, but the night was so black all he could see was his own reflection in the glass.

"It's that chief clerk of mine," Safar said. "He can't resist a bribe. I'd get rid of him, but the extra money he earns dishonestly makes him so efficient I have the best kept schedule of any administrator in Esmir."

"You could have refused," Leiria said. She gave him a teasing smile. "But I suppose you're as curious to see her as every man in the city. It's said she's quite beautiful."

"I never know when the event is the result of bribery, or duty," Safar said. "It's easier just to go to all of them. Linger an hour or so for appearances' sake, then slip off."

"And it doesn't hurt that she's beautiful," Leiria said.

Safar laughed. "And notorious," he said. "Don't forget that."

Leiria laughed with him, a lovely and exotic woman in her own right in her best dress uniform.

But Safar took note she was unusually inquisitive that night.

And her training session at the palace had been that same morning.

Interesting.

*   *   *

Nerisa saw him come in.

The rain had made the guests tardy but after a time she'd despaired Safar would be among the later arrivals. It had been a difficult evening, doing her best to be a charming and witty hostess to a group of strangers, while at the same time preparing herself for the moment when he arrived.

She didn't want to him think she'd come all this way because she required something. The Lady Fatinah was quite capable of taking care of herself and didn't need a man—even though he might be the Grand Wazier—to fend for her. No, she had a duty to perform. A too long delayed duty.

As for her girlish crush on Safar, it was years ago and was, after all, just that—girlish. Safar was kindly enough at the time to see it and not humiliate her.

She determined when they met she'd be as calm and cool as everyone expected the Lady Fatinah to be.

Then she saw him at the door. One minute the entryway was empty, the next a liveried servant was leading him in.

Someone pointed her out to him and he raised his head and he smiled as their eyes met.

Nerisa was lost.

His eyes were just as blue as she remembered.

*   *   *

Safar was stunned when he saw the woman approach. The Lady Fatinah was every bit as beautiful as people had said. Perhaps even more so in her stunning black gown, cut low to reveal a pearly bosom. The dress clung to her, showing off her long slender figure.

But her face was a cold shield when she came close, hand outstretched to welcome him. The coldness put Safar off, as did her thin smile. This was clearly a woman out for the main advantage, he thought. His clerk had taken a bribe and that was that.

Then their fingers touched and Safar felt her shiver. He looked into her eyes—saw the dancing flecks of gold. He saw her lips turn up in a familiar crooked smiled.

"It's Nerisa, Master!" Gundara hissed from his breast pocket. "Nerisa!"

But Safar had already seen and known. He was in shock, seeing little Nerisa raised from the dead to come back as the beauteous Lady Fatinah.

Nerisa gave his hand a warm, firm squeeze.

She whispered, "Don't give me away." Then, loud enough for all to hear, "How kind of you to visit my humble home, Lord Timura."

Safar murmured a suitably polite reply.

"I fear we've started without you, My Lord," Nerisa said, pointing at the tables of food. "Why don't we dispense with formalities and join the others before you starve to death?

"Perhaps, if you are still in a generous mood, we can have a little chat later and get to know one another."

Safar came unstuck enough to make an awkward bow. In a daze he let a servant lead him over to the banquet area.

Only when he sat down did he realize he'd left Leiria in the entryway without orders. He turned his head and saw her looking in his direction, her face like stone. He whispered a message for a servant to carry to her, saying she could join the other bodyguards in the pantry. But when the message was delivered he saw Leiria give a furious shake of her head, hiss something back, then exit into the storm.

When the servant returned Safar wasn't surprised at her reply: "Please tell his Lordship thank you, but I shall wait in his carriage."

This was not good.

Then he heard Nerisa laugh—that natural earthy laugh breaking through her facade—and he forgot all about Leiria.

*   *   *

The rain had made the banquet late, but it also caused it to break up early. The guests streamed out, saying they had a lovely time but Her Ladyship would understand that with the storm they had to hurry home.

Nerisa murmured polite good-byes, but the whole time her attention was fixed on Safar, tarrying in an out-of-the-way corner near the verandah. It was as if all the years between them had collapsed into but a few days or weeks. Old emotions were new again, swift torrents hammering against her mature resolve.

She called herself a fool, thinking it was only the stress of the meeting churning up silly emotions. And even if she did still have tender feelings for him, Safar had never shared those feelings. He'd only been kind to an orphan waif. Kindness did not equal love.

Once again she steeled herself and when the last guest was gone she strolled over as casually and easily as any great lady going to greet an old, dear friend.

But when she reached him he leaped to his feet, saying, "By the gods, Nerisa, I thought you were dead!"

And he crushed her into his arms.

*   *   *

Outside, Leiria huddled in the carriage, peering through the curtains. Even in the downpour she could make out Safar's familiar figure pacing in front of the wide glass verandah doors.

She saw another figure approach—a woman's slender figure.

Lightning crashed, momentarily blinding her.

When her vision returned she saw Safar and the woman embracing.

*   *   *

The last vestiges of Methydia's gentle spell of forgetfulness vanished when Nerisa came into his arms.

A thousand and one thoughts and emotions burst forward, while another thousand and one crowded behind, demanding to be heard.

But all he could say was, "Nerisa, my little Nerisa."

He kissed her hair, her cheeks, the tears flowing from her eyes, crushing her against him as if the tightness of his embrace would keep her from turning into a ghost and wisping away.

Then their lips met and the embrace become something else altogether.

It happened so abruptly there was no time for questioning, much less surprise.

*   *   *

Nerisa melted against him, weeping and murmuring his name. She was in a dream, an old sweet dream, and her Safar was holding her close, kissing her, whispering endearments. Passion firing them both beyond control.

She opened her eyes and saw her major domo's shocked face reflected in the glass of verandah doors. But she didn't care and she waved a curt dismissal just as Safar swept her off the floor.

And she said, "Yes, yes, please, yes," and somehow she directed him to her rooms.

Then they were in the big soft bed, tearing at each other's clothes.

*   *   *

"After I fled Walaria," Nerisa said much later, "I became a caravan lad."

She smiled at the memory, nestling deeper into Safar's arms. "I always did play a good boy."

Safar gently caressed her. "You wouldn't have such an easy time of it now," he said.

Nerisa giggled. "Actually, it became a problem fairly quickly," she said. "I suddenly bloomed, as the old grannies gently put it. One day my breeches didn't fit over my hips. The next, I was bursting the seams of my lad's shirt. I had to bind myself down and get looser clothes."

"Did no one ever suspect?" Safar asked.

She shook her head. "Never. Oh, I got a few odd looks once in awhile. But that was the extent of it. Second glances, nothing more."

Safar said, "That leaves a great leap from caravan lad to the rich Lady Fatinah."

"I suppose it does," Nerisa answered. "Although it didn't seem like it at the time. I had some money. The gold you gave me. I invested a little of it in some of the caravan goods, made a good profit and invested more."

Nerisa laughed. "I found I had a talent for merchanting. All those years as a little thief served me well when it came to picking out bargains and quality goods.

"After a time I had enough to become a minor partner of a very wealthy caravan master."

"Lord Fatinah, by any chance?" Safar asked.

Nerisa made a face. "It's true he was named Fatinah," she said. "But he was no lord. He was a merchant, nothing more. Old, fat and kindly. At least I thought he was being kindly. He treated me like a son."

Another laugh. "As it turned out, he merely had a weakness for handsome boys."

262

Safar stirred. "You mean, he . . . ?"

"He . . . nothing," Nerisa said. "Fatinah was an honorable old man. He believed it unseemly to take advantage. I never even knew his feelings toward me . . . or the boy he thought I was . . . until just before he died. Then he confessed all. Swore he loved me. And handed me a will, saying I was to inherit all."

"That's when I became a woman . . . and his widow. The will would never have stood, otherwise. No one would understand, much less believe, that he'd give such a fortune to a mere boy. So I invented our marriage. Paid certain sums to certain people to draw up the necessary documents. No one ever questioned an old man would be fool enough to give his money away to a grasping young woman.

"Even so, the rumors started that I'd killed him. Especially after I purchased the necessary background to make him a nobleman."

"No one ever questioned that?" Safar asked.

Nerisa came up on an elbow, that crooked grin of hers playing on her face. A smile that brought a pang of love to Safar's heart, rather than its lesser cousin, Fondness.

"If you play the royal," she said, "and you play it well, no one questions anything. Especially if you have money.

"Besides, in these times there's so much chaos all of Esmir is turned upside down. I took advantage of that chaos, running caravans into places no one else dared go. I suppose I made a profit on the troubles of others. But I brought them what they needed. Bought what they no longer had use for. And consoled myself with the thought that I'm Misery's child.

"I believed I had a right."

"I suppose you do," Safar said. "Once I'd have said otherwise." She smiled at this. "But there are so many greater thieves in this world, thieves who will steal dreams. Thieves who break you. Thieves who would kill all you love, require you to watch, then kill you as well.

"And then steal your heart out of your body to make a sorcerer's meal."

Nerisa embraced him—twining arms and legs about him. Made her body as soft as she could for a shield that would protect him and comfort him from all the devils tormenting him.

She was Nerisa, the thief of Walaria, and she would allow no man she loved to come to harm.

✻   ✻   ✻

Later she took him into the nursery to meet Palimak. The child was awake, hazel eyes reflecting the candle she carried.

Nerisa picked the child up, wrapping his favorite crib blanket close around him. He was a tubby little thing with dark hair, olive skin and pearly milk teeth.

"This is Safar," she said to the child. "The one I've been telling you about all these months."

She made a nervous smile at Safar. "This is Palimak," she said.

"My son."

Palimak turned his chubby little face to look at Safar. He kicked his feet in delight and smiled.

His eyes lit up and with a shock Safar saw the hazel turn to a glowing yellow.

Demon yellow!

Nerisa's heart plummeted when she the look on her lover's face.

Safar managed a faint smile and held out a hand. Palimak grabbed his foremost finger and squeezed.

"He's strong!" Safar said, dredging a compliment from the depths of his confusion.

Nerisa turned her face to Palimak, hiding her feelings. "Of course he's strong," she said. "Aren't you strong, my Palimak? The strongest little boy in the world!"

The child gurgled pleasure. Then he threw up, soiling himself and Nerisa's sleeping gown.

"Oh, you bad boy, you!" Nerisa scolded. "Here I'm trying to show you off and you play the little pig."

Then she burst into tears.

Safar sat beside her, putting his arms around both of them.

"Why are you crying?" he asked. "Children make messes. That's what they do! Besides making you love them, of course.

"Ask my sisters what a mess I was! No. Come to think of it, don't. They will tell you in excruciating detail what a dirty little boy I was."

Instead of calming her, the words infuriated Nerisa.

"That's not why I'm crying!" she said. "As you know very well!"

She reached into her gown, drew out an object and threw it on the bed.

"Here!" she said. "Here's your damned old knife."

Safar stared at it. It was the silver dagger Coralean had given him long ago.

Nerisa wiped her eyes, pulling herself together. "That's why I came here," she said. "To return the dagger. It's yours. It was wrong of me to keep it. And I was a fool, a stupid, weak fool, to deliver it to you myself instead of sending a messenger."

Palimak stared to cry, which made Nerisa angrier. "There, you see what you've done!"

Safar was confused. "What have I done?"

"I saw *that* look on your face," Nerisa said. "You think he's a monster! A half demon, half human freak.

"Well, be damned to you. I've had my pleasure. I've had my girlish dream. Safar Timura, my great ideal. The man who had so much kindness in him he could understand anything and anyone." She laughed bitterly. "I should have known better. And it's a good lesson for me.

"Now Palimak and I will be on our way. And to the Hells with you! And to the Hells with me for letting you make me into a fool!"

Safar started to get angry himself. "This is hardly fair," he said. "The least you could have done is warn me. At least you could have—"

A voice broke in: "Shut up, shut up, shuutt uppp!"

Safar swatted his tunic pocket. "Just stop it," he said. "I'm not in the mood to hear you argue with Gundaree."

The little Favorite leaped out of his pocket onto the bed. He put his hands on his narrow hips.

"I am *not* telling Gundaree to shut up," he said.

His eyes swept over Safar, then Nerisa, then Palimak. Back to Safar again.

"I am telling *you* to shut up, Master," he said. "And you too, Nerisa."

He sighed. "You were the first one to give me sweets in a thousand years," he said to Nerisa. "And you," he said to Safar, "have been a decent master, as masters go. Otherwise I wouldn't say a thing.

"If you both insist on making stupid human mistakes, why should I care? But I guess I do. So I'm saying, Shut up!"

"What mistakes?" Nerisa asked.

"He thought you had a husband," he said to Nerisa. "A demon husband."

"She thought you didn't want a little monster on your hands, much less a woman who would sleep with a demon."

"I don't have a husband," Nerisa said. "Demon or otherwise. Palimak is a found-ling. An orphan. Like me."

"And I don't care who you slept with, or didn't sleep with." Safar said. "It's none of my business. As for me thinking Palimak is a monster because he's part demon, why nothing could be further from the truth.

"He's a child. I like children. Ask my mother. Ask my father."

"There, you see?" Gundara said. "Wasn't that easy?"

He hopped onto the bed, growing larger. He chucked Palimak under the chin. The child gurgled in pleasure.

"Why don't you leave him here with me?" Gundara said. "Go back to the bedroom and do whatever you think is necessary to apologize to each other."

The little Favorite paid no attention to the murmurs between the two lovers. Nor did he turn to watch them slip out of the room. His entire focus was on the child with the glowing yellow eyes.

"What a handsome little thing," he said. "Eyes just like mine. Do you know how to talk yet?"

Palimak burbled and wriggled his little arms and legs.

"I guess not," Gundara said.

He made himself smaller and hopped onto the child's chest. He made funny toad faces and Palimak laughed, eyes glowing brighter.

"Do you know how to say, shut up?" Gundara said. "Go ahead. Try it. Say—Shut up. Shut up. Shuutt uuppp!"

And Palimak spoke his first words, "Shut up!"

"That's my boy," Gundara said. "Won't your mother be surprised in the morning?"

"Shut up, shut up!" the baby cried, "Shut up, shuuut uuppp!"

*   *   *

"It's my understanding," Kalasariz said, "that Lord Timura and this Fatinah woman have been in each other's company for weeks."

"That is so, My Lord," Leiria said. She turned to Protarus. "Lord Kalasariz' under-standing comes from my daily reports *to* him, Your Highness," she said. "Reports you ordered, Sire."

Protarus smiled. "I wanted to hear it from your own lips, Leiria," he said.

"Then you have heard it, Majesty," she said. "Other than for the hours of the busi-ness day, Lord Timura and Lady Fatinah have not been apart since the night they met."

"Doesn't that trouble you, Leiria?" Kalasariz asked. "It was my impression that you and Lord Timura have been lovers for some years."

Leiria shrugged. "It was my duty," she said. "The king knows that."

Protarus chuckled. "And an unlovely duty it was," he said to Kalasariz. "My friend Safar may be Grand Wazier of Esmir, but he is not so grand in bed." Then, to Leiria, "Isn't that true, my dear?"

"I have little experience with men, Majesty," she said. "But you are such a lion, sire, I was spoiled for any other."

Protarus roared laughter. "You see how it is?" he said to Kalasariz. He wiped his eyes. "When I bed a woman, she *stays* bedded, dammit! You should hear the weeping in my harem when I choose who is to enjoy my royal embrace and who must wait until another night."

Kalasariz grinned. "All of Esmir knows of your prowess, Majesty," he said.

He regarded Leiria. The moment he'd first seen her cast adoring eyes on Safar he'd known he could make use of her one day. It was his fine fortune Safar had betrayed her, giving Leiria good reason to seek revenge. Otherwise, kingly orders or not, he wouldn't have trusted her reports about Safar's activities.

"I don't think we have any further need for you at this moment, Leiria," he said, dismissing her. "You may report to me at the same time tomorrow."

Leiria touched hand to sword hilt and bowed in the military manner.

"Very good, My Lord," she said, and exited.

Protarus stared after her, thinking. Then he said, "This Fatinah must be an amazing creature to have Safar so spellbound."

"She is *quite* beautiful, Majesty," Kalasariz said. "I wouldn't mind giving her a tumble myself."

"I doubt if you'll have the opportunity," Protarus said. "Lord Timura has asked me for permission to wed her."

Kalasariz eyebrows rose. "Will you give it, Majesty?"

"I don't see how I can deny him," Protarus answered. "It's a routine request my courtiers are required to make by law. I've never said no to anyone yet."

"But we know nothing about this woman, Majesty," Kalasariz said. "This fact alone should make us be wary. My spies have sought information about her all over Esmir. To no avail. Apparently she just suddenly appeared one day. A rich noblewoman no one ever heard of before."

"And she has a child," Protarus said.

"Yes, but whose child is it, Majesty? That too is a mystery."

"I can't imagine any man wanting to wed a woman who was bred to another," the king said. "Beautiful though she may be."

"My sentiments exactly, Majesty," Kalasariz said. "Considering everything else, it tends to add to my suspicions."

"You think she is dangerous?"

"I know of no other woman like her in Esmir," Kalasariz said. "Somehow she's made herself extremely rich. From all reports she becomes richer by the day through shrewd business dealings. She answered to no man, at least until she entered Lord Timura's life. And it's my guess she doesn't answer to him either."

"Do you think she advises him?"

"That would be a safe assumption, Majesty. She's certainly a strong willed woman. And ambitious."

Protarus stirred, rapping his rings against the throne.

Then, "Yes, she would be, wouldn't she? She has my Grand Wazier in her thrall. What next?"

"Yes, Majesty," Kalasariz said. "What next?"

CHAPTER TWENTY SIX
WHERE THE RAVENS WAIT

The Grand Palace of Zanzair was a place of haunted chambers, cries in the night and conspiratorial whispers blowing like dry winds down the dark corridors. It reeked of centuries of intrigue and betrayal. Much blood had been shed over the years and there were places where the stone floors still bore murder's black stain.

Many kings had risen and many had fallen in that palace, but there were no noble monuments to mark their passing. Assassins were the dark messengers of each reign's end. A royal head posted at the main gates marked each beginning. And the first to praise the new monarch's name were feasting ravens.

Now Iraj Protarus was king and the intrigue and betrayal continued as before. Safar could smell the danger when he walked through the big main doors, sentries coming to attention and saluting the Grand Wazier. There was a sulfurous stink of dark magic in the air and under his formal tunic the stone idol sparked warning.

There was nothing unusual about Safar being summoned to a meeting with King Protarus, but as he strode through the palace—Leiria a few paces behind—many eyes turned his way. Some looked speculative, some glinted hatred, and some—the largest number, he hoped—appeared sympathetic.

As he approached the door of Iraj's private quarters it came open and three beings, their backs to him, bowing and humbly excusing themselves to "His Gracious Majesty" made their way out.

A sentry closed the door and they turned, each reacting in a different manner when they saw Safar standing there.

The first, Kalasariz, was cheery. "Good morning, Lord Timura," he said. "I hope this day finds you well."

"Well enough, thank you," Safar said, nodding at the hammer-faced spymaster.

The second, King Luka, was arrogant. "Grand Wazier," he said, only those two words and a nod of his demonly head noting Safar's presence.

Safar nodded in return, but said nothing.

The third, Lord Fari, was nervous. "How good to see you, Lord Timura," he said. "It's been long since I've had the pleasure of your company. Perhaps you would grace my humble home for dinner some evening?"

Safar dipped his head in a slight bow. "It would be an honor to be your guest, My Lord," he said.

Fari quivered, a jolt of alarm showing in his yellow eyes. "Quite, quite," the old demon said. "Of course, you are always so busy with your duties as Grand Wazier I suspect, alas, it will be a long time before you are able to attend."

"I'm never too busy for you, Lord Fari," Safar said. He couldn't resist the tease.

Fari clacked his talons together, distressed. "I'll have my clerk speak to your clerk," he said, "and arrange a convenient evening."

"Thank you, My Lord," Safar said, making another slight bow. "I eagerly await your kind invitation."

The sentry appeared, motioning for Safar to enter the king's chambers. He made his polite farewells to the three and went in—leaving Leiria waiting in the hallway outside.

Iraj was at his desk, looking over some reports. At least he appeared to be. His head was down, paper documents were in front of him, but his focus was on one spot instead of sweeping across words or numbers, betraying his pretense of being totally absorbed in his royal duties.

Safar cleared his throat and Iraj's head came up. He smiled. But his eyes seemed cold.

"Ah, there you are, Safar," he said. "Get a drink. Make yourself comfortable."

Safar sat and poured himself a cup of brandy from the spirits' service on the desk.

Iraj pretended to go back to the report, but his bejeweled fingers gave him away, rap, rap, rapping on the arm of the chair.

Finally, Iraj nodded, slapped the report down and raised his head to regard Safar.

"This is a little difficult for me, Safar," he said. "But I need to speak to you man to man—and as a friend."

Safar felt the stone idol glow warmer, uncomfortably so.

He smiled, saying, "Always, Iraj."

"It's about this marriage request of yours to the Lady Fatinah."

"What about it?"

"Are you sure this is wise, old friend?" Iraj asked. "I understand she is a beauty. And I congratulate you on your taste. But marriage!"

"I love her, Iraj," Safar said. "In Kyrania, marriage almost always follows love."

Iraj gave a nervous laugh. "*That* was Kyrania," he said. "You're no longer a common potter's lad. You are the Grand Wazier—second only to me in importance. You can have any woman you want. For your bed, or for marriage for that matter."

"I know that, Iraj," Safar said. "And it's Lady Fatinah I choose for both."

"But she may not be suitable for you," Iraj said, "beautiful though she may be."

"To me she's more than any potter's lad, as you put it, could possibly deserve. Meaning, she loves me too. What other requirement should I ask of a woman?"

"Here's what I think," Iraj said, leaning across the desk. "This is a mere romantic attachment. You know you have a weakness for such things. Remember Astarias? You thought the sun rose and set on her. You declared your love to the mountains. And even asked her to be your bride."

"She laughed, if you recall."

"This one didn't laugh," Safar said.

Iraj studied Safar for a moment then, "All I'm asking is that you reconsider."

Safar started to speak. But Iraj raised a hand to stop him.

"I know you're stubborn, Safar," he said, "so don't answer just now. Think on it a day or two and we'll talk again.

"I'm asking you to do this for me as a friend."

Safar bit off automatic refusal. "Very well, Iraj," he said. "I'll do as you ask."

He wouldn't change his mind, but agreement gave him time to figure out what was wrong and how to get around it.

Safar tried make a joke of the situation. "If Auntie Iraj wants a two-day cooling off period, she'll get it."

Protarus didn't respond. His eyes seemed glazed, as if he were elsewhere.

They snapped back to alertness. "Well, that's one problem dealt with easily enough," he said, forcing a light manner. "On to the next."

"Which is?"

"I'm afraid it's another delicate matter, my friend," he said. "So try to keep an open mind, as you did before."

"I will."

"It's this business about the casting," Iraj said. "Asking the gods what the future holds."

Inwardly, Safar groaned. Outwardly, he let a wry smile play across his face.

"So that's what my colleagues were doing here," he said. "Why, I'd thought they'd all gathered to sing my praises to their king."

Iraj frowned. "No one said anything against you," he said, curt. "I wouldn't allow such a thing."

Safar recognized the lie for what it was. "Of course, you wouldn't, Iraj," he said. "After all, we're blood oath brothers. And no man of honor would let another speak against his blood oath brother."

Iraj gave him the steadiest of gazes. "Never," he agreed. His cheek twitched. So he added, firmer still, "Never!"

"So what new suggestion did my friends have about the casting?" Safar asked.

"Fari proposed a compromise," Iraj said. "Make it two years, instead of one. My subjects will take just as much heart at that. Two years in not such a long time to wait for the Age of Great Blessings."

"Oh, so it's got a name now, does it?" Safar said. "The Age of Great Blessings?"

"Call it anything you like," Iraj said. "So long as it sounds positive. The point is, we want to say—quite firmly—that things will get better by and by, if only we make suitable sacrifices to the gods and be patient."

"I'll give you the same answer I gave before, Iraj," Safar said. "I won't lie. An extra year won't make it less of one. Or three, or five, even."

Protarus looked alarmed. "Five years!" he said. "You don't think it'll last that long, do you?"

"I have no idea," Safar said. "And that's the point. No one does. Not a bone caster, entrails reader or stargazer in your kingdom could say. All the signs are blank. As if there were no gods listening."

"That's ridiculous," Iraj said, features flushing. "Of course they're listening. Why else am I on this throne? Who guided me here but the gods? There's the Demon Moon. The comet ascending. Your vision long ago. All those things point to a decree from the Heavens themselves!"

Safar knew better than to argue. Iraj had fixed on this "divine destiny" idea when they were boys. To dispute it would be pointless—and dangerous.

"Whatever the reason," he said, "the gods are silent just now."

"Just say it for them, then," Iraj urged. "Say all will be well in two years. It's as good a guess as any."

"I can't," Safar said.

"It would offend your precious honor," Iraj scoffed.

"Something like that," Safar answered.

"Fari doesn't have that problem," Iraj said. "He told me he used to do such things for Manacia all the time."

"And look where that got Manacia," Safar said.

Iraj glared at him. "That has nothing to do with it," he said. "I was talking about honor, not Manacia."

"Well, if it doesn't trouble Fari to lie," Safar said, "then let him do it. He can oversee the whole thing. Feasts. Sacrifices. Prayers. Then the big lie. Let me know what date you decide on so I can be sure to be absent."

"That's damned foolishness!" Iraj shouted. "You're my Grand Wazier! Everyone will think you're opposed and are making yourself absent to show disfavor."

"That does pose a problem, doesn't it?" Safar said.

"Well, let's not have one, then," Iraj said. He'd calmed himself. He flashed his most winning smile. "Just do as I ask, Safar. A favor for a friend."

"Don't stake our friendship on this," Safar warned. "It would be a grave error to let it come to that."

Iraj trembled in fury. For a moment Safar thought he would lose his temper.

Suddenly, Protarus relaxed. He sighed deeply, emptied his cup, then sighed again.

"What a difficult man you are, Safar Timura," he said. "As immovable as the mountains themselves."

"I take no pride in it," Safar said. "It's only how I was raised."

"Then thank the gods," Iraj laughed, "that I only made one friend in Kyrania. Otherwise I would have been driven quite mad by now."

*   *   *

"There can only be one explanation for it, Majesty," Lord Fari said. "The Grand Wazier has clearly gone mad."

Protarus looked surprised. "Safar mad?" he said. "Why, he's always been the most stable of individuals. Oh, he has some silly flaws, of course, like that Hadin obsession of his. But madness?"

The king, led by Fari, Luka and Kalasariz, was moving along a narrow corridor toward the chambers containing what had once been King Manacia's Necromancium. The atmosphere was dank, the air smelled of embalming fluids and their bootsteps sounded unnaturally loud as they approached, making all seem very surreal.

"If I may say so, Majesty," Fari said, "madness is an affliction all wizards should guard against constantly. I am very old and know of what I speak. I've seen many a young mage overcome by the powerful forces he must reckon with. He forgets all true power resides with the king and he merely manipulates the spirit world for his monarch's benefit. After all, the king rules by Divine Decree. That is the nature of things, as the gods revealed to us long ago."

Luka snorted. "What else could you call it but madness?" he said. "Only a madman would play such a dangerous game. This is no ordinary monarch he's dealing with. But the King of Kings. Absolute monarch of all Esmir."

"What really troubles me," Iraj said, "is his attitude that somehow I want to harm my subjects. My whole purpose—my whole life—has been dedicated to the exact opposite. I want nothing but good for everyone. I truly do seek an Age of Great Blessings. Peace and plenty for humans and demons alike.

"Why, I remember telling him something almost exactly like that years ago when we were boys. And I've certainly done nothing but become stronger in that resolve.

"I consider it my holy duty."

"The root of the problem, Your Majesty," Kalasariz said, "is that Lord Timura has become not just mad, but power mad. This is not speculation, Majesty, but fact supported by your very best spies.

"Lord Timura has said time and again that he is more popular than Your Majesty. He believes he is revered by all your subjects. And that he should be king, instead of you.

"This is why he refuses you, Majesty. He holds his own reputation as more important than your own."

Iraj was seething when they entered the Necromancium. Rather than needling that anger further, the three conspirators changed their manner, pointing out different objects of interest.

Fari, the old demon wizard, took the lead.

"You see this, Majesty?" he said, showing him a flask covered with magical symbols.

"It contains a potion that would enhance even your mighty abilities with women. One drop in a glass of wine and you could pleasure a hundred maids."

Next, he displayed a small purse. He upended it and a handful of rare gems poured out. "With the proper spell, Majesty," he said, "these gems can become many. I mentioned their existence to Lord Timura, saying they would help solve your financial difficulties, but he declared them black magic, evil magic, and commanded me to say nothing."

Then he picked up a skull with the unmistakable shape of a wolf. "This is a shape-changer's amulet, Majesty," he said. "Used wisely it could give you amazing powers. Magical powers, Majesty. Which I hesitate to suggest, is the only thing Your Majesty lacks.

"Why, with magical powers, Majesty, you would have no need for wizards, other than to perform rote duties."

"Than I'd be like Alisarrian," Protarus murmured.

"Yes, Majesty," Fari said. "You would be master of both worlds. Temporal and spiritual."

"And I'd have no need for Safar," Iraj said.

Fari shrugged. "I hadn't thought of that," he said. "Lord Timura is such a mighty wizard it prevents such thinking.

"But I suppose it's true. You would have no need for him." He chuckled. "Or me either, for that matter. Except, of course, I'm more than willing to tutor Your Majesty in the magical arts."

"And Safar wouldn't?"

Another shrug. "You would be the best judge of that, Majesty," he said. "After all, you *have* been friends for many years."

Iraj pressed the point. "If that were the case," he said, "*I* could declare the Age of Great Blessings."

All three conspirators showed surprise.

Then, "I suppose you could, Majesty," Fari said.

"Indeed," said Luka.

"Why not?" posed Kalasariz.

"I must think on this," Protarus said. "I don't want to react too swiftly. That way leads to errors and disappointment."

"That is a truth that should be engraved on stone, Your Majesty," Kalasariz said. "A pause, well used, is what separates the good from the great."

At that moment a shrill noise sounded. All four heads, two human, two demon, swiveled to the source of the sound. It came from a small alembic, made of jewel encrusted crystal, which sat upon an ebony stand. The alembic had a large bulbous stopper which was flashing a purplish light.

Luka displayed his fangs in a most lascivious grin.

"Wait until you see this, Majesty!" he said.

Iraj was puzzled. "See what?"

"We had a small entertainment planned for you, Majesty," Fari said.

"Actually, it was completely unscheduled," Kalasariz added. "Everything depended upon luck. We prayed it would happen when you were here to see."

"I hate to repeat myself," Iraj said. "But . . . see what?"

Chuckling, the three conspirators guided the king over to the alembic. As soon as he came close the noise stopped and the flashing light became a steady glow.

"Look into it, Majesty," Fari said. "I guarantee you'll be delighted at what you see."

Iraj stared at the alembic, an expectant smile playing on his lips.

Then an image formed.

The king gasped. "By the gods," he said, "she *is* beautiful!"

*　　　*　　　*

Nerisa thought she heard voices. She stirred in her tub, head rising from the languorous waters. She looked around and saw nothing unusual in the huge marble bath chamber. It was hazy with perfumed steam rising from the sunken tub—large enough for four Nerisas to splay their limbs comfortably and wriggle them about to feel the water's gentle massage.

When she was certain there was no one around—and the voices were the product of her languid imagination—she eased back into her bath, breathing a long luxurious sigh.

The Lady Fatinah might have been a woman of immeasurable wealth, but she'd spent the short years of that nobility on the dusty caravan track gathering her wealth. Before she'd merely been Nerisa—a dirty orphan child who'd snatched a bath in cold rain barrels set beneath tenement gutters.

Abubensu had boasted of her mansion's view, praised the nursery he'd had remodeled to her exacting specifications, but he'd never said anything about the bath. When Nerisa had discovered it she'd whispered a fervent prayer of thanks to whatever god had sent such splendor her way.

Nerisa captured the huge sponge floating on the water. She reached over to the ledge and picked up the ornate bottle of bathing oils—one of many gifts she'd received from the guests who'd attended her welcoming banquet. The liquid inside was a deep purple, so rich in oily texture that it nearly glowed.

She withdrew the bulbous stopper, dribbled oil on the sponge, replaced the top, then smoothed the delicious, perfumed liquid over her body. Nerisa breathed another long sigh. She'd never felt so clean, so pampered, so—

The thought broke off as once again she thought she heard voices.

She let the sponge float away and looked up. Once again there was nothing and no one to be seen.

Then she heard a high-piping voice and smiled.

A moment later Scani came in, Palimak perched on her hip.

"Lord Timura is here, My Lady," the nurse announced.

"Thank you, Scani," Nerisa. "Tell him I'll be with him when I've done with my bath."

Scani bobbed a curtsy. "Yes, My Lady."

Nerisa smiled up at the child.

"And how is my darling Palimak?" she said.

The child's finger jabbed out—pointing directly at her.

"Shut up!" he said.

Scani was shocked. "Don't speak to your mother like that," she scolded.

Again, Palimak pointed, but his finger was at a lower level.

"Shut up!" he said again. He sounded angry.

"Hush, child!" Scani said. "Young lord or not, old Scani will peel your hide if you keep talking like that."

"Pay him no mind," Nerisa said. "He's just trying to get attention. If we ignore him he'll stop."

But Scani was upset. This was a blow to her skills as a nursemaid. "I don't know where he got such language, My Lady!" she said. "Those are words I most certainly never use."

"Shut up!" Palimak broke in.

Then he wriggled and kicked so fiercely Scani was forced to lower him to the floor and let him go.

"Stop that, Palimak!" Scani cried.

But the child paid no attention. On his hands and knees, he skittered across the wet marble floor. He stopped at the edge of the bath.

His eyes glowed yellow as he regarded the bottle of bath oils.

"Shut up!" he demanded.

He slapped at the bottle, rocking it.

"Shut up, shut up, shuutt uppp!"

And then, to the shocked amazement of the two women, he gave the bottle such a blow that it slammed against the edge of the tub.

Glass shattered in every direction.

*   *   *

Iraj reeled back as the image exploded in his face.

"The little whore's son!" he shouted.

Then he looked at the alembic, saw it was quite whole, and realized no harm was done.

He laughed mightily, slapping his thigh in glee. "It was almost as if the little bastard knew we were spying on his mother," he chortled.

His three new friends laughed with him.

"Tell me, Majesty," Kalasariz said, "wasn't she as beautiful as you've heard?"

Iraj glanced at the alembic again. His mouth suddenly went dry as he recalled the vision of Nerisa floating naked in her bath. He could almost taste her woman's scent rising on the perfumed steam.

"Yes," he said, voice rough.

"Even I was moved, Majesty," Luka said. "And I'm a demon and have little appreciate for the female human form."

"She seemed a dish more fit for a king," Fari said, "than a man of such common breeding as Timura."

Iraj's eyes narrowed. "What are you suggesting?" he asked.

"Suggesting? Why, nothing, Majesty," Fari said. "I was only commenting on the obvious."

"Lord Timura *does* claim to be His Majesty's most ardent friend and supporter," Kalasariz said to the others.

"That's certainly true," Luka said. "He's told us all that often enough . . . When it suits his purpose."

"Perhaps it's time you tested that friendship, Majesty," Kalasariz said.

"See how deep his feelings for you really are."

Protarus licked dry lips. His fingers rapped against the alembic's stopper—thinking, rap, rap, thinking.

Then he nodded—hard. His decision was made.

"As I see it," he said, "Safar's left me with no other choice."

*   *   *

"In the past," Safar said to Nerisa, "Iraj always listened to what I said. He didn't necessarily take my advice, nor did I always act as he wanted, but there were no hard feelings over it. At least none he showed."

It was night and the two were curled up on Nerisa's bed, the sleeping Palimak between them. The child had been restless since the incident in the bath the previous day, his sleep plagued with nightmares. At Safar's urging Nerisa had brought the child into their bed and now he was sleeping peacefully, thumb stuck firmly in his mouth.

"We don't *have* to become man and wife, Safar," Nerisa said. "I'll be your concubine, if you like. Or, since I'm a woman of means, you can be mine."

Safar smiled, but the smile didn't linger long.

"There's much more behind this than our nuptials," he said.

Nerisa nodded. He'd told her about the great lie Protarus was demanding of him, and the conspiracy he suspected was being hatched by Luka, Fari and Kalasariz.

"I was just making a silly jest," she said.

"For some reason," Safar said, "he's taken a sharp turn off the road we were both traveling on. And I don't know how to move him back."

Nerisa shivered. "I feel like a devil just perched on my grave," she said. "When I was girl on the streets of Walaria I always took that feeling as a warning sign. I don't know how many times I bolted—for no reason other than that shivery feeling—then saw the thief catcher creeping down the alley."

"Gundara has been howling danger since I left the palace," Safar said. "He advises me to flee."

"Then let's do it," Nerisa said, suddenly fierce. "Leave everything behind us and flee immediately. We won't lack for money. I have gold cached all over Esmir."

"I can't," Safar said.

Nerisa peered at him. Then, "I suppose it'd be pretty difficult giving up being Grand Wazier," she said. "It's hard to imagine having so much power."

"That means nothing to me, Nerisa," Safar said. "It was never anything I wanted, much less sought. Why, my fondest boyhood dream was to succeed my father some day as the greatest potter in all Kyrania."

"Then let's go to Kyrania," Nerisa said. "You talked about it so much in Walaria that it seemed a paradise to me. We'll go together. I'll be your wife, a simple village woman, with Palimak on my hip and his sister growing in my belly."

Her eyes glistened. "That was always *my* fondest dream, Safar," she said. "So why don't we both make those dreams come true?"

He took her hand and said, "I wish I could, but the Fates have decreed otherwise."

And then he told her the tale of two women—one a vision in Alisarrian's cave, the other a living woman, Methydia, a powerful witch and visionary in her own right.

When he was done he said, "Both insisted Iraj and I must travel the same path together. And at the end of that road is the answer I seek. The answer to the riddle of Hadin."

"Well, I'm no witch," Nerisa said, "and I'm certainly no vision in a cave. But it's plain to me Protarus has strayed off that path. You said it yourself. You said he'd taken a sharp turn and you didn't know how to get him back on the same road again."

"Did you ever think that maybe the road has ended? For the two of you, I mean? And *you* must go on, leaving Protarus behind in whatever madness he makes for himself?"

"Yes," Safar said, almost a whisper. "I'd thought of that."

Then he said, "But Iraj isn't mad. He's only king, which is a kind of madness in itself, I suppose. I remember I told him that a long time ago."

"Still," Nerisa. Then firmer, "Still!"

Safar thought a moment, then said, "I'll try one more time. We're supposed to meet again tomorrow. I owe him that one last chance."

"You don't *owe* him anything," Nerisa said. "It's the other way around, Safar. I wish you could see that."

Safar shrugged. "I can't help how I feel."

He looked down at Palimak, then back at her, brow furrowed with worry.

"What disturbs me most of all," he said, "is that both of you are in danger because of me. If Iraj acts badly he'll come after you as well as me.

"I think you should leave first thing in the morning."

Nerisa, a sensible woman, agreed. She had the responsibility of Palimak after all.

"There's a village at the crossroads about twenty miles outside of Zanzair," she said. "I'll have Abubensu get a carriage ready. I can tell him I'm considering an investment in the area, which isn't far from the truth. It looks to be a promising place."

"I know the village," Safar said. "If all goes well I'll send a message for you to return. And if doesn't, I'll meet you there."

"One of my caravans—bound for Caspan—will be crossing the desert in a day or so," Nerisa said. "We can go with it."

Palimak stirred. His eyes came open, a golden glow in the dim light.

Suddenly he screwed up his face and started crying.

Nerisa comforted him. "Everything's okay, little one," she cooed. "Mother's here. "She won't let anyone hurt you."

*   *   *

Outside the mansion, Leiria crouched in the shadows watching the house.

She heard a flutter of sound and her head snapped around to mark it.

It was a raven on the prowl, big wings spread to catch the evening air. The raven circled the mansion grounds, then it turned and flew off toward the palace.

It soared higher and higher until it disappeared in the red glare of the Demon Moon.

Leiria's eyes returned to the house. Deep inside she heard the child cry.

She thought she'd never heard such a lonely sound.

CHAPTER TWENTY SEVEN

ESCAPE FROM ZANZAIR

Iraj paced the royal chamber like a captive lion, golden hair flowing from under his crown like a mane, beard jutting forward like a lion's snout; his eyes were narrowed, lips stretched back over his teeth as if in a snarl.

Safar stood in the center of the chamber watching him pace, feeling the anger build.

"I could command it," Iraj said. "I could require you to make the casting."

"Yes, you could," Safar said.

"Would you obey?"

Safar breathed in deeply. Then let it out. "No."

"Even if the penalties were most severe?"

"Even so."

"I could strip you of your title and fortune," Iraj said.

"I understand that."

"I could even take your life," Iraj said. "Are you so set in your refusal that you'd risk it?"

"Let me answer this way," Safar said. "If you were in my boots and felt your honor was at stake, how would you answer such a threat?"

Iraj paused. "I didn't threaten," he said. "I was only pointing out a fact."

"Still," Safar said, "how would *you* answer?"

"It's not the same. *I* am Iraj Protarus!"

"And *I* am Safar Timura!"

It was not an answer sculpted to please. Iraj glared at Safar, who stood there calmly, manner mild, but will just as strong. The king broke first, spooked by the strange glow in Safar's eyes.

He resumed his pacing, saying, "I'm told you think you are more popular than I am."

Safar lifted an eyebrow. "I'd brand that a lie," he said, "but it's too stupid a charge to deserve the name."

Iraj whirled. "What? Now you dare to insult me?"

"I don't dare anything," Safar said. "But if you believe such a claim, it's no insult, but the truth."

Iraj's fury suddenly turned to anguish. Tears welled up. "Why do you insist on defying me, Safar?" he cried. "We are friends. No, more than friends. More even than blood oath brothers. I swear that I love you more than my mother, more than my father, more than any son born to me."

"I can only answer that with another question," Safar said. "If you love me, why are you pressing so hard to make me violate a thing I hold most sacred?"

The anguish reverted to fury. "Because I am your king!" Iraj thundered. "And I find it necessary to ask this of you for the greater good of Esmir!"

Safar said nothing—there was no reply to make.

Iraj's manner returned to normal. He shook his head, as if saddened. "And still you refuse," he said.

"I do," Safar answered.

"What if I made this a matter of friendship?" Iraj asked. "You pleaded with me not to before. But we *do* have a blood bond between us. We swore we would give the other anything that was asked—freely and without hesitation.

"If I asked out of friendship, would you comply?"

"Whatever I did," Safar said, "it'd be the end of our friendship. If I agreed, it would my last act as your friend. If I refused, you'd consider our bond broken. Either way it would be over.

"Are you willing to risk that, Iraj?"

Protarus laughed bitterly. "It would be the only thing in my life I haven't risked," he said.

"Family? Hah! I killed my uncle. And slew his wives and his children too so they wouldn't sprout into enemies.

"The honor of my clan? Yes, I risked that from the very beginning. For if I had ever stumbled and fallen, the name Protarus would have been shamed for all history.

"Fortune? Bah! I am like you in that, Safar. I know I tell little lies to myself now that I am king and can have anything I want. It's habit, like drinking too deeply and too often. But I risked one fortune after another on the road to Zanzair. Every palace I looted I risked in the next toss of the dice to win another.

"Life itself? No one would deny that I've proved my willingness to cast it down as the price of a challenge. Why, I've nearly thrown it away many times just for the thrill of it."

Safar suddenly remembered Iraj's headlong race down the Kyranian mountainside to confront the demon raiders. It seemed like such a pure act at the time. The act of a storied hero. And for what? To save a merchant's caravan? A caravan carrying not a soul Iraj knew or cared about. And there was not an innocent among them—not a babe, not a maid, mother, granny, or man who if you met them would wring pity from your heart.

Then he remembered his own mad dash in Iraj's wake. He saw it clear. Saw the snow crusted boulders leaping up in his path. Saw the demons with fangs and talons and terrible swords. Saw their steeds who fought like great cats. And he felt it. Felt the fear icing his veins. Felt the demon magic crackling with power he never knew was possible. Felt the anger when he saw Astarias being dragged through the snow by her long black tresses. Felt the cold, distant satisfaction of his first kill.

He looked at Iraj and for the first time truly understood the man he'd been following for all these years. With that knowledge came a small understanding of himself. It arrived with a pang of disappointment. Like Iraj, he'd been a creature of events. A creature who'd cried holy purpose when there was only self at heart. Made himself a man who stretched his head above others, falsely ennobled by the vision of Hadin.

For the first time since this confrontation had first roused itself, Safar wavered. What did it matter? In a world of lies, what was one more? Magic was no holy thing. He was no priest with a godly cause. He had no temple, no altar. And the gods themselves were silent on the matter. Why *not* do as Iraj asked and declare an Era of Great Blessings? He could say it, then work like the devils from the Hells to make it so.

Then it came to him to do otherwise might destroy the man he'd called friend. A man who had only one thing left to risk in the chest that made him human—Iraj's claim of friendship with Safar.

He almost said it, almost relented, almost opened his lips to speak.

But Iraj said, "And finally, there's friendship. My love for you. That I haven't risked. Am I willing? I can't say. The first question I have to ask myself before I do, is if that friendship, that love, is returned? Is it real?

"Or have you been playing me false all these years?"

"You know I haven't," Safar said.

"Do I?" Iraj asked, an awful smile growing on his face. "Do I now?"

"Of course, you do," Safar said. "So we're arguing. We've argued before. We'll argue again. We're different men, so we hold different opinions. But they are merely differences between friends."

"I tested you once long ago," Iraj said. "If you recall, you didn't do well at that test."

Safar shrugged. "I was a boy in lust," he said. "It meant nothing."

"I also said someday I might test you again," Iraj went on. "I think that day has finally come."

"You mean the casting?" Safar asked. "You want me to lie to prove my friendship?"

He was about to say, very well, then, I'll do it. But Iraj shook his head, cutting him off.

"No," he said. "You claim that as a matter of honor. I won't ask you to soil it. A man of equal honor would never require such a thing of his friend."

The statement caught Safar by surprise. Was it over? Had he succeeded?

"So here is the test, Safar Timura. The man who claims to be my friend. It's a small test. One that should give you no trouble."

"And that is?" Safar asked, alarm rushing back.

"I gave you a woman once," Iraj said. "A virgin I greatly desired for myself. Astarias.

"And now I ask the same of you, although she is no virgin and is therefore the lesser gift."

Iraj looked deep into Safar's shocked eyes.

"Give me Lady Fatinah," he said. "I want her for myself."

"How can you ask that?" Safar said, dumbfounded. "You *know* she is to be my wife."

Iraj shrugged. "You can have her back when I'm done with her," he said. "And still marry her if you like. There's no shame in following a king in his pleasure.

"You liked Leiria well enough. Now that I think of it, that's two women I've given you. Two, Safar!

"I ask only one in return."

"This is foolish, Iraj!" Safar cried. "Even if I would consider such a thing—which I wouldn't—she's not mine to give. She belongs to herself."

"I imagine Astarias and Leiria felt the same way," Iraj said. "But that didn't stop you."

Struck to the quick, Safar struggled for an answer. Before he could, Iraj drew an object from his pocket.

"Here," he said, "I'll even sweeten the bargain, although why this should be a bargain is beyond me. Our oath was to give freely, no questions asked."

Iraj dropped the object into Safar's open hand. He glanced down and saw a small golden amulet. A wondrously formed horse dangling from a glittering chain.

"Coralean gave me that a long ago," Iraj said. "It was my reward for saving his caravan. You remember, don't you? You received a magical dagger at the same time."

Safar remembered very well. That same dagger, whose image was Nerisa's crest, was tucked in his belt.

"Coralean said someday I would see the perfect horse. A warrior's dream of a horse. And all I had to do was give this amulet to its owner and he would not be able to refuse me.

"Well, I never found that horse, Safar. But never mind, I'm sure it's there."

He clasped Safar's numb hand around the amulet.

"This is yours now, my friend. I give it to you for the woman. Why, it isn't even an equal exchange.

"For what mere woman could ever match such a wondrous steed?"

Silence followed. A silence where murder crept out of the shadows. Safar had anger enough to call it closer. He had the opportunity—they were alone in the royal chamber. And he had the weapons, the dagger in his belt, the blasting magic at his fingertips. He fought down the violence, nearly gagged on it. If he did act, terrible reprisals would certainly follow.

And at this moment Nerisa and Palimak would be making their way to the village at the crossroads, and safety. If Safar slew Protarus they'd never reach it. He had to play for time. It was the only way.

Before he could stumble out some sort of answer, Iraj said, "I'm afraid you've waited too long to reply, Safar.

"You failed the test."

Protarus abruptly turned away and strolled toward a small private door leading out of the chamber.

He paused at the door. "But I'm not so hard a man that I won't give you another chance," he said.

"Send Lady Fatinah to me tonight. And all will be forgiven."

Then he was gone.

*　　　*　　　*

As soon as he'd cleared the palace grounds Safar ducked into an alley and shed his cloak of office. The rich costume, emblazoned with the symbols of Esmir's Grand Wazier, was kicked into a dung heap. Beneath the cloak he'd worn the plain rough tunic and breeches of a common soldier. Then he hurried off, head low, trying not to move so fast he'd draw stares. Even so, he soon came to the vast demon quarters that sprawled all the way to Zanzair's rear gates. Demon females peered up from their washing to watch him go by. Demon kits shouted insults, or crowded close to beg. And big demon males loomed out of taverns to issue drunken challenges at this human worm who dared walk their streets alone.

Safar paid them no mind, averting the eyes of the females, shaking off the young beggars and sidestepping the challengers.

His goal was a small shabby stable near the rear gates. He'd risen before dawn that morning, made a few hasty additions to the plan he and Nerisa had discussed the previous night, then gone home to pack some necessities before his servants arose. Afterwards he'd taken his best horse to the stable by the gates. He'd left it with the sleepy-eyed stablemaster, along with enough coins to ensure the animal's care, but not so many as to arouse suspicion.

The whole time he'd prayed luck would be with him and the preparations would be unnecessary. He'd thought the first sign of that luck was Leiria's absence either at the mansion or his home. He'd assumed she was attending one of her "training sessions"—the transparent ruse Protarus and Kalasariz had used so their spy could report to them and receive her instructions.

As he approached the stable he thought at least that one bit of luck had held. If it hadn't he would've been forced to incapacitate Leiria in that same alley where he'd shed his cloak. Or, worse, be required to slay her. Safar had strong doubts he'd be able to do such a thing, no matter what the cost. Spy or not, Leiria had crept into his heart long ago and held a small piece of it.

There was no one about when he entered the ramshackle building. He called for the stablemaster, but no one answered. So he fished out a few coins, laid them on a work bench within easy sight and picked his way to the back where his horse and gear waited.

He froze in front of the stall. His horse was already saddled, bags strapped to the back, sheathed sword hanging by its belt from the pommel. On either side of his mount were two others—both saddled and ready. But ready for whom? He moved closer and suffered another jolt. Both horses were his!

Straw rustled and he whirled, dragging out the only weapon he had, the small silver dagger.

Leiria stood there, mailed and fully armed. He nearly lurched at her with the dagger, but pulled back in time. Just as he'd feared he lacked the necessary hate.

"What are you doing here?" he demanded.

Leiria held out her hands to show they were empty. He looked down and saw her sword was still in its sheath.

"I'm here to help you, Safar," she said.

Safar barked laughter. "So I see," he said with heavy sarcasm. "But to where? My grave?"

"I don't blame you for thinking that," she said. "But you've got to believe me when I say I've never done or said anything to harm you. I told you once long ago I'd never betray you, Safar Timura. And I never have."

"What do you call spying?"

Leiria's eyes were pleading. "If I didn't give the king and Kalasariz what they wanted," she said, "they would have replaced me with someone else. Someone who didn't love you, Safar. And you know that I do. Even now, when your heart is with another woman."

Safar thought he saw truth, but he was desperately afraid he was seeing what he wanted, not what really existed.

"Besides," Leiria said, "you never did anything wrong. You've never been a traitor. Never conspired. What did it hurt to tell them about your innocent excursions, friendly meetings, or all the long nights you spent studying books of magic? There's one thing I didn't tell them, however. I said nothing about the child. About Palimak."

"What are you saying?" Safar said. "They know he exists. It's no secret."

"They don't know he's part demon," she said. "You kept it from me but I saw, Safar. I saw his eyes. What do you think Iraj would've imagined if he'd known that? His Grand Wazier in the arms of a woman with a monster for a child? Palimak's no monster, but that's not what Iraj would've thought. Especially after Kalasariz and Luka and Fari got to him. Whispering all kinds of disgusting things."

"I thank you for that, at least," Safar said. "But it doesn't matter anymore. If I were you I'd get away from me just as fast as you can. Iraj and I are finished!"

"I know that, Safar," she said. "You were finished before you met this morning. It'd all been decided. Iraj never had any doubt you'd refuse him. He just needed an excuse to bring you down. To declare Safar Timura a criminal. To blacken your name. He's afraid of you, Safar. He thinks you are his rival for his kingdom and the love of his subjects.

"But most of all, my dear, dear Safar, he's afraid and jealous of your magic."

She paused a moment. Saw the suspicion vanish from his eyes. Saw those eyes turn from icy blue to the color of the lake in far Kyrania.

He said, "I'm sorry about Nerisa." He shrugged. "I never meant it to happen."

"I know that," Leiria said.

"I thought she was dead."

"I know that too."

"I'm ashamed to admit that I've treated you badly."

"Never mind," Leiria said. "There's no time for apologies or remorse now, my love."

She took a deep breath, then said, "Hold on tight as you can while I tell you what's happened. I would have said it first, but I knew you'd think it was a trick. A trap.

"Nerisa and Palimak never left. They are still in Zanzair."

"What?" Safar's voice came like a cry.

"She was betrayed by Abubensu," Leiria said. "The carriage never arrived. He delayed her with lies until it was too late to find another. Now there are guards outside her home. Not many, but she knows they're there so she doesn't dare leave."

"How much time do we have?" Safar asked.

"I don't know," Leiria said. "A few hours at most. They would've moved sooner but it's you they want most of all. Besides, they have to gather their nerve and their forces to oppose you. You can be sure when they come it'll not be just with soldiers, but with Fari's best wizards and witch sniffers.

"That's how much they fear you."

Leiria indicated the horses. "Everything's ready. We have only to ride."

*   *   *

And ride they did. A mad clatter of iron hooves, shouted curses and cries of alarm as they dashed through the streets. They burst through the busy market place, scattering shoppers and knocking over stalls. They tore through parks, leaping hedges and showering mud. But when they came to the hill leading up to Nerisa's mansion they hauled the horses in, dismounted as quietly as they could, and hid them among some trees.

Then they crept up the hill in full daylight, using every rock and stump and bit of brush for cover. A young nurse with two young charges in tow saw them and hurried away. A gardener came on them while they were lying in a hedge and Leiria took him captive as gently as she could and bound him with leather laces from her harness.

There were four guards patrolling the grounds. Three demons and a hulking brute of a human.

They killed all four, quietly and efficiently.

Then they were at the door.

"I'll get the horses," Leiria said and she turned and ran back down the hill.

The door came open and Nerisa rushed into Safar's arms.

"I was afraid you'd never come," she said. "And I was more afraid you would. It's you they want, not me."

"I wish that were true," Safar said. "But when the king condemned me he condemned you as well.

"Now, quick! Get Palimak. We have to flee!"

Then they were out on the broad lawn and Leiria was thundering up, leading two horses behind her.

Safar took Palimak while Nerisa mounted. The child was silent, trembling. Eyes flashing from yellow to hazel and back again.

Then Nerisa was fully mounted and she reached down to take the child.

Safar was handing him up when Gundara suddenly shouted, "They're coming, Master! They're coming!"

He whirled, clumsy with the child still in his hands. Down the hill he saw helmed demons and humans kicking their mounts up the road. Then he heard the bay of the witch sniffers and saw the devil hounds bounding in front of the troops. He felt a blast of magic and reeled back, stumbling against Nerisa's horse, which shrilled and shied away. He heard her shout to him to hand up the child.

But there wasn't time, there wasn't time.

Another blast, stronger than the first, came at him like a great wind, shriveling the grass with its heat.

He managed a blocking spell, but diverted only part of it. He turned to protect the child, catching the force with his back. He felt it sear through his clothes, gritted his teeth against the pain and he heard Gundara shout, "Shut up!" and Palimak echo, "Shut up!" and then the pain was gone.

He set the child down and came about, clawing at his pocket. The witch sniffers were almost on him now, but he had time to hurl the pellets and they exploded, sheeting fire and smoke.

The devil hounds were scattered by the blast, shrieking in fear and pain.

Smoke clouds—red and green and yellow swirled all around.

Then he heard the thunder of the approaching troops and through the smoke he saw Leiria, sword in hand, charge into the mass, cutting left and right, leaving demon howls and human screams in her wake. She broke through, then wheeled her horse and came crashing back, her killing sword releasing rivers of blood.

And now Nerisa was off her horse and beside him, armed with nothing but a whip. A witch sniffer leaped out of one of the smoke columns, slavering jaws yawning. It came so fast it almost had him, but Nerisa lashed out with her whip, slicing through those open jaws and the creature's face became a gory mask and it slammed to the ground. So close that Palimak hit it with his tiny fist, crying, "Shut up! Shut up!"

Nerisa scooped Palimak off the ground. Slinging him on her hip, she held him with one hand while she whirled the whip with the other.

Then the air shrilled and a dark swarm of arrows came lofting towards them.

But they were slow, so very slow. They reached the apex of their flight then down they came, down, down and down.

Just as they struck, Safar hurled himself on Nerisa and the child. His body, not magic, was their only shield. He heard them strike all around him, thought for an instant they'd been saved by a miracle or incompetence. Then he grunted as one buried itself in his thigh. Grunted again when another struck his shoulder. He hurt, by the gods he hurt, but he didn't care because he could feel Nerisa's warmth against him. Hear Palimak crying beneath her. And he knew they were safe.

He rolled away, purposely and painfully breaking off the arrows against the ground.

Safar came to his feet, calm and strong and gathering more power with each breath.

He slipped the dagger from his belt. Casual, as if he had all the time in the world. With cold interest he noted Leiria savaging the soldiers. She was here, there, everywhere, darting in and out, dealing out death as if it were the sweetest of gifts. But she was tiring, as was her horse. He saw the animal stagger once, saw her sword arm droop and the effort on her face as she forced it up again.

Then the great spell came, just as he knew it would. He could smell Fari, that damned old demon, behind it. Ah, and there was a little bit of Luka there. A whiff of arrogance. And Kalasariz? Where was he? He sniffed again, caught the sewer stench of conspiracy. There you are, you whore's son. But Fari would need more for this spell.

He'd need Iraj.

Safar imagined them tucked safely away in some dark room of the palace. The Necromancium, most likely. Fari was a cautious old fiend and wouldn't trust his wizards to drag Safar down. So just in case he'd create a mighty spell. He'd take a drop of blood from each. And build on the innate power all conspiracies hold. He'd take one from Luka for his poisonous hate of his father. One from Kalasariz, to confound. One from himself for real magic. And finally, one from Iraj, for there is nothing as deadly as friend against friend.

Asper had taught Safar that.

Then Fari would mix the blood in a potion. A potion he would've labored long and hard on well before this conspiracy had come into the open. And then they'd drink. Each passing the cup on to the other.

Poor Iraj, Safar thought. He probably didn't know the potion would seal him to the others forever.

Then Fari would cast the spell. But what spell would it be?

Ah! What else?

The Force of Four!

Another lesson learned from Asper.

He shouted for Gundara who leaped out onto his shoulder.

The little Favorite chattered a spell, head darting this way and that, looking, looking . . .

He jabbed a finger to the east. "There, Master!" he cried.

At first all he saw was the glare of the Demon Moon above the palace. Then he saw a shape take form. It looked like a wolf's head. A wolf with long fangs like a demon's. Baleful eyes moving. Searching.

Then the wolf saw him. It bayed in hellish joy and shot forward, head growing larger as it came.

But it wasn't the head Safar feared. It was the killing spell coming like a desert storm behind it. So strong it was impossible for him to stop.

Safar pointed the dagger at the wolf's head, the tip glittering blood red from the moon.

He made that his center. Then he cut to the side, once for Luka. Another slice. Twice for Kalasariz. Again. Thrice for Fari. And then the fourth—for Iraj.

Then he aimed the dagger at the center again. Right between the wolf head's glaring red eyes.

He felt the force of its gathering hate. Felt the first buffet of searing magical winds.

He put all of his might, all of his will behind the dagger tip.

And he shouted—"*Protarus!*"

There was a clap of ungodly thunder and the wolf head shattered. He heard a distant howl. And then the sky was empty and the air was still.

He looked around and saw the troops fleeing down the hill. Leiria was coming up to him, leading her horse, which was bleeding heavily from many wounds.

"There's more of them, Safar," she said. "You can see from the edge of the hill. Hundreds of soldiers. They're milling about now, gathering their nerve. But they'll come soon enough. This isn't over yet."

"I couldn't kill him," Safar said. "I hurt him, but I couldn't kill him. There wasn't time. "

"Iraj won't give you another chance," she said.

"Then let's not give *him* one," Safar said.

He turned to find Nerisa, saying, "We'll head for the village just like we—"

Nerisa was sprawled on the ground. There was an arrow through her breast, blood stain creeping across her tunic.

Palimak was kneeling beside her, weeping and blubbering over and over again—"Shut up, shut up, shut up!" as if he were trying to silence Death himself. And perhaps he was.

Safar felt nothing. He was too shocked to grieve, too numb for thought. The only sensation was the cold stone in his chest where his heart had once lived.

He felt a tug at his sleeve. "We have to go, Safar," Leiria said. "I'm sorry she's dead, but there's nothing we can do."

Her voice sounded distant—like a gull crying above a great sea.

Then it came closer, clearer. "Safar! They'll be here any minute."

Still, he did not move.

Leiria rushed over to Nerisa's body. Gently she picked up Palimak, soothing him, but awkwardly in a soldier's manner.

She carried the child back to Safar and pushed him against his chest. Safar didn't react and so she grabbed each arm in turn and folded them across the boy, forcing an embrace.

"They'll kill the child, too, Safar," she said. "Nerisa's child!"

Safar came unstuck and clutched the weeping Palimak tight.

"I won't let them," he said. "I'll kill that whoreson, I swear I will!"

"Killing will have to wait, Safar," Leiria said. "We have to get away first."

And so that is what they did. They rode off the hill, Leiria leading the way and Safar carrying Palimak. Exactly how they escaped, he'd never be able to recall. He remembered only the shouts of soldiers behind and to the side of them. The sound of shutters and doors slamming as they clattered through the streets. Screams and blood at the city gates. The countryside whipping past. Switchback trails, splashing in creeks, hiding in woods.

Finally they arrived at the village where Safar and Nerisa had planned to meet.

There Safar came alive again. His heart was still stone, but he felt a growing heat. It was hate that brought him alive, desire for revenge.

He sent Leiria on with Palimak. Perhaps she argued, he couldn't remember. There was only a vague recollection she'd return on a certain date. Soon as she was gone he forgot the date.

There was a large stream running through the village. Safar searched the banks until he found a small clay bed of the purest white.

He gathered what he needed and mounted the hill that rose above the village. He could see Zanzair from that hill. See the palace where King Protarus sat on his throne and ruled the land.

Safar spread out the things he needed. He gathered wood and lit a small fire and when it'd burned out he stripped to his loin cloth and covered himself with ashes.

He cut the first slab of clay with his silver dagger and started on the model of Iraj's great palace.

And there he sat, day into night, and night into day, mourning Nerisa and planning his revenge.

EPILOGUE
THE RECKONING

The spell was ready.

All his hate was gone. Contained, now, in the model of the Grand Palace.

He'd conjured up every bit of bitterness and made each into a monster. Some he enclosed in the gilded turrets. Others in the smooth domes. Each parapet bore a devil's visage. Anger, betrayal, murder and lust, on and on until the whole palace was ringed with the faces of hate.

In the bowels of the palace, deep, deep within, where the only sounds were the cries of tortured things and the clank of the chains that bound them to their pain, he placed the greatest hate of all. And that was what had been done to Nerisa.

Satisfied, he looked up from the model. Shimmering under the Demon Moon he could see the real Zanzair, the real Grand Palace where Iraj Protarus sat upon his golden throne. He wondered what Iraj was thinking, what he was seeing as he looked out over his teeming court. Who were his friends, now? Which were his foes? Iraj could hurl the greatest army at the gates of that riddle and never seize the answer. All the mailed men, all the horned demons, could not bring it down.

Safar recalled a riddle from Asper's book:

> *"Two kings reign in Hadin Land,*
> *One's becursed, the other damned.*
> *One sees whatever eyes can see,*
> *The other dreams of what might be.*
> *One is blind. One's benighted.*
> *And who can say, which is sighted?*
> *Know that Asper knocked at the Castle Keep,*
> *But the gates were barred, the Gods Asleep."*

Safar took one last long look at the gleaming city and glorious palace that had been another man's dream. He turned away.

And would not look again.

Only the final touches remained to make the spell. He surrounded the model with the dried branches of a creosote tree. They had an oily smell, not pleasant, but not unpleasant either. He sprinkled powders all around, concentric circles of red, green, yellow and black. He made a wide patch of all the colors just in front of the gate. And in that patch he first pressed the silver dagger, making the impression firm and deep. Next, the horse amulet, pushing hard so the stallion seemed to rear up from the mark of the blade.

When he was finished he cleaned the dagger and amulet, scouring until every speck of powder was gone. Then he put them carefully away in his saddle bags.

At the crest of the hill a spring trickled from beneath a large boulder, making a shallow pool where the boulder's weight leaned hardest. He stripped and washed himself, ash-colored rivulets coursing off until the pool was black.

He stepped out, skin gleaming in the morning sun, the pool a dark mirror of sorrow he would leave behind.

Then he dressed with care, clean tunic and breeches and a wide leather belt cinching his waist. He stamped on his boots, buckled on his spurs and then looked around to see what he should do next.

But there was nothing to be done.

So he sat on the boulder and waited, although he couldn't remember exactly what he was waiting for.

He thought of Kyrania. It came to him on a fresh breeze of imagination, blowing off The Bride's Veil, clean and full of spring's promise. He saw the valley's broad thawing fields with green sprigs bursting through white. And the orchards shaking off winter, swelling knots on the branches where clusters of cherries and peaches and apples would soon appear. He saw the sleepy-eyed boys leading the goats to pasture, the pretty maids giggling and posing as they passed, the watchful grannies grumbling warnings as they knocked winter's grime between the washing stones. Out on the lake the birds were returning, filling the skies with the sound of courting and challenge. He saw the hearth smoke pouring from the gray-slated rooftops and smelled roasted lamb, picked with garlic, and bread from the oven and toasted cheese crusting by the fire. His saw his family at table, mother, father and all his sisters laughing and gossiping and spooning up his mother's thick porridge to gird them against the day. He heard Naya bleat that she wanted milking and his mother shouting—

"Wake up, Safar, you lazy boy!"

Safar's head jolted up. He heard the sound of horses approaching and he smiled when he saw Leiria riding up the path, leading another horse behind her. She had a sword at her hip and Palimak strapped on her back, cooing and gurgling at the world from his little basket stuffed with soft blankets.

Leiria's brow was creased with worry, but when she saw his smile the creases vanished and she smiled back, sweet hope blooming in her dark eyes like the buds bursting from the fields of Kyrania.

She cantered up to him, smile widening.

Then she looked over at the model of the palace, surrounded by dry brush and voltive powders, and the pearly smile melted away.

"Are you ready?" she asked, a tremble in her voice.

Safar answered with a question. "What day is it?"

"Why, the day I said we'd return. The day of the feast when Iraj declares the Era of Great Blessings." She gestured down the hill. "All the villagers are talking about it."

Safar nodded, remembering his final instructions to Leiria. This was the day she was supposed to return if she could.

"Then I'm ready," he said.

"It's a good thing," Leiria said, "because if you weren't I would've knocked you on the head and taken you away tied to the back of the horse."

Safar could see she wasn't joking.

"He still hunts me?"

"All of Esmir hunts you," she said. "His troops are scouring the countryside dreaming of the fat purse your head will fetch."

Safar laughed. "I've been here all along," he said. "Twenty miles from his gates."

"Don't feel so clever," Leiria replied. "On my way I saw a patrol heading for the village. I rode with them for awhile. The sergeant told me there's rumors of a mad priest living in these hills who is none other than Safar Timura in disguise."

She shrugged, the smile coming back. "Fortunately he didn't think much of the rumors and was going to inspect a few other places before coming here."

Safar looked up at her, searching—for what he didn't know.

"Are you certain you want to do this?" he asked. "You could leave now. You could give me the child and ride on and find a much better life."

"Shut up!" Palimak cried. He was looking at Safar, hazel eyes turned to demon yellow in his delight at finding him here. "Shut up, shut up, Shuuut Uppp!"

And Safar heard Gundara answer from the nested blankets. "Shut up yourself! I'm tired of shut up! All the time, shut up, shut up, shuuttt upppp!"

Leiria laughed, horse skittering to the side at the loud sound of it.

"There's your answer, Safar Timura!" she cried.

And so he broke a jar of oil over the palace model and surrounding brush. He lit the brush, blew the fire into life until it roared.

Then he leaped on the horse and they rode away.

As they clattered past the startled villagers there was a thunderclap from the hill. A moment later there was another clap—from a great distance, but louder, as loud as if the gods themselves had awakened.

Then the whole northern sky was a sheet of flame so hot the Demon Moon vanished in the brightness.

But they didn't look back. They didn't pause and wait for the sky to clear and see the molten place where the Grand Palace of Zanzair had once stood. Where kings had come and kings had gone since times most ancient.

And where the last king—the King of Kings—Iraj Protarus, Lord Imperator of Esmir, greater even than the Conqueror Alisarrian, abode his destined hour and went his way.

Home was a thousand miles or more distant. But Safar could see it beckoning, a hazy, welcoming vision hanging just before his eyes.

He led them hard and fast across deserts and grasslands and wide rocky plains sprawling to the mountains of his birth.

To far Kyrania.

Where the snowy passes carry the high caravans to clear horizons.

The place he should never have left.

The place where this tale ends.

Wolves of the Gods

*For Rita & Avi Schour
and Linda & Jonathan Beaty*

One moment in annihilation's waste,
One moment, of the well of life to taste—
The stars are setting and the caravan
Starts for the dawn of nothing—oh, make haste!

> *The Rubaiyat of Omar Khayyam*
> Edward Fitzgerald Translation

Part One
Wizard In Exile

CHAPTER ONE
TO DREAM OF WOLVES

Up, up in the mountains.

Up where Winter reigns eternal and her warriors bully earth and sky.

Then higher still. Climb to the reaches where even eagles are wary. Where the winds cut sharp, paring old snowfields of their surface to get at the black rock below. Where moody skies brood over a stark domain.

Yes, up. Up to the seven mountain peaks that make the Bride and Six Maids. And higher . . . still higher . . . to the highest point of all—the Bride's snowy crown where the High Caravans climb to meet clear horizons.

Where the Demon Moon waits, filling the northern heavens with its bloody shimmer.

It was at the cusp of a new day; the sun rising against the Demon Moon's assault, the True Moon giving up the fight and fading into nothingness. It was spring struggling with late winter. A time of desperation. A time of hunger.

Just below the Bride's crown a patch of green glowed in defiance of all that misery. The green was a trick of nature, a meadow blossoming from a bowl of granite and ice. The winds sheered off the bowl's peculiar formation making a small, warm safe harbor for life.

But safe is in the eye of the beholder. Safe is the false sanctuary of innocent imagination.

And in that time, the time that came to be known as the Age of the Wolf, safe was not to be trusted.

Three forces converged on that meadow.

And only one was innocent.

*   *   *

The wolf pack took him while he slept.

He was only a boy, a goat herder too young to be alone in the mountains. He'd spent a sleepless night huddled over a small fire, fearful of every sound and shadow. Exhausted, he fell asleep at first light and now he was helpless in his little rock shelter, oblivious to the hungry gray shapes ghosting across the meadow and the panicked bleating of his goats.

Then he jolted awake, sudden dread a cold knife in his bowels.

The pack leader hurtled forward—eyes burning, jaws reaching for his throat.

The boy screamed and threw up his hands.

But the ravaging shock never came and he suddenly found himself sitting bolt upright in his bedroll, striking at nothingness.

He gaped at the idyllic scene before him—the meadow glistening with dew under the early morning sun, his goats munching peacefully on tender shoots.

There wasn't a wolf in sight.

The boy laughed in huge relief. "It was only a dream!" he chortled. "What a stupid you are, Tio."

But speaking the words aloud did not entirely still Tio's thundering heart. Nor did it lessen his sense of dread. He stared about, searching for the smallest sign of danger. Finally his eyes lifted to the heights surrounding the small meadow. All he could see was icy rock glittering beneath cheery blue skies.

The boy laughed again and this time the laughter rang true. "You see, Tio," he said, seizing comfort from the sound of his own voice. "There's nothing to harm you. No wolves. No bears. No lions. Don't be such a child!"

Tio and his older brother, Renor—a big strapping lad who was almost a man and therefore, Tio believed, feared nothing—had brought the goats up from Kyrania a few days before. Then one of the animals had been badly injured and Renor had left the herd with Tio while he hurried down the mountainside for help with the goat strapped to his back.

"You only have to spend the one night alone," Renor had reassured him. "I'll be back by morning. You won't be afraid, will you?"

Tio's pride had been wounded by the question. "Don't be stupid. Of course I won't," he'd said. "What! Do you think I'm still a child?"

Tio's boldness had departed with his brother. Soon he was agonizing over the slightest unfamiliar stir. Then at dusk he'd had the sudden feeling he was being watched. His imagination had conjured all sorts of monsters intent on making a meal of a lonely boy. He knew this was foolish. Kyranian boys had been guiding the herds up into the Gods' Divide for centuries. The only harm any had ever suffered was from a bad fall and this had occured so rarely it wasn't worth thinking about. As for voracious animals—there weren't any. At least none who lusted for human flesh. So there was nothing at all to fear.

Tio had repeated these things to himself many times during the night, as if chanting a prayer in the warm company of his friends and family in the little temple by the holy lake of Felakia. It did no good. If anything, the dreadful feeling of being watched only intensified. Now, with the sun climbing above the peaks and flooding the meadow with light, Tio's boldness returned.

"Such a child," he said again, shaking his head and making his voice low in imitation of his brother's manly tones. "Didn't I say there was nothing to be afraid of? What did you think, stupid one? That the demons would come and get you?" He snorted. "As if Lord Timura would allow such a thing! Why, if a demon ever showed his ugly face in Kyrania, Lord Timura would snap his fingers and turn his nose into a . . . a . . . a turnip! Yes, that's what he'd do. Make his nose look like a turnip!"

He giggled, imagining the poor demon's plight. He held his own nose, making stuffed sinus noises: "Snark! Snark!" More giggling followed. "The demon couldn't even breathe! Snark! Snark!"

Then he had a sudden thought and his laughter broke off. Tio remembered his dream hadn't been about demons, but wolves. He glanced nervously about the meadow again, smiling when he saw it was peaceful as ever.

"Wolves don't eat people," he reassured himself. "Just goats. Sick goats. Or little goats. But never people." He picked up the thick cudgel by his side and shook it in his most threatening manner. "Wolves are afraid of this!" he said bravely. "Everybody says so."

Satisfied, he munched a little bread and cheese then settled back on his bedroll to await his brother's return—the stout cudgel gripped in his small fists.

A few moments later exhaustion took him once again. He fell into a deep sleep and the stick fell from his hands and rolled onto the grass.

*　　　*　　　*

Graymuzzle was anxious for her cubs. Her teats were aching and swollen with milk and she knew her pups would be whining for her in their cold den. Graymuzzle's hollow belly rumbled and it wasn't only in sympathy for her young. Weeks had passed since the pack had made a decent kill.

It had been a hard winter, the hardest and longest in Graymuzzle's memory. First disease and then fierce storms had wiped out the herds in her old hunting grounds. The wolf pack, with Graymuzzle leading them, had ranged for miles searching for food. They'd been reduced to digging deep into the snow to claw up maggoty roots. When winter had finally ended, spring brought scant relief. The weather remained treacherous, going from calm to storm with no warning. Vegetation was sparse and there was little meat on the bones of the few deer and goats they'd found.

Graymuzzle used all her skills, won over twelve hunting seasons, to feed her pack. She took them high into the mountains, looking for meadows with sweet grass and fat herds. None of her old tricks worked and by the time her cubs were born the pack had been reduced to six wolves so scrawny their faces seemed to consist entirely of muzzles and teeth. The rest had died on the trail—her mate of many years among them. Still, she'd managed to eat enough to make milk for her cubs. Her packmates had seen to that, checking their own hunger to share their food with her; thus assuring the pack's future.

They crouched in the heights above the meadow, bellies grumbling at the promised feast below. The wolves had spent most of the night in their hiding place, whining eagerly whenever they'd heard a goat bleat. To their surprise, however, each time they'd risen to move in for the kill Graymuzzle had leaped to block them. Snapping and nipping at their heels until they obeyed her and sank down onto the cold ground again.

Graymuzzle sensed a wrongness. She didn't know what it was—there was no smellsign in the air; no sound that couldn't be traced to an innocent source. Still, she felt as if something was watching. Not her. Not the pack. But the boy and the goats in the meadow below. Whenever she moved forward her hackles rose of their own accord in warning. Graymuzzle was an old wolf, a careful wolf, who had learned to trust her deepest instincts. So she waited and watched.

Now dawn was breaking. The morning was bright, the air without the slightest taint of strangeness. Whatever it was that had troubled her was gone. She could see the goats grazing in the meadow and the sleeping figure of the boy sprawled behind the low stone walls of the windbreak. There was nothing to fear. No reason to hesitate.

She yawned. It was a signal to the others and when she came to her feet they were waiting.

Graymuzzle slipped out of the hiding place and trotted down the rocky path—her packmates at her heels.

A moment later she felt the soft wet meadow grass under her pads. Heard the wind sing a hunter's song as she quickened her stride, smelled the strong goat smell as she rushed her first bleating victim.

Then lighting cracked—bursting from the ground in front of her, exploding rock and turf in every direction.

And all she'd feared during the long night of hunger howled out of nothingness to confront her.

*   *   *

Tio could hear the goats bleating. He was awake, but he couldn't open his eyes. He tried to move, but a heavy weight crushed down on him so hard he could barely breathe. He heard growling and bleats of pain.

You must get up, he thought. The wolves are coming, Tio! You must get your stick and drive them off. Get up, Tio! Get up! Don't be such a child! What will Renor think?

He forced his eyes open.

A nightmare shape rushed at him. All burning red eyes and slavering jaws. Long fangs stretched out to take him.

Tio threw up his hands and screamed.

CHAPTER TWO
UNDER THE DEMON MOON

The wolf leaped for him and Safar shouted, scrabbling for his dagger.

He rolled out of bed, landing in a crouch; bare toes digging into the rough floor for balance, dagger coming up to strike.

He blinked out of sleep, then gaped about in amazement. He was standing in an empty room—*his* room! There was no wolf, there was no threat of any kind. Instead he was presented with the most peaceful of scenes—the morning sun streaming through the bedroom window, spilling across his writing desk where the cat was sprawled across his papers basking in the warmth. The window was open and he could hear birds singing and smell the fresh breeze coming off the lake.

Safar turned away from the strong light, dagger hand sagging in relief. He came out of the crouch and suddenly found himself shivering in his thin nightshirt.

Nothing but a damned dream, he thought. Safar padded over to his desk, set the dagger down and poured himself a goblet of brandy. He drank it off, shuddered at the sudden heat rising from his belly and started to pour another. The cat stared at him, an accusing look in her eyes. She was only irritated for being disturbed but the look make Safar feel guilty for entirely different reasons.

He glanced at the brandy jug and made a face, thinking, you've certainly been doing a little too much of *that* of late, my friend. But the nightmare had been so realistic he only felt a little guilty when he gave in and poured himself "just a bit more" to calm his racing heart. Safar had dreamed he was a small boy, alone on the mountain, with a wolf pack closing in. He'd awakened just as they were attacking—the pack leader rising on its hind feet and its front legs turning into demon arms, reaching for him with razor-sharp talons.

At the last moment, as he hovered between dream and consciousness, the wolf's mask transformed into a human face. Long snout retreating into a strong human jaw, sharp brow broadening and rising into a human forehead, a human mouth with human lips parting to speak . . . and it was then that he'd awakened . . . just before the words were spoken.

Safar set the tumbler on its tray, wondering what the dream beast had been about to say. He snorted. Don't be ridiculous! The brandy's got you. It was a dream. Nothing more.

He glanced down at his notes, a scatter of linen pages peeping out from under the cat who had gone back to sleep. Yes, nothing but a dream. Brought on, no doubt, by the long fruitless night he'd spent poring over the Book of Asper. Trying to make some sense of the ancient demon wizard's musings.

And yes, he'd imbibed a bit too much and worked a bit too late. The last thing he'd read before he'd fallen asleep was another of Lord Asper's warnings, maddeningly couched in murky poetry.

What was it? How did it go? Oh, yes:

". . . the Age of the Wolf will soon draw near
When all is deceit and all is to fear.
Then ask who is hunter and who is prey?
And whose dark commands do we obey?
With the Heavens silent—the world forsaken—
Beware the Wolf, until the Gods awaken . . ."

Safar sighed. It was no wonder he'd dreamed of wolves. Too much brandy and Asper's poetry was a certain recipe for nightmares.

He put the jug down, found a robe, shrugged it on, then stuffed his feet into soft, hightopped slippers—a habit he'd formed during his years at the court of King Protarus. Felt-lined comfort on a chilly morn was only one very small luxury of many he'd enjoyed in his days as Grand Wazier to the late, unlamented by him, King of Kings.

Once Safar had possessed more palaces than there were cusps in the Heavenly Wheel. The finest food, wine, clothing, jewelry and women were his for the asking. Men and demons alike bowed when he passed, whispering his name for their children to hear and remember. Safar missed none of this. The rough, healthy life of Kyrania—the remote, high mountain valley of his birth—was all he'd ever really wanted. In the greater world he was Lord Timura, a wizard among wizards. A man to be to be feared. Here he was merely Safar Timura, son of a potter and now village priest and teacher to giggling school children. A man whose main faults were a citified taste for warm slippers on a chilly morning and possibly, just possibly, a bit more of a desire for strong spirits than was good for him. The only spoiler was that his fellow Kyranians called him by the title King Protarus had bestowed on him. So even here among the people he loved, the people he had known all his days, he was called Lord Timura.

As for women—Safar glanced at the tangled covers of his empty bed—well, he hadn't had much luck in that area. Oh, he supposed he could wed just about any maid in the village if he so desired. He was barely in his third decade of life, after all. Taller than any man in Kyrania and stronger than most. In the past women had called him handsome, although his blue eyes in a world of dark-eyed people made some nervous in his presence until they had been in his company for a time.

He was also quite rich. Thanks to Lieria he'd fled Zanzair with enough precious gems in his saddlebags to match even the greatest miser's measure of immense wealth.

Since he'd returned to Kyrania the young maids had buzzed about him like ardent bees, making it known they were available. A few had even made it plain that marriage wasn't necessary and they'd be satisfied just to share his bed. Scandalous offers indeed in puritanical Kyrania. In the early days, when Leiria still graced his bed, many an old Kyranian woman's tongue had been set clucking whenever she passed. In the moral double-standard favored in Kyrania, Safar was not blamed. A man will do what a man can, was the motto. And it is a woman who must preserve respect for Dame Chastity.

Now that Leiria was gone, Safar's mother and sisters were constantly conspiring to get him betrothed to a "decent woman."

Safar had gently eluded their little traps. To tell the truth he thought it unlikely he'd ever marry. He had good reasons for this, although he didn't mention them to family and friends. It was his secret shame. A secret he'd mentioned only to Leiria, who'd told him he was insane. Insane or not, Safar was convinced he had caused the deaths of two women who had loved him and broken the heart of a third.

Safar frowned, remembering Leiria's final words on the subject . . .

*   *   *

297

. . . It was their last night together as bedmates. Neither had spoken of this, but it was understood between them. Leiria had come home that day after a long ride in the hills. She'd been in a reflective mood, but full of single-minded determination at the same time. Safar had watched in silence as she gathered her things, then whistled up a boy to get her horse and a pack animal ready for the morning.

Finally she'd hauled out the brandy and they'd both gotten gloriously drunk and had made love until they'd fallen asleep. But an hour so later they'd both awakened, made love again, slow and full of secrets and depths neither could decipher, much less plumb. Then they'd talked. Retold old stories about shared adventures. About the time the Demon King Manacia thought he had them cornered and they'd sprung a trap on him instead. And the trick they'd pulled on Kalasariz, who had seized Kyrania with a demon army. And then the even better trick they'd played on the demons to free the valley.

They talked until it was almost dawn.

And then Safar said: "I'm sorry, Leiria. I know I said that once before, but this time I have even more—"

"—Six years ago," Leiria interrupted.

"What?" Safar said, confused.

Leiria nodded. "Yes, it was six years ago almost to the day. I remember we were in the stable near the east gate of Zanzair. You didn't know if I was friend or foe and you were thinking about killing me. By the Gods, you were stupid! To ever think I'd ever hurt you!"

"Yes, and I'm sor—"

Leiria put a finger to his lips, silencing him.

"Let's not make it three times," she said. "Twice is once too many. I deserved the first 'sorry.' Back when we were in the stable and you were doubting me. But I don't want, much less deserve, the second.

"As always, my love, you reach too deep for guilt. Be sorry that you ever doubted me. I'll keep that. I'll put it away for some weepy hour when I need to drag it up, along with as many others as I can. There's nothing I like more than a good cry on the eve of battle. It loosens the sword arm wondrously.

"As for any other 'sorries,' I say camelshit! You didn't break my heart, Safar Timura. I broke my own heart. It was a good lesson for a naVve soldier. And it was also something every person needs for the future. Man or woman. If you're wounded early in life it gives you something to reminisce about when nobody thinks you are worth a tumble.

"So, camelshit! Safar Timura. You didn't break my heart, anymore than you killed Methydia or Nerisa!"

"You have to admit," Safar said, guarding the odd comfort of familiar guilts, "that if they hadn't met me they'd be alive today."

"That's ridiculous!" Leiria said. "They were on whatever road the Fates decided. Sometimes you're ambushed. Sometimes you turn it around and ambush your enemy instead. Either way, you're on the same road the General commanded you to take. So you do your job. March when they say march. Fight when they say fight. Rest when they say rest. And when you're resting you pray to all that is dreaded in the Hells they keep for soldiers that you meet somebody you can love. Methydia and Nerisa had that, Safar. And if they were alive today they'd both give you a piece of their minds for feeling sorry for them. They weren't the kind of women who could bear that sort of thing. If their ghosts were to speak they'd tell you exactly what I'm going to tell you now. Which is this:

"Almost no one ever really experiences love, Safar. You get bedded. You get warm. Maybe you even get a sort of intimacy. I don't have much experience at such things, so I can't really describe what I mean. I've only been with two men in my life, after all—you and . . . Iraj. And yes, I loved him too . . . once. And that's my own 'sorry.' Hells! I have more sorries than I care to think about when it comes to Iraj.

"Sorry that I didn't see who he really was. Sorry that I gave him everything I had to give. Sorry that for a moment, however small, I really did think about betraying you. One thing I'm not sorry about. You killed him. And good riddance to Iraj Protarus. The world is a better place without him.

"So don't you feel guilty, Safar Timura. Especially not about the women who have loved you.

"I speak for all of them!"

That was the end of the conversation. They cuddled for awhile in silence. Then Leiria rose, bathed, and dressed in her light armor.

He didn't watch her leave. He stayed in his room, head bent over the Book of Asper. He heard her ride away. Heard the clatter of her armor. The creak of her soldier's harness. And just before the sounds faded from hearing he thought he caught a whiff of her perfume on the morning breeze.

In his whole life he'd never encountered a scent that lingered so long and lonely . . .

✻   ✻   ✻

Safar shook himself back to the present, thinking, no matter what Leiria had said, his hesitation would remain. It would be a very long time—if ever—before he chanced being the cause of harm or sorrow to another woman. But guilt, large as it was, had only a supporting role to play in the drama that made up Safar Timura. To him it seemed whenever his emotions came into play it exposed him—and, more importantly, his purpose—to danger.

Take love, for instance. The last time Safar had declared himself to a woman . . . say her name, don't dodge the pain of that old wound . . . her name was Nerisa.

Nerisa was a former street urchin who grew to became a woman of beauty, wealth and power. These three things—but mostly it was his love for Nerisa—had brought him into conflict with the king. And Iraj Protarus had used that love to find a weakness to betray Safar. The incident had ended with Nerisa's death and Safar's bitter repayment. The epilogue of the tale saw Safar kill Protarus and bring down his empire.

He'd fled the glorious demon city of Zanzair, leaving palace and riches behind in the flames that had consumed the city—flames evoked by the great spell he'd cast to slay Iraj.

Six years had passed since that day. A little longer, actually, since it had been several months since the day Leiria had noted the tragic anniversary. Six years of relative peace—at least in Kyrania. In the outside world things were much different.

Safar went to his bedroom window and looked across the beautiful valley he called home. His house—a narrow, two-story cottage set on a hillside near the cherry orchard—overlooked the dazzling blue waters of Lake Felakia, named for the goddess whose temple was now in his care. On the lake he could see fishermen casting their nets. In the rich farmland surrounding the glistening waters men and women were tending the green shoots that were just now poking their heads from their warm blankets of soil to greet the spring sun. In the distance two boys were driving a herd of goats up into the mountains to the high meadows where the lush grasses made their milk sweet. The shouts of the boys and bleating of the goats drifted to him on the breeze flowing down the mountainside. It was an idyllic scene, which Safar doubted could be matched anywhere in the world.

Yet his thoughts were not on the beauties of his native valley that morning. Or even—after he'd stirred through the pot of guilt—were they permanently fixed on Leiria, Methydia or even Nerisa.

He was still troubled by the dream that had awakened him. It was no ordinary nightmare. It was so strong an experience he wondered if it might actually be a vision. But there was no magical scent lingering in the nightmare's aftermath, so he was fooled for a time, thinking that maybe it really was only a dream. So when Safar looked through the window he barely saw all the beauty that so beguiled the rare outsider who visited Kyrania. Instead he focused on all the troubles the beauty hid.

Three poor harvests in a row, followed by harsh winters, had sorely tested the people of Kyrania. They had lived in ease for so many generations they were ill prepared for the hard times that had descended on the world in recent years.

The income from the great caravans that had once crossed the Gods' Divide from Caspan to Walaria and back again each year had ceased. Kyrania suffered from this. Yet once again in the age-old Kyranian story, Safar's people didn't suffer nearly as much as everyone else.

In the outside world—the world beyond the foothills of the Gods' Divide—all was chaos.

Protarus' shattered empire had turned Esmir into a confusion of petty kingdoms, so weak they couldn't keep the bandits off their own roads, so unstable that any bold warrior prince with an army at his back could easily step into the gap left by the mighty Iraj. Kyrania was cut off from the rest of Esmir, so Safar couldn't be certain that such a prince hadn't risen.

In the past, news would have come through the great merchant princes who knew the route over the mountains to Kyrania. But they were either dead, or huddled at home praying the chaos would soon end.

Safar thought it unlikely their prayers would be answered anytime soon. If at all.

He looked north and saw the Demon Moon—a silver comet trailing in its wake—rising over a mountain peak. As long as that moon ruled the heavens, he thought, plague and war and hunger would ravage the land. From his studies he knew things were likely to get worse, not better. Someday the Demon Moon might reign over lifeless seas and plains and mountains. The world, Safar believed, was slowly poisoning itself—shedding humans and demons and animals and plants as if they were so many parasites, like lice or ticks or aphids.

Once Safar had thought he might find the answer—the means to end the abysmal reign of the Demon Moon. It had been this search that had brought him to Protarus' court and all the terrible things which followed. Now, after more than six years of study and magical experiment, Safar was starting to wonder if he had been a fool from the very beginning. And that there was no answer to the riddle.

That damned old demon, Lord Asper, claimed the gods were asleep in the heavens and didn't care a whit about the fate of human or demonkind.

Safar eyed the brandy jug, thinking, if Asper were right, why should he, Safar Timura, care?

He picked the jug up, thinking, why should *I* fight the natural course of things? The gods must hate us, he thought. From what Safar had seen in his three decades of life the gods had good reason to abandon this world to its fate. Humans as well as demons were masters of misery, striking out at themselves as much as at others.

He started to pour himself one more drink, thinking, to the Hells with them all! If that's what the gods want, who am I to say nay?

Then he heard a small voice in the other room:

"You show him!"

Another voice protested.

"No, no, you show him!"

"He'll get mad."

"No he won't."

"Yes, he will."

"All right, all right. I'll do it."

Listening, Safar smiled, thinking—There's your reason, my friend!

He heard his son call, "Come here, father! Come and see quick!"

Safar laughed and went into Palimak's room. He entered cautiously, not knowing what he'd find.

The smell hit him first.

It was like something had died, then risen from the dead just short of complete mortification. It was more redolent than flesh. It was more like . . . Then smell shock became vision shock and Safar jumped back as a huge creature lumbered toward him.

"Surprise!" Palimak shouted.

The creature confronting him was buttery yellow with holes running through it so huge you could see to the other side. One of those holes opened—Safar imagined it might be a mouth—and then he knew he was right when the creature spoke:

"Cheese!" it said in a deep bass voice. Or at least that's what Safar thought it said. And then he was sure because it spoke again, saying: "Cheese!"

It waved clumsy arms at him, like an clockwork toy from a child prince's chest of pleasures.

Safar buried a smile, then made a motion and the creature froze in place.

Palimak clapped his hands, chortling, "What do you think, father? Isn't it good?"

He was a handsome boy, not quite eight, with curly brown hair and a slender body with long legs and arms splayed across the bed. He had a long elfish face, with rosy cheeks and skin so fine it was almost translucent. At the moment his normally hazel eyes were huge and golden—dancing with magical fire.

"Well? Say it!"

Safar put on a solemn face and examined the creature, trying not to laugh, which was difficult because behind Palimak was a small, green creature, doing its best to keep out of sight. It was an elegant little figure—about three hands high—dressed in fashionable tights, tunic, and feathered hat. It had the body of a man, but the face and talons of a demon. The creature was Gundara, Safar's Favorite. Gundara knew he was in a great deal of trouble with his master, ducking behind the boy, teeth chattering like a monkey's and giving him away.

Safar ignored Gundara for the moment and observed his son's creation. It wasn't yellow all over as he'd first thought. It also had brown, loaflike arms and legs that bore neither hands or feet. And it was indeed, shaped like a man—a stick figure with a big ball for a body and a smaller ball stacked upon that for a head.

Safar couldn't quite tell what the creature was made of. He sniffed the air. "What's that?" he asked.

"Guess!" Palimak demanded.

Safar looked past the boy to glare at Gundara. "Come out here," he said.

Gundara grumbled and hopped out onto the bed. "It wasn't my fault, Master!" he said. Suddenly his head swiveled around, little eyes fixed on a small stone turtle sitting next to Palimak.

The turtle had the mark of Hadin painted on its back: a green island, outlined in blue, and on that island was a red mountain with a monster's face spewing flames from its mouth.

Gundara's long delicate demon's tongue flickered out, and he said, "You just shut up, Gundaree. You hear me! Shut up!"

"That's not nice," the boy admonished Gundara. "You shouldn't say shut up!"

Gundara was hurt. "You used to say it all the time, Little Master," he said. "'Shut up,' were the very first words you spoke. Why, I remember when—"

"Never mind that!" Safar broke in. He pointed at the moldy, man-high thing. "What's this?" he asked Gundara.

Gundara hung his head. "Cheese, master," he muttered. "Just like it said." And he lowered his voice to match the creature's, intoning, "Cheese!'"

Despite himself, Safar laughed. For just as Gundara said, the magical creature Palimak had created really was made entirely of cheese—other than the legs and arms, which he now realized were made of bread.

"It's breakfast, father!" Palimak piped. "See. I made you breakfast!" He wrinkled his nose. "Although, maybe it doesn't smell too good."

"I told him not to use the stuff under his bed, master," Gundara said. "But he wouldn't listen. I said, 'that's somebody's old snack . . . some dirty little thing's old snack. Some dirty little thing who sneaked under the bed to eat." Gundara glared at the stone turtle. "I won't mention any names, but we all know who I mean."

Palimak clapped his hands. "Gundaree!" he shouted. He grinned at Safar. "Gundaree likes eating under the bed, father," he said. "And he likes his cheese, really, really old." The boy pinched his nostrils to show just how old Gundaree preferred his cheese to be.

Gundaree was Gundara's twin. The two of them had dwelt in the stone turtle for at least a millennium. A gift from Nerisa, the idol and the Favorites it contained had been created in Hadin—a world away from Esmir. Whoever owned the idol had the decidedly mixed blessing of the twin's magical assistance. They had a constant war going between them, making it quite disconcerting for whoever was their current master. The only consolation was that they couldn't appear at the same time before normal beings. Gundara serviced humans, Gundaree demons. Only little Palimak—who was part human and part demon—could see them both at the same time.

Mischievous as they were, their magic was very powerful and Safar had ordered them to protect Palimak. The boy kept the idol with him at all times, giving him a permanent set of child minders and magical playmates.

At the moment Gundara was doing his best to appear the innocent above all innocents.

"I warned Palimak, master, " he said. "I told him, 'Oh, no, you shouldn't use that smelly old stuff to make a breakfast spell, Little Master. Your father will be angry.'"

"You never said that!" Palimak protested.

"Yes, I did!"

"You taught me the spell!"

"No, I—"

Safar clapped his hands twice. The first won him silence. The second commanded the collapse of the cheese beast. There was a *pop!* and it returned to its original, disgusting shape, which was a small mound of old cheese and bread piled on the floor. Safar swept the mess up and dumped it out the window, counting on Naya, the old goat who made her home in his yard, to make short work of it. Then he mumbled a cleansing smell, snapped his fingers and the air in Palimak's room was sweet again.

When he turned back Gundara had vanished—fleeing into the retreat of the little stone idol where he would, no doubt, continue his argument with Gundaree.

Palimak sighed. "I'm awfully tired," he said. "Making breakfast is hard work."

"I suppose it is," Safar said.

"The hard part was making the Breakfast Thing talk," Palimak said. "I thought that'd be a really, really Big, Big Surprise!" He spread his hands wide to indicate just how amazing the effort was.

"It said, 'Cheese!'" Safar said. "You can imagine how surprised I was. I've never had breakfast speak to me before."

Palimak hung his head. "I'm sorry it was so smelly, father," he said. "There's some good cheese in the kitchen, but Gundara said I couldn't get out of bed until you woke up." He shrugged his shoulders. "There sure are a lot of rules in this house," he said.

Safar aped the sigh, making it long and dramatic. "I guess there are," he said. Then he shrugged—again mimicking Palimak. "But what can we do? Rules are rules!"

"I suppose you're right, Father," Palimak said with weary resignation. "What can we do? But I'd sure like to know who makes up all those rules!" He yawned. "Well, maybe I'll go back to sleep for a little while."

Palimak made a magical motion and soft dreamy music floated out of the stone turtle. He hugged his pillow tight, yawning again. "Wake me up when it's time for breakfast, father," he said.

Then he closed his eyes and went to sleep. Lips trembling with his last words. The child went from wakefulness to sleep in less time than it took for a heart to beat. Safar smiled at the boy, watching how the sun streaming through the window lit up his milky skin. Palimak positively glowed and Safar could see, deep, deep, under the child's skin, the faint gleam of bluish green. Demon green. And his little hands, clasped together, had pointy little nails, so paper thin you could only tell they existed because of the darker blush of the pink skin beneath them. When Palimak became excited and forgot himself those pointy little nails could hook out like kitten claws and accidentally draw blood from an unwary adult.

Palimak possessed amazing magical powers for his age. Although he called Safar "father," the boy was a foundling, a child of the road, whom Nerisa—an orphan herself—had taken pity on and adopted. Safar had assumed responsibility for Palimak's care after Nerisa had died, raising him as if he were his own. How a demon and a human—bitter ancestral enemies—had come together in love to make the child was surely a tale of complexity and tragedy. Unfortunately, Nerisa had died before she could tell Safar much about what she knew of Palimak's origins and as the boy had grown older it had become increasingly difficult to explain that his all-wise father should be ignorant about something so important.

Safar tucked a blanket around the boy and returned to his rooms, purpose renewed. He washed, dressed—leaving on his soft slippers—and ate a little yogurt and drank cold strong tea left over from the day before. A village woman would bring breakfast soon, so he had a little free time before Palimak would be thundering around.

He slipped behind his desk and retrieved the little book from beneath his notes. It was an old book, curled and dry and quite small—no bigger than a man's hand. It was a master wizard's book of dreams. The musings of Lord Asper, who was perhaps the greatest wizard in all history. Asper had lived long ago and in his old age had started recording his thoughts and discoveries. The old demon's writing was so small that Safar found it more comfortable to use a glass to read. There was no order to the book, making it even more difficult for the reader. A theoretical phrase or two about the possibilities of mechanical flight might find itself on the same page as an elaborate magical formula whose only purpose was to keep moths away from a good wool cloak.

Maddening as it was, all that was known about the world was contained between its brittle covers. And all that wasn't cried for recognition's ink.

Safar opened the book at random. On one page was a large sketch of the world—showing the two halves of the globe in a split ball. The four major land masses were inked in, but as actual formations, rather than the usual stylized maps of Safar's time that showed the turtle gods carrying the lands across the sea. The names of the continents were inked below each drawing. Floating in the Middle Sea was Esmir, the land where Safar lived. To the north was Aroborus, to the south, Raptor. Last of all was Hadin, on the other side of the world—directly opposite Esmir.

Hadin, land of the fires, the place where Safar believed the great disaster that was slowly consuming the world had begun.

He had seen Hadin in a vision long ago—handsome people dancing on an enchanted island under a threatening volcano. The volcano erupting, hurling flame and death. The dancing people were gone in the first few moments, but the volcano continued to spew huge poisonous clouds charged with such magical power that it had seared Safar through the vision. Since that time nothing in the world had been the same.

And it was Safar's obsession and self-sworn duty to somehow unravel the mystery of Hadin and halt the disaster.

Asper had seen the same disaster, not as it was happening, but in a vision hundreds of years before the incident. The coming death of the world—no matter that it was far in the future—so disturbed the old demon that he had made an abrupt shift in all his thinking. It was as if a blindfold had been lifted from eyes, he wrote, and suddenly "Truth was lies/and lies were truth . . ."

It was then that Asper began the greatest work of his life. Old age sapping his strength, bitter realizations stalking his dreams, he raced against Death's imminent arrival in an ultimately futile effort to solve the riddle that was the coming end of the world.

Near the end, during a moment of great despair, he had written:

Wherein my heart abides
This dark-horsed destiny I ride?
Hooves of steel, breath of fire—
Soul's revenge, or heart's desire?

Not first for the first time, Safar wondered what particular incident had caused Asper to write such a thing. After long study it was plain that Asper faced much opposition at the end of his life. He was speaking heresy after all. Uncaring gods asleep in their heavenly bower. A world doomed. And the greatest heresy of all—that humans and demons were not so different. He even speculated that the two species, who were historic enemies, were originally twins—the opposite sides of a single connubial coin.

Safar was both a wizard and a potter. The wizardly side of him tended to question everything. The potter's side demanded practical proof as well. He still had many questions about Asper's theories. But as far as practical proof went, he only had to look at Palimak, a child of the two species. What greater proof could one need to show that demons and humans had once supped the milk of a common mother?

Like Safar, Lord Asper had been forced to flee his enemies. Unlike Safar he had no home to return to and had wandered the world for nearly twenty years. Before he died—Safar guessed he lived nearly three hundred years, ancient even for a demon—Asper had visited all four continents and had made notes and drawings of his experiences and conclusions. In Aroborus, for instance, he spoke of trees that ate meat and could uproot themselves to chase down and trap their prey. On Raptor, Asper said, there was a strange birdlike creature that was nearly twelve feet high. It couldn't fly and hunted in packs, cornering its victims to hammer them down with huge, ax-shaped beaks. On Hadin Asper told of a once great civilization containing both humans and demons that had destroyed itself in a religious war so fierce only barbarians remained among the ruins.

It was at this point that the riddle of Asper truly began. The old wizard had suddenly, and without explanation, left Hadin. There was a great gap in months, possibly even in years, between the time of his flight—Safar guessed he was escaping something—and his arrival at a small island in the Caspan Sea about two hundred miles off the coast of Esmir. The island, Safar learned from his research, was the mythical birthplace of Alisarrian The Conqueror, who had welded demons and humans together under one rule many centuries before.

Safar eyed the brandy jug, sighed, then turned back to the book. Once again he looked at the small map of the world. And once again he traced the lines showing Asper's travels. His flight from Esmir to Hadin and back. Beneath the map was a tiny sketch of the island where Asper ended his days.

The island's name, scrawled in red ink, was Syrapis.

Musing, Safar said the name aloud—"Syrapis." Then, "I wonder what Asper sought there?"

Suddenly his fingers itched with a powerful desire to touch the drawing of the island—a need as strong as a thirsty man's obsession for water. His fingertips touched the paper and a surge of energy flowed up his arm.

There was a *boom!* of distant thunder and a sharp *crack!* of lightning quite near.

Suddenly all was blackness and his hair rose up on prickling roots.

CHAPTER THREE

THE WIZARD'S TOMB

Safar felt a great force seize him, lift him up, then hurl him away.

He flew through darkness—so far he lost all sense of motion and direction. Then he was falling, plunging, an eerie voice whispering in his ear, "Down and down and down. Down, and down and down . . ."

And then he just . . . *stopped!*

There was nothing between the two feelings of falling and stopping. One moment his insides were rising up and the next moment he felt hard ground under his feet and the comforting sensation of weight. Still, all remained blackness and he had no idea where he was. All he knew was that it was someplace hot and dank. Perspiration flooded from his pores, soaking his clothes. Under his feet, still shod in slippers, he could feel heat rising from the rocky floor. And then far off he thought he heard the sound of dripping water and he wondered if he might be underground.

He stayed quite still, trying to get his bearings. As he was about to probe the darkness with his wizard's senses he suddenly heard rustling all around him—like dry insect wings. He also heard whispering, or at least what he thought was whispering—he couldn't make out the words.

Then he heard, quite clearly: "Sisters! Sisters!"

The voice was like sand polishing glass. Keeping his head motionless, Safar forced his eyes toward the source of the sound. He saw two large red holes burning through the darkness—floating a good ten feet above the ground.

It spoke again—"Sisters! Awake, sisters!"

The voice came from just below the red holes. Safar's heart quickened as he realized they were huge eyes and the voice was likely coming from an equally enormous mouth.

Then someone, or *something*, answered, "I hear, sister!"

The words had the same sand against glass sound to them. But harsher. And he realized the voice was coming from directly above him! It was all Safar could do not to look up.

Others answered: "I hear! I hear! I hear!"

The voices came from every direction and the darkness bloomed with a ghastly garden of many glowing red eyes.

Then the first voice said, "I smell a human!"

A harsh chorus answered, "Where? Where, sister, where?"

"Here with us!" was the reply.

Horrid shrieks filled the air: "Kill him, kill the human, kill him!"

Talons and scaly bodies scraped against stone, heavy wings flapped from above and there was a great gnashing of teeth. Burning eyes rushed about like huge fireflies fleeing an oncoming storm. Safar needed no magical help to keep absolutely still in that chaos of hatred. His blood turned to ice, his heart to stone and his breath fled from him like an escaping ghost.

Then he realized they couldn't see him. The realization was small comfort, especially when next he heard a shout:

"Silence, sisters!"

It was the first voice, the commanding voice. And it got the silence it demanded.

A pause, then, "Where are you human? Show yourself!"

Safar had the sudden hysterical desire to laugh. It hit him so quickly it was all he could do to bite it off. Show himself? Did she think he was insane?

She also must have thought he was deaf as well, because she said, "You have nothing to fear from us, human! We like humans, don't we sisters?"

"Yes, yes, yes," came the chorused reply. "We like humans. We like them all!"

"We would never hurt a human, would we sisters?"

"Never hurt, never, never!"

Silenced followed, as if the creatures were waiting for Safar's answer.

When it didn't come, the commanding voice said, "You are insulting us, human! You should speak and show us your trust. Speak now, or we will forget our love of all things human. You will suffer greatly for angering us."

Another long pause, then Safar heard: "Sisters! I think I smell him over here!"

The voice came from quite near. Safar heard heavy talons rattle on stone and a snuffling sound, like a large beast following a strong scent. He knew he had to do something quickly before he was found.

The idea jumped up at him and he knew he couldn't wait and think it through, because with thought would come fear and fear's hesitation would be the end of him. He made a spell and clapped his hands together and roared:

"Light!"

And light blasted in from all sides, nearly knocking him over with the sudden shock of it. He had been blinded by darkness before, now he was blinded by its white-hot opposite. There were awful screams of pain all around and then his vision cleared and the first thing he saw ripped his breath from his body.

The beast towered above him, enormous corpse-colored wings unfolded like a bat's. It had the stretched out torso of a woman with long thin arms and legs that ended in taloned claws. There was no hair on its skull-like head and instead of a nose there were only nostril holes on a flat face shaped like a shovel.

Safar nearly jumped away, but then he realized the creature was too busy screaming in pain and clawing at its eyes to be a threat.

He was in an enormous vaulted room, filled with blazing colors. Great columns, red and blue and green, climbed toward glaring light then disappeared beyond. The room was filled with hundreds of death-white creatures, some crouched on the floor howling pain, others hanging bat-like from long stanchions coming out of the columns. They twisted and screamed, horrid flags of misery blowing in a devil wind of conjured light.

Safar spotted the one he wanted. Again he shouted, his magically amplified voice thundering over the wails.

"SILENCE!"

The shrieks and screams cut off at his command, and now there was only moaning and harsh pleas for "Mercy, brother, mercy!"

Safar paced forward, moving through the writhing bodies until he came to the throne. It looked a great pile of bones—arms and legs and torsos and skulls stacked in the shape of an enormous winged chair. As he came closer he saw the bones were carved from white stone. The creature who commanded that grisly throne was like the others, except much larger. A red metal band encircled her bony skull to make a crown. Unlike the others, however, the creature was silent and although she was hunched over, claws covering her eyes, she made no outward show of pain.

Safar stopped at the throne and said loudly for all to hear: "Are you queen to this mewling lot?"

"Yes, I am queen. Queen Charize." As she answered she couldn't help but raise her royal head, carefully keeping her eyes shielded. "I command here."

"You command nothing," Safar replied, voice echoing throughout the chamber, "except what I, Lord Timura of Kyrania, might permit."

Queen Charize said nothing.

"Do you understand me?" Safar demanded.

He made a motion and the light became brighter still. The creatures shrieked as their pain intensified. Even the queen could not stop a low moan escaping through her clenched lips.

"Yes," she gasped, "I understand."

"Yes, Master," Safar corrected her. "You will address me as Master."

The queen gritted her fangs in protest, but she got it out: "Yes . . . Master!"

Safar motioned and the light diminished. There were gasps of relief as he dimmed it until the room was merely a soft glow. But no one rose or uncovered her eyes. Dim as the light was, it was still too painful for the sisters of darkness to bear. He could also smell the fear in them. They knew that if their new master was threatened, he could instantly retaliate.

To make certain, Safar said, "You may be queen here, but that doesn't mean you actually have wits to rule elsewhere." Queen Charize hissed indignation. Safar laughed to grind in the humiliation. "Hiss all you like," he said. "Just so long as we understand each other. I've already formed a spell that will turn you and all these filthy things you call subjects into dust. I only have to cast it. It would take a word, no more."

This was a lie. As far as Safar knew there was no such spell. But his days with Methydia's circus had taught him how to lie most convincingly.

"I will do as you say . . . Master," the queen answered. "On my word, no one will harm you."

"Fortunately," Safar said, "I don't need to test your word.

"Now, tell me, what is this place? And what do you do here?"

The queen answered simply. "We are the Protectors," she said.

"And what, pray tell, are you the protectors of?"

The queen's head jerked in surprise. If this human wizard, this Lord Timura, was so powerful, why didn't he know the answer? Safar didn't give her a chance to scratch his pose further.

"Well, answer me!" he demanded.

"Why, as all know on Syrapis," she said, "we are the Protectors of Lord Asper. And this is his tomb."

The answer so surprised Safar he nearly lost control of his spell. Syrapis? This great vault was in Syrapis? And what was this about Lord Asper? Protectors!? Protecting what? Asper had long been dead.

What happened next surprised him even more. The queen began chanting in a harsh whisper:

"We are the sisters of Asper,
Sweet Lady, Lady, Lady.
We guard his tomb, we guard his tomb,
Holy One . . ."

The other creatures joined her in a harsh chorus, as if coming from the grave. It seemed to be a prayer to some goddess, but coming from those throats of malice it made a mockery of all that was holy.

They sang:

"We take the sin, we take the sin,
Sweet Lady, Lady, Lady.
On our souls, on our souls,
Holy One."

Safar thought, if these creatures had souls he didn't want to meet the god who made them. Then he felt a dry, spidery web drifting over him and he realized they were trying to trap him in a spell.

His own spell was weakened and the light dimmed further. The creatures began to stir.

Safar saw the queen's great red eyes come up from the shield of her claws like twin suns rising over the sharp peaks of the Hells. But he only laughed and clapped his hands, bringing the light back to its most shocking brightness, nearly more than even he could bear.

The prayer song collapsed into shrieks of torment. He ignored their pain and turned his back on the queen, who was squirming on her throne in such agony he was confident he had little to fear from her.

He looked around the gaudy room, shielding his eyes against the glaring light, until he saw a raised dais not many paces away. The dais supported a large black coffin, shaped like a demon. Emblazoned on its lid in blood-red paint was a hauntingly familiar shape—a winged snake with two heads, poised to strike. The sign of Asper! This was the burial place of Lord Asper himself. The source of all the wisdom Safar sought.

But how had these evil beings come to infest the Master Wizard's tomb? Safar had no doubt that Queen Charize's claims of being Asper's Protector were lies. Just as the prayer song had been a lie.

Amazed as he was, Safar kept his wits about him. He wouldn't make the same mistake twice. Tightening his control on the spell of light, he went to the dais and climbed the steps, being extremely careful not to stumble and lose concentration. When he was a few feet away, he felt the buzz of magic.

The snake heads came alive and shot toward him, then stopped. Still buzzing, but more a buzz of recognition than warning.

Asper knew him!

An odd thought came—How strange! Why should *he* recognize me?

Then he saw another familiar symbol on the side of the coffin. It was the outline of the island of Syrapis, exactly the same as the one in Asper's book—although much larger.

His fingers tingled with the sudden desire to touch the symbol. He mounted the dais steps, hand outstretched, so taken by the notion he forgot the warding spell. The light began to dim. He paid no attention, drawing closer and closer to the symbol of Syrapis. As the light dimmed still more, he heard Queen Charize mutter commands and her subjects rising up behind him, dry insect wings stirring old dust from the floor. Still he ignored them, climbing higher until the coffin was within his reach.

His fingers moved toward the symbol of Syrapis. He thought, I only have to touch it and all will be explained.

Words came to him, he didn't know from where, and he whispered, "Wherein my heart abides/This dark-horsed destiny I ride?"

And a whispered reply came back—"Khysmet!"

His journeying hand froze. What was this? Who was speaking? And what did he mean?

Was it Asper's ghost?

"How do you know me, Master?" Safar asked.

And the ghost whispered: "All wait for thee, Safar Timura. From Esmir to far Hadinland. Come to me, Timura. Come to Syrapis!"

"But how shall I come, Master?" Safar asked. "Syrapis is a long journey across the sea."

And the ghost said: "First to Naadan, then to Caluz. That is the way to Syrapis."

"But what if I fail, Master?" Safar asked. "What if by some accident I am killed?"

"Then send the Other," replied the ghost.

"Other?" Safar asked. "What Other?"

Just then he heard the queen shout: "Kill him!" And the creatures closed in on him.

But he didn't care. If only he could know the answer, it didn't matter . . . death didn't matter . . . nothing mattered but the knowledge he was certain was waiting to be revealed in one blinding flash, brighter even than the light he'd used to keep the Protectors at bay.

"Tell me, Master!" he shouted. "Who is the Other?"

His fingertips were scant inches away from the sign of Syrapis when he heard another voice shouting:

"Father! They're coming, father! They're coming!"

It was Palimak's voice.

A small hand plucked at his sleeve, dragging his fingers away.

"No!" Safar shouted. "Noooo!"

"Father!" Palimak's voice insisted. "They're coming! The men are coming!"

Asper's chamber vanished and Safar found himself in his bedroom again. He was clutching the edge of his desk, staring at the open page of Asper's book. The drawing of Syrapis still beckoning.

He turned, seeing Palimak next to him, tugging at his sleeve.

"Something awful has happened, father!" the boy said.

Palimak pointed out the bedroom window. "Look!"

Dazed, so sick to his stomach he wasn't sure he could hold its contents for more than a moment, Safar raised his head and looked.

Through the window he saw six men approaching his house, bearing a litter. And on that litter was a small, frighteningly small, human form. He didn't know who it was, because blood-soaked blankets covered the features.

"It's poor Tio, father," Palimak said. "I think the wolves got him!"

CHAPTER FOUR
THE WOLF KING

The skies were somber, the lake ashen, when they sent little Tio to his watery grave. The village was draped in black and the winds came off the Bride's slopes cold and moaning, black bunting flapping like the tongues of so many ghosts.

All of Kyrania was in shock that one so young and innocent had met such a horrid fate. The mourning women wailed and tore their hair. And all the men got drunk and swore vengeance. Against whom, no one was certain.

Safar presided over the funeral ceremonies, casting cleansing spells and leading the village in traditional prayer.

And everyone sang:

"Where is our dream brother?
Gone to sweet-blossomed fields . . .
Our hearts yearn to follow . . ."

When the song was done, Safar and four temple lads fired the boat and pushed it away from the lakeshore. The mourners watched in silence as the funeral craft, festooned with yellow ribbons, was pulled this way and that by errant winds. Black smoke trailed through the curling ribbons and everyone wept in relief when the boat bearing Tio's remains finally halted in the middle of the lake. This was lucky for Tio's spirit. Everyone had worried the misfortune he'd suffered in this life would follow him to the next. The boat burned to the waterline and then wind-driven waves slopped over to hiss and steam in the flames. The boat sank slowly, smoke and steam columning up into heavy gray skies. Then it was gone.

Safar's heart sank with the boat. He thought of the dream he'd had only yesterday morning. The dream of wolves in which he'd witnessed Tio's death.

Suddenly his hackles rose and chill fingers of danger ran up his spine. Palimak suddenly clutched his hand.

"Somebody's watching, father," the boy whispered. "And he's not very nice!"

Safar felt eyes boring into him—eyes from nowhere and everywhere. He squeezed Palimak's hand. "I can feel it too," he said. He kept his voice easy, but with just a tinge of concern. "And you're right. He's not very nice."

"What should we do, father?" Palimak asked. "I don't like this! It isn't right! Watching people, and . . . and . . ." He shrugged. "You know . . . *Looking at everything!*"

Only Safar and Palimak were aware of what was happening. Their fellow mourners were solemnly engaged in singing songs and beating their breasts to help speed Tio's ghost to the Heavens.

"I could use your help with this, Palimak," Safar said. The boy's face brightened, worry lines vanishing.

"Do you have a trick, father?" Palimak asked, flashing a sharp-toothed smile.

"I certainly do," Safar said. "But it won't work unless you help me."

He felt the remainder of the child's tension vanish. Now the ominous presence seemed only a game.

Palimak giggled. "We'll get him! Really, *really* get him!"

His gusto was alarming. Safar remembered his own blood-thirsty ways as a child and forced himself to stanch a sudden, unreasonable feeling of parental concern.

"Yes," he said, "we're going to surprise him. Maybe even hurt him . . . but just a little bit. Enough to make him sorry."

Palimak drew in a deep breath, gathering his concentration. And then, "I'm ready, father."

Safar nodded. "Here's what we'll do," he said. "Let's make ourselves really hot! Let's be so hot he feels like he's looking right at the sun. Can you imagine that?"

"That's easy," Palimak said.

"Not that easy," Safar warned. "I want you to think really, really hot. Hot as you possibly can."

Palimak chortled. "We'll burn him!" he said. "That'll teach him!"

Safar started to add a few more words of caution, but then Palimak's eyes started to glow and the air crackled with a surge of magical power. Hells, the child was strong! Safar leaped in to catch the surge and blend with it. Then he gained control, added his own power, and focused their combined strength like a magnifying glass intensifies the rays of the sun.

He smelled the stink of ozone and then the air became hot and heavy and it was difficult to breathe. He heard Palimak cough. And then from far away he heard a howl of surprised pain. Like a wolf who had just sprung a steel trap.

Then the eyes were gone—snatched away—and all was normal again.

"Will he come back?" Palimak asked.

"I don't know, son," Safar said. "But we'll have to be careful."

Then the crowd descended on him and he was shaking hands and commiserating with the family as if nothing had happened.

The following night he called an emergency meeting of the village elders.

First they heard from Renor, Tio's older brother. The men's eyes became moist as they listened.

"It was only for the night," Renor sobbed. "I didn't think there was any danger, or I wouldn't have left him there. I'd have taken him with me and made the herd fend for itself!"

Safar, a master of old guilts, said, "You had no reason to act differently, Renor. That is the way things are done in Kyrania. Boys have always taken the herds into the mountains to learn how to be on their own and act responsibly. That was what you were doing with Tio." He waved a hand at the others. "All of us have had that first time experience of a night alone on the mountains. It's a tradition—a necessary tradition."

The other men muttered agreement. "My brother did the same for me when I was a lad," said the headman, Foron, who was also the village smithy.

Renor wiped his eyes, trying to regain control.

Safar's father, Khadji, leaned in. "Tell us the rest, son," he urged. "Then you can go home to your family. They need your strength now."

Renor nodded. "On the way down the mountain," he said, "I didn't see anything to worry about. And I was looking, believe me. I mean, I had an injured goat on my back, didn't I? No sense giving some big cat ideas, or reason to think *I* was the goat. Tio has . . . had . . . a good imagination. I knew he'd be frightened. So I didn't even wait until morning to go back up the mountain. I just left the goat with my father and set off again."

The young man said he'd made good time on the return, but then it became too dark, the trail too treacherous, and he was forced to make a cold camp a few hours from the meadow.

"I couldn't sleep," he said. "I was worried about Tio the whole the time so I got up before first light—I didn't even eat—and set off to meet my brother."

Finally he came to the meadow. "It was like walking into a nightmare," he said.

The ground was torn up, barely a blade left untouched, and there was a huge smoking crater in the center. There was blood everywhere and the mangled remains of animals strewn about the field made it look like a giant's butcher shop. Renor ran for the shelter and there he found Tio's body, ripped so badly he barely recognized him. Next to him was a big gray she wolf, also torn to pieces.

"I couldn't figure out what happened," Renor sobbed. "I went mad for a bit. I rushed all around the valley and the hills calling him, 'Tio! Tio!' He didn't answer, of course. But I couldn't believe what had happened. I kept thinking of my mother and father. And of Tio, poor little Tio who never did a wrong to anyone. Then I became angry, stupidly angry, and I ran all over the meadow looking for something to kill. But everything was already dead. Goats and wolves . . . all dead."

"I don't understand," said another of the Elders. "How could they *all* be dead? Goats and wolves alike?" The man was Masura, who was second in command and no friend of the Timuras. A prissy fellow, Masura considered himself the ultimate word in village morality.

Renor shook his head. "I don't know," was all he said.

Safar remained silent during the discussion. He had an idea what was at the end of this bumpy trail of logic, but he thought it was important the Elders find it for themselves.

Foron scratched his grizzled chin. "If the wolves killed Tio and the goats," he said. "Tell me—who killed the wolves?"

"Maybe it was another pack," Masura suggested. "But stronger, much stronger."

"That doesn't make sense," Safar's father said, drawing a hot glare from Masura, who disliked being contradicted. "I've heard of such things, of course. Wolves attack other wolves all the time. But only when they come on the same prey. And then the weaker wolves run away as soon as they see all is lost. They don't stay around to be killed."

Foron agreed. "You're right, Khadji. Also, once the others took flight, the stronger pack wouldn't chase after them. After all, the object would be to eat goats, not to fight other wolves."

"There's another thing that was strange," Renor said, breaking in. Then he ducked his head and blushed, embarrassed by having interrupted the headman.

"Tell us what you saw," Safar said, gentle as he could. "We have to know everything."

"Well, it wasn't what *was* done," Renor said, "but what wasn't done that bothered me. I mean—nothing was eaten. All the bodies were ripped up, but they weren't gnawed on . . . or anything. They were just . . . I don't know . . . torn apart!"

"Sorcery!" Masura exclaimed. "Of the foulest kind." He glared at Safar as if he were responsible for all the foul magical deeds in the world.

All eyes turned to Safar. "I suspect you're right," he said. "In fact, if you think about it closely, you'll see there is no other reasonable explanation."

The house became so silent Safar could hear the ticking of the roof beams and the scuttle of insects hunting in the cold hearth. The men only looked at him with fearful eyes.

"What could it be, my son?" Safar's father asked. "And what have we done to deserve such a curse?"

"The whole world is cursed, father," Safar replied. "It isn't just us. Down on the flatlands people are suffering greatly, as you know. And there are all sorts of magical beasts plaguing them. I once dealt with a creature who had a whole region under its thrall." He was thinking of the Worm of Kyshaat, whom he had defeated some years before.

The Worm was just the first of many manifestations to infect the world.

Safar sighed, mourning the end of his people's innocence.

"What should we do about this . . . this . . . creature, Lord Timura?" Foron asked.

"Exorcise it," Safar said firmly. "That's what I did before." He turned to Foron. "If you'll provide me with a guard I'll go up into the mountains tomorrow and see what I can do."

As frightened as everyone was they were so angry at what had happened to Tio that Safar was deluged with volunteers to accompany him. He held them off, preferring to hand pick the party in the light of day.

Then he said, "If you will excuse us, Renor, I'm sure your family is anxious to see you."

The young man looked startled, then realized Safar was politely indicating he should leave. Safar turned back to the group when he was gone.

He hesitated. There was much he had to say, but his thoughts were disorganized. The emergency had left him little time to consider the vision of Asper's Tomb. Still, he knew one thing: he had to leave Kyrania. If there was any chance to stop the magical poisons blowing on the winds of Hadin, he would find it in Syrapis. Before he left, however, he had to protect them as best he could.

So absorbed was he in his musings, he forgot the others. His father's voice brought him back.

"What is it, son?" he asked. "You seem as if you wish to tell us something."

Safar started to speak, then shook his head.

"Let it wait," he said. "We can discuss it later."

*   *   *

There was heavy fog upon the mountain when Safar entered the meadow where Tio had been killed. The mist was so thick it was like a midnight garden; wet, heavy cobwebs breaking before him, then clinging and trailing behind. He was accompanied by five of Kyrania's best men, including Sergeant Dario, the village's elderly fighting master, as dangerous at seventy as when he'd fought on the Jasper Plains fifty years before. Guiding the group was Tio's brother, Renor.

"Better let us secure it first, me lord," Dario said. He tapped his sharp, beaked nose. "Don't smell nothin' amiss. And the old sniffer never failed me all these years. But like I always tell the lads—better a good professional look around than blind guessin'."

Safar stopped a grin and nodded solemnly. Dario was a proud little man—short, bowlegged and so skinny and wrinkled he looked like a whip made of snake hide. His only concession to age was a tendency to be a bit loquacious. Even so, he was no figure of fun as he motioned to his men and they fanned out. He gave another signal and they all disappeared at once—slipping through the fog like ghosts to investigate the meadow.

It was cold and Renor wrapped his arms about his heavy coat and stamped his feet.

He started to speak, but Safar shushed him.

He took a small pot from his cloak and set it on the ground. Then he withdrew a little silver tinder box, lit a wick and pulled the stopper from the pot. Oily, orange-tinged fumes coiled out, heavy smelling, like overripe fruit. Safar quickly inserted the smoldering wick into the fumes. Flames sheeted up and a great trumpet blared.

It was a great hammer of a sound, smashing against the foggy shield. Then there was the indrawn whop! of an implosion as all moisture was drained from the atmosphere and air rushed in from all sides to quarrel over the vacuum left behind. The fog vanished, showing Dario and the others creeping forward, looking a little foolish as they turned to gape at Safar and Renor.

Safar pointed past them. "Over there!" he said, indicating the blackened crater in the center of the meadow.

The men revolved to look and it was if the force of their eyes let loose nature's darkest side. With sight came smell, and the odor of the goat corpses drifted across the torn up ground and the men had to turn their faces away to gasp for sweeter air.

Safar made a magical gesture and a slight breeze blew through, infused with the smell of violets. Dario nodded at him, made his mouth into an "O" as he drew in fresh air, then shuffled forward to the crater. He peered inside.

"There's nothing here, me lord," he called back.

Safar concentrated, radiating a cautious "find and flee" spell across the meadow. It was a difficult exercise. The rocky encirclement forming the meadow also made a natural cup that urged spells to flow back to their source.

The group had returned to his side by the time he was done.

Safar shrugged. "As far as I can tell, sergeant," he said, "it's safe. Hells, there's barely a sign of the magic that was done here. Certainly nothing to exorcise. Whatever spirit visited this place has either gone or is in such deep hiding that I can't find him."

His words were hardly reassuring—nor were they meant to be. Dario and the others scanned the area, nervous. A few moments before they'd been full of fire, set on vengeance. Now they were wondering if anyone . . . or thing . . . was examining them, measuring them for the grave.

It was Renor who broke the mood. He drew himself up. "I'm ready for whatever they're after," he said.

His comment made no outward sense, but it resonated deep into the cavern of last resorts, where all threatened things retreat to make their final stand.

Dario nodded—a downward jerk of his sharp features, like an ax cutting through. "Sure we are," he said.

Warmth spread through them all like a comforting wine as the villagers, including Safar, drew on their common strength.

It was then that the first wolf howled.

This was a howl from the earth. A hunting howl, ululating across the glen, then turning sharper, higher, victorious, as the Hunter found its prey.

There was not a man standing on that bloody meadow who did not know in his heart the Great Wolf was calling, and that its hungry call was meant for him.

A moment later another wolf howled in reply; a huge creature from the sound of its baying, but not as large as the Great Wolf. Then another acolyte of the fang joined the first two. And then another, until the whole meadow rang with their ungodly song.

The howling stopped as suddenly as it began. Only a deathly silence remained, a void almost as frightening as the devil wolves.

Dario coughed—hard and harsh to choke up the phlegm of fear. "I was never the sort what opposed an orderly retreat, me lord," he said in a gruff voice. "Assumin' the circumstances called for it."

Dario jerked as the howling resumed—even closer than before. The old warrior forced himself to relax and then he smiled, carved wooden teeth making an old man's splintered grin.

"What I'm sayin', me lord," Dario continued, ignoring the howls as best he could, "is that right now appears to be one of them circumstances I was talkin' about. For retreatin', I mean."

Serious as the situation was Safar couldn't help but laugh. "I don't think you'll find anyone here who objects to such a strategy," he said.

The laughter calmed the other men. They all grinned and nodded. Safar gestured toward the trail they'd taken into the meadow.

"You can have the honor of leading the retreat, sergeant," he said. "But go as quickly as you can. Don't look back. Only forward. And don't pay any attention to anything that might confront you. Just charge on through. Do you understand?"

Dario licked his lips, then nodded. He formed up the group, young Renor in the center, and at Safar's signal he charged, moving at an amazing pace for one so old. The others had to strain to keep up.

Safar followed until he reached the meadow's edge. There he calmly halted and shed his pack. He unbuckled it, drawing out a half dozen small stoppered bottles. He waited, the howls growing louder and closer.

Then he saw them—gigantic wolf-like shapes bounding out of the rocks. There were four of them, twice the size of a man. They were a misty gray, like fog, but so lightly formed Safar could see through them.

Safar picked up one of the bottles, hefting it in his hand. It was filled with a silver liquid tinged with purple—wolf bane mixed with mercury. It was heavy for its small size. He tossed it from hand to hand like one of Methydia's circus juggling balls.

And he intoned:

> *"Wolf, wolf,*
> *Trickster,*
> *Shape changer—*
> *Bane*
> *Of our existence . . ."*

He hurled the bottle.

It sailed through the air, falling a good twenty feet before the charging spectral pack. Safar turned away, shielding his eyes, just as the bottle struck. Great sheets of purple flame exploded. He heard satisfying howls of pain and rage. He scooped up the other bottles and ran after Dario and the others.

For fifteen paces or so the only sound was the ringing in his ears from the explosion and the terrified yowls from the ghostly wolf pack. Then he heard the eerie, commanding cry of the Great Wolf ordering the pack to follow. It echoed through the small meadow, was pinched in by the frozen rock, and then blasted forward to sear his back.

The ghost wolves, however, recovered almost immediately and he hadn't taken more than five paces before he heard the sound of their running feet just behind him.

They were so close he didn't have time to stop and aim. He hurled a bottle over his shoulder as hard as he could, digging his toes into the ground with such force that he practically levitated as he flew down the trail, sliding where it curved toward a cliff edge and sending a shower of ice and frozen pebbles over the side. He fought for balance, hearing the debris tumble down a frightening distance and the sound of his howling pursuers drawing near. Then the bottle struck and the explosion was so forceful he almost went over the edge himself. He recovered at the last moment, boot heels skittering at the cliff's edge as he hurled himself to the side and back onto the path.

Again he heard the yowls of pain. Again he heard the Great Wolf howl for his spectral pack to follow. But from the sound of the baying pack there was a more comfortable distance than before.

Safar caught up to the others as they entered a canyon, shrouded on all sides by a thick, clinging fog.

He heard a growl then a grinding and he shouted, "Faster!" And everyone threw caution away and ran as fast as they could. But it wasn't quite fast enough to avoid the huge boulders that rumbled into their midst. Safar heard someone scream and turned just in time to see one of his fellow Kyranians fall beneath a huge rock. It crushed his legs, then bounced away down the mountainside.

Dario shouted a halt and as the men hastily lifted up their moaning, badly wounded friend, Safar swept about and hurled two more jars into the surrounding fog. He aimed blindly, but he heard shrieks of pain and knew he'd struck his mark.

Then they were running again—on and on, until all their strength was gone and they could run no more.

Safar and Dario directed the group to a clump of snow-covered boulders, where they sat their injured friend down and turned to meet the pursuing horror.

To their immense relief there was only fog and silence. After a moment or two Safar probed the mist with his senses. He found nothing.

The Great Wolf and his ghost pack were gone.

*   *   *

They crouched in their camp all that night and set off at first light. It was a cheery day, with only the Demon Moon hanging on the northern horizon to remind them that this was not the most delightful place in the world to be. Birds were singing, fawn were dancing in the forest and small animals darted underfoot.

No one was fooled.

They could hear heavy bodies moving through the underbrush behind them and knew they were being trailed. Even so, they reached Kyrania by late afternoon with no further incidents.

Everyone was too tired to do more than report the barest details of what happened. Still, those details were harrowing enough to rouse the village into mounting a guard at all the main entrances to the valley.

Safar collected Palimak from his parents' house. The boy ran into his arms, sobbing as if he had undergone an unpleasant ordeal. When Safar asked what was wrong he didn't speak, but only clutched him tighter. Palimak was silent on the short walk home. He ate little of his dinner and went to bed without complaint.

Late that night Safar was awakened from a dreamless sleep. His limbs were heavy, yet his mind sang with urgency. He forced his eyes open and saw Gundara crouched on his chest.

The little Favorite was frantic, clawing at his nightshirt. "Hurry, Master!" he cried. "The boy! The boy!"

Safar groaned out of bed, fighting rolling waves of lethargy. He grabbed his little silver dagger and staggered to Palimak's room.

He paused at the door, fighting the strange weariness. Gundara was perched on his shoulder, fangs chattering in fear.

Safar looked inside.

A tall man stood over the sleeping child. Flanking him were gigantic wolves, reared up on their hind legs.

When the man saw him he smiled and said, "Hello, Safar."

The wolves growled menacingly.

"Silence!" the man commanded. "Can't you see I'm speaking to my friend?"

It was Iraj Protarus. Back from the dead.

CHAPTER FIVE

THE RETURN OF IRAJ PROTARUS

She rode in from the north, keeping the Demon Moon at her back and staying well within its long shadows. Her horse's hooves were muffled, as were her weapons and armor. The night wind was up, moaning through trees and gullies so the only discernible sound was the occasional creak of her harness, or the faint rattle of pebbles when her horse misstepped.

Leiria drew up when she neared the bend where the first sentries should have been posted. She knew where they'd be because it was Leiria herself who had reformed Kyrania's methods of guarding the approaches. She'd not only drawn up the map but had trained the sentries. She'd also imposed an orderly system for challenges and knew what passwords the lead sentry would use when he demanded if she were friend or foe. The plan was that as the approaching party or parties considered the response, two other guardians of the trail would move in on opposite flanks. If she appeared threatening, they'd cut her down with their crossbows while she was still focusing on the lead sentry.

That was the plan—as foolproof as anyone could make it. She'd drilled her charges thoroughly, warning all the while that the fools she was attempting to guard them against were on their side.

"If the enemy presents himself," she'd told Rossthom, the man she'd schooled to take her place when she left, "it's safer to assume he isn't a dimwit. If he's to be worth anything at all as a potential enemy, he'll have scouted your defenses before the approach. He'll know very well who is the greatest dullard on your side. The one most likely to fall asleep. The one who favors a nip or three on the jug to keep off the chill. When you issue your challenge he'll pause to consider for an arse scratch or two, while his best men cut your laggard friend's throat. By the time you repeat the challenge his entire force will be on you."

Rossthom had heeded her well—and to a lesser degree, so had her other charges—so she was quite disappointed when no one challenged her when she came to the barricade. Her disappointment deepened when she found Rossthom's bloody remains sprawled next to the barricade. There were no marks on the muddy ground so she knew he'd died without a struggle. There were only his footprints and the depressions his body made as he flopped about while his attacker slit him from stem to stern.

Leiria dismounted and considered the situation. She thought it quite odd there was no sign of the enemy's approach. As carefully as she searched, there were no other marks on the ground. It was as if Rossthom had been attacked from above. She searched further and found the corpses of the other two sentries. Once again, there was no spoor left by the enemy.

She led her horse into a grove of trees overlooking Kyrania. In the light of the Demon Moon the fields and homes were quite clear. A few chimneys glowed, a few candles were guttering down in distant windows and far off she could hear a young rooster mistake the Demon Moon for dawn and crow an eerie welcome.

All in all, everything seemed quite peaceful. If it weren't for the dead sentries she might have thought her mad rush to Kyrania was not only a waste of time but a humiliating one at that.

Since she'd left Safar's side she had been making a decent if precarious living by selling her sword. Only a few weeks ago she'd been wriggling into the comfortable post as captain of a minor king's guard. The pay was good, the king's ambitions small and she had a comfortable room with a soft bed, easy access to the privy and a fireplace to warm her on a winter's night.

Then one night she'd had a dream. The dream had started well enough—she was in Safar's arms, snuggling up after making love and drifting off to sleep. This was a planned dreamed, a dream she'd conjured on many a night to carry her away from a difficult day.

On that particular night, however, the dream continued on. She found herself being pulled into another embrace. She went willingly, sleepily enjoying the caresses of her re-awakened companion. Then the arms holding her were suddenly somehow unfamiliar—but familiar—at the same time. It was not an embrace she welcomed. Leiria felt as if she had been drugged and had awakened in the arms of a monster.

In her dream, she opened her eyes and saw it was not Safar, but Iraj preparing to mount her. She shouted, catching him by surprise, then gripped his hair and flung him to the side. She came to her feet, grabbing a candleholder for a weapon. Iraj rolled away just in time as she hurled it at him and the heavy base thudded uselessly into the feather mattress.

Her sword was lying next to the bed where she always kept it and she snatched it up just as Iraj rose from the floor.

Except now it wasn't Iraj she was facing. Instead she was confronted by an enormous wolf! She slashed at it, but the bed between them was too wide and the wolf too agile.

Then it turned to her, red eyes boring in. The wolf opened its jaws to speak. She was too numb to be surprised when she heard Iraj's voice issuing from the wolf's mouth.

"Slut," it hissed. And, "Whore!" Then, "I gave you to Safar Timura. Now I want you back!"

Naked as she was, those words armored Leiria in the strongest mail. "I was given once," she said. "I won't be given again. Back, or otherwise."

And she hurled herself across the bed, slashing with all her might.

Then she was sitting up in bed, striking with her fists at nothing but innocent darkness.

Instead of confusion, however, Leiria had one thought fixed in her mind—Safar was in danger. She didn't question this thought, much less dwell on the nightmare. Her soldier's instinct said this was so and therefor she acted.

Two hours later she was riding for Kyrania. She didn't even bother to tell her employer, the king.

Now, looking down at the peaceful scene, she wondered for an instant if she'd gone mad. Love mad, that is. Had the dream been nothing but an excuse to be in Safar's presence once again? Admit it, Leiria, she said to herself, you still love him. But then she thought, No, I'm over that. If there's any love, it's because I love him as a sister loves a brother.

Then she had the skin-crawling awareness that there must be a spell on the trail to make her feel so confused about her mission. Behind her were dead sentries. Ahead of her was a seemingly peaceful village. Only a fool wouldn't realize that it didn't add up.

She moved closer to the hill's edge. Just below she could see Safar's home peeking out of the cherry grove that was Kyrania's unofficial boundary. There was a strange silvery glow streaming out of one of his windows. She frowned, remembering the layout. The light was coming from Palimak's room. At any other time she would have thought the child was up to some magical mischief.

But not this time. Not this night.

She loosened her weapons, took up her horse's reins and led it quietly down the trail.

*   *   *

Iraj turned back from his charges, sneering at Safar. "And what a *friend* you proved to be, Timura," he said. "To think I once swore a blood oath with you."

Then his eyes met Safar's and there was a long, frozen moment as the two enemies regarded each other from across the room. The only sound was the harsh breathing of the wolves and Gundara's frightened whimpers from his perch on Safar's shoulder.

Even through thick lenses of hatred, Safar could see that Iraj was as handsome as ever—muscular frame draped in black, white teeth glittering through his golden beard. A simple crown of black onyx encircled his flowing locks. But his eyes were fiery red—red as the Demon Moon. Red as the wine he'd shared with Safar when they'd pledged eternal friendship and brotherhood. Red as the blood that had stained Nerisa's snowy breast when Iraj slew her. And now Iraj had returned to threaten the life of the one he loved most. A sleeping child—half demon, half human—named Palimak.

Blood infused with shape-changer's hate, all senses heightened to the painful extreme—it was all Iraj could do to check his murderous rage. Safar's obvious good health and strength infuriated him. Safar should be diseased and mutilated, with barely strength to draw breath for what he'd done to Iraj. At the same time, Safar's strange blue eyes penetrated his heart and saw his shame and guilt, which made Iraj fear him—and hate him even more.

Safar exhaled and the moment came unstuck, slamming his emotional gate shut before those old wrongs could overwhelm him. Revenge was an unpredictable sword that cut in all directions. It was enough for Safar to recognize that Iraj was his enemy—an enemy so powerful he'd risen from the grave to confront him.

Quick—so quick Old Man Time Himself couldn't take its measure—Safar formed the killing spell and his little silver dagger rose to blast Iraj back into whatever hells he came from. The two wolves sensed the danger. As he formed the spell they growled and as the dagger rose they gathered to leap—long fangs dripping, claws anxious to rip out his heart.

They'd be fast, Safar thought, but not fast enough.

Iraj's mind, however, was racing ahead of the killing moment. He knew Safar, knew him well, and could see his enemy consider the murderous possibilities. Safar blinked, deciding, and Iraj immediately knew what he'd do next.

Iraj instantly visualized the action from Safar's point of view. Safar would attack Iraj first. Then the wolf on the right. Finally he'd whirl to confront the third creature. But it'd be too late and Safar would be ripped from throat to groin. However, in the killing the wolf would also die. Except Palimak would be safe and that's all that would matter to Safar.

Yes, Iraj thought. That's his greatest vulnerability. The child.

Safar had the spell set and had all but cast it when Iraj raised a cautioning hand. "Beware, Safar!" he said.

Instantly, he turned on his companions, shouting, "Hold!"

And they held, snarling and gnashing their fangs. Eyes sparking in terrible frustration.

Safar stayed his hand as well. The dagger point dropped, but he only had to raise it less than an inch to hurl his spell.

"Consider before you act, Safar," Iraj said. He gestured at Palimak, who stirred in his spellbound sleep, moaning as if suffering a bad dream, saying, "Anything you do against me is certain to harm the boy."

Gundara stirred uneasily on Safar's shoulder. "He speaks the truth, master," he whispered. "One wrong move and Palimak is doomed."

As low as he'd spoken, Iraj's hearing was so acute he overheard. He smiled, saying, "If you won't heed me, heed your Favorite. And I promise you the child will not only die, but will suffer greatly in the dying."

Safar let the dagger point dip lower. It wasn't a surrender, but it was an admission of momentary defeat.

Small as the gesture was, Iraj was thrilled by it. His overcharged shaper-changer's emotions frothed over and he couldn't help the wild laugh that exploded from his throat.

Safar winced. "You look better than you sound, Iraj," he said. He was surprised when he realized he hadn't meant to be sarcastic, or wounding. It was simply a natural comment between old friends. Or old enemies, as the case seemed to be.

"Never mind what I sound like," Iraj snarled. He knew very well the laugh seemed like that of a jackal and felt humiliated by showing that weakness. It spoiled his momentary thrill of victory.

Grinding to gain the upper hand again, he said, "You should be worrying about what I want instead of thinking up empty insults."

"Very well, then," Safar said, evening the game by making his voice and manner mild, "What *do* you want with us?"

Another jackal bark. This time purposeful. "Why, I only want your misery, my friend," Iraj replied. "Whatever injures you is my pleasure." He nodded, indicating the wolves. "Or should I say, *our* pleasure! When you tried to destroy me, they were also injured most severely."

He gestured at the wolf on his left. "You remember King Luka, I presume?" Then to his right. "And Lord Fari?"

Safar remembered them *very* well. Luka had been the crown prince of Zanzair before he'd conspired with Iraj to overthrow his father, King Manacia. Fari had been Manacia's chief wizard and Grand Wazier. In their original forms both were not men, but demons.

"Where's Kalasariz?" Safar asked, dry. He was speaking of the old human spy master who had been his nemesis for many years. "It's my fondest hope he's absent from this impromptu party because I killed him."

Iraj let his eyes widen in mock surprise. "Of course you killed him, my friend," he said. He motioned, his gesture taking in himself and the others. "You killed us *all!* However, as you can see we've risen from the dead. Including Kalasariz. He's busy elsewhere and sends his regrets and apologies that he had to miss this reunion."

"Call him forth, then," Safar said. "I promise you this time there will be no messy resurrection."

As he spoke he let the dagger tip rise. He felt the weapon turn warm in his hand. He didn't have to look to know the point was white hot as if it had just been lifted from a forge.

Iraj saw what he was up to and laughed.

*　　*　　*

Leiria was rocked to the core when she peered through the window and saw Iraj.

Braced as she was by the dream that had driven her to Kyrania, she wasn't prepared to see her old lover in the flesh.

In the first shock wave of recognition her practical side was hurled into a gully of confusion. Battered logic rose to demand that her senses were badly mistaken. You're dreaming again, this practical side argued. In fact the whole thing is a dream. You never quit your post, much less rushed off on an insane journey to rescue Safar.

Nothing else made sense. Iraj was dead, wasn't he? Hadn't she seen his palace explode into flames with her own eyes? As well as the city surrounding it? Safar's spell was so powerful that nothing or no one could have escaped it.

She rubbed her eyes but the vision remained. Iraj was still hovering over little Palimak, two giant wolves standing on their hind legs on either side. Safar was still motionless in the doorway, Gundara chattering with fear on his shoulder. She saw the little magic dagger glowing in Safar's hand. She noted the ridge of concentration on his brow and knew he was gathering his strength to strike.

Mind racing with a thousand possibilities for action, all suicidal, she bent closer to listen.

*　　*　　*

"Let me tell you what I learned about dying," Iraj said to Safar, very calm as if the burning dagger presented no threat. "To begin with, it isn't necessarily fatal." He laughed again, bitterly. "Now isn't that a good jest?" he said. "One that few could make. Unfortunately for you, I am one of those few. And I owe it all to them."

Another gesture at the wolves. "Thanks to them we were already exploring . . . how shall I say it . . . new forms of life? Or afterlife, if you will. And when you struck we were able to escape into one of those forms—Shape-changers!"

Iraj was crackling with inner fire. As he spoke he seemed to grow larger, shoulders broadening, chest deepening, head rising almost to the ceiling. It wasn't posturing, but a spell he was making with the help of Fari and Luka. He was using that spell to strike fear into Safar's heart, attempting to hammer his enemy into submission.

He smiled, his long teeth making him look like a wolf. "We can move in and out of this flesh at will. It's a bit painful, but after time you learn that pain gives strength as well as pleasure. There's more hope in pain than you might guess, Safar. You can see things, horizons and possibilities you never dreamed of before. As a boy my greatest dream was to be King of Kings. Well, I achieved that dream. But great as it was, once won, it was nothing. I felt hollow, Safar. Empty of all achievement, even though I'd matched my boyhood hero, the Conqueror Alisarrian."

Protarus saw the dagger in Safar's hand waver. The spell was working! He pressed harder, pushing against Safar's defenses with all his might. The dagger point dropped lower still and it was all Iraj could do to keep from smacking his lips in anticipation.

Instead he gestured at the wolves who were Luka and Fari. "My friends saw this. They understood even more than I—even more than you—what I truly sought." He leaned closer, his breath hot on Safar's face. "Now, I can be King of Kings of *both* worlds—magical as well as mortal. I suppose I should thank you for opening the way for

321

me. My ambitions, my dreams, have always been greater than the flesh that could hold them."

The spell was so strong that Safar—who was already stretched to the breaking by his twin effort to protect Palimak plus hold Iraj and the wolves at bay—was nearly overcome. Gundara sank sharp claws into his shoulder, hissing, "Master! Master!"

Safar rallied, beating back the spell. He said, "If you are so all powerful, Iraj, why don't you just do away with me now? Kill me. Kill the child. Blast Kyrania to dust with your most powerful spell. What's stopping you?"

Iraj forced laughter. He was shocked at Safar's swift recovery. This wasn't how it was supposed to work! On his right Fari growled, urging him to keep on.

"Think about it," Iraj said, swiftly trying to repair the spell. "The only thing that held me back from true greatness before was my lack of magical abilities. You were the one whose powers were so awesome even demons feared you."

"That's hardly my fault," Safar said, mentally brushing aside the spellweb. Looking for his chance. "I was born with those talents. And you weren't. What more can I say?"

"Still," Iraj said, "you could have given me those powers. They could have been a gift to your oath brother and king." He gestured at Luka and Fari, who growled at his motions. "They were certainly willing to give me such a gift. Why wouldn't you?"

"You won't believe this," Safar answered, "but even if I'd wanted to, I didn't know how. Not safely, anyway. With these two—plus Kalasariz—you formed the Spell of Four. Very powerful. But also a two-edged sword. It is dangerous not only to others, but to yourself. You don't realize it now—perhaps you never will—but the pact you made was your downfall. I did nothing to you. Not really. True, I made a spell of destruction. But it depended upon your own nature for it to work."

"You're right," Iraj said. "I don't believe it."

Safar shrugged. "I didn't think you would."

"As for destroying my kingdom," Iraj said, "it was only temporary. Even as we speak my armies are putting it back together again."

Safar ignored this. "You still didn't answer my first question," he insisted. "Why all this talk? It's really quite unlike you, Iraj. Why not just kill us now?"

"The answer is simple, Safar," Iraj said. "I'm here to collect your powers." He nodded at Palimak. "And the boy's."

Now, Safar thought. Now! And he let himself sag a little, as if in spell-induced shock.

Iraj's temples hammered with sudden elation. He gestured at the sleeping child, grinding in his perceived advantage.

"My friends and I are perfectly willing to drain those powers from your dying bodies. And put them to better use." He shrugged. "The result would be rather weak, but it'll do, it'll do. Alive would be better, of course. And with your full cooperation it'd be better still."

"You'd still kill us," Safar said. "Eventually."

Iraj barked humor. "Oh, I promise you that, old friend. As I said, I owe you much. But if you surrender now, I'll let the boy live."

"That's no bargain," Safar said, pretending unconcern. "I'd still be dead."

Iraj frowned, as if deeply concerned at an impasse that did not exist. "But I require the boy alive. He's the key ingredient to what I need to secure my new throne." As he spoke, he and his Brothers of the Spell poured all their powers into their assault on Safar's will.

"I know the child's just a foundling," Iraj continued. "So you probably don't have any deep feelings for him. You won't suffer greatly when I tell you we intend to make the boy's life as miserable as possible. And believe me, there's nothing about misery I don't know, Safar Timura."

Safar let a soft moan escape. Iraj grinned, excitement so great that he lost control of his human shape and a wolf snout suddenly erupted from his face.

"What luck!" he growled. "You *do* love the boy, you poor sad fool." He sniffed the air, licking his chops. "Marvelous," he growled. "I can already taste your pain."

Iraj sniffed again, liked what he found even more, and drew in a long breath, shuddering from the infusion of fear and servile misery Safar was pumping into the atmosphere.

I am small and weak, Safar thought, and you are large and strong. Mercy, Lord, mercy. If I must die make it swift. Mercy, Lord, mercy. And spare the child. I beg you, spare the child. Mercy, Lord, mercy.

Iraj gloried in the rich scent of Safar's humiliation. Grinned at the sour sweat running off of him in streams. It made a quite a heady concoction.

When he relaxed his guard Safar struck.

It wasn't his strongest spell. In fact, it was rather weak. But it was the best he could do without killing Palimak in the backblast.

A fiery arc leaped from his dagger point to Iraj's crown. There was a flash of light and a howl of pain as Iraj was hurled back by the force of Safar's attack, slamming against the far wall.

Hoping against all the odds Safar turned to his left, aiming a second blast at the demon wolf who was Lord Fari.

"To Palimak!" he shouted to Gundara.

The little Favorite leaped from his shoulder onto the bed.

Fari was almost on him when Safar let loose the next sorcerous blast. But it was weak, too weak and the demon wolf shrugged it off and kept coming. From the corner of his eye he could see Luka leaping for him. Just beyond Iraj was rising up, shaking off the affects of Safar's attack.

Then he felt a heatshudder as Gundara threw a protective shield over the spellbound Palimak.

He reached deep for his strongest spell but even as he formed it he knew he was too late.

All was lost but he kept going, praying his enemy would make the smallest mistake or misstep.

It was a foolish prayer because there were claws scything toward him and the euphoria of certain death leaked into his brain, numbing him for the shock.

Then there was a thunder of hooves bearing a chill war cry and the house shook as an enormous weight struck the wall.

Safar's three attackers stumbled about in surprise as the whole wall crashed inward—showering them with debris—and they hurled themselves to the side just as a mailed warrior on horseback smashed into the small room. And then everything was a confusion of flying hooves and slashing sword and shrill battle cries.

Iraj and his demon/wolves were flung apart. They roared in pain and fury as horse and rider whirled about, barreling into them.

Safar leaped back through the doorway as the horse swerved toward him. He glanced over at Palimak's bed and saw the boy was still asleep; Gundara crouched over him, his shielding spell keeping bed and boy miraculously untouched by the chaos.

Safar turned back to the melee. He had his killing spell ready but there was no clear target. A slight miss and his rescuer would die as well.

Then the equation became simpler as the two demon/wolves were driven through the shattered wall and horse and rider plunged after them. And then there was only Safar and Iraj, who was coming up from a pile of debris. As Iraj rose a powerful light radiated from his body. He began to transform into a giant wolf, black as a starless night with the fires of the hells in its eyes.

The wolf turned its huge head toward Safar, maw coming open. Their eyes met . . . and held for what seemed like an eternity. It was only a moment but it was time enough for an arc of recognition to leap between them. It was like two souls brushing together—souls from another place and another time when they were just boys, fast friends, with only clear horizons before them.

Then hate rushed back and Safar let loose his spell.

He meant to kill and held nothing back but when his sorcerous bolt struck there was a white hot flare, a loud crack of overheated air, and when his eyes cleared the demon wolf who was Iraj had vanished.

Cursing, Safar sagged back against the shattered door frame. Iraj had escaped unscathed. And he was certain to return—in one form or another—with even greater forces than before.

Safar looked over at Palimak and knew a small bit of joy when he saw the boy was still sleeping peacefully as if nothing had happened. There was debris all around the bed and spatters of blood on the lower frame.

Gundara stood over the boy, chest puffed up under his elegant little doublet, standing as tall as he could, a sharp-toothed grin gleaming in his little demon's face.

"Never fear, Master," he said, bold as can be. "Gundara is here."

Safar sighed and nodded his thanks.

He heard the clatter of hooves and the creak of harness and looked up to see the mounted warrior canter up to the gaping hole that had once been a little boy's bedroom wall.

The warrior reached up with a mailed glove and swept the helm away.

Safar was too numb for surprise and he barely reacted when he saw Leiria grinning down at him.

"Are they gone?" he croaked, exhaustion overcoming him.

"Vanished, is more like it," Leiria said, still burning with the odd joy battle fever can cause. "Good thing, too. They were coming at me from both sides and I thought I was in for a helluva fight. Then, *poof!* they disappeared."

At that moment Palimak sat bolt up in bed. He rubbed sleepy eyes and looked all around him, noting the destruction of his room.

He looked up at Safar, still a little dazed, a worried frown creasing his brow.

"I didn't do it, father," he said. "Honest, I didn't."

CHAPTER SIX

THE COUNCIL OF ELDERS

The funeral ceremony for Iraj's victims was depressingly easy to arrange. The village was still draped in black from mourning Tio. The wailing women's cheeks were well oiled for tears. This time, however, there were no swaggering louts shouting vows of revenge.

If Tio's death had shocked the villagers, the toll they now faced was beyond shrieks and tears and shouts. Besides the three murdered sentries Leiria had found, there were six others who had been surprised and killed by Iraj and his companions.

When the dawn came and the bodies were discovered there had been so much blood they couldn't keep the children from seeing it. After Safar pronounced the funeral prayer and the boats were fired and launched, many of the young people became hysterical with grief. They clutched each other and wept, shouting the names of their dead friends. It was a scene that would haunt many a dream for years to come.

As soon as he could Safar retreated into the little temple. But there was no peace to be found in the dusty silence of his inner chambers. Solitude makes misery larger, not smaller, Safar thought. And when you are truly alone there's no one to curse but yourself. He was exhausted from his encounter with Iraj, so tired his limbs were ungainly weights and the air itself seemed formed of the thickest clay, resisting his every motion. It was as if he had been stripped of all spirit and will, leaving him so weak that if Iraj had suddenly appeared Safar would have surrendered gladly.

It made him ill prepared when his father entered the chamber, shamefaced and shuffling.

"You are my son," he said, avoiding Safar's eyes. "But it is my duty to speak to you not as a father, but as a member of the Council of Elders. Forgive me, Safar, for what I am about to say. It's their words, not mine, that I must speak. And you should know it is only out of courtesy that the Council is allowing me to carry them to you so the insult might be lessened."

Safar nodded. "That was good of them," he said. If there was sarcasm in his manner, it was unintended.

His father stiffened. "Safar Timura, son of Khadji and Myrna Timura, it is the wish of the Council of Elders that you report immediately to the Meeting Lodge. There you will wait while the Council considers the recent tragic events and the part you played in them. You have the right to address the Council before their final decision is made. However, you may not be present while that decision is being discussed. Do you understand?"

"I understand," Safar said.

Khadji's formal pose collapsed into that of a worried and awkward father.

"You know I'll speak up for you at the meeting, son," he said.

"Of course you will," Safar said, feeling like a child pretending to be an adult so he could reassure his parent.

Khadji added to the awkward moment by suddenly leaning forward as if to embrace him, then pulling back at the last instant, embarrassed.

"Your mother and sisters send their love," he said. Then, lower, "To which I add mine."

"Thank you father," Safar said, realizing the reply was weak, but under the circumstances it was the safest one he could manage.

He saved his father and himself further embarrassment by becoming occupied with a misplaced sash. While his eyes were lowered he heard his father let loose a long sigh of frustration.

It was a sigh best ignored, so Safar drew himself up, squaring his shoulders. "Tell the Council," he said, quite formal, "that I will be honored to attend them. And will abide by whatever wise action they deem necessary."

Khadji's eyes welled with tears. He stepped back, fighting for control. Unlike Safar, he was not a self-assessing man, so he didn't understand the difficulty he had with his son. A man of strong beliefs, rights and wrongs, blacks and whites, he assumed it was some glaring fault in the clay he was made of and berated himself for his failings. Safar had inherited many of his father's flaws. On sleepless nights, when good deeds are cracked in guilt's jaws to find the sinful center, he'd added greatly to that score. Still, he was a wizard with an instinct for striking for the truth and sometimes he was even lucky enough to find it. So where his father turned away, Safar looked deeper. Over time he'd come to understand that Khadji suffered from the ancient curse of all master potters. Under a potter's hands clay is a spirit demanding form and life. It also wants to be useful. It requires a purpose. What's more it insists that purpose and beauty be combined. To achieve this unity—which all potters desire above all else—perspective must be maintained at any cost. A potter loves the clay as deeply as any being can love. Yet he can never declare it. He must not let the barest hint of it come through. Above all things a master potter must keep his distance or he will lose his vision, hence control. Or else what he loves will become an ugly thing that bursts in the kiln at the first firing.

Unfortunately, Safar thought, understanding has less value than a beggar's bowl when it stands alone, leaving him with nothing to offer when he looked across the chasm between himself and his father.

So he said, "How is little Palimak?"

His father laughed, more in relief than anything else.

"He thinks it was all a great adventure," he said. "He's even forgotten he was asleep the whole time." Khadji shook his head in grandfatherly amusement. "When I saw him last he was sitting in your mother's lap trying to make up a poem about the great boy hero, Palimak Timura, who drove away a hungry pack of wolves."

His father laughed again and Safar laughed with him. Then before the humor could lapse into an uncomfortable silence he used the skills he'd learned as a man of the royal court to send his father away feeling as comfortable as he could under the circumstances.

It didn't make Safar feel any better. However he looked at it, the Grand Wazier and Chief Wizard of all of Esmir had just dismissed—however politely—his own father from his presence.

*   *   *

Safar stood outside the meeting lodge while the Elders debated his fate. The village was silent, doors barred, windows shuttered. Even the dogs had been taken in and the only sound—other than the buzz of discussion going on inside the lodge—was the harsh sawpit song of a young cicada in lust.

At first he paced, then he realized the whole village watched through those closed shutters, and he stood as still as he could, trying his best to strike a noble pose. It made him feel clownish, like a young acolyte waiting to be punished for some bit of mischief. So he fussed with that pose, shifting from noble to manly unconcern and all the other contortions people go through when they know they're being watched but must pretend otherwise. In his days as a circus magician, Methydia, who had turned witchery into a crowd pleasing art, said the greatest trick when squaring off before an audience was to find something natural to do with your hands. It was a lesson he'd thought he'd learned, but as he waited for the elders' decision his schooling hid giggling in a corner while he shuffled his hands this way and that, feeling foolish, but not knowing what to do about it.

Leiria came hurrying down the lane, clutching a large jug in one arm. When she saw him she grinned and hoisted the jug onto her head. She walked toward him, exaggerating the swing of her hips so even in a soldier's costume of metal and leather she looked like a fetching village lass coming up from the well who'd rather tarry with the lads than go home to her mother. When she reached him she maintained the pose, swinging the jug down and coming up on her toes to offer it to him.

"I hope everybody is watching," she whispered.

"Wish granted, madam," Safar said. "No magic required."

He drank the cold well water as if it were the finest wine, surprised at how thirsty he was. When he lowered the jug Leiria stepped away, relaxing into her normal flat footed stance—right hand resting on the hilt of her sheathed sword.

"They could never figure out if I was a soldier or a slut," she said. "If anyone ever had the nerve to ask, I might have been more tempted to stay here."

"How would you have answered?"

"Simple. I'd have said, 'If truth be known, sir,' assuming it was a sir who asked, 'If truth be known, sir, I was once captain of the Imperial guard. But I was also once the king's whore. So I can claim both titles, sir. I stand before you, soldier and slut together. Lips and sword, sir. Lips and sword.'"

Safar laughed. "That speech sounds like it's had a bit of practice."

"I used it on my last master," Leiria said. "But I told him only one was for hire. I could tell he'd be trouble if I didn't put him straight at the beginning, so I made him guess which was which. Lips or sword? He could see right off the penalty'd be severe if he guessed wrong, so he took the safe road and hired my sword. And that was that!"

A loud voice from the meeting lodge interrupted them. They turned to listen in, but although they could tell it was Safar's father speaking, they couldn't make out the words. Then the voice stopped and the buzz continued.

Leiria was disgusted. "This is stupid."

"I'm not that sure it is," Safar replied. He was so tired almost anything seemed to make sense. "I told them exactly what'd happened. Iraj came here looking for me. And for Palimak. From their point of view the boy and I are responsible for the deaths of many fellow Kyranians."

"So what are they going to do about it?" Leiria asked. "Exile the two of you? Cast you out? As if that's going to solve anything."

"Maybe it will," Safar said wearily. "If we leave, maybe Iraj will let them be."

Leiria sneered. "That's ridiculous!" she said. "Iraj would never be satisfied so easily. He'd want to lay waste to the village as well." She snorted. "Typical leadership! Doesn't matter if you're talking about the leaders of the grandest city or smallest hamlet. They're all the same. I came to the conclusion long ago that to be a leader you must first drink the Wine of Stupidity. Followed by a hefty slug of the Brandy of Forgetfulness. And then a nice tot of Trivial Answers To Questions No One Asked for a nightcap."

She jabbed a finger at the lodge. "They know Iraj. He lived here when he was a boy. They sheltered him when he needed them most. It was Kyrania who brought Iraj here, not Safar Timura. You were only a boy, what did you have to say about it?" Another finger jab at the lodge. "I'd wager anything that your precious Council of Elders held a vote on whether Iraj was to be invited. Any trouble they have with him now comes from that decision.

"So who is to blame? The former members of the Council of Elders? Or Safar Timura, a young lad in a village so small you and Iraj were bound to meet?"

Safar made a wry grin. "You have a way of putting things in such simple terms," he said.

Leiria smacked her sword hilt. "Not so simple that they aren't true," she said. "Any ordinary person could see it. Those silly old men are in there trying to decide who to blame. Which will end up being you and Palimak. No doubt about that! Meanwhile, they're ignoring the real problem. Which is that Iraj *will* return—and in full force.

"Hells, the only reason they're meeting for so long is that they're faced with harming one of their own. Palimak will be easy for them. Half demon, half human. Bad luck all around and who else could be to blame? What they'll probably do is ignore you entirely and banish Palimak."

"But anyone who knows me would understand what that'd mean," Safar said, bewildered. "Which is that I'd have to leave as well. Adopted or not, half-breed or quarter breed, I'm responsible for the child."

Leiria rose up on her toes and gave him a quick kiss. "Of course you feel that way," she said. "That's why I fell in love with you. I didn't need the presence of Palimak to know that's how you would act if some sort of thing like that ever occurred. That's why I came back.

"Unless you missed it, Safar Timura, I have returned! Which in my mind—being the only mind I possess—is a damned remarkable thing and you are one hells of a lucky fellow!"

She raised her head and looked Safar straight in the eyes, catching them and holding them so there would be no misunderstanding. "But it's not for love," she said. "At least not *that* kind of love. I'm not only over that, but I've gone on."

Safar nodded. He had an odd feeling of sudden relief . . . and regret. "No need to be upset," he said, rather lamely. "I'm not expecting anything, or asking anything of you."

Leiria slapped her sword, angry. "Dammit, Safar Timura, that's not what I mean at all! I'm your friend. Ask me anything. That's what I want . . . maybe all that I ever really wanted. But ask me, dammit! Ask! Or go to the hells along with the whole damned world you're worried about!"

Safar didn't know what to say. He tried to make a weak joke out of the situation. "You never give me a chance to thank you," he said. "You keep saving my life before I can even shout for help."

Leiria nodded toward the lodge. The meeting had ended and his father was standing in the doorway beckoning him. "They're ready for you," she said. "The question is, are *you* ready for *them?*"

Safar's mind suddenly cleared. Resolve returned. Which had been Leiria's intent from the beginning.

"I'm ready," he said. "Now I know what to do."

✳   ✳   ✳

Safar didn't wait for the Elders to settle into various poses of wisdom. He struck first. "I know you've already made your decision," he said, "but I *also* understand I have the right to speak before the ruling is announced."

A swift glance around the silent room showed him he was right. Except for his father, they all avoided his eyes. "All of us are not in agreement," his father said hotly, glaring at the other Elders. "So yes, son, a speech in your own defense would be most appreciated."

"But a vote *has* been taken, has it not?" Safar asked.

"Yes it has, Lord Timura," said Foron, the chief elder. The look on his face was that of someone who had tasted something unpleasant, but was required by circumstance to take another bite. "A vote *has* been taken. Your father was in the minority."

"Then I have absolutely no intention of defending myself," Safar said.

"Please, son," his father protested.

Safar raised a hand, begging his silence. "But I *do* insist on my right to speak."

"This is most unusual," Masura grumbled. "Not in the rules at all."

There were loud exclamations of agreement and disagreement. The Elders' debate still had them stirred up. Foron thumped the ceremonial pot in front of him. It made a booming sound like a large drum. Everyone obediently stopped. Safar noted with minor interest the speaker's pot had been made by a Timura long ago.

"Seems simple enough to me," Foron said. "In Kyrania all citizens can say what they want, when they want. Lord Timura is a citizen of Kyrania. Let him talk."

Masura tried to protest. "But this is a formal meeting of—"

"Oh, be silent!" Foron said. "We're not judges in some king's royal court. This is a village, not a city. Everyone knows Safar. Hells, most of us are even third and fourth cousins to him. Let him talk."

There was instant silence. Even those opposed to Safar were chastened. Masura opened his mouth to protest, caught the heavy scent of disapproval, and stopped.

Safar said, "No matter what your decision—be it in my favor, or not—I will leave Kyrania tomorrow!"

Khadji cursed and there were sounds of shock all around, even from the majority who had called for Safar's banishment. How could a Kyranian willingly leave his home? This was the blessed land. The Valley of the Clouds where Kyranians had lived for as many generations as there were stars in the sky. Where the Goddess Felakia reigned, rewarding them with her bounty because they were her chosen people. The people of the High Caravans.

Safar raised a hand for silence. "My decision," he said, "has nothing to do with these proceedings. Or any of the tragic events that have occurred. In fact, when we last met I was going to announce my departure. But it didn't seem the right time, what with all the panic over Tio. I was, however, going to ask permission to leave Palimak with you." He nodded at his father. "Under my parent's care, of course. The journey I have in mind is rather dangerous for a child."

The journey he was referring to was his half-formed, and therefore unspoken, plans to somehow make his way to Syrapis and investigate the vision in the demon wizard's tomb.

Masura snickered. "You must think we're fools," he said. "First, to believe that you'd already intended to leave us. Secondly, that we'd harbor that devil's—"

"Be careful, Masura!" the headmaster broke in, eyeing Khadji, who was about to come across the room after Masura to make him eat the insult. "This is no time for loose talk!" Foron turned to Safar. "Most of us like the lad, Lord Timura," he said. "At the time we would've granted your wishes." He shrugged, "But things have changed since then."

"What cowardly words!" Khadji broke in. "Say it plain, Foron. You voted with the majority—which consists of everyone but me!" He turned to Safar. "These cunning devils voted to exile Palimak," he said. "But not you. They figured if they banished him, you'd have no choice except to go with him."

Safar buried a smile. How right Leiria had been. Only now did he fully appreciated her subtle efforts to arm him against the elders, and to shoulder duty's burden and march on. A duty Safar was just beginning to make out. Dim as the outlines were, the undertaking would be enormous. If not impossible.

He had to go carefully, or he would stumbled at the first step. "Never mind them, father," he said. "It doesn't matter anymore. Because when I leave I'm taking Palimak with me."

There were murmurs of relief among the Elders. The issue was being settled for them. Possibly they could even forgo the announcement of the ban, which would be been controversial in the extreme. The Timura clan was as popular as it was influential.

It was the perfect time for Safar to play the next piece in a game whose rules he was making up as he went along. "I have only one request to make of the Council," he said.

Foron smiled broadly. With the pressure off he was eager to please. "Ask anything you like, Lord Timura," he said. "How can we help your journey? Is it supplies you need? Animals to carry them? Tell us exactly what you want from us and it will be provided."

"I want you to come with me," Safar answered, flat.

There was stunned amazement, which shattered as everyone shouted at once, some saying Safar must be insane, others that maybe he'd been misunderstood and should be given the chance to explain. Safar waited the small tempest out, noting the majority against him was hardly solid. Even though in effect they'd voted to banish him, Masura's trick of putting the vote against Palimak had only gone so far. Lord Timura had spoken. Mysterious as his intentions might be, they were used to listening to him with enormous respect.

At the proper moment Safar raised a hand and got silence. "Here's how I see it," he said. "I'm sure most of you think if Palimak and I leave, Iraj will ignore Kyrania and follow us."

Most of the men nodded agreement; that was the general feeling. "I mean no disrespect," Safar said, "but if you all think that, then you'd better spend a bit more time examining your logic. Because there is no way under the Demon Moon that haunts us all that Iraj will be satisfied with just my blood and Palimak's."

The Elders stirred as this truth sank in. "You all know as well as I," Safar continued, "that anyone who helped Iraj at any time will suffer for it. This is his nature. Kyrania once sheltered him from powerful enemies. Believe me, he'll destroy Kyrania for knowing he was once so weak that he needed our help."

"But he was just a boy," Foron wailed, the wail giving away the fact that Safar's logic had already smashed his own. "There's nothing for him to be ashamed of. We never harmed him."

"Neither did Tio," Khadji growled, "and look what happened to him!"

Cold dread filled the room and the men shivered at the memory of Tio's ravaged corpse.

Safar said, "There only one course. And that's to flee!"

"But where should we flee to, my son?" Safar's father asked, anguished.

Safar bowed his head. "There is a place I know," he said. "A place where we may all be safe. For awhile, at least."

Masura snorted again. "Bah! Why are we wasting our time with this? Read the child Palimak off the village rolls! Banish him! None of you but I had the nerve to make it Safar Timura we're tossing out. But we all agree it'll have the same purpose. Boot out the boy and Safar will follow. Then life can get back to being normal. No more damn demons stalking our hills, no more wolves killing our children, no more anything but sow our crops, tend our goats and face each season with as much cheer as the gods will allow. This is how we've always done things. I see no reason to change. And I sure as hells am not going to listen to foolish talk about leaving the place of my fathers."

A long silence followed this outburst. However, as embarrassed as everyone was by Masura's rude behavior, Safar could sense that most of the men agreed.

Before anyone could speak there came a familiar sound—caravan bells! Everyone stirred. Could this be? It had been ages since a caravan had visited Kyrania.

A boy burst through the door, shouting, "Caravan! Caravan!"

CHAPTER SEVEN
THE CARAVAN MASTER

The Elders rushed outside, Safar at their heels. Doors and shutters banged open as the excited villagers rushed from their homes, blinking at the wondrous animal train rattling into the main square.

It wasn't a large caravan—there were only a few camels and llamas and perhaps six ox-drawn wagons—but it was a magnificent thing to see on such a sorry day with all the banners flying, bells jangling and animals bawling. Everyone knew it would bring news from the outside world. People laughed and shouted, thinking the news must be good, else how had the caravan made it through?

Leading the cavalcade was a huge bearded horseman who rose up in his stirrups to bellow: "Greetings, O gentle people of Kyrania. It is I—Coralean of Caspan—who once again begs your hospitality!"

The Kyranians became even more excited, repeating the name to their neighbors as if they hadn't heard for themselves. An immense smile split Coralean's big face. He was an amazing sight; armored vest buckled about his rich merchant's robes, an immense sword dangling from his waist, his beard all bedecked with colorful ribbons.

"Coralean's heart is bursting with joy," he boomed, "that his old friends remember him with such kindness. He comes to you out of a wilderness of great trouble and sorrow. There was many a night when he didn't believe he'd live 'til dawn. And there was many a dawn when he doubted the blessed night would come again."

He thumped his mailed chest and it resounded like a ceremonial drum. "But here he is! Coralean, in the flesh! And damned be the eyes of all the devils who tried to strip it from me for their supper."

"What news?" someone shouted. Others took up the cry. "What news? What news?"

Coralean waved the questioners down. "Later, my dear people, I will tell the stirring tale of what has befallen this old dog since last we met." He shaded his eyes, searching the crowd. "But first Coralean must speak urgently with his old friend, Safar Timura. Will someone send for him, please?"

Safar stepped forward, the crowd parting to let him through. "Here I am, Lord Coralean," he said. "It's good to see you after so many years."

Safar was smiling, but he was not as overjoyed as the others. He liked Coralean, owed him much for past favors, but he knew the old merchant too well to trust him completely.

When Coralean spotted Safar he leaped off his horse and engulfed him in a mighty embrace, booming, "Safar, my old friend! How glad I am to see you!"

He pounded Safar's back, raising dust and a cough. Then he leaned forward and whispered, "You must call the Council of Elders together immediately!"

"I bring word from Iraj Protarus!"

*　　　*　　　*

Once again the Elders gathered in the Meeting Lodge. This time it was to learn what the future had in store for *them*.

"Coralean would rather the gods had ripped his tongue from its roots," the caravan master said, "than be forced to speak the words I must say to such dear friends. I am here at the orders of King Protarus, who waits with an army not two days hence. The King sends his heartfelt greetings to all his dear friends in Kyrania and begs forgiveness for the misery caused by his struggles with the traitor, Safar Timura."

"Here now, I'll not have my son spoken of like that!" Khadji protested.

Safar patted his arm, silencing him. "Coralean means nothing by it, father," he said. "Those are Iraj's words, not his." He smiled at the old merchant. "Go on, my friend."

Coralean placed a meaty hand of sincerity across his chest. "I have sons and daughters of my own, so I understand full well that my words are wounding. As everyone knows, Coralean has the softest heart of any man in Esmir. Am I not easily moved to tears by a sad tale? Do I not shower charity on every beggar from Caspan to old Walaria? Why, the list of Coralean's generous deeds for the less fortunate could fill volumes, I tell you. Volumes!"

He looked fiercely about the room as if expecting argument. None came. "Nevertheless," he said. "I would be shunning my duty to you if I softened King Protarus' words, injurious though they may be to my old friend, Khadji Timura.

"The King commanded me to say he has no ill feelings toward the people of Kyrania. In truth, he says he has great love for them and fondly recalls the days when he was a lad and lived among you. He said he means no one here any harm. And he only asks that you lay down your arms and pledge your fealty to him. If you do this, he will reward you all greatly when he visits you with his army. And he will give much gold to the families of the young people who died in Kyrania's service to help compensate them for their great loss."

"What of Safar?" Khadji demanded. "And Palimak? I assume we're supposed to hand them over to Iraj as part of this . . . this . . . whole extortion!"

Coralean looked him full in eyes, then nodded. "As you say, my friend. As you say."

There was a touch of bitterness in Safar's laugh. "You've arrived with your message at exactly the right time," he said. "It seems that my fellow Kyranians have decided to exile me. And the boy, too."

Coralean stroked his beard, examining the faces of the other men. "That explains it," he finally said.

"Explains what?" Khadji asked.

"Why no one but yourself protested when I maligned your son," he replied.

Masura broke in. "Excuse me, Lord Coralean, but do you believe King Protarus speaks the truth? Will he spare Kyrania if we do as he demands?"

More beard stroking from Coralean. Then he nodded, "That's certainly what the King promises."

"But did he speak the truth?" Masura prodded again. "Come, my lord, you must have an opinion."

"Why, I have many opinions, my friend," the wily old caravan master said. "Sometimes my opinion is this. Sometimes it is that. All strongly held views, mind you. Coralean bows to no man when it comes to firm opinions."

Masura was exasperated. "And what is your opinion right now, please?"

Coralean grinned. "That you should seek an opinion other than mine, my good fellow. Better yet, form your own. This is the wisest advice I can give you."

He looked over at Safar. "I'm returning to Caspan when I leave here," he said. "You'll understand if I don't ask you to accompany me." He laid a hand on his breast. "Our King would not be amused."

"You're assuming that I intend to flee," Safar said, "rather than sacrifice myself to Protarus."

"Coralean admires bravery," the caravan master said. "He admires it above all things, save one," he tapped his head, "and that's a canny nature. It's a useful tool for cowards and heroes alike."

"What of Iraj?" Safar asked. "How did he seem to you?"

Coralean shrugged. "I can tell you very little," he said. "I'm not permitted to actually see him. They blindfold me and lead me into his chambers. There he addresses me. Asking for the news or commanding me to perform some errand. In return, I am given free passage through the lands he controls. What's left of his kingdom, after . . . uh . . ." he glanced at Safar, "you and he had your disagreement."

He shook his head. "If only someone had consulted Coralean. I could have negotiated a settlement that might have avoided this whole catastrophe."

"It wasn't a business dispute, my friend," Safar said.

"Nonsense," Coralean replied. "Everything is business. The world would be a much better place if only everyone realized it."

"He wanted too much," Safar said, surprised at the heat in his voice.

Coralean shrugged. "It was just a matter of price," he said. "And neither of you could see it because you had no one like Coralean to advise you." He sighed. "But what can be done about it now? We must all go on as best we can."

There was a time when Safar would have been angry at Coralean's remarks; reducing betrayal and murder to a simple business dispute and from there to cross price. He would have shouted, he would have railed. He would condemned Coralean as a hypocrite with a miser's cold lump of gold for a heart. But it was only a small moment, so small that it wasn't worth considering. He'd been a firebrand student of magic in Walaria—flirting with honey-candied idealisms like purity and truth. Then Asper had taught him there was a lie behind every truth and a truth behind every lie.

And so he said to Coralean, "You speak wisely, old friend. In the end good business is satisfaction for both sides, with the spice of promised profits on a greater scale in the future."

Coralean tapped his head. "It is a great thing to know," he said. "But unfortunately it is not always something that is acted upon." Another big grin split his face. "This is why Coralean, who is a poor man with many wives and children to feed, is not so poor as some of his competitors."

"I'm glad we understand one another," Safar said. He made a motion taking in the assembled Elders—his father included—their faces clouded with bewilderment. "All of us understand!" Which made the looks become even more bewildered.

"This is good," Coralean said. "Understanding is a virtue I praise above all others."

He plucked a long, fat leather-bound tube from his belt. It had hinged stoppers of brass on either side. He casually flipped it from end to end, then handed it to Safar.

"Here," he said, "a gift from Coralean to seal his side of the bargain."

Safar eyed him, but the old pirate's face was blank. He unsnapped one end of the tube, peered inside, then unscrewed a thick sheaf of parchment papers. He fanned them out, the other men bending close to look.

"Why they're maps," Foron said. "What do we need with maps?"

Coralean shrugged. "Worthless things," he said, "if you plan to stay in one place. But if you intend to travel, why I expect you might find them of some value."

"These are caravan maps," Safar said. "Worth a fortune to any trader."

"You will note," Coralean said, bending forward and poking at one of the maps, "the detail of these maps. They show all of Esmir, including the most secret trading routes favored by peace-loving merchantmen like myself. Why bother with bandits and greedy local overlords if you can skip them out by choosing another path? And if one were being followed by a fierce competitor, why you could quickly shake him off by using an unexpected route."

Safar quickly scanned the maps, which showed in detail the whole northern region—from the Gods Divide to the port of Caspan where ships might be for hire to get him to Syrapis. He also marked the cities Asper had said he must visit on the way—Naadan and Caluz. It would be an extremely difficult undertaking, only made possible by the many hiding places along the route which were detailed on the maps.

He rolled the maps up and slipped them back into the tube. "What do you desire in return?" he asked.

Coralean slapped his knee and roared laughter. "Why isn't obvious, my good friend? I want your favor. If someday I stand before you a ruined man, I'll expect your help."

Safar made a thin smile. "In case things don't work out for Iraj, you mean?"

Coralean shrugged a mighty shrug. "Who can say what the morrow will bring, brother? At the moment, Iraj Protarus seems to have the upper hand. He's regained a good portion of his kingdom and nothing seems to stand in the way of his winning all of it back. Few kings dare defy him and those that do are guaranteed a horrid end.

"Also, his magic, I'm told, is most powerful. I've even heard rumors that he is a shape changer. Wolf and man in the same body. This could be true, it could be false. However you look at it, rumors are bad for business. And if he *is* a shape changer, why, how does an honest businessman know if he'll abide by his word? Did I make a contract with a man, or a wolf? Or something in between?"

Coralean sighed. "And so I come to my dearest friend, Safar Timura, for whom I have done many favors in the past. True, he is a wizard. But a most amiable one who has never meant old Coralean anything but the best. I'm sure a man as great as that will understand Coralean can do the bidding of Iraj Protarus and still look out for his good friend."

Now it was Safar's turn to slap his knee and roar laughter. "You win either way, right? No matter who loses, you win?"

Coralean made a long face. "I suppose you could look at it that way," he said. "But it would spoil the spirit of the bargain. I truly hope you win, Safar Timura. I doubt if you will, but there is a slight chance, considering that Iraj lost out to you once before. You will appreciate, I hope, the elegance of my bargain."

He gestured at the maps. "Coralean gives you freedom! In any direction you choose to take. I ask only your word in return. Your word that someday, if required, I may call on your favor."

"Consider it a bargain, my friend," Safar said. "And no hard feelings if it doesn't work out my way."

Coralean beamed. "I am most pleased!" he said. "I made a wise investment in you when you were young and I paid for your education in Walaria." He brushed his hands together and rose heavily to his feet.

"Please, gentlemen," he said to the Elders, "I hope you will forgive Kyrania's oldest and dearest friend, but I must be on my way. Please make my apologies to your people, but the caravan must not tarry. We're off to Caspan where Coralean's wives wait with much anxiety for his return. I'll leave some fine food and drink for you all, in hopes that you will toast Coralean's health. Bull that I am, I will need it desperately for my loving wives when they welcome me home."

Safar rose with him and Coralean grasped his hand, squeezing hard. "Before I depart, I will send a runner to Iraj's camp with my report. Unfortunately, the runner I have in mind—alas, the only man I can spare—is rather elderly and infirm, so it may take a little time for him to reach the king."

"What will the report say?" Safar asked.

"Coralean is not a man who lies," he said. "I will tell him that I delivered his proposal. And the Council of Elders is presently meeting to consider his magnificent offer."

"How much time do you think we have?" Safar asked.

Coralean shrugged his apologies. "Not much for you," he said. "But quite sufficient for me. I am a minor spot for Iraj to consider. His thoughts are full of you, so it isn't difficult for me to slip out the side door while he's thinking."

He made a face. "What can I say? I have a family to care for. Children enough to fill a villa with Coraleans and wives anxious to produce more." He sighed. "Few men appreciate the burdens I bear. The responsibilities are endless."

"Do you really believe," Safar asked, "that Iraj will wait two days or more for your messenger?"

Coralean lumbered to his feet. "That's another reason I must hurry on my way," he said. "Your former master *has* been known to apply a little pressure when he's negotiating. So if you will forgive me, my dear friends, I must say goodbye and make haste!"

The old caravan master stepped forward and embraced Safar in a great bear hug. "Good fortune, traveler," he said, in the age old blessing of the road. "Good fortune!"

Then he was gone.

Chaos followed as the Council of Elders turned into mere men—and frightened men at that! They all gathered around Safar, shouting questions and opinions and any nonsense that came into their heads. It was plain to them now that Iraj would attack no matter what they did.

Safar felt his energy creeping back, and with it, his confidence.

"Call all the people together," he said—no, he commanded, his old authority of office settling onto his shoulders like a royal robe.

"We must act now, or all is lost!"

CHAPTER EIGHT

BONES OF FORTUNE

They were the People of the Clouds; the men, women, lads and maids and wailing babes who made up Kyrania. When they gathered in the old stone fort there were just a little over a thousand of them. For many generations they had lived apart from the rest of the world. They lived up, up in that bowl of fruit and blossoms they called home where no evil could easily reach them.

But at long last darkness had descended and they were blind and stumbling, not knowing what to do.

Although he was one of them, Safar steeled himself against all empathy as they filed silently into the arena. There was no time for wasted emotion or leisurely debate by the tradition-bound Council of Elders.

If his people were to survive he must rally them to accomplish the impossible. First, they must defend themselves against Protarus. Second . . . Well, he'd get to what came next—the most daunting task of all—if they lasted the night.

He watched his people stream into the old fort and take their places on the big parade ground, pounded smooth by generations of young Kyranian boys who had trained here to defend their homeland. The fort had been built long ago, perhaps even before the time of Alisarrian, and only the battered walls and the remnants of ancient stone barracks were left.

Safar had dressed with care for the occasion. He was wearing his most glittering ceremonial robes. Never mind he no longer held the office, the robes were the ones he'd worn at King Protarus' most important court functions when Safar had been Lord Timura, the second most powerful man in all of Esmir. Upon his breast were all the medals and ribbons and awards Protarus had granted him for his many services.

He felt no sense of irony, much less guilt, as he raised his hands for attention, acting as much a king as Iraj. He'd forced himself to swallow a hefty draught of manipulative leadership. And now he had to act. The late afternoon sun made his robes glow, leaping off his medals and dazzling the crowd. Instead of friends and family, he made himself think of the gathering as an audience, with a group attention he could capture, then form to his will like good Timura clay into a good Timura pot. Adding to his regal display was Leiria, who stood next to him on the raised platform, the steel and leather of her harness and weapons burnished to a dazzling gloss. Between them was Palimak. He was dressed like a little soldier, complete with toy sword, breast plate and helmet.

As Safar gathered his mental forces, Palimak sensed the crowd's bewildered mood and whispered, "I like this father! I can make them do anything I want."

Thank the gods he said it a bare moment *before* Safar cast the amplifying pellet to the stone. Otherwise everyone would have heard. Instead, all they noticed was Leiria clapping her hand across Palimak's mouth, saying, "Sshhh!"

Just then the magical pellet burst and her admonishing "sshhh!" echoed loudly across the field. There was weak laughter from the crowd, who assumed Palimak had merely said something childishly clever.

Safar grabbed the moment and built on it.

"If Iraj Protarus heard that laughter," he proclaimed, voice resounding across the arena, "he'd be quaking in his boots. After all he's done, the people of Kyrania can still laugh at the antics of a little boy."

There were more chuckles, stronger than before.

Safar lifted his head as if to address the heavens. "Do you hear that, O Mighty King?" he roared. "Do you hear the spirit of the People of the Clouds? We are not afraid! We stand proud and defiant before you!"

Shouts of approval greeted this. Faces brightened, shoulders straightened and people lifted their children high so they could see better.

Safar smiled broadly at his audience, clapping his hands in congratulations. "That's the message we want to send to Iraj Protarus," he said. "He may do his worst, but our spirits will remain unbroken!"

This time nearly the entire crowd roared in agreement. Some even shook their fists at the skies as if Iraj were hiding in the clouds. Only some of his enemies on the Council of Elder appeared unmoved. They were knotted about Masura, whose face was swollen with fury because Safar had upstaged him and gone directly to the people. Safar was determined to change that look.

When the noise died down he said, "We're going to need that spirit in the days ahead, my friends. The future of all Kyranians depends on your strength.

"Nay, the world itself depends on it!"

There were murmurs and puzzled looks but Safar pushed on. His next words, he knew, would dash the little enthusiasm he'd won.

"Brave as you all are," he said, "you will need to be braver still. At this moment we are stalked by a great enemy. A royal enemy who has somehow escaped from the grave to become the king of the shape changers. He and his minions have killed innocent Kyranian children and young men."

Safar gestured at Masura and people turned to look at him. "I know you have all heard the controversy regarding those tragedies. It's said that the only reason Iraj Protarus brings such bloody actions to our peaceful valley is because he seeks revenge against me."

Masura jerked his head in dramatic agreement. Safar ignored him, signaling Leiria to lift Palimak high for all to see.

"You've also heard that Iraj demands we hand over this child," he said. "This is a child you all know. A child who is an orphan of the storms that ravage the outside world."

Not understanding the seriousness of the situation, Palimak kicked his heels in glee and shouted to the other children in the crowd—his playmates. "Look at me!" he laughed. "Look how big I am!"

Some people joined his laughter. But not enough, not nearly enough. Safar pressed on.

"It's true that Iraj demands my head," he said, "just as it's true that he requires you to hand over little Palimak. And if I thought for one minute that Protarus would spare you, pass the people of Kyrania by to savage other poor, helpless souls, I would march down the mountain to his camp and throw myself and Palimak on his mercy."

A few people, Safar's family among them, shouted, "No, no! We'll fight him. We'll never give you up!"

Safar smiled, pretending it was resounding chorus of majority approval. He took Palimak in his arms. "I'm overjoyed by your support, my friends," he said. "Palimak and I thank you for your loyalty and love."

Saying this made it so in many hearts and this time the cheers were louder as he passed the boy back to Leiria. When he turned back to speak the crowd grew quiet in anticipation.

"Unfortunately, the issues aren't so simple. The fact is, Iraj Protarus will not be satisfied until every Kyranian, from our oldest, most respected leaders down to our newborn babes are wiped from the face of Esmir. This is what we face, my friends. Not choices, but certain annihilation. This is how Iraj Protarus plans to repay you for your generosity to him when he was a boy."

Murmurs of fear ran thought the crowd. Even Masura looked grim-faced with sudden worry. Harsh reality was gradually boring through his vanity.

Meanwhile, Palimak was greatly moved by Safar's words. "Let's fight him, father," he cried. His shrill voice carried across the arena as if he were a giant's child. "To the death!" He raised his toy sword in defiance.

Fully half the crowd joined in the cheering that followed. Fired by a child's boldness, they roared for the chance to give battle and somehow bring Protarus down. Masura, however, seemed to have regained his composure and with it much of his former stupidity.

When the crowd sounds faded, Masura shouted, "You have no right to speak, Timura! You and the boy have been banished by order of the Council."

Since the vote hadn't been announced, some people were taken by surprise and started muttering among themselves. Masura and his supporters took advantage of the confusion, shouting, "Don't listen to him!" and "He's just trying to save his own skin."

Safar cracked another capsule of amplification, then spoke, voice so strong it drowned out his foes. "People of Kyrania!" he thundered, flinging his arms high. "Heed me!"

Everyone froze. Even Masura was cowed by the thunder of his voice. "Whether I leave or whether I stay, Iraj Protarus will come this night to slay you in your beds! Unless you act with me now, that is your fate. If you doubt me . . . then witness this!"

He snapped his fingers and there was a crack! like a glacier rock exploding in a campfire. At the same time his other hand shot out, snatching at the air. There were gasps of amazement as he drew first one long yellow bone, then another, from thin air.

Safar made a great show of it, displaying the casting bones for all to see. He fanned them out and a thousand pairs of eyes were compelled to count them, one, two, three, four, five!

Safar chanted, feeling his power growing over them with each word he spoke:

Has the day falsed us?
Promising nights
With strong shutting doors?
Did the light halt us?
From seeing skull eyes
Dark and void?

The bones made a ghastly rattle as Safar hurled them onto the platform. Two thousand eyes followed their progress, saw them bounce and scatter. The crowd was deathly silent as Safar peered long and hard at the ivory pattern.

"Will Iraj come?" Palimak asked, posing the question for all.

Safar raised his head. He looked first at the crowd, then Palimak, finally, straight at Masura. The man's eyes were bright with fearful suspense, his defiance smothered in Safar's hypnotic spell.

He stretched the moment to the fullest, then whipped out his silver dagger and jabbed its point at the jumble of bones. "Speak, O great spirits!" he commanded. "What is your answer?"

He waved the dagger and the bones floated off the platform. He motioned again and they reformed themselves, shifting from one pattern to the next, until finally they formed the skeletal head of a giant wolf.

"Speak!" Safar again commanded. "Speak!"

There were wild shrieks of alarm as fire burst from the wolfhead's empty sockets. The big jaws grated open, unleashing a blood-chilling howl! Suddenly, the head flew forward—straight at Masura! Howling and snapping its jaws.

Masura ran away, screaming, "Help me! Help me!" But everyone fled from his path, crying out in fear. At just the right moment Safar jabbed his dagger at the head and an explosion ripped the bones apart and they vanished into nothingness.

"There is your answer, my friends!" Safar shouted. "Iraj will come! The Fates have decreed it!"

Masura realized he was safe and fell to his knees, babbling, "Save us, Lord Timura! Save us!"

First Masura allies joined in, then the rest of the crowd, all shouting, "Save us, Lord Timura! Save us!"

Safar had won. The victory disgusted him.

Another sin to add to his ledger.

*   *   *

It was a warm night, a night that drew roiling mists off the lake. Under the Demon Moon the mists made ominous shadows, deep oranges and reds bleeding through fantastic black figures that spilled over hollow and hill and got caught up in the branches of trees where owls waited to hoot at darkening skies.

In the village all the homes were shuttered and dark. The chimneys were cold, the cobbled streets empty and the only sound was the belly rumble of a llama and the long soft tramp of its feet.

Renor was leading the llama, an old thing who had seen more of life than she liked but pressed on anyway from habit. She was carrying a heavy load of thorny brush that shifted painfully from side to side as she walked. The llama groaned and Renor dodged just in time as she tried her best to step on his foot.

"Don't bother complaining, Granny," Renor said. "I won't feel sorry for you no matter what you do." He shook his head at the swaying burden on her back. "I did my best to tie it down tight. But you blew yourself up like an old horse and now all the knots are loose. It's your fault, not mine."

The llama swung its head to the side, there was a rumble in its guts, and then it coughed up a good spit. Once again Renor dodged to the side and a stream of smelly stuff splattered against an alley wall.

"Threats won't do you any good either, Granny," Renor said, brushing away the few drops that had spattered onto his cloak. "You'll still have to carry this load all the way to the fort. And if there's time you'll have to go back and fetch another."

The llama grumbled in protest, but Renor was unmoved. "I don't know why Lord Timura wants all this wood," he said, "but if he says to fetch it, and the more the better, then we'd *better* fetch it!"

They rounded the corner and Renor saw the dark shape of the fort looming out of the gathering gloom. The llama stopped its complaining and quickened its pace.

"Ho! So you go quickly now, do you?" Renor said. "You think your day's work is over. Lazy old thing." He looked up at the Demon Moon, growing deeper red as night rushed in. "I sure hope you're right," he grudged. "I don't want to go back out into this again."

He thought of the huge mound of brush and timber already piled in the center of the fort. When he'd delivered his last load Captain Leiria had been directing people to spread the wood out into some kind of design. No one seemed to know its purpose. Only that Lord Timura had ordered it done and so they were doing it. Just like Renor and a score of other village lads were unquestioningly scouring the countryside for wood. Lord Timura had said it was to protect them from Protarus and after seeing the magical wolfhead chase after Masura, nobody was going to argue.

Personally, Renor hadn't needed any convincing. After what had happened to Tio and his adventure by Lord Timura's side in the meadow, he was burning for revenge. He imagined himself advancing on a cowering devil wolf, spear raised to strike.

Just then the llama bawled and Renor almost jumped out of his skin. The animal surged forward, breaking into a fast lope. Renor shouted at it and ran to grab the load, which was tilting dangerously to the side. As he reached for it he heard an ungodly howl.

The young man whirled and his breath froze in his chest when he saw the four huge gray shapes bounding toward him.

Renor turned and ran, scrabbling his sharp work knife from his belt. Behind him the four creatures shattered the night with their howls. He ran faster, catching up to the llama. Renor slashed at the ropes and the load fell away. The animal stumbled, bawling in terror, but he yanked on its halter, helping it keep to its feet.

"Run, Granny, run!" he shouted and the llama leaped away.

Heavy bodies, moving at a frightening speed, were closing on him.

Renor was only twenty feet from the fort entrance, but the beasts were coming on so fast it might as well have been a thousand.

Then he saw a figure leap from the ruined walls. It was Lord Timura! Safar landed in front of the entrance.

"Get down!" he shouted.

Renor dropped to the ground, bracing for the scything claws he was sure would follow.

Then there was a sound like the wind and a hot breath whooshed! over his body. Behind him the howls turned into yips of pain.

Renor looked up and saw Lord Timura beckoning him.

"Come on!" he shouted. "I can't hold them for long!"

Renor scrambled up and ran for it. He turned his head and saw a wall of hot light. Just beyond the four wolf shapes howled in pain and rage.

Then he was sprinting past Lord Timura into the safety of the fort.

People rushed to him, shouting what was wrong and was he all right and other such nonsense. Struggling for breath, Renor pushed them away and turned to see what was happening.

Just as he did he saw the wall of light—some sort of magical shield—vanish and the four wolf figures crashed through.

Lord Timura backed up quickly and at the same time Renor saw Captain Leiria and some men pushing a big cart of wood into the entrance.

"Now!" Lord Timura shouted and someone threw a burning torch onto the wood.

The wood caught and there was a great blast of white light, blinding Renor. Then his vision cleared and he saw the wagon was engulfed in eerie flames that sparked and shot off long tongues of fire.

Beyond the flames, which seemed to have sealed the entrance, Renor could no longer hear the howling.

A small hand tugged at his cloak and Renor looked down to see little Palimak standing beside him, his toy soldier armor glittering in the fire.

"We're safe now," he said. Still, he had a worried look on his face. "But I think they'll come back pretty quick."

It was like an omen, because as he spoke the howling resumed.

*   *   *

Safar crouched in the little tent, assembling his magical arsenal by candlelight. He was mixing herbs and votive powders in a strange little pot with a five-sided mouth, working quickly and expertly in the near dark. He was used to such difficulties. When he'd been a young acolyte in Walaria he'd often lacked the price of lamp oil and so he'd had to practice his spell making under similar conditions. Although it had been much more pleasant to hear the watchman call the hour, rather than listen to the incessant howling outside the fort.

Never mind he was fairly certain Iraj and his friends were merely waging a war of nerves while they gathered their strength for the next attack. If that were the intent, by the gods it was working. The awful sound of the howling had everyone's nerves stretched taut. Safar had the village busy with a myriad of tasks, trying to keep their minds off the four savage creatures bounding and baying about the walls. The Kyranians went about their duties silently, whispering prayers to the Lady Felakia.

When the attack came, Safar had no idea how much force Iraj could muster. The only thing he was sure of was that it would be entirely magical. Coralean had no reason to lie when he'd said that Iraj's army was two days distant. Safar guessed it was even farther away than that—the terrain they had to cover was all treacherous mountains. Also, if there'd been an army behind him, the massacre of Kyrania would already be over. No, tonight would be a night of horrors meant to intimidate the villagers. To soften them up for his army.

To help in his work Iraj had three of the most cunning creatures in the history of Esmir. Two had been demons in their previous forms and therefor magical by birth, although Prince Luka was nowhere near as powerful as Lord Fari, who had been chief wizard to several generations of demon kings. Iraj's other ally was the human spymaster Kalasariz, who had no natural magical powers but was so ruthless and clever he hadn't needed them. The three had preyed on Iraj's many weaknesses, promising him even greater powers then being the *mere* king of kings of all Esmir. The result was The Spell of Four—the shape changer's spell—that bound them together forever.

Safar poured a silvery liquid into the pot, whispered a chant until the mixture began to bubble, then set it aside for his next task. He slipped five heavy-headed war arrows from a bundle and dipped them into the liquid one by one.

The defensive spell he was concocting was much weaker than he'd like, but he had no choice. With over a thousand people to protect he was going to be spread very thin. A more powerful spell—a spell capable of doing any real harm to Iraj but still safeguarding the villagers—would be impossible to maintain.

His preparations done, Safar opened his wizard's pouch and lifted an amulet out by its leather thong. It was made of some rare black stone that had been carved into the shape of a wondrous horse. The amulet had once belonged to Iraj—a gift from Coralean for saving his life. Safar had received the silver witch's dagger at the same time and for the same reason.

He remembered the moment as if it were yesterday, instead of nearly twenty years before. Safar and Iraj had been mere lads then. Even so, they'd first warned and then rescued Coralean and his caravan from a marauding army of demon bandits who'd broken out of the Forbidden Desert.

The gifting had come at a meeting of the Council of Elders and both boys had been bursting with pride as Coralean praised them.

Safar slipped back in time, remembering . . .

"First, I must thank my friend Iraj," the caravan master said. He took out a black velvet pouch. Iraj's eyes sparkled as Coralean withdrew a small golden amulet. It was a horse—a wondrously formed steed dangling from a glittering chain. "Some day," Coralean said, "you will see the perfect horse. It will be a steed above all steeds. A true warrior's dream, worth more than a kingdom to men who appreciate such things. The beast will be faster and braver than any animal you could imagine. Never tiring. Always sweet-tempered and so loyal that if you fall it will charge back into battle so you might mount it again.

"But, alas, no one who owns such a creature would ever agree to part with it. Even if it is a colt its lines will be so pure, its spirit so fierce, that the man it belongs to would be blind not to see what a fine animal it will become." He handed the horse amulet to Iraj. "If you give this magical ornament to that man he will not be able to refuse you the trade. But do not fear that you will be cheating him. For he only has to find another dream horse and the man who owns it will be compelled to make the same bargain when he gives him the amulet."

Tears welled in Iraj's eyes and they spilled unashamedly down his face as he husked his thanks and embraced the caravan master. "When I find that horse," Iraj said, "I promise that I will ride without delay to your side so you can see for yourself what a grand gift you gave me."

A great chorus of howls, louder than before, broke through Safar's reverie and he jolted back to the present. He checked the arrow tips, but the potion smeared on them was still damp. A few more minutes and he'd be ready.

Safar glanced down at the amulet. Iraj had never found that horse. He remembered that Iraj had cursed Safar for that failing, as if he were to blame. Then he'd hurled it into Safar's face, demanding that he take it in payment for Nerisa. At that moment the war between them had begun.

"Ah, well," Safar said to himself, taking comfort from the sound of his own sighing whisper. "Ah, well."

He tested the arrows again. They were ready.

Safar gathered them up, along with a sturdy bow, and slipped from the tent to confront the night.

*   *   *

Leiria gritted her teeth as the next chorus of howling began. It was a sound that first pierced the ears, then jabbed the brain with hot spear points. All around her the villagers crouched down in misery. Some wept and covered their heads to drown out the sound, while others held their heads high in stoic defiance.

Palimak stirred beside her. She'd promised Safar that she'd guard the child until the danger had passed.

"If I were bigger," he said, "I could magic their howls right out of their throats." He lifted up both hands, cupping them into paws like a cat's. Needle point claws emerged from his fingertips. "I'd do like this . . ." and he slashed the air with his claws . . . "and cut those howls right out!"

Not for the first time, Leiria felt a shiver when confronted with the demon side of the child's nature. Claws and glowing eyes are damned hard to get used to! She wondered, also not for the first time, if she would've been able to adopt the child as her own as Nerisa had done. The thought of Nerisa made her feel momentary resentment. The woman had remained her rival even beyond the grave. Then she remembered her resolve and smiled at the lapse. She and Safar were friends, not lovers. So there was nothing to resent.

Then the howling stopped. The silence came so abruptly it was like falling off a cliff into nothingness. Leiria tensed for danger, one arm going around Palimak.

"Look, Aunt Leiria," the child said, "there's my father!"

Her eyes swept left and she saw Safar walking from the small shelter to the raised platform in the center of the field. People called out to him as he passed and he had a quick smile and word of reassurance for each of them, but he never paused, always moving easily and quickly along towards his goal. Leiria remembered when he'd done the same at Iraj's great court in Zanzair, giving cheer to his followers while hurrying to an appointment with the king. Except then he'd been moving through a dazzling royal chamber instead of a makeshift campground full of frightened peasants and their flocks.

Palimak struggled to get up. "I'd better go help him," he said.

Leiria gently pulled him back, saying, "Your father said you had to stay with me."

Palimak frowned. "Well, maybe he did," he admitted. "But I still think I ought to help. This is going to be a really, really hard spell. Maybe harder than he thought. I can feel it all the way over here."

His voice was mild, but Leiria could tell he was worried and a little angry with her for holding him back. His eyes were beginning to glow yellow and his little pointy claws were emerging unbidden.

"But if you disobey your father," Leiria said, "you might spoil his spell. I mean,

342

what if he's so worried about you that he can't concentrate? Then what'll happen?"

Palimak sighed dramatically and slumped down. "I suppose you're right," he said. Then he brightened. "But we can be his . . . his . . . reserves, right?" he said. "Like they do in the army?"

Leiria chuckled. "That's exactly right," she said. She patted her sword. "We'll be his brave and loyal reserves. I'll provide the steel." She nodded at the stone turtle clutched in his hand. "And you can provide the magic."

Palimak chortled. He lifted up the little idol. "Did you hear that, Gundara? We get to be reserves. You too, Gundaree. Won't that be fun?"

There was no answer, at least any Leiria could make out. But Palimak seemed satisfied so the two little Favorites must have heard. She looked up and saw Safar mounting the platform, waving to the crowd, while at the same time directing some men who were quickly encircling the platform with a pile of wood. That circle was the center of a great four-pointed star also made of wood. Many barrels of oil, magically enhanced by Safar, had been poured on the wood, as well as on the mounds of additional wood scattered strategically about the field.

It would be a strange kind of fight, Leiria thought. Logs and bundles of brush instead of spears and swords. Like Palimak, she wished she could join Safar. Perhaps even more so. Finer feelings aside, Leiria had been Safar's personal bodyguard for many years. She'd turned away assassins' knives in the dark and had even charged into battle with him to protect his back.

Safar's orders, however, had been quite plain. If he failed—and all was lost—she and the two Favorites were to carry Palimak to safety. The child, he said, must survive at all costs. He'd entrusted her with one other thing, nearly as precious, he said.

Leiria patted her breast pocket. Inside was a small book, the Book of Asper. She was to keep that safe as well.

"Give it to the boy when he's old enough," Safar had said. "He'll know what to do once he's read it."

Just then, Safar made a gesture and green flame and smoke burst from the earth. The crowd went silent. Not a child cried, or a goat bawled. And when next Safar spoke his voice rang out like a great temple bell.

Leiria leaned forward, swept up like the rest.

※   ※   ※

"Gentle people," Safar said, "the moment is upon us, so listen to me closely. You will need courage and boldness this night, but you will also need your good common sense. No one here has had experience in magical battle, but I can assure you it isn't much different than the ordinary kind. There'll be lots of noise, smoke and confusion. The trick is to concentrate on your duties, whether it's to help me or assist a child or sick family member. Pay no attention to anything else and we'll be just fine when this is all over."

Safar saw all the wise nods his remarks drew, but he also saw the glazed, wide-eyed look in them that comes from facing a nightmare. He wondered if any of them really understood what he was saying. Hells, he wondered if they were even capable of hearing what he had to say.

As he struggled for words to break through their fear Iraj launched the first attack.

CHAPTER NINE
ESCAPE TO SYRAPIS

He was only a boy, too young to be alone in the mountains and he came out of the night crying, "Help me, Renor! Help me!"

The boy was a ghostly figure whose plaintive cry cut into every human heart gathered in the fort. His father collapsed, his mother shrieked and his brother shouted, "Tio! Tio!"

Kalasariz laughed as he manipulated little Tio's ghost. He put all the pain he could into its voice as it cried, "Help, me, please! Help me!"

He fed on the crowd's hysteria, straining to conjure up more ghosts. Kalasariz was new to shape-changer's magic and he found it difficult to concentrate.

Then Renor ran to the top of the fort's walls and clawed at the sky, weeping and flailing at nothingness in his effort to help his brother.

Kalasariz laughed again and made stronger magic.

Nine other ghosts faded into being.

They were the slain Kyranian sentries, with Rossthom at the their head, pleading with all their families and friends, "Help me, please help me!"

Now the crowd in the fort went from hysteria to blind madness. To Kalasariz' delight they rushed the walls wailing comforts to the dead.

The spy master's blood boiled with delight. As he liked to tell Luka and Fari—his demon rivals for influence over Protarus—native intelligence was more important than magical prowess. Even with his lesser magic, he could accomplish much by simply knowing his target's weaknesses.

He gloried at the agony he'd caused, drawing in more power from that pain and adding other little touches to his handiwork, like a bloody scar on Tio's face and a gory stump on Rossthom's right arm where a hand used to be.

Kalasariz struggled mightily and gave them all a voice, crying, "Help me! Help me!"

He basked in the misery, his black spirit wallowing in it—sinking and rising then sinking again in the heady musk.

And then he heard a voice shout, "Kalasariz!"

His spirit head jerked down, looking from sky to ground for the source of the shout—spectral eyes honing in like an eagle owl hunting a squeaking rodent. When he found the source of the squeak he would blast it from existence. But instead of a puny creature his eyes fell on a tall man with fiery blue eyes that cut across the great distance to sear his heart.

It was Safar, posing on a stone platform in the classic frieze of a bowman, heavy weapon bent tip to tip, string making a high-pitched whine as the flaming arrow leaped from the bow.

Kalasariz loosed his own killing bolt, but the fiery arrow speeding toward him made him jerk, spoiling his aim, and he desperately flung himself to the side.

In the fort Safar heard the boom! of his arrow exploding, heard Kalasariz wail, then swiveled, grabbing up another arrow as his eyes swept the skies for his next target.

Behind him, a huge gray wolf leaped onto the walls. The creature's claws gripped the rough stone and there was a flash as the wolf transmuted himself into demon form.

It was Prince Luka, eyes aglow, fangs bared, sword lifted high. Although people screamed warnings it was almost too late for Safar, who whirled, falling and firing at the same time. A tongue of flame arced from Luka's sword, but Safar's own arrow exploded simultaneously. He heard Luka shriek then felt pain sear his own back as the prince's bolt blasted close overhead.

He came to his feet with difficulty, stifling a groan as he picked up his third arrow and fixed it into his bowstring.

Lord Fari watched Safar shuffle in a clumsy circle, pain-dulled eyes searching for the next point of attack. But the canny old demon wasn't so foolish that he'd mistake his enemy's stumbling show for real weakness. Safar was hurt, yes, he could see that. But how badly? Long ago, when Safar was the prize jewel in Iraj Protarus' crown, Fari had noted Safar's talent at showmanship. It was a thing that Fari, who was a purist when it came to sorcery, particularly disliked in him. Still, he had grudging admiration for the way Safar used his magical theatrics to convince the entire royal court, demon and human alike, that he was a most powerful wizard truly deserving of the title Grand Wazier.

So Fari assumed that much of Safar's present difficulty was a sham to draw him out.

Instead of leaping onto the walls of the fort, Fari crept up on them. He put his spirit self into its demon presence and scrambled to the high point at the ruined gate. Then he made his spell, chuckling at his cleverness as he did so.

Even Leiria, who had seen all the terrible things a soldier could see, was shaken by what happened next. The stone walls of the fort came suddenly and horribly alive as the rubble was transformed into small mountains of gore that moved and squirmed and streamed torrents of blood. People screamed and fled this way and that, bouncing from one horror to the other. Then pustules of gore bloomed on the walls and each pustule became a face and each face was a Tio or a Rossthom or any of the other slain sentries.

But this time instead of begging for help, the ghosts snapped at their friends with long teeth and spewed obscenities.

Leiria gathered up a struggling Palimak and was preparing to flee when Safar fired his arrow.

Automatically her eyes followed its fiery flight and she saw it was hurtling toward the north corner of the wall. There were dozens of human faces there, shouting filth or begging for assistance.

Then she saw the target and the moment became quite still. Just below center, between two faces that were both Tio's, she saw Lord Fari. The demon was scowling with concentration, putting all his clever old ways into the apparition that was the wall of blood.

Safar's arrow flashed toward that face and Leiria had a jolt of pleasure when she saw Fari's yellow jaws widen with fear.

Then, crack! as the arrow struck. Flame running all around the walls. And then they were nothing but blank stone again. Leiria saw a spot of blood where Fari's face had been and prayed that Safar had done heavy damage.

On the platform Safar took his time as he fitted the fourth arrow into his bow. Iraj would be next, he thought. But from which direction would he strike . . . and in what manner?

The answer came in a great shout from above: "Safar!"

It was Iraj's voice and Safar's head shot up and he saw the face of the Demon Moon suddenly split down the middle and yawn open like a gigantic mouth. A ghostly cavalry charged out of that mouth, lead by a mighty warrior in golden armor.

It was Iraj.

And he shouted a challenge—"Safar!"

Iraj yanked back on his horse's reins and the huge ghost animal reared up, pawing the night, sparks shooting from its hooves.

Then horse and rider plunged down toward the fort, a horrid cavalry of demon riders sweeping after them.

Safar fired and the arrow arced toward Iraj. It exploded just in front of him and there was a blinding flash as magic collided with magic.

Iraj paused, but only for an instant. Then he and his demon riders continued their charge.

In the fort the crowd shrieked in terror. But Safar paid no attention to their panic. As calmly as he could he swept up his final bolt. As Iraj and his spectral army closed in he whispered the spell that brought the arrow into fiery life.

He drew back, aiming for Iraj, then at the last moment he swiveled and fired the bolt into the dry mass of wood encircling the platform.

The oil-soaked fuel ignited with an enormous blast that nearly hurled Safar off the platform into the roaring flames. He teetered on the edge, but recovered his balance just in time.

The soles of his feet prickled with the intense heat and his scalp hair bristled like so many hot needles. He smelled scorched cloth and knew it came from his own robes. They smoldered at the hems and sleeves and the smoke curled up to bite his eyes.

But now it was Safar's turn to laugh. He saw flame tongues leap across the arena, shooting along the paths of wood he'd laid out, leaping from place to place until the entire arena seemed to be engulfed—with Safar and the blazing platform at its center. The whole mass finally combusted into a blazing pentagram of magical flame that smashed upward like a massive shield.

It caught Iraj and his cavalry in midstride, lifting them up and up, hurling them back at the Demon Moon.

A clap of thunder, then the sky turned white. The white shattered and became snowflakes that drifted down and down until they struck the pentagram shield blazing over the arena and flashed out of existence.

The sky was empty and there was a momentary quiet as the crowd sagged in relief. Then the air was rent with cheers as the Kyranians congratulated themselves and Safar for turning back such a deadly force.

Safar shouted to them, his voice thundering across the arena. "It isn't over yet!" The cheers vanished, swallowed by this bad news. "Iraj will be back," Safar warned. "But we'll be ready for him, my friends! We'll be ready!"

Then he shouted orders and a select group, Renor among them, sprang into action. They ran to the spare piles of brush and fed them into the flames. The fiery pentagram took on new life, soaring brighter and higher, forming a sparkling shield above the fort . .

Iraj came again. As did Kalasariz and Luka and Fari. But each time the flaming pentagram hurled them back. Safar shouted orders until he was hoarse, urging his fellow villagers to feed the fires, whipping them past exhaustion while hour piled on hour and still the attacks were unrelenting.

Many horrors were lived that night. Many threats were posed, many ghosts were roused, but somehow Safar and the villagers managed to turn them back. They burned all the gathered wood, then broke up the carts and ripped off their clothes to feed them into the magical fires.

They were exhausted when dawn finally came and the attacks ended. The pentagram was nothing more than an ugly black smudge with foul smelling heaps smoking and sputtering in the morning's wet chill. People shuddered with relief and collapsed to the ground. There were no choruses of self-congratulation. The enemy had been defeated, yes. But all knew the defeat was temporary. Iraj would return, but now he'd be backed by a real army, not specters in the sky.

Safar slumped on the platform and looked around at all the spiritless people. It was as if they had been the losers, instead of Iraj. Even so, he had to rouse them, enthuse them, convince them that all was not lost. Then somehow he had to prepare them for a challenge far more daunting than Protarus and his army of demons and wizards and human savages. To do this he would have lie to them, manipulate them, then keep on lying and manipulating until either the goal was achieved or they were all dead.

Suddenly the whole thing seemed hopeless. His people's weary despair had infected Safar and now his plan seemed foolish, impossible in the extreme.

A voice cut through, "We haven't much time, Safar."

He looked up. Leiria was standing there, a sleeping Palimak in her arms. Her eyes were red from the smoke, her armor blackened. But her back was straight, shoulders square, and there was a gleam of determination in her tired eyes.

She nodded at the slumbering Kyranians. "We have to get them up and going," she said, gently lowering Palimak to the platform. There he curled up to sleep on, the stone turtle clutched between grimy paws.

"We have maybe two days at the most," she continued, "before Iraj shows up with his whole damned army."

"I know that," Safar said, a little sharp.

Leiria snorted. "Good for you," she said. "Now, would you mind enlightening me about what we're supposed to do next? All you've said is that somehow we're going to make an entire village of over a thousand people disappear." She chuckled. "I know you are a wizard above all wizards, Safar Timura, but that's magic I'm going to have to see to believe."

As she spoke, Leiria returned the Book of Asper. The sight of the book and the buzz of sorcery when he put it away firmed his resolve. A greater tonic, as always, was Leiria's presence. Her attitude had always been, show me the mountain and we'll both figure out how to climb it together.

Safar slipped Coralean's maps from his belt. "Actually, there's no magic to it," he said, unrolling the maps. "Well, not much, anyway. It's more of a trick, really. Sleight of hand, except with two thousand hands."

"That's still one hells of a trick," Leiria said.

"Not when you consider that Iraj will be dragging along of tens of thousands of soldiers," Safar said, "plus baggage trains that'll stretch from one horizon to the next."

He showed her one of the maps. "Look here," he said, tracing a finger north from the Gods' Divide to the Great Sea. "There are so many canyons and hills and secret roads and trails between Kyrania to the Port of Caspan we could hide a small city of people, much less a village."

Leiria studied the map, eyes narrowed. Then she nodded. "It could be done," she said. Leiria glanced over at all the people collapsed on the ground. "But I don't know if it can be done by them! They've lived in one place all their lives. They know nothing about life on the road, much less life on the road with the dogs of war on your heels."

"We can teach them," Safar said. "If you're still willing to help me, that is. A sensible person would laugh in my face and walk away with her skin still safe on her bones."

"I told you before, Safar," Leiria said. "That I'm with you. No matter what. So we've got two thousand miles or more between us and the sea. So there's who knows how many hundreds of sea miles more to go to reach Syrapis. And us not knowing if there'll even be ships to hire in Caspan to take us there."

She grinned. "If that's what his lordship wants, that's what he gets!"

They both laughed, although Safar's laughter was weak. Already his mind was running ahead.

Between skirmishes, Safar had managed to tell Leiria about his vision in Asper's tomb. Although he'd held some things back—like the mysterious side trips to Naadan and Caluz. He had two reasons for his silence. First, if it became too difficult he might skip them entirely and head straight for the sea. More important: whenever he'd been about to relate exactly what Asper's ghost had said magical alarms went off. All his sorcerous instincts warned him that by telling all he'd be putting Leiria in grave danger.

Safar was especially worried about mentioning Caluz. He knew something about the region from his days in Iraj's court. It was strange place where mysterious forces had been at work for eons.

"Come to me through Caluz," Asper had commanded. But Safar dreaded the moment of decision—if they lived to see it—when he finally reached the road that led to that dark region.

Lost in thought, he was surprised when he heard Leiria say, "There's only one thing that worries me, Safar."

"What's that?"

She indicated the villagers. "Maybe they can do it. Maybe they can't. The thing is . . . how are you going to convince them to try?"

"Magic," Safar said.

And he heaved himself to his feet and started getting ready.

*   *   *

An hour later, washed and refreshed, Safar once again stood before his people, Leiria and Palimak beside him.

Exhausted as the Kyranians were, they seemed to sense hope in the air and their faces were bright with expectation.

Safar cracked an amplifying pellet, then spoke: "You fought well and bravely, my friends. I'm sure that even now Iraj Protarus is cursing your courage and nursing a battle-sore behind!"

The laughter was weak. No one had to tell these people that Iraj wasn't done with them. Methydia used to say that the best way to get an audience in your palm was to make a dream for them . . . and keep them reaching for that dream. But first, she'd said, you have to scare them. Well, Iraj had done that unpleasant little job for Safar. Unfortunately, he needed to scare them in a whole different way.

"But I didn't rouse you from your well-earned rest to praise your courage, my good people," Safar said. "Besides, everyone knows that courage is something no Kyranian lacks."

Faces brightened, especially among the young bravos like Renor. He saw them flex their muscles and swagger from side to side.

"But it's another brand of courage I want from you today," Safar continued. "One that calls for even greater sacrifices than before."

The crowd stirred, a little fearful. What was he talking about? Wasn't dealing with Iraj Protarus enough?

"Not just your lives, but the lives of untold millions are at stake. In fact, the very world we stand upon depends on you, the Goddess Felakia's Chosen Ones, the People of the Clouds, the People of the High Caravans."

Safar definitely had their interest now.

"Behold!" he shouted, making a gesture and his magical dagger leaped out of nothingness into his hand.

Then, quieter, "Let me show you the world of the future, my friends. Even if by some miracle we could make Iraj Protarus and his forces vanish from Esmir, this is what the world would look like in not many years."

Safar made a circular motion with the knife, as if cutting a hole into the air itself. The crowd jumped as a fierce wind blew, shrieking through the hole he'd made.

Then a miniature tornado leapt off the dagger point. It swirled madly about the platform for a moment, then steadied, spinning in place like a top.

"Behold!" Safar shouted again and there was a loud pop! as the little tornado suddenly disappeared. The air where it had been shattered like glass, leaving a great dark hole gaping into nothingness.

There were gasps and fearful cries all around as everyone realized there was more than a blank void beyond the jagged edges of the hole.

"Look, my friends," Safar intoned. "Look hard and deep. See the world as it will be. With or without Iraj Protarus."

They looked and it was a terrible sight. A familiar range of mountains beckoned from the other side. It was the Bride and her Maids, but they had been shorn of all their glory and stood there black and wind-torn under a lunatic sky. There was not a patch of snow, tree, or blade of grass upon the range.

The scene shifted and there were fearful shouts as the crowd suddenly found itself looking down into the barren valley that had once been Kyrania. There were no fields or homes, or even the holy lake of Felakia.

Then the ground seemed to move and people shouted in horror as they realized that millions upon millions of scaly insects made up the floor of their beloved valley. They swarmed over and under each other, feeding on rock and dust.

Just as everyone thought they could stand this nightmare no more Safar clapped and the scene vanished, the hole was healed and everything was the same as before.

"That is what we must prevent from happening," Safar said. "Only we can do it. Only the people of Kyrania have the will and the means. But to accomplish it, you must come away with me. You must come out of the clouds and walk the land and swim its rivers and climb its hills. We must walk until the land ends and there is only sea. And then we must find boats and cross that sea until we come to a new land, a place of safety and peace."

He jabbed at the air with his dagger point and again it shattered. But this time, instead of darkness, a warm yellow light poured out. Everyone looked and this time the gasps and shouts were of marvel, instead of fear.

A glorious island, looking like a wondrous emerald lizard, rose out of a shimmering blue sea. It had thick forests and high mountains on its back, with soft white clouds caught in the peaks. Silver streams coursed down the mountain slopes, leaping over cliffs and boulders and sending up fantastic rainbows from their spume.

"Friends and family," Safar said, "I give you Syrapis! The island of dreams!"

He clapped again and the vision dissolved. Safar turned back to the crowd. He took note of the faces. Some people's eyes were alight with the wonder they had beheld. These mostly belonged to the young. Others appeared withdrawn, suspicious. These mostly belonged to the old. Among the vast majority, however, was a mixture of the two, plus confusion.

Palimak piped up. "Was that our new home, father? Is that where we're going to live?"

Safar answered as if he and the child were alone, instead of surrounded by a thousand people. "If it pleases our friends to do so," he said.

"Is Syrapis very far?" the boy asked.

"Yes, son," he said, "it's very far. Farther than anyone has ever been before."

"If it's so far," he asked, "how will we ever find our way?"

Safar pulled the tube of maps from his belt. "Lord Coralean gave me these," he said. A quick side glance showed that Coralean's name was having a great affect on the Kyranians. All of it positive.

"These are secret maps that only caravan masters possess," Safar said. "They show every road and path in all of Esmir."

He raised his head slightly, making sure all heard. "You know how great a friend Lord Coralean is to all of us. He gave us these secret maps to save us from Iraj Protarus."

"Secrets!" the boy exclaimed, eyes glowing yellow in delight. "Does that mean if we go down those secret roads and paths no one will be able to find us? Even that . . . that . . ." Palimak automatically scanned the crowd for his grandmother's face. The words he had in mind would surely earn him a scolding. "That . . . wolf thing, or man thing, or whatever he is. He wouldn't be able to find us, would he?"

"It would be a pretty hard thing for him to do," Safar said. "And if he found us, we could always lose him again."

"Then what are we waiting for, father?" Palimak asked.

He turned to the crowd, putting his hands on his hips, looking like a circus midget in his little uniform.

"Who wants to go to Syrapis with us?" he shouted. "You get secret maps and a chance to save the world, and . . . and . . ." He spread his hands wide as if encompassing a huge world of wonders . . . "Everything!"

Everyone was laughing now, enjoying the show. In their laughter, Safar knew he'd found acceptance.

Palimak, however, wasn't satisfied. He stamped his little foot.

"You're not answering!" he shouted. "Who wants to go?

"Who wants to go to Syrapis?"

Part Two

Khysmet

CHAPTER TEN
THE COURT OF KING PROTARUS

The man's face was a bloody mask. "Please, master, please," he moaned, "we din't know no better, honest to th' gods we din't!"

Luka flicked a talon, making a greater mess of the man's face. "What a slimy little human you are," he said. "Everyone knows that Safar Timura is a desperate criminal, so why bother lying?" He flicked again and the man's shrieks echoed across the gloom that was the royal tent. "Even if I believed you, it wouldn't save your life. Your continued existence isn't at stake here, you filthy thing. Only how much pain you can bear before I send you on your miserable way."

Iraj shifted in his throne. Although Luka prided himself on his interrogation techniques, with lots of blood and moaning for entertainment, the king was clearly bored. As a shape changer some concentration was required to retain one form or another—whether human, or giant wolf. Iraj's concentration was visibly shattered by the proceedings; his body parts kept shifting back and forth from animal to human. Hand became claw, face grew a snarling muzzle, then crunched back again.

"Please, master!" the victim begged.

Iraj made a wolf snout. "Please, master, please!" he mocked, his voice a perfect imitation of the tortured villager's. His human face returned. "What a sniveling lot of fools I have for subjects. Always begging, never giving."

He turned to Fari, who sat to his left in a lower and smaller throne. "Tell my scribes," he said, "that in my next decree the phrase 'Merciful Master' is to be removed from my signature titles. King of Kings, Most Exalted Emperor of Esmir, Lion of the Plains, etc., etc., and all the others should be quite sufficient."

"Noted, Your Highness," the old demon wizard said. "All will be done as you say. And in that spirit, I propose that we examine your other titles more closely as well. For phrases like 'Peaceful Protector,' and 'His Benevolence,' which would also be suspect."

Iraj agreed. "Peace, mercy, and benevolence are out," he said. "My subjects need to have a clear idea of who I am. That's the key to good leadership. And I blame you and Luka and Kalasariz for not reminding me of this."

Fari bowed, beating his breast to show his own quick acceptance of guilt. "It's as you say, Majesty," he said. "There's been too much talk of peace and mercy of late and we ought to end it."

Iraj was calmed and became fully human in appearance. "Exactly, Fari, exactly!" he said. "And by the gods it's undermining my kingdom and I won't put up with it any longer."

He gestured, his hand transforming into a claw to indicate the grisly scene before him. Besides the man Luka was tormenting, there were five others chained to stakes. All of the townspeople were horribly maimed, with only their soft moans and the quivering of their tortured flesh to show they were still alive.

"This a perfect illustration of my point," Iraj said. "They all begged for mercy, screaming and farting at every little poke Luka gave them . . . and what do we get for our pains?" Another wide gesture, paw becoming a hand again. "Nothing but a great deal of wasted time because we are unsure of their respect for me.

"I tell you, Fari, we're losing far too many taxpayers to get at the truth! If I learned anything from Safar, it was that! I mean, genocide is all very well for an ordinary king recapturing an ordinary kingdom. But if you want to be truly great, you must pay a mind to the royal treasury."

Fari bobbed his big scaly head with the ease of one who had tended to the moods of many kings. "I agree entirely, Majesty," he said. "All your wishes will be put into force immediately."

"That's good, Fari," Iraj said. "We don't want to give out too much hope, you know. Another thing I learned from Safar is that hope is a coin more precious than any metal, including gold. So let's give out hope sparingly, if you please. Let's make it count."

Across the tented room, Luka did something to the prisoner again and the sound of his pain rasped against the scab of Iraj's boredom.

"Enough!" he shouted. "Enough! This exercise is making no progress whatsoever . . . No matter what we do, the fellow's only going to repeat what the others said."

"As always, your Majesty," Lord Fari replied, "your instincts are on target. This is the township's mayor, after all. And I don't know why Prince Luka left him for last. In my experience the post requires a good deal of moral cowardice, so the truth and pulled fingernails will out, as they say."

He made a lazy wave at the mayor, who was gibbering protests and squirming against his restraints as Luka delicately cut his flesh away. "In the end he'll confess to the same thing as the others. He'll claim that Lord Timura and his ragtag army of villagers arrived one day and forced the town to sell him food and supplies. He'll say they had no choice but to comply. And that he is as surprised as we are that Lord Timura insisted on payment."

Fari hefted a small sack of gold in his talons. "Our friend paid quite handsomely too."

"So what's the point in listening to this fellow's whining, then?" Iraj demanded. He raised his voice so Luka could hear. "Kill him and be done with it!"

The prince shrugged, cut the mayor's throat, then ambled back to his seat on Iraj's right, wiping his talons on a rag as he went and dropping it to the ground. Luka had no doubt that his work had been discussed by the king and his old rival, Fari. So he automatically protested.

"I understand your impatience, Majesty," he said, "but we should have probed deeper. After all, we still don't know where Lord Timura went when he left this township. We don't even know which direction he took."

He rattled his talons on the arm of his chair. "One thousand people, gone, vanished. Or at least that's what these fools told us." He indicated the chained forms. "Someone had to have seen what happened," he said. "A thousand people just don't disappear. There's no wizard in the world who could do such a thing."

"Whatever the explanation, my prince," Fari said, "this is hardly the first time Lord Timura has accomplished the trick. When we showed up in Kyrania with the army, all we found was a smoking ruin. The homes and fields were burned, so there was nothing for our soldiers to scavenge. And all the people had vanished."

Iraj glowered at the memory, wolf jaws grinding in frustration. "Where could they have gone?" he growled. "They were there two days before."

Fari shrugged. "That remains a mystery—as Your Majesty is well aware. Our trackers found the northern trail they took through the mountains from Kyrania. But once into the desert they lost it in a warren of rifts and barren canyons so complicated only a devil god could have been the creator."

He indicated the map board posted near their thrones. All the major cities, Naadan and Caspan included, were clearly marked. As were all the known roads and byways.

However, unlike the special maps Safar had received from Coralean, none of the secret caravan tracks were shown. From the point of view of Iraj and cohorts, there was nothing but an impassable wilderness in those areas.

"Not only our trackers, but all my wizards have been confounded ever since," Fari continued. "We've been hunting Lord Timura for *months* without success. Sometimes he reappears at a town or city with a band of raiders to resupply his people. But when our troops reach there, he's vanished again without a trace. The next time we hear of him weeks have passed and somehow he's several hundred miles away."

To Luka's immense displeasure, Iraj smiled at Lord Fari. The demon wizard's calmly put litany of what was already known soothed the king somewhat and his face was back to normal.

"You have summed up our difficulties most succinctly, my lord," Iraj said. Then he immediately grew angry again, glaring at Luka. "At least Fari's using his gods given mind," he said. "Unlike some fiends I know."

Fari openly gloated at the demon prince. And Luka thought, you'll never change, you old fraud. First my father, now Protarus. Always posing as the all wise one, trying to appear superior at my expense.

But what he said, was, "Lord Timura will make a mistake by and by, Highness. They always do. It's the nature of such things."

Fari shifted tactics and nodded in wise agreement, "Quite true, my prince," he said to Luka. "Quite true."

But he was thinking, you're just like your father, you young fool. Nothing but cold porridge for brains.

Iraj's dark mood returned and he glowered at them both. Such useless creatures, he thought. Always quarreling and backstabbing. Telling lies to win his favor. If it weren't for the unbreakable Spell of Four that chained them all together, he'd have them taken out by his soldiers and beheaded. *That would shut them up once and for all!*

"Enough excuses!" Iraj rumbled. "The point is we've failed. Despite the fact that I've had an entire army pursuing these peasants. Why, I'll soon be the laughing stock of all Esmir."

You already are, Luka thought, wishing not for the first time that it was he who wore the crown.

But all he said was, "I'll fetch some more prisoners, Majesty. Perhaps we'll have better luck with the next batch!"

Iraj slammed his fist on his throne arm! "Nonsense!" he roared. "All of it, nonsense! You've turned my tent into a charnel house for nothing!"

He leaned forward in his throne. "Let me make myself completely clear, brothers mine," he said. "We must have this man, Safar Timura, and his ridiculous child. And we must have them immediately. I will brook no more excuses, do you hear me?"

"We hear, Majesty," both demons muttered, bowing their heads and hating him and each other.

Just then there was the sound of bootsteps, sentries snapped to attention and Kalasariz was ushered into the big tent that was Iraj's traveling palace. The spy master was leading an old woman by a long chain that was locked about her waist.

"I've brought you a little present, Majesty," Kalasariz said, yanking the chain hard so the old woman stumbled. "For your afternoon pleasure, if you will."

Iraj was so surprised that his lower face erupted into a wolf's snout. "What kind of present is this?" he growled. "A skinny old woman with bones so brittle I'd choke on them."

"I'm not for eatin'!" the old woman exclaimed. "And if yer thinks yer gonner get any fun from tormentin' a poor old soul like me, yer gots 'nother think comin', Majesty! I'm so frail that if yer touched a hair on my head I'd up and die on yers."

"How amazing," Luka murmured. "The gift talks. Not very well, but it's amazing just the same."

"And now that's she's seen us," Fari said, "we'll have to kill her. How tiresome. Like she said, she's so elderly she'll be no sport at all."

Kalasariz ignored his enemies, addressing his rebuttal directly to Protarus. "She isn't for sport, Majesty," he said, "but for gain. And as for seeing us, it surprises me that ones so perceptive as Prince Luka and so intuitive as Lord Fari haven't noted the woman is blind. Ergo, she isn't here for killing, but for your Majesty's possible edification."

Kalasariz shot quick gloats of victory at Luka and Fari, thinking, There you go, you sons of pig lizards. Root around in that trash and see if I've left anything tasty behind!

Iraj peered at the woman, noting for the first time her disfigured eyes, which were entirely white as if they had been permanently rolled up into her head. The king's wolfish features dissolved into something quite human, featuring the same bright and handsome smile that had once won him so many ardent friends and supporters.

"She really is blind," he said, smile growing broader. "I like this. Now the question is entirely open on whether we kill her or not. It's been a long time since precedent was challenged."

Iraj leaned an arm on his throne, cupping his chin in his palm. He studied the old woman for a moment, noting that although her dress was stained with dirt, the material was quite expensive. "Tell me, Granny," he said, "What do you have to say about all this?"

"Same as I said 'afore, Majesty," she replied. "Old Sheesan ain't for killin'. And never mind I'm blind. Don't take eyes to know yers're shape changers. Old Sheesan can smell the wolf in yer!"

"Let me kill the old bitch, then," Prince Luka said. "Since there's no longer a question of her lack of sight saving her."

The old woman snorted and turned her blind face toward Luka. "Beggin' yer pardon, Lord," she said, "but that'd be about the stupidest thing yers could do. Yer should count yer blessin's that I'm even here 'afore yers."

Kalasariz laughed. "It's true," he said. "We didn't capture her, you know. She turned herself in and demanded to see someone in charge." He tapped his breast. "Which is when I stepped in."

He turned to Iraj. "In case you haven't noticed, Majesty," he said, "the woman is a witch. She claims she can use her witchery to help us track down Safar Timura."

Luka and Fari made derisive noises, displaying rare agreement. Iraj made no comment, but he stared at the old woman in disbelief.

Finally, he said, "Are you saying that this hag can do what all of us combined haven't been able to accomplish?"

Kalasariz started to speak but the old woman beat him to it with a prolonged bout of cackling and coughing.

"Hag, you say?" she chortled. "Just an old bag of bones with a hank of hair on top. That's what'cher thinks of me, does yer?"

Then she composed herself, crossing her arms over wizened breasts. "All's it'll cost yers is a purse of gold, Majesty," she said. "A nice fat one, if yer please. And I'll deliver Safar Timura to yers soon enough."

"I can't believe I'm listening to this," Luka said. "An old woman dares to ask a price for what she should give us freely. What is Esmir coming to? Is there no dignity left in this court?"

"If it's dignity yer wantin', Me Lord," the old woman said, "it'll cost yers *two* purses, not one. Dignity spells don't come cheap, 'specially when I gots some fiend like yerself fer a client. No insult intended, I'm sure. I'm only speakin' the facts, here." She sniffed at the air and wrinkled her nose. "Shape changers make such a stink," she went on. "Can't do nothin' 'bout that. Even if yer was to give me three purses of gold."

While Luka was choking on this insult—to the vast enjoyment of the others—the witch turned her blind face to Iraj.

"Purse a gold's me price, Majesty," she said. "But most of it won't be fer the likes of me, if it gives yer comfort. Be lucky if I can keep a coin fer meself, as matter of fact. The rest'll go to me dear sisters of the crucible."

Iraj gawked at her, then he looked at Kalasariz. "What in the blazes is she talking about?" he asked. "Purses of gold and sisters of cups, or whatever. Is this a jest, my lord? If it is, it's in damned poor taste."

The old woman started to speak again, but Kalasariz yanked viciously on the chain, silencing her.

"It's quite simple, Majesty," the spy master said. "This remarkable woman is not a thing of beauty, I admit; or at least not in any conventional sense. She's beautiful enough, however, when judged by her position and talents.

"It seems that this . . . this . . . creature . . . is quite an influential person in her own sphere. It so happens that Old Sheesan is an elder in the Witches' Guild, which has members in every city and hamlet in Esmir.

"What she proposes to do is to contact every member of her Guild, promising fat rewards for any and all sightings of Safar Timura. The earlier we get notice, the richer the reward. Finally, if a witch should trap Lord Timura, or one of his key people, there will be a special bounty above and beyond all other rewards."

Old Sheesan raised a finger. "And I'll be wantin' commissions on all's a them," she said. "Includin' the bounty."

"What a greedy thing she is," Lord Fari said admiringly. "But she makes such good sense I'm inclined to recommend it." He bowed to Kalasariz. "A remarkable find, my good fellow. My congratulations."

"Well, I don't like it at all," Luka grumbled.

The old woman sniffed. "What's not to like? A bit a gold gets the whole sisterhood in yer camp. Witches all over Esmir'll be on the lookout for this Safar Timura feller. And they'll be at it day and night, I tells yer. Day and night. Sniffin' ever stranger comes to their village, tossin' bones or lookin' into their crystals for some sign of him.

"Time's are hard for witches just now. What with droughts and plagues makin' money so scarce. Use to get a bit of silver for yer spell makin'. Curin' boils, or castin' the evil eye and such. Now, yer lucky if yer can get a skinny chicken for yer pot. Which is why yer gettin' us so cheap, Me Lords. A whole army of witches for a single purse of gold."

At first Iraj had been merely amused by Old Sheesan, but the more she talked the more amusement dissolved into intense interest. As he stared at her, Iraj suddenly caught a flash of someone quite different than the toothless hag standing before him. It was as if curtains were momentarily parted to reveal a shimmering creature of incredible beauty. Then the curtains closed and the image was gone.

The old woman cackled knowingly—as if she had just shared a great secret with the king.

Iraj gripped the throne arms, so overcome by emotion that his wolf snout erupted through his face.

"Woman," he said, "if you bring me Safar Timura's head I will make you richer than any queen."

The old woman giggled, sounding remarkably girlish. "Imagine that," she said, primping her greasy hair. "Old Sheesan a queen!"

And Iraj thought, yes, yes I can imagine.

CHAPTER ELEVEN
MISSION TO NAADAN

The demon glared down at Safar, fangs bared, yellow eyes narrow with suspicion. "State your business, human!"

Safar staved off nausea as the soldier's foul breath washed over him and forced his most jovial smile. "Profit and entertainment, sergeant," Safar said. "If not the first, why we'll settle for the second. Especially if it comes with ale."

Beside him, Leiria smacked her lips. "I hear Nadaan makes the best ale in all Esmir," she said.

The demon soldier peered at her, noting her dirty mail and even dirtier sword. His eyes swept on, taking in the ox-drawn wagon and the three heavily-laden camels. Besides Safar and Leiria, who were both leading horses, there were four other humans—a driver for the wagon and three men to tend the camels. There was something decidedly shabby about the group. Their clothes were unkempt, the animals' fur was clotted—even the canvas covering of the wagon was filthy.

The demon snorted in disgust. "You call this a caravan?"

Safar sighed, leaning against the portable barricade blocking the road. Five soldiers—three of them human and all wearing the uniforms of Protarus' troops—guarded the barricade. About a mile beyond were the Naadan city walls.

"It's a long story sergeant," he said. "And not a very pleasant one, either. A year ago I was sitting pretty. A dozen wagons, a score of camels plus horses and men and . . ." he glanced at Leiria, lowering his voice, " . . . And I had a proper guard, if you know what I mean. Six outriders and a retired captain of the king's own to lead them."

He let his voice rise again. "But you don't want to hear my tale of woe, sergeant. Times being what they are, there's hundreds of poor merchants just like me all over Esmir. So broke we clatter like a glazier's cart on a badly cobbled street. All we ask is a chance to get back on top again. Hell's, I'd settle for just staying even!"

The demon shrugged, massive shoulders rising like mailed mountains. "What do I care, human? You and your entire shabby lot can turn into dust and blow across the desert, for all it means to me."

He jabbed a taloned-thumb at the gates of Naadan. From beyond came the caterwaul of bad music and the babble of a great crowd. "Besides, rules'r rules. If you wanna to sell your trash at the Naadan Fair you gotta have a permit. No riffraff allowed. And that's my job—to keep out the riffraff."

Once again his eyes swept Safar's ragged outfit, but this time his look was more meaningful. "Smells like riffraff to me," he said.

Safar slipped a fat purse from his sleeve. He gave it a good shake so the silver rattled.

The demon's long, scaly ears perked up at the sound.

"Are you sure we can't come to some sort of arrangement, sergeant?" he asked. "Hmm?"

*   *   *

As they came to the city gates Leiria cantered closer to Safar. "You're getting to be such a good liar," she teased. "Aren't you ashamed of yourself?"

Actually, he was. As far as Leiria and the others knew they were in Naadan on a routine raiding mission. Which was far from the truth.

"I'm not ashamed one bit," Safar laughed. "But I am damned thirsty. In fact, before we get down to the business of robbery why don't we try some of that famous Naadan ale?"

Leiria wrinkled her hose. "I was just looking for something nice to say," she laughed. "Actually, I hear their ale tastes like mare's piss," she said. "But he looked like the sort of creature who liked mare's piss, if you know what I mean."

She made a rueful face. "Guess I'm getting pretty good at lying myself."

Safar flinched and looked away so she didn't see the guilt in his eyes.

*   *   *

Inside the gates all was madness. It was the last day of the fair and the streets were packed with revelers. Traffic was a great drunken weave with no apparent purpose or goal. There were tribes and villagers from all over the vast high desert region. There were painted faces, scarred faces, veiled faces, faces with filed teeth, faces pierced with jewelry, and, yes, even a few faces that would have been ordinary except they stood out among so many exotics.

Until recent years the Naadan Harvest Festival—which the fair celebrated—had been a minor event that drew only nearby farmers and herdsmen. It certainly hadn't been large enough to entice Methydia to stop with her circus when she and Safar had passed this way. The circus had instead gone to Silver Rivers, a much larger and richer town and many miles distant. But a series of disasters had reduced Silver Rivers to a ghost city, where the only inhabitants were bandits. Silver Rivers' misfortune, however, had been Naadan's good luck. Five years of rich harvests—so rare in recent times that it seemed a miracle—had turned the city into a thriving center of life and commerce.

The once sleepy water hole in the middle of the Northern Plains now enticed people from hundreds of miles around—including Safar Timura and his band, who quickly unburdened themselves of their paltry caravan by simply walking away from it. Sharp-eyed thieves led the wagon and animals off before Safar and the others had melted into the crowd. Just as the shrewd demon sergeant had noted the caravan was worthless. The goods were trash. The animals spavined. They were all surplus booty from an encounter that had gone badly for a group of seedy bandits.

"So much for my debut as a merchant prince," Safar joked, after they'd all found a grog shop and had ordered up mugs of cold wine. "Shed my whole caravan and didn't earn a clipped copper for my troubles."

Renor, who had been driving the wagon, snorted. "Oh, I don't know about that, sir. We couldn't throw the stuff away or bury it because it'd give us away. And the animals were not only useless, but eating us out of hearth and home. Hells, we made a profit just by getting rid of them."

He took a long happy drink from his mug. "Least, that's how I see it, Lord Tim—" and one of his companions elbowed him before he could get the whole name out.

Realizing he was in the middle of a packed bar, and someone might overhear him, Renor blushed and ducked his head. "Sorry," he said. "I'm not used to so many people about."

A man staggered into their table, sloshing his drink all over them. "That's what I tole him," the man roared into Safar's face. "An' if he dares say the same thin' to me again, while I'll spit in his face! The dirty son of a . . ." and then the man realized Safar was a stranger and his voice trailed off. He burped and pulled back. "You're not my friend," he said, surprised. Then he shrugged. "Just don't tell nobody, right?"

"Right!" Safar said and the man staggered away. He turned back to Renor. "No need for sorries," he said. "In this place we're as safe as in the middle of a forest."

Unnoticed by them, across the room the drunk suddenly straightened. He looked back at Safar's table, measuring with sober eyes. Then he smiled and exited the tavern whistling a merry tune.

Back at the table, Safar refilled everyone's mugs, saying, "You're in charge of this little expedition, Leiria. Why don't you give us our orders now so we can drink up and be on our way?"

Leiria nodded. "This should be fairly simple," she said. "Easier than most, as a matter of fact, because we have a good map of Naadan, thanks to that little trove of maps we got from Coralean.

"You've all got your copies, right?" The men all nodded, but just the same they patted their pockets to make sure. "And you all know which area you're to do your snooping in, right?" More nods.

"Fine. Now, here's what to look for. If you have barracks in your sector, check to see how many beds they have. That'll tell us the exact number of soldiers on hand during normal times. My guess is that most of the soldiers we're seeing are here temporarily for fair duty and will be gone within a day or two.

"Also, if there are any storehouses in your area of search, see what kinds of grains, food, clothing, etcetera are inside. The more portable the better. Pay close attention to this, because we want to have a good shopping list drawn up when we show up here with our army to talk things over with the king. Quintal, I think his name is.

"We also need first hand knowledge of all the ways in and out of the city. Maps are good, but they aren't always up to date, or even accurate when they are. We don't want to have to beat a hasty retreat, then find that the gate we're heading for—a gate clearly indicated on our map—has long since been covered up. Or was just a royal architect's dream that never got funding."

She looked at each man. "Is that all clear? You understand what you're supposed to do and how to do it? I know we've gone over it all before, but I want to make sure. We can't afford any mistakes. Protarus' soldiers are none too bright, but they can be as error-prone as they like. For us one mistake might be a death sentence."

Everyone said they understood. Then, to avoid suspicion by getting up and leaving en-masse, they drifted away one-by-one, until only Leiria remained. She stared at him, eyes narrowed with sudden suspicion.

"What's going on, Safar?" she asked

"Going on?" Safar said, all innocence. "Why, what ever do you mean?"

She kept staring, eyes ferreting for some sign beneath Safar's bland features. Finally she sighed. "Never mind," she said. "I'm sorry I asked."

And then she was gone. Safar caught a serving wench by the elbow and ordered up another jug of wine.

His assignment was to investigate the city's central arena where the sporting matches were going on—and to get a close look at the Naadanian king. At least that's what

Leiria thought. Actually, Safar's mission was much more difficult.

Asper had bade him to go to Naadan. For what purpose, he hadn't said. Safar grimaced, wishing the master wizard had given him the smallest hint of what he was supposed to accomplish in Naadan. All Safar could think to do was go about his thieving business and pray for a sign.

Then the wench came with the jug and he set about the impromptu task of restoring his confidence. He settled back in his chair and let the warm sounds of the tavern flow over him. It had been a long time since he'd been in such easy company. When he was a student in Walaria his happiest hours had been spent at the *Foolsmire*, a tavern catering to the student trade that was known for its cheap wine and even cheaper books.

Safar took a big gulp of wine, enjoying the feel and taste of it going down. Strange thing—he remembered liking wine in those days, sometimes in excess if truth be known. But he didn't remember *needing* it. This wine he definitely needed.

And with good reason, he thought. At one time, the odds against him ever reaching Naadan had seemed insurmountable.

He drank his wine, remembering . . .

*   *   *

It was an epic flight, an odyssey of terror. Panic lurking like cliff edges on every side as Safar used all his tricks, plus inventing scores more, to keep himself and his charges alive and out of Iraj's clutches.

The first days were so desperate that Safar didn't have much memory of them. Everything was a blur of hysterical people and animals and badly packed baggage trains careening from one mountain pass to another. Safar had a vague route in mind to confuse their pursuers, but it was all Leiria and her scouts could do to keep the Kyranians on the right track.

The journey might have been made easier if Safar could have commanded the leading party—his presence alone tended to calm people. But out of necessity he had taken up position well in the rear with Renor and his friend, Sinch, to assist him. He peppered the trail with magical spells and traps to confound the enemy. He also triggered a whole series of avalanches, blocking not only the passes they'd pushed through, but all others as well so Iraj's scouts couldn't tell which way they'd taken.

Luck was also with them. As they were coming out of the mountains into the northern wastelands an unseasonable storm roared in from the Great Sea, hammering the ranges with icy blizzards and bringing all of Iraj's forces to a miserable halt. Meanwhile, the Kyranians were safely in the rocky foothills and Safar and Leiria only needed to keep the villagers moving through the heavy rainstorm.

When the rains stopped they found themselves in a bleak landscape of blasted stone. Oddly formed peaks burst out of blackened ground that was cut by hundreds of ravines and gullies, many so deep and broad and filled with storm-swollen creeks and rivers it took days to negotiate them.

It was in these badlands that Safar performed the greatest non-magical tricks of his life. Food was scarce and water came only in amounts that were treacherous—swift moving streams that could sweep away a wagon and its contents, or tracks that remained waterless for day after throat-parching day. To shake off Iraj he relied on Coralean's maps of all the secret caravan routes that crept through the north country from the Gods Divide all the way to Caspan and the Great Sea. All the main trade centers were also well-documented, including routes meant to avoid the clusters of bandits that prowled the outskirts of civilization.

The sheer number of Kyranians, plus their lack of experience on the road, nearly defeated Safar at the start. Fortunately they had reached the relative safety of the badlands, with all its switchbacks and secret trails, before Safar was overwhelmed by the sheer logistics of the expedition.

When they'd abandoned and burned their village, the Kyranians had fled with little thought of what they ought to carry away with them. Some households tried to transport all their worldly goods—from kitchen stoves to festival dinner service. Others only snatched icons off the wall, cats from the hearth seat and lucky cicada cages made of dried reeds that buzzed like supportive orchestras when the insects sang their songs of romantic longing. The Kyranians pressed everything into service that could carry weight for their flight—from lumbering ox-powered freight wagons down to sledges drawn by goats. They also tried to take all their animals—goats by the hundreds, oxen by the score and llamas and camels by the dozens. Even favorite horses long retired from toil were brought along. The consequence of this chaos was an enormous unwieldy mass of people and animals spread all over the landscape. Heavily-ladened wagons broke down, animals scattered and were lost, one pregnant woman and a several elders died of exhaustion.

But when all seemed lost, Safar dug keeper into his sack of leadership secrets to rally his people and put steel back into their spines. The villagers stripped themselves down to the barest necessities, burying tons of abandoned goods and household items in places where Iraj's scouts couldn't find them. When they set out again they were a disciplined force that got better with each passing day. Thanks to Leiria and Sergeant Dario, most of the young men were being turned into a skilled fighting unit, so they had little to fear from bandits and rogue soldiers.

When supplies ran low Safar used Coralean's maps to find secret routes to the richest towns and cities and after he'd raided them the Kyranians were able to vanish with ease into hidden passes and deep ravines.

To keep his people going, Safar dangled the vision of Syrapis before them—a paradise to replace the one they'd lost. Meanwhile, he kept edging them toward Naadan. The city was to the north, as was the Great Sea, so no one guessed his intentions.

It didn't hurt that Safar wasn't that sure of them himself. However, after worrying on that bone until it was splinters, he gave up. Frustrating as it was, he had to let the winds of fate carry him where they would—as long as they headed north. To keep his will focused he reduced everything to a simple mantra: Naadan, Caluz, Syrapis. Naadan, Caluz, Syrapis. Naadan, Caluz . . .

. . . Syrapis!

He wondered what waited for him there. Prayed that whatever it was, it would at long last answer the two questions that had haunted and driven him his entire adult life:

What was killing the world?

And how could he stop it?

*   *   *

Safar downed his wine and poured another. At the rate he'd been traveling, he thought, he'd die of old age before he reached that fabled isle.

What was Asper's line? Oh, yes, " . . . All who dwell 'neath Heaven's vaults . . . live in dread . . . of that monster, Time . . ."

Monster, indeed.

He got up to leave, nearly stumbling over a skinny little crone who had been leaning, unnoticed, against his table.

"Pardon, Granny," he said politely. But as he spoke he felt a sudden prickle of magic sniffing along his skin.

The crone grinned a toothless grin, saying, "Alms, master. Alms for a poor old woman."

Safar kept his features mild, showing no reaction to her witch's magic. He cast a spell to ward off her snooping, fishing in his purse for a few coppers to cover his actions.

"Here you go, Granny," he said, plopping the coins into her outstretched claw. "Make your prayers sweet for me tonight."

He moved on, pushing through the crowd until he reached the door. As he went out he turned sideways to peek at the witch's face. She looked most disappointed. Just beyond her he saw a familiar figure. It was the drunk who had bumped into his table not long before.

You don't need a Master's License from Walaria University to figure that one out, he thought as he walked down the street. Obviously, the witch was looking for him and that fake drunk was in her employ. Iraj had offered a fortune for Safar's head and this wasn't the first time he'd encountered reward seekers. They were easily spotted and avoided, so normally he didn't trouble himself. However, he'd never encountered a bounty-hunting witch before and it made him wonder if some new element had been added to the game.

By the time he reached the arena he'd decided it was only a coincidence that this particular reward seeker was a witch. He bought a ticket at the gate and went inside, putting the crone from his mind. He did go more cautiously, however, his magical senses wary for more signs of danger.

The highlight of the Naadan Fair was the wrestling tournament, an ancient sport taken to a high art in this region. Hundreds competed in the opening matches but their numbers were whittled down as the festival progressed until the final day when the last two men competed for the championship.

Safar bought a bowl of hot peppered noodles from a vendor and joined the specta-tors in the stands. Some were cheering the action on the big grassy field, but others paid no attention at all—gossiping or eating or scolding unruly children, while on the field several pairs of beefy champions grappled with one another, heaving and hauling as they attempted to hurl their opponents to the ground. In Naadan wrestling matches often went on for hours before a winner was decided, so the spectators behaved accordingly, becoming only fully absorbed at key moments in the matches.

While Safar ate his noodles he casually searched the stands until he found the wide stone box with its gaily colored awning shading King Quintal and his family. The royal box was just across from him, so he could see the king quite clearly. He was a big man, a once muscular man who had gone to fat. His face was puffed and red in the places his gray-streaked beard didn't cover. While around him his children and wives cheered the match, the king watched sullenly, drinking deeply and frequently from his cup.

"Looks like the king's drunk again," said the man sitting next Safar. He turned and saw a pleasant little fellow with a pudgy face and a wine-stained robe. "Seems like Quin-tal's always drunk these days."

Pudge Face lifted up a leather bag and shot a stream of wine down his throat. He wiped his mouth, cleaned his hands on his robes, which were of a rich material, then said, "Bad example for our children, if you ask me."

He offered Safar the wine bag. After he drank, Safar passed it back, saying, "Glad I'm not king. Can't think of a more boring life. Being a good example, I mean."

Pudge Face chuckled. "No chance of that for me," he said. "But I never wanted to be champion, much less king. Got a nice little shop, a good wife and five hard-working daughters to keep it running while I do what I like." He slapped the wine bag. "And what I like is *this*."

Safar glanced around at the crowd, many of whom were as red-faced with drink as Quintal. "I'll wager Naadan is as silent as a temple vestry when this festival is over," he said.

Pudge Face laughed. "Whole city will be passed out for at least a week," he said. "Nothing, but nothing gets done after a harvest festival. Nobody on the streets, that's for sure, unless they're on their way to a healer to get something for their sick heads and bellies. Hells, even the taverns are closed because the innkeepers are as bad off as the rest of us."

Safar was delighted with this intelligence. The festival was officially over tonight. That would give him a day or two, if needed, to track down the answer to Asper's mysterious command. It'd also make the supply raid much easier. They could ride right up to the king's palace and face him unopposed. The escape ought to be just as easy. Few would see them go and those who did would be in no shape to follow.

The crowd burst into cheers and Safar looked up to see the reason for the sudden mass interest. Out on the field there were only two wrestlers left. Their victims were being helped away by officials in flowing red robes with yellow sashes and high-topped boots.

The victors were huge men, wearing only short leather breeches with wide belts. Their bodies were streaked with so much blood that it was hard to tell the difference between them and the losers who had already been carried off the field. They stumbled as officials led them into the center of the field for the final match. The crowd shouted its appreciation and everyone seemed to be scrambling to get a bet down.

"What's going on?" Safar asked his new friend.

"This is what we've been waiting for!" Pudge Face said excitedly. "Finally, we're going for the championship! Won't be long and we'll see who's the new Titan."

He pointed at the wrestlers. One was entirely bald, the other shaggy as a bear. "The hairy one's Butar," he said. "The other's called Ulan. He's the most popular wrestler in Naadan. And favored in this match. Hells, Ulan could be king himself one day. Which would be a big improvement over Quintal, that's for certain."

"What's the prize?" Safar asked, wisely skirting the political issue of who'd make the better king.

"Whoever wins today," Pudge Face said, "gets to put Brave Titan in front of his name. He'll also be rich for life. Plus, this year, there's a special prize. To thank the gods for it being such a good harvest year."

At that moment Safar felt a tingling sensation against his chest and his hand came up unconsciously to touch the horse amulet dangling beneath his shirt. To his surprise it was quite warm and was growing warmer by the minute. He clutched it, wondering what was happening.

Just then six riders dressed in flowing, calf-length robes, rode onto the field. They appeared to be some sort of honor guard and they pranced about showing off to the crowd. What they were presenting soon became apparent as two men trotted out, leading a magnificent horse onto the field.

Safar felt a shock jump from the amulet to his skin and he nearly cried out—not from pain, because the shock was more surprising than hurtful. His entire attention was suddenly fixed on that horse.

It was the most remarkable animal he had ever seen. Safar was a man of the mountains and no great horse lover. Plainsmen like Iraj, who spent their lives on horseback, practically worshipped the animals. To Safar they were merely useful creatures under certain circumstances—circumstances rarely met in the snowy passes of the mountains. He liked them well enough and had even encountered a few with interesting personalities. On the whole, however, he thought a good goat or llama was far more valuable to a Kyranian.

But this creature seemed to exist on an entirely different plane than all other animals of its kind. He was almost godlike in beauty, so handsomely muscled he seemed like a great work of art from a master sculptor. He was tall, taller than any horse Safar had ever seen. He was the color of fresh cream, a deep and glossy off-white so full of depths he seemed to glow. His feet were black, as if he wore short boots on his hooves and he had a lighting bolt of black on his handsome forehead.

He ignored the crowd as he came out, giving off an aura of royal aloofness. When he came to the center he tossed his head high and pawed the ground as if he were anxious to be off on more important business than mere adulation.

Then Safar had a second shock as the horse turned his sculpted head and looked in Safar's direction. The look flew across the distance and found him and he had a sudden feeling of warm and glad recognition. It was as if two souls had met and in the meeting an instant bond had been formed.

Safar whispered, "Hello, old friend!" And the horse rose up on its hind legs, pawing the air and shrilling a glad greeting.

And he thought, this is it! This is what Asper wanted me to find.

Then all was confusion as the horse was led to the side and trumpets announced the final match. The last note had barely faded away when Ulan The Bald rushed his opponent. It was as if the sight of the horse had given him new life and he grasped Butar by the belt and hoisted him off the ground. The crowd screamed in ecstasy as all the days of suspense ended in a quick, breath-bursting second as Ulan slammed his opponent onto the ground. Trumpets blared, drums rolled and big kites of every color were launched into the sky, carrying exploding fireworks in their tails.

Safar didn't see any of it. He was concentrating solely on the horse, who stood patiently in solitary splendor at the far side of the field.

"Now we'll see if there's going to be a challenge," Pudge Face said.

Safar, half in a daze, turned to him. "What do you mean?"

"Anyone can challenge the champion," he said. "At least that's the fiction. In a minute the king's gonna ask the crowd in if there is anyone among us who can best Ulan." Pudge Face took a drink, laughing at the same time and making a bigger mess of his robe. "As if any of us could outwrestle a Brave Titan!"

"What happens if someone does?"

Pudge Face laughed again. "Don't be ridiculous," he said. "These men are not only giants, but they train all their lives. They know all the tricks."

"Still," Safar said, "what if such a thing occurred?"

"Then they'd win the title, plus the riches, plus the horse. But if you're considering some sort of wager, keep your money in your purse, my friend. No challenger has ever defeated a champion in the history of the games."

Pudge Face looked over at the horse. "More's the pity," he said. "A stranger could keep the horse for his own."

"What do you mean?" Safar asked.

"Well, this particular horse is meant for sacrifice. That's Ulan's gift to the gods."

Safar jumped at this, as if stung. But the little man didn't notice. He'd just tried to take a drink but found his wine sack was empty. He sighed, regretting his generosity. But that couldn't be taken back, so he looked across the field at the horse and gave still another sigh, but deeper. Sometimes life seemed so terribly unfair.

"Ah, look at that!" he said. "I'm as religious as the next person. Praise the gods once a week and try to do right in between. But the sight of that beautiful creature prancing about so proud ... and knowing the poor thing's fate ... is enough to make you wonder if the gods are right in their heads.

"Does our heavenly family really want to see this handsome creature handed over to thin-lipped priests with sharp little knives?" He shuddered. "Holy purpose or not, what a horrid fate for something so magnificent."

He turned to Safar. "With a little drink in you it makes you wonder if the gods even—"

Pudge Face stopped in mid-flow. The seat beside him was empty!

As Safar raced down the stairs he didn't notice the old crone reach through the crowd to snatch at his tunic with her long nails. He only felt resistance and he tugged hard. The fabric ripped and the witch snatched back a claw full of shredded cloth. He ran on, while behind him the witch chortled in glee.

"It's him!" she cackled. "I jus' know it is!"

Out on the field, Safar trotted toward Ulan. The officials stood back, incredulous. Who was this lowly creature who dared challenge a Brave Titan? Safar stripped off his shirt and as he ran the amulet bounced on his chest. Each time it struck he felt a warm glow. It was such a strong feeling that any misgivings dissolved before they were fully formed.

As he approached Ulan he heard the stallion whinny and he saw the two minders grappling with the animal, who was struggling mightily against the ropes.

Then he was standing before Ulan, who grinned at him through bloody gums and shattered teeth. Ulan stared down from a great height. Safar was tall for a Kyranian, but Ulan took him by at least a foot. Safar was slender, but broad of chest and shoulder. Against Ulan he seemed puny, a weakling with wrists that could be snapped easily and a slim bow of a backbone that could be crushed under Ulan's mighty feet.

The wrestler's bloody grin grew wider. He rose up, blowing his body out to intimidate his opponent. His brow beetled, making his eyes as small as spear points. He clapped his horny hands together, making a sound like thunder.

"Who are you, little man," he intoned, "to challenge the great Ulan?"

"All I want is the horse," Safar said, trying to throw his enemy off the mark. "You can keep everything else after I defeat you."

Ulan's big head split in two and he guffawed a great guffaw. "You can wish in one hand and defecate in the other and you'll soon see what comes out in the balance," Ulan said.

An official locked a wide belt around Safar's waist. "You know the rules," he said.

Safar shook head. "Actually," he said, "I've never done this before."

Both the official and Ulan were incredulous. "What a fool you are, little man," the wrestler said.

The official shrugged. "It's your life," he said to Safar. "You can do what you want with it." Then: "The rules are simple. Kicking, punching, gouging, neck breaking, whatever, are permitted. The fight ends when one man lifts another off his feet by the belt, then throws him to the ground. Getting knocked to the ground or slipping and falling doesn't count for anything. Got it?"

Safar gulped. "I think so," he said.

The trumpet blared and Ulan advanced on Safar, enormous arms outstretched to catch him whichever way he dodged.

Safar cast a spell of confusion and leaped to the left. Ulan lofted a clumsy swing, missing with a blow so strong that Safar heard the punch explode the air as it sailed past his head.

Ulan made a lumbering recovery and Safar grabbed him by the big leather belt and heaved.

Ulan looked down on him, amused. He spread his feet and became a weight that could not be moved. "Heave away, little man," he mocked.

Safar gasped, but it was like trying to pick up a mountain.

Then a blow like an unleashed siege machine sent him flying. As he sailed through the air he heard the stallion nicker in alarm. It gave him strength and as Safar hit the ground he tuck-rolled to his feet.

The Brave Titan of Naadan bellowed and swept down on him like an avalanche.

CHAPTER TWELVE

SAFAR IN CHAINS

Uh, oh!" Palimak said. "Looks like my father's in trouble."

"Let me see! Let me see!" Gundara demanded, pushing forward.

"Will you please!" Gundaree complained. "You are such a rude Favorite! Mother would be so displeased!"

"Just shut up about Mother!" Gundara shouted. "You hear me? Shut up!"

Palimak, who was crouched on the tent floor peering into a wide, silvery bowl, looked up at them with an expression of utter disgust on his elfin face. The two Favorites could only appear together in his presence. But they squabbled so much sometimes he wondered if it was worth the extra strength he got from them.

"Stop your arguing this instant," he said, copying the scolding tones adults used when chastising him.

Gundara pointed at his twin, tiny demon's face all screwed up in outraged innocence. "He wouldn't let me see," he whined.

Gundaree sneered, his little human face a portrait of lordly condescension. "I only asked him kindly not to shove," he replied.

Palimak sighed. "Why do you two always make everything so hard?" he said. "Now, look. There's plenty of room for everybody." He pointed to one end of the bowl. "You stand here," he said to Gundara, making his high child's voice as commanding as possible. "And you can stand over there," he told Gundaree, indicating the opposite side. "And hurry up, please. I told you my father is in trouble. Big trouble!"

Chastened, the Favorites obeyed. When they were set Palimak waved his hand over the bowl and a cloud of blue steam hissed up.

Gundaree sneezed. "What an awful odor," he said in cultured tones.

"Just shut up and look," Palimak said.

"Don't say shut up," Gundara admonished. "You're not supposed to say shut up."

Palimak snorted, but didn't reply. Instead he peered into the bowl. The smoke vanished and the whole inside of the bowl became a miniature of the Naadan Stadium. The audience cheered from the stands, which ran all along the side of the bowl. At the bottom was the grassy wrestling field where his father grappled with Ulan.

"I wonder why he's fighting?" Palimak mused.

"Who knows why the Master does anything?" Gundaree said. "Except, show him an impossibility and he'll attempt it."

Gundara winced as Ulan struck again and Safar was knocked backwards. "Ouch!" he said. "I'll bet that hurt!"

"We have to help him," Palimak said.

"That's all very well and good," Gundaree said. "But the question, Little Master, is how?"

*   *   *

Safar scrambled to his feet, dodging just as Ulan reached for him. He came around, joining his fists together into a club. He swung, connected with Ulan's kidney and heard a satisfying grunt of pain.

But the giant wrestler was used to much worse punishment and just as Safar was forming another spell of confusion a huge hand snatched out and caught Safar by the belt.

The crowd roared. The final moment had come. Now that Ulan had a grip on Safar's belt all he had to do was lift him off the ground then slam him into the earth. That would certainly be easy enough—compared to the massive Ulan, Safar was less than a feather.

Safar heard the horse shrill as Ulan hoisted him on high.

Without warning a great wind swept into the arena and bowled them both off their feet. Safar landed on top and he heard the breath whoosh out of Ulan. Some kind of miracle had just occurred, but Safar wasn't thinking about miracles just then. Instead he was backing up as fast as he could because Ulan was already bounding to his feet.

Another blast of wind struck, this one bearing rain. It hit them like a tropical torrent and in moments the whole field was turned into a slippery river of mud.

Ulan kept coming, looking like a sea god as he burst through all that rain. He didn't look so godlike when he reached for Safar, skittered in the mud and fell backward, sending up a dirty spray that struck Safar full in the face.

Safar sputtered, rocked back and then his feet abandoned him and it was his turn to go arse over hearth kettle.

He tried to rise but it was like walking on a boatload of fish and he was flailing wildly, arms and legs going every way except the intended direction. Safar finally rested on his back. Through the heavy rain all he could see was the hazy outline of the cheering crowd.

Safar sensed Ulan moving toward him and he flopped over, pushing himself to his hands and knees. He found himself looking straight into the wrestler's giant face. The Titan of Naadan was also on his hands and knees—nearly incapacitated from laughter.

"What a match, little man!" Ulan roared. "A match that will never be repeated in a thousand years. Nay, ten thousand, if the world should live that long." He reared back, muddy hands gripping Safar by the belt. "Unfortunately, it's time for this match to end, my small friend," he said.

And he lifted Safar over his head, then gently dropped him to the ground.

Safar had lost.

Ulan was helping him to his feet when the rain stopped as suddenly as it began.

The crowd cheered and the wrestler pounded his back, knocking the wind from him. "What a brave little man you are," he said. "But let me give you some advice. If you should visit us next year, don't try it again."

"Believe me, I won't," Safar promised. "I feel as if I've been run over by a freight wagon."

He smiled at the big man, but his thoughts were on the cause of his sudden madness. Safar glanced over at the horse who was looking straight at him, head jerking up and down. The animal's hide was shining from the rain, sun dancing on the high gloss. Safar sent a silent promise that he'd be back no matter what and the horse seemed to understand for it reared back and pawed the air, whinnying loudly.

"Here, what's this?" Ulan shouted.

Safar turned to see a group of guards descending on him. Rough hands grabbed his arms and twisted them back behind him.

"This is no way to treat a challenger!" Ulan roared. He stepped forward, threatening.

"Don't do anything you'll be sorry for, Ulan," said one of the men—an officer from his rank tabs. "We have reason to believe this man is a great criminal. Wanted by Iraj Protarus, himself."

Ulan stopped. He looked at Safar with sad eyes. "Is this true, little man?" he asked. "Are you indeed a criminal? If you're not, speak up! You have won the respect of Ulan, the Titan." He gestured at the guards, all strong, tough men. "And I will break their heads for insulting you."

Safar sighed. "Don't get yourself in trouble over me, friend," he said. "I'll be fine after all this is straightened out."

As they dragged him away a familiar old woman came scampering up. "Yer've just made this old granny a rich woman, Safar Timura," she cackled. "Thankee very much fer that!"

*   *   *

"Oops!" Gundara said.

Gundaree grimaced. "What a terrible development," he said.

Palimak groaned. "What'll we do?"

Gundara shrugged. "Not much we can do," he said. "Oh, well. He was a good Master, as masters go." He saw Palimak's sad face and try to cheer him up. "But we still have you, Little Master."

"Now, there's a silver lining if I ever saw one," Gundaree said in his mocking voice. "I'm sure Palimak is just *so* pleased to hear the news that he's about to inherit."

"Oh, shut up, you!" Gundara grumbled. "I was only trying to be thoughtful."

"What if we made it rain again?" Palimak said. "Except this time, we don't let it stop." He stretched out his hands. "For a long, long time."

"What good will that do?" Gundara asked.

Palimak frowned, thinking. "Well, if it keeps raining . . . they can't do anything to him, right? And they can't send anybody to tell that damned old Iraj, either. I mean, if we make it rain hard enough the roads will be too muddy. Then Aunt Leiria will have time to rescue my father."

"I don't know if I'm up to it," Gundaree said. "I'm faint from exhaustion as it is. Rain isn't easy. Especially a prolonged rain."

"What a puny," Gundara scorned. "Tired out from a little cloud squeezing."

Gundaree slapped his forehead in exasperation. "Why must you always contradict me?"

"I don't," Gundara said.

"Yes you do."

"No I don't."

"You're contradicting me now."

"That's because you're stupid, stupid!"

"What about this?" Palimak broke in. "If I get some bread and cheese for you, Gundaree. And some honeyed figs for you, Gundara. And you ate them all up. Why, you probably wouldn't be tired anymore, right? And we could keep on making it rain."

Both Favorites were delighted at this solution.

"I must say, Little Master," Gundaree commented, "you *do* have the makings of a

369

most remarkable diplomat."

Palimak frowned. "What's a diplomat?"

"I'm not sure," Gundara said. "But I think it has something to do with always having lots of nice treats for your Favorites."

Palimak snorted. "That's ridiculous. Who'd make up a word to mean something like that?"

"Some very wise men, Little Master," Gundaree said. Then, to Gundara, "Amazing how sensible you can be sometimes, brother dear."

"Oh, shut up!"

*   *   *

The guard aimed his crossbow straight into Safar's face. He fingered the trigger that would send the bolt crashing forward. "Don't try anythin' funny," he said, "or I'll put this right between your eyes!"

Safar rattled his chains and laughed. "What am I supposed to try?" he said. "You've got me shackled, manacled and chained to my bench." He indicated the others in the cell. "Plus, I'm surrounded by six crossbowmen who have been commanded never to leave my side."

The guard beetled his forehead, looked at Safar who was weighed down with twenty pounds of chain, then at his companions who were all relaxing on barrels that had been dragged into the cell for makeshift seats. They were grinning at him, amused.

"Jus' remember what I said," he growled. But he lowered the bow.

"Yer better watch out, Tarz," one of the men teased. "He might bust outta all them chains and kiss yer!"

"Aw, stuff a dirty loincloth in it," Tarz shot back. "He's a wizard, ain't he? Wizards can . . . well, you know, do stuff." He thought. Then, "Real bad stuff, too." He nodded, firm.

"If I really were a wizard," Safar said, "why would I be here in chains? Why would I allow myself to be captured?"

Tarz shrugged. "How the hells do I know?" he said. "Maybe yers messed up. Made a mistake, like. Makes no never mind to th' likes of me."

Safar had no answer for this. The man, dumb oxen that he was, had hit the nail squarely. Safar had "messed up" as the man said. And at the present time there was nothing he could do about his dilemma.

Outside thunder crashed and rain drummed against the steel roof of the cell compound. Thank the gods for the rain, Safar thought. Or else he'd already be on the road to wherever Iraj was camped. Then he smiled to himself. Thank the gods, indeed! And here he was a man who firmly believed the gods were all asleep and paying no attention to human affairs. It was enough shake a man's faith in his disbelief.

He glanced at Tarz and the other men who perched on their barrels quietly talking among themselves. Very well, he thought, however he'd come by whatever time the storm provided, he'd best start putting it to some good use.

Safar examined his surroundings. His cell was one of twenty contained in a single story stone building with a steel roof and heavy bars on all the windows and doors. The whole building had been emptied of prisoners, mostly rowdies arrested during the festival. The six guards normally assigned to oversee the compound were now gathered in Safar's cell to provide air-tight security.

He shifted, sneaking looks at the heavy padlocks on his chains. Those he could open. As for the rest, they probably wouldn't be that difficult once he was free of the chains. If he started gesturing and muttering spells he'd have six crossbow bolts in him at the blink of an eye.

Then he felt the amulet grow warm on his chest and he thought of the fantastic stallion who was destined to be sacrificed when the rain stopped. He had absolutely no doubt now that the horse was the reason Asper had sent him to Naadan. He had to act quickly, or all would be lost. All I need, he thought, is some small advantage. A means to divert their attention so I can cast a spell. It wouldn't take much for one man. But six!

He felt a tickle on the back of his hand and he looked down to see a mosquito getting ready to drill. Safar was about to brush it away, then realized the sudden clatter of chains might accidentally get him drilled by something much worse than a mosquito's beak.

Then necessity wed inspiration and he quickly made a fist, trapping the mosquito in the tightened skin. He closed his eyes, pretending to sleep, but instead he was focusing inward, making his mind slender and sharp like the mosquito's beak. He pierced an artery and went snaking along through his own blood stream suddenly filled with the knowledge of all the loops and turns so he was ready when he shot into the heart, felt the immense pressure of contraction, then was released and hurled onward. He raced to the place where the mosquito's beak came through and then he released his fist and let the insect draw his spirit self up along with the blood.

His world became a place of powerful odors and strange lights and images, but somehow it all made sense when he realized *he'd* become the mosquito. And he wasn't a he, but a She! And this she was ravenous. She could smell the hot blood all around and it was driving her mad with hunger. Safar tightened control and gave her a mission first. A mission that had to be accomplished before she could feed.

The mosquito buzzed through the cell bars, vertical massifs from her point of view, gleaming with oily moisture. She called to her sisters, a high pitched whine of a song. A song of a place of plenty, where the prey was huge and slow and clumsy. And full of hot blood, rivers of it, torrents of it, floods of the stuff of life.

They came to her, lifting up from stagnant pools in the nooks and crannies of the cell house. First by the scores, then by the hundreds. Her song grew louder, clearer, and the little mosquito larvae in those pools burst wings and legs through skin and became full grown adults who joined their sisters by the thousands. She led them all to the cell, a swarm so thick with flying insect life that it looked like a black wall moving along the corridor. They were all singing together now, singing the blood song and the sound of them all was a shrill skin-crawling wail.

At that moment Safar snatched his spirit self back and he became fully aware, eyes opening just as the guards were turning to see what was happening. He made a quick warding spell as the hungry black cloud swarmed into the room and attacked. The men slapped at themselves, cursing. Then the slaps became frantic and the curses wild. More mosquitoes poured in, all ignoring Safar and going for the guards. They were rolling on the floor in agony now, or curling up into balls of pain.

Safar came to his feet, chains rattling in odd counterpoint to the mosquitoes' song. He made a simple spell, then clapped his hands together, shouting, "Sleep!"

The guards all sagged, unconscious. The black cloud of insects settled onto them, covering them like a blanket. But this blanket was alive and ravenous, draining them of their blood.

Safar took pity on them. He quickly whispered an unlocking spell and the chains fell away and the cell door clacked open. Then he snatched a torch from its bracket, whirled it around his head until it was sparking and shouted, "Begone!"

He hurled the torch to the floor, white smoke exploded upward and outward, filling the cell with a harsh, oily odor. Then the smoke cleared away and all the insects had vanished. The guards were sprawled out on the floor in whatever position the sleep spell had caught them.

Safar smiled at them. "Pleasant dreams," he said and slipped out into the corridor.

He went to the main door, barred inside and out for extra security, and peered through the peephole. It was night and the rain was so heavy he couldn't make out the guard post at the main gate. When he'd entered the compound he'd seen a dozen soldiers led by a lieutenant. He'd assumed they were to secure the outside of the small prison in case someone tried to rescue him. At the moment, Safar guessed, those soldiers would be huddling in the guard shack sipping tea and trying to keep dry and warm. He'd counted on that when he'd worked the mosquito spell, figuring they wouldn't hear the cries of their victims. So far it looked as if he'd guessed right.

He motioned and both locks, inside and out, fell away. He cracked the door a few inches, saw no one about, and went out, shutting and locking the door behind him. With luck his escape wouldn't be noticed for a few hours until the sleep spell faded and the guards woke up and found him gone.

The rain was falling so hard he was soaked through within seconds. He made his way gingerly across the muddy ground, trying to work out a plan of action for when he reached the guard shack. He still needed another bit of luck to complete his escape. Actually, he needed more than a bit. He strongly suspected that to overcome twelve soldiers a mosquito just wouldn't do.

When he got close he heard a thump and a groan, then the sound of a heavy weight splashing onto the muddy ground. Safar had frozen at the first sound, pulling back into a dark recess. He heard bootsteps going into the yard and tried to make himself smaller.

Then he saw a familiar form leading four men toward the cell building.

He sagged in relief.

It was Leiria!

CHAPTER THIRTEEN
THE BLOOD PRICE

The priest chanted a prayer, swinging his censer by the chain, lid clack-clacking, incense smoke billowing through the altar room.

King Quintal gagged on the smoke, making the painful throb in his temples drum harder and he cursed the very gods the priest was invoking. Quintal was sick—sick with fear, sick from too much drink and trebly sick from enforced sobriety on this most horrible of mornings.

Two other priests joined the others in sing-song prayer, adding their censer smoke to the too-sweet perfume that already infused the air.

Quintal shouted, "Get on with it you pack of shrieking eunuchs!"

The head priest protested. "But Your Majesty, this is a solemn occasion. Everything must be properly purified."

"Well, I'm purified up to my behind," Quintal roared. "My bowels are bursting with your damned purity. If you want to keep your head you'll get that horse out here right now. Let's kill it, and be done with it!"

The frightened priest issued orders and a moment later the stallion was brought out by sweet-faced boys dressed in white robes. The executioner followed, a broad ax resting on his shoulders.

Sick as he was, Quintal couldn't help but admire the animal. Besides its classic form, the stallion seemed quite calm. Not placid—his head was up and his eyes were alert. Confidence, that's what it was. Despite circumstances that would panic most animals, this one acted as if it were in complete control of the situation.

To Quintal's right a bulk as large as his own stirred uncomfortably. It was Ulan, sitting in the traditional place of honor. He was also the sole public witness to the event. Other than the principals, the sacrificial chamber was empty. The room was large enough to hold several hundred and normally it would be packed with dignitaries and honored guests. The priests began to pray over the horse and Ulan shifted again, the ornate seat groaning under his weight.

"I don't like this, Majesty," he grumbled. "Don't seem right to kill a great horse like that. And in such a hurry, too. With nobody around, so it's like we've got no respect for him."

Quintal flushed, angry, but he bit off a royal curse. Ulan was the most popular man in Naadan. Not only was he a Brave Titan, fresh from victory, but he was well-known for his many kindnesses to the poor, his temperate lifestyle, and for speaking up when ordinary people were wronged. In short, he was Quintal's rival for the throne. And if the king wasn't careful he find himself deposed.

Quintal pretended sympathy. "I know, I know," he said. "I've been in your place—declared Brave Titan of Naadan with all the honors and glories. And you want your friends to see. And your family, too. They'll all be proud and damned disappointed as well they can't be here."

"I don't care about that!" Ulan said. "Killin' the horse is what bothers me. I already offered to put up a sacrifice double his value. That should satisfy the gods. I won him fair. And I oughta be able to do what I like!"

It was all Quintal could do to keep from calling the guard to punish Ulan for his impertinence. But he needed the wrestler's support. Especially now.

"I can't take a chance on pissing off the gods," the king said. "Especially right now!"

Ulan was not mollified. "So why're we doin' it this way, Majesty?" he asked. "In secret and all. Like we're ashamed of something. I don't like the smell of this!"

Quintal looked about to see if anyone could overhear him. Then, desperate to win Ulan's backing, he leaned closer to say, "I'll tell you what's happening. But I've got to swear you to secrecy."

"Done," Ulan said. "You've got my word as a citizen, brother wrestler and fellow Brave Titan."

Quintal hesitated, then said, "A terrible thing has happened. Safar Timura has escaped."

Ulan gaped. "How?"

Quintal sighed. "It doesn't matter how. He just did. I haven't told anyone other than my closest advisers, otherwise the whole city'd be in a panic."

Ulan grimaced in painful understanding. "When King Protarus hears about it they'll be the hells to pay."

"Exactly. I haven't sent runners out to tell him yet. I'm trying to decide what to do and how to portray it. But I can't delay much longer because Protarus will think I've conspired with Lord Timura."

He pointed at the horse. "That's why I'm doing this so quickly and so quietly. My priests tell me the faster we make the sacrifice, the faster we get the gods' blessings. Which we'll need when Iraj Protarus hears what's happened. But my generals said if any kind of crowd was gathered together—especially a crowd of such important Naadanians—word was sure to get out. Then we'd have public hysteria on our hands at the same time Protarus showed up."

Ulan frowned. Like most Naadanians of late, he thought Quintal a drunken fool. Now, it seemed he'd become dangerous as well. If Iraj Protarus was about to pay a visit with blood in his eye, they ought to be doing more to get ready than killing a poor horse in some stupid secret ceremony. Ulan was never one to keep his deep-felt beliefs silent.

The big wrestler was weighing a reply, when a voice broke through: "Perhaps I can solve your problem, gentlesirs!"

The men jolted around and saw Safar standing there, hands on hips, wizard's cloak thrown back to show a gleaming breast plate, steel blue eyes boring out from a face darkened by the desert sun.

Then a second jolt as they saw the tall warrior woman standing by his side, crossbow cocked and ready. Behind her were at least ten other bowmen, all poised to strike.

Quintal jumped as the executioner saw the group, let out a berserker's roar and charged, swinging his ax over his head.

Leiria fired and the bolt dropped him in midstride and he crashed to the floor, dead.

Ulan was coming to his feet, but Safar stopped him with a shouted, "Hold, friend! I mean you no harm!" The giant wrestler sagged back.

Safar turned to Quintal, saying, "I'm sorry for that man. He was only trying to protect you. Now, let's make certain no one else makes such a tragic error. Tell your people to keep quite still and when our business here is done we'll be on our peaceful way."

Quintal gave the orders, although he saw it wasn't really necessary. The priests and boys were frozen with fear. Then the horse nickered, pulled free and trotted over to Safar. To the king's amazement the two seemed to know one another. They acted like old friends, too long apart. Safar touched the horse, hesitant at first, then it snorted with joy and nuzzled him. Safar patted and stroked and whispered into the horse's ear.

Then he looked up, blue eyes moist. "Does he have a name?" His voice was husky.

"Khysmet," Quintal said. "He's called Khysmet."

Safar's eyes widened. The vision in Asper's burial vault leaped up and he once again heard Asper's ghost whisper, *Khysmet!* He blinked in sudden realization.

He smiled, patting the big stallion, "Khysmet. Khysmet. Yes, now I understand!"

Then, to Quintal, "This is why I'm here. For Khysmet."

Dazed, Quintal waved a hand. "Then take him!"

"We're not thieves," Safar said. "I don't intend to steal him." He turned to Ulan. "Besides, he belongs to you."

"I'm with his Majesty," Ulan said. "If that's what it takes to get you out of here, he's yours. We've got troubles enough on account of you. Call him a gift, call him anything you want. Just take him and go!"

"Actually," Safar said, "I had a trade in mind." He lifted the horse amulet from his neck. He came forward, Khysmet trailing him like a big dog.

Safar handed the amulet to a puzzled Ulan. Then puzzlement turned to surprise. "It's warm," he said. "Like it's been toastin' next to the heart."

"It's an old witch's charm," Safar said. "The story is that whoever owns it will someday find a great horse, a magical horse." He nodded at Khysmet. "Like him." The horse rubbed its head against him like a cat. "As you can see, that part is true. So the next part must also be true." He indicated the amulet. "Someday you'll find such a horse and the owner will have no choice but to trade it for the amulet. And so on and so on."

"Who cares?" Ulan snapped. "Don't matter one way or the other if it's magic or not! Iraj Protarus is maybe gonna come down on Naadan like a hammer 'cause of you! Thousands of innocent people could die for somethin' that wasn't their fault!"

Quintal groaned and Ulan turned to him. "Isn't that right, Majesty?" he said. "Naadan's in big trouble all because of—" The rest was cut off when he saw Quintal slumped over in his throne.

"Ah, hells!" Ulan said. Ignoring Leiria and her warriors, he stalked over to the throne and bent to listen to Quintal's chest. After a moment his head came up and he announced grimly, "He's dead! Guess this was too much for him." He straightened, shaking his head. "Can't say as anybody'll be sorry. Even his kids didn't like him much."

Before Safar could speak, the high priest wailed, "But who will speak for us now, Ulan? Who will plead for us to King Protarus?"

Ulan thought a minute, then thumped his chest. "I will!" he said. "I'll tell Iraj Protarus what happened here! And if wants a head for revenge, he can take mine. And godsdamn his eyes!"

"I can help you with Iraj," Safar said.

Ulan peered at him. "Oh, yeah? How?"

Safar pointed at the amulet around Ulan's neck. "That used to belong to him," he said.

Ulan jumped, snatching at the amulet. Safar laughed. "Don't worry, I came by it honestly. Though not the way the charm is normally supposed to work."

"So what about the amulet?" Ulan growled impatiently. "How will that help?"

"Give it to Iraj as a gift," Safar said, "and all will be forgiven. I guarantee it."

Ulan stared at him, hard. Then: "You've got no reason to lie about that. So I'll take your word for it. But don't expect any thanks."

"I don't," Safar said, taking Khysmet's reins and preparing to lead him away.

"One other thing," Ulan said.

"What's that?"

"If you're ever in this region again . . ."

"I'll give Naadan a pass," Safar finished for him.

"Yeah," Ulan said. "Like that!"

✳   ✳   ✳

The escape from Naadan was slow going. Supplies were low in the main Kyranian encampment and Safar had tarried long enough to force Ulan to sell him all the goods they could haul away. Now there were so many wagon and camel loads of food and other badly needed things that they had a fairly large train. Plus there was a herd of goats and fresh horses to tend, so they barely made it into the hills by nightfall. Safar didn't know how much time they had. He assumed the worst. Ulan was clearly no fool and Safar suspected the new king would send runners to Iraj the moment they cleared the gates.

Once in the hills, Safar and his companions only rested a few hours. They set out again before dawn, using the stars to guide them and the Demon Moon to light the way. Their goal was the main camp, where all the villagers were well hidden in a woody ravine.

When first light came Safar dropped back to the rear of the column, where Leiria and her best men were positioned.

Leiria waved at the rumbling wagons and slow-moving camels. "We'll be a week at this pace," she said. "We never counted on the expedition taking that long."

"We'll be fine," Safar assured her.

"Are you soothsaying, or just trying to make me feel better?" she said, but she said it

375

with a smile.

"Neither one," Safar said. "I was merely expressing my faith in you, Leiria."

"Then we're lost for certain," Leiria laughed.

"I'm supposed to be the wizard in this group," Safar said, "but you're the one who's had all the magic." He nodded at Renor and the other men, weapons at the ready, alert for any danger. "They were all just farm lads and goat herders not many month ago," he said. "But you've turned them into a real force to be reckoned with. As professional a group as I've ever seen, even when Iraj was at his peak."

"It wasn't that difficult," Leiria said, with not a trace of false modesty. "In a way they're better than professionals. They have a greater reason to fight than money or ambition." Once again she indicated the caravan. "They're fighting for their own. You can't ask for a better goad than that."

Safar agreed and was about to praise her more, when she said, "All right, Safar, you've got your horse . . . Khysmet . . . and you've rather belatedly told me that he was the reason we were in Naadan. That it wasn't just a routine raid. Fine. Wonderful. Asper speaks and we obey, whether we know we're obeying or not! Now, what else are you holding back?"

"I can't say," Safar replied. "I've already told you why."

Leiria groaned. "I know! Wizard business!"

"It's not that simple," Safar said. But before he could go on Renor whistled a warning.

They turned to see an ominous cloud of dust puffing up on the horizon.

Leiria examined it with expert eyes. "Not that big a force," she said after a moment. "But it's coming up fast."

Safar frowned, concentrating until he caught a whiff of purpose in the oncoming cloud. "I think it's a scouting party," he said. "Iraj's men, that's for certain."

"Doesn't look like there's enough to mount any kind of serious threat," Leiria said. "I'll get some men together and ride out and meet them. Make them sorry for being so stupid."

Safar started to agree, then hesitated. "That's not necessarily a good idea," he said. "You'd have to catch or kill them all. If you failed, Iraj would be able to pinpoint us exactly for the first time since we left Kyrania."

Leiria was irritated. "What are we supposed to do," she said, "let them follow us all the way back to camp?"

"What are your chances of getting them all?" Safar asked.

Now it was Leiria's turn to hesitate. After a bit, she sighed and shook her head. "Not very good," she admitted. "They're most likely Iraj's best scouts. They'll be smart. They'll be fast. And they'll never forget that mission takes precedence over all else."

Safar nodded, then said, "Give me your water."

Leiria was startled. "Water? What are you talking about."

"I have an idea," he said. "Their prime mission is to capture me, right?"

"Rii-ght." Leiria wasn't sure where this was going.

"Fine, then I'll ride out to meet them," Safar said, "wag my tail and get them to chase me. I'll lead them off in some other direction, lose them, then meet you either on the trail or if it takes longer, at the encampment."

Leiria gave him the hells for even thinking of the idea. But Safar persisted and in the end she saw he was determined.

Safar patted the stallion. "Besides," he said, "I've been wanting to give Khysmet his head and see what happens. Both of us have been going crazy with this slow pace."

"One fall," Leiria warned, "and you're done for."

"We won't fall, will we Khysmet?" Safar said to the horse. The stallion whinnied and pawed the ground. "I don't think it's possible for him to stumble," Safar said to Leiria. "I can't explain how I know this. I just do."

"Great," Leiria said, "You get to play and I get to trod along the common path."

Her voice was heavy with sarcasm but Safar could see it was to cover real worry. "What a lucky man I am," he murmured, "to find a friend like you."

"Just you remember that, Safar Timura," Leiria scolded as she handed over her water bags. "If you let something happen to you I'll track down your ghost and kick its behind from here to Hadin."

Then Safar was riding away, looking like a warrior prince on his great horse.

A large piece of Leiria's heart went with him.

CHAPTER FOURTEEN

HORSE MAGIC

Iraj dreamed of horses—a great wild herd flying across the plains. He sailed with them, moving at breathtaking speed, the air full of fresh spring currents, the horizon a joyous thing of blue skies meeting lush green earth. He felt like a boy again, a fully human boy with innocent dreams and youthful yearnings.

He was skimming just above the herd, which moved in graceful unison like a flock of birds flying to some glorious home that was free of all earthly cares.

Iraj quickened his pace, moving along the herd until he came to the leaders. There were two of them, the first creamy white, the other hearthstone black, and both were so magnificent he loved them at first sight. The black was a fiery mare, the white a tall, noble stallion.

He chose the stallion and settled down, down, and just as he touched the world spun and he suddenly found himself crouched in a canyon, the stallion standing next to him. Now the horse was saddled and harnessed and he was holding the reins loosely in one hand.

Iraj heard the sound of fast-moving riders and he knew his enemies were hunting him just over the ridge. He didn't know or care who that enemy was, but he thrilled at the prospect of an encounter. The horse nickered, sharing his excitement. Laughing, Iraj came to his feet and vaulted into the saddle.

Astride the horse he felt strong and swift, a man who feared nothing. The horse was magic under his hands, moving with easy fluidity. It was as if he were part of the animal and it was part of him.

Blood sang in his ears and he shouted in glee as he and the horse surged forward. They practically flew up the steep sides of the canyon, dust and rocks boiling behind them as they plunged up and up and then they were over the rim charging across a hilly plain.

When he spotted the scouting party he brought the horse to a skittering halt. Iraj was startled at the animal's quick obedience. He'd barely touched the leather straps and the horse had stopped on a skinned copper. It was as if the action had been communicated by thought alone. Now the stallion stood trembling under him, ready to charge into the fight, or turn and run like the winds.

Iraj waited, keeping a rein on his own high-pitched emotions. He felt wonderful. Full of life and spirit and clean purpose. Gone were the ravenous urges of a shape changer. He had no overpowering lust for blood and misery. No fiery dreams of grand thrones and bowing subjects. He didn't even hate his enemies who were thundering toward him. He only wanted to bedazzle them, confound them. That would be enough to make a joyous victory.

He patted the horse, soothing it as the scouting party came closer. There were twenty: six main scouts astride fast horses in the lead, and eighteen demons, bristling with arms and riding the huge, cat-like beasts that could take a charge and turn it back with their ferocity.

When the scouts were near enough to see him, Iraj raised his fist high in challenge. He stood his ground until he heard excited shouts of recognition: "It's him! Don't let him get away!"

At the last moment Iraj wheeled the stallion and raced away across the plain, the soldiers in thundering pursuit.

It was a ride like no other and Iraj whooped in joy as they sped over rocky ground as if it were meadow grass, leaping wide ravines as if they were merely narrow clefts. Sometimes he got too far ahead of the soldiers and he had to turn back to swoop just outside of their range, then wheel and charge away again.

He led them far from the main track, through rough hills, barren valleys and dusty canyons full of tricky switchbacks and false trails. He never stopped, riding on through the night, the horse never tiring under him. The scouts grew weary, their animals ready to drop. Laughing at their plight, Iraj gave them no mercy, prodding and teasing whenever they tried to rest.

He rode that way for many a day, until he finally abandoned the soldiers, exhausted and lost in the middle of a desert.

A few hours later he came to a small wooded area with a creek running through. A tall willow shaded a pool where the creek widened. He dismounted and led the horse to the pool for a cool drink and shady rest. The two of them drank long and deep, a warm feeling of comfort and satisfaction shared between them.

Iraj splashed water on his face, breaking the mirrored surface with his cupped hands as he sluiced dust and grime from smooth cheeks.

Strange, he thought, I remember a beard.

Curious, he peered into the water and saw a wavery reflection floating up at him. He couldn't make it out at first, but then the surface calmed and the image resolved itself.

With a shock he realized he was looking at the face of Safar Timura!

*   *   *

Safar jolted back, nearly losing his balance and falling into the water. Khysmet nuzzled him, wondering what was the matter.

"It's nothing," Safar said, stroking the soft nostrils. "I'm just tired, I guess."

Even so it was with some trepidation that he leaned forward again to peer into the water. Floating there was the reflection of his own smooth features.

A moment before he would have sworn an oath that he'd seen the face of Iraj Protarus staring back at him. The illusion, surely caused by exhaustion, had been so strong he'd even felt a beard under his fingertips when he washed.

Ridiculous as the notion was, Safar was vastly relieved. To calm himself he washed and groomed Khysmet, then gathered some sweet grasses for a treat. He also found berries all fat and full of juice and he fed them in alternating handfuls to Khysmet and himself.

Then he slept. It was a sound and dreamless sleep and when morning came he felt refreshed and full of energy. Khysmet evidently felt the same, for he pranced about and kicked up his heels like a colt. Safar was eager to get into the saddle and be on his way. He had many miles to cover before he reached home. Although it was nothing more than a tented encampment soon to be on the move again, home was how he thought of it and so home it was.

As they cantered out of the woods, Safar thought of his wild ride—the ride that seemed as if it would never end. Khysmet snorted, tossing his head, as if sharing the memory and enjoying it equally. Then Safar thought of the soldiers he'd left in the desert. They were so exhausted and so lost he doubted they'd survive. To his surprise he felt not one pinch of pity for them. They'd chosen the wrong side and too bad for that.

It was a cold, just so, feeling and it was discomforting how easily it sat upon his soul.

And he had a flash of awareness of what it was like to be Iraj.

*   *   *

In Iraj's most private quarters the king paced the room, fighting to control his emotions and retain his human form. He kicked at the pillows and snarled at a terrified serving wench to fetch him some wine and make it quick or he'd tear her heart out.

The dream was gnawing at him. Although to call it a dream would be an exaggeration, because Iraj never slept. That was one of the things he missed most about his previous life. Sleep, blessed sleep. As a shape changer he only dozed, or, as Fari explained it, he entered a neutral state where he was vaguely aware of his surroundings but was resting.

Iraj knew all this, but he still thought of the experience as a dream. And it had left him with a feeling of great loss. Normally, if normal it could be called, Iraj's neutral state was full of quick, bloody images mixed with snatches of voices; some screaming, some wailing, some babbling, some shouting in fury. When he came "awake" he was angry, always angry and the only relief was causing pain. The greater the pain the closer he came to a state of—joy? All that had somehow been welded to his overweening ambition and combined into a ferocious desire to always be on the move—doing something, crushing something, killing something.

It was like a furnace, Iraj thought, an immense furnace straight out of the hells that could never be satisfied.

But the dream, ah the dream, if only he could capture it and make it into a potion then drink it down and quench that angry fire.

Wine was thrust into his hand and he drank and paced and drank some more, letting the dream spill out. The horse! That magnificent creature, a plainsman's treasure unmatched by any Iraj had ever seen. And the ride! By the gods that was a chase to end all chases! Iraj chuckled, remembering how he and the horse had fooled the soldiers. Most of all he remembered the feeling of being whole and human again—the sense of freedom so strong it was like being lifted up to the skies.

Then he came to the uncomfortable part, the part that had smashed him out of his dream into dismal reality.

He thought of the moment when he'd stared into the pool and seen Safar's reflection instead of his own. Everyone knew dreams sometimes had deep meaning, but what was that all about? The strangest thing was although seeing Safar had been a shock there had been no feeling of hatred for him. And for certain Iraj hated Safar with passions only a shape-changer could know. Iraj hated him now as he paced and thought and wondered, thinking, if he had Safar in his grasp at this moment he'd rip off his limbs and devour them before his still living eyes.

However, for a brief span, just as Iraj was recovering from his surprise at seeing Safar, there was no hate. In fact, the first thought he had was being glad that he'd met an old friend in his dream.

He was still worrying that bone an hour later when Kalasariz begged an audience. The spy master entered, cool and smooth as ever, with only a few spots of wolfishness to show his inner excitement.

"I bear good tidings, Majesty," he said. "Our witches' net has proved itself already. There's still some rough spots, such as communications, to burnish, but I do believe we are on the right path with this."

"A sighting of Lord Timura?" Iraj asked, nerve endings burning with interest and he remembered his bargain with the strange witch known as Old Sheesan.

"Better than that, Majesty," Kalasariz said. "A witch over in Naadan not only sniffed out Lord Timura in a festival crowd of thousands, but she was able to alert the authorities in time so he could be captured."

Caught by surprise, Iraj's wolf snout erupted from his face. "You mean, we have him?" he snarled.

Kalasariz sighed. "Unfortunately, he was able to escape, Majesty," he said. "His magic was too strong and his kinsmen were too clever for the local king. Disappointing perhaps, but only when looked at from a certain angle."

"And how should we look at it?" the king growled. "How can Lord Timura's escape be viewed as anything other than abject failure?"

Kalasariz had been ready for this. "Why, Majesty, Old Sheesan only just set up the witch network. And already we have proof that no city in your kingdom is safe for Lord Timura." He shrugged. "Nest time we'll get him! We only have to improve the response of the local authorities. They have no experience in dealing with wizards."

"You'll see to that?" Iraj demanded.

Kalasariz smiled. "Gladly, Majesty," he said, "except I fear I'd be treading on Prince Luka's territory. He's in charge of dealing with local authorities, if you recall."

Iraj looked at him coldly. "You've certainly managed to wriggle off that hook," he said.

Kalasariz acted hurt. "Why, Majesty," he said, "you've misconstrued my intent. I was merely reporting what I thought was the best news since this whole exercise began."

Iraj decided to ignore this large chunk of dissembling, saying, "Tell me the details. Exactly what happened in Naadan?"

Kalasariz reported as fully as he could, from the tavern encounter to Safar's strange challenge of the wrestler, Ulan, to his capture and eventual escape.

"Now, here's where it really gets interesting, Majesty," he said. "We nearly had him twice. The Naadanian messenger was on the road to this camp and luckily encountered one of your scouting parties a few miles from Naadan. They went in pursuit."

"Yes?" Iraj said.

Kalasariz took a long breath. This was another dangerous area to be bridged. Then, "Well, I can't say what happened exactly after that. The soldiers never returned. I suspect they were ambushed by Lord Timura's forces."

Iraj was rocked by the news, his features becoming more wolflike. Not at the defeat. He was thinking of the dream, the mad chase into the desert. The soldiers—his soldiers!—in pursuit. Could this be true? Had it been a vision, not a dream?

"There's another way Prince Luka can aid our cause," the spy master went on. "We should post similar scouting units in each city, backed by sufficient troops to prevent another ambush. Then we don't have to leave things to chance."

Iraj was drifting now, not really paying attention. He was thinking of the dream in a completely different light, which had an odd calming effect on him.

It was a human hand that he waved at Kalasariz, saying, "Yes, yes, tell Luka to do all that."

"And the witch, Majesty?" the spy master asked. "Old Sheesan? Shall we increase the reward? I'm a great believer in financial incentive."

"Fine," Iraj said absently. "Double it if you like." He paused. "And send for the witch. I want to speak with her."

"Yes, Majesty, it will be done, Majesty, just as you say." Kalasariz hesitated. He'd won every point thus far and was willing to try his luck once more. "One other thing, Majesty."

"Say it."

"Prince Luka informs me he plans to punish Naadan for allowing Lord Timura to escape."

"Whatever he decides," Iraj said.

"Yes, Majesty," Kalasariz said, "except Naadan is such a rich area—one of the few bright spots in your kingdom that can pay real taxes, instead of chickens and scrawny goats. And the king who was responsible for letting Lord Timura get away—King Quintal—suddenly died. He was probably scared to death. Ulan the wrestler is king now."

Iraj shrugged. "Luka knows my views on that issue. I assume he took them into account when he made his decision."

"Yes, I'm sure he did, Majesty," Kalasariz said, "and I meant no criticism."

He slipped an object out of his sleeve and held it up for Iraj to see. "However, I don't think he took this into account, Majesty," he said.

Iraj goggled at the object. It was the horse amulet he'd given to Safar long ago! Hurled it at him, actually, in his anger at Safar's defiance over the woman, Nerisa.

"King Ulan sent this to you as a gift, Majesty," Kalasariz said, "and he begs you to spare his people."

Iraj took the amulet with trembling hands. He had no doubt the spy master knew the tale behind the amulet. But Kalasariz could have no idea that it now had even deeper meaning.

"It's true," Iraj murmured. "The horse really exists."

"Pardon, Majesty?" Kalasariz asked.

Iraj shook his head. "Leave me."

"But what about Naadan, Majesty?" the spy master asked. "Shall we spare them?"

Iraj snarled, "Yes, dammit! Now get out of my sight!"

Kalasariz left, vastly pleased with himself. He cared nothing about Naadan's fate. However, he'd just won a major victory over Luka by having his orders reversed.

When he was gone, Iraj hung the amulet about his neck. He felt the warm glow of its magic against his chest. Once again he was astride the great horse running free with the winds. The reverie ended with a crash and he shouted for his officers.

They came running and he issued orders to break camp immediately. He would march within the hour, never mind there wasn't time to rouse the whole army. "They can catch up to us later," he said, dismissing the men.

The furnace in his belly was burning full force. He knew exactly where to go to pick up Safar's trail. Somewhere outside Naadan there was a canyon where Safar had lain in wait for his soldiers.

Iraj had no doubt he'd recognize the spot the moment he saw it.

*   *   *

Palimak felt like he was swimming in camel curds, which he hated more than anything, especially if the milk camel had grazed in an onion field and then it was really awful because all the onion juice seemed to concentrate in the curds. Grandmother Timura said it was good for him and made him eat it anyway, but why was she making him swim in the stuff? It was thick and slimy and hard to swim in and he kept on bumping into big pieces of curd and then he'd sink down and down and get it in his nose and mouth.

Then he thought he heard voices. He wasn't sure whose voices they were but he heard his name so he turned over on his back and floated on the curds to listen.

"Palimak's been sick since the storm," he heard his grandmother say. He knew she wasn't really his grandmother, although she acted like one and talked like one and cuddled like one, and scolded like one, so that's what he called her.

The same with Grandfather Timura and that's who he heard talking now. He heard him say, "We've been scared to death. First it was a fever, which seemed to hit when the rain stopped."

"I got the fever down just fine," his grandmother said. Her voice quavered. "Then he went to sleep and we haven't been able to wake him up." She sniffled, trying to hold back tears. "It's been more than a week, now."

Someone answered but Palimak couldn't tell who because he sank under those stupid curds again and he was swimming and swimming and then he was whirling around and around in all that onion tasting stuff and then . . . Nothing. A long, long time of nothing. Then he smelled incense, except not just one kind because there were so many layers of scent—rose and sage and lemon and cinnamon—that it was like he was smelling a rainbow . . . if only you could break off a rainbow hunk and put it in an incense burner. Then he sensed light and he heard someone chanting, but they were whispering so he couldn't make out what the chant was all about.

He thought, talk louder, please! and just like that someone said, "Wake up, Palimak!"

The boy opened his eyes to find his father bending over him. His threw his arms around his Safar's neck, crying, "Oh, father, I'm so glad to see you!"

Safar hugged him back and told him what a good boy he was, and brave too, and other things like that until the world was whole again.

Then Palimak remembered and became alarmed. "What about Gundara and Gundaree?" he asked, fumbling around his bedclothes for the turtle idol. "They've been sick too!"

"Don't worry," his father said, slipping the turtle from his sleeve. "I had to take care of you first." He laid it on Palimak's chest. "Just leave it there for awhile," he said. "Before you know it they'll be out here driving us crazy again."

Palimak giggled. "They will, won't they," he said. "Saying 'shut up, shut up' all the time." Then he remembered something else and the giggle turned into a full-bodied laugh. "You sure looked funny in all that mud, father," he chortled. "Falling down, splat! And that big wrestler, boom, splat!"

"So you were the one who made it rain," his father said, laughing with him.

"Sure," Palimak said. "Well, not just me alone. Gundara and Gundaree helped too. It was pretty hard to do. You have to sort of catch clouds and keep squeezing them to get all the water out." He made wringing motions with his hands. "And then you have to blow real hard to make a wind." He puckered his lips to demonstrate. "At first it was fun. Then we had to keep going and going until you got out of that dungeon and it wasn't fun anymore."

He shrugged. "I guess that's why we got so sick," he said. "But it was worth it. You escaped, right?" More giggling. "All those mosquitoes!" he said. "That was really, really *disgusting*, father. Would you show me how to do it someday?"

"Soon as we can find some mosquitoes," his father promised. Then, "When you're well again," he said, "perhaps we'd better talk about doing great big spells, like making it rain. You can see for yourself that it can be very dangerous."

"It was the only way I could help," Palimak said.

"I know, son, and I thank you for it. You were very brave and very smart and you might even have saved my life."

Palimak squirmed with pleasure. "Did I really save your life, father?"

"Absolutely," Safar said. "And I wasn't criticizing you for doing it. I was only saying that you have to learn how to be careful about that sort of magic. We have to go slowly, son. Sometimes you'll even have to help me keep up with you. Even though you're still a boy, there's things you can do that I can't." He smiled. "Like making such a big rainstorm!"

"Oh, sure you could, father," Palimak said, feeling quite manly in his reply. "You're much stronger than me!"

"Only because I'm older, son," his father said. "And I've studied very hard all my life. You'll catch up to me one of these days. Plus more. Much more."

"That's because I'm half demon," Palimak said with much satisfaction. "It's better than just being one or the other, right?"

"That's right, son," his father said.

Palimak had a sudden thought. "What about the horse?" he asked, worried. "Khysmet, right?"

His father looked surprised. "Yes, that's his name."

"Is he here? Did you bring him back?"

"He's outside the tent eating a big basket of corn and rye."

"That's good," Palimak said, quite solemn. "He deserves it after riding around all over the place."

His father frowned, then, "Did you see that too, son? Me on Khysmet and the soldiers chasing us?"

Palimak hesitated, then, "I guess I did, but not the same way I saw you in Naadan. It was after I got sick and I had these strange dreams. One of them was you and Khysmet."

"That was a vision, son," his father said. "Not a dream. I was wondering when you'd start having them."

Palimak wasn't listening. He was thinking of something else. "The really, real strange thing was that you weren't always on Khysmet," he said. "Sometimes somebody else was riding him."

His father's blue eyes narrowed. "Who, son? Who else did you see."

Palimak remembered and his heart gave a bump. "It was Iraj Protarus, father!"

✻   ✻   ✻

"I'm no wizard," Leiria said, "but that sounds worrisome to me."

Safar nodded. "Exactly why I wanted to talk to you before the meeting," he said. "There's no sense getting everyone alarmed when I don't know what it means myself. I'm sure Palimak had a vision. And in that vision he definitely saw me playing my little game with Iraj's scouts. But I don't know what to make of him seeing Iraj as well. Hells, that might not even have been part of the vision. Perhaps it was a dream attached to the vision. It happens sometimes. It's the magical equivalent of the tail on a kite."

"We'd be safer assuming the worst," Leiria said. "Although only you know what that could be."

Safar thought a moment, jumping from worst case logic point to the next and so on, face growing grimmer with each leap. The moment he'd proposed that Ulan give the amulet to Iraj, he'd known that he was making Iraj's task easier. Still, with so many lives at stake he had no other choice. He considered the gloating witch in the arena who had torn off a piece of his cloak. That, too, might help Iraj. On the other hand, the magic of human witches was weak. It would take an extraordinary sorceress to make any use of it. And those were very rare, indeed. Still . . . still . . .

"The safest thing," he said finally, "would be to run as far and as fast as we can."

"You think he'll track us here?"

"Taking the bleakest view, yes."

"Then that's what we should do," Leiria said. "Run." She sighed. "At least we're ready for it," she said. "We're supposed to move out at first light."

"True," Safar said, "but we just might want to change which way we go and how." He unsnapped the map case from his belt. "We'd better get the route plotted before the meeting. Otherwise our beloved Elders will want to debate the issue for a week."

"Honestly, Safar," Leiria said, "I don't know why you put up with them. I know the Council of Elders is a proud Kyranian tradition and all that. But they aren't organized for this kind of life. They've rarely had to decide on anything more important than when to let out the pigs and geese to keep the streets clean.

"This is war and they're just not suited for it. You need to organize some kind of military leadership. People who can think quickly, argue when its time to argue, and no matter what they think to shut up and fall in to march with the rest of us when the final decision is made."

"You don't understand, Leiria," Safar said, unrolling the maps and picking through them. "This is the system we've always had. I'm loathe to interfere with it, much less change it. We're nomads now. But I hope that doesn't last much longer than a couple of years. In Syrapis, with luck, we can start a new life. A new Kyrania. If we set up some sort of military command it might be hard to change things back to the way they were."

He grimaced. "From what I've seen of most places, with all the kings and generals, it's nearly impossible to get rid of them once they're installed."

Leiria pointed at the maps. "Even so, the Elders don't get to choose now, do they?" she said. "I mean, we're going to work the whole thing out in advance, right? Then you'll convince them they thought of it themselves. Why, you're already leading them by the nose. So what's the difference?"

"Simple," Safar said, "I don't like doing it."

Leiria thought a minute, then smiled. "To split a hair like that, Safar Timura," she said, "your conscience must own a damned sharp sword."

* * *

In the tent with the Elders, Safar spread out the map and placed a stone on each corner. He moved casually, although inside his anxiety was mounting. After studying the maps he knew exactly where they had to go next. He didn't like it, but it was the only thing to do. The moment he'd been dreading for months had arrived.

"It seems to me," Safar said to the Elders, "that Naadan was very lucky for us. For the first time since we left Kyrania we have enough supplies to last us for several months."

"Only if we live off the land," the always argumentative Masura replied.

Khadji growled. "I suspect that's what Safar meant and you know it, Masura," he said. "The supplies we have on hand, plus living off the land. That's how we've been doing things for close on to a year!"

Masura grumbled. "I just want to make sure things are clear to everyone," he said.

"Actually," Safar said smoothly, "I did mean that, my friend. And I'm glad you brought it up. We don't want to miss anything and the supply situation is just the sort of crucial mistake we want to avoid."

Satisfied, Masura gave Safar's father a dirty look as if to say, see, I was right to ask. Your own son says so.

The headman, Foron, peered at the map. He put one finger on the ink blot that marked their current position and another on Kyrania. There wasn't much distance between them.

"I don't like that," he said.

Then he measured the distance to Syrapis. He grunted with effort as he made the stretch. It was two thousand miles away. "I like that even less," he said.

Foron scratched his head. "What if we took advantage of our luck to really cover some ground?" he said. "Instead of dodging and ducking and hiding out all the time, we could make one long dash for it."

Masura coughed. "We'd never make it all the way to Syrapis," he said.

Safar gave his father a signal and Khadji groaned. "For the gods sake, Masura," he said. "Foron wasn't saying anything of the kind. He meant we should try to get as far as the supplies will take us."

Khadji moved to the map, just as he and Safar had planned, and studied it. He pretended to search for a moment then put his finger on the prearranged spot.

"My guess is we wouldn't need new supplies until we reached here."

Everyone craned to see, including Safar who acted as curious as the rest.

"It's the Kingdom of Caluz," said the headman. Then, to Safar, "Have you heard of that place, Lord Timura?"

"Only that they have a famous temple there," he lied. "I once approved funds for a temple restoration project in Caluz. For the life of me I don't remember anything more about it. However, it must have been a rich area to possess such a temple."

Safar thought, if they only knew! He hadn't even told his father why Caluz had to be the choice. After finding Khysmet in Naadan, Safar had greater reason than before to heed the words of Lord Asper's ghost: *Come to me through Caluz!*

"If Caluz is that rich," he heard his father say, "then we can get new supplies without much trouble."

Everyone murmured agreement and the decision was made. There would no ducking and dodging and hiding in the months ahead. Instead they would strike straight for Caluz and resupply there.

"Actually," Safar observed, "Caluz might be the last place we have to raid." He indicated the map. "A short run from Caluz should put us at the Port of Caspan. On the shores of the Great Sea."

The headman smacked fist into hand. "Then it's on to Syrapis!" he exclaimed.

"Well, there's a sea to cross first," grumbled Masura. "Don't forget that!"

The men roared laughter and teased Masura—which had been Safar's intent all along.

Then wine was passed around and everyone drank to the journey ahead.

*   *   *

Two weeks later Iraj's army entered the wooded ravine where the Kyranians had camped. It was night and the sky was alight with the thousands of torches they carried to show the way.

The Kyranians had gone to great pains to wipe out all signs of their presence, but an advance party of Iraj's scouts had found an iron horseshoe nail, which led to the uncovering of the thrown shoe itself. From there it was only a matter of more detailed searching and enough other small signs were discovered to give the Kyranians away.

Now the army was coming, led by Prince Luka and his demon cavalry of mailed warriors astride the great cat-like horrors they used for mounts. Behind them was a huge armored elephant bearing King Protarus' royal howdah, all gold and bejeweled and with blood red curtains drawn tight so the king could not be seen. The king's army sprawled back from there, starting with his royal guard of crack troops, both human and demon. There were archers and slingmen, demons who fought with giant battle axes and short spears, fierce human tribesmen who fought on horseback with crossbows they could fire at the gallop, and long curving blades so sharp they'd slice through chain mail as if it were paper.

The army stretched for miles, torches and lanterns all gleaming in the night, back to the farthest reaches where the big supply wagons groaned like captive giants put to the rack.

In the howdah Iraj sniffed the air with excitement, wolf's snout bristling. Old Sheesan cackled in the corner, waving a scrap of cloth about like a tattered flag. "I paid her handsomely fer this," she said. "But it's right off Lord Timura's cloak, so it's worth ev'r bit a gold I could scrape together."

Iraj licked his chops and tossed her a purse of gold. "I'll give you another," he said, "if you can sniff out his spoor."

If the old witch only knew, he thought, she could get a cartload of gold from him as a reward. In all these months this was the closest he'd ever come to finding Safar. First he'd retraced the route he'd taken in the vision, finally coming to the desert spring where he'd seen Safar's reflection. His plan had been to have his scouts follow Safar's trail to the main Kyranian encampment. But his old nemesis had been too canny, using both physical and magical tricks to obscure his passage. Several times his hopes were raised when he'd caught the scent of the great dream horse he'd ridden in the vision. It was the amulet that made this possible, heightening his powers to pick up the stallion's musk. Then some spell of Safar's would interfere and the scent would be gone, his hopes dashed.

It was then that Kalasariz had showed up with Old Sheesan in tow and the witch had presented him with the scrap of cloth she said would put him on the trail again. Iraj had his doubts—the dirty old hag was hardly a figure to inspire confidence—but he'd given her the chance and now he was vastly pleased with himself for doing so. Using the cloth and her witchy powers—which even Fari had grudgingly admitted were "most remarkable . . . for a human!"—she'd picked up Safar's trail and carried it many miles forward until Safar confounded them again with another trick.

The trick, however, proved to be flawed. Iraj had merely scoured the area in a twenty mile radius and this time luck was with him, not Safar, and his scouts had stumbled on the ravine.

Yes, Old Sheesan had proved her value. In his wolfen state it was difficult for Iraj to think deeply. Even so, he felt an sense of affection for her and even . . . trust? That was strange! Iraj had only trusted one man in his life—Safar. And look what that had gotten him! Still, every once in awhile, when the witch was in repose, he caught a glimpse of that remarkable creature he'd seen for an instant when they'd first met. Who was this woman who called herself Old Sheesan? Was she a beautiful woman hiding behind an ugly facade? Or a filthy old hag through and through . . . and the glimpsed visions of beauty a product of his imagination?

Just then he heard a voice whisper in his ear, low, and musical and full of seductive promise: *"Together . . . together . . . we can achieve all . . . together . . ."*

He jolted around, but only saw the witch sniffing at the scrap from Safar's tunic, beaked nose twitching.

She lifted her head, cackling triumphantly. "This is his place, yes it be, Majesty," she chortled in voice totally unlike the whisper he'd heard. "Lord Timura slept here, ate here and he left it not long ago. The scent's that strong, it is. Not more'n two weeks gone, is Old Sheesan's guess, Majesty."

Iraj concentrated, transforming fully into his wolfen state. He strained to catch Safar's spoor, but he didn't have the witch's powerful magic nose, with a long lifetime of experience to separate and interpret what she sniffed.

Suddenly the amulet glowed, so hot it nearly scorched his chest and he growled with delight at the pain, pressing it tighter against his wolfish hide to feel all the more.

Then Iraj caught the spoor of the great dream horse and he lifted his head and howled with delight.

CHAPTER FIFTEEN
THE SPIRIT RIDER

Once out of the wilderness the Kyranians dared the main caravan tracks for the first time since they'd fled the Valley of the Clouds. They were amazed at the pace they could maintain, averaging nearly thirty miles each day—a distance a trained army would covet. What's more, they were able to command the entire length of that thirty miles. With scouts ranging far ahead and behind their control was extended even farther—a hundred miles or more.

It was Safar's practice to alternate between both scouting parties when they were on the road, seeing little of Palimak and the rest of his family during that time. Sometimes he found himself too far away from the caravan to rejoin it at night and would miss seeing them altogether for days at a time.

He regretted this, particularly when it came to Palimak whose boyish experiments with magic could be worrisome. He'd learned, however, that even a wizard couldn't be all places at all times so he locked the feeling away with all the other regrets that make up a life.

Thanks to Khysmet, he was at least enjoying these lonely but necessary missions more than in the past. It was not only a joy—and sometimes a breath-taking thrill—to ride him, but the stallion was remarkable company as well. Like an old friend, Khysmet knew all his moods and how to deal with them. When Safar became absorbed in thought, usually about what might await him in Caluz, the horse took control of the journey. Uncannily guessing the route Safar intended and becoming extra wary, sensing that Safar's mind was far away from present dangers.

Once when Safar was digging into Asper's book for a spell he could use in a swamp he became so absorbed in the demon wizard's theories he forgot where he was. When he became aware again he was startled to find himself on the other side of the swamp. Somehow Khysmet had found the way even though it was riddled with pits of quicksand deep enough to swallow a team of oxen, wagon and all.

Khysmet also proved to be a bit of a practical joker and Safar had to be wary when he squatted by a stream to drink, lest Khysmet butt him into the creek. When Safar came up out of the water sputtering and swearing Khysmet would rear back, snorting and pawing the air in delight.

There was also a strange kind of magic emanating from Khysmet. Oh, he couldn't suddenly sprout wings and fly, or scratch out a spell with his hooves like a witch's goatish Favorite. But on a long run, just when Safar felt he could no longer go on, he'd feel a sudden surge of energy and purpose radiating from Khysmet and then he could continue on for as long as it took to achieve his goal. As for the stallion, Safar had yet to see his limits.

There was the smell of the earth in Khysmet's magic: tall plains grasses golden in the sun; swarms of bees and locusts swooping this way and that, all of a single mind though there were thousands of them; small birds darting through the insect clouds to feed; and sharp-eyed hawks and eagles floating above it all, watching for their chance.

Safar strayed so far away from the others that Leiria admonished him, saying it was his duty as their leader to keep himself safe. Safar knew she was right, but despite several promises to stay close he kept forgetting and giving Khysmet his head and then there was no telling how many miles he might travel before he remembered his last promise.

One day she swore she'd stay with him herself and she brought along a spare horse so she could switch back and forth to keep them both fresh. By nightfall she'd worn out both animals and herself and it was all she could do to prop herself up to eat when dinner was ready.

Safar had gone to some trouble for her, catching a brace of pheasants and roasting them over the fire with wild herbs to sweeten the flesh.

She sighed, saying, "This is when I miss palace life. All those servants to tend your every need. If we were in Zanzair right now, I'd snap my fingers and order up strong wine and a good massage and then I'd have them carry my poor boneless body to the bed, where'd they'd tuck me in for the night."

"I can help you with the wine," Safar said, popping the stopper off a flask and pouring her a cup. He handed it to her, grinning. "I'd best not offer my services as a masseur. Not if we want to remain just friends, that is."

Leiria laughed. "A lot of good it would do you," she said. "I'm so tired you'd be sleeping with a corpse."

"There's nights when that wouldn't stop me," Safar joked, "and let's just say this is one of those nights."

Leiria gave him a look. "You don't want to start something you can't finish, Safar Timura," she said. "So don't tease a woman who still has delicate feelings for you."

"I know that, my dear, dear Leiria," Safar replied. "It's only how I'm feeling tonight, which I can't help."

Leiria yawned, sleep suddenly very hard to resist. "We need to find you a woman, Safar," she said. "We need to . . ." and she fell asleep in midsentence.

Safar watched her for awhile, admiring her clear strong features and inviting figure. He thought of the days—and nights—when they were lovers, then the memories became too disturbing and he rolled up in his blanket and tried to follow her into sleep. He drifted for a time, thinking of nothing, then he heard Khysmet nicker, soft, not in alarm, but calling, calling . . .

. . .And Safar was astride Khysmet, riding through a soft wood full of trailing ferns and sweet mosses. The air was misty, almost raining. They came upon a small glen filled with wildflowers and nourished by a musical brook.

Khysmet whinnied and Safar saw something moving through the mist and then it swirled away and the most marvelous woman he'd ever seen floated into view. The mist parted more, like a veil being drawn back, and with a shock he saw she was riding the remarkable black mare he'd seen in the vision.

Then his eyes were drawn back to the woman. She was achingly, exotically beautiful. She had long limbs and ebony skin with long waves of hair tumbling to her waist. She was nearly naked, wearing only a loin cloth and a light chain vest that swung open as she rode, showing her long torso and small, shapely breasts. She had a bow over her shoulder, along with a quiver of heavy arrows. Strapped to her waist was a short, broad-bladed sword.

Khysmet snorted, shifting back and forth as his blood warmed at the sight and scent of the mare. Then the rider and her steed sensed their presence and froze. Both turned to peer through the mist.

Safar felt a thrilling jolt as his eyes met the woman's. They were large and dark and full of wary interest as she examined him in turn. Her face was long, with high cheekbones, brows like black swallow wings, a slender nose slightly hooked over a sensuous mouth.

He saw that mouth twitch with humor and then the woman raised her hand to him as if in greeting.

Safar waved back and started forward, Khysmet quivering under him, filled with burning thoughts of getting closer to that mare.

The woman laughed—it was a rich husky laugh, a laugh out of the deep places in the forest, full of mystery and delight and no little danger. She wheeled the mare about and plunged back toward the wood and the mist swallowed her up. Safar heard the laughter trailing behind her and he urged Khysmet forward.

The stallion didn't need the urging and he exploded after the mare, crossing the meadow in a single jump and plunging into the mist.

It was a delicious chase, a chase full of thrills and near encounters that only added to the fire burning in both man and horse. The mare was Khysmet's equal and the woman was more than Safar's match when it came to pure riding. She led him on a merry hunt through the forest. Sometimes she'd let him draw near then dash away under branches so low Safar was nearly swept off, while she ducked down and easily evaded them. Or she'd disappear for so long he'd be hurled into depression thinking he'd lost her, then she'd burst out of a grove, hold the mare just long enough for Safar to get near, then wheel and dash away again.

Finally they came to the forest's edge and the mysterious horsewoman cantered out. There was a long patch of narrow ground bordered by a steep cliff. Safar's heart tripped when he saw she could go no further.

Then she turned her mare to face him, dropping the reins as if to show the chase was over. The mare nickered for the stallion and Khysmet trotted forward, eager to join her.

The closer Safar came, the more beauteous and exotic the dark stranger seemed. Her long arms and legs were remarkably graceful. Her ebony skin gleamed as if it were burnished and her smile was a bright welcoming light. But it was her eyes which captivated him most, so wide and dark and full of humor.

When he came within twenty feet or so, she raised her hand again. "Please stop," she said, in a voice that was low and full of warmth.

Safar did as she asked but his heart was with Khysmet, who grunted in protest when he reined him in. He obeyed but with great reluctance and once again Safar was struck by the horse's strength of purpose. Any other stallion would have thrown Safar off and hurled himself upon the dancing mare.

"So you're the famous Safar Timura," the woman said. She looked him up and down and seemed to like what she saw. "I must say, I'm certainly not disappointed."

"Who are you, my lady?" Safar asked. "Please grant me the boon of your name."

She laughed and shook her head. "Why, I can't tell you that," she said teasingly, "for if you knew it I could deny you nothing."

Safar's mouth became dry, his throat parched as a desert thicket.

The woman tossed her head, tresses floating in the wind. "Oh, but I probably shouldn't worry about that," she said. "If I were pleasing to look upon, perhaps I'd have reason to worry. But as it is . . ." a graceful hand swept down and up, indicating her lovely form . . . "I fear I'm too plain for one such as you."

"Who said you were plain?" Safar said. "Tell me and I swear that great liar will soon lack a tongue for so offending you."

Another musical laugh. "Only my sisters, Safar Timura, and it would be a vast relief if I had sisters without tongues. They're such dull-witted chatterboxes. But I think my mother would object, so, alas, I must refuse your kind offer to rid them of the means to torment me."

"I am the one in torment, my lady," Safar said. "To be kept in ignorance of one such as you is the deepest of miseries. If you can't find it in your heart to say your name, at least tell me your reason for being here. Are you lost? Is there some way I can assist you?"

Her ripe lips twisted in amusement. "Lost? I think not. A Spirit Rider is never lost!" A small laugh. "Although one of my sisters was confused for a month or two. But that's because she dallied with a handsome lad and forgot her duty. My father punished her—much too mildly in my opinion."

Safar goggled. Spirit Rider? He'd never heard of such a thing.

"As for assisting me," she continued, "it's my duty to assist you, Safar. My father sent me to warn you of grave danger."

Now it was Safar's turn for amusement. "Danger? How unusual." he said dryly. "What, pray tell, could be a greater danger than Iraj Protarus?"

The woman frowned, "Protarus? I don't know this name." Then her face cleared. "Ah," she said, "you mean the strange one who pursues you."

"The very one," Safar said.

"I can't say if you will survive this Protarus fellow," she said. "He's a shape changer in league with other shape changers so it's impossible to predict the outcome."

"Then I repeat the question, my lady," he said. "What could be worse than Iraj Protarus?"

"You will meet it in Caluz," she said. "There you will face a challenge as great as the shape changer and all his armies."

Safar's heart raced. "But I must go there!" he said harshly. "Lord Asper commanded it!" Intuitively he knew she understood who Asper was.

"Of course, you must!" the woman exclaimed. "Otherwise you'll never reach Syrapis."

"Then what's the sense of the warning?" Safar asked. "I already know Caluz is dangerous."

"It's much worse than you think, Safar Timura," she said. "Whatever preparations you have in mind—double them!"

"I will," Safar said.

"One other thing," the woman said. "My father bade me to say that what you seek to defeat your enemy—this Iraj Protarus, I presume—can be found at the temple in Caluz."

"You mean the oracle?" Safar asked. "The Oracle of Hadin? I know something about—"

She stopped him with a raised hand. "I can say no more. Go to Caluz just as you planned," she said. "Accomplish what you intend to accomplish. But remember, Safar Timura, in Caluz all is not as it seems. Seek the truth beyond the veil of lies."

Suddenly the woman and the mare began to fade. "I have to go," she said.

"Wait!" Safar shouted.

She shook her head, becoming fainter and fainter until she was like a ghost. She waved to him.

"Farewell, Safar Timura," she cried, then turned the mare and plunged toward the cliff.

The woman and her steed were translucent, now. At the cliff's edge the mare leaped high.

The woman shouted, "Until we meet again!"

"Where shall we meet?" Safar cried after her. "Where?"

She vanished, but her answer was left floating in the air:

"Syrapis!"

Safar came awake with a start. Across from him, Leiria was still sleeping peacefully. He glanced at the campfire and was surprised to see it exactly the same as when he'd fallen asleep. The vision had seemed so long, yet only a few seconds had passed.

He rose quietly and went out to where Khysmet was tethered. The stallion perked up his ears as he approached, but he stood quietly, as if his thoughts were elsewhere.

Safar laid his head against the horse, stroking the sensitive nose. "Were you there?" Safar whispered. "Did you see?"

Khysmet huffed and stamped his feet, switching his tail back and forth.

Leiria called out. "Is something wrong, Safar?"

"No, Leiria," Safar answered. "Nothing's wrong. Go back to sleep."

He stroked Khysmet. "Syrapis," he whispered. "Syrapis."

*   *   *

Palimak was bored. Day after day he rode with the small group of wagons making up the Timura family caravan with little to do but get into mischief. The roadside scene passed so slowly and with so little change that the smallest thing became major entertainment. A rodent dashing across the track, an ox lifting its tail to defecate and birds taking a dust bath were among the more stirring sights he'd seen that day.

It wasn't so bad for the older children, he thought. They got to run around the wagons, or dash off into the fields to explore and play games. Sometimes they'd disappear all day and wouldn't catch up to the main caravan until nightfall. Oh, how he wished he could go with them. Why one of his cousins had seen a bear and her cubs just the other day. Now, wouldn't that've been something to see? Maybe he could've made a pet of one of the cubs, or at least played with it a little, What really offended him was that his cousin was a girl. This made life seem even more unfair.

There was little privacy when on the road, so he couldn't play with Gundara and Gundaree as much as he'd like. The Favorites hated it when so many people were around and tended to be grumpy when he summoned them. Always complaining that people could peek into the covered wagon anytime they wanted.

To Palimak it seemed as if he was always getting into trouble, especially when he played with his magic. Although he never meant any harm, sometimes things just didn't go as planned and he was always being scolded as if he'd done it on purpose.

He was still sulking over an incident earlier in the day. After his grandmother had put out the wagon fire he'd explained quite plainly that he'd only been trying to help. But she didn't listen—they never listened!—and he'd gotten the scolding of his life and was banished to the smelly old supply wagon.

"Now, let's see what mischief you can get up to in there, Palimak Timura," his grandmother had said in her most scornful tones. "I'm sorry there's nothing but moldy flour and wormy corn to occupy your Lordship. Now maybe you'll have time now to think about all the heartache and worry you're causing me."

"I'm sorry, Grandmother," he'd said in his most contrite manner. Unfortunately, she wasn't so easily soothed.

"I'm sorry, I'm sorry," she mocked. "When I'm in my grave from the worry you've caused me *you'll* know what sorry really is!"

Palimak poked a finger at a damp floursack. He didn't know what she was so upset about. It hadn't been that big of a fire, after all. And he could easily have put it out himself. If he could've remembered the fire putter outter spell, that is.

He still didn't know what had gone wrong with his experiment. The whole idea had originated with his grandmother's and aunts' complaints about how dark it was in the wagons. There was always a lot of mending to be done and they said they were going blind from sewing in such dimness. Because of the danger of fire and the roughness of the road no one was permitted to burn an oil lamp while the wagons were moving.

Bored as he was, Palimak became intensely interested in their difficulties. Interest turned to a child's concern for his loved ones. What would his grandmother do if she were blind? And his aunts, what if they couldn't even see their children to kiss them? So he'd turned his agile little mind full force on the problem.

Instinctively, he went at it backwards. What was the result he wanted? That was easy, he wanted light without having to burn anything. There were two ways to go at that, he'd decided. The first would be to take the light out of the fire and throw the fire away. You could then pour the light into bowls, or something, or even glass jars with stoppers on them so the light couldn't escape if it were so inclined. Probably the jars would be best, he thought. For reasons he couldn't explain he imagined light might be pretty rebellious and would always be trying to run away.

The second method would be to somehow trap the light. You could catch it in some kind of net, or whatever, as it ran away from its source—the sun or a campfire—then you could store it in great big casks with spigots like wine barrels. Then whenever you needed some light all you had to do was turn the spigot and fill up a jar.

He could envision his grandmother and aunts with jars of lights all around them, sewing away with no trouble at all and praising him for being such a smart and thoughtful little boy. The image pleased him immensely and he worked even harder.

He'd quickly dismissed the idea of trapping light and storing it. The trouble with light was that it was even runnier than water and much thinner so you'd have to have really big, big barrels, maybe even bigger than a house—which was the largest object he could imagine—to hold just a little bit. Which wouldn't last very long either, so that was really stupid. Fine, then. He'd try to separate the light from fire and see what happened.

This feat proved to be surprisingly easy. Oh sure, Gundara and Gundaree helped, but it was his idea and he'd done most of the real work. One night after everyone had gone to sleep he'd filled a bowl with oil, lit it with a candle, then summoned his Favorites. After a few false starts due to the usual quarrels between the two, he'd cast the spell.

"Come out, little light," he crooned. "Come and play with Palimak. We'll have lots of fun and good things to eat and you won't have to smell that stinky oil all the time. Come out, little light. Come out and play with Palimak."

He scooped his hands forward, skimming across the wavery fire and to his amazement he suddenly had a double palmful of light spilling onto the tent floor. It made little glowing puddles with scattered drops all around. Then the light began to fade—running away, as Palimak thought of it—and he quickly turned a jar upside down over the largest puddle. Inside the jar the light was only a soft glow at first, then it suddenly became much brighter.

Palimak clapped his hands with glee. He'd done it! He looked over at the bowl of oil. There was no light coming from it now. But he could smell the burning oil and when he put his hand close he could still feel the heat of the fire.

That night Palimak slept the peaceful sleep of a smart little boy, a kind little boy, a boy who'd just saved his grandmother and aunts from blindness. He'd smiled to himself as he slept, the jar of light clutched in his arms, dreaming of all the hugs he'd get and all the nice things they'd say about him.

When he awoke the light was gone. Palimak was in a panic trying to figure out what had happened. The stopper was on tight. The spell he'd used to enforce the jar's light-holding properties was still strong. Then he'd looked at the bowl of oil and saw that it was empty and the invisible fire was no longer burning.

Palimak frowned. It seemed obvious that although he'd separated the light from the fire, some connection had remained. When the fire had burned up its fuel the light in the jar had gone out. Well, that was no good. You still had the same problem as before, which was that you can't have a fire in a moving wagon. But, wait! Nobody said anything about *outside the wagon.*

Palimak had labored until late that night working on the solution. The next morning—this very morning, in fact, this most boring of all days with its almost squashed rodent, stupid oxen and dusty birds—he'd put his plan to its first, and final, test. A brass burner was suspended beneath a rarely used wagon. A fire was lit, a small one so no one would notice. Light went into a jar. And the jar was hidden under Palimak's coat until the caravan set off and he was alone in the wagon. Then out it came, glowing very nicely, although maybe only enough for one person to sew by. So what? That was no problem! He could make a jar for each of them, being sure to hang the same number of burners under the wagon. Then when the light got dim all somebody had to do was jump off the wagon, toss more fuel into the burners and the light would be strong again. Palimak figured he'd volunteer to do the jumping off to start with. Later on someone else could do it, like that cousin of his who thought she was so smart because she'd seen a bear with its cubs. As if anybody couldn't do that!

It would have worked just fine too, Palimak thought, if the driver hadn't gone over that bump. And the bottom of the wagon had caught fire. Real fire you could see and smell and which could burn everything up! Palimak was trying to think of a spell to put it out when his grandmother came running from her wagon and beat it to death with a wet broom. Scolding and punishment followed swiftly.

Deep in the gloom of his supply wagon exile, Palimak gave a long, heartfelt sigh. It was so unfair. The more he thought about it, the sadder he became. So sad he thought he might even let himself cry, although he was probably too old for that and if somebody saw him he'd never get to run in the fields and play just like everybody else.

A tear was leaking down his cheek, with more due to follow, when his grandfather opened the back flap and jumped into the wagon.

"If you're not busy, son," his grandfather said, "I could use a little help."

Palimak hastily wiped the tear away and composed himself. "I'm not busy," he said. "What do you want me to do, grandfather?"

"I'm taking over the lead wagon," Khadji said. "We just added a new ox to the team and she's so green she's going to need some watching. I can't mind the road and her at the same time. Not very well, anyway. And I thought I could use a real good pair of eyes to help me."

"I've got real good eyes, grandfather," Palimak said, spreading the lids wide and looking this way and that. "See?"

"You're just the man for the job," his grandfather said and in a few minutes Palimak was ensconced on the seat of the lead wagon, glaring for all he was worth at the worrisome ox.

"Now, I feel much better," his grandfather said, cracking his whip to get the team moving. "No telling what a green animal will get into its head."

"But she's white, grandfather," Palimak said, pointing at the young ox. "Why do you keep saying she's green?"

Khadji buried a smile and pretended to examine the ox, which, as Palimak had said, was white as snow. "Hmm," he said. "Now that you mention it, she *is* white. I must have been looking at her in the wrong light. Thanks for pointing that out to me, son. I might have missed it."

Palimak was disappointed. "Then you don't need me to help you watch her anymore?" he said. "Since she's white, I mean. And it's the green ones that give you all the trouble."

"Oh, white's worse," Khadji said. "Much worse than green. Give me a green ox any day, but spare me the white." He gave Palimak a nudge. "You just watch her extra hard," he said. "Now that we know she's white."

Palimak glared at the ox even harder, so hard his eyes started to burn. "Why don't you take a little rest for a minute, son," Khadji said when he noticed the boy blinking fiercely. "I think she'll be all right for a mile or two now that she knows you're along."

The boy relaxed, easing closer to his grandfather and enjoying his company. A long silence followed. It was comfortable at first, but then it extended and expanded, making room for alarming thoughts, like the unfortunate matter of the wagon he'd set on fire. His grandfather stirred and Palimak had the horrible thought that Khadji was about to bring up the subject. Which was just awful. Everything was so peaceful and nice but it was going to be spoiled by another scolding. And maybe other punishment, as well. You could never tell with adults. They were like, like . . . the white ox, which his grandfather said was worse than even the green ones and you never knew what they'd do next.

By way of preamble his grandfather hawked, then turned and spat into the dust and Palimak knew he was in for it.

"I don't know about you," his grandfather said, "but ever since we took the main track I've been going crazy with boredom."

Palimak gaped in surprise. "Me too!" he said.

"I don't want to dare the gods for more trouble than we already have," his grandfather continued, "but when we were running and hiding all the time at least things were interesting. Sure, we might have been caught by Iraj, but that just made it more exciting. Our minds were always busy thinking up new things, or tricks, or guessing what Iraj might be up to." He glanced at Palimak, smiling. "Right?"

"Right!" Palimak nodded hard for emphasis.

"So here we are on the main track," his grandfather went on, "and they tell us we're making excellent time. Thirty miles a day!" He snorted. "Feels more like a thousand before the day is done."

He shook his head. "Nothing to do and all day to do it in," he said. "It's hard to bear sometimes, I tell you. Very hard to bear."

Another sigh, this one longer. "In fact," he said, "I'm feeling like that right now. Like I can't stand it anymore."

He paused, as if thinking, then, "Here," he said, "take over for a moment, will you?" And he handed Palimak the reins.

The boy was stunned at this display of trust. He straightened up and tried to snap the reins. It came out as a disappointingly slow wave that died before it reached the first oxen, but his grandfather nodded in approval.

"That's the way to do it," he said. "Nice and gentle. A wise driver is careful not to frighten his animals."

Heartened by the praise, Palimak sat taller still. Khadji fumbled in his pocket and took out a small lump of moist clay wrapped in oil cloth.

"Here's what I like to do to keep from getting bored to death," his grandfather said, working the clay between his hands.

Palimak gaped as his grandfather squeezed and pinched, turning out one little figure after the other—a goat, a bear, an ox and even a camel with such a long neck and silly expression on its face that the boy burst out laughing.

"May I try?" he asked.

He'd seen Khadji and sometimes even his father make pots and jars and dishes. All useful things, but dull as mud as far as Palimak was concerned. It'd never occurred to him you could create such interesting figures.

"Why not?" Khadji said. He fished another oil cloth packet from his pocket. "I've been saving this for something special," he said. "So far I haven't thought of anything, but maybe you can."

He traded the reins for the packet and watched from the corner of his eye as Palimak opened it. The boy's face brightened when he saw the unusual color of the clay. Instead of a dull gray it was a lustrous green, so deep that it was almost black when looked at from certain angles.

"It's beautiful!" the boy breathed. He looked up at Khadji. "Can I make anything I want?" he asked. "Anything at all."

"Of course you can," his grandfather said. "It's yours, now."

Palimak stared at the clay long and hard. Then his face cleared. "I know!" he said. And he started squeezing and molding in the clay.

"What're you thinking of making?" Khadji asked.

"I can't tell you," Palimak said with a sly grin. "But I'll give you a hint. It's a surprise for somebody.

"A really big surprise!"

CHAPTER SIXTEEN
PALIMAK'S REVENGE

Kalasariz moved cautiously through the night forest, keeping a discreet distance between himself and his quarry. His shape changer senses were tuned to their highest pitch and he could smell the sulfurous odor of the witch clinging to the brush lining the narrow trail. It was so powerful it nearly obscured the king's spoor, that mixture of fresh blood and old graves that marked all shape changers.

Behind him, sprawled on a great field, the army slept. Except for a few key sentries—all in the pay of Kalasariz—no one knew the king was out this night.

The spymaster seethed as he followed the king and Old Sheesan through the forest.

Unless they were of his own making, Kalasariz detested all mysteries. And this midnight journey certainly fit that definition.

He wasn't as worried about what they were up to as he was at being left out. From the outset he'd given Old Sheesan explicit orders she was report every word and movement the king made when in her presence. This was the main reason he'd introduced the witch to Protarus. He was much more interested in knowing his king's most secret thoughts than he was in finding Safar Timura.

The witch, however, had proven to be cannier than he'd thought and now he was losing control. Old Sheesan's reports had become perfunctory, vague and of little value. She hadn't started outright lying to him yet—other than lies of omission—but he suspected she'd begin soon enough. And then he'd have to go to a great deal of bother and no little danger in getting rid of her.

The forest's edge reared up with no warning and Kalasariz nearly gave himself away as he stepped out onto open ground into the light of the Demon Moon. Hastily, he pulled back and found cover. He stayed quite still for a moment until he was sure no one had noticed him. Then he gently parted some branches and peered out.

Old Sheesan and the king were walking along a narrow strip of barren ground that seemed to be edged by a cliff. The forest was silent so the spymaster could hear the swishing of the witch's robes as she moved and the creak of Protarus' battle harness. They paused at the edge of the cliff. The witch gestured at a point on the ground.

"More magic there," Kalasariz heard her say. "A woman, methinks."

"A witch?" Protarus asked.

"No, she weren't no witch. Somethin' else, for certain. I can't quite put me finger on it."

She turned and pointed back at the forest where Kalasariz was hiding. He was so alarmed he nearly fled. But then she said, "Both of 'em come through there. Lord Timura was on that horse that's been givin' yer Majesty fits of envy. The woman was on a mare—and that was somethin' special too. Animal magic all over the place."

"Yes, yes," Protarus said, sniffing eagerly at the air. "I can smell it myself!"

The witch chortled. "Soon yer won't need the likes of Old Sheesan to ferret out mischief," she said. "And then where will this poor old granny be?"

"She won't be poor at any rate," Protarus said. "Not after all the gold I've been dumping in her lap."

"Gold's not ever'thin', Majesty," the witch said. "Least that's what they say. Although they leave out the part about exactly what's missin' that gold won't cure."

Kalasariz made a mental note to find out where the witch had hidden all this gold she was talking about. If he removed her little treasure cache she'd be more dependent on him.

"Anyways," the witch went on, "they came out there and rode up to the cliff where they stopped to palaver awhile. Then Lord Timura went off that way." The witch pointed to the most distant edge of the forest.

"What about the woman?" Protarus asked.

"I don't know," the witch said. "There's no sign of her after that. It's like she rode her mare off the cliff, or somethin'. Whatever she did, she didn't go with Lord Timura."

"Is that all?" Protarus asked, impatient. "When you urged me to go with you tonight you said you'd made a great discovery. Where is it? I see Safar's trail, which we've been following all along, so that's certainly no 'great discovery.' He met a woman! So what? A romantic interlude, I suspect. He's probably tired of Leiria by now and wanted something different. Again, so what? As for the woman's disappearance, if I don't care about the woman, then what do I care what happened to her?"

"Yer got it exactly, Majesty," the witch replied. "A romantic inter-lude! Yes, indeed, that's what Lord Timura was up to." She gave a nasty giggle. "In more ways th'n one, yer old granny suspects."

She gestured wide. "There's lust in the air, that's for certain," she said. "A prancin' stallion and a willin' mare. A lusty young man and a hot-blooded maid. What could be more natural, like? Then add magic: the man's a wizard, the maid's maybe a witch. Stir the pot well, mixin' in the horse and the mare, both magic too, and we gets us a delicious broth, yer Majesty.

"We're gettin' close to Lord Timura, Majesty. Catch up to him within a week, is Old Sheesan's guess. And yer needs to be prepared when that time comes, if yer don't mind me sayin'."

"What's to prepare for?" Protarus asked, curt. "I have an army. He only has a few hundred peasants."

"But he's slipped yer grasp afore, Majesty," the witch said. "So he might do it again. More important—how's he gonner fight back? Ferget his soldiers, good or bad. Don't matter. Neither does yer army. We're talkin' about a wizard, here. Most powerful wizard in all Esmir, some say, demons included.

"Why, it's said it was Timura The Wizard that brought down Zanzair, Majesty. And yer had a bigger, meaner army then. And yer weren't a shape-changer, neither, was yer, Majesty? That's how bad he hurt yer, ain't it? Hurt yer real bad he did, this Timura the Wizard and if yer ain't careful, he'll get yer again!"

"And you have a solution, I take it." Protarus said.

"Indeed I do, yer Majesty," she said, lifting up her blind face to him. "I can give yer power over him when yer meets. We can make a spell here and now that'll do it."

"Then cast the spell, woman," Protarus demanded. "Get on with it!"

"That's all I needed to hear, Majesty," the witch cackled. "Yer had to order it, first!"

With that she raised her hands and began to twirl. Around and around, like a slow moving top. In his hiding place, Kalasariz snorted in disgust when he saw her raggedy robes rise up and show her bony knees. Then she went faster, turning still faster, and both Kalasariz and Protarus gaped as she became a blur. The blur began to glow, radiant sparks flying off into the night. Then the witch slowed and the blur took form.

Kalasariz gasped. For instead of an ugly witch there was a wondrous woman standing before Protarus. She was pleasing of form and face, with long golden hair and a gossamer gown of black that displayed all of her beauty.

The spymaster heard a growl of lust, thought it was his own being voiced, then realized it was Protarus.

The witch laughed, but instead of a harsh cackle it sounded like tinkling bells. "Come to me my sweet," she said, voice silky and smooth. "And we shall make such a spell!"

She opened her arms and Protarus gave a great howl and bounded forward to take her.

Kalasariz crept away. Before he'd been angry and worried. Now he was merely frightened. He had to come up with something quickly, before the witch had complete control over the king. What really frightened him was that it might already be too late.

If the spymaster had tarried he would have seen greater reason to fear the witch.

After she had drained Iraj of all his strength, she made herself more beautiful still, curling up to him, whispering poisoned words into his ear.

"You are a mystery to me," she said. "You are so strong, so wise, and yet you allow yourself to be guided by fools."

Iraj stirred. "If you mean my spell brothers," he said, "I don't have any choice."

The witch cuddled closer, pressing her luscious form against Iraj. "Is that what they told you?" she asked. "That once the Spell of Four was cast, you were locked to them forever?"

Iraj sighed. "Yes," he said. "Forever."

"I can show you how to be free of them," she said. "I can teach you how to break the chains."

Even in lust, Iraj's suspicions were aroused. "Why would you do this?" he asked. "What is it that you expect in return?"

"Only to be your queen, Iraj Protarus," the witch answered. "I have waited a lifetime for one such as you. I have powers—more power than any witch in all of Esmir. But I want more. You understand what I mean by that, don't you? To want *more*?"

"Yes," Iraj whispered. "Yes!"

"Together," she said, "we can have it all! Together we will at last be satisfied. But first . . . we must set you free from the Spell of Four."

Iraj turned to her, eyes bright with hope. "How?" he asked. "Show me!"

"First we have to catch Safar Timura," the witch said. "It would help to have the child, but it isn't absolutely necessary."

"Teach me now!" Iraj demanded. "I don't want to wait!"

The witch giggled. "So impatient!" she said. "Just like that stallion after the mare!"

He tried to take her again, but she avoided his embrace, saying, "First swear to me that you'll make me your queen."

"I swear it," Iraj said huskily. As he spoke he felt a strange sensation burn through his body and knew a magical pact had just been made. This was one promise he'd have to keep.

Sheesan smiled, eyes aglow with victory. "When the time comes to confront Lord Timura," she said, "you must make certain that your Spell Brothers are close by. The casting will not only free you, but kill them, as well as Timura. Do you understand?"

Thrilled at the prospect of all his enemies being destroyed at one blow, Iraj nodded eagerly that he did.

"Go on," he urged. "What's next?"

Laughing, the witch drew Iraj into her arms again and they made even wilder love than before. When they were done she bathed him with cool water from a forest stream. And when Iraj was entirely human—too spent from lovemaking to be overcome by his shape-changer's side—she taught him the spell.

He was amazed at how simple it was.

✻   ✻   ✻

Leiria watched the horizontal smear of light inch toward her. The smear broadened and deepened as it came, like a slow moving storm creeping along the earth.

"No doubt about it," she said to Safar. "It's Iraj. The way he's going he'll be on to us within a week."

The two were crouched on a hill overlooking a swift moving river crossed by a sturdy bridge wide enough for two large freight wagons to pass with room to spare.

"He's moving more quickly than I expected," Safar said. "With an army that size I thought the most he could do was keep pace with us."

"It's because he's marching all night," Leiria said. "I was on a campaign with him once when he used that trick. We'd set out at dusk and march until late morning. Then hole up in the afternoon to rest. Surprised the hells out of the enemy when we showed up at his door two weeks before we were expected."

"Why didn't you tell me about that trick before?" Safar asked, a bit exasperated.

"You had enough worry on your mind," Leiria said. "Besides, there's nothing we could've done about it. We're going as fast as we can. Scary stories wouldn't make us move any faster."

Safar sighed. "I suppose you're right." He studied the horizon a little longer. Then, "How long can he keep that kind of thing up before he exhausts his army?"

Leiria shrugged, then gestured at the approaching light. It was bright enough now to obscure the lower heavens. "In this case," she said dryly, "he's in little danger of that."

"Let's do our best to give him a nice long rest," Safar said. He pointed at the bridge. "Remove it and his engineers will need at least a week to bridge the river. From the map of this area, there's no other place to cross for miles."

"And I suppose O Great Wizard," Leiria teased, "that you have some amazing magical spell that will do the job."

Safar laughed. "Absolutely," he said. "I call it fire. Perhaps you've heard of it? It's especially effective on wooden bridges."

"My, haven't we been jolly lately," Leiria said. "If I didn't know better I'd say there was a woman involved."

When he didn't answer Leiria looked up sharply and caught him blushing. He muttered something unintelligible, mounted Khysmet and cantered down the hill to the bridge.

Leiria puzzled over this as she hurried to catch up to him. Had she somehow stumbled on a little secret? But that didn't make sense. Where would he meet a woman way out here?

* * *

Gundara and Gundaree were perched on a keg of honey, sucking on their fingers while they watched Palimak fuss over his masterpiece.

"Looks like a dog," Gundara said. "If you put some ears on it, that is."

"It's not a dog," Palimak scorned, "and it doesn't have any ears because I haven't made them yet."

Nevertheless, the next thing he did was form small pointy things on the odd-shaped lump of clay.

"Oh, *now* I understand," Gundaree said. "You're making some sort of an animal. Yes, now that I look at it that way I can see four legs, a tail, a neck, and I suppose that's some sort of head, right?"

"With ears," Palimak said, showing him.

"The ears were my idea," Gundara sniffed. "Pretty stupid dog, if it didn't have ears."

"I detest dogs," Gundaree said. "Filthy creatures. Always sniffing around our little home."

"Remember the one that made water on us?" Gundara said.

Gundaree shuddered. "Like it was yesterday, instead of six hundred years ago."

"It was seven," Gundara corrected.

"Six," insisted Gundaree. "I remember because our master was—"

"I *told* you," Palimak broke in, "that it's not a dog!"

He held up the object. "It's a horse! See?"

Both of the Favorites studied the object, scratching their heads.

Finally, Gundaree said, "I can see why you asked for our help. I hate to say this, Little Master, but your skills as a sculptor need a bit of honing."

"I still say it's a dog," Gundara said. "A big black dog."

"Maybe a little more green than black," Gundaree said.

"All right, it's a greenish blackish dog," Gundara said. "But it's a dog just the same."

"I don't care what you *say* it is," Palimak scolded. "I thought horse when I made it, so it's a horse. I even put a horse hair in it from Khysmet's tail."

He picked up a sharp twig and poked holes in the clay for eyes. He examined his work and nodded in satisfaction. "All I have to do is write my name on its stomach," he said, flipping the clay over and sketching the letters with the stick.

Palimak plumped the "horse" down on the wagon bed. "Now, we can make it pretty," he said. "Make it so he can't help himself when he sees it and he'll just have to pick it up! Then he'll flip it over ..." Palimak demonstrated, turning the clay so the belly and writing was exposed. " ... And when he spots my name he'll read it aloud."

"And that's when the surprise comes in?" Gundara asked.

"You guessed it!" Palimak said. "That's when the surprise comes in!"

*   *   *

Kalasariz watched the engineers hoist the last timber in place and start to nail it down. In an hour or so the bridge would be complete and the army could march again. As he considered the rough but sturdy structure that spanned the raging river, he couldn't help but feel grudging admiration for the king.

Not long ago, when the scouts had returned with the news that the bridge had been destroyed, Kalasariz thought the task was hopeless and the canny Safar had foiled them once again. To his amazement, Iraj had been vastly amused.

"It's good see you in such humor, Majesty," the spy master had said. "Enlighten me, please, as to its source so I can join in your laughter."

"Safar just made a mistake," came the reply. "He's playing to my strength."

"To your strength, Majesty?"

"Yes, to my abilities as a general. And there's no man or demon who can match those."

Then without further explanation he'd shouted to an aide, "Call the chief of engineers! Tell him his life depends on how quickly he obeys my summons!"

A few moments later a badly frightened old demon had stumbled into the tent to get his orders.

That had been four days ago. Now Kalasariz watched that very same demon crouch with the work crew, closely overseeing the finishing touches. What Iraj had done was order the bridge built while they marched. Freight wagons were cleared out for the carpenters to work and the bridge was built in parts and by torchlight as the army moved on through the night. By the time they'd reached the river it was nearly done and only a little more time was needed to erect it over the stumps of the old stanchions the previous bridge had stood upon.

Kalasariz heard horses approaching from the other side of the bridge and looked up to see a group of weary scouts coming in to report to their officers. It was ironic, Kalasariz thought, that the first group to cross the new bridge was coming from the opposite direction.

But the spymaster wasn't here for humor and certainly not to admire Iraj's brilliance. He smiled to himself as one of the scouts saw him and made a signal unnoticed by the others. Very good, Kalasariz thought, nodding to acknowledge his spy. Then he signaled back. They'd meet in an hour at the usual place.

One and a half turns of the glass later he was back in his tent examining an object under his brightest lamp. Gleaming up at him was the small figurine of a black horse, so beautifully wrought that it could only have been produced by a master potter. He turned it over and made out the name sketched in the hard-fired clay.

"Palimak," he read. The spymaster's eyes glittered. It was from the boy—the half-breed Iraj was hunting along with Safar.

The figurine was not only beautifully fashioned and fired, but it buzzed with gentle sorcery, as if it were meant to be a magical pet. The child was obviously some sort of prodigy. Not only in magic, but in the arts as well.

What great luck, Kalasariz thought. Somehow the boy had lost a prized, personal treasure. One he'd made himself, so it would be of incredible value to Fari and his wizards. It was a direct magical link to Palimak—and where the boy was, Safar would be nearby.

I'll present it to the king myself, Kalasariz thought. I'll wait a day or two and pretend I found it abandoned on the road. Which is where the scout said he'd found it. He said it was lying next to a broken keg of honey and the whole ground was so swarming with ants he'd almost missed it. Kalasariz would tell the same tale, but with himself as the hero. It wouldn't solve his problems with Old Sheesan, but it would put him in such favor with Protarus that her advantage would be slightly lessened.

In Kalasariz' world slight was a great victory. Slight could be made into a gap and the gap could be widened into a ravine. Slight had won many battles for him in the past and in crucial moments when his life had been at stake, slight advantages had saved his neck.

He was about to send a messenger to the king to beg an audience when a second thought crept in. Kalasariz always heeded such things, placing second thoughts above even slight advantages as plums to his trade. Second thoughts kept you wary, second thoughts gave you special insights, second thoughts kept you alive when all else failed.

What if there were some trick to this? What if Safar Timura's mind was behind the crafting of this magnificent creation? That made more sense. Lord Timura was a master potter as well as a wizard, after all. The more he thought about it, the more this scenario seemed likely. Even a child was unlikely to lose such a beautiful magical toy. He'd keep it close to him always, checking for it when he went to sleep, looking for it first thing when he awoke and patting his pockets wherever he went to make certain it was still there.

If this were a trick he could be ruined. However, if it wasn't and he didn't present it to the king opportunity might be lost. Never mind that if the king found out he'd withheld any kind of a clue, ruin would be the most pleasant thing that would happen to Kalasariz. Yes, he'd bless the possibility of mere ruin from his chains and beg to be lifted to such a high plane as the king's torturers worked on him.

They wouldn't kill him. He was bonded to Protarus by the Spell of Four so they couldn't make away with him or the king would suffer as well. As would Fari and Luka. But they could keep him barely alive. Keep him imprisoned in perpetual pain with one of Fari's spells.

Then the solution came. Old Sheesan! Ever since the night he'd seen her reveal her true self to Protarus, he'd pondered how to regain the upper hand. After the initial shock, his old confidence had returned.

A wily master of setting plots within plots, Kalasariz had never met his match in sheer cunning. Well, Safar Timura, possibly. But he didn't like to dwell on that. But this woman—this witch—was not Safar Timura. He didn't care how much magic she possessed. Kalasariz had something better—a mind full of so many tricks and turns that he could confound mere magic and run her as easily as he ran all his spies.

He sent a messenger to the witch, politely begging her attendance.

A few minutes later she joined him in his quarters to examine the figurine. She turned it about in her hands, feeling every inch of it, blind face furrowing in concentration.

Finally her brow cleared. "It's jus' as yer guessed, me lord. Made by the boy, Palimak, himself." She rubbed scratched letters on the belly. "Don't need to see the name to know it's his work." She tapped her nose. "I can smell him, I can."

"And it's of some use to you, I hope?" Kalasariz asked.

She cackled. "Sure it is," she said. "All kinds of spells to get at a body if yer gots somethin' real personal of his. Shrivel his head or his parts, assumin' he's old enough to have parts, that is."

"Excellent, excellent," Kalasariz said.

He took the figurine from her, pulling slightly to make the greedy old thing give it up. Blank as she kept her face, the spymaster had long experience in reading hidden things so he could tell she was seething with jealousy.

Good. Now for the next part.

Kalasariz wrapped the clay figurine in a piece of silk, then, to the witch's immense amazement, he put it back into her hands.

"Perhaps you wouldn't mind delivering it to the king," he said. "I'd consider it a personal favor if you would."

Old Sheesan was instantly suspicious, just as he knew she'd be. "Why the likes of me?" she asked. "Why not take it to him yerself. Yer deserves the credit fer findin' it."

"Actually," Kalasariz said, "much as I'd like to be involved I can't. I came by it by means I wouldn't want to get around."

"'Specially the king, right?" the witch said, knowing he was talking about revealing the extent of his network of spies.

Kalasariz laughed, wagging a finger at the witch. "It's not nice to pry in other people's business," he said. "But you did get the general idea of my problem."

Her suspicions satisfied, the witch made the figurine vanish into her raggedy cloak.

"I'll see he gets it, I will," the witch said. "And thanks fer thinkin' of Old Sheesan, me lord. Yer've made a better friend than yer know."

"That was uppermost in my mind, Madam," the spymaster replied. "Uppermost."

Old Sheesan made a remarkable transformation when she entered Iraj's tent an hour later. Instead of a cackling hag, she was once again the beautiful, sensuous woman Kalasariz had seen in the forest. And just as before her blindness was miraculously "cured."

She curled up against the king, purring like a sleek cat. When he fumbled for her she laughed a musical laugh and drew away.

"Wait," she said in a most melodic voice. "I have a surprise for you."

"A surprise?" Iraj asked, vastly pleased. Kings and queens are like children when it comes to gifts. "What is it?"

She handed him the cloth package containing the horse figurine. "Oh, just a little thing I found on the road," she said lightly. But her eyes, which were a deep shade of violet, danced with excitement.

Iraj unwrapped the package. He reacted strongly when the fantastic miniature of the black horse was revealed.

"What's this?" he said, trembling with excitement. "Is it from the boy?"

"Turn it over and see for yourself," the beautiful witch said.

Iraj flipped the horse upside down. He immediately saw the clumsily scratched letters.

He spelled them out. "P-A-L-I-M-A-K." Iraj grinned, wolfish teeth gleaming.

"Palimak!" he said aloud.

*   *   *

Safar and Leiria were once again hidden on the hill overlooking the bridge. They'd been bitterly disappointed Iraj had foiled their plan so easily and now they were frantically wracking their brains for some other means to stop him.

"This is the only place for miles where we can do any good," Leiria said, not bothering to whisper.

Although Iraj's army was at rest, there was so much activity going on no one could hear them. Off in the night they could hear armorers hammering, animals bawling and supply sergeants barking at their lazy charges.

Safar peered at the big tent set up in the middle of the camp. Iraj's flag flew overhead, fluttering in the light of the Demon Moon.

He shook his head, grim. "There's nothing that can be done," he said, getting to his feet. "Come on. We'd better catch up to the others and warn them."

At that moment a large explosion rent the air. The two turned to see a fiery shower bursting into the night sky.

Iraj's tent was in flames and frantic men and demons were rushing from all over to put it out

Leiria could barely keep from doing a dance. "What incredible luck!" she hooted.

Safar was thoughtful, examining the dancing flames. "It wasn't luck," he said at last. Then he smiled. "Someone's been up to some mischief again," he said.

"Palimak?" Leiria asked, incredulous.

"Who else?"

*   *   *

Palimak and his Favorites were peering at the small lump of clay he'd pinched off the original before he'd made the horse.

Suddenly it flared and Palimak yelped with glee. "We got him! We got him!" he shouted. He smacked his knee with a small fist. "That'll teach that mean old Iraj Protarus!"

Then the bit of clay shattered into dust. Palimak's joy turned to dismay.

"Do you think he's still alive?" he asked.

Gundaree stroked his handsome chin, examining the patterns of clay dust on the floor. "I fear so, Little Master," he finally said.

Gundara was looking over his shoulder. "But we killed somebody," he said, trying to sooth Palimak's feelings. "At least we did that."

"So what?" Palimak said, still gloomy. "It was probably just some stupid soldier."

"It wasn't an entirely cheerless event, Little Master," Gundaree said. "We did manage to hurt the king. Enough to keep him out of action for awhile."

Palimak brightened. "That's all right, then," he said. "Maybe we didn't kill him, but at least we slowed him down."

*   *   *

Kalasariz watched with much satisfaction as the burial party carried the still-smoking remains of Old Sheesan to the river and dumped them in without ceremony.

In the medical tent he could hear Protarus howl in pain as Lord Fari treated his burn wounds with magical ointments and spells.

403

"I want that child found and killed!" the king shrieked. Another howl of pain, then, "No, don't kill him! I'll skin the man or demon alive who harms a hair on his head!

"I want him for myself, do you hear? I want him for myself!"

Once again the spymaster whispered thanks to the dark god who'd overseen his birth. Without the native caution of second thought, it might have been Kalasariz' body that was being so roughly treated.

Oh, sure, the spymaster was sorry the hunt for Safar would be delayed while the king healed. But in his opinion—the only one that ever really counted to Kalasariz—that was a small price to pay for survival.

There was also a bright side—possibly even outweighing the near disaster. At least I rid myself of that witch, he thought.

He looked down at the roiling river and saw a blackened lump of flesh snagged on the shore. A freshwater crab scuttled out from a hole in the bank, snatched the flesh up in its claws and dashed out of sight.

Good riddance, you old bitch, Kalasariz thought. Then he strolled into the night, humming to himself while his agile mind searched for new plots to hatch.

Part Three

Covenant of Death

CHAPTER SEVENTEEN
INTO THE BLACK LANDS

Three weeks out of Caluz Safar led his people into a region so desolate, so barren that even vultures shunned the ashen skies. Black peaks vomited sparks and sulfurous smoke over a dark, cratered plain littered with gigantic heaps of rock. Here the Demon Moon shone strong and bright, casting strange shadows that seemed like pools of old blood.

Tornadoes rose up like disturbed nests of dragons, roaring from one end of the plain to the other, destroying everything in their path. The craters proved to be entrances to deep caverns and at night millions of bats swarmed out. They hovered in dense black clouds, then flew away to some distant promised land where plump insects abounded. The bats returned each dawn, descending into the craters in great swirling columns as if they were being sucked into the Hells.

Everyone became fearful, starting at the slightest sound, continually casting nervous glances over their shoulders, trembling hands never far from a weapon. Although surrounded by hundreds of fellow villagers, each person felt oddly alone and vulnerable to the vagaries of evil chance.

Then they began to run low on supplies, especially feed for the animals. In the long, sustained dash to Caluz there had been little chance for the animals to forage. Now the stores of fodder were dangerously scarce and there was no place to stop and let the beasts fill up on the bounty of the fields. Nothing grew in that bleak land where even a thorn could not take root.

The alarmists on the Council of Elders wanted to abandon some of the wagons, killing and butchering the oxen, then drying the meat so they'd be certain to have enough food to reach Caluz. Their reasoning was that the wagons and animals could be replaced when they reached their goal.

Safar successfully argued that it was too great a risk. "What if something happens in Caluz that prevents us from buying more?" he'd said. "Then we'd be caught in a trap of our own making."

Actually, he was fairly certain there'd be no chance at all of replacing the wagons and animals. But if he told them what he really knew about Caluz he'd be hard pressed to keep them from running like the Hells in the other direction.

If truth be known, it wouldn't have taken much for Safar to join them in mad flight. From the moment he stepped foot into the Black Lands his wizardly senses had been assaulted by sudden magical disturbances—a rippling of the surface of the otherworlds, that made him feel unsteady, sick to his stomach. On a few occasions he was hit by a feeling of the deepest foreboding that something quite terrible was going to happen if he continued and it was all he could do not to order an immediate retreat.

If it weren't for the memory of the mysterious and beautiful Spirit Rider who'd come to warn him in the vision, he might have succumbed. True, she'd said he faced grave danger in Caluz. However, she'd also confirmed the necessity of the visit. The two things combined to give form to the dangers they faced. Thus strengthened, he was able to cast shields to protect the other Kyranians from the worst of the rogue spells that made all seem so hopeless.

Palimak didn't seem to be as affected. The boy's growing powers seemed to shield him from the worst. Since they'd entered the black lands Palimak's eyes were a constant glowing yellow and Safar could feel currents of power flowing from him.

Most surprising of all, the boy had a fairly good idea about what was happening.

One night Safar rode in from a scouting mission and found Palimak lying awake waiting for him. When he entered the tent the boy held up a finger urging silence.

He pointed at the stone turtle, whispering, "I just got them to sleep." He put a pillow over the idol, made a magical gesture to soften sound, then said in a normal voice, "There. That ought to do it."

"What's wrong?" Safar asked.

Palimak shrugged. "Gundaree and Gundara don't like it here," he said. "I don't either, but what can you do? Like grandfather says, 'this is the way the road goes so you just have to put up with it.'"

Safar nearly pinched himself. The boy frequently sounded like a miniature adult, but this was beyond the wisdom of a good many of the full grown adults in the caravan.

"You seem to be learning a lot from your grandfather," he said.

"Oh, sure," Palimak replied. "I was surprised myself. I didn't know he knew so much, being kind of old and everything." He frowned. "I don't mean old is dumb, but sometimes it is pretty cranky. And cranky people don't seem to think very well. They just get mad for no reason and say 'get out of here,' instead of trying to find out what's happening."

Safar smiled. The child was plainly speaking of his grandmother, who tended to have less patience with the boy. How ironic. When Safar was a child it was his mother who was full of understanding and his father who, in Palimak's words, was "pretty cranky."

He held out his arms and Palimak scrambled into his lap and snuggled against him. He stayed there for a time, breathing deeply and Safar remembered the comfort he'd felt in his own father's arms many years ago.

Then the boy rose up, saying, "Is it a machine that's doing it father?" he asked. "Making everything feel so bad, I mean?"

Safar was mildly surprised. "How did you guess?"

"Oh, it wasn't so hard," Palimak said. "I was just thinking about what could be causing all that bad magic and I couldn't see a person doing it. You know, like a wizard or a witch. Even a whole lot of them together couldn't keep on making so much magic all the time. So then I thought, maybe a machine could do it. A great big machine."

He shook his head. "The only thing is, why's it doing it? It's just sort of shooting off lots and lots of power and a whole lot of spells that don't seem to do anything for any special reason. Except make people feel really bad. Why would a machine want to do that, father?""

Safar hesitated, then said, "I suppose I'd better tell you, so you know what's ahead. But first you have to promise to keep it a secret."

Palimak was excited. "I'm good at secrets," he said. "Ask anybody. Ask Grandfather, even. He'll say I never, ever tell." Then he frowned. "Except I guess you can't ask him or anybody else," he said. "'Cause they'd know there was a secret, which would spoil the whole thing."

"Don't worry," Safar said, smiling. "I'll take your word for it."

"Does Leiria know?" Palimak asked.

"Some of it. But she's the only one. I didn't want to frighten people."

"Is Caluz a bad place, father?" the boy asked.

"I'm afraid so, son," he said. "You've seen how everything looks around here. I honestly didn't know it would be like this. So I have to think that Caluz might be worse."

"Is that where the machine is?"

"Yes."

"And that's what's causing all this?"

"There's other things involved, but yes, it's mainly the machine."

"But if Caluz so is so awful, why are we going there?"

"There's an oracle we need to visit," he said. "For reasons so important that I think it's worth the risk we're taking."

"Will it help us with Iraj?"

"I'm not sure. Possibly. But that's not my sole purpose."

He saw the boy's puzzled look. Safar knew he was wondering what could be more important than escaping Iraj Protarus.

"I'll tell you the story," Safar said, "and then maybe you'll understand."

He settled back, remembering when he'd first heard of Caluz and its oracle. "It started long before you and your mother came to Zanzair looking for me," he said. "I had just been appointed Iraj's Grand Wazier . . ."

*   *   *

. . . Day was fading to night and from his hilltop home Safar could see the oil lamps blooming all over the ancient city of Zanzair. The dying rays of the sun danced on the gold demon-head towers of the Grand Palace, where Iraj had been recently crowned king of all Esmir. He had made his main court in the old demon seat of power to symbolize that he was king of demons and humans alike. Even so, with an influx of humans seeking opportunity in the capital of the young and progressive king, Zanzair remained stubbornly demon. It was a place of mystery and secrets that were already swirling about the throne just as they had in the days of the demon kings. Safar had learned quickly to trust no one and always to mind his back. So when one of his gate guards became ill and was replaced by a stranger from the royal barracks, Safar decided to keep an eye on him to see if there was some hidden purpose behind the illness and the replacement.

He noticed right away the fellow was erratic about who he would admit to see Safar and who he wouldn't. Safar's duties were wide and in this climate of constant double dealing he need to keep his door open to anyone with legitimate business. He'd admonished the man the night before, so he was particularly watchful that day, peering out his study window whenever he heard someone approach.

At first everyone seemed to be properly handled, then Safar saw a man approach riding a little donkey. He was a tall man, with an unkempt beard and dusty, much-patched robes. He made a comical figure as he approached, sitting crossways on the donkey's back, sandals dragging across the cobbles. The guard barred his way and although the man argued strongly, Safar could see his employee's mind had been made up and nothing the visitor could say would sway him.

An argument ensued. Safar couldn't hear the details at first, but then the visitor lost his temper, shouting, "How dare you treat me in this manner! I am a priest, I tell you! Here to see Lord Timura on important business!"

The guard responded by shoving the man toward his donkey and ordering him to leave. At that moment Safar decided if the guard were a spy, he was not only an incompetent one but rude to boot, so he sent his majordomo to intervene. A few minutes later the guard was summarily dismissed and the visitor was brought to Safar's chambers.

"Please accept my apologies, kind sir," Safar said, "as well as the hospitality of my house. Anything you desire is yours. Food. Drink. A bath and a place to sleep. Whatever you require."

"I require nothing, My Lord," the man said, "other than to beg your attention on a matter of utmost importance."

Nevertheless, Safar sent for refreshments and a servant with hot towels and perfumed water and waited until the trail grime had been wiped away and the man was sitting in a comfortable chair with a glass of brandy in his hand.

"Now, speak to me," Safar said after the man had taken his first drink and he'd seen color flood his cheeks. "Tell me of this urgent business."

"I am called Talane, my lord. A priest in the temple of Caluz. The High Priest has sent me all this way to tell you of the calamity that has befallen us and to plead for your assistance."

He gestured at his raggedy robes, which when examined closer still retained the faint symbols of a priest's robes. "You would never know to look at me, lord, but I started out for Zanzair over a year ago with an entourage of scholars and soldiers and wagons loaded with rich gifts to place at your feet. Alas, after many misadventures on those bandit-infested roads I now possess only these robes. The wagons are gone, the soldiers dead or vanished like the cowards many of them were. As for the rest of my priestly colleagues, only I survived to complete the journey."

Immensely interested, Safar urged him to continue. Not long before he'd encountered a reference to Caluz in Asper's book. The demon wizard had speculated that the area was a source of much natural magical activity. Word had come from the human lands that a fabulous temple had been erected at a place in the Black Lands where two rivers joined. It was said to be near a small village named Caluz. The temple, Asper said, was shaped like an immense turtle and it rose out of the place where the two rivers became one. Water rushed through the center of the turtle, he said, rotating a huge wheel which in turn operated magical machinery inside the temple, sending out a constant stream of spells that nourished the spirit as well as the land.

There was one other thing Asper had said about the temple.

"Forgive my ignorance, holy one," Safar said, "but wasn't Caluz once known for its famous oracle?"

Talane nodded. "It still is, my lord," he said. "It's called The Oracle of Hadin."

Safar felt something move in his pocket, then a little voice whispered, "Ask him about the turtle." It was Gundara, stirred from his home by the mention of Hadin.

"What did you say, my lord?" Talane asked. "Something about a turtle?" He sighed and took a sip of his brandy. "I fear my ordeal has affected my hearing. All of a sudden your voice became quite faint."

Safar pretended to cough. "My fault," he said. "A chill coming on, I think. But, yes, I did use the word turtle. I was referring to your temple, where the Oracle keeps her home. Isn't it in the shape of a turtle."

"Yes, my lord. It's in honor of the turtle god who carries Hadin on its back. That's on the other side of the world, you know."

"That's my information as well," Safar said dryly.

"Sorry. Of course you would know that. I'm told you are a great scholar. A learned man as well as a master wizard."

Gundara snorted. "If he only knew!" the little Favorite whispered.

Talane gave Safar a look of sympathy. "The chill again, my lord?"

Another cough. "Yes. Forgive me." Safar gave his pocket a warning tap. Once more and Gundara was in for it.

"I'm sure you also know of the old tale that there is a holy force—you would probably call it magical—that runs between Hadin and Caluz. Like a river running straight through the world."

"I've heard that tale before," Safar said. "Although never in detail." Actually he had only just guessed it. The priest's comments, plus Safar's years of studying Asper had led him to the conclusion. Talane told him about the temple and the great wheel inside that had churned out magical spells for many centuries.

"Our land was once a poor place," he said, "a bleak place of wild storms and mountains that spat fire. But then a holy man, whose name is lost to us, found the magical springs running under the place where the rivers join. No one knows what he did there, but somehow word got out and other holy men came. The first man vanished, the others stayed and built the first temple—the one standing now is much larger and more powerful. They cast spells to bless the land and when the wheel began to turn a miracle resulted. The land became rich, the weather tame, the mountains silent."

"And the oracle?" Safar asked.

"Yes, the Oracle of Hadin came into being during that time. People came from all over Esmir to consult it. Even Alisarrian made a pilgrimage on his way to conquer all of Esmir."

"She gave him a glowing forecast I take it?" Safar asked with a touch of sarcasm. Methydia had taught him that there were notorious frauds in the oracle profession.

"Actually, my lord," Talane said, "it is written that the Oracle warned Alisarrian he would someday be betrayed by those closest to him."

Which is exactly what had happened to Alisarrian—betrayal, death and the eventual destruction of his kingdom. At that moment Safar began to take the Oracle seriously.

"What do you require of me?" he asked. "As the Grand Wazier I can authorize many things to assist our priests. Construction funds, increased temple subsidies, scholastic endowments. That sort of thing."

Talane lowered his head as if in shame. "What we need, my lord," he said, "is a means to make the wheel stop!"

Safar was surprised. "But why would you want to stop something so wondrous?" he asked. "The very source of all your happiness and wealth."

"It is now the source of the greatest misery, lord," Talane said bitterly. "Something terrible has happened. Only bad spells, malicious spells, are being churned up now. Our fields are barren, our newborn deformed and one of the mountains has even begun to spit fire."

"I'm desolate to hear of your people's misfortune, holy one," Safar said, "but what's the difficulty? Why can't you stop the wheel on your own?"

"Perhaps we could have done it once," Talane said. "But now anyone who approaches with such an intent is killed the moment he touches the wheel."

"What does your oracle say?" Safar asked.

Talane sighed. "Only that she warned us this would happen and we didn't listen."

"Perhaps you'd better tell me exactly what happened," Safar said.

The tale was a simple one of human greed's many victories over common sense. It happened some years back—about the time, Safar guessed, he'd had his youthful epiphany in the mountains above Kyrania. Talane said one day the Oracle summoned all the priests. When she appeared she was weeping, which frightened everyone. She said a great disaster had occurred in Hadin. And that tragedy would have so great an affect on the world that she couldn't see the future after a point not many decades hence. What she *did* foresee was that Caluz would be among the first to suffer. Their only hope, she said, was to prepare for the worst. Store food and drink and carefully husband all their resources in hopes they could weather the bad times to come. But most of all, she urged them to stop the wheel. Her final warning came as a great shock to everyone. Oh, they'd been frightened by her dire predictions and mysterious remarks about the disaster in Hadin. But in reality those things seemed so distant, so surreal, they couldn't imagine them.

The wheel was a different matter. All they could see was that the moment it was

411

halted all the good things that made Caluz so rich would stop as well. Fortunes were at stake and important men were not pleased when the priests brought them the news. A great argument ensued, settled when the king ordered a royal commission to meet and study the Oracle's remarks closely. Perhaps the priests had misinterpreted her. Maybe she meant some other wheel. All kinds of alternatives were suggested, each one more foolish than the others. Years passed, the commission continued to meet, but nothing was ever done. Early on a young priest was so scandalized by the blasphemy against the Oracle that he attacked the wheel with an ax. He'd chipped a large hunk of one blade off before they stopped him and carried him away to the dungeons.

"That's how we know it was once possible to destroy the machine," Talane said. "But when a team of engineers tried the same thing two years ago, every man was blasted on the spot by some mysterious force. All seven were killed, may their ghosts be at rest."

Safar thought a moment, then said, "I can't see how I can help you find a solution from such a distance, holy one. I'd need to visit Caluz and consult with your High Priest and best scholars. I'm not opposed to making such a journey, mind you. Even if I were so unfeeling that I didn't sympathize with your plight, I have personal reasons to come. Unfortunately, it will be several months before I can take leave from my king."

Talane became agitated. But not over the delay. "Oh, but you must not come, lord!" he said. "The Oracle warned us you would want to, but she said you must stay away at all costs."

Safar's eyebrows shot up. "Why is that?"

The priest made a weary shrug. "She didn't say. Oracles aren't always that forthcoming, you know. But she was most insistent. She said you shouldn't come until the machine is stopped."

Safar was mightily confused. "I don't understand," he said. "You want my help, yet at the same time you say I'm barred from giving it. What other way can we halt that wheel?"

Talane took a deep breath, then, "By changing the course of the rivers that drive it."

The rescue project Caluz proposed was not only costly, but an enormous engineering feat. Two rivers had to be forced to leave their natural beds and find a new course to the sea. Safar spent many hours with the priest, who came armed with facts and figures and memorized plans that he sketched on scraps of paper as he talked. In the end Safar was convinced it could be done.

Several weeks later Talane departed for Caluz with royal promissory notes and decrees calling on neighboring cities to provide all necessary assistance. Safar and the priest said their final farewells at the main gate. Outside the walls they could hear the caravan master cry his last warning that he was ready to depart.

"There's one other thing I should tell you, my lord," Talane said. "Forgive me for withholding it, but I wasn't clear on the Oracle's meaning. I was already ladened with so many confusing things to relate to you that I feared it would only make explanations more difficult."

"Tell me now then, holy one," Safar said.

"The Oracle said to tell you this: 'He who seeks the way to Hadin must first travel through Caluz.'"

Talane scratched his head. "It still doesn't make any sense to me, lord," he said. "Do you know what she means?"

Safar shook his head. "No. But I hope to find out one day."

*   *   *

Palimak stirred in his lap and Safar looked down to see if the boy had wearied of his story. Instead, Palimak's eyes were huge and glowing with interest.

"Imagine that!" he said. "Making two whole rivers change which way they go." Outside a volcano rumbled with pent up gases and his elfin face turned serious. "I guess it didn't work," he said. "The machine's still going."

"Actually, it did work," Safar said. "They labored for several years building dams and digging an alternate bed for both rivers to flow into. The wheel stopped and the bad magic with it. The people of Caluz sent me many proclamations of thanks and praise. I even had a note from Talane saying the city was going to honor me by naming a day after me. I don't know if they did, because not much later I was fleeing Zanzair with you and Leiria. And I haven't heard anything since."

"Something must have happened, father," Palimak said, "because the machine's going again."

"Apparently," Safar said, "all that work turned out to be just a temporary fix. We'll find out what happened when we get to Caluz."

Palimak was alarmed. "But what about the Oracle's warning?" he asked. "If the wheel's going, you might get hurt. Or even . . . you know . . . killed or something!"

Ever since Asper's ghost had bade him to travel to Caluz Safar had considered that point himself. But he smiled at the boy, saying, "Don't worry. I know a lot more about such things then I did in Zanzair. A wizard gets stronger as he ages. Why, think about how much more powerful you are now then when we left Kyrania. You've made storms from small clouds, saving my life, I might add.

"And that trick you played on Iraj was masterful. It gave us valuable time to get away."

Palimak frowned. "That's what everybody says. And I guess maybe I'm a hero, like I wanted to be. They're all saying, 'Oh, Palimak, you're such a brave boy! And 'How can we ever thank you enough.' Things like that. But, I don't know. I don't feel very good about it."

He gave Safar a look of great frustration. "I was trying to kill him, father!" he said. "That's how it was supposed to work. But it didn't. It was sort of like the rivers. A temporary fix."

Safar ruffled his hair. "That's all we needed," he said. "So it doesn't matter."

Actually it did matter to Safar, but not the way Palimak might have thought. He was secretly glad the boy had failed. Evil as Iraj might be, Safar thought his murder would be too much for a child's soul to bear. There would be plenty of opportunity in the years ahead for such scars to accumulate.

"Will you let me help you in Caluz, father?" Palimak asked. "I'm really strong, just like you said. See?"

He flexed one of his little arms by way of demonstration. Safar smiled and felt the small lump of muscle. To his surprise it was hard and sinewy and quite unchildlike.

"You certainly are," Safar said. "I was nowhere near as strong when I was your age."

Palimak shrugged as if indifferent but he was secretly pleased. "I think it's because I'm part demon," he said matter of factly. "They get stronger faster, right?"

"Right," Safar answered.

"Stronger in magic, too, right?"

"Right."

Palimak's face turned sly. "Then you'll let me help you, right?"

"Right again," Safar said.

The boy looked startled. Had his trick worked? Then he became concerned.

"Do you really mean that, father?" he asked. "Or are you just saying it and then you'll make up a reason later why I can't?"

"Yes, I really do meant it, son," Safar said. "To tell the truth, I was sort of counting on it. That's why I told you the story, so you'd be ready when we got there."

Palimak's face lit up with supreme pleasure. "Will it be dangerous?" he asked.

Safar turned serious. "Very dangerous, son. So you have to pay close attention to everything I say. No more little tricks and experiments on your own, right?"

"Right!" Palimak said. "Right, right, right. And three times right makes it so!"

＊　　　＊　　　＊

Sergeant Dario eyed the road ahead. The old Kyranian fighting master was not pleased with what he saw, or actually, what he couldn't see. They'd been traveling for weeks on the barren plains of the Black Lands, but as forbidding as they were, he thought, at least a man had an uninterrupted view of any danger he might face.

Here, however, the great caravan road narrowed to accommodate a passage hewn straight through a mountain. Dario figured it had once been a natural ravine which was widened by gangs of slaves working for some greedy king determined to bring the caravans to his realm.

Whatever the origins, Dario definitely didn't like the way the road snaked into the dim passage, then vanished entirely beyond the first bend.

"If I was thinkin' of settin' up an ambush," he said to Leiria, "I'd pick somewhere's in there. You could trap the whole damn caravan."

"I was thinking the same thing," she replied. She looked up at the towering, blank-faced mountain. "I wish there were a route around it, or over it," she said.

Dario leaned away from his saddle and spit, which Leiria had learned over many miles was a signal that he was thinking. His leathery old face, which drooped like a jowly dog's, was a permanent, emotionless mask he kept for the world. But Leiria could see a glint of worry in his eyes as they darted this way and that, probing the depths of the passage.

Finally he settled back in his saddle. "Had a cap'n once't," he said, "who knew all there was to know 'bout ambushes, 'cept for one thing. And that killed him so I never did find out what he was missin'. Make a long story short, he taught me what he know'd afore he ate that arrow, so I'm a pretty fair hand at ambushes."

Leiria laughed. "Except for the kind that got the captain," she said.

Dario grimaced, which was his way of smiling. "Hells," he said, "there's always one more for a soldier. One more hill to climb. One more meal you ain't gonna eat. One more sword lookin' for your guts. Same with ambushes. There's always one more waitin' somewhere's that's gonna get you."

Leiria laughed. "Isn't that the truth! What's the old barracks' saying? No matter how bad the shit gets, it's only the second worst thing that's going to happen to you."

Dario grunted his enjoyment. Then he gestured at the pass, saying, "Why'nt I slip on in there, Cap'n, and see what's what? Maybe you could sorta linger a bit behind me to guard my back."

Leiria nodded agreement. "Wait up a minute," she said, "until I talk to the boys."

She trotted back to where the other scouts, including Renor and his friend, Seth, waited. She told them the plan and then said, "In all likelihood we're worrying about nothing. But if we should trigger an ambush the last thing I want is for any of you to come running to our rescue. Leave one man here to watch and the rest of you ride to the main column for help. Renor, you're in charge, so you choose who's going to stay and who's going to ride. Got it?"

"Yes, Captain," Renor said, squaring his shoulders as if suddenly feeling the weight of command settle on to them. "But, how about if I send somebody back now, so Lord Timura and the others will know what's going on up here?"

"Good idea," Leiria said, feeling a flash of pride at how far Renor had come since Kyrania. He was going to make one fine soldier someday—assuming he lived long enough. "In fact, instead of waiting to see if we need help, ask Lord Timura to send up a platoon now just in case."

She rode back to the pass where Dario was stripping himself and his horse of all unnecessary weight. She did the same, then they helped each other tie rags around their horse's hooves to muffle the sound. When they were ready she nodded at Dario to proceed.

The sergeant grimaced a smile. "If somethin' happens," he said, "tell my old woman to put a jug out for my ghost tonight. Way I hear it, dyin's damned thirsty work."

And then he rode into the pass.

She waited until he reached the first bend. At his signal she moved slowly forward. Dario took up temporary position at the bend, keeping watch in both directions until she reached him. While she stood guard he moved to the next point, scanning the high walls of the canyon for any movement.

They leapfrogged like that, going deeper and deeper until the light became so dim that all was in shadow and they relied on hearing and instinct more than sight. The high canyon walls were old and rotting, showing dark wounds where they had given away to tumble down onto the road.

There was no wind and the air was hot and stale. Sound was intensified, almost unnatural; the horse's muffled hooves seemed like distant drums, their breathing harsh and gasping like a dying beast's, and once in awhile some far off landslide would break, sounding like slow rolling thunder.

Sweat trickled down Leiria's back, increasing the prickling sensation she'd experienced after passing the first bend. She felt as if she were being watched, a sensation she'd normally heed. But the atmosphere was so bleak she thought it might be her imagination. Adding to her wariness was the fact that there was simply nowhere for anyone to hide—no perches on the faces of the cliffs, no rubble so dense or high enough to provide cover. Each section of road they cleared should remain cleared. It was only common sense.

Then she saw Dario signal frantically. She halted the horse and swiftly fit an arrow into her bow.

Dario held his hand, keeping her in position. She saw him lean forward, as if listening.

Then she heard it—the heavy, measured tread of many boots. Dario reined his horse back, quickly slipping an ax from his belt. He came slowly, eyes forward, listening to the tromp, tromp, tromp of the approaching boots.

Suddenly, from behind her she heard the same measured tread. Leiria came about, heart hammering at this impossibility. She lifted her bow, staring at the bend, waiting for the first face to show.

The boots came closer, moving in from both sides as if closing some gigantic pincer with Dario and Leiria in between.

She sensed Dario at her side and they moved together, the noses of their horses pointing in opposite directions.

The sound of marching boots grew louder and louder until they were like kettle drums. Then a great horn blew, the boots went stamp . . . stamp . . . stamp . . . three times, hard on the last, and stopped.

Silence.

Then the air shimmered and out of all that nothingness appeared a long column of huge, mailed warriors. Their skin was white as death, lips blood red, and their eyes were great empty sockets as black and deep as caves.

Leiria took a chance and glanced behind her. And her eyes confirmed what mind and heart knew.

The pincers had closed.

They were surrounded.

CHAPTER EIGHTEEN
THE ROAD TO CALUZ

Lord Fari watched with mild amusement as the soldiers tormented the two prisoners. A man and a woman, both stripped naked, were staggering between two ranks of cheering warriors. One side was human, the other demon, and they were hurling rocks and sticks at the couple, trying to drive them toward one group of soldiers or the other.

The game would go on like this, with some interesting variations, until the prisoners had been ripped to pieces. Then those pieces would be used in stirring games of fiendish polo, pitting mounted demon and human teams against one another as they whacked gory parts about the field with clubs made of bone.

It was all great innocent fun, Fari thought, and he was pleased to see the young soldiers engaged in such vigorous, morale-building activity.

The woman fell a few feet from the demon side and long talons reached for her. She screamed, dragging herself away, long trails of blood raking along one thigh where they'd caught her. The soldiers roared laughter, giving the woman time to stagger to the middle of the wide gap between the ranks of tormentors. They howled louder still when she fell next to the man and he embraced her with bleedings arms trying to comfort her.

"Oh, good show! Good show!" Fari cried, rapping his skull-topped cane against the ground. Beneath him, a husky demon slave shifted patiently under Fari's bulk, alert to his lord and master's every movement.

There was a lull in the game as wineskins were passed about to slake all that happy thirst and Fari sent a runner with a bag of gold to add to the stakes and the excitement.

The rough playing field was set up on the edge of the Black Lands where Iraj had camped his army while he considered his next move. Fari frowned, absently reaching out a taloned hand—instantly filled with a cup of wine by a demon maid who was as comely as she was attentive.

Actually, time for consideration had little to do with the king's planning. Protarus was in one of his moods again, so black no one dared come near him except his slaves and they had no choice in the matter. He'd already killed more than a dozen for infractions so small even Fari was startled. Lord Fari was known to have hard views about spoiling slaves. He even approved of the occasional act of casual violence to keep them anxious to please. Besides, a slave on a gibbet in front of your house was a good thing for an enemy to see when he came to visit.

There was no similar artifice in Iraj Protarus' actions, however. He didn't even kill them out of anger, Fari noticed. It was more like a fly had been buzzing about, interrupting his melancholia. It was a melancholy so deep and so dark the king seemed to find a strange comfort and escape in it, as if sorrow were a thick, warm coverlet he drew over him to blot out the world. Then came the buzz of the fly—a smile when he didn't want to see a smile, a solemn face when he wanted a smile—and he would flick it away. Claws erupting from his hands, snatching out a throat, then becoming hands again as the king returned to his thinking, eyes only blinking when the body struck the floor.

Protarus had been like that since the attempt on his life by the boy, Palimak. Fari scratched his horn with a long, contemplative talon. It had been a very good spell, he thought. One that even he, a master wizard, could admire. The only error the child had committed when he'd composed the spell was to leave a link between the giver of the amulet and the taker. So when the king spoke the word "Palimak" aloud, triggering the spell, it was the witch who took most of the killing force, not the king.

The king had suffered enough physical harm to delay the march for several weeks while his wounds healed. He'd been left with only one scar no magical treatment could erase, even when applied to the self-healing body of a shape changer. It was a small scar that lifted one corner of his lip into a permanent smile. It wasn't a sneer or a grin, but a sly tilt that made you wonder if he knew some secret that did not bode well for you.

As time went by it soon became apparent the king had suffered a deeper wound. Without warning, he'd suddenly fall into a black mood and call the army to a halt, only to retire the into the depths of his harem. When the mood ended he'd suddenly rise up and order the march to resume, cursing at the delay as if it were the fault of others.

The consequence was that they were far behind Safar Timura and his refugee caravan. So far the magical trail they were following was very weak and would soon fade out entirely. And Lord Timura would have eluded them once again—possibly for all time. The forced hunt could only go on for so long. Eventually, either all the supplies would be exhausted or the kingdom would become so neglected Protarus would have to pause to put things in order.

For the first time since the hunt began, Lord Fari didn't care. It didn't matter to him if they won or lost the race. He had different goals now. Goals which only coincidentally involved Safar Timura. In short, Lord Fari had a new view on things, a new way of thinking. Shorter still, he was thinking only of himself.

The game resumed with a blood-curdling scream as a rock struck the male captive. Fari glanced up, red demon's tongue flicking out at the prospect of renewed amusement. This time, however, he found himself bored. The man and the woman were barely conscious, so there was little sport. Fari snorted. The youth of today, he thought, have even less patience than they have imagination. Some other torments should have been used well before now. The trick was to keep the game alive and interested as long as you could.

Fari hoisted himself up on his cane. It was something he no longer needed—the transformation to shape-changer had rid him of all the ailments old demons suffer. But he used the cane anyway, out of habit, and as a badge of authority. He strode away, his slaves scrambling to keep up. The one who served as his stool ran the hardest. When Lord Fari decided to sit, he would sit. The slave's most constant nightmare was that he wouldn't be there, hunched on all fours and steady as a rock, when Lord Fari took it into his mind to rest.

Fari climbed a short hill, stopping at the crest and leaning on his cane to take in the view. His slaves scrabbled around him, the stool ready to leap into any position, the shade unfurling the wide umbrella over Fari's horned head, the fan swishing the air with her feathery plumes, the maid at the ready with cup and jug. Spread out behind him were guards and runners and bearers carrying small comforts he might desire while taking the air.

Fari glanced back, taking rare notice of his entourage. The king had more, he thought, much more. So many to tend his whims it beggared the imagination. Fari shrugged. What did it matter? It was better to be Grand Wazier than king. He gazed out at the Black Lands, where tornadoes rutted a ghastly terrain and volcanoes spat their fire, poisoning the air with their stench. To Fari it was a place of beauty and promise that soothed his old demon's soul.

When Lord Fari first saw the Black Lands he felt as if a veil had been lifted from his eyes. For too long he had been held in the grip of the wild emotions and sensations of a shape changer. It was difficult to think clearly, to plan beyond the immediate goals and challenges. A demon of more two hundred feastings, he had seen many kings come and go. He'd survived them all by always being attentive to their moods, guessing which way they would leap next and racing ahead to that point so he could be there when they lighted. Not unlike the living stool Fari now sat upon. Court intrigue was second nature to the old demon. Many a knife had been aimed at his back by his rivals. Many a deadly plot hatched with Fari's removal at their core.

He was not a fiend normally driven by emotions of any kind—other than fear, that is. Fear alone was to be trusted. Fear kept a fiend wary. Fear could see into shadows. Fear could creep around corners unnoticed. Fear could read the lips of whispering conspirators. Fear could divine the deepest thoughts of a king. Fear had been with him as long as he could remember. It was his father, his mother, his brother and sister and most loyal friend. Fear was his lover whom he ardently embraced every hour of every day.

When he looked out over the Black Lands and felt the constant pounding of magic gone wild, Fari realized he had been without fear for much too long. He'd allowed himself to be overcome by his shape changer's heart where only bloodmust raged. Fari felt a little ashamed of himself when he realized that. The old Fari, the Fari who had kept his head while thousands of others were losing theirs, would have made better use of the new powers he'd gained when he became a shape changer.

It was Fari who was the architect of the Spell of Four, after all. It was Fari who'd drawn Prince Luka and Kalasariz into the conspiracy to seduce the king into the shape changer's bond that had saved them all from Safar Timura's great spell of revenge, which had turned Zanzair into a molten ruin, killing all but the new brotherhood Fari had formed. The trouble was, he had forgotten his original intent. At the time it had seemed as if he were losing control. Safar Timura was the Grand Wazier, not Lord Fari. What's worse, Timura was such a powerful wizard Fari had no hope of competing against him. It was no secret. Everyone knew it. And in the game of Grand Waziers, second best is a shadow away from an assassin's blade.

The old demon sighed and lumbered about, his entourage shifting with him, those who might impede his view falling to the ground to let him see what he wanted to see. The king's banner—silver comet collapsing onto the red demon moon—hung limp over the huge pavilion that housed his court and quarters. From the hilltop Fari could see the three smaller pavilions that made a half moon frame for the king's traveling palace. One was his. The others belonged to Prince Luka and Lord Kalasariz.

Each had his own fear, his own driving ambition. Each sought not just to find favor with the king, but to control him. To master him. To Lord Fari it only seemed right and just that it should be him. But how to go about it? How to slip past the canny Kalasariz? And Luka. What about him? His hate for Fari was long and deep. His ambition also burned brighter, because Prince Luka wanted nothing less than to be king himself. Something Fari could never allow him to achieve. It suddenly occurred to the old demon that Luka and Kalasariz might naturally seek an alliance. He wondered if they'd realized it yet. He wondered if their minds had become clear before his own.

He snorted. Not likely. He was not only wiser and cannier, but he possessed more magic than any of them. But then he thought, Just in case, my dear Fari, just in case . . . you'd better plan for the worst.

Then he straightened as he thought of a course of action. He'd begin with the king. All else should follow after that. First he had to shake the king from his melancholy. He needed to put the hunger back into Iraj Protarus. To rouse the hunter from his sleep.

A final, piercing shriek caught his attention and Fari looked over at the field, a smile curling up from his fangs. The soldiers had finished off the victims and were gleefully ripping them to pieces so the next game could begin. Actually, he thought, they'd done quite well. Considering their two captives were so young—barely in their teens—it was really quite a feat to keep them alive so long.

Then he saw a tall demon holding up the heads, the greatest prize of all. Many cheers greeted this gory sight.

Lord Fari grinned as the idea dawned. He rapped his cane for one his aides.

He tossed him a purse of gold, saying, "Buy me those heads."

✻   ✻   ✻

Renor and Sinch sat easily in their saddles, nibbling on dried fruit while keeping a casual watch on the entrance to the pass. They'd neither heard nor seen anything amiss since Leiria and Dario had set out to investigate the Caluzian Pass.

Renor chuckled. "Old Dario had me about ready to wet my breeches with all that ambush talk," he said. "But I guess that's all it was—talk." He stretched, yawning. "At least he's not wastin' our time for a change. We get to rest up while he and Cap'n Leiria scout the trail for us."

"I don't know if it was such a big waste of time," Sinch said. He waved at the dark entrance of the pass. "Sure looks like ambush pie to me. And the only way to find out is to dig into it." Despite his comments, Sinch felt a sense of great ease and cheer.

"The sergeant's a good sort, don't get me wrong," Renor replied. "He just goes on and on, is all. You've got to listen to the whole history of the Tarnasian Wars, or some such, before you come to his point."

Again he stretched and yawned, really enjoying it. For the first time since they'd entered the Black Lands Renor felt safe and quite comfortable sitting here talking his friend about nothing in particular.

"Oh, I don't know," Sinch laughed. Actually, it was more like a giggle. "Depends on what sort of story he's telling. Like the kind you wouldn't want your little sister to overhear. The other night he told me one about an old lamplighter in Walaria. Did you hear it?"

Renor laughed in anticipation. "No, I haven't," he said. He nodded at the pass. "Nothing happening there. So go ahead."

Sinch chortled, remembering the jest. "Anyway," he said, "there was this old lamplighter in Walaria named Zenzi. And old Zenzi had been lighting lamps faithfully in one neighborhood for nearly thirty years. And now it was time for him to retire and collect his pension from the king.

"Comes his last night and when he gets to the first house the family comes out with food and drink and a few silvers to thank him for all his years of service. Same thing at the next house and the next. Everybody liked Zenzi, so they were piling on the gifts and making his last night something really special.

"Then he comes to the last house on the street and a slave comes to fetch him, saying her mistress wanted to speak to him. The slave takes Zenzi by the hand and leads him into the house and up the stairs, where he is pushed into a bedroom, the door closing behind him.

"You can imagine his surprise when he sees there's a beautiful woman waiting for him—dressed in nothing but a filmy gown and a big smile. 'My husband is away for the night,' she says, real sultry, then she takes him to bed and they make mad passionate love. The greatest love poor old Zenzi had ever experienced. Then the woman claps her hands and the slave brings in a wonderful dinner of the best kabobs and sherbet and all the other delicacies the rich get, but Zenzi had never tasted before. When he is done the woman pours him some fragrant tea.

"Zenzi starts to reach for the cup, then notices a copper coin sitting beside it."

"'Pardon, my dear lady,' Zenzi says, 'but everything has been so wonderful. The hours of love. The food. The drink. Everything. But what's this copper coin for?'"

"The woman smiled and said, 'Well, yesterday I told my husband this was your last night after thirty years of service. And I asked what we should give you. And my husband answered, 'Screw Zenzi. Give him a copper!' The woman shrugs. 'The dinner,' she says, 'was my idea!'"

Renor roared laughter, slapping his thigh and looking quite unsoldierlike when Lord Timura came riding up on his great stallion, accompanied by thirty men.

"I thought there was an emergency here," he said, blue eyes fierce under his dark brows. "Instead I find my best men lolling about like tavern sops. Laughing and making merry."

Renor shook his head, amused. "This is a pretty funny situation if you think about it, my lord," he said, chuckling. "Here we are telling jokes—dirty ones, at that. And then you ride up and—"

"Where's Captain Leiria?" Safar barked, breaking into Renor's babble. He glanced around. "And Dario! Where's Sergeant Dario?"

Renor grinned and motioned toward the entrance. "Checking out the pass, Lord Timura," he said, choking back laughter. "To see if there's . . . ha ha ha . . . an ambush! Ha ha ha."

Sinch snorted laughter. "Did you hear the one about the guys who ate the frogs?" he asked.

Safar slipped his silver dagger out. He mumbled a spell.

Renor shook his head, laughing so hard there were tears in his eyes. "No," he said.

"Well there was this plague of frogs, see . . . And—"

Safar sliced the air, casting his spell, and the two young men were suddenly left gasping and flailing the air as if they'd been drenched with icy water.

Renor was the first to recover. His eyes were wide with shame and fear. "I'm sorry, Lord Timura," he said, voice trembling. "I don't know—"

"Never mind, lad," Safar said gently. "It wasn't your fault. Now, join the others. You too, Sinch."

The young men did as he said. At Safar's signal everyone formed up and checked their weapons and gear.

He turned back to the entrance of the Caluzian Pass, probing with his magical senses. Khysmet chuffed and shifted under him, as if he too were investigating. Safar pushed harder. It was difficult to "see" in the constant hail of wild magic that pelted the Black Lands, but whoever had cast the spell of amusement on Renor and Sinch had left a faint trail. In Safar's magical vision it looked like a silvery path left by a snail. But it faded away just before it reached the first bend in the road.

To Safar it seemed obvious that whoever, or whatever, had tricked the young scouts was trying to keep their attention away from what was happening down that dark avenue through the mountain. Not for the first time he wished he had Gundara with him. The little Favorite was an expert at snooping out such things.

He gritted his teeth, forcing his mind away from what might be happening to Leiria. And Dario, oh yes, mustn't forget Dario. But it's Leiria, dammit, Leiria! She has no stake in this whole thing . . . except for me. Then Khysmet pawed the ground and Safar jerked back. He knew immediately he was being seduced by another sort of spell and he shook it off like clinging moss. Quickly, he raised a magical shield over himself and his men so there could be no other such surprises.

Safar leaned forward, patting Khysmet and whispering, "Who needs a Favorite?" The horse jerked its head up and down as if agreeing.

Then, without a thought passing between them Khysmet moved toward the pass and Safar signaled for his men to follow.

They made their way much as Leiria and Dario had done—leapfrogging from one cleared section of road to the next. Although the passage was narrow, it was still wide enough to carry caravan wagons and so Safar had little concern he might encounter an overwhelming force. There was plenty of room for him to deploy his men in strength, and either fight their way through or retreat to safety, dealing out much death and injury to whoever opposed them.

Khysmet moved easily over the rubble-strewn ground, finding firm footing in places where the other animals stumbled. Safar was left free to concentrate solely on the task at hand. His eyes pierced every shadow, his hearing was acute and his magical senses kept up a slow sweep for any sign of danger.

It came without warning—the heavy tread of many boots marching toward them. Khysmet whinnied alarm and Safar heard his men shout. With a start he realized the sound of marching came from both before *and behind him!*

As the air shimmered he scrabbled for a blocking spell, mind yammering that there had been no sign of a magical attack, but it was coming just the same.

Then he saw what Leiria had seen: long columns of huge mailed warriors marching toward him, closing the jaws of the trap.

He reared back to blast them, praying he had the right spell. But just before he struck he heard a shout:

"Safar!"

Safar blinked. It was Leiria's voice.

She called again. "Over here, Safar!"

He looked in the direction of her voice, then realized he could see through the warriors as if they were ghosts.

And there, just beyond, he saw a small golden pavilion. And in that pavilion, sitting at their ease before a table filled with food and drink, were Leiria and Dario.

Leiria waved to him. "Just push on through, Safar," she said. "They're harmless. Come and meet our hostess."

✳   ✳   ✳

Lord Fari fussed with the heads, pushing a stray curl away from the woman's dead eyes, wiping a spot of blood from the man's pale lips.

"Perfect, your Majesty," he said. "Just perfect. We couldn't have asked for better heads."

Protarus gloomed at him from his throne, eyes hollow, features slowly changing from man to wolf to man again. Scarred lip twitching in all forms.

"What's so special about these heads?" he asked in a deadly voice.

"Exactly what I was wondering, Majesty," Prince Luka said.

He glared at the old wizard, who stood between the two posts that held the heads. "The king is ill," he said to Fari. "Why are you disturbing him with such nonsense?" And he thought, what an old fool you are. I've been waiting for you to slip. Now I'll boot your arse the rest of the way down the stairs.

Fari sneered at Luka. "His Majesty will soon be able to judge for himself whether this is nonsense or not," he said. And he was thinking, You haven't a brain in your noggin, my prince. You were bred to fight, not to think. Your father was right not to trust you.

Kalasariz shifted his glance from one demon to the other, highly amused at the barely disguised hate between them. He kept silent—ready to jump to whichever side most benefited him.

Protarus motioned. "Get on with it," he said. His voice, however, was less threatening than before. The game between Fari and Luka had sparked his interest more than Fari's urgent call for a meeting.

"My mission tonight is most vital, Your Majesty," Fari said. "If I am successful in my experiment we will know the whereabouts of Lord Timura within the hour."

Iraj shifted in his throne, black mood momentarily abated by this news. His features becoming wholly human.

Luka sneered, exposing many rows of gleaming fangs. "I suppose the heads are going to tell us," he said. "We've tried that sort of thing before. But Timura's shields are too strong to get past."

"That's true, Lord Fari," Protarus said, mildly amused. He was thinking of various torments he could apply to the old demon after he failed. "It's never worked before. Why now?"

Fari raised a talon, looking a bit like an old demon school master. "In a moment, Majesty," he said, "all will be clear."

He busied himself with the heads, taking jars of magical oils and powders from the stand beside him and sprinkling the heads.

"For most of this hunt, Majesty," he said, "Lord Timura has been dashing all over the landscape. Going in first one direction, then another, then back again. It made it more difficult to find him, because we couldn't determine his eventual goal."

"He had no goal," Luka snorted. "Except to live another day. He's running, that's all."

"Do you think that's true, Majesty?" Fari asked, daubing a bit of ointment on the woman's head. "Does this sound like Lord Timura? You know him best."

Protarus frowned. "Not one damn bit," he said, surprising himself a little by his answer. "Safar always has a goal. A direction."

Luka was alarmed. "Well, of course he has some eventual goal, Your Majesty. But that's only to find some place of permanent safety for his people."

Kalasariz thought it time to insert a neutral comment. "He has been moving generally toward the northwest," he said. "Taking in all miles traveled, that is."

"That's most likely accidental," Luka protested. "We're the ones doing the driving. He's fleeing in the only direction left open to him. Which just so happens to be northwest."

But to the Prince's dismay, Protarus had already gone past that point. "I wonder what he's looking for?" he mused. "What's in that region?"

Fari pretended to be busy, hiding a smile as he poured golden oil over each head.

Kalasariz thought it was safe for another neutral answer. "Eventually, Majesty," he said, "there is only the Port of Caspan. And then the Great Sea."

Luka took heart, smacking one taloned fist into the other. "Exactly!" he said. "In the end, there's nothing but the sea. And if we keep going like we are we'll have him pinned against it. With nowhere to go."

Protarus shook his head, his scarred smile making Luka's heart jump. "Not likely," he said.

"There's one thing we've all overlooked, Majesty," Fari said. "I blame myself for not seeing it before."

"What's that?" the king prodded.

"Until a few months ago everything Prince Luka just said appeared true. Lord Timura was behaving exactly as described. Dashing this way and that with no other apparent purpose than to escape us.

"Then everything changed. Just before the, uh . . . " he gave Protarus a sympathetic look, " . . . the uh . . . most unfortunate attack on Your Majesty . . . he leaped onto one road. And then stayed on that road, never varying his direction or using his usual tricks."

Kalasariz cleared his throat. "Actually," he said, "it happened after Naadan. We tracked him to the ravine. He tried to escape, but we had the, uh . . . the uh . . ." he glanced at Protarus "the, uh . . . Lady Sheesan to help us. Then he got on this road and went like the hells."

"He must have made some kind of decision in Naadan," Protarus said. Then he grimaced, remembering the magical stallion. "Or maybe even before. Perhaps he meant to go to Naadan all along. And then . . . and then . . ." He shrugged. "My logic takes me no further. So he travels through the Black Lands. What does that tell us? Nothing."

He sighed, adding, "Except that Safar is as brave as ever. We have two hundred wizards with us. He has only himself. And yet he dashes across the Black Lands while we stand here afraid to set our toes in it."

"It's the machine, Majesty," Luka pointed out. "We know that somewhere out there a great magical machine has gone wild. We have to be sure we have the right spells before we proceed. It's the prudent thing to do, isn't that right, Lord Fari?"

The old demon brushed away Luka's desperate clutch to rejoin him on the side of safety. "I don't think our esteemed Majesty wants to hear about prudence right now, My Lord," he said.

Kalasariz, the most cautious of men, agreed. "Bold action is the only course," he said, aligning himself with Fari. Thinking, you cunning old foul-breathed devil. I just know you have something up your sleeve. Now, let's see it.

He was startled when the king, as if reading his thoughts, said, "Let's see it, Fari! What are you leading up to?"

"Why, the heads, Your Majesty," Fari said, "The heads." He gestured at the completed pair. "Beautiful, aren't they?" He said this as if they were the greatest works of art, instead of two ghastly things with dead eyes and slack mouths.

Luka found reason to murmur appreciatively, as did Kalasariz. The king only frowned, impatient.

"It's like this, Your Majesty," Fari said. "The Black Lands have confounded us for a few days, no doubt about it. But they also give us an opportunity. With all the magical insanity raging out there, it's highly unlikely that Lord Timura could maintain his usual shields. Why, all my wizards together couldn't do it and as great as Lord Timura's reputation might be, I suspect he's met his match with that machine.

"So he'll be going naked, as it were. Using all his powers just to throw up a small ring of protection around his people. There's nearly a thousand of them, if you recall, Majesty. That is an enormous amount of people for one wizard to shield, especially in the Black Lands."

He gestured at the heads. "These people were captives from a nearby village. They were born and raised next to this region, continually bathed in all the sorcery leaking out. They had no magic of their own, of course, but when I saw our soldiers making sport with them, it came to me that they would be very sensitive to it." He shrugged, "That was my guess, at any rate. Subsequent experiments proved my theory."

"Now I understand," Kalasariz said, smiling, feeling pleased he'd jumped in the right direction. To seal his position he hastened to explain, whether anyone needed the explanation or not.

"Lord Timura is not only vulnerable to a casting," he said, "but those are the ideal devices for the casting spell."

"As always, My Lord," Fari said, "you are most astute even in matters that aren't your expertise."

"You are too kind, My Lord," Kalasariz murmured.

Luka said nothing.

"Enough!" Protarus barked. "You're mooning over each other like a pair of harem girls. Do the casting, dammit! Let's see what Safar's up to!"

＊   ＊   ＊

Safar goggled at the scene, not sure which was real and which the apparition. The threatening horde of warriors, or Leiria and Dario laughing and waving in greeting.

Then he had even more reason to goggle as a large figure rose from the table, saying, "Welcome to Caluz, Safar Timura. We have been waiting many a year for your visit."

The speaker was female—a demon female. And as she spoke she made a motion and the ghostly soldiers vanished.

She was a spectacular sight. Even taller than a large male demon, she was dressed entirely in red—a red gown of the finest Sampitay silk; red shoes beneath that gown with the sheen of a rare jewel. Her talons were painted red, as were her lips curling up in a red painted demon smile above fangs like spears. A ruby crown was set upon her jutting forehead—just above her ivory white demon horn, which was decorated with red magical symbols.

Big as she was, demon as she was, none of these things were the true reasons for Safar's amazement. What had his complete attention was her gown, which was embroidered with a startlingly familiar decoration. The winged, two-headed snake that was the sign of Asper.

She came toward him and Safar whispered assurances to Khysmet, who was still uneasy, then swung off the saddle to greet her.

Safar had never been aboard a ship, but in his imagination the demon queen—for her bearing left no doubt she was a queen—looked like a ship as she came to him, red gown billowing like great sails. Despite her size she was incredibly graceful, moving with smooth and sweet femininity. An odd side of him, a primitive side most men would rather not discuss, took note of her remarkable figure. She was large, yes. A demon, yes. But her shape was the perfect hourglass that dumbfounds all human and demon males.

When they came together, pausing for the formal greeting, Safar felt shamefaced, like a boy.

She held out her claw, dainty as a maid, saying, "I am Hantilia. Queen of Caluz. And chief priestess to the Oracle of Hadin."

＊   ＊   ＊

In Protarus' court Lord Fari was making his final preparations.

"I'll need your help, Majesty," he said. He motioned to the others, Prince Luka and Lord Kalasariz. "All of you must help. To ferret out Safar Timura we need the full powers of the Spell of the Four."

Everyone leaned forward, concentrating, as Lord Fari made magical motions over the heads, chanting:

> *Speak, my Brother.*
> *Speak, my Sister.*
> *Speak, O creatures of the Shades!*
> *What road does Timura take?*
> *What goal does he seek?*
> *And what is his heart's desire?*

Soul numbing shrieks shattered the air as both heads came alive. Their eyes burned with pain and they screamed to the heavens as they relived their final moments on the sporting field. Their anguish was so deep that it pierced Iraj's shape changer's heart and struck at the core that was still human.

Their wails echoed throughout the royal chamber, hammering at his ears and rattling the small, scarred thing he called a soul. He wanted to shout at Fari to end their agony and his misery, but he clipped it off, gagging on guilt. To do otherwise would show a dangerous weakness.

Then, thankfully, Fari waved a claw and the wailing stopped. Two pairs of haunted eyes turned to regard the demon wizard.

"Speak, my sister," Fari chanted. "Speak, my brother. Grant us this boon and we shall release you from all your cares."

The woman spoke first, voice quaking with pain. "He is near!" she said. "He is very, very near!"

Then the man, in equal agony—"Yes, he is near! Run my friend, run from these devils!"

The woman shouted—"No, don't run! Please don't run! Save us, Safar Timura! Save us!"

Fari chortled. "What willful heads," he said to Iraj and the others. "No matter. They're very young and so it's to be expected."

Then, to his victims—"Lord Timura can't hear you. And even if he could, there'd be no help. You are in our care, my lovelies. Only I can help you. Now speak. What road does Timura take?"

And the woman said, "The king's road."

"What king?" Fari pressed. "Tell us his name."

"Protarus," the man croaked.

"Timura and the king," the woman said, "travel the same road."

Fari was clearly puzzled. Luka, seeing slender hope, said, "I knew this was nonsense from the start."

But Protarus shouted, "Silence, you fool!"

The outburst surprised Iraj as much as the demon prince. Mysterious as the answers were, they made ghostly, skin-prickling sense.

Emboldened, Fari continued. "What goal does he seek?"

"Hadin," the woman said. "The Land of Fires."

And the man said, "Two were together. But now there is one."

Iraj shuddered as the words unleashed memory's flood. Suddenly he was a boy. And

Safar was with him, casting the demon bones to see what the future held.

He remembered the red smoke hissing up, rising like a snake. Then out of the smoke a mouth formed, curving into a woman's seductive smile. Then she spoke, and he could hear the words clear echoing down the long corridor of years:

"Two will take the road that two traveled before. Brothers of the spirit, but not the womb. Separate in body and mind, but twins in destiny. But beware what you seek, O brothers. Beware the path you choose. For this tale cannot end until you reach the Land of Fires."

Then he was jolted back to the present as Fari asked the final question:

"What is his heart's desire?"

And the woman said, "Love."

And the man said, "Hate."

And Fari shouted, "Answer clearly, or I'll blast your souls to the Hells!"

But once again Iraj could glimpse cloudy meaning and the two words, "love" and "hate" churned about in his guts.

Kalasariz spoke up. "Some of my spies are like that. Ask the time and they count the grains of sand in the glass. Perhaps our questions are too general."

Fari took heart and tried again. "Tell me brother, tell me sister, where is Lord Timura now?"

"Caluz," the man answered.

Fari was pleased. "Who does he seek there?"

"The Oracle of Hadin."

"Now it makes sense!" Kalasariz said. He turned to Iraj. "There is a famous oracle at Caluz. Called the Oracle of Hadin, I believe."

Fari could see his victims were tiring. He wracked his brains for a last question.

Then, "Tell me brother, tell me sister, what is Lord Timura's purpose in Caluz?"

The answer came in a ghastly chorus: "To kill the king."

Then their eyes went lifeless, their lips slack, and blood gushed to the floor.

Fari turned to address the king, rattling his talons in glee. But when he saw the state Protarus was in, he kept his silence. He noticed Kalasariz and Luka were also staring in wordless fascination. The king was flickering from one shape to the other at a blinding rate, claw and maw and handsome human profile winking in and out of existence.

Iraj knew his emotions were an unchecked torrent, but he couldn't help himself. The announcement that Safar sought his death had unaccountably ripped him from his moorings. He suddenly felt as if he were the hunted, instead of the hunter. He knew this made no sense. Safar was the deer, Iraj the bowman. Still, he'd felt a chill run down his spine when the words were spoken: *"To kill the king."*

Then fear turned to mad outrage. This was betrayal! Safar was his friend! How could he possibly plot to assassinate a friend? Never mind that Iraj tried to kill Safar long ago and had sought his death since. Never mind that Safar had struck back furiously, nearly killing Iraj and destroying his kingdom. Deadly blows had been exchanged many times over the years. Safar Timura was clearly his enemy. But why did Iraj still feel he was also a friend? A friend bent on betrayal and murder?

All these thoughts and emotions stormed about his heart and brain, then anger took root and bloomed into a mighty tree, spreading strong branches of rage all through his body from toe to nape.

With anger came cold reason and purpose and fully human now, he rose to his feet. Golden beard and head and crown glowing in the torch light. He was Iraj Protarus, by the gods! The King of Kings. Lord of the Shape Changers. Greater even then the Conqueror Alisarrian, who was a mere mortal, wizard though he had been.

"We all owe you a great debt, my lord," he said to Fari, who visibly preened, not caring if Luka or Kalasariz noticed. "Now we know not only exactly where Safar Timura is hiding, but we know that Caluz has been his goal all along.

"Timura is not a man to just run and hide. He was mountain born and people who live so high above us all have courage and will bred into them. They breathe air so thin it would make you faint. I lived among them once, so I know. I was weak and light-headed for days before I found my footing. In fact, I think that's the reason for it. The reason Safar and his Kyranians have managed to defy us for so long.

"It's the air, dammit! And I curse myself for missing it all this time. I'm a man of the plains. The air is thick and healthy on the plains. Now water, that's scarce and all our wars rise from that. But water is nothing compared to air. Can you imagine living in a place where you had to fight for the very air to sustain you?"

No one answered. The king's anger made speech unwise.

"They can also see! Oh, by the gods can they see! Up in that eagle's nest they called Kyrania, they could see the most amazing horizons. Horizons so distant they confounded me. Me, a simple man of the plains where all is flat and you drown in the air and you can't imagine what it really is to see. All the way around you—all the time. That's what separates Kyranians from ordinary mortals. The power to see.

"That's another thing we must remember. Safar is the greatest Kyranian of them all, for he can see the future. And sometimes I think he can imagine more. If there is a place that lies beyond the future, Safar can see it.

"But he has to kill me first." The king slammed his throne over, shattering the wood against ground.

He turned to Fari, who was frightened, no longer so desirous of the king's attention.

"Tell me, Lord Fari," he said, his tone fearfully close to the one the demon had used addressing the heads, "And tell me true. Does Safar have to kill me to get to Hadin? Isn't that what your heads were telling us?"

Fari called on all his skills to slip to a middle course. He shrugged.

"Who can say, Your Majesty?" he said in his most oily voice. "Our casting was not plain on that point."

The king merely nodded, so Fari braved thinner ice. "We should be practical about this, Your Majesty," he said. "Hadin is so far away it was known as World's End by the ancients. Surely, this place is out of anyone's reach.

"Far-seeing though he may be, I think it would be wiser to surmise that Lord Timura's goal is more reasonable. Forget about World's End. Think of Esmir, only. It would be far seeing enough of Lord Timura to conclude that his answer was in Caluz. In the center of the Black Lands where a magical machine has gone wild.

"He must overcome the devil machine, the desolate land, the low spirits of his people—everything—to consult with the Oracle of Hadin. And there he must pray that he can find a means to kill the most powerful king in history."

He snorted. "Come, now, Your Majesty! That is seeing very far, beyond not only the future, but hope itself. And as for the business with the air, Highness, I think he's breathing something very thin indeed to conjure up such an impossible task."

"Here, here," Luka said, making the king smile and gaining back a bit of grace.

"Lord Fari speaks wisely, Majesty," Kalasariz said, tipping a wink at the old demon that meant, 'We *must talk.*'

Although no plan had been set, the unholy three, as Iraj had come to think of his brothers, acted as if victory had already been won. They called for food and drink and music and dancers to celebrate. Iraj tilted his scarred lip, making them believe he was fooled by their actions.

Oh, but he was cold, so cold. Damnation he could see it clear. Like Safar could see distant horizons.

Iraj was no fool—even though he was a king, and kings, it is said, make the grandest fools of all. He knew what was going on. His brothers of the spell conspired against one another and they all conspired, separately and together in various alliances, against him. Sheesan had warned him about that.

He felt a pang, thinking of that strange, beauteous witch. How could she have borne appearing like such a crone, when she had been a woman of such beauty and wonder. She had her own designs, of course—some of which she'd even admitted. But that hadn't bothered him. Iraj had learned early that no one addresses royalty without base motives. Even Safar, pure, humble, "I'm only a potter's son," Safar, had something he wanted when he joined Iraj in his mission. He wanted Iraj's power. Safar was jealous because Iraj Protarus was favored by the gods! Destined at birth to be king of kings.

But what was it Safar claimed he wanted? Oh, yes—to save the world. What a *lie* that was!

Iraj scraped at his chair with a heavy ring, smiling at his false brothers as they drank and made merry jests about the human and demon maids who danced for their pleasure. They pretended to chatter happily about their king, their wise, strong king, and how they would stretch every tendon in his effort. Talking about this plan of attack and that.

Fari was saying something about gathering all his wizards to cast a spell to protect them all from the wild magic of the Black Lands. Luka was laying plans to create the greatest mounted shock force in history. As if the Kyranians were the half million demons Iraj once defeated to gain his crown, instead of a handful of hastily trained peasants. And Kalasariz— Damnation! Safar warned me about him, I'd better be careful—Kalasariz was slipping up to Fari, saying this and that and glancing in Luka's direction. What Iraj would have to watch for was when Kalasariz looked in his direction.

In some ways Luka and Fari were easier to understand, he thought. They were demons. Conspiracy came easily to demons. But Kalasariz—oh, be careful of Kalasariz—was of a different cut. The least of which was that he was human. And humans, Iraj thought, were superior to demons in hatching a conspiracy.

I should know, he thought. I am the result of conspiracy—from whom my father would bed on a royal night, to my mother's scheming against his harem. His mother had been a gentle sort, loathe to use poison. But when it came to her son and dreams of being mother of a clan leader, her hand was steady when she poured.

Iraj's mother had taught him about secrets. Keep your own counsel, she'd said, no matter who tells you what is closest to their heart. They are lying. Know this, son, and build greater lies and you will be safe.

Iraj had such a secret. He'd guarded that secret more closely than even his love for his mother. If she were here he'd lie to her face and know she'd be proud of him.

His secret was that thanks to the witch who desired to be his queen, he had the means to break free of the loathsome bond he'd made with these fiends. He ached for the moment when he could cast the spell she'd taught him and destroy them.

But first he'd have to catch Safar. Oh, yes, I must not forget—and his scarred lip twitched—the child, Palimak. Before she died the witch said the child wasn't really necessary. Although the spell would be more powerful if Iraj had them both—like the heads on Fari's stake.

Then I can be free, Iraj thought. Free!

A winsome demon maid pranced in front of him. She was half again his size and of a form he'd only killed before, not caressed. But he suddenly found himself desirous of her and so he motioned and she came to him, pressing strange but somehow familiar parts against him.

He plunged into her embrace, thinking, I wonder what Safar is doing now?

I wonder how he finds Caluz?

CHAPTER NINETEEN
THE VEIL OF LIES

Leiria and Dario waved their wine cups and chorused—"Long live Queen Hantilia!"

Then Leiria whacked Safar on the shoulder, saying, "What do you think of Queenie, here?" She made curving motions with her hands, then winked. "Nice package, don't you think?"

Dario whacked his other shoulder, then leaned in, sloshing wine into his boots. "She likes you, me lord," he stage whispered. He hiccuped, covered his mouth, then said. "Couldn't help but—hiccup!—notice."

Safar smiled, then turned to Queen Hantilia. "Are they drunk or in your spell?" he asked.

"A little of both," the queen answered. She flicked up two talons—rather daintily, Safar thought, considering each was a curved ruby dagger six inches long. "First, you'll have to admit that the wine *is rather good.*"

She toasted Safar and drank. He eyed his own glass, cast a spell to search for ill intent, found none, and so he shrugged and drained his glass. It was delicious, as if all the fruits of the Valley of the Clouds had been turned into the rarest of wines.

"Ambrosia!" he sighed. He hooked the jug onto the table, asking, "Shall we have a little more?" She nodded, and Safar refilled their cups.

Leiria and Dario started sniggering and whispering to one another like excited children.

"Now that we have the drunk issue settled," Safar said, "tell me about the spell."

The demon queen shrugged, well rounded bosom lifting her gown most delightfully. "It's completely harmless," she said. "I just didn't want them to have to worry until I talked to you."

She gestured, saying, "The same with them." His men, hardened scouts all, were sprawled next to their horses, laughing and drinking wine served by giggling maids, many of whom were demons. They wore red robes like Hantilia's, although not as fine, also bearing the twin-headed snake symbol of Asper.

"Trust me, it's a harmless spell," she said. "Their troubles and worries have been momentarily interrupted. That's enough to make anyone drunk—no wine required, my dear Safar. And I promise you there will be no ill effects when they awaken."

Safar glanced around and saw that other than the maids, the queen had no guards, no royal entourage. "I could lift the spell myself, your highness," he said, half-teasing, "and cast a few of my own. Then the tables would be turned. And it would be you and your servants who would be in *my* thrall." He smiled. "I'd make it as pleasant as possible, of course."

Hantilia lifted a claw to her mouth, covering pealing laughter. It was quite musical, Safar thought. Strange that a demon should sound so melodious.

"But you are already in *my* thrall, my dear, dear Safar," she said, chuckling. "Haven't you noticed?"

Safar drank a little more wine, measuring his faculties as he did so. The queen spoke the truth, he thought. He sensed danger, but he felt cheerful about it. He found her company most . . . stimulating? And he was anxious to learn more.

"You're right," he said. "The wine is good. The spell is good. No harm intended."

Hantilia smiled. "And the company?" she asked archly. "Do you find that pleasant as well?"

Safar grinned, raising his cup. "It was boorish of me not to praise my hostess," he said. "Yes, I find the company most charming. Mysterious though she may be."

Hantilia held out a claw. "Come with me, Safar Timura, and all will be revealed." She gently took his hand and led him toward a shale outcropping bulging from the cliff face. "We'll start with Caluz."

Safar glanced down the caravan road. "I thought it was in that direction," he said, pointing. "Through the Caluzian Pass."

Hantilia shook her head. "That way was barred by the Guardians long ago," she said.

Safar puzzled. "The Guardians?"

"Those ghostly warriors who greeted you," the queen answered. She pointed at the many cave mouths that pocked the walls of the passage. "For generations the people of Caluz buried their mightiest heroes in those walls. They are called the Guardians because their ghosts protect the city from any who might come against her."

Safar made a face. "So they aren't harmless," he said.

"Not at all," Hantilia replied. "As you would soon have learned if your intent was other than peaceful."

Then without further ado she waved at the outcropping and Safar felt a jolt of magic. "Open," she commanded—and the rock face dissolved into a misty curtain.

"This is the new road to Caluz," she said. "In fact it's the only one. Even with the Guardians assisting us, we've had to close off the other pathways to defend ourselves from the nasty business going on these days."

For some reason this comment had a false note to it. But before he could consider further, she let go his hand and stepped through the mist, vanishing. Safar hesitated, glancing back at Leiria and Dario, who were still happily under the spell. He followed.

Safar felt a slight chill, then a tingling sensation and suddenly he was shielding his eyes from a bright sun. There was a warm breeze carrying the scent of flowers and ripening fruit. His wizard senses were also pleasantly entertained with fragrant spells carried on gentle magical breezes.

"Once again, Lord Timura," Hantilia said, "welcome to Caluz!"

His vision cleared to be treated to a marvelous sight. They were standing at the crest of a road that curved down to meet a small, graceful valley. There were farms and fields and wooded hills nourished by two rivers that ribboned down from high blue mountains. On a bluff near where the rivers joined there was a beautiful city, all silver with a grand palace towering over the walls.

Below the castle was the Temple of Hadin—a huge stone turtle crouched at the end of a peninsula where the rivers met to form a single stream. The turtle was identical to the miniature idol that was home to Gundara and Gundaree down to the red painting on its back of a volcanic isle topped by a fire breathing demon. Blissful magic streamed from the temple, churning out spells of health, happiness and prosperity.

All in all Caluz seemed a wondrous place where birds always sang, butterflies sweetened the air and its inhabitants happily tilled the fields, tended the markets, or fished the rivers.

As he looked, the warning from the Spirit Rider rose up and he heard her whisper, *"In Caluz, all is not as it seems. Look for the truth beyond the veil of lies."*

"How perfect this world is," Safar said. And then he couldn't resist adding sarcasm: "The only thing missing is a fat pink cloud hanging over the rivers."

Hantilia grimaced. "I told them you'd ferret it out soon enough."

"I suppose the real Caluz is down that road you told me was barred," Safar said.

Hantilia frowned. "Yes, it is. I'm sorry I lied to you." She shrugged. "My priestesses and advisors were afraid you would turn back if you knew the truth. Immediately, that is. I assure you I had no intention of keeping it from you for more than a few days."

"You mean, until I had brought all my people here," Safar said. "All one thousand of them."

Hantilia sighed again. "Am I so transparent?" she asked.

"No," Safar said, "it's only that I've had much experience with royalty. Even when they have the best of intentions, kings and queens have a certain way of thinking. I merely followed that route."

He laughed. "Also, wouldn't I be fairly dim-witted if I didn't notice such things as the absence of certain large celestial bodies." He pointed to the bright blue sky. "Such as the Demon Moon." Hantilia said nothing. She only looked more embarrassed. "Finally," Safar said, "there's the machine itself." He pointed at the great turtle idol. "That is certainly not what's causing all the misery in the Black Lands."

"Actually, it is," Hantilia said. "Except what you are looking at is a manifestation of the real machine. A mirror image, so to speak. It's the result of a spell the Oracle cast just as Caluz was being destroyed." She waved at the city and the pleasant valley. "As is all this."

"What of the original inhabitants?" Safar asked. "Such as the priests who asked my assistance long ago."

"They're all dead, it grieves me to say," Hantilia replied. "But you'll be pleased to hear a few of the former inhabitants escaped here. Into this false Caluz."

Safar perched on a rock, then took off his cloak and placed it on a flat spot next to him. He motioned to Hantilia. "Why don't you make yourself comfortable," he said, "and tell me the tale? From the beginning, if you please."

Once she was settled she said, "Just as I told you, I am Queen Hantilia and I really do rule here. I'm also chief priestess of the Oracle. But it wasn't always so. I am a pilgrim like you, Safar Timura. My kingdom was in a distant land, a realm so small and so peaceful that when Manacia was king of the demons he barely knew we existed.

"There, I was also the high priestess of the Cult of Asper."

"Pardon," Safar said. "I've never heard of such a thing."

"There are few of us," Hantilia replied, "but our origins go back very far." She nodded at the temple. "For instance," she said, "one of our myths is that Lord Asper discovered the magical properties of this place and set the forces in motion that led to the creation of the temple and the machine.

"But back to my tale. Scarce as we were, when the barrier fell between demon and human lands the way was opened for our religion to spread. Soon there were small groups like us all over Esmir. We mingled together, humans and demons, all in the spirit of Asper's teachings."

Hantilia blushed—her skin turning a deeper shade of emerald. "Some even became lovers. A few married. Fewer still managed to bring forth a child."

Safar's heart bumped. Hantilia saw his reaction and said, "You have one such child with you, I understand. The Oracle spoke of him."

"Yes," Safar said. "His name is Palimak."

Hantilia frowned. Then her brow cleared. "Ah, now I understand. It is in the Walarian tongue. Palimak means promise, does it not?"

Safar nodded. "Yes."

"A lovely name," she said. Then—"It is quite likely the child comes from just such a union as those I described. In fact it is impossible for it to be otherwise. And I'll tell you why.

"When the Demon Moon rose and ill befell the land many of us were forced to flee our homes because of sickness and starvation and evil things crawling out of the earth. My kingdom was one of the early victims and my people and I became refugees, wandering Esmir, finding our living where we could. The others of our cult did the same. Many did not survive. I suspect Palimak was the child of such a couple—demon and human—who met with misfortune during that time and he eventually came into your care. Someday you must tell me that tale."

Safar bit into the bitter memory of Nerisa and grimaced. "Someday," was all he said.

The queen saw his discomfort and steered her remarks past that desolate trail. "The day arrived when things were at their worst," she said. "I didn't know how I would find food and shelter for my people. Then the Oracle appeared to me."

"The Oracle of Hadin?" Safar asked.

"The very one. You'll meet her soon enough. At least I pray you will agree to such a meeting. But to go on. The Oracle appeared and commanded me to make my way to Caluz. She said the fate of the world depended on it. I learned later she made many such appearances to members of our cult throughout Esmir.

"Soon all of us were streaming toward Caluz. Our strength grew as we came together and the journey was made easier because we no longer had to fear bandits. We arrived in Caluz just before it collapsed. The city was in a panic because the Oracle was issuing dire warnings. But the Caluzians only became more hysterical with each passing day. And so all the things she urged them to do were left until it was too late."

Safar frowned, remembering the old Caluzian priest who'd told him his people were of that temperament. "The last I heard," he said, "the city leaders were going to divert the rivers, which would effectively shut off the machine. It seemed like a good plan to me. What went wrong?"

"The Demon Moon," Hantilia said. "No one took its tides into account. At the time the plan did seem like an artful solution. After the dams were built and the new channels dug the machine fell silent for a long time. Then the influence of the Demon Moon became more powerful.

"The river tides began to rise, overflowing their banks. This went on day after day, the floods reaching higher each time. The people filled bags with sand and stacked them along the riverbanks trying to halt the flow. Finally the currents jumped back into their original courses and the machine returned to life. This time worse than before."

"I saw the Black Lands," Safar said. "I saw what the machine has done."

"As I said," the Queen continued, "the Oracle warned of the disaster all along. She'd urged a course of action, but only the priests listened. This is when I arrived in Caluz with my followers. And at the pleadings of the priests—and the Oracle's command—we did all we could to help construct her spell."

Hantilia paused, lines of sadness creasing her face. She wiped an eye with her claw, then said. "I have seen many things in my life. Horrible things. But the day we cast the spell overshadowed all the horrors I'd seen before. It is too painful a memory for me to recount.

"Suffice it to say, Caluz was destroyed and the priests all died nobly, staying until the end so the rest of us could escape."

She gestured at the lovely scene that was the false Caluz. "And we've been here ever since. Waiting for you."

Safar sighed. "What do you want of me?" he asked.

The Queen's eyes glittered. "Only to save our lives, Safar Timura," she said. "For without your help all of us will be dead within the month."

*   *   *

Leiria was mortified. Although her memory was hazy from the moment she met Queen Hantilia until the spell was lifted many hours later, she had flashes of seeing herself and Sergeant Dario behaving like two tavern sots.

"I don't like this," she said to Safar, who was riding beside her on Khysmet. "We're trusting everything to a complete stranger."

Safar chuckled. "You're only embarrassed," he said. "Don't be angry with Hantilia."

"I'm not angry!" Leiria snapped. "I just don't know the bi—uh, know anything about her. Oh, I understand the spells were the gentlest way she could handle us. And that certain things were done because the Oracle of Stupid Hadin wanted it that way. So I have nothing to hold against her. In fact, I quite like Hantilia. For someone I only met, that is."

She suddenly grinned at Safar, a devil's glint in her eye. "Although a certain friend of mine—who shall remain nameless, but whose seal bears the letters S.T.—seems to have gotten a great deal more out of that first meeting than I did."

"Ouch!" Safar laughed. "Come on. You're just jabbing at me to relieve your own frustration. Go back to being embarrassed. See if I care. You're right. You were a total fool and should be ashamed of yourself. There. Chew on that, my sweet Leiria."

"You can't get off that easily," Leiria parried. "Admit it. You're attracted to her."

Safar blushed. "A little," he said.

"Even though she's a demon, right?"

Safar's reply was a muttered, "Right."

Leiria snickered. "Now you know how Palimak was made," she said. "First hand, or claw, or whatever."

Another mutter—"Whatever." Then, firm—"Do you feel better now, my dear Leiria? After putting me in my place?"

"Sure I do," Leiria said, eyes dancing with fun. "But what about you? And Hantilia? What do you intend to do about it?"

Safar squared his shoulders. "Nothing," he said. "Except note it as a curiosity of nature."

"Don't make me laugh," Leiria chortled.

"You are laughing."

"Well, who wouldn't?"

"All right! All right!" Safar snapped, switching moods with Leiria. "Let's talk about something else. Something depressing and morbid like your premonitions of doom and betrayal."

"I didn't say that," Leiria retorted. "I only said we were trusting an awful lot to someone we don't know. We're fetching the entire caravan to Caluz. Or whatever that place is. You say there's two of them, I'll take your word for it. Anyway, we're throwing ourselves on the mercy of these people." She shuddered, remembering. "And those . . . Guardians! I'll never forget how helpless I felt when I realized they were all ghosts. And

433

they could hurt me, but I could do nothing to them!"

"Don't worry about the Guardians," Safar said, matter of factly. "I can take care of them."

"Sure you can, or at least I believe you when you tell me something like that. You're a mighty wizard, and all. But we'll still be outnumbered. They can overwhelm us at will."

"That's true," Safar said, "but you're forgetting something. They need me to stop the machine."

Leiria became angry. "I just don't want you to get killed, Safar!" she said. "That's all. What's down in that damned temple? Who is the Oracle? She could be the great devil queen of all devil queens, as far as we know. What if it's a trap?"

Safar started to laugh. "Thanks," he said. "I feel much better now."

"What are you talking about?"

"You just reminded me of the worst thing that could happen."

"You're damn right. Death is what could happen."

"No, the worst thing that could happen is that we'd be killed by Iraj."

Another laugh. "And can you imagine how angry he'd be if we died in Caluz before he could catch us? If I could see his face just as I died, I'd go to my grave a happy man."

"I never thought about it like that," Leiria said, smiling. "You're right. It does make you feel better."

They came to the top of a rise and reined in to let the others catch up. Some miles away they could see the caravan crawling across a barren plain to meet them. It was late afternoon—the worst time of day in the Black Lands—and the heat was intense, the air thick with sulfurous fumes from the distant volcanoes.

"At least the air is sweeter in Caluz," Leiria said. "They'll be glad of that."

Safar didn't answer and she turned to see him drawn up stiff, peering hard at the caravan.

"What's wrong?" she asked.

"I'm not sure," Safar said. He pointed. "But look at that crater. Just to the left of the wagons."

Leiria found the crater. Although large, it was only one of hundreds scattered across the plains. The road skirted them all, so after a time she'd grown used to their presence.

"I don't see anyth—" Something swirled in the entrance and she broke off.

Then the swirl became an immense cloud of bats flying out of the crater—rising in a thick column.

Leiria relaxed. "It's just the bats," she said. "They fly out every night about this time."

"It's . . . not . . . just . . . the . . . bats!" Safar gritted. Then he shouted, "Come on!"

As he charged down the long hill he had a flicker of memory of another such time. Iraj had been with him then.

Racing down the snowy pass to save the caravan.

*　　　*　　　*

Palimak was dreaming of the machine. He was asleep, almost in a stupor from the heat, and in his dream he saw the machine as a huge turtle, a gigantic clockwork toy with immense snapping jaws and it lumbered toward him on mechanical feet.

He jumped into a lake and made himself a fish and swam away. But the turtle came after him and its legs became like revolving oars and it churned through the water at an amazing speed. He swam faster, fast as he could, but the turtle got closer, closer, jaws snap snap snapping, snap—

"Wake up, Little Master!" came a voice. "Wake up!"

Palimak's eyes blinked open and he saw two small frightened faces hovering over his chest—Gundara and Gundaree.

"What's wrong?" he mumbled, rubbing his eyes.

"Can't you feel it?" Gundara said. "Something's watching!"

"And it isn't a very pleasant something, either," Gundaree added. He shuddered. "Kind of oily."

And that was it! Palimak could feel it, feel something watching, something big, something mean and something . . . oily! But thick. Real thick. And hot! How could it live and watch and be so hot?

"Let's go!" he said, jumping up.

The two little Favorites fled back into the stone idol. He pocketed it and leaped out the back of the slow moving wagon.

The Timura wagons were about half way down the long line, herd animals straggling behind the last wagons with boys driving them along. Beyond them was the rear guard. Perhaps twenty armed men. Up front—past the lead wagons—was another force of fifty. In between and along the both sides of the road, people and children walked, talking listlessly in the heat, burping babies, or flicking sticks at goats and llamas to keep them together.

Palimak stood in the road, letting them pass by. He turned, searching for the source of his discomfort. Then he caught it. On the other side of the road!

He ducked under a camel, swatting its jaws as it tried to snap at him like that damned turtle. Oops! Shouldn't say damned. It made Grandmother mad.

Then he saw the bats streaming out of the crater. He looked up at the huge black cloud swirling above the caravan. Normally the bats flew away. But this time they were staying in the same place! Millions of them!

"Is it the bats?" he asked.

Gundara's voice came from his pocket. "It's not the bats!"

"*Definitely*, not the bats!" Gundaree added.

"Quit repeating everything I say!" snapped Gundara.

"I wasn't repeating. I was emphasizing."

"Oh, shut up!"

"Don't tell me to shut—"

Palimak slapped his pocket. "If I get killed or something," he said, "you'd better learn to like oily stuff. Because that's what your new master's going to be. Big and oily!"

"And hot," Gundaree said. "Don't forget hot!"

Palimak sighed, "Okay, he's hot! But where is he?"

Then he caught it. A filthy presence at the crater's edge. About fifty feet away. And he could feel it oozing out.

"There he is!" Gundara said. "We'd better get you out of here!"

"Lord Timura will kill us if we let something happen to you!" Gundaree added.

"What spell should we use?" Gundara asked his twin.

"I'd suggest running," Gundaree said. "We can think of one while we're running!"

"Good idea. Do you hear that, Little Master? Run! Run like the Hells!"

But Palimak was already running as fast as his little legs could go. But he wasn't running away. He was racing toward his Grandfather, who was driving the lead Timura wagon.

"Grandfather!" he shouted. "We have to get out of here!"

Khadji heard the boy and turned to see Palimak running toward him. "What's wrong?" he shouted.

Palimak twisted his arm to point, still running. "Back there! It's coming!"

Khadji jumped off and swept the child up. He was startled to see his eyes glowing fiercely yellow and he could feel the boy's sharp little claws biting into his arm.

"What's coming?"

Palimak calmed himself down, eyes flickering back to normal. "It's a great big magic thing, Grandfather," he said, spreading his arms wide as he could. "And it's going to get us all if we don't run."

He squirmed to be freed and Khadji let him go. He landed lightly on his feet, like a cat.

"Quick, Grandfather!" he shouted. "Sound the alarm!"

"Calm down, son," Khadji said. "Let's see what it is that's bothering you."

He looked around, saw the bats, smiled and looked down at the boy. "It's just the bats," he said. "They won't hurt us."

Palimak stamped his foot. "It's not the bats!" he snapped. He pointed at the crater. "It's in there. And it's coming out and you'd better blow the stupid horn!"

He saw his grandfather flush with anger and realized he wasn't getting through. To Khadji he was just a little boy who'd suddenly become very rude.

But there wasn't time to fool with that adult stuff. He didn't have time to argue or explain. He knew what he could do, suddenly felt the knowledge and power to go with it. Still he held back, reluctant to take action. This was his Grandfather, after all!

"Please, Grandfather," he said, "Please, please, please. Blow the horn!"

"I'm losing my patience with you, young man!" Khadji said in the tones adults used when they'd had enough.

"I'm sorry, Grandfather," Palimak said.

And then he cast the spell, right hand shooting out, claws uncurling from his finger tips, eyes glaring yellow.

Khadji twitched as the spell hit him, stiffening to his full height. He looked down on his grandson with fond eyes. Such a wise little boy.

"Please blow the horn, Grandfather," Palimak said as nicely as he could.

"Sure, son," Khadji said, a broad smile on his face. "Right away!"

Khadji jumped up on the wagon and grabbed the long warning horn that every family leader kept nearby at all times. He blew three blasts—the signal for everyone to go like the blazes and ask questions later. Palimak knew this wasn't the best plan of escape, but it was all he could think of. Other horns picked up the warning and joined in the cry. People shouted, whips cracked, animals bawled, and the caravan surged forward at a much greater speed.

Khadji smiled and waved happily at Palimak as he drove the wagon away. The boy waved back, feeling very bad about what he'd done.

"All right, Little Master," came Gundara's voice, "so you don't like running. I hope you can think of something pretty quick."

"Frankly," Gundaree added, "we're out of suggestions."

CHAPTER TWENTY
BEAST OF THE BLACK LANDS

Palimak walked slowly back to the crater. Wagons and animals streamed past, people running beside them, horns blowing, camels bawling, geese shrieking, children wailing, parents shouting, a whole cacophony of panicked flight.

As fast as they were moving, he could tell it wasn't fast enough.

It was getting darker and oil lamps and torches flared into life, so the caravan became like a stream of stars flying low across the land. A passing wagon hit a rut and a lamp came flying off, shattering against the ground to leave a small pool of flaming oil.

"This thing is hot," Gundara said, "but he doesn't like fire."

"Fire is absolutely not one of his favorite things," Gundaree added. "Apparently he's rather vain about his appearance."

And then a great voice shouted: *"Hate!"*

It echoed across the bleak plain, striking lightning on the highest rocks. Overhead, the immense swarm of bats shrieked and Palimak's heart jumped so high he thought it was going to fly out of his throat.

Again came the shout: *"Hate!"*

And then Palimak was trying his best to catch and swallow his heart as the crater began to bubble and froth, foul steam rising to meet those shrilling bats.

A scum formed, cracked and then a mighty head emerged, all tarry and stuck this way and that with the white bones of angry things that had died long ago. Skulls made its eyes. Ribbed spines its nose. And its mouth was a graveyard clutter, opening wide, bone dust expelled in a cloud as it shouted:

"Hate!"

It rose out of the crater, shoulders following head, then arms and trunk and limbs, climbing higher and higher. A massive black tarry beast, all pitted and scarred with oil bursting from those scars and bleeding down the sides.

The creature's head moved slowly, looking for the cause of its terrible wrath.

Then its eyes, all aboil with grinning skulls, fixed on Palimak.

*   *   *

Safar rode full out, urging every ounce of speed he could from Khysmet. Even so, when he saw the beast rise from the crater to confront Palimak he feared he'd be too late.

Far below he could see the crush of fleeing people and wagons and animals race up the hill toward him, flooding the road from bank to bank like a solid wall of onrushing water. He'd never break through to get to Palimak.

He saw a narrow trail to the side that looked like it might lead in the right direction. He shouted for Leiria to meet the panicked horde and guide them, then turned down the trail, praying he'd made the correct decision.

*   *   *

Palimak was frozen with fear. His whole being fixed on those ghastly eyes and bony mouth splitting open into a horrible smile. In the background he could hear sounds of panic as the caravan fled the horrible presence.

Then Gundara said, "You should have run, Little Master."

And Gundaree said, "It isn't nice to say, 'I told you so.'"

"Shut up!" Palimak shouted to them both, breaking from his trance.

He ran to the pool of flaming oil. He made a scoop of his hands and skimmed through the heart of the fire. The light came off, spilling out in beads, but Palimak quickly make a glowing ball of them, holding the ball firmly between his hands.

And the beast shouted—"YOU I HATE YOU!"

Palimak jumped, burning himself on the invisible flame, but he kept his concentration. Pulling up the spell, putting together all the parts of it—light and fire, it was hard, a lot of pieces don't fit. Hurry! Hurry! Don't pay attention when he shouts. So what if he's close—oh, boy is he close!

"Listen to me," he said to the Favorites. "Remember the spell we practiced? Fire follow light?"

"That's a good spell," Gundara said.

"I don't know if I feel like it," Gundaree grumbled. "He said 'shut up' to us. Which was a very rude thing to say."

An immense shadow fell over them. Palimak hunched his shoulders, holding the ball of light close to his stomach.

"I apologize, all right?" he said. "Sorry and double sorry. Now, do it!"

He turned—looking up and up, head craning back, feeling like such a small boy. Standing beneath a living mountain of tar and bone. So close that when the pustules of oil broke they ran down the smoking skin to pool at his feet.

The creature's breath was a hot, foul wind of gritty magic blasting away at his senses. But he closed his eyes and stuck out his chin taking the wind full on his face.

And he chanted:

> *"Palimak, Palimak,*
> *Here I come!*
> *Demon boy,*
> *Or people boy—*
> *Guess which one!"*

He threw the ball of light as high he could, casting the spell, feeling Gundara and Gundaree push in behind it. Blowing it bigger and bigger until it looked like a watery sun when it crashed into the beast's face.

Dazzling light splashed into the creature's eyes and he reeled, screaming as if the light had been acid.

And Palimak shouted, "Fire follow light!"

The Favorites fed him their powers and Palimak's right hand speared out, pointing finger becoming a long, sharp talon. There was a searing from within as the fire leaped from the oil pool to his body, then shot out of his talon, racing to join the light.

A huge blast followed as the two forces were rejoined and the beast roared in pain, stumbling back, head bursting into flame. It beat at its skull trying to put the fire out, but then its hands caught and it was shouting and wailing in agony. Flailing and screaming helplessly.

"Got you!" Palimak shouted.

"I wouldn't be too sure about that, Little Master," Gundara cautioned. "You might have just made him madder."

"Maybe you'd better consider running again," Gundaree added.

To his horror, Palimak saw the beast had managed to put out most of the flames and was recovering.

What would he do now? The spell had left him drained and he was frightened that even if he could think of another spell he'd be too exhausted to cast it.

"Wait!" Gundara said with sudden excitement. "Here comes help!"

He no sooner spoke than a score of mounted warriors rushed onto the field to do battle. Shouting Kyranian battle cries they charged the beast, firing arrows and waving swords and battle axes.

"Let's think about that running option again," Gundaree said. "There's just enough time."

Still, Palimak didn't budge. Frightened as he was, he'd determined to make a stand.

"Such a stubborn child," Gundara said.

"I'm definitely going to tell his father," Gundaree said.

For a moment it looked as if the mounted charge was having some affect. Pierced by arrows and spears and slashing blades, the beast shrilled pain, bleeding oil from many wounds.

"*Hate!*" It shouted. "*Hate!*"

Then it suddenly drew itself up, towering three times the height of the warriors. The beast's mouth yawned open, a great black hole ringed by white skeleton lips.

First smoke belched out, thick, evil-smelling clouds that burned the eyes and seared the lungs.

Then it vomited boiling oil. A great steaming river of it, splashing over the attacking men.

Their cries were terrible, but only a few caught the full blast. They were left groaning on the ground, while the others wheeled about and fled.

*　　　*　　　*

High above, Leiria had commanded a position at a bend in the road, shouting into dazed faces, smacking panicked men with the flat of her sword.

"Get them in order! Get them in order!" she shouted, hauling the calmer ones out of the crowd and pointing at the hysterical mass.

Gradually, some order took form as her deputies waded in to straighten out the confusion. Then a camel reared up, frightened and bawling and lashing out with its front feet. It came down, nearly smashing over a wagon, but people caught the rim and tilted it back up. As it crashed to the ground the camel panicked even more, roaring in fear and trying to bite anything in sight.

Leiria leaped over two men who were scrambling to get away from those flat, deadly teeth.

The camel's head snaked toward her, eyes wide and glazed, bloody gums and teeth exposed in a panicked snarl.

Leiria ducked, letting the head sweep past her, then jumped for the rear.

She caught the animal as it came about, jabbing the camel in the hind quarters with her sword. It bawled and galloped up the hill, caroming off of several wagons, bowling over a few people, then disappearing from sight.

Leiria turned, shuddering relief. Then she saw the beast and the fleeing men. Saw the wounded flailing on the ground.

And Palimak, very small, very alone, looking up at the beast.

They was no way she could reach him. Groaning, she looked this way and that, wondering:

Where is Safar?

The beast looked down at the injured men and horses. He held up a tarry hand, belching wreaths of smoke.

"*Kill later you!*" he thundered. "*First kill hate!*"

He stepped over them, coming toward the road, eyes sweeping the ground for his small enemy.

Then once again the beast settled its awful eyes on Palimak. Bone cracked as its mouth opened into a ghastly grin.

"I'm going to miss you, Little Master," Gundara sniffed.

"It'll be a thousand years before we find somebody as nice as you," Gundaree added.

And the beast shouted—"*Hate! You I hate!*"

It stomped forward, ground rumbling under its weight and Palimak conjured up all the power he could find. The Favorites rushed to help him, squeezing out every drop of sorcerous energy, but it was only a slim trickle and Palimak felt as if he was lifting an infant's fist against a giant.

He heard someone shout his name and he turned to see a glorious sight charging toward him. It was his father and Khysmet flying across the plain, the red Demon Moon grinning behind them.

"Pa-li-mak!" his father shouted, voice stretching across the distance between them, long and slow and sweet like grandmother's taffy. "Pa-li-mak!"

And the beast said, "*Hate! Kill you hate!*"

An immense hand swept toward him, tarry fingers the size of ancient swamp stumps, opening wide to grasp.

Palimak closed his eyes.

Then there was a rush of sound and sensation and a hand grabbed him by the collar.

He was lifted up, but so slowly, hells it was slow! Like he was coming up from the same dreamlike depths where the giant turtle had pursued him. Someone—someone he loved, someone who loved him possibly even more—was heaving, kicking, fighting the heavy drowning weight, turtle jaws going snap, snap, snap, kicking hard for the surface.

The dream shattered and everything sped up. Real sensation returned, but in quick jerks—A rush in his ears. Snatched from the ground. Beast spitting Hate! Blistering splatter across his legs as he was snatched to safety. Then all was normal—but upside down normal—as he opened his eyes and saw the ground racing past beneath him.

It nearly made him sick.

He tried to rise, but his father pushed him down with one hand as Khysmet plunged away—contorting his body as he dodged from side to side. Palimak felt like a huge ungainly weight that shifted wildly as Khysmet avoided attack. He saw torrents of smoking oil shoot past, curl into them, then be hurled away as Khysmet changed course, bending as if he were double-jointed.

Then his father reined Khysmet in and the halt was so sudden Palimak's stomach hit an unforgiving wall. Acid contents splashing about, then racing for his throat.

His father dropped him to the ground and he fell on his knees, spewing.

Palimak wiped his mouth and looked up. His father's eyes were bluer and deeper than he'd ever seen them. Wells of blue, dark seas of blue, so sad and all-seeing in the moment passing between them that Palimak nearly wept.

His father spoke. "Stay there, son. I'll be back as soon as I can."

He held the reins tight as spoke, steadying Khysmet who was pawing the earth, anxious to get on with it. Then he whistled to the stallion and they whirled in their tracks and charged back to face the beast.

"Get ready," Gundara said.

Palimak fell from safety to fear so fast he thought he was going to throw up again.

"Ready for what?"

"As I see it—tell me I'm wrong if you think differently . . ." Gundaree said, so slow in his reply that Palimak thought he'd go mad, watching his father and Khysmet plummet toward the hideous creature. " . . . but in my view we have two choices."

"Run," Gundara broke in.

"Yes, we could run," Gundaree said, impatient with the interruption, but keeping his temper so he could make his point. "Running is still a very good idea," he said. "A course we've urged all along."

"I hope you tell your father that," Gundara said, "because he's going to be really mad when this is all over. And it wasn't our fault."

"Never mind fault," Gundaree said, such an uncharacteristic statement from him that Palimak's attention was riveted. "The point is, we're looking at life and death, and who our new master is going to be if something isn't done right away. The beast is stupid. I don't mind that. We've had stupid before. But he's also really, really dirty. An affront to all civilized beings. I definitely do not want that . . . that . . . *thing*, for a master!"

Palimak saw his father closing on the beast, the huge, hideous figure turning to fix on them.

"Soooo, if we're not going to run—" Gundara began . . .

" . . . Which we still advise—" Gundaree poked in . . .

" . . . We might consider helping the Master," Gundara completed.

And the beast shouted, *"Hate!"*

Palimak saw Khysmet rearing up, hooves slashing the air, bolts of lightning cracking out. He saw his father reach behind him, scrabbling at the saddle, then plucking a javelin from its sheath beneath the cantle lip.

As his father reared back to throw, he saw the javelin tip flare. The flare leaped to join the crackling fire from Khysmet's hooves, shooting up toward the beast.

Palimak dug down, clawing past layers he never knew existed, finding untapped reservoirs of magical power. The effort took everything the boy had and he fell to his knees.

"Now!" the Favorites shouted in chorus.

The beast was reaching for his father when Palimak cast the joining spell.

He was so empty he had no mind, no soul of his own. Everything was focused on the spell. He leaped onto the spell's back, clutching as tightly as he could, magical winds buffeting his face. Palimak collided with his father's spell, burst through the walls, then was swept onward and upward at a heart-stopping speed.

Then he entered a never-never state where he was floating like a high meadow moth on a spring wind. He could see all the parts of his father's spell, a wondrous flock of soaring birds with more colors, it seemed, than there were rainbows in the world to make them.

Palimak turned, relaxed and lazy, still speeding along, but feeling easy about it. Time to think. Time to consider. Time to marvel at the complex beauty of the spell, but marveling more at the elegant simplicity of its core.

His father's spell made him feel as if he'd just lost his childhood. Everything before this moment had been a game. A silly little boy amusing himself.

Now he could see what real magic was. See it and admire it through the eyes of an adult. He was confounded and excited at the same time. Tone deaf at one moment, acute musical hearing the next, with all those magical notes spurting out like a harp played by a madman. But then it all made sense. He could see it, hear it, feel his bones throb with it.

Magic as it should be.

And he thought: So that's what it's like to be a wizard!

His father shouted a warning and Palimak kicked away just in time, spirit self plunging back into his mortal form. Then he was a small boy again, watching the white hot spear sink into the beast's face.

It thundered agony, grasping the magical spear between both mighty hands. The beast heaved, screaming louder still, then there was a great blast of light and the beast exploded into flames. The force was so great it hurled Palimak away and for a moment he thought he was his spirit self again, flying with the sorcerous winds. Then he struck, landing heavily on his back, the air knocked out of him.

He fought for breath, desperate to get up, to get moving before the beast struck back.

Then he found his father standing over him and relief rushed in along with returned breath and he shuddered in all the air he could hold. Safar knelt beside him, trying to smile to cover worry and feeling his limbs for signs of injury.

When Palimak could speak again, he asked, "Did we get him?"

Safar glanced over his shoulder at the scattered pieces of the beast. Hot tarry lumps, big and small, with white bits of shattered bone showing through.

He turned back. "We sure did, son," Safar said, scooping him up. "As good as any pair of wizards could."

Palimak grinned weakly, proud to be included. A moment later he was aboard Khysmet, nestled against his father and they were riding slowly after the caravan—back in order now and climbing the hill.

He was tired but his mind was abuzz with all kinds of thoughts and possibilities roused by his experience.

"I want to learn to be a real wizard, father," he said. "Like you."

"I've already been teaching you, son," Safar said.

Palimak frowned. "Maybe so," he said. "But I don't think I've been listening real well." He sighed. "There's so much to know," he said, thinking of the elegance of his father's spell. "So I'd better hurry and learn before I get too old."

Safar chuckled but didn't answer. Then a sudden thought struck Palimak and his eagerness turned to dismay.

"I think I'm going to be in big trouble," he said.

"I kind of doubt that," his father said. "You're the hero of the hour, son. You saved the caravan."

Palimak shook his head. "But I had to do something really bad," he said. "I was mean to my grandfather."

"He'll forgive you," Safar said. "Whatever it was."

"He wouldn't listen to me," Palimak went on. "So I put a spell on him and made him do what I said."

Safar looked down at him, his eyes unfathomable. Palimak thought he even looked a little sad. Then he saw a glitter in the depths.

"When I was going to wizard's school," Safar said, "they had a special class for first year acolytes called 'The Ethics of Magic.' Naturally, it only lasted a week, and no one ever attended." He snorted humor. "In fact, it was the only class at the Grand Temple of Walaria where students were expected to cheat. You could buy the tests from the teacher for six coppers. Four if you were on scholarship."

"Did you cheat, Father?" Palimak asked. "Did you buy the test?"

"I confess I did, son," Safar said. "I didn't have any choice. The master of the course didn't attend either and the only way you could take the test was to buy it with a set of answers. But I did feel guilty about it. And I suppose that's the best you can do. Keep a good, healthy sense of guilt at hand."

"And then still do what you think have to do?" Palimak asked, troubled at this new and very difficult world being revealed to him.

Safar squeezed his arm. "That's the closest to the truth that I can get," he said.

"But what about the gods?" Palimak protested, thinking of the lessons he learned at the Temple in Kyrania. "Don't they tell you that one thing is right, and another thing wrong?"

"I've never had one tell *me*," Safar said. "Only their priests. And priests are no more honest than the rest of us. Maybe even less, since there's so much temptation about when you make your living from sin."

Palimak was amazed. Each level of this larger world obviously became more complicated and confusing the higher you climbed. Or maybe he was going down. Maybe to know wasn't up, but down, down, and then down some more. All the way down a long flight of dark stairs that descended forever.

He looked up at the boiling skies of the Black Lands and the grinning Demon Moon.

"What's wrong with the gods, anyway?" he said, a little angry and self righteous. "Can't they see? Can't they warn you? Are they asleep or something?"

Palimak felt his father suddenly tense up. What had he said wrong? Then Safar relaxed.

"I'll tell you a riddle," he said. "When you figure it out, you'll know as much as anyone in the world about what the gods are up to."

"I'm good at riddles," Palimak said. Then he frowned in exaggerated demonstration. "Go ahead," he said. "My riddle machine is all the way on."

And so Safar recited the Riddle of Asper:

> *"Two kings reign in Hadin Land,*
> *One's becursed, the other damned.*
> *One sees whatever eyes can see,*
> *The other dreams of what might be.*
> *One is blind. One's benighted.*
> *And who can say which is sighted?*
> *Know that Asper knocked at the Castle Keep,*
> *But the gates were barred, the Gods Asleep."*

Palimak listened closely, setting his sharp little mind to work on the pieces. But no matter how hard he tried, the puzzle refused to make itself clear. Finally, he gave up.

"I suppose you have to think about it a real long time," he said.

"I suppose so," Safar answered, dry.

"Do you know the answer, Father?" he asked.

Safar shook his head. "No I don't son," he said. "No I don't."

Then from overhead came the cry of many bats and Safar looked up to see that the black swirling cloud was still there. Except now the bats seemed more excited than before, shrieking and flapping excitedly as if suddenly disturbed.

"What's wrong with the bats?" Safar asked.

Palimak yawned, exhaustion suddenly overcoming him. "Nothing, Father," he said. "It was never the bats!"

He fell asleep, but Safar kept his eye on the bats as he rode along, wondering at their odd behavior.

*   *   *

Far away at the edge of the Black Lands, four giant wolves prowled a hilltop. A great spellfire swirled in the center of the hill, shooting off sparks and spears of flame. The wolves paced about the fire, sometimes on all fours, sometimes on hind feet, growling and grinding their teeth.

Their huge glowing eyes were fixed on the heart of the spellfire, where an image of the Black Lands wheeled about. They were looking down from a great height, gaping crater to one side, a wide track running along it. They could see the blasted remains of the beast. And far up ahead the lights of a caravan were winking on, curving up a long hill.

But immediately beneath them, trotting along the track after the wagons, was the sight that had them growling with delight, shape-changer's hunger stoked into hot-bellied pain.

It was Safar Timura, riding a magnificent horse, carrying a sleeping Palimak in his arms.

Then Timura looked up—staring right at them. It was so sudden they were startled and drew back, growling warnings as if Safar's image were about to attack.

The image became clouded and confused as their spell concentration weakened.

"Kill him!" they snarled. "Kill his brat! Kill his bitch woman!"

The creature who was Iraj Protarus recovered first, roaring at the image, "Enough! I've seen enough!"

And the image shattered.

*   *   *

Safar's hackles prickled as the huge black swarm of bats suddenly broke apart. Their cries were wild, hysterical, as if they had been asleep and now danger had suddenly awakened them.

Then, just as quickly as it began, the hysteria ended and they formed up again and flew off in an orderly fashion. A great long, blunt-tipped arrow aimed out of the Black Lands.

Safar shivered and at the same time Khysmet quickened his pace.

The hunters were out and it was time to get off the road.

*   *   *

Iraj paced the edge of the hill, staring out into the Black Lands, scarred snout moving this way and that as he searched the barren plains.

In the background he could hear his spell brothers howling orders and his great army muscling into life. Demon steeds shrieked and clawed at one another as their masters booted them into formation. Humans threw their shields over their shoulders and settled their battle harness and weapons for the march. Cooks and supply men were scattering the campfires and loading the wagons. Demon and human whores fought each other for space aboard those wagons, slapping or comforting frightened children and kits, depending on their temperaments.

Iraj ignored all this, searching the glowing skies beneath the Demon Moon. The wait seemed interminable. His anger and blood lust grew by the minute.

Then he saw it—the huge cloud of shrieking bats, streaming out of the Black Lands.

His senses exploded into exquisite life and he howled in joy at the sight. Then the bats were overhead, wheeling about the sky, once, twice, three times. Then they flew off

444

again, heading back the way they had come.

Like an unleashed bolt Iraj charged forward, bounding down the hill after them, howling for his prey. His spell brothers charged after him, fanning out to sweep up anything and everything in their great snapping jaws and deadly talons.

Behind them came Protarus' army. The first elements had already topped the hill and were pouring down the other side. They were led by five hundred mounted demons, their spears making a deadly forest, their battle cries ululating across the lightning blasted terrain.

Within moments the whole plain was swarming with men and demons—led by the four immense wolves who were their masters.

It was a juggernaut aimed straight at Caluz.

CHAPTER TWENTY ONE
DARK PARADISE

After a year of desperate flight and miserable camps, the Kyranians fell into the embrace of Caluz as if it were the softest and deepest of pillows. They were warmly welcomed, with hundreds of people and demons streaming out to greet them with gifts of choice food and delicious drink and all manner of clothes and goods to replace their trail-worn things.

Queen Hantilia provided them with a large, lightly wooded field to make their temporary home and supplied them with every luxury imaginable, until soon the field seemed more like a pleasure camp for royalty enjoying a few weeks in the bracing outdoors. They settled into colorful pavilions filled with thick carpets and pillows. Cheery cooking fires were scattered among the pavilions, each with tables and benches so the Kyranians could imagine they were at home, gossiping and sharing leisurely meals.

Portable bath houses were set up along the river and the Kyranians reveled in an orgy of hot soapy baths, soaking away months of grime in steaming kettles big enough to hold a family. Then they all donned their new clothes and strolled through the trees, or along the nearby river bank, feeling clean and without care.

Special attention was paid to the soldiers and horses hurt in the encounter with the beast. The Queen sent her best healers to treat them with magical herbs and ointments and soon they were up and about, injuries fading, enjoying their new home as much as the rest.

Every day was a glorious day in Caluz. The sun always mild, the nights pleasantly cool and the remarkable absence of the Demon Moon made everyone feel as if a large weight had been lifted. Children played, lovers swooned, mothers and fathers enjoyed many stolen moments alone, as did the grandparents. At night those who could make music made it and everyone danced and sang away their troubles.

It was a grand holiday for one and all—except Safar, who disappeared for several days of intense conferences with the Queen and the top Caluzian priests and scholars. His absence only made everyone's mood lighter. For a short time they could forget about Iraj Protarus, prophecies of a doomed world and their desperate journey to far off Syrapis. Safar was dealing with such things. And when he decided what they should do next he'd come and tell them. Who could say when that would be? So let's enjoy life, grab what we can from it for the dark days will return soon enough.

Yet there was a ragged edge to their joy. Snatched as they were from a place where fear had become ordinary, the Kyranians went about their pleasures at a frantic pace. Leaping from one activity to another. Always glancing over their shoulders, waiting for the predestined shadow to fall.

Only Palimak and Leiria were unaffected. Only they saw the mirror cracks in the perfection that was Caluz. Leiria because she was a soldier and had a soldier's healthy suspicion of all things. Palimak because he was a newly serious boy, a self-appointed wizard's apprentice to his father, whom he was worried would leave him out of the main action. Whatever that was going to be.

One evening while they were walking together along the river looking for a likely fishing spot they came upon a small park with a dozen or more Caluzians—both human and demon. Some were taking the air alone, some in company, and there were several family groups with children or kits.

As soon as they saw the two Kyranians they all rushed over to bow and smile and murmur greetings. Saying, "How is the Lady Leiria this evening?" Or, "Does the Young Lord Timura find himself well, we pray?" And "May the blessings of Lady Felakia be with you!"

As they spoke they spontaneously handed the two little gifts, a bracelet or necklace for Leiria hastily stripped off by the owner, a small top or a ball for Palimak, willingly given by smiling children. Leiria and Palimak made polite replies and tried to fend off the gifts but it was no use, so they stuffed them in their pockets, thanking everyone and grinning until their jaws ached.

A moment later the Caluzians all chorused farewells and trooped off, pleasant laughter trailing in their wake.

Leiria looked about the empty park. "They certainly left in a hurry," she said. "I feel like we brought something odorous to a party."

Palimak snorted. "They're just so nice they make me sick!" he said. "But they never really want to talk to you. Or play with you. They just say, 'How are you, Young Lord Timura?' And 'May the gods be kind to you!' Things like that, but soon as you try to say something back they pretend they're busy, or going someplace in a hurry, and run away."

"I thought I was the only one to notice that," Leiria said. "I went into the city the other day and you should have seen the fuss everyone made over me. Then they suddenly melted away and all of sudden the street was empty and people were closing their doors and shutters.

"The same thing happened when I went into a tavern to get a drink and some company. At first they were all my friends, buying me drinks and welcoming me to Caluz. Next thing I knew the tavern was empty and the innkeeper was making excuses about having to close up early."

"What's wrong with them, Aunt Leiria?" Palimak asked.

"I don't know, my dear," she answered. Then, thinking she might be neglecting her auntly duties, she tried to sound more kindly. "Maybe they're all just very frightened and trying to put a brave face on things. The gods know they have a right to their fears. From what your father said they're under some curse and don't have much longer to live, unless he helps them."

"Maybe . . ." Palimak said doubtfully. He thought a minute then said, "What if they have to be really nice and happy all the time because that's the way the machine wants it? What if they don't have any choice?"

He waved at the idyllic scene around them, taking in twittering birds and flitting butterflies. "Look at it, Aunt Leiria!" he said. "*Everything's* too nice! It's not natural. It has to be the machine!"

Reflexively, Leiria turned to look upstream at the great stone turtle squatting over the place where the rivers joined. Water poured out its mouth, thundering into the wide basin below, sending up a mist laced with many rainbows.

For a moment she thought she saw something. A flicker of another scene laid on top of this idyllic vision, but black like a shadow cast. In this, the turtle god was the size of a mountain with lighting crackling on its back. And instead of water pouring from its mouth, there was a river of fire. Then the vision vanished and all was the same again.

At first she thought she was imagining things, but then Palimak said, "Did you see it, Aunt Leiria?" His voice was excited with just a touch of fear. "Did you see it?"

"Yes," she said, almost in a whisper. "I saw!"

* * *

High above in Queen Hantilia's silver palace Safar was having his own problems.

He paced the lush waiting area outside the Queen's courtroom, a little red-robed serving maid trotting behind him with a silver decanter of wine to fill the glass he clutched in his hand. Behind the closed doors he could hear the low murmur of the Queen's aides, discussing his request. A request he had made three days before and still had no answer.

His mind was buzzing with all manner of questions and half-formed conclusions. Many of them quite similar to Leiria's and Palimak's.

Yes, the Queen and her subjects were strange, yes, the wonderland spells emanating from the Temple of Hadin were too good to be trusted, and, yes, the citizens of Caluz faced eventual doom from the machine and had every reason to be frightened in the extreme, but somehow they spent their days with pleasant smiles pasted on their faces as if life could be no sweeter.

Safar paused at the window, which looked out over the Temple of Hadin. If he could have seen far enough he might have spotted Palimak and Leiria strolling along the path by the river. He sipped his wine, thinking, piling still more questions on his plate.

For instance, there was the matter of the twin Caluzes—one good, one evil—which made things complicated to the extreme. When he'd queried the Queen's wizards and scholars about the phenomenon, they became blank-faced, uncomprehending. Their own situation was too complex to fathom, much less factor in such minor things as the cause of it all. Their main worry was that Safar would refuse, or be unable to help them. So they coated every difficulty with such a sweet layer of honey Safar came to doubt most of what they said.

In the courtroom there was a hush as the Queen spoke and Safar turned his head to listen. But her voice was so low it was swallowed by the thick silver doors that closed off the chamber.

Safar let the serving maid refill his cup, giving her an absent smile by way of thanks.

Hantilia was as serene as her subjects, he thought, but seemed more willing to speak her mind. Her magical resources were great, so she wasn't quite as affected as the others by the dream-spinning machine. Possibly it was because she was spinning so many of her own—and all were aimed directly at Safar. It was an innocent thing, an unconscious thing, or so he supposed. Although she was a demon and he was human, she found him attractive and was sending out many signals and spells that made her alluring. How he should or would react remained to be seen.

He pushed all this aside for another time—if there ever was to be such a time. There was urgent business to attend to before he began to plumb this and the other mysteries of the odd mirror worlds that made Caluz.

Safar resumed his pacing. He'd rarely been so frustrated. He'd expected to be rushed off to the temple immediately where he would consult with the Oracle he'd come so far to see. The queen said the Oracle of Hadin and all her people had been waiting for his arrival, so one would think they'd be just as anxious for the foretold visit to begin. Except there was apparently more to consulting the Oracle than just marching into the temple and announcing his presence. He was told there were elaborate purification ceremonies that had to be performed first. Ceremonies and spell castings that would take a week or more. So he was bathed and oiled and suffered so many hours in incense filled rooms that he felt like smoked meat.

Meanwhile, he fretted and gnawed at his growing worry that all would be for naught.

Uppermost in his mind was what to do about Iraj. The question wasn't if his enemy would show up, but when. The flash of awareness Safar had caught of Iraj's presence had been very strong—as if Protarus had been newly energized, stronger in purpose and determination than ever.

Safar would just as soon not be here when Iraj and his spell brothers showed up with their vast army.

The only reason he had tarried in this cursed place was because Asper's ghost had said the way to Syrapis was through Caluz. How this could be, he didn't know. But he had to take the chance. Safar was more convinced then ever that only in Syrapis would he find the key to the disaster that was overtaking the world.

The disaster blowing on poisoned winds in far Hadinland.

The serving maid offered more wine. Safar hesitated, then shook his head, no, and returned his now empty cup.

He smiled, thinking, many things besides Iraj Protarus could stop him from reaching Syrapis. Life being what it is he might even choke on a wine cork and that would be the rather foolish end to the saga of Safar Timura, son of a potter who rose to become the king's chief wazier, only to die trying to get at his drink.

Just then, while he was grinning at his own imagined clownish demise, the doors boomed open and a troop of robed priestesses with serene eyes and pleasant smiles came to escort him into the Queen's presence.

He tried to read Hantilia's expression as he approached the gilded throne, but all she presented was a sweet smile on her oddly—to him—beautiful demon's face. He also couldn't tell from the atmosphere of the courtroom if a decision had been reached. The Caluzians only watched his progress down the main aisle, murmuring little pleasantries as he passed.

"My dear, Lord Timura," the Queen said after he'd reached her and bowed his respects. "Please know that we've given your proposal our full attention. We've discussed it for many hours. But, frankly we find ourselves in a great quandary."

"What could be so difficult, Majesty?" Safar asked, keeping his tone as formal and distantly polite as hers. They'd met many times since his arrival, but always in more intimate surroundings. "I only want to make a casting—under the close guidance and full assistance of your best mages—to determine when we can expect Iraj Protarus.

"I've not only promised, but shown magical proof that he will be unaware of this casting. It will in no way draw his attention, or the attention of his wizards."

Safar raised his hands, turning them palm up. "What could be simpler than that?" he asked. "Or more vital? After all, you must be as concerned as I am that an army will soon show up to knock on your doors."

"I don't agree," the Queen said. "We are well hidden. How will this Protarus find us through the secret gate? You saw for yourself how well hidden it is. Only the cleverest wizard would ever find it, much less unravel the spell locks."

"Don't make that mistake!" Safar said, emphatic. "Believe me when I say that Iraj will find the way. It may take him awhile, but he has more than enough magical resources at his command."

"You forget the Guardians," the Queen said. "They will protect us now, as they always have. Nothing has ever managed to get past them! Only those we favor are permitted through, such as pilgrims and innocent wayfarers escaping the Black Lands."

"And I'm telling you that you don't know what you're facing," Safar said, deliberately letting some of his anger show. "Iraj Protarus is an enemy who once conquered all of Esmir. And he's quickly bringing it back under his command. He will hammer your Guardians into ghostly dust and crack your gates open and spill you out like an egg.

"Finally, Your Highness, this something I simply must insist on. If no one here will take the threat seriously, I'll have to gather my people and leave before Protarus arrives. And there will be no meeting of Safar Timura and your blessed Oracle of Hadin, a meeting that I am now beginning to think was a big mistake on my part for ever even thinking about."

Safar's bluff got the result he intended. There were gasps in the courtroom. The Queen gave him a look of great concern, clutching her robe at the breast. "But you don't understand, my dear Lord Timura," she said. "We aren't refusing you out of some mean-spirited motivation. Our survival is at stake as much as yours, after all. The real fear is that the casting will ruin everything we've done. You're almost ready for your meeting with the Oracle. What if your spell conflicts with the magical preparations we've already made?"

"Why didn't someone say that was the worry, Your Highness?" Safar asked, bewildered. "Why all this unnecessary secrecy? Let me meet now with your best scholars and we'll have the answer within the hour."

The Queen shook her head, no. "I'm sorry," she said. "That isn't possible. You would have to delve into things that are forbidden for you know in advance."

"I've never seen a situation in which ignorance is good for anyone, Majesty," Safar said sharply. "And if this decision is final, I really must take my leave. My people and I will be on the march again by tomorrow at dawn."

"But where will you march to, my dear?" the Queen said, finally calling his bluff. "There is only one way out of Caluz. And that's the way you came. Back through the Black Lands to face an oncoming army. As I said before, the road ahead is blocked. What I kept from you then was that we sealed it because it leads right into the heart of the real Caluz, the mad Caluz, the Caluz where no mortal could possibly exist for more than a few moments."

He caught an odd note in her tone as she spoke the last, but when he tried to catch her eyes she averted them.

"So you see, Lord Timura," she said, "there is no escape for your people. They are trapped here, it grieves me deeply to say, along with my own subjects. And what happens to us will happen to them."

At that moment Safar fully understood the nature of the trap he'd been drawn into. And if he failed in his mission here, there was no getting out.

"I'm sorry, Safar, my dear," Hantilia said, low. "But you see how it is?"

Safar saw. Just as he saw there was no malice intended by Hantilia or anyone here. It was just so.

"All of us came here at great cost," she went on. "It was and still is a holy mission. We must trust and we must believe, or everything is lost. Not just for us, but for the world itself. Perhaps it's made us a bit mad. I'm sure you think that when you see us smile when there is only reason to weep."

Safar thought they probably all were mad, including Hantilia. Then it came to him there was more to it than that.

"When we cast the spell that made this place," Hantilia said, "the Oracle warned us we would not be the same as before. She said we would leave part of ourselves in the real Caluz, the city we fled."

Somewhere in the courtroom someone giggled. There was an hysterical edge to it. Hantilia nodded toward the sound. "It's easier to bear than weeping," she said, "so I suppose we can't complain."

Safar knew he was defeated. He had no choice but to go on. "When will I see the Oracle?" he asked.

"In three more days," the Queen answered. "After I have undergone my own purification. I won't be able to see you until then."

"What about the boy?" Safar asked. "I'll need Palimak, you know."

"When I send for you," she answered, "bring him along. He'll only need a few hours of preparation."

Safar stared at her, realizing there was still a great deal more he didn't know.

He made one more attempt. "There is one other thing I'd like to ask," he said. "Something that has mystified me more than anything else."

"And what is that, my lord?" the Queen asked.

"You are all adherents of Asper," Safar said. "You wear robes with his symbol—the two-headed snake. You speak his name with zealous reverence. You even describe yourselves as members of the Cult of Asper. True?"

"Quite true," Hantilia said. "But what is the question?"

"Why is it none of your are curious about what I know of Asper?" he asked, noting the sharp reactions all about. "I have studied him most of my adult life. I doubt there is a mage in all Esmir who knows as much about his teachings as I do. I've even shown some of you his book, which I have in my possession."

He slipped the little book of Asper from his sleeve and held it up. "This is quite rare, you know," Safar said. "I got it at great personal cost. And yet none of you have asked to see it. I would have thought you'd have a team of scholars and clerks awaiting my arrival so you could copy down his words."

Hantilia sighed wearily, then said, "We are forbidden to speak of it to you. I can say no more."

"Yes, but do you have anything like it?" Safar pressed, waving the book. "If not, do you possess any artifacts from Asper at all?"

Another long silence, another shake of the Queen's head. "Again," she said, "I am forbidden to answer."

"Yes, yes, I know," Safar said, not hiding his disgust. "Have patience and all will be revealed."

Hantilia sighed, then leaned forward from her throne. Safar felt her cast the gentle spell that made her perfume headier, her presence soothing with just a hint of sensuality. But he pushed it away. She drew back and for a moment he thought she was offended. Good, he thought. That's how I meant it.

Then she sighed again. "It's the best I can do, Safar," she whispered. "Please trust me."

*   *   *

Safar was in a dark mood when he entered the Kyranian encampment. It was made fouler by the holiday spirit in the air, music and dance and hilarious chatter in the face of what he knew to be a most questionable future. Khysmet caught his bad temper, laid his ears back and nipped at the barking dogs.

They made a gloomy pair riding through the camp and when people saw them they stopped what they were doing—music and laughter cutting off in mid-peal—and stared as they passed, faces turning dark with worry. His kinsmen's plummeting emotions startled Safar from his mood and he felt guilty for being the cause of it.

He could see the dread in their eyes that maybe he'd returned to announce their brief stay in paradise was ended and they must once again resume their fearful journey.

Safar hastily pulled on his old entertainer's personality, waving and laughing and shouting jokes and words of cheer. Khysmet did the high step as if born to the circus march and soon everyone's joyous mood returned. He pushed on, smiling until his lips ached, until he came to the place where his family had set up camp.

All his sisters and their husbands were gathered about a big, rough plank table, eating and making merry while the children played games under the trees. In a little potter's shelter his mother and father were making small clay necklaces as gifts for the young ones—painted jesters, with skinny limbs and peaked hats riding jauntily over long beaked noses. Toys in the shape of the Jester God, Harle, were an ancient favorite of Kyranian children.

His mother, who was running leather thongs through holes bored into the caps, was chatting gaily with his father when Safar rode up and dismounted.

When she saw him her face lit up she dropped what she was doing. "It's Safar, Khadji!" she cried. "Come home just in time!"

She ran over and embraced him while his father looked fondly on. "We're having a celebration, dear," she said. "And I was so hoping you'd come."

Myrna pulled back, eyes shining. "Thanks to you," she said, "we're safe at last. And in such a beautiful place! Why, it's almost as beautiful as home!"

Safar didn't know what to say, so he embraced her and murmured the usual loving evasions sons and daughters use when they believe one of their parents has lost all touch with reality. Such as, "I'm happy that you're happy, mother, dear." Or "Yes, I've missed you too."

And so on until his mother rushed off to fetch him a plate of the tastiest morsels from the feast. When she was gone, he eyed his father, who was painting smiling faces on the toy jesters.

"You've made your mother very happy coming home today, son," he said. "She and your sisters worked hard on this feast."

"What is she celebrating, father?" he asked, still smiling, still trying to hide his concern.

"Why, our deliverance, son," his father said brightly. "Didn't you hear what she said?"

Safar was finally tested too far and his smile dissolved. "Of course I did," he said. "But that's ridiculous."

To his surprise his father's eyes seemed to glaze over and like a child shutting out harsh words it didn't want to hear he started humming a bright little tune.

Safar kept going, trying to break through. "For the gods sake, father!" he said. "No one's been delivered. No one's safe. You know that as well as I do. Why are you letting mother think differently?"

But the whole time he spoke his father kept up the humming. When Safar finally realized he wasn't getting through and gave up, Khadji broke off and resumed his side of the conversation.

"It's such a relief to all of us that you found this place, son," Khadji said. "To think we no longer have to go all the way to Syrapis to find our new home. The people here are so wonderful and generous. Why, I heard only yesterday that the Queen was selling you a good bit of land so that we can rebuild Kyrania right here."

He blinked back tears of joy. "You can't imagine how proud you've made your mother and me," he said.

Safar gave up. It was clear his family and friends had been afflicted with the same insane but merry spell as the Caluzians. He would have to do something about that soon, but just now he didn't have the heart. So he hugged his father and kissed him. Then his attention was drawn to the pile of completed jester necklaces. He picked one up to examine it and felt a faint buzz of mild magic.

"Where did you get the clay for these, father?" he asked. "They're quite . . . uh . . . unusual."

Khadji pointed up the river. "There's a nice bed of it around the next bend," he said.

He grabbed some up from a pail, skilled fingers forming another jester. "Palimak discovered it," he said. "And I must say I've never seen clay as perfect as this. A nice neutral gray color, not too sticky, not too spongy, and it fires in no time at all. And not one shattering out of the scores I've already made."

Khadji scratched his head, thinking. Then he smiled. "In fact," he said, "it was Palimak's idea to make these jesters for the children." He chuckled. "Such a thoughtful boy."

Safar narrowed his eyes when he heard that. He looked down at the large pile of completed jesters. There were also several trays of others ready to go into the oven. Plus, Khadji was painting several dozen more.

"There's a lot more here," he pointed out to his father, "than there are Timura children."

More chuckling from Khadji. "Well, after we talked about it for awhile, it seemed like such a good idea that we decided to make enough for everybody."

Safar goggled. "*Everybody?*"

Khadji nodded, firm. "Before we're done every Kyranian, down to the newest infant, will have one. The best of luck from Harle, the king of luck, hanging about our necks.

"Now isn't that a grand gift for everyone?" his father asked.

Safar nodded absently, puzzling over all this. What was Palimak up to? "Sure, father, sure," he said.

"Well, it's nice talking to you son," his father said. "But I'd best get back to it. I've got more than a thousand of these to make."

He started getting busy, pinching out more jesters and laying them on a firing tray. Becoming so absorbed in his work he seemed to forget his son's presence. Safar gently took his arm, stopping him. His father blinked at him, awareness coming back.

"Where is Palimak, father?" Safar asked.

Khadji again pointed up the river. "At the claybed," he said. "He's with Leiria, so you don't have to worry. They're fetching more material for the jesters."

Safar just smiled, gave his father another hug, and swung up on Khysmet. "Tell mother," he said, "that I'm off to see Palimak. And to save us some of that delicious food."

His father didn't hear him. He was humming merrily again, totally absorbed in his work. Safar shrugged and headed up the river.

He eventually found them standing on a hill, supervising a half dozen willing lads who were digging up buckets of clay from the river.

"Be sure and clean it real well," Palimak admonished two young men who were washing the debris from the clay.

"You there," Leiria called to another group. She pointed to several pails of finished clay. "Grab a couple of those buckets and trot them down to Khadji. He should be getting pretty low by now."

The lads took all this with such good nature that Safar was immediately suspicious.

When Palimak and Leiria spotted Safar they both jumped in startled guilt. Palimak ducked behind Leiria.

"I take full responsibility," Leiria said. She said it boldly, but he detected a quivering note of embarrassment.

Safar sighed and pointed at the working youths. "Let them go," he said wearily.

"Yes, father," Palimak squeaked. Then, his voice a little firmer, "But you have to let me do it my way. If they wake up too quickly they're going to feel pretty bad."

"Go ahead," Safar said.

Palimak ventured out from behind Leiria enough to wave a hand at the boys. "You're suddenly all feeling very tired," he said, trying to sound commanding. The boys all stretched and yawned. "That's good," Palimak praised. "Really, real sleepy." More stretching and yawning. "So now that you're so sleepy," Palimak said, "you all decide to go home and take a little nap. And when you wake up you'll feel just great and you won't remember anything."

The young men all nodded, then put the buckets down and wandered back toward the encampment, yawning and mumbling sleepily as they went.

"Don't worry about them, father," Palimak said. "They'll be fine." He gestured at the buckets of clay sitting by the shore. "Besides, we were almost done anyway."

This brought a hot glare from Safar. "Ooops," Palimak said, clapping a hand to his mouth.

Leiria groaned. "I wish you hadn't said that."

"We have a awfully good reason, father," Palimak said. "Honest."

"He's right," Leiria said. "We do."

"Go on," Safar said, climbing off Khysmet. He patted the animal, drawing on its powers of patience. "I'm listening. And it had better be as good as you claim."

Palimak swallowed hard, but Leiria had a completely different reaction. She blew. "Listen here, Safar Timura," she said, standing tall and hooking her thumbs into her sword belt. "In case you haven't noticed, everybody here has gone insane. They are in hap-hap happy land, where the bees don't sting and the wolves graze on grass like the lambs."

"I noticed," Safar said, gritting his teeth. "But that doesn't give—"

Leiria stomped a boot. "That doesn't give you the right," she said, "to come storming in here to dump a camel load of grief on us, after being gone for the gods know how long, and not a word from you, by the way, and we're here with all these crazy people not knowing what to do."

Safar was rattled by this verbal assault. "Still," he said, "you have to admit—"

"Admit nothing!" Leiria stormed on. "What if something happened? What if Iraj attacked right now? Everyone would just stare and giggle while his army cut them down!"

Now it was Safar's turn to be stung by guilt. "You have a stronger point than you realize about Iraj," he said. "But, honest to the gods, couldn't you have waited?"

"I repeat my last question, Safar Timura," Leiria ground in. "What if something happened?"

"It really is a good plan, father," Palimak made bold to say. "I got the idea when I found the clay."

He pointed at the gray, dug up pits at the river's edge. "Leiria and I went fishing right over there. Which is how I found all that fantastic clay."

Palimak glanced at his father and decided a self-serving aside might be called for here. So he made his eyes rounder and more innocent as he said: "Grandfather has been teaching me ever so much about clay, father. And I've been doing my *very best* to learn all I can. And so that's why I noticed the clay right off. All because of my wonderful, wonderful grandfather, who I love more than anything anyone can mention at all. So you can imagine, father, how bad I felt when I put a spell on him. *Again!* I mean, that's twice, now. And I knew you'd be mad, because I was mad at myself, but like Leiria said, what were we going to do?

"Nobody would listen to me. They wouldn't even have listened to Leiria. They're all crazy, father! Just like Leiria said. So we had do something! And I figured out what to do soon as I saw that clay. I was looking at how the water comes out of the turtle. You really ought to take a close look at that turtle, father, because it is really, really strange.

"Anyway, I saw right off the clay was not only the kind of stuff grandfather thinks is the absolute, absolute, best, but it also had a little bit of magic in it. And I that's when I got the idea!"

"You should have waited," Safar said again, but rather glumly, with little force to it. "I could have talked to my father. And those lads. I could have spoken to them and convinced them with little trouble to help us make those amulets."

He shook his head. "I know what you're up to. You were going to supply everyone with an amulet of the jester—and that was clever, Palimak. But perhaps a little too mature." He looked pointedly at Leiria.

She blushed. "Guilty," she said. "I'm an outsider. Outsiders noticed things. And one of the first things I noticed about Kyrania is that the tots are crazy about anything to do with Harle, the Jester God."

Leiria gave him a defiant look, tilting up her chin. "Since adults are only children in not so pretty skin," she said, "it only seemed logical that it would be a figure loved by everyone. From children to the gray hairs."

"And at the proper moment, I presume," Safar said, "Palimak was going to cast a spell to wake everyone up to a most unpleasant reality."

Leiria nodded. "It was acting for the greater good," she said. "We were thinking about saving lives."

"That's right, father," Palimak piled on. "For the . . . what did Leiria call it . . . oh, yeah–'The Greater Good.' Sure! That's what we were doing." He threw his shoulders back, intoning, "Acting for the greater good."

"Oh, bullocks' dung!" Safar snorted. "You've both gone as mad as the others!"

He dropped Khysmet's reins, wheeled about and stalked away, muttering, "I'm raising a despot! Befriended another as well! And I'm responsible! By the gods above, if they are awake and listening, please strike me dead on the spot!"

Leiria and Palimak trailed along, shrinking at his mutters. Although they knew they were right, so was he—perhaps even more so.

As Safar stalked up the hill he thought, what a ridiculous, quite human situation this was. It was certainly worthy of Harle, who had a darker sense of humor than most realized. What a joke we all are, he thought. Struggling with silly moral points while the whole world melts about our ears. I'm Palimak's moral mentor, hammering away at rights and wrongs as if they were real. As if they meant a damn. As if the gods were suddenly going to stir in the heavens and take notice that one small person, on one small world, was sticking to his moral principles. Principles supposedly handed down from on high and thereford objects of much heavenly interest.

He recalled a fragment from Asper:

"Why do I weep?" he'd asked.

And Asper's answer, after a few other rhymed musings was:

"I weep because Harle laughs!
So why not laugh instead, my friends . . .
And make the Jester's tears our revenge?"

So Safar laughed. Laughter poured from him, bursting like a pent-up flood suddenly released after much hammering on humor's gate.

He doubled up, holding his sides, wracked with laugh after laugh. What was he worried about? What did it matter if his son, aided by his best friend and former lover, cast spell nets of enslavement over his father and mother and innocent Kyranian lads? It was well meant, that was all that mattered. We're only trying to save the world, here. So we bend things a bit for the "greater good." What's the harm in that?

And wasn't he doing worse?

And wasn't he going to ask even more?

Palimak and Leiria caught up to him. They watched in silent amazement as he choked and gasped laughter.

Then he stood up straight, wiped his eyes and chin, and said, "I love you both, anyway."

He continued up the hill, taking the last few steps to the summit with his arms draped over both of them. He was still laughing, although not so uncontrollably. Just little outbursts, with chuckles building and falling in between. They grinned crazily, not knowing what he was laughing at and if they had they wouldn't have understood. But they grinned anyway. Grinned in empathy, strangely sorry that whatever they had done had made him laugh like this.

When they came to the top of the hill Safar paused to catch his breath. Below them was a broad field decked with many festive banners. And in the center of that field was a huge tent shot with bright, dazzling colors.

A familiar voice thundered from that tent, chanting a joyous, heart-wrenching refrain:

"Come one, come all! Lads and maids of Alllll ag-es! I now present to you—Methydia's Circus of Miracles!

"The Greatest Show In Esmir!"

CHAPTER TWENTY TWO
THE GIFT FROM BEYOND

Palimak was circus struck. All his cares, all his troubles, all his toils smashed away by a lightning storm of the senses—color and music and smell and thrilling action crashing here and there and everywhere, all seeming chaos.

His attention, no, his whole being was snatched from one amazement to another, each sight a new experience exploding all that had come before.

But it couldn't be chaos because everything seemed to have a direction, a goal, a point, a moral, a story with heroes and villains and a beginning and middle and end. It was madness—delicious, soul-satisfying madness—but most of all it was orchestrated madness.

Commanding it all was the circus ringmaster, a fantastic, muscular dwarf with a lion's skin tossed over his magnificent torso like an ancient hero.

He had an incredible voice that reached everywhere and everyone, booming and intimate at the same time.

At the moment he was lit by a brilliant pool of light. And he was shouting:

"And now, without further ado, we present our star attraction. A wonder of all wonders.

"A gift from the heavens!"

Music blared and the dwarf gestured—hand coming up slowly, dramatically, commanding complete attention. A slowly opening fist, reaching for the heavens, promising entire volumes of mysteries that were about to be revealed. Music somehow sliding under all that anticipation, lifting it higher and higher on a rhythmic out-rushing tide of drums and pipes and strings all running toward the Mother Moon of imagination . . . and beyond.

And all the while the dwarf was saying, "Only the gods themselves could have created the wonder you are about to see, my friends. A marvel, a mystery, unveiled before your very eyes.

"Look, my friends. Look high above! Look to the heavens themselves!"

As he spoke the music and the gesturing hand crept up to the penultimate point and all eyes were fixed on the dwarf's fist as it came fully open.

Palimak jumped as cymbals crashed and a shower of sparkling bits burst from the dwarf's mighty hand, shooting up and up, carrying Palimak and the whole audience with it to the very top of the tent. It hung there for an agonizing moment, swirling and boiling like a troubled, many colored cloud, slowly forming a glittering curtain of suspense. Seemingly held up only up by the building music.

And the dwarf said, "Ladies and gentlemen, lads and lasses, beings of all ages, I present to you the one, the only . . ."

A skillful pause as the music reached its climax . . .

And then, in an enormous voice that filled the tented arena:

"Arlain!"

Cymbals crashed and the curtain burst, shattering in every direction.

Palimak, along with the entire audience, gasped as all was revealed and they saw a glorious figure dancing high above them on a wire so thin it was nearly invisible.

And the dwarf roared:

"Arlain!

"She's half dragon, half woman, my friends! And oh, what a woman she is! A great beauty, a wonder, known in every nook and cranny of Esmir. Thousands, tens of thousands, have been thrilled and fulfilled by her wondrous feats."

As he spoke fiery bits rained down on the performer and Palimak oohed and ahhed at the sight—a blazing shimmer settling on Arlain like a cloak, setting off her startling body. She was a heady, enthralling sight for everyone, but especially a small boy. For beside the scraps of see-through gossamer Arlain was clothed only in the tiniest of breast coverings, plus the merest scrap of a modesty patch about her loins. The covered part was all too human. The rest of her was just as striking and oddly seductive—an elegant white dragon who breathed fire through pearly fangs and lips, exploding all the particles drifting about her.

Palimak was instantly in love. He could see nothing, feel nothing but the presence of the strangely beautiful Arlain. And amidst all his mental bewilderment one thought leaped out from the rest: She's just like me! Except she's half dragon and I'm half demon. Other then the Favorites, Gundara and Gundaree, Palimak had never seen a being quite like himself.

The boy sat between his father and Leiria, hypnotized by Arlain, the audience's wild applause flowing over him.

He'd never attended a circus before, although he'd often tried to imagine one. The moment he entered the tent—before he'd even seen Arlain—Palimak's wildest circus imaginings became pale things. Not worth ever thinking about again.

It was a place of giddy lights and wonderful music, a place of mystery where performers did impossible things—flinging themselves across amazing heights, disappearing and appearing in clouds of fantastic smoke, hilariously costumed clowns—six of them—clambering out of a box too small for even one.

There was a turbaned snake charmer whose horn seemed to contain the sounds of all instruments, from strings to drums and pipes. But his snake was even more incredible. It rose six feet above the basket, weaving in time to the music, and it when it turned its head in Palimak's direction he gasped when he saw a man's face. Then there was the acrobat clown—a husky, seemingly normal person, except that he had a very small head, which he would continually lose—literally! The head tumbled off his shoulders and into his hands. Then you could see it still attached by a long rubbery neck and the acrobat would pretend to fumble to get it back on, his eyes and mouth contorting into a series of faces, each more comical than the other. Best of all was the master of ceremonies, the dwarf with the muscles of a giant, who spun the tales, leading the audience from one breath-taking act to the next, plus performing in half-a-dozen roles at the same time.

Palimak was stunned by all these amazements. They seemed magical, but yet there was not one bit of real magic being used. Otherwise he would sense it. The whole idea of this illusion without sorcery swept him away to the Land of the Circus!

The relief of being freed from his normal cares made him feel as light as a balloon rising in clear Kyranian skies. Although he was small, the weight of the world had been heavy on his slender shoulders. He was only trying to do his best but there were so many newly discovered shouldn'ts and oughto's—with many moral gradients of dark to light in between—that sometimes he thought it was a conspiracy concocted by adults to keep children in their place—whatever that might be.

Here in the circus, however, everyone was equal. On either side of him his father and Leiria were reacting like children, laughing and clapping in glee.

For a moment he became more aware of the audience, looking around and seeing they were all Caluzians, both human and demon, from infant to granny, completely fixed on the performance. This led to him to the realization that there was some other strange kind of magic in the air. The members of the audience all fed on one another's excitement and joy, becoming a warm, quivering whole reacting as one to the events in the big center ring. It was also the first time he'd seen honest emotion from the Caluzians. What he noticed most, however, was their laughter. He strained hard to think what was different about it. As close as he could get was that it seemed to come from someplace real—a sort of a home for laughter. And this gave shape and form to their laughter instead of the hazy, spell-induced giggles he normally heard.

Thinking this made him suddenly feel very alone, apart from everyone else, examining them, looking at them through the pale, cold glow of his demon side. It was unsettling and his belly lurched. He wanted badly to rejoin them, to be once again part of that warm, quivering mass that made the audience.

Then he saw Arlain and got his wish.

Safar watched the emotions play across Palimak's face, grinning in memory of his own first introduction to the art of entertainment. It was long ago and far away, but it was this very same circus. Methydia's Flying Circus, except they no longer flew and Methydia, alas, was dead.

Even without the wondrous Methydia—who had been not only a great diva, but a powerful witch—the performance was every bit as marvelous as Safar remembered. Arlain was dazzling, witness Palimak's enchantment. And there was his old mentor, Biner, the massive dwarf, who had taught him everything he knew about showmanship and illusion. And he was pleased to see Elgy and Rabix—the snake charming/music act—were just as skilled as ever. No one would ever guess that it was the snake who was the "brains" behind the act. Poor Rabix had the mind of a mouse, playing his instrument wonderfully, but following Elgy's commands. Finally, there was Kairo, he of the small detachable head and almost superhuman acrobatic talents.

Safar didn't know how his friends came to be here, although somehow he wasn't that surprised. Circus people had a way of showing up in the most amazing places and at the most interesting times.

*   *   *

Leiria was as entranced as anyone, but she couldn't help looking over at Safar, trying to imagine him as one of the performers.

It was surprisingly easy. His face was alight, shedding years of care and she could suddenly seem him as a dashing young showman, dressed in tights and a swirling cloak, stealing the hearts of all the women with his magical feats and athletic derring-do.

In the center ring there was a romantic aerial ballet going on, with moody lights and contemplative music.

Music that allowed uneasy memories rise to be examined in a less hurtful light. Bursting pin bubbles of a regret you could savor and enjoy like a rare and effervescent wine. The kind of wine once tasted with a lover. And you remembered its flavor like you remembered the touch of his body.

She imagined Safar, innocent and free. A handsome young performer whose eyes were only on her as he moved from one seductive act to the next.

And she had the dreamy thought: I'd have liked to have known him then. Who knows? Perhaps things would have worked out differently.

Then the music made a sharp change and two clowns rushed out into the center ring.

And Leiria snorted, thinking, Will you be serious, woman! When Safar came into your arms it was to mourn Methydia.

Methydia!

Your first dead rival.

And the damned owner of this circus!

Methydia had not only been Safar's lover but his teacher as well—as only a skilled older woman can teach a young man.

For a fleeting moment Leiria imagined she was a wise, gray-haired beauty, coiling around a youthful Safar.

Then she laughed aloud at herself. No one noticed. They were too busy howling at the clowns—Arlain chasing Biner about the ring, shooting sheets of fire at the seat of his pants.

458

Leiria joined in, laughing at Biner's comic yelps and leaps, letting the circus take her away.

*   *   *

Palimak stood before his new goddess, blushing and gulping and wishing mightily that he knew a spell to untie his tongue so he could speak.

Arlain looked down at him, a delighted smile lighting her dragon's face. "My goodneth," she lisped. "You're tho handthome! Jutht like Thafar!"

Palimak's tongue came unstuck. "I'm not really his son," he said to his instant humiliation and regret. He thought, what a stupid, stupid, thing to say! Not his son! What must she think of me?

They were in the wardrobe tent, a warren of trunks and costumes and circus props, with a long bank of mirrored makeup tables on one side cluttered with cosmetics and paints and colorful masks. Safar and Leiria were at the far end of the tent, surrounded by Biner and the other members of the circus. It was a glad reunion and there was much laughter and drinking and shouted remembrances of shared adventures on the road.

A moment before Palimak had been safely buried in the middle of that chaos, much fussed over by one and all, but it was so noisy and everyone was so excited at seeing his father, he only had to smile and nod in return. If he said something stupid it didn't matter, because no one could hear him anyway. But then Arlain, who had cooed and gushed over him even more than the others, had drawn him aside "tho we can talk." He was thrilled, then he was chilled, and when he stood before her—alone with this perfumed goddess at last—and opened his mouth he'd made a complete ass of himself.

Palimak struggled for words to set his mistake right. He said, "I mean, I am his son. But, uh, not his son. I'm kind of like . . . you know . . . adopted. I don't know who my real father is. Or my mother, either."

As soon as he was done he gave himself a mental kick. Arrgh! That was just as stupid, he thought. If not stupider!

He hung his head and kicked at the tent floor, not having the slightest idea what to do or say next. He just wanted to escape before she started laughing at him.

Arlain saw his distress and sank gracefully down on a wardrobe truck, lovely white tail tucking around her legs as she sat, her eyes now closer to Palimak's level.

"Tho I gueth we have thomething in common," she said.

Palimak's head jolted up. "What?" he asked.

Arlain sighed. "I don't know who my parenth are either," she said. "I'm an orphan. Jutht like you." She shrugged. "I think my father dropped me when he wath changing the netht."

Palimak forgot his embarrassment. "Were you adopted too?" he asked, feeling very sorry and very protective of her.

"Yeth. But not by very nithe people," she said. She glanced over at Safar, who was engrossed in a story Elgy, the human-charming snake, was telling. "You're really lucky to have a father like Thafar."

Palimak threw his shoulders back, smiling and proud. "He's the best father any boy could have," he said. "The best in the whole world!"

"That'th what I always imagined," Arlain said. "From the firtht time I met him." She leaned closer, a fellow conspirator. "I had a thecret cruth on him, you know," she said. "But don't tell anybody I thaid that. They'll teathe me. And I don't like to be teathed."

Palimak promised he wouldn't. "I don't like to be teased, either," he added with such solemnity that Arlain couldn't help but giggle again.

459

This time, however, a bit of smoke puffed from between her lips along with a few flames.

"Oopth!" she said, covering her mouth with a dainty paw. "I'm thorry! Thometimeth I get all exthited and forget I'm a dragon. And I accithidentaly thet thingth on fire! I'm tho clumthy, you wouldn't believe it! People get tho mad at me!"

Palimak was absolutely charmed by this confession. Arlain suddenly seemed less intimidating. More like an older sister with ordinary foibles, instead of a gorgeous, distant idol.

"I accidentally set my grandmother's wagon on fire once," he said, trying to make her feel more comfortable. "You can't believe how mad she got!" He sighed. "I guess it's hard for people to understand that you can't always help it."

"I uthed to worry about it all the time," Arlain said. "But now I don't worry tho much. I wath born thith way! Half one being, half another. Nothing I can do about it. I mean, nobody athked me if I wanted to be born."

She looked at him, smiling a smile that melted his heart. And then she said, "I thuppoth it'th the thame with you."

Palimak's eyes widened in astonishment. "How did you know?" he asked.

Arlain pretended confusion. "Know what, my thweet?"

Palimak ducked his head, suddenly embarrassed, although he didn't know why. He wanted to speak, but there was a knot in his throat that wouldn't allow it. He coughed, trying to clear a suddenly constricted throat.

Arlain said, "I'm thorry, I couldn't hear you," as if the cough was a statement.

Her voice was so kind Palimak chanced an answer. Head still down, wanting to get it over with in a quick mumble, but forcing himself to make his words clear.

He said, "How did you know that I'm . . . well . . . uh . . . what do you call it . . . special, I guess . . . Yeah. Special. Like you."

He wanted to say more, but his throat constricted. He coughed again, trying to fight past it, but what came out was still badly crippled.

"Except I'm half demon, instead of dragon. How could you tell? I try to be really careful because people get all upset when they find out. And not just human type people. Demons act the same way."

"You didn't do anything wrong," Arlain said. "I jutht thort of guethed. Maybe beingth like uth recognize each other right away."

She giggled, purposely letting a little smoke and fire leak out. But this time she didn't say, "oops," or apologize.

Instead, she said, "Not that you can't tell thoon ath you meet me," she said, hand moving gracefully through the air, going from dragon face to lush woman's body. "I can't hide who I am," she said. "It wath written all over me by my mother and father."

He nodded, but it wasn't a nod of understanding. It was an abrupt nod, a nod urging her to go on. To explain more. Mind full to bursting with questions, questions, questions. Questions he couldn't put a name to. Questions he didn't know he wanted to ask. A whole tangled fishing net of questions suddenly dragged from the depths and needing an answer. All boiling and roiling about, tantalizing silver flashes of questions, but nothing that could be picked out in all that frantic wriggling.

As his mind raced through all these things Arlain was observing him closely with her dragon eyes—wonderful eyes, eyes like an eagle, eyes that could see far and near and everything in between, eyes that could look into your heart.

Palimak desperately wanted to make some meaningful gesture—something that would show Arlain how close in nature and kind he felt to her. But he was only a boy and he hadn't the words, so in the end he blurted:

"Look at this!" Grinning and holding out a hand, eyes suddenly flaring yellow as claws needled out from his fingers. Then he leaned forward, blew on the claws and his breath became a swirl of colors—a magical imitation of Arlain's dragonfire—playing it across the claws, turning them this way and that as if in forge. Then there was a slap! as the colors burst and Palimak held up a hand that was quite ordinarily human again.

"See?" he said, a whole flood of meanings intended in that single word.

Arlain blinked—and to Palimak she caught all his meaning in that blink—then she clapped her hands in delight, making his heart leap.

"Oh, my goodneth grathiouth," she said. "That'th marveloth! You thould be in the circuth!"

Palimak goggled. "Really?" he said. Then, doubtful. "You're not just saying that to be nice, are you?"

Arlain drew herself up, dignified. "Thirtainly not! I know a born thowman when I see one!"

Then she leaned close and asked, "Would you like me to teach you?"

Palimak's eyes became very wide and very round. "Sure," he said, heart drumming, thinking of all the things he had seen at the performance, flipping through the thrilling feats and excitement, picking what he like best.

And he said, shy, "Could I learn how to be a clown?"

*　　　*　　　*

Safar glanced across the tent, smiling, a little drunk at the sight of Arlain and Palimak together. Biner, sloshing drink into their cups, followed his gaze, then back again, understanding and enjoying Safar's smile.

"Damnedest' thing 'bout the circus," Biner said, "is she always finds her own." He examined his cup, grinning at memories of old times. "Look at how it was with you," he said. "Layin' out in the middle of the desert, mostly dead, then the circus comes along, sees its kindred, and swoops you up. Next thing you know you're earnin' your keep wowin' them at the fairs."

"It seemed like a miracle at the time," Safar said, remembering Methydia's great airship sweeping across the desert toward him. Then he thought of what happened later—all the glorious circus adventures, the applause, the camaraderie, the long nights of loving and learning with Methydia.

And he said, low, "I guess it really was a miracle."

Across from them Leiria peeled laughter at some jest told by Elgy. The other performers joined in, waving their arms, spilling their wine, completely wrapped up in the party.

Safar looked at Biner. "Speaking of miracles," he said, "maybe you'd better tell me about this new one before we get too drunk."

"You mean how we come to be in Caluz?" Biner said.

"Exactly."

Biner eyed him, owlish, amusement in his eyes. "Some might call it a miracle," he said, "some might call it a coincidence." He tapped his head. "Some who thinks they know it all, call it smoke and mirrors." He made a grand gesture—"Illusion! But no matter how smart they think they are, how sharp-eyed, knowin' all the tricks, the circus always gets 'em. Pulls them in. Makes them want to believe so much they ignore the wires even when the lightman's drunk and you can see the glint plain as day."

Safar shook his head, amused. He said, "Either I'm really, really, drunk," he said, "or I'm not drunk enough. But somehow that makes sense."

Biner sloshed more wine into their cups. "In questions of drunkenness, lad," he said, "it's best to figure you ain't had enough."

They drank as Biner gathered his thoughts, then he said, "I'll give you the poster line first."

He grinned at Safar and said, "Methydia sent us!"

Safar nearly spewed out his drink.

Biner chortled. "Got your attention?"

Safar swallowed hard, wiping the spillover from his chin. And he choked, "Go ahead."

Ever the showman, Biner said not another word but climbed to his feet, hooking up the wine skin as he rose. He stumped away on his thick, short legs, leading Safar to a room off the main tent. Biner turned up an oil lamp and Safar saw the room was crowded with trunks. They were huge things, heavy with all sorts of circus gear, but Biner pushed them about as if they weighed nothing at all.

When there was enough room he perched on the lid of a vaguely familiar black trunk, covered with leather and bound by thick iron straps. He gestured at a place across from him for Safar to sit, took a slug of wine right out of the skin and passed it to Safar.

"Sad times," he sighed, "when last we met."

The sigh stirred bitter memories, carrying Safar back to another tented room where Methydia was laid out on a rough cot dying; Safar and others gathered about her. Outside a whole city was in flames, people weeping and wailing as Iraj's soldiers led them to their doom. Through the canvas doorway they could see the smoking ruins of the wondrous flying ship that was the heart, body and soul of her circus. All dead and dying now. Methydia clutching his hand and begging him to forgive Iraj, to go with him, saying it was his destiny. That it was for the good of all.

Safar was young, easily moved by death bed appeals, and he'd agreed. There were rare days that he didn't think that he'd made a grave mistake.

Then he heard Biner speak and he blinked back to the present to hear the dwarf say, "We wasn't much of a circus after that. Methydia gone. Airship burnt. No spirit in us. So we couldn't put any into the crowds. Our acts felt flat. No spark, no suspense. All of us just going through the motions.

"Not that we didn't care, we just couldn't do anythin' about it. Worse it got, the harder it got. And pretty soon we were hardly sellin' any tickets, cause the word had gone out of ahead of us that we weren't worth seein'.

"We wandered around like that, hittin' whatever fairs we could. Sometimes workin' for not much more'n our suppers."

Biner smiled at Safar, "Not that we were in danger of starvin', thanks to you. We had that fat purse of gold you gave us. Which is how we got through those times. Hells, maybe we would've woke up sooner if we didn't have that cushion. Maybe it made it easier to mope and moan and feel miserable. So instead of the best circus in all Esmir, we were the saddest.

"After awhile maybe you even start liking being miserable, although you don't know it."

Safar nodded. "I've felt that way myself," he said. "It becomes an odd sort of addiction. The emotional version of an opium merchant who loves his wares too well."

"Ain't that so?" Biner said. Then, "But one day we woke up. Threw away the pipe and opened our eyes to what was goin' on around us.

"It was at a performance, last show of the last night at a weevily little fair. You know the kind. Where the folks don't have much more'n corn dust in their pockets—and that's wormy."

Safar smiled. He remembered towns like that when he was in the circus.

"Anyway," Biner continued, "there wasn't but maybe twenty people in the house. And they were so bored even some of them were leakin' away. Then it happened. Right in the middle of the big clown act. Where Arlain's chasin' me around the ring, settin' my britches on fire?

"All of a sudden a kid start's cryin'. And I mean, really, cryin'! It was the most mournful cryin' you ever heard in your life. Like the world was endin' and the kid's scared and wants its momma but then he suddenly knows, way down deep, that when the world ends so does his momma and that is more than he can bear.

"It stopped me right in my tracks. I'm standin' there, ass on fire, but all I can see and hear is that kid, clutchin' at a raggedy woman beside him, bawlin', 'Momma! Momma!' My heart breakin' with every cry. And I'm not the only one. The whole audience is lookin' at him and pretty soon they're leakin' tears and behind me I hear Arlain say, 'Poor thing,' and I know she's cryin' too. And so were the others, Elgy and everybody. Like it was a funeral instead of a show.

"Then it hit me."

"Wait a minute," Safar said, "last I heard your ass was still on fire."

Biner laughed. "It sure was," he said. "And maybe that's what got me unstuck, because the first thing that hits me is that my behind feels like it's being grilled for supper. So I put it out. Stuck my butt in a bucket of water like I always do. And there's a hiss and the steam's risin' up around me and I start laughin' at myself. For the first time in ages I could see myself as a clown again, see in my head what a silly figure I was, squattin' in the bucket. Which, when you think about, is what most of us are doin' in real life—squattin' over our troubles without much of a clue that anythin' else is happenin' 'cause our attention is fixed on our sore asses.

"Then I think, well, we're all fools goin' to a fools' hell, so godsdamn it all!

"Damn everything but the circus!

"So I come up out of my bucket and I see that I'm no lonesome genius, because Arlain and the boys are thinkin' the same thing. We all smile at each other and I give the high sign and boom! Elgy and Rabix strike up the band and boom! we start all over again. Right from the top. The whole show. But this time we're playin' right to the kid.

"Every trick, every laugh-getter aimed for the kid, who's still cryin', still callin' for his momma, but after awhile his cries get quieter, tears goin' from a river to a trickle, until just when me and Arlain did the pants on fire number again the kid gets to laughin.' Startin' with a giggle, then a snicker, then an all out belly laugh that wouldn't quit.

"The whole audience is with us now, laughin' along with the kid. Havin' the time of their lives. Don't matter what waits for them outside, how bad it might be, how bad it might get, this is the circus. And when you are at the circus you are free and nothin' can get to you long as the music's playin' and the clown's are clownin' and Arlain is flyin' high over your heads, beautiful and makin' dreams come true in the air."

Biner's eyes misted over at the memory. Then he coughed, coming back. "Jump to the chase. We put on one hells of a show. Sent the folks home happy, especially that kid. Just like the old days. Afterwards, we sat up all night and gave each other hells for forgettin' we were circus people. It's not a trade, it's a callin'. Like a holy mission. And the harder the times the more folks need us.

"But most of all we talked about how ashamed Methyida would of been for forgettin' all that. So the next day we packed up the tents and hit the road again. Playin' the fairs and festivals like before. But this time we had purpose. This time we had heart. We were a real circus and it made all the difference in the world."

There was a respectful silence as both men contemplated circus mystique, passing the wineskin back and forth.

Then Biner winked, humor a bright splinter in his eye. "Guess I've given you enough of a buildup," he said. "Maybe I ought to get on to the feature act."

"I wish you would," Safar said, dry. "I bought the ticket for the big tease. Which was that Methydia sent you. If that's not the case, I want my money back."

"Never fear, my lad," Biner said. "This is an honest circus. The sucker—I mean, the honored customer—always gets what he pays for."

He lumbered to his feet, saying in his ringmaster's voice, "Ladies and Gentleman, lads and lasses of all ages . . ." hauling the trunk around until it stood out clear in the light, ". . . I now present to you—"

He stopped in mid cry, hand flourish indicating the trunk. Then he winked again and said, abruptly normal voiced, "Recognize it, lad?"

Light dawned and Safar nodded, excited, "It's Methydia's," he said.

"That's right, lad," Biner said, throwing back the top, revealing a bright jumble of costumes and small boxes and jars and packets and glittering bits of this and that. "It's Methydia's Amazing Trunk of Tricks."

"That's what she called it," Safar said, smiling at the memory. "Her Trunk of Tricks. If you needed to fix your costume, or your act, or even if you were sick, she could always find something in the trunk that did the job."

Biner started rummaging, tossing things aside, "Arlain came on this about a year or so ago," he said, talking as he worked. "We'd forgotten all about the thing and it got lost in all our gear. But then one day Arlain had a new idea for her act and she was lookin' for somethin' to help her out and while she was diggin' around she found Methydia's trunk.

"Well, she figured she was saved, because whatever it was she needed just had to be in this trunk. So she started going through it, just like I'm doing now."

Biner was near the bottom, sweeping out the last things. Then he turned, gesturing for Safar to come closer, saying, "And then she saw this . . ."

Safar looked inside. At first he was puzzled: the trunk was empty. Then in the center he saw a scrap of white lace, no bigger than a thumbnail and he automatically reached to brush it aside, but it stuck there, stubborn. He plucked at it, but it remained fast.

"Just give it a bit of a tug, lad," Biner advised.

So he did, pulling gently, feeling some resistance, then it started to give and he was lifting up a rectangular lid! He goggled at it, realizing it was dangling from the lace, then, wide-eyed, he looked down and saw the hidden compartment he'd revealed. It was about six inches wide and a foot long and lined with thick black velvet. Sitting inside, cushioned by the velvet, was a glass case.

Safar looked up at Biner, hesitant. "Go ahead, lad," the dwarf said. "Take her out."

Gently, Safar lifted out the case. As it emerged into the light it glittered and shimmered with color. Begging the eye to look closer and be amazed, so Safar did, heart tap-tapping like a cobbler's hammers, palms moist with excitement.

When he saw it he gasped like a boy.

"It's the Airship!" he cried, holding the case out to Biner as if he didn't know already. "Methydia's Airship!"

"Sure it is, lad," Biner said, a big grin lighting his ugly face. "A perfect replica from stem to stern."

And indeed it was, a wondrous ship with graceful decks dangling beneath two marvelous balloons that made it a creature of the air, rather than the sea. All in perfect scale down to the copper burners that in real life provided the lifting power.

The lead balloon bore Methydia's beauteous face, with huge exotic eyes and sensuous lips. Beneath it was the legend: "Methydia's Flying Circus of Miracles!"

"It's so real," Safar breathed, "I feel as if I'm on it."

"There's more, lad," Biner said. "You still ain't seen the whole show. Not by half!"

He pointed at the chest. "There's somethin' else in that compartment. Somethin' you missed."

Safar glanced where he was pointing and saw a small roll of white parchment with a blue ribbon tied around the middle and creased where the edge of the case had rested. He handed Biner the glass case and lifted out the scroll.

He slid the ribbon off and as he unrolled the message he could smell Methydia's perfume floating up from the parchment. It made it seem as if she had suddenly entered the room and all he had to do was turn around and see her warm smile.

Then the scroll was fully open, revealing a simple message written in Methydia's elegant, flowing hand:

> *"To Safar*
> *My heart, my love*
> *My life*
> *Methydia"*

"When we saw that," Biner said, "we knew the ship wasn't just a pretty model."

Safar raised his head, dazed. "What?"

"The airship, lad," Biner said. "It's not a toy! It's real, lad! It's real!"

CHAPTER TWENTY THREE
THE JESTER'S LAUGH

Safar goggled at the model of the airship, then at Biner, saying, "What do you mean, it's *real?*"

The dwarf shook his big head, laughing. "You're lookin' at me," he said, "like you think I just cut the last sandbag loose and now there's no tellin' when I'll ever come to ground again."

He put the glass case on the trunk between them. "Maybe you're right," he said. "Maybe old Biner has finally lost his way. Or maybe I was always lost, which is more likely the case. Point is, crazy or not, Arlain, Elgy . . . all of us . . . were so certain what Methydia's gift meant that we've scoured heaven and Esmir to find you.

"We almost gave up a couple of times, because with you on the run from Iraj—duckin' and dodgin' and keepin' out of sight—it seemed like we'd never track you down. Then a couple of months ago we ran into a party of those Asper heads."

"Asper heads?"

Biner grinned. "That's what we call Queen Hantilia and her crew. Not that they're not all nice beings and such. Hospitable as can be. And you couldn't ask for a better audience. Still you have to admit they're damned strange. Happy all the time, but there's something sad and maybe even a little desperate about them."

"So I've noticed," Safar said, dry.

"Anyway," Biner went on, "as luck would have it the group we met up with was late to the party. Or whatever it is they're throwin' here in Caluz. They were broken down on the road and we helped them out. Naturally, we noticed the robes they were wearin', with the Asper symbols on 'em. And just as naturally we knew you were real interested in anythin' to do with the old boy. So we asked and they babbled their heads off about the Oracle orderin' them all to Caluz. Not only that, they said the same Oracle predicted you would be there. That the stars and planets were all linin' up for a big show and you'd be the main attraction. A command performance, so to speak.

"Well, we all figured there were too many coincidences to sail over. And that crazy as those Asper heads might seem, we'd be damned fools if we didn't see what was what. Make a long story short, we went along with them."

He eyed Safar, chuckling. "So here we are . . . and here you are . . . so I guess those Asper heads aren't so crazy after all."

"Apparently not," Safar said, smiling. "And they're aren't enough words to thank you for what you've done. You risked your lives for me."

"Some of it was for you," Biner said. "But mostly it was for Methydia. It's what she would have wanted us to do." He hooked up the wineskin and drank. Then, "Now maybe I'd better explain about the airship bein' real and stuff."

Safar took the wineskin from him. "Wait'll I catch up to you," he said. "I think I'm going to need it." He drank deeply, wiped his chin, then said, "All right. I'm ready."

"Actually, it's pretty simple," Biner said. "But I won't begrudge a man a good drink whether he's goin' to need it or not.

"See, it's like this. Methydia always told us the airship was made by two old lovers each tryin' to get the better of the other. She had different versions of the story, dependin' on her moods, but they all pretty much worked out the same. Which was that the airship was built of a rare wood that was extra light, but still real strong, plus it was powered by special spells to help the burners lift the balloons."

"She also said it was one of a kind," Safar pointed out.

"You're as right as you can be, lad," Biner said. "But you weren't with us much more'n a year. So you couldn't of heard all the things she said on the subject. Like the real particulars on how the ship was made.

"The main thing was, she said it was cast from a model. In other words, a small version was made first. And the airship proper was made from that. We got the idea it was a big damn spell, somethin' that took days to cast. But we always thought she meant the big ship was copied from the model. Measurements taken, or whatever, and copied with saws and hammers and big planks of that rare wood.

"But soon as we found the model and saw that note we started thinkin' differently. She was obviously thinkin' of givin' this to you before she died. Waitin' for the right time, like maybe when you left the circus to go do what you had to do. And believe me, if Methydia thought this was important enough for a farewell gift, it wouldn't be any damned toy. She didn't hold with that kind of silliness and there was no way she'd picture you wanderin' around with a pretty glass case under your arm all the time just so you could remember her."

Safar touched the delicate crystal housing the model. "I see what you mean," he said, running his fingers along the edge. "I wonder how it works."

"She probably intended to tell you in person," Biner said. "Which is why there's no directions along with the note. Hells, we couldn't even get the case open. It appears like all one solid piece with no seams, much less a lid."

Biner sighed, eyes becoming moist. "I guess she wasn't figurin' on dyin' when she did."

Safar only shook his head. What could he say?

Then his fingers bumped against a small gold stud. There was a hot snap! of static and snatched them away. "Ouch!" he said, sucking on his fingers. Then he looked closer and saw a little red needle point sticking up from the stud.

"Hold on!" he said, excitement overriding the sad memories. "I think I see it!"

There were seven other studs arranged in a pattern. Gingerly, Safar pressed them one by one, but with the surprise gone the sensation was nothing more than a barely painful pinprick. As he touched each stud a red needle point popped up, just like the first.

Biner leaned closer to look. He scratched his head, puzzled. Then he brightened. "Maybe we have to link 'em, somehow," he said. "You know, like a wire or a thread, goin' from point to point?"

Safar nodded. "Let's try it."

He found a rough spot on his sleeve, picked a piece of thread free and pulled it out, snipping it off with his teeth when he thought he had enough. Then he wove the thread around each needlepoint until they were all joined together in a web of thread. He stepped back, waiting. Nothing happened.

Biner shook his head. "Maybe it's some kind of special pattern," he said. "Trouble is, unless you got lucky it could take years before you hit on the right one."

Safar smiled. "Fortunately," he said, "I know a quicker way to find out."

He slipped the little silver dagger from his sleeve and laid it across the web, chanting an old, reliable unlocking spell:

> *"Conjure the key*
> *That fits the lock.*
> *Untangle the traces,*
> *And cut the knot."*

Suddenly there was a hiss and the case filled with smoke. The top of the case snapped open and the sides fell away and the room was filled with the smell of a heavy incense.

The airship bloomed into life, tiny burners blazing, bellows pumping, twin balloons swelling, bigger and bigger until the ship lifted off the trunk.

"By the gods," Biner breathed, "it really does work! We weren't crazy, after all!"

Safar caught the model before it could float to the ceiling. Instantly it became lifeless again. He gazed at it, thinking this might just be the edge he needed against Iraj.

He cradled the airship in his arms as if it were the woman who'd loved him enough to make him such a gift.

And he whispered, "Thank you, Methydia. Thank you."

*   *   *

Queen Hantilia smiled down at the scene—Safar cradling the model, Biner grinning at his friend, trunks stacked along the canvas walls of the storage room.

"It's going exactly as we wished," she said to someone behind her.

A red-robed assistant moved closer, peering over Hantilia's shoulder at a hand mirror lying on the Queen's makeup table. It was a magical stage, lit by five red candles, where Safar and Biner played out their drama in miniature.

Safar's voice floated up, "Thank you, Methydia. Thank you."

The assistant giggled. "How sweet," she said. "And right on schedule, too, Your Majesty."

Hantilia waved a claw and the scene disappeared. "I'd rather allow things to boil a

467

bit more," she said. "So let's give it another day. Make some excuse for the delay that won't arouse suspicion."

"Yes, Majesty," the assistant said.

"It shouldn't be difficult," Hantilia said. "Even though we've forbidden it, I know Lord Timura will be simply bursting with spells he needs to cast." She chuckled. "This will make it easier for him to hide his work."

"Indeed, Majesty," the assistant said.

"And that will give us time," the Queen said, "to be absolutely certain everything is ready for The Great Sacrifice."

"All will be done as you command, Majesty," the assistant said.

Hantilia sighed. "What a pity," she said, wiping an eye. "He's such a handsome young man."

* * *

As Hantilia predicted, Safar was vastly relieved when news was delivered that the date with the Oracle had been delayed one more day.

Leiria, on the other hand, was suspicious. "If it were a bargain sword in a smithy's shop," she said, "I'd pass it by, thinking the price was so cheap it'd be certain to shatter at the worst possible moment."

The two of them were strolling along the riverbank, discussing Hantilia's message.

"I don't know," Safar said, "it seemed reasonable enough. Something went wrong during the purification ceremonies. So certain steps had to be repeated. That sort of thing happened all the time to the priests in Walaria."

"It still doesn't smell right to me," Leiria said. Then she eyed Safar. "And what about you?" she asked. "Why the big change? A couple of days ago you were worrying the bit to get on with it before Iraj showed up."

Safar shook his head. "I'm still worried," he said. "But as things stand now, if he did show up we'd be chin deep in a temple privy on feast day. To start with, all our people are wandering around in a Caluzian pink cloud and it'll be at least two days before Palimak's spell is ready. Then they'll have to be organized. Soldiers whipped into shape as fast as we damn well can. Some kind of rear guard action devised so we can escape. The wagons packed and ready, animals fed and watered and everyone set to go at an instant's notice.

"As it is now, most of the work is going to be on your shoulders, Leiria. I don't know what's going to happen when Palimak and I finally get to meet with the Oracle. Or how long we'll be away. Or, hells—let's face it—even if we'll make it back. So, it's going to be up to you, Leiria. Up to you—my dearest friend—and by the gods sometimes I think you must be crazy to put up with us all."

Leiria laughed. "I'm here for the flattery," she said. "What else?"

Then, more seriously, "Let's go back a bit on your list of to do's," she said. "I'm stuck fast on the part about escaping. And I have not one, but three questions. First, what escape? Second, how escape? Third, and most important of all, where escape?"

She looked around her—the gurgling river, the idealized blue mountains beyond, the exotic city gleaming on the hillside overlooking the great stone turtle.

"Hells," she said, "I don't even know where we really are!"

"Think of it as a big bowl turned upside down in the Black Lands," Safar said. "Everything under the bowl is happy and safe—for the time being. Everything on the outside is just like it was before."

"Except, maybe worse," Leiria said.

Safar nodded. "Except, maybe worse."

Leiria chuckled. "What kind of leader are you?" she said. "Where's the cheery words? Where's the lies that things will surely be better?"

Safar pretended to be hurt. "You should have more faith in me," he said. "Next you'll be doubting that I have a plan."

"Do you?"

Safar grinned. "Actually, no," he said. "But I'm working on it. Which is the main reason why I'm glad Hantilia gave us another day. Intended or otherwise."

"Oh, my!" Leiria said. "Coming around full circle and attacking my flanks, are we? Cutting off my argument with sneaky logic. Now, is that fair?"

"I never promised fair," Safar said. "I only promised a plan."

"Seriously," Leiria said. "Do you even have an inkling?"

"A few glimmers," Safar said. "To begin with Iraj will most certainly come through the same gate we used." He pointed east to the high shale cliffs that divided Caluz from the pass. "So we can't run in that direction."

"We could delay him at the gate," Leiria pointed out. "A small force could hold him there while the rest escaped."

"I like that," Safar said. "The first thing we should do then, is to take the airship as high we can and get a peek on the other side of the cliffs. That will give us an idea of how close Iraj is getting and how much time we have."

"But how do we get out of here?" Leiria said. "Which way do we run?"

Safar pointed north, toward a low range of mountains marked by two high peaks. "Through those peaks," he said. "Somewhere beyond those mountains is the Great Sea. If we bear a little west we ought to hit Caspan, where we can hire some ships to take us to Syrapis."

Leiria grimaced, saying, "Yes, but how far away is it? A week's journey? A month? And another thing, what's between us and the sea? More of the Black Lands? Rough trails or a broad caravan track? Coralean's maps aren't any help. The ones for this area are too old to trust."

"If we have time," Safar said, "we can use the airship to find out."

"Assuming you can figure out how to turn that model into a real airship, that is," Leiria pointed out.

"Exactly," Safar said. "Which is another reason we need time. With luck I'll have it worked out before I go. But chances are, once again, it'll be you—with the help of Biner and Arlain—who will be doing the looking. And mapping the escape route."

Leiria nodded. She was quiet for a moment, then she said, "I have to ask this. What if you don't return? What if you and Palimak don't make it?"

"Then you make it, Leiria," he said, giving her shoulder a squeeze. "And, please, get as many of my people as you can out of harm's way."

"Should I go on to Syrapis?" Leiria asked.

"It's the only place I know of," Safar said, "that will be safe for awhile."

"And after that?"

Safar face darkened momentarily, then he suddenly brightened. "What the hells' the difference?" he laughed. "To misquote a good friend of mine, the 'journey will probably kill you anyway.'"

*   *   *

Palimak eyed the cable doubtfully. It stretched from the platform he was standing on to another platform about ten feet away.

"Go ahead, my thweet," Arlain said, "We won't let you hurt yourthelf."

The cable was only about six feet off the ground, but to the boy it seemed much higher. Arlain was posted on one side of him, Kairo on the other.

"I don't know," Palimak said, "it looks kind of scary."

"Yez done jus' fine when she were lower, me boy," Kairo said. "Matter of fact, old Kairo's never seen anyone take to the wire so quick like."

"Letthon number one in wire walking," Arlain said, "ith that height doethn't matter. Anything you can do at ground level ith no harder than when you're all the way to the top of the tent."

Palimak giggled nervously. "Are you sure?"

"Thure, I'm thure," Arlain said. "I thtarted out the thame way you did. And tho did Kairo. Firtht you put the wire on the ground and thee that it really ithn't that thmall. It only lookth that way to the audienthe when it'th high up. Then you raith it off the ground a little wayth tho you can get uthed to the way it thwayth back and forth when you move."

"We gots yez up to six feet already," Kairo said. "After this—why, the sky's the limit! And that's a fact, me boy, not smoke blowin'."

Arlain glared at Kairo. "Pleathe!" she said. "Thome of uth are thenthitive about that word."

Kairo winced. "Sorry!" Then to Palimak. "But yer gets me point, right?"

Palimak eyed the distance again, gathering courage. Licked his lips. Nodded. "Right."

"Lovely!" Arlain said, waving her tail in excitement. "Let'th go, then. Thout out when you're ready!"

Palimak gulped. "Rea-dy!" he said, voice quavering.

He took his first step. The cable gave slightly under his weight, but remained steady.

"Keep yer toes pointed out," Kairo reminded him.

"Got it!" Palimak took another step. "Toes out and eyes aimed at where I'm going."

He took several more steps, gingerly at first, keeping his outstretched arms steady, resisting the natural but wrong-headed temptation to wave them about and overbalance himself. Arlain and Kairo paced with him, ready in case he should fall.

"Very good, my thweet!" Arlain said.

Taking heart, Palimak picked up the pace and to his immense surprise it suddenly became much easier to keep his balance.

"That's it, me boy," Kairo said. "When it comes to wire walkin' the sayin' is—'briskly does it . . . and slowly goes the fool.'"

Palimak had no wish to be a fool—or a "rube" in his growing vocabulary of circus words. A "rube," he gathered was lower than low. An ignorant, "cud chewing civilian"—another circus disparagement.

He blanked the surroundings from his mind and instead imagined himself strolling along a garden path. Before he knew it he found himself stepping onto the opposite platform. Palimak spun about, gaping at what he'd done. Then the gape became a bright beam of pride.

"Ta-da!" he shouted, raising his arms high in victory.

Arlain applauded, shooting a sheet of smoky flame into the air, while Kairo lifted his head high above his shoulders and cheered.

"Ithn't that wonderful?" Arlain crowed. "Lookth like we have a new member of the thircuth!"

Palimak goggled at her. "Really?"

"Abtholutely," she said. "And it couldn't come at a better time, ithn't that tho, Kairo?"

Kairo let his head fall into hands and pumped it up and down in an exaggerated nod. "That's the truth, me boy," he said.

Palimak giggled at the strange sight—the face grinning at him from its nest between Kairo's palms—long tubular neck snaking up to his shoulders. His body jerked and the head snapped back into its proper place.

"We've been short an act for months, now," he said, looking quite normal again.

Palimak clapped his hands in glee. "Wait'll my father hears the news," he said. "I'll be a circus man, just like him."

Then he looked at them, suddenly shy. "But maybe I'd better practice some more," he said. "If it's all right."

"Sure, yer can, me boy," Kairo said.

"Great," Palimak said. "But let me announce it first."

"Announthe away," Arlain said.

Palimak threw his hands wide, in imitation of Biner's ringmaster pose. "Ladies and gentleman!" he shouted. "Lads and lasses! Beings of all ages! Methydia's Flying Circus now proudly presents . . .

"Half boy, half demon, half fly and that's three half's rolled into one. Brought to you at . . . Enormous Expense!

"Palimak The Magnificent! Ta-Da!"

Then without warning he bolted out on the wire.

"Wait!" Arlain shouted, but it was too late.

In a blink of the eye Palimak was already at the midpoint of the wire while she and Kairo raced on either side of the cable trying to keep up. The boy nearly overbalanced in the center, swaying for a moment, almost looking down and losing it, but then he remembered to fix his eyes and mind on his distant goal and he kept moving, pushing through the momentary clumsiness, until he regained his balance, practically sprinting along the wire until he reached the other side.

Once again he shouted, "Ta-Da!" and made a flourishing bow to even greater cheers from his new friends.

"What'd I say?" Kairo cried. "The boy's a natural!"

"Let's go higher!" Palimak crowed, jabbing a finger at the dim heights of the circus tents. "All the way the way to the very, tip, tip top!"

"Thlow down, thweetneth," Arlain laughed. "You're going too fatht for uth."

"She's right, me boy," Kairo chuckled. "Besides, before we go any higher yer gots to learn the next most important thing about wire walkin'."

"What's that?" the boy asked.

"Yer gotta knows how to fall," Kairo said. "Because if there's one thing that's certain in this life, me boy, it's that someday, somehow, a body's gotta fall."

"The trick," Arlain added, "ith to not get killed when you do."

*   *   *

Gundaree bounced up and down on his chest, chanting, "Palimak's in luu-uve. Palimak's in luu-uve!"

"Shut up!" the boy snarled, pulling the pillow around his ears.

"Don't say shut up, Little Master," Gundara admonished. Then, to his twin, "Stop teasing him! It isn't nice!"

Gundaree giggled. "But it's the truth!" He wrapped his arms about himself. "Ooh! Arlain," he mocked. "I luu-uve you so much!"

At that, Palimak lost his temper. His eyes suddenly glowed demon yellow. He pointing a finger at the Favorite, who gleeped as a sharp claw emerged.

"I don't like that!" he said.

Gundaree's little demon face drooped into infinite sorrow. Even his horn seemed to sag. Big tears welled into his eyes. "I'm sorry, Little Master," he sobbed.

For a change Gundara didn't gloat over his brother's misery. From the look in the boy's eyes he thought it best not to draw attention to himself.

Gundaree sniffed, wiping his nose, and Palimak's anger dissolved. He felt ashamed of himself for frightening the Favorite.

"I'm sorry first," he said. "You were just playing. You didn't mean it and I shouldn't have gotten so mad."

The small crisis past, both Favorites brightened considerably. "Who cares?" Gundaree said. "We're back in the circus again, that's the point."

"The point indeed, lesser brother," Gundara sneered as only he could sneer—little human features elevating into high snobbery. "Instead of teasing our poor master, we should be instructing him." He turned to Palimak, face rearranging itself into something more respectful. "We learned some excellent circus tricks when we toured with your father. If I do say so myself."

"You *always* say so yourself, Gundara," his sibling mocked, hands on narrow hips. "And that's because you're only talking to yourself because you're so stupid no one is listening."

Gundara sighed. "I'm only glad our poor mother isn't alive to see what her son has come to."

"Don't talk about our mother!" Gundaree shouted. "You know I hatefttuh . . ." The rest was lost as Palimak clamped his pillow over both Favorites, shutting off the quarrel.

Palimak laughed at the muffled sounds of protest. "I should have thought of this before," he said. Then, "You have to promise to quit arguing, or I won't let you out."

He bent an ear close and heard mumbles of what sounded like surrender. "Good," he said, lifting the pillow away to reveal two very rumpled Favorites. "Now it's my turn to talk."

Gundaree, a stickler for tidiness, brushed himself off. "That wasn't nice," he said. "Pillows have feathers. And I hate feathers. They give me a rash."

Gundara plucked here and there, restoring a semblance of dignity. "If you wanted to speak, Little Master," he complained, "all you had to do is *ask!*"

"Then I'm asking," Palimak said. "You were talking about teaching me some circus tricks. And I wanted to ask, were they magical circus tricks? But you kept arguing and arguing until I thought I was going to go crazy because you wouldn't let me talk."

Gundaree shrugged. "Of course, they're magic. That's what we do, right? Magic. We're not sweaty acrobats, or jugglers, for goodness sakes."

"We do not like to perspire," Gundara sniffed. "Call it a fault, if you like, but we were made for royalty and perspiration and royalty don't go together at all."

"But you like to eat, right?" Palimak asked, rummaging around in his blankets.

Both Favorites eyed his fumbling, then licked their lips as the boy drew out a greasy sack of treats, saying they certainly did like to eat.

"Here's the deal," Palimak said, shaking the sack. Both Favorites slavered at the smell of good things wafting out. "I'll trade you a treat for every trick you teach me. All right?"

Gundaree and Gundara made enthusiastic noises of agreement and before very long they were stuffing their mouths, while stuffing Palimak's brains.

He worked them hard and he worked them late and before they were done both Favorites were fat, full and happily perspiring.

Palimak was so absorbed he didn't sense the dark figure that crept close to his tent to listen. Gundara and Gundaree noticed, but there was no danger so they didn't mention it. Especially since the figure was Safar. He stood there for nearly an hour, face a portrait of fatherly pride at the boy's newly discovered circus talents. Arlain and Kairo were right. He was a natural.

Then a light dawned in his eyes and his smile widened. The boy had just given him an idea. An idea that might solve two problems with one blow.

*   *   *

"Step right up, my friends," Safar shouted. "Don't be shy. Admission is free today, ladies and gentlemen. That's right. Free!"

Dressed in the red silk shirt and white pantaloons of a circus barker, Safar was manning the ticket counter, calling out to a crowd of bemused Kyranians. Behind him the circus had been set up in the open, complete with stands surrounding a wide ring, colorful banners blowing in the breeze, and trapeze and wire walking equipment slung from high poles. Half the stands were already full of Safar's fellow villagers, who were being entertained by the clowns. The rest of the Kyranians were either filing through makeshift gates to join the others or crowding around Safar's booth. He was thoroughly enjoying himself in his old role as a ticket seller, delighting at the looks of amazement he was getting from his kinsmen. None of them, even his own family, had ever seen this side of him.

He kept up the patter. "You heard right, my friends. I said free."

Safar slapped five coins on the counter. "Not five coppers, which is our usual price."

He made a motion and the crowd gasped as one of the coins vanished. "Not four." Another motion, another disappearing coin. "Not three . . . not two . . . not even—" He held up the remaining coin— "one clipped copper." Safar flipped it into the air and to the crowd's amazement it hung there, turning over and over.

Safar gestured and there was a bang! and the coin burst into colorful bits of paper. Everyone jumped at the noise, then applauded as the paper rained down on them.

When the applause faded, Safar jumped back into verbal action. "In just one hour, friends," he shouted, "you will see sights that have dazzled the greatest courts in Esmir. Thrills, chills, and sometimes even spills. A special performance. For Kyranians only. And all for free."

Safar held up one of Palimak's clay amulets—the Jester hanging from a leather thong. Next to him were several boxes filled with similar amulets.

"And that's not all you get, my friends," he cried. "Besides the most exciting performance you have ever witnessed, we have a special gift for each and every one of you."

He waved the amulet. "It's the Jester, ladies and gentlemen, lads and lasses. The Laughing God! The slayer of ill humored devils. The Lord of Luck! Prince of Good Fortune! All wrapped up in this lovely, magical amulet, guaranteed to ward off evil spells."

The Kyranians oohed and aahed at the gift. Scores of people pushed forward, waving their hands, begging Safar to give them an amulet and let them enter.

"No need to crowd, my friends," Safar shouted as he handed amulets out by the fistful, "there's plenty for all."

He stopped a blushing young mother, babe in arms, who was too shy to take more than one. "Don't rush away, my pretty. You're forgetting the baby. He gets one too." She gratefully accepted it and sped away to see the show.

Safar kept handing out the amulets, reminding people to put them on so "the Jester can get to work for you right away. Wasted luck is lost luck, my friends. Remember that!" The Kyranians streamed through the gates, amulets dangling from their necks and found seats in the stands. Soon the whole village was accounted for and Safar rushed away to change costumes.

The first act was about to begin. And he was the star.

*   *   *

Meanwhile—far away, but too close, too close . . .

Iraj raged against the Black Lands, driving his troops mile after mile until they dropped, exhausted; lifting them again by his will alone to go onward, onward to Caluz, pummeled by nature and magic gone wild.

As they marched the earth heaved under them, splitting and groaning open, eager to swallow whole regiments if they were fool enough to come near. Volcanoes shuddered and burst, tornadoes and sand storms lashed out with no warning. Vicious spells, insane spells, rained from the bleak sky like ash, burning spirit and skin until they thought they could bear no more.

But then Iraj would turn his wrath on Fari and his wizards, demanding countering spells, healing spells, spells that would put heart into his troops again. He worked Fari and the wizards even harder than the soldiers. A warrior by birth and inclination, he empathized with the demons and men who made up his army. Even through the cold view of a shape changer he still bled when they bled, hungered when they hungered. If he'd had any love in him left he would have lavished it on them—human or demon, all brother warriors together.

Wizards were a different matter. A creature of magic, Iraj distrusted all sorcery. A soldier at heart, he thought wizards and war magic were only necessary evils and he was disdainful of the soft-fingered spell makers, be they demon or wizard, who made up Fari's private corps. And that's what it was, a private army within an army, a very dangerous situation for Protarus if he let it go on.

For now he was letting it be, even going so far as to let Fari think he was in supreme favor with the king. Just as he allowed Kalasariz to believe what he wanted—and Luka the same.

Poor Luka. He thought he was out of favor now, the fool in Iraj's eyes. This was true as only a monarch can make things true, especially king to lesser king where every frown or sneer is an iron bolt to the heart. Soon, however, he would make the prince glad. Lift him high up in the royal favor of King Protarus. But at the moment he needed Fari and his miserable wizards, so it was Fari's turn to smile now, no matter how weary that smile.

Iraj took joy in demanding more from Fari and his sorcerers than he did from his troops. He ground it in, commanding more than they could give, then pushing harder and getting it after all. Spell by strength-draining spell from the wizards, blister by bloody blister from his soldiers, every moan subtracting another inch from his goal.

Even so, Iraj was a commander who led from the front, demanding as much from himself as the others, so no one had reason to complain they were being asked too much.

That night, while Safar was rejoined with his old circus mates, Fari and his sorcerers had cast yet one more spell to shield the army from the ravages of the Black Lands. It was only good for three hours at the most and now Iraj—in full wolf form—was charging across the fiery landscape, leading his army as far as he could before time ran out and they had to regroup to cast another protective spell.

A poisonous yellow fog was clamped upon the land and Iraj could barely see the cratered road before him as he bounded along on all fours. Behind him he could hear the

474

tramp of his army and over that the howls of Fari, Luka and Kalasariz, urging the soldiers to hurry, hurry, hurry!

For Iraj the most agonizing part of the ordeal was knowing that Safar and the Kyranians had passed this way before with seeming ease. Only one of his wagons had been found abandoned on the caravan track, while Iraj's army was losing several a day. Many of the king's animals had also died, or were too sick or injured to go on. Yet not once had they found even a lost goat from the Kyranian caravan.

He couldn't understand how it was possible for Safar to accomplish so much single-handedly and with no losses to speak of. Where did he find the will, much less the power?

His spell brothers—Fari, Luka and Kalasariz—had promised their king once Safar and the demon child were captured all their powers would be his. Then he would be not only king of kings, but the most powerful sorcerer in Esmir.

Once, that promise had been what drove him. Capturing Safar and taking his powers had been Iraj's obsession, his burning goal. But not any longer. Not since Sheesan. Now he had an even greater reason to bring Safar to ground. He had the witch's spell that would free him from his spell brothers forever. Then he could be a true King of Kings. A great emperor unchained from those foul creatures who had tricked him into spell bondage.

It was this new goal—a shining promise—that kept Iraj from falling into despair. But sometimes he couldn't help but wonder—what was it that kept Safar going? What did he see that Iraj didn't see?

And most of all, what did Safar want?

To Iraj, that had always been Safar's greatest mystery. Even when they were boys and fast friends he'd never been able to get Safar to admit his deepest desires. He kept saying he only wanted to remain in Kyrania and be a potter like his father and grandfather. Which had to be a lie, for how could someone as powerful as Safar be satisfied with so little?

Iraj's spell brothers said Safar wanted Iraj's throne. This made a great deal of sense—for what could be a greater goal for one such as Safar Timura?

Yet sometimes Iraj wondered. When his moods were the darkest and most foul he thought, what if they are wrong? What if that's not what Safar wants at all?

And if that were true—what in the hells could he want?

A hot blast of wind swept the yellow fog away. The Demon Moon was at its brightest and the barren landscape leaped up under its harsh red glow. Many miles distant Iraj could see the huge black range where the road ended. Just beyond, his officers and aides all agreed, was Caluz.

Blood suddenly boiling with eagerness to get at his prey, Iraj lifted his wolf's snout to howl. Just then the shield dissolved and the howl was strangled off by the thick yellow fog rushing in again.

Iraj gasped for breath, shifting into human form and rising on two legs. Then the wind shifted and it was easier to draw breath—big, gulping lungsful of the hot, foul substance they called air in the Black Lands.

He heard Fari roaring orders to his mages and turned to see twenty demons in wizard's robes lofting five spell kites into the sky, each so large that it took four strong demons to control them. The wind whipped the kites high into the air, lighting crashing all around them. Electrical fire ran down wires to the ground, where they were attached to large jars with magical symbols painted on them. The jars glowed with every lightning strike, slowly building up the spell charge. When they were "filled up," Fari and his wizards would create yet another shield to protect the army for a few more hours.

Iraj tugged at his beard, growing angry at the delay.

Then one of the kites broke free, wrenching groans from the wizards who knew they'd suffer Fari's wrath for the delay the accident would cause.

Iraj watched the kite fly free across the boiling night sky and he had a sudden yearning to fly with it, to sail away to a place where he could shed crown and scepter and become an ordinary man, with ordinary cares and ordinary dreams.

And then the thought struck him—isn't that what Safar had said he'd wanted all along?

Just then a bolt of lightning struck the kite and Iraj was suddenly, unreasonably, gripped in the jaws of despair. He groaned as the kite burst into flames and plummeted toward the earth, coming apart as it fell, shattering into thousands of fiery bits. Before the burning mass hit the ground a blast of wind swept it up again, carrying it high into the sky—like a meteor shower in reverse.

Iraj's hopes soared with it, climbing higher and higher, then pausing to hang just beneath the blood-stained heavens.

There it took on a strange form—a human-like figure with a familiar cap and beaked nose. All sputtering with multi-colored fire.

Then it dawned on him—It was the Jester. The playful god. And the Crown Prince of Luck.

Iraj smiled at the omen, confidence flooding back, making him feel stronger than ever before.

It was a promise, he thought, of things to come.

CHAPTER TWENTY FOUR

ASPER'S SONG

Biner stood in the center ring, resplendent in his dashing ringmaster's costume. "Ladies and gentlemen," he cried. "Lads and lasses of *all ages. Welcome to the circus!*"

The Kyranians were rapt, all wearing huge smiles, clutching their jester amulets and listening closely to Biner's every word.

"This is a special program today," Biner continued, "for all our Kyranian friends. So we won't begin the usual way. First off, I want to tell you that our little company has always held Kyrania dear to our hearts. We had the rare good fortune of meeting one of your sons long ago and heard all about you." He grinned. "That young man, by the way, is known to you as Safar Timura. Some might even call him Lord Timura. But when he performed with us he was known far and wide as 'Safar The Magnificent!'"

He chortled and the crowd laughed with him, especially Khadji and Myrna and the other members of Safar's family who had front row seats of honor.

"Can you imagine, Myrna," Khadji whispered. "Our Safar who was always so clumsy when he was little?"

"That was from your side of the family," Myrna teased. "From my side he got 'Magnificent!'"

Khadji pretended he didn't hear. "Quiet, please, Myrna," he whispered. "I'm trying to listen."

He pointed at Biner, who was saying, "It was a name well deserved, my good people. For as we all know our friend Safar is remarkable in many ways."

Led by Myrna and Khadji, the crowd made loud noises of agreement. Biner used the diversion to palm a handful of explosive pellets.

"So put your hands together, ladies and gentlemen, lads and lasses, and give warm welcome to the one, the only . . ." Biner made a dramatic gesture, at the same time flinging the pellets to the ground, shouting, " . . . Safar The Magnificent!"

There was a heart-stopping blast of fire and a cloud of smoke, red and green and white, burst up. The crowd gasped and all eyes were fixed on the thick, swirling mass. The smoke cleared and there were more gasps as three figures emerged, posing nobly on a small platform decorated with magical symbols. In the center was Safar, wearing ceremonial wizard's robes. On his right was Palimak, decked out in his miniature soldier's outfit. To his left was Leiria, proud and tall in her glittering armor. In her hands was the black box containing the model of the airship.

The stands exploded as all the Kyranians came to their feet, clapping and cheering their village heroes. Safar motioned to his companions and they all bowed together, boosting the applause to even greater heights. He'd lost none of his skills with an audience, knowing how to take people to the edge, then bring them back again just before exhaustion crept in, making them dull and less receptive for a performance. But this time he had to press them past that point—treating the opening of the show as if it were the last encore after a long evening's entertainment. He wanted them limp and receptive to all his suggestions, so when the cheering started to fade he turned, sweeping a hand out to indicate Palimak.

The boy had been well-rehearsed and he drew himself up and gave them all a snappy salute. It had its desired effect—another long round of thunderous applause. And when that began to diminish Safar immediately turned to Leiria. She held the black box over her head as if it were a trophy and although no one in the audience had the faintest idea what was inside, this triggered a new burst of cheering.

His eyes swept the crowd and he felt an all-too familiar pang of guilt when he saw all the happy grins pasted on their faces. Safar's first job was the complete opposite of what any circus performer desired. He had to turn those smiles into grimaces of misery. Then his gaze fell on his father and mother and he saw the merry insanity in their eyes. The machine's spell made them look foolish and his parents would rather be dead—much less miserable—than not to have all their considerable wits about them.

So he steeled himself and when he felt the audience reach its last dregs of energy he threw up his arms and shook his head, urging them to stop, saying, "Thank you, thank you, my friends. But, please. Please." His voice was magically amplified and had the ring of command, not pleading.

Then he brought his hands down and although there was no magic involved, it seemed like sorcery when the crowd noise sank along with his hands. And the people dropped into their seats with happy obedience. Their spirits were like soft clay waiting to be molded by him.

He whispered to Palimak, "Are you ready?"

Palimak glanced down, checking the two black dots on his sleeve. They weren't dirt specks, but Gundara and Gundaree shrunk to the size of fleas. "Ready, father," he whispered back.

Safar nodded and turned back to the crowd. "I hope you'll all forgive me," he said conversationally, "if I seem a little clumsy up here. It's been more years than I like to admit since my circus days." There were chuckles of understanding from the audience. "And if you can't find any forgiveness to spare," he added, "please don't blame my assistants." He smiled at Palimak and Leiria. "Anything that goes wrong will be my fault, not theirs." More chuckles.

Somewhere close by, Elgy and Rabix started a drum roll—low, but building quickly.

"And so," Safar said, "without further ado . . ." and his voice rose to a shout: "Let the show begin!"

Drums crashed like thunder and Safar stabbed at the sky with his silver dagger. All eyes jerked up, like puppet heads responding to a string. A single cloud, golden in the sun and ridged like a broken cliff face, floated overhead. A red beam of light leaped from the dagger point, lancing the cloud. Harp music swelled and the audience sucked in air as one, then let it out in a long sigh of wonder as a slender stream of golden light spilled from the cloud, arcing down like a waterfall. It fell on the platform and for a moment all was obliterated by brilliant light. People threw up their hands to shield their eyes. The harp music shifted to teasing pipes that made everyone smile.

Hands came down and wonder of all wonders the light was only a faint shimmer, like curtains of the sheerest yellow silk. Palimak stood alone on the platform, bathed by the golden light. The crowd gaped at him, because instead of a small boy, they were presented with a towering, but childishly slender figure, nearly twelve feet tall.

Palimak giggled nervously, which made the crowd laugh. Big as he was, the giggles made him seem like a harmless boy again.

Cymbals crashed and he shouted: "Is *everybody* happy!"

"YES!" the crowd roared back.

"How happy are you?" he cried.

"VERY HAPPY!" came the reply.

"That's good," Palimak said. "Because I'm going to need your help with this spell. All right?" There was an enthusiastic chorus of agreement.

"Great! Now, do you all have those amulets we gave you?" Everyone shouted that they did.

"Are you all wearing them? I mean everybody—especially the little kids like me, and the babies, too." There was much rustling and adjustment as the people all checked to see.

When he was sure they were ready, Palimak said, "Now I want you all to concentrate real hard while I say this spell."

He stopped. Shook his head. "Oh, wait a minute. I almost forgot. First you have to hold on to the amulets. Then concentrate. Got it?"

Nods all around. "Good. Now, listen real close while I say the spell."

He drew his toy sword and raised it high, chanting in his high, child's voice:

> *"Jester, Jester,*
> *What's the riddle?*
> *Up, or down, or in the middle?*
> *Jester, Jester,*
> *Tell us quick.*
> *Happy, to sad, what's the trick?"*

He waved his stubby sword and his eyes turned huge and demon yellow. A cold shudder rolled through the audience and Palimak no longer looked like such a comic figure. He seemed huge and forbidding—a giant child with a frightening grin and alien powers. The clay amulets suddenly turned uncomfortably warm and people tried to let them drop, but their hands had become unwilling fists, gripping the jester talismans tightly.

No one cried out, but there were low moans of fear that tore at Palimak, almost making him lose concentration. He saw his grandfather and grandmother and they were staring at him in terror. He nearly stopped right then, nearly turned to find his father and go running into his arms, begging him not to make him do this. It was awful. Everybody would hate him.

Gundara's voice shrilled in his ear. "Go on, Little Master! You can't stop now!"

And Gundaree added, "This was your idea, remember?"

Palimak bore down and got his focus back. Now, for the last part of the spell:

> *"I'm so sorry,*
> *I'm so blue.*
> *But a bad spell's got you,*
> *So what else can I do?*
> *Happy to sad,*
> *You're no longer glad,*
> *And I have to make you mad*
> *Because it's good for you!"*

He paused, gathering power from the Favorites, then he lashed out with his sword, shouting:

"Begone!"

He cast the spell and the sky immediately dimmed as a huge cloud moved over the arena. It was accompanied by a chill wind that rolled over the Kyranians, wet and clammy and tasting like salty tears. The villagers groaned as the machine's spell of gladness was swept away and cruel sanity returned.

There was a funeral-like wail as everyone realized they had been living an illusion. Dwelling for awhile in a mirage of happiness, while outside Iraj Protarus and his demon wolves waited, prowling and anxious to feed.

On the platform the golden light had vanished and Palimak was small again, a forlorn little boy, head hanging in shame because he had made his grandparents cry. Then Leiria and his father were embracing him and whispering words of comfort, which made him feel better—but only a little. Then they all took their places again, Safar in the center, raising his hands to address a much different crowd than he had faced only a few moments before.

"There's a lot of things I could say right now," he told them. "Beginning with how sorry I am I was forced to trick you. Such words, however, would be empty of meaning to you now."

His eyes moved from familiar face to familiar face, many of which were flushed and swollen with growing rage.

"Instead I want to caution you," he said. "I can see that many of you are angry with me and I don't blame you. Just be careful you don't turn it on yourselves. Soon you will all feel like fools for allowing yourself to become victims of the machine's spell. For that's all it was—a spell you had no control over. And that spell was caused by the turtle idol you all saw when you entered Caluz. It was the idol—a magical machine—that dulled your wits and feelings and made you insane."

This won some grudging nods from some people and a snort of understanding from his father, who had been glaring at him along with the rest. Of all the Kyranians, Khadji was perhaps the proudest of his ability to reason. To see things as they really are. Only Myrna was his match.

"What I want you to fix on instead," Safar said, "is who you are. Kyranians! The greatest and rarest of people in all the world. Many miles and months ago we set off from our homeland—not in flight. Not in fear. But on a holy mission to save all beingkind."

There were heartening murmurs of approval. Safar pressed on.

"But to accomplish this great deed," he said, "we must first guard our own lives. For if we perish, who will take up our banner? Who will shoulder our cause?"

The murmurs grew louder, especially from the young soldiers like Renor and Seth, who were spurred on by growls of approval from the grizzled Sergeant Dario.

"My dear friends," Safar said, building on that changing mood. "That is why I had to awaken you. We are faced with both the gravest of dangers and the grandest of opportunities."

Safar knew that when good and evil are placed side by side, human nature would instantly grab for the good and give less weight to the evil. So he wasn't surprised when he saw all the faces brighten as hope was suddenly raised from the dead at the news of "the grandest of opportunities."

"In a short while," Safar said, "I will be called to consult with the Oracle of Hadin. This meeting has been our purpose all along. This is why we had to face the terrors of the Black Lands to come here. For we have good reason to believe that many of the answers we seek will be revealed to us by the Oracle."

He saw frowns and knew his people were growing vaguely disappointed. They were expecting an instant pot of gold, instead of a possibly long wait for what might or might not be good news from some mysterious Oracle who might decide to have a cranky day.

Safar smoothly dealt up what they really wanted, saying, "But before that hour comes, my friends, I have a great miracle to show you."

He pointed at Leiria, who held up the long black box. "In there," he said, "is a great gift. A magical gift that will give us the edge we need against Iraj Protarus!"

Prickling with excitement, everyone craned their heads to look as Leiria ceremoniously presented the box to Safar. He opened the lid slowly, heightening the suspense.

Safar stomped his foot and there was a crack! as he set off a smoke pellet with his heel. Purple smoke obscured the platform for a moment, then it dissolved and the crowd gasped when they saw the miniature airship hovering just above his head. Safar gestured and the little furnaces sparked into life and the airship sailed about in ever widening circles, until it came to the edge of the grassy ring where it took up position and skimmed around the edges.

Everyone applauded. Khadji even cried out in recognition. The airship was vaguely similar to magical devices he had helped Safar with many years ago during the demon wars.

"That is only the beginning of the miracle, my friends," Safar said. "In exactly one hour we will cast a spell that will reveal an even greater wonder. To weave that spell I have asked all our circus friends to assist us. When you entered this arena you were promised a show—and a show you shall get!"

Safar raised his arms and shouted, "Let the circus begin!"

And *crack!* came another explosion of smoke. And boom! went the drums. Music blared and the airship swung about in a long arc. Then the ship plunged through the smoke, lifting it away as it emerged from the other side—as if drawing a curtain.

People rubbed their eyes in amazement. The platform was gone. In its place was a gigantic, blue-speckled egg. There was a low drum roll and the egg began to shake, harder and harder until cracks zigzagged through the shell. Then it burst open and a score of clowns rushed out, colliding and chasing and prat-falling about until the audience was roaring with laughter.

From high above came a wild cry and everyone looked up as Arlain, wearing the filmiest of silk costumes and little under that, swung out of the sky on her trapeze. She breathed long plumes of fire as she plummeted down. Then she was going up, and up, letting go of at the apex of her swing. Then somersaulting, once, twice, three times—shooting flames as she twirled. And at the last moment, hanging there, a breath from a fall to her certain death.

Then the trapeze bar came back and Arlain grabbed it and swung away to safety and thunderous applause.

*   *   *

"Quite spectacular," the Queen said as she viewed the scene through her mirror. "And I must say, the more I learn about our handsome young Safar Timura, the more impressed I become."

She waved at the scene in the mirror—Biner, bared torso rippling, performed an incredible feat of strength. "This is sheer genius!"

"How so, Majesty?" murmured her assistant. "Other than the obvious artistry of entertainment, I mean?"

Hantilia waved a dismissive claw at the mirror. "Oh, that's just a device," she said. "But our Safar is making that device do double duty. Possibly even triple duty, now that I think of it."

Her assistant frowned. "Your Majesty is obviously much wiser than one such as I," she said. "But I would hope my wits weren't so dull that I couldn't see at least one of the three."

Hantilia exposed her fangs in a smile and primped at her hair. "It's a good thing you don't, my dear," she said. "Or I would have to worry about you."

"I don't understand, Majesty."

"The genius I am speaking of," she said, "involves the art of manipulation. Which is what this circus is. Mass manipulation by a very powerful wizard. It's a good thing for his people that he has their best interests at heart. If he were a despot they would be his slaves."

Light dawned in the assistant's eyes. "I think I see the first, Majesty," she said. "He's using the circus to rebuild their spirits. Their morale, as they say."

"Very good, my sweet," the queen replied. "But there's more to it then mere morale. If you had looked closely at the Kyranians—after he took away their false happiness—you would have seen that many of them were on the verge of rebellion. Of outright mutiny.

"They felt, possibly even justifiably, that much of what they have endured is Safar Timura's fault. And they were ready to turn against the only one who can save them. But by the time this circus is over, they will be ready to charge through the gates of the Hells for him.

"Which is a good thing, considering what we have planned for them in the very near future."

"I can see that, Majesty," the assistant said, "but what else is Lord Timura accomplishing?"

Another gesture at the mirror—Kairo, balanced on a pole, juggling three clubs and his head. "All the acts you see are part of the spell he's building. From the silly to the sublime, he is the weaver, they are his strings.

"The egg was the first part of the spell. Followed by the clown acts to call on the Jester. Rebirth from the egg. Strength from the mighty dwarf. Fire from that marvelous dragon woman. And so forth. As the entertainment goes on you'll see what I mean—if you watch closely, that is, and use your imagination.

"He's also mixing the Kyranians—his audience—into his magical tapestry. So when he casts the spell, they will be wedded to it. Co-creators, if you will, of the final result."

"Which will be?"

Hantilia laughed. "Oh, wait and see," she said. "I don't want to spoil it for you."

*   *   *

Hantilia was only wrong about one thing. She'd imagined the spell as a weaving, but in fact there was no object of any kind in Safar's mind. He was concentrating solely on the image of a person—Methydia.

As the circus continued—one act of amazement followed by another—Safar watched and worked from the sidelines. He was disguised as one of the roustabouts hauling equipment and cables around during scene changes. As each performance reached its climax he lofted a spell on the applause that followed. In a way they were love missives to Methydia. Safar imagined her in the Afterlife—still the great diva—smiling through tears at all the adulation.

The idea for the spell was drawn from Asper. Long ago the demon sage had written:

> *"My love, Remember!*
> *If ever I am exiled from your sight,*
> *Know that with my dying breath*
> *I blew one last kiss and set*
> *It free on love's sighing winds . . ."*
> *To the place where Life and Death*
> *And things that never meet*
> *Are destined to unite."*

Safar had often wondered what had caused Asper to write such a song. Who was the object of this great love affair? What was the tragedy that had ended it? Had Asper ever cast the spell buried in the verse? It seemed to Safar there wasn't enough strength in the spell to achieve Asper's goal. Had the old master wizard used some sort of mass gathering to cast it like Safar was doing with the circus? If so, what had been the result?

He saw Leiria waiting in the wings. She was mounted on a fine horse, every inch the warrior ready to do battle—except for her face which was flushed with excitement. And possibly just a little fear. Safar thought, now, isn't it strange? If Leiria were risking her own life, instead of just an audience's scorn, there would not be one mark of emotion upon her face.

Safar conjured a spell of confidence and whispered it in her direction. Then he hurled a light bomb signaling the grand finale and rushed away under cover of its crowd—dazzling glare to join his friends.

Trumpets blared and Leiria charged into the ring, smoke and light bombs bursting all around. The audience cheered wildly when they saw the standard she was bearing—a blue lake framed by cloud-capped mountains. It was the flag of Kyrania, streaming bravely as she raced about the ring.

She was enjoying herself thoroughly, now that the stage fright was gone. The change had occurred so quickly she was sure Safar had something to do with it. One moment she'd been ready to humiliate herself by spewing her guts, then the sick feeling was gone and she was burning with eagerness to show off to the crowd. Except when she'd dressed up as a clown, Leiria had been miserable, fearing at any minute she'd make a fool of herself, ruining the performance and therefore the spell. For some reason, when she was disguised as a clown it didn't seem to matter. Any clumsiness only added to the fun. Soon, even that respite faded, as the moment approached when she would take center ring and lead off the grand finale. The closer it came, the more terrified she became. When she spoke her voice came in a croak and she had to keep a firm grip on her horse's reins to keep her hands from shaking.

Now her nerves were running with a joyful fire and she laughed, sweeping off her helmet and letting her long hair stream out behind her like the flag itself. The Kyranians cheered and stomped their approval—chopped off by the crack of magical lightning. Leiria, playing her part, suddenly reined in her horse. It reared back on its hind legs and another magical lighting bolt blasted into the ground just before it. The horse trumpeted, pawing madly, nearly throwing Leiria from its back.

Caught up in the drama, the crowd shouted a warning, pointing into the sky where thick black clouds had gathered just above the arena. But it was too late, as six figures with faces like snarling beasts swept out of the clouds, swinging down on trapeze bars to within a few feet from her, then letting go—turning once in the air—and landing like cats, instantly crouching, ready to pounce with their gleaming scimitars.

They charged and the crowd groaned as Leiria was forced to drop the banner to draw her sword and defend herself. Steel clashed in time to wild music as Leiria battled the beastmen. One of the black cloaked figures—short, but massive in girth—grabbed up the banner, roaring through his bear's mask. He displayed the flag to the audience, who hissed and booed and shouted threats as he waved the banner back and forth in victory. And, indeed, for a long, agonizing moment all seemed lost as the beastmen encircled Leiria, coming at her from every side. Magical lightning blasting in front of her each time she threatened to break free.

High above, obscured by the black cloud, Palimak peered anxiously through the gaps at the action going on below. Dressed in his soldier's costume, he was standing on a platform, anxiously awaiting his turn. Safar was beside him, snapping a safety wire to his belt.

"I wish I didn't have to wear that, father," Palimak said. "It doesn't look right!"

Safar chuckled. "You're sounding like a star already," he said. "Don't worry. No one will see it. They'll be too busy following the action."

Palimak giggled. "More smoke and mirrors, father?"

"That's right, son. More smoke and mirrors. With a hefty dose of magic—applied frequently and liberally."

Safar rubbed the boy's shoulders. "Relax. You still have a little time before you get your cue."

Palimak licked his lips and nodded. Then, "Do you think she'll come, father?"

"I don't know. I hope so."

The boy became suddenly shy, ducking his head and mumbling. "Did you . . . you know . . . love her very much?"

"Yes, I did."

His voice dropped lower. "More than . . . well . . . you know . . . my mother."

"Nerisa?"

"Yes."

Safar shook his head. "I can't say," he replied. "I don't know any way to measure such a thing. I hope to never find one."

Palimak relaxed, smiling. "That's good," he said. "Thanks, father." Vague as Safar's answer was, it satisfied him. Now he could turn his full attention on the job ahead.

He patted the stone turtle in his pocket, alerting the Favorites. His father gave him a hug, saying, "It's time, son. Break a leg!"

Palimak laughed, feeling warm all over—because he was now part of the family of entertainers who knew this really meant extra special good luck. You weren't actually supposed to get your leg broken, which the boy thought was a wonderful joke.

Then Safar jerked a chain that shut off the flue of the smoke generator bolted to the top of the pole some seven feet above them. He jerked another chain, which operated a spark machine bolted just below the generator. Sparks showered through the widening gap in the cloud.

"Go!" Safar shouted, casting a spell that formed the sparks into a lighting bolt that crashed into the ground below.

Heart hammering, Palimak stepped out on the cable, which sloped to a lower platform some fifty feet away. He whispered to the Favorites, "Better get to work!"

Then he let go and slid down the wire, shouting a shrill war cry.

Safar was right, no one noticed the wires when he made his entrance. All they saw was a brave little figure in golden armor—a bow clutched in one hand—flying out of the clouds—shouting defiance at the beastmen, who had all but toppled Leiria from her horse.

When he reached the platform, he quickly drew a golden arrow from the quiver on his back, fixed it into his bow and posed his best and boldest pose—which he'd rehearsed for hours.

Palimak fired and the arrow sped toward the beastmen. It struck near the massive leader, who was still displaying the standard of Kyrania. Smoke exploded and the beastmen shrieked in anger, whirling to face Palimak. The boy fired again and this time the chieftain dropped the banner in his scramble to get away from the exploding smoke.

The tide was turned and the crowd roared in delight as Leiria recovered and attacked from the rear, knocking beastmen aside, then leaning down in an amazing feat of horsemanship and scooping up the fallen banner.

The crowd went insane, cheering their heroes on. But Safar wasn't done with them yet. Another lightning blast rocked the arena and a frightening figure dropped out of the sky. It was Arlain, dressed like an assassin in form-fitting black with a gold sash about her waist, breathing long tongues of fire at the scene below.

The Kyranians screamed warnings to their heroes but the assassin was too quick, snatching Palimak from the platform and swinging away with the boy clutched in her arms.

She dropped to the ground and held the boy high for all to see.

"Help!" Palimak shrieked. "Help me!"

Leiria saw his plight and spurred her horse forward, but Arlain froze her with a shout:

"Surrender! Or the boy dies!"

Leiria sagged, sword dropping, bowing to the inevitable.

And that's when Safar struck! A huge blast shook the arena, raising a huge bank of smoke swirling with every color. Khysmet came charging out of the smoke, horse armor picking up the colors and shattering them toward the beastmen. Another blast rocked the heavens and a great black hole opened like a gate in the cloud above. Safar, dressed in gleaming white armor and carrying a white shield emblazoned with the snake-headed sign of Asper, soared out of the cloud, roaring:

"FOR KYRANIA!"

A wire so slender it was invisible to the audience carried him down to meet Khysmet, who was circling the arena, taking his measure of the beastmen. Sparks showered out and at the same time Safar punched the release lever on his belt and dropped into Khysmet's saddle as smoothly as if he had vaulted from a sturdy fence.

And then came the organized chaos of what Biner called "The Big TBF, my lad!" Meaning, The Big Finish. It was fast, it was furious, but also quite stylized and elegant. There was none of the fake gore favored by other circus troupes. Methydia would have never permitted such a thing. "People have troubles enough," she always said, "without being reminded of the terrible things that are done. Give it art. Give it drama. Give them a little sex, a little comedy, a clown chase. And then a nice bit of action, with a happy ending that will send them all home to sweeter dreams than they had before the circus came."

So that's what Safar did. He gave the Kyranians lots of action, but with no hidden pig's bladder of blood bursting when a sword stroke was made. The battle was one of daring acrobatics and high drama, with many illusions—some circus trickery, some magical spells cast by Safar—to tell the tale. In the end, Palimak was rescued. The three heroes regrouped. The villains were driven off. And the standard retrieved.

On horseback now, Safar, Palimak and Leiria turned to the crowd and in a flourish of trumpets announced victory over the forces of evil. Leiria waving the flag of Kyrania as fireworks shattered the black clouds away and the bright sun and sweet breezes swept through the arena again.

Any cheering that had gone before was nothing to what happened now. There were whistles and screams and shouts, hands imploding, feet stomping so hard the stands swayed and creaked. Then they all poured out of their seats and into the arena, surrounding the whole circus troupe which had come out to take its bows.

Someone shouted, "For Kyrania!"

And they all took it up as a chant—all thousand of them. Refugees, torn from a sweet land, standing in the center of the Hells, shouting:

"KYRANIA! KYRANIA! KYRANIA!"

Safar let the emotion carry him until it reached its highest point. The others must have felt it too. Leiria gave his hand a squeeze and Palimak whispered, "I'm ready, father."

A gesture from Safar brought the little airship sailing out of nothingness to soar above the arena. The crowd, as if sensing something, was suddenly silent, staring up at the magical airship. Safar cast the final spell, letting it ride up and up, like a trapeze racing to its apex.

He imagined Methydia. Her smoky almond eyes. Long black tresses streaked with silver. Cheeks bones dramatically high. Fruited lips parted in a smile. First he chanted the Balloonist's Prayer. The one Methydia had chanted every eve and every dawn:

> "Come to us Mother Wind.
> Lift us in hands blessed
> By the warm sun.
> We have flown high.
> We have flown well.
> Take us in your arms, Mother Wind.
> And when you are done,
> Set us gently on the ground."

Then he sang the words to Asper's poem:

> "My love, Remember!
> If ever I am exiled from your sight,
> Know that with my dying breath
> I blew one last kiss and set
> It free on love's sighing winds . . ."

He heard Palimak whisper/singing with him and smiled. Then the circus troupe and the crowd joined in, singing:

" . . . free on love's sighing winds
To the place where Life and Death
And things that never meet
Are destined to unite."

She came in a gentle wind off the river, at first nothing more than a gray wisp of fog. But it was a fog heavy with the scent of violets and soon it grew and took form. A face gradually emerging.

Safar sucked in his breath.

It was Methydia.

And she called, "Sa-fahrr."

The voice came from everywhere, but at the same time it seemed right next to his ear, saying, "Sa-fahrr . . . Sa-fahrr." Each like a long sigh.

And Safar said to the ghost, "I'm here, Methydia."

She saw him and smiled, nodding, "Safar. I see you, Safar."

He was nearly overwhelmed by the ghostly presence, her perfume and haunting voice unhinging him from his moorings. Then he saw the ghost frown—sad . . . disappointed.

Safar remembered. "Thank you for the gift, Methydia," he said. Then he held out empty hands, saying, "But I have nothing so grand for you, my love. I have only this . . ."

And he blew her the promised kiss.

He heard Methydia's deep-throated laugh of pleasure. Saw her ghost reach up with a wispy hand to mock catch his kiss. She held the closed fist to her lips—kissed it. Then opened her hand and blew . . .

Her ghostly kiss came on a heady breeze and Safar drank it in, sighing, nearly drunk with the wine sweetness of it.

Then the ghost said, "Farewell, Safar. Farewell."

And Methydia was gone.

Instead, yawning over their heads as large as any galley that sailed the Great Sea, was the airship. Transformed to full size by Methydia's ghostly kiss. The breeze singing in its lines, magical bellows pumping, fire gouting, twin balloons swollen and straining to sail away.

The Kyranians were overawed by the miracle. First there was a murmur. Then a low mutter of amazement. Then the mutter became a shouted chorus of:

"Kyrania! Kyrania!"

Biner pushed through the crowd to Safar. "By the gods," he cried, slapping him on the back so hard he was nearly bowled over. "We're ridin' the winds again, lad," he cried. "Ridin' the winds."

*   *   *

Queen Hantilia smiled through tears. "That was quite touching," she said, wiping her eyes.

She looked away from the scene in her mirror where the Kyranians, led by Safar, rejoiced. "I'm such an emotional creature," she said to her assistant. "My heart strings have always been plucked too easily."

"I must say, Majesty," the assistant said, "that the airship was quite a surprise. I never expected Lord Timura to do such a thing."

"He does have an amazing way of working his magic," the Queen replied. "Most of us mages just want to get the spell over with—and do the minimum required. In this case, the minimum would never have worked. Ghosts aren't easy to summon. And this Methydia was apparently a great witch—and those kinds of ghosts are hardest of all to deal with. Actually, I'm not sure anyone has ever managed what he just accomplished."

"Surely, the great Lord Asper, Majesty?" the assistant protested.

Hantilia rubbed her brow, thinking. Then she murmured, "Possibly. Just possibly." She looked at her puzzled assistant. "I'm only guessing," she said, "but part of that spell did have the ring of Asper to it."

"Pardon, Majesty," the assistant said, "but a little while ago you said that Lord Timura was attempting to accomplish three things. But you only named two. What, pray, was the third?"

The Queen gestured at the mirror, where Palimak was sitting astride Safar's shoulders, waving to the cheering crowd.

"The boy," she said. "The spell you just witnessed was a dress rehearsal for something much, much bigger. And the only way he can do it is with the boy."

The Queen sighed. "Another sad little tale in the making," she said.

She waved a claw at the mirror and the scene disappeared. "Send for Lord Timura," she commanded.

"It's time for the Great Sacrifice to begin!"

*　　　　*　　　　*

The Queen's messenger came and went and Safar retired to his tent with Palimak to get ready. They dressed in comfortable clothes—trousers, tunics, cloaks and boots—as if they faced a long journey, instead of just a short stroll to the Queen's palace.

They both carried small packs filled with magical devices and potions, as well several purses of various things hanging from their belts. Besides this, Safar had his silver dagger tucked into his sleeve and Palimak had the stone turtle containing Gundara and Gundaree tucked safely away in a large pocket inside his tunic. For weapons, Safar made sure they both had bows and a quiver of arrows. Palimak's bow was the one he'd used in the circus act, which Safar deemed more than sufficient to do the job.

As for swords, however, Safar made a little ceremony out of giving Palimak a steel blade that been especially cut down for him, as well as a knife to balance out his belt.

Palimak straightened, a few more years of added maturity furrowing his youthful brow.

Safar stood back to admire the figure he cut. "With you at my side, son," he said, "they don't stand a chance."

Palimak chortled with delight, eyes turning demon yellow with excitement. "Let's go get them!" he said.

With that they exited the tent to say their farewells.

The Timura family waited outside. Leiria stood a little away from them, holding Khysmet's reins, saddle bags packed and ready.

Safar's mother and sisters and female cousins fussed over them, weeping all the while, while his sisters' husbands slapped them both on their backs and wished them "gods speed."

When they came to his father, Khadji knelt and embraced the boy, saying, "I'll show you some new pottery tricks when you get back." As always, Safar's father had difficulty saying what he really meant.

Palimak patted him and said, "I can hardly wait, grandfather." Trying to sound really excited about the promise and that the shining adventures he believed awaited him would be boring delays for when that moment came.

Khadji nodded, then rose to face his son. He was frowning, a little ashamed. "I guess I haven't been much help to you these last few days, son," he said.

"It was a spell, father," Safar assured him. "Nothing to do with you. There's no fault."

"Still," his father said, "I'm not happy with myself." He straightened, looking at Safar squarely. "It won't happen again."

Safar covered a confusion of emotions by giving his father a bear hug, slapping his back and telling him everything was going to be "fine, just fine."

Then they pulled apart. Safar's father seemed about to say something—lips opening, a clot of words gathering to be blurted. The moment passed and he shook his head.

"Tell the Oracle she'd better treat you right, son," he said. "Or she'll have another Timura to deal with!"

"I will, father," he said.

Safar took Palimak's hand and they turned and walked to where Leiria waited with Khysmet.

"Biner and Arlain send their apologies," she said. "They're busy rigging out the airship and loading up the gear."

"Make sure they take those packs I set aside for them," Safar said.

"They were loaded first," Leiria replied. "I watched them do it myself."

In the distance they heard Sergeant Dario curse the laziness of an errant soldier. Safar smiled.

"Sounds like you have everything else in order, too," he said.

"Dario and I are being extra hard on everyone," she laughed. "We both figure they had their fun in Happy Land. Now it's time to whip out the rest of the softness in them."

"After all these months," Safar said, "I can't think of anyone who's still soft."

"Neither can I," Leiria grinned, "but you tell that to Dario! He thinks everybody's too soft. I swear, when he dies they'll make a special rank for him in the Hells. Tormentor in chief, or something."

The two of them laughed. Palimak joined in, although a little weakly since he wasn't quite sure what they were laughing at. From what he'd seen of Dario he deserved the title, so where was the joke? There were some drawbacks to getting older and Dario, he'd decided, was definitely one of them. He shuddered when he thought of the day he'd join the older lads in training under Dario's baleful eyes and snarled insults and orders.

He snapped his fingers, saying, "I'm not worried about this Oracle at all!"

Safar and Leiria stared down at him. "What did you say?"

Palimak blushed, realizing he'd spoken aloud. He shrugged and gave the child's universal answer: "Nothing."

Leiria gave him a hug. "No matter what happens," she said, "I want you to remember Auntie Leiria's First Rule of Soldiering—When In Doubt, Find A Big Rock To Hide Under."

More laughter, final good-byes, and Safar swung into Khysmet's saddle. He hoisted Palimak up behind him, blew Leiria a kiss and wheeled the horse to trot away.

Leiria stared after them, wondering if she'd ever see them again.

CHAPTER TWENTY FIVE
COVENANT OF DEATH

There was not a soul to be seen as Safar and Palimak rode toward the city. The fields were empty, the farm house chimneys cold.

When they came to the gates there was no one to greet them, much less challenge them, and when they entered the city it seemed more like a great mausoleum, with only ghosts to watch as they passed by shuttered windows and closed doors.

"Where is everybody, father?" Palimak asked, unconsciously whispering.

"I don't know," Safar said.

Then they heard faint music and even fainter voices lifted in song. The sound was coming from Hantilia's silver palace.

Safar nodded toward the sound. "I expect we'll have our answer soon enough."

He tapped Khysmet's reins and the horse turned toward the palace, hooves clip-clopping in eerie time with the song.

They paused at the open palace gates. Inside were hundreds upon hundreds of red-robed Caluzians—so many the Queen's grand courtyard was filled to the overflowing. Her acolytes made a great circle many beings deep and in the center was Hantilia—most regal in her Asper robes and golden crown perched above her demon's horn. She was sitting upon a glorious throne made of ivory studded with many colorful gems. It had a sweeping back rising to form the symbol of Asper—the two-headed snake, wings spread wide as if ready to strike.

Hantilia sat calmly, a beatific smile on her face, as her subjects sang:

> *"It is our fault, it is our fault,*
> *Sweet Lady, Lady, Lady.*
> *We take the sin, we take the sin,*
> *Holy One.*
> *On our souls, on our souls,*
> *Sweet Lady, Lady, Lady.*
> *No one else, no one else,*
> *Holy One.*
> *It is our fault, it is our fault,*
> *Sweet Lady, Lady, Lady . . ."*

It was a haunting chant that stirred deep emotions in Safar, although at first he didn't know why it should hold any meaning for him. Then he remembered the vision in Asper's tomb where Queen Charize had reigned over a nest of blind monsters. Charize had claimed to be the protector of the master wizard's bones.

Harsh-voiced memory recalled the monster queen's song:

> *"We are the sisters of Asper,*
> *Sweet Lady, Lady, Lady.*
> *We guard his tomb, we guard his tomb,*
> *Holy One . . ."*

Safar stared hard at Queen Hantilia, all his magical senses alert for the lie behind her subject's song. But there was none to be found.

Gripping the saddle, Palimak leaned back as far as he could to see around his father's bulk. The sweet voices of the great choir made him feel sorry for Hantilia's people. He didn't know why the chant should make him feel that way. It just did.

He listened as the chant continued its circuitous quest:

> *"It is our fault, it is our fault,*
> *Sweet Lady, Lady, Lady.*
> *We take the sin, we take the sin,*
> *Holy One.*
> *On our souls, on our souls,*
> *Sweet Lady, Lady, Lady.*
> *No one else, no one else,*
> *Holy One.*
> *It is our fault, it is our fault,*
> *Sweet Lady, Lady, Lady . . ."*

Then Queen Hantilia saw them and her smile broadened. She gestured with a crystal-topped scepter and the acolytes' voices faded to a whispered, *"It is our fault, it is our fault . . ."* on and on without stop.

Hantilia gestured again and the crowd parted to make a long avenue leading to her throne. Safar noticed there were crushed flower petals strewn over the path, scenting the air with their sunny corpses. He slipped off Khysmet and hitched Palimak forward into the saddle, then he took up the reins and led horse and boy down the flower-strewn avenue to meet the Queen,

When he reached the steps leading up to the throne he stopped and bowed low, tugging at Khysmet's reins, who dipped like a veteran parade horse. Palimak surprised himself by instinctively going with the current and he made his own pretty bow from the saddle.

Hantilia applauded, saying, "My! What manners! You must have been an elegant sight at Iraj Protarus' court, Safar Timura!"

She nodded at her whisper/singing acolytes. "I wish you had time to teach them what *real* manners are," she said. "Unfortunately, my court has always been so small and unimportant that my subjects never received much practice."

Safar made a small bow, but said nothing. It was the sort of royal statement wanting no comment. Hantilia was merely setting him at ease and it would be the height of rudeness—an implied insult to her people—to agree.

The Queen turned to Palimak who was not used to royalty at all and was a little frightened by this imperious being. Moreover, with Khysmet between him and the ground he was nearly at eye level with Hantilia and he had shyness to add to his fears for being such an obvious target of scrutiny.

The Queen said, "You *must* be Palimak. I've been looking forward to this meeting for quite some time." Her smile broadened. "For one so young," she said, "you cut quite a dashing figure on that horse."

Palimak just stared at her, blushing and feeling like a goggle-eyed, frozen-tongued babe. Her voice was warm and friendly, her manner seemed genuine. But the atmosphere had unnerved him—all those beings whisper/chanting, *" . . . We take the sin, we take the sin,/Holy One."* Except they stretched out the "Holy One" so it was "Hoo-llyy Won-ahh." With a long hum stretching the "ahh" even more so it all sounded like a funeral.

He felt a stir in his tunic pocket and Gundara piped up, using his magical voice that could be heard by no other. "Don't be stupid, Little Master. She's only a queen. And not a very important queen at that!"

"Our queen was much grander," Gundaree added. "Much, much grander."

"Even she had to get someone to wash her dirty underwear," Gundara said. "Just like any normal being."

"No one is so royal," Gundaree put in, "they don't need to change their underwear."

Palimak started to giggle, then came unstuck. He dipped his head, and in the manner of a courtier he touched fingertips to his brow, then his breast, saying, "Your Majesty is too kind!"

Delivered in his high boy's voice, feet dangling many inches from Khysmet's stirrups, his little speech stirred laughter in the Queen. She covered with a cough, so as not to embarrass the child.

"Fine manners seem to run in the family, My Lord," she said to Safar. "You raised him well."

"Thank you, Majesty," Safar murmured.

The Queen's attention was still fixed on Palimak so Safar said nothing more. The exchange between them gave him time to cast a few sniffing spells to see what Hantilia was up to. So far he'd had little success.

"It's a pity your mother couldn't see you now," she said to the boy. "She'd be very proud."

Once again Palimak's tongue froze. He gaped at her a moment, then managed to stammer, "Y-y-you kn-kn-knew my mother?"

"I believe so, my dear," Hantilia said, demon eyes glowing softly. "Although I can't be certain, the resemblance is amazing."

Safar forgot about his spells. He was as riveted as the child. Neither one noticed that the voices of the chanters had risen slightly. Singing, "*On our souls, on our souls/Sweet Lady, Lady, Lady.*"

And Palimak blurted—"My mother was human?" For some reason he'd always imagined his real mother was a demon.

The queen shook her head. "No, but even so, my dear, you are quite like her. Your eyes . . . the shape of your face . . . all very much the same. The more I look at you—even though she was pure demon—the more certain I become."

Hantilia leaned forward, examining him closer. She settled back in her throne. "Yes, I'm quite sure of it," she said. Then: "We called her Baalina."

"Baalina," Palimak said, rolling the name around, fixing it in his mind. "Baalina," he said again—but firmer. Then he looked at the Queen, expectant.

"She was the daughter of one of my royal attendants," Hantilia continued. "Everyone knew and admired Baalina. She was not only a great beauty, with many suitors for her hand, but she was also a very powerful and promising young sorceress."

She turned to Safar. "She was with us when the Oracle appeared and bade us to begin this journey." She sighed. "We had no experience with the road, you understand. Many of my people were lost during those early days. Including the Princess Baalina."

"Then you don't know what happened to her," Safar said. Although he was intensely curious—Baalina's talent for sorcery explained much about Palimak's extraordinary abilities—Safar asked the question more for his adopted son than for himself. The boy clearly wanted to know, but was afraid to ask.

"I can't say," Hantilia replied. "Although we heard several rumors. The most reliable was that she had been rescued by a young soldier. A human soldier. The story was that they fell in love. A child was conceived and born." She nodded at Palimak. "You, my dear." She frowned, trying to remember if there were any other details. Finally, she shook her head. "That's all I know."

"You mean, they could still be alive?" Palimak asked, voice trembling.

"No, my dear," Hantilia said, kindly as she could. "I don't mean that. All the tales I heard agreed on at least one thing—they died in some tragic incident. That, and the fact that the child was somehow rescued."

She smiled at Palimak, saying, "And now we know that's true, don't we, my dear?" Palimak nodded. To say more would have burst a dam of tears.

Safar eyed Hantilia. Why was she bringing this up now? Why hadn't she told him this tale before so he could break the news to Palimak gently, instead of possibly unnerving the boy on the very day when he needed all of his strength and concentration.

"We'll never be able to repay Your Majesty for this kindness," he said to the Queen. "My son has long wondered about the mystery of his birth. Now he knows for certain what all of the people who love him have guessed for many years. That his mother was the kindest and sweetest of beings. A princess admired by all."

Then, to Palimak, "Maybe when we get back from seeing the Oracle you can have a longer visit with the Queen and she can tell you more."

Hantilia gazed at the two. It was a touching scene—father comforting son as best he could under the most trying of circumstances. She sensed Safar was suspicious of her motives. She was sorry for that. She wished she could tell him that all she'd done and said had been either ordained or commanded. But she couldn't.

Meanwhile, the boy was looking at her expectantly. And so the Queen said, "Your father's right, my dear. We can have a nice long chat when you return. And that's a promise."

*   *   *

At that moment the first of Iraj's scouts reached the entrance to the Caluzian Pass. There were six of them, all demons, and all hand-picked for their magical skills as well as for their tracking abilities.

Like Dario and Leiria they instantly saw the danger of ambush. They could also sense the strong magic emanating from somewhere deep within the bowels of the passage. This time, however, instead of the spell of humor and giddy well-being that had greeted the Kyranians, a tremendous sense of dread and certain doom radiated out at them. The spell was so strong it leaked through the shields Fari and his wizards had cast to protect them.

Shivering and gnashing their fangs in fear, the scouts drew back until they were out of range. They regrouped, repaired their shields and considered. Courage regained, several of the younger scouts wanted to continue on. Huge rewards had been offered to the first scouts who picked up the trail of Safar and the Kyranians.

Their leader, however, was a scarred veteran of similar encounters when golden bounties had outweighed common sense.

"All the gold in Esmir," he said, "won't buy us a drink in the taverns of the Hells. Let some other fiend get rich, if he dares."

With that, he unsaddled his mount and settled down to wait for the rest of the army to catch up. He broke out a package of rations and started to eat, calmly ignoring the others who were heatedly debating the pros and cons.

In the end, rare common sense prevailed over greed. Grumbling about missed opportunities, they followed his example.

Deep within the passage hollow eyes peered out at the scouts. Pale lips parted in a ghastly smile of anticipation at all the blood that would soon flow.

Then the Guardian warrior lifted his spectral horn and blew.

Hantilia shivered. The warning was for her ears only and so no one else heard the Guardian trumpeting news of Iraj Protarus' approach. The Queen signaled her assistant, who was posted at the far end of the courtyard. Then she turned to Safar and Palimak, hiding her concern with a broad smile.

"It is time, my dear ones," she said "for us to bid you farewell."

Despite her efforts to hide it, Palimak caught the eddy of magic emanating from the Queen as she gathered her powers.

At the same moment Gundara whispered a warning, "Watch out, Little Master. Something's going to happen!"

Khysmet shifted under him, snorting and swishing his tail. Alarmed, Palimak glanced at his father, who gave him a slight nod—he'd noticed too. The boy felt something soft fall over him as Safar cast a shielding spell to protect them from betrayal. Nerves tingling, the boy glanced over at the Queen. The flame in her eyes burned brighter. Whether there was good or evil there, he couldn't say.

Then the acolytes lifted their voices higher, singing, " . . .*It is our fault, it is our fault,/Sweet Lady, Lady, Lady . . .*"

And Hantilia intoned, "In the name of the Mother of us all, I command the Way be opened!"

She gestured and the far wall of the courtyard dissolved before their eyes. Beyond was a flower-lined pathway leading down a graceful hill to where the two rivers met. And where the Temple of Hadin waited.

The Queen pointed a long claw at the temple. "Go!" she commanded. "The Oracle awaits!"

Safar didn't hesitate. It was too late in the game for doubts, or for second-guessing Hantilia's motives. He grabbed the reins and swung into the saddle behind Palimak.

He saluted the Queen. "Until we meet again, Majesty," he said.

Hantilia smiled at him and he saw tears gathering in her eyes. "Yes, Safar Timura," she said, forcing one last lie. "Until we meet again."

Safar flipped the reins and Khysmet started forward—the chanting crowd parting to let them through. He felt Palimak shudder.

"Are you sure you want to do this, son?" He whispered. "Say the word and we'll turn back now."

Palimak shook his head. "I'm not afraid for us, father," he said. "Just for them."

From her throne Queen Hantilia watched Safar and Palimak ride toward the gateway—and the flowered path beyond. Unlike Leiria, she didn't have to stop and wonder if she'd ever see them again. She knew better. The Oracle had been quite clear on this subject from the very beginning.

They reached the gate and Khysmet hesitated a moment, then pressed forward. The air shimmered and there was a faint pop! like a bubble bursting, and then the horse and its riders were gone. But she could still hear the clip, clop of Khysmet's hooves on the seemingly empty pathway.

The Queen gestured and the gateway closed. She turned to her red-robed acolytes.

"Let the Great Sacrifice begin," she commanded.

Their voices rose in a loud chorus and she joined them in song:

> *"It is our fault, it is our fault,*
> *Sweet Lady, Lady, Lady.*
> *We take the sin, we take the sin,*

Holy One.
On our souls, on our souls,
Sweet Lady, Lady, Lady.
No one else, no one else,
Holy One.
It is our fault, it is our fault,
Sweet Lady, Lady, Lady . . ."

Behind her the snake of Asper stirred into life, two pairs of eyes glowing blood red. Tongues flickering out to taste the air.

*   *   *

In the Kyranian encampment everyone heard the singing and stopped what they were doing, turning toward the city to listen.

"What in the Hells are they up to?" Leiria said to the group gathered about the airship.

The ship, which was straining against the strong cables that kept it earthbound, was crowded with crates of equipment that Leiria, Biner and the others had already loaded.

The muscular dwarf scratched his head. "Singing, I guess," he said.

Arlain, who was passing up a crate to Kairo, snorted. "Of courth, they're thinging!" she said. "Anyone with ear'th on hith head can tell that! The quethtion ith, *why are they thinging?*"

"I hope Safar and Palimak are all right," Khadji said. "I still think we should have sent a good strong force along with them . . . just in case."

Leiria sighed. "Once Safar gets a plan set in mind," she said, "there's no moving him from his course."

"Maybe it still isn't too late," Khadji said. "I could get Dario to gather up a few soldiers and go investigate."

"You won't hear me arguin'," Biner said. "For all we know those Asper heads have finally dropped their sand bags and gone starkers. He could be surrounded by a whole slaverin' bunch of them for all we know."

Leiria shook her head. "Much as I'd like to," she said, "we'd best stick to what we all agreed on. Which is to get everybody ready to run like the winds when Safar gets back." She pointed at the airship. "Plus, get that thing off the ground and do a little snooping to see what Iraj is up to."

"I thuppoth you're right," Arlain said, starting to hand up another crate to Kairo. "If we thtray from the plan now, we might all be real thorry later."

"I still don't like it," Khadji said. He looked around at the others, but they'd all returned to work, lifting and stacking and stowing the gear.

"I wish I could say something to make you feel better," Leiria told him. "But anything I said would be a damned lie."

*   *   *

Safar heard the gates crash shut and suddenly he was enveloped in darkness. There was a blast of heat, the choking smell of sulfur and long tongues of flame snaked out to devour them. Khysmet whinnied in pain and alarm, but Safar tightened his grip on the reins to steady him, at the same time throwing his cloak over Palimak.

He dug in his knees and the great horse charged forward. There was a feeling of resistance, a thick, oily stickiness dragging at them—then they burst through and found themselves charging down a rocky path, the Demon Moon gibbering overhead. Wild spells rushing in from every side with hungry mouths to devour them.

They were in a nightmare reversal of Caluz—a barren valley with black rocks ripping through hard, blood-red dirt where gentle fields filled with fat grains and fruited orchards had once reigned. The flower-bordered pathway was now a ruined roadway filled with razor sharp pebbles and limb-threatening potholes.

Ahead loomed the huge stone turtle that was the Temple of Hadin, straddling two roiling streams of inky water—a veritable sewer of greasy liquid spouting from its beaked mouth.

Drawing on Palimak's powers, as well as his own, Safar hurled up a shield to protect them from the insane magic of the Black Lands. Then he chanced a quick look behind and saw a blasted ruin where the Queen's palace had once stood—columns of foul-smelling smoke rising from the rubble.

The ground heaved under them and Khysmet nearly lost his footing, hooves scrabbling on loosened rock. Safar threw his weight forward and the stallion broke through, hurling himself down the steep roadway toward the temple.

Palimak peered through the folds of Safar's cloak and saw the temple growing larger as they raced toward it.

Then from somewhere a great horn trumpeted and suddenly the temple seemed to retreat.

He heard his father urge Khysmet on and he felt the stallion strain with effort for still more speed. But the faster he ran, the farther away the temple seemed to be. Retreating across the valley—rivers and all—until it was a mere pinpoint lying against the black mountains forming the most distant wall of the valley.

"It's a trick, Little Master!" Gundara squeaked from his pocket.

"To the right! Go to the right!" Gundaree urged.

Palimak nudged his father. "That way, father!" he shouted, pointing to the right of the distant temple.

Instantly, Safar veered Khysmet off the path and down a boulder-strewn slope. Now they were heading across the valley floor—appearing to angle away from the temple. They had gone no more than a few yards when the landscape shifted and once again they were closing on the huge stone turtle.

On either side of them the ground erupted like boils bursting and hot, oily liquid spewed out, flowing across their path.

Safar pressed his knees into Khysmet's sides and the stallion gathered himself like a giant spring, then leaped across the smoking streams. He landed with barely a jolt and sped onward.

Huge gray boulders hunched up in their path. Khysmet gathered himself to leap, then reared back as the boulders came alive. Rising up on saw-toothed insect legs—vicious heads beetling out from under the gray shells, pincer jaws scissoring wide.

Safar drew his sword, hacking at the nearest. There was a terrible shriek as he cut into the creature, splitting its shell. Khysmet trumpeted defiance, striking out with his front legs, crushing the attacking insect with his hard hooves.

Palimak struggled to free his own small weapon, but as it came out of its sheath a nightmare face reared up and mighty jaws snatched the sword from his hand. Safar slashed and Palimak heard another shriek, then the creature was gone.

He had time to see several other giant insects fall on their wounded brothers, tearing hungrily at the shells to get at the flesh beneath.

Khysmet carried them out of the bloody chaos and they were free, racing toward the temple—now only a few hundred yards away.

Just then the ground opened up under them and they were falling, Khysmet shrilling in fear and flailing his legs.

Below a huge mouth yawned wide and a long tongue lined with fangs shot out to take them.

*   *   *

In Hantilia's courtyard, the Queen came to her feet, throwing her hands high to beseech the heavens.

"Dear Mother!" she cried over the chanting acolytes. "Two innocents seek your counsel. Two innocents whose presence you commanded."

Behind her, the twin-headed snake of Asper reared up from her throne, wings spreading like a cobra's hood, venom dripping from its fangs.

And the Queen intoned, "Know them, Mother! Spare them! Keep them safe! Remember our bargain, dear lady.

"Take us in their stead!"

Hantilia stared up at the heavens, waiting. Arms spread wide to embrace her fate—and the fate of her followers. For the first time in many years she felt at peace. Her mission was done. What would be, would be.

Then lightning blasted from the skies. She felt a terrible, searing pain.

And all was darkness.

And all was peace.

*   *   *

Leiria was thrown from her feet by the force of the blast. She hit the ground hard, breath knocked out of her. She heard people cry out—some in fear, some calling to others to ask if they were all right.

Then she could breathe again, gulping in all the air her lungs would hold. Awareness returned and the first she noticed was that the air tasted like blood—as if she were suddenly transported to a gigantic meat market, with aisle upon aisle of freshly skinned animal corpses hanging from hooks.

She groaned to her feet, ears ringing from the blast, looking around the encampment with dazed eyes, expecting the worst. To her amazement no one appeared hurt. Like her, people were climbing to their feet, patting themselves for signs of injury, or soothing crying children.

"By the gods who hate us," she heard Biner exclaim, "would you look at that!"

She turned to find him pointing at the city—or at the place where the city had once stood. Now it was nothing but a smoking ruin perched on a blasted hilltop. Only the Queen's palace still stood—towers oddly twisted and sagging.

Leiria heard someone moan and saw Khadji, who was staring at the ruins, tears streaming from his eyes.

"Safar!" he groaned. "Safar!"

Leiria felt as if her heart had been torn from her chest. She raced for a panicked horse, grabbed its loose reins and vaulted into the saddle—wrenching the poor beast's head around until it faced Caluz, then digging in her heels, spurring it forward. She was halfway up the hillside before anyone else had wits enough to follow.

Leiria was a soldier who had seen many horrors, but there was nothing in her experience to brace her for the devastation she witnessed in Caluz. Other than the palace, not one building was standing. Everything, including the strong walls encircling the city, had been reduced to waist-high piles of rubble as if a gigantic hand had flattened them. The streets were buckled, pavement hurled up in every direction, making it difficult for the horse to walk, much less gallop at the pace she'd originally demanded.

By the time she reached the palace several others, including Khadji, Biner and Sergeant Dario, had caught up with her. They all paused at the open gates, fearful to look inside. Leiria spurred her horse forward. It whinnied in fear, eyes rolling wildly, mouth frothing, fighting her so hard that she finally gave up and dismounted. The horse bolted away as soon as she dropped the reins. Leiria braced herself and walked through the gates.

At first it seemed a peaceful scene. Hundreds upon hundreds of red-robed figures were lying on the ground—limbs and clothing all neatly arranged as if they had fallen asleep. Raised on a platform in the center of the courtyard was the Queen's ornate throne, presided over by the carved Asper snake. Slumped at the foot of the throne was the still body of Hantilia.

"Dead!" she heard Dario growl. "Ever' blessed one of 'em."

Numb, Leiria stalked forward, stepping over the robed figures, until she came to the throne and mounted the steps. She looked down at Hantilia's corpse, feeling oddly removed, as if looking down from a great distance. The Queen's features were peaceful. Smiling.

"Where's Safar?" she heard Khadji demand. "And Palimak! Where's little Palimak?"

Leiria glanced around the courtyard, picking over body after body, heart hammering at her ribs, expecting at any moment to discover Safar lying among them.

"I don't see him," she mumbled. "Or Palimak, either." She kept looking, wits dull as old brass. "And the horse," she said. "Khysmet. There's no way you could miss him!"

Someone caught her arm and she looked around and found Khadji staring at her, eyes desperate.

"Where are they?" he demanded, acting as if she were cruelly withholding information.

"I don't know," she said.

Khadji gripped her arm harder. "Do you think they're dead?"

"I don't know that either," Leiria said.

*   *   *

One moment Safar and Palimak were falling toward a ghastly death and then there was a great clap of thunder and suddenly they were trotting along the rocky floor of a huge cave, dazzled by the sunlight streaming through the entrance. There was the sound of bursting waves and a shallow river of foamy water rushed into the cave, hissing around Khysmet's legs as he splashed toward the light.

The light broke across them as they exited the cave and they found themselves traversing a peaceful beach—a cool, salty breeze blowing, while overhead gulls wheeled in clear blue skies, crying for their supper.

Khysmet was the first to recover. He snorted in surprise, then shook his head in delight at still being alive and trotted through the foamy surf toward a distant spit of land jutting out into a rolling ocean.

Palimak came out of his shock, peering out at ocean. "Is this real, father?" he said, voice croaking in wonder. "Or are we still in the Black Lands?"

Safar laughed and gave him a hug. "What a son you are!" he exclaimed. "One minute we're facing certain death. The next, we appear to be safe. And the first words out of your mouth are—'is it *real*?'"

Palimak flushed happily at the compliment. But his eyes were drinking in the vision of the rolling seas and gently crashing waves. A child of the mountains, he'd never experienced the ocean before.

He shook himself—not unlike Khysmet. Still the vision of an endless rolling horizon persisted, beckoning to him, calling with the voice of the gulls.

Again he asked, "Is it real, father?"

Safar threw back his cloak to catch the fresh breezes. "Real as can be, son," he said.

Palimak sighed relief. Then he frowned. "But where are we, exactly?"

Safar studied their surroundings—the ocean was to their left and to the right was a vast range of green mountains hugging the coastline. He mentally correlated what he could see with his memory of the maps Coralean had given them.

He pointed south at the mountains. Two peaks commanded the center of the range. "As near as I can tell," he said, "Caluz—and the Black Lands—are beyond those peaks." He nodded at the vast ocean to their left. "And that's the Great Sea," he added. "It could be nothing else. Near as I can tell, some magical way has been opened between Caluz and the sea."

The boy was only mildly surprised. He was still young enough so it didn't seem so strange that they'd been transported hundreds of miles.

He studied the vast oceanic distances for a moment, then said, "And Syrapis is somewhere out there?"

"Yes. I believe so."

"But it must be very far. How do we get there?"

"The same way we got here, son," Safar answered. "Magic."

Although his manner was sanguine, Safar was just as surprised as the boy. From the very beginning, he hadn't been sure what to expect. Even if he had let his imagination run free, he would never have dreamed such a thing could happen. He peered ahead, studying the small peninsula they were heading toward. A powerful wave of sorcery was emanating from that direction, pulling at them—urging them onward.

Safar was certain that the Oracle was waiting for them there.

Then Khysmet perked up his ears. He whinnied and quickened his pace. Up ahead, riding off the land spit, was a sight that made Safar's heart jump—a glorious woman with long ebony limbs and flowing hair trotted toward them on a spirited black mare.

The woman waved at them. Her laughter was sweet music floating on the ocean breezes and Safar forgot all caution.

"Do you know her, father?" Palimak asked.

"Yes," he answered, voice husky. "I know her."

Khysmet broke into a gallop and they skimmed across the sandy beach toward the woman.

Palimak felt a scratching in his pocket. Then Gundara spoke up: "Little Master! There's something you should know. I hate to contradict Lord Timura, but everything he's said about this place is wrong!"

"None of this is real, Little Master." Gundaree added. "Can't you feel it? We're inside the machine! And Lord Timura doesn't know it!"

At that moment the light suddenly dimmed and a freezing wind blasted off the seas.

And it began to snow.

Part Four

Spellbound

CHAPTER TWENTY SIX
IRAJ AND THE UNHOLY THREE

The first attempts on Caluz were a disaster.

Iraj sent one hundred hand-picked men and demons into the pass and not one returned. He sent a hundred more, setting up a throne post at the entrance—guarded by his toughest and most loyal troops—so he could closely observe everything that happened.

He saw nothing, but he heard more than enough to ice even his shape-changer's veins. There were trumpets and challenging shouts, the clash of weapons, screams from the wounded and a chorus of ghostly groans as his fighters breathed their last and shed their souls. Then all was silence.

There was movement at the mouth of the pass. Through narrowed eyes Iraj saw a lone figure stagger out. It was a man, bearing his weight on his spear, dragging the remains of a shattered shield behind him. It made Iraj glad the sole survivor was human. One of his own, as a matter of fact, from the make of his costume—spurred boots and baggy breeches, short bow over his shoulders, scimitar at his waist. An old soldier from Iraj's homeland on the Plains of Jaspar.

Iraj was deeply affected by the sight of the battered soldier. Old emotions, human emotions, emotions that had been long absent in his heart, surged into the light. First pity welled up, then homesickness, then guilt for allowing one of his own to be so mistreated. Iraj bolted from his throne and went to his kinsman, guards and servants scampering to keep up.

When he reached the soldier the man stopped, wavering, confused at having his way blocked. His eyes were wild, his face a bloody mask and when he finally noticed Iraj he shrieked and threw up his ruined shield to protect himself, spear point rising to counter-strike. Iraj jerked back, easily avoiding the spear. But then all his speed was called for as his guards leaped in to kill the man for daring to threaten the king. Iraj sent two big demons sprawling from the force of his blow.

"Hold!" he shouted, freezing the others in place. His retine goggled at him, desperately trying to decipher the king's intent. He ignored them, turning back to the old plainsman.

"Pardon, Cousin," he said gently as he could, "but you seem to be without horse." Meaning, in the argot of Jaspar, that the man was in great difficulty.

"Monster!" the man shouted, stabbing at the air with his spear. "You took my horse but you won't take me!"

Iraj brushed the spear aside and grabbed the man by the shoulders. "What's wrong with you?" he barked. "Have you gone mad?"

Then he saw his own reflection in the man's eyes—a great gray wolf rearing up—and he knew the reason for the man's fear—why, he'd called his own kinsman "Monster!"

Iraj concentrated, making his form as human as possible, and the old soldier suddenly recognized him.

The man fell to his knees, babbling. "So sorry, Majesty! Didn't mean to . . . I must've been mad to think . . . But it was awful, Sire! Bloody, awful! Nothin' but ghosts in there, I tell you! Nothin' but ghosts. You can't get a hand on 'em, much less a good poke with your spear . . ."

The man broke down, tears making a bloody track on his face. He shook his head.

"I'm . . . I'm . . . I'm sorry, Majesty. I have failed you!"

Iraj was powerfully moved by the sight of one his most faithful and long-serving kinsmen brought so low. Then the man drew himself up—turning from shambling wreck to a proud old soldier.

"Give me the knife, Cousin," he demanded, plucking at Iraj's belt for the curved knife hanging there, "so I can end my shame!"

Iraj let him take it, but as the soldier shifted his grip to plunge the knife into his heart he stayed his hand.

"This isn't necessary, my friend," he said. "You are not at fault this day! No failure can be laid at your feet." Iraj thumped his chest. "It is your king's doing, Cousin," he said. "Blame no other."

The man sagged in relief and Iraj caught him, slipping the knife from his hands and returning it to its sheath. He steadied the soldier, turning him toward the great pavilion that housed his traveling court.

"Come," he said. "Let us eat and drink and boast of the deeds of our youth. And when you recover your horse, your strength, we can talk about what went on this day."

The two of them—Iraj nearly carrying his charge—moved toward the pavilion. Without being ordered, servants ran ahead to prepare an impromptu banquet for the king and his new companion.

Iraj paused at the entrance to speak with his aides. "Send for the Lords Fari and Luka," he ordered. "And that bastard Kalasariz, if you see him about. Probably hiding under some rock is my guess. Tell them their king wishes to speak to them immediately!"

The aides rushed off to do his bidding. Iraj looked down at the old soldier, who seemed to be recovering somewhat.

"What is your name, my friend?" he inquired. "What do the other men of Jaspar call you?"

"Vister, Majesty," the man replied. "Sergeant Vister at yer service!" He tried to draw himself up in salute and nearly toppled over.

Iraj steadied him. "Let's get a few drinks in you, Cousin Vister," he said, "before you try that again."

As they strode into the pavilion the first few flakes of snow began to fall. Then the flakes became a flurry and the skies turned pewter gray. The snow fell harder—flakes the size of small pillows drawing a blanket of white across the stark terrain. Even the Demon Moon became diminished—an orange grin peering through the gray. Soon the entire encampment was buried in snow and the soldiers were turned out to dig paths to the tented barracks and clear the main road.

Fari and Luka arrived at Protarus' headquarters but were denied entrance while the King supped with Vister. Finally Kalasariz arrived, shivering in the cold despite the thick fur cloak he wore. He was surprised when he saw the two demons cursing and stomping about in the snow.

"What's the difficulty?" he asked. "Is the King in one of his foul moods again?"

"Who can tell?" Luka grumbled, horned brow made pale green by frost. He snorted twin columns of steam in the frigid air. "Foul or fair, all his moods seem for the worst these days."

Fari gestured at the Caluzian Pass, where several of his demon wizards were huddled miserably by the entrance tending smoking pots of magical incense.

"From what I can gather," the old demon said, "all our efforts have been brought to a massive halt so our master could talk over old times with some lowly sergeant." He shrugged, miniature avalanches of snow cascading from his shoulders. "It's a pity, really. All this snow is a great help to us."

Kalasariz frowned, then realized how much better he'd felt since the snow started. No more constant battering of wild Black Lands spells.

"I thought perhaps you had come up with some new shield," he said to Fari.

The old demon snorted. "Who has had the time for such experiments?" he said. "No, it's the storm that's doing it. As near as I can tell the snow blocks—or possibly even blinds—the machine at Caluz."

"Which means the devils inside that pass," Luka broke in, "ought to be ripe for the plucking. It's my guess that one more attack ought to knock them loose."

Kalasariz cocked an eyebrow, amused. "I assume you've told the King this," he said.

Luka barked laughter. "No, my Lord," he said, making a mock bow. "We were waiting for you to bless us with your esteemed presence. You seem to be in the greatest favor with our Lord and Master these days. We thought you could tell him for us."

Kalasariz grinned. "And wouldn't that make me the prince of fools," he said. "Especially when I know for a fact that neither of you are sure who exactly is opposing us in that pass."

"I really must speak to you at length someday," Fari said, "on your spying methods. Not even the flies in the latrines escape your notice."

"That's true," Luka said. "Sometimes I think you can see up our arses."

"Now you've guessed my secret," Kalasariz joked. "The flies are in my employ."

All three of them laughed—forming a temporary bond in this rare moment of shared humor.

Fari was old enough and wise enough to recognize opportunity first. "Let's speak honestly for a change, my brothers," he said. "Or should I call us the Unholy Three." He chuckled. "I've heard that name for us bandied about in the ranks. Rumor has it that the King himself calls us that behind our backs. However, no matter the intent of the fellow who originally coined the term, I think it fits us all quite well."

"The Unholy Three," Kalasariz murmured. Then he smiled. "I like that. I think we should keep it."

Luka snorted. "Forget the game playing, my Lord," he said. "Call us what you will. But please . . . get to the point."

Fari was careful not to take offense. "Very well," he said. "I'll dispense with pleasantries and reach down for the final sum of our woes. In a few minutes the King will call us before him. How shall we advise him?"

"How *can* we advise him," Kalasariz said, "when we don't know what's happening in that pass?"

"We *do* know it isn't Safar Timura or his Kyranians who are killing our soldiers," Fari said. "All my castings at least show that."

"Then Timura must have an ally," Luka said. The careful tone of the others had made him feel awkward. Unpolished. Definitely not royal. So he tried to be as smooth and diplomatic as he could when he said—"I know that's so obvious it may make me seem foolish to say it. However, knowing such a thing and understanding what it means are not the same. For instance, the King believes Lord Timura chose Caluz for his destination because he wants to form an alliance with the Oracle of Hadin." He shrugged. "This could be true. However, I've never heard of an Oracle with an entire army at its disposal."

"All excellent points," Kalasariz said.

"Yes, yes, I agree," Fari said, impatient. "But we're all forgetting we have an actual eyewitness to what occurred in that pass." He pointed at the king's pavilion. "And right now he's in there with Protarus telling him the gods know what! So how can we, uh . . . *guide* our master—if you understand what I mean—if we don't know what is being said? Much less his reaction to it."

There was an uncomfortable silence as each being considered. Finally Kalasariz said, "Let me start. To begin with . . . might I be so bold as to propose a truce?"

The others considered. Brows furrowing. Weighing what this might entail. The first— and by far the largest—was trust, which slowed down the thinking considerably.

Kalasariz hastened to fill the gap. "Only a temporary truce, of course."

Fari's brows climbed in approval. "Ah!" he said. "That might work."

"Yes, yes, it might," Luka agreed. "Go on, please."

"Well, as Lord Fari so wisely pointed out a moment ago," Kalasariz said, "King Protarus will summon us soon. None of us can predict how he will behave. What he will do or say. Except we do know this—no matter what passes, he will demand an immediate response."

He paused, looking each demon in the eyes by turn. "True?"

Luka nodded. "True."

"I most fervently agree," Fari said.

"So, to protect ourselves," Kalasariz said, "wouldn't it be prudent to see what transpires before we act? Then instead of each fighting the other . . . we can examine the situation calmly . . . rationally . . . without fear of attack from our own ranks. Finally, when we speak we should speak with one voice. None of us trying to win the advantage as long as the truce lasts."

"I can see much value in that line of reasoning," Fari said.

"As long as we remember the truce is temporary," Luka added. "There's no sense pretending it could be anything but that."

"No, there isn't," Kalasariz said, "In fact, why don't we make the truce for the duration of our visit? In other words, when we leave the king's company the peace will end."

A harried aide rushed out of the pavilion. "King Protarus calls, my Lords," he said. "Hurry, if you please! He's in no mood to be kept waiting."

To the amazement of the aide the three burst into laughter as one.

Then Kalasariz said, "Well, my Lords. What is your thinking? Are we in agreement?"

Luka eyed the aide, who was shuffling about, wondering what was being said. "What about him?" Luka said, jabbing a talon at the aide.

Kalasariz smiled. "Don't worry," he said. "He's one of my flies."

More laughter.

Then Luka stretched out his right claw. "To the Unholy Three," he mock intoned.

Kalasariz and Fari caught the spirit. "To the Unholy Three," they chorused, layering hand and talon with his.

Then, chuckling and shaking their heads, they stomped the snow off their boots and went inside to see what was in store for them.

Iraj was waiting—lolling in his throne, booted legs supported on the naked back of a comely slave. He was completely at ease—frighteningly so for the Unholy Three. He was in his human form and they'd rarely seen him in such control. Only the red glow of his eyes gave him away.

Sitting to his right—on a smaller throne—was the soldier, Vister. He was wearing only a clean white loin cloth and was being tended by several pretty human and demon maids, who had just finished washing him and were now rubbing scented oil into his limbs. In one hand he had a silver flask of wine, from which he took frequent pulls. In the other, he clutched a thick sandwich of roasted lamb with several large ragged wounds in it.

Heaters had been brought in when the storm began and the throne room was uncomfortably hot. Sweat poured from the soldier's body, mixing with the oils and coating his heavily muscled torso with an heroic sheen. Vister's age and experience were apparent in the thatch of gray hair on his battle-scarred breast.

When the Unholy Three were announced, Vister's head wobbled up to blear at them through half-closed eyes. He was drunk, he was exhausted, he was wounded in body and soul. The maids had to keep at him constantly, bathing away blood and sweat, changing the bowls of scented water frequently as they became discolored and fouled.

At first he didn't recognize them and waved a drunken hand. "Come and join us, friends," he shouted. "Me and my cousin, the King here, are havin' a party!"

Under Protarus' glare, the Unholy Three chuckled kindly, covering their reaction at being addressed so rudely. In normal circumstances Vister would have been beheaded before he finished the first sentence of his greeting.

Then the old plainsman's eyes cleared and he realized who they all truly were. He choked on a mouthful of meat, the wine he'd just taken to wash it down dribbling from the corners of his mouth.

He pushed weakly at the maids and tried to come to his feet, sputtering apologies.

"Please, my dear fellow," Kalasariz said smoothly. "Don't trouble yourself." As much as this foul peasant's manners turned his stomach, under the circumstances he had to be treated with the utmost respect.

"Yes, yes," Fari came in. "Don't interrupt your meal, my friend. You must replenish your strength after such a trying day."

"We salute you, brother," was Luka's skillful addition, touching ringed talons to royal brow, "for all you have suffered in our service."

Still, Vister was clearly overcome. He fell to his knees, babbling, "Please, Masters. I am not worthy!"

His words snapped Iraj's crossbow trigger. The King leaped from his throne, roaring, "Never say master to ones such as these! You are a soldier from the Plains of Jaspar! Worthy of any company!"

He helped Vister back into his seat, casting foul looks at the Unholy Three as if they had tried to humiliate the old soldier. Making much of the gesture, Iraj personally fetched up the flask that had fallen from Vister's hands, feeding the wine to him as if he were a child.

"There, there," he said. "Rest easy, Cousin. Your brave toil is done. Only honors await you."

Vister gurgled down the wine, eyes glazing over. Finally he pushed the flask away, wiping his lips and belching. A bold, drunken grin spreading over his features. Iraj patted him and sat back, coldly observing the Unholy Three.

"Speak to them, kinsman mine," he said to Vister. "Tell them everything you told me. Explain to them in the simple, common logic of a plainsman what they have been doing wrong."

Vister belched loudly. Then he said, "They're killin' too many of us, that's what!"

Iraj sneered at Fari and the others. "Do you hear, my brothers?" he growled. "The answer is as plain as the frowns on your ugly faces—which I have grown to despise more with each passing day. By the gods, you're killing too many of my soldiers! And I won't stand for it. Everyone knows how much I love my soldiers. Demons as well as humans, they are more brother to me than any of you. And be damned to your Spell of Four!"

He gestured at Vister, whose attention was now totally fixed on human needs. He was staring at either hand, trying to decide what to do next—bite another hunk off the sandwich or slobber down more wine. In the end he did both, biting and drinking, biting and drinking. Crumbs and dribbles of wine splattered his lap—the maids giggling and fussing over the mess as if it were all a marvelous jest.

Iraj turned his full attention on the Unholy Three. "I told Sergeant Vister that I—Iraj Protarus, his kinsman, his king, was to blame," he said. "And this is true. I am not only king, but king of all kings in Esmir, so it is only right that final responsibility must rest on my shoulders."

He paused dramatically, throwing an arm around Vister's shoulder. "However . . . *This* . . ." Aand he dabbed at one of Vister's wounds with a napkin. "*. . . This* was never my intent! I have made it plain from the very beginning that I dislike having the lives of my soldiers shed needlessly."

"I assume you are speaking of the pass currently in dispute, Majesty?" Luka said.

"Of course I'm speaking of the pass!" Iraj roared, eyes turning to red coals. "What else what would I be talking about? We've lost two hundred of our best so far. And not an inch of gained ground to show for it!"

He patted Vister. "Instead we have won only pain and torment for those I value most."

Luka wanted to laugh. Protarus thought nothing of hurling a thousand demons and men to their doom—if it won him what he wanted. But now he was presenting the face of an innocent. Posing as a king who wished only the best for his subjects and required little for himself—except for their kind opinion of him.

Fari rapped his cane and Kalasariz coughed, bringing Luka back to reality. Just in time he realized his wolf's snout was about to break through.

To cover, Luka bowed low and thumped his breast abjectly, murmuring, " . . . a misunderstanding, Majesty. The fault is entirely my own."

When he'd regained control over his shape-changer's body, he straightened, saying, "Your words have given expression to the confusion of all our most worthy ideas, Majesty." He gestured at Fari and Kalasariz. "The three of us were only just discussing this most terrible of affairs. And we all agreed that we have failed you, Sire."

Fari broke in. "Except, perhaps I am more to blame then the others, Highness," he said. "After all, this is sorcery we are fighting in that pass. And things involving sorcery are *my* responsibility and no other."

"I beg to differ, my great and good king," Kalasariz said. "Lord Fari and his wizards have done their utmost. It is *I* who is most at fault for not discovering what we were up against before we sent men such as this . . ." he nodded respectfully at Vister, who grinned like a baby and burped— ". . . correction, heroes such as this . . . into battle."

"Some of what you say is true, my brothers," Luka said to Kalasariz and Fari. "But in the end, it is *I* who direct all special missions. I should have been at the forefront . . . leading both attacks. But I listened to my cowardly aides who claimed the King would be badly served if I were killed." The Prince shook his head. "I'll dismiss them from my service the moment I return to my headquarters."

Vister croaked laughter and everyone swiveled to see him hoist himself upright on his elbow. "Sounds like we're gonna have a nice day o' executions tomorrow, lads," he said. "There's nothin' like a couple of whacked necks to fix a soldier's mind on his job, I always say." He leaned closer, elbow nearly slipping out from under him. Grinning at Luka. "Course, you'd be talkin' about officers and such, wouldn't you, Sire? Maybe that's not such a good idea. Neck whackin' don't come so easy with the officer class. Might not have the same affect it does down in the ranks. Maybe it wouldn't be so good for morale."

Then he lifted his haunches and farted.

Iraj slapped his thigh, howling laughter. "That's telling them, Cousin!" he said. "The truth—and from deep, deep within you, by the gods!"

Vister chuckled drunkenly, lifting the flask to his lips. Then he frowned, turning the flask upside down. Nothing came out. He shook it, frown growing deeper.

"It's empty," he said in a voice so mournful you'd have thought he was announcing the death of his dear mother. One of the maids traded it for a full one and he was happy again.

He drank, then thumped his chest. "I was the only one!" he said. "Me! Vister! The rest are dead and rottin' in that pass. We all went in. Like so." He wriggled his fingers, making walking motions. "Then along comes the ghosts and whack!" He chopped at the air. "Ever'body's dead . . . 'cept Sergeant Vister." He settled back in his chair, chuckling and drawing a maid onto his lap. "Now I'm guest o' the King! Ain't that a tale to tell!" He tapped just beneath his right eye. "And these are the eyes what seen it!"

"A marvelous tale indeed," Kalasariz murmured. He turned to Fari. "Pardon, my good Lord Fari," he said, "but it seems the good sergeant is too modest to tell his story more fully."

Fari nodded. "He's too tense, poor fellow," he said. "That's his trouble."

Luka took the cue. "Wouldn't it be prudent, Majesty," he said to Iraj, "to see if we could learn more?" He laid a ringed claw of sincerity across his breast. "Let the good sergeant be our teacher, Majesty. And we his humble students."

Kalasariz muttered from the side of his mouth. "A little thick, don't you think?"

"What was that?" Iraj demanded.

"I was only agreeing with Prince Luka, Highness," Kalasariz replied.

Now Fari was up to speed. "Yes, let this humble hero instruct us, Majesty," he said. "As all know, I have always been particularly sensitive to the lower classes. Like Your Majesty, I pride myself on listening most intently to their crude words of wisdom." He shrugged. "Of course, sometimes we need a little assistance to understand their meaning."

Iraj raised an eyebrow. "What's to understand?" he said. He turned to Vister. "Tell them what you told me, my friend. And leave nothing out."

Vister struggled upright and the maid slipped off his lap and resumed her place with the others. "Sure," he said. He snapped his fingers. "Nothin' to it! Simple as all the Hells! The problem is this, see. There's ghosts in that pass. Hundreds, maybe thousands of 'em. And they can kill you, but you can't kill them. And that's all there is to it!"

He gave Luka an owlish look. "So all's you officer sorts gotta figure out is how to turn the whole thing around. Like we get to kill them, but they don't get to kill us." He tapped his nose. "Simple as the nose on your face." He gave Luka another look and giggled. "Oops!" he said. "Didn't mean to speak outta turn there, Sire. You bein' a demon and all, I'm not so sure that's a nose you got stickin' out there. Could be another horn, for all's I know. No offense intended, Sire."

Luka dipped his head. "None taken," he murmured, thinking he'd like to rip this filthy human's heart out. Fari's cough and Kalasariz' sudden grip on his elbow helped steady him. He turned to Iraj. "As first field reports go, Majesty," he said, "that was most enlightening. But I, for one, would certainly want to know more."

"That's why I called you here," Protarus said. "To listen and learn." He turned back to Vister. "Tell it again," he said, "but in more—" a loud snore cut him off. Vister was sprawled his seat, head lolling on his chest, sound asleep.

Iraj chuckled kindly. "Let him rest," he said. "He deserves it. We'll question him later."

"Pardon, Highness," Fari said. "But what I had in mind will be much easier while he sleeps. What I propose is that we witness his travails first hand. I don't need much in the way of preparations." He indicated an ornate charcoal brazier that had been brought in to warm up the throne room during the snow storm. "In fact," he said, "I can use that for our stage." He pulled a pouch from his wizard's belt, opening it to sniff at the contents. He nodded in satisfaction. "I have everything we require, Majesty," he continued, "for all to be revealed."

Iraj studied the Unholy Three from beneath lowered eyelids. He appeared bored, but he was observing them closely—growing warier by the minute. At first he couldn't put his finger on what was bothering him. Then it came to him that the three were displaying remarkable unanimity. He certainly didn't feel violent waves of tension between them—which was by far the more normal state of affairs within his inner court.

For a panicked moment he wondered if they had uncovered his secret—the spell the witch, Sheesan, had given him that would not only destroy Safar, but free him from the Unholy Three. Were they were conspiring to foil him?

Then he relaxed. How could they know? Say what he might about his brothers of the Spell of Four, they had worked hard to bring him this close to his goal—the capture and ritual slaying of Safar and Palimak. If the Unholy Three knew about his plans, they certainly wouldn't have pressed so hard to bring them to fruition.

So—what were they up to? Were they seeking a means to break the bonds with him? That would certainly be the worst case conclusion he could make. But the more he thought on it, the more unlikely such a scenario seemed.

Very well. The best way to find out what was going on, he thought, was to give way to their suggestions and see where that carried him.

"Proceed, my lord," he said to Lord Fari. "Enlighten us all with your magic."

Fari bowed low, then quickly assumed command of the shapely maids tending Vister. Naked, except for modesty patches at their loins, gleaming with a faint film of perspiration from the overheated room, giving off the scent of the most remarkable perfumes, the female humans and demons made exotic magical assistants for the old master wizard.

Taking a lesson in magic as entertainment from Timura, the Lord Fari made the most of the maids' presence—drawing out and changing his spell so that it showed off their jiggling forms to the best advantage.

When he reached the penultimate moment he glanced at Protarus and was sorely disappointed when he saw how unaffected the king was. Instead of being flushed with excitement from all this mystery and magical erotica, Protarus sat boredly in his throne, fingernails tapping impatiently.

Fari hurled a handful of votive powders into the brazier and there was a flash of smoke, a swirl of colors. Despite himself, Iraj's pose of unconcern dissolved and he bent closer to see. Timura was right, Fari thought. The King can't resist magic, especially when accompanied by a little showmanship.

As Iraj stared into the brazier the smoke began to shape itself into a deep canyon with high walls. He heard Vister groan in his sleep and suddenly the throne room vanished and Iraj found himself sitting on a nervous warhorse, those steep walls now towering over him on either side. He was in the lead group of a tightly-packed force of men and demons moving cautiously through the Caluzian Pass.

Iraj felt somehow diminished. Weaker—not just in muscle and bone, but weaker of spirit, of self, of . . . he fumbled for the word, then it came in a flash—Authority!

He glanced down and found filthy leather breeches covering his legs. He raised a hand and saw something strange and gnarled and quite unfamiliar rise up—the hand of another man! And then it came to him that he was in Vister's body, reliving the moments leading to the second battle in the pass.

"Easy, Majesty," he heard Fari murmur. Voice close, but distant at the same time. "We are with you!"

"Yes, Highness," came another voice—Kalasariz'. "I am here."

"As am I, Majesty, as am I," he heard Luka say.

He looked at the mounted soldiers on either side of him. All were grizzled and filthy. Of the lowest of the low-ranking, be they demon or human. Fari and the others were among them, but he couldn't tell which was which.

He heard a clatter of falling stone and Vister's body jerked in alarm. Eyes probing here and there, every nerve screaming ambush, but nothing real to place the feeling on no matter how hard he strained his senses.

Then he heard a steady, tromp, tromp of many marching men and he twisted in his saddle, steadying his skittish horse, looking for the source of the sound. All around him the other soldiers were doing the same and the air was filled with whispered curses and clanking armor.

A great trumpet sounded—blasting through the narrow canyon and resounding off the walls.

Iraj/Vister whirled to the front, shouting and clawing for his sword when he saw the ghastly army march into view.

They were huge men, so heavily mailed they turned the pass into a solid wall of armor. Their flesh was pale, corpselike, their lips the color of blood. They had huge hollow eyes that seemed like the darkest and deepest of caverns.

He heard his companions cry out and draw their weapons. Attack orders were shouted and Iraj/Vister raked his horse's flanks with his spurs and charged straight ahead. All his sensibilities were hurled aside. His own life became insignificant as he joined the thundering cavalcade intent on slaughtering the enemy marching towards them.

He heard a hoarse voice shout: "For the King!"

And the others took up the cry—"FOR THE KING!"

Iraj/Vister found himself shouting along with his brother warriors and for a few seconds he thought the greatest thing he could ever accomplish would be to die for his king.

And then he thought, But, *I'm the King!*

At that moment he smashed into the armored ranks of the enemy.

The expected shock of collision never came. To his amazement his horse swept through the densely packed enemy ranks as if they didn't exist. Helmed faces rose up to confront him. His horse, a veteran of many such attacks, lashed out with iron hooves, screaming in panic when it encountered nothing except insubstantial smoke and air.

A huge enemy warrior lunged at him with a spear. Iraj/Vister tried to knock it aside with his sword, but like the horse, his weapon encountered nothingness and he was nearly toppled from the saddle from the force of his own blow.

They're ghosts! his mind screamed as he clawed himself upright, losing his sword in the process. Ghosts!

He righted himself just as the ghost warrior's spear caught the edge of his chain vest. The spear skittered across the links and he felt the all too familiar white hot sear as a sharp point needled through the links and cut into flesh. Experience as much as fear dulled the pain and Iraj/Vister kicked through, mercilessly raking his horse's flanks.

His body was violated many times during the charge through that ghostly mass. By the time his horse was cut down he had suffered many small wounds and lacerations. He'd fought hard, yet not one of his enemies had been harmed. Every blow he struck met no resistance. The enemy soldiers seemed to dissolve as he thrust and slashed at them.

In the end he relied on his professional skill as a horseman, dodging this way and that, avoiding many of the blows aimed at him. All around him his companions were being slaughtered by the score.

Then a javelin took his horse and the poor beast squealed and folded under him. Iraj/Vister tried to roll free, but his wounds made him weak and the horse rolled on top of him. Amazingly, he found himself lying under the animal not only alive, but still mobile. Several corpses propped the dead horse up just enough so that Iraj/Vister was sheltered from the one-sided battle raging in the pass.

All desire to fight was gone. Now it was all he could do to keep from gibbering with fear and giving himself away to the enemy.

He peered through a small opening and saw the last of his mates dragged from his horse by the ghost warriors. They forced him to kneel and one giant grabbed the soldier by the hair, while another sliced off his head. The execution was so close that blood sprayed Iraj/Vister's face.

Then all became blackness.

Iraj's eyes blinked open. He felt strength flood back into his limbs and he realized he'd been returned to his own body.

He was back in the throne room, the Unholy Three standing before him, studying his reactions through conspiratorial eyes.

Iraj coughed and sat upright, squaring his shoulders. "Very informative, my Lord," he said to Fari, making his voice casual.

Fari bowed. "Yes, Majesty," he said. "Quite informative indeed."

Luka said, "Give me the right spells to fight them, my Lord Fari, and I will clear the pass by tomorrow night." Then, to Iraj, "And it is my solemn vow, Highness, that not one drop of the blood of our soldiers will be shed without just cause."

Kalasariz suddenly felt left out—vulnerable. He was a spy master, not a warrior or a wizard. He had nothing of value to offer at this most crucial moment. Then he glanced over at Vister and saw that the old soldier was no longer snoring in his chair. Instead he was quite still, his face yellow and waxen.

Just then one of the maids noticed something was amiss and placed a hand on Vister's chest. She was too well trained to cry out—possibly drawing the wrath of the moody King Protarus. Nevertheless, big tears welled up in her eyes and she began to weep.

Kalasariz saw his opportunity and took it. "I fear, my Lord," he said to Luka, "that your promise to our king came too late for at least one of our most noble heroes."

He gestured and everyone turned to see Vister slumped in his chair, the maid weeping over his body.

"Unless I am mistaken," Kalasariz continued, "the good Sergeant Vister is quite dead." He looked pointedly at Fari, who was fuming at this early betrayal of the truce. "Apparently your spell was too much for the poor fellow," he said. "Although you assured us otherwise."

"Look here, Kalasariz!" Luka snapped, "it's easy enough to criticize when one—"

Iraj cut him off. "It so happens, my Lord," he rasped, "that our brother, Kalasariz, happens to be echoing the criticisms of your king!"

He rose from the throne and went to Vister, pushing the maids away and hoisting the body up in his arms, cradling the big soldier as if he were a babe.

"This is your fault, Fari," he said to the old demon. "And yours as well, Luka," he said to the prince, "for the reasons I gave before."

Fari and Luka, reduced to the Unholy Two, bowed, spewing many fervent apologies.

"Know this," King Protarus said. "The man you see in my arms was my kinsman, my cousin. He had followed me faithfully for many years over many miles and suffered much in my service. I do not take his death lightly. Do you understand me?"

Fari and Luka assured the king they understood quite well. Kalasariz said nothing, edging to the side to separate himself from the others.

"Go then," the King ordered. "Win me my victory, but remember this man. Remember him well!"

Kalasariz added his own voice with others, saying, "Yes, Majesty! All will be as you command."

All three bowed, then crept away.

Iraj watched them go, relieved. First, that their unity had once again been shattered. Second, that for the moment his secret still seemed safe.

He looked down at Vister's dead face. "They don't know a blessed thing, do they cousin?" he said.

Then he dropped the body into the chair. "See to it that he has a proper burial," he said to his servants, then strode away.

CHAPTER TWENTY SEVEN

SPIES ON THE WIND

"Steady!" Biner shouted. Then: "Launch!"

The ground crew let go the cables and the airship shot into the sky—furnaces roaring, the twin balloons taut till near bursting.

Leiria's stomach lurched at the unaccustomed feeling of weightlessness. She leaned over the side, fearing she was about to get sick, then saw the rapidly diminishing figures on the ground and felt sicker still. She closed her eyes, willing the sickness to be gone. She kept them closed for a long time, concentrating on the sounds around her—Biner's shouted orders, the aircrew's reply, the pumping bellows and roaring furnaces. And finally, the oddly melodic song of the wind strumming the great cables that held the ship to the balloons.

The sudden snowstorm had delayed the launch well past the chosen hour. Biner had held everyone at ready, ground crew poised at the cables, aircrew scrambling about knocking off ice. Meanwhile, teams of Kyranian volunteers shivered in the cold as they kept the area swept free of snow.

Then there'd been a brief respite as the sun broke through, revealing a small patch of blue sky and Biner had launched the ship.

Now Leiria was crouched on the steering deck, wishing for all the world that she could be somewhere else. Anything, even a charging horde of demon cavalry, would be better than this. At least she'd be on nice safe ground.

"I know what yer thinkin', lass," she heard Biner say. "That if the gods meant yer to fly, they'd a provided yer with the belly for it."

Leiria opened her eyes to find the dwarf standing next to her. She nodded weakly. "I would have thought wings," she said, "or at least a few pin feathers. But you're right. Whatever god made birds must've started with the belly."

She groaned to her feet, forcing herself not to look over the edge. "I think I'm going to live," she said. "Although I'm still not sure if I care."

Arlain came up, carrying a steaming mug. "Thith'll do the trick," she said. "Ith an old balloonitht cure for air thickneth."

Gratefully, Leiria drank. It was delicious—a thick, forthy elixir heavily laced with brandy. Her queasy inner world suddenly settled.

"Oh, that's much better!" she said. "My stomach's practically cheering."

"It's usually much smoother than this, lass," Biner said, taking her elbow and leading her over to the big ship's wheel.

"Here," he said, putting her hands on the wheel. "This'll give you somethin' to hold onto." He pointed to a mountain ridge off in the distance. "Keep her headed that way," he said.

Then to her great surprise and alarm, he bounded down the gangway to berate a lazy crewman.

"Wait," she cried, "I don't know how to–"

She bit off the rest as the dwarf vanished below. And she thought, if Biner wasn't worried, steering the airship couldn't be that difficult.

Leiria concentrated on the ridge, moving the wheel whenever the nose of the ship veered away from it. At first she tended to oversteer and the ship yawed widely from side to side. She kept expecting someone to come running to push her aside and take the wheel. When no one came she soon forgot about everything else but steering the ship and quickly saw the way of it.

The combination of Arlain's elixir plus having something useful to do gradually did its work, and before she knew it, Leiria was actually enjoying herself. The air was clean and bracing and there was an incredible sense of freedom that came from floating so high above the earth. They were sailing just above a thick cloud cover, blue skies and a bright sun, mountains stretching away in every direction as far as she could see. At least that's how it appeared for a time. About a half mile from the ridge Biner had aimed her toward, it began to dawn on her that something was wrong.

Instead of fleeing as the airship approached, the horizon grew closer. The sky in that direction was still blue, but the blue seemed more . . . *solid* was the only description she could think of. But not hard, like metal, but soft, like . . . like . . . some kind of cloth. And now that she thought of it, the cloth was moving . . . billowing . . . as if an immense window had been left open and the wind was pushing through the curtains.

Biner and Arlain must have sensed something was up, because they both came running up on the deck. As Biner took over the wheel, Leiria pointed.

"Look," she said. "Through there . . ."

She was pointing through the gap of what she thought of as "curtains." Biner cursed and Arlain covered her mouth in alarm. Glaring through the opening was the familiar, evil face of the Demon Moon.

The sight of their old celestial enemy was driven home by the heavy throbbing of a huge machine and the whiff of the foul air of the Black Lands.

"No use cryin' over spilt air," Biner said grimly. "Besides, we were half expectin' it ever since we started on this little spyin' trip."

"I thirtainly wath never exthpecting that again!" Arlain said, jabbing a claw at the leering moon. "Thomebody thould of warned me!"

"And then what would yer have done?" Biner said. "If we'd of spelled it out real plain—so we could be sure yer were scared sandless. I mean, Safar told us we were livin' in a false Caluz. That outside that little valley was the real world. Which is where we gotta go if we're gonna do any worthwhile eagleyein'.."

"I know that," Arlain sniffed.

"So, if we'd a painted a picture for yer," Biner went on, "and made sure yer knew we'd be in the Black Lands again, complete with Demon Moon and crazy sorcery, what would yer have done, lass. Decided not to go?"

"Don't be thilly," Arlain said. "Of courth, I'd thill go! I haven't been flying in yearth! You couldn't have kept me off thith airthip with a whole army of Demon Moonth!"

She sniffed. "But it thirtainly wouldn't have been impolite to *warn me!*"

"Listen," Leiria broke in. "I don't know you all very well. Maybe this little bantering between you is just your normal way of facing a dangerous situation."

She indicated the flowing curtain, which they were moments away from sailing through. "But while you've been talking, we've getting closer to *that!*"

Biner frowned at her. "So? That was the plan, wasn't it, lass?"

"Yes," Leiria said. "But we weren't supposed to do it naked!"

Biner slapped his forehead. "Damn! I fergot!"

He shouted orders and several big crewmen raced to break out several large kegs. It was a little too late, however, because they were just knocking the tops off the kegs when the airship sailed through the curtains and suddenly they were sweeping over a bleak landscape—a frozen plain pierced by huge, tortured black rock formations.

As they entered the Black Lands Leiria was wracked with sudden pain. Every joint and muscle ached and her head throbbed as if she'd been stricken by some dreaded plague. She heard Biner and Arlain moan and the harsh wrenching sound of a crewman coughing up his breakfast.

Safar had warned them about entering the Black Lands without a shield to protect them from the wild spells. He'd even provided them with the means to make one—the contents of the casks the crewmen had been opening.

Leiria forced herself off the steering deck, going down the gangway step by agonizing step, feeling as if she were carrying a heavy load of hot bricks on her shoulders.

She stumbled over the crewmen, who were writhing about the main deck, clutching their heads and calling for their mothers. When she came to the first cask she almost broke down, falling to her knees and cracking her head on the rim. Somehow she found strength and pulled herself up, blood streaming down her face from a cut. She dug out her tinder box, feeling like an old arthritic woman as she tried to light it.

Finally it caught, and she threw the entire tinder box into the cask, hurling herself backward just in time as flames and smoke exploded up and out.

Leiria stayed flat on her back, watching the smoke curl under the air bags, then flow around the sides until both balloons looked like immense white clouds. Gradually, as Safar's shield took affect, she felt better. For the second time in less than two hours, she thought she felt well enough to care if she lived.

She clambered to her feet, muttering, "Damned flyers! Not a brain in their heads!"

The crewmen were also recovering and she set them to work tending the casks. They were to wait until the first barrel burned out, then light the next, and so on until someone told them to stop.

She returned to the steering deck, expecting to find Biner and Arlain waiting with shamed expressions and many apologies.

Instead she found them intent on the scene below.

Leiria's eyes widened when she saw what they were looking at. Beneath them was an immense army, drawn up under a thick steaming blanket of snow.

She heard camels bawling and the racket of armorers pounding out dents in shields.

Rising out of the center of the encampment was a snow-covered pavilion topped by a waving banner—the Demon Moon with the Comet rising.

Iraj had finally caught them!

CHAPTER TWENTY EIGHT
THE ORACLE SPEAKS

"We're inside the machine, father!" Palimak shouted. But Safar had sensed the wrongness a moment before the boy's warning.

The air became very cold and gulls shrilled warnings overhead. The breeze coming off the sea carried the sudden stink of sorcery. Ahead of him the Spirit Rider wheeled her horse and charged away. Instinctively he knew this was no tease, no game of seduction in a dark wood.

He dug his knees into Khysmet and the horse leaped after the black mare. Both of them knew the threat came from behind—not ahead. Snow started to fall, then Palimak cried out his warning—"We're inside the machine, father!" Putting words to the half-formed thoughts in his mind.

There was a loud crash! behind them—so heavy it shook the ground.

Safar glanced around and saw huge white jaws reaching for them. Khysmet surged forward just in time, the jaws clashing together on emptiness. Safar turned his head away, but the creature's huge eyes—burning with the blue fires of some icy hell—caught his. He felt numb, his strength drained away by sudden cold. It took all his will to force his eyes away from the creature's and his strength flooded back the moment he was facing forward again.

The creature roared. Palimak tried to turn and see, but Safar leaned forward, blocking him, telling him, "Whatever you do—Don't look back!"

There was another crash—this one much closer. Khysmet stretched to his fullest, straining to gain more speed.

The snowstorm intensified and Safar lost sight of the Spirit Rider. All he could see was a snatch of the shoreline to the side and just ahead of him—chunks of ice hissing in and out of the mist on steely waves.

Again there was the sound of something heavy slamming down behind them. The ground quaked, but this time the beast didn't seem quite as close. At least he hoped so.

A large wave boomed in from the side and Khysmet veered from the shoreline to escape it. The mistake was evident within a few seconds. Without the shoreline to guide them visually, and the sound of the sea lost beneath Khysmet's pounding hooves, they quickly became lost in the blizzard.

Their enemy, however, had no such trouble. The crashing sound suddenly gained on them—coming closer than ever before.

Then a beacon flared well off to the left and Safar turned Khysmet toward the light.

He heard a marrow-freezing roar and a cold foul breath blasted across his back. Safar fumbled a small pouch from his belt, bit the drawstrings apart and hurled the pouch and its contents behind him—his shouted spell ripped from his lips by the storm:

> *"Fire to cold,*
> *Cold to fire.*
> *All hearts burn*
> *On Winter's pyre!"*

As he hurled the last words into the winds one of the beast's claws caught his cloak, pulling him back. He jerked forward against Palimak, feeling cloth and flesh tear.

There was a spellblast behind him, followed by the howl of some great beast in pain, and the claw was snatched away.

The beacon grew larger in his view and then he gradually began to make out the shadowy figure of the horsewoman racing ahead of him through the storm—a bright magical brand held aloft in one hand.

There was a violent crash behind him and he realized the ice creature had only been slowed momentarily by his attack spell and was pursuing him again. From the sound of its roaring—hate mingled with pain—it was back to full strength, more determined than ever to bring them down.

He heard waves crashing on both sides of them and realized they were now out on the narrow peninsula. Now there was no way open but straight ahead. And when they reached the end they'd be trapped against the raging open seas.

To gain time he repeated his previous attack, hurling the spell blindly over his shoulder. The action had even less effect than before—the creature had evidently learned from the first experience. Safar groaned in disappointment when the spellblast went off and all he heard was a sharp yelp of pain as their pursuer dodged most of the impact.

"Let me help you, father!" Palimak cried and Safar plucked the last pouch from his belt—reaching for the boy's strength to add to his. But there wasn't much there—he could feel Palimak's weariness, sense his struggle to add to Safar's powers.

Still, it was just enough, and when he cast the spell he heard a satisfying shriek from the beast.

He saw the Spirit Rider reach land's end, but to his surprise, instead of turning about she kept going, riding straight out onto the water's surface.

Safar put all his trust in the woman, riding after her without hesitation. Even so, as Khysmet plunged ahead, he braced to be swallowed by icy waters. The expected shock never came and a moment later they were racing across the boiling sea as if it were the firmest ground.

Behind them he heard the beast roar in frustrated fury and with every stride Khysmet took the roars became fainter and fainter, until they faded altogether.

The snow fell harder until everything above and below was obscured from view. He felt as if he were riding through a strange world where only the color of white existed—except for the beacon of light bobbing ahead of them as the horsewoman led them onward.

They rode like that for a long time. How long Safar couldn't say, except to note that Palimak had fallen into an exhausted sleep. Safar might have slept himself—he'd find himself dozing off, eyes closing involuntarily, then being jogged awake and seeing the ever-present beacon still moving ahead of them. Even Khysmet seemed to tire, his pace growing gradually slower as they went on.

Safar was shocked from his stupor by a loud rumbling sound. The sea heaved under them and Palimak snapped awake, crying out in fear—"Father! Father!" Safar was too busy holding on to answer as Khysmet shrilled surprise, leaping high into the air. Safar and Palimak were nearly hurled off when he landed—hooves skittering on what seemed to be a reef rising from the ocean floor. They were rocked from side to side, but still Khysmet managed to keep his footing.

For a moment all was still. Then a blast of wind sheered in from the side, sweeping the snow away.

They were presented with an incredible sight. Looming over the tiny, barren island they now found themselves on was the immense stone image of a demon. It had a long narrow face topped by heavy brows that arched over deep-set eyes. Whoever had designed the statue had given it a sad smile, which added to the effect of the deep-set eyes, making the demon seem incredibly wise.

Safar remembered the face very well. It had been carved on the coffin lid he'd seen in his vision long ago. It was the face of the great Lord Asper.

As they rode toward the statue Safar saw the Spirit Rider had stopped. She was waiting in front of a wide stairway that led up to the statue's open mouth—beacon still held high.

Khysmet perked up, whinnying at the black mare, who whinnied greetings in return. Safar's pulse quickened as they drew near.

The woman was just as beautiful as he remembered back in that moonlit clearing so many miles and months ago. Her face and form were so perfect she looked as if she'd been carved by a master artist from some rare ebony wood and her bright smile of greeting warmed the frozen lump deep in his heart.

She called out to him, "Only a little farther, my friend. Only a little farther."

Then she whirled the mare about, shouting, "This way to Syrapis!" And plunged up the broken staircase to disappear into the mouth of the statue.

Safar didn't have to urge Khysmet to follow. The big stallion lunged up the staircase after the mare and a moment later they were leaping through the opening.

There was a flash of white light. Then darkness—marked only by the distant beacon carried by the Spirit Rider. The beacon light steadied, then stopped.

Palimak whispered, "There's no danger, father. Everything's fine, now."

The light grew stronger then wider, until Safar realized it was no longer a beacon, but natural light shining through a cave opening.

A moment later they cantered out into soft sunlight. Safar blinked. The woman was gone! His heart wrenched in dismay. Under him he could feel Khysmet's sides heaving and knew the animal was just as deeply affected by the disappearance of the mare.

"We're not in the machine anymore, father," Palimak announced.

"What?" Safar was so dazed he barely heard.

"Gundara and Gundaree say we're out of the machine," Palimak said.

Safar glanced about. Gradually his surroundings sunk in. There was no island. No raging seas. No blinding snowstorm. All had vanished.

Instead, they were riding along a narrow mountain ridge, breathtaking vistas stretching out in every direction. To the south was a snow-dappled range of low mountains, marked by two familiar peaks. Caluz was beyond those mountains—and not so very distant. Safar could see a yellow tinge lying low on the horizon and knew it was from the poisonous atmosphere of the Black Lands. Further evidence were puffs of smoke from all the active volcanoes. He looked closely at the mountains the Kyranians needed to cross when he went back to fetch them. To his joy he saw the faint scar of a caravan track running between the peaks.

Even brighter news beckoned from the north. Not many miles beyond the ridge they were riding along was a shining sea. He could even make out a few dots of white that were sailing craft skimming across the peaceful waters. There was no sign of the snow storm he'd just experienced. The fields were green and summery. Far off he saw the curving slash of a road running along the shoreline. Beyond that was a dazzling city of the purest white.

Hovering over the city was a vast field of golden clouds—flattened so they looked like fabulous islands in the sky.

Caspan!

The last jumping off point to Syrapis.

Palimak's voice jolted him out his reverie. "There's someone waiting for us, father," he said, pointing to a little deer trail leading off the ridge and down to a little grove of trees. "Down there."

Safar tensed. "Is it dangerous?" he asked.

Palimak hesitated while he conferred in whispers with the Favorites. Then, "They're not sure," he said, scratching his head. "They go back and forth. It's all pretty confusing. The only thing they agree on is that we have to go there—no matter what."

Safar loosened his sword. "Let's assume the worst, son," he said. "Then we won't have any reason to be sorry later."

Palimak nodded, arranging his cloak and belt so he could reach anything that might be needed. Young as he was, the boy was now quite trail wise—speaking only when necessary. He quietly got himself a drink of water and a handful of dried dates to munch on.

Safar was pleased the boy seemed so alert, all signs of exhaustion gone. As for himself—well, he felt as if he'd been through the hells and back. Which, now that he thought of it, he *had.* Pity he didn't possess the restorative powers of the very young. He was only in his third decade of life. Right now he it seemed like five more had been added to that span by the ordeal.

He glanced up at the sun to mark the time. To his surprise he saw it was barely mid-afternoon. Which meant only a few hours had passed since they'd left Hantilia's palace. If he had been asked, Safar would have sworn at least a week had gone by. This was very powerful magic, indeed.

There was no time to ponder such mysteries. He needed a clear mind for whatever faced them down that trail. Taking a lesson from Palimak, he got himself a drink and something to eat. Except he chose a palmful of jerky and a hefty slug of wine from the flask at his hip. Refreshed, he turned Khysmet down the narrow deer trail.

The path was steep and deeply curved so it was impossible for the riders to see very far ahead. Also, the grove of trees below them was too dense for them to make out what it hid. Skin prickling, eyes shifting back and forth, Safar guided Khysmet down the trail.

There was no warning. They came around a bend, the path dipped, and suddenly they were trotting into the grove. A gentle sun streamed down through the tree, giving the light a holy cast. A musical fountain played in the center of the grove, mist rising from the playing waters to glow in the sunlight. The fountain itself was a scene out of the Book of Felakia—the goddess revealed in all her beauty as she bathed in a stream, dipping up a cup of water to pour over her marble tresses.

Other than the life-sized statue of the goddess there were no structures in the grove, only a few stone benches set about the fountain. It was the sort of place one might expect to find in a temple garden—certainly never in the middle of a forbidding wilderness.

Just then Safar spotted someone waiting for them by the fountain. His heart jumped in amazement.

"It's the Queen, father!" Palimak blurted. "Queen Hantilia!"

The Demon Queen, graceful and royal as ever in her flowing red Asper robes, raised a claw of welcome.

"Greetings, Safar Timura," she said. "I have waited long for this meeting."

Safar goggled at her. What in the hells was she talking about? Where was the Oracle? Most important of all—how did she get here? Meanwhile, the Queen was eyeing him, looking him over as if she'd never seen him before.

"I didn't know you'd be so handsome," she said. "For a human, that is." She turned to Palimak. "And you, young Palimak Timura," she said in her musical voice, "I mustn't neglect you. You are quite handsome as well. Handsomer than your father, if I may be so bold. It's the demon in you that makes the difference."

Safar slid out of the saddle. "Pardon me for sounding rude, Majesty," he said. "But you're talking nonsense. And before anything else is said, I'd appreciate it greatly if you answered a few questions. To start with, could you please explain how in the hells you got here!"

Hantilia laughed. "Be patient, my lord," she said. "And all will be revealed to the best of my ability."

She waved at a bench across from hers. "Come sit and rest," she said. "And take a little refreshment, please. You must be hungry and tired after your long journey." Another wave and the small table in front of the bench was suddenly filled with plates of delicacies and mugs of drink.

Safar started to object. He was tired of the Queen's constant evasions and pleas for patience. He wanted answers, by the gods! Safar took half step forward, then paused. For the first time he noticed how insubstantial Hantilia seemed to be. In fact, if he turned his head slightly he could see right through her to the other side of the grotto where the trees moved gently in the breeze in a shadow play scene tinted red by her robes.

"She's not a ghost, father," Palimak said. "Gundara says she isn't real. But Gundaree says she's sort of real." He shook his head. "They're not being very helpful today."

"What do you say, Safar Timura?" Hantilia said, again indicating the bench and the table of food. "Will you take a chance with me? You've taken so many just to get here, what could be the harm?"

Safar sighed, accepting whatever fate had in store for them. Palimak took the sigh as a signal and scrambled off Khysmet. They quickly unsaddled the horse and set him free to graze on the tender grasses fed by the playing fountain.

As soon as they sat down in front the table of food they became famished and fell to. Hantilia sat quietly while they ate and drank. To Safar's surprise the magical food was delicious—in his experience such things always tasted like paper forgotten in some musty nook of a old library. There was never any substance or nourishment to that kind of food—when you finished eating you realized there had been no meal at all and you were left feeling just as empty as before. The drink she provided was equally as marvelous. Safar's cup proved to contain a never-ending supply of a rich, earthy wine, while Palimak's was an ever flowing container of what he said was a delicious fruit punch.

When they were done and the world seemed much brighter than before, Hantilia said, "Ask your questions, Safar Timura. I've been waiting for many a day to answer them."

Safar eyed her. Things were beginning to make a glimmer of sense.

"You're the Oracle of Hadin," he said—a statement, not a question.

Hantilia chuckled. "What did you expect? Some sort of great, goddess-like figure descending from the heavens? If so, I fear you must be very much disappointed. To begin with, if you are a student of Asper, you'll realize there are no gods or goddesses about. They're all asleep, you know. Slumbering away in their celestial beds while the world is turned to ashes."

"I'll try again," Safar said. "Are you the Oracle I seek?"

Hantilia shrugged. "I'll have to do," she said. "The original Oracle is . . . dead, isn't quite the word for such a being. Dissolved, I suppose, is more descriptive. However you put it, she was destroyed when the Caluzians failed to halt the machine." She touched claw to breast. "I am her replacement, so to speak."

Palimak snorted. "Why didn't you just say so right away?" he piped up.

"Good question, son," Safar said. Then to Hantilia, "Do you have an answer?"

"A simple one, actually," she replied. "If I'd have spoken then it would have ruined the spell."

"What spell?" Palimak broke in. "I didn't sense any spell. Neither did Gundara or Gundaree."

"That, my dearest, is because the spell was cast after you left the palace," Hantilia said.

Her form suddenly wavered, weakening, until she seemed about to vanish. Then it firmed. Safar saw moisture in her deep-set demon eyes.

"Forgive me," she said, wiping away an escaped tear. "But I was thinking of what must have happened after you departed."

She paused to compose herself, then said, "The Hantilia you see before you, as you've no doubt guessed, is not a living creature. I suppose you couldn't call me a creature of any kind, living or otherwise. I am merely part of the overall spell—the Great Sacrifice, is what we named it. In reality—if there is such a thing—I and all my followers are dead."

Safar and Palimak were rocked by this statement. They also had no doubt but that it was true. Safar remembered when they left the courtyard Palimak said he felt sorry for Hantilia and the others. The boy must have sensed the tragedy about to unfold.

"It was necessary for us to sacrifice ourselves," Hantilia said, "for the final part of the spell to be cast. Otherwise there wouldn't have been enough power."

Safar reflected on their perilous journey and realized they never would have made it this far without some outside help. An enormous amount of help, at that, considering the magical snowstorm—which he now realized had been for their benefit.

"To be frank," the Queen continued, "I'm a little surprised my people and I had the will to act when the moment came." She sighed. "At times I wondered if we had all become insanely religious, like those strange cults you hear about in the wilder areas of Esmir."

"You said before that it began with a vision," Safar said. "Of the Lady Felakia appearing before you."

"I lied," Hantilia said. "Or at least my other self lied. I suppose there's not much difference. I'm truly sorry, but it was the easiest way to avoid uncomfortable questions I was forbidden to answer."

"Then what is the truth, Majesty?" Safar asked.

Hantilia indicated a large stone at Safar's feet. "Lift up the rock," she said.

He did as she directed and the stone came up like a lid. Beneath the stone, in a brick-lined hollow, was a packet wrapped in oil cloth.

Safar fumbled the package open, gasping when saw what it contained—an old, leather bound book emblazoned with the sign of Asper.

He leafed through the book with numb fingers. It was a much larger and fuller version of the battered little volume he'd carried with him for so many years. Like the other, it was annotated in the master wizard's hand.

An even greater surprise awaited him in what Hantilia said next.

"I am kin to Lord Asper," she announced. "A direct descendant, to be exact. His great, great—oh, I can't count how many greats you'd put before it—granddaughter. That book has been in my family for many centuries. It was handed down with specific instructions for its use when a certain day came—the doom Lord Asper predicted for the world. It was my misfortune to be the one chosen by the Fates to carry those instructions out."

Safar frowned—he believed her, but some of what she said didn't quite make sense. "How could Asper know of me?" he asked. "I'm more than aware that he was wise and far seeing—but what you are speaking of would require so much specific knowledge of the future it defies imagination."

"Oh, your name isn't in the book, my dear Safar," Hantilia said. "Although if you read deeply you'll see he predicted someone very much like you."

She chuckled. "However, I think he believed you would be a demon like him. Regardless, you're getting the wrong idea. There are no details in the book on exactly what to do when doomsday comes. As you said, how could he predict all the events that have occurred? However, there is a spell in the book we were instructed to perform when trouble began.

"When I cast the spell, I was immediately stricken with a terrible malady." She shuddered at the memory. "I was unable to move from my bed for many weeks and the whole time I suffered the most horrible visions. It's a wonder I wasn't driven insane. In fact, until you rode into the grotto just now I wasn't certain if perhaps I was insane. Anyway, when I recovered I knew exactly what to do—up to and including the Spell of the Great Sacrifice, which was the most important and frightening requirement. I don't know how this knowledge was passed on to me. The point is, the knowledge was there and I felt obliged to act on the plan."

She hesitated, then said, "Strange as it may seem, as time went by and different things happened, I suddenly knew what I had to do next."

Hantilia smiled wryly. "The appearance of the Lady Felakia was my own idea. Actually, when I was ill I *did* see her in my dreams. She was one of the nicer visionary beings to visit me. I built on that dream to convince my followers of the rightness of the cause. A lie, to be sure. One I'm quite ashamed of and my real self is probably suffering in the hells right now for that sin. And rightly so. But I had to turn my followers into zealots. For who else but a zealot would agree to shoulder the blame for the sins of all human and demonkind—and then commit mass suicide as penance?"

Safar thought of how he'd manipulated his own people to what he believed was for the overall good. He hadn't asked them to commit suicide . . . although perhaps he had. Look at the situation they were all in—trapped in the Black Lands with Iraj ready to pounce at any moment. The odds were so short it was a grim joke to call it anything else but suicide. Even worse, he wasn't done with his kinsmen yet. If they survived this test he'd have to ask even more from them.

"I see from the look on your face, Safar Timura," Hantilia said, "that you have some . . . experience, shall I say . . . in matters of manipulation to achieve your own ends."

"That I do, Majesty," Safar said fervently. "That I do." He collected himself, then said, "I assume you were . . . uh . . . created by your . . . uh . . . living self, correct?"

"There's no need to spare my feelings, Safar," Hantilia said. "The real me no longer exists. And this image you see before you will vanish in a short while. But, to answer your question—Yes. She created me. I was placed here to await your arrival. The Great Sacrifice, you see, could only be performed in Caluz. Away from the machine and the Black Lands. Part of the spell's intent was to open a portal between the Black Lands to the shores of Caspan, where I was to greet you and instruct you further."

"When I first met your creator," Safar said, "she told me it was vital that I destroy the machine somehow. Was that true, or only a necessary lie?"

"It was partly true," Hantilia said. "I don't know what was going through my real self's mind, since I wasn't there. But I suspect I told you that was my desire so you would think I had a selfish, and therefore believable, motive for my actions. After all, if I had told you I planned a mass suicide to assist you I doubt if you would have listened much further."

Safar grimaced. That was certainly the truth!

"However, it is no prevarication that the machine presents a dire threat," Hantilia continued. "Regionally speaking, of course, since what happens to Esmir is happening everywhere else. From what I've been able to determine the machine is an open wound between Hadin and Esmir. If it isn't stopped, Esmir will cease to exist in not many years."

"And if it is stopped?"

"Another decade or so will be added to Esmir's span." The Queen frowned. "But it won't do more than delay the inevitable. Unless you can find a solution to the disaster destroying this world, that is. Frankly, I have grave doubts you can succeed. When you study the book I gave you, you'll see that my ancestor, Lord Asper, had the same doubts.

"There's a chance to save the world. But a very slim one, indeed."

She gave another of her elegant shrugs. "Destroy the machine, or don't destroy it. That's up to you. You will most certainly have the power to attempt it, thanks to the Spell of The Great Sacrifice."

Palimak fidgeted on the bench. He was getting restless and a bit bored with all this talk of things that happened in the past. He was here for the future!

"When do we get to the Oracle part?" he asked. "You know, when you tell us what to do to get to Syrapis?"

Hantilia smiled. "Would now be soon enough?" she asked.

Palimak nodded. "Maybe we'd better," he said. "Gundara and Gundaree say we don't have much time. I'm sorry everybody is dead and everything. Especially you. But we're not dead and I get the idea that any minute now you're going to go—poof! And disappear. Forever, probably."

Safar frowned. Although his opinions were bluntly put, Palimak was right. Safar could sense the magical creation that was Hantilia fading in and out—growing a bit weaker with each cycle.

"How do we start?" he asked the Queen.

She nodded at the book he held in his hands. "Give it to the boy and let him open it," she said.

Safar did as she asked. Palimak held the book gingerly, a little nervous.

"Go ahead," Hantilia gently urged. "Open it, my dear."

"Which page?"

"Let the book decide," was Hantilia's only reply.

Palimak's brow wrinkled in puzzlement. "I'm not sure I understand," he said.

"Just open the book, dear one, and you'll see."

Palimak took a deep breath and squared his shoulders. But being a child he went at the task perversely, carefully choosing a point about a third of the way through the book. He tried to pull it apart, but the pages stuck together and the book insisted on parting in the center.

The boy peered closely at the pages, expecting a miracle, but seeing nothing but a few poems.

"What do I do now?" he asked.

"Read one of the poems," Hantilia answered.

He looked back down at the book, trying to choose, but the words seem to skitter across the pages.

Hantilia sensed his difficulty. "Don't try to pick one," she advised. "Just open your mind to all possibilities."

Palimak squirmed, impatient, wanting to tell her this was stupid. For not the first time, he wondered why witches and wizards didn't speak plainly. They always used such funny words that didn't really mean anything when he thought about them later. Like Hantilia saying he should "open his mind to all possibilities." How do you open a mind? It's closed up in your head, for goodness sakes. And as for "all possibilities," that was just plain silly. It didn't describe anything. Or maybe it was the other way around. Maybe it described Everything. Was that what she meant?

Suddenly, to his amazement, words took form and a poem practically leapt from the page.

"This is great!" he exclaimed. "What do I do next?"

"Read to us," the Queen said. And so he did, chanting:

> *"The Gods are uneasy in their sleep.*
> *They dream of wolves among the sheep.*
> *Brothers in greed, kin to hate,*
> *Wolves bar the path to Hadin's gates."*

As Palimak spoke the last words, red smoke whooshed up and he reflexively jerked his head back in alarm.

"It's all right, Little Master," Gundara whispered. "It won't hurt you."

Palimak nodded and sat quite still, watching the smoke curling up like a snake. Then lips formed in the smoke—full lips parting in a woman's seductive smile.

Safar instantly recognized that smile. He'd first seen it as a boy, except Iraj had been with him then. He leaned closer as the lips opened to speak. Safar heard a woman's voice say:

"There is a veil through which no sage can see. For there is no lamp to light the fates. Yet know that in the place where the heavens meet the hells—good and evil, foul and fair, life and death, are all coins of the same value. Spend them wisely, seekers, or spend them foolishly, it makes no difference to the sleeping gods. But do not hesitate, do not stray from your path. And remember above all things—what two began, three must complete."

The smoke vanished and the book snapped shut.

Safar looked up at Palimak, expecting to see wonderment on his face. Instead, the boy was sneering.

"If I ever make one of those things," he announced, "I'm going to figure out how to make it talk so people can understand what it means."

Serious as the moment was, Safar couldn't help but laugh. "If you ever do, son," he said, "you'll have witches and wizards with fists full of gold lined up for miles to buy one minute of your oracle's time."

"Maybe," Palimak said absently. Then his eyes brightened. He started to say more, but Safar made a signal and he stopped, looking over at Hantilia.

To the boy's surprise her form had faded so much that she was nearly a shadow. In a few moments she would be gone.

"I have one other thing to tell you before I go, Safar Timura," she said.

"Go on, please, dear lady," Safar said.

"You will need ships to sail to Syrapis," she said. "So you must travel to Caspan next. There is a friend waiting for you there who can help.

"But do it immediately. Haste is of prime importance. I can't stress that too much.

"You have three days at the most to make your arrangements and return to Caluz for your people. The portal will be closed after that."

"Who is this man?" Safar asked.

"He's called Coralean," she said.

Safar reacted, surprised. But before he could ask more, the Queen turned to Palimak.

"Answer me quickly, dear one," she said. "I have little time left. Back at the palace . . . Did my temporal presence tell you about your mother?"

"Yes," Palimak said, trembling.

Hantilia smiled. "Good," she said. "Good."

She raised a hand of farewell, barely visible now.

"Wait!" Safar shouted. Hantilia's form steadied. "What about the lady? The Spirit Rider who led us here? Who is she?"

"Lady?" Hantilia said, eyes widening in surprise. "I know of no lady."
And then she was gone.

CHAPTER TWENTY NINE
CORALEAN'S BARGAIN

As beautiful as Caspan had seemed from a distance, up close it was a horror. It was late afternoon when they reached the city. Plague bells were tolling and there was an awful stench of death rising from the great ditch encircling the city's walls—a sure sign even routine burials had been abandoned. The gates were wide open and people with the wild looks of refugees were streaming out, their belongings piled onto carts or on their backs. The walls, which had appeared so pristine white from the hills, were a filthy gray, marked further by crumbling stone and breaks in the wall due to civic neglect.

Palimak shuddered. "Do we have to go in there, father?" he asked.

"No, thank the gods," Safar said. "Coralean never liked city life. Too many people spying on you from alleys, is how he puts it."

They traveled a few miles more until they came upon a magnificent villa built on a hill that overlooked a graceful bay. In the dying sunlight Safar could see scores of white sails sitting off the coast and he idly wondered why so many ships were anchored in the same place.

As they approached the villa's gates—closed and barred against the coming night—Palimak suddenly said, "Look out, father!"

Before he could react a hard voice rang out from behind them. "Hold, stranger!"

Startled as he was, Safar knew better than to whirl around to see who was challenging them. He reined Khysmet in and sat quite still, whispering to Palimak that he shouldn't move a muscle. He heard heavy boots moving toward them, estimating by the sound that he was being confronted by at least half-a-dozen men.

Then three heavily armed thugs came into view, sidling up on either side. A crop-eared man grabbed Khysmet's reins while the others spread out, crossbows cocked and ready. Behind them, Safar could hear the other men cock their bows.

The scar-faced thug spoke to the others. "If the bastard moves, kill him! Don't wait for orders."

"What about the boy?" one of the men asked.

Crop Ear shrugged. "Kill him too."

Then he turned to Safar. "Talk," he commanded. "And you'd better make it good. We've got some graves down the bottom of the hill dug specially for liars."

Safar grinned down at the man. "It sure is good to see your ugly face again, Gitter," he said. "And I notice you still have one ear left. You're either a better thief than you used to be, or you've made good your promise to end your evil ways."

Gitter jerked back. Then he peered closer at Safar, an ugly smile slowly spreading across his face as recognition dawned.

"Ease off, lads," he ordered the men. "And, you, Hasin, run and tell the master Lord Timura's come for a visit."

*   *   *

"I once believed that Coralean was the luckiest man in the whole history of Esmir," the caravan master rumbled. "I thought that when the gods coined luck they must have kept back the fattest purse for Coralean's glorious arrival to this world."

He raised a crystal goblet in toast. "But now I know that I, Coralean, who has prided himself these many years for not only being lucky, but also on being rarely wrong in his judgment, was most grievously in error. You, my friend—not Coralean—won the fattest purse of all."

Safar clinked goblets with him. "Thank you for the words of hope," he said, "but I fear that when it comes to luck . . . I'm down to my last few coppers of the stuff."

They were taking their ease in Coralean's spacious study, which sat atop a specially built garden tower looking down on the bay. It was night. From the huge window Safar could see a forest of ships' lights playing on the waters. It was a peaceful scene, an idyllic scene, marred only by the face of the Demon Moon peering through a high cloud cover.

Both he and Palimak were bruised from the big man's hearty embraces of welcome. Coralean had then ordered his wives to see his visitors were fed, bathed and massaged with soothing oils. Palimak had fallen asleep during his massage. Now he was peacefully slumbering in a soft bed with silken sheets and perfumed pillows—the finest bed he'd known since he was a babe in Nerisa's luxurious care.

Coralean refilled Safar's goblet, then topped off his own. "I must confess I had grave doubts this meeting would ever occur. In fact, if I had any worthy competitors left, I would have suspected them of concocting a wild plot to diminish Coralean's hard-earned fortunes. Consider, my friend. A fellow in red robes and fiendish eyes shows up at my gates with news of your imminent arrival. It had been so long since I had heard anything of you, I thought you dead."

"We've been stranded in the Black Lands for quite awhile," Safar said.

"So you've told me. That also explains why I've heard nothing about Iraj Protarus' progress. It was as if his whole army had disappeared from the face of Esmir while hunting you. An impossibility, of course. Which gave Coralean hope that Safar Timura still survived. Otherwise our good king would be marching through these streets at this very minute, proclaiming victory over the evil Lord Timura."

"Which is why you listened to Hantilia's courier," Safar said. "Otherwise, Gitter would have planted him in your little garden of liars at the bottom of the hill."

Coralean grimaced. "What a world we live in, my friend, where a gentle man—a man who is loathe to kill a flea, who is, after all, only going about his honest purpose—could be forced to condone such deeds."

Safar buried a smile. Coralean was not a casually brutal man, but he had not made his great fortune by avoiding bloodshed. Many a new caravan track had been opened by Coralean over the years—all well-marked by the heads of bandits—and other enemies—stuck up on posts.

"But to return to our wild-eyed stranger in red," Coralean said. "He was not a man I would normally take seriously. I would have given him a few coins and sent him on his madman way. However, when he presented me with a bag of gold—a gift from his queen, he said—well, I felt obliged to listen. I'd never heard of this Queen Hantilia, but the payment was so unnecessarily large I thought only royalty could be that foolish. I think the crowns they wear are to blame. They squeeze their heads so tightly there's no room for common business sense."

Safar chuckled. Then, "I still find it amazing you believed him. If someone—even if it were the royal personage herself—told me that a fellow hunted in every corner of Esmir would show up at my door, dragging a thousand people behind him, I'd have declared them insane to their face and called in a guard to escort them from my presence."

Coralean stroked his beard. "Is it really a thousand, Safar?" he asked. "You really did manage to carry away your entire village? All of Kyrania? Without fatalities?"

Safar's face darkened. "I wish I could say no one died," he replied. "I'm to blame for many deaths in this mad contest I've been caught up in with Iraj. Besides war dead, many old people, who should have been sitting at home spoiling their grandchildren, have given up the ghost before their time." Then he smiled. "But there's still at least a thousand of us," he said. "More, I suspect, than when we started because so many of our women have given birth on the trail."

The old caravan master eyed him, considering. Then he nodded. "Now I understand why you never claimed credit for saving my life," he said. "You let Iraj take the greatest share of the glory. This puzzled me at the time, because I suspected what you had done but was loathe to embarrass you by asking for an explanation."

Safar blinked, seeing the mental image of a young Iraj leaping on the demon's back to rescue Coralean from certain death.

"It was Iraj who saved you," he objected. "Not me. No matter what has happened since you can't deny that he was once a hero."

"This is true, my friend," Coralean said. "Iraj was . . . and is . . . a brave man. And I think that once he had good in his heart. Coralean is the most ambitious of men and he truly understands how ambition, however well meant in the beginning, can turn the most charitable men into devils. So understand, I was not slighting that particular deed. However, we still would all have fallen to those demon bandits if an avalanche had not suddenly, miraculously, swept that band of fiends back into the hells they came from."

He oiled his throat with a sip from his goblet. "Coralean is a believer in many things. In repose, with his wives begging his favors, he is quite a romantic fellow." He snorted, sounding like a bull. "But I am always suspicious of coincidence. You must admit, Safar, that the avalanche was too convenient to be marked up to coincidence. Then I didn't know, although I suspected, that you were a wizard. Now you are alternately cursed and hailed as the greatest wizard in all Esmir. So confess, my friend. It was you who caused the avalanche, was it not? It was you who ultimately spared my wives the awful grief of losing their dear, sweet Coralean."

Safar grinned, mischievous. "I'll never tell," he said. "Was it chance, or was it purpose? Come now, Coralean. You'd never expect a wizard to reveal something like that!"

Coralean slapped his thigh. "Well said," he rumbled. "You should have been king instead of Iraj. With me to advise you, we would have built the grandest fortune the world has ever seen."

Safar turned serious. "Thrones or fortunes," he said, "mean nothing in these times. Perhaps they never did. Perhaps they never will. It's useless to speculate."

Coralean shrugged. "Speculation is my nature," he said. "Speculation is the sole reason I not only listened to the red robed one, but waited many days after my planned departure from Caspan to see if what he said was true."

He pointed to the bobbing ship lights. "I even hired ships on the doubtful word of an insane messenger, who claimed to speak for an unseen queen whose name had somehow escaped Coralean's notice."

Coralean paused to empty his goblet. "I told you I thought you lucky. Luckier even than Coralean. You are also wise. Not as wise as I am, to be sure, but that would be an impossibility." He tapped his head. "No, in wisdom I am your superior. Just as I am every man's superior when it comes to the art of pleasing women. Strong brain, strong loins, those are things that make Coralean, Coralean."

"I'll grant you both with no argument," Safar said. "Especially wisdom. Who else but Coralean would be calculating enough to remain Iraj's confident, but still place a wager on his worst enemy?"

Coralean grinned. "Only a portion of it was due to calculation," he said. "The rest was because of my deep feelings of friendship towards you."

"And my luck."

Coralean's grin widened. "And your luck. Especially your luck."

Safar nodded at the ships sitting offshore. "What happens when Iraj finds out what you've done?" he asked.

The caravan master grimaced. "Coralean has no intention of lingering in Caspan long enough to realize the depths of Iraj Protarus' wrath. My original intention was to seek retirement as far away as my gold would take me. My thinking was, once Iraj caught you he would start looking at men like me with suspicious eyes. And that would be my end. Once that decision was made, I didn't know where to run. Either Iraj would eventually find me, or I would die a trivial but agonizing death in the chaos that has afflicted Esmir."

Safar laughed. "Now I understand," he said. "You couldn't flee Esmir, because no one really knows what lies beyond the Great Sea."

"Except for you," Coralean said. "One of the things that madman told me was that you had a goal. A peaceful island you knew of far across the sea."

"Syrapis," Safar said.

"Yes," Coralean said. "Syrapis. I like the sound of it. A good place for business."

"You really are casting the dice, my friend," Safar said. "Things must be desperate for you."

"Desperate enough," Coralean replied, "to consider things that go against my generous nature. A lesser man than I might threaten to deny you passage on those ships if you did not agree to carry him away from this cursed place."

"I have no objection to your company," Safar said. "In fact, I welcome it."

Coralean refilled both their goblets. "Good, it's settled then. A nice bargain for both of us, with each thinking he got the better of the other, but not too much to injure friendship."

Safar started to speak, then hesitated, thinking. Finally he shrugged and dug an old map from his pocket.

"You gave me maps once," he said. "They saved my life and the lives of my people. Now, let me return the favor."

He unrolled the map, copied in his flowing hand from the Book of Asper. It showed the Great Sea from Caspan, to a large island many miles away.

Coralean studied it with an expert eye. "Yes," he said. "I see how to go."

Safar rolled the map up and handed it to him. "Here," he said. "Take it."

The caravan master was so surprised by this gesture that his mouth fell open and for a moment he looked like a huge, bearded fish.

His jaws snapped shut. "Surely you have another."

"No, that's the only copy," Safar said. "I have three days to accomplish what I have to do. If you don't see me by then, sail without us."

Coralean grinned. "How do you know I'll wait?" he asked. "Coralean is a man of his word, but sometimes urgent business forces a man of industry and ambition to make regretful decisions."

Safar looked at him, measuring. Then he nodded. "You'll wait," he said, flat.

"I suppose if I don't," Coralean pressed, "you will cast some wizardly spell of misfortune upon me, correct?"

Safar chuckled. "Another sort of question no wizard will ever answer, my friend," he said. "But let me tell you this. If I do, your wives will be the first to notice!"

The caravan master roared laughter, leaping to his feet to drag Safar from his chair for another tortuous embrace of Coralean friendship.

"What a man you are, Safar Timura!" he cried. "What a man!"

Then he broke away to refill their goblets.

"More drink, Safar," he said. "More drink. It's the only honorable way to seal a bargain between such like-minded brothers.

"To Syrapis!" he shouted, raising his glass.

"To Syrapis!" Safar replied. "And may we live long enough to see it!"

CHAPTER THIRTY
THE FACE OF MURDER

Luka was a fighting prince. Born of rape and murder, teethed on steel, he had carried his father's royal banner into scores of crucial encounters. Under Iraj, he had seen warfare on an even greater scale. When it came to the shedding of blood and the taking of life, Luka firmly believed he had seen it all. But when he led his shock troops into the Caluzian Pass all his previous experiences seemed like nothing.

The road through the pass was treacherous. The storm had left a thick blanket of snow in its wake, hiding the pits and broken rubble, turning them into traps for the unwary. Overhead, a threatening sky boiled with clouds that cast everything into intermittent shadows, making travel harder still. Even the demon steeds with their fierce natures and huge cat claws were sorely tested. Several suffered broken limbs and had to be destroyed before they'd progressed beyond the second bend.

Luka thought he knew what to expect. Fari's vision had given him a good look at the enemy he would face. Powerful spells had been cast to sheath their weapons so they would cut through ghostly flesh and parry ghostly thrusts. Even so, he was not prepared when the horde of warriors rose up to confront him.

The battle for the Caluzian Pass was to consist of three waves, of which Luka's was easily the most dangerous. He was to lead a shock force composed of his best cavalryfiends. His mission was to charge through and break the enemy formation. Under no circumstances was he to engage in fixed fighting or worry about what was happening behind his back. He was to charge and keep charging, leaving the next two waves of troops to deal with whatever was happening behind him. Not only that, but he must maintain his demon form to inspire his soldiers, thereby abandoning the extra magical powers and strength of a shape changer. In short, if the slightest thing went wrong he would be the first to fall.

Skilled as he was, brave as he was, Luka had no love of battle. As a prince his death was always ardently sought—on both sides. The enemy wanted his head as a trophy of their prowess. And in his own court so many would gain from his assassination that he had to be constantly on lookout for a knife in his back from one of his own soldiers. So he despised battles. Distrusted the motives of those who sent him to fight.

Killing, he firmly believed, was a dish to be enjoyed in private. It was like torturing an animal bound for the table—the greater the entree's agony, the tastier the dish. In other words, the fear and pain should be confined to the victim with no danger to the chef.

Luka was thinking of such things when he entered the pass and so he shouldn't have been surprised when he was stricken by a sudden feeling that he'd entered a kitchen where he was set to be the main course. Never mind that Fari had warned him—and armed him—against the spells of fear and hopelessness the enemy was sure to employ against him. A vision leaped into his mind's eye of a demon bound to a spit slowly rotating over a slow fire—twisting and screaming and begging his tormentors to end the agony with a swift and merciful death. The demon was Luka.

The prince might have been overcome there, the battle lost before it had even begun. But the moans and wails of his brother warriors jolted him to his senses. Cursing himself as a fool and a coward, he cast Fari's spell. There was nothing to mark one moment from the next. No fiery blast, no sorcerous smoke, only an immediate feeling of heavy shackles falling away—and then he was free.

His demon brothers shouted gleefully, as if they'd already won a great victory. Jokes and laughter ran through the ranks, punctuated by loud boasts from young warriors about what they'd do to the enemy when they found him. Luka was too experienced to be drawn in. He had no doubt this would be only the first of many spells hurled against them. And if his opponent was wily he would be saving the worst for last.

A dedicated survivor, Luka granted extreme cunning to his enemy. But he couldn't pause or turn back to study the extent of his enemy's perfidy. In such circumstances a prudent soldier, a soldier loath to have his fangs plucked from his lifeless jaws to make a necklace for some tavern wench, knows he has only one recourse—madness.

Luka signaled his buglers to sound the attack, unsheathed his sword, and raised it high—desperately driving away the memory of the human, Vister, in identical circumstances. Digging deep for all the courage, all the blind battle lust he could muster.

"For the King!" he shouted over the blare of the horns.

"For the King!" his brothers roared in return.

And with no enemy in sight they charged.

In the end, it was this act of madness that saved him.

As Luka came around the bend, honor guard lagging several paces behind him, his mount's claws broke through the snow's crust into a hidden pit. The beast stumbled, nearly foundering, Luka sawing on its reins and raking its sides with his spurs to bring it up. Hissing in catlike fury, the animal's head snaked around, long fangs bared to punish him. He leaned forward, whacking its sensitive nose with the flat of his blade to remind it who was master and who was slave.

At that moment the air was suddenly filled with the deadly song of the arrow and something passed over his head. He heard meaty thunks of arrows striking their targets, cries of the wounded, surprised coughs of those who would never breathe again.

He came up, raising his shield in time to deflect a second swarm, cursing Iraj for putting him in such a place. Shouting orders to rally his warriors out of the shock of ambush.

It was then that he saw the enemy. Time was knocked from its course and Luka's whole world became a long and frozen moment. Hundreds upon hundreds of ghostly warriors were marching toward him. There were no challenging roars, no shouted insults, no loud chorus of what would be done to them. He heard none of the words that give a normal army its voice. Curses that warriors are encouraged to shout when they advance on their foes. Shouts of bloody purpose crafted by bullying sergeants long ago and passed down from one generation of soldiers to the next. All calculated to shrink the enemy's courage and enlarge the imagined prowess of the aggressor.

Luka, who would have ignored such things like a fishing hawk ignores water when it dives for its prey, was unnerved by their absence. His entire existence was suddenly filled with the image of silent men, deadly men, marching in measured steps to crush his life away. The thud of their boots, the clank of their armor, hammering their purpose against his.

Fari's final words of warning crawled to the fore. "There is no single heart to this enemy," he'd said. "No single head we can lop off to defeat them. Each one will fight until the end. The only way to defeat them is to kill them all."

Luka forced himself to ignore the mass of advancing warriors. He fixed on one man—a huge ghost with hollow eyes and bloody lips—one step ahead of the others.

The demon prince spurred his mount forward, shouting for his soldiers to follow.

He had time for one long breath, then he was on them. The large ghost he'd aimed for hurled his spear with such force that it broke Luka's shield in two. He threw the shield away, slashing with his spell-charged sword. He had a moment's satisfaction of feeling his blade bite through ghostly flesh, seeing the man fall, mouth coming open to spew blood-red smoke, then he felt the shock of collision as his mount crashed into the advancing soldiers. That shock followed another and then another as his fiends waded into battle, cutting and jabbing, forcing their way through by the sheer weight of their massed charge.

Made vulnerable by Fari's spells, the ghosts no longer had the protection of shadowy afterlife. When they were struck they died, bloody smoke spurting from their mouths. Even so, they did not die easily. They fought with wild but still silent purpose. Luka killed many of them, but he saw just as many of his own soldiers die as well.

For what seemed like an eternity the struggle was stalled at the point of first collision. It seemed that every ghost who died was immediately replaced by another. Luka felt as if he were pressing against a huge wall. And no matter how hard he fought, the wall would not give.

Just when he thought all was hopeless, he sensed a sudden weakening. He pressed harder, driving his mount against the armored mass, crying out for others to join him.

Then the line broke and Luka burst through the first formation. A moment later he was surrounded by his own soldiers who were streaming through the gap.

Luka had enough time to see a second force—mighty as the first—coming toward him.

He charged, once again bracing for the shock of collision.

Then blood lust overcame him and he knew no more.

*   *   *

Biner turned away from the scene below, sickened by the slaughter.

"I can't watch anymore," he said to Arlain. "Got nothin' left in me guts to heave."

Hidden by the magical cloud cover, the balloon was hovering over the Caluzian Pass spying on Iraj's fight to take it.

"Poor devils," Biner said. "Dyin' once seems hard enough. But twice!" He shuddered. "Makes me skin crawl even thinkin' about it, much less havin' to watch! It's more'n a sensitive showman like meself can take."

Arlain stood well away from the railing, trembling, tears streaming down her face. She hadn't been able to watch at all.

"Ith it over yet?" she asked.

Biner nodded. "Almost," he said. "For awhile I was hopin' them Guardians wouldn't break. But they did. And then old Protarus hit 'em twice more. Mos' awful thing I ever did see—or ever hope to see. Protarus' fiends are down there now finishin' off what's left."

"Pleath!" Arlain protested. "Don't tell me anymore. All I think of ith what'th going to happen if thoth awful tholdierth catch uth."

Biner squared his massive shoulders. "They won't!" he vowed. "Not if old Biner can help it."

"If only Thafar would get back," Arlain said.

"Never mind Safar," Biner said. "He's either gonna make it or he ain't. We have to be ready either way."

"Maybe they won't find the gate into the valley," Arlain said hopefully. "Maybe they'll mith it and jutht keep on going."

Biner snorted. "Sure," he said. "And smoke don't rise, the wind don't change, and if you dump the balloons the airship'll just keep on flyin'!"

*   *   *

King Protarus was agitated as he approached the group gathered around Lord Fari. From the angry tone of the voices he heard echoing across the gory snow, the king was riding into the middle of a debate. It was an argument so heated the participants didn't notice the imminent arrival of the royal party.

Iraj pulled up his horse, raising a hand to bring his aides and guards to a halt. Pushing aside the reason for his agitation, he leaned forward, listening.

"This is insanity, Fari!" Luka was raging. "You're holding up the entire godsdamned army with all your second-guessing."

"I must agree with Prince Luka," Kalasariz said. "There's a time for caution and a time to strike onward."

Then their voices dropped to more normal levels and Iraj couldn't hear what was said. He let the shape-changer's side of him come to the fore, snout erupting, bones cracking and shifting horribly, forming the head of a giant wolf sitting on a human body. There were involuntary gasps of terror from his men and he snarled for silence.

With his heightened senses he could hear their words with startling clarity.

"How many times must I repeat myself," Fari was raging, "before you two fools understand what I am trying to tell you. Lord Timura's trail ends here. It does not continue on through the pass."

"Something must be wrong with your sniffers, Fari," Luka said. "And as always you are too stuffed with pride to admit it when your magic fails you. I'm the one who is most at risk here. I'm the one who nearly died I don't know how many times today. I am the one most likely to die as a result of your pride. But never mind that. The point is, this halt you ordered is not only likely to result in many unnecessary casualties, but also endangers the entire expedition. The longer we wait to clear the rest of the pass, the more time we give the enemy to regroup."

"And for Safar Timura to escape," Kalasariz put in. "Which is far more important. I guarantee you that if we bring him to ground, Protarus won't care how many of our soldiers' lives were wasted."

"I warn you both," Fari said. "If you prevail over me with the king Lord Timura has an extremely good chance of prevailing over us."

Kalasariz sneered. "You've underestimated this man all along, Fari. As have you, Luka. I have more experience with him than either of you. I first tried to kill him when he was nothing more than a ragged-cloaked student in Walaria with barely enough funds to pay for the crusts he ate. I even had him on the executioner's block. On his knees, mind you. His neck bent for the sword. He escaped despite what any rational fellow would judge as impossible odds against him. Just as he has escaped us countless times ever since."

Fari rasped laughter. "What's this?" he mocked. "You tried to kill Timura before? During a time when it was known to all he was the king's dearest friend. Why, it was my impression that you told the king you were Timura's secret ally in Walaria. You repeated that tale when we went to the king with charges that Timura was conspiring against him. A tale you told in the manner of a man who was shocked to learn of Timura's perfidy."

Kalasariz started to answer, but just then the three sensed Iraj's presence. They turned, gaping when they saw him, burying their reactions as quickly as they could.

Iraj kept his wolf's head intact for a long moment, making sure they'd worry about how much he'd overhead. The spy master, whose remarks gave him reason to have the most to fear, was the first to recover.

"Hail, O King!" Kalasariz cried. "Once again you have inspired us to win a great victory!"

Fari and Luka shouted similar bold words of praise.

Iraj resumed his human shape, flicking the reins for his horse to amble forward. He sat easily in the saddle as if he hadn't a care in the world, letting a sarcastic smile play across his face to heighten their tension. Inside, his emotions were boiling to a froth. There were two more battles he had to win before the day was done. First, Safar. Next, his spell brothers. To build confidence and bring his emotions under control he imagined Safar's corpse under his boot while he confronted these three—his final enemies. From this moment on he had to view everything as a sport. A sport in which Iraj Protarus, king of kings, had no master. With one hand he would display a whip of fear, with the other, a broad palm heaped with the gift of the king's favor.

As Iraj closed the distance between them Fari caught a whiff of the king's intent—plus . . . something else. Something he couldn't quite put a talon on, except that it did not bode well for him or his companions in conspiracy. In his long life Lord Fari had advised and survived many kings. It was his ambition that Iraj Protarus would be the last royal fool he had to suffer. A master wizard, a demon of incredible cunning, Fari knew every mask a king could present to his royal advisers. And in Iraj's face he read his demise. His old heart bumped over the rocky road of logic. It was the Spell of Four that chained Protarus to them. A spell that he had created and cast. A bond that could be rearranged—with Fari as the ultimate mechanic—but not broken. Then suspicion, his most faithful friend, crept into his bosom. The king has a secret, he thought. A secret that did not bode well for any of them.

Before Iraj came within hearing distance, Fari whispered, "Beware, brothers! If you want to live, be with me!"

"Bugger you!" Luka whispered. "We're in the right. You are most grievously wrong."

"Who cares?" Kalasariz hissed. The spy master didn't have to reflect on Fari's warning. He too, sensed danger. "New truce. Quick!"

"And let you be the first to stab me in the back?" Luka replied. "Bugger you as well!"

"Trust me!" Fari urged. "Or all is lost!"

"Truce, dammit! Truce!" Kalasariz said.

Iraj rode up before Luka had a chance to answer. On horseback Iraj towered over them, his crown sparkling with jewels and rare metals. Shoulders squared, head uplifted, that knowing, scar-twisted smile playing across his lips, making his face unreadable.

The king raised his sword to Luka in salute. "It is you who should be congratulated for this victory, my good and loyal friend," he said. "Your bravery is an example to us all."

As the demon prince bowed in humble thanks the sense of peril became so strong his skin pebbled and began to itch as if he were about to molt.

"I am not worthy, Your Majesty," he murmured.

"Don't be so modest," Iraj said. "It is you and you alone who deserves full credit. And to reward your great deeds I will give you the honor of leading my army onward to even greater glories."

Not far away Kalasariz' assassins were roaming the battlefield cutting the throats of the enemy fallen with magical knives. Making certain no Guardian would never rise again. Luka heard the tell-tale hiss of ghostly life fleeing the temporal world and reconsidered.

"Modesty has nothing to do with it, Your Majesty," he said. "The fact is, at this time it would be imprudent of me to assume such an honor."

Iraj let his eyebrows rise as if he were surprised at this statement. "Is there some problem?"

"Only one of indecision, Your Majesty," Luka said. He gestured at his companions. "At this moment we were debating the merits of what to do next."

Out of the corner of his eye Luka saw Fari and Kalasariz visibly relax. The truce was on.

"What's this?" Iraj said. "A disagreement? At such a crucial moment for us all?"

"Only a small one, Majesty," Fari said, wringing claws of humility. "My brothers think we should continue on until we reach the end of this pass. And, presumably, come upon Lord Timura waiting for us in Caluz. I, on the other hand, believe that some sort of trick has been played on us."

Further down the pass they heard a chorus of frustrated howls from a pack of sniffers. Fari nodded toward the sound. "Safar Timura doesn't wait for us there, Majesty," he said. "At least that is my opinion. I think we will only find the machine that has been bedeviling us since we entered the Black Lands. If I am right, many of us will die before we have time to turn back. And once again Lord Timura will most certainly be laughing up his sleeve at us as he makes his escape."

Iraj peered down at Kalasariz. Although he was smiling, his eyes were deadly. "And you, my lord?" he asked. "Where do you stand?"

"With Prince Luka, Majesty," Kalasariz said. He nodded at Fari. "No disrespect intended, of course. Only an honest disagreement among brothers who wish to serve you well."

Iraj already knew the substance of their disagreement. But he didn't know the reason. He brought himself up short. There were many perils in the double-think necessary to this game he played. Above all things, Iraj reminded himself, you have to remember that Safar must come first. Once that game was won, the end of these traitorous bastards would quickly follow. Before he shifted his attention, however, he made special note that once again his three opponents had overcome their personal animosities to oppose him as one.

Then he had another thought and his belly crawled. But what of his dream? The one that had been bedeviling him when he came upon these deadly conspirators. He gritted his teeth, remembering his terror. Yes, the dream. A dream within a dream so complicated it defied rational interpretation. And yet it was the sort of dream a man could relive in its entirety in the blink of an eye.

Iraj blinked.

And relived the dream . . .

*   *   *

He was only a boy, too young to be alone in the mountains. His name was Tio and he had spent a sleepless night guarding the goat herd against imagined horrors. Now he slept the sleep of the exhausted, the gentle dawn rising over the peaceful Kyranian mountains.

Iraj was a wolf, a great gray wolf, slipping across the meadow, leading his ravenous spell brothers to the kill. His plan was to slay the boy but leave the herd untouched. A coldly calculated murder intended to strike terror in the hearts of the Kyranians and undermine their faith in their vaunted hero, Safar Timura.

During Iraj's time with these people, who in his youth had shielded him against his enemies, he'd learned that wolves killed goats, not people. So poor little Tio, defenseless Tio, a child who whose death would wring pity from the hardest of hearts, would be his meat that day. He and his spell brothers would gut him, ravage him, and when the villagers came to investigate they'd find the goats bleating over the child's remains.

Then Kalasariz howled a warning, "Interlopers!" and Iraj spotted Graymuzzle and her starving pack descending on the goats. His rage was immediate and uncontrollable. How dare these wizened creatures plot to spoil his carefully wrought plan? His pent up shape changer's fury exploded and he charged into the pack, scattering them. All he could think of was "kill, kill," and so he killed and kept killing until there was nothing left alive on the meadow except Graymuzzle, trapped against a rock outcropping.

But as he went for her, instead of cowering and meekly accepting death, she suddenly roared in a fury as wild as his own. She leaped at him, slavering jaws snapping to do whatever damage she could before she died. Iraj caught an image of pups whining in a cave and knew the reason for her blind, suicidal attack. It made her death all the more delicious and his spell brothers crowded in close beside him to lap up her torment.

Ordering the others back, Iraj went to the little stone shelter alone, eager to feed on the child who waited there asleep. He rushed into the shelter, every nerve firing in delightful anticipation. Tio bolted up, screaming in terror, raising his puny goatherder's staff to protect himself.

Iraj bit the staff in two, then killed the boy.

Suddenly the child was sitting up again, but this time instead of screaming, he was smiling, and it wasn't Tio's face he was looking at. It was Safar's! A young Safar, the Safar he'd known long ago with those gentle blue eyes that could see the good in him.

Shocked and frightened to his core, Iraj reeled back.

Safar said, "So tell me, brother. How do you like being king?" And then he laughed.

Iraj recovered, more furious than ever, hysterically so, thinking how can this be, how can this be? Safar smiled the whole time he was killing him.

But he wouldn't stay dead. He kept rising, calling Iraj brother, his laughter becoming more mocking each time he died.

Finally, it was over and the corpse lay still under his paws and Iraj knew it would rise no more.

Exhausted, emptied of all emotion, Iraj stared down at the body.

But when he saw the youthful face staring up at him the horror came full circle.

For the face was his own!

✳   ✳   ✳

"Majesty?" Fari was murmuring. "Is something wrong?"

Iraj blinked and he was back in the Caluzian Pass, his spell brothers looking at him anxiously.

"No," he said, shaking off the dream. "There's nothing wrong. I was only considering our problem." He turned to Fari. "I've heard all sides of the dispute," he said. "Save one thing."

"Yes, Majesty?" Fari asked.

Iraj said, "What do you propose we do? Luka and Kalasariz say we should continue on through the pass. You say we shouldn't. But you haven't said what we ought to do instead. We can't just sit here scratching our heads forever in dumb amazement at Safar's latest trick. If, as you say, it is a trick."

Fari drew himself up, confidence restored. He said, "Majesty, if you we allow me two hours—three at the most—I think I can solve the riddle of the vanished Lord Timura." He pointed at a rock outcropping bulging from a nearby canyon wall. "His trail ends there. Our sniffers have searched and double-searched the area in all directions. But they keep coming back to this point."

"Go on," Iraj said.

"I suggest," Fari said, "that I be allowed to gather my wizards together and make a casting to find out exactly what happened."

Iraj looked at Luka and Kalasariz, then back at Fari, thinking. There was good logic on both sides. It was Iraj's nature to favor quick action. But on the other hand—Iraj chopped off further speculation and made his decision. And he said to Fari:

"Call your wizards!"

CHAPTER THIRTY ONE
THE FIGHT FOR CALUZ

Leiria thought the valley was particularly beautiful that day. Blue skies, sweet breezes, joyous birds swooping over fruited fields and babbling rivers. Looking down on them from the hilltops the city of Caluz shone under the gentle sun, seemingly full of promise and hope and welcome.

Leiria thought of the palace courtyard heaped with all the Caluzian dead and turned away, choking on bile.

The business awaiting her didn't make her feel any better. At the moment she was sitting at a small camp table going over last minute arrangements with Khadji Timura and Sergeant Dario.

"No one is very happy about this latest plan of yours, Leiria," Khadji said. "They want you to reconsider. Some of them are even demanding it."

Leiria sighed, shaking her head. Civilians! What could you do with them? They kept imagining orders were open to debate.

"Tell them no," she said.

Khadji frowned. "You really ought to at least hear them out," he protested. "Frankly, I'm in agreement with many of their complaints."

Leiria's eyes hardened. It was all she could do to keep from snapping his head off. Sometimes Safar's father could be a most difficult man. Then her lips twitched with a sudden urge to smile. And so is Safar, she thought. And his mother. And his sisters. Hells, all the Timuras were absolute mules. Even Palimak seemed to have caught the disease.

Calmed, she did her best to temper her words. "I don't know how many times we've been over this, Khadji," she said. "I thought we were in agreement. It might not be the best plan, but it's the only one that might, just might mind you, give us a chance."

"I'm with the Captain, here," Dario broke in. He nodded at the nearby field where young Kyranian soldiers were pawing through their gear, keeping some things, but throwing most of it away. "And you can tell the knotwits on the Council of Elders that so are my lads."

"You don't understand," Khadji said. "We've already lost our homes and almost all of our possessions. All we have left of our old lives are the few things we've managed to carry along in our wagons. Now you want us not only to abandon them, but to leave the wagons as well. Plus most of the animals. You're even begrudging us a few extra clothes."

"You can't eat clothes," Leiria said. "You can't fight with clothes. That's a lesson everyone should have learned by now."

Dario glowered at Khadji. "And you can't eat clay pots, either," he said, "in case that's what's really stuck in your craw."

Khadji blushed. "I'll admit that was on my mind," he said. "If only I could—"

Leiria put a hand on his. "Listen to me, Khadji," she said. "I promised Safar that if Iraj found us before he got back I'd do everything I could to see that as many of you as possible escape. I'm not trying to be cruel or unfeeling, but the way I've outlined is the best I can manage."

Drawing on her last reserves of patience, she went over the plan one more time. She'd divided the Kyranians into two groups—those who would fight and those who would run. The latter was by far the largest group, women and children and those too old or infirm to fight. When and if they got the signal all of those people, led by Khadji who had the maps, were to head for the mountains.

"Aim for those peaks," Leiria said, pointing at the twin pillars that towered over the range. "With luck, you'll find a track there to make things easier. Just make sure the track heads north to the Great Sea."

Khadji nodded. "There's a port at Caspan," he said. "I saw it on the map."

"Yes, Caspan," Leiria said. "Safar said we might be able to get some ships there. And I've given you the gold he left to hire them to take us to Syrapis."

"What about Safar?" Khadji said mournfully. "What about my son? And little Palimak! What about him?"

"I think it would be best if you put them out of your mind," Leiria said. "Concentrate on getting to those peaks. Then set your sights on Caspan. Let the rest of us, including Safar and Palimak, worry about how we're going to catch up to you."

Then she carefully explained the rest of the plan. As Khadji and the villagers fled, Sergeant Dario and the bulk of the soldiers would follow in their footsteps as shields.

Meanwhile, Leiria and a small force of their best soldiers would attempt to hold Iraj at the breakthrough point for as long as they could. When the inevitable rout came the survivors would fall back to join Dario. The strategy from there would be to fight a rear guard action—using every trick Dario and Leiria had drummed into the young men to keep Iraj from overtaking the refugees.

"Speed is our only real defense," Leiria said. "Iraj taught me the value of speed long ago. That, and surprise, win more battles than not. When Iraj breaks through he'll think his job is nearly done. In his mind all he'll have to do is overtake a caravan moving at the speed of the slowest group. Ox-drawn wagons and heavily laden people on foot. Which is why I want to leave all that behind and fool him at the start. We won't fool him long, but gods willing it will be just long enough."

To accomplish this, Leiria had ordered that everything be abandoned but the barest necessities. Anything the Kyranians took with them would be loaded on the goats and llamas and horses, with experienced mountain lads to drive them along. The old and the sick and the very young would ferried to safety on horses and camels.

Dario gave a sharp nod of agreement when she was done. "A fine plan," he said. "One of the best these old ears have ever heard."

Khadji wavered. "Maybe," he said. "Maybe."

Dario snorted. "No maybe to it," he said. "Quit chewin' on it, man, and swallow."

"I'll do my best to make them listen," Khadji said. "But I can't promise what their reaction will be."

Leiria's patience collapsed. "I'll make it easy for you," she said. "From this moment on army rules will apply to all situations."

Ignoring Khadji's puzzled look, she turned to Dario.

"Sergeant!" she snapped.

Dario stiffened. "Yes, Captain."

"You will tell your men that once the enemy is engaged anyone who disobeys my commands is to be killed on the spot. No questions. No excuses. No arguments. And no hesitation. Do you understand?"

Dario buried a grin and snapped a salute. "Yes, Captain," he growled. "And I'll make it my personal business they start with the Council of Elders."

Khadji goggled at her. "You wouldn't really do that!" he said.

She gave him the hardest look she could. "I swear on my friendship and love of Safar, your son, that I will do everything I say."

Before he could respond there was a loud explosion from overhead. Their heads jerked up and all eyes were immediately fixed on the airship sailing over the mountains into the valley. A bright green flare guttered in its wake. Immediately there was a second explosion as Biner fired off another of Safar's magical flares.

"Iraj has found us," Leiria said, flat. "Now we'll see who wants to live and who wants to die."

An hour later she was standing next to the outcropping that marked the magic gate into Caluz. A few feet away Renor and Seth were inspecting the weapons of the brave few who would make this last stand. Off in the distance she could see the Kyranians streaming out of the valley as fast as they could. It was the oddest caravan she'd ever seen. Bleating goats and llamas, light packs tied to their backs, were leaping ahead of the refugees, scrambling over the rocky path that led into the mountains. Old men and women swayed back and forth on bawling camels, infants clutched in their arms. Just behind them came the main group led by Khadji, followed by Dario and his soldiers, who were cracking whips and roaring for everyone to "hurry, hurry, hurry!"

And not once did she see anyone stop to argue. Leiria had only a moment's satisfaction. Safar would be pleased. Then she suddenly felt very cold and very alone. Was this how she would end? In this bedamned valley with no one to care and no one to mourn her passing? A knot rose in her throat and she suddenly felt very sorry for herself. If only she could see Safar once more. If only they could kiss one final time, she thought, it might all seem worthwhile. Then she became angry with herself for allowing such weakness. She swiped at a leaky eye, muttering all the curses at her command, lashing confidence and resolve back into life. It was difficult. Surprisingly so. Fear scuttled into her belly when she realized just how far and how deep her morale had plummeted.

Then she heard a shout from overhead. Leiria look up and saw the airship settling closer to the ground, Biner and Arlain and the other circus performers gathered at the rail to look down at her.

"We're with you, Leiria!" Biner roared in his loud, pure, ringmaster's voice.

Arlain waved to her, shooting a long, gaily colored stream of dragon flames from her mouth. Kairo tipped his head in salute, making funny faces. Elgy and Rabix played a stirring tune, filling the air and her heart with glad music.

Then they all leaned far out over the railing to chorus, "Damn everything but the circus!"

And she was no longer alone.

Laughing and weeping tears of relief, Leiria waved at them.

At that moment the ground lurched under her feet and the outcropping bulged outward as if under extreme pressure. Shale broke and Leiria ducked as debris showered down on the path.

Then all was still and all was silent.

Her temples pulsed in slow time with the beat of her heart. Once . . . Twice . . . Thrice . . .

Wolves bayed and she drew her sword, boots spreading apart into fighting stance. Renor and the other young soldiers gathered around her, their weapons at the ready, cursing loudly to control their chattering teeth.

Then the outcropping swung away on magical hinges and Leiria peered into the revealed darkness.

Nothing.

She looked deeper.

Still nothing.

And deeper still, nerves winding tighter, neck muscles cabling with tension, each second a water drop trembling to fall.

It was almost a relief when nothingness ended and the yellow-eyed demons scrambled out of the darkness to get her.

She shouted a challenge and braced herself to meet them.

*   *   *

This time Biner couldn't turn away. This time Arlain made herself watch. They saw the earth shudder, saw the gate swing open and then Leiria's shout reached out to chill them. To fix them on the scene below. They saw Leiria brace, saw her soldiers flow in to form a line—Leiria at its center. Suddenly a demon horde burst out of the gateway, ululating war cries shattering the air.

Then the two lines converged and Leiria was swallowed up in the chaos of battle.

"Now! Now!" Arlain cried. "Do it now!"

She lunged toward a pile of crates heaped near the railing. Biner stopped her, gently pulling her back.

"We have to wait," he said. "It's not time for our entrance."

Arlain heard cries of pain from below and trembled. "We have to help her," she pleaded.

"Not yet," Biner said. Then, to cut through—"Remember how we rehearsed it."

Arlain sagged, overcome by performer's logic, and turned back to the railing. Whispering the actor's mantra for strength: "Character, timing, plot, character, timing plot . . ." and so on as the tale unfolded beneath her.

She made herself think of it that way. A tale to be told in two acts. Act One: The villains attack. Heroes fight bravely, but are overwhelmed. Act Two: Heroes retreat, villains in pursuit, all seems lost. Cue The Forces of Good. Which was Arlain's cue, the circus' cue—the big It Was All A Clever Trick Surprise. Villains routed, heroes rewarded, cue the music—Happy Ending, ta da!

Arlain watched the horror below, doing a very bad job at keeping her actor's pose, visibly shrinking as the sights and sounds of battle increased. Awaiting her cue.

Leiria was a calm center to the storm raging about her. It was place where there was no fear or anger. No shrill relief when she parried a well-struck blow, no fierce animal enjoyment at slipping a guard and killing her opponent. She was a cold, calculating killing machine, ripping through every weak point her enemy revealed. And there were many. So many weaknesses she could end the fight now with a rallying cry for her men to charge the demons and seal the gap.

She and Safar had planned for this moment. The doorway between the pass and the valley was no more than two wagons wide. No matter how large the force Iraj hurled at them only so many could come through the gap at a time. A handful of determined soldiers would be enough to stop them. The problem was, this handful could only kill a finite number and with the enormous force opposing them it was only a matter of time before they were overwhelmed. To give the fleeing villagers any chance at all more time and more enemy casualties were needed.

Leiria kept her mind fixed on the plan, an impersonal observer of very personal events.

A demon towered over her, roaring in her face. Slicing at her with a huge battle ax and at the same time lashing out with a demon spell of hopelessness—the image of a cowering rabbit about to be carried away by an owl.

In theory it was an unequal contest. Demons had size, speed, and magic over humans. But Leiria was a former captain of Iraj's personal body guard, trained and blooded in all varieties of encounters—be they human or be they demon—and so these things meant nothing to her. She was doubly armed that day, as were all the Kyranians, with Palimak's necklaces. Which made it even easier to turn back the demon's spell so that He was the bleating rabbit, and She was the owl.

Whoosh! as the ax swung down.

Shriek! as Leiria's owl froze the demon.

Snack! Snack! and Leiria's sword parried the faltering blow.

Then another *Whoosh!* for her final stroke and then the sounds became very ugly as the demon fell, farting and shitting his last dinner, crying for his mother as Leiria stepped over him to meet the next ax.

On either side of her she heard Renor and Seth hoot with owl-like glee as they similarly dealt with their opponents. The hoot was taken up by the other young men, and they pressed forward, shrilling "hoot, hoot, hoot," killing and killing until the demon line began to waver.

Leiria was nearly overtaken by their blood lust. She saw hundreds of yellow eyes swirling in the darkness, howling for blood, hurling curses to diminish her.

Do it now! she thought. Do it now!

And she signaled the retreat.

Biner saw the Kyranian line waver, then break. He immediately shouted orders to dump the ballast and all hands rushed to the side to drop the sandbags.

The airship, suddenly relieved of weight, shot upward, climbing high above the battle scene. Clouds passed under the ship and the figures below became very small. Even so, they still kept their significance and Biner felt a mailed fist clutch his guts as Leiria made her dangerous maneuver.

To his amazement, it seemed to be working. When the Kyranians fell back it was as if a pent-up flood had been released and hundreds of demon warriors burst through the gate, swarming down the hillside after Leiria and her retreating soldiers. From his vantage point Biner could immediately see the grave error the demons had made. The error Leiria had been counting on.

As the enemy warriors rolled down the hill they suddenly found themselves milling about in a small valley—a dip in the terrain their officers had no way of knowing about. It looked like a bowl from the airship, a bowl quickly filling up with confused enemy soldiers who had only one way to go and that was straight up the hill to where Leiria stood her ground.

Leiria reformed her line and began firing arrows into their ranks to block the advance.

Biner waited until the valley was nearly brimming over with soldiers, then turned to Arlain and the others.

"Showtime folks!" he said. "Showtime!"

*   *   *

Leiria and her men were down to their last few arrows when the flaming crates and barrels came tumbling out of the sky.

"Get down!" she shouted, and everyone leaped for cover.

Just then the first crates struck and the ground was rocked by explosions. More immediately followed, a fast series of *whump! whump! whumps!* Leiria's whole world suddenly became very small as stones and clods of earth rained over her. Waves of heat followed each blast, searing her back. She hugged the ground, trying not to listen to the screams of the demons.

*   *   *

Iraj watched his panicked soldiers pour back through the gateway, crushing fallen comrades beneath their feet in their desperation to escape. His spell brothers were knotted around his traveling throne, stunned by the rout.

"I wouldn't call that a glorious first effort," he said dryly.

"It was merely a probe, Your Majesty," Prince Luka said, quickly trying to diminish the size of the defeat. "To feel out the enemy's defenses."

Iraj sneered at him. "Now we know," he said. "And the answer does not inspire my confidence in you."

"Pardon, Majesty," Kalasariz said, "but I don't think we should be too hard on our brave prince. Or make too much of what just happened. After all, how many times can Lord Timura withstand our assaults?"

"Kalasariz makes an excellent point, Majesty," Fari said. "Even now our wizards are preparing a spell that nothing can withstand. Not even Lord Timura."

Their gradually hardening unity disturbed Iraj. He had to get this over with before they discovered what he was up to. He had to get into that valley immediately. He had to defeat Safar. But he had to do it quickly so he could cast the spell that would free him from his spell brothers forever.

"Do it now," he said to Fari. "Get your wizards into that tunnel and do it now."

"But, Majesty," Fari protested. "We won't be ready for at least another—"

"Do it, Fari!" Iraj thundered. "Do it!"

*   *   *

Leiria surveyed the results of her victory. It was not a moment to savor—the valley had been turned into a enormous blackened grave, heaped with smoking bodies.

Behind her, she heard Seth and some of the other young men choking on the horror. She glanced up and saw the airship floating closer to the ground, the circus performers crowded along the rail looking down on the scene with haunted eyes.

Renor pushed up to her, his face pale and many years older than before.

"I hope I never have to see such a thing again," he said.

Leiria got herself under control. "You won't," she said. "Because next time it won't work."

She regretted the remark when she saw Renor's shock. He really hadn't had time to consider what they still faced.

"We'd better get ready," Leiria said. "I don't know how much time we have."

Just then she heard a familiar shout. She turned, heart leaping with joy when she saw who was riding to meet her.

It was Safar!

CHAPTER THIRTY TWO

SPELLBOUND

The moment their eyes met Leiria thought something was wrong. Safar was smiling, laughing, genuinely glad to see her, but he seemed withdrawn—as if he were hiding something. Even Palimak was strangely subdued, hesitating when she embraced him, then suddenly hugging her tightly as if he were afraid.

Then the soldiers and circus performers were crowding around shouting and babbling nonsense and the sense of wrongness was swept away in the happy reunion that followed. But the pall of death from the nearby battleground soon penetrated their happiness—a grim reminder that there was little time for such things.

Safar pulled everyone away, quickly explaining what had to be done next while he led them down to the field where the airship waited, straining at its cables.

"We have to move fast," he said, "before Iraj sticks his ugly head through that hole again."

Biner forced a grin. "And won't he be surprised when there's not a blessed soul waitin' for him."

Arlain shivered. "Thurprith?" she said. "What could thurprith a . . . a . . . *thing* like him?"

"It's Dario's surprise I'm thinking about," Renor said with a small laugh. "Imagine his face when he sees we're still alive. He probably thinks we're dead by now."

There was weak laughter at this, but there was a hard bite of hysteria to it. Safar put everyone to work stripping the airship of all unnecessary weight so they could board the ship and flee.

The sense of wrongness returned when Safar pulled Leiria aside.

"Walk with me," he said, taking her elbow and guiding her to a path that twisted down to the river.

Palimak walked next to her, still silent and oddly subdued. Khysmet plodded patiently behind, reins looped over the saddle horn.

Safar told her what had happened—about the distance-collapsing magical portal that waited on the other side of the mountains to carry them to Caluz, about the ships he'd hired to take them to Syrapis, and the agreement he'd made with Coralean.

Finally they reached the river bank, where Safar stopped. They were just a few hundred yards downstream from the peninsula where the Turtle of Hadin churned out its mechanistic magic.

When he stopped Leiria knew what was wrong. Especially when Palimak clutched her hand.

"You're not coming with us," she said—a statement, not a question.

Safar sighed. "I was getting to that," he said.

"But *why*, Safar?" Leiria cried. *"Why!"*

"There's no other way," he said. "I've already discussed this with Palimak. Ask him. He'll tell you—much as he dislikes admitting it."

Palimak's head dropped and he said, low and forlorn, "Father's right. There's no other way."

"But we're finally almost free of Iraj!" Leiria protested. "All the villagers—your family, your friends, everyone—are so far into the mountains now that he'll never catch them. In a few minutes we can join them, thanks to the airship. And then we're off to Syrapis with no reason ever to look back."

Safar shook his head. "I have to stop the machine," he said. "If I don't it will be the end of Esmir."

Leiria felt as if she'd just been clubbed. When she heard Safar's reason she knew there was nothing she could say or do—even if she had a tongue that coined only words of silver and a thousand years to argue in—that would change his mind.

Still, she had to try. "To hells with Esmir!" she said. "We were leaving here anyway."

"You don't understand," Safar said. "Actually, I didn't myself until after I spoke to Hantilia and got Asper's book. Some force—don't ask me *what* force, I can't yet say—is devouring the world from the inside out. I think of it as a voracious worm, a parasite, tunneling through the earth's belly looking for the weakest place where it can burst through and spread destruction. Hadin was the weakest point, the first place the worm broke through."

"And Esmir is next?" Leiria said.

Safar nodded. "Yes. At Caluz."

Leiria slumped, defeated.

"Don't worry," Safar said, trying to sooth her. "I have every chance of making it."

"Oh, of course you do," Leiria said, angry again. "In a few minutes several thousand blood-thirsty soldiers will be charging into this valley—led by four great wolves from the hells. While you're hammering away at that machine, or whatever you plan to do to disable it. And you'll be there all by yourself with no one to guard your back, or help you."

"Actually," Safar said with a thin smile, "I was planning on asking Iraj for help."

Leiria waved, dismissing the remark. "We don't have time for silly jokes," she said.

"It really isn't a joke, Aunt Leiria," Palimak broke in. "He has to have Iraj there or the spell won't work."

Leiria stared at Safar. The more she heard, the worse it became.

"Listen to me, Leiria," Safar said. "We really don't have as great a lead on Iraj as you think. He'll be in those mountains before the blink of an eye and everything we've done up to this point will be a tragic waste. I can delay him, perhaps even defeat him. Either way it will give my people the chance they need. When you catch up to them, use the airship to speed things up. All you have to do is get them to the top of those mountains.

Palimak can show you how to go from there."

"Please, Safar!" Leiria said. "Give me a chance to think. This is moving too fast and I don't know where it's going."

Safar put an arm around her. "The same place we've planned on from the beginning," he said. "Syrapis. But only if you do exactly what I tell you. Hear me out, Leiria. You have less than two days to get them through the portal before it closes. It shouldn't be too difficult—Palimak and I had no trouble getting back here. Even so, that's not much time to get to Caspan and meet Coralean."

"That's right," Leiria said, feeling numb. "Otherwise he'll sail without us."

"And he'd be insane to do otherwise," Safar said.

They heard people shouting and turned to see that everyone had boarded the airship and was ready to go.

"Aren't you even going to say goodbye to them?" Leiria asked.

"I wish I could," Safar said, eyes becoming moist. "But they'd only argue with me and there isn't time."

Leiria started to speak, but Safar stepped in, pulling her close. Crushing her to him, kissing her long and deep. A kiss of farewell. A kiss of regret.

Then he pulled away, saying, "See you in Caspan!"

Leiria nodded. "All right," she said. "Caspan."

She turned and started for the airship, walking slowly so Palimak could catch up after he'd spoken to his father.

Safar knelt beside the boy. "We've already talked about this," he said, "so you know what to do."

Palimak rubbed an eye. "Sure I do, father," he said, voice trembling.

"Do you have the book?"

Palimak patted the package in his tunic and nodded. "Yes, father," he said.

"And when you get to Caspan," Safar pressed, "what then? What did we agree?"

Palimak dodged the question. "I'm supposed to wait for you," he said.

Safar pressed harder. "Yes, but if it comes time to sail and I still haven't shown up—then what?"

Palimak started to cry, but Safar grabbed him by shoulders, stopping him.

"Then what, son?" he insisted. "Then what?"

Palimak sniffed. "We leave without you," he said.

Only then did Safar pull him close, hugging him and whispering that he loved him and calling him a brave boy, a noble boy, who could do all the things his father asked of him.

Finally, Safar stood up. "You'd better go, son," he said.

Palimak straightened his shoulders, trying to look manful. "Goodbye, father," he said.

He started to turn to leave, then stopped. "But what if they don't listen, father?" he asked.

"They'll listen," Safar insisted.

"Sure, but what if they don't?"

And Safar answered, hard—"Then make them!"

                    *   *   *

When Iraj stepped into the passageway he suddenly became frightened. Attack seemed imminent, danger a densely coiled spring ready to snap. He smelled the fear in his spell brothers and knew they were experiencing the same sudden cold dread. Never mind they were surrounded by a veteran guard of soldiers and wizards prepared to die to protect them. Never mind the passageway into Caluz had been declared safe—the enemy driven back.

The feeling of dread persisted, growing stronger with each step they took down the wide, torch-lit corridor. Where every wavering shadow seemed an assassin gathering to strike.

Moments before they had declared victory. The trouble was the victory had come too easily. True, Fari and his wizards had cast the mightiest of battle spells to clear the passageway—and beyond. They'd reamed it with magical fire, followed up by soul-shriveling spells no mortal could withstand. At the same time, expecting a counter-assault from Safar, they'd thrown up impenetrable shields designed to turn his own attack against him. Luka had quickly followed up, sending his best fighters rushing behind the spells to wipe out any force that remained.

Safar's expected counter never came and when the soldiers burst into the light on the other side, there was no one to meet them, with only the bodies of their own dead for evidence that any fighting had gone on before. Confident, Iraj had brushed aside all doubt and ordered his party forward to finish off Safar.

Now, as he moved toward the light shimmering at the end of the passage, all those doubts returned—and in greater strength. He thought, it's impossible . . . Safar couldn't have been defeated so easily. Then a second fear—what if he were dead? Iraj had to catch Safar alive, then kill him with his own hands or all his plans would be for naught.

Mind in turmoil, belly roiling with conflicting emotions, Iraj burst out of the passageway into dazzling light.

And found—nothing.

Iraj blinked in the strong sunlight, struggling to regain his bearings in the odd beauty of Caluz. All was serene, all was peaceful, but no matter where he looked he saw not one living soul.

He sniffed the air—Safar's spoor was so strong he knew he still must be there. His companions evidently agreed.

"It's only one of Timura's tricks," he heard Fari say.

"Yes, yes, a trick," Kalasariz agreed.

"A pitiful trick at that," Luka added. "There's no place he can hide that we can't find him."

Just then—on the hill directly opposite them—Iraj saw a lone horseman ride into sight. The man waved at him, almost cheerily, as if greeting an old friend.

It was Safar!

And he rose in his stirrups to shout: "This way, Iraj!"

Then Safar swung the horse about and cantered easily back down the hill as if he had nothing to fear in the world.

*   *   *

The airship hovered just above the mountain path, a sentinel for the last group of Kyranians streaming out of the Caluzian Valley to safety.

Palimak crouched in the observer's platform, watching the villagers pass under him. In a few minutes the airship would get the signal from Dario that all had crossed. Then it would be Palimak's duty to lead them through the portal to Caspan. He tried hard not to think about what would happen after that.

As the refugees passed by some of them spotted him on the platform. They cheered and waved and he forced himself to wave back, feeling like the blackest, the cruelest of liars. Because when they saw him they naturally thought Safar Timura was there, falsely raising their hopes that all was well.

He touched the package beneath his tunic—the Book of Asper. Suddenly the entire weight of world crushed down on him. What if his father didn't make it? What if his father were killed?

For a minute he couldn't breathe, then when he could he was overwhelmed by self pity. It wasn't fair! He was just a boy! Too young to be alone with so much sorrow, so much responsibility. How could they expect . . . and so on . . . and then a little voice piped up from his pocket:

"It won't be so hard, Little Master," Gundara said. "You can do it."

"That's a stupid thing is say," Gundaree broke in. "We're talking about saving the world, here!"

"Don't call me stupid!"

"Well, I don't know what else to call it. The whole thing's impossible no matter how you look at it. Saving the world, indeed! If I told Lord Timura once, I told him twice, there's no use. So why bother trying?"

Palimak broke in. "Gundaree?" he said.

"What, Little Master? How may I serve you?"

"Shut up, please!"

For some reason, he suddenly felt a little better.

*　　　*　　　*

Safar guided Khysmet toward the river shallows where he could cross over to the temple. The big stallion kept pulling at the reins, wanting to run, wanting to get the hells out of here before they were surrounded by all the known villains in the world.

Safar soothed him, saying "It's all right . . . it's all right . . ." Knowing all the while that it might very well *not* be all right! That any number of things might be happening right now, the least of which would be a swarm of arrows winging their way toward his exposed back.

To keep his nerve, Safar reminded himself that only two things could occur and he was prepared for both eventualities. The first—the worst—was that as soon as he had called out to Iraj, he would have four great wolves and an entire army charging down his back. This would be a very foolish thing for Iraj to do because Safar would make him pay with his life and still accomplish his purpose. Iraj was no fool and would know this, which led to the second possibility.

The possibility that allowed for Safar's survival, which made him rather prejudiced in its favor.

When Khysmet splashed through the shallows and still nothing had happened, Safar knew that Iraj had chosen correctly.

He started thinking he might live after all.

*　　　*　　　*

The Unholy Three immediately wanted to charge after Safar, but Iraj stopped them in place with a curt, "Hold!"

His command caught them in mid transformation. They were so surprised that they froze there, an ugly mixture of parts. Skin marred by erupting patches of fur, wolf snouts bursting under demon horns, shape-changer eyes burning out of deep pits. What monsters! Iraj thought, disgusted, horrified, at the sight of them. Then he saw himself in their ugliness and hated them even more.

Iraj pointed at Safar, who was riding down the hill toward the river. "Don't you think he *knows?*" he hissed, finger quivering. "Don't you think he's ready?" He fought for calm. "This is *Safar Timura*, you fools! If we charge after him we'll all be dead before we reach the top of the rise!"

While he was berating them his spell brothers had come unstuck and shifted back to their mortal forms. Good, Iraj thought. The weaker the better.

Fari sniffed the air, then shuddered as he caught the scent of all the killing traps Safar had conjured in their path.

"Your Majesty is certainly correct in his caution," he said. "Lord Timura may be trapped, but he can *still* bite."

Luka wasn't happy with this. He thought, no matter what that bastard Timura has up his wizardly sleeve, he can't stand up to a whole army. But Luka was wise enough to say nothing. He let Kalasariz beg the point and ask the diplomatic question.

The spy master nodded to his king. "We bow to Your Majesty's wisdom," he said. "Tell us what to do."

Iraj shrugged. "Follow him," he said.

✳   ✳   ✳

When Safar reached the temple grounds he dismounted and sent Khysmet on his way. He fed him a palmful of dates, turning away all the questions trembling on the whiskers of Khysmet's tender mouth as the horse nuzzled him. Whispering assurances all the while.

Then Safar drew away and said, "You know where to meet," and slapped him gently on the rump. Khysmet snorted, reared up, then came down to whirl and gallop away. In no time at all he was across the second river channel and heading for the meeting place they'd imagined together.

Safar glanced up and saw Iraj riding down the hill toward the temple. He started to count how many were with Iraj, then shrugged. At this point it didn't matter.

He swung his pack off his shoulder and dumped it upside down. Then he crouched beside the jumbled heap, sorted a few things out and soon had a little oil fire burning in a bowl. Safar heard the sound of many horses splashing across the shallows, but ignored them. Instead he pulled a small book from his sleeve and drew his little silver dagger to cut it up. He paused, looking fondly on his old friend, the little Book of Asper he'd carried with him since Walaria. He felt guilty about what he had to do with it. He almost wished Hantilia hadn't given him the second book—the one he'd bequeathed to Palimak. Otherwise he never would have thought of the spell.

The sound of horses cantering across the peninsula toward him broke the reverie. He started cutting up the book and feeding the leaves into the fire, chanting:

> "Hellsfire burns brightest
> In Heaven's holy shadow.
> What is near
> Is soon forgotten;
> What is far
> Embraced as brother;
> Piercing our breast with poison,
> Whispering news of our deaths.
> For he is the Viper of the Rose
> Who dwells in far Hadinland!"

He burned all the pages save one, which he kept back. Ignoring the sounds of soldiers dismounting and the approaching boots, he carefully twisted the page into a narrow stick, then lit the end. It burned slowly, like incense—smoke curling thinly from the glowing tip.

Finally Safar looked up and saw Iraj standing not ten feet away. Prince Luka was on his left, Fari his right, and Kalasariz leered over his shoulder. Framing them were at least a hundred soldiers, weapons ready, bows tensed for the killing command.

He paid no attention to any of them, fixing only on Iraj. Golden hair and beard blazing in the sun, royal armor gleaming, helmet under one arm, hand resting on the jeweled hilt of his sheathed sword. There was no doubt who was in command here.

Safar came to his feet, lazily twirling the burning stick between two fingers.

He smiled, saying, "So tell me, brother, how do you like being king?"

The words struck Iraj like a fire bolt fresh from the forge. The dream of the boy he'd slain, the boy who became Safar, with the gentle blue eyes that looked into his heart, whispering the question that had no answer. "So, tell me, brother, how do you like being king?"

"Enough of this nonsense!" Fari growled.

"Kill him now!" Luka demanded.

"Beware his cunning, Majesty!" Kalasariz hissed.

Safar twirled the burning stick of paper, still smiling, friendly, open, as if this were the most normal of meetings.

"Tell them, Iraj," he said, quite mild. "Tell them it's not as good for them as they think."

Iraj recovered. He smiled back, just as friendly. Just as open. It surprised him that it took so little effort.

"I already did, Safar," he said, with a small laugh. He tapped his head. "But sometimes they have trouble remembering the things I say."

"Oh, they listen," Safar said, returning Iraj's laugh. "We all listen! When the king speaks whole armies of clerks sift and sort his words so their masters can study them for their true meaning."

Iraj chuckled. "You mean they listen but they hear only what they want to hear."

Safar shrugged. "If had I put it that plainly," he said, "you never would have made me Grand Wazier. More words equals greater wisdom—that's what the priests taught me in Walaria."

Iraj snorted. "Priests! You know what I think of priests!" Another smile—reminiscing. "But there was one priest . . . old Gubadan."

Safar nodded, remembering the kindly schoolmaster who had overseen the unruly young people of Kyrania. Iraj and Safar had been the most mischievous of the lot, combining forces to bedevil him.

"What a windbag!" Iraj laughed. "But I liked him." He shrugged. "He was my friend."

"A commodity of great value," Safar said. "Even for a king." He gestured at Fari and the others. "Especially for a king."

Safar paused, eyes going back to Iraj's spell brothers. "Forgive me for not acknowledging you before, my lords," he said.

Then he addressed each one in turn, saying, "Greetings to you, Prince Luka," bowing slightly, waving the burning stick of paper, " . . . and you, Lord Fari," another bow, another wave of the stick, " . . .and, of course you, my dear, dear, Lord Kalasariz!"

He came up, spell nearly completed, turning to face Iraj.

"It seems that when it comes to friendship, Iraj," he said, "you have more reason than most to consider that homily."

One more bow, one more wave of the smoldering paper stick, and the spell was done. Safar gave himself a mental kick for thinking that. It wasn't done! This was only the end of the first act. He was only in the middle, the great sagging center of the tightrope. Now for the rest. He fixed his mind on his goal and prepared to move on.

Fari spoke up: "That was a very clever little spell, Lord Timura," he said. "It took me more time than my good reputation as a wizard can bear to unravel it. I assure you, however, that in the end, age bested wisdom. Look for yourself and I think you'll agree. Your spell has been effectively terminated."

Safar obediently concentrated, testing the magical atmospheres with his senses, confirming what he already knew, which was that Fari had fallen for Safar's spell-within-a-spell trick.

Calling on his most subtle acting abilities, Safar blinked with dismay—sinking the hook.

Another blink, then he forced a smile, making it overly wide and bold in a pretended attempt at recovery.

Barely controlling a trembling voice, he said, "We shall see, my lord, we shall see," as if he were supporting a bluff doomed at the first call.

Iraj observed all this, confidence growing by the minute. The game was going as he wanted, never mind Safar's spell, which he guessed was still in place regardless of what Fari had said.

He didn't need magic to sniff out his friend. The moment he saw Safar appear on the hill he knew his intention.

And when he heard his voice ring out, "This way, Iraj!" he knew it was more than a challenge. It was an invitation. An invitation that fit perfectly into Iraj's plans.

So he said, "Why don't we end this pretense, Safar? We've been friends—and enemies—much too long to be dishonest with one another. I am here for one reason, there is no other. And that reason is—"

"To ask my help?" Safar said, cutting him off.

He'd meant to be sarcastic, but when he saw Iraj's reaction he was surprised how close he'd come to the mark. He quick-sniffed the magical array against him. Double checked his defenses. Then he sensed it! A threat from Iraj he hadn't noticed before. He glanced at Iraj's spell brothers, noticing their growing awareness that something was amiss. And it wasn't Safar. It was—

"Listen to me, Iraj," he hissed, moving quickly, swiftly rearranging his plans. "You think I'm here to kill you. I won't deny it. But the main reason is to stop that machine!" He jerked his chin, indicating the stone temple. "Help me with it," he said. "Help me if you want to be free! That's what you want, isn't it? To be free?"

Iraj recoiled, shocked that Safar had guessed his secret. Shocked even more at the pitying look on Safar's face and the humiliating offer of rescue. So shocked he didn't notice Fari sniff the air, then stiffen in alarm.

Iraj shouted: "To the Hells with you, Safar Timura. I can free myself!"

All his pent up fury of emotions exploded and Protarus drew back to cast the spell.

But before he could act he heard Fari shout: "Betrayal, brothers!"

Then Luka: "Kill the king!"

And Kalasariz, crying "Kill them both!"

And then three great wolves rose up to ravage Iraj, so furious and strong in their combined wrath they caught him by surprise. His mind had been fixed on Safar, not the others, and now he saw the error.

Iraj had the sudden vision of the child he'd killed, the child in the dream who was only a boy, too young to be in the mountains. The child who was first Tio, then Safar, and he'd killed them over and over again until only one face was left.

His own!

And Iraj suddenly understood. Awareness struck like a thundering dawn over Kyrania. Despair instantly followed and he thought, This is it . . . I'm too late . . . I'm a fool from beginning to end . . .

Then the wolves rushed in and Iraj cast the spell, shouting: "Safar! Safar!"

Safar gathered in Iraj's spell. He was surprised at the strength of it. But he was even more surprised at the spell's suddenly changed intent. Iraj's cry of "Safar! Safar!" echoed in his head, resounding like temple bells. "Safar! Safar!" A shout of contrition.

Safar slammed the door to a torrent of conflicting thoughts and emotions. Working quickly, very quickly, he absorbed the power of the spell. Never mind Iraj. Never mind what was happening to him now. Never mind repentance, never mind forgiveness, never mind, never mind . . .

. . . Safar heard the wolves coming for him, their howls filling his ears, shriveling his heart. Coming so fast he realized he was taking too long and he fumbled at the complexity of the spell. Trying to put it together, knowing he was too late, too late, and he was only a boy, too young to be in the mountains and this was the end of him.

And once more he heard Iraj cry, "Safar!"

Suddenly he knew the answer.

Prayed he knew the answer.

He flung the paper into the air, shouting, "*Syrapis!*"

And the world became a white hot explosion.

CHAPTER THIRTY THREE

THE BECKONING SEAS

Coralean paced the docks, rumbling, "We must go, my friends! Hurry, hurry!"

And Leiria shouted, "By the gods, Coralean, you'll wait! Or I'll cut out your greedy innards to feed the fish."

Palimak listened to them argue, feeling cold and apart from the scene. He already knew the answer, but was too frightened to voice it. He turned away, looking out over the Caspan harbor where the hired ships were sagging under the weight of all the Kyranians and their goods. The airship hovered over the refugee fleet, engines fired up and ready to go.

Only three tarried on the shore, Coralean and Leiria, pacing and arguing and waving their hands, while Palimak listened, gathering his nerve to speak.

"We *must* wait for Safar!" Leiria said. Then she pleaded. "Just a little bit more, Coralean. Give him a chance."

She pointed at the distant mountains that ringed the port city of Caspan. A thick column of yellow smoke rose up from the lands beyond. "You only have to look at that," she said, "to know that he destroyed the machine."

Coralean nodded. "Granted," he said. "And we also have the word of several wise priests to support what our eyes want to believe."

"Then Safar must live!" Leiria said.

Coralean shook his shaggy head. "Alas, my good Captain Leiria," he said, "that does not necessarily follow. In fact, those same priests said when the machine was destroyed it was impossible for anyone to have survived the holocaust that resulted."

"Safar said he had a way," Leiria insisted. "He was sure he would live."

The caravan master sighed. "This quarrel grieves me deeply, Captain Leiria," he said. "Safar was my friend as well. And he was not so certain of success as he apparently led you to believe. Perhaps he was trying to spare you, which would be so like him. However—and this is a most important however—Safar and I agreed that I would wait for three days. Those three days have now passed. And so, tragic as this realization is to one so tender as I, we must assume that our good friend, our most beloved friend, Safar Timura, is dead. And we must carry on for him."

"To hells with your agreement," Leiria said. "Safar could be riding to us now." She gestured at a hill overlooking the harbor. "Any moment now he could appear over that rise."

Palimak's eyes went to the hill, praying with all his strength that what Leiria had said would suddenly be so. And his father would appear, sitting tall and proud on a prancing Khysmet. Both man and horse eager to face whatever the Fates had in store for them.

Then Gundara said, "He's not coming, Little Master."

"That's definitely true," Gundaree added. "No sign of him at all."

Palimak gulped back tears. Then he hardened himself. Squaring his shoulders and lifting his chin.

"That's enough!" he said to Leiria and Coralean.

The two turned to him, surprised at his sudden interruption.

Palimak said, "My father told us not to wait." He shrugged. "So I guess we'd better not wait."

He turned and started walking toward a skiff tied up at the shore. Leiria caught up to him, grabbing his arm.

"What's wrong with you?" she demanded. "We're speaking of your own father!"

Palimak looked up at her, smiling gently. Demon eyes glowing yellow as he cast the spell.

"I love you, Aunt Leiria," he said. "But we have to go to Syrapis."

And so they flew away on bully winds blowing all the way from far Kyrania.

Where up, up in the mountains the stars are setting and the High Caravans greet the Dawn of Nothing.

Up to where the eagle cries over a ruined land that was once a paradise.

Oh, make haste!

The Gods Awaken

For Cassie and Thomas Grubb
and
My friends in Washington State . . .
especially
Judy, Jon, Stormy, and Brian
and
To all my faithful friends in New Mexico
particularly
Sal, who changed my altitude

O threats of Hell and hopes of Paradise;
One thing at least is certain: this life flies.
One thing at least is certain, the rest is lies.
The flower that once has blown forever dies.

I sent my soul through the Invisible,
Some letter of that afterlife to spell,
And by and by it returned to me
To answer: I myself am Heaven and Hell.

Heaven but the vision of fulfilled desire.
Hell but the shadow of a soul on fire.
Cast onto darkness into which we—
So late emerged—shall so soon expire!

From The Rubaiyat of Omar Khayyam
Edward Fitzgerald Translation

Part One

Syrapis

PROLOGUE
ESCAPE TO SYRAPIS

And so they flew away on bully winds blowing all the way from far Kyrania . . .

It may have been the strangest, the saddest voyage in history. The People of the Clouds mourned the loss of their leader, Safar Timura, who had guided them over thousands of miles of mountains and deserts and spell-blasted blacklands to the shores of the Great Sea of Esmir.

A paradise awaited them across that sea: the magic isle of Syrapis, where they would make their new home far away from the evil beings who had driven them from their mountain village in Kyrania.

Safar Timura—the son of a potter who had risen to become a mighty wizard and Grand Wazier to a king—had sacrificed his own life so that his people might escape.

And now a thousand villagers were packed aboard a ragtag fleet of privateers, sailing to Syrapis and safety. High above them a marvelous airship flew over the silvery seas, pointing the way.

For many days and weeks the skies remained clear, the winds steady; and at any other time there would have been cause for a grand celebration. A feast of all feasts, with roasted lamb and rare wine, playing children and sighing lovers.

The world should have been a bright place, full of promise and joy. After months of terror, the Kyranians were free of Iraj Protarus and his ravening shape-changers.

But hanging over them was the Demon Moon—an ever-present bloody shimmer in the heavens. Reminding one and all of the doom Safar had predicted would befall the world. More haunting still was the memory of Safar. The handsome young man with the dazzling blue eyes and sorrowful smile.

Everyone wept when they learned that he had been given up for dead. The mourning women scratched their cheeks and tore their hair. The men drank and regaled one another with tales of Safar's many brave deeds, shedding tears as the night grew late.

Lord Coralean, the great caravan master who had hired the ships so that they could all escape together, spoke long and memorably about the man who had been his dearest friend.

Aboard the airship the circus performers—among them Biner, the mighty dwarf, and Arlain, the dragon woman,—worked listlessly at their tasks. They did only what was absolutely necessary: feeding the magic engines; adjusting the atmosphere in the twin balloons that held the ship aloft; manning the tiller to keep them on course.

Meanwhile, the decks grew shabby, the material of the balloons drab, the galley fires cold. It seemed impossible to them that Safar would no longer be at their side, amazing the circus crowds with his feats of magic.

Sadder still were Safar's parents, Khadji and Myrna, who had never imagined, even in their deepest night terrors, that they would outlive their only son. And his sisters mourned Safar so deeply they could not eat or sleep and if their husbands hadn't begged them to desist for the sake of their children, they surely would have died from sorrow.

Only four outsiders—a warrior woman, a boy and his two magical creatures—prevented the voyage from becoming a disaster.

When the privateers, seeing the poor morale of the Kyranians, conspired to seize them and their goods—planning to sell the people into slavery—the woman overpowered and slew the raiders' captain. While the boy—Safar's adopted son—combined his powers with those of the magical creatures to cast a terrifying spell that paralyzed the pirates with fear. And forced them into obedience.

The woman's name was Leiria. The boy, half human and half demon, was Palimak. And the creatures, twin Favorites who had lived in a stone turtle for a thousand years, were called Gundara and Gundaree.

Leiria and Palimak had made a promise to Safar Timura—a promise that they were determined to keep. And they would allow no one to stand in their way.

Then one day the lookout in the airship shouted the joyful news that land was in sight. And the little fleet finally came to the shores of fair Syrapis: the promised land.

Except, instead of milk and honey, they found an army waiting on those shores.

An army intent on killing them all.

But Palimak and Leiria remembered well their promise. So they roused the people and routed the army.

For three long years they fought the ferocious people who inhabited Syrapis.

And for three long years they searched for the grail Safar had urged them to seek.

They had many adventures, many setbacks, and many victories.

During that time Palimak strove mightily to educate himself. He scoured ancient tomes, quizzed witches and wizards. And he seized every spare moment to study the Book of Asper that his father had bequeathed to him.

For in those pages, his father had said, was the answer to the terrible disaster on the other side of the world—in far Hadinland—that was slowly poisoning all the land and the seas.

It was a race against extinction for humans and demons alike.

And in that race Palimak lost his childhood.

CHAPTER ONE

THE DANCE OF HADIN

Oh, how he danced.

Danced, danced, danced.

Danced to the beat of the harvest drums.

All around him a thousand others sang in joyous abandon. They were a handsome people, a glorious people; naked skin painted in fantastic, swirling colors.

And they danced—danced, danced, danced—singing praises to the Gods as shell horns blew, drums throbbed and their beautiful young Queen cried out in ecstasy. She led them, tawny breasts jouncing, smooth thighs thrusting in the ancient mating ritual of the harvest festival.

Safar danced with her, pounding his bare feet against the sand, rhythmically slapping his chest with open palms. While above him the tall trees—all heavily laden with ripe fruit—rippled in a salty breeze blowing off the sparkling sea.

But while the motions of his fellow dancers were graceful, Safar's were forced and jerky—as if he were a marionette manipulated by a cosmic puppeteer.

Madness! was his mind's silent scream. I must stop, but I cannot stop, please, pleaseplease, end this madness! Yet no matter how hard he battled the spell's grip his body jerked wildly on—and on and on—in the Dance of Hadin.

For Safar Timura was trapped in the prelude to the end of the world.

Beyond the grove, a dramatic backdrop for the beautiful Queen, was the great conical peak of a volcano. A thick black column of smoke streamed up from the cone. It was the same volcano that Safar had seen in a vision many years before. And Safar knew from his vision that at any moment the volcano would explode and he, along with the joyous dancers, would die.

Was this real? Was he truly on the shores of Hadinland, destined to be swallowed in a river of molten rock? Or was it just a night terror that would end if only he could open his eyes?

He'd had such dreams before. Once he'd dreamed of wolves and Iraj Protarus had risen from the dead to confront Safar with murder in his heart and a horde of shape changers at his back.

And, with a jolt, he thought: Iraj! Where is Iraj?

He tried to force his head around to see if Protarus was among the dancers. But his body wasn't his own and all he could do was prance with the others, slapping his chest like a fool.

He had no idea how long this had gone on. It seemed as if he'd been a barely conscious participant in a dance that went on endlessly. Yet there were moments of chilling clarity, such as now, when he would regain use of his mind enough to struggle against the mysterious force that held him.

It was a cruel clarity, because each time he knew the fight was hopeless. He'd struggle fruitlessly, then lapse into semi-consciousness.

Safar thought he heard Iraj's voice among the others and once again tried—and failed—to look.

Then he felt his senses weaken as if a drug were creeping through his veins to cloud his mind. He bit down on his lip, grabbing at the pain to keep his wits.

With the pain came a sudden memory of Iraj standing before him. Half giant wolf, half all-too-human king. Flanking him were Safar's deadliest enemies: the demons, Prince Luka and Lord Fari; and the spymaster, Lord Kalasariz. All bound to Iraj by the Spell of Four.

Yes, yes! he thought. Iraj! Remember Iraj!

And what else?

There was something else. Something that had brought him here. If only he could recall, perhaps he could escape.

The machine! That was it!

The image floated up: Iraj and the others bearing down at him; at Safar's back the great machine of Caluz. A hunched turtle god with the fiery mark of Hadin on its shell. It was a machine whose magic was out of control and if Safar didn't stop it his beloved land of Esmir would die an early death.

He fought hard to remember the spell he'd cast then to plug the sorcerous wound between Esmir and the deathland that was Hadin.

The words kept slipping away. Think! he commanded himself. Think!

And it came to him that the words formed a poem. A poem from the Book of Asper.

Asper, yes, Asper. The ancient demon wizard whose strange book of verse had predicted the end of the world a thousand years before. And who had speculated on the means to halt the destruction.

Safar felt sudden joy as the spellwords burst from nowhere:

> *"Hellsfire burns brightest*
> *In Heaven's holy shadow.*
> *What is near*
> *Is soon forgotten;*
> *What is far*
> *Embraced as brother . . ."*

He groaned as the rest of the words fled. Safar bit his lip harder, blood trickling down his chin. Remember, dammit! Remember!

But it was hopeless. The remainder of the spell remained agonizingly just out of reach in a thick mist.

Fine, then. Forget about the verse. Think of what happened when you faced Iraj. Remember that—and perhaps the spellwords will come.

His mind threw him back to Valley of Caluz. His enemies before him, the sorcerous machine behind. He was alone: Palimak and Leiria had fled on his orders, leading the people of Kyrania to Syrapis and safety. Safar had remained to stop the machine and destroy Iraj so he couldn't pursue the villagers.

And then what?

His life, he realized instinctively, depended on recalling what had happened next. No. Not just his life—the world depended on it.

Very well. He had cast that spell. He could remember that. But, wait. Something had interfered! What, or who, had it been? Iraj? Had Iraj cast a spell of his own?

That was it! Iraj had attempted to break free from the Spell of Four, which bound him to Kalasariz and the others. Iraj had surprised Safar with that powerful bit of magic.

A collision of spells.

An explosion.

A blinding white light.

And then what?

Safar dug deep for the memory. He could recall intense heat. Then blessed coolness. Followed by a long time of floating on what seemed like billowing clouds—as if he were aboard Methydia's magic airship.

Time passed.

How much time, he couldn't say.

Then he'd heard—from far below—pipes and horns and throbbing drums. And voices— many voices—chanting a haunting song. Safar didn't have to struggle to remember *those* words, for it was the same song the beautiful Queen and her subjects were singing now:

> *"Her hair is night,*
> *Her lips the moon;*
> *Surrender. Oh, surrender.*
> *Her eyes are stars,*
> *Her heart the sun;*
> *Surrender. Oh, surrender.*
> *Her breasts are honey,*
> *Her sex a rose;*
> *Surrender. Oh, surrender.*
> *Night and moon. Stars and Sun.*
> *Honey and rose;*
> *Lady, oh Lady, surrender.*
> *Surrender. Surrender . . ."*

Safar recalled twisting around and finding himself floating above a green-jeweled isle set in a deep blue sea.

Towering over the island was the volcano. He knew in an instant this was one of the islands that made up Hadin. But how could that be? Hadin was on the other side of the world from Esmir—the continental opposite of his homeland.

Had the violence of the spellcast hurled him so far?

Or was he only dreaming of his boyhood vision, when he'd foreseen the end of the world?

The song grew stronger, rising up to enfold him . . . *"Surrender. Oh, surrender . . ."* It drew him down like a netted fish. *"Surrender. Oh, surrender . . ."* Fear lanced his heart when he saw the dancing people of his vision and their lusty young queen. *"Surrender. Oh, surrender . . ."*

Panicking, he tried to struggle free, but the song flowed through and around him until he became a part of it. *"Surrender. Oh, surrender . . ."*

And he had no choice but let it take him. He fell into a stupor, floating downward.

Then he found himself among the dancers. Except, now he was one of them. Dumb and gaping at the nubile Queen. Warm sun on his suddenly naked back. His bare feet beating against the sand. Open palms slapping his chest in time to the music: *". . . Night and Moon./Stars and Sun./Honey and rose;/Lady, oh Lady, surrender . . ."*

Yes, that was how he came to be here. Safar suddenly felt quite calm—reassured that his mental faculties were returning. Only one small step was left. Once he retrieved the remaining words to the spell he'd cast in Caluz he could free himself.

Then excitement blossomed as another piece came: *" . . . Piercing our breast with poison,/Whispering news of our deaths . . ."*

Yes! That was it! Now, there were only two more lines. Two more and the spell could be broken.

Safar heard the Queen shout and he looked up at her—dismay poisoning his resolve—and his concentration was broken.

The Queen was crying out to her subjects, pointing at the volcano. The column of smoke was thicker, blacker and pouring out more furiously. Great sparks swirled in the smoke, showering upward like blossoms from the Hells.

Any moment the volcano would explode. Just as it had in Safar's vision. Just as it had . . .

A great shock rocked Safar to the core. Not the shock of the volcano's eruption—that was still to come. But a shock of realization that he'd lived and died in this very same scene hundreds of times before.

The volcano would erupt. A deadly shower of debris driven by typhoon winds. Followed by a river of lava that would kill any who survived.

Even those who fled into the sea wouldn't be able to swim or canoe out far enough to escape. They'd be boiled alive like shellfish in a roiling pot.

In the long ago vision Safar had only been a witness to these events. But now he was one of the dancers doomed to die not once, but an endless number of deaths until the world itself was dead.

Only then would his soul be released.

Just then the last two lines came to him: *" . . . For she is the Viper of the Rose/ Who dwells in far Hadinland!"*

But even as he reached for them, desperate to complete the spell, he knew he was nearly out of time.

Still, he rushed on—no time to hope, much less pray. He started reciting the spell: *"Hellsfire burns brightest/In Heaven's holy shadow . . ."*

Then it was too late.

And the volcano erupted.

But just before it did, he thought he heard someone calling to him: "Father! Father!"

Desperate, he cried out: "Palimak! Help me, Palimak!"

And everything vanished—except pain.

CHAPTER TWO

OF SONS AND LOVERS

Palimak peered over the railing, clutching his cloak against the damp chill as the airship slowly descended through the clouds.

Behind him he could hear Biner cautioning the crew in his rumbling baritone, "Steady, now . . . Keep her steady, lads . . ."

The clouds thinned and he could see the forbidding north coast of Syrapis: jagged reefs rising out of a stone-gray sea; a narrow pebbled beach ending at black cliffs that ascended to forested mountain peaks.

There came a rattle of chain mail and a faint breath of perfume as the warrior woman moved up behind him. "Over there," she indicated. "On the easternmost peak. Do you see it?"

The moment she spoke, Palimak spotted the castle. It was a black stone crown sitting atop the lowest peak, with eight turrets strategically positioned around the thick walls.

Palimak grimaced. "I see it, Aunt Leiria," he said. "But it doesn't look like how I remember it."

Leiria patted his arm. "That was more than three years ago," she soothed. "And you were on horseback, sitting behind your father."

Palimak shrugged. "I hope you're right," he said. Then he turned to the airship's bridge, where Biner held forth, directing the crew.

"Can you maneuver around the castle, Uncle Biner?" he shouted.

"Sure thing, lad," Biner called back. He barked orders and the crewmen scrambled around the airship's deck. Some tended the magical furnaces that pumped hot air into the huge twin balloons. Others checked the lines that held the ship's body suspended beneath the balloons. Still others spilled ballast to help stabilize the airship when Biner made the turn.

As they sailed around the peak, Leiria studied the fortress with a professional eye. On two sides the castle was protected by steep, rock-littered slopes. Obviously the rocks had all been piled up by the castle's human defenders.

One small stone hurled into the right place would set off an avalanche that would pour down on any ground troops foolish enough to climb the slopes.

The castle's front was just as steep and the road winding up to the gates was edged with low walls and a series of stone guard shacks, with slits for arrow holes.

The rear of the castle came right up to the edge of a sheer cliff shooting down to the hissing seas that beat against the little beach.

In the center—about twenty feet below the castle walls—a waterfall spilled out of a wide cave mouth. It fell hundreds of feet before it thundered into waves that crashed over the beach and against the base of the cliff.

"On the whole," Leiria said at last, "I'd rather defend it than attack it."

Palimak touched the hilt of his sheathed sword, eyes flickering demon-yellow. "I don't want a fight," he said. "We have more important things to do. But if that's what King Rhodes wants . . . " he grinned, displaying surprisingly sharp teeth . . . "That's what he'll get."

Leiria nodded approval. "I'm sick and tired of all these little Syrapian despots and their game playing," she replied. "They think the only purpose of a truce is to give them time to get behind you and stab you in the back."

Palimak shrugged—what would be, would be—and returned his attention to the castle.

The airship sank lower and he could make out the crowd waiting for them in the center courtyard. All eyes were turned upward to see the airship's approach.

He could imagine the amazement on their faces. The airship was a wondrous sight to behold, with the tattooed face of a beautiful woman on the front balloon. And the words "Methydia's Flying Circus" emblazoned on the other.

Methydia, dead for many years now, had been his father's lover and mentor. She'd rescued Safar from the desert and had let him join her troupe of circus performers while he had hidden from the Walarian spymaster, Lord Kalasariz.

The circus lived on in Biner, the muscular dwarf; Arlain, half fire-breathing dragon, half fabulous woman; Elgy and Rabix, the intelligent snake and the mindless flute player; and, finally, Kairo, the strange acrobat who could detach his head from his shoulders, tossing it about on the tether of his ropy neck.

In normal times, Palimak thought, they'd be preparing for a royal performance at the castle. Biner would've been stirring up excitement with his traditional bellow of: "Come one, come all! Lads and maids of All ages! I now present to you—Methydia's Flying Circus of Miracles! The Greatest Show On Syrapis!"

Palimak grimaced. The airship and circus troupe had spent more time than they liked acting as a military force, rather than entertaining. He was as sorry about that as Biner and the others. But what could be done about it?

From the moment Palimak and his fellow Kyranians had landed on Syrapis they'd been at constant odds with the violence-loving inhabitants of the island. How so many warring factions could be packed onto an island one hundred and twenty miles long and thirty miles across at its widest was a continuing and unpleasant amazement to Palimak when he was at his most depressed.

As if reading his thoughts, Leiria said, "Honestly, sometimes I think the Syrapians have got some sort of congenital war disease." She shook her head. "Remember how they greeted us at the beach that day? Olive branch in one hand, dagger up the other sleeve!"

Palimak sighed. "Poor father thought Syrapis would be a paradise for us all," he said. "A new home—maybe even a better home—than the one we left behind."

The yellow demon flecks faded from his eyes, leaving them sad and all too human. "Instead we landed right in the middle of about twenty wars all going on at the same time. Everybody in Syrapis hates each other. But now that we're here they finally have something in common—which is to hate *us.*"

His eyes misted slightly. "I guess things don't always work out the way you want," he said. "Even if you're someone as great as my father was."

Leiria wished she could give Palimak a comforting hug. But that would only make the boy feel awkward. Actually, he was a "boy" only in human reckoning.

The product of a romance between a demon princess and a human soldier, Palimak's demon side made him mature at a much faster rate than was normal for humans. At thirteen he was nearly six feet tall, although he hadn't filled out yet and was quite slender. Still, his shoulders were wider than those of most boys of his age and his broad-palmed hands had long, supple fingers. When he was angry or upset, sharp talons lanced from his finger tips like a cat's claws: a phenomenon so disconcerting that even Leiria, who'd known him since he was a babe, had never become used to it.

He also didn't act like a boy—except in rare moments when he allowed himself to relax enough to be playful. Or, blushingly so, when he was in the presence of a flirtatious maiden. Thank the Gods, Leiria thought, this part of his nature hasn't matured at the same rate as the rest of him. He had enough problems without adding sex to the equation.

Despite his youth, Palimak was the undisputed leader of the more than one thousand Kyranian villagers he and Leiria had led across the Great Sea to Syrapis and supposed safety. He had the strength of will and the charisma of his adoptive father. Backed by demon magic nearly as powerful as Safar's—who'd been the greatest wizard, demon or human, that Esmir had ever known.

During the three years since Safar's death and the Kyranians' flight from Esmir in a fleet of hired ships, Palimak had used all these attributes, plus a sometimes chilling ability for calculation, to keep the Kyranians from being overwhelmed by the fierce natives of Syrapis.

Palimak suddenly shifted. "There's the king," he said. Then he grinned. "Maybe Rhodes is going to keep his side of the bargain after all."

Leiria peered down at the courtyard. Though the airship still wasn't low enough for them to make out individual faces, there was no way she could miss Rhodes, ruler of Hanadu, the northernmost kingdom in Syrapis.

He was a giant of a man sitting on a huge, gaudy throne, placed on a platform in the center of the courtyard. The only other people on the platform seemed to be two liveried attendants. Leiria spotted a dozen or so uniformed soldiers' but they were scattered throughout the crowd, rather than being in any sort of military formation.

"That's a scene with peace painted all over it," Leiria said dryly. "I wonder why I'm not impressed?"

Palimak curled a lip. "Maybe it's because Rhodes is the last and trickiest of the bunch," he said. "And neither one of us thinks that after all this time he's finally going to roll over on command like a dog!"

Just then the crowd stirred and the sound of fierce martial music thundered upward. Banners waved, flags were unfurled and a hundred or more colorful kites took flight.

"I think that's our official welcome," Leiria said. "Either that, or a declaration of war." She was only partly joking, knowing from bitter experience how quickly the Syrapians could turn on the unwary.

Palimak patted the fat purse hanging from his belt. "I've got enough gold here to light up even King Rhodes' scowling face," he said. "With promises of more to come for his cooperation."

He laughed. This time it wasn't forced. "My father used to always say that if you sue for peace you'd better bring both swords and money. I didn't know what he meant then, but I sure do now!"

Rhodes was notorious for his greed: Palimak was counting on this in his bid for peace, as well as on the bloody defeat the Kyranians had handed the king's forces not one month before.

"My best bet," Leiria said, "is that any treaty we work out with Rhodes will be violated by spring."

Palimak laughed. "That long, huh?" Then, more seriously: "If this is the right place—the castle I saw when I was with my father that day—then all we need is a couple of weeks and a free hand. After that, King Rhodes can do whatever he wants—up to and including going to the Hells."

The airship had made a full circle and they were once again hovering just off the rear of the castle—the waterfall and the cave now in clear view. Palimak leaned far over the rail to get a closer look. The tide was running out fast, water retreating from the bottom of the cliff face at an amazing rate.

Palimak probed the atmosphere with his magical senses. Instantly, he felt a powerful force dragging at him, as if his spirit self was a bit of flotsam caught in that raging tide.

Instead of breaking away, he fought against the force, wave after wave of sorcery smashing over him.

Leiria was shocked at his sudden struggle, seeing the blood drain from his already pale features. Talons emerging to cut into the rail as he gripped it. She had an urgent desire to grab him and rip him away from whatever invisible enemy he was fighting.

But she steeled herself to remain a witness, knowing there was nothing she could do to help.

Then Palimak gasped. "There it is!" he said, voice shaking with effort. "The island! And the idol, too! Just the way I remember it!"

Leiria dragged her attention away from Palimak. Below, about a hundreds yards from the cliff face, a small rocky island was emerging from the frothy waves.

Towering over the island was an immense stone image of a demon, with a long narrow face and heavy brows arching above deep-set eyes. The sculptor had given the demon a sad smile, which added to the overall effect of making the demon seem very wise.

"It's Lord Asper!" Palimak breathed.

Magical tendrils reached out to take him and suddenly he was a small boy again, gripping Safar about the waist as the great white warhorse, Khysmet, bore them both through a blinding snowstorm. Behind them an enormous ice beast was closing in fast as Safar shouted the words of a protective spell.

"Let me help you, father!" Palimak cried out, adding his own magic to the spell.

Safar hurled a magical jar into the beast's path and Palimak heard an explosion, followed by a shriek of agony. Then he gasped with relief as he sensed the beast falling away. But he knew instinctively that this wasn't enough and the ice beast would soon be upon them again.

He peered around his father and saw the beautiful Spirit Rider racing ahead on a black mare. She held a blazing magical torch high to guide them through the storm. They were heading for the point of a narrow peninsula, waves breaking on either side.

To Palimak's amazement, the Spirit Rider didn't stop when she reached the end of the peninsula. Instead, she rode her mare right out onto the water, leaping across the surface as it were a broad, firm king's highway.

He felt his father tense and knew he was wondering if he should follow. Then Safar relaxed—decision made—and gave Khysmet his head. Immediately the stallion sprang across the water, running after the mare with no difficulty.

They rode like that for a time, hooves splashing in what seemed like shallow water, while on either side enormous waves boomed past. Soon the novelty wore off and Palimak dozed. He slept fitfully, waking every now and then to see the beacon still moving ahead of them.

Then Gundaree and Gundara were both shrieking in his ear. The two little magical Favorites, his ever-present guardians, were both crying out at the same time: "Beware, Little Master! Beware"

He felt a rumbling beneath him and he shouted a warning to Safar. But his father was already coming up out of his stupor, steadying them as Khysmet shrilled surprise and bounded high into the air. When he came down, his hooves skittered on slippery rock, but then the nimble-footed horse steadied himself and they were racing over stony ground.

At that moment a blast of cold winds swept in from the side, sweeping the snow away. Palimak gaped at the sight. Hunched over the little island they now found themselves on was a huge statue of a demon.

Palimak felt his father jump in shock, as if he'd been stung.

"Asper!" he said in a harsh voice. "It's Asper!"

As they rode toward the statue Palimak lifted his head and saw something loom up just beyond. About a hundred yards away was a tall, sheer cliff face, unmarked except for a wide cave mouth in the center. At the top of the cliff that was some sort of black stone structure. Palimak dully wondered what it was. Then he saw several turrets and he realized it was a castle.

Just then he heard the Spirit Rider shout and his head snapped back. He saw her poised on the mare, waiting at the steps of a wide stairway that led up to the statue's open mouth.

She shouted, "This way!" And plunged up the broken staircase to disappear into the mouth of the statue.

Safar didn't have to urge Khysmet on. The big horse leaped after the mare with such force that Palimak's grip around his father's waist was nearly torn away. A heartbeat later they were inside the idol and all was darkness.

There was a flash of light and he felt a shock shiver through his body, rattling his teeth. Dazed, he realized his father had vanished. And now Palimak was holding Khysmet's reins. More puzzling still, his hands were no longer those of a small boy, but were large and muscular.

Khysmet whinnied and Palimak instinctively leaned forward, ducking under the dim shape of a low overhang. From far ahead he heard the rhythmic pounding of drums. A great chorus of voices chanted words he couldn't quite make out.

Then, soaring over the chorus, he thought he heard a familiar voice. Recognition dawned and he shouted, "Father! Father!"

A voice full of agony cried out in reply: "Palimak. Help me, Palimak!"

At that moment a great explosion erupted, lifting him up and hurling him away on a hot fierce wind.

He burst out of the vision, gasping for air as if he had come up from the bottom of the sea itself.

And he was back on the airship again, Leiria's hand on his shoulder, eyes deep with concern.

Palimak brushed at his face, as if swatting away a fly. "By the gods," he said, hoarsely, "I swear I heard his voice!"

"Whose voice, Palimak?" Leiria asked. "Who did you hear?"

The young man's eyes were agonized. "My father's," he said. He shook his head. "It can't be possible," he said. But I think . . . somehow . . . somewhere . . . he must be alive!"

Leiria felt like the sun had suddenly decided to arise after a long, cold sleep. The ice jam broken, all the feelings she'd been holding back for so long flooded forth.

Safar! she thought.

Alive?

She clutched Palimak to her and wept.

CHAPTER THREE

THE SEA OF MISERY

All was pain.

Iraj had no body: no blood, no sinew, no muscle, no bone—much less skin to contain them.

And yet there was still pain.

In its torment, pain defined him. He was a writhing shadow of a soul on fire. A smoking stone in the guts of some howling devil dancing on the coals of the Hellfires.

If he'd had tears, Iraj would have wept them. If he'd had a tongue, he would've lapped up those tears to quench the awful thirst. And if he'd had a voice, he would've screamed for mercy. Yes, Iraj Protarus, who had never seen value in mercy, would trade his crown—and a thousand more—for one drop of pity now.

But who was there to pity him?

The gods?

Safar had once told him the gods were asleep and wouldn't answer even if the prayer were cast into the Heavens by a million voices. Safar had said many things like that and if Iraj had possessed a heart to break, or a heart to hate, he would have both loved and despised Safar now for all his wise words.

Safar Timura—enemy and friend. Friend and enemy. The one who had saved him. The one who had condemned him to this eternity of pain.

If Iraj had possessed the ability for amusement, he'd have finally known the true meaning of irony.

In his previous existence Iraj had been a shapechanger. Rabid wolf to black-hearted man, then back again.

And before that?

Images bubbled up to burst on the thick surface of his pain.

He was a boy again in Alisarrian's secret cave, swearing a blood oath of eternal loyalty to Safar. He was a young prince again, leading his armies against the demon king, Manacia, who threatened all humans with enslavement. He was King of Kings again, betraying Safar because he feared Timura would betray him first. He was a fiend again, avenging himself on Safar for the crime of uncommitted sins.

As each of these images took form, only to dissolve into a soul-searing froth, Iraj gradually emerged into an awareness that was somehow separate from the pain. It was like struggling from a molten sea to rest a moment in a world both familiar and yet alien.

He was only a lowly creature whose sole desire was to escape into death. But in his desperation to escape a more solid firmament was formed.

His first thought was: Where is Safar?

With this thought came heightened awareness: Safar was nearby! And he was also in pain. Satisfaction followed, but then he was pummeled by a further realization: Safar was not in as much pain as Iraj.

He pulled himself higher out of the sea of misery, determined to reach Safar. As he did so, Iraj sensed other creatures scuttling up behind him. Groaning things. Weeping things. Evil things.

Something like a tentacle wriggled toward him. Then a second. Then a third.

He knew who they were. When they had names, they were Kalasariz, Fari and Luka.

Iraj had escaped them once, but somehow they had followed.

Not voices, but images of voices, came to him like the dry scuttling of many insects itching across his memory. "The king! Where is the king?" And, "Here, brothers!" And, "Follow him! Follow him!"

Iraj gathered all his strength and flung himself forward, humping madly like a hunted worm.

He must escape. He must reach Safar.

Crying: Safar, Safar! Wait for me, Safar!

CHAPTER FOUR
THE BARBARIAN QUEEN

King Rhodes hefted the sack of gold in his big fist. "For another one of these," he rumbled, "you can be king of all Syrapis for all I care."

His bearded jaw swung open like hairy gates to make a yellow, broken-toothed smile. "'King of kings' is a title I've been hearing bandied about lately. If that's what you want, I won't stand in your way."

Rhodes was playing to his subjects, who laughed in appreciation at their king's jest, crowding closer to the platform so they could hear every word of the exchange.

Palimak snorted. "They tried that in Esmir," he said. "Didn't work."

There were angry mutters in the crowd. They didn't like Palimak's rude retort to their king.

Rhodes dug thick fingers into his beard to scratch at some irritation. "Clever answer," he said. He jerked a bejeweled thumb at a scrawny-looking nobleman at his side. "Only the other day I was telling my minister—Muundy here—what a clever young prince you are. Setting a fine example for me and my brother kings to follow."

Palimak couldn't help but notice the contrast between the rich stone set in the thumb-ring and the grime under the king's nails. He warned himself mentally to proceed with great care. It would not be wise to underestimate this man. Of all the kings of Syrapis, Rhodes was the biggest, the meanest, the most barbaric.

And yet he had more than mere cunning glinting behind those rheumy eyes. He was also obviously well-informed by his spies. His hinted knowledge of Palimak's past troubles with Iraj Protarus was firm evidence of that. One thing Palimak had learned, however, was that the only way to deal with Rhodes was from strength.

As Coralean—that canny old caravan master—liked to say, "Rhodes is either at your feet or at your throat."

"That's kind of you to say so, Majesty," Palimak replied, not bothering to hide his sarcasm.

He turned to Leiria, who was standing easy by his side, thumbs hooked over her belt. "When we get home," he said, "remind me to see about setting up a special school for the kings of Syrapis. We'll start with classes on regular bathing and grooming."

Leiria made a thin smile. She was barely conscious of the exchange, eyes flickering here and there for signs of danger.

Outwardly, Rhodes didn't take offense at Palimak's abuse. He guffawed, slapping a meaty palm against a thigh as thick as a pillar.

"What's the matter with you Kyranians?" he said. "Don't you like a good smell? A man's smell?" He frowned, pretending concern. "I worry about you, young prince. You bathe more than is healthy for you. Why, if you aren't careful, you'll catch a chill and die on us. What a pity it would be for you to let out the ghost so young. Just when we're getting to know and love you."

Palimak grinned sarcastically. "And my gold," he said. "You seem to love that as well."

Rhodes' heavy brows beetled into a frown. Another buzz of anger went through the crowd. Leiria shifted, deliberately letting her chain mail rattle in warning.

A stranger to King Rhodes' court, Leiria reflected, would've thought Palimak's impertinence foolishness of the first order. After all, the two of them were the only Kyranians on the platform with the king. And that platform—the same one they'd seen from the air not long before—was surrounded by hundreds of the king's subjects, who filled the open courtyard from wall to wall.

It was certainly an intimidating mob. Like their king, they were filthy. Food stains spotted their garments, some of which were actually quite well-made beneath the dirt. They were a large people; even some of the women were nearly six feet tall. The men sported fierce tattoos on their faces and many of the women had sharp filed teeth. Leiria suppressed a shudder.

It was rumored that Rhodes and his subjects were cannibals, although there was no real evidence of this. There was no doubt, however, that they collected the heads of their enemies. Many wore belts festooned with shrunken skulls, decorated with colorful ribbons worked into the hair.

At any other time this mob would have charged the platform and ripped Palimak and Leiria to shreds.

Leiria glanced upward. Circling overhead was the great airship. Bowmen lined the rails, arrows fixed and ready to fire. They were magical arrows, specially constructed by Palimak— with the help of Gundaree and Gundara—to strike and horribly burn any target they hit.

These, plus the other spell weapons Biner and the crew were armed with, were the only things that kept Leiria and Palimak safe. Rhodes knew from painful experience that any threatening move on his part would bring instant and massive retaliation from above.

Rhodes caught Leiria's glance and his eyes instinctively flickered upward, then back again. She noted a brief, uncontrollable twitch of fear.

Then the king recovered, placing a hairy paw of mock sincerity across his broad, mailed chest. "Here is the truth, young prince," he said to Palimak. "Spoken straight from this old heart. Despite our . . . ahem . . . difficulties in the past, I now find myself thinking of you as the son I never had."

Leiria saw a dangerous glow in Palimak's eyes: she knew he was thinking of Safar and was offended by Rhodes' remark. Sometimes she almost forgot how young Palimak really was. And with youth came a quick and deadly temper.

She broke in before things took a bad turn. "Pardon, majesty," she said to Rhodes, "but there seems to be something missing here." She looked pointedly around the plat-form. "Such as the matter of the hostage we agreed upon."

Rhodes turned surly. "What has this world come to?" he grumbled. "Not to trust the word of a Syrapian king! I see no reason for this hostage business. You have my personal pledge that this truce and all of its terms will stand."

"And one of the key requirements of those terms," Leiria said, "was that you would provide us with a hostage."

She turned to Palimak. "Apparently, King Rhodes still doesn't think we're serious, my lord," she said to him. "It's my advice that we leave now and allow him more time to reflect."

Palimak eyed the king. "Is that what you want?" he asked. "If you need more thinking time, I'm certainly ready to grant it. Meanwhile, the blockade will stand."

The blockade he was referring to was one of the main things that had forced Rhodes to the bargaining table. Coralean was at this moment standing off Rhodes' main port with a small but well-armed fleet of mercenary warships. Effectively bottling Rhodes' ships up and cutting off all trade with the outside world.

Rhodes sighed heavily. "Very well," he said. "If you insist." He turned and rumbled orders to one of his aides.

A few moments later there was a loud yowl—like someone had just been foolish enough grab hold of a tiger's tail! This was followed by a firestorm of shrill curses and threats.

Palimak heard someone rail, "Get your hands off me, you sons of flea-ridden curs! I'll claw your filthy eyes from your heads and your lying tongues from your mouths!"

Then he gaped as two red-faced soldiers stumbled onto the platform, dragging a biting, kicking, scratching bundle of fury between them. The men's faces and arms were dripping blood from wounds they'd already suffered in the struggle.

It took Palimak a full minute to realize that it was a woman, not a howling animal, that they were hauling before the king.

And what a woman she was! Easily as tall as Leiria, sinuously muscular like a great cat, tawny hair like a lion's and glittering diamond-hard eyes. She was half naked—someone had obviously tried to force her to dress and she wasn't having any of it.

The rich clothing, inlaid with gems and gold bead, had been ripped to shreds by her struggles, revealing an impressive expanse of shapely limbs. Only a narrow breast band and a scanty loin cloth guarded her modesty from full public view.

Not that she seemed to care. The woman was so angry, so bent on getting at the soldiers to rake them with her dagger-like nails, that the remains of her clothing were practically falling off her. Finally, after what seemed like a small eternity, the soldiers wrestled her over to the throne.

King Rhodes lumbered to his feet, drawing himself up like an angry bear. Palimak barely restrained a gulp. He knew Rhodes was big, but, by the gods, he hadn't known he was this big! Seven feet, at least. With shoulders as wide as a freight wagon.

"Stop this, daughter!" Rhodes thundered. "How dare you humiliate me in front of our friends."

Instantly, the woman ceased her struggles. But there was no fear in her as she quickly straightened up. She glared at the soldiers, who swallowed hard, gingerly let her loose and backed away.

The woman lifted her head to meet Rhodes' eyes, and sniffed imperiously, saying, "Balls to your humiliation, father dear! Balls, I say!"

She quickly and somehow regally pulled her tattered clothing around her. Making the rags seem like a royal gown.

"I am being treated like a slave hauled to market." She ran strong, slender fingers through her hair. "Worse than a slave, actually. Slaves have some value, after all. In this kingdom, it has become quickly apparent, a queen has no rights or dignity at all!"

Rhodes face went from purple to its normal drink-induced flush. He turned to Palimak and Leiria, grinning hugely and with relish.

"Allow me to introduce you, noble ones," he said, so mildly polite that they might have been at a fine dinner party, "to my daughter, Queen Jooli.

"Your hostage!"

Leiria coughed, recovered, then dipped her head. "Pleased, I'm, uh, sure."

Palimak could only stare. His entire vocabulary was stuck somewhere in the vicinity of the huge lump in his throat. Leiria jabbed an elbow into his ribs.

"Uh, yes," he croaked, "hap . . . uh . . . happy to . . . uh . . ." The rest was lost.

To Palimak's dismay, Jooli whirled about to confront him. She studied him, piercing gaze taking him in from toes to crown. Palimak suddenly felt very small and very young. Much like a minnow about to be swallowed by a large female-type fish.

At the same time a little voice whispered in his ear. "Beware, little master. She's a witch!" It was Gundaree, reduced to a flea speck on his shoulder. The moment he heard the Favorite's warning, Palimak felt a spark of sorcery leap across the space between Jooli and himself.

"So, *you* are to be my captor," Jooli said, in a voice dripping with belittlement.

Before he could react, she turned back to Rhodes. "What's happening, here, father?" she asked, equally sarcastic. "Have you been defeated by a child's army? Or is this one of your rude jests?"

Nonplused, Rhodes shrugged. "Just do what you are told for a change, daughter," he said. "Certain terms were required. And I met them. My honor is at stake here."

Eyes still on her father, Jooli stabbed a long finger at Palimak. "Bugger your honor, father," she said. "You can't really expect me to go with *him!*"

Rhodes snorted. "We've gone over this before, Jooli. As my eldest child, you are in line to succeed me. On the other hand, I'll be damned if a woman will ever take my throne."

He gave her a beseeching look. "Why wouldn't you marry any of the good and honest princes I've brought to your chamber, seeking your favor? It would've been so much simpler that way."

"They were all either boors or cowards, father," Jooli said. "What's worse, they were stupid. You expect me to confer a kingship on stupid men? And simper in their shadows, dropping dim-witted children by the dozen like a brood sow?"

Leiria struggled for self control. She felt like an unwanted witness to an intimate family fight—which this definitely was—and wanted no part of it. She wished mightily that Coralean were here. The wise old caravan master would've shut these people up with a few well-chosen phrases.

Palimak, although old in mind, was too young and out of his element for this sort of thing. Hells, Leiria knew *she* wasn't up to it and she was not only pushing the three-decade mark, but had been lover to a great king and in love with a mighty wizard. Plus a soldier commander in countless wars.

Rhodes brushed his hands together—a rare washing, if only by air. "*I'm* done with you, daughter," he said. "I've finally found you a duty you can't shirk. Your kingdom requires this sacrifice. You cannot refuse it!"

Jooli drew herself up and Leiria could tell by the narrowing of her eyes that she was about to skin her father alive verbally. It was time to stop this nonsense. There was much more important business ahead than their damned family squabble!

Leiria drew her sword—the distinctive rasp of metal riveting everyone's attention. Her steel-soled boots rang as she stomped forward, blade extended, point aimed directly at Jooli.

"What's this!" Rhodes shouted, taking a step forward. But at the same moment he looked upward at the hovering airship and all those drawn bows and hesitated.

Jooli fixed Leiria with a fierce glare. "Am I to be assassinated before my own father?"

she growled. Brave as her words were, she still shrank visibly before Leiria's determined approach.

Leiria swung the blade back as if to strike, then smoothly slid it forward, turning it from razor edge to flat passiveness. She stopped the sword just short of Jooli's heart.

"Do you, Queen Jooli," she said with all the solemness she could muster, "swear to give us your royal oath that you will give yourself over to captivity? And that you will not attempt to escape, or conspire to escape, while you are in our custody?"

"This is ridiculous," Jooli protested.

"Swear it, daughter!" Rhodes thundered.

Queen Jooli made a dramatic sigh. "Oh, very well," she said. She placed her hand on the flat of the sword. "I so swear," she said. She glowered at Leiria. "There, you have my parole. Are you satisfied?"

For just a moment, Leiria imagined she saw a glint of amusement in Jooli's eyes. And she wondered, was this all an act? If so, for what purpose?

Palimak finally found his voice. "We'd better get you on board, your highness," he said to Jooli. "I have other business with your father."

He signaled to Biner and immediately a large basket, dangling from a strong cable, began its descent from the airship.

"But what about my belongings?" Jooli said. "My clothing and personal things aren't packed."

"We'll provide you with clothing," Palimak said.

"But my crossbow and my sword," Jooli protested. "I can't leave them behind."

For some reason Palimak wasn't surprised that Queen Jooli so valued her weapons. He nearly relented, then remembered Gundaree's warning. If Jooli were a witch, the last thing Palimak wanted was a chance for the queen to slip sorcerous supplies into her baggage.

"You won't need them," he said.

Before Jooli could protest some more, the basket—tended by a burly crewman—was resting on the platform.

"Get in, your highness," Leiria said with no attempt at ceremony.

Jooli sniffed, then walked toward the basket. But before she climbed in, she turned to King Rhodes. "You're going to be very sorry for this, father," she said.

And then, assisted by the crewman, she climbed into the basket, which was raised swiftly away. There were sounds of amazement from the crowd as they saw the king's daughter disappear into the hovering airship.

In control again, Palimak swung about to address Rhodes. He slipped another bag of gold from his tunic, holding it out so the king could see.

"Before we leave," he said, "there's one other thing I want to do. And I willing to pay for it handsomely."

Rhodes' eyes glittered greedily at the proffered sack of coins. "Ask away," he said. "I'm sure we can come to some agreement."

CHAPTER FIVE
THE MAGIC STALLION

The black mare pranced maddeningly just out of reach as Khysmet thundered after her across the darkening plain, heart and loins charged with *must.*

Above, gray-knuckled clouds gathered in immense lightning-charged fists. A fierce wind drove him on—so heat-charged that long blue sparks flew off his snowy back. Beneath his hooves the cloud shadows rolled past like fast-moving waves.

Behind him poured a great herd of wondrous horses, including the fifty mares who were his wives. On this magic plain he was the king of the stallions and none dared stand in his way. He'd killed attacking lions with his mighty hooves, scattered packs of jackals intent on making a meal of his colts, humbled stallion rivals for his four-legged harem.

Nothing could be denied him on this marvelous plain that spread a thousand miles between two great mountain ranges. Nothing, that is, except for the fabulous black mare who refused to acknowledge his claim on her.

The mare had appeared only a few grazing periods before:

She came like a dream—just at twilight when the insects were rising in a thick buzzing mist off the sweet grasses. Birds and bats wheeled through those clouds crying joyously as they feasted on the fat insect bodies.

Khysmet was about to shrill the signal for the herd to move to the sleeping area he'd scouted earlier in the day: a little valley—cupped between four low-slung hills—that he could easily defend against night stalkers.

But then a cloud radiant with colorful insect wings parted and the mare pranced through.

As soon as she saw him she stopped.

Steam blew through her tender nostrils as she whinnied a greeting. Then she wheeled around and looked at him enticingly over her graceful shoulders.

Khysmet neighed in astonishment, rooted for a moment by the audacity of the strange mare. Then he dimly recalled her. They'd met in the Other World, where Khysmet had once lived with his master.

Except then the mare had been ridden by a tall woman as beautiful in human terms as was the mare to Khysmet's equine senses. He'd sensed her human beauty because upon spying the woman his master had suddenly tensed, radiating a rich musk of desire. A desire just as fierce as the heat lancing Khysmet's loins as he examined the mare.

Master and horse had pursued the mare and her rider, but after a long, teasing chase, they'd vanished. Much later they'd appeared again, this time to lead Khysmet and his master through a winter storm iced with sorcery and danger. The wild ride had ended with the mare and her mistress vanishing as mysteriously as before.

And now, here the mare was once more—sans rider.

Khysmet whinnied a command for her to hold, then trotted forward to claim her.

But the mare shrilled amusement and shot away, dashing across the plain into the gathering night. Khysmet pursued her for a while, but was forced to turn back to care for his herd. He spent a long night pacing the ground, trembling with the remembered scent of her.

At dawn, the mare returned to entice him once more, rearing up to whinny her seductive challenge, then dancing off with Khysmet in pursuit. No matter how hard he ran she always managed to stay comfortably ahead, until he was forced to give up the chase and turn back.

The next time she came, however, he was prepared. His herd leaders were ready for his signal and when he charged after the mare, they gathered up his harem and followed.

The chase went on all that day into the late afternoon.

Now, with the shadows of night spilling across the wrinkled stone brows of the far range, Khysmet had the sudden thrilling knowledge that the mare was tiring.

Her steps became faltering, her breathing labored—flecks of pure white foam flying off her nostrils.

And then she stopped and he shrilled his victory cry, sprinting forward to close the gap and take her.

But there was a flash of lightning and the human woman suddenly appeared, dropping from the sky to land lightly on the mare's back.

Surprised, Khysmet skittered to a halt. And then he and the mare and the woman became a living island, the herd flowing around them like a great animal river, thundering and shrilling as they raced onward, their king forgotten.

Then all was silent, except for the distant rumble of the herd's flight.

The woman's hand lifted gracefully, a single finger bending out to point at Khysmet.

He snorted, not knowing what to do.

Khysmet felt a tingling shower of magic—familiar magic. Magic that had once carried him into and through the maw of an icy hell.

The woman shouted, "Your master awaits!"

Then she and the mare whirled and leaped upward.

Khysmet leaped after them.

Up, up, up . . . until their pathway became the gathering stars.

In the glittering distance the Demon Moon shimmered in silent, bloody challenge.

Khysmet's mighty heart thundered in anticipation.

The call he'd waited so long for had finally come.

CHAPTER SIX
WHERE DARKNESS WAITS

Palimak crouched in darkness so complete it felt like he was being smothered in a damp blanket. There was no sound other than that of his breathing and the steady drip, drip of water oozing from the unseen ceiling just overhead.

It was painfully cold—like pincers squeezing his joints where they stretched the material of his woolen costume. Icy sea water made a thin, salty sheet on the floor of the tunnel, burning through the soles of his boots. The steel cap on his head, meant to ward off blows from swords or war clubs, was a painful halo of cold.

Suddenly, he felt as if all his energy was being sucked through the cap and he swept it off. The cap fell to the floor with a heart-jolting clang. At that moment a drip of freezing water plopped down and he jumped as if an invisible monster had clutched him by the back of the neck.

"No need to be alarmed, Little Master," Gundara said. "There's no one here."

"Except for the rats," Gundaree added. "You forgot to mention the rats."

"I didn't forget anything," Gundara snapped. "I just didn't want to make our master nervous."

"Maybe he should be nervous," Gundaree argued. "They're pretty big rats."

The two Favorites were each perched on a different shoulder and although they were invisible in the darkness Palimak could tell from their weight that they were full size—about three hands high.

"I don't care how big the rats are," Gundara said. "Our master is very brave."

"Maybe so," Gundaree said, "but there sure are an awful lot of them. And they're getting closer!"

"Stop it with the rats," Palimak ordered. "And get busy making a light."

"I was only warning you," Gundaree grumbled. "No need to snarl at me, Little Master."

"Honestly," Gundara said to his brother, "you're such a quarrelsome thing. I wish Mother had eaten you, like I told her."

"Shut up about Mother!" Gundaree snapped.

"I will not shut up!" Gundara stormed back. "You're nothing but a—"

"Light, please!" Palimak broke in.

"All right! All right!" Gundara said.

There was a low muttering from the two Favorites, then a clatter of little talons as they cast the spell. *Crack!* and a glowing ball suddenly appeared, hovering some six feet off the tunnel's floor.

"There's your light, Little Master," Gundara said.

Palimak started when he saw scores of small, furry bodies dart away—seeking the cover of the darkness that loomed just beyond reach of the dim, swirling light.

"And there's your rats," Gundaree said with some satisfaction. "Told you there were a lot of them."

Palimak suppressed a shudder. "Get rid of them," he commanded.

"You're supposed to say 'please,'" Gundara sniffed, acting hurt.

"Goodness, gracious," Gundaree said. "You'd think we never taught him how to be polite."

Palimak sighed. Bequeathed to him by his father, the two Favorites had watched over him since he was an infant—a mixed blessing despite their powerful magic.

Although they were twins, they were exact opposites in appearance. Gundara had the elegant body of a man, but the head and claws of a demon. Gundaree bore the face of a darkly handsome human perched on a demon's torso. Both were fashionably dressed in tunics, tights, capes and burnished boots. They were greedy, irritating, quarrelsome and had no use for anyone other than Palimak. Although they were commanded to obey him, it was no good arguing with them when they got into one of their moods.

"*Please!*" Palimak said.

"I'm *hungry!*" Gundaree complained.

"Pleases go down better with a few treats," Gundara added.

Suppressing a groan of frustration, Palimak dug into his pocket and pulled out a handful of sweets. The two Favorites quickly gobbled them up.

Gundara burped. "Is that all?" he asked.

"We're *still* hungry," Gundaree added.

"One more word," Palimak gritted, "and I swear I'll turn the two of you into big, fat, slimy slugs!"

The Favorites gulped, then leaped into action without further delay. They jumped to the floor of the tunnel. There was a purple flash and suddenly they transformed into two very large, very deadly cats.

The cats/Favorites darted forward into the darkness. An explosion of fierce yowls and frightened squeals soon followed. A moment later Palimak found himself dodging a stream of gray bodies as the rats bolted out of the gloom and ran straight for him.

"What the hells!" he shouted, as a monster rat ran up his leg.

He swatted it away. Then he kept on swatting, kicking and cursing as a veritable river of squealing rodent bodies flowed around him, over him and even between his legs, trying to escape the Favorites.

Then it was over and he stood angry and panting as Gundara and Gundaree calmly strolled back into the light in their original forms.

"They're gone, Little Master," Gundara piped.

Glaring, Palimak opened his mouth to give them a piece of his mind. Then he shrugged. What was the use? It was his fault for not being specific. Given more than one way to do things, the twins usually chose the route that gave their master the most trouble.

To keep the peace, he managed a "Thanks, boys," then got down to the job at hand.

Palimak motioned and the two leaped back onto his shoulders. He stalked onward, the glowing ball bobbing in front of him, lighting the way. Almost immediately, however, he was brought up short and to his dismay he learned the reason why the panicked rats had rushed him. The passage ended abruptly in a blank-faced wall

"Oh, we meant to tell you, Little Master," Gundara said, "the tunnel doesn't go any further."

Palimak was stunned. "What happened?" he croaked. "This isn't how it looked in either of the visions! There was an opening! I saw it clear as day. Both times!"

"There's one thing wrong, Little Master," Gundaree said.

"Two things, actually," Gundara added.

"Oh, shut up, you!" Gundaree demanded.

Palimak growled for silence and got it. He knew very well what his trouble was. Or he could take a damned good guess, at least. He should have realized at the start of his journey through the tunnel that it wouldn't be so easy. From the moment he'd entered the mouth of the Idol of Asper he'd sensed a wrongness. It felt like a place where the blackest of magic had been practiced a long time ago.

Although there was nothing visible present, he sensed the damp corpses of ancient castings. The sense of danger had been so strong that he'd sent Leiria and the other members of his party away while he cast his arsenal's strongest series of protective spells.

The danger had seemed to lessen. But no sooner had he and his guards advanced down the tunnel again than the feeling of danger returned, just as strong as before.

Although Leiria and the others had argued fiercely, he'd made them wait at the entrance while he explored further, casting cleansing spells as he went on so there'd be nothing to worry him when he retraced his steps.

After five hours of searching through the darkness—using up the magic in one lightball after another—he'd started to realize why King Rhodes had looked at him so strangely when he'd made his request.

"The idol?" he'd said, surprised. "No one goes into the idol!"

"Nevertheless," Palimak had responded, "that's what I want to do."

Oddly enough, King Rhodes hadn't questioned him further. And his eyes had seemed to gleam with mysterious pleasure when he'd granted permission.

As he studied the blank wall once more, Palimak again puzzled over the king's reaction. When he'd entered the tunnel and encountered the spore of the old spells, Palimak had assumed Rhodes was hoping some evil magical presence lurking within the passage would do the job the king had been attempting since the Kyranians first landed in Syrapis. Which was to kill Palimak.

But now Palimak had reached the end of the tunnel and there was nothing apparent that posed any danger.

Gundara suddenly tensed on his shoulder. "Beware, Little Master!" he said.

Palimak was startled. "What's wrong?"

"There!" Gundaree said, pointing at the wall. "It's waiting!"

"And it's really, really hungry, Little Master," Gundara added.

"Maybe we'd better get out of here," Gundaree said.

Ignoring them, Palimak drew his dagger, reversed it, and started tapping on the wall. There was a sound like the beat of a drum. The wall was hollow! And then suddenly, steam started wisping off the face of the wall.

Palimak ignored it and continued tapping.

CHAPTER SEVEN
QUEEN CHARIZE

On the other side of the wall Palimak's tapping echoed in a vast dark chamber.

Tap, tap. Tap, tap.

Then there was a sound of things stirring, like the dry wings of large insects disturbed in their slumber.

Tap, tap, tap.

"Listen, sisters," rasped a voice. "Someone's coming!"

Tap, tap.

"Silence, sisters," said another. So deadly in tone that if there had been human ears present the voice would have chilled the foolish bearer of those ears to the marrow.

And there was silence.

Except for: Tap, tap. Tap, tap, tap.

Echoing through the chamber.

Queen Charize stirred on her throne, examining the source of the sound. She was practically blind, but that made no difference here, since sight would have been useless in her underground kingdom of eternal night. Her senses of smell and hearing, however, were so acute that she could make out Palimak and the Favorites through solid stone.

Tap, tap. Tap, tap, tap.

The hammering produced the image of a tall, wingless creature, with two legs and two arms.

Tap, tap.

And little Gundaree and Gundara were displayed in her greedy mind. They were perched on the wingless creature's shoulders. Her nostril openings widened, sniffing the chamber's hot air. The scent carried through the pores of the stone, drifting like steam wafting through from the cold Other Side.

"I smell a human, sisters," she said.

There was a low, hungry muttering from the others. "Human! Human! Human!"

Queen Charize sniffed again. "And demon as well."

More muttering. Puzzled, instead of hungry: "Human *and* demon?"

The presence of both races together was astounding. Could it be the two beings on the creature's shoulders?

The answer came from the spoor rising through the pores of the stone. And all her highly-tuned senses told her the two beings were clearly magical. With no real form. They were creations, not true living things. Strange spirits whose origins were very ancient indeed. Charize smiled to herself. She could almost taste the presence of the long-ago sister witch who had made them.

Again she tested the air. Separating the human and demon scents. Tap, tap, tap. Form radiating an image on her brain. And then the scent was traced back to a single source—laid over the sound image of the wingless creature.

"A feast, sisters!" she chortled. "Let him in!"

There was a hungry muttering. Broken by one voice:

"Pardon, Majesty. But what if it's Safar Timura?"

The question was a hot dagger to the huge organ that served Charize as both heart and lungs. It had been a long time since she'd truly fed on a human's spirit and her intense hunger had interfered with her memory.

"How dare you speak the name of Safar Timura?" she rasped. "It is forbidden here!"

"Just the same, sister," came the voice. It was that of Tarla, her royal rival. "I must speak it for the good of us all. It was Safar Timura who nearly destroyed us, if you recall."

Queen Charize remembered very well.

Again came the sound from the Other Side: Tap, tap. Tap, tap, tap.

And there was a slip in awareness and she found herself back at that moment—some ten sheddings ago—when her most grievous enemy, the mighty wizard Lord Timura, had confronted her. Except, in this vision, she found herself in Timura's mind. Cloaked in darkness. Danger all around. She experienced both his emotions and her own at the same time.

Charize choked in disgust as her mind merged into the filthy body of the remembered other: She *was* Safar Timura! And she was surrounded by darkness and ghastly beings. And those beings were herself and her sisters!

*   *   *

Safar heard heavy talons rattle on stone and a snuffling sound, like a beast following a strong scent. He knew he had to do something quickly before he was found.

The idea jumped up at Safar and he knew he couldn't wait and think it through, because with thought would come fear and fear's hesitation would be the end of him. He made a spell and clapped his hands together and roared: "Light!"

And light blasted in from all sides, nearly knocking him over with the sudden shock of it. He had been blinded by darkness before, now he was blinded by its white-hot opposite. There were awful screams of pain all around and then his vision cleared and the first thing he saw ripped his breath from his body.

The beast towered above him, enormous corpse-colored wings unfolded like a bat's. It had the stretched-out torso of a woman with long thin arms and legs that ended in taloned claws. There was no hair on its skull-like head and instead of a nose there were only nostril holes on a flat face shaped like a shovel.

Safar nearly jumped away, but then he realized the creature was too busy screaming in pain and clawing at its eyes to be a threat. He was in an enormous vaulted room, filled with blazing colors. Great columns, red and blue and green, climbed toward glaring light then disappeared beyond. The room was filled with hundreds of death-white creatures, some crouched on the floor howling pain, others hanging bat-like from long stanchions coming out of the columns. They twisted and screamed, horrid flags of misery blowing in a devil wind of conjured light.

Safar spotted the one he wanted. Again he shouted, his magically amplified voice thundering over the wails: "Silence!"

The shrieks and screams cut off at his command, and now there was only moaning and harsh pleas for "Mercy, brother, mercy!"

Safar paced forward, moving through the writhing bodies until he came to the throne. It looked like a great pile of bones—arms and legs and torsos and skulls stacked in the shape of an enormous winged chair. As he came closer he saw the 'bones' were carved from white stone. The creature who commanded that grisly throne was like the others, except much larger. A red metal band encircled her bony skull to make a crown. Unlike the others, however, the creature was silent and although she was hunched over, claws covering her eyes, she made no outward show of pain.

Safar stopped at the throne and said loudly, for all to hear: "Are you queen to this mewling lot?"

"Yes, I am queen. Queen Charize." As she answered she couldn't help but raise her royal head, carefully keeping her eyes shielded. "I command here."

"You command nothing," Safar replied, voice echoing throughout the chamber, "except what I, Lord Timura of Kyrania, might permit."

Queen Charize said nothing.

"Do you understand me?" Safar demanded.

He made a motion and the light became brighter still. The creatures shrieked as their pain intensified. Even the queen could not stop a low moan escaping through her clenched lips.

"Yes," she gasped, "I understand."

"Yes, Master," Safar corrected her. "You will address me as 'Master.'"

The queen gnashed her fangs in protest, but she got it out: "Yes . . . Master!"

✳   ✳   ✳

Tap, tap. Tap, tap, tap.

The sound brought Charize back to awareness. It was just in time, because as her great head jerked upward she sensed danger.

Not from without, but from only a few feet away where Tarla was sidling closer. Charize could smell the hate musk on her rival's breath. Hear the faint clatter of talons reaching for her throat.

The queen slashed with her mighty claws. There was a cry, the sound of a falling body; then the heady scent of death filled the chamber. And Tarla was no more.

Excited whispers came from her subjects as word was passed on what had happened.

"Are there others, my sisters," came Charize's deadly voice, "who wish to challenge me?"

The whispers died.

Silence.

Except for the *tap, tap, tap* from the Other Side.

And then the remembered humiliation of the incident with Timura combined with the shock of Tarla's recent bold attempt at regicide to force a decision. Charize had to show them who ruled here. A raw display of power was required to silence those who had favored Tarla.

"Let him in, sisters," she said. "And we will feast!"

✳   ✳   ✳

Palimak pressed an ear against the wall, listening as he tapped with the haft of his dagger. *Tap, tap, tap.*

All his senses were focused on the hollow echo that came back to him. The space behind the wall was quite large, he guessed. More of a chamber than just a rift in the rock's surface. Also, it was obviously a place that was quite warm. Witness the steam rising off the stone.

Getting ready to make another sounding, he shifted and felt a scratch against his cheek. He drew back, noticing a raised ridge on the otherwise smooth wall.

"What's this?" he asked.

On one shoulder, he felt Gundara shiver. "I don't like this place, Little Master," he said.

"Maybe we should leave," Gundaree added.

"Is there danger?" Palimak asked.

Frightened as he was, Gundara could not help a snort of derision. "We said it was hungry, Master," he pointed out.

Gundaree's teeth were chattering. Still, he managed to add, "And it wants to eat *us!*"

Palimak ignored their fear. "Make the light brighter," he said.

"Are you deaf, Little Master??" Gundara said. "Didn't you hear us tell you to leave as fast as you can?"

"Do as I ask," Palimak said. Then added, "Please."

"All right, if that's what you want, Little Master," Gundaree said. "But don't blame us if you end up in the belly of some nasty thing."

"I won't," Palimak said.

The two Favorites muttered a little chant, the ball of light grew brighter and Palimak was able to see the raised area of the rock more clearly. It was a carving of a winged snake with two heads, its tongues flickering out to taste the air.

"The sign of Asper," he whispered.

At that moment the Favorites cried out in unison: "Look out, Master!"

There was a low rumble, then a loud grating noise, and as Palimak stepped back the wall began to shift in its moorings. Palimak drew his sword—double-arming himself by readying a defensive spell. But then the wall stopped moving. Foul-smelling steam hissed through an inch-wide opening between the wall and its stone frame.

He waited, whispering a spell to turn the awful odor into something more bearable. The Favorites were silent, which he supposed was a blessing. But the lack of their usual chatter was unnerving.

Palimak had rarely seen them so afraid before. During grave danger to himself their usual attitude was a cheery resignation that they'd receive a new master if the danger proved fatal to Palimak. Sure, they'd miss him. Perhaps even mourn him a little. But the fact was that after a thousand or so years they'd become fatalistic about the many short-lived creatures who had been their masters. What would be, would be. In this case, however, their attitude was far from indifferent.

Palimak probed the darkness for some sign of the danger that was worrying them. He didn't doubt its existence. Gundara and Gundaree were never wrong about such matters. But all he could sense was the spoor of the long-dead magic he'd encountered when entering the tunnel.

Once again he looked at the twin-headed snake symbol of Asper. Unconsciously he reached out to touch it. But as he did so he had a quick mental flash of something—a horrible something—leaning forward in anticipation. Its enormous fangs exposed in a wide grin.

At that moment the ball of light sputtered and died and all became darkness. There was a subterranean rumble, then the heavy grating of stone against stone: he sensed that the door was opening wider.

Palimak took a deep breath and stepped through.

And then there was a loud, echoing *boom!* as the door slammed shut behind him.

CHAPTER EIGHT
ESCAPE FROM HADIN

Oh, how he danced. Danced, danced, danced. Danced to the beat of the harvest drums . . .

Safar fought against the spell's fierce grip. He groaned with effort as the cosmic puppeteer manipulated the strings, forcing him through another performance on the doomed stage that was Hadin.

All around him his eternal companions pranced and sang, giving themselves over joyously to the harvest queen's song: *"Lady, O Lady, surrender/ Surrender . . ."*

Smoke once again columned up from the volcano that formed a backdrop for the dancing queen. Showering sparks flitted through the black smoke in seeming time to the music.

Any moment now history would repeat its terrible cycle and Safar would once again experience the soul-searing death of flesh, bone and spirit.

But now there was a difference. And with that difference came hope. It seemed to him that he'd regained awareness more quickly than the other times he'd been resurrected in the eternal hell that was Hadinland.

And now he was armed not only with the words of Asper's spell, but also with the memory of Palimak charging out of the mist of some Spellworld on the muscular back of Khysmet.

Of course, it could all be merely another awful manifestation of the eternal damnation that he'd been flung into when he'd first cast the spell back in Esmir. In fact, he had no proof that the original spell had worked. He had only a vague feeling of success. For all he knew the poisons might still be pouring through the magical portal that linked Hadin with Esmir.

Another worry—what about Iraj? What had happened to him? Safar had a skin-crawling suspicion that his old enemy lurked nearby. Perhaps not exactly in the Spellworld of the doomed Hadin. But close. Very close.

He tried to concentrate. Tried to push his magical senses into places where he thought Iraj might be hiding. But he was so caught up in the spelldance that he could only keep prancing like a naked clown.

"Lady, O Lady/ Surrender . . ."

Slapping his palms against his chest. Pounding time with his bare feet in the hot sand.

For a frightening second he nearly lost control—and with it his will to cast the spell that he prayed would free him.

Then he heard the distant thunder of the volcano building toward its fiery climax. The queen turned to observe the eruption and then shout her belated warning to her doomed flock. Just as she had hundreds of times before.

Grasping for all his strength, Safar quickly began to chant the words of Asper's spell:

"Hellsfire burns brightest
In Heaven's holy shadow.
What is near
Is soon forgotten;
What is far . . .

*   *   *

Iraj struggled higher onto the rock.

Or at least he imagined it as a rock. Just as he imagined the soul-burning sea behind him to be something that could be described as a "sea." Never one for deep reflection, Iraj had no sense of the metaphysical, much less words to describe it.

All he knew was that he could hear Safar's voice. And although that voice came from a place he couldn't see, he was certain it was quite close.

There it was now:

" . . . Embraced as brother;
Piercing our breast with poison,
Whispering news of our deaths . . .

Iraj knew instinctively that his enemy was preparing to escape.

And he was determined to escape with him.

Iraj flung himself higher, ignoring the pain as he flopped onto the rough surface. At the end of the rock was a blue-gold shimmer of light. He thought he could make out movement in that light. Gigantic shadows, dancing to a rhythm he couldn't hear.

Safar was one of those shadows.

He was sure of it.

Iraj reached . . . reached . . . reached . . .

*   *   *

The primitive creature that was Kalasariz saw Iraj moving and cried out to the others. "The king," he rasped. "Follow the king!"

Racked by pain, he heaved closer to Iraj.

Behind him the two wormlike things who were Fari and Luka heard his call. Desperately they forced their bodies after him.

*   *   *

Lava was already rolling down the sides of the volcano when Safar chanted the last lines of the spell:

" . . .For she is the Viper of the Rose
Who dwells in far Hadinland!"

A great cloud of black smoke burst from the mouth of the volcano. The queen and the other dancers screamed in terror.

Safar braced for the mighty blast of hot breath that he knew would follow.

But just then he heard a shrill animal cry. With that cry came power over his own limbs and he sagged—nearly falling to the sand. It was as if the puppet strings had been suddenly cut.

There was another shrill trumpeting and he staggered to his feet. With difficulty, he turned on numb limbs and his blood thrilled when he saw an amazing creature charging across the beach.

It was Khysmet! White coat gleaming silver in the sun.

Safar didn't stop to think where he had come from, or how. Somehow he got the strength to move forward. Then to run on legs that felt like dead stumps as he staggered across the sand to meet the stallion.

When he reached him, he gathered all his strength and threw himself on Khysmet's broad back.

The horse swung around and sprinted for the shoreline where the waves crashed over a tumble of black rocks.

At that moment the volcano erupted.

An enormous blast of burning hot wind smashed against them.

But instead of dying, they were flung high into the air.

Safar had a sensation of soaring. Then he felt Khysmet plunge forward. It was as if the stallion had suddenly grown wings and they were hurtling across a flame-washed sky.

Behind him he heard someone shout: "Safar!"

It was Iraj's voice.

Safar bent around, but there was nothing to see except the smoking ruins of the island.

Then he felt something sear his chest and he cried out in surprise and pain. It seemed to burn through flesh and bone, then pierce his heart like a fire arrow.

And then the pain was gone as quickly as it had come.

Khysmet trumpeted joy, surging forward with even greater speed.

Safar was too weary to feel anything now. He collapsed on the horse's back, letting his friend carry him away to wherever he wanted to go.

Still, he couldn't help whispering, "Free, free." And then he thought he heard a faint echo: *"Free, free."*

Stupefied by exhaustion, he barely registered that echoing voice.

Then darkness seized him and he knew nothing more.

CHAPTER NINE
DEATH SONG

Palimak was surrounded by huge red eyes that glittered at him hungrily through the darkness. He couldn't move; his limbs were like stone and each breath came with great difficulty.

His mind was a chaos of half-formed thoughts. Where was he? Who were these creatures? Why had he ignored the advice of his Favorites? And what in the hells had possessed him to step through that door in the first place?

Although the inky-black chamber he found himself in was sweltering hot, a chill ran down his spine as he realized that "possession" wasn't too far off the mark.

He'd entered because he had been compelled. Some powerful force had reached through the very rock to seize him and bend him to its will. Deafening him to his survival instinct's loud clamor of alarm.

Gundara and Gundaree were silent. From the absence of weight on his shoulders, he guessed they'd shrunk to their smallest size, hoping they wouldn't be noticed.

He heard a heavy body moving toward him and he raised his eyes to see the largest of the burning orbs coming closer. By the gods, he wished he could see more!

Although, perhaps it was just as well he couldn't. From the lumbering sound of the body and the fact that the creature's eyes were several feet above his head, Palimak realized that the beast must be enormous.

With that jumble of frightened thoughts came an idea: These creatures feared light! If someone had asked him how he knew this, he couldn't have answered. The knowledge just suddenly bloomed in his consciousness: to escape, all he had to do was conjure up another ball of light.

Desperately, Palimak tried to signal the Favorites—sending his thoughts out through the well-oiled mental channel between them. Their disappointing answer came racing back. That avenue of escape had been slammed shut by the same powerful magic compelling him to enter the chamber. The spellcaster had factored in its own vulnerabilities and had made sure that no light spell at Palimak's command would work within these chamber walls.

Strong magic rippled the dank currents of sweltering air as the huge red eyes moved closer.

Palimak dug deep for strength. But with a shock he realized that merely keeping the life forces burning in the tomb of his spell-frozen body had drained his powers. He couldn't even open his mouth to speak, much less scream.

The beast paused in front of him, its breath like a foul wind issuing from an open grave. Then it moved slowly around him, as if measuring Palimak for that very same grave. Finally it returned to the front, huge eyes widening even larger—two red orbs ready to swallow him up.

Then the beast spoke. "This creature is a puzzle to me sisters," it said. Rasping though it was, Palimak detected a feminine quality in the voice. "From all outward signs it is human," the voice continued. "But there is also a demon scent to it. Demon and human and in the same body. How could this be?"

A low mutter swept the chamber—many low voices echoing: "How could this be? How could this be? How could this be?"

The beast's voice rumbled with what Palimak thought might be laughter. "No matter, sisters," it said. "Human or demon, it will taste just as fine."

"As fine . . . as fine . . . as fine," came the echoing reply.

The hungry edge in all of those voices nearly swept away Palimak's will to resist. But he strained mightily to make one last desperate effort.

Then it was like a gate opening, and power burst forth. His whole body tingled as it awakened. A burning sensation afflicted his eyes, as if they'd been struck by hot sunlight. He closed them. The pain vanished and when he opened them again the night-black darkness had dissolved into a dusky gloom.

Surprised as he was by this just-in-time return of his powers, he still didn't move. Towering over him was a nightmare figure—grave-devil white with outstretched wings so wide they seemed like they could enfold a score of Palimaks. Behind the beast were similar creatures, slightly smaller, but just as heart-stoppingly ghastly.

The beast bent its terrible head until its eyes were at Palimak's level.

It said, "Before I eat you—whether you be human or demon—I'll gift you with my name. It's none other than Queen Charize you will honor with your flesh. Queen Charize who will suck up your marrow. Queen Charize who will savor your soul. So make yourself ready, little one. As ready as you can."

As Charize spoke, Palimak's eyes flickered left and he saw a high altar with a half-dozen steps leading to the top. Resting on that altar was an enormous coffin whose lid was sculpted into the shape of a demon. Emblazoned on the sides of the coffin was a golden twin-headed snake with outstretched wings.

Immediately he knew what it was: the long-lost tomb of Lord Asper!

This was the place he had sought from the moment he'd set foot on Syrapis. Long ago his father had told him the tale of his visionary visit to the chamber of horrors ruled by Queen Charize. And of the coffin he'd found there—a coffin containing, Safar had been certain, the body of Lord Asper, as well as many secrets.

It came to Palimak that if only he could reach the coffin he would be safe. And with that knowledge came the odd feeling that he was not fully in command of his mental faculties. It was as if some older, wiser being had entered his body. A being of cool cunning and calculation. He felt strong and coldly superior. Magical power coursed through his veins.

He spoke, a touch of sarcasm coloring his tones. "Pardon, royal one, for defiling your ears with my puny voice. But before I die I would demand a boon from you."

Surprised, Charize stepped back, barbed tail curling like a giant scorpion's.

"What's this?" she growled. "You can speak?"

A sound like mistral winds hissing through the poisoned thorns of a devil tree stirred the cavern: "He speaks, sisters, he speaks!"

Palimak shrugged, which surprised the monster queen even more. Her spell should have rendered him not only speechless, but immobile as well.

"It's a small thing," he replied. "I open my mouth and words present themselves." He glanced at the queen's horrid minions who were whispering to one another, uneasy at his ability to shake off the effects of Charize's spell. "The important thing isn't whether or not I can speak," Palimak continued, "but whether you will grant me the boon I've requested."

Queen Charize had recovered her wits. "Boon?" she said scornfully. "Why should I grant you a boon?"

Palimak frowned. "Are you the Queen Charize," he asked, "who claims to be ruler of the Sisters of Asper?"

The question surprised him as much as it did Charize. Where had it come from? And why was his voice deeper, his words formed from an experience and a knowledge beyond his ken?

"Claim!? Claim!?" Charize roared. "How dare you speak such words of doubt?" Her talons clattered angrily. "Now, your death will not be so easy, foolish one. You will linger in exquisite agony before I eat you."

Palimak's instincts begged him to scream pleas of Mercy, lady, mercy. Instead, he amazed himself by finding the courage to smile.

"If the gods will my death, so be it," he said. "Painful though that death may be."

He managed even greater nerve and wagged a finger under the queen's flaring nostril slits. "But I'll die knowing you are a great liar," he said. "Claiming a throne you don't deserve."

The queen's barbed tail shot toward him, poisoned hook aiming for his heart. Palimak wanted to jump away, but he steeled himself. A heartbeat later he was rewarded as the hook point stopped scant inches from piercing his breast.

Charize glared at him, clearly confounded by his boldness. All around her the other creatures hissed in wonder at their queen's hesitation. Whispering, "Is it true? Is it true? Does Charize lie?"

At that moment Palimak spotted the bloody corpse of one of her subjects, sprawled near what he thought might be her throne. Several of the beasts were gathered next to the corpse and it seemed to him that they were the ones leading the chorus of doubts. In his misfortune, had he in fact been fortunate enough to have stepped into the middle of a palace revolt?

"Who are you to dare brand Charize a liar?" the queen roared. "Tell me your name before I kill you."

"Why, I am Prince Timura," Palimak answered. "Perhaps you'll find that name familiar. Hmm?"

Gasps of terror echoed through the chamber. "Timura! Timura! Timura!"

Charize's great jaws unhinged, but not to attack. Instead she was in shock. Then her jaws snapped shut as she fought to recover her dignity.

"Now, you are the liar," she said. "I have met Safar Timura. And you are not him. He was fully human. There was no demon blood running through his veins."

"Actually, I'm his son," Palimak said. "Disbelieve that at your own peril."

Charize managed a sound that Palimak took for forced laughter. "What a fool you are," she said, "if you think you are a danger to me."

"Perhaps I am a fool," Palimak said. "Test me and we shall see. But I promise you this: one of us will be dead before the test is done. And I strongly doubt that it will be me." He chuckled. "My father told me what a coward you were. How he bested you with the simplest of spells."

Charize clacked her talons in annoyance. "It was a silly trick, nothing more," she said. "You will notice I didn't fall for the same trick this time. My spell made you powerless to bring light into this chamber!"

Palimak snorted derisively. "You silly creature," he scoffed. "I don't need light. I am part demon . . . as you noticed. And with my demon eyes I can see you and your sisters quite well."

He surprised himself when he said this. Until the moment he opened his mouth, Palimak hadn't realized what had happened. Raised among humans, he had kept the demon side of himself at bay for most of his young life. It was a part of him that he feared. A side that he believed was capable of shameful cruelty. However, he now realized it was the demon side that had saved him. Somehow, when fighting to win his powers back, he'd broken through to his demon self and this was what he was using to confront Charize.

As this realization ran through his mind, it also came to him that there was more to it than that. Far more than just his demon powers were available to him. Suddenly, he felt as if his father was quite near. This notion took him by such surprise that he nearly turned his head to see.

But the chamber abruptly became silent and he quickly shifted his full attention back to Charize. A moment before she'd been wavering between waiting to find out more about her new enemy and killing him on the spot.

As he looked up, he saw that indecision end as she drew back a mighty claw to gut him where he stood. Unfortunately, there was nothing Palimak could do about it. This was Charize's lair, after all. And on her own ground there was no magic he knew of that was powerful enough to do more than slightly wound her before he died.

Palimak instinctively went for the bluff. He struck quickly, conjuring up a spell that would be quite painful, but would actually do little damage.

Charize gasped as the spell hit her and jumped back. Before she had time to think,

Palimak laughed at her.

"That's just a small sample of what I can do," he said. "Threaten me again and I shall turn you into ashes." He gestured at the others. "I'm sure your sisters have wearied of your rule and will thank me for killing you. So don't make the mistake of thinking I am vulnerable merely because I am outnumbered."

The other creatures muttered. From their tone, Palimak could tell that his bluff had struck the target dead center. None of them would mourn if Charize fell.

Unsure of her ground, the queen decided to play for time. "You asked a boon, small one," she said. "What is it?"

Palimak nodded, as if satisfied the danger had passed. "I entered this chamber," he said, "because I seek the tomb of Lord Asper. My father told me it was here and bade me pay homage to him."

Charize snarled. "You entered this chamber," she said, "because I compelled your obedience. There was no free will involved in your decision."

Palimak shrugged. "The more you speak," he said, "the more convinced I am that you are a liar."

He turned, as if he were about to stroll easily away through an open gate, instead of being confronted with a thick stone door. He even raised a hand, as if to cast a spell that would open it. He was mildly surprised when he saw that his hand looked barely human. His sharp claws were so fully extended that his fingers were misshapen. His tongue reflexively moved around inside his mouth and he found long sharp fangs instead of blunter human teeth.

An odd part of him wished he had a mirror to peer into, wondering what his face looked like. How much of a demon had he become?

"You didn't answer my question," Charize said. "What is your boon?"

Palimak turned back. "Why, only to pray before Lord Asper's tomb," he replied.

Charize nodded her mighty head at the dais. "Go pray," she said. "But know that you will pray your last, little one. For you will not leave this chamber alive."

Palimak felt a spark of fear. She'd finally guessed he was bluffing. And was only letting this charade play out long enough to satisfy her followers.

He hid this knowledge and strode calmly over to the dais and mounted the stairs. He didn't have the slightest idea what he was going to do next. It seemed there were two liars in this chamber. Palimak was the first—Safar had most certainly never told him to pray at Asper's tomb. He was only working off a vague notion that once he reached the tomb there might be a chance of escape.

The second liar was Charize—just as he'd claimed. Palimak had studied the ancient Book of Asper Safar had bequeathed to him long and hard. And he doubted strongly that the old master wizard had left creatures such as Charize and her sisters to guard his resting place.

If Asper had truly intended such a thing, there'd have been broad hints about it in the book—the latter pages of which were filled with the demon's thoughts on his approaching death. He'd known his illness was fatal and had worried that despite all his efforts, no one would find his tomb and the secrets it contained. Secrets that might save the world from the disaster he'd foretold.

When Safar had visited here in his vision, Asper's ghost had commanded him to come to Syrapis. Since Safar's death had prevented this, Palimak was determined to take his father's place.

As he knelt before the tomb the world shifted slightly and Palimak remembered his wild dream ride on Khysmet, his father shouting to him for help. And he thought, but is he really dead? And, if not, how can I save him? And what is it I'm supposed to save him from?

Charize rumbled, "What are you waiting for? Pray!"

Her voice jerked Palimak back to a chilling reality. If he didn't come up with something quickly he'd soon be dead himself. Palimak bent his head over the twin-headed snake that was the symbol of Asper.

In the background he heard Charize lift her monster's voice in song:

"We are the sisters of Asper,
Sweet Lady, Lady, Lady.
We guard his tomb, we guard his tomb,
Holy One . . ."

Although the sound of her voice was like broken glass scraping against stone, the song was strangely familiar. It became even more so as Charize's subjects joined her in a blood-curdling chorus:

"We take the sin, we take the sin,
Sweet Lady, Lady, Lady.
On our souls, on our souls,
Holy One."

Out of Palimak's memory crawled the courtyard scene in far-off Caluz, where Queen Hantilia and her subjects sang a similar song. In Hantilia's case the song was a call to sacrifice, a mass suicide for the greater good of Esmir and the world at large. But the same song rang shrill and evil when Charize and her devil horde sang the words in their banshee voices.

". . . On our souls, on our souls,
Holy One."

It was a harsh melody of despair that nearly ripped Palimak from his moorings. All his confidence dissolved and his life suddenly seemed like it was dangling from the slenderest of threads in the Fates' holy loom. And he thought: Help me, father! What shall I do?

At that moment what sounded like a great drum boomed from someplace close by.

And Asper's golden snake came alive.

Part Two

The Return of Safar Timura

CHAPTER TEN

BETWEEN WORLDS

Safar jarred awake, the thundering sound of an enormous drum booming in his ears. At first he thought that he was back in Hadin and the harvest drums were commanding a new performance.

Then relief flooded in along with awareness as he realized he was still astride Khysmet who was racing across a starlit sky. No more would he be forced to dance the mad dance of Hadin under the erupting volcano.

He was free!

Yes, but free for what? The question came from nowhere. And for some reason it frightened him. Where was he going, and why? What fate awaited him?

Other sensations flooded in. The first was the knowledge that he was now fully clothed. He flexed his limbs and felt a familiar weight, then glanced down and saw he was dressed in the same battle gear he'd worn when he'd faced Iraj and his minions back in Caluz. To his delight, he even felt his sheathed sword slapping against his thigh as Khysmet soared onward.

Reflexively, he touched his belt and found the small silver dagger waiting there—the magical witch's knife Coralean had given him long ago.

Then he heard the drum again and lifted his head. Off in the distance—moving at the same speed as Khysmet—was a bobbing torchlight. He whispered a sightspell and the image grew clearer. A spark of joy ran through him when he saw the glorious black mare and the familiar figure of the beautiful Spirit Rider.

Safar grinned and was pleasantly surprised how good the smile felt. It had been a long time since he'd worked those muscles, that was for certain. And now that he understood who had saved him, the "why" didn't matter as much as before. Khysmet whinnied as if in agreement.

Safar glanced around, trying to guess where he might be. The first thing he noticed was the absence of the blood-red Demon Moon. He'd already figured that he and Khysmet were in some sorcerous betweenworld. Asper had postulated the existence of such alternate worlds in his book. He'd even performed some experiments whose results were promising, although not final proof.

Absently, Safar ran some magical calculations in his mind. Although they didn't lead him to any useful observations—much less a discovery—it was eminently satisfying to use his brain again for so elegant a purpose.

For a long while he'd felt like nothing more than an enslaved animal. Like a poor dumb ox tethered to a grain wheel, going round and round with no will save that instilled by his master's whip.

He looked out at the Spirit Rider, torch held aloft, ebony skin gleaming in the starlight. A base side of him ached to catch her and enfold her in his arms.

By the Gods, it had been ages since he'd felt such life!

Then once again he heard the thunder of the big drum. This time the sound was followed by a long hiss, like that of an angry snake. The sound continued: boom! . . . hiss . . . boom! The rhythm was vaguely familiar. And then the identity of the sound came to him. A man of the high mountains, he'd had scant experience with the sea. But that was what it sounded like: a rolling sea striking some coastline, then drawing slowly back to gather strength to strike once more.

He looked down and saw a sparkling night ocean beating against a shore. Another sightspell increased his perspective and he saw a huge stone idol rising out of the booming surf.

Safar recognized the figure immediately. It was Asper.

Syrapis was just below!

The Spirit Rider and her mare plummeted downward. The mare whinnied for them to follow and Khysmet trumpeted a note of agreement.

Down and down.

Down and down.

Down!

*   *   *

"Something's wrong," Leiria said. "Palimak's been gone too long."

"Aye, lass," came Biner's rumbling reply. "I was thinkin' the same thing myself."

He shifted his bulk, bringing the heavy club up. It was Biner's favorite weapon—a thick-headed club sprouting a needle-forest of horseshoe nails.

His action triggered Leiria's decision. "Let's go," she said, starting down the tunnel.

Biner followed, along with the dozen Kyranian soldiers who had volunteered for the expedition.

Leiria had been reluctantly hanging back for well over an hour. Palimak had commanded them to wait, which was something that Leiria—a woman of action—was never very good at. Except when the waiting involved ambushes, of course.

She'd always been supremely patient when it came to tarrying by a trap set for an enemy. In such cases she enjoyed herself as much as any sane person can take pleasure in the foul art of warfare. During an ambush one could visualize the enemy's approach. See the canny noncom in charge of the attacking squad pause to study the terrain ahead. But you had been so clever—and this was the greatest thrill—covering all traces of the ambush that it was as if you were a trickster ghost. And a small fire of delight would bloom in your bosom as the noncom decided to ignore the prickling hackles at the back of his neck and advance to his doom.

But there was no pleasure of any kind standing idly by while someone else went about a possibly dangerous errand. Especially since Palimak—in Leiria's professional opinion—had been a bit too quick handing out orders. He'd merely said that she and the other members of the party must wait while he explored the tunnel. No arrangements had been made for emergencies. And in Leiria's mind, Palimak's delayed return certainly fitted the definition of an emergency.

That was the trouble with having such a youthful commander. Usually Palimak listened to her soldierly advice. Also Coralean's, when it came to matters of money or diplomacy. And Biner's, when the mission involved an aerial expedition.

However, this admirable trait tended to be tossed right into the slop hole when he was confronted with a threat that required his magical powers—which was Palimak's own area of expertise. It was then that the arrogance of youth overtook native caution and he tended to rush into the sorcerous breach without further thought.

Leiria moved swiftly along the tunnel, the flickering torchlight picking up signs of Palimak's passage: boot depressions in the salty silt on the floor, or the glitter of wet marks on the wall where he'd leaned.

Otherwise, she saw nothing except the occasional lone rat that panicked at their approach and dashed through their legs. About half an hour earlier a thick swarm of rats had descended on them—frightened, Leiria guessed, because they'd been cornered by Palimak and had no other way to flee.

Leiria was not a squeamish woman, but being confronted by all those dirty, squealing little beasts had unnerved her. She had taken no satisfaction from the near-hysterical curses of Biner and the others as they had fought off the wave of rodent intruders. When it was over, she'd felt humiliated by her own instinctive reactions. Perhaps this had been the main reason she'd finally decided to wait no longer and investigate what had happened to Palimak.

They splashed onward through the cold passage for many minutes, pausing only to recharge the pitch on their torches from the wide-mouthed jars of the stuff they'd packed along for that purpose.

Then they came around a corner and were brought up short by a thick stone wall that blocked all other progress.

"What's this?" Biner barked.

He looked back along the passage, searching for other openings, even though he knew very well there were none.

"Where in the hells did he go?" he wondered.

Leiria ignored the question, scanning the wall, looking for a break.

Nothing.

Then she spotted the twin-headed snake symbol carved on the wall. It glowed in the light when she held the torch close. Leiria put an ear against the stone, listening.

Immediately, she heard someone cry out in alarm "It's Palimak!" she shouted at the others. "He's in there!"

She threw herself against the wall. She rebounded, cursing in frustration, shoulder numb where she'd struck the stone. Even so, she prepared to hurl herself against it again.

But Biner stepped in front of her. He swung the club against the wall with all his strength. There was a loud crack! as a piece of rock broke off.

He swung again.

And again . . .

*   *   *

The Asper snake came alive, leaping off the face of the coffin, twin jaws hissing, long fangs lancing out for the strike.

Palimak jumped back, shouting and scrabbling for his sword. But he caught a bootheel on one of the steps and tumbled awkwardly to the ground.

Still, he managed to roll to one side, drawing back his sword to strike.

"Don't, Little Master, don't!" Gundara cried.

The warning came just in time to stay his hand. The Asper snake loomed over him, growing larger and brighter. Heads striking this way and that. Long tongues of flame shooting from its mouths.

"It's on our side, master!" Gundaree shrieked in his ear. "Our side!"

Palimak heard a deep moan of pain and swiveled to see Charize holding up a huge clawed hand to shield herself from the bright light.

The Asper snake swooped about the vast cavern, sparks showering off its long tail as if from some kind of reptilian comet.

Charize's monsters howled in agony, colliding with pillars as they ran this way and that, or smashing against the vaulted ceiling itself as they flew blindly away on their huge wings in their desperate effort to escape the intense light.

Palimak heard Charize scream in fury and pain and as he came to his feet he saw her rushing toward her throne. A enormous bone-white scepter leaned against one arm. Instinctively, Palimak knew it was some kind of weapon.

And then he knew it was because Gundara shrieked, "Run, Little Master, run!"

But there was no place to run, except after Charize, so he charged her, sword outstretched.

It was an unequal contest. Despite her bulk, Charize moved with amazing speed, great wings flapping so that she was carried forward in great hops.

Still, Palimak was right on her horned heels when she reached the throne and grabbed up the scepter.

He struck, but his sword bounced off the scaly armor of her back. Her tail lashed out, sending him flying and he crashed to the ground, dazed.

If Charize had gone after him then it would have been all over. But evidently she saw him as a lesser enemy and focused her wrath on the Asper snake.

Palimak heard her roar words in a language he didn't understand and a bolt of blue flame exploded off the tip of her scepter. It struck the snake full force. The creature hung in the air for long seconds, both heads hissing and wriggling in agony.

Another blast of blue fire from the scepter crashed into the beast. This was followed by an enormous explosion of pure sorcerous energy.

Charize's sisters shrieked in pain as the blinding light burst over them.

Palimak came to his feet, rubbing burning eyes. Then his vision cleared and he saw that the Asper snake was gone and the chamber had returned to its former gloom.

Charize was the first to recover. She shouted to her subjects, "Kill Timura! Kill him!"

Slowly, they formed around her. Then they advanced, Charize at their head.

Palimak backed up, feeling like a fool as he waved his puny sword before him.

"It's been nice knowing you, Little Master," Gundara squeaked.

"Oh, shut up!" Gundaree snapped. "We're going to be eaten too, you stupid thing!"

For a change Gundara did not reply. For some reason the lack of argument between the twins frightened Palimak more than any other experience in his young life.

Then his heels bumped against the bottom of the stairs leading up to Asper's coffin. Charize's jaws widened into a terrible grin. Her sisters tittered in ghastly amusement.

"And now, little one," Charize said. "And now . . ."

CHAPTER ELEVEN
BLOOD AND DARKNESS

Queen Charize leaned forward, one great claw stretching out to slice Palimak's life away.

He cut at her with his sword, but she only laughed and slapped it aside.

At that moment an enormous drumboom resounded from behind Charize and her army. They jolted about to see what this new threat might be. The boom was immediately followed by the trumpeting cry of what Palimak swore was a horse.

Then there was the thunder of hooves and a shouted war cry.

Palimak gaped as some invisible force burst through the line of monsters, hurling them aside.

There was a skitter of horse's hooves, another war cry, and then two more creatures fell to the ground, gutted and fountaining blood.

Then Palimak thought he heard someone shout, "Palimak! To the tomb, Palimak!"

It was Safar's voice.

His father's voice.

Without hesitation Palimak whirled and rushed up the short flight of stairs to the coffin. He was too numb to be surprised when he saw that the huge lid had been thrown open.

The mummified corpse of an enormous demon stared blankly out at him. He had time enough to see that it was dressed in black wizard's robes decorated with bejeweled symbols. Then he heard Charize hiss orders and he came about to do battle.

The beast that was Queen Charize roared at her sisters to close in on the invisible force. At the same time she struck out blindly with her scepter. A blast of blue light shot out, but she must have missed because the magical light hammered at nothingness.

Although for just a moment Palimak thought he could make out the shadowy figure of an armored warrior astride a great stallion.

Then the vision was gone and everything became a strange, violent shadow-play as Charize and her sisters battled the invisible force.

He saw a line of beasts form before Charize, saw that line bend as the force cut through them. Then the way was open and Charize clubbed at the air with her scepter.

Palimak heard a heavy thump and a groan as her scepter struck something.

There was a long pause, as if the attacker were struggling to recover, then the moment broke and Charize roared defiance, charging forward.

He heard a meaty thunk, saw Charize stop in mid-charge. And suddenly a red line jagged across her throat.

Charize toppled over, huge head falling to one side—bony skull held only by a thread of gristle—and she crashed to the floor.

There was a shocked silence as Charize's sisters stared down at their queen's lifeless body. Then that silence grew longer and more thoughtful as both Palimak and the creatures realized that the horseman and his steed were no longer present in the chamber.

First there was a shuffle—many claws and talons clicking against the stone.

Then a single whisper: "Who will be queen?"

That whisper became a chorus, "Queen? Queen? Queen?"

And the first voice began to chant:

> *"We are the sisters of Asper,*
> *Sweet Lady, Lady, Lady . . .*

The others took up the chant, turning on Palimak as they did so.

> *" . . . We guard his tomb, we guard his tomb,*
> *Holy One . . ."*

And Palimak had the soul-shivering realization that the battle for royal succession would be fought over his body.

*   *   *

Thwack! as Biner once again assaulted the wall. His club blow did so much damage that Leiria had to shield her face against the shattered rock that exploded outward. Even so, a sharp piece of stone cut her hand and the blood started to flow.

Leiria ignored the wound. What's a little blood, even if it's your own? She studied the results of Biner's work. Strong as he was, mighty though his blows might be, he'd only managed to hammer out a shallow depression into the wall. At this rate, hours would pass before they broke through—assuming Biner didn't wear himself out first.

There was one dubious victory his efforts had won—the depression made a kind of funnel that magnified the sound on the other side. They could hear plainly the clash of battle raging in the chamber beyond.

"Dammit, Biner!" Leiria growled. "This isn't working."

Biner didn't waste his energy on a reply. Instead, he drew back the club once again—planting his feet far apart and bunching his big shoulders in readiness for the blow.

"Here, let me help you," came a woman's voice.

Startled, Leiria turned to see Jooli standing there. Flanking her were the Kyranian soldiers who were gawking at King Rhodes' daughter. Apparently they'd been so surprised to see her, that they had let her walk right through their ranks.

Biner—stopped in mid swing—glared at her. "What're you doing here?" he demanded.

Jooli gave a throaty laugh. "Not making a fool out of myself, that's for certain," she said.

Leiria was angry. "I don't know how in the hells you escaped your guard," she said, "but I don't have time for you. Get your royal behind out of here before I thin-slice it for rations!"

"I'm a witch," Jooli said, answering Leiria's unasked question. "Right now the guards on your airship think I'm tucked away nice and cozy in that tiny closet of a cabin you gave me."

Biner was furious. "I don't care if you are the witch of all witches!" he roared. "Remove yourself from my sight, woman!"

Jooli chortled. "You have more muscles in your head," she mocked, "than you'll ever get in your body."

She took a step forward. Leiria started to block her, but there was something about Jooli that gave her pause. Leiria quite liked Biner. But sometimes he *did* tend to let his brawn get in the way of cool thought process.

Just as he sometimes used his big voice—even more startling because it came from the body of a dwarf—to hammer down people it wasn't always wise for him to overpower.

Jooli plucked the club from Biner's fingers as if it were a feather. He was too surprised to react. Then she made a gesture at the wall with her free hand. And she chanted:

> *"You are stone!*
> *You were sand.*
> *You are strong!*
> *You were weak.*
> *Strong to weak.*
> *Weak to sand.*
> *Sand to dust!"*

On the last line she leaned forward and gently tapped the stone wall with the club.

With barely a sound the entire thing collapsed, making a two-foot-high pile of dust on the floor.

Leiria didn't waste any thought on Jooli's amazing feat of magic, much less her motives for being here.

The only thing she cared about was that the wall that had been barring her way was gone. And now she was staring into a deep, black emptiness.

Although sight was absent, hearing was plain. There was a whispering of many voices. Harsh voices. Alien voices. Growing louder and louder, until the words rang clear:

> "*We are the sisters of Asper,*
> *Sweet Lady, Lady, Lady . . .*"

Then she heard Palimak shout: "Get back!"

Leiria hurled her torch deep into the dark cavern. There was a flare as sparks scattered in every direction.

She caught a glimpse of nightmare creatures—enormous things, with long fangs and vampire wings—then the torch guttered down.

"More light!" she shouted to the others.

And she charged through the opening, sprinting toward the place where she'd caught a brief glimpse of Palimak's pale face.

As she ran she heard Biner bellow orders. More torches arced into the cavern. Spears of light crashed against the floor, scattering flame in every direction so that the chamber became like a night sky lit by a meteor swarm.

Ungodly screams came from all around her, as if she'd burst into a nest of banshees.

She collided with a massive body, struck out blindly with her sword. An exploding torch revealed a horrible figure towering over her. As her sword bit into flesh she had time to realize that the creature was cowering in agony.

Warm fluid splashed her arms then she stepped around the creature and kept on running—dodging or slashing at any shadow that got in her way. The images revealed by the hurled torches seemed jerky, unreal, as light gouted, then died, then gouted again.

A smaller shadow loomed up and a stab of light came just in time for her to stay her hand: she saw Palimak—eyes wild, sword stained with gore.

"Leiria!" he cried, voice full of relief.

She leaped to his side, whirling to see a shadow army of shrieking beasts advancing on them. From far across the chamber she heard Biner bellow his war cry, followed by sounds of fighting. The others had joined the battle.

"They fear light!" Palimak shouted, at the same time dodging a huge claw striking out at him from the darkness.

Leiria lopped at the claw, sharp sword cutting through flesh and bone. And she heard a satisfying howl of pain.

"All I need is a little time," Palimak cried out, "and I can stop them!"

Knowing he meant to cast a spell, Leiria tried to give him the time he needed, chopping and thrusting in every direction. But there were too many of the creatures and after a moment Palimak broke off his efforts and joined her in the fight.

Even so, the fight was clearly turning against the Kyranians. She could hear Biner and the others trying to fight their way through. But her limbs grew weary and each blow seemed to have less effect. The torches were all guttering out and the chamber seemed to grow darker and more deadly by the minute.

Then she heard a wild ululation and a tall, slender figure vaulted over a knot of beasts.

There was a blast of light and the creatures howled, shrinking back. Leiria had time to see a shattered pot of burning pitch on the floor.

The light from the fire dazzled her for a moment, but as the flames died—too quickly! too quickly!—she saw that it was Jooli who had vaulted to their side.

She'd found a pike somewhere and was jabbing at the beasts in the guttering light as they recovered and pressed forward for the kill, mad with pain and hatred.

Jooli leaped up beside her, then turned, her shrill ululating war cry sweeping away Leiria's weariness.

The two of them attacked the beasts full force and it was if they had been a fighting team for years, instead of only a few minutes.

Jooli's pike would thrust at a creature, running it through to the backbone. While at the same time Leiria's sword would slash and cut at any who dared the defensive gap Jooli's attack would leave open.

Then Leiria would dance forward, doing awful damage with her sword, Jooli at her back, lancing pike giving Leiria the room she needed to maneuver.

Even greater damage was done when they would fall back, the creatures surging forward to take them. Their very numbers making them easy targets for the steel snake-like strikes of sword and pike from the two warrior women.

Still, the numbers were so unequal that Leiria knew they couldn't last much longer. And she could tell from Biner's shouts and the sounds of fighting across the chamber that his attack was stalled.

Just then she heard a dry crack! and a cry of alarm from Jooli.

Leiria glanced to the side, but in the stormy twilight of the chamber she couldn't see what had happened. All she knew was that suddenly she was ringed by snarling beasts, talons reaching out to take her.

Leiria struck at a shadowy claw, felt the blade bite, then she was flung back, her sword swept away.

Stone steps cut into her backbone as she fell, knocking her breath away.

And she sprawled there helpless, without even enough fight remaining to kick and bite and claw with her nails.

Two enormous red eyes loomed over her. She saw the glint of long fangs reaching for her throat.

Her mind raged in fighting fury. But she didn't even have breath enough to curse her enemy before she died.

Just then she heard Palimak shout: "Light!"

And suddenly a hot white light seared into being.

It was so bright, so blinding, that Leiria wasn't sure whether she'd been saved, or if she had been killed and her ghost was seeing the fiery entrance to the Hells.

CHAPTER TWELVE

SAFAR RETURNS

Light delivered victory, but it came at a terrible price.

The creatures, with their pale, death-worm skins, cowered on the floor of the vast chamber. Their howls of agony from the light were so intense that even Leiria, the most battle-hardened of soldiers, was moved by pity.

They were like flies in a cruel boy's insect collection—pierced through with needles of light. Pinned to the floor, their immense wings flapping feebly as they circled those impaling shafts on all fours, shrieking in pain and begging for mercy.

After Leiria had recovered she clambered to her feet and saw Jooli rising from the place where she had fallen—tossing away her broken pike. Blood leaked from a shallow arm wound where a talon had caught her.

About twenty feet away she saw Biner, surrounded by the other members of the Kyranian party, transfixed by the sight of the groaning monsters. The Kyranians were covered with blood, but when they unfroze from the shock and started to move Leiria sighed in relief when she realized that little of the blood was their own.

Biner came up to her, shaking his big head. "What do we do with them, lass?" he asked. "Make them prisoners?"

Before she could form an answer out of the chaotic thoughts and feelings racing through her mind, Palimak stepped down from what Leiria realized for the first time was a dais.

Behind him she saw the great coffin sitting on the platform—the mighty sarcophagus that was also the source of all that brightness. For out of its open lid spilled a blazing river of light, filling every nook and cranny of the chamber with an intensity that forbade the existence of even the smallest shadow.

The coffin light framed Palimak, silhouetting him larger than life. As intense as that light was, Leiria could see his eyes huge and glowing with magical fires. She saw the long talons arcing out from his fingers. And when he opened his mouth to speak she shivered at the sharp teeth he revealed—almost like fangs.

His ears seemed to have points that were more pronounced than normal. And his pale skin appeared more translucent than usual, with a green cast just beneath the surface. It was as if, she thought, another Palimak were ready to burst through. His demon side. Which was a Palimak she wasn't so certain she wanted to know.

And then she thought, No, it is a trick of the magical light. He's still my little Palimak. My dear little Palimak. The strange child I carried away from Zanzair on horseback. Chortling the first rude words taught to him by Gundara and Gundaree, "Shut up, shut up, shut up!"

He had been still oblivious to the fact that his mother, Nerisa, had just been killed by Iraj Protarus. Or that Iraj and his soldiers were hunting him now, bent on putting Safar, Leiria and the child to the sword.

Palimak turned to her, blazing eyes commanding. But when he spoke, his voice was a soft, almost mournful, counterpoint.

"We have to kill them, Aunt Leiria," he said. "I'm sorry to make you do this, but I don't think we have any choice. They're worse than any nest of vipers."

He drew in a deep breath. "Vipers, at least," he said, "have a purpose that's not so different from ours. No more terrible than ours, anyway. They have to eat, they have to breed and protect their young. And they only harm us if we threaten those needs and wants."

He gestured at the corpse of one of the beasts. It was much larger than the others, its head sheared from its body and fallen to one side. Eyes glaring hatred even in death.

"That's their queen," he said. "Queen Charize. And she was an evil thing, a hateful thing. And her purpose was something I still really don't understand."

He pointed at the open coffin. "That's Asper's tomb," he said. "I think there's promise there. Hope there. Father said there was, at any rate. And Charize was trying to subvert it. Turn it into an evil force for her own uses."

Palimak picked up his sword, which he'd dropped while making the light spell. He advanced toward one of the cowering creatures, talons retracting into his fingers. Fangs turning back into human teeth again. Eyes transforming into something more human with each step he took.

He looks so sad now, Leiria thought. And she wondered how hard it must be for him to wear a cloak of human form after living in the steel-hard skin of a demon.

He raised the sword high. "Mercy, master!" the creature shrieked. "Mercy!"

Leiria thought she heard Palimak groan in sorrow. But perhaps it was only a result of the muscular effort it took as he brought the sword down and cut off the creature's begging. Then, without pause, he went to another and took its life. Then another, and another . . .

Reluctantly, Leiria retrieved her own sword and joined in the slaughter.

After she'd killed her first victim, Biner, Jooli and the soldiers joined in. But just as hesitatingly. Whereas before they had fought and killed with a will, now they just struck out blindly, trying not to look at the poor, mewling things who were their victims.

Sometimes they stopped, sick of themselves and the gods for requiring such a thing. But Palimak urged them on, saying his light spell wouldn't last much longer.

In the end Charize's underground kingdom sank in a welter of gore. A place where the Butcher King had set up market with enough corpses to feed the greatest of cities. Except no one would ever feed on this flesh, so in their deaths Charize's subjects were denied even that most basic honor. They would putrefy here. Unwanted, unneeded, and mourned only in the nightmares of Leiria and the others who would most certainly never boast of their victory in this place. Because it was mass murder, nothing more.

So went the false Sisters of Asper. And as Leiria slew her last she remembered their refrain: *"We take the sin/ We take the sin./ Lady, Lady, Lady."*

The words would remain with her for the rest of her life.

* * *

Palimak could feel himself transforming. Sharp pin-prickles stabbed his skin as if he'd just been caught out in a lightning storm in the High Caravans of Kyrania. Hair like barbs in his skull. Eyes so dry it was painful to blink. The air was oppressive, crackling with energy.

He felt like he was two animals stuffed into one skin. One was cold logic: what was required, must be done. The other wanted to weep in empathy for his enemy. As he struck another scaly head from its shoulders, he thought, What if this were me?

Gradually, the softer side—the human side, he realized—superseded the first. And each killing blow became more difficult. No, that wasn't correct. It wasn't harder to kill, but it took more passion. He had to conjure up hate to power his muscles as if it were a magical spell. He had to hate these things to kill them. Invest them with all the deviltry the human world could imagine that he could deliver the blow.

And when he was done and there were no more creatures left to kill, he stood panting over the last corpse. Blood singing for more. Mind horrified at what he had done.

It was then that he realized he was fully human again. It was then that he realized he'd been fully demon before.

And on the whole, he thought, he much preferred the demon state.

Palimak mentally shook himself. Appalled at that thought. He was human, dammit! More human than demon!

Wasn't he?

Palimak buried this doubt. Triggered an avalanche of excuses and rationalizations, plummeting so quickly down that mountain of emotions that all other thought was smothered.

He looked at Leiria and saw . . . what was it? . . . relief? . . . in her eyes. Glanced down at his hands and saw that the claws had retracted into . . . normal? . . . human fingers. And then the rest of him felt human as well. Body and mind. Mind and body.

And there was blood everywhere he looked. Blood that he had spilled.

He felt sick and wanted badly to flee from this place.

Then he threw his sword away. By the Gods, he didn't want that blade in his hand anymore! It felt filthy. Defiled. And he was glad to be rid of it.

He also badly wanted to get out of this chamber. To seal its horrors off from the rest of the world with the largest boulder he could find.

A small voice chattered in his ear. "The coffin, Little Master," Gundara said. "Remember Asper's tomb."

And Gundaree added, "That's why we came here, wasn't it?"

Mind swirling with weariness, Palimak turned to face the tomb. The light spilling out was so hot and bright that he had raise a hand to shield his face. He was vaguely aware that Leiria and the others were watching him; probably wondering if he were possessed, so forced were his movements. But he didn't have the strength to voice reassurance.

He made a weak gesture, but the light only barely dimmed. It was still too hot to approach and he didn't have the strength to make a better spell.

"I'm hungry!" Gundara announced. It sounded loud in his ear, but Palimak knew from experience that the others couldn't hear.

"Me too," Gundaree added. "I want something sweet to eat. Like some honey cakes."

"With syrup all over them," Gundara put in. "Yum, yum."

"I don't have any honey cakes on me at the moment," Palimak said, too tired to worry that his human friends would think he was talking to himself. He patted the pocket where he kept their treats. "Maybe some currants. But that's it."

"They probably have pocket lint on them," Gundaree sniffed. "I hate lint!"

"Besides," Gundara said, "currants give me gas. You can't imagine what it's like living in a stone turtle when you have gas all the time."

Palimak couldn't help but grin. In the middle of all this blood the twins remained true to form. They were safe now, that was all that mattered. Base needs came first, bless their greedy little souls.

"I'll get you some honey cakes when we get back to the airship," Palimak promised.

Gundara sighed. "All right. If that's how it has to be. I guess we can't do anything else."

"But I want doubles," Gundaree insisted. "You have to promise doubles. Plus some really old cheese. Smelly as you can get it."

"Doubles it is," Palimak said. "And all the smelly cheese you can eat."

Once again he gestured, but this time he felt a surge of extra power from the Favorites. The light dimmed until it was bearable enough for him to look at the coffin straight on.

He clumped up the steps, boots heavy, feeling like he was walking through mud. But as he advanced up the stairs the Favorites were giggling to themselves, as if they had a great secret. Palimak figured they had something up their sleeves to get further promises of treats.

Then he was at the coffin.

He peered inside, expecting to see the mummified remains of the demon wizard, Lord Asper.

Instead a man, wearing the very same robes Asper had been entombed in, stared blindly up at him.

And the twins chorused: "Surprise, Little Master! Surprise!"

It was his father . . .

Safar Timura!

Palimak blinked, stunned.

Then Safar's eyes came open. His lips moved, forming words.

In a haze of unreality, Palimak leaned forward to listen.

"Khysmet," Safar whispered.

Then a hand came out, gripping Palimak's tunic and drawing him down with surprising strength.

And Safar said, insistent, "Where is Khysmet?"

CHAPTER THIRTEEN
THE WITCH QUEEN

It was near the end of day when the king's spies brought him the news. Rhodes hurried out to his castle's seaward wall and clambered up onto one of the big ship-killing catapults that defended this portion of his fortress.

According to his spies, Palimak and his party had left the warrens of the Idol of Asper and were now carrying a strange burden to the airship.

The catapult—hewn from the largest timbers in Syrapis—made a difficult climb for a man of Rhodes' bulk and he gasped curses at his underlings. But the curses were really directed at himself for the sloth that had turned his once muscular body into such a wheezing mass of fat.

This was the reason, he thought, that Palimak and the Kyranians had been able to best him. He'd not only allowed his body to become larded, but his mind as well. He'd grown lax—and by example had allowed his subjects to become lax. His own mother had belabored Rhodes when he was a prince for his lazy tendencies.

Barbarian though he might be, Rhodes had a good mind and a natural instinct for strategy, plus an unerring eye for spotting his enemy's weaknesses.

He was also blessed with formidable strength and speed, especially for someone so large. At birth he'd been over fifteen pounds, which would have made for a difficult delivery if his mother had been a normal woman. But she came from a race of overly large people—not quite giants—and Rhodes' entrance to the world through her wide hips and iron womb had been rather routine. If passing a cart horse could ever be called routine.

This combination of superior size and mental acuity had made Rhodes an easy winner over the other petty kings and queens in Syrapis. That was what had made him lazy, he thought. It had been too easy. And when Palimak and the Kyranians had arrived he had not been prepared for their new forms of warfare.

Rhodes finally reached the top of the catapult and peered over the walls to see what his enemy was up to. Across from him, hovering over the little island that was home to the Idol of Asper, was the airship. Not for the first time, envy gripped him as he gazed on that remarkable machine.

It was this magical device, he thought, that had been the key to the Kyranians' many victories over him and his royal Syrapian cousins. If only he had been blessed with such a thing the tale might have had a different ending. The humiliating scene in the courtyard two days before would not have happened. Instead it would have been Palimak and that bitch warrior woman of his who would have suffered the shame of defeat.

He lapsed momentarily into a reverie in which the two of them were being dragged before his throne to be condemned to the nastiest agonies that Rhodes' best torturers could devise.

Rhodes brought himself up short. No time for imaginary pleasures. He must be stronger than ever before. He must spy out his enemies' doings and look for the weakness that might deliver them into his hands.

He saw the tide was turning below. Waves were already beginning to wash over the island. In an hour or so there would be no dry ground. An hour after that the idol itself would disappear beneath the creamy froth of the waves.

He gestured and an aide handed him a spyglass. Rhodes peered through it and made out Palimak directing four soldiers who were swaying up a large, mysterious object. What in the hells was it?

He adjusted the focus, following the object up as it rose in the net that enclosed it. Was it some sort of box? And what was that carving on the lid? Then he realized it was shaped like a coffin. If so, it was a very big coffin indeed. Large enough to hold a man twice Rhodes' size, that was for certain.

Once again he studied the carving on the lid. Just before the coffin came level with his eyes, he realized what the carving was. It was a demon! Not only that, but the demon's face had the same features that were carved into the stone idol.

It was none other than Asper! He was certain of it. Then the coffin rose out of sight and a moment later the airship crew were muscling it over the rails to the deck.

Heart thundering, mind whirling with questions, Rhodes swung his glass back down to the island. Two men were carrying a stretcher down the stairway that descended from the idol's head. On the stretcher was a tall man, dressed in black robes. Rhodes couldn't tell if the man was conscious, but he noted with interest how tenderly his stretcher bearers treated him. A man of importance, no doubt. A man beloved.

This impression was underscored when he saw Palimak and the woman general rush over to the stretcher. Palimak gripped one of the man's hands. While Leiria bent over to kiss him. Then the stretcher was placed in a net, which was swayed up to the airship.

Rhodes followed its progress, then nodded with satisfaction when he saw the dwarf who captained the airship and his first mate, the exotic dragon woman, personally assist the crew in getting the stretcher aboard. Whatever the identity of the man, he was obviously of enormous importance to the Kyranians.

Rhodes had never seen him before, but that in itself didn't mean anything. There were many Kyranians he had no knowledge of. What gnawed at him was that his spies had never brought him word of someone of such obvious importance. Did the Kyranians have a secret leader? Someone of far greater importance than Palimak, whom everyone had been led to believe was the supreme commander of the Kyranians?

Was this fellow, the object of such respect and affection, the secret power behind Palimak's throne? The reason why one so young could perform so many remarkable feats of warfare and magic? If so, what had happened to the mystery man? Why was he in the stretcher, obviously ailing or injured?

A spark of hope flared in Rhodes' chest. If his suspicions were correct—and the man *was* their secret leader, then his weakened state might weaken the Kyranians as well.

He lowered the spyglass and quickly clambered back down the catapult. Excitement made the return trip much easier. Rhodes needed advice to take advantage of this vulnerability—assuming that's what it was.

And the best person who could provide it was his mother, Clayre, the beautiful witch queen of Hanadu.

Later, Rhodes would berate himself for not tarrying a bit longer on his catapult perch. If he had, he'd have seen his daughter, Jooli, unfettered and armed, making her way out of the idol's entrance and hurrying down the stairs. And he might have wondered why the Kyranians were allowing their hostage such freedom.

*   *   *

Aboard the airship, so many tears of joy flowed at Safar's miraculous return that they would have filled an ocean.

"He'th alive!" Arlain sobbed, smoky rings issuing from her dragon's mouth. "Thafar hath come back to uth!"

Biner honked emotion into a kerchief, then knuckled moisture from his eyes. "Methydia would be so happy," he said, "to see the dear lad with us again."

Renor and Sinch, mere striplings when the exodus from Kyrania had begun but full-grown young men now, knelt by the stretcher, crying unashamedly.

"If only Dario could be here," Renor said. "He always insisted Lord Timura was still alive." Dario, dead two years now, had been the grizzled warrior who had trained and drilled all the young men of Kyrania.

Soon all the other crewmembers and soldiers were kneeling around the stretcher, sobbing prayers of thanks to the Lady Felakia—goddess patron of Kyrania—for returning Safar to them.

In the background, Elgy and Rabix piped music, while Kairo did a little dance of happiness, tossing his head from one hand to the other.

Leiria and Palimak clutched each other, sobbing uncontrollably.

During all this, Safar was quite still. Eyes closed, breath coming in little gasps. Oblivious to everything around him.

Then a breeze came up, making the airship's lines buzz. Leiria shivered, feeling the sudden cold, and broke out of the cocoon of happiness.

"Let's get him into the cabin," she said. "Before we make him sick with all our affection."

She and Palimak picked up either end of the stretcher and carried Safar into the luxurious main cabin that had once been the quarters of Methydia, the long-dead witch who had created the airship and circus. And who had been Safar's lover.

Jooli, a total stranger to Kyranian affairs, watched from the outskirts of the little crowd, wondering about this man who was the cause of so much love and unashamed emotion.

The only thing she was sure of was that whoever he might be, the fellow was an immensely powerful wizard. Even unconscious, exhausted and ailing, the magical rays radiating from him were so intense that her own sorcerous abilities were nearly overcome.

He must be a good man, she thought, otherwise these people would not be so overjoyed. If he were a tyrant—like her father—they might have abased themselves, but only out of fear. Except, powerless as he now was, they would have been more likely to have cut his throat before he regained cruel consciousness.

An act Jooli had seriously contemplated herself upon occasion, when she'd come upon her father in a drunken stupor.

Then, just as the stretcher disappeared into the cabin she caught a strange eddy in the magical waves the man gave off. It was something not so good and not so kind and certainly not worthy of adulation. She tried to sniff it out, locate its source. It seemed to come from the mysterious wizard. But for some reason she couldn't fathom, it was also apart from him.

Something . . . not evil . . . not exactly that, at any rate. But redolent of fiery ambition and greedy hunger.

Then she lost the scent and by the time the cabin door closed Jooli wondered if it had been her imagination. Nothing more than a cynical reaction to all that outpouring of love.

She sniffed the air one more time and found nothing amiss. Jooli shrugged. Yes, that was it. Only her imagination.

A moment later Biner thundered orders and the crew rushed to the lines and the engines.

Then Biner cried, "Put some muscle into it, lads! The folks at home will want to hear this glad news! Safar Timura is with us again! By the gods, from here on out it'll be, 'Damn everything but the circus!'"

And the airship swept away on chilly winds, heading for the new kingdom of Kyrania.

The place Safar had spun into a dream for his people so long ago.

*　　　*　　　*

Rhodes tromped down many long flights of stairs to his mother's chambers.

She made her salon in the deepest reaches of the castle. Past the grain and wine stores, paltry now after the series of losing battles with Palimak Timura. Below the furthest dungeons where Rhodes imprisoned men and women who opposed his reign but who were too important in kill outright. Beneath the realm of the royal torturers, who gleefully plied rack and hot pincers in his majesty's service.

Below the treasury—which Rhodes loved even more than his harem. The treasury was guarded by his best and most loyal soldiers, who were paid three times the normal rate to ensure that loyalty.

Here he had experienced both his highest joys and deepest despair. Shuddering in pleasure during those times when he had heaped rich ransom and tribute chests into its crowded recesses. Weeping like a mourning woman as his wars with Palimak drained it to a puny thing, with only a few chests of jewels and gold left.

Only yesterday he'd deposited the two sacks of gold Palimak had given him to sweeten the treaty and to gain his favor for the Kyranian expedition into the Idol of Asper. When he'd added the fat coins to his store it had eased his humiliation a little bit. It had even given him slight hope that someday the tables might be turned: Palimak defeated, gold and gems once more flooding into the chamber.

As Rhodes walked past the treasury, guards snapping to and saluting, he had a moment of regret that he couldn't tarry there and run Palimak's gold through his fingers. Imagining that each coin was a piece of flesh wrested from Prince Timura's body.

Scores of torches lit the marble receiving area marking the entrance to his mother's apartments. The walls were decorated with enormous murals—pastorals extolling the many beauties of Syrapis.

On their surface the compositions radiated peace and harmony with nature. But if one looked closer there were little horrors in each mural that changed their whole meaning. A seascape, with Syrapis' most picturesque shore in the foreground. A burning ship in the far background, a winged monster scooping up sailors from the sea and devouring them. A vineyard, where handsome lads and pretty maids played lusty games beneath ripe grape clusters, drunk with the joy of the harvest wine. In the distant corner, a demon king leading his fiends in an unspeakable orgy of torture of those same lads and maids.

Rhodes thought they were quite nice, although he was wise enough not to have similar murals in his own chambers. Beauty, apparently, was in the eye of the beholder. And what Rhodes beheld and loved would have given nightmares to even his cruelest soldiers.

The chief of the witch queen's eunuch guard greeted him, twitching his head in a perfunctory bow and asking him to wait while Rhodes was announced to his mother. The eunuchs were all enormous men—the chief guard was almost as large as Rhodes—thick slabs of muscle beneath even thicker slabs of fat. Except their muscles were diligently exercised, whereas Rhodes had done nothing at all for a long time except eat, drink and shed tears over his starving treasury.

When he was granted permission to enter, Rhodes walked into his mother's salon with some trepidation. Mighty ruler of Hanadu though he might be, his mother was a powerful influence over him. She wasn't exactly the power behind the throne, but what she wanted she generally got. And her son lived in fear for her favor. Something he had been out of for a long time now. Specifically, since he'd lost his first battle with Palimak.

Queen Clayre had been his father's third wife—taken to seal an alliance. Big as she was, she was perfectly constructed in proportion: long shapely legs and arms, a marvelous bosom and an hour-glass form. When Princess Clayre had wed his father that beauty—flowing out of such a large package—had made her a rather exotic bride and his father couldn't get enough of her in their early days. At least, this was what Rhodes' mother frequently told him, as her body slaves gathered round to make her up and clothe her in robes which fairly flowed over a still near-perfect form.

Rhodes doubted that she exaggerated very much. To this day Queen Clayre was considered one of the most beautiful women in Syrapis. She was also renowned for her lusty appetites and took young lovers frequently and casually. She was quite discrete, however, surrounding herself and her ladies in waiting with eunuch guards whose loyalties were fierce and unquestioning.

It was one of those guards who greeted the king as he entered the chamber. He was quickly turned over to the chief eunuch who led Rhodes into her presence. He didn't announce the king, instead putting a finger to his lips to ask the queen's son for silence. Rhodes looked across the ornate chamber and saw his mother bent over her spelltable that was littered with ancient scrolls which were piled next to little jars filled with magical potions and powders.

Only the center of the table was clear. Although Rhodes couldn't actually see, what was there, he knew very well what it contained. Set into the table was a large area with tiles of pure gold, all encrusted with gems and arranged to form a pentagram.

Clayre seemed to be studying one of the parchments, glancing once in a while at the pentagram, then nodding as if to confirm her speculations.

She was dressed in the finest robes, all decorated with the magical symbols that declared her the High Priestess of Charize. Around her neck was a many-layered necklace made of black pearls. Some years before, six men working from tide to tide—day in and day out—had shortened their lives by many years to gather the pearly parts that made up his mother's necklace.

As Rhodes dutifully waited for his mother's attention, he saw sparkling red lights leap from one strand of the necklace to the next and back again, as if the pearls were alive with some inner force. Which, of course, they were, since Queen Clayre was a powerful witch.

Rhodes worried at a hang nail, thinking about his mother. Daughter of a minor king, she should have had little influence over his father's court. But she had proved to be a genius at harem intrigue. Within a few years of her only son's birth she'd removed her two rivals.

One by hired assassination—or, at least, that was what palace rumor said. Rhodes knew for a fact that his mother had used magic, plus her feminine charms, to work her will on one of her rival's sons. And it was that son who had slain his own mother, then committed suicide after he'd come out of his trance and seen what he had done.

The other rival she'd killed herself, smothering the woman with a pillow while the rest of the harem watched. Even the big eunuchs guarding the harem didn't dare interfere, because by then everyone feared his mother.

The two murders had made Rhodes crown prince, although this claim was disputed by his half-brothers and half-sisters who had been borne by his father's other two wives. But Rhodes' mother worked hard to ensure his succession.

She put together a salon that welcomed the best athletes of the time. And she spent her money freely to buy the wisest scholar-slaves available in Syrapis. These athletes and scholars Rhodes teachers for his body and mind throughout his young years. And their wise words were backed up by his mother, who taught her son everything she knew about court politics.

At six, Rhodes could lift the fifty-pound stone shot that was favored for the mobile catapults. At eleven, he'd stalked his twenty-year-old half-brother—and his main rival to the throne—from one trysting place to another. His rival had a weakness—a fatal weakness as it turned out—for other men's wives. As a matter of fact, Rhodes had finally caught his brother at the very seaward wall he'd perched upon to spy on Palimak.

Just to the right of the base of the catapult was a little alcove. A sheltered altar to some minor god, whose name no one could remember. It was also a favorite meeting place for lovers.

As Rhodes waited nervously, he thought about that fateful day. Drawing strength from the memory. He grinned as the image rose up of the honey-tongued weakling who had opposed him so long ago. The mother of Rhodes' princely rival had been an ambitious second wife. She'd named her son Stokalo after the legendary Syrapian prince who had been banished by his cruel father but who had eventually returned from the sea to win back his rightful throne.

Stokalo was strong, but not so strong as Rhodes. He had an agile mind, a mind schooled in warfare by Rhodes' father, who favored Stokalo even after the life had been choked out of Stokalo's mother by the offending pillow. But he was not so smart as Rhodes, who as a boy used to humiliate him in games of chess.

Rhodes thought of that day when his sibling, angry over a defeat, had laid himself wide open for elimination. He'd sent a message to his most recent lover—the young wife of a great general. The message said that they were to meet at the seaward wall where the fun would commence. Naturally, a spy who favored Rhodes had gotten a glimpse of that message and had passed on the news.

So the thirteen-year-old Rhodes had raced to the alcove ahead of the sinful couple. Lurked in the shadows until Stokalo was fully engaged—his lover pinned against the wall, gown hoisted above her hips—and then had crept up behind them.

A meaty hand grasped his brother's neck and a heavy knee jammed into his backbone, breaking it as easily as if it had been a twig in a drought forest. The woman had been too panicked to scream and had only moaned, cowering against the wall, as Rhodes lifted up his brother's dead body up and hurled it over the side.

He had thought about killing the woman on the spot—eliminating the only witness to the murder. Instead, he'd given her a chance to live or die and she'd chosen the wiser course.

First, by servicing the young Prince Rhodes. Second, by claiming that she'd inadvertently witnessed Stokalo's suicide while taking an evening stroll to catch the air.

Rhodes stirred a finger in his dirty beard, aroused by the memories of the means he'd finally used to eliminate Stokalo's former lover not many months later.

But before he could relax into that treasured memory, his mother coughed. He glanced up, starting when he saw her beckoning him.

As he approached, she said, "I have news, my son. Both fair and foul."

Her eyes were glowing, full of witchy power—making her appear even more beautiful than usual. "The foul news," she went on, "is that Queen Charize is dead. Slain by Palimak Timura."

As that disaster smacked him in the gut, Clayre waved it away as if it were nothing. Chortling in her rich, deep, earthy voice.

"The fair news," she said, "is that I've found someone better to replace her. Several someones, actually.

"And what they hate, above all things, is anyone named Timura!"

CHAPTER FOURTEEN
THE COUNCIL OF ELDERS

Rhodes stared at his mother for a moment. His shock at her announcement that Queen Charize—the true source of Hanadu's strength—was dead gradually subsided as the rest of her words rang through.

The monster Charize was dead. Not so bad by half if the rest of what she had to say was true. But what was this about an alliance? With powerful figures who shared his hatred for Palimak Timura?

Rhodes grinned. "Good news, indeed," he rumbled. He looked about the room. "Where are these wise men? Bring them out so I can greet them properly."

Clayre gestured at the golden tiled pentagram in the center of the spelltable. Rhodes peered at it, as if expecting to see something. But it was empty.

"They can't be summoned so easily," she said. "They want certain assurances. Assurances, I'll warrant, that you'll be glad to grant."

"Anything!" Rhodes breathed with deep feeling. "As long as they'll deliver Timura into my hands."

Clayre stared at him a moment, as if measuring her son's commitment. Finally she said, "I'll need to cast some rather complicated spells. And there are certain sacrifices we'll need to make to appease Charize's ghost. Give me a a week or so—a month at the most—and the bargain can be sealed."

Although he was filled with curiosity, Rhodes didn't question his mother further. Magic made him nervous. It was something he had no talent for, so it was something to be distrusted. One of his secret regrets was that he hadn't inherited his mother's sorcerous abilities. Instead, they'd skipped a generation to favor his oldest child, Jooli.

He'd never liked Jooli. If it had been up to him he'd have drowned her at birth. After all, his first-born should have been a son. A male heir who no one would doubt was the rightful person to succeed him to the throne. Increasing his dislike of his daughter was the early talent she'd shown for things that only a man should have possessed. Strength, speed, skill at arms.

But what had sealed his dislike was the revelation that she was a witch. His mother had informed him of it one day and for a time had tutored the child. All went well for a while and then his mother had reported in great disgust that Jooli had suddenly turned away from her and would have nothing more to do with her grandmother.

Rhodes had chastised his daughter, but although she was quite young she spoke her mind quite plainly. And she had made it very clear that she had no intention of entering into a spell bargain with Queen Charize, much less help provide the steady stream of sacrificial victims the monster queen had required of Hanadu for time immemorial.

The reasons Rhodes and Clayre hadn't removed Jooli long ago were complicated since they involved the bloody diplomacy Syrapis was known for. Further complicating things was the fact was that Rhodes had found it necessary to not quite withhold his blessing of Jooli as his rightful successor.

This was why he'd ordered her to become a royal hostage to Palimak. And it was his heartfelt desire that when the time came to break his treaty with the Kyranians Jooli would be the very first victim of young Timura's wrath.

His mother impatiently rapped bejeweled fingers on the spelltable, snapping Rhodes out of his reflections.

"Yes, mother?" he asked.

"I didn't summon you," she pointed out, "so I assume you came here for some purpose."

Rhodes nodded and proceeded to tell his mother about what he had seen while spying on the Kyranians. The enormous coffin bearing Asper's image and the mysterious man who had been carried out of the idol on a stretcher, a man whom all the Kyranians seemed to worship.

Queen Clayre was troubled, frown lines marring her beauty. "This does not bode well," she said. "The coffin was clearly Asper's."

Rhodes frowned. "That's ridiculous," he said. "How could the Kyranians have taken it from Charize?"

"I told you she was dead," Clayre reminded him. "And that Prince Timura was the cause of her death. Which should give us even greater reason to be especially wary of him. If he could kill Charize, he is even stronger than we feared."

Again, she rapped her rings on the table. "Possibly," she said, "it has something to do with the man you saw them remove from the idol."

Rhodes didn't answer. None of this made sense to him.

"Which means," his mother added, "that this alliance with these . . . ah . . . Timura-haters I mentioned, might be a better idea than even I'd imagined. In fact, I now think their offer has everything to do with the appearance of the mysterious person you observed."

Then she sighed, as if suddenly weary. "Leave me, my son," she said. "Let me reflect on this."

She offered a cheek, which Rhodes dutifully kissed and he started for the door.

But just before he left the room a gleam of light caught his attention. He glanced over to the mural just above his mother's spelltable, which was where the glimmer had come from.

The mural was an idealized painting of Hanadu during ancient times when, legend said, Lord Asper had lived in Syrapis. There was the castle, a bit smaller, not quite so imposing as the fortifications Rhodes had built. In the foreground, riding down the winding road leading out of the castle was a troop of soldiers, wearing archaic armor. At their head was the king—a handsome man of middle age. He was flanked by women warriors—his daughters the scholars said.

Rhodes had always admired the pictures of the king's daughters. Strong, fierce, all remarkably beautiful. Many times he'd dreamed of bedding those warrior princesses. Particularly the ebony-skinned woman who rode next to the king on a stunning black mare. The two of them made a fiery, intriguing pair, so full of life they practically burst out of the mural.

He'd studied that mural many times over the years, so it came as a huge surprise to him that there was a detail present he apparently hadn't noticed before.

Just ahead of the column was a fabulous white stallion. Rearing up before the black mare and her rider. Hooves striking painted sparks in the air.

He peered closer, wondering why he hadn't seen that magnificent horse before. Something in the back of his mind also wondered if those sparks had been animated a second ago. The reason why his attention had been drawn to the familiar mural.

"Is there something else?" his mother asked.

He almost spoke. But then, as he gazed at the mural it came to him that maybe he hadn't noticed the stallion before because he had always been so intent on the king's shapely daughters.

This was not something a son discussed with his mother. "No," he said. "There's nothing more."

"Very well," she said. "I'll call for you when I know more about our new allies."

King Rhodes nodded and exited the room.

*   *   *

It was a strange homecoming for Safar. He was barely conscious when he arrived at New Kyrania, the mountaintop home his family and friends had carved out in their wars with the Syrapians.

Of this time he had only vague recollections of bells and pipes and songs sung in praise of someone the villagers must have loved dearly or there wouldn't have been such a grand celebration. He didn't connect that someone with himself.

He had vague impressions of his mother, Myrna, his father, Khadji, and all his sisters gathered about his bed. In the background was the tall figure of a strange person who reminded him of Palimak but who was too old and self-possessed to be the boy he remembered.

Also in this dream—for that was what he thought it was—stood Leiria. Beautiful as always. Strong and steady in her armor. A rock for his homecoming—if that was what this dream was about. And in that dream Leiria stepped through the throng and kissed him—and ah, what a kiss it was. And he felt such regret for steeling himself against that love before.

And in this odd otherworld of Safar's consciousness, he remembered their meeting. A warrior woman, one of Iraj's personal bodyguards, given to him by his former friend. He recalled his guilt about that act—which had required his acceptance. An even greater guilt, since it was against all Kyranian principles and teachings that one human being could be given to another. And he remembered their first days of lovemaking, when he was mourning Methydia's death and he had used her to soothe his grief.

What a sin that had been. Even though she'd whispered to him during their embraces that she didn't mind if he was thinking of another.

Regret upon regret as he recalled what a friend she had become. Sacrificing everything to save him from Iraj. Not once displaying jealousy about Methydia, nor especially about Nerisa, the little Walarian thief who had grown into the love of his life.

What had been wrong with him? Why hadn't he realized that Leiria was above all others?

Such a sin. Such a sin. So extreme the gods would never forgive him.

And then he thought, but the gods are dead!

And that was followed by—Every woman I've ever loved suffered tragically for knowing me.

I'm not worthy.

This is why I've been condemned to dance eternally to the deadly music of Hadin.

And then he feared that at any moment he would suddenly hear the harvest drums resume their throbbing and once again the wild spellsong would compel him to dance, dance, dance. Palms slapping naked chest. Bare feet pounding the sand. On and on while a thousand others danced beside him. The beautiful harvest queen leading them on.

And the volcano ready to erupt!

But after a while, when nothing happened, he dared to wonder if somehow the cycle had been broken.

Then one day the stranger who looked like Palimak bent over Safar, pressing cool cloths on his forehead. The smell of healing incense tickling his nose. The stranger whispered words of affection, asking if there was anything he required.

He tried to speak, but his lips were numb. There was something very important he needed to say. But the words wouldn't come.

The stranger said, "What is it, father? What do you require?"

Maybe this *was* Palimak. Although it seemed unlikely, because the Palimak he remembered had been quite small. But the terrible yearning in his heart pushed him past these doubts.

So he answered, "Khysmet! Where is Khysmet?"

And he lapsed back into unconsciousness.

＊　　　＊　　　＊

The Council of Elders had not met for several years. In fact, the last time they'd been together had been in Esmir when Safar had cajoled them into entering the Blacklands. For a long time, dire circumstances—such as a dead run to escape Iraj Protarus—had prevented such a gathering of Kyrania's most prominent men.

An attempt had been made to bring that traditional ruling body together after they'd landed on Syrapis, but Palimak had blocked it. A youthful witness to their endless, and, in his view, foolish debates, he'd decided to dispense with that form of village government the first time the question had arisen.

Supported by Coralean, that canny old caravan master, as well as by Leiria and the other members of the Kyranian army, he'd not so gently pushed them aside. Forming instead a loose counsel of advisers, which included Biner, Arlain and the other members of the circus troupe.

Constant warfare, plus an unbroken string of victories, had kept the Elders quiet. These men—who'd once tried to exile Safar and Palimak—held little standing with the other villagers. And those who had occasionally dared to contest Palimak's will had found themselves in a very small minority.

Once in a great while Palimak had even used the force of magic to compel the Elders to obey his commands. Actually, it wasn't so much obedience as a sudden, magically induced desire on their part to follow where he led.

At first he'd been ashamed of these tricks. His father had drummed into him the value of village democracy, where all views were accounted for and compromises made. On the other hand, when he and Safar had separated in Caluz, another message had been delivered. It was up to Palimak, his father had said, to lead the Kyranians to safety while he remained behind to confront Iraj.

And when Palimak had pleadingly asked what he should do if they refused, Safar had answered harshly, "Then make them!"

So that was what he had done, from that moment on the Esmirian shores of the Great Sea when they had all demanded to wait for Safar's return. And Palimak, believing his father dead, had cast the greatest spell of his young life, forcing them to wait no longer and flee to Syrapis.

Since then his guilt had subsided. Now he had become accustomed to being their prince. Practically a king—although never in the history of Kyrania had its people been ruled by royalty. So when Foron, the chief of the Elders, had come to him demanding a meeting, he'd been quite irritated. Who needed these stupid old men?

But what could he do when even his grandfather, Khadji, supported Foron's request?

And so three days after they'd borne the ailing Safar to New Kyrania, Palimak convened the Council of Elders to let them have their say.

He'd expected only long windy speeches praising their native son Safar Timura and welcoming his return to the bosom of his people. Perhaps a declaration of a special feast day to celebrate it.

But that was not how it had turned out.

Masura, leader of the loyal opposition, spoke first. "I'm a blunt man," he said, "so I won't shilly-shally around the point. Which is this: The miraculous return of our beloved Safar Timura—your *stepfather*—proves what I have always suspected. That you have been lying to us all along!"

The young man made note of the way Masura underscored Palimak's questionable status as Safar's adopted son. He reflected briefly on Masura's hypocrisy; this man had not only opposed Safar but had been the leader of the group trying to exile him.

"I really think we should use words that aren't so incendiary," Foron said, in minor admonishment. "Accusations of lying are a bit strong, if you ask me."

Palimak said nothing, only raising an eyebrow at Foron's weak defense. In the past he'd always been a strong supporter of the Timuras and certainly no friend of Masura.

Then Foron turned his gaze on Palimak. "However, in Masura's defense," he said, "I must admit there is understandable concern about *certain things.*"

"Such as?" Palimak asked.

"You told us he was dead!" Masura accused, voice shaking with emotion. "You convinced us to abandon him in Esmir. Lies! All lies, which has now been proven!"

Palimak glanced at Khadji, expecting some support from his grandfather. To his dismay, he saw the old man nod in sad agreement.

"It's true, my grandson," Khadji said. "We all protested. But you insisted."

"And that's another thing," Masura broke in. "Why was it that a boy was able to insist on anything? And why did we just nod our heads and shuffle on board the ships, leaving our beloved Safar behind?"

"You didn't leave him behind," Palimak pointed out. "We found him here in *Syrapis*. I found him, actually. So you have no point."

"It was the work of some devil," Masura insisted. "I just know it was. How else do you explain your . . . unusual . . . influence over us. You wave a hand and everyone does your bidding."

He leaned closer, face dramatically lit by the traditional council fire. "Perhaps I spoke in error," he said, a wide sneer greasing his face. "Maybe it wasn't some devil's work—but a *demon's* work!"

He glanced around at the others, smiling grimly when he saw they had taken his point—Palimak's status as a half-breed.

"I say there should be an investigation," he said. "A special committee appointed by the Council of Elders to decide once and for all if this . . . this . . . demon's spawn . . . has possessed us. To make us do terrible things, such as abandon our dear friend, Safar Timura."

"That's not unreasonable," Foron agreed. "Eliminating certain insulting terms, of course. Such as 'demon's spawn.' Palimak is one of us, despite his background. We should treat him as such."

"He's a good boy," Khadji said. "He's always been a good boy. I can attest to that." The he sighed. "However, there are certain questions I have myself."

He glanced at Palimak. "No offense, my boy." Then back to the council. "I'll support an investigation—as long as it's not biased, of course."

The others murmured . . . of course, of course. And before Palimak knew it Foron was lifting up the white kid's-leather sack that held the voting markers. He upended the bag and dozen or more tiles spilled out; half were black, indicating a no vote, while the other half were white, meaning yes.

Palimak's blood went to high boil. He'd had enough, dammit! Betrayed by his own grandfather, by the gods! Although a small part of him whispered there was some truth in what they said. But to the hells with that! He'd done it for their own good, hadn't he? Only doing what his father had asked.

On his shoulder, the speck that was Gundara whispered in his ear, "We're ready, Little Master. Just say the word!"

Palimak's fingers stole into his pocket, touching the bit of magical parchment he kept there for just such emergencies. All he had to do was withdraw it, toss it into the council fire and a heady smoke would fill the room, making the men insensible. Then, with the help of his Favorites, he'd cast the spell that would make them pliant to his will and he'd send them on their way.

The spell would make them forget the confrontation. And he could easily create some clever bit of fiction to fill the gap in their memories. Such as the festival honoring Safar, the arrangement of which he'd originally thought was their purpose.

Then sudden self-disgust rose in his gorge. And his hand was empty when he yanked it out of his pocket. He got to his feet.

"Go right ahead," he said. "Have your investigation. I'll abide by the will of the majority."

Ignoring the shock on their faces and the mutters of surprise that swept the room, he stalked out of the chamber.

It's up to my father, now, he thought. And with that thought a feeling of immense relief washed over him.

CHAPTER FIFTEEN

THE CALL OF HADIN

Leiria watched Coralean pace the room, big bearded head bent in concentration as he listened to Palimak explain what had happened at the meeting of the Council of Elders. She could hear quarrelsome voices outside, coming from the market place.

Normally, the disputes would be about the prices and quality of the goods being offered. But now—although the exact words weren't distinct—she knew the voices were lifted in heated debate about the future of the Kyranians in Syrapis.

Since Safar's return and Palimak's abdication of responsibility, politics had reared its head, showing its ugliest face. Everyone seemed to have their own strongly held opinions, with no views shared in common. It was minority against minority and as a result the only rule was that of chaos.

When Palimak was done, the wily caravan master sighed deeply and shook his shaggy head. "Coralean is not a man who easily passes judgment on another," he rumbled. "But I must confess, young Timura, that all you have told me is deeply troubling to this weary old heart." He thumped the massive structure that was his chest.

Then he fixed Palimak with his fierce eyes. "But, my headstrong friend," he went on, "it is with the greatest regret that I must tell you that a grievous error has been made. And I fear it is you who have committed it, though it pains me to point out the mistake.

"You should never have allowed the Council to convene, young Palimak. Failing that, you should have used all your wiles to prevent the outcome of that meeting. I blame myself for not being here to advise you. But, alas, I was busy with those pirates who call themselves ship captains."

"But what the Elders suspect just happens to be true," Palimak replied, voice weary from lack of sleep. "I *did* force my will on them before. I did use magic to make them see things my way. Not once, but many times."

He looked over at Leiria with sad eyes. "I even did it to you, Aunt Leiria," he said. "You would never have left Esmir if I hadn't cast a spell on you. You'd have waited there until the hells turned to ice before you abandoned my father to the Fates."

"I know that," Leiria replied. "And I can't say your actions don't bother me when I think on it. However, we now know Safar never would have showed up. The wait would have been futile."

"But he wasn't dead," Palimak said. "I was wrong."

"And he wasn't in Esmir, either, was he?" Leiria said. "It was in Syrapis that we found him. There's no doubt in my mind that if you hadn't forced us to come to Syrapis, inspired us to defeat Rhodes and the others and then led us into that horrible chamber, we never would have found him. Don't ask me how he got here. I'm no sorcerer, so I couldn't say."

Palimak smiled bitterly. "Well, I am a sorcerer," he said, "and I can't tell you, either."

He gestured at the immense coffin crammed into one side of the tower room that he used for his quarters. "The first time I looked inside I saw the remains of a demon. There was no mistaking that corpse for anything but. Not just his looks, but the sheer size of him."

Palimak shook his head. "I've never seen a demon so large," he said. "Besides that, the demon looked exactly like the pictures and statues of Lord Asper. So that's who I think was in there. Not my father, but mummified remains of Asper."

Coralean stroked his beard. "You've said that the next time you looked Asper was gone and instead you found the ailing body of my dearest friend, Safar Timura: correct?"

"Just as you say," Palimak replied.

"A mystery indeed," the caravan master said. "One designed to confound even one such as Coralean. A man who has seen more things than most."

He turned to Leiria. "How is our Safar?" he asked. "Has his condition improved?"

She brushed away the sudden moisture in her eyes. "No, it hasn't," she said.

For three weeks, Leiria had helped Safar's mother and sisters nurse him. Spoonfeeding him broth, which he instinctively swallowed without ever regaining consciousness. Bathing the body she knew so well; except it was uniformly tanned from head to toe, which was most odd. It was as if he'd been naked under a hot sun for a long time. Also, other than what grew on his head, he was completely hairless. His face, his chest, his limbs, his groin.

Then, not long ago, he'd started to sprout a beard. But instead of coming in dark, like the hair on his head, it was golden. Since Safar had always kept his features smooth she'd shaved him, puzzling over the yellow hairs.

Also, his eyebrows and the hair on his head seemed lighter. Although that might have been from the sun that had toasted his skin. Stranger still, this morning, when she'd given him his sponge bath, she'd seen a little golden nest of hair beginning to form in his groin.

She'd wanted to ask his mother and sisters about it. But Leiria had never been Safar's wife, only his former lover, so she hadn't managed to summon the nerve to ask such an intimate question of the prudish Kyranian women.

"There's no need to mourn, my beautiful Captain," Coralean said. "Safar will be back with us in spirit as well as body soon enough." He tapped his head with a strong, thick finger. "Coralean knows it here." He thumped his chest. "And here."

"He's spoken a few times," Leiria said. "So that gives me hope. Except he always says the same thing." She shook her head. "He keeps asking, 'Where's Khysmet?' I wish could answer him. I keep thinking—if I could suddenly produce Khysmet he'd recover. But of course, that's a hopeless task. The last time we saw Khysmet was with Safar in Caluz. My guess is that he was probably killed when Safar destroyed the Idol of Hadin."

She paused, reflecting on the enormous explosion they'd all witnessed from the distant shores of the Great Sea. She shuddered. "Nothing could have survived such a calamity," she said.

To her surprise Palimak said, "I'm not so sure of that. My father did." He paused, thinking. Then, "I told you what happened in Charize's chamber. How, when all seemed lost, what I thought was my father's ghost engaged those monsters. But it wasn't a ghost, was it? Because we later found my father alive in Asper's tomb."

"Yes, yes, but we were talking about the horse," the caravan master said, displaying rare impatience.

Palimak sighed. "The whole incident all seems like a terrible nightmare now. So I can't say for certain. But it seemed to me that during the battle I heard Khysmet. You all know that trumpeting sound he made whenever there was a fight?"

Leiria and Coralean nodded. They remembered it very well. Especially Leiria. She couldn't count the number of times she'd followed that wild cry into always-victorious battle.

"Well, that's what I heard," Palimak said. "Or maybe it's what I wanted to hear. I can't say."

"Are you telling us there's more to this mystery?" the caravan master asked. "Poor Coralean's brain, agile as it is, has not been able to unravel the knot of Safar's sudden resurrection, much less these other things you suggest."

"If you did hear Khysmet," Leiria said, "where is he now? Where did he go?"

Palimak groaned in frustration. "I don't know," he said harshly. "But every day that goes by, I wonder if I didn't make a big mistake by not searching Hanadu for him, instead of leaving so quickly."

Always a woman of action, Leiria said, "Let's return to Hanadu and see. It's stupid sitting around here wondering about something we can't prove unless we go there in person. And if we do find Khysmet, maybe Safar will recover."

Angry shouts echoed from the market place. Coralean peered out and saw the Elder,

Masura, haranguing the villagers. His words weren't distinct, but they were obviously causing a heated debate. People were jabbing fingers at one another, defending whatever stand they had taken.

He turned back, face dark with displeasure. "Coralean is not the sort of man who usually advises delay," he said. "Direct action has always been his motto, as you both well know."

He jabbed a thumb at the window. "However, it's Coralean's considered opinion that this would not be a good time to undertake another expedition to Hanadu. There's too much discontent in our ranks. King Rhodes is no fool and would be certain to sniff out our weakness. Then we'd have another war on our hands."

He grimaced. "With so much disunity, Coralean fears that the outcome of such a war might not achieve the same happy result as before."

"I'm not sure we have anything to lose," Leiria said. "It's my guess that his spies have already informed his hairy majesty that we're at each other's throats."

"Possibly so," Coralean replied. "But to hear a thing from a spy is not the same as knowing it in your heart. Spies are notorious tellers of falsehoods. They lie for gold. Or they lie to please their master, telling him what they think he wants to hear.

"Sometimes spies do both. Fattening their purses and getting in their master's good graces at the same time. King Rhodes knows this, so he'll wait until he has absolute proof before he moves against us. And it is Coralean's view that it would be foolish for us to provide him with the proof he seeks. Let him labor for it. And if the gods are kind to us, our problems will resolved by then."

Palimak sighed. He felt like a child. Confronted by forces he didn't understand and certainly wanted no part of.

"If only my father would get well," he said. "He'd stop this squabbling. He'd know what to do!"

Coralean studied him. Then, "Although Safar has returned to us, it's still up to you, my young friend," he said. "You must act. We can't wait for your father's recovery. It saddens Coralean deeply to say this, but there's a chance Safar might never recover."

"But he has to!" Palimak moaned. "I can't force people against their wills any longer. I never liked doing it. And I don't want to start again."

Leiria fixed Palimak with a hard look. She said, "This is a rotten time, Palimak Timura, to develop a conscience."

"Our beautiful captain has hit the target in its tender center," Coralean said. "The troubles we are having now with the Council are nothing compared to the evils we will face very soon."

Palimak raised a questioning eyebrow. "What could be worse than this?"

"As you know, I've just returned from negotiations with our hired fleet," Coralean said.

"They want more money?" Palimak asked. "That's easy enough. We've plenty of gold and jewels in the treasury."

The caravan master snorted like a bull. "Of course they want more money," he said. "Mercenaries always want more money. It's in their greedy natures to wring the sponge dry, then press it again in case there's a speck of moisture left. But our new worries aren't on account of money. Coralean has had the distasteful task of dealing with such men many times during his long, illustrious career. Sea pirates, land pirates, they're all the same.

"I reasoned with them. Thumped the heads of a few captains. Slipped their lieutenants a little gold to foster insurrection. And eventually arrived at terms favorable to us."

Leiria eyed him. "So what's the problem?"

"Waterspouts," Coralean said.

Palimak and Leiria gaped at him. What in the blazes?

Coralean nodded. "Yes, indeed, my friends. Waterspouts," he continued. "'The biggest damned waterspouts in all creation,' is how one captain put it. One of them appeared right off the coast of Hanadu. According to the captain, who swears he hadn't had a drink in a week—a lie, of course, but no matter—this particular waterspout was over a mile wide. And powerful! Strong enough to pull the biggest ship under. At least, that's what the captain said."

Coralean plucked a leather-covered flask from his belt and drank deeply of the wine it contained. He handed it to Palimak, who shook his head. Then to Leiria, who nodded absently and drank as deeply as the caravan master.

"I questioned a sampling of common seamen from the other ships," Coralean said, "and they confirmed the tale. As a point of fact, the spout forced the fleet to put out to sea for more than a week."

Coralean sighed. "Thank the gods Rhodes didn't know that, because there was a time when the blockade we have established along his coast did not exist."

"But now the fleet's back, right?" Palimak said. "So there's nothing to worry about."

"Oh, you couldn't be farther off the mark, young Timura," Coralean said. "The fleet's back. The blockade once more intact. But I fear—and more importantly those pirates fear—that new manifestations will occur. Sailors are the most superstitious of men, as you well know.

"But it seems they have reason for their nervousness. For similar waterspouts have been reported in the seas between Syrapis and Esmir. There's news that a dozen fishing boats disappeared just off Caspan. Sucked down by a waterspout, I'm told."

"But why should we worry?" Leiria wanted to know. "Waterspouts can't get us on land. And if the sea off Syrapis breaks out in them like plague rash, it doesn't matter if all the ships light out for deep water. We might not be able to land at Hanadu, but neither can Rhodes send a raiding party to our shores. Who needs ships, if Nature Herself forms a blockade?"

But Palimak immediately understood what Coralean was getting at. Ghostly fingers chilled his spine.

"It's not King Rhodes he's worried about, Aunt Leiria," he said, his voice trembling. "Or, really even the waterspouts." Then, to Coralean. "Isn't that right?"

Again, the caravan master sighed heavily. "Indeed it is, son of my dearest friend," he said. "Safar predicted the end of the world long ago. He said the gods were asleep and no longer concerned themselves with human, or demon, affairs. I didn't believe him, at first.

"But look what has happened to Esmir! Despite his valiant efforts to destroy the machine at Caluz—plugging the magical breach between Hadin and Esmir—the poison has continued to spread. The seafarers tell me much of Esmir is now uninhabitable. That people are fleeing to the coast in tremendous numbers."

He pressed his hands against his temples, as if in pain. "It is my fear," he said, "that this poison will soon spread to Syrapis. And then what will we do? The waterspouts are quite possibly the first sign of such an occurrence."

Just then they heard a rooster crow. Surprised, for it was midday, they turned their eyes to the window. Another cock joined in. Then another. Somewhere a donkey brayed and horses whinnied. Then all the dogs started to bark.

They looked at each other, wondering what was happening. Palimak opened his mouth to speak.

At that moment the earthquake struck!

There was no warning. The floor heaved under them. Coralean was flung against the window and nearly toppled out. Leiria snatched at him, pulling him back.

The floor heaved again. Leiria was hurled backward, still holding on to Coralean. They fell heavily to the ground. The massive stone fortress swayed like a fragile sailboat in a storm.

Palimak found himself lying on the floor, staring up at the ceiling as an enormous crack shot from one side of the room to the other. Stone shattered into sand and rained down on him, but he couldn't rise. It was as if a gigantic weight was holding him down. All he could do was shut his eyes against the falling debris.

He heard screams from the market place. Rock grinding against rock. Glass and clay jars bursting. Large objects hurled to the ground from great heights. Animals bawling in pain and fear.

And then, as suddenly as it had begun, the earthquake ended.

Silence hung like thick velvet drapes. The atmosphere was filled with dust, sparkling in a wide burst of sunlight streaming through the enormous hole in the wall where the window had been.

Then the silence was broken by the sound of movement from across the room. Palimak and the others turned and gaped at the sagging door, which had been half-torn from its hinges.

A wild-eyed figure staggered through the doorway. It was Safar.

"It's Hadin!" he cried. "It wants me back!"

And he collapsed to the floor.

CHAPTER SIXTEEN
UNDER THE DEMON MOON

Kalasariz floated above the golden-tiled plain, which stretched away from him on all sides for what seemed like an enormous distance.

For the first time in what seemed like eons, the spymaster was without pain. He felt strong and confident—mind as sharp and clear as it had ever been.

He knew that he was still quite small; that the plain was actually a table, with a tiled center. And that the enormous face bent over him was that of a normal-sized human woman. A witch, actually. Who at this moment was mumbling the spell that would break the last link of the magical chains that had imprisoned him for so long.

Beside him, Luka and Fari were whispering to one another. He couldn't hear what they were saying, but he had no doubt that they were conspiring against him. Prince Luka and the Lord Fari disliked one another intensely. But as demons they were united in their hatred of all humans—especially Kalasariz, who had been their rival from the beginning.

The moment the witch cast her spell, they would attack him. If Kalasariz had possessed a face, he would have smiled that thin cold smile that tens of thousands had feared for so many years.

For the spymaster had plans of his own. Plans that included Luka and Fari only in a small, but possibly delicious, sort of way.

It was a pity things had to be as they were, Kalasariz thought. Although he loathed the two demons, it wouldn't have prevented him from working with them as an equal.

Unlike Luka, he'd never envied Iraj Protarus his throne. Nor had he ever shared Fari's jealousy of Safar's former title of Grand Wazier to the king.

All his adult life the spymaster had been content to remain in the background. Letting others wear the trappings of power, while he steered the course. The only person who'd ever aroused the green-eyed beast in his bosom had been Safar Timura. And that was because Safar had quite different ideas on how Iraj should rule his kingdom. Nor did Safar's plans include Kalasariz in any role—especially not that of the power behind the throne.

Complicating Kalasariz' enmity for his rival was the strange hate/love relationship between Safar and Iraj. Before they fell out the two had been boyhood friends. Blood-oath brothers. But so what? What was a blood oath when a grand kingdom was at stake?

As the spymaster thought about these things it suddenly came to him that perhaps the reason he'd failed in his fight against Timura was because of Kalasariz' own lack of ambition. Maybe he'd been a fool all those years being content to be the power behind the throne.

Perhaps by relying on kings to do his work, instead of acting directly on his own behalf, he'd sown the seeds of his own failure.

The spymaster started getting excited. What a new and interesting way of looking at things!

Above him, the witch shifted position and Kalasariz put these thoughts aside to be examined more fully later. He had to keep his wits about him for what was coming next.

Although the spy master's smallness prevented him from clearly making out what the witch was up to—all things were so enormous that he couldn't see past the immediate details in front of his face—he smelled burning incense and guessed she was moving to the next part of her spell.

Beside him, Luka and Fari stirred restlessly. They were silent now. Conspiracy completed, he suspected. Waiting their moment.

Kalasariz had no idea how he and the others had come to this place. When Iraj had grabbed onto Safar's magical robe-tails, Kalasariz had instinctively followed. Leaping into the trough of his sorcerous wake, carrying Luka and Fari with him.

Then Iraj and Safar had disappeared and Kalasariz had found himself hovering between darkness and light, Fari and Luka mere specks of existence floating nearby. For some reason they were even smaller than he was and quite weak. And so when they heard the witch's voice summoning them, it was Kalasariz who had answered. And it was Kalasariz who had negotiated with the witch.

She would give them substance. A place in this world. In return, they would join her in her struggle against her deadliest enemy—Palimak Timura. The three agreed most enthusiastically. For wherever Palimak was, they'd find Safar. And wherever Safar was, they'd find Iraj—their errant brother of the Spell of Four.

Iraj had broken the spell's link, condemning them to puny existences that the most insignificant insect would not envy. Their only hope was to find Iraj again and bring him under their power.

Fari, who had been a master wizard in his previous existence, had explained that this time the bond could be reformed differently. Since Iraj had violated the Spell of Four, it was no longer necessary to make him the kingly center.

"All we require is his essence," Fari had said.

"His essence?" Kalasariz had puzzled, not certain what he meant. "How do we accomplish that?"

If Fari had owned lips, he would have smacked them. He answered, "We eat him!"

This answer had inspired the glimmerings of what Kalasariz now believed was turning out to be the greatest plan in his career.

The witch's indistinct mumbling ended. The huge head drew back, long hair stirring like a great forest in a summer storm.

"Make yourselves ready," she commanded.

She gestured, mountain of a hand slicing downward.

But as it descended, Kalasariz whipped around to confront Luka and Fari. He had time to see them coming forward, then there was a white-hot flash that blinded him. Even so, he didn't hesitate but surged forward.

There was a slight sting, then another, as he engulfed first Luka, then Fari.

Thunder boomed and he felt an enormous weight crushing downward. The weight eased. Became . . . normal? He opened his eyes and found himself staring into the glittering eyes of the witch. They were at his level.

The spymaster looked down and saw he was kneeling on the table. The golden-tiled center almost completely covered by one knee.

He was gripped by a delight so fierce it verged on hysteria. For a moment he considered stepping off the table and removing the witch before she became too much of a bother.

Then he thought better of it. From the negotiations, she hadn't seemed the type to leave an opening.

"I can put you back the way you were with a snap of my fingers," Queen Clayre warned. "So I wouldn't move too quickly, if I were you."

"I wouldn't dream of it," Kalasariz said with a smile.

The queen grimaced. "Where are the others?" she asked.

Kalasariz covered his lips as he burped politely. He said, "I ate them."

The queen frowned at him a moment, head turning to one side, ear cocked as if she were listening. The frown turned to a smile. Then a laugh.

"Oh, that's very good," she chortled. "You've consumed your enemies, but they still exist inside you. They're your slaves now. With no will of their own."

"We didn't get along very well," Kalasariz replied. He hesitated, then decided it was best to be truthful. "Circumstances forced us together. But when you were working your spell I got the rather strong impression that they were planning to end our partnership."

"But you acted first," Clayre said.

"It seemed the prudent thing to do," Kalasariz said.

He glanced about the room, noting with mild surprise that everything was in disarray. Chairs were knocked over. Broken glass and clay jars were scattered across the rich carpets, which were also stained by spilled liquids. A shelf of books had been dumped over. And everything was covered with a thick, fine dust.

"What happened here?" he asked.

The queen shrugged. "Nothing to concern yourself about," she said. "Just an earthquake." She waved a dismissive hand. "I was anxious to work the spell, so I didn't bother getting a few slaves in to clean the mess up."

Kalasariz thought this was a very interesting admission. Obviously, time was of the essence to the witch. It was a good thing to know. If she was facing some self-imposed deadline, then he could drive a harder bargain.

"What exactly is it you want me to do?" he asked.

"Help my son regain the royal mantle he deserves," she replied.

The spymaster smiled. "You've certainly come to the right person for that," he said.

*　　　*　　　*

Palimak sat by his father's bedside all that night. Safar's breathing was labored. Sometimes he would twitch and moan. But mostly he was still, dragging in each breath, then letting it go in a long sigh as if there were a heavy weight on his chest.

Twice he became suddenly rigid, the pulse in his throat visibly throbbing. He'd whisper, "Khysmet!" And then his body would relax and the labored breathing would begin anew.

Outside, even the nightbirds and insects were silent. Everyone and everything had been exhausted by the earthquake. Fortunately, no one had been killed and although many had been injured, those injuries mostly consisted of cuts, scrapes and minor bruises. The damage to the buildings was spotty. Some walls had collapsed in the fortress and several homes had been destroyed.

However, the earthquake had arrived at a lucky time. It had been a fine day and most of the Kyranians had been outside. Now everyone was so weary from cleaning up the debris and treating the injured that they were fast asleep.

Palimak studied his father's sleeping form. The Demon Moon was shining through the window, bloody red light pooling on Safar's chest as if he were horribly wounded.

He thought about his father's sudden appearance in the doorway after the earthquake. His wailing cry that Hadin wanted him back. Instinctively, Palimak knew these were not the mad ravings of a sick man. If someone had asked him what Safar had meant, he couldn't have answered. Not precisely, at any rate. But he strongly sensed that Coralean's report of the waterspouts in the Great Sea and the desolation overcoming Esmir had something to do with it.

As did the earthquake.

For the eighth time that day, he withdrew the Book of Asper his father had entrusted to him when they had parted three years before. He placed the book's spine in one hand and let the pages fall open as they pleased.

He peered down at the page that had presented itself. And, just as it had seven times before, the same poem showed him its face:

> *There is a portal,*
> *Through which only I can see.*
> *There is a secret,*
> *I dare not breathe.*
> *Under the Demon Moon there*
> *Is thee and me.*
> *And then there is no more*
> *Of me and thee.*

Frustrated, Palimak snapped the book shut. The eighth appearance of the poem in as many attempts was certainly no accident. But what in the hells was that damned Asper getting at? And how could he have conjured such a reoccurrence from the distance of a thousand years or more?

If only his father would awaken and explain to him what the poem meant. A wave of self-pity swept over him. He thought, It's not fair! I'm only thirteen years old. Other children my age spend most of the day at school, or at play. Or doing minor chores, like tending the animals. He brushed away a tear. Then steadied himself. It just was, that's all.

Fate had decreed it long ago when the parents he'd never known had met and had fallen in love. A human father and a demon mother. Both dead now. Mercifully, perhaps, all things considered. At least they wouldn't be forced to witness the end of the world.

And then he thought, And they don't have a chance to save it, either.

He felt a tingling sensation and his gaze was drawn to the window which framed the evil face of the Demon Moon.

It seemed to be summoning him. Calling him. He heard a harsh voice whisper, "Pa-li-mak! Pa-li-mak! Pa-li-mak!"

The moon's pull grew stronger. So strong it felt like his scalp was being lifted from his skull.

His head ached with a rhythmic pounding hammering from within. And with each drumbeat—for that is what the hammering seemed like—the pain intensified until he thought he could bear it no longer.

Then once again he heard his father moan, "Khysmet!"

Safar shifted in his bed. There was a metallic ring as the silver witch's knife fell to the stone floor. To Palimak's pain-intensified senses it sounded like a sword clashing against a shield.

Joints aching, he retrieved the knife, then found his gaze drawn to the red moon-glitter reflecting off the blade.

They'd found the knife while undressing him and had placed it under his pillow. It was Safar's most prized possession—given to him by Coralean for saving the caravan master's life. Palimak started to slip it back under the pillow, then hesitated when an image caught his eye.

Once again he peered at the shiny surface of the blade. He saw eyes staring back in the dagger-shaped reflection. For some reason they didn't appear like his own. Still, they seemed familiar.

The pain in his head was so intense it was difficult to think. His emotions were as dull as his thoughts. The rhythmic pounding made everything seem distant, unreal. He turned the blade and saw other portions of the reflection. A slash of a wide forehead. Another of what seemed to be a square, bearded chin.

How strange!

He blinked and the reflection seemed to shift and then became a mirror image of himself.

The pain vanished. It was as if all the agony had been contained in a cask of water and then someone had knocked out the plug and it had quickly drained away.

Now the knife shone silver instead of red. Palimak looked up and saw the Demon Moon had risen above the top of the window frame. The soft glow of the morning sun gleamed through.

Palimak was surprised he hadn't noticed the passing of so many hours. One moment it had been late night. Then he'd stared into the knife's surface and all that time had collapsed.

He didn't remember falling asleep. How could he have, with all that pain—and its sudden, blissful release? But it seemed to be the simplest and therefore the most logical explanation. It also accounted for the strange image he'd thought he'd seen reflected in the knife blade.

Yes, that was the answer. He'd fallen asleep.

*   *   *

With dawn's arrival, Palimak started putting his plan into action.

First he got out the little stone idol and summoned the Favorites. The boys were usually cranky in the morning, but he had some sweets ready for Gundara and some very old cheese for Gundaree. They munched on the treats, quarreling with one another between bites, but he kept pulling tasty bits from his pockets until they were more or less settled down.

Palimak turned his attention to the task at hand, fishing various magical items from a leather purse: six tiny pots filled with special oils; small packets of sorcerous powders, each of a different color; a jar of an alcohol-based elixir, in which he'd dissolved powder made from ground ferret bones; and finally, a little mirror.

He drew magical symbols on the floor, using a quick-drying paint for ink. While he worked, Gundara and Gundaree hopped up on Safar's bed.

"The old master looks pretty sick," Gundara observed in cheerful tones.

"Maybe he'll die," Gundaree put in, partly stifling a yawn with his hand.

"You two are such ungrateful wretches," Palimak said. "Three weeks ago he saved your worthless lives. Now you're all but getting ready to bury him."

"I only said he looked sick," Gundara protested. "Gundaree was the one who talked about dying."

Gundaree put hands on his slender hips. "What's wrong with that?" he demanded. "Death happens, you know. When you get to the bottom of the Scroll of Life, that's it!"

He made a cutting motion across his throat. "Finished. End of story. It's the same for everything that lives. Fish do it. Sheep do it. People do it. And demons do it. Although I suppose fish and sheep don't have very interesting stories on their Scrolls."

Gundara leaned against Safar, relaxing. "I don't know about that," he said. "I met a fish once who had a pretty interesting life. It was maybe six or seven hundred years ago, not long after we were stolen by that witch."

Gundaree shuddered. "Why do you have to bring her up?" he protested. "That witch was a terrible mistress. Maybe the worst ever. You're going to spoil my whole day by making me think about her."

"I was talking about a fish, not the witch," Gundara said. "That great big fish they served up at her birthday banquet. It was still alive, remember? And they were cutting off strips to make fish bacon."

Gundaree grinned. "That was great bacon," he said, licking his chops as he fondly recalled those fishy snacks.

"I wish you'd stop interrupting my story," Gundara grumped. "While you were eating that poor fish, I was talking to him. About how he used to live at the bottom of the sea and had more female fishes than you could shake a fin at. And all the adventures he had fooling the sharks and the sea snakes."

He shook his head, marveling at the memory. "What a fish he was!" he said. "A fish above all fishes."

"You ate him too," Gundaree said. "After you made friends with him and promised you'd free him. You got in there too and ate the fish bacon as fast as the cooks could fry it up."

"It seemed like the polite thing to do at the time," Gundara said. "I didn't want to insult him. Let him think he didn't taste good."

Gundaree hopped up on the bed with Gundara. He studied Safar's face for a moment. "I still think he looks like he might die," he said. Another yawn. "If I weren't so sleepy, I'd feel bad about it."

Palimak did his best to ignore them. They were what they were and there was no way anyone would ever change them, much less warm up their cold little hearts. Usually they didn't bother him that much. In fact, their dark humor appealed to the demon side of him.

He couldn't help but smile at his own hypocrisy. The truth was, if they hadn't been talking about his own father, he might have found their conversation pretty damned funny.

The rueful smile made him relax. He arranged the pots on the floor, making a six-pointed star with the mirror in the center. He sprinkled powder from each of the packets into the oil pots, then lit them with a candle.

Multi-colored smoke hissed up, filling the chamber with a sweet, heady odor.

Gundara and Gundaree made gagging sounds of protest, but he paid them no mind.

Next, he took out his father's dagger, reversed it, and rapped the mirror with the butt. The mirror shattered. He rapped again, breaking it into smaller pieces. Then he stirred the glass bits with the tip of the knife, mixing them up.

Palimak squatted back on his haunches. "All right, boys," he said. "I'm ready for you now."

Grumbling, Gundara and Gundaree hopped back down on the floor.

"This isn't going to work," Gundara said. "He's too sick."

"You might kill him," Gundaree added. "Did you ever think of that?"

"Besides," Gundara said, patting his little belly, "I'm too full to work."

"Enough!" Palimak barked, finally letting his weariness get the better of him. "I've fed you, pampered you, and listened patiently to your mewling."

His eyes glowed demon yellow. "If you don't want to work, then by the gods I'll seal you in your stone house and throw it into the deepest part of the sea I can find. And you can argue with each other and the damned fishes for a thousand years, for all I care!"

The two Favorites went through an instant change in attitude.

"We were only jesting, young master," Gundara said, flashing his white fangs.

"Yes, yes, only a joke," Gundaree put in. "We'll help you all we can."

"And, I must say," Gundara added, "the old master really is looking much better."

Palimak motioned, and the Favorites leaped up on his shoulder and shrank to flea-size specks.

He concentrated on the bits of shattered glass, breathing deeply, taking the incense smoke deep into his lungs. The spell he'd chosen came from a poem of Asper's his father had recited to him long ago.

Palimak chanted:

> *"Wherein my heart abides*
> *This dark-horsed destiny I ride?*
> *Hooves of steel, breath of fire—*
> *Soul's revenge, or heart's desire?"*

Suddenly, the shattered glass reformed into a mirror. A swirling image appeared on its surface.

Palimak felt dizzy and he gripped his knees as if he were about to fall.

He heard his father whisper, "Khysmet! Where is Khysmet?"

There came a thunder of hooves.

And Palimak was swept away.

CHAPTER SEVENTEEN

DEADLY BARGAIN

Rhodes was in an ugly mood when he tromped down the stairs leading to Queen Clayre's chamber. Who in the Hells was king here, anyway? So what if she was a witch? So what if she was his mother? How dared she think she could summon him with an imperious snap of the fingers. Didn't she know he was busy?

The earthquake had done extensive damage and he'd spent half the previous day and the entire night, plus most of today, overseeing the clean-up and rescue work. Twenty-two dead. Fifty-three more buried in rubble and possibly dead. No matter that they were only slaves. They were valuable, dammit! Brawny workers and comely women all; plus half the women were pregnant, and therefore worth double.

Rhodes did not deem himself fortunate because there had been no deaths among the citizenry. They'd only suffered injuries—two hundred minor, forty-six, serious. Pity some of his courtiers hadn't been killed instead of the slaves. In his estimation they were all a needless drain on the kingdom's treasury.

He would tell his mother all this, then give her a good piece of his mind for interrupting his labors digging out the collapsed slave quarters.

But when he came to the closed door leading into his mother's rooms, the king paused, stricken first by doubt, then by weakening resolve. Feared by thousands—no, tens of thousands—Rhodes always found himself undergoing a transformation in Clayre's presence. He was a brave man. A king who always led his troops from the front even in the fiercest battle. But when his mother spoke his nerve fled like kitchen beetles when a torch was lit.

Adding tension to this particular visit was the knowledge that his mother had been working on the plan they both had agreed would turn the tables on Palimak Timura and the Kyranians. He thought it was a good plan. Fortuitous circumstances had delivered the means into their hands. Three powerful devils who had appeared the moment after Queen Charize was killed by Palimak. Devils they could enslave and use against the Kyranians.

Still, he had grave doubts about the part he was supposed to play. Then Rhodes thought, be damned to magic! Why can't we just do things the old, honest way? Such as slipping a spy into Palimak's quarters and slitting his throat?

His mother, sensing his presence, called out: "Come in, my son. We're waiting for you." Cursing under his breath, Rhodes entered.

Across the room—looking more beautiful than ever—his mother was regally ensconced in her wide-backed, pillowed throne. Standing in front of her was a tall man, who turned as Rhodes entered. The man had features as pale as death and he was so thin that his long face looked like a skull. His eyes were flat black—giving away nothing. He smiled when he saw Rhodes and the king thought he'd never seen such a terrible smile. Thin lips made a long red gash in the pale face.

The man nodded his head in what could have been taken for a slight and oh, so imperious bow.

"Good afternoon, majesty," the man said in deep tones. "It's a great honor to finally meet you." He held out his hand.

Rhodes was furious at this gesture. How dare this . . . this . . . common creature . . . offer such an intimate exchange as touching hands with the King of Hanadu!?

"Go ahead, son," his mother said. "Take his hand."

Rhodes was not only going to refuse, but his hand instantly went to the hilt of his sword. By the gods he'd cut this swine's heart out and have it roasted for supper! But, strangely, his hand swept past the hilt, rising of its own accord to find the stranger's.

"My name is Kalasariz, majesty," the spymaster said as their fingers touched. "And I understand we're about to have a great deal in common."

And then he laughed. Rhodes nearly balled up his fist to smash that laugh out of the man's head, when a shock ran up his fingers—lanced along his arm, then burst into his heart.

The king clutched his chest, but then the pain was gone. And he found himself staring into empty air.

Kalasariz had vanished!

The astonished king scanned the room. "What in the hells!" he exclaimed. "What happened to that son of a whoremaster?"

Clayre smiled gently. "Don't you remember our plan, my son?" she asked. "He's inside you now. A supremely powerful force at your instant command."

Kalasariz stared out at the queen through Rhodes' startled eyes. He could feel the king's throat constrict in fear. His heart trip hammering, his veins and nerves running with ice.

The spymaster experienced the king's shudder of agony. The licking of dry lips, then an embarrassing stutter, as Rhodes said, "I . . . I . . . You didn't warn me, mother!"

"I thought it would be less of a shock, my dear," Kalasariz heard Clayre reply through the king's ears.

This is a good body, the spymaster thought. And he quite liked the mind. Although it was filled with confusion now—shot with more fears than a brutally violated maiden. But he sensed the sharpness of the king's brain, and the cunning, oh, the cunning, it was like finding a honeycomb in a bitter wilderness. It wasn't so cunning as the thinking organ that Kalasariz had himself been blessed with. But it would do. It would do.

He whispered to Rhodes, *Do not trouble yourself, majesty. I am a very discreet fellow. I will do nothing to interfere with your natural functions. I'm only here to advise. And to add to your already inestimable powers.*

To his surprise, the heart he shared with Rhodes went from trip-hammer to hysterical pounding. The ice in the king's veins switched to shocking fire. And he realized that his "voice" had unnerved Rhodes, coming from within as it did. Funny, came a thought as an aside. Funny, how Kalasariz had imagined his own lips moving, his vocal apparatus making words, but the entire process had been mental. Much faster than real speech.

So fast, in fact, that he could react and suggest new things with a speed that outpaced the sudden relaxed feeling growing in Rhodes' bladder. There was no way Kalasariz would permit the shared embarrassment of Rhodes pissing their pants.

So he said, *When the time comes, majesty, I'll help you kill your mother.* Various of Rhodes' organs became calmer. Kalasariz went on: *She's been telling you what to do for far too long now. Using her magic to keep you under her thumb. It's not fair, you know. A mother should allow her child to be the man he truly is. I saw it right off. The instant I entered your body.*

There was a tremble when he mentioned the part about body entering so Kalasariz hastened to add, *This is a temporary solution for both our problems, majesty. Your mother forced me into this situation. But rest assured, as soon as we accomplish our common goals, I have a plan to properly separate us into two delightful human beings again.*

Unconsciously, Rhodes opened his mouth to reply. Kalasariz quickly jumped in. *Say nothing to me now,* he advised. *Wait until we are in private and we can learn to communicate together without giving our conversations away.*

Rhodes nodded. He got the message. His heartbeat calmed and his breathing became more gentle.

Queen Clayre glared at Rhodes. "Why are you nodding your head like a fool?" she demanded. "Are you listening to me? Have you heard a word I've said?"

And to Kalasariz' immense satisfaction, Rhodes replied with the utmost calmness: "Yes, mother. I hear."

Then Kalasariz internal "sight" was jarred as the king's eyes moved to the side and focused on a large mural. The spymaster saw an army marching out of a mountaintop castle. And at the head of that army was a mounted warrior armored like a king. On either side of him were women warriors—princess generals, Kalasariz guessed by the banners they flew. One of the princesses was dark-skinned and rode the most magnificent black mare Kalasariz had ever seen.

It's just a painting, he thought. Why is the king so interested? Is he a lover of fine art? Or horseflesh? Or both? He quickly became bored with Rhodes' attention to the mural and attempted to turn his thoughts away to some proper planning. Maybe he'd snoop around this new body a bit to see just how well things worked. Maybe he'd talk the king into visiting his harem tonight. It had been a long time since Kalasariz had enjoyed the embrace of a woman.

But the king's fixation with the mural was so strong that Kalasariz couldn't tear his own mind away.

He felt Rhodes' vocal chords open and once again experienced the rumble of the king's voice.

"What happened to the horse, mother?" Rhodes asked, finger lifting to point at the mural.

Queen Clayre turned her head to look. Nothing caught her attention, much less caused her any surprise. She turned back to her son.

"What horse?" she asked.

Kalasariz felt the king's heart quicken. "I saw a white stallion there," he said, still pointing. "Right in front of the black mare. It was rearing up on its hind legs."

The queen snorted impatiently. "I've lived with that mural my entire adult life," she said. "And there was never a white stallion in it."

"But I only saw it a few days ago!" Rhodes protested.

"You were imagining things," Clayre replied. "It comes from drinking too much. Which I've warned you about many times. It doesn't do for a king to lose his wits to wine."

Rhodes opened his mouth to argue, but Kalasariz moved in. *Never mind the horse, he advised. We can talk about it later.*

The king suddenly relaxed. "I'm sorry, mother," Kalasariz heard him say. "I was obviously thinking of a different mural."

But in his mind was a blazing image of his mother tied to a stake, flames leaping up around her as she writhed in agony.

Very good, majesty, Kalasariz thought-whispered. *A most appropriate image. And I'd be pleased to help you make that dream come true. But only at the proper time, hmm? We have other business to attend to first.*

As if she had been listening in, Clayre said, "We have pressing business to attend to, my son. Business I think you will quite enjoy."

With a flourish she placed a small wooden container on the table. It was made of some kind of rare dark wood—polished and giving off a pleasing scent. It had hinges made of white gold, with a tiny lock also of white gold.

"I made this two years or so ago," the queen mother said, eyes narrow as she poked something into the lock—a minuscule key, Rhodes supposed. "About the time you lost your first battle to the Kyranians." Her voice dripped with accusation.

The king flushed at the humiliating memory. The Kyranians had presented a much smaller force than had the Syrapians. But as Rhodes and his army had marched into the valley the Kyranians had occupied, the airship had appeared overhead.

It was Rhodes' first experience of aerial bombardment and on nights when memory of the incident kept him awake until dawn, he recalled in vivid and frightening detail the fire raining from the sky. The screams of his men set ablaze. The smell of burning flesh. The shock of realization that his army had turned tail and was running down the hill. Men hurling their shields and weapons away in their haste to escape.

"It wasn't my fault," he muttered.

"Of course it wasn't, my son," Clayre said, waving her hand airily, as if the notion had never entered her head.

Then her voice hardened. "I can understand it happening the first time," she said. "There was the surprise of a new and mighty weapon. But it kept on happening, didn't it? Every time you faced Palimak Timura in battle. It was the same old story. He'd draw you into a trap. The airship would show up.

"And once again the Kingdom of Hanadu would suffer a humiliating defeat because the king was too stupid—or too cowardly—to come up with a solution."

Rhodes burned with fury and embarrassment. Kalasariz said nothing to soothe him, curling himself up in a little ball of indifference just beneath the king's heart. Wisely staying out of the confrontation.

Clayre opened the box and took out a strange multi-colored object. She placed it on the golden tiles in the center of the table.

Rhodes puzzled over it for a moment, then realized it was a diorama of the Kyranian stronghold. It was a perfect replica, from the forested peak it sat upon to the old stone fortress his spies had identified as the place where Palimak and his key people were ensconced. Below the fortress was the village proper, market place in the center, slant-roofed homes spread out on either side.

Rhodes studied the terrain with a professional military eye, searching out the weak points.

Then his frown deepened. "If this model was made two years ago, mother," he said, "then how have you managed to put in details my spies didn't map out until several weeks ago?"

He pointed at the turreted gatehouse guarding the entrance to the fortress. "That's where Palimak has set up his command post and sleeping quarters. Two years ago it was in ruins. And my spies have only just reported its reconstruction."

The witch queen chuckled, in that maddeningly condescending manner she had. "Either my spies are better than yours, my son," she said. "Or your spies work for me first—and you—second."

Clayre gave him an amused look. "If I were you I'd decide in favor of the former, because the latter would only put you to unnecessary anguish and work. This is not the time to dispose of all your spies, you know. You'd have to train a whole new crew."

Another chortle. "And you still wouldn't know if they were yours or mine."

Rhodes lost all patience. "What exactly do you want, mother?" he snapped. "All my young life you said your greatest desire was for me to be king. But now that I'm king you seem to do everything to subvert me."

Clayre pretended to be shocked at his charges. "Me?" she mocked. "Subvert you? My only son? My heart's desire?"

She placed an insincere palm across her shapely bosom. "Why, I only want what is best for you. I have no other ambition but to see you become king of all Syrapis. Is that not our family's destiny? A destiny I have sought from the moment I learned the story behind that painting?"

She indicated the mural of the mounted king and princesses. The gesture took some of the heat out of Rhodes. Clayre supposed it was because of the strength of her argument. Actually, it was because Rhodes had remembered the white stallion.

Where had it gone? Dammit, he hadn't been drunk when he'd first spotted it! His brow wrinkled as he wondered if his mother had commanded one of her artist slaves to paint the horse out, just to bedevil him.

Kalasariz stirred. Something was going on. Rhodes was thinking about that horse again. And what was this about mural-painting slaves?

Clayre asked, "Do you recall the tale, my son?"

Rhodes shrugged. "Yes, mother," he said. "I remember it very well."

"Even so, perhaps I should tell it again to refresh your memory," she said. "And also for the benefit of our new friend who resides within you."

But to Kalasariz' disappointment, Rhodes chose this time to dig his heels in. "If you please, mother," he said, "let's leave it for another time. I've much to do, what with the earthquake. Besides, I'm far more interested in what you intend to accomplish with that."

He pointed at the diorama. "How will it help in our fight against Palimak Timura?"

Clayre frowned, clearly irritated at her son's impatience. Then she shrugged, "Very well," she said. "I'll leave the story for another day. As for that model, I'd intended to use it as a focal point for a spell I cooked up with Charize. A bit of magic that would cause the Kyranians no end of trouble and more than a few deaths. With luck, it might have even resulted in the rather gruesome demise of Palimak Timura himself."

The witch queen sighed. "But Charize's own death put paid to that plan. As I said before, alone I don't have enough magical strength to perform the necessary sorcery."

She smiled. "But that was yesterday's disappointment. Today, the sun is shining brightly and our hopes are reborn. For now we not only have the assistance we require, but a whole new plan to bedevil our enemies."

"When do you want to start?" Rhodes asked, assuming correctly that his role as host to Kalasariz meant his presence would be needed.

Clayre motioned at the table. "I'm never one to put off a devilish deed that needs to be done," she said. "So why don't we begin now?" She gestured for him to approach the table.

Rhodes obediently moved forward. Then he hesitated. "There's only one thing," he said.

"And that is?" Clayre asked.

"Have you forgotten your granddaughter is being held hostage by the Kyranians?" He pointed at the model. "What if this spell endangers Jooli?"

The witch queen raised an eyebrow. "Do you really care?" she asked.

Rhodes shrugged. "Not particularly," he replied. "She's always been more of a bother than she's worth."

"My sentiments exactly," Clayre said. "As granddaughters go, she certainly lacks a certain . . . well, reverence." Her attention returned to the model. "Now, let us begin."

And she started to weave her spell. Inside the king, Kalasariz wriggled with delight. It was good to be back on a winning side again.

The only thing troubling him was that Rhodes didn't seem very enthusiastic. Was it because of this Jooli person? The one Kalasariz guessed might be the king's daughter?

If so, perhaps his reluctance was understandable, even though Rhodes plainly disliked his own child. Although Kalasariz had little empathy for people stricken with parental love, he had a professional understanding of that all-too-human malady. The spymaster had relied on it many times as a lever to get his own way.

Then he caught a stray thought from Rhodes. And, dammit, he was still wondering about that horse! That's the trouble with kings, Kalasariz thought. They can't seem to keep their minds on the job at hand. Important tasks. Like killing people!

A blue light formed over the model of the Kyranian stronghold. Tiny figures began to appear. Men and women. Children and animals. And then the figures came to life!

Clayre said, "One thing I noticed about Palimak and his friends when they were visiting Charize is that they absolutely hate and fear rats."

She placed a cage next to the now-living model of the Kyranian stronghold. Inside was a large gray rat. She poked it with a long needle and it squealed in pain and fury.

Clayre laughed as it attacked the bars of the cage. "I'll give them rats," she said, "like they've never seen rats before!"

And then she opened the cage and the enraged rodent leaped onto the model.

CHAPTER EIGHTEEN

HORSE MAGIC

Leiria watched the crowd of angry villagers march up the hill from the market place. She leaned easily on her spear, smiling as if they were only a few friends coming to call for dinner, instead of an unruly mob in the making.

She whistled a casual little tune. Behind her Renor and Sinch took her signal and slipped through the gatehouse entrance. They shut and barred the door. As planned, they would take up position inside in case things really got out of hand and the crowd took it into its minuscule group mind to break through.

Besides herself, she had only Coralean—who stood at her right—and five other soldiers loyal to Palimak.

"I think we can manage well enough," she said to Coralean. "There's only a hundred or so of them."

"Sometimes there's profit in violence," the caravan master said. "Although, as all who know Coralean would confirm, I loathe to engage in that sort of business. Unless, of course, there's no other way of conducting one's affairs. After all, a good family man must consider the well-being of his wives and children. And only the greatest liar in the world would cast doubt on Coralean's dedication to his family."

Leiria nodded at the approaching crowd. "Do you see any profit there?" she asked.

Coralean stroked his beard, considering. Then he shook his mighty head. "They have nothing of value," he said. "Only their own foolish thoughts."

Leiria sighed. "I'm afraid this is turning out to be one of my least favorite days," she said. She glanced up at the empty sky. "I wish Biner and Arlain were here with the airship," she said. "That'd sure keep this group peaceful."

The circus troupe had taken the airship out on a routine surveying expedition. There were no decent maps of Syrapis and Leiria had been intent on filling that gap since their arrival on the island. Unfortunately, the latest mission had coincided with what appeared to be turning into an uprising.

"It is probably for the best they aren't here," Coralean said. "Our Kyranian friends hold the circus folk in awe. And if Biner was forced to act against them on our behalf, they'd lose all influence over them."

He shrugged his massive shoulders. "Only two people can truly help us in these circumstances. Safar, who is ill. And Palimak, who is unavailable."

When Leiria had risen this morning she'd found a note waiting for her from Palimak. He'd said he was involved in a long and dangerous job of spellcasting. Under no circumstances was anyone to disturb him or enter Safar's room.

Leiria had checked the door to the room and found it barred. She'd smelled the faint scent of magical incense and ozone wafting through the crack under the door. She knew from things that Safar had said in the past that if she ignored Palimak's wishes, it might result in the deaths of her two friends.

Then she'd received a much more disturbing message from Masura—who'd apparently overthrown Foron as chief of the Council of Elders. The new headman said that he and the other villagers demanded an immediate hearing. Since she didn't dare disturb Palimak to get help, she'd politely asked Masura for a delay.

The headman, however, was evidently so intent on a confrontation that he'd sent back a note refusing her request. He'd even had the temerity to threaten herself and Coralean with immediate expulsion.

The result of this heated exchange of paper was presently being played out in the mass march on Palimak's headquarters.

Leiria heard a faint scraping noise and turned to see Jooli climbing out through one of the fortress's windows. The royal hostage dangled by her fingertips for a moment, then dropped lightly to the ground. She casually brushed herself off and strode over to join Leiria and the others.

"You shouldn't be here, majesty," Leiria said.

"Just call me Jooli," the young queen said. She nodded at the crowd coming up the hill. "This doesn't look like the best time to stand on court formalities."

Leiria looked at her through narrowed eyes. "Whatever I call you," she said, "the point is that you are supposed to remain in your quarters. We're responsible for your safety."

Jooli chuckled. "How safe will I be if your friends have their way? I doubt if those people will honor any agreement you have with my father."

"She does have logic on her side, Captain," Coralean pointed out.

"I'm also bored to tears," Jooli put in.

She stretched her long arms and worked her shoulders, getting the stiffness out of her muscles.

"I could use a bit of exercise," she said. "And I thought perhaps your fellow Kyranians would provide it."

Then she indicated Leiria's sword. "Loan me your blade," she said, "and I'll stand with you."

Leiria hesitated. Queen Jooli had mystified her from the very first meeting. She clearly despised her father. Had been instrumental in freeing Palimak and Safar from the monsters in the cavern. And had spent her short term as a hostage acting more like one of Leiria's warrior companions than the daughter of their greatest enemy.

At that moment Leiria realized she'd grown to like Jooli. And was possibly even beginning to trust her.

She drew the sword and handed it over. "Have at it," she said.

Jooli smiled, took the sword and gave it a few experimental swings. "Nice balance," she said. Then she turned to face the villagers, who were nearing the top of the hill.

Naturally, Masura was leading the crowd. But Leiria noted with extreme interest that only four other members of the Council of Elders were present. Foron, the ousted former headman was notably absent. Obviously, Masura's victory was far from unanimous.

Then she heard a commotion and saw another group approaching the crowd—angling in from a path that village boys used when taking the goats to pasture. It was a much smaller group, but it included Khadji Timura, Safar's father, and Foron. Several other influential villagers were also present.

"With fortune," Coralean observed, "wiser heads might prevail."

Jooli snorted. "If not, I'd be happy to lift a few of the stupider ones from their shoulders."

Leiria said nothing. The prospect of killing people she'd fought beside and had lived with for several years was depressing, to say the least.

The two groups met. Although she couldn't make out what he was saying, Leiria caught the gentle sound of Khadji's voice. A renowned potter, Khadji had been much respected long before his son's accomplishments had won him so many honors. Foron joined in, as did the others, and the conversation grew animated—much hand-waving and point-making gestures.

Then Masura's voice rose above the others. "We're through listening to the Timuras! I say we drag Palimak out here and make him answer for his crimes!"

There was a roar of approval from Masura's followers. They shoved Khadji and the others aside and continued their march up the hill. The crowd was working itself up, shouting oaths, sliding over into mass hysteria.

"Get ready," Leiria warned.

And there was a creak of leather battle harness and a rattle of metal as her people braced for the onslaught.

*　　*　　*

Queen Clayre chuckled at the scene before her—the tiny figures of Foron's mob charging toward Leiria's small group.

"Well, well," she said. "Apparently we have some new friends among the Kyranians to assist us. It's so much easier to make magical mischief if people hate each other!"

King Rhodes' attention was riveted on the drama unfolding in the model of the Kyranian stronghold. He'd never realized the Kyranians were so divided. By the gods, if only he had a few troops present, he'd wipe them out with ease!

Then he frowned. Where was Palimak? He peered closer and couldn't find a trace of his enemy. Then he spotted his daughter lined up with Captain Leiria and Lord Coralean, waiting to hurl back the mob.

"What's Jooli doing helping them?" he rumbled.

"Never mind that now, son," Clayre advised. "I need your full attention to cast this spell."

"Be damned to her!" Rhodes growled. "She has no business getting involved."

The soothing voice of Kalasariz came from within. *Don't trouble yourself, majesty. All who betray you will be punished. This I swear to you.*

With Kalasariz sending out calm feelings, Rhodes relaxed and once more started concentrating on the spell.

Meanwhile, Kalasariz was loving every minute of this new and most powerful experience. He could feel the tingling of Clayre's magical energy coursing through the king's veins. And within his spirit self he could sense the agony of the creatures that were Fari and Luka as they leaped about to do his bidding. It was a delicious feeling to witness his enemies humbled so. They were less than insects in this new world he'd carved out for himself.

Clayre muttered spell words, sprinkling powders over the model.

The blue light intensified as she continued to weave her deadly spell.

*　　*　　*

As the crowd approached, Coralean made one more attempt to settle things peacefully. He stepped forward, raising his hands high. So powerful was his personality that the crowd came to an immediate halt and fell into silence.

"People of Kyrania," he said, his big voice carrying to the most distant edges of the crowd. "All of you know in your heart of hearts that Coralean is your oldest and dearest friend. And I call upon your affection for me—and upon our long and profitable association—to hear Coralean's words."

There were murmurs of agreement in the crowd. Masura glowered, furious at the caravan master's effect on the others.

"Please, my dear friends," Coralean continued, "do not shame yourselves this day. Do not sully Kyrania's long tradition of peaceful discussion and compromise. It is this quality of yours that has most endeared you to me over the years. A quality that I hold in the highest esteem."

Masura shouted: "The time for talk is over! We've had enough Timura trickery."

Coralean looked hurt. "Do you accuse me, Coralean, of anything but honest intentions, my friend?"

"You're no friend of mine!" Masura shouted. "You're nothing but a paid toady of Palimak Timura!"

There was a flash of steel as Masura suddenly drew a blade from beneath his cloak and leaped forward to strike the caravan master down. So unexpected was his attack that even Coralean, an experienced fighter and agile despite his size, was caught unaware.

He threw up an arm in surprise and Masura aimed his blade at the caravan master's exposed heart.

But Leiria was quicker, jumping between Masura and Coralean. She felt a hot, stinging sensation as Masura's short sword cut into her arm. But she turned with the blow, catching the main force on her body armor. Then she grabbed Masura by the throat and hurled him backwards.

"Assassins!" Masura screamed. "Assassins!"

Only a few people had seen his attack. Most believed it was Leiria who had struck first.

Chaos erupted and the screaming mob surged forward.

*   *   *

Rhodes watched in joy as the Kyranian mob attacked his most hated enemies. He burned in even greater delight in anticipation of what would come next.

Kalasariz shared his delight, soaking up the hot juices flowing through the king's veins. Meanwhile, he whipped his little slaves into a frenzy, driving Fari and Luka to greater heights of pain. Drawing on the powerful magic their agony produced.

Queen Clayre shouted, "Now!" and stabbed an elegant finger at the model of the Kyranian fortress.

Kalasariz felt the pull of her powerful magic and delivered his own pent-up sorcery in twin hammer blows of energy that blasted through the king's eyes.

The blue light hovering over the model turned white hot, then burst. Fiery particles rained down on the melee below.

*   *   *

It was Jooli who caught the first hint of danger. A man was lunging toward her and she parried his sword thrust and kicked his legs out from under him.

But as she turned to confront the next attacker her hackles suddenly rose and her hair stood up on her scalp like hot needles.

Instinctively she looked upward and saw an enormous blue cloud floating overhead.

The cloud was shaped like the face of a beautiful woman—a familiar face with two enormous eyes that glowed with evil power.

"Beware!" Jooli shouted. "It's my grandmother!"

No one heeded her warning. They were too busy fighting.

In the next instant all that changed. A lightning bolt shot from cloud to ground.

There was an enormous, ear-bursting crash and suddenly the air was filled with fiery particles raining out of the sky.

Someone screamed in pain as a particle settled on his flesh. Then another person cried out as his hair caught on fire.

The two victims broke from the crowd, running wildly, blindly away. Shouting, "I'm on fire! I'm on fire!"

The crowd scattered under the deadly rain, people diving for any shelter they could find.

"With me!" Jooli shouted, whirling and running for the shelter of the stone overhang that protected the door.

Leiria, Coralean and the others knotted in beside her. Pounding at the door for Renor and Sinch to let them in. Mistaking the hammering for the mob trying to get in, the two young guards ignored their entreaty.

Then, as suddenly as it had started, the hot rain stopped. People peered out from their hiding places—farm carts, trees, big clay jars they'd upended.

"What in the Hells—" Leiria began.

"She's not done with us yet," Jooli broke in, cutting her off.

"Who are you talking about?" asked a bewildered Leiria.

"I told you—my grandmother," Jooli snapped. "Queen Clayre." Then, as if it would explain everything, "She's a witch."

"What do we do?" Leiria asked.

"Wait and see what happens next," Jooli advised.

But even as she answered she was digging through her own mental book of spells, searching for a defense. Feeling helpless even as she did so. The power of her grandmother's attack had surprised her, humbled her. She'd had no idea that Queen Clayre possessed such abilities.

At that moment the ground turned spongy under her feet. It started to crumble and she jumped away, shouting a warning to the others.

She whipped around to confront whatever new threat Clayre had in store for them and saw a large dark hole in the ground where she and the others had been standing. Then glowing red dots appeared in the hole. The air suddenly took on a sharp, foul scent of rodent droppings. There was a scurrying and a squeaking—and then hundreds of large rats poured out of the hole.

Coralean booted one rat and slashed at another with his sword. Shouting in surprise as it dodged his cut and leaped onto the blade itself and ran up his arm. He hurled it away, splattering its body against the fortress walls.

But then others swarmed up at him and he cursed and swatted at the squeaking tide. Leiria and the soldiers fared no better. The numbers were overwhelming and they soon found themselves being driven back, dripping with blood from the many bites they suffered.

Jooli cast the only spell she thought might prove effective, but it flattened in the air like a burst goatskin bag.

Screams came from every direction and she could see where other holes had suddenly appeared, pocking the hill like an ugly skin disease. Thousands upon thousands of rats poured out of the holes, attacking the Kyranians with a stunning ferocity.

Fleeing people stumbled, then were quickly overwhelmed by the rodents who went for the most vulnerable parts—snapping at eyes and throats and lips. Slashing ears into bloody ribbons.

Jooli leaped up onto a low wall, clubbing rats away with the flat of her blade. Leiria used her spear to vault onto the wall and they stood back to back, protecting one another against the horrid tide.

But the rats kept coming and Jooli felt her strength slipping away at a frightening rate.

She knew she couldn't last much longer.

*   *   *

Rhodes danced up and down, shouting in glee as the rats overwhelmed the Kyranians. Kalasariz did his own little ghost dance inside the king, thrilled at this easy victory.

Even the inscrutable Queen Clayre let some true emotion leak through, saying "Good show!" as a big rat leaped over Leiria's head and sank its teeth into the back of Jooli's neck.

But then there came a sound like a thunderclap and the fortress door boomed open.

And now it was Queen Clayre's turn to cry, "What's happening?"

*   *   *

Leiria heard Jooli shout in pain and she whirled about, plucked the rat from Jooli's back, snapped its neck and threw it away. A rodent jumped on Leiria's leg, digging in sharp claws and teeth. She smashed it off with her fist, then caught another in mid-leap on her spear point.

It was then that she heard the thunderclap, followed by the crash of the big fortress door slamming open. She looked up, dazed. And beheld a most wondrous sight.

Charging out of the fortress was Safar, mounted on Khysmet! Palimak was seated behind his father, gripping his waist. Safar was waving a long curving sword that glowed like a golden beacon.

And he shouted in a great voice: "Come the winds! North and South! East and West! Come! Come the winds!"

There was a roaring sound, like a distant sea gathering its strength. Then the roar became a wail, then a giant banshee shriek.

The next thing Leiria knew, she was being hammered by fierce winds blasting over her from all sides. She grabbed Jooli and the two women toppled off the wall to take shelter behind the stonework.

Leiria raised her head to see—wind-borne grit lashing her face and scouring her helmet like a sanding machine gone mad.

At first all she could see was the glowing tip of Safar's sword. Then the atmosphere seemed to steady and she could make out the dark, funneling cloud that swirled around man and horse and boy. The banshee sound suddenly changed to shrill squeaks and she saw the rats being lifted off the ground and hurled into the sky.

Thousand upon thousands of them, swept into the heavens, to disappear into the great blue cloud that had a woman's face.

Then the cloud tore apart and was gone.

The wind ceased. And all was silent.

Rhodes shouted in surprise as the model of the Kyranian fortress exploded.

And then thousands of rats were falling from the vaulted ceiling of his mother's chambers. Squealing in fear and anger.

It was as if a rodent hell had opened its gates and let loose a vicious tide of fur and claws and teeth.

Clayre stood frozen in fear as the first of the rats went for her. Then she screamed in terror.

Quickly, Rhodes grabbed his mother, lifting her off the ground. Then he rushed up the stairs, Clayre under one arm, smashing rodents under his heavy boots.

He got her through the door, turned, and slammed and barred it, squashing several rats as they tried to slip past.

The king set his mother on her feet. "What a mess!" he said, then turned his back on her and staggered to his chambers where he collapsed on his bed.

He slept for three days straight and not even Kalasariz could arouse him.

Then he got up, called for food and ate like a war horse. When he was satisfied, Kalasariz spoke to him from within, saying, *You seem quite calm, majesty, considering all that has happened.*

Instead of answering the question, Rhodes said, "Was that Safar Timura? The big man on the white horse?"

Yes, Kalasariz replied. *You can see why he's given me so much trouble over the years. He's a very powerful wizard.*

Rhodes thought a moment, then nodded as he made up his mind. "I want that power," he said."

Then you shall have it, Kalasariz vowed. *We'll just consider your mother's first effort a noble but failed experiment.*

"I have no problem with that," Rhodes said. "I'm not one to give up easily."

He paused, then, "That stallion Safar was riding?"

Yes, what about it?

"That's the steed I was talking about," Rhodes said. "The horse I saw in the mural when I last visited my mother. And then it was gone. Vanished!"

Perhaps we should examine that mural more closely, Kalasariz suggested.

And so Rhodes revisited his mother's chambers. While he'd slept, the rats had been exterminated by poisonous spells. Their bodies were still being hauled away by slaves when he entered his mother's rooms. Clayre was nowhere to be seen. She was probably off somewhere in borrowed quarters, nursing her wounded pride.

"The mural's just over here," Rhodes said, lighting a torch and carrying it to his mother's throne.

But when he looked up his jaw dropped in astonishment.

There was no sign of the mural. The wall was completely blank.

CHAPTER NINETEEN

HOMECOMING

Safar's homecoming was a glorious celebration that lasted a full week. There was much singing, feasting and sacrifice to the Goddess Felakia. Sparkling fireworks filled the nights, dazzling kites of many colors the days. The whole mountaintop was thick with the heady scent of roasting kabobs and spiced fruits and perfumed rice. Wine flowed in rivers and everyone was drunk from dawn to dawn.

His parents and sisters fussed over Safar, weeping and laughing in relief that he was with them once again. Men thumped his back and called him brother and hero. Women offered themselves, swearing they would do anything he desired—with no betrothals asked in return. Coralean gave him a treasure chest filled with exotic gems and rare coins struck by kings in distant lands.

His circus friends staged a fabulous performance in his honor. Biner dressed in his best ringmaster's uniform to direct from the ground as Arlain and Kairo performed many wondrous feats on wires strung from the high-floating airship to the ground. Arlain in her skimpiest costume, breathing long tongues of fire. Kairo juggling his detachable head along with a flaming sword. While Elgy and Rabix played stirring music specially composed for the show.

During all these events Khysmet was always nearby, flowers woven into his mane and tail by pretty Kyranian maids. Palimak sat at Safar's feet, feeling light as a feather, now that he no longer had to wear the heavy mantle of leadership.

Leiria was perhaps the happiest of them all, standing permanent guard at his side. Her burnished armor shining almost as strongly as the internal glow of her overflowing heart. She was joined by the fiercely loyal Renor and Sinch who made certain Safar was safe from all who approached.

With no discussion, Jooli made herself part of this group. She appeared one morning and took up position beside Leiria. It seemed so natural that no one questioned her right.

Safar made only one speech during this time. On the first day he called all the villagers together to purify the mountaintop of the last vestiges of Clayre' sorcery. Afterward, he told them how overjoyed he was to be home again. Although he didn't say where he had been, it was understood by all that Lord Timura had suffered much for them. He congratulated his friends and family for successfully negotiating the Great Sea and making a new home in Syrapis, despite many difficulties and personal sacrifice.

Finally, he begged them to pardon Masura and his supporters for their actions. Left unsaid was that until Safar's miraculous appearance the majority of the villagers had sided with Masura. Everyone seemed quite anxious to forget that ugly little truth.

Safar said he understood and even agreed with the concerns of the Council of Elders. However, these were perilous times that called for extraordinary measures when it came to leadership.

Here he drew Palimak close to him, praising him before the entire assemblage for all that he had done to protect the people of Kyrania. And for so faithfully carrying out all Safar had commanded.

This simple and loving declaration banished any doubts that might have remained among the villagers about Palimak's role since their flight from Esmir. Coupled with the pardon of Masura and his supporters, everyone was so relieved that they wiped their minds of all grievances, real or imagined.

Yet all that gladness was an illusion. Safar knew he would soon have to make his people face a terrible truth: all they had suffered and all they had endured was nothing compared to with the dark days to come.

But he allowed them this brief time. Let them dance, dance, dance, as he had in the endless nightmare of Hadin.

Meanwhile, he would marshal his strength and resources and play the deadly waiting game.

*   *   *

Deep in the wine-dark night, Safar paced the room. Filling one whole side was the great empty coffin of Lord Asper. On the wall above the coffin was the mural that had once graced Queen Clayre's chambers.

Here was the glittering castle and the mysterious King of the Spirit Riders leading his army into battle. There were his warrior daughters, each more beautiful than the other. In front of them was the most beautiful of all—the ebony-skinned princess on the midnight-black mare who had appeared several times over the years to warn Safar, or lead him to safety.

It was all a maddening puzzle. A labyrinth of hidden meanings. Safar had little memory of what had happened since his escape from the past and future dreamworld of Hadinland. There were only impressions, swirling like stars in a drunken sky. There was the wild ride on Khysmet. Quick snatches of the battle with the monster queen in her underground lair. A hazy period of illness, when he sensed he had been knocking on Death's door. Then Palimak had appeared astride Khysmet and they were hammering together at a stony surface.

The surface finally gave way and he suddenly found himself bursting out of the wall of this very room. And then he was charging out of the fortress on Khysmet to meet and defeat the plague of rodents attacking his people.

Safar stared at the mural. He remembered being a momentary part of the ancient painting—sitting astride Khysmet with Palimak, whispering for him to remain quite still while the spell he'd cast continued its course.

He was peering out into the room of the witch queen, Clayre. Nearby was her son, King Rhodes—ruler of Hunan. They were bent over a table, concentrating on something. What it was, he couldn't see. But he could feel the intense flow of magic arcing back and forth between them.

Then it came to him that Rhodes wasn't a true part of that magic. He was only a vessel, with a sorcerous something within.

Safar dug deeper, investigating this oddity. He caught the whiff of a familiar scent. It carried him all the way back to his student days in old Walaria. By the gods, it was Kalasariz!

He'd defeated the canny spymaster several times before, but he kept arising like a vengeful ghost to bedevil him. Somehow he'd taken up residence within the king.

There was still more. What was it? Who was it? Then he sensed the lesser presences of Prince Luka and Lord Fari—Iraj's old demon companions of the Spell of Four. Kalasariz had somehow turned the tables on them. Now they were his much-abused slaves.

However, that left a major question unanswered. There was Kalasariz, Luka and Fari. That made only three.

What had happened to the all-important fourth—Iraj Protarus?

Safar had strained mightily, but couldn't find a single trace of the man who had once been his dearest friend but was now his bitterest enemy. Had Kalasariz managed to kill Iraj as well? That didn't seem possible. Wily as Kalasariz was, Iraj was not one to go so easily.

As Safar had pondered this, Palimak had cast the remaining portion of his spell and they'd been hurled across a spectral world into the Kyranian fortress.

Safar sighed heavily, still caught on the horns of the dilemma of Iraj. He turned away from the mural, which Palimak's spell had transported with them. There were too many questions, each requiring him to follow completely different roads, so it was unlikely a single answer could be found that would satisfy everything.

A line from the Book of Asper crawled into memory: *"All that is Without is Within . . . And all that is Within, is Without . . ."* Safar smiled. Once again he was confronted with another murky verse from Asper that seemed to have meaning. But the meaning defied penetration. No help there.

He strode over to a mirror, and for the first time in what seemed an eternity, viewed his own face. There were the familiar features. The blue eyes, the long chin, the strong nose. He was richly tanned from his time under the hot Hadin sun. No answers there, either, my friend.

Safar touched his chin. There was a bit of a morning stubble. Safar got out his razor, stropping it keen for a shave. Idly, he noticed the stubble was golden instead of its usual dark shadow.

When he'd bathed last night he'd noticed the same was true of the hair on his chest and privates. There were also several wide golden streaks running through the dark hair on his head. Obviously, so much time being naked under that burning sky had bleached him out—possibly forever.

The rest of his body seemed unaffected, except he was more muscular than before. Some good had come from his time in Hadin. He'd always been strongly built, but now his chest and limbs were heavier, more defined. And now that he was well he felt like he was filled with a never-ending supply of energy. This was a definite bonus. For he'd need all the strength he could summon for the hard days ahead.

Safar soaped his face and started shaving. He paused a moment, staring into his own eyes as if they belonged to another, wiser man. And he asked that other man, *Where is Iraj?* But no answer came from this silly exercise.

He chuckled at his foolishness and continued his ablutions.

*   *   *

In his hiding place, Iraj suppressed outright laughter.

He was so close to his enemy that if he had a knife he could catch him unaware and kill him. Of course, he'd need hands to hold that knife—which was something he lacked at the moment. In fact, he had no body at all. And wasn't it odd that he didn't miss it?

Then again, maybe it wasn't so strange. In Iraj's previous existence as a shapechanger he'd known constant pain. Especially as he moved through the agony of assuming one form or another. Bones cracking. Skin stretching and transforming. Internal organs boiling in a sorcerous cauldron. Brain and nerves on fire as they were bombarded by over-intensified sensations.

No, this was much better. The spirit form was a perfect container for the hate he felt for his enemy. What was more, as a spirit he could be patient in the extreme. And patience was a quality that Iraj had never possessed before.

Here he would wait—just out of his enemy's sight. He would watch all that occurred and, at the proper time and the proper place, he'd strike.

Poor Safar.

Sentence had already been passed and he didn't know it.

CHAPTER TWENTY
STORM OVER SYRAPIS

The monsoon season struck Syrapis full force. Even the natives said it was the worst in recent memory.

First came the stultifying atmosphere, settling over the island like a thick, uncomfortable blanket. Breathing was accompanied by a wet rattling of the lungs. Old people and babes were most affected by this and Safar and Palimak were kept busy night and day treating a host of respiratory ailments.

This was accompanied by a series of heavy rainstorms that drenched everyone to the bone. Clothes never seemed to dry. Small wounds became huge weeping sores. The animals developed mange and other skin diseases. Goat milk and cheese became a precious commodity as the mother goats' teats dried up.

Next came the crops. The Kyranians had brought seeds and cuttings from their high-mountain homeland. Over the past few years the Esmirian plants had done well in the mountain fortress the Kyranians had chosen for a home. But the monsoon brought a dampening sickness with it. Roots of young plants were pinched off by the disease. The older plants were stricken with a mysterious fungus. Gray patches would suddenly appear on the leaves and within only a few days the plants would wither and die.

Lightning was a constant peril. Striking without warning even on those rare days when the skies were blue and empty. Parents taught their children to make a small presence if they were caught out in a lightning storm.

They were taught to crouch down, head between their legs, being sure to keep their weight balanced only on their toes. The idea being to make as little contact with the ground as possible. They were also told to stay away from fences during a lightning strike. And if caught out in a wooded area, to get under the shortest tree. For some reason the Lightning Gods favored the tallest objects on which to concentrate their wrath.

The airship was grounded the whole time and there was no surveillance while the monsoon storms lasted. Safar and Palimak weren't too concerned about this vulnerability, reasoning their enemies were just as hampered by the storms as they were.

Safar, however, was concerned about the mercenary fleet they'd hired. Besides the airship, it was this sea force that had kept King Rhodes bottled up. Coralean was dispatched, along with a strong guard, to make certain the pirate captains remained loyal.

Meanwhile, Safar spent all his spare time pondering his next move. He told Palimak and Leiria about his enslavement to the spell of Hadin, his escape and the subsequent disappearance of Iraj.

"I suppose we'll unravel those mysteries in good time," Safar said one night. "But at the moment the thing that intrigues me most is that mural."

He indicated the painting on the wall. "I wonder mightily what the story is behind that. Who was the king? And what of his daughters? Especially the dark-skinned woman on the black mare. When her ghost visited me she said she was a Spirit Rider. And that she was commanded to lead me to Syrapis. For what purpose, I don't know."

"Maybe it has something to do with Lord Asper's coffin, father," Palimak said. "To me, that's as big a mystery as the mural. One moment I saw his mummified corpse. And then he was gone. To be replaced by your living body."

"I have an inkling of what happened to Asper," Safar replied. "It's my theory that the coffin is a gateway between here and Hadin. Unless I'm in grievous error, we basically traded places."

He thought a moment, then added, "At least, it is was a gateway. It's closed now. And there's no way of reopening it again."

Outside, the intensity of the rainstorm increased, furiously pounding on the shuttered windows.

Leiria shivered. "Give me a sword, a spear and a shield and I'll fight any enemy you put in my way," she said. "But all this talk of magical gateways, missing corpses and Spirit Riders is unnerving."

Palimak said, "About the mural, father . . ."

"Yes?"

"Why don't we talk to Queen Jooli?" he asked. "Maybe she can tell us its history."

Safar considered his suggestion. Jooli was nearly as big a puzzle to him as the magical mysteries he was attempting to unravel. He still thought it odd that a hostage should so completely switch her loyalties.

Yet he sensed he could trust her implicitly. She clearly hated her father, just as her sympathies were clearly with the Kyranians. Perhaps it had something to do with her witch's powers. Had she learned something through magic that had opened her eyes?

There was only one way to find out.

"Send for her," Safar said.

A few minutes later Jooli came into the room, still sleepy-eyed from her bed. Twin lightning spears crashed outside, light flaring through the shutter panels. Mixing with the wavery light of the torches sputtering in their brackets on the wall.

Jooli was wearing a long, soft gown and in the sudden intensity of light her slender figure was outlined through the rich cloth. At the same time Safar caught the scent of her perfume—delicate flower blossom. He was startled at her beauty, realizing this was the first time he'd seen her out of armor.

He started to speak and found his voice had grown husky. It had been a long time since he'd been with a woman and she'd caught him off guard with her earthy presence. He cleared his throat to cover his embarrassment and bade her to sit and take some wine with them.

They talked casually for a time, drinking wine and remarking that the storm seemed to be subsiding. Safar noticed that Jooli was eyeing him speculatively, no doubt wondering why she'd been called here. He felt a gentle touch of magic as she sniffed about to see if there was any danger. When none was found, the subtle probing quickly vanished.

Jooli spoke first, going directly to the heart of things. "I suppose you're all wondering about me," she said. "Wanting to know why I'm acting like such a willing hostage. And why I seem so disloyal to my father."

"I suppose you're even asking yourselves if it's some sort of trick. Suspecting, maybe, that any day now I'll reveal my true colors and stab someone in the back."

The rain made a gentle patter now and Safar smiled. "No one thinks that of you, Jooli," he said. "It's apparent to us all that when we found you, we found a friend. Although I must admit that I'm mystified how we came to be so fortunate. Until you came here to live, you knew nothing about us."

"That's not quite true," Jooli said. "You see, Safar Timura, I've been waiting for your arrival ever since I was a girl."

There was a long silence as everyone in the room wondered at this startling remark. A sudden wind blew up, crashing against the shutters.

Palimak's eyes jerked toward the mural, then toward Jooli. His demon senses prickling with awareness. He muttered, "Yes, it makes sense."

Safar said, "Apparently my son is much more astute than I am, Jooli. Which doesn't surprise me. In not too many years our roles are sure to be reversed. And he will be the teacher and I his willing student. But please enlighten me. So I'll possess the same knowledge as my son."

"I'm only guessing, father," Palimak said, blushing. Safar was his hero and he didn't want to discover any chinks in his armor, much less think of himself as superior in any way.

Once again, the storm's fury lessened. The pounding at the shutters became a faint, tap, tap, tap.

Safar chuckled. "Let's see how good a guess it was, son," he said. "Go on, Jooli. Please explain."

Jooli nodded. "Gladly. I've been waiting for the right moment and it's finally here. However, first I need to tell you a little about myself. So, if you'll forgive a rather lengthy approach . . ."

"We have all the time in the world, Jooli," Safar said. Then he grimaced, rueful. "Although that might not be as long as we wished."

"I know something about that, too," Jooli said. "The gods asleep. The Demon Moon. Hadin. The end of the world."

As if on cue one of the shutters came loose, crashing back and forth with the wind. Palimak jumped up to fix it back into place.

Safar acted as if nothing had happened to disturb them. "This is getting more and more interesting," he said mildly. "Go on."

Without preamble, Jooli said, "I am the oldest of my father's children. I am also the best warrior in Hunan. This is no boast, merely a statement of what is so. I have natural abilities, plus I've trained long and hard at the art of warfare. As you've no doubt noticed, in Syrapis a leader must be a noteworthy warrior, or she wouldn't be able to hold her kingdom much past the coronation.

"Regardless, in my view I am the rightful successor to the throne of Hunan. There is no law in our land forbidding a woman ruler, so my claim to the crown is certainly not without merit."

The wind took on a sighing note, whispering many sad things. And Leiria murmured, "But your father is reluctant."

Jooli laughed, not without bitterness. "When it comes to my father," she said, "*reluctant* is such a mild term. 'Over my dead body' is more the way he puts it. Although lately he's dropped that phrase. Imagining, I suppose, that I might take him up on it. Anyway, he's done his best over the years to marry me off to one prince or another. Hoping to get me out of the way and make a key alliance to boot.

"He's also tossed me a royal bone by giving me the title of 'Queen,' and a few hundred acres of farmland to rule so I can have an independent income and satisfy my cravings for leadership by ordering the cows and harvest crews about."

Outside, there was a lull in the storm and everything became very quiet.

Safar frowned, then said, "You don't seem the sort of person to be ruled by overweening ambition. Do you really want the crown of Hunan so badly you'd take up with your father's enemies? Or is there another, much deeper reason?"

Jooli gave him a long look. Then she hoisted her wine cup, drained it, hooked the jug and refilled her cup. She gave a long sigh.

"Yes, Safar Timura," she said, "I do have a deeper reason. And as it so happens, I'm driven by the same foolish desires as you. In short, I want to wake up the gods and save the world!"

Safar nodded, then said, "Good. Now, tell us about the mural."

Palimak gaped in surprise. Leiria stifled laughter when she saw his expression. The poor boy had really believed he had guessed something his father was too slow to realize. She didn't say anything to him, but she thought, It's time you understood, little one, that Safar always knows! Then a sad caveat came to her: Except when it's a personal matter. When it came to love, Safar was as ignorant as a splay-footed plowboy.

Jooli said, "Yes, the mural. I've just about reached that point in my story. But one moment more, please."

"You can have as many moments as you desire," Safar said.

"You can't fully understand," Jooli said, "until I tell you about my grandmother—Queen Clayre. Queen Mother Clayre, to be more exact."

The lull ended with a loud crash of lightning, followed by a torrent of rain that slammed into the old stone fortress, shaking it.

Jooli glanced at the trembling shutters, then back at Safar. She said, "My grandmother's a witch, as I told Leiria before—rather alarmingly when all those damned rats appeared. And I've made no secret that I'm a witch as well."

She smiled first at Safar, then at Palimak. "As if I could keep such a thing from two such powerful wizards."

Palimak blushed. Safar's face remained a bland, albeit friendly shield. Leiria's eyes narrowed. The flattery wasn't called for. Then her features relaxed as she realized that Jooli was nervous. The female artifice was only reflexive. She thought, As if you haven't foolishly reacted that way yourself upon occasion! Then she saw Jooli's eyes darken as she realized her error and gave herself a mental kick. It made her like the woman even more.

The slip seemed to make Jooli concentrate more on her tale. She bowed her head, speaking so low her words could barely be heard over the storm.

She said, "At one time my grandmother was training me to take her place as Queen Witch of Hunan. I was about five years old when she first brought me into her chamber. It was shortly after my mother died."

Jooli stopped speaking for a moment. Then she shook her head, saying, "I've often thought she poisoned my mother. But that's another tale that has nothing to do with what has occurred since."

Safar gently picked up her wine cup and gave it to Jooli to drink. She sipped the wine, nodded her thanks, and continued.

"My grandmother introduced me to all the mysteries over the next few years," she said. "I was a good little girl who never gave her elders cause for concern. I did what I was told, when I was told. And then one day I saw the mural."

She gestured, indicating the painting on the wall. "Oh, I'd seen it before, of course. Even wondered about it. It's such a romantic scene. A noble king. Warrior daughters at his side. Marching off to do battle against what you instinctively knew was a very powerful and evil enemy. I was especially struck by the dark-skinned princess who led the procession. She was so beautiful, so brave, on that great black mare!

"I made up heroic little stories about her in my mind, substituting myself in her place. Once I asked grandmother about the mural, but she became very angry and said I was asking too many stupid questions. That it was just a painting, nothing more.

"But on this particular day I was alone in her chambers. She was off about some sort of business, I don't recall what. And as I gazed at the mural I started thinking that it couldn't be just a painting. It had to have some special meaning. I got up and went into the hallway, where there were other murals. They're still there, as a matter of fact. And they are frightening things! Ugly things! You've never seen them, but if you had you'd know what I mean when I say they look like they were created by some devil from the hells.

"I learned later that this description wasn't so far off the mark. The originals were done long ago by a great artist—a wizard—in the employ of that ancient king." She motioned at the golden-mailed king in the mural.

"But my grandmother used those murals for her own purposes," Jooli continued, voice harsh. "At one time they were all beautiful pastorals that lifted the spirit. But she painted over portions of them, inserting nightmarish, sinful scenes. Despicable things. They make me ill just thinking of them. And then she used the altered murals to create black spells against her enemies. I learned later that her bargain with Charize, the monster queen, made all this possible.

"For some reason, she never touched the mural that now sits in this room. I don't know why. But I think she's afraid of it."

Safar asked, "Can you tell us anything about the people depicted in the mural?"

Jooli smiled. "I certainly can. In fact, I met the dark woman. She is a creature of the mural. It was she who told me about you and your holy mission. She bade me to wait for your appearance in Syrapis. And to do everything I could to ensure that your mission is successful."

Safar was stunned. "You mean she only exists in that painting?"

"Quite so. Now, at any rate," Jooli said. "She and her family lived hundreds of years ago. They were rulers of Syrapis when Lord Asper arrived here from Hadin. They watched over him while he labored over his books, seeking an answer to the disaster that would someday overtake the world. And when he died, they created the idol and the death chamber you found his coffin in. Asper made the coffin with his own hands when he knew his death was near."

"What about Queen Charize?" Palimak asked. "How did she and her monsters end up ruling Asper's chamber?"

"My grandmother said that she was Asper's Favorite. He came upon her in Hadin and although she was evil, her magic was so strong that he used her to help cast his most difficult spells. Before he died, he enslaved her and set her to guard his tomb.

"But over much time she managed to break his spell and free herself. There are some who say that Charize is responsible for all the warfare in Syrapis. That she and her minions set human against human to feed on our misery."

Jooli shrugged. "I don't know how true that is," she said. "In my experience people don't need that much of a reason to kill one another. I do know this, however. In order to live and create her sisters she required someone in the outside world to help her. And, in recent years, my grandmother was that person."

Palimak grinned, demon eyes glittering in delight. "Now that Charize is dead," he said, "it'll make it damned hard for your grandmother."

Safar sighed. "Maybe so," he said. But his tone was doubtful.

He was thinking of the new being Queen Clayre could now rely upon. The creature that was Kalasariz who dwelt in King Rhodes. He didn't say anything, because he was loath to tell Jooli what Rhodes had become. Even though she disliked him—perhaps even hated him—it would be a difficult thing for a daughter to bear.

He decided to wait for a more appropriate time. The tale Jooli was telling was already having a great effect on her. Her features had become pale and drawn, eyes sitting in bruised hollows. He changed the subject.

"What of the Spirit Rider?" he asked. "Could you tell us of your meeting with her?"

Jooli nodded. She was growing weary. Not so much because of the talk, but because of all the memories that had come flooding back as she spoke to her new friends.

Somewhere far off a dog howled and she realized the storm had finally ended. Silence cloaked the room as she gathered her strength.

And then she drank down her wine and began the tale . . .

CHAPTER TWENTY-ONE

JOOLI'S SONG

She was a lonely girl of less than ten years. Her limbs were long and lanky like a young colt's, and she could scamper up a tree like a mountain goat. And she could run like the winds, sprinting past even the fastest boys in the Kingdom of Hunan.

Jooli was full of fire and curiosity, but inside there was an emptiness created by the loss of her mother. An emptiness made deeper and sadder still because of her father's neglect. And so it was that when her grandmother took Jooli under her wing, at first she went gladly. Looking for love even more than the knowledge of the world that she so craved.

The Queen Mother's chambers were a frightening place for a child. The light was dim and wavery, with guttering torches sending off a greasy smoke. There were little scratching and squeaking noises coming from the moving shadows produced by the light.

Shelves were lined with books marked with strange witch's symbols—red scorpions, fanged snakes and pinched monster's faces. Glass jars filled with preserved animals and human body parts added to the grave-like feeling of the chilly room. And there was the heavy scent of sorcerous ozone, mixed with the torch smoke and heady incense that left the metallic taste of old blood in her mouth.

But she put a brave face on it, going eagerly to her grandmother's chambers every time she was called. Doing her best to ignore the fearsome atmosphere. Paying close attention to all her grandmother taught her.

Although Clayre was a cold, unfeeling woman, the child simply thought this was merely her grandmother's way and believed in her heart that she was loved. Why else would the Queen Mother pay so much attention to her?

Jooli was thrilled by the gradual exploration of her magical side. Her grandmother said she had talents no one else in Hunan had—other than Clayre, of course. And she boasted that there were few people in all Syrapis who could perform any magic—and most of them were very weak.

Only Clayre and Jooli were so blessed, the queen mother said. She said it was a talent passed by blood through the women of their family, but always skipping a generation. Clayre's own daughter—dead many years now—never displayed magical abilities. And neither Clayre's mother. It was Clayre's own grandmother who had introduced her to the witching arts.

She said that although there were years between them, she and Jooli were like sisters. "Sisters of the Oath," as she put it. Exactly what oath, she didn't explain. Then one day her grandmother summoned her and put her to the test.

Clayre placed a small doll on the table. It was dressed in the clothes of a courtier and had a pinched little face carved from an apple that had then been dried in an oven, painted and lacquered.

Jooli giggled when she examined the face and realized it was modeled after her father's cranky old Grand Wazier. King Rhodes thought highly of the man—he was as parsimonious as the king and always looking for ways to add coin to the royal treasury. Lately, he'd complained of the "unwarranted expenditures" that went to pay for the Queen Mother's care.

Clayre loved her luxuries and was constantly adding to her collection of jewels and fine clothing. Goat's milk and expensive oils were used in her bath. The purest henna and rarest powders for her make-up. These things, along with the high prices for her witch's potions, had caused the Wazier to question the money she spent. Her son fervently supported the old man.

"Why, I could pay for a month's rations for a battalion with what it costs to keep you, mother," he'd said.

Jooli'd heard her grandmother complain about the Wazier, but hadn't thought about the controversy very much. She only knew the old courtier didn't seem to like children and complained bitterly when she got underfoot. Once she'd dropped a sweetmeat on the floor, getting it grimy. So she'd thrown it away. The Wazier had seen this and had berated her for wasting food. He'd lectured her for a half-turn of the glass, making her cry.

And so when she saw the doll with the Wazier's funny face and her grandmother had said they were going to play a little joke on him, she'd giggled and eagerly agreed to help.

"We're going to try something very special together, dear," Clayre said, drawing the child to her magical table. "But I'll need you to concentrate with me, ever so hard. Can you do that for your grandmother, my sweet?"

Jooli agreed without hesitation. Her grandmother's voice was so gentle, so loving, she thought she'd never been so happy since her mother died.

On the table was a toy executioner's platform, complete with a masked doll bearing an ax, and a little bench for the victim to kneel over and expose his neck.

This didn't bother Jooli very much. Executions were quite common in Hunan and there was always a fantastic party atmosphere at them, with treats for the children and puppet shows and all sorts of wondrous things to get the crowds in the mood to witness the evildoer receiving his just punishment.

Jooli clapped her hands in delight. "We're going to give him a pain in the neck!" she crowed. "That's perfect, because that's what he's always calling me."

She frowned. "Although once he said a bad word, instead of 'neck.'"

Clayre smiled and Jooli noticed an odd glitter in her eyes. "That's exactly what we're going to do, my sweet," she said. "Give him a pain in the neck!"

Jooli frowned, suddenly concerned. "But it won't hurt too much, will it?" she asked. "He is pretty old, after all, and maybe that's why he gets so cranky. Maybe his bones hurt or something."

"Don't worry, dear," Clayre said, "it'll only hurt a little bit. And after that—why, he'll never suffer again." She chuckled. "You won't find him so cranky after we play our little trick on him."

Mollified, Jooli helped her grandmother prepare the spell. Following Clayre's directions, she set four gray candles, pebbled with black, around the toy platform. When Jooli lit them with a taper, they gave off a purplish, sweet-smelling smoke.

She sprinkled a white powder up the little steps that led to the executioner's bench. More powder was dribbled on the bench, then smeared on the tiny ax held by the toy executioner. Finally, using a pen dipped in glistening black ink, Clayre had Jooli draw a circle around the Grand Wazier doll's neck.

She got a little of the ink on her fingers and Clayre made her stop and wash them carefully with vinegar before they proceeded.

"Otherwise it will make your fingers burn when we cast the spell," her grandmother explained.

Jooli's eyes widened. "Will it make his neck burn too?" she wanted to know. "I wouldn't want to really, really hurt him, or anything."

"No more than a sunburn, dear," Clayre replied. But she said it a little quickly, although Jooli didn't think about that until later.

When all was ready, Clayre gave Jooli the doll. She told her to pretend it was the real Grand Wazier and to make the doll walk up the steps, then bend over the executioner's bench. Four tiny cuffs fixed to the bench were locked around the doll's hands and feet.

Jooli did as she was told, but after she arranged the doll, Clayre wasn't satisfied, saying, "We need to stretch his neck a bit, dear."

As she spoke, she tugged on the doll's dried apple head, drawing out more of the cloth neck and tucking in the collar of the robe so the inky mark Jooli had made was fully exposed. She told Jooli to focus all her attention on the task at hand. And to repeat everything Clayre said.

Then she sang:

> "We are the sisters of Asper,
> Sweet Lady, Lady, Lady . . ."

In her high, piping voice, Jooli chanted:

> "We are the sisters of Asper,
> Sweet Lady, Lady, Lady . . ."

Then Clayre sang:

> We guard his tomb, we guard his tomb,
> Holy One . . ."

And Jooli repeated:

> We guard his tomb, we guard his tomb,
> Holy One . . ."

Then the chamber's dim light faded even more until it became quite dark. The golden tiles glowed into life, bathing the executioner's platform in an eerie light. A ghastly face formed on the tiles, floating there as if caught in a watery mirror.

"Welcome, Sister Charize," Queen Clayre intoned.

Jooli was frightened and started to draw away. But Clayre pulled her back.

"Speak with me, child!" she commanded. "Repeat all I say!"

Then Clayre said again, "Welcome, Sister Charize." And she tugged at Jooli's arm to do the same.

Jooli quavered, "Welcome, Sister Charize."

Although she certainly didn't mean it! This horrible creature with its long glistening fangs and scaly face was certainly not welcome anywhere near her, as far as she was concerned.

"We have a boon to ask, dear Sister," Clayre said, tugging once again at Jooli's arm to prompt her.

And so, against her will, Jooli repeated, "We have a boon to ask, dear Sister."

The beast's jaws opened and a voice like rough sand on a washboard said, "Is this the girl we spoke of, Sister Clayre?"

Jooli's racing heart skipped a beat. Was this . . . this . . . Thing! . . . speaking of her?

Then she knew the answer, because her grandmother said, "None other, Sister. She goes by the human name of Jooli."

Red eyes turned on little Jooli, who felt as if they were boring holes into her soul. "And is she ready to take the oath, Sister?" Charize asked in that terrible voice.

"Indeed she is," Clayre replied. "And the boon I ask is her initiation into the Sisterhood." Clayre indicated the toy platform and dolls. "All is prepared. We only need your assistance to complete the spell."

There was a silence as the face floated over the scene. Then Charize chuckled. It was an awful sound.

She said, "Ah, I see. The king's Grand Wazier. What a nasty little man. I'd be pleased to grant your boon and welcome the girl into the Sisterhood. Proceed."

"Thank you, Sister Charize," Clayre said. Then to Jooli: "Concentrate, my sweet. And we'll all cast the spell together."

And she sang:

> *"O, join us together who now are apart.*
> *Make us an arrow aimed for his heart.*
> *We are his pain, we are his hot blood.*
> *Spilled on the ground in a great raging flood!"*

Charize joined in, rasping:

> *" . . . O, join us together who now are apart.*
> *Make us an arrow aimed for his heart . . ."*

Trembling, Jooli piped in her clear voice:

> *" . . . We are his pain, we are his hot blood.*
> *Spilled on the ground in a great raging flood!"*

To Jooli's horror the dolls on the bench suddenly came alive. The wazier doll screaming and struggling against his bonds. The executioner doll running forward, lifting his blade high to strike. And *whack!*, the head came off! And the white powder was transformed into a torrent of blood flowing across the platform and down the steps.

Jooli shrieked in horror. She broke away from her grandmother and bolted from the room, Clayre angrily calling after her to come back. But Jooli closed her ears to her grandmother's commands and ran to her room where she hid under her bed all day and all night.

The next morning, Clayre sent a burly slave to fetch her. Jooli protested, but it was no use. The slave grabbed her by the feet and dragged her out from under the bed. On the way to Clayre's chambers they passed the Grand Wazier's room. To Jooli's relief, she heard him groaning in pain. At least he was alive! She got a peek into the room and saw him sprawled on his bed, a bloody bandage around his throat. Puzzled doctors were in attendance.

As she was rushed down the stairs to her grandmother's sanctum, the ghastly murals on the walls took on new meaning to Jooli and she was even more terrified when she entered the chambers. Thankfully, her grandmother was absent—off on some errand. The slave told her to sit and wait Clayre's return. He disappeared up the stairs, leaving her alone. Suddenly, she gripped her neck—wondering if her grandmother was making a Jooli doll. Was her head about to be lopped off?

Just then, a soft, sweet voice called to her: "Joo-lii! Joo-lii!"

Startled, she looked around. But there was no one else in the room.

Again: "Joo-lii! Joo-lii!"

There! It came from behind her. She turned, but all she could see was the beautiful mural of the King and his warrior daughters. Then a light glittered in the armor of one of the princesses. It was the dark-skinned woman on the black mare! Jooli leaned closer. Her eyes widened and she saw the woman's hand move. The princess of the mural was waving to her! Beckoning?

And she saw the lips move and heard: "Come to us, Jooli!"

The child stretched out her hand. There was a gentle tingling sensation and suddenly there was a roaring in her ears. The ground heaved under her, but she wasn't afraid. And then she was flying through the air, her arms around the narrow waist of the Sprit Rider. The wind blasting in her face as they rode the black mare through a starry sky.

She peered around the Spirit Rider's shoulder. Far away she saw a glorious golden city. The city of the mural: The ancient Kingdom of Hunan!

Jooli lived there for a year. It was the happiest year of her life.

She paused in the telling of her tale. A mischievous smile graced her lips.

"While I was there," she said, "they taught me a song. They called it the 'Song of Safar Timura.' Would you like to hear it?"

Everyone said they would. And this was the song she sang, in a high clear voice that made her audience laugh and cry and sigh:

> Colored lights play, smoky mist swirling low;
> Two indistinct figures catch spotlight's glow,
> Bow in the center as breathless crowd waits
> For the fates to decree, On with the Show!
>
> On gyring wheel 'neath Kyranian sky
> Vessels take shape under artisan's eye.
> Master's young son laughs to magic the clay;
> 'Cross Black Land afar spins circle awry.
>
> In wizard's den on high mountain tor,
> Protarus unveiled, mighty conqueror.
> Demon-fang casting the perils disclose
> That brothers of spirit must stand before.
>
> The road divides, leads to glory or doom
> Writ by silver stars and the crimson moon.
> One to Walaria, wizardly school'd
> By generous caravan master's boon.
>
> Protarus, the bloodier path does take
> Crush spirit and flesh, an empire to make.
> Victor triumphant, but victim of war
> Honor held captive for cruelty's sake.

Spell-magic and wisdom the potter gain,
While dancers of death whirl 'neath burning rain.
Swift thief, young girl, bears a talisman strong
A gift to fight fire with love's brighter flame.

Upon the ages-blackened turtle's dome
The map of journey's danger, fiery home
Of Hadin's mountain; hell of earthly end?
Can valor save what Asper saw to come?

Within, the Favorites sleep, then wake to see
Their master, strong Safar, whose prophecy
Demands they heed Iraj's deadly call
The wizard's vision calls relentlessly.

Which high-born son's path must evil beware,
Child of the mountain or war chieftain's heir?
Both stride with power, yet wisdom's undone;
The gyre off-balance, the gods unaware.

Above! Converge the signs of Khysmet's paths:
Demon moon portends empires' bloody clash,
Sky-borne circus, star-crossed, young wizard bears,
While Hadin's bellows raise the fiery ash.

Iraj, icon of Alissarian
To restore the kingdoms of Two to One
Ensorcels his soul to confound Safar
Can brothers' blood oath be ever undone?

Demons, cold allies, he marches before
By compact with hell, now bound evermore.
The potter's dreams shaped like clay on the wheel
Lie shattered in pieces by the Unholy Four.

Desert sands to mystic Caluz soon lead,
Place of Hantilia's astonishing deed.
Great turtle, apostate, artifice bent,
The wheel of Hadin's malevolence, Heed!

The wolf's stride lengthens, the chase faster make,
Speed sorcery's evil and sword's bright hate
Sharp as the arrow in Nerisa's breast
And will doom be sealed when the gods awake?

Two paths, divergent, 'cross sinister seas
Might alchemy meld to one Destiny.
A race to gain mighty Asper's abode
Syrapis' secrets behind fierce Charize.

Three for the quest to battle Esmir's woe
Banner'd with courage against demon foe
Wizard, warrioress, and magical child
Will only the three be allies enow?

But wait! Now Four! Joins a mysterious queen
Once hostage, once ally, spirit-realm seen;
Her journey now meet, now merge with the One
All to quench Hadin and birth Asper's dream!

Leave mem'ry of past, and future esteem
Soul forfeit if need, the champions deem
To leap to battle, by honor full-armed,
By courage and love, the world to redeem.

And now, tent brightens, the spells lightly fall;
The next act awaits the ringmaster's call.
Biner steps forth, gleaming eye and sly grin:
"Damn everything else, the circus is all!"

CHAPTER TWENTY-TWO

TRUMPET OF DOOM

Jooli paused at the end of the song, weary from reliving the memories of her youth.

Safar and the others applauded her, which did much to lessen her weariness.

"If you let Biner hear your voice," Safar said, making Jooli blush, "he'll recruit you for the circus and make you a star performer."

When they were settled again, Jooli said, "As I mentioned, the time I spent in that magical kingdom was the happiest year of my life."

She took a long drink of wine to restore her energies. "Actually," she said, correcting herself, "it was only a few minutes in real time. If anything in this world can be called real, that is. But in the spirit world of the mural it was a year. And in that year I was not only healed, but armored against my grandmother's designs."

She shook her head. "I wouldn't have survived if the Spirit Rider hadn't rescued me."

Safar stared at the mural, his mind a meteor shower of thoughts, ideas, questions. Although the mural was only a thin wash of paint on stone, the people portrayed seemed full-bodied and alive. Especially the Spirit Rider, with her haunting beauty and beckoning hand. Posed on the fabulous black mare as if she were about to fly away.

He forced calm on his spirit and turned to Jooli. She was staring at him with an odd look of expectation in her eyes.

"Tell me her name, please," he said.

Jooli nodded, as if she knew he'd ask this. "Princess Alsahna," she said. "And her father's name was King Zaman. The last king to rule all Syrapis. And the grandson of the great Alisarrian."

Safar felt like he'd been hit by a chariot-wheel spanner. "By the gods," he said, "can this be true?"

Jooli started to protest, but he stopped her with a raised hand. "I don't doubt your word, Jooli. Of course it's true. It's only that this revelation makes things so clear, so simple that it . . ."

He let the rest trail off. Excitement building. Then: "Alisarrian was Asper's student, correct?"

"Correct," Jooli said, surprised at Safar's intuition. "His teachings were the foundation of Alisarrian's greatness. Not only as a general—a conqueror—but as a sorcerer."

"But later, Alisarrian spurned Asper's ideas. King Zaman said this was the reason for the break-up of Alisarrian's kingdom after his death."

Safar boiled with excitement. He'd learned as a schoolboy that Alisarrian's death had led to the bloody human-versus-demon wars in Esmir. And that Lord Asper, the old demon master wizard, had been part of the committee of wizards who ended those wars by creating the Forbidden Desert that divided the two species for centuries. Ended only in Safar's time when the demon king, Manacia, broke the spell and invaded the human lands. Which led, in turn, to the rise and fall of Iraj Protarus. Who worshipped and emulated Alisarrian as if he were a god.

But then Safar came full circle and his excitement ended with a great emotional crash, plunging him into depression.

What did any of this matter? It only confirmed what the histories already hinted at. Of interest to scholars, to be sure. Except in a short time there would be no scholars, much less history for them to ponder.

Jooli said, "It was while I was with Princess Alsahna that I learned about Hadin. About the end of the world. And about you, Safar Timura."

"I noticed she used my name—and many other names familiar to us all in the song she taught you," Safar said.

Jooli nodded. "But it was you she mainly spoke of. The princess said you were the only one who could change the course of history. That someday you would come to Syrapis to learn Lord Asper's secret. And that I was to help you find it."

Palimak snorted. "Which secret?" he said sarcastically. "My father's had me studying Asper's secrets since I was a toddler. Why, the first words I learned to read were from the Book of Asper. He might have been a mighty wizard and all. But he makes everything so mysterious that there's literally thousands of secrets. And it's not even that big a book!"

Safar smiled, remembering Palimak's long-ago complaint that the world of magic was unnecessarily vague and complicated.

"If I ever write a Book of Palimak," the young man said, echoing Safar's thoughts, "every word will be as plain as the nose on your face. And it won't be written in poetry, that's for certain. Why, I'll bet Asper spent more time and energy looking for a rhyme than he did putting down his thoughts."

"You could very well be right, son," Safar said fondly. "I've often thought the same thing, especially when studying Asper. Whose words are murky, to say the least. The only thing is, poetry does reduce a complicated thought into something more manageable. And as for magic, verse helps focus your mind on the spell."

"If you two don't stop it, I'm going to scream!" Leiria broke in, disgusted. "Debating the merits of verse in magic isn't going to get us anywhere. Except dead from boredom!"

She pointed at Jooli. "The woman just told you something that to my poor, dull, soldierly mind is pretty damned important. So ask her, please! What secret was she supposed to help you find?"

Jooli rose. "It's easier to show you than tell you," she said.

She went to the huge coffin of Asper, beckoning the others to join her. She positioned them around the coffin: Safar at the carved head, Palimak at the feet, herself and Leiria on either side.

Jooli grinned at Palimak. "I'm afraid you're going to have to put up with a little more murky poetry," she teased.

Palimak only nodded. He could feel the magic radiating from the coffin. But it was a very strange sort of magic—whether for good or ill, he couldn't say.

Safar had a different reaction to the magic. To him it seemed amazingly familiar—as if he'd come upon his own footprints in the snow.

He studied the carved features of Asper. They seemed almost lifelike—the long demon fangs, pointed ears, heavy horn over a much-wrinkled brow. Deep-set eyes made of rare red gems that glittered in the torchlight. He seemed so incredibly wise and sad—contemplating a grim future.

Then Jooli raised her hands to cast the spell and Safar bent closer, eager to see what happened next.

Jooli chanted:

> "The Gods dream awhile of me and thee:
> Demon and Man alike in our Hate.
> Come sound the trumpet for all to see:
> Darkness and Light, twin rulers of Fate!"

Safar heard a long, deep sigh, like that of an old ghost set free of his bonds. The torchlight dimmed, then flared anew—much brighter than before. Asper's gemstone eyes became two ruby-red spears of light.

Jooli leaned forward, passing her hand through the beams, chanting:

> "Yes, come sound the trumpet
> Before the Castle of Fate.
> And there you'll find Asper
> At Hadin's last gate!"

Safar heard a sound like the tumblers of a enormous lock turning over. Then a click! And the red beams vanished and the carved jaws gaped wide. For a brief moment Safar thought the demon had come alive and was about to speak. Then he saw that the open mouth offered a passageway.

He started to reach, then hesitated—looking up at Jooli.

She nodded, encouraging him. "Go ahead. Reach inside."

Safar slipped his hand into the opening, felt something there, and drew it out. Puzzled, he held the object up for all to see.

It was some sort of seashell. About eighteen inches long, spiraling from its finger-wide tip to its bell-shaped opening. Its colors were various shades of orange and white, all very glossy as if the shell had been fired in a pottery kiln. He thumped it experimentally and found that it was hollow.

Then he realized the shell was very much like the conch shell horns the musicians played in Hadin. Except long and narrow like a . . .

"A kind of trumpet?" he asked Jooli. "Like the one in the spell verse?"

"The very same," Jooli replied.

Safar started to raise it to his lips, then hesitated. "Shall I try it?" he asked.

"I don't see why not," Jooli said. Then she laughed. "I've been waiting for this moment since I was a girl at Princess Alsahna's knee!"

In his hiding place, Iraj burned with curiosity. He was anxious to get on with whatever was going to happen next.

Palimak caught a whiff of strangeness. He sniffed the atmosphere with his magical senses, but couldn't trace the source. It must be the coffin, he thought. And turned his attention back to his father, who was lifting the shell trumpet to his lips.

Safar blew and the most wondrous music issued forth. It was as if a whole orchestra of musicians were playing—pipes and horns and silver-stringed lyres. With a single wild wailing trumpet swooping above and through and below all the notes like a glad hawk set free on the winds after a long period of captivity.

On the wall the mural shimmered. Then not only the painting but the entire wall dissolved. Except instead of looking out on a Syrapian night, they were gazing across bright rolling seas.

A tall ship danced over the waves, graceful sails billowing in a balmy breeze. Playful dolphins and flying fishes leaped high in its wake, making the whole a joyous scene. The ship flew a flag bearing the symbol of Asper: a twin-headed serpent, borne on jagged-edged wings. And soaring above it all was the unmistakable silhouette of the circus airship, suspended beneath its two painted balloons.

Safar lowered the shell trumpet, but the music kept playing—growing more haunting, more compelling. Each note beckoning them to follow.

Palimak saw familiar figures moving about the tall ship's bridge.

"Look, father!" he said in awestruck tones. "Don't you recognize them?"

"It's us!" Safar said.

Jooli pointed at a slender figure in armor. "I'm there, too," she said, pleased and amazed at the same time.

"I wonder where we're going?" Leiria marveled.

Safar indicated the red moon hanging low on the horizon. "There's only one course that puts the Demon Moon so low," he said. "We're bound for Hadin."

Leiria was startled at how grim he sounded. She looked at him. His face was pale, blue eyes hollowed and bruised.

Then the scene vanished to be replaced by the hard, blank surface of the fortress wall. And the mural of the Spirit Rider was gone.

Safar turned to them, slowly straightening his shoulders as if steadying a weighty burden. "Oh, well," he said, smiling brightly. "It's not as if I didn't know that I had to go back."

Palimak caught the worry hiding beneath the false surface of cheer. "It'll be different this time, father," he said. "You were in some kind of spellworld before. It's wasn't the real Hadin."

"I know," Safar said. But he was shaking his head slowly, uneasy.

"Maybe we're looking at this the wrong way," Leiria offered.

The world and everything in it could go to the Hells, as far as she was concerned. She'd do anything to spare Safar further agonies.

"How do we know that wasn't a false vision? Something concocted by Charize and her monsters?"

"It wasn't," Safar said. "To begin with, Charize had nothing to do with the mural. That's clearly Asper's work. Just as it was clearly Lord Asper's intent for Princess Alsahna—whom I've always thought of as the 'Spirit Rider'—to help me discover a way to keep the world from destroying itself.

"As you can plainly see there is no sense denying—or fighting—our fate." He drew in a long breath. "We must go to Hadin. And as quickly as possible."

Palimak became frightened. Not for himself, but for his father. Suddenly he saw him as a driven, tragic character. Doom was written all over his features.

"Let's not be so hasty, father," he said. "I think we ought to look into this some more. You know . . . Study the auguries . . . Re-read the Book of Asper. After all, Hadin is on the other side of the world! Thirteen thousand miles away. We need to look for other answers before we decide to do something so drastic."

"Palimak's right," Leiria said. "We can't just abandon everything and everybody in Syrapis. Think of your family and friends. You brought them so far. And now you're going to leave them again."

Desperate, she turned to Jooli. "Tell him," she said. "Tell him there must be another way. Another answer!"

Jooli gave a sad shrug. She quite liked Leiria and Palimak and was loath to disappoint them. But what could she do?

"Princess Alsahna was quite clear," she replied. "The only one who can decide is Safar Timura."

At that moment the floor heaved under them. The earth shock was so great that they were hurled flat.

It was like riding a giant bucking horse and they found themselves clinging to any surface they could dig their nails into.

Objects crashed to the ground, shattering. Plaster and stone rained around their ears.

Outside, people and animals panicked, screaming and bellowing in fear.

Then, as suddenly as it had begun, the earthquake ended. And all was still and all was silent as they braced for another shock.

Finally, they realized it was over.

Safar was the first to his feet. He looked around, surveying the damage. Furniture smashed, stone walls cracked, the floor split right down the middle.

"There's your answer," he said. "We go to Hadin!"

In his hiding place, Iraj knew fear. He'd just escaped from that awful place. He fought for calm.

Safar was right. There was no other choice: they had to return to Hadin.

Part Three
Bound for Hadinland

CHAPTER TWENTY-THREE
THE CRY OF THE TURTLE

Safar stood on the bridge of the tall ship watching the green rolling seas froth into white spume as they parted before the wooden prow. Hungry birds followed in their wake, filling the air with their gleeful cries as they swooped on fish stunned by the ship's swift passage.

From above he could hear Biner shouting orders to the airship crew. And—more faintly—the roar of the magical engines that kept the balloons taut and the airship aloft. He smiled, remembering just how much fun it was to be a member of the airship's crew. Everyone would be rushing to perform the tasks Biner set, laughing and joking with one another as they sailed through azure skies.

The atmosphere would be the direct opposite of what he'd experienced thus far on the tall ship. The vessel—named the *Nepenthe*—was the best that Coralean could provide from the mercenary fleet. Although Safar was no sailor, it certainly seemed sound enough.

But the crew was sullen, the captain harsh and when orders were given the sailors were slow to act. To Safar they also seemed deliberately clumsy—fouling lines, tangling sails and generally making an unnecessary mess of things.

Sooner or later he would have to do something about this state of affairs. However, at the moment he was content just to get the voyage started. He consoled himself, thinking he had thirteen thousand or more miles to bend matters—and the captain—to his will.

Some consolation! By the gods, if there were any other choice he would've taken it. To begin with, he dreaded the voyage's goal. Of all the becursed lands in this becursed world, Hadin was the last place he wanted to visit. Secondly, as far as he knew such a voyage had only been accomplished once before: by Lord Asper many centuries ago when he'd journeyed to Hadin and back again.

No wonder the captain was moody and the sailors unwilling. Safar was paying them handsomely—many times more than they'd ever received before in their seafaring careers. He'd also promised rich bonuses when the voyage was complete.

However, these men had never strayed far from Esmir. Venturing only to the not-so-distant islands, such as Syrapis. They were ignorant men, had sometimes even worked as pirates, and had little knowledge of the wider world. But, ignorant as they were, in their many voyages they'd experienced first-hand what the scholars of Esmir had only speculated about.

Safar watched a great sea turtle swim frantically away from the path of the ship. It was a huge creature—big enough to seat a large man on its broad shell. Possibly a hundred years or more in age.

He smiled ruefully, thinking this was how all but the wisest scholars and priests saw the world they lived in. According to Esmirian myth, the world was borne on the back of a sea-turtle god. In turn, the continents that made up the world were carried by lesser turtle gods.

There were four such continents—confirmed in Asper's voyages. First there was Esmir— which in the language of the ancients simply meant The Land, or The Earth. Then Aroborus, the place of the forests. The third continent was Raptor, the land of the birds. A place they wouldn't visit until their return voyage.

Last of all was Hadin, land of the fires: a continent shattered by the forces at work there into a vast island chain that crouched at the bottom of the world.

The place, Asper said, where he waited at "Hadin's last gate."

Of course, Safar didn't think Asper would actually be waiting there. The old demon had been dead for a thousand years, after all.

Nor was Safar certain that he'd truly find a solution to the world's ills once he reached Hadin.

However, despite his uncertainties Safar was driven to act. His entire adult life had been devoted to this mission. And many had suffered and died as a result of his obsession to halt the poisonous cloud that was slowly killing the world.

And he had no doubt many more would meet similar fates before he was through.

To accomplish his goal, Asper said Safar would have to awaken the gods. Exactly what this meant, or how he'd go about it, Safar was far from certain. He'd have to wait until he arrived in Hadin to find out.

Safar wondered how his people would fare during his absence. Even if he were successful it was unlikely he'd survive the experience and return to Syrapis to find out. Would they prosper? Would they find happiness again? The happiness lost to them when he'd led them from their ancestral home, Kyrania—the Valley of the Clouds.

As he pondered these unanswerable questions his mind floated back to the last night he'd spent with his family, friends and fellow Kyranians.

*   *   *

Safar had invited all the Kyranians to a farewell feast, although only his closest confidants were aware of its purpose.

Long tables were set up in the main courtyard of the mountain fortress. Colorful lanterns were hung all around giving everything a cheerful atmosphere. The tables were heaped with every dish and delicacy he could manage to assemble in the short time he'd had to prepare. And the finest Timura jugs were set out, full of wine and beer and cold goat's milk sweetened with honey—this last for the children.

First Safar put on a little show to entertain the Kyranians and brighten their spirits. With the help of Biner and the other circus folk he performed many astounding acrobatic feats, spiced with glittering displays of magic.

Biner and Arlain put on their clown costumes and wowed the crowd with their most humorous antics. Safar also performed horse tricks with Khysmet, showing off the stallion's uncanny abilities.

Finally, when he thought the moment right, he asked them all to gather round for an announcement. There were more than a thousand Kyranians, so he had to stand on a table for all to see. He cracked a magical amplifying pellet so that no one would miss his words.

"My dear friends," he said, "the time has come to speak to you on a matter of the utmost importance."

Immediately his mother and sisters burst into tears. His father, face pale, straightened his shoulders and tried to look stoic. But it was hopeless, for several tears could be seen running down his cheeks. Safar's family had been told of his plans and could no longer hold back their emotions.

Everyone looked at them, a sense of dread chilling the air.

"I stand here before you with a grieving heart," Safar said. "I've known all of you my entire life. And we have been through so much together—good times and ill. So it is with great sadness and much reluctance that I now tell you that I must take my leave.

662

"Perhaps forever."

There was a stunned silence. Followed by shouts of, "No, Safar! It can't be! Stay with us! We love you, Safar! We love you!"

Safar bowed his head, letting the outpour flow over him until it was spent.

"Thank you, my friends," he said, eyes glistening with barely checked emotion. "But you must understand this isn't something I want to do. When I was a boy herding the village flock through the passes of the Gods' Divide I was given a sacred trust. And I cannot refuse what I have been called to do."

Foron leaped onto the table with him. "Please, Safar," he said. "You must listen to us. You are a great man. Still, you are only a man. You cannot prevent what the gods desire. Forget the outside world. Remain with us."

He made a sweeping gesture that took in the fortress and the mountains beyond. "This is a paradise, Safar. Just as you promised back in Kyrania. We had to fight for it, to be sure. But this is a wonderful place.

"Look about you, my friend. Look at all the plenty. There are fish in the sea begging to be netted. Forests full of game, rich earth eager for seed and fat herds of goats to be milked or slaughtered. And the mountain air is so clear and clean and sweet it's like drinking wine when you breathe."

"All you say is true," Safar replied. "But there are forces at work that will soon end this paradise. It will be destroyed, just as Kyrania was destroyed."

Foron shook his head. "No one doubts your wisdom, Safar," he said. "But in this one thing I must tell you that you are wrong. I can't believe it's necessary for you to leave us in order to fight whatever evil it is that threatens us all. Again, I beg you—remain with us.

"Allow us to fight with you. And if we win, what gladness. And if we lose, so be it. At least we'll all die together."

The crowd took up a chant: "Fight, fight, fight. Fight together!"

Safar let them chant for a time, then raised his hand for silence. When he got it, he said, "I wish with all my heart that what you said was true. But it isn't. Please let me show you so you can see for yourselves."

He gestured for Foron to step down. When he'd done so Safar said, "First, I beg you to send the children away. What you are about to witness is not a sight for young eyes."

After the children had gone—the babes borne away by the village grannies—Safar called again for everyone's attention. When he had it, he drew the shell trumpet from beneath his cloak. People gaped at it. They'd couldn't imagine the sea creature that had once inhabited the marvelous shell.

As he raised the trumpet to his lips Safar took a deep breath. And then he blew, long and hard.

Once again the sounds of the wondrous magical orchestra filled the air. The Kyranians murmured at the beauty of the music. Then they gasped when they saw the Spirit Rider suddenly appear on the fortress wall, shimmering like an apparition. Then, once again, the mural and the wall dissolved into nothingness.

As the solid stone dissolved there were loud cries of alarm as the Kyranians found themselves looking *down* on a yawning emptiness. It was as if they were at the edge of a sloping cliff and were to fall into a terrible abyss.

People clutched each other, the tables, the benches—anything to prevent themselves from plunging into the unknown.

Safar himself didn't know what was going to happen next. And when the music and then the scene changed his nails dug into his palms until they bled.

First came the familiar throb of the harvest drums. The conch shells wailing. The rhythmic slap of bare feet on sand and open palms on naked chests. And then they were looking down on the beautiful people of Hadin dancing before the smoking volcano. Their lovely harvest queen leading them in song:

"Her hair is night,
Her lips the moon;
Surrender. Oh, surrender.
Her eyes are stars,
Her heart the sun;
Surrender. Oh, surrender.

Her breasts are honey,
Her sex a rose;
Surrender. Oh, surrender.
Night and moon. Stars and Sun.
Honey and rose;
Lady, oh Lady, surrender.
Surrender. Surrender . . ."

Then the volcano erupted and the Kyranians screamed and turned their eyes away as the island people died their agonizing deaths.

Thankfully, the scene finally dissolved, giving way to a myriad of bubbling lights of many colors. The music took on a playful note and when the living picture realized itself, they saw an old sea turtle swimming comically over and through rolling waves of dark emerald.

There were a few giggles of relief. Some of the younger men and women cheered loudly for the turtle.

Another shift in the music occurred as the turtle came to land and painfully climbed onto a black rocky shore. There were birds everywhere, birds of all possible varieties.

A studious young Kyranian made an educated guess and shouted the name of this country: "It's Raptor—the land of the birds!"

Several scholarly men and women in the crowd murmured agreement.

The instruments took on the musical personalities of birds they saw. Some soaring with haunting cries. Some whistling melodious mating tunes. Some hawking and chattering over rocky nests. And everywhere there was the peep-peep-peep, of new life. Nestlings calling for their mothers and fathers to "feedmeloveme, feedmeloveme, feedmeloveme . . ."

But just as people were smiling, nodding in empathy at this feathered life, a huge green poisonous cloud swept over Raptor. Enormous ghostbats, shrilling and hungry flew out of the cloud. Followed by shrieking reptiles on leather wings.

Once again the Kyranians had to turn away at the killing horror that was visited upon the land.

This time no one laughed when the turtle paddled frantically away.

Now came the music of forests and rivers. Innocent song of clear-flowing creeks, mossy ponds and flowered paths that wound through an exotic jungle. Sweet pipes carried cooling breezes through the branches of every sort of tree imaginable. Wise oaks, foolish pines, swaying willows and forest giants lifting their aged heads into the very clouds.

They saw all the things the music spoke of and more. The scholarly youth proclaimed the land as Aroborus, the place of the forests. But no one had to hear him to know the answer.

Their attention was riveted on the turtle, pausing just off a gentle, sandy beach. Its blunt head and sad eyes lifted to the skies. Then the Kyranians groaned as the poisonous cloud swept in, bearing all the horrors they'd seen before.

The turtle paddled away, so weak she could barely negotiate the slow-rolling seas.

Now the music took on a hard, desperately driving note. Shimmering scene dissolved into shimmering scene, one after the other. But each one had the same subject: the turtle swimming and bobbing on endless seas. Sometimes the water was the deep green that indicated of enormous depths. Sometimes it was bright blue and cheery. And sometimes it was slate-gray and forbidding, with glistening icebergs shot with eerie rainbow colors: layers of purple and pink and green and sapphire-blue.

And always, in the background, was the poisonous cloud sweeping over the endless oceans. Fish turning up white-bellied, dead in its passage. Seals and otters and even enormous whales shriveling to the bone as they breathed their last.

Dead birds plummeting from the sky in such numbers that it seemed the heavens had become an avian graveyard, opening up to rain a torrent of feathered corpses.

Finally, the turtle climbed up on a pebbled beach. It barely had the strength to pull itself from the foaming surf. By now, no one was surprised when they recognized the long, curving shoreline. It was the same place where the Kyranians had landed three years before.

Someone—it wasn't the student—voiced the name in a low, drawn-out hiss: Syrapis!

The turtle struggled, using the last of its strength to dig a shallow nest with its flippers. Then it squatted over the hole and began to lay its eggs. Each one membrane-white, turning to ivory as it met the air and fell into the hole. The shadow of an embryo turtle showed through the thin shell.

The turtle covered the eggs as best she could, shoveling pebbles and sand. Then she lifted her head and saw the killing cloud drifting overhead.

A single tear formed, then fell.

And the turtle died.

The music stopped and the fortress wall re-formed itself. Leaving a silence moist and thick and twisted like the rough blankets kicked off in a nightmare that refuses to end. As before, there was no sign of the mural.

All eyes turned to Safar. He thought he'd never seen such haunted looks. Such fearful looks. So much begging and pleading for rescue—for deliverance.

Although not one word was said, the silence was like a shout.

Safar said: "Do you see? Do you finally see?"

And they did.

*　　　*　　　*

Safar leaned against the rail, the *Nepenthe* leaping and bucking under him as it turned and caught the wind for Hadin.

He saw the turtle paddle over a ten-foot wave. Disappear into its trough, then climb the watery incline on the other side.

A light hand touched his shoulder. It was Leiria's.

She watched the turtle's progress with him for awhile. And just as it became a dot on the horizon she whispered, "Gods speed, my friend. Gods speed!"

CHAPTER TWENTY-FOUR

THE KING'S SPIES

The old goat strained wearily at the harness, hauling a little cart over the broken pavement. Aboard the cart was a legless beggar dressed in the rags of a soldier. Crying, "Baksheesh! Baksheesh for the blessing of the gods!"

The beggar was moving through the tawdry harbor district of the Syrapian town of Xiap, so his pleas for alms went unheeded. A drunken sailor spat at the beggar when he offered his bowl, a single coin rattling against the battered tin sides. A syphilitic whore mocked his injuries, wondering aloud what else he had lost besides his legs.

But the scar-faced beggar ignored the insults, switching the goat's flanks to keep moving. And all the while he cried his plaintive, "Baksheesh! Baksheesh for the blessing of the gods!"

He was making his way along a pot-holed freight road that ran alongside the docks. Out in the Bay of Xiap were twelve of the thirteen tall ships that made up the Kyranian naval force. Several lighters were moving toward the docks, ferrying sailors on liberty to a night of debauchery.

If a suspicious man had been following the beggar he might—just might—have caught the slight jerk of the wounded veteran's head when he noted the missing ship.

And if that same distrustful fellow had stayed close to the cart after that he'd have seen the beggar switch the goat into a quicker pace. Making straight for a seedy waterfront tavern—still rattling his bowl, still crying his cry, but with much less intensity.

The beggar pulled up in front of the tavern, anchored the goat with a rope tied to a heavy stone and hoisted himself off the cart onto knee stumps padded with leather. He had brawny arms and muscular shoulders, so he hopped up onto the porch with ease—bearing his weight on blocks of wood clutched in each fist.

A moment later he was through the door and swinging himself familiarly along a narrow passage between the rough, ale-stained tables.

The place was nearly empty and he had no trouble picking out his favorite spot. He grabbed the edge of the bar and swung himself up onto a stool with acrobatic agility.

The laconic barkeep grinned at him through blackened stumps of teeth. "Mornin', Tabusir. Bit early for the grog today, ain'tcha?"

"Thirst don't know th' time o' day, Hazan," Tabusir said. "'Sides, th' pickin's been sweeter'n a whore's smile on payday."

He slapped a silver coin on the bar. "Got this one right off," he said. Tabusir shook his purse. Hazan's eyes glittered at the jingling music of minted coin. "Primed th' pump for six, seven more."

Hazan grew friendlier still, filling a tankard to the brim and planting it before Tabusir. "Yer the luckiest beggar I ever seed," he said in most respectful tones. "Most of the lads get nothin' but empty bellies in these parts."

"It's me charmin' ways," Tabusir laughed. "Plus I spin a good yarn 'bout how I lost me legs in th' service of th' good King Rhodes. Fightin' Hanadu's enemies and all."

He shrugged. "Course, it don't hurt that th' yarns be mostly true."

Tabusir rapped the coin on the bar. "Yer lookin' thirsty, too, Hazan. Buy one fer yerself outta this."

Hazan poured one for himself with pleasure. "Yeah, yer sure did yer share, Tabusir," he agreed. "Nobody can deny it. Least, not in front of me, they can't. I'd box their ears for insultin' such a good friend."

Tabusir nodded toward the open door—and the harbor waters beyond. "Speakin' of th' enemy," he said, "better start waterin' down the ale. Saw a whole mess of 'em headin' out from th' fleet."

Hazan grinned broadly. "Music to a hard-workin' barkeep's ears," he said. "Lads musta got bonuses, or somethin'."

The barkeep shouted up the stairs to wake the whores and bargirls. Then he turned back to Tabusir. "I wouldn't tell this to nobody else, Tabusir," he said in low tones. "But bein' as yer such a good friend . . . I ain't *that* sorry that the Kyranians took over this here port.

"We was sewer-dirt poor when Rhodes was still runnin' things in Xiap. But ever since the blockade, why, times have shined, they have. Paid all the bills, got a nice line of credit with them tight-fists suppliers. And I'm even thinkin' of knockin' out some walls and puttin' in more tables."

He nodded at the stairs, where the women were already tromping down, sleepy-eyed and cranky at being awakened so early. "And some more beds, too. Lots more beds!"

Tabusir pounded the bar and laughed as if Hazan had just told the greatest jest. "Ain't that th' truth," he said. "Only goes to show that sometimes it pays to lose th' war!"

Hazan joined in the laughter. Then they heard the loud voices approaching and a moment later the first wave of enemy sailors burst into the room. And they kept coming. And coming. Until Hazan and the women were hard pressed to keep up with the various desires of all the lusty, thirsty sailors.

Tabusir made himself companionable. Buying drinks, telling jokes, nodding in sympathy when the sailors griped about their officers who overworked them without mercy. Most of them said they preferred their previous lives as pirates. Although they allowed the pay in their former careers wasn't as good—and was certainly more chancy.

"But at least a pirate's a free man," one sailor said. "And he's got a say in how the ship's run. But all we do is drill and train and patrol. Like we was in a *real navy, or somethin'*."

The name that seemed to come up the most was that of Lord Coralean—a name well-known to Tabusir. And the drunker the sailors got the more they cursed the caravan master. As near as Tabusir could make out, Coralean was generous with his gold, but was entirely too domineering for these men—all criminals who'd fled Coralean's brand of regimentation long ago.

"It's even worse since he cut out the *Nepenthe* and sent it off on some godsforsaken mission," said one sailor, who sounded a little more educated than the others. "Now we have more area to patrol and they're working us like slaves."

Although he didn't show it, Tabusir was most interested in this bit of information. It answered the question about the missing ship. He plied the man with more drink and when the fellow tried to hire the services of a pretty whore and came up short of cash, Tabusir kindly made up the difference.

In return, he learned some things that turned those few coppers into a fat purse of gold.

*　　　*　　　*

Miser though he was, King Rhodes did not begrudge a single coin of the eventual reward he gave the handsome young spy. Why, it was easily worth half his treasury.

Although he certainly didn't tell Tabusir that when he stood tall and straight before him, delivering his news.

"I confirmed the report in several other taverns," Your Majesty," Tabusir assured him. "And then I went up the coast to visit some other ports and the story was the same."

Kalasariz stirred in his nesting place within the king. *Press him some more*, the spymaster said to Rhodes. *Safar Timura is a very cunning man. It could be one of his tricks.*

"My only hesitation," Rhodes said to Tabusir, "is that you seem to have come by this information so easily. This isn't just a leak of the Kyranian plans, but a damned big flood-gate you have opened."

Tabusir nodded. "That's a good caution, Your Majesty. And I thought the same thing myself. Which is why I visited those other places, instead of coming directly here. The thing is, Majesty, these sailors have no loyalties. They're for hire to the highest bidder. And no matter what their superiors might say, they don't feel beholden to any master or cause."

Kalasariz mental-whispered: *Even so . . .*

Rhodes took the cue. "Even so, the events you described could have been staged for our benefit. And purposely leaked to the sailors."

Tabusir shook his head. "Forgive me, Majesty, but I don't believe so. The story was given out by Lord Coralean that *Nepenthe* was only assigned a different mission—a mission that still involved the blockade. The idea was that the *Nepenthe* would become a roving ship, going wherever the captain thought necessary to stop any supplies or weapons getting through to us.

"However, one of the *Nepenthe*'s crew was badly injured shortly after she took sail. The captain thought the sailor was dying anyway and sent him back."

Kalasariz wasn't satisfied. *That's pretty damned humane, of the captain, don't you think, majesty?*

Rhodes agreed. "Why didn't the captain just let him die?" he asked Tabusir. "And throw the body over the side. That's what I'd do, rather than risk security."

"So would I, Your Majesty," Tabusir said. "But sailors are very superstitious. Especially this lot. I think the captain didn't want to spook the rest of the crew. Or, maybe it was Coralean. In either case, they thought it best to accept the risk. The injured man looked *near* as dead. How could they know he'd have a miraculous—and, for them, unlucky—recovery?

"In fact, Majesty, the man was a malingerer and a coward. First, he hears that the *Nepenthe* is sailing away from Syrapis for parts unknown. Then the Kyranian airship joins them. Coward though he might be, the man's no fool. It's obvious to him that if the Kyranian land forces are willing to part with the airship, something desperate—and quite dangerous—must be in the wind.

"So he injures himself—but not that badly—and takes a potion to give him a fever. So he'd look like he was at death's door. It's an old sailor's trick—well-known to this band of criminals.

"Then the moment he's returned to the fleet he takes an antidote. Recovers. And then goes off with his companions to drink and talk like, well . . . like a drunken sailor, Majesty!"

Kalasariz mental whispered: *Admirable logic!*

Rhodes nodded. "Well done!" he said to Tabusir. He took a heavy, gem-encrusted ring from his finger and gave it to the young spy. "Take this to the Treasurer," he said with a wide smile. "And turn it in for whatever it's worth."

Tabusir was well pleased. He dropped to the floor and knocked his head against the pavement, thanking Rhodes profusely. Then he took his leave.

But just before the guards escorted him out, he turned back.

"Pardon, Majesty, but there's one other thing . . ."

"Yes?" Rhodes asked.

"There's a tavern at the port run by a man named Hazan."

"What of him?" Rhodes wanted to know.

"He's a traitor, Majesty," Tabusir said. "And no friend of Hanadu's."

Rhodes shrugged. "What do I care what a lowly tavern keeper thinks, or does?"

Tabusir nodded. "I understand, Majesty. Only . . . I was thinking . . . if you were to quietly do away with him . . . then substitute one of your spies . . . Well, the tavern is an excellent place for intelligence, Majesty, and . . ."

He let the rest drift away. It was too obvious, in to his mind, and might bore the king.

"That's good advice, young Tabusir," Rhodes said. "I'll think on it." And he waved a hand, dismissing him.

Tabusir bowed low and exited.

Kalasariz said: *I quite like the cut of that fellow. Reminds me of myself when I was just getting started in the spy business.*

Rhodes said, "Should I promote him?"

Yes, yes, Kalasariz replied. *An excellent idea. But we should keep him close to us, hmm? He'd be useful for, shall we say, very personal errands?*

The king thought this excellent advice. Then, armed with Tabusir's intelligence, he descended the long dark stairs to consult his mother.

CHAPTER TWENTY-FIVE

THE IMPS OF FOREBODING

For several weeks all was peaceful aboard the *Nepenthe*. The ocean was calm, the wind a sailor's dream. Brutar, the aptly-named captain of the ship, eased off on his men and the crew became less surly and settled into a somewhat more orderly routine.

The sea teemed with life. They sailed through enormous schools of fish, some of which were quite exotic and so colorful it was like sailing through a magical artist's pallet. Reds and greens and yellows flowing by in an endless stream.

Once they saw a huge crocodile chasing the fish and the colors spurted in all directions as they fled its gaping jaws.

The birds became so used to the *Nepenthe* that they grew quite tame—settling on the rails and mast spars within easy reach. The sailors thought this a good omen and started feeding them by hand.

It became a common but always comical sight to see a burly, scarred ex-pirate cooing over a seahawk as he tenderly fed it bits of biscuit and salt-beef.

Leiria and Jooli kept busy exercising the young Kyranian soldiers who had joined the expedition. Leiria and Palimak had hand-picked the lads, being sure to include Renor and Sinch who had proved themselves in many battles and were corporals now. She'd also brought along Sergeant. Hamyr, a grizzled old warrior with much experience to keep all the lads in line.

There'd been so many volunteers that Safar had assembled the entire army to console all those being left behind. And to remind them that the safety of their families and friends was at stake.

Safar suspected the sight of the twenty crack soldiers being put through their paces by the two magnificent warrior women had a little to do with the more friendly attitude of Captain Brutar and his crew.

Not only was the Kyranian equipment the best they'd seen, but the fighting tricks that the Kyranians displayed were enough to give any potential mutineer pause.

And, of course, there was the ever-present airship hovering over the *Nepenthe.* Some of the sailors had witnessed Biner and his circus folk in battle in the past—raining death from the sky—and word soon spread that they were to be feared even more than the soldiers.

Every once in a while Safar trotted Khysmet out of the comfortable stable he'd had specially constructed for him. First he'd have the men create a small arena on the main deck, covering the wood with a thick layer of sand to make the footing easier for the stallion. Then, with the help of Leiria and a few of the soldiers, he'd put on a thrilling one-horse cavalry display.

Weaving and bobbing in the saddle, while wielding a wooden sword. Ducking completely beneath Khysmet and coming up on the other side, like a warrior from the great plains of Esmir. Or rearing the stallion back onto his hind legs and letting him paw the air with his steel-shod hooves as if Khysmet were fighting off attacking infantrymen.

It always made for a good show and further strengthened the wary respect the sailors had for the Kyranians.

After awhile Safar felt confident enough to leave the *Nepenthe* and spend some time with his old friends aboard the airship. Sometimes Palimak came with him, sometimes Leiria or Jooli. But he always made certain that at least two of his commanders remained on the ship to keep watch on the seamen.

Traveling in the airship took him back to the carefree days of his youth when Methydia had rescued him from the desert. He recalled those times while scudding through empty skies like a cloud, watching the world pass beneath his feet. Standing at the rail, looking down at the small, sea-bound figures aboard the *Nepenthe.* Or simply sprawling on the deck, surrounded by friends and talking over old times and adventures.

The circus folk never forgot their true life's purpose, which was entertainment. They were always rehearsing or trying out new tricks. Sometimes Safar would join them and for an hour or so he could imagine he was one of them again. Sailing across Esmir, staging shows at festivals, fairs, small towns . . . wherever the winds took them.

It was only during these impromptu moments that Safar could forget the nature of his mission and the heavy responsibility he had to all those who'd agreed to help him. But more than anything, it made him forget how alone he was.

It was a state of being that was entirely his own fault. Ever since his escape from the spellworld he'd kept a careful emotional distance from everyone. Especially from Palimak and Leiria. He made sure he was never alone with either one of them. He wasn't certain why he found this necessary, except that he was edgy about engaging in talk that went beneath the surface.

Safar could tell they were both a little bewildered by this, although they hadn't had a chance as yet to think on it and be hurt.

Sometimes, late at night, he'd think about his dilemma. Pick and poke at it like a child toying with a small wound.

Oh, he loved them both, there was no doubt about that. And there was nothing he wanted more than to embrace his son and be a father to him once again. Or to draw Leiria close and seek her kisses and warm comfort again as he had so many years before when they had been lovers.

But for some reason he felt awkward with them—no, not awkward. That was definitely the wrong word. What was it then?

And then one night the answer came to him: He felt as if he'd somehow betrayed them.

But why? This made no sense. He'd never done anything to harm them. And would never dream of doing so.

Or would he?

When he thought that, he became fearful. Alien to himself. As if there were another part of him—a part he'd never known about before—that lurked in the shadows . . . waiting. To do what, he couldn't say. Except this other part had no love for Palimak and Leiria. And did not want the best for them.

As soon as he thought that he suddenly became very calm. The strangeness vanished and he drank down his wine, feeling whole again.

Odd, how the mind played tricks on itself when the wine was deep and the hour late.

*   *   *

Other people noted Safar's forced solitude. One of them was Jooli.

She found herself powerfully attracted to this strange man with eyes as blue as the seas they sailed upon. Back at the Kyranian fortress she'd seen the young women approach him, but to no avail.

At the time it had puzzled her that Safar was able to resist their advances. On the other hand, she didn't sense that he preferred men or boys over women.

Not that this would've seemed odd to her. In Syrapis, there were many men who quoted the old saying: "Women are for babies, boys are for pleasure."

Just as there were many women who sang the merry little tune: *"It is our duty, misses,/ to breed a mighty army;/ but we save our best kisses/ for our sisters who bliss us;/ and know all men to be barmy!"*

Since they'd met, Jooli had given Safar no indication of her interest. After all, it would be unseemly for a royal person to express such sentiments—unless she was certain they'd be returned.

However, during the early weeks of the voyage, when she'd consumed more wine than normal, Jooli had found herself pacing the deck outside her stateroom as restless as a she-tiger in season.

She kept thinking how handsome Safar was. The dark, curly hair. The boyish grin. The startling blue eyes beneath mysterious brows. The ripened lips. The strong neck and torso. And those cursedly graceful legs, revealed when he carelessly crossed them and his tunic rode high.

Adding even stronger spice was the magnetic aura of his wizardry. She'd never met anyone who possessed such powers. To embrace a man like that would be like embracing a storm. Witch joined to wizard loin to loin. The images were a sleep-disturbing aphrodisiac of the worst sort.

One night she encountered Leiria on the deck, who was doing a bit of pacing of her own. Immersed in her own hot-blooded thoughts, Jooli at first didn't recognize the similarities of Leiria's symptoms.

Casual talk soon turned more personal. "I'm not one who impresses easily," Jooli said. "But I've certainly grown to admire Lord Timura."

"There's much to admire," Leiria agreed. "Good people are never disappointed when they come to know him better. You can't go wrong if he gives you his friendship."

671

Jooli nodded. "I thought as much." She hesitated, then, "I'll be blunt," she said. "Woman to woman, I find it strange that no one shares his bed. Is he some sort of priest who has taken a vow of celibacy?"

Leiria smiled. "Nothing like that," she said.

Jooli frowned. "He has no wife?"

"No."

"No one he's betrothed to?"

"Never in his life."

Jooli hissed with exasperation. "What's wrong, then?" she asked. "Every man of his rank and prestige I've ever known had whole harems to pleasure them."

Leiria's eyes took on a faraway look as she thought about this. Absently, she said, "Safar could have that as well." Then she nodded, as if coming to a conclusion. "But he's definitely a one-woman man."

Then Jooli noticed moisture forming in her friend's eyes when Leiria added, "He found that woman a long time ago. But she died."

"If you mean Methydia," Jooli said, "I've heard that tale from the circus folk. But I also got the idea that although he loved her—and she loved him—it wasn't a permanent thing. An older woman . . . a sorcerous mentor . . . a passing fancy for the two of them."

"That's true," Leiria said. Her voice was soft, memory going back over the years to her first meeting with Safar. Then, so faint Jooli could bare hear her: "Although I didn't realize that in the beginning."

Leiria's eyes hazed over as her mind flashed back to that time so many years ago . . .

*   *   *

When Leiria awoke she found herself nestled in the crook of Safar's arm. Ever so gently, he was trying to disentangle that arm. Feeling warm and loving, she smiled at him. Pulling him closer, wanting to give him more of what they'd enjoyed all night. But Safar was tense. She sensed that he felt like he was betraying another.

Safar disengaged from her politely, but firmly. "I have duties to attend to," he said.

At first Leiria pouted. Then she giggled and got up, saying, "I mustn't be selfish and take all your strength, my lord."

Faint as his answering smile was, Leiria loved it. The intensity of her feelings surprised her. Not long before she'd been the warrior concubine of King Protarus. How could she fall in love with another so quickly? Embarrassed, and confused, Leiria arose hastily and pulled on her clothes.

But she couldn't help but comment, letting words flow without guard. "You called out another woman's name in the night," she said.

Leiria made certain her tones were light, but she couldn't hide the hurt. She saw Safar's eyes flicker, sensing her pain. And she loved him all the more because of that.

Safar said, "I'm sorry."

Leiria forced an oh-so-casual shrug. "I don't mind," she said. "It's good that your heart is faithful."

She kept her head down to hide emotion, pretending to concentrate on her harness and weapons. She said, "The king has ordered me to comfort you and guard you with my life."

Then Leiria raised her head and she couldn't help revealing the tears welling in her eyes. "The king orders," she said with deeply felt conviction, "but I do it gladly."

She straightened, every inch a royal warrior. She said, with all the conviction she could muster: "I will guard you and I will be this other woman for you for as long as you like."

Leiria almost took her leave with that. But she found there was one more thing it was impor-

tant for her to say. "*Perhaps someday,*" *she said, desperately fighting to keep her voice from trembling,* "*It will be my name you speak instead of . . . hers.*"

And then Leiria fled.

*   *   *

Leiria came back to the present, feeling Jooli's eyes on her. "The woman's name was Nerisa," she said. "Safar loved her and she died tragically."

She shrugged. "What's more tragic is that Safar believes it was his fault. Just as he thinks that he is to blame for Methydia's death."

"Is there any truth to it?" Jooli asked.

"None at all," Leiria said. "But Safar's like that. He takes on guilt faster than anyone I've ever met."

Jooli eyed her. "You're in love with him, too," she said.

Leiria blushed. She said, low, "Yes. We were . . . lovers once."

"And he sent you away," Jooli asked, "because of his guilt?"

Leiria wiped an eye. "No, I sent him away," she said. "Or I left, at any rate. But it was because of his guilt, yes."

"And now you wished you hadn't?" Jooli asked.

Leiria only nodded.

"What are you going to do about it?" Jooli prodded.

Leiria shook her head. "Nothing," she said. "What's done is done."

Jooli put a hand on her shoulder. "Sister," she said, "thank you for keeping me from making a big mistake."

She looked Leiria straight in the eye. "Let me return the favor by giving you a word of advice. You are wrong, sister. You were wrong then and are wrong now. And when the right time comes, be sure to correct the mistake. And you'll both be happier for it."

Then she turned and walked back to her cabin. Leiria stared after her, too surprised to answer.

*   *   *

"Something's wrong with my father," Palimak said.

He was lying on his bunk, arms behind his head, the two Favorites perched on his chest nibbling sugar rolls and cheese.

Gundara belched. "Of course there's something wrong with him," he said. "He's a master, isn't he? Masters always have worms in their brains." Another belch. "Present company not included, of course."

"Speaking of worms," Gundaree said. "I found a nice fat one in a biscuit the other day. It was dee-lish-shous! Better than old cheese."

"You're such a disgusting thing," Gundara sneered. "How can you stand yourself?"

"Worms, worms, worms," Gundaree said.

"Stop it!" Gundara shouted. "You're making me sick!"

"Big fat juicy ones," Gundaree continued. "Worms in your sweets. Worms in your sugar buns. Worms, worms, worms!"

"Shut up, you!"

"Don't you say shut up! You shut up!"

"Shut up, shut up, shut—Ouch!"

Gundara rubbed his backside. Palimak had just given it a stinging flick with his finger. "Why'd you do that?" he whined. "I wasn't the one talking about worms."

673

"And I didn't say shut up first! You—ouch!"

Now it was Gundaree's turn to rub his tender behind.

"Do I have your attention now, boys?" Palimak asked.

The twins muttered, "Yes, Little Master," while rubbing their rears.

"Now, I was talking about my father," Palimak said. "There's something wrong, but I can't figure out what it is. Ever since he got back, he's been acting . . . well . . . I don't know . . ." He shrugged . . . "Strange, I guess."

"Seems the same to me," Gundara said.

"Me too," Gundaree agreed.

"Why are you asking *us*, Little Master?" Gundara wanted to know. "We don't care how people act. People are people, which is pretty stupid."

"Yeah," Gundaree said. "People are sometimes stupid one way. Sometimes stupid another. So it's all the same to us. Stupid is stupid. What more is there to know?"

Palimak sighed, trying not to become impatient. He fed them more sugar buns and cheese to shut them up.

"I was talking about magic," he said. "Could something have happened to him in that spellworld that somehow affected him?"

Gundara shrugged. "Sure, it could have," he said. "But it didn't."

"How do you know?" Palimak asked.

Gundaree snickered. "There he goes, just like people. Acting stupid."

"I'm also part demon," Palimak reminded him.

Gundara belched loudly. "What's the difference?" he said. "Stupid with fingers, or stupid with talons. Still stupid."

"All right," Palimak said. "I'm being stupid. But if I'm so stupid, how am I supposed to know unless somebody tells me."

Gundaree giggled. "That's our job," he said. "Stay with you always and tell you when you're being stupid."

"Not that you ever listen," Gundara said. "Lots of times we say, 'Run, Palimak, run! Run for your life!'" He gave Palimak an admonishing look. "But you don't run. And someday they're going to catch you. Mark my words!"

"I'm marking them," Palimak said. "But you still didn't answer my question. Why am I being stupid about my father?"

Gundaree gave a long and weary sigh. "Because, Little Master," he said, "if something magic was going on we'd *know it, right? And so would you. You're a wizard!*"

"But you're both better at that kind of thing than I am," Palimak said. "Much better. The witch who made you gave you heightened powers so you could protect your masters." He pointed at the door. "Why, if something that meant me harm was walking toward this at cabin this very minute, you'd both know. And warn me. Right?"

Gundara shuddered. "Something's coming, Little Master!" he suddenly squealed.

"Stop fooling around," Palimak said, getting irritated. "I'm serious about this!"

"And so are we!" Gundaree cried. "Look out, Little Master, here it comes!"

And at that moment Palimak heard a heavy body thump against his cabin door.

CHAPTER TWENTY-SIX
CORALEAN

Coralean was tossing fitfully in his bunk when he heard the scratching at his cabin door.

He'd spent a miserable day both cajoling and threatening his fleet captains, all of whom had been stricken with jealousy over the handsome sums paid to the crew of the *Nepenthe.*

Never mind that none of them had actually wanted to join Safar on his mysterious mission. Never mind that the camel had been let out of the stable and now everyone knew Safar's mission was a dangerous around-the-world voyage with minimal chance of success.

The mere thought that other men were enjoying fatter purses than theirs was more than those pirates could bear. They wanted more money, they wanted it now, or they would lift the blockade on King Rhodes.

In the end, Coralean had used all his persuasive powers to get them to agree upon a lesser sum. Although he'd sweetened the contracts with promises of bonuses for every month spent on station patrolling the Syrapian coast.

The problem was that Coralean was uncertain how successful he'd actually been. Blockade work was incredibly boring, sailing up and down one sector day and night with only occasional breaks for debauchery at free ports such as Xiap.

These men were used to action and now that Syrapis was more or less pacified they were all yearning for their former lives—lives that had been spent plying their trade as thieving cutthroats.

In a way, he didn't blame them. Coralean was just as bored. He was also bitterly disappointed that he couldn't have sailed with Safar. That's where the action would be, no doubt about it. Moreover, he worried that without his skills as a negotiator—won through many years of running caravans across the wilds of Esmir—Safar's chances of success would be much less.

But, he thought, what other choice did his dear friend have? Safar needed wise old Coralean at home in Syrapis commanding the naval fleet that kept the Kyranians safe from the quarrelsome kings and queens of Hunan. Especially that devil Rhodes. That eater of camel dung. That intestinal worm of deceit.

There was no telling when and where Rhodes would strike next.

The caravan master snorted. Just let him try! Coralean, former bull of the land, was now the bull of the sea. If Rhodes launched an attack he wouldn't stand a chance against wily old Coralean!

That thought alone should have sweetened the caravan master's sleep. But he had other, more immediate, frustrations. He ached for the comfort of one his wives. Unfortunately, of the twenty-three women who constantly praised him as husband and lover, he'd only taken Eeda with him on this trip to the fleet.

Eeda was his newest bride. Barely eighteen, she was younger than many of Coralean's fifty children. Lusty and adventurous in bed, Eeda was so sweet-tempered that only one or two of his wives appeared jealous. And he had no doubt he could cure that jealousy when he returned home, bearing gifts of jewels, rich cloth and his ardent attention.

At the moment, however, Coralean wished mightily he hadn't delayed his husbandly duties. Upon his arrival at the fleet, Eeda, poor thing, had taken ill. Apparently she was newly with child and suffered from that sickness of early pregnancy. The result was that she had taken to her bed—leaving Coralean alone in his.

Not that he begrudged her the rest.

Was not Coralean the most understanding of husbands, who doted on his wives? Did he not see to their every need, even anticipating such niceties as insisting that each one should always have a private room that they could retreat to in times such as these?

Coralean groaned and turned uncomfortably in his bunk. Wishing that sometimes, just sometimes, he wasn't such a mighty bull of a man. Whose powerful seed took root so swiftly and easily that he had to deny himself the most important of all his pleasures.

It was at that moment he heard the scratching at his door.

Ah ha! he thought. It must be Eeda. Her sickness had passed and now she longed for the strong, lusty arms of her bull, her Coralean.

Eagerly he rose from his bunk and went to the door, white sleeping shirt swirling around his massive frame like a tent battered by the desert winds. His hand went to the latch, but just before he threw back the lock he hesitated.

What if it wasn't Eeda? What if it was someone who meant Coralean harm? One of Rhodes' spies, perhaps. It would be difficult, but not impossible, for an assassin to swim or row the two miles from Xiap and slip on board under the cover of night.

How would the assassin know which cabin was Coralean's? Again, a not impossible task. Perhaps the killer had a colleague aboard. These men were pirates, after all. To them, Coralean's life was worth no more than the coin he could keep heaping into their palms.

One of them might not have been completely satisfied with Coralean's bargain and high have decided to get as much as he could all at once by betraying the caravan master to Rhodes' hired killers.

Coralean's lust turned to anger. A man of many enemies—none of which he believed he deserved—he had not lived so long by ignoring his instincts.

Again, he heard the scratching. But this time, instead of sweet Eeda, he imagined a sharp-faced killer with a dagger poised on the other side of the door.

Coralean snatched up his sword and at the same time ripped the door wide. A figure was crouched on the floor and the caravan master's blade was swinging down, ready to split the assassin in two, when he heard a small cry of terror.

"Lord and master!"

It was Eeda!

Coralean caught himself just in time and stayed the blow.

His heart hammering from what he'd almost done, Coralean leaned down and drew the girl to her feet.

"I'm so sorry, little one," he said, embracing her. "I didn't mean to frighten you. How can you ever forgive your Coralean? Who believed his dearest wife was an assassin at his door."

To his surprise, Eeda hissed, "Silence," and pushed him back into the room. She whirled, softly shut and latched the door, then turned back.

"They're not at the door yet, my lord husband," she whispered. "But they'll be here soon!"

Coralean frowned. Lovely and young as Eeda might be, she was the daughter of a wild Syrapian chieftain. And was well-experienced in matters of the assassin's knife. Taking her word that danger was afoot, he hastily drew on his clothes.

"Who are these men, dear one?" he rumbled. "And how do you know what they plan?"

"Earlier my illness chilled me, lord husband," she said. "And so I had closed the little round window in my cabin. But then I began to feel feverish and longed for fresh air.

So I opened the window, hoping there might be a sea breeze. The window was so small, however, that the breeze was faint. So I put my face close to get all the air I could."

The caravan master slipped his boots on. "Go on, dear one," he said. "Tell Coralean what happened next."

"As you know, lord husband," she continued, "my cabin is below the captain's. And his little round window was open too."

"It's called a porthole, dear one," Coralean corrected her. Eeda was very much a landswoman and had no experience with terms of the sea.

Eeda shrugged. "Thank you for instructing me, lord husband," she said.

But her tone was just sharp enough for Coralean to realize she wasn't thanking him at all. The caravan master warmed even more to her. What a sassy wench she was!

"Pray continue, little one," Coralean urged.

Eeda nodded, catching the implication of an apology. Which was as far as Coralean would ever go with one of his wives.

"I heard the captain speaking to some other men," she said. "I don't know who the other men were, but I could tell right off they weren't crewmen. And from their barbaric accents I was positive they were from Hunan."

"Rhodes' men!" Coralean growled, buckling on his sword.

"None other, my lord husband," Eeda said. "My dear lord father was a prince unsurpassed by any in the number of men he hated. But of all his enemies, he despised King Rhodes the most."

"Another reason for Coralean to admire your father," the caravan master said. "Now, tell me, dear one. Did you hear what these men planned?"

"Yes, lord husband," Eeda replied. "They intend to kill your soldiers. Then capture you and hold you for ransom."

"Let them try," Coralean growled, hand going to the hilt of his sword.

"I believe I said they intend to," Eeda pointed out. Poking at Coralean's manly pride a little harder than perhaps a good wife should. The caravan master frowned, but said nothing. "You should also know that this isn't the only ship in danger. Several of the other captains have also thrown in with Rhodes. Or at least that's what I heard one of the men claim."

Her pretty brow furrowed as she thought of something else. "About that man, lord husband," she said. "The captain used his name. It was Tabusir. Lord Tabusir. And it was my impression that this conspiracy was his idea. And that he has much at stake with King Rhodes to see it's carried out properly."

Just then, Coralean heard bootsteps thundering overhead. Then the wild cries of surprised, brutally awakened soldiers as Tabusir's assassins attacked them in their sleep.

He started to buckle on his armor, preparing to rush up on deck and join the fray. But then he heard the sound of many men coming down the stairway, then along to corridor to his door.

Overhead, the sounds of the fighting had ceased. He could be of no help there.

"Pardon, lord husband," Eeda said.

And he looked down to see that she'd found his battle ax. She pointed at the porthole.

"Perhaps you could make the little round window bigger with this," she said.

"By the gods, woman, you are a wonder!" Coralean roared, not bothering to hide his voice from his enemies.

Eeda blushed and bobbed her head. "Thank you, my lord husband," she said prettily.

Then she drew a dagger from her bodice and stood guard at the door while Coralean hacked at the "little round window" until it was large enough for him to pass through.

The men were breaking down the door when he grabbed Eeda by the waist and hurled her through the enlarged porthole.

And just as the last door plank exploded inward and the men poured into the cabin, Coralean forced his own bulk through the hole and fell into the dark waters below.

As he emerged sputtering to the surface two small, strong hands grabbed him by the collar, pulling him under again.

Coralean kicked up, trying to get a breath, only to be pulled under again.

Finally, he yanked the hands away, grabbed a slim figure about the waist and got his head above water to drag in a shuddering breath.

"Forgive, me lord husband!" Eeda cried. "But I cannot swim."

Above, he could hear men shouting in the cabin from which he'd just escaped. "He's gotten away! After him!"

There was a thunder of boots on the lower deck.

"Take a breath!" Coralean commanded Eeda.

The moment he felt her chest fill with air he dived back under the water, pulling a frantic Eeda with him.

Arrows and spears rained into the water after him.

Coralean held Eeda tight with one arm and kicked deeper. Following the bow, he swam under the ship to emerge on the other side.

"Get on my back," he whispered to Eeda.

Quickly, she did as he directed and he kicked away from the ship, strong arms powering them through the waves.

Behind him he heard the cries of his enemies as they spotted him again. But he ignored them and kept swimming, heading for another ship about a quarter-mile away.

He prayed they wouldn't have sense enough to lower boats and pursue him until it was too late.

His prayers were answered as he heard the splash of arrows falling nearby. They were going for the quick kill, but it was night and the glowing red Demon Moon made the light tricky.

If Dame Fortune smiled they'd keep missing until he was out of range.

She must have had two heads that night, because while one smiled, the other frowned. For although he and Eeda escaped the arrows, they heard the sounds of fighting as they approached the other ship. Obviously, there was no refuge to be found there.

Coralean stopped, treading water, while he looked around to see what his next move ought to be. There was a fire burning on the next closest ship, so he knew that was no good.

Be damned, this meant three ships had gone over to the enemy!

Eeda gently tugged his collar for attention. "Look, lord husband," she whispered. "To the left!"

Coralean paddled around and saw an empty boat bobbing about fifty yards away. Apparently it had broken loose from the ship during the early stages of the fight.

He struck out for it and soon he and Eeda were hauling themselves over the side. Coralean didn't waste any time. Quickly, he found the oars and started rowing. Big muscles bunching and easing, sea-water and kelp streaming from his head and beard as from some burly god arisen from the depths of the ocean.

A half-hour later he was crouched under the broad stern of the *Tegula*, straining to hear what was happening on deck. He heard men talking, but their voices were so low that he couldn't make out whether they were friend or foe. Whoever they were, the boarding nets were in place so they obviously knew something was happening.

Eeda tugged at his sleeve, signaling. Coralean turned to see that the flames aboard the ship that had been on fire had been put out. Now its sails were going up and it was moving away—heading out to sea. The other two ships were already under way and were nearly clear of the bay.

Cursing and so angry he was prepared to face alone whatever foe awaited him aboard the *Tegula*, Coralean started to draw his sword. But the scabbard was empty, the sword lost in the long swim.

Just then, Coralean heard the splash of oars and he lumbered about in the small boat, grabbing up an oar for a weapon. Eeda had her dagger out, ready to fight beside him.

Then a harsh voice called out: "Make one move, you flea-bitten Rhodesman, and you'll be eating my arrow for supper!"

Coralean's heart leaped with joy when he heard the broad accent of a Kyranian soldier.

"We're safe, lord husband!" Eeda cried.

And she threw her arms around him, nearly toppling them both into the sea.

✻   ✻   ✻

Several hours later, Rhodes and his three ships were standing just off the narrow tip of Syrapis. A stream of boats churned out to meet them. Each carried an oil lamp hoisted on a pole and the effect was like a rare string of pearls from his treasury bobbing on dark waters.

These boats, however, were more valuable to Rhodes than a whole chest of pearls. For each was loaded with soldiers, weapons and stores enough for many months.

The king strode happily up and down the deck of his command ship—the *Kray*. Within a few hours he'd have five hundred crack troops crammed into his ships. And then he'd be off well before the Kyranians sniffed out his plan.

His only disappointment was that he hadn't been able to capture Coralean. But that didn't matter now. Even that canny old devil wouldn't suspect what Rhodes was up to until it was too late.

When they heard the news of the king's raid on their ships, the Kyranians would think Rhodes was planning an invasion of their territory by sea. They'd scramble as fast as they could to bolster their defenses. And then they'd send all their ships and men down to meet him.

Only to find he wasn't there.

Thinking of their bewildered faces when they finally learned what he was up to, Rhodes couldn't contain a chuckle. By the gods, sometimes it was good to be king!

Within him, Kalasariz shared his pleasure—reveling in the hot juices of victory. *Brilliant, Majesty, brilliant*, he said in that whispered inner voice that Rhodes had become quite at ease with.

And it won't be long, Majesty, Kalasariz added, *before you'll shine with even greater brilliance. When we've cornered and crushed Safar Timura and that fiend he calls his son!*

Rhodes nodded vigorously, oblivious to the nearby Tabusir and his other officers who wondered what the king was doing, muttering and nodding to himself. Was he drunk?

Then Clayre's voice cut through, spoiling the king's good mood. "Son, son! Come at once. I have need of you."

"The old bitch!" Rhodes growled low.

Do not trouble yourself, Majesty, Kalasariz soothed. *Once we have the Timuras, we won't need her anymore.*

And Clayre shouted, "Did you hear me, son? I'm calling you!"

Mood restored, Rhodes chuckled again and started for the Queen Witch's stateroom.

And he cried brightly, "Coming, mother!"

CHAPTER TWENTY-SEVEN

CREATURE COMFORTS

Don't open the door, Little Master!" Gundara whispered.

"It's *definitely* not a good idea!" Gundaree chimed in.

Once again, Palimak heard a heavy thump against his cabin wall.

"What is it?" he asked.

"Something really, really mean," Gundara replied.

"And hungry," Gundaree added. "You forgot to mention that."

"You *always* say that," Gundara sniffed. "Mean things usually are hungry. That's what makes them so mean."

Palimak put a finger to his lips, shushing them. He motioned and the two Favorites leaped up on his shoulders and perched on either side of his head.

He put his ear against the door, listening. Nothing.

No, wait! He thought he could make out a creaking noise. It reminded him of thick boughs settling in a tree. Very strange.

Palimak opened mental gates to his demon side and his senses became more acute. Beneath the sound of the settling boughs he heard a slight clicking. Like a beetle? No, not that. Then more clicking. Was there more than one?

Cautiously, he sent out a magical feeler. He caught the vibrating aura of a single being. But what kind of a being, he couldn't tell.

He slipped the astral tentacle out further, gently feeling around.

First there was a warning buzz of magic. Then suddenly something white-hot burned his senses and he snatched the probe back.

"It still doesn't know you're awake, Little Master," Gundara whispered.

"That was just its armor," Gundaree explained.

Palimak noticed he was dripping with sweat. And it wasn't from fear or tension. The cabin was definitely getting warmer.

Then his demon hearing picked up a rustling sound, like a breeze disturbing an old pine. Followed by more clicking sounds. All very faint.

"It's trying to talk to me and Gundaree," Gundara said.

"But it doesn't want us to wake you up," Gundaree said.

"Go ahead and answer," Palimak said.

Evidently they did, because he felt a tingling sensation run up his spine and his hair stood on end. Followed by another heavy thump against the wall. And the sound of the whispering pines and insect-like clicking.

Then silence—the waiting kind where stillness takes on a shadowy presence. The room grew warmer, the atmosphere dank from the sweat pouring off Palimak in rivulets. Finally:

"He doesn't seem so mean now, Little Master," Gundara said.

"Not mean at all," Gundaree added.

"But he's still hungry," Gundara said.

"So what?" Gundaree said. "You can't blame somebody for being hungry."

"That's true," Gundaree said in singular agreement. "I'm hungry right now, as a matter of fact. And it's making me feel mean."

"What does he want?" Palimak said, paying no attention to the last.

"Oh, nothing much, Little Master," Gundara said. And Palimak could almost hear the shrug in his voice.

"Except he wants us to help kill you," Gundara added.

Palimak raised his eyebrows. But said nothing.

"He promised us all sorts of nice things if we agreed," Gundaree said.

"And he also said we wouldn't have to work so hard all the time," Gundara put in.

"He sure sounded like a pretty nice new master to me," Gundaree said.

"What did you tell him?" Palimak asked.

"Oh, that we'd think about it," Gundara said.

"Good," Palimak said. "We need to stall for time."

"Except, maybe we really will think about it," Gundaree threatened.

"The snacks around here haven't been too good lately," Gundara said.

Palimak ignored this last exchange. The Favorites had been his lifelong companions. And although they could be nasty, quarrelsome little things, in their thousand years of existence he was the only friend they'd ever had. Besides, their loyalties were bound to whoever possessed the stone turtle that was their home.

He wiped perspiration from his eyes and looked around the cabin, trying to figure out what to do. Magic was out. The intense heat, he realized, was the by-product of a spell meant to smother his abilities.

And it was doing a good job of it, too! Even the idea of sorcery made him feel weary.

A direct physical attack would also be doomed. Whatever the thing was, it was huge and most certainly prepared to deal with Palimak on a one-on-one basis.

"Why doesn't he just break down the door and kill me himself?" Palimak asked. "Why does he need you?"

"Because you can still use us to make magic and fight him," Gundara said.

This surprised Palimak. "Aren't you two affected by his spell?"

"Little Master's being stupid again," Gundaree said.

"He certainly is," Gundara said.

"Stop it!" Palimak hissed. The heat and tension were making him impatient. "Just answer my question."

Gundara gave a long sigh, like a child pressed by an adult to explain the painfully obvious.

"Magic is what we're made of, Little Master," he said. "Don't you know that?"

"Oh," Palimak said, feeling very stupid indeed.

The Favorites were spirit folk, composed entirely of magical particles. Safar had explained this to him years ago. He'd used the analogy of a clay jar filled with water. A human or demon wizard was a jar containing a certain amount of sorcerous "liquid." Whereas spirit folk were the jar itself, plus all it contained.

"If his spell could take away our magic," Gundaree continued for his brother, "then we wouldn't be here. We'd be dead."

"Sorry," Palimak said. "I didn't mean to get angry."

"That's all right, Little Master," Gundara allowed in a rather grand manner. "We know you can't always be perfect like us."

There was another thump at the door. Then a cracking sound as something heavy leaned against it. He could see the planks bending inward under the weight.

"He's getting mad, Little Master," Gundaree said. "He wants our answer now, or he's going to come in anyway."

"Stall him some more," Palimak said.

The twins resumed their odd communication with the creature, filling the air with whispering and clicking noises.

Whatever lies they told seemed to work, because soon the planks groaned as the weight was removed and they resumed their original shape.

Even with the help of the Favorites, Palimak knew he didn't have enough sorcerous strength to live through an encounter with the creature. Which meant the only avenue open was escape.

He glanced at the open porthole—the only exit from the cabin, other than the door. Steam from the overheated room was wisping out into the night like a fog.

For a moment, he considered climbing out and dropping into the sea. Then he dismissed that idea. The ship was under full sail and Palimak would swiftly be left behind to drown.

It was starting to come down to a choice between a watery grave or being eaten alive.

As if on cue, Gundara whispered, "I'm hungry!"

"Me too!" Gundaree said.

Absently, Palimak fished a biscuit from his pocket and broke it in half. A wriggling worm fell to the floor. Palimak looked at the worm, then at the two biscuit halves, then at the door. A hazy idea started to take form.

"What kind of a creature is he?" Palimak asked the twins.

"Oh, he's sort of like a tree," Gundara said. "Except he doesn't have any leaves."

"And he's sort of like an animal," Gundaree said. "Except he doesn't have any skin or bones."

"But he's got ever so many teeth," Gundara said.

"They're all over his branches," Gundaree added. "Lots and lots of teeth in lots and lots of little mouths, all with long, sharp tongues."

"I'm sorry we can't be more helpful, Little Master," Gundaree said. "But it's hard to describe something that's both an animal and a tree."

"And we really wouldn't help him kill you," Gundara said.

"Never!" Gundaree agreed.

A slight pause, then: "Now can we eat?" Gundara asked plaintively.

"I want the worm!" Gundaree said, smacking his lips.

"Not this time," Palimak said. "I need that worm."

He squatted, took out his dagger and cut the worm in half.

"Poor thing," Gundara observed.

Gundaree sneered at his twin. "What's wrong with you?" he asked. "It's only a stupid worm."

Gundara wiped away a solitary tear. "But she seemed so happy in that biscuit," he said. "And now look at her. One part's a head without a tail. And the other's a tail without a head."

"I'll soon fix that," Palimak said, placing a wriggling piece on each side of the door.

Then he crept silently to his bedside and fetched a pitcher of water back to the door. He crumbled up the biscuit halves, mixed them with the water and made two lumps of dough. From these he formed two credible dough men, complete with legs, arms, heads and faces with simple features.

"I get it," Gundara said. "They're sort of like the cheese monster!"

He was referring to one of Palimak's boyhood experiments that had worked well enough to get them all into trouble with Safar.

"Something like that," Palimak agreed.

Then he indicated the still-moving worm halves. "Get in," he ordered the twins.

"Yuk!" Gundara said.

"Yum!" said Gundaree.

Palimak pointed at Gundara. "Just do as you're told."

Pouting and muttering under his breath, Gundara stomped over to his worm half, held his nose, then vanished inside.

"You next," Palimak said to the lip-smacking Gundaree. "But don't you dare eat it!"

The Favorite's smile was replaced by a look of outrage. He kicked at the floor, grumbling, "I never get to have any fun!"

But he did as he was told and vanished into the piece reserved for him. Palimak pressed a worm half into each doughman and set them on either side of the door.

Then, very slowly and quietly he slipped the latch.

Heart hammering so hard he was sure the creature could hear it, he tiptoed to his bunk, stripped off the blanket and tied one end to a stool.

He placed the stool under the porthole and grasped the free end of the blanket.

Then he said to the twins: "All right. Tell him to come in!"

CHAPTER TWENTY-EIGHT
ATTACK ON THE NEPENTHE

Safar was surrounded by four enormous wolves with glowing eyes and slavering jaws. They were reared back on their hind legs, towering nearly two feet over him. Their front legs ended in long, sharp, demon-like claws.

He was pinned by powerful magic and couldn't move as they stalked in for the kill. His mind gibbered, How can this be? I destroyed them, dammit! I destroyed them all!

From somewhere nearby he heard beasts ravaging flesh and breaking bones between strong jaws. He could smell the stench of blood and offal from their victim. And then a shiver of helpless agony shook him to the core as he heard the victim scream:

"Help me, father! Help me!"

It was Palimak. Crying and flailing as the beasts ate him alive.

The wolves were so close now that Safar could smell the carrion on their breath. If only he could break free. If only he could fling himself at them. Or sear them with a spell. The battle would be brief and would end in his death. But that was far more preferable than living and hearing Palimak's tormented cries.

The king wolf—the largest of the four—rasped laughter at Safar's predicament. And then he spoke with Iraj's voice.

He said, "Here we are, together again, old friend."

The wolf that was Iraj gestured and a goblet appeared in his claws. It was a fragile thing with such beautiful designs carved into its surface that Safar shuddered to see such artistry despoiled. It was like being forced to watch some piece of filth ravish your sister.

The king wolf raised the goblet in a mocking toast. "To my blood brother, Safar

Timura," he said. "Long may he die!"

Then he drank the contents down and hurled the goblet away to shatter on the ground. The other wolves growled in satisfaction.

And Palimak screamed, "Help me, father!"

The king wolf chuckled, then mimicked the cry, "Help me, father!"

His head snaked down until his eyes were at Safar's level. Huge and afire with hate. "What's wrong, Safar?" he asked. "Why don't you help him?"

He gestured back into the darkness. "There's still some of him left. If you act quickly, you might be able to save an arm or a leg."

Safar tried to speak, but no words would come.

The king wolf tilted his head. "What's that?" he asked. "I can't hear you."

Safar gathered all his strength and, gasping with effort, he croaked, "Stop!"

The king wolf acted surprised. He said, "Is that all you can say after all these years? Stop? Why should I? You're the one who started this. Why don't you stop? Then perhaps we can be friends again."

And Safar croaked, "Please!"

Instantly, the wolf started to transform. There was an awful popping of joints as his limbs moved violently in their sockets. His snout retreated, his eyes and ears shifted position, his gray fur dissolved.

And Safar found himself staring into the handsome human face of Iraj Protarus.

"You see, Safar?" Iraj said, hands sweeping down to indicate his transformed body. "You see what I'm willing to endure for you? And a simple 'please' was all it took."

He turned to the other wolves. "Am I a reasonable king, or am I not?" he asked.

The other wolves growled agreement that His Majesty was the soul of gentility and kindness.

Iraj grinned at Safar, dark eyes flashing with amusement. Golden hair and shapely beard beaming in a sudden shaft of sunlight.

"Do you really want to save Palimak, brother?" he asked. "What would you do to spare him?"

And Safar groaned, "Anything!"

Iraj nodded, sharp. "Good," he said. "Now that we've agreed on a price, shall we start again?"

And he waved a hand and suddenly Safar found himself standing above a snowy pass. He was back in Esmir, high in the mountains called the Gods' Divide. He could hear caravan bells jingling and could see a wagon train—Coralean's wagon train—winding toward the white peaks known as the Bride and Six Maids.

Iraj was beside him and he was young again, a boy of seventeen. And Safar was young too, with supple limbs and a heart like a lion's. Iraj pointed at two canyons that bisected the caravan track.

"The demons," he said.

And Safar saw the two forces of mounted demons waiting to ambush the wagons.

"What shall we do?" Safar asked.

Iraj laughed, drawing his sword. "Warn the caravan," he said. And he started running down the mountainside.

But in midflight he turned his head and shouted back. "Oh, I almost forgot. This time Palimak is with them!"

And he ran on, leaping over icy boulders, crying, "Follow me, brother! Follow me!"

Safar ran after him. Bounding down the steep slope, heart bursting, mouth full of ashes. He had to reach the caravan. He had to warn Coralean.

But most of all, he had to reach Palimak in time.

Except the harder he ran, the more distant became the caravan. His legs grew weary, his breath short. But he struggled on, slipping in the snow. Desperately fighting to keep on his feet. But then falling, falling . . . hearing the war cries of demon bandits as they attacked. And it was too late, too late, and he could hear Palimak scream:

"Help me, father. Please!"

And the last thing he heard was Iraj laughing.

*　　　*　　　*

Safar shot up in bed, clawing at the blankets, Iraj's laughter still echoing eerily from his dream. He was soaked to the skin with sweat and he shivered in the cold night air.

He could hear the low rumble of the magical furnaces that powered the airship and the fluttering of the balloons in the wind. But he didn't make the mistake of thinking what he'd experienced was only a dream and sagging back in relief.

To be sure, some of it was a dream: The wolves, Iraj, plus the repeated caravan incident from his boyhood.

He had no doubt, however, that Palimak really was in great danger. The atmosphere fairly crackled with a dark, brooding force. He had a sudden sense of looking into a huge demonic eye and seeing Palimak reflected in the surface of its iris.

Safar leaped from his bunk, hastily pulling on clothes. He rushed outside, buckling his sword belt as he ran. There were only a few crewmen about—the rest were asleep. But on the bridge he spotted Biner at the wheel. Safar raced up the stairs to his side.

"Where's the ship?" he shouted. "Where's the *Nepenthe?*"

Biner knew at once something was wrong and didn't waste time asking for details.

"About a mile back," he said. "On the lee side."

Safar bolted to the rail to look. The seas were running like an incoming tide over a sandbar. Short, frothy waves speeding past; foam faintly pink under the bright Demon Moon. He made out the billowing sails of the *Nepenthe* just where Biner had said she'd be.

"Get back to the *Nepenthe!*" he shouted to Biner. "And get everybody up."

Biner went into instant action, roaring, "All hands! All hands!"

Other orders followed and the night crew got busy adjusting the steering sails as Biner muscled the wheel over—turning the airship in a wide arc.

The soldiers and the rest of the crew poured out onto the deck. Leiria, followed by Arlain, rushed up to the bridge. Professional that she was, Leiria was already dressed to fight—boots, buckler, short tunic with a weapons belt buckled about her small waist, a bow in one hand and a quiver of arrows thrown over one shoulder.

Arlain, who never wore that much in the way of clothing except in the coldest of weather, wore only a revealing sleeping gown thrown over her startling-beautiful body. But she was wide awake and prepared for battle. Claws extended. Sparks and smoke leaking from her dragon's mouth.

"What's wrong, Safar?" Leiria shouted over the wind.

"I'm not sure," he replied. "Except that Palimak's in some kind of trouble."

Leiria didn't ask any more questions. She only nodded and raced over to the soldiers. Barking orders for them to get into position. The long days of drilling paid off and everyone moved like well-oiled clockwork. Within a few scant minutes, they were all ready.

Arlain's great eyes glowed in fury. She loved Palimak like a doting older sister. Both the product of inter-species mating, they'd been close friends from the moment they'd met.

"If anybody hurth him," she said, "I'll roatht them in their thkinth!"

685

Safar only hoped they had skins to roast. Other than the fact that powerful sorcery was involved, he didn't have the faintest idea what he was up against.

But all he said was, "Make sure the boarding lines are ready."

Leaking smoke through her nostrils, Arlain hurried off to do his bidding.

Safar leaned far out over the rail, patience barely under control as they tacked toward the *Nepenthe*. Biner bellowed orders as they fought the wind.

Finally they were hovering directly over the tall ship.

"Let's bring her down, Biner," Safar said. "But keep it quiet, please."

Biner nodded. The airship's best defense *and* offense was surprise. After all, who would ever imagine an attack from the skies? He signaled for runners and started a relay of whispered orders. The magical engines were cut so the only sound was the gentle buffeting of the wind against the big balloons.

Then, slowly, cautiously, the crew started bleeding air from the balloons and the airship drifted down toward the *Nepenthe*.

Safar peered at the shadowy deck as it rose toward him. He could only see a few small figures moving about. With the weather so mild, night watches on both the *Nepenthe* and the airship were kept to a minimum so everyone would be fresh in an emergency.

Everything seemed quite peaceful. The crewmen's movements were leisurely. And only the most necessary lanterns were lit—a normal practice aimed at conserving oil for the long journey.

Then Leiria was at his side again. "I don't see anything," Safar said. "But I know they're there!"

Leiria remained silent, running experienced eyes over the ship and the surrounding seas.

Then she pointed. "There's something odd along the port bow," she said.

At first all he could make out were eight dark, twisted shapes hanging off the ship. They looked inanimate, like logs of stressed timber with the branches still intact.

Then he saw thirty—possibly forty—other similar shapes bobbing in the ocean next to the ship. It was if the *Nepenthe* were sailing through debris from a lumber mill. Although there was no land for miles, it was entirely possible the cast-off wood had been carried far out to sea by a swift-moving river.

Safar wondered why the crew couldn't hear the ship bumping into the logs. They ought to be fending off the debris with poles before the hull was damaged.

Leiria said, "Did you notice how the ones in the water are moving *with the ship?*"

At first he didn't understand what she meant. But as the airship drifted lower he realized the logs seemed to be clinging to the sides of the *Nepenthe*.

Then he noticed movement from two of the eight shapes hanging from the bow. And it wasn't in reaction to the ship heaving through the waves.

Safar slid his dagger out. Whispering a spell of clarity, he cut a wide circle in the air. The area he'd inscribed began to glisten in the Demon Moonlight as if it were window glass coated with a thin film of oil.

Looking through it, everything became magnified as if through the overly large lens of a ship's telescope.

"What in the Hells?!" Leiria blurted.

Which was Safar's exact reaction. For what they both saw with startling clarity were devils' spawn incarnate. Clinging to the sides of the *Nepenthe* were huge living creatures with bodies that looked like dead, twisted tree trunks.

He increased the magnification and could see that each trunk had scores of arms and legs with the appearance of fire-blasted branches and twigs. And each woody limb was pocked with dozens of small mouths, like leeches. And each mouth contained a long barbed tongue and was rimmed with several rows of sharp fangs.

At that moment Safar heard a chorus of clicking sounds, like an army of hungry land crabs advancing across a beach. It was apparently some sort of signal, because the eight creatures hanging from the bow suddenly swarmed onto the deck of the *Nepenthe*, while the platoon of beasts still in the sea scrabbled up the sides of the hull to join their leaders.

The air magnifier collapsed as Safar raced over to Biner to whisper the news. The were so close to the *Nepenthe* that the slightest sound might have given them away.

Biner signaled his runners and swiftly the word went out for everyone to "Prepare for boarding." All over the airship the soldiers and crewmen tensed for the final order.

Safar hurried back to the rail, where Leiria waited. She'd drawn her sword and wore an odd grin on her face that looked like she thought something was amusing, but it was actually her fighting expression. He'd seen that same grin remain on her face during the bloodiest of battles as she cut down the charging enemy.

Before readying his own sword, he slipped an amplifying pellet from his pocket. He had to warn the *Nepenthe*. Unfortunately, that warning couldn't come until the last possible moment. Otherwise their surprise counter-attack would be spoiled.

Safar waited, nerves taut as lyre strings. Heart pounding against his ribs. He could see the first group of tree creatures closing in on the unsuspecting crewmen. The second, much larger group was starting to climb over the railing to the deck.

Then, as the ends of the airship's boarding ropes brushed along the *Nepenthe*'s deck, he cracked the pellet, and shouted: *"All hands! All hands! We're under attack!"*

The amplifying spell made his shout into that of a giant's. The words thundered into the night and were repeated over and over again:

"All hands! All hands! We're under attack!"

Safar didn't wait to see the effect of his warning, but leaped immediately for a boarding rope. He caught it and slipped several feet, burning his hands. The pain went unnoticed. He only let go and plummeted to the deck, landing in a crouch and coming up swift as a cat.

His sword came out and he charged the creatures, some of whom were whirling about to face this unexpected attack from the rear.

Leiria was at his side, shrilling her wild battle cry.

Behind him, he heard the shouts of his soldiers as they plunged off the airship into battle. Biner's roar of fury sounding over all but Arlain's blood-chilling dragon shriek.

Safar felt incredibly powerful and fast, as if he suddenly possessed the strength of two men. He leaped for the nearest tree beast, his jump carrying him twenty feet.

The creature towered over him by at least four feet. Long, gnarled branches filled with gnashing teeth lashed out at him, but he slashed them off with his sword.

A greenish white liquid splattered on the deck, where it hissed and bubbled. A few drops splashed his sword hand. He could feel it sear his flesh but his bloodlust was so hot he didn't care.

He chopped at the main body, felt his blade sink deep. The creature toppled to the deck, limbs and branches flailing, all the teeth chattering wildly.

Except it didn't die! Somehow the creature fought on, lashing out with its deadly branches!

A shadow reared up behind him. He turned, knowing it was too late, but desperately striking out at his attacker.

Branches enfolded him, pulling him down onto the deck. They held him there, sharp teeth ravaging his back.

Then the creature suddenly let go, falling away and he rolled over to see Leiria hacking it with her sword. Leather armor hissing as it took the brunt of the spurting acid sap.

From far off he heard Khysmet shrill his battle cry and the sound of splintering wood as the big stallion broke through the walls of his stable to join the fight.

Then he heard Jooli's shout and the cries of the Nepenthe's crew as they boiled up onto the deck.

Leiria jerked Safar to his feet and they stood side by side as an enormous tree beast scrabbled for them, huge roots serving as feet. All its branches lashing out like thick, nail-studded whips.

The fury of its assault drove them back and it was all they could do to keep out of the way of its flesh-eating limbs.

Then Khysmet suddenly appeared behind the creature, rearing up on his hind legs then plunging down with his sharp hooves.

There was a crack! as the beast split in two.

Safar vaulted onto Khysmet's back and held out a hand for Leiria. She jumped up behind them and they plunged into the fray, striking out in every direction.

The *Nepenthe* was still under full sail and the ship's deck made a heaving, slippery battlefield. It made no difference to Khysmet who launched himself like a mighty lion, biting with his great teeth and raking the creatures with his hooves.

However, even with the entire crew and all the soldiers of both ships engaged, the fight was not going well for the Kyranians. The tree beasts simply wouldn't die, but fought on with undiminished ferocity no matter how many wounds they suffered.

Even their hacked-off branches remained deadly, whipping around men's legs and tearing into them with their teeth.

And the only cries of pain Safar could hear were human.

And the only dead he saw were his own.

CHAPTER TWENTY-NINE

WITCH WORLD

King Rhodes and his mother were quite enjoying the battle for the *Nepenthe.*

Floating just above her golden-tiled table was an exact duplicate of the events taking place hundreds of miles from their own ship. Shimmering on her table was the night sea with the choppy waves, foam tinted pink by the Demon Moon.

A miniature of the *Nepenthe* boomed through those waves under full sail. Hovering over it was the airship, boarding lines dangling down to the deck. And all along the *Nepenthe*'s deck were the tiny figures of the Kyranians struggling valiantly but hopelessly against the tree beasts.

They could even see Safar and Leiria, swords slashing this way and that, rage across the deck on the broad back of Khysmet.

"Oh, good show, good show!" Rhodes declared as one of the creatures swept Leiria off the stallion and onto the glistening boards.

Peering at the scene through the king's eyes, Kalasariz reacted with equal glee. Of all the many people and demons he hated, Leiria was quite high on his list.

He'd been unsure of the plan when Clayre had proposed it only a few days before. Now that it was coming to fruition—with the deaths of Safar and Palimak apparently imminent—he liked it so much he was beginning to become a little envious that it wasn't a plan of his own making.

As the battle for the *Nepenthe* raged, Kalasariz reflected back on the day Clayre had had her sudden inspiration.

*   *   *

Stealing the ships was his idea, of course. It was the kind of sneak attack Kalasariz had mastered many years before when he was one of the three rulers of Walaria.

The pursuit of Safar was also his idea and it had taken all his cunning to convince Rhodes and Clayre this was a goal superior to their own.

The king and his mother would have been content to use the ships to launch a new invasion of the Kyranian fortress in Syrapis. Life long island dwellers, their idea of empire fitted exactly the shoreline boundaries set by the Great Sea.

And so when Kalasariz offered them the world as their kingdom, they were at first hard put to stretch their imagination beyond the spit of sand and rock that was Syrapis.

Eventually his silky powers of persuasion had fired their ambitions. All they had to do was get their hands on Safar and Palimak—it didn't matter if they were dead or alive—and supreme power would be theirs. Power that even the gods might envy.

The only worm in the apple—and this he hadn't mentioned—was that he also needed Iraj Protarus. Kalasariz was only guessing that wherever Safar was, Iraj would be nearby.

One thing he was fairly sure of was that once he got his hands on Safar's corpse some sort of spell could be devised to locate his former king.

With Iraj in the spymaster's power, Kalasariz could rid himself of his two barbarian allies. And then he would rule absolutely. And alone. Once he had been content to share power, or even to manipulate from the shadows behind a throne.

But since he'd arrived in Syrapis to take up residence in Rhodes he'd undergone a spiritual transformation that quite excited him.

Kalasariz now truly understood that kings and allies could not be trusted—unless your boot was firmly planted on their throats. And the only way to assure himself of that happy state of affairs was to wear the royal mantle himself.

As for his plan, in the beginning the only trouble was that Safar would be difficult to catch. The *Nepenthe* had a head start of many days and it would require more luck than skill to corner the Kyranians. Once that was accomplished, however, defeating the Timuras would be simple. It would be three ships, all packed with crack troops, against the *Nepenthe*'s puny forces.

Even the airship wouldn't give Safar much of an advantage, because Kalasariz fully intended to strike when all the Kyranians were on land, taking on supplies and water.

But to surprise Safar, they needed to catch him first. Kalasariz hadn't known how go about this, but thought it best to sail after the *Nepenthe* as fast as they could and hope for some storm or other accident to delay the Kyranians long enough to overtake them.

It was his experience that good fortune usually tended to favor the hunter rather than the hunted.

Clayre, however, had other ideas. Such as creating a delay through sorcery, rather than trusting to chance. Even with the newly-won magical powers that Kalasariz now possessed—thanks to the meal he'd made out of Fari and Luka—he didn't see how it could be done.

The distance was too great, he reasoned. Plus, they didn't know the exact position of the *Nepenthe.*

The beautiful Queen Witch solved that soon enough. First she dug out a roll of ancient parchment. It was a copy of Asper's hand-drawn map of the world, which the demon wizard had composed during his travels. She'd gotten it from Charize, the false guardian of Asper's tomb.

"I never thought I'd have any use for this," she said. "However, there are some faint traces of magic in it left over from Asper. Enough to cure a wart, perhaps, but no more. Regardless, I make a habit of never throwing anything magical away, so I put it aside just in case."

She also had another surprise up her sleeve. "Bring me the gold Palimak Timura gave you," she commanded her son.

This stung Rhodes' most vulnerable part—his greedy heart.

"That gold is mine," he said. "If you want to buy something, use your own funds. I give you a large enough allowance, the gods and my treasurer know. Besides, I earned that gold the hard way."

His face darkened at the memory of Palimak and Leiria standing before him, gloating at his defeat.

"It was the most humiliating thing that's ever happened in my life," he said. "And there isn't gold enough in the world to make me forget it."

This, of course, was a gross exaggeration. Rhodes would do anything for money and power.

As witness his eager willingness to sacrifice his own daughter, Jooli.

However, Kalasariz quite understood his point. Although gold itself had never been that important to him—except for the power it contained—he was equally avaricious in other ways.

Kalasariz also knew what it was like to suffer humiliation at the hands of a Timura. He had several scores to settle with Safar on that account.

Even so, Kalasariz suspected there was more to Clayre's request than a need to buy magical supplies. She'd been quite specific, as a matter of fact. It was Palimak's gold she wanted. Not just a random purse of the stuff from the king's treasury.

He stirred in his nest, signaling Rhodes that he was about to communicate. When he had the king's attention, he said, *I know she's a greedy bitch, Majesty, but perhaps there's more to her request than meets the eye.*

Rhodes' frown deepened, but Kalasariz felt the king's nerve cords relax and knew he'd gotten through. But first Rhodes had to hear his mother out.

"Why do you always insist on arguing with me about ever little detail, son?" she said. "Your father was of the same quarrelsome nature and look what it got him."

"Dead," Rhodes replied, a little nastily.

"That's right, dead," Clayre agreed.

She sighed, thinking about her former husband. "I swear," she continued, "no matter what I said, your father had an argument against it. Why, we could have been talking about a haunch of venison and if I said it was gamy, he'd claim it was sweet. And he never listened to me. Never! It was as if he had his ears plugged with wax every time I came into his presence."

Clayre smiled in gentle reflection. "But in the end, I certainly unstopped his ears, didn't I? Unfortunately, a corpse can't hear. Still, I made my point clear to his ghost."

Rhodes barely suppressed a shudder. Curious, Kalasariz tapped into his memories. He caught an image of Clayre pouring hot poisoned oil into the ears of her sleeping husband. Immediately, his admiration for Clayre increased.

A difficult woman she might be, but one couldn't deny she had a sense of humor.

Clayre gazed on her stubborn son. "So, I ask you again, my son," she said, "to kindly bring me Palimak Timura's gold. Hmm?"

Rhodes bristled at the implied threat. "Or what?" he asked.

And Clayre replied, "Or I can't help you find the ship, that's all. What else did you think I meant?"

"Never mind," Rhodes said. "I'll get the gold."

When he returned with the purse, Clayre dumped the gold out on her magical table. She sorted through the coins, eyes narrowed in concentration. Finally, she held one up.

"This will do," she said. Then she dismissed the others with a wave. "You can have these back."

Puzzled, but relieved, Rhodes quickly scooped up the coins and returned them to the purse. One fell to the floor so he got down on his hands and knees and crawled about until he found it.

Kalasariz was irritated to the extreme. This was not proper behavior for a king. But he said nothing. His object was to make Rhodes think of him as his dearest friend and he had to be careful not to appear judgmental. Ah, well, he thought. Living inside another person certainly had its burdens—even though the host did do all the physical work.

"Why did you choose just that one coin, mother?" Rhodes asked after he'd tucked the purse away.

"Because it carries the strongest scent," she replied. "Apparently young Palimak held it more than the others. Perhaps he even bit the coin when he first received it to make sure it was pure gold. In any event, he's left very heavy traces of his aura behind for us to make use of."

Then, with no further explanation, she unrolled the parchment map and placed it across the golden tiles. Four stubby black candles were stuck at each corner to hold it down. The gold coin went in the center.

"Now, help me with this," she said.

Rhodes obediently approached the table. While she concentrated, Kalasariz stoked up his own magical fires, lashing the imps that were Fari and Luka with red-hot whips until their sorcerous energies boiled over and flowed into his own.

This was Kalasariz' favorite part of his new-found skills at performing the business of magic. The two demons were hateful creatures who had worked long and hard to bring him down. Their agonies gave him pleasure of such extremes that it bordered on the sexual. Which in his present form was the best he could do, since the only way he could enjoy the mating act these days was through Rhodes' activities.

And the king was such a rutting brute, with no style at all, that his amorous exploits only whetted Kalasariz' appetite.

As he focused his powers, adding them to Clayre's considerable strength, he saw the coin begin to move. The movement was hesitant at first—a barely perceptible tremble. Then it shifted left a few inches, then right, then to the center again.

Another trembling hesitation, then it shot below the center point and came to rest.

Clayre waved a hand at the coin and it slowly transformed in shape, size and color until it became an exact duplicate of the *Nepenthe*, sails billowing in a spirit-world wind.

Then she broke the sorcerous connection and Kalasariz relaxed.

Rhodes leaned over the table to get a closer look, and through the king's eyes Kalasariz could see that the ship sat a little south of a large land mass, with small tree-like squiggles inked in.

"They're just off Aroborus," Clayre said. "The land of the forests."

"Now that we know where they are," Rhodes asked, "how do we delay them?"

"Never fear, my son," Clayre said with supreme confidence. "I'll think of something."

*   *   *

Kalasariz gazed fondly at the tiny figures of the tree beasts as they ravaged the Kyranian forces, driving them across the deck of the *Nepenthe.*

Clayre had been as good as her word and then some. Drawing on the Land of the Forests for inspiration, she'd created a unique and cunning enemy to delay and perhaps even destroy Safar Timura and his allies.

Kalasariz noted that Leiria was still down, barely holding off one creature, while Safar—seated on his white stallion—fought desperately but futilely to reach her.

Suddenly, he saw Jooli burst onto the scene, armed with a spear. She set the butt onto the deck and vaulted over several beasts to land at Leiria's side.

Then she jabbed at the beast that was attacking the Kyranian warrior, driving it back long enough for Leiria to come up and hack it down with her blade.

"You have to admit," Rhodes rumbled in fatherly admiration, "that my daughter is one hells of a soldier. Too bad the bitch whelp turned traitor and joined the other side."

But Clayre did not share his pride, grudging though it might have been. She became furious at the sight of her granddaughter.

"I'll fix her," she snarled.

She drew a long, sharp pin from her hair and rubbed it vigorously on the sleeve of her silken witch's gown. Kalasariz could feel the energy growing until magical sparks shot off.

Then Clayre jabbed the pin down at the tiny figure of Jooli.

But as the needle point descended, Kalasariz, whose attention had been fixed on his old enemy, saw Safar sheathe his sword. He pulled an object from his cloak that the spymaster couldn't quite make out.

When he raised it to his lips, however, Kalasariz realized it was some sort of horn.

And just as Clayre thrust the needle at Jooli, Safar blew through the horn. The sound blasted through Clayre's cabin as if it were made by some gigantic trumpet.

The Queen Witch gasped in shock as she saw two strange apparitions rise up through the golden tiles. The figures were vaguely familiar, but she didn't have time to think where she'd seen them before.

Then something was lofted up at her.

Instinctively, she ducked.

And then a great white light flared, blinding everyone in the cabin.

A moment later, when their vision cleared, the living seascape had vanished.

Only a dark smudge on the golden tiles remained to mark the spot where the battle for the *Nepenthe* had raged.

Rhodes whirled to face the witch. His features were swollen and red with anger. He'd seen exactly who those two magical creatures were.

"Dammit, mother," he roared. "I told you so! Maybe it's about time you started listening to me!"

Clayre was astounded. "Why, whatever are you talking about, son?" she asked.

"The mural, mother!" he snarled. "You said not to worry about it. But by the gods who torment us, it's come back to haunt us again!"

CHAPTER THIRTY

IN THE DARK SEAS

When Safar realized Leiria was gone it was as if his heart had been pierced by an arrow. One of the enormous creatures loomed up, deadly branches slashing in to take him. But he didn't care. In that terrible moment of agony only Leiria mattered.

It was Khysmet who saved him, wheeling about and kicking through all those chattering teeth and thorny tongues to knock the tree beast away.

Coming out of his shock, Safar saw Leiria lying on the deck, desperately cutting and jabbing at the huge creature towering over her. One blood-smeared leg was caught in a slender, snake-like branch and she was being drawn slowly toward the beast's twisted trunk.

Safar kicked Khysmet and they charged forward, only to be hurled back by three other creatures who moved in to block the way.

Hard as he and Khysmet fought, they kept losing ground to the living wall of pain.

Then he saw Jooli vault to Leiria's rescue. As she jabbed at the tree beast with her spear, Leiria slashed away the branch gripping her leg and then the two women joined together to drive the creature off.

It was then that a strange sensation came over him. To Safar it seemed as if he split in two and another part of him—a spirit self—was standing off at a great distance watching the progress of the battle. He could even see himself, astride Khysmet, fighting along with the others.

Although the view was godlike, his emotions were intensely human—frightened that all his friends would soon die unspeakably horrible deaths.

Then his spirit self heard a voice whisper, *Safar, Safar.*

It came from quite close—just at his ear. He even imagined he could feel warm breath stir his hair.

And then the voice came again, whispering, *Look to the heavens, brother!*

He looked up and saw nothing but the night sky. A cloud bank partly obscured the Demon Moon, dimming its red light. Surrounding it were only the stars—cold and pitiless as always.

Then he noticed a faint golden shimmer beyond the night. As if the darkness was a thin black veil drawn over a sheen of some ethereal surface.

Reflected in that sheen was the dim outline of two enormous faces. He couldn't make out who they were, only that they were watching.

And then there was motion. A disturbance. First it pierced the golden surface. Then the black veil that was the night.

A long, slender needle of flame pushed through and descended toward the *Nepenthe.* His eyes followed its course, the needle growing thinner, sharper, hotter.

And then, with a jolt, he realized it was aimed directly at Jooli!

Suddenly, his spirit self vanished and he was back in the midst of the battle. Slashing and cutting as the three creatures closed in on him and Khysmet.

But now he knew why he was losing this battle.

Fighting all natural instinct, he ignored the long tendrils of death reaching for him and sheathed his sword.

With forced calm he drew out Asper's shell trumpet. And lifted it to his lips and blew.

The sound was world-shattering. As if a thousand war trumpets—set close by—blared all at once. Everyone on the ship—including the creatures—froze, as if they'd been suddenly turned to stone.

Floating high above the *Nepenthe* he saw the mural of the Spirit Rider. It was hazy, ghost-like and of enormous size. Then he saw the beautiful Princess Alsahna and her black mare come alive.

The Princess shouted, "For Safar!" and horse and rider soared out of the mural into the night sky. They charged, up and up—Alsahna pulling a javelin from a loop on her saddle.

And then, just before they reached the golden shimmer, the Princess hurled it at the Watchers.

An intense white light flared, then was gone. Taking with it the faces of the Watchers, the shimmering gold surface and the ghostly mural.

Now there were only the cold stars and the grinning Demon Moon to observe what followed.

Immediately, Safar sensed a subtle shift in the atmosphere. And then a settling. It was as if the very particles that made up the air had rearranged themselves into a more normal pattern.

But he could still hear the sounds of battle and human cries of pain and defiance all around him.

A long, thick branch filled with chattering teeth reached for him. Safar roared in a fury and slashed it away. Then he kicked Khysmet forward, cutting at the beast's trunk with his sword.

But this time, when the blade bit the creature screamed and died!

All over the ship the besieged humans experienced similar results.

Biner, spattered with blood from dozens of cuts, swung his great club, bursting a tree-beast in two. He shouted in glee as it writhed in agony, then grew still.

Arlain hissed a long tongue of fire at one of the creatures. To her delight it burst into flames, then toppled over the rail into the sea.

Kairo the acrobat clung to a boarding rope and swung along the deck, slashing at the creatures with a sword. Amazed that this time they remained where they fell and didn't get up again.

Renor and Sinch netted their attacker, then slung it over the side.

Leiria and Jooli had found ropes. Together they lassoed one of the creatures, toppling it. Then, with sword and spear, they slew it where it fell.

But even without the magical assistance of Clayre and Kalasariz, the beasts were not easily defeated. It took an hour of furious fighting and many tricks before the humans had killed them all and hurled them into the sea.

As Leiria and Jooli dealt with the last one, Safar and Khysmet thundered up to them.

Safar shouted, "Have you seen Palimak?"

Leiria's heart jumped as his question sunk in like a wide-bladed spear. Dismayed, she shook her head: no.

Safar leaped off Khysmet and raced toward the stairwell leading down to Palimak's cabin, Leiria and Jooli at his heels.

He didn't bother with the stairs, but jumped ten feet to the passageway below. Immediately he saw a large, ragged hole where the door to Palimak's cabin had been. He also heard movement—a dry scraping sound—and knew another of the tree-creatures lurked inside.

Leiria and Jooli had joined him by now and he signaled silence. Then the three of them crept down the passageway, weapons ready.

When he reached the cabin he peered inside. Lying in the wreckage of the room was one of the beasts. Many of its branches had been ripped away and its trunk had enormous chunks torn from it. The creature was weak and dying.

Heart racing, Safar looked about the cabin and saw no sign of Palimak. He sagged against the broken doorway, overcome by grief.

It was Jooli who finally killed the beast, running it through with her spear. Leiria called for help and several crewmen came to drag the thing away and dispose of it.

By the time it was gone, Safar had recovered some of his sensibilities. And with them came hope.

"Palimak wouldn't die so easily," he said.

"Of course not," Leiria agreed, soothing herself as much as Safar. "Perhaps he managed to get out of the cabin."

Safar winced and shook his head. "I heard one of the crewmen say that no one has seen him since he went to bed."

He studied the cabin, looking for some sign. At first all he could see was the broken debris—smashed furniture, shattered bunk, scarred walls and deck. Then he spotted something peeping out from under a ruined plank.

Safar lifted the plank away, revealing a strange little object in the shape of a man. He squatted down to examine it more closely.

"It's been molded from dough or something," he said to Leiria, who was looking over his shoulder. He touched it. "It's still wet," he said.

There was an impression in the belly of the dough man where a navel might be. There was slight movement in the depression so Safar gently pulled the dough away from the edges. To his surprise he found what appeared to be part of a still-living worm. At the same time his magical senses caught a faint spark of sorcery.

Safar grinned. This was Palimak's work.

"It's a cheese beast," he said.

"What?" Leiria asked. "I thought you said it was made from dough."

"Never mind," Safar said.

He moved some other planks and found another dough man, but this one was missing a leg. However, he found the worm's other half wriggling within. An idea of what Palimak had intended started to come to him.

"Over here!" Jooli said.

Safar turned to see her pulling a blanket through the porthole. She held it up and he saw that one end of the blanket was tied to a broken stool. Jooli placed it across the port-hole, measuring. The stool was larger by several inches than the opening.

"He used the blanket to hang outside the cabin," she said, "so the creature couldn't get at him."

Safar came to his feet. "Go tell the captain to turn the ship about," he said to Jooli.

Then, to Leiria: "Ask Biner to get into the air as fast as he can. Palimak is out there someplace—and I mean to find him if I have to search every inch of sea from here to Aroborus!"

*   *   *

Palimak tightened his grip on the blanket. He said to the twins, "All right. Tell him to come in!" And he dived head-first through the porthole.

Slender though he was, he stuck at the hips and found himself in the ridiculous position of hanging half in and half out of the cabin, his posterior facing the monster as it burst through the door.

A fit of hysterical laughter nearly overcame him when he had a sudden vision of the creature gaping in astonishment when confronted with such a rude view of his victim.

But the chattering sound of many teeth spurred him onward and he kicked himself through the rest of the way.

Palimak plunged out into the night, then was brought up short by the blanket rope as the stool rose up to slam across the porthole.

He hung there a moment to recover, swaying with the motion of the ship. Then he spun about, got his feet against the hull and pulled himself up hand over hand until he could see through the porthole.

His first sight of the creature took his breath away. Its twisted, blackened trunk. Scores of branches and minor limbs waving madly about. All pockmarked with hundreds of little mouths filled with sharp, chattering teeth. And it was huge. Standing just inside the cabin—the wreckage of the door hurled to one side—its jagged-edged top was jammed against the ceiling.

It was also looking for him—turning slowly, first this way, then the other. Long barbed tongues tasting the air like a nest of snakes hunting their prey. Any minute now, it would make the connection between the stool jammed against the porthole and the whereabouts of its intended victim.

Palimak concentrated, drawing on all his powers. Opening the gates to his demon side and feeling the strength pour in. His nails grew into talons, cutting through the blanket, making his grip catlike and more assured.

He felt his canine teeth lengthen until the sharp points hooked over his lower lip. And his eyes burned in their sockets, turning a blazing yellow that cast twin beams of light onto the hull.

He hissed the spell words remembered from his boyhood. Foolish words, composed by a child. But the moment he said them he felt a surge of magical energy well up. He called out to the twins, using his mental "voice" to urge them to join him in the spell.

They replied in unison, their spirit voices like little bells—We're here, Little Master! We're here!

And boom! he cast it. Thunder crashing against his spirit ears as he hurled it into the cabin. And boom! boom! the little dough men containing Gundara and Gundaree jumped to their feet, swinging around to confront the beast. They were on either side of him, so small and made only of moistened bread crumbs that it would be laughable even to think the word "surrounded," much less use it.

But then they started growing and growing until they were the same size as the monster. And they were strong, so strong—dough flesh hardening into the consistency of steel—that they weren't laughable any longer.

And there was nothing funny at all when the creature realized it had been tricked and closed with them. All those deadly branches whipping out to embrace and kill the Favorites.

The three strange beings locked in battle. Crashing about the cabin, shattering everything in sight. The only sound was the destruction. There was not one roar of fury or agony from any of the creatures.

For Palimak it was like watching three mute giants fighting it out in an arena too small for any of them to escape.

As the fight raged, Palimak tried to shout a warning to the crewmen on deck. But his shouts were swept away by the heavy sound of the wind and crashing waves.

Even so, it didn't seem to matter. Because, ever so slowly, the twins gained the advantage. Hardened flesh impervious to all those teeth, they ripped off limbs and gouged out hunks from the beast's thick trunk. Greenish-gray acid splattering everywhere to hiss and burn wood and cloth.

Finally they had the creature pinned to the floor and were tearing at the jagged top Palimak imagined as a head. He thought it was over. The beast's movements growing weak, as if it were dying.

Then, suddenly, it surged up. Strong and fresh as when the fight had begun. And the furious battle commenced again.

And again.

And again.

Each time the twins got the creature down it somehow found new strength to fight on. The minutes dragged on like each was a year. And slowly Palimak and the twins began to weaken.

He dug deep for more strength, finding just enough to make one last desperate attempt to call for help. But this time he made the shout magical, calling for Safar:

"Help me, father! Help!"

For a brief moment Palimak thought there was an ethereal connection. A stirring of the magical atmosphere. So he clung to the blanket harder, directing the twins to continue the fight as long as they could.

After what seemed like an eternity he heard his father's voice raised in a thunderous cry:

"All hands! We're under attack!"

And Palimak laughed. Help was on the way. But then from the deck he heard cries of pain and the sounds of battle. Khysmet shrilling his battle cry, shattering the walls of his stable with his powerful hooves. And then the shouts of Leiria and Jooli and Biner and Arlain.

All of them fighting just as desperately as he.

Then the twins cried out, Help us, Little Master! Help us, please!

And that was the end of it.

Clinging with one hand, Palimak fished the stone turtle from his pocket and raised it high. He called for the twins and the turtle suddenly glowed as they fled into it.

Through bleary eyes he saw the doughmen collapse, then shrink to their original size. And the monster started turning again, hunting him with those flickering snake tongues.

Palimak returned the turtle to his pocket. And let go of the blanket.

Cold, salty water enveloped him. He kicked his way to the surface and when his head emerged he could see the *Nepenthe* moving away from him.

He saw a rope dangling from the side, trailing in the water and he swam after it. Arms and legs churning furiously. He nearly caught the rope. But then, weary, so weary from the battle, he slowly fell behind.

Then he could swim no more.

Palimak rolled over on his back and floated. The sounds of the fight on the *Nepenthe* growing fainter and more distant by the minute.

Finally, there was silence—and he knew he was alone.

Then he heard a stirring and Gundara and Gundaree hopped up on his chest.

"Please, Little Master, don't give up!" Gundara said.

"It would be awful if you drowned, Little Master," Gundaree added.

Palimak couldn't help but smile. "It's nice to finally know you care," he said.

"Of course we care, Little Master," Gundara said.

"If you drown," added Gundaree, "then we'll sink with you."

"And then we'd have to live on the bottom of the sea for ever and ever," Gundara said.

"I can't think of anything more boring," Gundaree put in. "Although it might not be so bad if we could find some nice fat sea worms."

"That's disgusting," Gundara said. "You stupid worm eater!"

"Shut up, Gundara!"

"No, you shut up!"

Palimak was too tired to intervene. And he floated along under the Demon Moon, wondering how long it would be before he drowned.

The twins voices echoed across the empty sea like strange gulls that cried, "Shut up, shut up, shutup!"

CHAPTER THIRTY-ONE
BLOOD AND MAGIC

When the king is unhappy, the sages say, all must suffer. And Rhodes was not a happy king. Standing on the bridge of the *Kray*, lashed by wind and rain, he watched grimly as his chief executioner applied an ax to the exposed neck of an unfortunate sailor.

The offense: laughing at the king's clumsiness. Oh, the fellow protested he hadn't seen Rhodes slip and fall on the slick deck and was only laughing at a comrade's jest. And never mind that the comrade had supported his friend's innocence, swearing that neither had witnessed the royal mishap; and that the jesting and the laughter it drew was a mere coincidence.

If the king's mood had been brighter he might have shown mercy and spared the friend's life. After all, Rhodes appreciated loyalty to a comrade as much as any man. A tongue plucked from the liar's mouth with hot pincers would've sufficed as punishment.

On a feast day, or his birthday, he might even have reduced that sentence to a hundred lashes with the cat, followed by a bath in vinegar and salt.

However, Rhodes had just come from a quarrel with his mother and there was never any question that both men would have to die.

Usually, he would've enjoyed the proceedings: various tortures, performed by the executioner, so ingenious that both men were brought to the brink of death. Then their revival by a special elixir whose recipe had been the executioner's family secret for several generations.

And, finally, two satisfying whacks of the ax, with the cutoff heads posted on stakes as a warning to all potential transgressors that the king's dignity must be preserved at all costs.

Sadly, Rhodes' heart was so troubled that not even these delights moved him.

All hands had been ordered on deck to view the executions. Soldiers and crewmen, ship's officers and royal aides standing silent and miserable in the rain as first one, then the other head was removed.

When the second head fell and rolled across the deck, Rhodes saw one of his men turn away and retch.

"That soldier!" Rhodes snapped at Tabusir, who hovered nearby. "I want his head as well!"

"Which one, Majesty?" Tabusir inquired mildly.

The king stabbed out with a bejeweled finger, indicating a uniformed drummer's lad. Too young to grow a beard or to steel his heart against the troubles of another.

"I'll have no man in my army," the king said, "who can't stand the sight of a little spilled blood."

Tabusir didn't point out that the soldier was probably no more than thirteen summers old. And after two beheadings the pitching deck was running with so much blood mixed with rainwater, that it splashed over the men's boots like spillage in a heaving slaughterhouse with stopped-up gutters.

Perhaps there was just a twinge of sympathy for the lad in the spy's heart. Or perhaps it was a pang of doubt at the king's judgment. In either case it was apparent from their gloom that none of the assembled men were happy about the executions. And maybe it was merely due to a spot of indigestion. After all, he'd eaten a hearty, heavily-spiced meal just before the day's bloody entertainment.

Whatever the reason, Tabusir swallowed his rising bile and snapped a salute so military-perfect that even in a drenched uniform he looked crisp and professionally eager.

"Immediately, Majesty!" he said.

Then he strode briskly off to collect two guardsmen. Moments later the surprised drummer's lad was dragged from the ranks and delivered to the executioner.

A mutinous murmur swept across the ship, silenced by growls from sergeants and bosons. Only to be aroused again by the lad's screams as he was forced to kneel on the gory deck.

"Please! Please!" the boy cried. "I did nothing! Nothing!"

Both the pleading cries and the angry muttering stopped abruptly when the ax fell and the boy's head plopped to the deck.

Immediately, Rhodes felt much better. "Three's a charm against all harm," he murmured to himself, reciting an old nursery jingle. He smiled, trying to remember the rest.

From inside him, Kalasariz spoke up, finishing the doggerel: . . . Four's a chore and to all a bore;/ Five's a sty, not a pig alive;/ But six is a trick of the very best mix!

Rhodes chuckled, to the vast relief of all the aides gathered about him. Even these battle-hardened men worried that the executions were an ill omen and bad for morale.

"That's good!" the king said aloud. "That's very, very good!"

Thinking he was speaking to them, his aides all murmured that, indeed, Majesty, the executions had been a remarkable performance.

Inside him, Kalasariz said, Thank you, Majesty. But it is you who deserves the greatest credit for thinking of these executions. I always found that a mass beheading was a lucky way to start a new venture. It both pleases the gods and chastens the men.

Rhodes nodded agreement, but this time he used his internal voice to reply, saying: It's amazing how much wisdom can be found in a nursery rhyme. From a child's mouth, etc.

At that moment, Tabusir came trotting up. "All has been done as you commanded, Majesty," he said, snapping another crisp salute.

"Excellent work, Tabusir," Rhodes said.

He pulled the smallest ring from the collection on his fingers and tossed it to the spy as a reward. Tabusir caught it and bowed low, murmuring artful words of appreciation.

"Now go fetch three more," the king said. "And deliver them to the executioner with my compliments."

Skilled as he was in covering his true feelings, Tabusir's gaze flickered. "Pardon, Majesty," he said. "But which three do you desire?"

Rhodes shrugged. "Doesn't matter," he said. "Choose who you like. The main thing is that I want six heads posted on the main deck."

Then the king turned and strode from the bridge, saying, "Lucky number, six." Then, in a sing-song voice, he added, "Six is a trick of the very best mix!"

And he roared with laughter, stomping down the passageway to his mother's quarters. As if on cue, the squall suddenly ended when he disappeared from view.

Stunned by the king's behavior, all the men were careful to keep blank faces and did their best not to meet each other's eyes. One of the aides, a jowly, red-faced colonel named Olaf, tried to pretend for all of them that everything was quite normal.

"It's good to see the king in such high spirits again," he said to Tabusir. "You are to be congratulated for such excellent service to His Majesty."

His smile was friendly, but jealousy glittered in his eyes. Seeing it, Tabusir only bowed his head slightly in thanks.

Olaf made the mistake of continuing. "Although I certainly don't envy you your next task," he said with a smirk. "It's not going to make you very popular with the men."

He turned to the others. "Isn't that so, gentlemen?"

There were murmured agreements, some louder than others.

He turned back to Tabusir. Laughing, he said, "Tell me, young man, how do you plan to choose three more victims? By lot? Or will you make them draw straws?"

Tabusir pretended honest puzzlement. "I'm not sure," he said, his face worried. "But I'll come up with something."

"You'd better think fast," Olaf said, amused at Tabusir's predicament. "When the king wants heads he tends to be most impatient."

"Is that so?" Tabusir replied. Then he frowned, as if musing. "I've been trying to place your face for some time, Colonel," he said. "Then it came to me. Weren't you the officer who refused my commission a few years ago?"

Olaf's eyes widened in sudden fear. Jowls trembling, he said, "Oh, it most certainly wasn't me!"

Tabusir examined the man's face with deliberate slowness. Olaf couldn't help but let one hand steal up his chest to touch his fat throat.

"Are you sure about that?" Tabusir asked. "I'd swear you were the man. I rarely forget a face."

"No! Truly!" Olaf squeaked.

Tabusir made an elaborate shrug. "Ah, well, then," he said. "I suppose it's a case of mistaken identity." Then he bowed low. "My apologies, Colonel for begging an end to this most delightful conversation. But I must be off to find the king his heads."

Another bow. "With your permission, of course."

Olaf made a weak-fingered wave, babbling, "Yes, yes. You must not tarry. You have the king's commission!"

Tabusir strolled away, leaving a group of very shaken officers in his wake.

He looked up at the clearing skies, thinking, What an excellent day this has turned out to be.

*   *   *

In his mother's quarters, Rhodes was thinking the same thing as Clayre made an apology so rare that no matter how hard he racked his brains, he couldn't recall another such incident.

"I humbly beg your pardon, my son," she said, "for being the cause of our quarrel. You were right to worry about the mural and I should have listened to your concerns."

Rhodes was about to press his advantage and make her grovel more before accepting her apology, but Kalasariz hissed a warning and he thought better of it.

"It's a thing of the past, mother," he said, forcing magnanimity. "We'll not speak of it again."

He paused, giving Kalasariz time to suggest how to proceed. Then he said, "Have you figured out how the mural disappeared from your chambers, mother?"

Clayre sighed. "I'm afraid not, my son," she said. "Nor do I know how it came into Safar Timura's possession, much less how he managed to use it against us."

She raised a golden wine cup to her beautiful lips and drank sparingly. Then she said, "The trouble is that the mural was there for so long that I'd quite forgotten it. Oh, I had heard stories. Stories that I believed were myths. That the mural depicted the first great king of Syrapis and his daughters. One taleteller even had it that the king portrayed was the grandfather of Alisarrian."

Clayre took another sip of wine. After a moment of reflection, she said, "Although I thought these tales were only myths, I must have sensed some truth in them. For it is the only one of the ancient murals in my chambers that I did not use or alter in any way for my magical purposes. And although it does not excuse my forgetfulness, it does explain why I put it from my mind."

The Queen Witch placed the goblet down quite firmly, her eyes growing fierce. Her fabulous looks so intensified by the emotions roiling within that even Rhodes was stricken by his mother's beauty.

"But I promise you this, my son," she said. "Before this journey is done I will find a way either to nullify the power of the mural or use it to use it our own advantage."

Both Rhodes and Kalasariz were relieved to hear this. "Do you think we can continue the expedition with some hope of success?" the king asked.

"Without a doubt," Clayre said.

Then she waved at her gilded table, where the map was still pinned against the tiles by the four black candles. The replica of the *Nepenthe* now sitting a few hair's breadths from the coast of Aroborus.

"I can also report that our efforts were not completely unsuccessful," she said.

Rhodes looked carefully at the scene and gradually he detected slight movements in the ship. A little fluttering of the sails. An almost imperceptible pitch and roll of the hull. Then he realized that the ship was not quite touching the parchment of the map. And that it actually rested on seas so faint that a flicker of the eye would make them vanish.

"The last time," Clayre said, "my only mistake was that I tried to interfere. It was Jooli's fault, really. Honestly, that girl could drive the most patient of people mad. Still, I shouldn't have tried to kill her. That's what alerted Safar Timura to our presence."

Again, she raised the chalice and sipped. And she said, "I won't make that same mistake again. As you can see, I've got a very weak spell working for us now. One that's impossible for our enemies to detect and yet we'll still be able to follow them."

"That's certainly good to hear, mother," Rhodes said. "But don't we still have the problem of catching them? I mean, our delaying tactics didn't work, correct?"

Clayre smiled, her perfect features glowing with delight. "Actually, they worked quite well," she said. "Naturally, it would've been nice if we could have ended the race quickly by killing them. On the other hand, we've accomplished the next best thing."

"Which is?" Rhodes asked.

The Queen Witch's lovely smile twisted into an ugly, gloating expression.

"Which is that they've lost that little bastard, Palimak," she said. "He fell off the ship and fools that they are, they're searching for him now."

She pointed at the miniature *Nepenthe*, which had moved half an inch down the coast of Aroborus.

"If the winds stay with us," she said, "we ought to catch them within a week!"

The prospect of victory excited Rhodes. But the hope that Palimak might be dead made him positively tingle.

But then Kalasariz spoke, his mental whispers dousing Rhodes' joy as effectively as a large pail of cold water. He said, *Remember, we need the boy's body. Just as we require Safar Timura's. Otherwise you will not achieve your dream of taking their powers to overwhelm your enemies—especially your mother.*

The king's mouth went dry. He grabbed up the wine flask and drank down half its contents. His mother observed this with barely concealed disgust.

"But what if he has drowned, mother?" he asked, voice thinning with tension. "What if he fell into the sea and sank to the bottom? That'll do us no good!"

"Corpses don't sink, they float," she said. "And if he floats, I'll find him, never fear. And if he didn't drown . . ."

She paused, turning to gaze upon the *Nepenthe* with eyes as fierce as a demon's.

"If Palimak didn't drown," she said, picking up where she'd left off, "by the time I'm done with him he'll curse the gods he holds most holy for sparing him from the sea!"

CHAPTER THIRTY-TWO
EEDA'S SECRET

Coralean had never felt so sick in his life. From the shelter of the bridge he could see the storm-driven waves boom under the *Tegula*, lifting her up, up, up, then dropping her down so far his stomach thought it had found a new home, lodged at the back of his throat.

Torrents of rain lashed the ship in a never-ending fury. Great seas burst over the sides, flooding the decks until they were waist-high and the men had to go about their duties with safety lines tied about their waists.

Captain Drakis checked the sails with a critical eye to make certain there was just enough canvas spread, but not too much. Then he studied the compass heading and nodded in satisfaction.

"She's right on course, me lord," he said. "Lucky thing we caught this storm. If she holds, we'll cut the lead that scurvy dog Rhodes has over us by half or more."

Coralean gulped back bile and forced a smile. "Surely the gods must love the name of Drakis," he said with false cheer. "Considering the bonus I'll be blessing you with when we overhaul the king."

"Aye, that be the truth, me lord," Drakis replied. "Luck's favored the Drakis family far back as even me granny can remember. Even when we was lubbers not one of us ever went hungry more'n a day or three.

"Just when we'd be down to thinkin' old boot leather'd make a lovely meal, the gods'd send along a drunk with a fat purse and a skinny neck, if ya know what I mean."

Coralean's stomach did a somersault that was only partially inspired by the heaving deck. Seasick as he was, his imagination seized on some poor sod staggering out of a tavern to spew his guts and having his throat cut by one of Drakis' relatives.

I must be getting old, he thought, to let such flights of cutthroat fancy affect me. The Coralean fortune, after all, was not built by men who shrank at the idea of spilled blood. How many bandit heads have you cut off yourself to post on the caravan trail as a warning to others? And how many murderous competitors were buried by the trail after they tried to ambush you?

In all honesty he had to admit the difference between deaths caused through honest commerce and outright theft was slight. His mind started to wobble further down that disturbing path and he pulled himself up, realizing it was a by product of his illness. Besides, Drakis was looking at him, wondering why he hadn't answered.

"Coralean knows from personal experience what you mean, Captain," the caravan master replied. "In fact I was just reflecting on my youthful career as a raider. One day in particular stands out. It was when I won my first big stake into the caravan business. Why, we cut so many throats that day we . . ."

And he went on to spin a marvelous and detailed lie. Sick as he was, Coralean told such an artful tale of murder and deceit that the pirate captain's eyes shone with admiration. Believing himself fortunate to be admitted into the awesome presence of such a cold-hearted thief as the great Lord Coralean.

All of the captains and sailors in the fleet thought Coralean was not only as much a rogue as they were but was actually better than themselves at the craft of crime. And certainly far more cunning.

It was one of the ways he'd kept his hold over them. A steely grip he had to keep more secure than ever if he were to save Safar from being overtaken and ambushed at sea by Rhodes and his three stolen ships.

Coralean had not been fooled by the Hunanian king's ruse. A man who had won several fortunes by never underestimating his enemies, he'd not wasted one minute thinking Rhodes' intentions were to use the ships to stage an attack on the Kyranian stronghold.

Which was what the Council of Elders had believed when he'd brought the news to them of the betrayal off the port of Xiap. They were all for rushing the army down to the beach where Rhodes was most likely to come ashore.

Fortunately, Safar's father, Khadji, quickly saw Coralean's logic. Especially after the caravan master revealed that their old enemy Kalasariz—who had once seized Kyrania with a horde of demons—had shown up in Syrapis and joined Rhodes.

Leaving Coralean to argue with the Council, Khadji had led a lighting raid on Hunan and brought back several captured officers. Rhode's men were as greedy as their king and all it took was a little creative bribery to get them to spill the details of his plan.

Immediately all opposition to Coralean's proposal to chase down the king and rescue Safar and Palimak had collapsed.

Now he was only three or four days behind Rhodes. He had all nine remaining ships at his disposal, plus a large force of Kyranian soldiers spread through the fleet. All of them well-warned and alert to the possibility of another attempt at betrayal.

If even a single sailor showed mutinous intent, he'd be cut down and thrown over the side to the sharks.

The image of sharp teeth tearing into human flesh and blood-frothed water rose up in Coralean's mind and his belly staged another rebellion.

"Is somethin' wrong, me lord?" Drakis asked, concern in his voice and a gleam of something quite different in his eyes. "Are you feelin' under the weather this day?" He waved at the straining sails. "It's only a little blow. Nothin' to set a *real sailor's belly to quarrelin'.*"

The last thing Coralean wanted was a display of weakness in front of Drakis, the most respected of the pirate captains in the fleet. Especially a weakness of the seagoing variety.

"It's not my innards that are rebelling, captain," the caravan master lied. "As all men know, Coralean has a belly worthy of a cast-iron pot. Why, a fellow once tried to poison me with lye and I drank it down and called for more."

He gripped his forehead between mighty fingers and squeezed. "It's my poor head. I blame it on that keg of brandy my wife served me last night. I only drank a gallon or so for a nightcap before bed. Still, it seems to have given me a fierce headache."

He sighed. "The price of getting old, I warrant," he said. "I used to drink a whole keg without effect and sleep like a babe in his mother's arms."

Drakis was instantly and honestly sympathetic. Under the pirate's rules of manly behavior too much drink was a completely acceptable excuse for any number of things, up to and including taking an ax to your own family.

"It musta been a bad batch of brandy, me lord," he said. "Or maybe the keg was broached and some sea-water got in. Hells, I've gotten sick meself from that sort of thing!"

"It did taste a little salty," Coralean said, frowning.

Drakis nodded vigorously. "See, what'd I tell you? It's the brine that's makin' your head hurt!"

He placed a hand on one of Coralean's massive shoulders. "Whyn't you go below and take a rest, me lord?" he suggested. "I'll send you a keg of my own private reserve to help you sleep. Couple quarters of that, mixed with a little sugar, and you'll sleep like that babe you was talkin' about and wake up feelin' right as rain. That's my prescription."

Coralean grinned. "Thank you very much, Doctor Drakis," he jested. "I'll take your good advice and go below to my cabin."

Then, calling on his last reserves of willpower, he fought down another wave of seasickness and took his leave, reputation intact.

*   *   *

Eeda was waiting for Coralean when he entered the spacious cabin.

"Oh, my poor, dear lord husband," she said when she saw his pale face, "you don't have your sea legs under you yet, do you?"

The caravan master groaned, letting all pretense vanish. For reasons not quite clear to him yet, he felt more comfortable in Eeda's presence than in that of any of his other wives.

"I fear not, my pretty one," he admitted. "At this moment, your beloved bull, Coralean, feels more like a foundling calf, sick from wanting his mother."

"Here, my lord husband," she said, handing him a steaming goblet. "Drink this and you'll feel much better."

Coralean sniffed the fumes. It was brandy laced with fragrant spices. Still he hesitated, saying "I don't know if I can, little one," he said. "Even brandy may not sit well on this traitorous belly of mine."

Eeda put on a charming pout. "Oh, please trust me, lord husband," she said. "I used to make this for my father when he was feeling less than himself. And it always worked such wonders that he called it a miracle potion direct from the gods."

"I doubt if even a miracle can help me, sweetness" Coralean said. Then, moved by her pout, he relented, saying, "But I can refuse you nothing, pretty one. Although it might result in the God of Death, himself, paying a visit to carry poor Coralean away."

He drank the potion down, shuddering as it hit bottom and bounced several times. Then he smiled as the bouncing stopped and warmth and good cheer flooded through his body, banishing the sickness.

"Why, I feel better already," he said, surprised. He looked at the dregs in the cup. "What was in that marvelous elixir, my precious one?"

Eeda smiled prettily. "Oh, a little of this and a little of that," she said. "Along with a large dose of magic."

Then she gently pushed him to his bunk, unbuckling his belt and helping him with the fastenings of his clothing. A moment later he was seated and she pulled off his boots, then his breeches and shirt. Like a helpless child he submitted to her tender ministrations, letting her pull a sleeping gown over his head to cover his massive body.

He sighed blissfully. She'd even warmed the gown with a hot iron.

"You're not sorry you brought me with you, lord husband?" she asked as she pressed him down onto the bunk and pulled up the blanket.

"Even though it nearly caused a revolt in my harem out of jealousy," he said, "I've yet to regret my decision."

"And a wise decision it was, my lord husband," Eeda said. "Although your other wives are paragons of character and strength—and beauty, of course, since all your wives are perfection itself. Reflecting your good taste in women. But as it turned out, only I had the good fortune to be born blessed with the means of assisting you."

Coralean chuckled. "What a surprise that was," he said. "I never dreamed when I married you that you were a witch. Why didn't you tell me before?"

Eeda blushed. And somehow, although she was sitting on the bunk and her head was above his, she managed to look at him through lowered eyes, charming him through and through.

"Oh, I'm only a little witch, lord husband," she said. "Nothing to boast about. I can cure minor ailments, such as your sickness. And cast one or two spells that don't amount to much, but which you might find useful in your mission."

"Pardon, my sweetness," Coralean said, "but you didn't answer my question. I asked why you didn't tell me about this ability before—never mind your opinion of its worth."

Eeda hung her head. "You promise you won't be angry with me, lord husband?" she asked. "I couldn't bear it if I disturbed your serenity by being the cause of any irritation."

"How could I be angry with such a pretty thing as you?" Coralean said. "Go on—tell all. And I, Coralean, swear upon my children's souls that I won't become even slightly angry."

After a moment's hesitation, Eeda said, "Well, my lord husband, I was afraid if I said anything you wouldn't marry me. Most men are not so generous and forgiving of their wives. Just as most men would—dare I say it?—feel intimidated by having a wife who had powers they themselves did not possess."

"Bah!" the caravan master exclaimed. "Other men are not like Coralean." He thumped his big chest. "As all know, I have the strength and wisdom of many. How could I ever feel my manhood was being called into question by mere magic? Which, as you say, doesn't amount to much in any case."

"I must confess it is stronger than it was before," Eeda said. She patted her still-flat belly. "I think it's because I am with child. There are those who say a pregnant witch comes to possess abilities far above her normal state."

Coralean frowned. "Your delicate condition was one thing that almost made me decide against your request to accompany me," he said. "This is a perilous mission, there's no denying. But Coralean has faced such dangers before—too many times to enumerate. However, not once did I risk one of my wives. Who are all dear to me. Why, Coralean holds his wives and children as his most precious possessions!"

Perhaps Coralean caught Eeda's quick flash of irritation at his description of his women and children as possessions. Or perhaps he only sensed it without consciously realizing. At any rate, he instinctively corrected himself.

"Not that a human being—at least one not born or sold into slavery—can truly be called a possession," he said magnanimously. "A treasure, perhaps. But not a possession."

He smiled broadly, feeling good about himself. As if he'd given her a rare gift by all but admitting an error.

Eeda smiled as if in appreciation, but he noted the smile vanished a shade too quickly. She plucked at a loose thread on the blanket and he got the idea that she hadn't taken kindly to his admission.

Finally, she murmured, "You are most gracious, lord husband."

But she said it without feeling, as if speaking words she did not mean. And for the first time in his active career as husband and lover, Coralean became unsure of himself. What, pray, had he done to offend her?

Then, changing the subject, Eeda said, "I've nearly completed my project for you, lord husband. Are you still too ill or weary to examine it?"

"No, sweetness," he replied. "I'm feeling much better, thanks to your tender care—and your miracle potion, of course. Why, it's a wonder your father ever allowed a daughter as valued and useful as yourself to depart his household."

Another quick, cold smile and Eeda rose and went to the writing table to fetch back a piece of parchment. Coralean examined it with exaggerated interest, wondering how he could climb out of the hole he'd dug, instead of deepening it with every word he said.

The parchment had once contained only a dashed-off and highly inaccurate sketch of Safar's intended journey. Safar had drawn it absently while describing his plans to Coralean and Khadji just before he'd left. There were scratched-in mileage figures on the side—all guesses—meant mainly to help determine the type and quantity of the supplies Safar would need.

He'd thrown it away when the meeting was over, but Myrna, Safar's mother, had saved it as a souvenir—just as she saved all of her scholar son's cast-off scribblings.

She'd remembered it when Eeda had asked if there was something personal of Safar's she could have as an aid in casting a spell to locate his position. Armed with the sketch, Eeda had labored hard in the days that followed. Making many false starts, but gradually working out a magical method.

At first, as Coralean studied the parchment he could see little difference from the original. Then he noticed faint lines—appearing like the marks of an artist's brush moistened only with water, which had since dried.

Still, he was bewildered—uncertain of Eeda's intent. "You'll have to explain this to me, my sweet," he said. He shook his mighty head. "Sometimes, I must confess, your beloved husband—sage that he might appear to be—is not as wise as he makes out."

The caravan master immediately became alarmed at this admission of weakness. "But only *sometimes*," he hastened to add. "Such as when I'm weary, or have not regained my sea legs. For as even Coralean's enemies will admit, lying jackals that they are, when it comes to wisdom, no man—"

Eeda put a slender finger to his lips, shushing him. Coralean saw the coldness had vanished from her eyes and her smile was once again tender and loving.

"Say no more, please, lord husband," she said softly. "Lest you spoil the gift you have just given me."

Coralean didn't have the faintest idea what she meant, but he took her advice and said no more. Although he was not always wise he was never a fool, and so he let it rest, thinking understanding would most likely come later.

Then she plucked the parchment from his fingers, saying, "Here, let me show you, lord husband, what I have done."

Eeda took a small pouch from an inside pocket in her robe. She dipped two fingers into the pouch and drew out a pinch of glittering green dust. This she carefully sprinkled on the parchment.

"As you know, dear lord husband," she said, "I've tried many spells, but all have failed. Partly because I was afraid to spoil the parchment, making it useless to us forever. And partly because I am young and lack experience in such things. However, this morning I attempted something new. A spell of my own invention. I was only waiting for your return to test it."

Eagerly, Coralean sat up in his bunk, pushing pillows behind him. "Pray, continue, O wisest of women," he said. "Coralean is but a young, ardent student crouched humbly at your pretty feet."

Eeda gave him a sharp look, but then saw he was not attempting to make a feeble jest at her expense. It was only his way of speaking and there were no hidden meanings or insults. Once again her eyes softened and her smile became gentle.

She held the parchment up to her lips and blew. Coralean heard a sound like temple chimes swaying in the breeze. The green dust flew away, sparkling in the cabin's dim light, and hung suspended in a cloud.

Then faintly, ever so faintly, Coralean could see Safar's face forming in the cloud. He looked sad and careworn. His lips moved, forming a word, but no sound issued forth.

However, the canny old caravan master, a past master at eavesdropping on his competitors, was quite skilled at reading lips.

"Safar said, 'Palimak'," Coralean whispered. "Palimak!"

Then Safar's face—and the green cloud—vanished.

Eeda held up the parchment for Coralean to see. A thin green line was now etched on its surface. It ran in a long arc, following the trade winds from Syrapis all the way to Aroborus, where it stopped.

"That's where he is now, lord husband," Eeda said, tapping the place where the line ended.

She glanced at the mileage figures Safar had scratched on the side. "Shouldn't he have made better progress than this?" she asked.

Coralean nodded, brow knotted in worry. "Yes," he replied. "His plan was to bypass there and strike for the islands beyond, where he would take on water and replenish his provisions. His thinking was that there was so little known about Aroborus it wouldn't be wise, or safe, to tarry there."

"I wonder why he stopped?" Eeda said.

Coralean shook his big head. "There must be something wrong," he said. "And whatever that wrongness is—it has to do with Palimak!"

CHAPTER THIRTY-THREE

IRAJ'S SONG

The search for Palimak was stalled half the night by a swift-moving rainstorm that first reduced visibility to only a few yards, then became so strong they were forced to heave to and lay out a sea anchor to hold position.

As Brutar, the captain of the *Nepenthe*, said: "If we let the blow take us, we'll never find the place where the lad went off."

Biner took the airship above the storm, circling in the cold, thin air until just before dawn when the storm passed on to bedevil the lands beyond.

Then they resumed the search, retracing their path beyond the point where the battle with the tree-creatures had begun. Safar sent out two longboats to help scour the area, with Leiria and Jooli taking command of each of them.

Although he had little experience at sea, Safar was a skilled hunter—as were all Kyranians—and he used an old trick the mountaineers used to employ when speed was paramount—such as finding a lost child after a blizzard had passed, obliterating all trail signs.

But instead of human trackers he used the *Nepenthe* and the airship. The tall ship started in the center and circled outward, while Biner started at the most distant point and circled inward toward the center. This way the same area was scoured twice in a very brief time period and there was little chance of missing Palimak if he were still afloat.

Although he didn't say anything, Safar could tell by Captain Brutar's dark expression that he thought the search was pointless after so many hours had passed. Like most sailors, Brutar and his crew could barely swim—if at all—and thought Palimak had most probably drowned not long after he had jumped from the ship to escape his pursuer.

Brutar's expression became darker still when he saw how infested the area was with sharks and sea crocodiles. Fins constantly criss-crossed the calm seas, while hungry reptilian eyes poked just above the surface, looking for opportunity.

Once they came upon an enormous crocodile fighting with two equally huge sharks over bloody remains.

Leiria and Jooli moved up in the longboats as the terrible fight raged. Then dispatched all three of the creatures with their longbows.

To Safar's relief, the remains proved to be not human but the corpse of a serpent whose body was twice the girth of a man's.

Finally, Captain Brutar made bold to approach Safar. Embarrassed, he hawked and spat over the rail.

Then he said, "Beggin' yer pardon, me lord, and it pains me somethin' awful to say this to a father what's boy has gone missin'. In this old salt's opinion the lad's a goner and that's for certain. We can hunt 'til the Hellsfires burn themselves out and we won't find nothin' but what we already found—which is nothin'!"

Safar shook his head. "He's still alive," he said. "And if I have to, I'll turn the sea upside down and shake it out to find him!"

Brutar sighed. "Dammit, man," he said, "yer talkin' like we was lookin' fer a worm in a biscuit. Knock it 'gainst a table and the worm falls out, real easy like."

He made a wide gesture, taking in the long, empty horizon. "The sea ain't no biscuit. And the lad, bless his soul, ain't no worm livin' and eatin' in its natural born home. This is the sea, man. Which means she'll even kill her own!"

The captain braced for an argument, but was prepared to stand fast. Personally, he didn't give a thin fishbone about Palimak, much less about Safar's tender fatherly feelings. He wanted to get on with the voyage and either collect his promised bonus or toss Safar and the Kyranians over the side if for some reason the bonus wasn't forthcoming.

Actually, it was his cherished dream to accomplish both—collecting the money and ridding himself and his crew of this pesky lot once and for all. And get back to honest pirating, instead of fighting another man's enemies for pay.

However, instead of arguing, Safar's eyes lit up. He slapped the captain on the shoulder, saying, "Thanks, Captain! You may have just solved the problem!"

And he rushed away, leaving a bewildered Brutar staring after him. What in the hells had he said to be thanked for?

Safar burst into Palimak's ruined cabin and quickly found the doughmen as well as the two pieces of worm, which still showed faint signs of life. Then he sped to his own quarters where he dug out a wine jar, emptied the contents into a basin and knocked off the jar's narrow mouth with the blade of his silver witch's dagger.

Next, he waved the dagger over the worm parts and cast a regeneration spell. Sparks leaped off the point and each piece grew the part it was missing. A moment later there were two whole worms wriggling across the table. Safar imprisoned them with an overturned cup, then went on to the rest of his preparations.

After moistening the doughmen with wine, he formed them into a single ball. Then, with his skillful potter's fingers, he sculpted a single doughman of his own. Except, instead of Palimak's rather clumsy figures, this one looked like a tall, slender, broad-shouldered youth.

Using the dagger point Safar pricked in the features and in scant minutes Palimak's face appeared like magic—although it was art, not sorcery, that Safar used.

He slit the belly, pressed the worms inside, then smoothed over the wound. The Palimak doughman went into the wine jar, whose mouth was sealed with wax. He paused, taking in a deep breath to clear his mind. Now he was ready for the spell.

He went up to the main deck, the jar cradled in one arm. Leiria was already there, face pale as death, thinking the search had been called off. Jooli was just clambering on board from the longboat. Safar signaled the airship for Biner and Arlain to join him. And when all were gathered at the bow he asked their assistance in casting the spell to find the lad they all loved.

When he thought their minds were all fixed on the single goal he gestured, and burning incense appeared in his hand, filling the air with its heady scent. He heard murmurs from behind him, where Brutar and the crewmen watched, fearful of the wizardry he was about to perform.

Then, drawing on Asper for inspiration, he whispered:

> *"When in your mother's womb*
> *You did dwell;*
> *Tarrying between love's tomb*
> *And life's Hell;*
> *Did you ever wonder if the fearful Path*
> *Where you tarried*
> *Was close or distant from Fate's wrath?*
> *Or were you carried,*
> *Into this world not knowing*
> *From whence you came*
> *Or where you were going;*
> *Bound for Nowhere on winds of pain?"*

Then he threw the jar into the rolling waves. It bobbed about for a moment, then retreated swiftly as the ship sailed on. A great shark's fin cut in front of it. Everyone held their breath, whether from the sight of the shark or in anticipation of the spell, Safar couldn't say.

Suddenly, the jar reversed course. As if powered by a mighty sail it shot forward against the waves, moving past the ship's bow, then heading steadily away to the thin green line on the horizon.

Safar pointed. "That's where he is," he said. "In Aroborus."

And then he gave orders to set sail and follow the magical device to wherever it might lead.

٭ ٭ ٭

The shores of Aroborus were a dazzling green, as if some wastrel god had cast emeralds from Heaven's treasure house into the sea. The wind blew fragrant, carrying the heady scent of spices and fruited vines. Clouds of birds wheeled in the sky, filling the air with their mournful cries.

The wine jar came to rest on a wide beach of white sand, pebbled with broken shells of many colors—swept up from the sharp coral reefs that ringed the narrow-mouthed bay. Somehow the jar had been swept over the reefs unscathed. But at no point was there a place the longboats could get through, much less a tall ship the size of the *Nepenthe.*

Safar could see the wine jar bobbing in a tidepool and for the life of him couldn't imagine the circumstances that would have allowed Palimak to reach the beach unscathed.

Brutar said as much, pointing out that common reason said if the lad had made it this far alive, he surely would've died when he was hurled against the reefs to be shredded by their razor edges.

"Makes me shiver just to think about it, me lord," he said gloomily. "The poor boy comin' so close to safety, like. Gettin' his hopes up when he saw dry land. Then bein' 'et up alive by them reefs, like he'd run into a school of sharks."

He sighed. "And ain't it a wicked world we was born to, me lord," he said, "to allow such an innocent lad—a lad loved by all—to come to such a terrible end? Makes a simple man like meself question his faith, it does.

"Damned priests are al'ays sayin' the gods smile on the good folk who mind their laws. But if truth be known it's the bad 'uns who al'ays get through this life the easy way, ain't it?"

Worried as he was, Safar had to bury a smile at this speech, coming as it did from the lips of a committed cutthroat and pirate. Not that he entirely disagreed with Brutar's philosophy. Which was that under the unspoken laws of the heavens, it was the wicked, not the meek, who endured and prospered. While priests made themselves and their client kings rich and powerful by preaching the opposite to the masses.

It reminded him of a blasphemous drinking song from his days as a rebellious student in Walaria. He'd taught it to Iraj after they'd joined up again and it had become Protarus' favorite ditty.

He sang it whenever they got together in private to drink and talk as equals. As young brothers of the blood oath, whose sworn common goal was for the good of all.

An image rose up in his mind—so strong, so real, that it swept away the terrible present and replaced it with the pleasant past. In his mind's eye he could see Iraj sprawled on thick pillows. The slender waist of a nubile wench clasped in one hand, a cup of cheer lifted in the other.

And he was singing, the remembered voice so real it strummed Safar's own vocal chords. He had the odd feeling that if he opened his mouth it would be Iraj's voice that came forth, instead of his own.

Although he didn't humiliate himself in front of the others, he let the scene play out in his mind. Then suddenly he lost all sense of time and place, waves of peace and half-drunken joy thrilling his imagination as the man who was once his friend sang:

710

> *"Rich man, poor man,*
> *holy man, thief.*
> *The rich get heaven,*
> *the poor man grief.*
> *Alms for the holy man,*
> *To the thief, baksheesh!"*

Then the other Safar—the Safar of the vision—joined in, slapping his knee in rhythmic time and singing the chorus:

> *"Oh, there's dancing on the altar*
> *For those who do not falter.*
> *Sin and gold for the bold.*
> *To the meek, lash and halter . . ."*

And then Leiria's voice cut through, bursting the vision like a knife thrust into a swollen bag of wine. And all the images spilled out, weakening him as if they were his life's blood.

"Are you all right, Safar?" she was saying.

He gasped, sucking in air like a man rising from watery depths, and emerged into the painful present. The wine jar still bobbed in the tidepool, but with Brutar nowhere to be seen. Instead of the captain, it was Leiria standing before him, looking up at him with worried eyes.

Safar coughed. Then he managed to nod, but the movement was jerky, clumsy. "Yes," he croaked. "I'm fine."

He glanced about and saw that Brutar was some twenty feet distant, standing with some of his officers. Safar had no recollection that they'd parted.

"Are you sure?" Leiria asked. And for the first time, Safar realized she was whispering so the others couldn't hear.

"A few minutes ago," she continued, "you were talking to the captain, then you suddenly turned and walked off as if he'd angered you."

"I'm not angry at anyone," Safar said, puzzled. "Why should I be?"

Leiria put a gentle hand on his arm. Its loving warmth seeming to act as a catalyst to cleanse the remaining dregs of unreality from his mind.

"Actually," she said, "when I came up to see what was wrong, you were smiling. You looked so peaceful I hated to disturb you."

She made a faint motion with her head to indicate Brutar. "But I didn't want them to get the idea their commander had suddenly gone mad."

"I was only thinking," Safar said. "About . . . well, it doesn't matter now."

He knew this was an insufficient explanation, but was uncomfortable about saying more. Especially since it involved Iraj, whom Leiria hated with a passion.

"Whatever it was you were thinking about," she said, "I'm glad it made you smile. It's been a long time since I've seen you look so happy."

She moved closer, soft breasts brushing against him. Familiar perfume and fragrant breath rising to fill him up like wine.

And they were suddenly just a man and a woman—lovers from another time and place come together once more.

Safar had the overpowering urge to embrace her and kiss her. To carry them both away to the bower of joy they'd once shared together.

Only the presence of Brutar and the crew kept him from acting on his impulse.

Leiria shuddered, aching for the embrace. "You can come to me anytime you like," she whispered. "I won't send you away again."

"I know," Safar said, voice rasping with effort.

Hurt came into her eyes. "But you won't," she said, nearly weeping.

"I want to," Safar said. "But I can't."

The hurt softened. And she recovered, smiling sadly. "For the old reasons?" she asked.

Safar nodded. "And more," he said. "There's . . . there's . . . something that . . ." and he gave up the struggle and broke off the rest. "I can't explain," he said again.

"Will you ever tell me?" she whispered.

"Yes," he said. The answer started as a lie but, brief as his reply was, by the time he spoke the word it became a promise.

Leiria smiled and, hidden from the sight of the others by his body, she blew him a kiss.

Then she turned and for the benefit of the onlookers laughed loudly as if he'd just told a fine jest. It must have worked for Brutar was visibly relieved.

The pirate captain turned to his officers, chuckling as if he'd overheard the joke, saying, "You see. Lord Timura was only a bit tired from worryin' and bein' up all night lookin' for his boy."

Safar squared his shoulders, again accepting the weight of all the burdens he'd escaped, however briefly.

"We'd better get going," he said to Leiria.

"Yes, we'd best," she said, but her tone was regretful.

Safar pushed emotions aside and got to work. He'd already decided how to proceed and immediately signaled for Biner to prepare to take him away. A moment later a large basket was cranked down from the skies.

Before he ascended to the airship with Leiria and Jooli, Safar sent for Renor. The young soldier approached, his ever-present companion, Sinch, at his heels.

"Biner's going to land us on the beach with the airship," Safar said. "I don't know how long it's going to take to find Palimak, or what dangers we might encounter, but I want you to be on the alert for my signal."

"Don't worry, Lord Timura," Renor said. "We'll come running the moment you send for us."

Safar patted his shoulder. He was quite fond of the young Kyranian, who had suffered and borne up under much since the days when they had all been forced from their homeland. His little brother had been the first victim of Iraj's assault—slaughtered in a high mountain meadow in the Gods' Divide.

"I never worry about you, Renor," Safar said. He grinned at Sinch. "Or you either, Sinch. Except for your tasteless jokes, of course."

Sinch blushed, pleased that the great Lord Timura remembered such a personal thing about him.

"I'll have a dozen more ready, my lord," he said, "for when you get back. I know you love a good joke."

Safar smiled in appreciation. Then he said, "The only thing that really worries me is Captain Brutar and his pirates. I want you both to be on your guard in case they decide to forgo the bonus and play the traitor."

Renor nodded. "I'll get all our boys together," he said. "Drill them in full armor and all. That ought to put the fear of the gods into those pirates. They're just rabble and they know they can't stand up to real soldiers. And if that doesn't work, we'll already have our weapons at hand to teach them some lessons about loyalty."

Safar approved this plan, issued a few more orders to cover details they hadn't discussed before, then took his leave.

Half an hour later Safar was retrieving the wine jar from the tidepool. A squad of Kyranian soldiers stood by for his orders, while Leiria and Jooli scoured the beach for some sign of Palimak.

From above came a whoosh of air and the throb of the magical engines as Biner took the airship aloft. The plan had been thoroughly discussed and the system of signals worked out. Now all Safar had to do was find Palimak.

"Over here, Safar," Jooli shouted.

He hurried to her side, Leiria joining him.

Jooli pointed at several impressions in the sand "Footprints," she said. "Although they're too faint for me to make out who they belong to."

Safar knelt, fishing out his silver dagger. He waved it over the impressions, muttering a spell. The sand shifted, moving only a few grains at a time and gradually the footprints took form, standing out deep and clear.

They were human prints—long and narrow with well-formed toes. The only thing out of the ordinary were tiny marks like hooks springing from the toes. Not hooks but talons, Safar thought. Which could only mean one thing. Relief flooded in.

"It's Palimak," he said.

Safar looked up at the forest bordering the beach. The trees were so dense they might as well have been castle walls. Then he saw the break of a narrow avenue leading into the woods.

"He went that way," he said, rising.

They followed the footprints a short distance along the beach, Safar stopping every now and again to work his magic.

Then, suddenly, the distances between the tracks started lengthening. Each footprint far in front of the other.

"He's running!" Leiria said.

"Yes, but from what?" Safar said.

Heart racing, he looked about the beach, but saw no other signs.

"I don't know what's happening," he said, "but we'd better hurry."

Then he called for the soldiers and they all plunged into the dark, ancient forest of Aroborus.

CHAPTER THIRTY-FOUR

THE RAVENOUS SEAS

Little Master's getting tired," Gundara observed from his perch on Palimak's shoulders.

"That's too bad," Gundaree said. "We still have a long way to go."

"I'm all right," Palimak gasped. "I'm just thirsty, that's all."

He was lying more to himself than to the Favorites. Trying to stay afloat in the increasingly choppy surf was difficult. Palimak only had his tunic, which he'd turned into water wings, to support him. He'd kept his breeches on, although their weight made things more difficult. But, except as a last resort, he was loath to shed them as he had his boots.

It had nothing to do with modesty. Naked and alive was better than clothed and dead in even the shyest person's rule book. He had a few items in his pockets and hanging from his belt that might better his chances of survival once he reached land. Such as a knife and his waterproof wizard's purse, which contained all sorts of useful things.

More importantly, he needed a pocket to hold the stone turtle, otherwise the Favorites would be lost to him. Even if he could do without them, as irritating and cold-hearted as they could sometimes be, Palimak would never condemn his mischievous friends to an eternal prison at the bottom of the sea.

"You should have told us you were thirsty, Little Master," Gundara said.

"We can do something about that!" Gundaree put in.

"Then do it, please!" Palimak croaked, throat sore and raspy from all the salt-water he'd taken in.

The Favorites directed him to put his head back as far as he could. Then they hopped onto his forehead and crouched down to suck up sea-water. To his surprise they drew in enormous quantities, blowing up like little toads.

Gundara signaled for him to open his mouth and then both of them expelled the water in a torrent so heavy he had to swallow fast to avoid choking. Transformed in their bodies, the water was amazingly clear and sweet, like fresh spring water mixed with honey.

"Enough!" Palimak finally sputtered and they stopped, resuming their perch on either shoulder.

He took in a few deep breaths and suddenly felt his strength coming back. Most likely from the nectar the Favorites had expelled along with the water. He wondered idly if perhaps spirit folk were like bees, processing what they ate into honey.

"Thanks," Palimak said. "I didn't know you could do that."

"You never asked," Gundara pointed out.

"There's lots of things we can do," Gundaree added, "that you've never asked about."

"If any of them include a way of getting us out of this fix," Palimak said, "now's the time to speak up."

The Favorites thought for a moment.

Then Gundara said, "Well, if we could make you small enough, maybe we could fit you into the turtle with us."

"But first we'd have to make the turtle float, like a little boat," Gundaree pointed out.

"I already thought of that!" Gundara sniffed. "I'm not stupid, you know."

"That's not what our mother said," Gundaree replied.

"She never!" Gundara protested.

"Sure, she did," Gundaree said. "The last time we saw her she said Gundara was the stupidest—"

"Please, please, please!" Palimak broke in. "I'm dying here, in case you've forgotten. And if I go, both of you go!"

"Little master has a good point," Gundara said.

"I'll stop if you do," Gundaree said.

"Truce?"

"Truce!"

When they were quiet, Palimak said, "We were talking about getting me into the turtle and then making it float."

"Two very good ideas, if I do say so myself," Gundara said.

"The tide's going in," Gundaree said. "So that means we'd end up on dry land in no time."

Hopes stirring, Palimak said, "Let's get started, then. What do you want me to do?"

This was greeted by dead silence. Frustrated, Palimak said, "Come on! We're wasting time!"

"There's nothing to start, Little Master," Gundara said.

"But you both said they were good ideas," Palimak pointed out.

"They are," Gundara said. "But they were only theories."

"And, unfortunately, we can't actually do either one," Gundaree said.

Palimak groaned. Some day the Favorites were going to be the death of him—literally.

"The best thing to do is keep swimming, Little Master," Gundaree advised.

"Except maybe a bit faster, before the shark catches up to us," Gundara put in.

"Shark!" Palimak exclaimed.

He stopped treading water, paddling about to look. He saw nothing but the empty Demon Moon-lit seas.

"There's two of them, actually," Gundaree said.

"And a crocodile," Gundara added. "Don't forget that."

"I didn't want to scare the Little Master," Gundaree said. "Two sharks seemed bad enough."

"What should I do?" Palimak gasped, trying to hold back panic. "I can't outswim any of them!"

"That's certainly true," Gundaree admitted.

"We have such a smart Little Master," Gundara said. "Too bad he can't swim as fast as he thinks."

"Even if he could," Gundaree said, "he'd never get away from the sea serpent."

"Sea serpent!" Palimak cried. "Where?"

"Oh, he's about thirty feet below us," Gundara said.

"He's not sure yet if you're food," Gundaree said. "But he's starting to get the idea."

Just then, off in the distance, Palimak saw a huge fin break the surface. It started to circle him—slowly, almost lazily. A moment later another popped up, circling in the opposite direction.

He couldn't see the crocodile, but he knew it'd remain so low on the surface that his first sight would be its jaws opening wide to take him.

As for the sea serpent, he'd never spot it. The thing would probably just wriggle up to grab him by the legs and pull him under.

Palimak had been in trouble many times before, but never had he been so thoroughly trapped. His panicky mind churned for inspiration but was continually interrupted by images of being eaten alive by one—or all—of the big sea carnivores closing in on him.

Meanwhile, the Favorites were conferring. Palimak was too frightened to make out what they were saying, but he supposed it was a discussion of the dubious merits of being trapped beneath the sea, with no possibility of a new master coming along to rescue them for several thousand years—if ever.

Finally, Gundara said, "We have an idea."

"Not another damned theory!" Palimak groaned, imagining the sea serpent examining his dangling legs with hungry interest.

"Oh, no," Gundaree said. "It's not a theory. This idea we can actually do something about."

"Maybe," Gundara cautioned.

"All right . . . maybe," Gundaree grudgingly admitted.

"But it's worth a try, at least," Gundara said.

"I suppose so," Gundaree agreed. "And if it doesn't work we could always try the other idea."

"What other idea?" Palimak asked.

He felt as if he'd been cast into some other world, a surreal world. A world where his impending death could be discussed so casually. While less than fifty feet away the circling sharks were closing slowly in.

And although it might only have been his imagination, Palimak thought he could see the knobbed eyes of the sea crocodile poking up a few feet within the circles.

And the serpent—oh, damn the serpent! Let him eat the leftovers! Palimak suppressed an hysterical giggle.

"Never mind the other idea," Gundara said.

"Absolutely!" Gundaree agreed. "It'll only make you mad."

"Fine, fine!" Palimak moaned. "It's forgotten. Now, please do something! I wasn't born to be somebody's dinner."

"That's not quite true, Little Master," Gundara said.

"Yes," Gundaree said. "Don't you know that *everybody* is somebody's food?"

"Not necessarily right away, you understand," Gundara said. "But eventually. It's life's most important lesson, you know."

"Our mother used to sing us the most wonderful lullaby that sums it all up," Gundaree said. And he sang:

> *"Everybody's somebody's food.*
> *Everybody's somebody's slaything.*
> *And though it's very, very rude,*
> *Everybody's somebody's food!"*

Gundara wiped away a tear at the memory. "Mother was such a marvelous teacher," he said.

"Oh, gods!" Palimak groaned, seeing one of the sharks make a short dash toward him. "Please, hurry and do something!"

Perhaps it was because they saw the shark make its dash, or perhaps it was only because they'd run out of things to say. Whatever the case, to Palimak's massive relief he sensed the comforting buzz of a powerful spell being cast.

He suffered one more moment of fear as suddenly there was a surge just beneath his feet—so strong it rocked him in the water. In reaction, Palimak's body spasmed and talons shot out from his fingers *and* his toes—ready to do futile battle.

There was another surge and a huge slime-covered body bumped against his, tossing him to the side.

The water boiled and he paddled furiously to keep afloat. Then an incredibly long and thick snakelike body burst from the water. It kept coming and coming like a wagon train all tied together.

He heard a wild howl of fear and caught a glimpse of the sea serpent's head as it leaped over him—fang-rimmed mouth so wide it could swallow a small boat whole.

Then several other bodies collided with his and he went under, pawing madly to regain the surface. The tunic water wings were ripped away. His talons lashed out in every direction in a desperate, instinctual, defensive effort.

The claws caught on something—he didn't know what—then ripped along dense flesh as the creature powered past him without pause.

A moment later he was on the surface, vomiting brine, too overcome to see what was happening.

"We did it, Little Master!" Gundara cried. "We did it!"

Palimak steadied himself enough to see the sea serpent racing away. A wave hit him and he went under again. But when he resurfaced he had time to catch sight of the two sharks leaping high into the air as they pursued the serpent.

Then a strong eddy rocked him as the crocodile swam past, its muscular tail slashing through the water, barely missing Palimak.

He was so astonished at not being attacked that he forgot to tread water and went under once more. But this time when he pulled himself up he did it slowly and without panic.

Palimak started treading water, clearing his eyes. To his astonishment and supreme delight he saw the sharks and crocodile speeding away after the panicked sea serpent. All jumping high out of the water to achieve maximum speed.

"What did you do?" Palimak gasped.

"It was easy, Little Master," Gundara said.

"We made the sea serpent think he was food," Gundaree explained.

"And we made the sharks and the crocodile think he'd taste better than you," Gundara continued.

"Like the song we just made up," Gundaree said. "You know: 'Everybody's somebody's food . . .'"

"I wish you'd shut up," Gundara said. "You're making me hungry and everything the Little Master has in his pockets for us to eat has been spoiled by the water."

"I won't say, 'You shut up, too,'" Gundaree replied in a surprisingly reasonable voice. "We still have that truce, right?"

"I'm sorry," Gundara said to his twin. "I forgot about the truce. Which we really need right now."

"That's all right," Gundaree said. "I know you didn't really mean it. You were just distracted because of the storm and all."

This time Palimak's heart descended to his bowels, forming an embarrassing lump of fear.

"What storm?" he asked.

At that moment rain pelted down. And a strong wind exploded the calm, whipping up waves of fearful height.

"That storm, Little Master," Gundara answered.

"What with the sharks and the crocodile and the sea serpent," Gundaree said, "we didn't think it was a good time to mention it."

"But there's still good news, Little Master," Gundara said. "We're really, really close to land right now."

From a distance, Palimak could hear the sound of waves booming across an obstruction.

"Is that a reef I hear?" he asked.

"You're so smart, Little Master!" Gundaree said. "That's exactly what it is. A big, sharp coral reef."

"You'll probably be torn to pieces by it," Gundara said. "But at least you won't have to worry about us."

"That's right," Gundaree said. "This time when you're killed we won't be stuck at the bottom of the ocean."

"We'll be washed up on the reef," Gundara further explained. "And only have to wait maybe a hundred years or so before a new master finds us."

"Doesn't that make you happy, Little Master?" Gundaree asked. "Knowing we won't get bored?"

Palimak's heart jumped as realization sank in.

"You mean," he said, "that you don't have the faintest idea on how to get me over that reef?"

"Well," Gundaree said, "we *do* have some theories . . ."

CHAPTER THIRTY-FIVE
JUNGLE MAGIC

The moment Safar plunged into the jungle he knew he'd made a potentially fatal error.

Biting insects swarmed up all around him. Above, there was an explosion of wings and a chorus of shrill warning cries as birds took flight.

There was a scatter of motion in the trees, like errant winds bursting forth in every direction and he saw enormous apes swinging away from his entry point, jabbering simian curses.

A huge snake fell in his path, rising up on threatening coils, spitting poison at his eyes.

But all his alarm bells were already ringing and he brought his shield up just in time for the poison to splatter against it.

Jooli shouted something he couldn't make out, but he instinctively leaped to the side and an arrow from her bow pinned the snake to the ground.

Leiria rushed in, severing the snake's head with her sword. It fell on the black leafy ground, hissing and spitting its poisonous hate.

Safar heard shouts of dismay from the soldiers and whirled around to see thorny vines and branches shooting forth to bar the entrance into the jungle.

Somewhere not far off an ape hooted in triumphant glee.

Safar raced to the closing gap, hacking at the vines with his sword. Leiria and Jooli crowded in to help. But as fast as they cut, the vines grew back at double the speed and thickness.

Then he heard an explosive *pop!* and two large insect eyes appeared out of nowhere, only inches from his face.

Crying a warning to the others he stumbled back, only to find himself caught in the sticky tendrils of a frighteningly strong web.

He fought his way out, then slashed at the thick strands entangling Leiria and Jooli.

Freed, they dashed out of the gap, which healed itself with such blinding speed that soon there was no sign of the path by which they'd entered.

Instead, Safar found himself confronted by an enormous black spider—big as a royal banquet platter. Poison oozed from large fangs set in a mouth large enough to grip a child's head.

Several strands of web shot out of tubes along its bloated body. The thick threads wrapped around branches on either side of Safar and the spider rushed along them to attack.

Jooli's arrow hissed past Safar's ear, knocking the spider to the ground and killing it. But then other spiders—just as big and fierce—popped out of nothingness and scuttled toward them.

Safar ordered a hasty but orderly retreat along the narrow path. The squad of soldiers led the way, wary of new dangers. Jooli acted as rearguard, firing arrow after arrow into the spiders, while Leiria and Safar used their swords on those that got through.

Gradually, the number of spiders diminished and then they seemed to vanish altogether. Safar called a halt to reconnoiter but, as far as he or any of the others could tell, there were no other paths except the one they'd taken.

The trees were so tall and dense it seemed like twilight under their canopy instead of the middle of the day. The forest was strangely silent. There were no bird or insect sounds. Even the apes were quiet. It was hot and humid and the air smelled of rotting things.

The Kyranians moved on, treading lightly and keeping their voices to a whisper.

Then Sergeant Hamyr, who was a bit older than the other soldiers and a skilled tracker, found Palimak's footprints in the carpet of decaying leaves.

"At least we know we're on the right trail," Leiria observed.

"The question, of course," Jooli said, "is whether it'll eventually take us out of this place. After we find Palimak, that is."

Safar shrugged. "If we can't find a way to walk out," he said, "all we have to do is start climbing." He gestured at the towering trees. "Biner is ready to pick us up with the airship anytime we're ready."

There were murmurs of relief from Sergeant Hamyr and the others. Rattled by the events of the past hour, they'd forgotten the fall-back plan.

"We can also rely on Biner to send us reinforcements if we need them," Safar added—further comforting his soldiers.

He patted a hefty pouch on his belt. "I have plenty of signal powder. So I only have to find an open space, or get high enough into the trees, to let Biner know what's happening."

Everyone felt much better after that, talking in normal voices and enjoying a quick meal of parched corn and dried goat flesh which they washed down with good Kyranian wine mixed with honey and water.

Refreshed and with their spirits restored, the expedition continued—following the narrow path that wound through the gloom like an uncoiling snake.

However, Safar was not as unconcerned about their situation as he'd made out. Dead magic permeated the forest. Rather than coming from a single source, the magic seemed to radiate from all sides as if the very trees were inhabited by unfriendly spirit folk.

Quietly, he cast some warding spells and hoped for the best. Moments after he'd finished, Jooli slipped up to his side.

"You can feel it, too?" she whispered so the others wouldn't hear.

Safar nodded. "But I've taken some precautions," he said.

"As have I," Jooli said. "Except I don't think any of our spells are strong enough."

"That's because we don't know who or what we're guarding against," Safar said. "We're both working blind."

He gestured ahead, where the path curved around a vine-choked tree, saying, "Unless I'm well off my mark, I think we'll find out soon enough. There's something waiting for us just past that point."

Jooli's eyes narrowed as she concentrated. Then she nodded. "You're right," she said. "But I can't make out what it is. Everything seems . . . I don't know, scattered."

That was exactly how Safar would have described the strange waves of magic he sensed. It was as if they were made up of many sorcerous particles with no particular center or purpose, but had only been brought together by coincidence.

"We'd better investigate before we walk right into some sort of trap," Safar said.

"Why don't I go ahead," Jooli asked, "while you watch my back?"

Safar agreed and called another halt. He told the group there were some unexplained disturbances he and Jooli needed to investigate, playing down the danger and making it seem like a routine precaution.

Leiria knew what he was up to. They'd fought together so many times that even the subtle system of signals they'd worked out over the years was unnecessary. She sensed what was happening before he had a chance to tug his earlobe or straighten his sword belt.

Instantly, she took appropriate action. "If Jooli's going to play witch when she takes point," she said, "we'll need plenty of hard steel behind her, not just more magic."

Leiria spread the men out along the trail, spears and swords at ready. When Jooli signaled to begin, they all moved forward—Safar lagging back, alert to magical attack from both the front and the rear.

When she reached the tree that marked the bend in the trail Safar saw Jooli hesitate, then lean forward to concentrate. He'd become familiar with her sorcerous spoor and caught the tingle of her magic as she probed the area beyond.

Safar added his own powers to her work and found nothing to be alarmed about.

The he saw her shrug and step forward.

Immediately, the air around her began to glow. Although he caught no scent of magic—threatening or otherwise—Safar opened his mouth to call a warning.

Then the glow became a cloud of colorful butterflies that circled her for a moment, then swept along the path just above the soldiers' heads. Except for quick glances, no one paid them the slightest attention—not even pausing to admire this swirling rainbow of flying insects.

Leiria and the soldiers were so tensed for possible danger that the butterflies' beauty escaped them.

Jooli turned her head and called back, "Everything's fine. I'm going on." Then she disappeared around the bend.

Leiria was the next to cross and once again a cloud of butterflies appeared, circling her briefly before flying down the trail. She too signaled that all was well and that she was proceeding.

Sergeant Hamyr followed, leading the soldiers around the bend, absently brushing at a third swarm of the marvelous butterflies.

Safar paused at the tree. He studied the ground, then examined the massive roots that rose twenty feet or more before they joined the trunk.

He saw a large snake, thick as a man's body, moving slowly up one of the roots. But its attention was fixed on a monkey, sitting silently and peacefully on a limb, grooming itself.

Other than the snake, he could see nothing that might endanger him. Nor could he see where the butterflies had come from.

He heard Leiria call to him, her voice calm and reassuring. So he stepped forward, alert for the slightest disturbance.

And nothing happened. No odd shimmer of the atmosphere. Not even a single butterfly rising up, much less a colorful swarm.

He went around the bend and some distance away saw Leiria and the others squatting on the trail, peacefully munching on rations and slaking their thirst.

Leiria waved to him. "It's all right, Safar," she cried. "Come and have something to eat and drink."

Then Jooli called out. "We found more of Palimak's footprints."

Safar hurried forward, anxious to see.

Without warning, the ground shifted under him. He fell heavily, hands shooting out to catch himself.

But when he landed, instead of the leafy jungle trail he found himself gripping hot, bare ground.

And all around him he heard hundreds of voices roar: "Kill, kill, kill! Death to Safar Timura!"

Safar came up, bewildered—but automatically reaching for his sword. He found himself standing in a large arena made of hard-packed red earth.

And instead of the jungle and his waiting friends he saw hundreds upon hundreds of shouting, painted savages—all pounding the ground with the butts of their spears. Horns blared, drums thundered and somewhere a big cat screamed in fury.

From behind he heard the heavy slap of feet racing toward him and he whirled, sword coming up. But then he froze, gaping.

For charging toward him was a half-naked youth. Brandishing a long spear aimed straight at Safar's heart.

It was Palimak!

And the crowd roared: "Kill, kill, kill! Death to Safar Timura!"

CHAPTER THIRTY-SIX
THE FOREST OF FORGETFULNESS

Even over the whistling wind and hard-driven rain, Palimak could hear the waves boom against the reef. Dimly he made out their jagged line—the boiling surf dyed pink by the grinning Demon Moon.

He tried to back-paddle, but the tidal current was too strong, sucking him inexorably toward the reef.

"To your right, Little Master!" Gundara cried.

Palimak obediently turned his head and saw a thick black object lifting up in the curl of a wave.

"Swim for it!" shouted Gundaree.

Palimak struck out for the object. One stroke. Two. Three. And then he was drawing close and could see it was a gnarled, twisted log, with a dozen or more limp branches trailing behind.

Palimak reached for it, then caught a glimpse of a horribly familiar set of teeth grinning out of the trunk.

Fear lanced his heart and he snatched his hand back, nearly drowning as he went under in a desperate effort to kick away from the tree-beast.

He came up, choking and sputtering, pawing at the water to stay afloat.

"Don't worry, Little Master," Gundara cried. "It's dead!"

"Well, it's almost dead, anyway," Gundaree quibbled.

"Never mind that!" Gundara said. "Get up on it before you drown, Little Master."

It took all of Palimak's faith in the Favorites to comply. Gingerly, he caught hold of the tree creature. He felt a faint flutter of life and heard the weak clicking of teeth.

Doing his best to still his quaking nerves, he flung himself across the trunk. He dangled there for a moment, skin instinctively shrinking where it touched the creature's rough surface.

"Sit up on it," Gundaree ordered.

Shuddering, Palimak did as he was told—throwing a leg on either side until he was straddling the dying beast. Then he saw one of the fang-rimmed mouths snap open near his crotch and almost flung himself off into the sea again.

But Gundara hopped down onto the trunk, pulling a kerchief from his tunic pocket. He stuffed it into the gaping mouth.

"Eat that, you stupid thing," he said. The Favorite turned back to Palimak. "See, we told you it would be all right," he said.

"Sort of all right," Gundaree cautioned.

"Well, I guess we still have to get him over that reef," Gundara admitted.

Palimak shivered. "You mean, we're not done yet?" he asked.

"Oh, no," Gundaree said. "That was just the first part of the idea."

"The easiest part," Gundara added.

If crawling up onto one of these awful monsters was the twins' idea of easy, Palimak didn't even want to think about what was coming next.

Then he flinched as one of the tree creature's trailing limbs thrashed back to life. It rose from the water, hung there for a moment, then started to curl toward him—several small mouths opening to expose chattering fangs.

"Oh, pooh!" Gundaree said. "Honestly, some *things don't know when they're dead.*"

"Cut it off with your knife, Little Master," Gundara advised. "It's hard to concentrate with all that chewing noise."

"The stupid thing's making me hungry," Gundaree complained.

Numb, Palimak pulled out his knife and lopped the branch off. It fell into the sea and sank out of sight.

"Let's get on with it, please," Palimak said, returning his knife to its sheath. He nodded at the reef. "We're getting awfully close."

"I don't know," Gundara said doubtfully. "Are you sure you can stand up that long?"

"Maybe it'd be better to wait until the last minute," Gundaree put in.

"Stand up?" Palimak croaked. "What do you mean, stand up?"

"Well, how else are you going to jump over the reef?" Gundara asked.

"Maybe he knows how to jump sitting down," Gundaree said to his twin.

"Well, maybe he can," Gundara said doubtfully, pulling on his chin. "Although I've never seen him do it. Even in the circus."

Palimak was aghast. "Have you two lost your tiny wits?" he demanded. "I thought you were going to use magic. Not have me do something that's not only impossible but ridiculous to even think about."

"Of course, we're going to use magic," Gundaree said.

"That's what we *do*, remember?" Gundara put in.

"Except you have to help a little bit," Gundaree said.

"By standing up on the tree-creature . . ." Gundara began.

" . . . And jumping when we say so," Gundaree finished.

"Trust us," Gundara said. "It'll work."

"And even if it doesn't," Gundaree added, "you were going to die anyway. So what's the harm in trying?"

"We'll be all right either way," Gundara said. "Since we're so close to the beach we won't be stuck at the bottom of the sea like we would've been before."

"That makes me feel a whole lot better," Palimak said sarcastically.

"Such a kind Little Master," Gundaree replied. "Always thinking of us!"

Palimak was a hair's breadth from saying to the hells with it and revolting. But then he thought, what else can I do but trust them? He also remembered their trick with the four sea carnivores. If they could pull that off, why not this?

"All right," Palimak said grudgingly. "I'll do it."

"Isn't he brave?" Gundaree said to his twin.

"He sure is," Gundara said. "Bravest master we've ever had."

"Except Sakyah, the demon," Gundaree said. "He was *awfully brave.*"

"That's true," Gundara said. "He just couldn't jump very well."

Alarmed, Palimak asked, "You mean you've tried this trick before?"

"Sure we did," Gundara said. "And it almost worked, too."

"Poor Sakyah," Gundara said. "He wasn't such a bad master."

"Better than that witch who got us next, at any rate," Gundaree said. He sighed. "If only Sakyah could have jumped a little better. It would've saved us *so much trouble!*"

"Never mind Sakyah," Palimak snapped. "In case you haven't noticed, it's my tender skin you need to start worrying about."

Both Favorites took note of the reefs, now no more than fifty feet away. Huge waves crashed over them, then withdrew to reveal a vast expanse of sharp coral.

"Maybe you should try standing up now, Little Master," Gundara said.

"That way you'll have a few seconds to get used to the balancing part," Gundaree added helpfully.

Heart pounding, Palimak gingerly climbed to his feet. The tree-beast swayed in the water, but he managed to steady it, thanking the gods for Arlain's lessons in acrobatics.

"That's very, very good, Little Master," Gundara said.

"Now, get the turtle out of your pocket," Gundaree said.

"What am I going to do with that?" Palimak asked, bewildered by this new instruction.

"Well, just as you jump," Gundara said, "you have to throw it."

"We'll be inside, so don't worry about losing us," Gundaree added.

Burying his suspicions about this last instruction, Palimak dutifully got the stone turtle out of his pocket. Immediately, the two Favorites disappeared inside the talisman.

The reef loomed up, the storm-driven sea thundering against it. Then hissing like an enormous nest of disturbed snakes as the water retreated, revealing a massive, dripping cliff face studded with spears of coral.

Palimak fought for balance as he was drawn up, up and up. And then a huge wave flung him forward.

He plummeted down the side of the wave, heading directly for the coral reef! Feet skittering on the slippery surface of the tree-beast, outstretched arms wavering, the stone turtle clutched tightly in his right hand.

Then he was rising, surf boiling up to his waist, the reef top coming first to eye level, then higher until he could see a small bay on the other side—edged by a broad, rain-battered beach.

For a brief moment he thought he was going to make it. That the dead tree-beast, with him upon it, would be flung to safety on the other side.

But then he saw jagged rock rushing forward and knew he was going to be slammed against it.

"Throw the turtle, Little Master!" Gundara shouted.

"And jump!" Gundaree cried.

Palimak hurled the turtle as far as he could. Then closed his eyes and leaped.

He was never quite sure exactly what happened next. The moment he jumped, the trunk of the tree-beast struck the rocks. He had a brief sensation of flying through the air.

Then of falling to his certain doom.

But just before he struck, what felt like an elastic tether suddenly jerked him forward. He heard Gundara and Gundaree shouting at him, but he couldn't tell what they were saying.

Then he was plunging into the water on the other side of the reef, desperately striking for the bottom where he thought the voices of the Favorites were coming from. Clutching onto the magical tether as a guide.

Suddenly the stone turtle was in his hand again and he struck out and up for the surface. He had time to suck in air before another wave caught him, hurling him toward the beach.

Then his head struck something hard and all became shooting stars of pain against a black, velvety night.

When he came to, Palimak didn't know how long he'd been unconscious. He was lying face down in wet sand, mouth full of grit, hot sun scorching his back, the stone turtle gripped in his right hand.

And the Favorites were jumping up and down on his shoulders, shouting hysterically:

"Get up, Little Master! Get up! Get up! Get up!"

Palimak spat sand and moaned, "I can't. Gods, I hurt all over!"

"You have to get up, Little Master!" Gundara pleaded.

"It's coming, it's coming!" Gundaree cried.

He groaned and forced himself to his knees, brushing sand from his face. Then he heard a furious roar and sudden fear swept away all feelings of pain and weariness.

Hurtling along the beach toward him was an enormous lion's head. Seemingly supported by an invisible body that left no tracks in the sand, the maned head was carried about five feet off the ground.

The lion's eyes were fixed on Palimak and it was roaring in fury, exposing fangs the length and breadth of heavy spear blades.

Palimak needed no further persuasion from the Favorites. He jumped to his feet and ran for the jungle.

A narrow opening through the dense trees seemed to promise safety and he swerved toward it, practically diving through the leafy portal when he reached it.

Palimak stumbled, heard another roar—this one seeming to come practically at his heels—and he recovered, sprinting along the dimly-lit path as fast as his demon-powered muscles would carry him.

The lion was so close that he didn't have time to stop and climb a tree. He ran onward, praying his strength and breath would hold out.

Then he came to a sharp bend in the trail, forced by a great tree surrounded by thick roots that towered many feet above him.

"Stop, Little Master, stop!" the twins shouted in unison. "It's a trap!"

But the lion roared at the same time, its foul breath washing over his shoulders.

Naked fear spurred a panicked leap and in less than a heartbeat he was hurtling past the sharpest part of the path's bend.

There was a burst of colorful lights, then a tingling sensation that shivered up his body from toes to crown. He fell heavily, landing on hard-packed ground.

Palimak remained there, hot sun scorching his bare torso. And he wondered why his heart was beating so hard and why his breath was so labored—as if he'd run a great distance at top speed.

But he had no memory of this, much less of the reason for it.

Many other questions came flooding in. He heard hundreds, possibly thousands of people cheering all around him.

Who were they? And why were they cheering?

There was also this shrill chattering noise in his ears. What was that all about?

And then he felt a stone-hard object in his pocket—jammed between the ground and his upper thigh. For some reason the object was important to him, although he couldn't say why, only that he was relieved it was still there.

Palimak thought, I wonder where I am?

And then came another, most disturbing thought: I wonder *who I am?*

Confusion mixed with growing alarm. For the life of him, he couldn't think of his name. It didn't help that all those people were shouting and those two hysterical voices chattering alien words in his ear wouldn't stop. He just wished everyone would shut up and give him a chance to figure it out.

Shut up, shut up, shut up, he thought. Odd, how those words seemed so familiar and served to make him feel better. He mouthed them: *Shut up, shut up, shut up! It was like a tonic, settling his nerves.*

Then a strong hand clutched his. And a deep voice said, "Rise, Honored One."

Palimak let himself be drawn to his feet. He found himself facing a broad, sun-blackened chest. He looked up—then up some more, neck craning back—until he saw a huge lion's head sitting upon on a man's thick, muscular shoulders.

"Good day, honored sir," Palimak said mildly, feeling not one twinge of fear at this oddity. "Who might you be?"

"I am King Felino," the lionman said.

"Very nice to meet you," Palimak replied. Then, frowning, he asked, "Pardon, Majesty, but am I supposed to know you? I hope you don't mind my rude question, but I seem to have lost my memory."

Instead of answering, the lionman handed Palimak a spear. Red ribbons were hung from its haft, looking like streams of blood.

"This is for you, Honored One," King Felino said.

Palimak nodded. "If that's my name," he said, "I quite like it: Honored One. So much better than the only other name I can think of, which is Little Master."

He grimaced. "I keep hearing that name in my head. 'Little Master, Little Master' these voices keep saying. And I do wish they'd stop."

Palimak looked around and noted he was in a broad arena made of hard-packed red earth. Surrounding the arena were hundreds of half-naked people. Faces painted with gaudy colors, teeth filed to points.

And they were all shouting: "Kill, kill, kill, kill!" as they slammed their spear butts against the ground.

Palimak looked at his own spear, then at the lionman. "Am I supposed to kill some-body with this?" he asked.

"It is your duty, Honored One," King Felino answered. "You must save your people."

Palimak nodded. "That's a pretty good reason," he said. "First sensible one I've heard all day."

Then he wrinkled his brow. "A little earlier somebody advised me to jump and although that seemed like a terrible idea at the moment, I did it anyway. And I guess it must've worked out. Because here I am, ready to do my duty and all."

Just then the voices in his ear rang louder and this time he could make out the words: "It's a trap, Little Master! A trap!"

Reflexively he glanced around the arena. "I don't see a trap," he said to the voices. Then, to the lionman, "Do you see one?"

"It is time, Honored One," King Felino said.

"That's good," Palimak said. "Because I'm starting to get tired of just standing here and doing nothing but listen to these crazy voices."

Again, he scanned the arena. "If you don't mind me asking, Majesty," he said, "exactly who and where is this person I'm supposed to kill?"

The lionman lifted his long, brawny arm, pointing. "There," he said.

Obediently, Palimak looked where the lionman pointed. At first he didn't see anything except empty arena.

Then, in the center, there was a burst of bright light. Followed by an enormous swarm of colorful butterflies exploding out of nothingness.

Puzzled, he thought, I don't see anything but butterflies and they hardly seem worth killing.

And the voices in his ear jabbered, "It's a trap, Little Master. A trap!"

"Oh, shut up with your trap," Palimak said, getting really irritated. "Can't you see I'm busy looking for somebody to kill?"

At that moment a man popped out of thin air and plunged to the ground. He remained there for a moment, as if recovering from shock.

The crowd's shouts grew louder: "Kill, kill, kill!"

"There's the villain, Honored One!" King Felino thundered. "The black-hearted enemy of your people—Safar Timura!"

Then he roared his lion's roar, quickening instant hate in Palimak's heart.

As the enemy rose to his feet, Palimak lifted the spear and charged.

And Palimak thought, Die, damn you! Die, Safar Timura!

CHAPTER THIRTY-SEVEN

WITCHCRAFT

Ordering Jooli and the others to remain in place, Leiria rushed back along the trail to the point where they'd seen Safar vanish.

She cursed herself as a fool for not remaining at Safar's side at all times, no matter what the circumstances. Leiria had watched him come around the bend, then pause as if something was troubling him. She'd even called to him to say there was nothing to worry about.

Then—right before her eyes—he'd mysteriously disappeared. There'd been no disturbance or hint whatsoever that something was going to happen. He'd just vanished into thin air.

Now, bared sword ready, Leiria was determined to take on a whole army if necessary to wrest Safar from the clutches of whatever threatened him.

But when she came to the place where she'd last seen him there was no sign of what had occurred.

Cautiously, she retraced Safar's steps—the prints of which were mingled with hers and the others—about a hundred feet back down the trail. Still nothing. She returned to the bend where they'd lost sight of him and examined the area more closely.

The only thing she found were the scattered bodies of scores of dead butterflies. This was quite puzzling. As far as Leiria could recall she hadn't seen a single butterfly since they'd entered the jungle. More determined then ever, she once again retraced the trail. Studying every inch of the ground for some sign of Safar.

Meanwhile, Sergeant Hamyr had stumbled on a new mystery.

"Look here, Your Highness," he called to Jooli. "Young Lord Palimak's footprints ain't here no more!"

Jooli strode over to Hamyr who crouched, studying the ground. He looked up at her, bewildered.

"They were here, plain as day, a couple of minutes ago," he said, making a wide circle with his finger to surround an empty spot on the path.

He tapped the center with heavy emphasis. "Right damned here, they were," he said.

"And there were others, too," he continued, pointing down the trail ahead. "But those bastards ain't there, either! You saw them, right? Or has some son of a flea-bitten goat snuck up to steal my wits?"

Grim-faced, Jooli absorbed the news. "Yes, I saw them," she said. "Unless my wits have been stolen as well."

"Where'n the hells did they go, then, Your Highness?" he asked, voice pleading. "Nothing but damn, rotted jungle trash far as the eye can see!"

"Let me take a look, sergeant," Jooli said, motioning Hamyr aside. "And then maybe I can answer the question for both of us."

Sergeant Hamyr made room and Jooli crouched before the circle he'd scratched in the leaves. She fumbled in her witch's pouch, which hung from her belt, and found a small oilcloth packet, marked with magical symbols.

Jooli opened it and sprinkled a small quantity of purple dust into one palm. Then she blew gently across her open hand, the dust streaming out to settle on the circle.

"There it is! Right where it was before!" Sergeant Hamyr exclaimed as Palimak's distinctive footprint faded into view, thinly painted purple by the magical dust.

It remained there a moment, the dust stirring into motion as if bringing the footprint to life. Then it vanished, dust and all.

"It's gone again, by damn!" Sergeant Hamyr cursed. He looked at Jooli, scratching his head. "Do you know what in the hells is happening, Your Highness?" he asked.

Jooli nodded, face grave. "It's a false trail, sergeant," she said. "Laid by witchcraft."

Sergeant Hamyr was aghast. "You mean some wrinkle-teated witch played us the fool?" he said.

Then he reddened as he remembered Jooli's abilities and made a hasty apology. "Beggin' your pardon, highness," he said. "I guess I stuffed my boot in my mouth, heel and all!"

"No apology necessary, sergeant," Jooli said. Despite the circumstances, she couldn't help smiling. "Although I can't speak for the witch, who may or may not possess a wrinkled bosom. As a matter of fact, this witch could be a wrinkle-teated he, instead of a she."

The sergeant goggled. "I thought a witch was just a wizard in female dress," he said.

The other men had gathered around and were listening in. Although this was hardly the moment for a general discussion on gender sorcery, Jooli noted that their interest was taking their minds off their current problems.

So she said, "The difference is in power, plus the source of the magic. Witches generally get their power solely from nature and make greater use of plants, animal matter and talismans. Wizards rely somewhat on nature, but they can also draw energy from the spirit world."

She shrugged. "Generally speaking, this makes wizards like Safar and Palimak much more powerful than witches. But not always. And not in all cases."

Jooli gestured, taking in the surrounding jungle. "In this place a witch would be very strong indeed."

She started to explain that the jungle was full of animal spirits and magical plant life, but decided not to.

No sense frightening them so much they'd need a change of breeches the next time an ape hooted.

"Anyway, that's the theory," Jooli said, rather weakly.

Just then Leiria strode up, interrupting the conversation. Jooli's immediate reaction was relief that she'd be able to avoid some uncomfortable questions. But when she saw Leiria's expression all the worry returned.

"No sign of Safar?" Jooli asked, praying that her guess was wide of the mark.

Leiria shook her head—so much for the power of prayer.

"Not a trace," she said. "I couldn't find a clue about what happened."

She hesitated, frowning. "Except for one small thing. And maybe I'm just a drowning woman grabbing at straws. But I did find some dead butterflies on the trail. Hundreds of them. At the very spot where he vanished."

Sergeant Hammer said, "That don't seem right. Ain't seen a butterfly since we walked into this godsforsaken forest. And I got pretty sharp eyes."

He turned to the other soldiers. "How about you men? Seen any butterflies lately?" All the soldiers said they hadn't.

Jooli's eyes lit up with excitement at Leiria's news. "Show me," she said to her friend.

Leiria led them all back to the place where Safar had been seen last. She took the precaution of posting the men on both sides of the curving trail so they couldn't be taken unaware.

Jooli, meanwhile, was studying the heaps of dead butterflies. After she got over the surprise of their numbers, the first thing she noticed was the amazing variety of colors.

In her experience, butterfly swarms were always composed of the same shade. And if there *were differences, they were so minor that they went almost unnoticed.*

She started to sort them by color—reds, blues, greens and so on. Which was when she came upon her second discovery. No two seemed to be quite the same! Butterflies that were mainly blue might have touches of orange, or purple or red. While those that were red might be tinged or spotted with green, or brown or yellow.

And the more the she tried to break down the colors further, the more it became apparent that each individual butterfly was startlingly different from the others.

"If I hadn't seen it with my own eyes, I wouldn't have believed it possible," Leiria said after Jooli had demonstrated her discovery.

"It isn't," Jooli said. "Except through magic."

"Surely either you or Safar would have noticed if someone had cast a spell," Leiria said. "Safar's always told me that he can, well, feel it happening. Like the hackles going up on the back of his neck, or something."

Jooli nodded agreement, saying, "When Safar and I first entered the jungle we both cast spells to alert us to sorcerous danger."

She sighed. "Except we both agreed that since we didn't know what we were up against, the spells might not do us much good."

Jooli grimaced. "But this was a complete failure!" she went on. "I've never experienced anything like that!"

"Apparently, neither had Safar," Leiria said. "And yet it happened."

As the hopelessness of the situation sank its barbs deeper into them, Leiria was overcome by angry frustration. "By all that's holy," she said, "when I find out who is responsible for this, I'll spill their guts on the ground and serve up them up on a platter!"

"There's a slim chance," Jooli said, "that I might be able to grant your wish."

"How?" Leiria asked.

"By recreating the spell," Jooli said.

Leiria eyes burned with fury. "Then do it!" she demanded. "Show me this villain's face!"

"That's exactly my intention," Jooli said.

And she immediately got busy with her preparations.

First, she swept all the butterflies into a large pile. Then she spread her cloak out on the ground and upended her witch's pouch so that she could sort through the contents. As she worked, Leiria paced next to her like an angry she cat.

To calm her friend, and also to relieve her own tension, Jooli talked while she worked.

"When I was a girl learning the basics of magic from my grandmother," she said, "the whole thing seemed like such a huge, complex mystery that it was a long time before I could do even the simplest spell."

Jooli smiled, reflecting. "But my grandmother was a very patient woman," she said. "And an excellent teacher. Strange, isn't it? That even someone as evil as she is could still have good qualities?"

Leiria snorted. "Reminds me of a certain king I used to know," she said. "Iraj Protarus! King of Kings. Brutal lord of all he surveyed. And yet, he was a dreamer once. A man of good intentions, I think. And sometimes he could be quite gentle and forgiving."

She sighed. "It was greed that changed him. Not greed for money, but for power. And a man who thinks like that can't understand others might not want the same thing. That's why he ended up hating Safar so much. He couldn't believe that Safar—who in many ways had once shared his vision—had never ceased being a dreamer."

Jooli laughed. "Similar to my grandmother," she said, "but not quite the same. I think she caught the greed disease while still in her mother's womb."

Leiria shuddered. "It almost makes me feel sorry for her," she said.

Jooli looked up at her. "Don't," she said. "That's another thing she's good at. Making people feel sorry for her so she can gain the upper hand."

Then she returned to her work, choosing certain little packets and vials and putting them aside.

"Anyway, I was talking about the complexity of magic," she said. "What my grandmother taught was that witchcraft was really quite simple and logical. Almost childishly so. In fact, sometimes it helps to think like a child and not let adult narrow-mindedness infect you."

She got out a small cup and started measuring various powders and liquids into it. "The first thing I learned was to truly imagine a thing. Which isn't that difficult for a young girl. It was easy to imagine a favorite doll in every detail. Or a sweet I particularly liked.

"And it was also easy to imagine things I dreamed of being able to do. Like winning the affections of a handsome boy. Or beating a bully in a wrestling match."

Leiria laughed. "I should have been born a witch," she said. "Bullies are easy. I've whacked more than my share. But I've yet to unravel the mysteries of the male race!"

"It wouldn't have helped," Jooli said, sharing her laughter. "When it comes to men, witches are no better at it than normal women."

Briefly forgetting her worries, Leiria asked. "What was the next thing you learned?"

"The Law of Cause And Effect," Jooli replied as she began mixing the foul-smelling brew in her witch's cup. "Which means, quite simply, every effect has a cause and every cause has an effect. Fire makes heat. So if the effect you want is fire, you only have magically to cause heat."

She indicated the cup. "If I added a drop or two of a certain elixir I have," she said, "we'd get an enormous bonfire." She wiped sweat from her brow. "Although in this awful humidity I don't know why we'd want to."

Gingerly, Jooli poured the mixture into a small clay vial, then plugged it with a little cork stopper.

"And that elixir I mentioned," she said, "leads to the next law of magic. Which is: Like Produces Like. The elixir is made from the root of a plant whose flowers are fiery red and look quite like flame. Also, the root itself is quite hot to the taste.

"Long ago some clever witch figured out that if it looked like fire and behaved like fire it might be the perfect thing to cause the effect of fire."

"It sounds easy," Leiria said. "Although there must be more to it than that. Otherwise anybody could be a witch."

"The theory is simple," Jooli said. "But the practice requires a special gift you are either born with or not. Also, only a few witches have really good imaginations. Which is the most important secret of magic.

"You have to be able to imagine a thing in perfect detail—break it down into all its parts and put it back together again—before you can achieve your goal."

"What about prayer?" Leiria asked. "Most people believe that if you pray to the gods and they favor you, miracles can be performed."

"Most people are also deluded fools, my friend," Jooli said. "Because if you are depending on prayer for rescue, you might as well call in the dogs to urinate on the fire for all the good it'll do you."

Leiria nodded. "Safar's of the same opinion," she said. "Except he thinks the gods are asleep and not paying attention. And even if they were awake, he doubts if they'd care."

Leiria's worries flooded back with the mention of Safar's name. "What about this witch?" she asked, pointing at the dead butterflies. "How good do you think she is?"

"Actually, I think we're dealing with a male witch," Jooli said. "I'm only guessing, of course. But my guesses are usually accurate.

"As for his powers, I can't say. His spell was clever enough. He trapped Safar and probably Palimak too with it. On the other hand, this jungle is his home. And even a very weak witch—or wizard—is hard to beat in his own home."

Leiria slapped her sheathed sword. "Then it is my wish and fondest imagination," she said, "that when we encounter this fellow it will be blades, not magic, that'll win the day. And I'm not boasting when I say I've met only one swordsman in my life who could best me.

"Except that was long ago and I've had a great deal of practice killing people since then. So I don't think it'd come out quite the same way."

Jooli's eyebrows arched. "Iraj Protarus again?" she guessed.

Leiria nodded sharply. "The very same," she replied.

"I'd like to see that fight," Jooli said.

Leiria smiled, but without humor. "Consider yourself invited," she said.

Jooli rose, saying, "Enough girl talk. Let's find out what sort of stuff this witch is made of."

She went to the piled-up butterflies and placed the clay vial in the center. Next she got Leiria to help her surround the colorful mass with dry sticks, carefully placing them in the shape of a pentagram.

Then she stood and dusted herself off. "If this works," she said, "we'll only have a few seconds to act."

"I'll get the men ready," Leiria said.

Jooli shook her head. "The original spells trapped two people," she said. "We'll have to strike the same balance. So I'm afraid it's down to just you and me against whatever is waiting."

"That sounds like damn good odds to me," Leiria joked.

She called for the soldiers and filled them in on their plan. They were all disappointed at being left out of the fight. But Leiria cajoled them, stroking their egos, and told them how vital it was for them to remain here and stand guard.

"Ah, then we're expectin' more action, right?" Sergeant Hamyr said, pleased.

Leiria clapped him on the back. "Count on it," she said.

Then she joined Jooli at the pentagram.

"Ready?" Jooli asked, drawing her sword.

Leiria nodded and drew her own. "Ready," she replied.

And so Jooli cast the spell.

A sheet of flame shot up, momentarily blinding them. Then the flame shattered in a soundless explosion. Bursting into thousands upon thousands of fiery bits of color. It was like all the rainbows in the world had been gathered together, then smashed apart with a giant's hammer.

Slowly an enormous face formed within the hot shower of color.

It was the face of a lion. His huge cat's eyes glared at them. And then he roared.

Leiria and Jooli shouted their war cries and charged!

CHAPTER THIRTY-EIGHT

SLAY GROUND

Safar stood frozen in the center of the arena as his own son rushed toward him—a spear aimed directly at his heart.

The arena thundered with the shouts of a savage audience urging Palimak to "Kill, kill, kill! Kill Safar Timura!" Underscoring the wild, blood-demanding chorus was the marrow-freezing roar of a mighty lion.

Caught on the horns of a nightmare dilemma, Safar was helpless to act.

The cold, outraged wizard side of him commanded self protection at any cost. Automatically digging for the ultimate, death-dealing spell to cut Palimak down in his tracks.

But in the place where all love dwells another part of him demanded the ultimate parental sacrifice—to die so that his son might live.

And then, from the narrow gulf between death and survival, came yet a third, most desperate voice: *Kill him, brother! cried the voice. Kill him or all we worked for together is lost!*

Safar had the sudden vision of a world strangling in its own poisons. Of corpses heaped to the heavens. Of seas turned into barren deserts littered with bleached white bones. Of howling devils fighting to suck out the last bit of marrow from life itself.

And with that vision came the nearly overpowering urge to slay his son. Ghostly commands shot through his body making his nerves and muscles twitch in reflex.

The killing spell flooded into his mind unbidden—numbing his will to resist.

Palimak was almost on him. So close Safar could hear Gundara crying, "Stop, Little Master, stop!"

But the boy ran onward, eyes burning with murderous hate.

The heavy spear blade was only inches from Safar's heart. At the same time his killing spell coiled like a hissing cobra, ready to launch.

He had no doubt which would strike first. In less time than it took for a heart to beat, Palimak would be lying dead at his feet. And Safar would be standing over him, the bitter victor.

A man whose soul would carry the blackest mark of all: the sin of a father who had slain his own son.

But as Asper once wrote: Between thought and action lies a shadow. And in that shadow dwells the true power of choice. Of free will. The only real blessing the gods of creation bestowed on humans and demons alike. A gift to leaven the curse of this too-brief life.

So, at the last possible instant, Safar snatched up this power and used it as a bludgeon to slay the spell-cobra before it could kill his son.

And as he braced for the thrust of the spear blade, he whispered, "I love you, Palimak."

Then a hot, searing shock smashed into his body.

A thousand painful colors exploded in his brain.

He had a brief sensation of falling and then he collided with the ground.

Soft, leafy ground.

The moist smell of humus and rotting things.

Familiar voices murmuring in his ear.

Safar raised his head, bewildered that he was still alive. And he saw that he was back on the jungle trail. Sergeant Hamyr and the other Kyranian soldiers standing above him.

And a few away was the unconscious body of Palimak, the spear still gripped in his hand.

*   *   *

Leiria saw the red dirt crashing up at her. She twisted in mid-air and tuck rolled to her feet, sword slashing at a blurred claw reaching for her throat.

She felt the sword strike hard iron, then slip and bite into soft flesh. She heard a lion's soul-satisfying roar of pain and danced to the side as another iron claw lashed out at her.

But then her heel slammed against a ridge in the ground and she toppled backward, twisting to keep her sword arm free and falling heavily on her side.

The iron claw rang as Leiria parried the next blow. But her fall had left her in an awkward, indefensible position. She caught a glimpse of her opponent as he rushed in, roaring in delight at his advantage.

From the shoulders down he was human—a near-giant clothed only in a loin cloth, which bulged as if he were equipped like a bull. His bare torso rippled with slabbed muscle. His arms and legs were thick as trees. Heavy iron claws were gripped in each mighty fist, one of which streamed blood from her initial blow.

From the neck up he was a lion. His huge cat's eyes glowed with fury. His powerful, spine-snapping jaws were spiked with whiskers like steel cables. All framed by a bristling yellow mane that fanned out like mighty wings.

As the claw came down she rolled to the side just in time and the hooks buried themselves in earth instead of in her flesh. But her back was exposed and she kept rolling, desperately trying to get out of the lionman's long reach.

Then Leiria heard Jooli's shrill war cry pierce the air, followed by the lionman's howl of surprise, and she exploded to her feet—back still exposed but turning, shifting her sword to her left hand so that she could draw her long-bladed knife.

In fighting position once more, Leiria saw Jooli fling herself to the side to avoid the lionman's charge. Blood ran down his bare back, gory evidence of Jooli's lunge to rescue Leiria.

Shouting her war cry, Leiria raced to join her friend and soon they had the lionman pinned between them.

Big as he was, fiercely strong as he was, he was no match for the two warrior women. Only his long reach and ferocity kept them from closing in for the kill.

Gradually, they wore him down. First Leiria would lunge, forcing the lion man to face her. But then she would backpedal as he charged, fending off his blows.

At the same time Jooli would dash in and attack his exposed back. And the positions would be reversed, with Jooli backpedaling as Leiria sprinted into striking distance.

The battle raged for an hour before a strangely silent crowd of savages. They only gaped as their king streamed blood from a dozen wounds, his roars growing weaker with each timed attack.

Then the lionman stumbled and went to his knees. At that moment, Leiria thought she had him. She lunged at the lionman, blade aimed like a spear at his exposed neck.

But it was only a feint and he suddenly exploded upward. She still would have had him, would have buried her sword in his chest, but the lionman had escape—not continued battle—in mind.

He dodged to the side, then bounded away, racing for the big double gates at the far side of the arena.

Leiria and Jooli went after him. Although he was amazingly fast for his size, they were faster and were soon closing on him.

As he neared the gate the lionman roared an order. Leiria saw the gates swing open and thought he was going to try to escape outside.

Instead, she heard bellows of rage and she dug her heels in to stop her headlong charge, shouting a warning to Jooli at the same time.

Both women halted, moving together for protection. Jooli had time to say, "What in the hells?!" and then six strange figures burst through the open gates to join their king.

They were nearly as tall as he, but with broader shoulders and wider backs. From the neck down they were men. But above they sported the mighty horned heads of fighting bulls. They were all armed with huge spiked clubs as thick as a ship's main mast.

The bullmen fanned out around their king. Then, with him in the center, they advanced—their bellows echoing across the arena.

Suddenly, the crowd came to life. They cheered wildly, then took up the chant: "Kill them! Kill, kill, kill!"

Jooli said, "Looks like we're in for a long fight, sister."

Leiria smiled, then said, "On my signal, we go for the king, agreed?"

"Agreed!"

And so Leiria gave the signal and they charged.

*　　　*　　　*

Safar forced a brandy-laced potion through Palimak's lips and he came awake, choking and sputtering. When his son had caught his breath, Safar gave him the flask and he took a long swallow.

Palimak closed his eyes and shuddered as the restorative did its work. When he opened them again relief flooded Safar's veins as he saw sanity had returned.

The young man was pale and shaken from his ordeal. Then, with a start, reality took hold.

He embraced his father, saying, "Thank the gods you found me!"

Moved by the sight of father and son reunited, the soldiers scraped the ground with their boots. Sergeant Hamyr wiped away a tear with a battle-hardened hand.

Then Palimak drew back. "I had a terrible dream, father," the young man said. "I was in this arena. And a man with a lion's head gave me a spear. And you were on the other side of the arena and the lionman—"

"It wasn't a dream, son," Safar broke in. "But never mind that. We have things to do. And they have to be done in a hurry."

Palimak was horrified. "Do you mean it was real?" he asked, voice quivering. "Did I really try to—"

Once again, Safar interrupted. "Please, son," he said. "It wasn't your fault. And we can discuss the whole thing later and I'll prove to you that it wasn't. Just take my word for it right now. All right?"

Palimak nodded weakly. "All right," he said.

"We have to get back to that arena immediately," Safar said. "Leiria and Jooli are in grave danger. Do you understand what I'm telling you?"

Again, Palimak nodded. "I understand," he said.

Safar helped him to his feet. He motioned to Hamyr who stepped in to belt a sword about Palimak's waist. Then he gave him a tunic and a spare pair of boots which the young man hastily pulled on.

"Are you hungry?" Safar asked when he was dressed.

Palimak shook his head. "I couldn't eat," he said. "I'd get sick to my stomach." He motioned at the flask, grinning weakly. "But maybe some more of that."

Safar gave the brandy to him and he drank it down. When he was done he drew in a deep breath, then squared his shoulders.

"I'm fine now," he said.

Safar turned to the soldiers. "Leave your packs here," he said. "Just take your weapons. And the moment we get there, don't stop to think. Or look around and wonder where in the hells you are. Just fight, all right?"

The men all said they understood.

However, Sergeant Hamyr made bold to ask, "Pardon, Lord Timura, but can you tell us exactly who we'll be fightin'?"

Safar chuckled. "The enemy," he said.

Hamyr nodded, smiling. "Ah, the enemy. That's good to know. Thanks, me lord."

"You're welcome, sergeant," Safar said.

Then he led them down the path to a large black patch that had been burned into the ground by Jooli's spell.

It hadn't taken him more than a few minutes to figure what she'd done and he was quite impressed with her feat. Her action had not only saved him and Palimak, but had also pointed the way for Safar to work some magic of his own.

The spell she'd cast had also weakened the witch's portal so much that he'd be able to return to the arena with Palimak and the entire squad of soldiers. Plus Leiria and Jooli would be able to remain with them, adding two excellent swords to the fight.

Especially Leiria's blade, he thought fondly. She's worth half an army all by herself.

Meanwhile, Palimak was studying Jooli's magical spoor. Gundaree and Gundara also whispered interesting hints in his ear.

After a moment he turned to Safar, saying, "I see how the spell goes together, father. Let me help you."

Safar clapped him on the back. "Sure you can, son. The more we can put behind this, the better," he said.

Palimak raised a hand. "Wait a minute," he said. "Gundaree and Gundara have a suggestion." Palimak said.

He bent his head, listening. Then he grinned. "It's a pretty good trick," he said to Safar. "Something that'll really put a curl in that damned King Felino's mane!"

Safar chuckled, recalling just how evil the minds of the two little Favorites could be. "Wonderful," he said. "The only caution is that I'd rather capture him if we can. I want to find out what's behind all this."

Palimak nodded agreement and Safar got to work setting up the spell. Using his silver witch's-dagger he scratched a pentagram in the ashes. In the center he sketched a lion's face.

He stepped back, raised his arms and spreading them wide, concentrated on his goal. As he did this he felt Palimak's power, backed up by Gundaree and Gundara's energies, flow into him.

And he chanted:

"To fly and fly and grace the skies
In numbers even gods could not add.
We conjure a thing to bedevil a king
And drive a foolish man mad."

Then he clapped his hands together and thousands of butterflies burst up from the pentagram, flying free and high into the towering trees.

"Arm yourselves," Safar shouted, drawing his sword.

Blades scraped from their sheaths and suddenly the jungle vanished.

And they all found themselves standing in the center of a huge arena, a battle raging not far away.

While all around them a thunderous crowd chanted its bloody anthem: "Kill, kill, kill!"

CHAPTER THIRTY-NINE

BUTTERFLY STINGS

In their first charge Leiria and Jooli came within inches of killing King Felino.

The lionman and his bellowing cohorts had clearly believed the two women would be so terrified when confronted with such an overwhelming force that they'd squeal in feminine dismay and beat a panicked retreat.

But Leiria and Jooli launched their surprise attack with such speed and ferocity that the lionman and his forces were caught flat-footed.

If he'd had his wits about him, the king would've drawn Leiria and Jooli in by falling back so that his bullmen could fan out on either side, then slam the trap shut in a pincer action. Instead, they wasted precious moments gaping at the two warrior women charging down on them, allowing Leiria and Jooli come to within reach of their goal—the king himself.

Leiria was even thinking of throwing the last dregs of caution to the winds to launch herself and her sword at the lion-headed enemy.

Belatedly, the king realized what was happening. He jerked back, roaring orders. The two bullmen closest to him clumsily lumbered forward to close the breach, mighty clubs swinging up.

Leiria's sharp blade slashed out at her opponent, taking his weapon hand off at the wrist. The bullman bellowed in pain, lifting up his stump to stare at the red life spurting out of him, then toppled to the ground and died.

Jooli made similar short work of the horned warrior she faced, running him through with her blade, then spinning around in mid-stride to free it and continue her charge.

Leiria struck out at the exposed Felino, who barely parried her sword with an iron claw, then roared in outrage as her blindingly fast return stroke nicked his side, drawing blood.

Jooli was only one pace behind and saw her chance. She hurled her knife over Leiria's shoulder. It spun once in mid-flight and she had a momentary thrill when she saw the heavy blade slamming toward the lionman's chest.

But at the last possible moment one of the king's guards threw his big body in front of Felino and took the blade himself.

Then the three remaining bullmen charged in and Leiria and Jooli were forced to retreat to keep from being overwhelmed. But as they backpedaled they made two of the bullmen pay for their crimes by dealing out shallow wounds to them both.

Despite their retreat, the women were in an excellent position for a counter-attack. With three of the six bullmen dead, two others wounded and the uninjured one reluctant to press the advantage regardless of Felino's roars, they only needed to regroup, then charge again.

Dripping blood from his side and his back, Felino drove his dispirited army of three after the women with roared insults and threats. The crowd had once again fallen into a strange silence—as if the sight of their king's humiliation had robbed them of their voices.

Acting as a single unit Leiria and Jooli skidded to a halt. Shouting war cries, they pretended to charge again and their attackers hastily scrambled back, nearly overrunning Felino.

The two women took advantage of the moment to catch their breath and check their weapons. Leiria gave Jooli her spare knife to replace the one she'd lost in the bullman's back.

She grinned at Jooli, eyes savage with bloodlust. "It's good to fight with you, sister," she said—the ultimate compliment from Leiria.

"My pleasure," Jooli said, equally as charged by the battle.

"One question, though," Leiria said. She pointed at the bullmen who were being harangued by Felino. "After we've killed them, how in the hells do we get out of here?"

"I've been thinking about that," Jooli said. She chuckled. "Maybe we can use the lionman's ears for a spell."

Leiria laughed. "Consider it done," she said as she stropped her blade on her leather harness.

Then she gave the signal and they both sprang forward to renew the battle.

King Felino immediately turned and fled, leaving his bullmen to face the warrior women without his help. Leiria and Jooli tried to go after him, but the three bullmen blocked their path.

"Coward!" Jooli shouted after the king, trying to wound his pride enough to make him return.

Leiria joined in, shouting, "What's that bulge in your loin cloth, your highness? Cotton wadding?"

"In the military, squads are traditionally composed of six soldiers," Leiria pointed out. "But I won't quibble. If you're right, how does it help us?"

Before Jooli could answer there was an ear-splitting roar and Felino came bounding out, leaping over the lizard-headed center group to take command. He seemed re-energized. His wounds were freshly bound.

"Kill!" he roared. "Kill, kill, kill!"

Immediately, the savage audience that ringed the arena exploded into life. Screaming, "Kill, kill, kill!"

"It was nice knowing you, sister," Leiria said, bracing for the coming assault.

Then King Felino gave the signal and exploded forward—leading his warrior menagerie down the field against the women.

*　　　*　　　*

It took Safar only an instant to size up the situation. Some fifty yards away a ring of howling monsters had Leiria and Jooli surrounded. The two were fighting valiantly, but were being slowly ground down. The lionman, King Felino, raced around the outer ring, exhorting his soldiers to "Kill, kill, kill!"

And scattered around the battling mass were many dead or dying animal-headed soldiers—bloody evidence of Leiria's and Jooli's stubborn resistance.

Safar cracked an amplification pellet against the hard red ground. And when he shouted the war cry of his people it thundered across the arena, drowning out the shouts of the crowd.

"FOR KYRANIA!" he bellowed as he raced forward.

"FOR KYRANIA!" came the echoed chorus from Palimak and the other men as they charged after him.

Stunned by the magically amplified cries, King Felino whirled about to stare at this new threat. His lion's jaw gaped wide when he saw his vanished enemies, Safar and Palimak, sprinting toward him backed by the small but heavily armed cohort of Kyranian soldiers.

Some of his soldiers also turned to gape and were punished for their lack of attention when Leiria and Jooli leaped forward to cut them to ribbons.

Felino recovered from his shock and shouted orders. Half his force whipped about to confront the new enemy, while the others pressed in on the two warrior women.

As the Kyranians waded into the melee, Safar leading the way, Palimak held back a little, waiting for his chance to cast Gundara's and Gundaree's spell. He parried blows but didn't press the fight—slowly circling the massed group to get close to King Felino.

A strange sensation of unreality fell over him. While everyone else was fighting for their lives, filling the air with shouted oaths, war cries and screams of pain, he felt quite cool, his mind acutely sharp; soaking up every detail of the battle.

He thought it quite interesting to note that Sergeant Hamyr's face wore a wicked grin that never changed, no matter what fortune might bring him. Whether he dodged a potentially killing blow, dealt one of his own or was hard-pressed by a skilled adversary, the grin remained the same.

It was also interesting, he thought, that although Leiria and Jooli had only met recently they fought like a smooth, single unit—as if they had been soldiering together their entire adult lives.

Most interesting of all was the way his father fought. Safar had always been a skilled warrior. Taller and more muscular than most Kyranians, he was also quite strong and fast. Today, however, it seemed to Palimak that his father fought on a higher level than ever before.

His swordplay was a thing of agile beauty. Far better than it had ever been before. Quite possibly nearly as good as Leiria's swordsmanship, which was so superior to that everyone else that most warriors considered her to be in a class consisting of one. Although Leiria always said there was one man—Iraj Protarus—who was her equal, everyone thought she was only being modest.

But now it seemed that another had entered that rarefied realm. Incredibly, that man was Palimak's father. He wondered how Safar had made such an improvement. Was magic involved? Or was it something else? Palimak thought the whole thing was very strange and added it to the other oddities he'd noticed about his father since his return.

Just then, Gundara whispered, "There's that stupid old king!"

Palimak looked up and saw Felino backing toward the gates, two enormous lizardmen guarding his retreat.

Suddenly, Palimak heard a familiar war cry and Leiria broke through, Jooli protecting her back as she charged the king.

"Leiria's going to kill him, Little Master!" Gundaree cried.

Sure enough, without missing a step, Leiria cut down one of the lizardmen, leaving Jooli to deal with the other as she raced toward Felino. The king raised an iron-clawed fist to defend himself, but Palimak could see it was too little and too late. The lionman was doomed.

"Stop her, Little Master!" Gundara cried, reminding him that Safar wanted to capture the king alive.

Palimak shouted, "Leiria, don't!"

She heard him and hesitated, breaking her stride and sword blow. To Palimak's horror, that moment's pause gave Felino just enough time. He smashed her sword aside and leaped toward her—great iron claws outstretched to slash her life away.

Palimak cast the spell, fearing the distance was too great and that he'd be responsible for the death of the person he loved above all others—except for his father. Leiria had practically been his mother, caring for him since he was a babe in arms. Carrying him in a sling across her back while she alternately fled and fought the soldiers that Iraj had sent after them.

Perhaps it was that love, combined with the fear of loss, that gave the spell enough strength to collapse the distance. Or maybe it was because he was in a magical arena carved out by Felino's sorcery that gave his own sorcery added power. Or possibly it was only blind luck.

Whatever the reason, the instant Palimak hurled the spell he knew the rightness and power of it. Like most of the Favorites' magic, the spell was dead simple. On their instructions, he'd scooped up a handful of the ashes left over from Jooli's casting. They'd spat in it and had directed him to mold the ashes into a grimy little ball.

It was this insignificant piece of dirt that he threw at the snarling lionman. At the same time he chanted in unison with the Favorites:

> *"Butterfly wings,*
> *Where have you gone?*
> *Butterfly wings,*
> *Who did you wrong?*
> *Promised honey*
> *And that's not funny!*
> *Sting, sting, sting,*
> *Butterfly wings.*
> *Sting,*
> *And sting,*
> *And sting!"*

Palimak's aim was more accurate than he could ever have hoped. The ash pellet struck Felino in the eye and instead of smashing Leiria down, he roared with pain, throwing his iron claws aside to rub his wounded eye.

At the same time there was an explosion of colorful light and thousands of butterflies popped out of nowhere.

They circled the injured lionman, buzzing like angry bees. Palimak saw long, barbed stingers emerge from their abdomens as they were magically armed by the Favorites' spell. Then they attacked, swarming all over Felino, thrusting their stingers into him by the hundreds.

The lionman ran about, flailing the air hysterically. Begging the now-silent audience to help him. Then he fell to his knees, covering his head in a futile effort to protect himself from the painful stings.

Palimak strolled casually over to him, an amazed Leiria several steps behind. He stood over the lionman, repeating the spell chant:

> *"Butterfly wings,*
> *Where have you gone?*
> *Butterfly wings,*
> *Who did you wrong?*
> *Promised honey*
> *And that's not funny!*
> *Sting, sting, sting,*
> *Butterfly wings.*
> *Sting,*
> *And sting,*
> *And sting!"*

Now Felino was completely covered with the beautiful but deadly butterflies. Thrusting their abdomens forward to deliver their poison. Then fluttering away to let another take their place. Felino collapsed to the ground, moaning and barely able to move.

When he was certain the lionman was completely helpless, Palimak waved his hand and the butterflies vanished.

"I don't know what just happened," Leiria said "Except I think you saved my life."

Ashamed, Palimak blushed. "I'm sorry, Aunt Leiria," he said. "Actually, I almost got you killed. I shouldn't have shouted at you like that."

Leiria clapped him on the shoulders and said, "Never mind." Then she directed him to the main battle, where Safar was dealing the last blow to the last opponent. His sword cut through a jackalman's throat, sending the barking head flying across the arena. The rest of the beastmen were either all dead or dying.

"I've never seen Safar fight like that before," Leiria said in her cool professional manner. "If he practices a bit more he'll be good enough to give me trouble."

"I was thinking the same thing," Palimak said. "Maybe he's got some new kind of magic."

Leiria frowned. "I don't know," she said. She started to say more, but then broke off as Safar approached them, wiping blood from his blade and returning it to its sheath. He looked down at King Felino, eyes hard and blue as newly-forged steel.

"Now let's see what this fellow has to say for himself," he said.

Safar plucked out his silver dagger and gestured. Flames burst out all around them. And the blood-stained arena, along with its silent audience, vanished. And they were suddenly back on the jungle trail again. The softly moaning lionman shivering on the path before them.

There came a series of soft popping sounds, like a child making bubbles in his cup of goat's milk, and Palimak saw Hamyr and the other Kyranian soldiers appear.

They all breathed sighs of relief and collapsed on the ground. But they only stayed like that for a few moments. After the men caught their breaths they started rummaging through their packs to dig out rations and wine to stoke up their energies in case danger should once again rear its head.

Palimak didn't see where Jooli came from. She was just suddenly there, walking up to the stricken lionman.

"If it's of any help to you," she said to Safar, "he seems to favor the number six. Maybe it has something to do with his magic. Maybe it's coincidental. Either way, I thought I'd better mention it."

Safar nodded, stroking his chin. With some surprise, Palimak noted the stubble of a golden beard sprouting from his face. Their ordeal had gone on so long Safar hadn't had a chance to shave.

And once again Palimak wondered about the changed color of his father's hair. Previously, he'd attributed it to bleaching by the sun. Now he wondered why a normally dark-haired person would grow a light-colored beard. It didn't make sense. He glanced at Safar's head and saw that what had once been dark hair, albeit streaked with gold, was now entirely blond.

Like the sudden improvement in Safar's fighting ability, something seemed wrong here. On the other hand, maybe it was only his imagination.

Then his father spoke and the doubts were forgotten. "Let's get His Highness aboard the airship," Safar said. "And we can question him at our leisure."

Everyone agreed with his thinking and so he sent up a green flare to signal Biner.

A half-hour passed and there was no sign of the airship. Frowning, Safar shot off another magical flare. Again, there was a long, fruitless wait.

Finally, Leiria said, "We'd better get back to the beach the best way we can. Biner's either asleep or in big trouble."

"Biner *never* sleeps when he's on watch," Safar said. "And neither does Arlain."

"I know," Leiria replied grimly.

A few minutes later they had the barely conscious King Felino tied to a litter and were dragging him along the trail as they retraced their steps through the jungle.

CHAPTER FORTY
GODDESS OF THE HELLS

Queen Clayre paced her cabin, waiting for news from the Hells that her secret plot against Safar and Palimak Timura had succeeded.

From the cabin adjoining hers she heard the muffled sounds of a man moaning in pain. She smiled in pleasure, thinking that in her case the news didn't have to travel very far. Only the door to her suite separated her from one small, particularly nasty corner of the nether world.

Above her came a flurry of barked orders and the slap of bare feet as the sailors raced across the vessel's deck to do the bidding of their officers.

Safar's ship had been spotted and even now her son and his minions were beating windward to catch the Timuras by surprise.

Clayre snorted derisively. She had little faith in her son's ability to bring the Timuras down. Even though the stolen fleet was packed with more than enough soldiers to overwhelm the Kyranians, in her mind Rhodes had failed before when he'd held even better odds.

And then he'd been engaged against the boy wizard, Palimak. Not a sorcerer of Safar Timura's enormous strength and cunning.

Clayre heard more sounds of pain and moved to the cabin door. It was open a crack and she could peek inside. Spreadeagled across her table was a half-naked sailor, his loins covered by cut-off canvas breeches. Bound and gagged, blood streaked his bare torso and legs as if he'd been lashed.

Some invisible force seemed to be tormenting him and he twisted against his bonds, causing the table to shift a few inches. Then he gave a strangled cry and went inert as he fell unconscious.

Excellent, Clayre thought. The spell is working. She turned away from the door and resumed her pacing, reviewing her plan.

After Clayre's first effort with the tree-beasts had failed she'd decided to seek help from a higher power.

By this, she did not mean the Heavenly gods. In her decidedly less than humble opinion the gods were useless things noted for not sticking to their bargain no matter how rich the sacrifice. The deities who ruled the Hells were much more trustworthy.

Charize, her mentor in sorcery, had speculated that the Heavenly gods were asleep and paying no mind to worldly affairs. Charize had postulated that this was the era for monsters and devils like herself.

Moreover, she'd said, there was an excellent opportunity to replace the gods in the minds of humans and demons with more realistic objects of worship.

"The worlds we reside in are quite cruel," Charize had observed. "Pain is the destiny of all living things. And this pain is not even relieved by death. Note the poor miserable ghosts who wander everywhere, bemoaning their fates.

"As if Fate had ever truly offered anything better. It would be kinder—and more delicious to us—if mortal creatures understood that everlasting pain and disappointment make up their eternal future.

"As I tell all my sisters, your prey's submission is such lovely sauce to be served up with a good, suffering marrow bone."

During Clayre's sessions with the monster queen she'd learned—and gloried in the learning—that during this period of inattentive deities, helpmates such as herself were not only spared misery but also got to feast at the wondrous table of hopelessness.

"And even if Asper is correct and things do eventually change," Charize had said, "and the gods should ever awaken, they have no loyalty to mortals. After all, corporeal beings are mere playthings to be tormented for the personal enrichment and enjoyment of the gods.

"So there will still be much for us to feast upon. But I think we should eat while the eating is good, and be damned to Asper and the gods. The longer we can delay their return, the better. And perhaps we can even prevent it altogether."

In the meantime, Charize recommended regular sacrifice to the Goddess of the Hells, Lady Lottyr. An unholy deity who had no love for mortal kind and who made it her practice to mix beasts with higher life-forms to achieve her aims. As false prophets of Asper, it was Lottyr's praise that Charize and her sisters had sung during their observances:

"... We take the sin, we take the sin,
Sweet Lady, Lady, Lady.
On our souls, on our souls,
Holy One ..."

The Lady Lottyr was the hellish shadow-goddess of her heavenly twin, the Lady Felakia. To whom her human and demon worshipers attributed all good things.

Charize had scoffed at Felakia's goodness. She firmly believed that good, as represented by the Lady Felakia, was only the feeble sister to evil, whose cause Lady Lottyr championed.

"Lord Asper was badly mistaken," she used to tell Clayre. "Because when the gods decided to allow the death of the present world it was only because they preferred the heartier taste of evil to the weak soup that the bones of good make.

"Ultimately, only Lady Lottyr can provide such wonderfully tormented souls. Made more delicious by their misery. All aged by their ethereal corpses being hanged on the butcher hooks of the Hells."

Despite the claims of friendship—and the revelation of many magical secrets—Clayre had never believed that Charize had her best interests at heart.

And so Clayre's emotions had been decidedly mixed when Palimak had killed the monster queen—the worshiper of Lady Lottyr. On the one hand, she'd been freed of Charize and her influences. On the other, Clayre's personal magic was much weakened without Charize's assistance.

Kalasariz had provided some of the answers to her dreams. He'd not only defeated but had digested his enemies. Enormous power was in the offing. Power Clayre was determined to control.

The spymaster had first proposed that he enter her own body. An offer Clayre immediately distrusted and refused.

Let Kalasariz possess her son. She could deal with Rhodes, no matter how much he might be influenced by Kalasariz. She had no doubt Kalasariz and Rhodes were plotting to make her their slave eventually by eating her soul—just as Kalasariz had devoured the demons, Luka and Fari.

Clayre snorted. Let them make their silly plans to betray her!

The main flaw in their plot was that they first had to defeat her enemies. And when the moment came for them to turn against her, she'd be ready. In fact, she was already building the spell to turn the tables on them—as well as widening her contacts in the spirit world.

But it was in the Hells that Clayre had found her greatest source of strength.

The Queen Witch glanced at the slightly open door, smiling at the memory.

The Hell Goddess Lottyr had been more than willing to join her conspiracy. No expensive sacrifice had been needed. Only the pledge of Clayre's immortal soul. A thing she did not value and so was eager to turn into coin for her hellish bargain.

And now, while her son's three-ship fleet closed in on the single Kyranian expedition ship, Clayre had already overreached him.

Somewhere in the jungles of Aroborus the Lady Lottyr's sycophant was confronting Safar and Palimak in a magical arena specially constructed for their doom.

Of course, the goddess of the Hells had also warned Clayre the first attempt might fail.

"As a sorcerer," she'd said, "Safar Timura is as close to a miracle as any of us can imagine. Although he is a mere human, his magical abilities are far beyond those of any being I have ever encountered. Even the demon master wizard, Lord Asper, would pale if put beside Lord Timura.

"Our main weapon is that Safar does not yet realize his full power. He's limited by his own imagination. But each time he tests those limits he overcomes them and gains more confidence and strength.

"I never believed it possible he could escape the otherworld of Hadin Future. But somehow he managed it. And now he is back to bedevil us, with abilities much greater than before."

Since her last session with Lottyr, Clayre had formulated many questions that hadn't occurred to her when she'd first conjured up Lottyr's presence.

For instance, Kalasariz had told her more about Safar's strange love/hate relationship with Iraj Protarus. Although the spymaster had not been completely forthcoming, Clayre had surmised that the unknown whereabouts of Iraj Protarus troubled him greatly. And that he was basing all his hopes on finding and overcoming the former king of kings by capturing and killing Safar Timura.

He'd even let slip the magical term that still bound him to Protarus—The Spell of Four. Clayre had done some research on this spell. But there were few magical texts available to someone stuck in such a provincial place as Syrapis.

However, it wasn't hard to figure out that the spell involved shapechanging. And that four participants were required to form that spell. Obviously, Kalasariz had once been one of those four. But he'd managed to break loose and now two of his spell partners had become his slaves. And the fourth, whom he was desperately seeking, could only be King Protarus.

As she paced the cabin, Clayre wondered where the final, most valuable link could be. At this point it was only a matter of curiosity. But if her attempt on Safar and Palimak failed, the question—and its answer—might surge to the forefront.

Who was Iraj Protarus? What were his aims, his goals? And, finally, where was he?

And if found, could Clayre make a bargain with him that would be beneficial to them both?

Her thoughts were broken by renewed moaning from the adjacent cabin. Her heart leaped in anticipation. Finally! She hurried to the door and slipped inside.

The sailor was a mass of horribly moving color. He was covered with hundreds of butterflies—fixed to him like winged leeches—and he jerked and twitched as their tiny mouths devoured his flesh.

Near the table was a net made of golden strands of silk. Quickly, Clayre picked it up and threw it across the man's body.

There was a single muffled scream, an explosion of intense light, and then Clayre hastily pulled the net away.

Hundreds of bloated butterfly corpses fell to the floor, their wings making a rainbow carpet of death. And the sailor was gone.

In his place was a huge spider-like creature, nearly three feet high. A fabulous form curved out of its throbbing, bulbous body. It had the torso of a beautiful woman, but fixed to that torso were six arms and six heads held aloft by long, graceful throats.

Each lovely face was identical—alabaster skin, high cheekbones and dark, flashing eyes. The mouths were full-lipped and red. And when they parted they displayed sharp white fangs, tipped with emerald drops of poison.

Clayre bowed low. "Greetings, Lady Lottyr, Goddess of the Fires," she said. "And thank you for blessing this worshipful one with your exalted presence. May I be so bold as to ask the news?"

The heads all spoke at once, making a strange chorus of identical voices—all melodious, like royal courtesans skilled in the arts of theater and song.

"The news is neither fair nor foul, sister," said the six voices of Lottyr. "Our first attempt on the wizard, Safar, and the demon boy, Palimak, was only partly successful. We captured them. And engaged them in sorcerous battle."

Clayre was confused. "But that's wonderful news, O Goddess," she said. "If we captured them, then victory is ours. And all our efforts will soon be rewarded."

The six long graceful arms waved in unison, slender hands arcing like posing dancers. "Unfortunately, the Timuras managed to escape, sister," Lottyr said. "And they also captured my slave, King Felino. No doubt they will soon put him to the torture in an attempt to learn our plans."

"Forgive me for suggesting any doubt of your words, My Lady Lottyr," Clayre said, biting back bitter disappointment, "but you said the news was neither fair nor foul. Yet the events you describe seem to have little good in them. Is there something this ignorant one is missing?"

Musical laughter issued from the six mouths of the goddess. Then Lottyr said, "I cautioned you once before, sister, that our first attempt might not entirely succeed."

It was all Clayre could do not to snap. She calmed herself. "You said the Timuras escaped," she said. "Forgive me, but the only conclusion I can draw from that answer is that we had no success at all."

"Oh, but we did, sister," Lottyr said. "As for their escape, you must share some of the blame. It was, after all, your granddaughter, Queen Jooli, who assisted them."

Clayre gritted her teeth. Be damned to that girl! "I'm sorry to hear that, goddess," she said. "And you were correct in saying I am at fault when it comes to Jooli. I should have killed that child long ago."

More laughter from the goddess. "Do not despair, sister," Lottyr said. "You'll have your chance to rectify that soon enough."

She paused, graceful arms waving, then she said. "Also, the man we used for the sacrifice wasn't satisfactory. He was too weak to bear the pain long enough."

Again, Clayre was stricken with guilt. Something she was quite unaccustomed to. The sailor had been suffering from some illness and she'd used the excuse of treating him so there'd be no suspicions of her intent.

"Next time I'll make certain the victim is quite healthy, Lady," Clayre vowed.

"Excellent," the goddess said. "Also try to find someone younger. Virility is the spice of life, you know. And of death."

"I'll do that as well, Lady," Clayre promised with a smile. "As a matter of fact, I've had my eye on some of the younger men in the crew for my own purposes."

"Lovely," the goddess said, giggling musically. "Then we can share."

"Pardon, Lady," Clayre said, when the giggling subsided. "But you said we did meet with some success in this encounter. What might that be?"

"The most important thing," the goddess replied, "is that I found the answers to several questions I believe you were thinking of asking me."

Clayre's eyebrows rose. "Yes?"

"To begin with," said the goddess, "I've learned the whereabouts of a certain king. His name is Iraj Protarus."

Clayre clapped her hands in delight. "That's wonderful news, my goddess," she said. "Wonderful news, indeed!"

*   *   *

An hour later, secure in her new-found knowledge, Queen Clayre sent for her son.

King Rhodes tromped into her cabin, full of protests and bluster. "By the gods, mother," he thundered, "have you lost all your senses? You know damned well I'm getting ready for battle! And yet you insist on interrupting me."

"Oh, the battle," she said, suppressing a yawn. "I'd forgotten about that."

"How could you forget?" Rhodes fumed. "This is the chance we've been waiting for ever since we left home!"

Clayre ignored his anger. She waved a hand airily. "Have you managed to catch up to Safar Timura's ship yet?"

Rhodes thrust a thick finger at her port window. "It's just over the horizon. We're going to heave to for the night, ready our defenses, then attack at dawn."

"How clever of you, my son," Clayre said. "Or should I say, how clever of Kalasariz. You couldn't have done this on your own, the gods know."

Rhodes, thanks to some mental prodding by Kalasariz, kept himself from exploding. He sighed heavily.

"What is it you want, mother?" he asked.

"Nothing much," Clayre said. "Just the loan of one of your younger sailors to help me with a little task here. A nice handsome lad would be best. Someone with a good, virile physique."

Rhodes glared at his mother. "Since when did you start thinking I was your whoremaster?" he demanded. "Get your own bedmate and be damned!"

Clayre smiled, quite unmoved by his words. "If you continue to insult me, son," she said, "I won't lift a finger to help you during the battle. Without my magic things might not go so well as you wish."

Once again Kalasariz had to surge forth to keep Rhodes from losing his temper.

Finally, after an intense internal debate with the spymaster, the king said to Clayre, "Very well, mother. I'll get you your lad. He'll be here within the hour."

As he turned to go, Clayre said, "Oh, by the by. I mentioned that I needed this boy on loan?"

"What of it?"

"I misspoke," Clayre replied with a shrug. "When I'm done with this fellow I fear they'll be nothing left to return."

"Whatever you say, mother," Rhodes growled.

As he exited, he made sure to slam the door.

"Such a temper," Clayre said to herself. "Just like his father."

CHAPTER FORTY-ONE
BATTLE FOR THE NEPENTHE

Queen Clayre should have had more faith in her son. Although he was no mighty wizard like Safar, he was a skilled general and a cunning adversary.

He hadn't wasted a moment of those many weeks at sea pursuing Safar and Palimak. His men were trained to the highest degree of readiness. And, after consulting with Kalasariz about Esmirian weapons and tactics, he'd come up with several tricks to stack the odds even more in his favor.

And so, as the pearly dawn crept up over the horizon, he approached his task eagerly and with supreme confidence. His first goal was to trap the *Nepenthe* against the coral reefs that lined the Aroborus shore.

With his ship, the *Kray*, in the center he spread his little fleet out windward of the Kyranian vessel to cut off any possibility of escape. Then, working in the half-light, he crammed every launch he possessed with soldiers.

Using muffled oars, the launches moved out ahead of Rhodes' ships, trying to get within easy striking distance before they were discovered.

Although Rhodes wasn't too worried about that possibility. At Kalasariz' urging, he'd asked Clayre to cast a spell that would fuddle the Kyranians' minds until it was too late. From all appearances her spell seemed to be working, for as the longboats approached there wasn't the slightest sign of life aboard the *Nepenthe*.

To the king's immense delight, the Kyranian airship was nowhere in sight. Clayre had warned him that her spell could only creep along the water and blanket the *Nepenthe* and thus would have no effect at all on the sky warriors.

Although Rhodes was fairly certain the airship would show up once the battle commenced, his hope was that his main task would be completed before he had to engage the flying vessel. But even if this hope proved false he was well prepared for the airship's arrival.

Within the king, Kalasariz wallowed in the juices of Rhodes' pleasure. In his mind's eye he saw Safar Timura led before him in chains. He imagined the elaborate torments he'd apply to Safar's body and soul. Whips and racks and bone crackers for the flesh. The sight of Safar's loved ones—the bitch woman, Leiria; the demon boy, Palimak; his mother and father and sisters—all tortured and humiliated most gruesomely, then murdered before Timura's eyes.

Kalasariz' emotions were so intense that his joy boiled over, flooding Rhodes' veins. Feeling his own senses sharpened by the pleasurable turmoil within, Rhodes couldn't help but laugh aloud. Fortunately, Tabusir and his other aides weren't close enough to hear, but only noticed their king's broad smile. He's in a good mood, they all thought, their own morale lifting along with Rhodes' own spirits.

The king whispered, "Are you thinking what I'm thinking, my friend?"

And Kalasariz lied: *That soon we'll be rid of your mother, my lord, and then nothing can stand in our way.*

"Exactly," the king said. "But I was also imagining some particular tortures we might apply before we kill her. She's such an awful woman. You have no idea what it's been like to be in her thrall all these years. It's kept me from being the true king I deserve to be."

Shifting focus, Kalasariz said, *There's not much I don't know about imposing agony on miscreants, Majesty. When the time comes, perhaps you'd be interested in my views on that most absorbing subject.*

"Oh, I would, I would," Rhodes replied, his imagination running wild about all the things he could do to repay his mother for her hateful treatment of him.

Then he saw the first of the longboats drawing near the Kyranian ship and pulled himself back from the contemplation of such delights. If he wanted to achieve his dreams, discipline was now required.

"Friend of mine," he said, "it's time to concentrate out energies. For I do believe I already hear the sweet song of victory."

Kalasariz said, *You are king and I am your glad servant. Give the signal, Lord, and let us engage the enemy together!*

And so Rhodes motioned to his officers. Who passed the word down. A signalman hoisted yellow flags and the heavy-weapons crews on all three ships went into action.

With a clatter and a rumble big catapults were run out on their wooden wheels. There were ten such weapons per ship—thirty in all, with skilled crews to man each one. Once run out and anchored into place, there was the groan of twisted sinew cords as they were wound down against their counterweights. Followed by the muffled thud of catapult arms settling against thick leather pads.

The next stage, loading the catapults, was tricky. A special fiery material, based on a formula Kalasariz had passed on and which Rhodes thought of as Esmirian Fire, was kept in furnaces placed next to each weapon.

Once the material was loaded into the catapult's scoop it was necessary to fling it at the intended target as quickly as possible, or the weapon itself might catch fire.

Although Rhodes had personally drilled each crew, still there had been several accidents—something he wanted to avoid repeating at all costs once the battle commenced. And so he'd worked out a simple system of signals so that all the catapults could be loaded and fired simultaneously on his command.

When all the crews reported that their weapons were ready and only needed arming, Rhodes took his time before issuing the order. Once again he surveyed the scene. All the longboats were in position—about a hundred yards off the *Nepenthe*, which was still unaware of the danger. There they would wait until the bombardment was over, then they'd rush forward to board the ship and seize it.

The king looked left, then right, noting that his ships were in proper order.

"Very good," he said.

And he gave the order to load and fire.

Immediately thirty furnaces roared into life as their doors were slammed open and the hot material inside hungrily sucked up the salty air. Then came the grind of shovels against coals as the loaders dug their wide-bladed instruments into the green-glowing mass of Esmirian fire.

Followed by a long steady hiss from each catapult as the loaders heaped the sparking emerald flames onto the wet leather pads lining each catapult's scoop.

The moment the fiery mass touched the scoops, the crew captains triggered their weapons and the huge catapult arms slammed forward.

And thirty fiery green balls arced toward the sleeping *Nepenthe*.

*   *   *

Aboard the Kyranian ship Renor was caught in the throes of a nightmare. In his spell-induced sleep he dreamed he'd stumbled into a quagmire and no matter how hard he struggled, it was drawing him down, down, down.

What made the nightmare worse was that at the same time he sensed danger creeping up on him from the outside world. But, as with like the imagined quagmire, the more he fought to come awake the more the spell entangled him.

Nearby, Sinch and the other young Kyranian soldiers were experiencing similar nightmares. Some of them had been on watch when Clayre cast her spell and now they were slumped unconscious on the deck, twisting and groaning in fear. While their comrades who had already been asleep found themselves mired even deeper in their nightmares.

All around the ship the officers and crew were also struggling against Clayre's magic. The least influenced was Captain Brutar, who'd gone to bed so drunk that the fumes from his heavy load of liquor seemed to lessen the spell's effects.

Instead of a nightmare the pirate captain was enjoying a dream in which Safar and the other Kyranians had been overpowered by his crew and looted of their valuables. Now he was tossing them into the sea. Pausing after each one plunged into the shark-infested waters to enjoy the humor of their frantic struggles.

He was fantasizing about holding Leiria and Jooli back for his further enjoyment when the first fireball struck the ship and exploded.

The impact hurled him out of his bunk onto his hands and knees. He remained there for a moment, fighting the alcoholic fog to regain his wits. Then another fireball hit, although this one failed to explode.

Cursing, Brutar struggled to his feet. It was then that he smelled what every sailor the world over fears the most—smoke!

He raced for his cabin door and hurled it open, practically ripping it from its hinges as he shouted, "Fire! Fire! Fire!"

When he stumbled up on the bridge it took him a long, bleary-eyed moment before he realized that no one was rushing to answer his call. To his amazement he saw one sailor curled up at the base of the ship's wheel, sound asleep. Not far away was the officer of the watch, also asleep.

Brutar lumbered around, seeing several other sailors scattered about the main deck, all sleeping fitfully. Then he saw smoke and fire raging near the center mast, green flames licking up the thick spar toward the sails.

He was too stunned to be angry. Never in his life had he seen such a sight. Slovenly pirates that his men were, no one had ever fallen asleep on watch and lived to tell the tale. To his further amazement he spotted several of the young Kyranian soldiers slumped on the deck, also unconscious.

What in the hells was going on?

Then Brutar heard a loud whoosh! from above and he looked up to see a large green fireball arc over his head to plunge, hissing and steaming, into the sea.

It was then that he became aware of the line of longboats moving toward the *Nepenthe*, all filled with heavily armed soldiers. In the distance he saw three familiar ships drawn up, and firing on the *Nepenthe* with huge catapults.

The ships, he immediately realized, were from the fleet he'd left back in Syrapis many weeks before he'd begun this ill-fated voyage.

Brutar did what any right-thinking pirate captain would do under the circumstances.

He ripped the white shirt from his back and ran to the rail, waving it frantically at the approaching soldiers.

"Ahoy, the longboats!" he shouted. "We surrender, gods dammit! We surrender!"

* * *

In what had to be the twentieth time in less than half an hour, Biner shaded his eyes with a broad palm and peered out over the waving green sea of treetops that was the Aroborus jungle.

And the same three questions chewed at his mind like a dog nipping uselessly at fleas. Where in the hells was Safar? Had he found Palimak? And, finally, when would they signal him to pick them up?

He kept telling himself that the constant worrying only made the hours drag on like a closely-watched sand clock, where time was measured by each slow-falling grain.

Safar hadn't really been gone that long, after all. He'd only spent yesterday afternoon and the night in the jungle. It was unlikely that he'd have searched for Palimak in the darkness. Instead he would have made camp until morning. And, now that dawn had broken, Safar, Leiria and the others were probably only just now grabbing a quick bite before resuming the search.

Logical as this line of thinking was, it did nothing to dispel the sense of dread that had been with Biner all through the night. It was one those feelings he'd learned to trust long ago. As the circus ringmaster it was up to him to make certain that all the equipment was as safe as possible. And that all of his people were healthy and concentrating on their performances.

A loose wire could send an acrobat like Arlain plunging to her death. Something as small as a toothache could break someone's focus during a particularly dangerous feat, with disastrous results.

Superb performers like Kairo tended to hide their ailments—the show must go on, and all that—and it was up to Biner to spot their weaknesses and then convince them to drop the most dangerous portions of their acts.

And then there was the audience—Biner's most important responsibility. Improperly tended fires could set the tent ablaze. Poorly constructed viewing stands could collapse. Children had a tendency to get lost in the marvelous confusion of the circus and then turn up in the most perilous situations.

As Methydia always used to say, if there were a weight hanging from a frayed rope or an untended hole in the ground, a child was certain to wander into the danger zone.

Also, there were always the rowdies, petty criminals and sometimes even cut-throats who preyed on Biner's guests. Which in his mind was the definition of an audience: honored guests to be protected and welcomed into his home, Methydia's Flying Circus.

And so Biner had spent a fretful night worrying about that vague feeling of unease he'd always heeded in the past. He'd driven everyone crazy, snooping about the airship, seeing that everything was just so. Several times he'd roused the crew to repair things that could have waited until morning.

But mostly he'd paced the deck, peering endlessly into the night, searching for some sign of Safar. Chilled by the knowledge that his sense of dread had never failed him before. Wondering fitfully what would go wrong.

As always, when the answer finally came it was from an unexpected direction.

Arlain's voice rang clear in the early-morning air. "Biner! Over here!"

He whirled about and he saw her standing in the aft section of the airship. She was waving furiously at him, smoke hissing from between her teeth—a sure sign of agitation in the dragon woman.

Quickly, Biner tied off the ship's wheel, then raced down the gangway and across the deck to where Arlain stood.

"What is it?" he asked.

She pointed a long talon at the shimmering gray of the distant sea. "I thaw thomething, Biner!" she lisped, great eyes wide with concern. "Thomething really, really thtrange and thcary!"

Just then a huge green fireball lofted high into the air—hanging at the airship's height for a second—then flaming downward like a meteor in a crisp mountain sky.

"Did you thee it!" Arlain cried. "There it ith again!"

Biner gaped at the sight, wondering for a bewildered moment of indecision if both he and Arlain were suffering from delusions because of their worry for Safar and Palimak.

Then another green fireball arced high. And another. And another.

Realization sunk in. "It's the *Nepenthe*!" Biner bellowed. "Someone's attacking the *Nepenthe*!"

And he sprinted back to the bridge, shouting orders to the crew.

Moments later the airship was turned about and they shot off for the *Nepenthe*, magical engines steaming and boiling at their greatest heat.

Jooli hacked at the thorny barrier with all her might. But, just as before, every barbed vine she cut was immediately replaced by several others, shooting off the main branch.

Beyond the barrier was the beach and freedom from this awful jungle.

At least the spiders haven't reappeared, she thought, as she hacked once more at the thorny vines.

Then Safar shouted, "Get back!"

She leaped away, fingers instinctively clawing madly at her hair, thinking that the huge spiders had returned after all.

But then she saw Safar loft a small clay jar into the air. It smashed just beneath the vines. A sheet of flame shot up, scorching the underbrush. Light from the outside world burst in. Then, to her dismay, she saw new vines inching forward to cover the exit to the beach.

In a calm voice, Palimak said, "It's working father. One or two more might do the trick."

And then she noticed just how thin and weak the new growth was. Palimak squatted and started mixing another batch of blasting elixir, while Safar fished a second clay jar from his pack.

Their flight through the jungle had been maddeningly slow. Scores of spells had been hurled at them. But each time either Safar, Palimak or Jooli had cast counter-spells, blocking their force.

Once a troop of enormous apes had threatened them, but Sergeant Hammer and the Kyranian soldiers had quickly driven them off with a barrage of arrows, backed by curses as heated as the obscenities the apes had voiced.

But then night had fallen. Just as Biner had surmised, they'd decided to camp out until first light. Leiria had suggested that perhaps they ought to signal Biner to lift them out, but Safar had been opposed.

Gesturing at their bound captive, King Felino, he said, "Someone very powerful is supporting this fellow. Let's call her Queen X. Although I suspect from the spoor that 'queen' is a lesser title. Maybe a minor deity. Maybe not. Time will answer that. However, it's my guess that if we involve the airship before we escape this jungle we'll be giving our Queen X an opportunity to work even greater magic."

He grinned down at Felino, who was tied securely to the large litter they'd used to drag him through the jungle. He was also securely gagged with a dirty strip of rag torn from Sergeant Hamyr's breech cloth. An indignity the good sergeant had insisted upon. The gag was to keep their prisoner from shouting orders to any of his minions who might have followed.

"Isn't that so, Felino?" Safar said. "Isn't she just waiting for us to let down our guard? And wouldn't she just love to cast her spell-net over the airship?"

Felino could only grunt through the gag. Muffled as his response was, it didn't take a great deal of imagination for Jooli to recognize several filthy expressions.

"My, my," she said. "Such language from a king."

Leiria burst into earthy laughter. "I've known some kings better than I like to admit," she said. "And this fellow is nothing when it comes to royal curses."

Her jibe silenced King Felino for the remainder of the night. A silence he'd maintained when dawn broke, poking silvery beams down through the close-set trees.

The remainder of the trip to the thorny barrier had taken surprisingly little time. This was in the nature of journeys, Jooli thought. Slow to get there, quick to return.

Then she and Leiria and the soldiers had taken turns standing in the narrow avenue, hacking at the regenerating growth. While Safar and Palimak conferred on a magical solution.

Jooli felt left out of their endeavors. She was a witch, wasn't she? A damned good witch, even if she said so herself. Why wasn't she being consulted?

And then she realized there was no insult intended. It was merely a father and son attempting to make some sort of personal contact after a long period of mutual fear for the safety of the other.

The other thing she noticed was that every once in a while a strange tiny creature would appear on Palimak's shoulder. Apparently none of the others could see it. And even through her own sorcerous lens the creature was quite hazy. Obviously it was some sort of magical creature.

Whatever was going on, powerful magic was being discussed and worked. Despite her empathy for a father and his son, this rankled her even more.

By the gods, she wanted to be included!

And then, as she stepped back from her latest attack on the thorn barrier to catch her breath and wipe perspiration from her brow, Palimak rose to his feet and came over to her.

Without one trace of condescension, he said, "Pardon, Aunt Jooli, but could you help us with this?"

Jooli was amazed. And honored, in an odd sort of way, that Palimak had added the honorific of "aunt" to her name. Instead of all those dreary royal terms like Your Highness, Your Ladyship, and so forth.

Leiria smiled at her as if she knew what was running through Jooli's mind.

Hells, Jooli thought, I'm an aunt to this remarkable young man! What could be better than that?

And then Safar said, "I'm really sorry we've left you out of this, Jooli. The thing is, I recognized your grandmother's hand in this. Her spoor is mixed with that of the deity I call Queen X. And I was reluctant to put you in opposition to your own kin."

He grinned, blue eyes warm and friendly. "Will you forgive me?" he asked. "It wasn't Palimak's fault. He urged, but I resisted. I guess I'm just so much of a family person—being Kyranian and all—that I thought it might cause you pain."

"Nothing to forgive," Jooli said gruffly, surprised at the sudden emotion roughening her voice.

"And if you really need help, I'd be pleased to offer it. Especially if it involves my grandmother. Believe me, there's no love lost between us."

She joined them in their efforts, quickly catching the sense of the spell they were working. And also, after some concentration, she picked up the scent of Queen Clayre's magic—a too-sweet perfume underlying the acrid stench of fire.

Jooli knelt down and brushed aside leaves to make a bare patch of ground. As she talked, she made a sketch with a twig.

"My grandmother likes to use a special table for her magic," she said, drawing the table. "It looks like this . . . also, the center is inlaid with golden tiles in the shape of a pentagram."

She sketched in the tiles, making the lines much deeper to give a three-dimensional effect. "Whatever or whoever this deity is that she's made her bargain with, chances are she's been summoned through those tiles."

Jooli looked up at Safar. "If we can break the contact between them—for only for a few seconds, even—we might be able to get through that barrier."

"How do we do that, Aunt Jooli?" Palimak asked.

"Grandmother is a very strong-willed woman," Jooli said. "Even when she's ill, she refuses to acknowledge it. However, there is one thing that drives her mad."

"What's that?" Safar asked.

"Capsicum," Jooli replied.

Safar's eyebrows shot up. "You mean, like pepper?" he asked.

"Exactly," Jooli said. "Pepper. The hotter the better. She doesn't even have to eat it. The mere presence of capsicum dust gives her a horrible reaction. She swells up like a balloon, her sinuses desert her and she gets a terrible rash all over body. She's a very vain woman, you know. So the rash probably angers her more than anything."

"I don't have anything with pepper in it," Safar said. He glanced around the jungle. "Maybe we can find something here . . ."

"It's not necessary," Jooli broke in. She grinned. "When I was a girl and made up my first witch's kit I made sure to include powdered betel pepper in it." She grinned. "It was the best way I knew to keep my grandmother at bay."

Palimak laughed. "That's a great trick," he exclaimed. "If you can't beat them, sneeze them to death!"

Jooli fished out her kit and found a packet of betel powder—it was orange with streaks of yellow. She handed it to Palimak.

"Add this to your next batch of blasting elixir and see what happens," she said.

Still laughing, Palimak did as she suggested, mixing the betel powder into the foul mixture in his portable wizard's bowl. Then he poured it into the small clay container that Safar gave him, jammed in the cork and handed it over to Jooli.

She hesitated. "It's your trick, Aunt Jooli," he said. "You deserve the honors."

Laughing with him, Jooli accepted the elixir. She cleared everyone from her path and held the jar high.

"Take this, grandmother!" she shouted.

And she hurled the jar. This time, the sheet of flame was even higher and hotter than before. A strange giddy sensation overcame Jooli. She had the sudden flash-vision of her grandmother sneezing and was struck with a fit of girlish giggles.

Laughing like a fool, but not caring, she shouted, "Let's go!"

And she charged through the wide opening created by the explosion. The others followed, dragging Felino's litter behind them and laughing with her. Only Safar and Palimak knew what was so funny, but everyone was so relieved they'd finally broken out of that dank jungle that they laughed anyway. Wheezing and gasping as they trundled out on the beach.

But then they heard the thunder of battle and the laughter died.

And they all looked out to sea, gasping in shock at the sudden realization.

The *Nepenthe* was on fire. Its deck swarming with soldiers in enemy uniforms, trying to put out the flames.

Surrounding the vessel were three other ships, all engaged in battle. But it wasn't the *Nepenthe* they were fighting. Whatever had happened there was long over. One only had to witness the prisoners in Kyranian uniforms crowded into the bow and under enemy guard to realize that.

This battle was going on elsewhere. Huge green flaming arrows—each easily twice the size of man—were being fired into the skies. Battery, after battery of them, shooting off in steady time.

And their target was the airship, hovering over the *Nepenthe* and fighting a losing battle. One of the arrows had struck the bow and they could see some of Biner's crew desperately trying to put out the blaze.

King Felino finally worked his gag free. And now it was his turn to laugh.

"You've lost, Safar Timura," he gloated. "Surrender while you can!"

CHAPTER FORTY-TWO
DARK VICTORY

Biner was doing his damnedest to outmaneuver the enemy fleet, and to extinguish the fire raging in the bow of the airship. If it spread to the engines the whole airship would explode.

The ringmaster called on his deepest reserves of calm. Never mind that the show was a disaster, he and his people would continue to perform until the last fat clown provoked laughter and the curtain closed.

His orders were issued in his grand ringmaster's voice. A presentation of things to come for the audience, filled with all sorts of subtext for the performers.

"Turn left," he boomed to the wheelman. Unhurried, but crackling with authority.

"Drop the port ballast," he roared to the port crew, calmly demanding their urgent but measured action so the airship could rise above the next arrow shot.

"Put some soap into that water, sir!" he bellowed to the captain of the fire-fighting team.

And the fire captain quickly, but without panic, added soap to the water barrels that fueled the hoses his men were playing over the leaping green flames. It seemed a long time, but soon thick suds shot out over the fire, quenching it.

Biner heard Khysmet trumpet from the aft section of the ship. The great stallion was housed in a temporary stable, waiting for his master's return. The excitement of the battle, plus his concern for Safar's absence, had worked the horse up into a fury and he was kicking at the wooden partition that held him.

To his relief, he saw Arlain running to the stable to calm the animal. Khysmet was much enamored of the dragon woman and would be sure to respond to her gentle ministrations.

He turned back to the task at hand. "Bombardiers, are you ready?" he shouted to his attack crew.

The signal came back that the sacks of magical explosives were set in their bays. The formula for the explosives had been worked out by Safar during their final flight from Esmir. Palimak had later added a trick or two of his own, guaranteed to devastate the most hardened enemy.

These explosives had been the key to the Kyranian occupation of their little piece of Syrapis. During Safar's long exile in the otherworld of Hadinland, it had been up to Palimak to lead the way against all those hostile forces.

Biner had been shocked when he'd realized that hatred seemed to be the natural state of things in Syrapis. This was an emotional environment he'd never understood. In his mind and experience, people—and even demons—were all the same. An audience was merely an audience. Most were sweet, but some were sour. And turning sour to sweet was his life's work.

He was a gentle giant in a dwarf's body. Short of stature, massive in girth and especially in heart, he believed down to his very bones there was no audience he'd ever met whose spirit couldn't be transformed—if only for two hours—into goodness.

And so the vicious, hateful attitude of the natives of Syrapis completely mystified him. Although he'd performed before thousands, possibly tens of thousands of people in his career, the Syrapians were like no others he'd ever met.

Arlain and the other circus performers felt the same and so although they were fighting for their own survival in Syrapis—as well as for that of the Kyranians—they despised this new, anti-human role they were forced to play.

Now they were being called upon to play that role once again. The *Nepenthe* had been overwhelmed by an enemy force. Biner had immediately recognized the uniforms of the attacking soldiers as being those of Hanadu, the kingdom ruled by Rhodes.

Biner could only guess why Rhodes had followed the Timuras to this far-off place. He supposed the king's purpose was to block Safar's mission to Hadinland. Why Rhodes should want to do this, however, was a complete puzzlement.

The only thing Biner knew for certain was that he had to stop Rhodes. At the moment the only way he could see to accomplish this was to bombard the longboats carrying the enemy troops. To bombard the *Nepenthe* itself would be useless, and would endanger the lives of the Kyranians still on board.

However, the huge fire arrows being launched by the three enemy ships were doing a damned good job of keeping him from that objective.

His maneuvers were designed to carry him above their reach, yet still be close enough to assume some accuracy. To maintain his calm, he imagined the action as raising a diving platform to its maximum height, while still giving the acrobat a good chance of hitting his watery target.

He was studying a group of longboats clustered near the *Nepenthe* as a possible target when he heard Khysmet whinny his shrill cry. A moment later Arlain came rushing up.

"Over there, Biner!" she cried, gesturing wildly toward the shore. "It'th a thignal from Thafar!"

Biner swiveled his glass in the direction she was pointing. And there, rising from the beach, he saw a green flare. Fearing some new trick to draw his attention away from the battle, he backtracked the flare's path until he came to a small group of people standing near the water's edge.

One of them was clearly Safar.

"Hard about!" he shouted to the crew. "Set a course for the beach!"

∗   ∗   ∗

Leaving his friends to tend to the battle, Safar spent just enough time with Khysmet to let him know his master was back for good.

Then he hurried to Methydia's old stateroom, where Jooli guarded their bound captive, King Felino. While waiting to be picked up by the airship she'd hastily briefed Safar about her magical observations in the arena.

"They seemed obsessed with the number six," she'd said.

That was good enough for Safar to make some quick deductions. Suddenly, he was quite certain of the identity of the mysterious Queen X.

In the cabin he gave Jooli a stick of magical charcoal and directed her to draw a six-pointed star on the deck, with Felino at the center. Each star point, he also told her, should bear the likeness of one of the animal warriors they'd faced. A lion to start with, followed by a jackal, an ape, and so on.

Jooli quickly caught on to what he intended and got to work.

Meanwhile, Safar flipped through the pages of the Book of Asper for clues to the proper spell.

He started with the Lady Felakia, the patron goddess of his people. In the most ancient Kyranian myths it was said that the beautiful goddess of purity and health was once wooed by the god Rybian, the maker of people and demons.

Legend had it that the Lady Felakia spurned Rybian's attentions and during the long lovers' siege he became bored and pinched out all the races of humankind and demonkind from the pure clay of Kyrania. The same clay that had made the Timura potters a modern legend; their work through generations was highly valued all over Esmir.

To Safar, however, the key was Asper's claim that humans and demons were born of "a common womb." In other words, never mind the myth of what Rybian had wrought, but pay close attention to the mother.

The demon master wizard had a theory regarding the subject. It was outlined in a poem that began:

> *"In the days of heavenly love and lust*
> *A wicked sister of the pure and just*
> *Conspired to win the heart of our maker . . ."*

In Asper's scenario, the Goddess Lottyr—who was the Hellsish shadow sister of the Lady Felakia—crept into Rybian's bed one night when he was drunk and through guile got him to impregnate her with his heavenly seed. In the morning, when he'd realized what he had done, the god ripped the seed from Lottyr's womb. Then implored the Lady Felakia to accept it into her own. Otherwise, he said, the creatures he had created would all be condemned to eternal lives of torment in the Hells.

In a night of godly passion, Asper said, Rybian wooed Felakia and she finally relented and accepted his embrace and his seed. From these two unions were born all the creatures of the world, including humans and demons.

Safar had never paid much attention to this portion of Asper's text. In both poetic form and mythical content it was quite out of character for the cynical old demon, who consistently warned that the gods were asleep and that the fate of both humans and demons was of little concern to them.

But when Jooli mentioned her own theory of numbers his mind plunged back to his student days in Walaria. He'd discovered Asper's book in the forbidden private library of the high priest, Umurhan.

There were many other volumes in that library to which his curiosity had also been drawn. One of them was a text on Hellsish magic, whose cover bore the drawing of a strange, six-headed, six-armed goddess of the dark worlds. He'd later learned it was the portrait of the evil Lady Lottyr. Shadow sister of the Goddess Felakia.

Although Safar was adamantly opposed to the practice of black magic, as a scholar he was quite familiar with all of its aspects. He was not only schooled in the spells involved in that terrible art, but was skilled in casting their counter-spells to protect himself.

This was how he had defeated Iraj Protarus and his minions when they had tried to destroy him and his people with the shapechanging Spell of Four. Safar doubted he had the power to similarly defeat the unholy deity that was the Lady Lottyr. But maybe, just maybe, he could slow her down a bit.

Finally, he found Asper's poem on the subject. It was one of his strangest verses. Written as if he, himself, had once encountered the dreaded Goddess of the Hells.

He called Jooli to show her. She smiled when she saw the poem. And with much feeling, she read Asper's words aloud:

> *"Deep in the Hell Fires I spied*
> *Rybian's false-hearted bride.*

> *Six heads and arms had she,*
> *And beauty enough to bedazzle me.*
> *Through the Sixth Gate I fled,*
> *Soul quaking in fear and dread.*
> *Up, up through the world's core,*
> *At my heels that Hellish whore.*
> *To the unfeeling Heavens I cried,*
> *'Where's the lamp, where's my guide?'*
> *Of all, only Felakia deigned to speak.*
> *And those holy words I now repeat:*
> *'If it's my sister, Lottyr, you wish to smite,*
> *In the lion's eye, seek the light.'"*

When she was done, Safar shook his head. "I never knew what Asper was getting at before," he said. Then, grinning, he pointed at Felino. "But there's our lion," he continued. "And what we need to do couldn't be plainer."

The lionman roared in fury, twisting futilely at his strong bonds. "You fools!" he cried. "You poor, weak fools! You'll never defeat the goddess!"

Jooli only laughed. "I'll fetch a torch," she told Safar. "That ought to be light enough."

But as she turned, Felino suddenly howled in agony.

"What in the Hells?" Safar exclaimed.

As Jooli turned back she saw the veins in the lionman's body swelling as if they would burst. His eyes were bulging from their sockets.

Then his jaws fell open and the strange, melodious voice of a woman issued forth. Although it was strong, it had a distant, echoing quality to it—as if it were coming from the bottom of a deep cavern. Neither Safar nor Jooli had any doubt who the speaker was.

"How dare you defy me, Safar Timura?" said the voice of Lottyr. "You have bedeviled me from the start of your puny, mortal life. Asper defied me and in the end I made him suffer for it most grievously. And now you make bold to follow in his doomed footsteps? Beware what you wish for, Safar Timura. For some day I may grant it, just as I granted Asper his wishes."

The voice stopped and Felino slumped against his bonds, dead.

Safar suddenly felt exhausted—as lifeless as those lion's eyes radiating nothingness from Felino's head.

He heard Jooli wail, "What do we do now, Safar?"

But he just shook his head. He was out of answers.

At that moment, Palimak burst into the cabin. "Father!" he cried. "Come and see! It's Coralean! With the whole damned fleet!"

Renewed hope leaped into Safar's breast. He and Jooli rushed out of the cabin to see what Palimak was talking about.

And when they got to the rail overlooking the battle scene it was like a vision granted from the heavens.

Nine ships were converging on Rhodes' little fleet of three. Safar immediately recognized the center ship, the *Tegula, which flew Coralean's coat of arms.*

Safar didn't know where his old friend had come from, or how he'd guessed Safar was in trouble. All he cared about was that the tide of battle had been transformed. Rhodes' longboats full of soldiers were rowing as fast as they could back to their mother ships.

And it was going to be a long pull for them, for even now the enemy ships were turning tail and fleeing, with four of Coralean's vessels in hard pursuit.

Directly beneath the airship, the *Nepenthe was sinking. But he could see one of Coralean's ships converging on it to take off the survivors. Many of whom wore the uniforms of the young Kyranian soldiers Safar had left behind.*

Already Biner was shouting gleeful orders to his crew to lower the airship so they could assist in the rescue effort.

Leiria fell into Safar's arms, laughing with joy. Everyone else whooped in glee, hugging or slapping each other's backs.

Just then, a strange feeling came over Safar. It seemed as if he'd suddenly become another person—standing slightly away—observing the scene. All the happy people, with his other self, his Safar self, at their center. Leiria clasping him tight.

And he thought, in an inner voice that was not his own: *Well done, brother. Well done.*

Then he was back in his own body again, trembling with alarm. He pushed a bewildered Leiria away and ran to the place where he thought his other self had been standing.

There was no one there, only a stack of empty ballast sacks. He looked about, but saw nothing out of the ordinary.

Leiria came up to him, concern in her eyes. "What's wrong, Safar?" she asked.

Still dazed, Safar nearly blurted something about Iraj. But he recovered just time.

"Nothing," he replied. "I'm just a little tired from the excitement, I guess."

She started to embrace him again, but Safar held her off as gently as he could. For some reason he felt that if touched her it would be a violation of her flesh. That if she knew him for what he was, she'd feel sullied. But that, like his bitten off response, also seemed insane.

Safar stood quite still for a moment, the world spinning around him. Finally, the mad whirling stopped and he felt whole again.

What now he wondered. What now?

And then the ghost voice intruded once again to answer: *We go to Hadin, brother. Just as we planned all along.*

At that moment Safar knew the answer to a much deeper question. Now he knew where Iraj Protarus had gone.

The deck of the airship rushed up to smite him. And then all he knew was darkness.

Part Four
Goddess of the Hells

CHAPTER FORTY-THREE
THE TWO KINGS

Safar was trapped in the prelude to the end of the world.

And oh, how he danced.

Danced, danced, danced.

Danced to the beat of the harvest drums.

All around him a thousand others danced in joyous abandon. They were a handsome people, a glorious people, led by their beautiful young Queen who cried out in ecstasy.

Beyond the grove, a backdrop to the Queen, was the great conical peak of a volcano. And he knew that at any moment the volcano would erupt and that Safar, along with the joyous dancers, would die.

Was this real? Was he truly on the shores of Hadinland, destined to be swallowed in a river of molten rock? Or was it just a night terror that would end if only he could open his eyes?

Open your eyes, he thought! Dammit, man! Open them!

And then, with a jolt, he thought, Iraj! Where is Iraj? He tried to look around to find him but then Palimak's voice intruded, calling:

"Father? Father? Open your eyes, father!"

And he thought, Oh, yes. I know where Iraj is now.

So he opened his eyes. Or was it Iraj who opened them for him? Never mind. That was something they would have to sort out later between themselves.

The main thing was, his eyes were open now.

But all he could see was darkness. He blinked, but the darkness stubbornly remained.

Alarm crept in, but he pushed it away. Obviously, there was a reasonable explanation. It was probably night and Palimak most likely kept the room dark so as not to disturb him. He could sense Palimak bending over him.

"Where are we, son?" he asked.

"We're in Hadin, father," Palimak replied.

"So soon?" Safar asked, although he was only a little surprised.

"You were unconscious a long time, father," Palimak said. "You had us pretty worried, what with the fever and all. But that's broken now, thank the gods. Jooli and I took turns treating you during the whole voyage."

Safar nodded understanding. "I dreamed I was trapped in that other world again," he said. "Dancing on the sands of Hadinland. I suppose it was the fever that caused it."

"Do you feel well enough to get up now, father?" Palimak asked. "Coralean has some people waiting to see you. They're all most anxious."

The young man paused, then—with amazement in his voice—he added, "It's a delegation from Hadin. They say you are their long, lost king."

Safar was astounded. "King?" he asked. "How could I be their king?"

Inside him, Iraj stirred in his nest. He said, *I told you long ago, brother, that we were both destined for great things. And here is final proof. We are kings of a people we never even met!*

Safar wanted to tell Iraj to shut up. His presence inside Safar's body was all too disturbing as it was without Iraj prattling in his ear. Safar felt confused, dazed, as if he had not quite awakened from a terrible dream.

He brushed his face with his hand, attempting to wipe away the confusion. Then he realized Palimak was trying to give some sort of explanation about the people who believed Safar was their king. He nodded, pretending he'd heard the answer.

He said, "I'll get up, son. Just bring me some clothes. And some water to bathe in."

Then he chuckled and said, "And please bring me a light. I'm not a cat, you know. I can't see in the dark."

His request was met by a long, frightening silence. "Did you hear me, son?" Safar pressed.

Palimak's voice shook when he answered. "I heard you, father." Another long pause. Then, "But it's broad daylight out, father. You shouldn't need a light!"

Inside him, Iraj jolted in shock. *What's this?* he demanded. *Are we blind? Or is this the boy's idea of some cruel jest? By the gods, I'll have him . . .*

Safar slapped his own breast, cutting Iraj off. He had to think, dammit! What was happening to him? Was he going mad?

"I must have misheard you, son," he said at last. "It's not really daytime, is it?"

He reached out desperately and Palimak clasped his hands in a tight grip. "Tell me it's night, son," he pleaded. "Tell me!"

Safar felt wet drops fall on his cheek. Was Palimak crying?

"Can't you see me, father?" Palimak begged. "I'm right here in front of you. And it's daytime, with a bright shinning sun. Honest to the gods, it is!"

Palimak's panic had the reverse effect on Safar. He became quite calm. If he was blind, so be it. Maybe he'd regain his sight later. Maybe not. The main thing was that there were far more calamitous events than his own personal misfortune that needed to be dealt with.

He patted the young man's hand. "Never mind, son," he said. "I'm probably just suffering from some sort of shock. Caused by the illness, no doubt. I'm sure I'll soon recover my sight. It's a temporary ailment, nothing more."

When Palimak replied, his voice was steadier. "Aunt Jooli told me about Lady Lottyr—the Hells goddess," he said. "Maybe the illness was something she caused."

"That's the answer," Safar said, hope growing. "Lottyr's at fault. Well, then. Now that we know the cause all we have to do is come up with some sort of spell to counter her. Couldn't be simpler."

He struggled upright, Palimak putting an arm behind his shoulder to help. After a brief moment of dizziness, Safar felt amazingly strong and full of energy. That was an incredible relief, for deep down he'd worried he'd be physically unfit as well as blind.

"If you'll help me wash and dress," he said to Palimak, "I'll attend to this delegation you mentioned."

He grinned. "Can you imagine?" he asked. "*Me, a king! Nothing could be more amusing.*"

Palimak told him to wait in bed while he went to fetch the things he'd need. Safar listened to the departing footsteps and the sound of the door opening and closing.

When he was sure he was alone he said, "We're going to have to work out some better means of communication, Iraj. I can't just have you charging around with your every thought and confusing matters. Otherwise, they're going to think I've gone mad."

Inside him, Iraj laughed. He said, *You've always been a bit mad, Safar. As have I. Still, you have a point. We'll need to figure out something. However, I must warn you: if you intend to tell this delegation from Hadin that you are* not *their king you'll get no cooperation from me. Never forget, there's not one crown at stake, here, but two. Hadin will have two kings, not one, if I have anything to say about it!*

Iraj's last words hit Safar like a hammer. *Two kings of Hadin! Immediately, he remembered a riddle from Asper's book. He'd always known the answer to the riddle would be crucial. But he'd never guessed just how much he'd be personally affected by it.*

Iraj suddenly found himself awash in Safar's hot-blooded excitement. *What's going on?* he demanded. *Your thoughts are too confusing to make out!*

Safar answered by reciting Asper's riddle aloud:

> *"Two kings reign in Hadin Land,*
> *One's becursed, the other damned.*
> *One sees whatever eyes can see,*
> *The other dreams of what might be.*
> *One is blind. One's benighted.*
> *And who can say which is sighted?*
> *Know that Asper knocked at the Castle Keep,*
> *But the gates were barred, the Gods asleep."*

Iraj thought a moment, then said, *So, we're the two kings, right?*

"That's what it would seem," Safar replied.

Clever fellow, that damned old demon, Iraj observed. *You were always going on about him, but I never paid much attention. Now it seems the old boy had this thing charted from the beginning.*

Safar didn't reply and Iraj suddenly realized he was concentrating on something else.

What are you doing? he demanded? Frantically, he scrabbled for the protection of his sorcerous nest. *If you try to kill me,* he said, *I swear you'll suffer for it!*

Safar's reply came from quite close. Frighteningly so. And he didn't speak aloud, but used a newly discovered inner "voice."

Don't worry, Safar said. *I'm not trying to kill you. I'm just climbing down there so I can "talk" to you without speaking aloud. Funny, being blind made it easy. I sort of turned my eyes inward and found you.*

Iraj didn't believe him. *Don't lie to me,* he said. *I know very well you'd like nothing better than to see me dead. After all, if I were in your position I'd do the same thing.*

That's the main difference between the two of us, Safar replied. *You always thought I desired the same things you did. That's never been the case. You wanted to be Esmir's King of Kings. I had no such ambitions.*

Don't fool yourself, brother, Iraj retorted. *All you ever wanted to do was save the world. Tell me that's not as insanely self-centered as my own wishes. Come on—Safar The Savior! No god appointed you to such a world-shaking role? You did! I was there, remember? And at the same time, boy that I was, I anointed myself the future King of Kings.*

I won't quarrel with you, Safar said. *Arguing about details won't get us anywhere.*

Iraj sneered. *You're afraid to admit I'm right, that's all.*

Safar sighed. *Let's deal with this later,* he said. *I'll admit you're right about one thing. When I first realized what was happening I decided to figure out a way to kill you, without killing myself. But now I realize we're fated to play this game out together. And the only way either one of us is going to survive, much less realize our goals, is to cooperate.*

Agreed, Iraj said.

Truce, then? Safar asked.

You have my word, Iraj said.

Safar nearly said something sarcastic about the worth of Iraj's word, but bit it off.

Instead he said, *Then let's go greet our new subjects, brother mine. And find out all we can about what's going on.*

Done! Iraj said. *I'll give you my strength and you give me your magic and nothing can stand against us.*

Ever the conqueror, Safar sighed.

I won't quarrel with that, brother, Iraj said. *Conquering is my destiny.*

CHAPTER FORTY-FOUR

THE ISLAND QUEEN

When Palimak left Safar's cabin he was so stricken with fear and grief at his father's condition that he fled to his own quarters before anyone could stop him to ask when Safar would emerge.

He had to think. He had to get his emotions in check before he told the others that his father was blind. Considering his own reaction, Palimak had no doubt that unless he handled the situation carefully everyone would panic.

Although he'd only recently turned fourteen, Palimak knew they all looked up to him as someone much older and wiser than his years. Despite the fact that demons matured at a faster rate than humans, both emotionally and physically, right now the human side of him ruled and he felt like a mere child incapable of handling such a burden.

He mixed himself a weak solution of water and sweet wine to settle his nerves. But when he took a sip the drink had the opposite effect and he rush to a basin to empty his stomach.

Then he wiped his face, washed out his mouth with mint water and sat on his bunk to think . . .

* * *

. . . The voyage from Aroborus to Hadin took many weeks. And although the seas were strange and filled with danger, the journey was without incident.

Even so, everyone kept looking over their shoulders for the reappearance of Rhodes and his fleet. Though they'd only suffered the deaths of two young men in the fight with Rhodes, all the Kyranians were grief-stricken at this loss.

Safar's collapse added even more tension to the atmosphere.

Coralean was all for turning back to Syrapis, reasoning that with Safar in a coma the mission had no head, and therefore no purpose.

Many of the other Kyranians agreed, but Palimak—supported by Leiria and Jooli—insisted that they press on. Safar had undergone such trials before, Palimak said, and given time and careful nursing, would likely recover.

It was Eeda, however, who turned the tide of opinion. Although she was young, her words were wise. She was also quite visibly with child, which gave even more depth to her appeal.

"Back in Syrapis," she said, "we all saw what is going to happen to this world if Lord Timura doesn't reach Hadin in time to intervene. I don't want my child born into the doomed land we saw in Lord Timura's vision. And I don't think you want to condemn your dear families to such a horrible fate."

Coralean spoke for the others when he argued, "That's all very well and good, dear wife. But Coralean must speak plainly when he warns that the chances of success appear small. If Safar doesn't recover—or worse, should he die—where will we all be then?

"Hadin is a land unknown to us all and may be filled with many enemies. If our fates are perilous, wouldn't it better to face those perils surrounded by our friends and families, rather than among strangers?"

"Forgive me for seeming quarrelsome, lord husband," Eeda replied. "But I, for one, would rather die bravely facing the unknown. With some hope—however slight—that we can cure this world of its afflictions.

"For me, the alternative is to cower like some lowly insect while unknown forces drag myself and my child—as well as my dear husband—to certain death. Why, in the vision Lord Timura revealed to us, there might not even be anyone left to bury us and sing our souls to the heavens once we are gone."

A long silence followed this powerful argument. But Coralean, a man who could see all sides, felt it his duty to point out other dangers.

"What of that devil Rhodes?" he asked. "Somehow he has eluded us. He has three ships loaded with soldiers. What if he is even now returning to Syrapis to launch a surprise attack on our homes to revenge himself for his failure here?"

Palimak replied, "I think my grandfather, Khadji Timura, is well able to protect our people against Rhodes. When you left Syrapis to help us, that was the plan you worked out with everyone, wasn't it? And once you'd found us, you told them all that you were to proceed to Hadin, leaving the safety of our people in my grandfather's capable hands."

There was another long silence. No one—especially Coralean—could argue with that statement.

It was Biner who then put paid to the discussion and spiritless mood by rising up from his place and declaring:

"Damn everything but the circus!"

Arlain and the other show people leaped to their feet and joined the ringmaster in a fabulous impromptu performance.

Palimak rushed to help them. And although there were no stretched wires, or tents, or costumes and make-up, they all brought the circus to life on that bare deck.

Incredible feats of acrobatics dazzled one and all. Stirring music from Elgy and Rabix lifted glum spirits. This was followed by a frantic clown chase—with all the circus people joining in—that soon brought roars of laughter to all the people. Laughter that echoed over the endless wine-dark seas, making them seem like a natural and friendly part of the act.

Flying fish leaping high, as if laughing with the crowd. Grinning dolphins gamboling in the ships' wake, playing like merry children in a watery nursery.

It was those people and those actions that kept the voyage from collapsing at the start. And although the cheer was short-lived because Safar remained in his coma, the closer they all came to Hadin, the more determined everyone became to complete the journey.

After Safar's condition, the main worry was Rhodes. Had he returned to Syrapis? Or was he lying ahead somewhere, ready to ambush them?

Biner made several long flights in hopes of catching sight of Rhodes. But the king and his minions were never seen. After a while everyone assumed that he had sailed back to Syrapis and that it would be their friends and families at home who would have to contend with him. This was worrisome, to be sure, but it also meant that Rhodes was no longer their responsibility.

Then, one day, Hadin announced its presence.

Normally, seafarers first become aware that they are nearing land when they notice subtle shifts in the currents. Also, the water color changes as the sea floor gradually rises, or a river makes itself known by the silt carried off by outgoing tides.

These things often present themselves many days before land itself is sighted. There are other signs, such as birds who normally live on shore but which hunt the deeps for food. Also, the variety of fish might change. Even more telling is an abundance of plant debris—floating logs with fresh branches still intact, or clumps of estuary weeds uprooted by a storm and swept out to sea.

With Hadin, however, the announcement was much more stark and more than a little frightening.

As they sailed, the Demon Moon sank lower in the sky until it rested just on the horizon. And there it remained for the remainder of the voyage. Only it seemed to grow larger as each mile passed beneath their bows. And soon it appeared as if they were sailing directly into its grinning mouth.

The color of the moon also changed from blood red to an eerie orange, giving the sky a strange and foreboding cast.

Next came the expected change in the color of the sea. Except that this change came without warning. One morning they awoke to find all the seas were painted a ghastly gray-white. The smell of rotting sea life was intense, coming from the hundreds of dead fish floating on the surface.

One of the sailors dipped up a bucket of water and examined the grayness. Although he didn't know the cause, a grizzled old salt said it was pumice—no doubt thrown into the sky by an erupting volcano.

If anyone doubted his word, they soon sighted huge gray hunks of the chalk-like substance—some as large as great icebergs. But most were the size of small rocks and they bumped along the sides of the ships making it sound like they were moving through a slurry of gravel.

Off to their left they saw a thick column of black smoke rising above the horizon and had no doubt that it was an active volcano—the source of all that pumice.

The fleet captains started to fret that one of the large pieces of pumice would damage the ships, possibly even sinking them, and they urged the Kyranians to turn about.

But Coralean put each captain under guard and forced them to go on.

The following morning the situation improved dramatically. For suddenly they sailed out of the gray waters into sparkling blue seas, full of active fish life. Then the normal happy signs of approaching land made themselves known—floating plant life, hunting birds and several great sea lizards swimming toward traditional nesting grounds.

And two days later, under a bright cheery sun, they sailed into a graceful bay with broad beaches and rich orchards of palm trees waving in a gentle breeze.

In the background of this idyllic scene was a towering volcano. It appeared peaceful, since there were only fluffy white clouds gathered about its conical peak. Terraced farms ran halfway up its sides, followed by lush greenery and then a sprinkling of trees near the top. A winding road cut through the farms, disappearing between smaller peaks.

Palimak was aboard the airship when they came upon Hadin. And when he first saw the beaches, palm trees and the volcano it reminded him of his father's description of the spirit world Hadin from which he'd escaped.

The differences, however, were remarkable. There were no naked dancing people. No resounding shell horns and harvest drums. And the volcano was far from threatening. In fact, it looked like a place where everyone had enjoyed a rich bounty of life for many generations.

Then he saw a group of about twenty people standing near the largest palm orchard. He borrowed Biner's spyglass to examine them.

The first thing that struck him was how handsome these bronzed people were. They were far from naked, much less painted, but their costumes were minimal. Short breeches for the men, with flower garlands decorating their bare chests. And tiny skirts and bright-colored breast bands for the women, who also wore flower garlands in profusion.

Brief as the costumes were, they were quite rich in coloring and design. It didn't take any ponderous thought to surmise that their brevity had more to do with Hadin's hot weather than with how civilized the people were.

A tall, regal woman stood in front of the group. When Palimak focused on her he was stunned by her beauty. Her costume was visibly richer than the others—more colorful and embroidered with what appeared to be gold and gems. A crown of fabulous flowers ringed her brow.

From this, as well as her bearing and the deference the others showed her, Palimak had no doubt that she was in command.

As he watched, the young queen made an imperious gesture and several men lifted large shell horns and blew. A loud but melodious note sprang forth. Both the shape of the horns and the sound reminded Palimak of Asper's magical horn Jooli had given to his father. The only difference was that no spell was created by these horns. There was only the lovely trumpeting music of warm welcome and invitation.

Immediately he rushed to the stateroom where his father was sprawled on a pallet, pale as death. Although he was unconscious, his presence was still powerful. Wild bits of magic sparking in the atmosphere as he twitched and moaned in his sleep. Caught in the throes of a living nightmare about whose content Palimak could only speculate.

He found the shell trumpet and raced back out on deck. There he planted his feet wide and blew an answer.

No magic issued forth, much less the Princess Alsahna—the Spirit Rider—on her magnificent mare, charging into the ethereal mist to confront the enemy. Nor had that been Palimak's intention. He didn't have Safar's power to master the horn, much less cause the appearance of the Spirit Rider. However, he intuitively knew that this was the best way to respond to the call of this island queen.

Palimak was surprised at the pleasing music he made as he blew through the horn. He'd feared that without practice the sound would be more in the realm of squawks and squeaks. Instead, melodious notes poured forth and when he lowered the horn he saw the queen and her court respond—pointing up at the airship in amazement.

"Take her down, Biner," he shouted.

Immediately the dwarf bellowed orders. Ballast was dumped, the engines went silent and at the same time there was the hiss of air being bled from the twin balloons.

They descended. Floating lower and lower to the dazzling white sands of the beach . . .

*   *   *

Palimak dragged himself out of his reverie. Important people were waiting for Safar's appearance. But first he had to explain his father's blindness to Leiria and the others. They'd be shocked, but he had to get them over that shock as quickly as he could.

Queen Yorlain was waiting and history stood in the balance.

CHAPTER FORTY-FIVE
HADINLAND

Blind as he was, Safar made a striking first appearance before Queen Yorlain and her court.

Dressed in his best ceremonial robes, he rode Khysmet across the sands to where the island queen waited in a portable throne made of rare fragrant wood, decorated with exotic flowers.

Leiria and Jooli walked on either side of Khysmet, their mail burnished to a high gloss. Palimak, dressed in a princely costume, led the way—walking several paces before the snow-white stallion.

Marching behind them was the entire Kyranian contingent. More than a hundred soldiers were spread out in ceremonial procession with Coralean at their head. Mounted on a tall horse, the caravan master was bedecked in flowing robes. Beside him, riding a dainty bay, was Eeda, who was also dressed in her finest. Despite her advanced pregnancy, Eeda looked lovely in her bejeweled gown, her face shining with excitement.

Overhead, the airship circled the beach, stirring music from Elgy and Rabix floating down to enthrall one and all.

Safar held Khysmet's reins loosely, trusting the horse to be his eyes. Once again he marveled at the mystical communication between horse and man. He only had to focus on a thing and Khysmet seemed to flow with his thoughts, anticipating his every need.

Although Safar couldn't see, Iraj's ethereal presence in his body made his senses doubly acute. Every sound was magnified, but not painfully so. Every scent was sharp and clear. The slight breeze fanned his face, making his flesh tingle with increased awareness of his surroundings. He also felt extremely strong and fast, his muscles throbbing with Iraj's added power.

As they approached the queen, Safar heard the murmurs of amazement from her courtiers. Deep inside, Iraj chortled in delight. He said, *They know a king when they see one, brother. But what they don't know is that there are* two *of us!*

Safar didn't need a signal from his friends to know when he was close enough to stop. The knowledge just suddenly came to him—and at the same time to Khysmet—and the stallion came to a halt, tail lashing, flanks quivering in anticipation.

He allowed a moment for drama before he spoke, turning his face this way and that as if his eyes were sweeping the scene. At the same time he soaked up the sensations, building a picture in his mind.

It was all too familiar. The sound of the palms stirring in the breeze, the hiss of the seas. The feel of the warm sun beating down. The smell of ripening palm fruit—and the distant, acrid odor of the volcano, mixed with the heady scent of the queen's exotic perfume.

Inside Safar, Iraj shuddered as he too recognized their surroundings, as well as the identity of the woman before them. He felt the quickening beat of Safar's heart and whispered a warning: *Steady, brother! It was a warning meant as much for himself as for the man whose body he shared.*

Safar nodded, then lifted his head to speak—centering his eyes on the place where the queen's sweet scent was the strongest.

"Greetings, Majesty," he said. "My people and myself will be forever indebted to you for your gracious welcome to your shores."

He heard a surprised gasp, then graceful movement as the queen rose from her throne.

"But why *wouldn't* I welcome you, King Safar?" came a puzzled voice. "Don't you know me? Am I not your sister in misfortune? Have we not danced together in the Vision of the World's End countless times in the past?"

Safar gave a long sigh as answers to questions he hadn't even known existed came rushing in.

"Yes, I know you, Queen Yorlain," he said. "But what I didn't know was that you shared the vision that has been tormenting me since I was a boy."

There was a pause as the queen considered his answer. Then she asked, "You mean, you have sailed from the other side of the world without truly understanding what was happening and what you must do to intervene?"

"What knowledge I have," Safar replied, "comes only from visions, oracles and the Book of Asper." He smiled ruefully. "Wondrous events and learned objects to be sure. But you must admit, none of them are noted for their clarity."

"And yet you came," Yorlain said, voice tinged with awe. "Although you were blind to the world's true needs."

For a moment, Safar thought she'd seen through his ruse. That she knew he was blind, although he'd pretended otherwise. Instinctively, this worried him. He didn't know why, but he felt it was important that he keep his disability from her. But her next words made him realize she was speaking about blindness figuratively and that his secret was still intact.

"Please forgive my ramblings, Majesty," she said. "I'm only happy that you've come at all. That we can look upon one another as ordinary mortals, instead of as slaves of that awful vision."

For an answer, Safar only smiled and bowed low in the saddle. The next question, however, brought him up sharply.

"But where is your brother king?" she asked. "The Holy Lady Felakia was quite clear that two kings would come to Hadin to awaken the gods. Two royal brothers and a child born of human and demon parentage."

Thinking quickly, Safar said, "The child you spoke of is now a grown man. And he stands there before you." He gestured at the place he was certain Palimak stood. "His name is Palimak, my adopted son."

"And the other?" Queen Yorlain pressed.

Safar tapped his breast. "My brother is with us in spirit, Majesty. And at the right moment he will make his physical presence known to you as well."

Inside him, Iraj murmured, *Excellent answer, Safar. But you always were good at turning a lie on its head and making it the truth. Hmm?*

Safar ignored this. Evidently the truce he and Iraj had agreed upon didn't include insults. He still had no idea how he was going to deal with his old enemy, much less present him to Yorlain when the time came.

More worrisome—on a personal level—was how Palimak and especially Leiria would react when he told them about Iraj. Worse still, he hadn't allowed himself to dwell on the living horror inside him. At the moment, the only course of action he could think of was to delay the inevitable as long as possible.

Queen Yorlain said, "I pray your brother doesn't wait too long, Majesty. The time is near when we must act."

"I promise you, Highness," Safar replied, "that we'll both be ready. There's nothing to concern yourself about as far as my brother's appearance is concerned."

"Very well, then, King Safar," Yorlain replied. "Let us lead you to your castle. All has been prepared for the work you must do there."

Safar was puzzled. "What castle?" he asked.

"Why, the Castle of the Two Kings," she said, mildly surprised. "Didn't Lord Asper mention that in his writings?"

Safar remembered the line: "*. . . Know that Asper knocked at the Castle Keep/ But the gates were barred, the Gods asleep . . .*"

He smiled. "Asper only commented on it indirectly," he said. "But I think I understand now what he was getting at. At least in part, that is."

"Will you come with us then, Majesty?" Yorlain asked.

Safar hesitated. "What of my friends and soldiers?" he asked.

"There's ample room, Majesty," Yorlain said. "Actually, it is a castle without inhabitants. A ghost castle, so to speak. No one has lived there since the days of Asper, although it has been kept in good repair."

Once again, Safar bowed low in his saddle. "Lead the way, then, O gracious queen," he said.

There was a rumble of wheels as attendants led a light, two-wheeled chariot across the sands. It was drawn by a matched pair of magnificent ostriches, standing over seven feet high. Safar heard Leiria and Jooli murmur in amazement and wondered what they were seeing.

Then the queen mounted her chariot. She gave the signal and to the sound of blaring shell horns and rolling drums the ostriches started off, drawing the chariot after them.

"This way, father," Palimak called.

But Khysmet was already moving, following the strange procession. Coralean bellowed orders and the Kyranian soldiers stepped out smartly.

"Do you see the castle?" Safar asked Leiria. He didn't remember one being here.

"All I see," Leiria replied, "is a big damned volcano. Which just happens to be the way we're going!"

*   *   *

Not far away, in the shadow of a small uninhabited island, King Rhodes and his three ships were drawn up in a little bay protected on three sides by high cliffs.

The ships looked different than before. Their hulls and sails had been painted or dyed a grayish blue to match the seas. The figureheads had been removed from the prows and all bright metal objects had been daubed with tar so that they wouldn't glitter.

In short, Rhodes' pirate captains had ransacked their brains for all the tricks of their criminal trade to obscure the ships from casual view.

Even more effective, however, was the spell Queen Clayre had cast with the powerful support of the Lady Lottyr. The spell made the ships completely invisible to prying eyes, such as those of the crew of the airship that had searched for them during the whole long voyage from Aroborus.

The goddess of the Hells had also aided them in other important ways, such as ferreting out the intended route of the Kyranians. And so it was, that when the Timura fleet drew up at the main island a few short sea miles away, King Rhodes and his ships were already hidden in the little bay.

Even now, the king's troops were camped on shore getting ready for the coming surprise attack. Grizzled sergeants strode among them as they cleaned and repaired their weapons and armor. Although their rations were necessarily cold so campfires wouldn't give away the army's presence, the food was plentiful and Rhodes encouraged them to eat their fill and build up their strength.

He'd also captured a native fishing vessel and had tortured the crew until they'd been emptied of every scrap of knowledge about Hadin that they contained. The four men had then been turned over to Clayre to feed her spellfires and keep Lottyr satiated.

Now, as the Kyranians marched in procession toward the mysterious Castle of the Two Kings, it was Rhodes who saw the edifice first.

In Clayre's cabin, the king leaned forward to study the living diorama of the main island that shimmered on his mother's spelltable. He could see the small figure of Queen Yorlain in her chariot, leading Safar and his people up off the beach toward the volcano.

A road began just beyond a thick grove of palm trees. It shot straight toward the volcano, then wound up its terraced sides—moving past tiny people working in the fields. The road continued through a series of small peaks, then dipped down into a wide, green valley cupped in the volcano's lap. A shallow blue lake filled one side, rippling along a rocky shore.

In the center of the valley—set on a peninsula that jutted into the lake—was a great golden castle surrounded by enormous walls. Within were several domed palaces, surrounding a massive keep that towered over all.

A second, lower wall ringed the castle's outer perimeter and Rhodes could clearly see the six gates that allowed traffic to pass to and from the castle. And a wide road leading past the domed palaces to the keep, where he knew Safar would take residence, since it was the greatest stronghold in the entire castle.

Looking through the king's eyes, Kalasariz examined the diorama with equal interest. Except for the castle, the valley reminded him slightly of Kyrania, which also featured a lake. The plant life was also different and Kyrania was set high in snowy mountains, instead of in the lap of a volcano. But those things aside, the number of similarities were surprising.

Clayre frowned at the scene. "That castle is going to be troublesome," she said. "It may even make our job near impossible."

"Why is that, mother?" Rhodes asked, mildly amused at Clayre's foray into his world—the world of tactics and strategy and fortifications.

She snorted in disgust at her son's imagined stupidity. "Isn't it obvious?" she said. "Once the Kyranians get inside those walls there'll be no getting them out!"

Rhodes chuckled. "That's one way of looking at it, mother," he replied.

"What other way is there of seeing it?" she demanded.

Another kingly chuckle. "That once the Kyranians enter the castle," he said, "they'll have a hells of a time getting out."

He pointed at several places, saying, "We just have to put troops here . . . and here . . . and maybe a few siege engines over there . . . and we'll have them thoroughly trapped."

Rhodes made a fist. "Then all we have to do is squeeze."

Clayre nodded, even smiling a little—pleased at his explanation. "But what about the Queen and her people?" she asked. "They certainly seem to be on Safar Timura's side. Surely she has more soldiers at her command then we possess."

It was Rhodes' turn to snort. "They won't be any match for my boys," he said. "We'll swallow them up and spit them out in no time."

Then he saw the tiny image of the airship rising toward the valley. He jabbed a finger at it.

"That's my main worry," he said. "That damned airship again! It can bombard the hells out of us during the siege while we're sitting helplessly in the open."

Clayre turned to her son, smile broadening. "I've been thinking about the airship," she said. "I even discussed the situation with our patroness, the Lady Lottyr."

"What was the result, mother?" Rhodes asked, hopes growing.

"That we won't have to worry about the airship much longer," Clayre replied.

"That's good news, indeed," Rhodes said.

"I'll need a few days to get things set up," Clayre cautioned. "So don't move too swiftly and give yourself away before it's time to act."

Rhodes shrugged. "No bother there, mother," he said. "I need a few more days myself before *I'm* ready."

Clayre nodded understanding. "You're waiting on Tabusir?" she asked.

"The very one," Rhodes replied.

CHAPTER FORTY-SIX

THE HELLS MACHINE

On the surface it was a glorious procession. The beautiful queen, posing nobly in her ostrich chariot, led the way up the long winding road that climbed the volcano. Flower petals covered the road and they gave off a marvelous scent when crushed by the passing parade.

But the higher Palimak climbed the more worried he became. Some of his worries were natural—his father's blindness made him feel he'd once again had to shoulder a burden much too heavy for one so young.

Reason told him this wasn't the case—Safar's blindness in no way diminished his wizardly powers. Nor did his father seem to be affected physically apart from his sight problem. Actually, he seemed much stronger than before.

However, Palimak could not shake off the sensation that something was very wrong—both with his father and with the journey itself. He couldn't get a grip on what was troubling him.

Hadin's air was so full of wild bits and flashes of magic that he couldn't trace the source of what was troubling him. Some of it came from Safar, some from the queen and her courtiers, but most seemed to emanate from the road ahead, and from the towering volcano.

Stirring music still wafted down from the airship, as Biner followed the procession on high. There was more to Biner's choice of music than mere pomp and ceremony. It was also a signal that all was well as far as the lookouts aboard the airship could see. If any danger was spotted, Elgy and Rabix would begin playing fierce music full of trumpets and war drums.

As the procession moved along the road, farmers in the terraced fields stopped their work to see what all the noise was about. Clad in loin cloths and broad-brimmed straw hats to shield them from the sun, they all radiated a feeling of the inner peace that comes from tilling the land.

Then the queen led them around a sharp bend. Along one side were hundreds of nearly naked beggars all crying for alms and bemoaning their infirmities.

Palimak dropped back to tell his father about the beggars—although the loud cries they made surely enlightened him to what was going on. Safar nodded, then called for Renor and Seth who trotted up with large leather saddlebags bulging with silver coins. At Safar's signal they began scattering the coins to the beggars.

Safar had come into the queen's presence well prepared for any eventuality. Although he couldn't have anticipated the journey they were now on, he had guessed that they would encounter the kingdom's poor.

"There are beggars in every realm," he'd said. "And whenever and wherever royalty is welcomed, the beggars turn out to test the visiting king's generosity. So if we want to make a good impression on this queen, we'd better be ready for her beggars."

And ready they were, with hundreds of silver coins being tossed into the air by Renor and Sinch. The two young soldiers went at their task eagerly, as if they were fabulously rich and dispensing their own wealth instead of Safar's.

They joked with the beggars, who all crowded around, blocking the road.

"Here's some for you, pretty lady," Sinch said to an old woman—pushing the laughing mob back so she wouldn't be shut out.

The toothless granny cackled with delight, both at the coins in her palm and the handsome young man who'd given them to her.

"Pretty yourself," the old woman said. "I'd rather have yer warmin' me bed than take your money!"

Sinch laughed with much good nature, giving the granny a kiss on her dirty cheek.

A legless man in a push cart knuckled his way forward, crowding close to Khysmet. Renor stepped in to block his way gently and tossed three silver coins on the beggar's cart.

The man opened his mouth to thank Renor, displaying rotting teeth and a short stump of a tongue. The wet smacking sounds of thanks that came from his mutilated mouth were a horror to someone of Renor's inexperience. Like all Kyranians he'd lived such a sheltered life in the mountains that such things were unknown to him.

Renor suppressed a shudder. Then he felt overwhelmed by guilt for his reaction and pressed two more coins into the beggar's hands.

More horrible noises followed as the legless one pushed in closer. Another beggar stumbled over him, making him lose his balance and reached out wildly, grabbing Khysmet's tail.

The stallion grunted in protest at the rude handling, jerking forward. Several long strands of snow-white hair pulled loose: the legless beggar waved them in Renor's face and spewed more obscene sounds, as if the horse hairs were a fabulous gift.

To Renor's surprise, he heard Palimak shout to him: "Hold that man!"

It was as if all of Renor's brains had run out of his head, because for the life of him he couldn't figure out what Palimak was asking. He gaped about, dismissing the amputee from his mind to look for a man with all his parts.

Then Palimak came rushing up. "The beggar!" he shouted. "The one in the pushcart. Where did he go?"

For the life of him, Renor couldn't figure out why Palimak would be upset about someone so unfortunate that he even lacked legs. But he looked around as he was commanded and to his surprise he realized that the man he'd been ordered to find was gone.

In his stead other beggars were crowding in, crying, "Alms! Alms for the poor!" And, "Baksheesh! Baksheesh!"

Then he heard Safar call out, "Palimak! Get over here right away!"

And then the whole column became a confusion of soldiers and beggars that tied the road into a knot of chaos.

Tabusir was a patient spy. He didn't mind waiting for his prey to come to him. As a matter of fact, he quite enjoyed the wait, planning many plans, anticipating the split second of enjoyment that came when he snatched a secret from beneath the very noses of his enemies.

Then there was the escape to dream about. The greater thrill was to slip away undiscovered and keep the secret of the encounter deep within your breast. Less exciting was to be discovered and to have to wrest yourself from the wrath of the discoverers.

Oh, to be sure, there was the thrill of the chase. But Tabusir had always considered a chase to be the result of his own failure to remain unobserved.

As all spies know, the ultimate value of a secret diminishes in proportion to the number of people who know it. And it is vastly diminished if the enemy realizes his secret has been revealed.

And so it was that when Palimak shouted, "Hold that man!" Tabusir felt diminished. He'd spent three days and two nights waiting for his chance to steal the secrets of the Timuras.

His scant knowledge of the local customs and dialect had only made his planning more exciting. All he knew came from the fishermen Rhodes had captured and tortured. Although Tabusir considered himself a master at language and its local nuances, the screams and groans of men in pain was no way to learn it.

Instead, he'd concentrated on the looks of the men. Ignoring their pain-twisted countenances, he had focused on their thick dark hair and sun-bronzed bodies. One of the men was toothless and his painful babble could barely be understood. This was what had given Tabusir the inspiration for his disguise.

If he pretended he couldn't speak, Tabusir reasoned, then he wouldn't be able to give himself away by using a faulty accent. To make sure people would think he was mute, he made a little device to fit over his tongue which gave it the appearance of being a stump. To further revolt anyone looking at him, he blackened his teeth with charcoal so they looked as if they were rotting.

Then all he had to do was dye his hair and stain his body with walnut juice so he'd look like a native and be able to mingle with the other beggars of Hadin. The cart, which he'd carried with him from Syrapis for just this purpose, had a false bottom that hid his legs.

Tabusir had landed on the island at night and had hidden the little boat among some rocks. Then he'd waited for Safar's arrival. It was the main topic of conversation among all the beggars. There was much excitement and anticipation of how charitable the great King Timura would be. Everyone also knew their queen would escort Safar to the Castle of the Two Kings and there was much dispute over the best place to wait for him.

When the day finally came, Tabusir followed the other beggars up the long road and took his place among them. When they'd seen his mutilated tongue no one questioned Tabusir's right to be with them.

As the grand procession moved past the beggars it had taken the sharp-eyed spy only a few minutes to realize that Safar was blind. It was the way Timura carried himself that'd given him away: a certain stiffness of the head, with the eyes staring blankly forward no matter what happened.

For instance, when he'd called his two men forward to disperse the silver coins, he hadn't looked at them when they came running up. Nor had he looked left or right as the beggars crowded close, crying for alms and singing Safar's praises.

The moment he caught Safar out, Tabusir had realized that even if he came up with nothing else for his king Rhodes would be mightily pleased with the outcome of Tabusir's mission. The spy smiled in anticipation of the fat purse of gold he'd receive as a reward.

Rhodes had also directed Tabusir to try to get his hands on some personal item from either Safar or his great horse. The coins the soldiers had dispensed might not meet that qualification, since there was a chance Safar himself had never handled them.

So he'd gone for the stallion, pretending clumsiness, then grabbing a few long hairs from the animal's tail as he struggled to regain his balance.

But then he'd heard Palimak shout and his perfect mission had been spoiled.

Now, as he sprinted down the road toward the place where he'd hidden his boat, he burned with resentment. What could have given him away? How had his clever disguise failed him? Then it came to him that Palimak—well-known for his powerful wizardry—must have used magic to ferret Tabusir out. Yes, that was the answer: Magic.

Still, it didn't make him feel any better. Perfection was his constant goal and Palimak had marred that perfection. But then, as he pulled the boat from the rocky cove, he wondered why no else had pursued him? It didn't make sense. Palimak had somehow discovered Tabusir's presence and yet he hadn't sent anyone after the spy.

Tabusir pondered on this while rowing toward Rhodes' island hideout. The only answer he came up with was that something more important must have distracted Palimak.

The spy cursed himself for running away so quickly. He should have found a hiding place nearby to see what was so important to the young prince. As he thought about this he recalled Safar shouting something to Palimak. But Tabusir had been too busy getting away to hear what was being said.

He stopped paddling. For a long moment he seriously considered turning back. He could easily adopt some other disguise and again attempt to get close to the Timuras. But then he thought of Palimak's magic and decided against this plan. The young prince would be wary now he knew an enemy had come within assassination distance of his father.

Tabusir started paddling again. He wouldn't tell Rhodes about being discovered. There was no sense in spoiling his king's respect for his abilities.

It would be enough to inform Rhodes that Safar was blind. Then hand him the hairs he'd stolen from the stallion's tail.

Tabusir's failure would remain his own little secret. Thinking of it that way made him feel a whole lot better.

But then the good feeling vanished as he once again wondered why the Timuras weren't pursuing him.

He paddled onward, cold fingers of dread running down his spine.

*   *   *

Rushing to answer Safar's call, Palimak pushed through the crowd of beggars to his side. Renor and Sinch accompanied him, shouting for the other Kyranian soldiers to help them untangle the mess.

"Gundara and Gundaree just spotted a spy, father!" Palimak said. "It's one of the beggars. A man without any legs. Or at least he's pretending he doesn't have any legs. But he's getting away, so we have to act fast if we want to catch him."

"Forget about the spy, son," Safar said. Although his voice was calm, Palimak sensed extreme tension. "We'll worry about him later," Safar continued. "There's something much more important happening."

Palimak frowned. "What is it, father?" he asked. "What's wrong?"

But no sooner had the words left his mouth than he felt a heavy, throbbing presence roil the magical atmosphere. All the wild bits of magic suddenly coalesced into a single deadly entity. An entity that was neither animate or inanimate. It just was. A soulless thing that somehow had a purpose.

"Can't you feel it, son?" Safar demanded. "It's a machine. Just like the one in Caluz!"

Then Palimak remembered that fearful machine from the Hells and said, "Yes. I can feel it."

He looked up at Safar, mouth dry. "What do we do, father?"

And Safar replied, "There's nothing we can do—except go on!"

CHAPTER FORTY-SEVEN
WHERE LOTTYR WAITS

When the procession topped the rise overlooking the Valley of the Two Kings the intensity of the machine's magic struck Safar with full force. He threw up a hand, as if protecting his face from a blazing sun.

In his nesting place Iraj was shaken to the core by the magical storm and its effects on his host. He said to Safar: *Aren't you going to do something about this? You could make some kind of shield, like the one you used in Caluz.*

At the same time, Palimak cried out, "We need a shield, father! But I don't know how to make one."

Jooli too was suffering from the magical blast. "Is this a trick, Safar?" she asked. "Has the queen led us into a trap?"

Meanwhile, Eeda was pushing her mount forward, Coralean at her heels. Her face was twisted in agony from the sorcerous assault.

"Please, Lord Timura," she begged. "We must do something. I fear for the life of my unborn child."

Safar had rarely felt so frustrated. He knew where the machine was. As he turned his blind face from side to side he could easily spot the point of the heaviest magical concentration. But without visual coordinates to support him he was helpless to cast the shielding spells.

"Patience, my friends," he said as reassuringly as he could. "I need to think."

Jooli guessed what was happening. She'd been as shocked as the others when Palimak had informed them of his father's blindness. However, as Palimak had assured everyone, magic rarely required the power of sight. He had said that Safar's wizardly powers were unaffected by his infirmity and they could proceed as planned.

But Jooli's deep studies of magic, plus her instincts, told her this situation presented a unique problem. To build a shield one not only needed to know the location of the danger, but also the location of everyone you wanted to protect. To accomplish this the sorcerer needed eyes.

"Tell us what to do, Safar," she said. "We want to help you."

Palimak and Eeda quickly came to the same conclusion and urged Safar to instruct them. Meanwhile, the machine's assault was slowly draining everyone of their energies.

Safar realized he didn't have much time to act. If only he could see, the danger could be countered within seconds.

Iraj rose up, saying, *Give me your eyes, brother. I can give sight to both of us!*

Safar hesitated, fearful of allowing Iraj the slightest control over his body.

A bolt of magic struck Eeda and she groaned in terrible pain, gripping her pregnant belly. "Please, Lord Timura," she cried. "Please!"

Safar relented, opening a gateway for Iraj to scramble forward. At the same time Safar's whole body crawled with sensation—like little worms of pulsating energy wriggling a burning path along every vein, every nerve.

And then the whole world became an explosion of colorful light. It was so sudden and painful that he cried out, jamming palms into his outraged eyes. Then the pain passed and he opened his eyes and saw the Valley of the Two Kings for the first time.

At first it was all cool greens and hot oranges, bordered with gray blues and varying shades of purple and pink. Then the image steadied and he saw the golden castle, with its towering keep, sitting in the center of a valley very much like Kyrania.

Except there was more raw orange land than ever existed in the valley of his homeland. It surrounded the castle—earth, hard-packed by hundreds of wagons and feet. Then the green farmland and pines so fragrant he could smell their sharp, fresh scent on the breeze.

And a lake, a lake as glorious as Lake Felakia in far Kyrania. Blue and cool and beckoning. The purples came from the diffused sunlight shining on a bank of coned mountains that fringed the great volcano of Hadin. The lesser purples and pinks radiated from the skies and clouds that framed the whole scene.

Safar tried to focus his eyes on the castle keep, where he knew the magical machine was housed. Instead, against his will, his head bent back—eyes running up the sides of the volcano, where a small dark puff of smoke burst out to mingle with the white clouds that surrounded it.

Panicked, he tried to force his head back down to view the castle. But to his horror he realized Iraj had taken full control of his body. And his head bent back further to take in the airship circling overhead—pleasant music playing as if nothing had gone wrong.

He tried to open his mouth to shout a warning to Palimak. But Iraj only swallowed, forcing Safar's words back down into his gut.

Iraj, speaking with Safar's voice, said, "Apparently my problem has passed. I can see again."

Renewed hope acted as a temporary balm, easing everyone's suffering. Leiria laughed aloud, clutching Safar/Iraj's hand, murmuring, "I'm so happy, my love."

But to Safar, a prisoner in his own body, the sensation of her warm, loving touch came from far away. And her voice seemed even more distant.

Iraj, commanding Safar's body, squeezed Leiria's hand. And, speaking in Safar's voice, he whispered, "Let me feast them on you tonight, Leiria."

Leiria gave Safar/Iraj a startled look. Then, to Safar's dismay, her eyes flashed gladness and she smiled warmly, asking, "Are you sure, Safar?"

And Iraj replied, "Yes, I'm sure."

Then he sent a mental command back to Safar, saying, *Cast the spell, brother. Before this damned machine gets the better of us!*

Despite the growing danger, Safar hesitated. Somehow he had to regain control of his own body.

Sensing his conflict, Iraj said, *Do you want to bargain with me over your friends' lives, brother? And even if I agreed, considering our past history together, do you trust my word?*

Just then Eeda gasped, swooning in her saddle. Coralean steadied her just in time.

His big booming voice shattered Safar's indecision. "You must act, Safar!" he said. "Before it's too late for my Eeda!"

Iraj said to Safar, *You see how it is, brother? Now, quickly, tell me what to do.*

And so Safar told him to get out the little witch's-dagger, which was hidden in the right sleeve of his cloak. Then he told him to cut a large imaginary circle in the air. Iraj followed his instruction—a little clumsily since he was unused to such actions. Then Safar fed him the words to the shielding spell he'd used so successfully in the Blacklands during the march to Caluz.

In Safar's voice, Iraj chanted:

"Sever the day,
Shatter the night.
Keep at bay,
All sorcerous plight.
Bedevil the devils
Who speak in flame
And dance and revel
In the Goddess's name."

There was no outward sign of the spell's effect. Only heaving sighs of relief from Palimak and the others as the shield slid silently and invisibly into place—folding the entire Kyranian contingent into its protective cloak.

Queen Yorlain had turned her little ostrich chariot around and was coming back to see why Safar's column had stopped. Iraj leaned forward in the saddle and Khysmet obediently trotted forth to meet her, snorting at the strange feathered steeds drawing her onward.

Iraj gloried in the strong, easy movement of the stallion. A man born and bred to Esmir's Great Plains, there was nothing he loved more than a good horse. But Khysmet was more than just a horse—he was magical. Using his mental voice, Iraj said to Safar, *I once dreamed I was riding Khysmet. Now that dream's come true.*

Safar remembered the dream, which he'd experienced too in that mysterious spiritual connection he seemed to have with Iraj. He said, *Never mind the dream. Let me have my body back. Or I swear I'll make you suffer for stealing it.*

Iraj's answer was a sarcastic laugh. Then he reined Khysmet in as they came up to the queen.

"What is the trouble, Majesty?" Yorlain asked.

Iraj gave her a sardonic look. "You didn't mention the spell," he said, a tinge of accusation in his voice.

Yorlain's beautiful eyes widened in surprise. "But I thought you knew," she said. "Did not the great Lord Asper warn of the killing spell? And propose the protective shield that is its answer?"

Safar whispered to Iraj, *Asper only mentioned the Blacklands and Caluz. He said nothing about Hadin. Tell her you were not informed of the killing spell, but still knew how to counter it when you came up against it.*

Although he was desperate to turn the tables on Iraj and retrieve his body, Safar realized that under the circumstances he had to cooperate with his old nemesis. And as long as Iraj was in control, Safar would have to guide his fingers as they pieced together the dangerous puzzle that was Hadinland.

Iraj gave Yorlain his most charming smile. And although it was Safar's mouth he was stretching and Safar's teeth he was flashing, his potent personality blazed through.

"I must have missed that part," he said to the queen. "At the time there were some very nasty fellows on my heels. So I only read about the shield, then ran like the Hells for cover."

Then he leaned closer, murmuring, "Visionary that he was, poor Asper must have been a very old demon. For he didn't mention you, my queen. A vision above all visions."

Swept away by Iraj's dash, Yorlain blushed and tinkled musical laughter. "Be careful, Majesty," she said. "Or I might get a false idea about your intentions."

Iraj bowed low in the saddle. "How could I be false," he said, "when confronted with such truly wondrous beauty?"

Meanwhile, Palimak and the others had caught up with them. Leiria overheard the flirtatious exchange and was wounded to the quick. Jooli caught it as well and placed a sympathetic hand on Leiria's shoulder.

"Pay it no mind," she whispered. "He's just sweetening her up because we have need of her."

Leiria shrugged off the hand and straightened—shoulders squaring like the warrior she was. "Safar doesn't say things like that unless he means it," she whispered bitterly.

Jooli said nothing in reply, but only watched with growing disappointment and sadness for her friend as a Safar she'd never seen before preened and postured for Yorlain as if he'd suddenly gone into heat.

Palimak stared at his father, wondering what he was up to. It must be part of his plan, he thought.

Meanwhile, Gundara and Gundaree were chattering in his ear: "Beware, Little Master! Beware!" But he was still feeling shaken and a little dizzy from the effects of the killing spell and found it hard to pay attention.

He gave a cursory glance around, sending out weak magical probes that encountered nothing. Assuming the Favorites were still worrying about the spy, he muttered for them to be quiet until they had privacy to talk.

Once again, Iraj bowed low in the saddle and bade Queen Yorlain to lead the way. Then, just as the queen cracked her little whip for the ostriches to proceed, he glanced over at Leiria, catching her eyes.

He grinned hugely, then shrugged, as if to say, Life has its strange little twists, doesn't it, dear?

Safar saw Leiria's hurt through Iraj's eyes and struggled madly to regain control of his own body. But Iraj was beginning to learn the ways and weapons of his new position and shot a searing inward blast at his prisoner.

Safar jolted as if he'd been struck by lightning. When he recovered, he tried once again to free himself. And the answer was another hot bolt of punishment.

He withdrew into the nest Iraj had once occupied. Nursing his wounds, while his mind ran wild with hate and half-formed thoughts of revenge.

An hour later the castle gates clanked open and Yorlain escorted the Kyranians across the bridge through the cheering crowds of her subjects.

And they all shouted, "The king has come! May the Gods save us and the king!"

Then she took them to the castle keep and Safar had recovered enough to marvel as the huge, iron-bound doors yawned wide to admit them. These were the very same doors, he thought, that Asper had said he'd knocked on without reply.

The old demon wizard's words echoed in his mind: ". . . *Know that Asper knocked at the Castle Keep, But the gates were barred, the Gods asleep.*"

The first thing he saw when the doors swung open was a wide courtyard. Straddling that courtyard was an enormous stone turtle. Flames exploded from its horny mouth. There was a great open grate in its belly and heavily muscled slaves were shoveling whole cartloads of fuel into the furnace within.

Safar noticed that the fuel was similar to the magical stuff the airship's engines used. But just then wild magic suddenly blasted through and he was forced to quickly repair, then strengthen the shield.

One part of his brain noted that he could act without Iraj's cooperation—perhaps even without his knowledge. But the other, larger part focused on a hellish emanation from the Keep itself.

Yorlain whispered orders to her aides, who rushed to open the final barrier—an enormous iron gate with bars as thick as a man's thighs, armed with sharp, spear-like points.

And as they were cranked up, heavy chains rattling against unseen gears, Safar saw a long dark tunnel. A blaze of light, no larger than his palm, winked at the other end.

Yorlain waved them through, getting out of her chariot and walking beside Khysmet.

As they moved into the darkness, both Iraj and Safar heard Yorlain say, "There are those who claim this was once the mightiest fortress in all the world. A thousand years ago, when the last kings ruled, it survived a legendary siege that lasted twenty years or more.

"Ten thousand demons hammered at these gates, but to no avail. If I recall correctly, Lord Asper himself led the last charge and was turned back with terrible casualties."

"What war was this?" Iraj asked. And Safar listened closely for Yorlain's answer.

"My scholars tell me it was an ethnic war of sorts," the queen replied. "Hadin was once populated by people of many races. Also, there was a large colony of demons who lived peacefully among us for centuries. Some say the demons were once so plentiful that one of the ruling pair of kings was a demon.

"I don't know if that's true, since it was so long ago that only the tales survived. There are no records. Regardless, when the slaughter reared its head everyone who was not exactly like . . ." She hesitated, trying to put genocide into passable words. Then: "Well, people without dark hair and dark eyes were condemned and executed as enemies of the state. Of course, the demon king had long since been executed, so that was no bother to these barbarians.

"Then came time to cleanse ourselves of the demons. It was about then that Asper came to our shores, warning of a cleansing of the entire world. Not just of demons . . . or of people like us . . . but of all living things.

"Naturally, no one listened. We all believed the gods were on our side, just as the demons claimed the gods were with them. Asper, of course, said the gods were asleep and we were all doomed.

"But the words of an old wizard don't amount to much when beings want blood, so everyone turned against him. And they drove him away during the long siege that the demons mounted against the humans.

"In the end, the defenders of the castle keep not only prevailed, but sallied forth to engage the demons in several decisive battles."

Sighing, Yorlain shook her head. "If you traveled throughout Hadinland you wouldn't have to ponder long on the result of those battles. For you would not find a single demon on any island throughout the continent. We killed them all and praised ourselves as saints for the killing."

During Yorlain's history lesson, Iraj's military brain drove him to inspect the tunnel's defenses. Here and there were patches of diffused light coming from above and he looked up to treat himself—and Safar—to a view of heavy grates with enormous iron pots set on swivels hanging over them.

Safar needed no explanation from Iraj that in wartime these pots would be filled with boiling oil or molten lead that could be tipped over to scald and kill anyone daring this passage.

Along with Iraj, he also took careful note of the series of gates spread along the tunnel. Smaller than those barring the entryway, but not by much, these gates were cranked up as they approached. Just beyond each gate were other windows of diffused light, with hot pots guarding them.

It took little imagination to see their purpose. Invaders would be tricked into sending troops into the tunnel. Gates would be slammed shut on each side, trapping them for the boiling oil or molten lead.

Finally, they came out of the tunnel into pure high-mountain light. Yorlain led them around a deep pit that had been constructed only a few yards away from the entrance to the fortress.

Iraj glanced inside the pit and both he Safar saw its purpose. A nest of pointed iron spikes was set in cement in the bottom. Gray, frosted demon skeletons were impaled on many of those spikes. Safar didn't have to hear all of Yorlain's words to know that the ancient bones dated back to the great siege.

At last they came to the keep proper. Iraj dismounted and led Khysmet inside, hooves echoing in the vast interior.

It was then that Safar experienced the strongest blast of machine magic. There was a rumble and a whirl that tore him from his center.

Yorlain said something, but he couldn't make out her words. And the magical storm was so intense that even Iraj was shaken. Eyes moving toward the source, carrying Safar's vision with them. Then fixing on a huge pentagram made of golden tiles.

Like Claire's table, Safar thought. And then that thought was ripped from his mind.

For the magic emanating from the pentagram was so powerful that all his senses were confounded. It was as if a thick fog had descended. A painful fog containing many barbs and poisoned hooks like a deep-sea devil fish.

Once again, he strengthened the shield spell. Putting all his energies into it. Wishing he had Palimak, or even Jooli or Eeda to help. But buried within Iraj he was barred from all contact with them.

Then he got the shield up, took scant notice of the fact that Iraj had also been injured by the spellblast, and concentrated on the colorful work painted within the pentagram.

It was an eight-pointed wind-rose. And on each directional spear was painted the form of one the major gods. Safar sent mental commands for Iraj to investigate.

To his surprise, Iraj caught his sense of urgency and let his eyes sweep from familiar figures such as the Goddess Felakia and the rest. Eyes moving onward, from one god or goddess to the other, until they came to rest on a wide red spear that was turned inward, pointing to the center.

And painted on that spear blade was the exotic, six-faced form of the lady from the hells.

The Goddess Lottyr.

Each face was more beautiful and yet more malevolent than the next. Painted flames shot from every mouth.

And as Safar looked at them through eyes that Iraj had provided he saw the flames bubble and move.

A terrible searing blast shot through Iraj, who moaned and shrunk in his own boots from the fiery assault. Safar felt it too, but quickly turned the attack back against its origin.

Somewhere in the gloom of the castle keep he heard a ghostly shriek.

Then the assault ended. But he knew it wasn't for long.

He mental whispered to Iraj, *This is the center. The center to the Hells. And it is through here that we must attack!*

Iraj asked, *How much time do we have, brother?*

And Safar replied, *Almost none at all.*

CHAPTER FORTY-EIGHT

THE TEMPEST

That night, thick black storm clouds gathered over Hadin. At first they scudded in a few at a time, then they arrived with increasing frequency until even the face of the Demon Moon was obscured.

King Rhodes landed his forces in that darkness, crossing from his island hideout to Hadin on longboats with muffled oars. He ignored Safar's nine ships, which were anchored in the little bay. Tabusir had assured him that all but a few Kyranian troops had left the ships to march with Safar and Palimak.

When Rhodes mounted his planned attack on the castle he also knew he'd have nothing to fear from the pirate captains. Once they saw which way the battle went, they'd be clamoring to join Rhodes in return for a few purses of gold.

As soon as Rhodes hit the beach, he sent shock troops forward to secure the road and silence any stray soldiers or farmers they encountered.

Meanwhile, his longboats returned to the island and began the onerous task of hauling the portable siege engines to the shore.

His mother arrived with the last group, hissing curses at her slaves as they clumsily loaded her magical table onto her royal litter. All the gilded decorations had been daubed with lampblack so they wouldn't glitter if struck by a chance beam of light.

"That's my favorite litter," she complained to Rhodes. "And now you've ruined it with your stupid soldier tricks. You're going to have to commission me another one when we return home."

"You're the only one of us who's not walking, mother," Rhodes pointed out. He'd left all the horses behind for transport after the siege was in place. "You're the one who insisted on bringing your litter along. Plus six useless slaves to carry you!"

Clayre sniffed. "Some people would think you'd show more gratitude to me," she said. "After all, it's *my* magic, not your precious army, that will defeat Safar Timura."

Kalasariz knew hand that she spoke the truth. Clayre had spent hours with the Lady Lottyr casting spell after spell to pave the way for the battle.

He whispered from within: *Please, Majesty. Promise her anything to shut her up! You're never going to have to deliver, remember?*

Rhodes took the advice. Sighing, he said, "Very well, mother. You'll get your new litter as soon as we return home."

"Nothing shabby, now," Clayre warned. "You know how tight-fisted you can be."

"Spend what you like," Rhodes said. "I'll give you a blank warrant on the treasury."

Clayre's eyes narrowed suspiciously and Rhodes realized he'd gone too far. "But half the cost will have to come out of your allowance," he hastened to say. "So don't go wild with the design."

Clayre's suspicions vanished. Rhodes' caveat was much more in character. For a flickering moment she'd wondered if her son had matricide on his mind. But on reflection, that didn't make any sense. To be sure, Rhodes had no love for her. Just as she had none for him. However, they did need each other. One held the hereditary crown, the other the magical means to secure it.

"Don't cheapen your gift by bargaining with me about its price," Clayre said. "I'll pay ten per cent, no more."

"Twenty," Rhodes said.

Clayre shook her head sadly. "You are so mean-spirited," she said. "Just like your father. But for the sake of family peace, I'll agree."

The Queen Witch had her own murderous designs. She'd discussed her hateful son with Lottyr, who had promised to aid her when the battle with Safar Timura was won. Further lessening her suspicion was her own good mood: Many magical tricks had been planned to confound the great Safar Timura.

All she had to do was bear with this barbarian lout who called himself her son for another day at the most, and then the tables would be turned once and for all!

Through the king's eyes, Kalasariz observed Clayre's shifting moods. He knew what she was thinking. He'd had his own private discussions with the Goddess Lottyr and was well aware of the Queen Witch's plans and the agreement she'd made with Lottyr.

But what neither she nor Rhodes realized was the Goddess had ambitions of her own. Ambitions that only Kalasariz could satisfy at this most historic moment.

He laughed to himself, thinking how surprised Rhodes and Clayre would be when they joined Fari and Luka in his belly.

Then he had only to capture Iraj and he'd no longer be the power behind thrones, but the throne itself.

King of Kings. Lord and master of Lottyr's worldly realm. For a single, spine-chilling moment he recalled an old Esmirian saying he had once been fond of quoting: "The deadliest poison ever made came from a king's laurel crown."

But then he dismissed this once-favored saying as nonsense. It was only a thing he used to repeat to soothe his pride when Esmir was ruled by fools like Iraj Protarus.

And as Rhodes massed his troops and organized his siege engineers the spymaster dreamed of powers he'd never held before.

Forgetting another most pertinent Esmirian saying: "When the king's spy plots his own coronation, he must first conspire against himself."

*   *   *

In the Castle of the Two Kings, Safar's warning of impending doom shook Iraj from his kingly posturing. A man of many flaws, he'd been momentarily overcome by his weaknesses.

After a long time of being denied even a human body, he'd reveled in his power over women. Never mind that Leiria believed he was Safar—and it was Safar whom she loved—he'd been anxious to master her with his lust. Never mind that Queen Yorlain thought him her handsome savior, he'd been overcome by the idea of adding another queenly notch to his bedstead.

Once he'd been a man—a princely warrior of the Great Plains—whose very smile and ardent looks could bring women into his bed like nubile mares trotting over the hills to the wild stallion's trumpeting call.

Then he'd been a shapechanger, a creature bound by an evil spell, whose lust could only be slaked by murder and blood. As a great wolf he'd delighted in the carnage of the harem of victims he'd kept. But in those rare moments when his human side had crept in, he'd despaired at all the torment he'd caused.

And yes, on occasion he'd even condemned himself for his betrayal of Safar, his blood brother and friend. But those moments were so rare, so fleeting, that they were easily replaced by rationalizations that it was Safar who was the betrayer, not him.

The saintly Safar who claimed that he never wanted anything but to save the world from itself. The lucky Safar, whose encounters with women had always been marked by a deep friendship and love that had always been denied Iraj.

Nerisa, the little thief who had stolen a great treasure for Safar, only to die at Iraj's orders. Methydia, the beautiful witch who had doted on Safar, only to be slain by one of Iraj's soldiers. And then Leiria—fantastic, lovely Leiria—who had once belonged in the literal sense to Iraj. But he'd given her away to Safar on a whim of false friendship and now she loathed her former master and thought only of Safar.

Thoughts of revenge flooded in. He couldn't kill Safar without taking his own life. But he could make him suffer for past wrongs. Just for starters, he'd torment Leiria by seducing the queen, making her think her lover had betrayed her with another. Next he'd seduce Leiria, then cast her out like scraps from the table.

Deep in his nest, Safar also brooded angrily over past wrongs. He too schemed of ways to strike back at Iraj. His anger was so great that he even considered black spells that would burn Protarus to the core. Only the fact that he would suffer too stayed Safar's hand.

Then he realized that Iraj's madness was stirring up a poisonous froth of bodily juices that were affecting him dangerously and might very well drive Safar over the edge as well.

He had to calm down. He had to focus on the tasks ahead—the *least* important of which was to free himself from Iraj's prison.

And that moment must wait until after he had confronted the Hells awaiting him in the Goddess Lottyr's machine.

※   ※   ※

Gundara said, "It isn't Lord Timura, Little Master!"

And Gundaree added, "Well, it *is* Lord Timura, but it's not exactly him."

Palimak frowned. "What in the Hells are you two talking about?"

Gundara said, "It's kind of difficult to explain, Little Master. See, somehow Iraj Protarus got inside your father's body. We think he was hiding there and maybe even Lord Timura didn't know. For a while, anyway."

"But then your father went blind," Gundaree came in, "and he needed King Protarus so that he could see and so your father let him out. And now your father's trapped inside his own body and Protarus is in control of everything!"

"We're just guessing about the blind part," Gundara added.

"But it's a pretty good guess," Gundaree said. "Like always."

Palimak considered. Although what the two Favorites had said was very strange, if you assumed their guess was right many things started to make sense.

Like his own perceptions of wrongness about his father, including the odd change in his hair coloring from dark to streaks of gold. If Iraj, who was a blond, had made himself into a magical parasite inside Safar, might not his presence have influenced his father's hair coloring?

It also explained Safar's bewildering and boorish behavior with Queen Yorlain. Which in turn had wounded his Aunt Leiria. His father would never commit either of those acts.

He nodded, accepting the twins' theory.

"What should we do about it?" he asked. "Can we come up with some sort of spell to purge Iraj from my father's body?"

"That'd be hard!" Gundara said.

"Really, really hard!" Gundaree put in.

"And even if it worked, we could kill them both," Gundara added.

Palimak saw his whole world collapsing under him. Everything that was good had turned out to be evil. His own father was trapped inside the body of the murderous Iraj Protarus!

"It would be easier to think of some kind of solution," Gundara said, "if we had something to eat."

"That's very true, Little Master," Gundaree said. "Thinking is hungry work."

Absently, Palimak fished sweets from his pocket and fed the Favorites. In his mind, past moments shared with his father were being blown about by gusts of nostalgia.

Palimak's first memory, so vague it might not even be real but a thing made up from tales adults tell their children, was as a baby held in Leiria's arms.

He was looking at his father over Leiria's shoulder. She was mounted on a snorting, ground-pawing warhorse and Palimak was tied in a sling about her back. Thumping against her chain mail as the horse moved. And there was his father, seen for the first time: tall and dark with fiery blue eyes that melted into softness when they settled on his adopted son.

There were a whole host of other memories: The cheese monster; the battles against the Great Wolf, Iraj Protarus; the flight across the badlands; the race through the Machine of Caluz; but especially the long talks late into the night as Safar patiently and gently taught his son the theory and practice of magic.

Then, with a start, he remembered a riddle his father had once posed. He'd said that if either of them could ever answer this riddle from The Book of Asper then many things might become clear.

It was the Riddle of the Two Kings: *"Two kings reign in Hadinland./ One's becursed, the other damned./ One is blind, one's benighted./ And who can say which is sighted? . . ."*

"I know it!" Palimak shouted aloud. "I know the answer!"

Gundara covered his fangs with a paw and burped politely. "The answer to what, Little Master?", he asked.

"The Riddle of the Two Kings!" Palimak said. "My father and Iraj Protarus are the two kings!"

"Of course they are," Gundaree said, brushing crumbs from his tunic.

"Didn't you know that, Little Master?"

"But don't you understand?" Palimak said. "That means we shouldn't do anything. The last thing that ought to happen is for us to interfere."

Gundara yawned. "That's fine with me, Little Master," he said. "It sounded like a lot of work, anyway."

Gundaree curled up in a little ball. "Wake me when it's time for dinner," he said to his twin. "All this doing nothing has tired me out."

*   *   *

"Thoth cloudth look pretty bad, Biner," Arlain said.

Biner nodded, brow furrowed in worry. "Ain't that the truth, lass," he said. "Some kind of blow brewin', that's for certain."

They were hovering hundreds of feet above the Castle of the Two Kings, the volcano barely visible as the clouds swiftly drew a veil over the Demon Moon.

"We're too clo'th to that thing," Arlain said, indicating the volcano. "If a thtorm whipth up, we could run right thmack into it."

"Maybe we'd better get to ground," Biner said.

He turned to shout orders to the crew, but just then he saw—or thought he saw—movement along the rim of the valley.

"Take a look there, lass," he said to Arlain, pointing at the deeper shadow where the road came over the rise. "Do you see somethin' on yon road?"

Arlain's dragon eyes were sharper even than the proverbial eagle's. This was only one of many reasons for her incredible acrobatic skills. In a darkened tent she could see a thin guy wire as if it were broad daylight. A fire breather, her vision was also unaffected by sudden flashes of the pyrotechnics the circus used to wow the crowds.

She turned her head to where Biner was pointing, dragon's tongue flickering between pearly teeth as she concentrated.

Many miles away, Queen Clayre's litter was being carried over the rise by her slaves. Careful as they'd been to obscure the gilded ornamentation with lampblack, a small speck of blackening had been knocked off when one of her slaves had brushed against it.

Just then, lightning from the gathering storm flared in the sky, reflecting off the exposed gilding. It was only a tiny spark of light, but it was more than enough for Arlain.

She not only saw the reflected light, it helped pinpoint the entire shadowy column coming over the rise.

"Tholdierth!" Arlain hissed. "Lot'th of them!"

Instantly, Biner roared orders to the crew, commanding them to fly over the approaching enemy. And as the airship turned about, he issued other orders to prepare for bombardment.

Meanwhile, Arlain shot off a red flare to warn Safar. But a strong wind suddenly blew up, casting it far away.

Biner grabbed the wheel, steadying it against the buffeting. But he'd no sooner steadied the craft then another heavy gust hit, driving the nose off course.

He started to curse the vagaries of nature, but then a squall hit full force, drenching him with what seemed like tons of water.

The wheel broke free from his strong hands, spinning wildly, and the airship was whipped about until the heavy winds were hitting it square on.

There were *pings!* as cables broke, lashing out with deadly force in every direction.

No one was hurt, but two of the cables snaked up to pierce a balloon and air squealed out as the airbags quickly deflated.

"Get her down!" Biner roared to his crew. "Get her down before she crashes!"

CHAPTER FORTY-NINE

SECRETS UNMASKED

When the first spear of lightning struck, Tabusir saw its reflection flash from Clayre's litter and raced to intercept her.

The queen gave him a terrible look as he ran up, so he aped surprise and made a hasty bow as if he'd accidentally stumbled into her presence. Using his sleeve, he quickly smeared lampblack over the bare spot to dull the glitter.

Fortunately, the queen was busy with some task. He caught a brief glimpse of her head bending low over a golden table, then the litter moved past.

When she was gone, he looked up into the darkening heavens and saw the airship swinging swiftly around. The cause of its movements was so obvious that even an apprentice spy would have known that Rhodes' troops had been spotted and the king's surprise attack was now no longer much of a surprise.

Rhodes was about a hundred yards away and Tabusir sprinted forward to warn him. But he'd taken no more then six steps when he heard Clayre shout something in a mysterious language.

The shout was followed by a sudden blast of wind blowing from nowhere. It was so strong that it knocked Tabusir to his knees.

But his heart was full of glee as he looked up and saw the airship spinning out of control. Then it steadied and began a hasty descent to the ground.

The air became still and the silence was as thick as the gathering clouds. Then a whole dragon's nest of lightning snaked from sky to ground in a series of *crack, crack, cracks!* Soon came the shock wave of rolling thunder, so powerful that it felt like a physical blow.

Another long silence set in, only to be broken by Rhodes' roared orders as he drove his men forward. He was so busy that Tabusir had to wait a full hour before he could approach with the news that they'd been discovered.

By then all the men and siege engines were in place and Rhodes only shrugged after he'd heard Tabusir out.

"It doesn't matter now," he said. "All we have to do is wait out my mother's storm, then attack."

And with those words a heavy rain began to fall. Then a steady, driving wind whipped into the valley and Rhodes and his soldiers huddled on the ground, drawing oil-skins over their heads.

Tabusir crouched beside the king, the wind-driven rain hammering against his waterproof hood.

The mud and the storm should have made him miserable. Instead, his excitement grew hour by hour, as he eagerly awaited Clayre's promise of a peaceful dawn.

* * * * * * *

Safar and Iraj were also not that surprised when Biner stomped in out of the storm with his news.

"Arlain spotted a column of troops comin' over the rise, lad," Biner said. "She thinks it's that devil King Rhodes. But I don't know. Seems unlikely to me, since we haven't heard one peep out of him for weeks."

Then he stomped his boots and shook himself like a great shaggy dog, spattering water all over the castle's royal chamber.

Iraj started to take offense at his behavior, but Safar hissed a warning that this was a friend of his and Iraj quickly turned an imperious frown of disapproval into a warm smile.

With Safar coaching him, Iraj replied, "We've never doubted Arlain's eyes before, Biner. We'd be fools to start now."

Biner nodded. "Aye, you're right about that, lad," he said. "Nothing we can do about it now, though. The storm's so fierce not even a giant could stand upright under those winds. We covered the airship as best as we could and we'll just have to hope that the wind lets up enough for us to get outside and keep the fires goin' in the engines."

Iraj poured a goblet of brandy for the ringmaster, saying, "This storm isn't natural, my friend. There's enough magic stink in it to rival a Walarian offal ditch. I think the tempest is the work of Queen Clayre. That's why it's so powerful. And when morning comes we'll find ourselves surrounded by Rhodes' entire army."

Biner snorted angrily. "What's wrong with that rube?" he growled. "He's got more flea-bitten ideas than a circus geek! Why can't he be satisfied with his own kingdom and leave us alone? Why did he have to follow the likes of us to the end of the freakin' world?"

Safar mental-whispered advice to Iraj, who replied, "Maybe we'd better send for the others, so I can explain what we're up against to everyone at the same time."

Biner grunted agreement and went to the door where Renor was standing guard to tell him to pass the word that everyone was wanted in Safar's chambers.

Soon they were all gathered before Safar, the wind whistling wildly outside and the rain hammering a heavy drumbeat on the castle's thick walls. All the shutters had been barred against the fierce tropical storm, making the room uncomfortably warm.

Iraj/Safar gave each guest a warm welcome. There was Queen Yorlain, seated upon a small ornate throne fetched in by her slaves. Also Coralean, immense beside the tiny Eeda. Leiria entered, looking drawn and troubled as if she'd had difficulty sleeping. Jooli was at her side, full of concern for her friend and casting odd looks at Safar, then at Leiria and back again.

Sergeant Hamyr, along with Renor and Sinch, attended as representatives of the Kyranian soldiers. Then there were Biner and Arlain, who came to speak for the circus folk.

Finally there was Palimak, who was pale from worry. The closeness of the atmosphere made the young man feel as if everything might not be quite real—like a dream threatening to spill over into actual life. As he watched his father greet each person, he burned with the desire to shout out his great secret: *This man was is impostor!*

In reality it was Iraj Protarus in Safar's body and he was falsely commanding their respect and rapt attention. But this wasn't totally true and besides, Palimak had promised himself that he wouldn't interfere unless it became absolutely necessary.

With much difficulty, he choked back the words that crowded into his thoughts demanding to be spoken.

Safar, speaking through Iraj, quickly summed up what Arlain and Biner had discovered. Then he said, "It's my strong guess that the storm will end at dawn. And Rhodes will immediately throw everything he has against us."

Queen Yorlain sat bolt upright in her throne. "What a fool this king is!" she said. "Doesn't he know the Castle of the Two Kings is impregnable? We can withstand months, nay, even years of any siege he can mount!"

"It's not quite that simple, Your Highness," Iraj/Safar replied. "To begin with, I doubt you've stocked the castle with all the weapons and supplies necessary to withstand even a short siege."

Yorlain started to protest, then hesitated. Finally, she said, "Unfortunately, your words have struck to the heart of our dilemma, my king. We barely had time to prepare for your coming, much less gird ourselves for war."

Biner thumped his chair arm with a mighty fist. "Never fear, me lad," he said. "We'll get the airship up at the crack of dawn and bombard Rhodes' filthy hide to the hells!"

"As always, your instincts are right on target, my good and trusted friend," Iraj/Safar said. "However, I suspect Rhodes has something planned for the airship. That's what this storm is probably all about. Clayre most likely created it to ground the airship.

And it would be most unwise for us to underestimate our enemy and to doubt that he has a follow-up plan to deal with the airship when the storm passes."

"I see what you mean, lad," Biner said. "But I still think we ought to get into the sky as quickly as we can."

"It'th the only plathe the airthip ith thafe, Thafar," Arlain pointed out. "On the ground we're helpleth."

"Then we should take that into consideration in our plans," Iraj/Safar said.

Leiria broke in, saying, "The moment the storm lifts—never mind if it's dawn by then—we ought to hit Rhodes and hit him hard. Nothing big. Just a nasty little in-and-out surprise attack that lets him know we have teeth."

"Wonderful!" Jooli exclaimed. "My father's a good soldier—an excellent general and planner. He also depends heavily on surprise. On the other hand, he's terrible at anticipating his enemy's response. That's his greatest weakness. And if his enemy has some kind of quick reply ready, it rattles him something fierce."

Coralean laid a hand of sincerity across his broad chest. "As all know, I am a great believer in the art of negotiation," the caravan master said in his booming voice. "The weapons of war are most necessary in this sad world the gods have cast us into. However, talk has won more battles than any war. And at the very least, talk has allowed defenses to be strengthened whilst the enemy perused a seemingly weighty bargaining proposal."

"In other words, we strike first as Leiria suggested," Iraj/Safar said. "Followed by a flag of truce to discuss the situation to death while we build up our defenses. Is that what you're thinking?"

Coralean started to answer in the affirmative, but Eeda tugged his sleeve, winning his silence. He smiled fondly at her as she spoke.

"If my lord husband permits," she said, "I can accompany him and cast some small—and quite subtle—spells of confusion to help draw the negotiations out." She patted her rounded belly. "Even that great bitch Clayre won't suspect me because I'm obviously weak from being with child."

Then, realizing the insult, Eeda blushed deeply and turned to Jooli. "I'm sorry," she said. "That was an unforgivable thing to say about your grandmother."

Jooli laughed, waving away the apology. "I've called her worse," she said. "Besides, it's true. She is a bitch of the worst order. And may all the mother dogs of the world forgive me for slighting them."

Meanwhile, Sergeant Hamyr was having a few quiet words with Renor and Sinch. When there was a lull in the conversation, he said, "Me and the lads here," he said, "crave th' honor of first blood."

He turned to Leiria and saluted smartly. "In other words," he said, "we'd be pleased to be in your troop, Cap'n, when the gates open in the morn."

Leiria laughed aloud, her dismal mood swept away by the bright prospect of battle. "Consider it done, sergeant," she said. "We'll all go out together and give King Rhodes' scrotum a good squeeze!"

There was laughter all around, even from Queen Yorlain, who at first struggled mightily to keep her serene dignity. But eventually she giggled, then tittered, and finally exploded in earthy guffaws.

Drinks were poured and toasts were made. Iraj/Safar laughed and drank along with the others—but the whole time each man was considering much deeper thoughts.

Both were finding the war parlay immensely interesting. Their interest, however, had little to do with the nuggets each person in the group had to offer. From Leiria's proposal of a surprise counter-attack to Coralean's idea of false negotiations.

There was an internal understanding that was beginning to take root in each man.

Iraj realized he was deferring to Safar on all matters involving personalities and magic. While Safar instinctively gave way when Iraj was discussing military tactics and strategy.

As the conference reached its climax, to be followed by false pre-battle levity, each man became more impressed with what could be accomplished when they cooperated with one another—without hesitation, or second guessing.

Although neither man asked for a renewed truce, they ceased their internal struggle with one another. Iraj hoisted a goblet of brandy and drank it down. And Safar found himself enjoying the drink, along with the peacefulness that followed.

Then Iraj's attention was gradually drawn to Leiria. Her color was high with excitement, eyes dancing. And then, to Safar's alarm, he felt heat rising in the body Iraj controlled. Legs that had once belonged to him, but now were no longer his to rule, moved toward Leiria.

Leiria looked up as Iraj/Safar approached and through the eyes Iraj provided Safar could see hope and love and pain and fear, all mingled together.

She dared a trembling smile of greeting and Safar could feel words that were not his own ghosting up for Iraj to speak. He did not have to wait to hear them to know they would be soft words, sweet words, and all of them traitorous to the core.

Prisoner though he was, Safar suddenly became aware that he still had a few small powers over the body that had once been his. He frothed up a bitter concoction from his belly and as Iraj opened his mouth to speak, acid flooded into the back of his throat.

Iraj felt the strong bile rise and it was all he could do not to spit. He swallowed hard, tried once again to speak, but only found more acid waiting to be coughed up.

And Safar said, *Leave her be, brother! Leave her be!*

He left Iraj no choice but to turn away. But through his enemy's eyes Safar saw Leiria's face fall and the hurt shoot through her as she thought that Safar had spurned her.

Although he could no longer see her reaction, he knew that most likely darkened as Iraj turned his attention on the lovely Queen Yorlain.

Again he felt the lust rise—even stronger than before. Yorlain smiled up from her throne, eyes full of equal heat and the promise of parted lips pressed together and twined bodies tossing on and on throughout some fated night to come.

Smooth, seductive words came into Iraj's mind—so full of must that Safar could practically hear them spoken aloud before they were uttered.

At the same time Iraj clamped on a more powerful physical control to prevent Safar from blocking him and spoiling his fun.

Except, as Iraj bent low to murmur his words, Yorlain's eyes suddenly hardened.

And she said, loud for all to hear, "You and your people are most clever, Highness. But there is far more to be concerned about than this coming battle with the barbarian, King Rhodes. In the scheme of things, he is nothing compared to with what is about to commence."

As she spoke there was a rumble beneath them strong enough to make the castle sway. And from a distance there came another, stronger rumble, followed by a short, explosive blast.

Then silence. A silence permeated by the gas stench of the volcano coming to life.

Yorlain said, "Did you forget the dance, Lord Timura? Did you forget the agony that awaits us all?"

And Iraj/Safar replied, *"We didn't forget!"*

For a moment a frown spoiled Yorlain's beautiful face. Then she recovered and her features became blank.

"Two kings are required," she said, "to halt the doom Lord Asper has predicted. I see you—King Safar Timura. But I don't see the other king you promised. Dare I think that you might be lying to me? And if so, to what purpose? For you will die, along with me, your friends—and, indeed, the entire world.

"What say you to that, Safar Timura?"

At Safar's suggestion, Iraj bit back a sneering regal reply. He shrugged as if unconcerned.

"I told you before, Your Highness," he replied, "the other king will be with us shortly."

Yorlain laughed, "Come now, Majesty," she said. "You're toying with me. Why don't you admit it? Why don't you come right out and confess that *he* is with us now?"

Then her eyes started to glow and at the same moment the room darkened so that the only light was that cast by her eyes, framing Iraj/Safar like footlights in a theater.

Outside came another rumble and explosion and the volcanic stench grew stronger.

Safar and Iraj found themselves suddenly frozen by her eyes. And from some place close by they heard drums and horns and the rhythmic slap of bare feet dancing in sand.

Then they felt their wills draining away as they heard ghostly voices lift in song:

> *"Her hair is night,*
> *Her lips the moon;*
> *Surrender. Oh, surrender.*
> *Her eyes are stars,*
> *Her heart the sun;*
> *Surrender. Oh, surrender.*
>
> *Her breasts are honey,*
> *Her sex a rose;*
> *Surrender. Oh, surrender.*
> *Night and moon. Stars and Sun.*
> *Honey and rose;*
> *Lady, oh Lady, surrender.*
> *Surrender. Surrender . . ."*

The others in the room heard nothing but the rumble of the volcano. But they were transfixed by the strange sight of Safar standing frozen in the pool of light cast by the queen's shining eyes.

Then the area around his body started to shimmer and his form became hazy, less substantial.

Palimak suddenly realized what was happening. He leaped to his feet, drawing his knife.

At the same time the Favorites caught the deadly magical scent and shouted a warning.

But Palimak was already driving forward—sprinting past the startled onlookers.

And then he grabbed Yorlain by the hair and slit her throat!

She fell to the ground, flopping horribly. But not one drop of blood came from the gaping wound.

Leiria cried, "What have you done, Palimak?"

He didn't need to answer—for in the next moment there was a loud thunderclap and the ghostly figure of the Goddess Lottyr rose from Yorlain's corpse.

All her many mouths howled fury, poison dripping from her sharp fangs. Her six arms waved violently as if she were going to attack.

Eeda and Jooli recovered quickly enough to join Palimak's protective spell.

Then there was a bright flash of light and she was gone.

Iraj/Safar suddenly jerked, coming out of their trance.

Palimak stepped over Yorlain's body to confront the strange thing his father had become.

"Tell them!" he demanded. "Tell them who you are!"

The thing that wore his father's body only sighed.

And when it replied it spoke in the voice of Iraj Protarus: "Safar always did say you were a bright lad."

It was Leiria who first understood what had happened. She would have recognized that voice in a cave black as midnight.

She gasped in shock. "It's Iraj!" she cried.

And she drew her sword and charged.

CHAPTER FIFTY
PRELUDE TO WAR

Kalasariz never slept. Sleep was something that had been lost to him many years before when he'd pledged himself to the Spell of Four and became a shapechanger along with Iraj, Fari and Luka.

The spell had been broken, but in his new entity as a spirit-world parasite living within King Rhodes' body he was permanently wide awake.

Unlike his former spell brothers, the spymaster considered this a blessing. In his previous existence he'd always hated the moment when the gods of slumber commanded his obedience. His father had been a seventh-generation priest. More to the point: his very name, Kalasariz, was the Walarian term for priest.

His mother had been a temple harlot enslaved to the priests and he had been seeded during a priestly orgy whose purpose was to cleanse sins by sinning. And to create sons for the priests to adopt and rear for their own holy purposes.

Kalasariz had soon learned he was better at ferreting out secrets to use against others than he was at religious scholarship. Better still was to forge those secrets into lies of solid gold. And Kalasariz had eventually sold out his own father with false charges that he was a heretic so that he might win his mantle as the supreme spy of all Walaria.

But deep inside Kalasariz he was still the son of a priest. And when he slept all his subsequent lies and murders sat heavily upon his soul. And so he'd always feared the night, because with it came terrible dreams of his transgressions, followed by imagined punishments for those sins.

Worse still, over the years those nightmares became increasingly and horribly complex because of all the enemies he'd made in his long career.

And so it was that when sleep overcame King Rhodes and he tossed and turned fitfully through the storm, dreaming bloody dreams much like those that had once afflicted Kalasariz, the spymaster was gleefully awake and guilt-free. Plotting his plots and conspiring in his conspiracies.

The best thing of all about his sleepless state was that he could keep constant control of Fari and Luka, who were enslaved in his ethereal belly. He kept their agonies constant and hot, so they didn't have time or energy to conspire against him.

Therefore, when Lady Lottyr came to him, spitting curses about Safar Timura and Iraj Protarus, Kalasariz was bright and alert and well aware that the goddess had suffered a defeat.

She called the incident in the castle a mere "setback," but he knew that this was only a hasty bit of fiction her pride had composed to lessen her humiliation. Failure and defeat dripped from every word she spoke.

"It was that demon brat Palimak who caught me out," she said. "Otherwise I would've crushed those fools who believe themselves to be the two kings Asper predicted would come."

Her six visages were terrible in their murderous beauty. And even though her visit to the spymaster was meant to be made in secret, she was so agitated that Rhodes would've been alerted to her presence if he had been awake.

Surely he would've caught the internal roiling Lottyr's frustration caused when she spoke to Kalasariz. The spymaster's ambitions might have been badly harmed by this royal realization.

In all his days Kalasariz had never met another person—except for himself—as rightfully and unerringly on target as Rhodes was when he became suspicious.

Well, maybe more: There was Queen Clayre. Whose own suspicious nature made her son look like a naVve peasant. But Lottyr had made her own false bargain with Clayre and had also cast certain spells that had dulled the witch's wary senses.

Lottyr laid out all the plans she'd heard the Kyranians discuss while she'd commanded Queen Yorlain's body.

"They'll attack the moment the storm ends," she said. "They're hoping to wound you severely, then withdraw. Negotiations will follow—all aimed at drawing things out long enough for them to strengthen their defenses."

Kalasariz asked, "Have you informed Clayre about their plans?"

"No," Lottyr answered, "but I intend to the moment I leave you. And when Rhodes awakes, I want you to instruct him."

A canny master of lies and half truths, Kalasariz knew very well that Lottyr had sworn to another bargain with Clayre. The goddess admitted as much when she spoke her puny lies, saying her pledge to Clayre meant nothing, while her promises to Kalasariz were solid as gold.

But which bargain would the goddess keep? Kalasariz knew better than to trust to chance for the outcome.

And so he said, "I have the advantage of long experience with Safar Timura. And also with Iraj Protarus. They've never been defeated—especially when the two of them put their minds together."

Lottyr was angrily abrupt. "What of it?" she asked harshly. "They are nothing compared to me—the greatest goddess of the Hells!"

"Forgive me, Holy One," Kalasariz said, "but I'm only trying to point out that in any physical fight Safar Timura and Iraj Protarus are the likely victors. That is their history. Neither one has ever failed—even against each other. Timura defeated Protarus at Caluz. But Protarus, from what you say, now rules Timura's body. Tentative though that dominance may be.

"From what you've also said, they've made a pact with each other to oppose you. Isn't that so, Holy One?"

"Why are you spewing all this defeatist sewage at me?" Lottyr demanded, her twelve eyes burning with suspicion. "Do you *want* Timura and Protarus to win?"

"Absolutely not and forgive me if I gave you that impression, Holy One," Kalasariz hastened to say. "However, you have asked my best advice. And it is my sad duty to say that my advice is for you to prepare for Rhodes' and Clayre's failure."

Lottyr pealed chorused laughter, her six voices echoing so strongly that they resounded through Rhodes' bones and the king kicked and swore in his sleep.

She waited until he rested again.

Then she said, "Know this, Kalasariz: when the dawn commences, it will be not one, but two battles Safar Timura and Iraj Protarus will have to fight."

And then she was gone. There was not even a flicker between her presence and her absence. One moment she was there, the next she wasn't.

In the distance the volcano rumbled into life. There was a heavy blast and an intense, fiery light poured into the king's pavilion.

Rhodes suddenly sat up, rubbing his eyes. Sleepily, he asked, "What's happening? Is there an attack?"

Kalasariz replied, "Go back to sleep, majesty. There's no reason for alarm."

And so Rhodes fell back on his soft pallet and slept.

*   *   *

Despite the tempest, Clayre was resting peacefully when the Lady Lottyr came to her.

But as soon as the Queen Witch sensed the goddess's presence she bolted up from her pallet.

"Is everything all right?" she asked.

And Lottyr said, "All is ready, my dearest one. I've only come to you to make assurances."

"What of my son?" Clayre asked. "Are we ready for him as well?"

Lottyr replied, "It's just as we planned, Clayre. At the dawn, when the first enemy arrows fall, your son will die."

Reassured, Clayre smiled. "It'll be good to be rid of him," she said. "He always was just like his father."

*   *   *

Despite his demon strength and speed, Palimak was no match for the infuriated Leiria.

He jumped in front of her to stop her charge against Iraj/Safar, but she only ghosted to the side and kicked his legs from under him.

Worse still, Jooli was on Leiria's heels, her own sword in hand to back up her friend. But Palimak snagged out a hand, demon claws scything out, and caught her by the ankle to bring her painfully down.

None of this mattered. The instant Leiria came within striking distance, she fed all of her hate for Iraj into the sword blow she struck.

Except, in mid cut, she saw that it was Safar she was also about to kill. One part of her wanted to halt the deadly blow. The other demanded that she ram her blade through Iraj's guts.

Between Palimak's feeble intervention and Leiria's hair's-breadth hesitation, Iraj stepped in, taking full command of Safar's body.

Safar almost used his own powers to slow Iraj down, but then he realized Iraj was only using his half-empty brandy goblet for a weapon and released all of his physical energy.

In that moment of hesitation he had three questions that were answered swiftly.

The first was the question of his own survival. If Leiria killed Iraj, Safar would die as well. However, that was of little importance to him. After all he'd experienced and all the people he believed he'd made suffer, death would be welcome. He ached for Leiria's slashing blade as a release from his guilt.

The second was that if Leiria succeeded the whole world was doomed. Except now Safar found himself beyond worlds and the fate of all living things. Let it happen, he thought. We deserve whatever comes!

The third cause of hesitation was that Leiria would never be able to forgive herself for what she'd done. Safar thought, She loves me! And then he thought, by all that is holy, I love her too!

And so Safar let Iraj have his will.

The killing sword came in and Iraj, moving like lightning, stepped lightly into its sweeping arc, crashing the brandy goblet against the blade.

The goblet shattered, the sword went to the side, but all this was nothing to Leiria. She only shifted her grip, so that both her hands were on the sword's haft. Then she swung with power enough to cut a stone column in half.

But Iraj only continued his forward motion, stepping within the blade's path and grabbing Leiria by the throat with immensely strong fingers.

He squeezed and brought her choking to her knees.

"I am the only mortal—man, woman or demon—who can best you in a fight," Iraj said to her in his own voice. "Now, please remain quite still while I explain my intentions."

Leiria's answer was to drop her sword and draw her knife, thrusting it at his exposed belly.

With his free hand Iraj caught her attacking wrist, putting so much pressure on it that she had to let it fall. Then he maintained the pressure there, just at the bone-breaking point.

And Iraj said, "Leiria, I love you more than I have ever loved another." Then he laughed bitterly. "That's not saying much, as I'm sure you understand. But I beg you, not because of my love but because of Safar's, to hear us *both* out!"

Leiria, face purpling from the grip Iraj had on her, nodded. And both Safar and Iraj understood she was making a promise.

Iraj released her and she fell back. And he said for all to hear, "Speak to them, Safar. Tell them what we have planned."

Then he relinquished all control over his brother/enemy and Safar found himself standing in his own body again, while Iraj curled up into the spirit nest he'd vacated.

But as before, Safar was quite blind. He knelt down beside Leiria, guided by her perfume. He reached out to touch her face. She flinched, but then relented as his blindness became apparent.

"Is it really you, Safar?" she asked, voice tremulous.

"I swear it is, Leiria," he replied. "And if you don't believe me, think back to the last time we saw each other in Esmir. Do you recall how we parted?"

Leiria nodded, then remembered that he could not see. And she said, quite softly, "Yes."

"I told you then that I planned to get Iraj's help to stop the machine in Caluz," he said. "Isn't that right?"

"I thought you were making a dark-humored joke," Leiria said as the memory of that sad day came flooding back. "I thought you were just sacrificing yourself to save us."

"As you know now," Safar said, "I did win Iraj's help. Although it was against his will. Well, only partly so. He wanted desperately to break the shapechanger's spell and escape Kalasariz and Fari and Luka. And I gave him the means to do that."

"Is that how he ended up in your body?" Leiria asked.

"It's not so simple as that," Safar said, "but it's close enough. The main thing is, I didn't realize then that I truly did need Iraj's help. Not just to stop the machine in Caluz, but to end what is happening here."

"But how did he end up controlling you instead?" Leiria asked.

"I let him," Safar said. "We both need eyes to do our work. And he can give us sight." He smiled. "Of course, being Iraj, there were lies involved. And betrayal."

"And you're going to let him take over your body again, aren't you?" Leiria said.

"Yes," Safar replied. "I have no other choice. To awaken the gods and end this misery, Iraj and I must enter the hells and face Lady Lottyr. And we'll need eyes to do that."

Then he embraced her and kissed her, murmuring words of love. Leiria wasn't certain whether he meant them, or was only trying to comfort her.

Finally, Safar rose to his feet. Palimak came to him, hugging him fiercely.

"Isn't there something I can do, father?" he asked, tears welling up.

"If you mean about Iraj," Safar said, "there's nothing you can do. But he and I will need every scrap of your strength to face the coming day."

Then he pushed Palimak gently away. He waved blindly to Coralean, Biner, Arlain and the others. And gave them a crooked smile.

"I won't say goodbye, dear friends," he said. "Because I'll be close to you until the end. I only ask that you trust me. And you must trust Iraj as well."

Everyone was weeping, but they all murmured that they would do as he said.

Then Safar opened the gates to Iraj, who once again assumed control. Iraj/Safar blinked his eyes as sight returned and light flooded in.

"Now it's my turn to address you all," Iraj said in his own voice. A voice that made them all shiver. "And the first thing I have to say is this:

"In the morning we'll have not one, but two battles to fight!"

Part Five
Into The Hells

CHAPTER FIFTY-ONE
THE BATTLE BEGINS

Clayre and Lottyr brought an end to the storm just before dawn. Rhodes immediately sent his men out to gather up any farmers who had survived the tempest and had them put to the sword.

When first light came it revealed that the whole valley was in ruins from the storm: trees ripped up by the roots, farmhouses roofless or smashed, the fields and crops a muddy mess.

The lake was filled with debris, including thousands of dead fish, white bellies turned upward to greet the red Demon Moon as it rose over the volcano, grinning its ghastly smile.

As for the volcano itself, a large gash had been ripped from its cone by the previous night's activity. Small black clouds puffed upward, looking like storm clouds; from his hilltop command post Rhodes could smell the acrid stench drifting in with the breeze.

The volcano made his men nervous, so Rhodes called for his priests and they cast the bones to show that all was well. This relieved Rhodes as much as his men. For although the Lady Lottyr had promised him the volcano was no threat, he was not entirely convinced the goddess didn't have plans which might not necessarily include his own survival.

What convinced him even more than the casting was that, just as Lottyr had predicted, the Kyranians kicked the castle gates open not long after the first rays of the sun spilled into the valley.

As they came screaming out to confront his men, Rhodes chuckled in delight.

Did he have a surprise for them!

He signaled the counter-attack and at the same time passed the word to his engineers. And as he sprang his trap on the attacking Kyranians, the bombardment of the Castle of the Two Kings began.

✳   ✳   ✳

Jooli burst through the castle gates, Sergant Hamyr and a contingent of twenty men right behind her, shouting their fierce war cries.

Just past the bridge she saw a bristle of pikemen surging forward to meet her. Behind them were archers and she could hear the *twang!* of their bows as they fired.

But she and her men were moving too fast for the archers and as the arrows lofted she waded into the pikemen, cutting men down left and right as Hamyr and the other Kyranians bunched in around her, then muscled outward to break the pack apart.

As she'd expected, her father's soldiers broke ranks too easily and began to retreat. But it was an orderly withdrawal. Not a flicker of panic as the pikemen moved back and the archers threw down their bows and drew swords.

They weren't true archers. None of their missiles had found a mark. But they were excellent swordsmen and they gave Jooli and her men a vigorous fight as they backed up along the road.

Far off, she saw her father's command-post banner waving in the morning breeze. She aimed for it, shouting orders to Hamyr and the others to redouble their efforts.

They overran the retreating men, stopping only to cut the throats of those who had fallen. As Iraj Protarus had warned, most of the men were feigning wounds and were only waiting their chance to leap up as Jooli passed so they could attack her from the rear.

Despite these precautions, with every step Jooli took she could sense her father's trap closing, pinching in from the sides, while leaving the way open to the fluttering command flag.

Any minute now the men she knew were lying in wait on either side of the road would spring up to overwhelm her. Even as she cut a man down she cast a spell of confusion to addle the brains of her hidden enemies.

But she knew that however great her efforts, soon it would be a case of too little and too late.

And she thought, Where's Leiria? Where's Leiria?

*   *   *

In the courtyard of the Castle Keep, the circus folk were desperately trying to get the airship aloft. Huge siege arrows fell all around them, sheeting green flame in every direction as the crew laboriously filled the twin balloons with hot air.

The axiom of all balloonists is that anything that can go wrong will strike in threes. And Biner's difficulties were further proof of that already well-worn prophecy.

First, the fierce storm had forced them to take refuge in the castle. The couldn't tend to the airship's engines and without fuel, the magical fires had gone out. In order to refill the balloons Biner had to waste an enormous amount of time heating up the engines.

Secondly, as the huge balloons slowly filled, straining against the lines, several cables snapped. They'd been badly stressed by the previous day's battle against the tempest and everyone had been so tired that they hadn't checked the obvious danger points.

Thirdly, the rudder had been damaged—another flaw that had gone unnoticed.

Biner and Arlain blamed themselves, not the crew, for these oversights.

As Arlain said, "I thould have been wat'thing. I'm your thecond-in-command, Biner, and it'th all my fault."

But Biner, a perfectionist to the core, cursed only himself for his shortcomings. Never mind the soul-rattling disclosures of Safar's dual identities. Never mind that he hadn't slept for two days. He was at fault, dammit.

It was the ringmaster's duty to oversee all things, and to anticipate all potential problems. And, by the gods, Biner had fallen down on his job.

So, as the explosive arrows slammed in from the skies, it was Biner who constantly threw himself into the most dangerous tasks. Shoveling fuel into the engines while others fought fires on the decks on the airship.

Dodging the scything release of broken cables, while clamping new ones in place. Once his tunic caught fire while he was heaving new ballast sacks into the airship.

Arlain beat the flames into submission while Biner continued to work, driving the crew to complete a hasty patch-job on the rudder.

Despite the brave and frantic work of Biner and the rest of the airship crew, for a time it seemed that all would be lost. The siege arrows kept falling closer and closer, marching their way across the courtyard as Rhodes' engineers gradually corrected their aim.

One arrow—as thick as a sideshow fat man's waist—slammed into the bow of the airship, igniting the well-oiled deck.

Arlain led a crew of foam-spraying fire fighters into the breach, but the flames became so intense that they drove everyone back except for Arlain. Hot flames licked all around her pearly body as she pumped foam on the blaze.

If it had been a circus act instead of real-life danger, the audience would have been thrilled at the erotic vision she presented. A fantastic female body, clothed only in a modesty patch at her thighs and two tiny dots over her breasts, sucking flames into her flat dragon's belly while she shot foamy spume onto the main fire from the hose that she held between her dragon claws.

But it wasn't an act and the fire drove her back, licking all around her fabulous form as she fought stubbornly on.

Then Eeda appeared, running out of the gates of the Keep, waving her arms as she composed a fire-quenching spell, her pregnant belly swelling her tunic to the bursting point. She looked as if she was going to deliver her child at any moment as she hastily cast the spell.

A fierce cold wind suddenly blew into the courtyard, killing the flames. Then the wind was gone.

"Get up as fast as you can!" Eeda shouted to Biner and Arlain. "I don't think I have the strength to do it a second time!"

Biner and Arlain needed no further prodding and minutes later the airship shot up into the sky just as a new barrage of fire arrows fell.

And Eeda dashed back into the relative safety of the Keep.

*   *   *

Coralean had a deep sense of foreboding as he waited at the edge of the golden-tiled pentagram. Events were moving so swiftly that he felt he barely had control. Looking at the figures of all the gods and goddesses portrayed in the fabulous wind-rose that the pentagram contained didn't help.

Particularly the portrait of the Goddess Lottyr, whose arrow pointed in a direction opposite to the others—straight at the painted flames of the Hells.

Behind him, six Kyranian pikemen were prodding Yorlain's aides across the chamber, hustling them toward stairs that led down into the dungeons.

Meanwhile, in the center of the wind-rose, tail lashing, muscles trembling in anticipation, stood Khysmet.

Iraj, wearing Safar's body and speaking in Safar's voice, said, "Easy, friend. Easy."

Then he vaulted into the great stallion's saddle. He leaned down to offer Palimak a hand up, but the young man gave a grim shake of his head and jumped up behind him without assistance.

Khysmet whinnied eagerly, stomping his hooves on the wind-rose.

Iraj chuckled to himself when he saw Coralean's worried face. Speaking in his own voice, he said, "There's no sense fretting, old friend. Safar and I were either born for this moment or doomed to it. You just concentrate on Rhodes and leave the Hells to us."

The caravan master sighed heavily and said, "If Coralean had a copper coin for all the times he was advised not to worry, Your Highness, he'd be even richer than he already is."

Iraj laughed. "Why is it that every phrase you speak dwells so much on profit?" he asked, half jokingly. "There's more to this world than money, don't you know?"

Now it was Coralean's turn to laugh. "That was always your trouble, Majesty," he said. "You think of profit as a base thing. A dirty thing. Whereas I, Coralean, know profit to be a thing of the utmost beauty. For profit is at the heart of all mortal endeavors.

"As a merchant sage once said, 'It is profit that drives all civilization.' How true, how true. For isn't it profit that makes kings—and lack of the same that ruins them? And does not profit allow the artist to make art and the musician to make music?

"More to the point—if you and my old friend Safar Timura win this day, why, the whole world will profit from your victory. So don't mock profit, majesty. But, praise it to the heavens!"

Palimak, confused and angry over the dual identities with which he was confronted, broke in,snarling, "Never mind the talk! Let's just cast the spell and get on with it!"

Just then Eeda hurried into the chamber, pale and obviously in great pain. "Forgive me, lord husband," she said, "but our child is coming!"

The news badly shook Coralean and he instantly swept Eeda off her feet into his arms. "We must find a midwife," he cried.

"Nay, nay, lord husband," Eeda said. "I can do this myself—if you will help me."

"Of course I'll help," Coralean said, voice weak. "What shall I do?"

"The child's birth can help the spell," Eeda said. "So, please, just place me on the floor. And let me—and your coming son—do our magic."

Inside Iraj, Safar quickly caught Eeda's intention. He rose up out of his nest, urging Protarus to wait until the proper moment. Eeda's bravery also broke through Palimak's reserve and he, too, whispered for Iraj to hold.

Coralean placed Eeda gently on the floor and ran to fetch pillows and blankets to make her more comfortable. As he pushed pillows under her, she cried out, gripping his hand fiercely.

Then she shouted, "He's coming, lord husband! He's coming!"

As she writhed in the throes of birth agony, Safar gave the signal for the spell-casting to commence.

And drawing on all of Palimak's powers, along with those of the Favorites, then combining them with Eeda's magic, Safar forged these spellwords:

> *"Eight winds blow, eight winds bend;*
> *Is it life or death these winds portend?*
> *And where hides the Viper of the Rose?*
> *And what dread secrets shall we expose?*
> *Into the Hells, our souls cast forth,*
> *East and west, south and north.*
> *North and south, east and west.*
> *The gods awaken, ah, there's the test!"*

Through Iraj's eyes, Safar saw Eeda jump as if she'd been struck with a lightning bolt. Then Coralean was holding up a bloody, crying little thing.

And then the whole floor gave away beneath Khysmet and Safar found himself falling through darkness toward a great, fiery light.

CHAPTER FIFTY-TWO
SPIES AND OTHER LIES

Rhodes was so intent on his daughter's charge that he didn't notice the airship soar out of the castle grounds. Jooli was sprinting toward his command post, smashing through every defense and cutting down every man that got in her way.

Her shrill war cry ululated up the hill, making his blood run cold. Even though she was still at a great distance, he believed he could see the fury and hate in her eyes. All concentrated on her father.

Running with her, the Kyranian troops were also taking a terrible toll on his men. And although he knew Jooli was only prolonging the inevitable—and his trap would close any second—the ferocity of her attack struck fear into his heart.

Brave though he was, Rhodes was so guilt-ridden by his treatment of his own flesh that for a moment he imagined her hot vengeful blade plunging into his breast.

"Get her! Get her! Get her!" he shouted to his officers.

Panicked by their king's hysteria, they ran around shouting confused orders to their underlings.

Only Tabusir kept his head. He walked quickly but purposefully to Clayre's litter. The spy had a duty to perform that he was looking forward to eagerly.

Clayre saw him coming and smiled a thin smile. Although she not only distrusted Tabusir and disliked him intensely, she'd been worried for some time now that her son was playing her false.

Her mind constantly ran wild with conspiratorial possibilities. Foremost among them was that Rhodes might make a last-minute alliance with her granddaughter, Jooli, and that the two of them would turn against her.

And even if this possibility was only the product of a fevered imagination, what if that was how it turned out? No matter their bitter past history, they were still father and daughter.

If Jooli survived her father's trap and struck a bargain with him Clayre had no illusions about what would happen next. A powerful witch, as well as a superb warrior, Jooli would make certain her grandmother didn't survive the day.

As guilt-ridden as her son over her treatment of Jooli, Clayre became fearfully obsessed with her granddaughter's intentions.

She had to be sure, no matter what the cost.

And so during the storm she'd sent for Tabusir, that most corruptible of corrupt men, and had dazzled him with gold and seductive promises.

Clayre was a beautiful woman and a rich woman who had years of practice in all forms of seduction. She'd only needed a little gold and a few hot-blooded hints of pleasures to come to convince the spy to join her.

And now she was not disappointed when the moment of Jooli's death neared and Tabusir came to her just as they'd planned.

When she saw him, she quickly turned her thin smile of satisfaction into one of erotic warmth. And she bedazzled him with her beauty as he dropped to his knees and made suitable gestures of loyalty and obedience.

"You are such a pretty fellow," she murmured to him in her most alluring tones. "Kneeling there so handsomely before me you fair make my poor heart leap."

Tabusir knocked his head against the ground, saying, "I am but a man, Majesty. A worshipful man, burning with love for you. If only I dared take you in my arms and kiss you!"

"Soon, my handsome one, soon," Clayre said, only partly lying. "Pray be patient. For I yearn for you as much as you yearn for me."

Then she drew the spy up, looking full into his eyes. Delighting at her effect on him as he seemed to quiver and quake with desire.

She drew a long tube from her bodice and handed it to him. "I've made this for my son," she said.

And he pulled the two halves apart, revealing a sharp dart. Tabusir started to test the point with his finger, but she stopped him, saying, "Don't touch the point, my dear. It's poisoned, you know."

With a brisk intake of breath, Tabusir snatched his fingers away just in time. He glanced down and saw that the needle-point of the dart was smeared with a yellowish paste.

"One prick of the dart will do," Clayre said. She pointed down the hill, where Jooli and the Kyranians were hammering their way through her son's lines.

"If my granddaughter should win through," she said, "there's a good chance she'll try to turn my son against me. If this happens, you only need to get close enough to the king to throw the dart.

"It won't kill him, for, as I told you last night, that is not my desire. But it will immobilize him—freeze his body and his will—until we decide what to do with him."

Tabusir examined the dart closely. Marveling at its handworked design. The Lady Lottyr's face had been carved on one side. And the needle's shaft had been lovingly stropped many times before the poison was applied.

"But what of Queen Jooli?" Tabusir asked. "Even if we remove your son, she'll still be a threat."

"Never mind Jooli," Clayre said. "I have plans to deal with her. It is my son who worries me the most."

Actually, it was Kalasariz' presence inside her son that terrified her. The king and the cunning spymaster made a formidable combination. Naturally, she said nothing of this to her new ally.

Smiling, Tabusir leaned close to Clayre, whispering, "I am yours to command, my queen. But might I beg of you one kiss to steel my nerve and send me on my way?"

Clayre thought, Why not? Tabusir really was quite handsome as well as clever. Of course, after he attacked her son, he'd have to be put to death himself for treating a member of the royal family in such a manner. Still, there was no harm in a kiss, was there?

And so she kissed him, full and deep. She was delighted when she felt Tabusir shudder.

But as she gently pushed him away, he whispered, "Here's a gift, Majesty, from your loving son."

And he rammed the poisoned dart into her soft, heaving breast.

Instantly, Clayre become immobilized—freezing into a living statue. Her expression was one of great surprise.

"You see, Majesty," Tabusir said. "After I spoke to you last night, I reported to your son. And he made me a much better offer."

He kissed her immobile face, rudely crushing his lips against hers.

Then Tabusir turned away and strolled off to see how the king was faring against his daughter.

*   *   *

Leiria ground her teeth impatiently as she waited for Rhodes to spring his trap on Jooli. From her hiding place in the rubble of a destroyed farmhouse she watched her friend lead the charge through the castle gates.

Sequestered in other nearby places were fifty Kyranian soldiers, all aching to join the battle.

On either side of her were Renor and Sinch and she heard their gasps of alarm as several enemy soldiers confronted Jooli. Then they sighed in relief when the warrior woman easily cut them down.

"Silence!" Leiria hissed. "You'll give us away!"

Not that she blamed them for displaying their youthful tension. She was damned tense, herself. They'd all crept out into the teeth of the storm several hours before dawn.

Drenched to the bone, buffeted by fierce winds, they'd had to fight a battle with the elements long before they were set to engage Rhodes. In the end they managed to set up a perfect double ambush—finding hiding places on either side of the road that Jooli would use.

And they were well back from the positions Leiria knew the king's soldiers would take when they made themselves ready for Jooli.

She hated to admit it, but the whole thing had been Iraj's idea. A master tactician, Iraj had immediately guessed what Rhodes would do after Lottyr reported back to the king that the Kyranians planned a surprise attack the moment the storm ended.

With Queen Yorlain as her slave, Lottyr had obviously overheard every detail of their planning session in Safar's quarters.

"He'll have a surprise attack of his own planned," Iraj had said, using his own voice. "But we'll be ready for him!"

"With me as bait for the trap?" Jooli had asked, eyes glowing at the prospect.

"Exactly," Iraj had said.

Leiria shuddered at the memory of that odd scene. Iraj's voice issuing from the lips of her lover. It had made her feel filthy all over.

She pushed those thoughts away. This was not the time and place for such weaknesses. But she couldn't help wondering for just a moment if she and Safar would ever have a life together.

Leiria bit her lower lip, using the pain to wipe that question from her mind.

Hells, most likely they'd all be dead by the day's end!

She concentrated on Jooli and her soldiers. Saw them fight their way along the road, leaving dead and wounded men in their wake. Saw the shadowy forms of Rhodes' troops creeping in from every side. Saw the defiant flag of Rhodes fluttering over his command post far up the hill.

Then, as Jooli and her troops reached the bend in the road, Leiria saw the enemy soldiers leap up on every side of her. She heard them shout shrill battle cries as they closed the trap.

"Now!" Leiria cried.

Drawing her sword she leaped to her feet and gave the signal that triggered Iraj's double trap.

*　　　*　　　*

Rhodes gaped like a village fool when he saw Leiria and her men suddenly leap up and attack his men from behind.

"Where the hells did she come from?" he shouted.

But there was no one to answer, for his officers were as stunned as their king to see such a perfect plan foiled.

It was all over in a few moments. There were terrified shrieks of surprise from his own men, mingled with the clash of steel against steel as the Kyranians worked their awful will.

And then the ambush site was reduced to a bloody mess of soldiers groaning their last, while the Kyranians stood around, leaning on their swords and laughing or slapping one another on the back, no doubt saying what clever fellows they all were.

He saw Jooli and Leiria meet, embracing like sisters. Then turning to look up the hill in his direction. He saw Jooli point straight at him and had no doubt about what she was saying to Leiria.

Rhodes turned and caught sight of Tabusir standing nearby, as stunned by the turnabout as everyone else.

"Send for my mother!" Rhodes shouted at the spy, all his fears and anxieties spilling over the cliffs of reason.

Tabusir gawked at him. "But, Majesty," he said, "your mother can't come, remember?"

"What did you do? What did you do?" Rhodes babbled, drawing his sword.

"Only as you asked, Majesty," Tabusir replied, edging backward, trying to get out of the king's range. But two officers moved in on either side, grabbing him by the arms.

"Please, Majesty!" Tabusir begged, feeling his carefully built world suddenly crumble beneath him. "I only dealt with your mother as she would have dealt with you. I only did what you commanded!"

"Damn you!" Rhodes roared. "How dare you turn my own words against me? I am the king!"

And with one blow he cut off Tabusir's head.

Then he raced to his mother's litter, his men leaping away when the saw the agony in their king's eyes and the bloody sword in his hand.

Clayre was all alone in her litter. Her slaves had already fled, taking with them every valuable they could find in their haste to escape the king's wrath when he learned that his mother had been murdered.

Her silk robes were gone, rent from her frozen body, and she was half naked. Her purse and jewelry were absent. And her magical table was shattered, the gold-tiled pentagram having been ripped from the very wood it had been fixed into.

Even the litter itself hadn't gone unscathed—gilded decorations and jewels had been torn from their settings.

Falling on her and embracing her, Rhodes cried, "I'm so sorry, mother! So sorry! I slew the villain who harmed you!"

But when he felt her stone-like flesh he leaped back, as if she were a leper.

And he shouted: "I need you, mother, more than I have ever needed you before! Please, please help me!"

But the only answer was the startled look frozen upon Clayre's face. And the poisoned dart sticking out of her chest.

Rhodes fell to his knees, weeping.

Inside him, Kalasariz sniffed the blood of failure and rose from his nest like a great white shark shooting out of the sea's cold, dark depths to seek his moment of gory opportunity.

He had the demons, Luka and Fari, crying in his belly, but he was hungry. Oh, so hungry.

And the Lady Lottyr whispered from someplace close: *You were right, Kalasariz. The king has failed.*

The spymaster said nothing in reply, but only ghosted toward the throbbing souls she was offering him, like pearls set in sweet oyster flesh.

First he gulped down Clayre and, oh, she was good and, oh, she was tasty. He felt the fires in his belly explode with increased power and energy. Then he found the soul of Rhodes, which was still weeping for his mother. And that soul was even more delicious and more power-giving than Clayre's.

He felt strong, so strong. And his mind, which he'd always prized above all things, became all-seeing.

Kalasariz/Rhodes whirled around, bellowing to his men. They fell to their knees before his awful majesty.

And Kalasariz thought, *This is good. This is very, very good.*

Coming up the hill he saw Coralean riding a huge horse. The caravan master was so immense that his feet dragged along the ground. He had a small woman in his arms. And she held a bundle that Kalasariz couldn't make out.

Marching on either side of Coralean were Leiria and Jooli, their armor sheening under the Demon Moon. Their troops behind them—Kyranian troops. Eager for the final kill.

And beyond them, hovering over the cone of volcano, Kalasariz could see the fabulous airship floating free. Ready to move in at a moment's notice and bombard King Rhodes' positions.

Kalasariz felt a flicker of disappointment. He'd come so far. Dared so much. But now, on the eve on his ultimate victory, had he already been defeated?

And the Lady Lottyr whispered, *I promised you two battles, Kalasariz. And it is only the second one that truly counts.*

Kalasariz felt hope rise like a mighty spear in his fist. And, already knowing the answer, he asked, *Who do we fight?*

And the Lady Lottyr replied, *Safar Timura and Iraj Protarus. They're waiting for us now at the gates of the Hells!*

The spymaster's hunger burned brighter at this prospect. And he said, *Let's fight them, then.*

But at that moment he heard a cry, coming from far away. It was like that of a newborn infant demanding new life.

He asked, *What's that?*

The Goddess Lottyr replied, *Only a child, Kalasariz. Nothing to worry ourselves about.*

But he was worried. And as the whole world shimmered about him, slowly dissolving, he heard the child cry once again.

Then he found himself striding along a broad beach, sword in hand. He heard drums throb and horns blow, then the voices of singing people.

Kalasariz found them dancing naked under towering palm trees, singing praises to a beautiful queen who led them in their dance. Beyond he saw the volcano, black smoke and angry sparks sputtering into the skies.

He knew he was still in Hadin, but it was a different Hadin. The armies and the ships didn't exist here. Just these dancing people and the volcano that looked as if it were about to blow.

The Lady Lottyr whispered to him, *Wait here!*

And so he waited, leaning on his sword and watching the people dance. Feeling strong and confident in King Rhodes' body. Powerfully cloaked in the magic radiating from his belly, where his enemies danced a quite different dance than the one that seemed to please the island people.

Kalasariz also didn't need to ask the goddess who they were waiting for.

He knew damned well it was Safar Timura and Iraj Protarus. The spymaster laughed aloud at the prospect.

      *   *   *

When Jooli came up the hill, trotting beside Coralean's horse, she was only mildly surprised when her father's soldiers stepped out of the way, bowing to her respectfully.

These men knew her—she'd once been their queen. And if her father finally admitted defeat she'd be their queen once again.

Then she smelled the stink of magic and quickened her pace, moving ahead of Coralean toward a knot of officers gathered around what she knew to be her grandmother's litter.

They were pale and trembling when they saw Jooli, but not out of fear of her. The men parted as she strode forward, Leiria close behind—sword drawn to protect her friend's back.

When Jooli saw what had happened she froze in her tracks. Both her father and her grandmother were dead. Clayre was sprawled in her litter, while Rhodes was slumped on the ground.

One of the officers said, voice trembling, "It wasn't us, Majesty! They did not die at our hands!"

Jooli said nothing, but only shook her head. She knew quite well no mortal had slain this pair.

And then, while she was struggling for an answer, the corpses started to fade and to shimmer with a strange light.

"Get back!" she shouted to the men.

They didn't need her warning and were already scrambling away.

Then the light grew brighter and the corpses became fainter still.

There was a double crack as magical forces split the air—and the bodies were gone!

Jooli turned to Leiria. "It was the Goddess Lottyr who did this," she said, almost in a whisper.

She was keeping a heavy check on her emotions. It was no time to test her feelings about her father and grandmother.

And she added, "But they aren't really dead. Well, not as you and I know death."

"Where are they, then?" Leiria asked.

The ground rumbled beneath them and several soldiers shouted. "The volcano! The volcano!"

Jooli slowly turned, then pointed at the cone-shaped mountain. Thick smoke was boiling forth and lava was flowing down its sides.

"There," she said.

Leiria was bewildered. But then she became even more confused when Coralean called to them in his big voice.

"Eeda wants to speak to you!"

They went to her where she was nestled in her husband's brawny arms, the infant whimpering at her breast.

"Safar has need of us," Eeda said, voice weak but urgent.

"What should we do?" Leiria asked, fear clutching her heart.

Eeda gestured at the volcano. "The airship," she said. "We must get in the airship. It's the only way to save him."

Immediately, Leiria sent a signal for Biner to descend. Meanwhile, Jooli told her father's men to flee as best they could.

"Get back in your ships," she said, "and sail like the hells for Syrapis. I'll meet you there, by and by, and we'll put the kingdom into order."

The men didn't need to be told twice. They ran, shedding armor and weapons and never looking back when another blast shook the volcano.

Leiria gave the Kyranians similar orders. She was only going to keep Renor, Sinch and Sergeant Hamyr with her. The rest were told to get back to the ships and tell the pirate captains to stand far off from the island.

"And if we don't make it," she added, "return to Syrapis and tell our friends what happened here."

Then the airship was down and the others were boarding it.

Leiria ran to join them, praying that this time she wouldn't be too late.

CHAPTER FIFTY-THREE

INTO THE HELLS

They plunged through hot darkness, the sound of what seemed like heavy whips whirring and cracking on every side. Far ahead of them they could hear the muted boom of big metal drums and the distant wail of hundreds of tortured voices.

Red tongues of flame flicked out at them and Khysmet swerved in mid-flight, dodging most of the hot spears. The big stallion shrilled in fury as one blast hit him, then steadied his course and flew onward at an even greater rate of speed.

Palimak felt a searing pain across his thigh but took heart from Khysmet's example and ignored it, concentrating solely on the transport spell he'd created with his father and Eeda.

They were plummeting deeper and deeper into the bowels of an immense sorcerous machine with nothing except the transport spell to guide them.

Enormous unseen gears groaned somewhere in the darkness. They were driven by what Palimak imagined to be huge clattering chains that powered the hellish machine in its mysterious, yet clearly evil purpose.

Gundara and Gundaree chattered fearfully in his ear, crying, "Look out, Little Master! Beware! Beware!" in a never-ending chorus of warnings.

He couldn't see any of the dangers that were stalking him—he could only sense fierce presences looming up with gnashing teeth and rattling claws and the stink of old carnivores.

Khysmet never stopped, only swerving from side to side like a swift-moving eagle, somehow always avoiding the danger.

All of Palimak's instincts shrieked for him to draw his sword and defend himself. But there was nothing to see except for an occasional cloud of hot sparks drifting up to meet them.

A verse from Asper came to him—leaping crazily into his mind and crowding out the fearful sensations.

Palimak chanted it, adding the old demon's powers to the transport spell:

> *"Into the Hells my soul did fly;*
> *Not knowing if we'd live or die.*
> *But then it returned with this reply:*
> *No truth in Heaven, only lies, lies, lies!"*

Palimak felt his strength return, his fears vanish. And the cold demon side of him opened like a yawning gate.

He felt his claws arc from their sheaths and he felt powerful and ready for any monster that dared approach.

And just then—looking over the shoulder of the creature who wore his father's body—he saw a large red ball of light appear. It was as if they were nearing the end of an incredibly long tunnel.

He'd seen a bright light when the tunnel had first opened, but then it had been swallowed by darkness.

Palimak looked closer, gripping Safar's tunic tighter with his claws. Features began to appear on the ball of light. Familiar features.

It was the Demon Moon!

*   *   *

Iraj gloried in Khysmet's fierce ride through the jaws of the Hells. Blood on fire, body burning with the joy of impending combat, he felt like he could take on the gods themselves.

And when the monsters came scrambling through the darkness, with only the beat of their leather wings and gnashing teeth to give them away, he laughed aloud at Khysmet's swift change in course, foiling their charge.

The awful sounds of the great machine and the distant wails of agony only made his bloodlust burn hotter.

He didn't know what awaited them at the end of this magical ride through the spirit world, but he also didn't care.

His enemy was there, that was enough.

What enemy?

Did it matter?

Never!

Only show me your face, he thought. And you'll curse the day you chose Iraj Protarus for your foe!

Then, far below, he saw the Demon Moon. Khysmet was flying straight toward it.

Is this where my enemy waits? he wondered. Then he thought perhaps it was the moon itself that opposed him.

He laughed, thinking, What a marvelous boast for a man to make: I was the one who slew the Demon Moon!

*   *   *

Buffeted by the storm of Iraj's emotions, Safar kept a tight rein on his own. He didn't care a damn for the dangers lurking in the darkness, nor did he allow himself to marvel at Khysmet's skillful flight.

His whole being was focused on the transport spell. He hoped Palimak was doing the same.

Several times he sensed his son's attention falter and the spell weakening under his grasp.

Safar wished mightily that he could speak to Palimak. He had a good idea what his son was going through. To know that his father's body had been invaded by another, much hated presence. Feeling somehow betrayed, but without reason or evidence to support that feeling. Putting his faith and trust into a stranger's hands—hands that had previously done their best to kill him.

Once Safar almost asked Iraj to let him voice words of comfort to Palimak. Then he realized that this would only make things worse.

For how would Palimak truly know it was his father speaking and not Iraj Protarus?

Then the young man suddenly seemed to become stronger than before. Safar caught a whiff of demonic magic and knew that Palimak had transformed himself—giving free rein to his demon side.

And Safar wondered, At what cost, my son? At what cost?

Then Iraj said to him, *Get ready to fight, brother! We're at the final gate!*

And Safar saw the bloody face of the Demon Moon rear up, with its death-mask grin.

Khysmet trumpeted a challenge and Iraj reached for his sword.

Safar said, *Wait, brother! It's not yet time for steel!*

And at that moment the moon's face burst into a violent sheet of flame. The hot blast smashed Khysmet back and they spun over and over, the stallion fighting desperately to right himself. Iraj and Palimak clawing for purchase.

Finally, Khysmet kicked himself aright.

"Go!" Iraj shouted, digging in his heels. "Go!"

And the stallion swooped toward the hot flames.

Safar hissed, *The trumpet! We need the trumpet!*

Iraj immediately plucked the shell horn from his tunic, lifted it to his lips—and blew!

Safar put all his magical energies into Iraj's breath. And the sound was like a thousand war trumpets shouting in unison.

A pale light bloomed, swelling larger and larger. And then the beauteous Spirit Rider burst out of the light on her glorious black mare.

Princess Alsahna turned in the saddle, waving her sword. "This way, Safar!" she cried.

And she and the mare charged straight into the flames.

Khysmet bellowed lustily at the sight of the mare and charged after her.

Then they were surrounded by a sea of fire. Great boiling waves of flame bursting in from all sides. Bone-scorching spears of fire cracking out of those waves.

The heat and the pain were so intense that it was all Safar could do to keep himself from screaming out, I surrender! I surrender!

Iraj shuddered with the pain, crying, *What's this, brother? What's this?*

And Safar felt Palimak's claws tighten, spearing through his tunic and into the flesh. He thought he heard his son shout, "Father! Father!"

But he realized that Palimak was actually urging them on, crying, "Onward! Onward!" And even in all his pain, Safar felt supreme pride at his son's bravery.

Then he saw the Spirit Rider charging back. The black mare rearing up and pawing the air.

Blue spears of light shot from her hooves, driving the flames back. And opening a passage through the boiling red sea.

Then the Spirit Rider whirled her mount about, shouting once again for them to follow, and charged out of sight.

Khysmet surged forward and there came a *crack! crack! crack!* A series of explosions so loud Safar felt like the bones of his shared body were about to burst.

And then everything became hazy. And everything became quite still.

And the only sounds were the boom of a slow, gentle surf, the rhythmic throbbing of sweet harvest drums, and a thousand glad voices lifted in song:

". . . Lady, oh Lady, surrender.

Surrender. Surrender . . ."

CHAPTER FIFTY-FOUR
THE VAMPIRES OF HADIN

The haze lifted and Safar found himself striding across warm sands. Khysmet was no longer with him, nor was the Spirit Rider.

In the distance he could clearly see the handsome dancing people of Hadinland. And there was their fabulous queen, bronzed hips and breasts heaving in the harvest dance.

Above the whole scene loomed the volcano. Beckoning and threatening at the same time.

Safar felt suffused with renewed hope and energy. His sight had returned and he was once again in full control of his body.

He felt so strong he barely noticed his armor. If the fates decreed his death, he thought, this was how he wanted to meet it.

"Welcome back, brother!" came a familiar voice.

And Safar looked to his left and saw Iraj striding beside him. Bedecked in burnished, kingly mail, Protarus was as young and handsome as when he'd first taken to the conqueror's road. His golden hair and beard glistened in the bright, tropical sun. And his smile was glad and innocent, as if he'd been washed of all his sins.

"The question is," Iraj said, "after all that has happened between us, are we still truly brothers?"

Safar wasn't sure how to answer. Wasn't clear in his feelings. And even if he had been capable of such clarity at this particular fates-colliding moment, he wasn't sure he ought to answer.

And then:

"I'm here, father," came another voice.

Safar looked to his right and saw Palimak, tall and slender, with shoulders as wide as the spreading branches of a new oak tree. His eyes glowed with demon fires and his claws were ten glistening daggers.

Palimak smiled, exposing long, double-rowed demon teeth. And even as Safar looked he saw his son's face transform, the forehead bulging, the demon horn bursting through. And his skin toughened and deepened in color until it was an emerald green.

The boy sadly flicked out his long demon tongue and asked, "Do you still love me, father?"

Again, Safar was confounded. But for an entirely different reason. How could Palimak ever doubt he loved him? Had he been such an unfeeling father that his own son—never mind he was adopted—doubted his love? Under any circumstances? Demon or human, or half-way in between, what did it matter?

Palimak was just Palimak.

Then it came to him—the same was true of Iraj!

And Leiria, oh, yes, Leiria; he loved her too.

Safar said: "All my words are poor. You ask if I love you, son. Of course I do. I always have and always will. And you, Iraj. You ask if I am your friend. And my answer is the same. Even in my hate I loved you."

Then he pointed at the glowering, fire-spitting volcano.

"There is the doomspell that has driven us all these years. And if we manage to destroy it we'll awaken the gods.

"But I must warn you both it's unlikely that the gods will thank us. I think they'll curse us instead and make us suffer for what we've done."

Iraj said, "Be damned to them, brother! What can they possibly do to me that I haven't already done to myself?"

Palimak snorted agreement. "I don't care what the gods think. They may have created this world but we're the ones who must make a life here the best we can!"

Safar laughed. "Very well, then," he said. "Let's have at it!"

Iraj slapped him on the back. "Good, it's settled. Now, brother, let's hear your plan."

He gestured at the dancing people. Just beyond them, standing behind Queen Yorlain, was the bulky figure of King Rhodes, leaning easily against his sword.

"What's the best way," he asked, "to make these fools beg for mercy?"

Safar grinned ruefully. "Actually," he said, "I don't have a plan. Nor do I have any magical tricks up my sleeve. Just my sword to put with yours."

"And mine," Palimak whispered, drawing his weapon.

Iraj roared laughter. "Then be damned to us all!" he shouted.

And with that he charged the dancing people, bounding across the rolling sand dunes on his way to meet whatever the fates had in store for him.

Feeling as foolish and frightened as he had years before when he charged after Iraj down the snowy passes of the Gods' Divide, Safar ran after him.

He heard Palimak shout something, but he couldn't make out the words. And a moment later his demon son was sprinting past him, closing on Iraj.

Safar put on speed to catch up, leaping over dunes and showering sand in his wake as he raced onward.

Soon he was up with them, Iraj and Palimak only a few steps ahead.

But then he smelled the thick, rusty scent of blood. And he knew it to be his blood and Iraj's blood and Palimak's blood.

The scent was delicious—soul-satisfying. And then he realized he was smelling their scent through the hungry senses of others.

Then the dancers all turned to confront the three charging warriors.

They smiled, exposing long canine teeth. And they shouted in glee as their prey ran into their arms.

And Safar finally realized who the dancers really were: emotional and physical vampires, who sucked out a man's soul along with his blood.

And they sang:

"Surrender . . . surrender . . ."

And all his will left him. To be replaced by a fabulous narcotic-like joy. He wanted to be with them again. He wanted to be ruled again.

Oh, how he ached to dance.

Dance, dance, dance.

Dance to the beat of their hungry hearts . . .

And more than anything else he desired to expose his throat, his wrists, his every blood-pumping, pulsating vein and artery to their fangs.

Just beyond them, Queen Yorlain danced, thrusting her hips, harder, harder. Making him lust for surrender all the more.

But then he saw Rhodes, leaning on his sword and laughing through his thick beard.

Damn you! Safar thought. Damn you!

And he was released from the death spell that bound him and he started dealing out death of his own.

Beautiful people, ugly-spirited people, all dying under his sword.

Evil as they were—long teeth reaching to suck the life from him—Safar cried out in agony with each killing sword stroke. As if each mortally wounding blow were struck at himself, instead of his enemies.

Yet, to his wonder, it was his enemies who died, not Safar Timura.

And they died so easily. Their flesh was soft, their defenses weak.

And they fell away, fell away, with each stroke of his sword.

And blood—so much blood—was released by his blade.

The dancers didn't shout or scream, but only chanted his name as he killed each one of them.

"Safar, Safar, Safar. Safar, Safar . . ."

On and on, dying and spouting his name along with their blood.

Then he was stumbling over the bodies Iraj and Palimak had left in their wake. And mortally wounded men and women—so beautifully formed one and all that it made their wounds and impending deaths seem especially abhorrent.

And they all moaned: "Safar, Safar, Safar. Please, Safar!" Until it drove him mad.

What did they want of him? They were his enemies. They were monsters and vampires and all the evil things a mortal could imagine.

But as he slew them they all begged him in voices he could not resist: "Safar, Safar, Safar. Please, Safar."

"Enough!" he shouted. "Enough!"

But it was too late because he and Iraj and Palimak had killed them all.

He shuddered, thinking he was going to become ill—except it was a spiritual, not physical, ailment. And through his sorcerous eye he saw a thousand souls float toward the volcano.

The black clouds grew thicker and seemed to form lips. And then those lips inhaled and he was knocked to the ground by the resulting tornado.

The twister ripped across the island, sucking up the souls of the dead.

On his knees, Safar looked up and saw hundreds upon hundreds of bright souls being carried into the gaping cone of the volcano.

And they were all crying, "Safar, Safar, Safar! Please, please, please, Safar!"

Finally, everyone was dead—the beach littered with corpses. And Safar saw Iraj and Palimak advancing toward King Rhodes.

Queen Yorlain stood in front of him, her face lit up as if she were finding heavenly glory instead of impending death.

She cried, "Safar!"

And Rhodes shouted, "This is the end of it all!"

Then he cut her in two and she fell to the ground, sighing and crying, "Safar, Safar, Safar!"

And her soul was swept away with the others.

The potter's son felt so small and insignificant at being the cause of all these people's deaths. His own soul withered as if it had been dashed by a freezing wave from the cold seas of the far, far north.

Then Rhodes bellowed defiance.

And he stood up, straight and tall and bearded and barbarian-strong. He waved his sword, shouting, "Come to me, little ones! Come to me!"

Safar ran forward, as did Palimak, but Iraj was many steps ahead of them.

But just before Protarus reached his enemy, lightning stabbed from the sky and the earth rumbled and shook under them.

And Rhodes started to transform, growing larger and larger, until he was the size of giant—three times the height of a man.

Safar gaped, but not at Rhodes' transformation. Because as he grew all his features became a stormy landscape of constantly changing images.

First it became the beautiful, evil face of his mother—Queen Clayre.

Then this changed—bursting apart in a bloody welter—to transform into the grinning demon features of Lord Fari.

And that face twisted and broke and bled to make the royal features of Prince Luka, the demon prince.

Then a shatter of light momentarily obscured the monstrous figure.

And finally, standing before them, waving a mighty sword, was Kalasariz!

Sudden realization of what was happening dawned and Safar shouted a warning to Iraj, who was almost on the giant.

But it was too late.

CHAPTER FIFTY-FIVE
THE GODDESS LOTTYR

When Iraj saw the enormous figure of Kalasariz towering over him, he knew he had been well and truly trapped.

He struck out futilely with his blade as Kalasariz' gigantic hand reached down to pluck him from the ground.

The spymaster held him at eye level, grinning terribly with that thin, cold smile.

"Welcome back, Majesty," Kalasariz mocked. "Your brothers have sorely missed you."

In the spymaster's eyes Iraj could see the reflections of the faces of Luka and Fari. Flames leaped all around them as they twisted in agony.

"We made a pact once, Majesty," Kalasariz continued. "Do you recall it?"

Iraj remembered it very well—it was the Spell of Four, which had once bound him to these creatures in a foul bargain. He'd escaped it for a time, but now his grievous error of the past had returned to haunt him.

He wanted to cry out to Safar to save him, but he knew there was nothing his friend could do.

"I feel compelled to tell you, Majesty," Kalasariz mocked, "that things have changed since we were last together. Then you were the king and we were your slaves. But now it is I, Kalasariz, who shall rule."

Iraj forced laughter. "Don't be a fool, Kalasariz," he said. "You aren't fit to be king. You don't have the guts, much less the will."

The spymaster's thin smile spread wider. "We shall see, Majesty," he said. "We shall see. With the Goddess Lottyr supporting me, however, I doubt I'll have much difficulty adapting to my new role."

And with that he drew Iraj toward his mouth, meaning to bite him in two. At the same time, his eyes glowed with magical power as he exerted all his strength to bring Iraj once again under the thrall of the Spell of Four.

Iraj tried to struggle and break free, but the spell slowly spread its force through his body, sucking away his will to resist.

Then he heard Safar whispering to him. Not from without, but from deep within. As if he were once again coiled in Iraj's breast.

And Safar said, *I'm here, my friend! Together, we can fight him!*

A fierce surge of energy burst through Iraj's veins and just as Kalasariz's maw spread wide to kill him, Protarus thrust his sword inward and then up with all his strength.

The blade speared through the roof of the spymaster's mouth and then plunged into his brain.

Kalasariz bellowed in agony, ripping Iraj away with his giant's hand and dashing him to the ground.

A red curtain of pain swept over Iraj. More pain than he had ever felt in his life.

Then the pain vanished and Iraj found himself sitting in the cave of Alisarrian The Conqueror. He was with Safar and they were boys again, swearing never-ending friendship and taking the blood oath.

"Someday I will be king of kings," he told Safar, "and you will be the greatest wizard in history. We'll make a better world before we're done, Safar. A better world for all."

Safar smiled agreement and started to answer. But suddenly he seemed quite distant and he started to fade away. He spoke, but Iraj couldn't hear what he was saying and he became quite frightened.

"Speak louder, brother!" Iraj shouted. "I can't hear you!"

Then once again, Safar spoke from within him. And he said, quite clearly, *Farewell, brother mine. A great dream awaits us. And the sooner we get started, the sooner that dream will begin.*

The words made Iraj feel quite peaceful. And he was content.

"Farewell, brother," he replied. "Farewell, my friend. Until we meet again."

And then the cave vanished and Iraj dreamed of horses—a great wild herd flying across the plains.

He sailed with them, moving at breathtaking speed, the air full of fresh spring currents, the horizon a joyous creation of blue skies meeting lush green earth.

On and on he sailed. Skimming just above the fabulous herd.

Flying toward horizons that would never end.

*   *   *

"It's not over yet, father, is it?" Palimak said. And Safar looked up from his friend's crushed and lifeless body to meet his son's eyes.

Palimak's demon face didn't seem strange to Safar. It was as if that face had always been there, waiting to get out. And now that Palimak had transformed into his true self, Safar only loved him the more.

"You're right, son," he replied. "It isn't."

Then they both heard two horses whinny in the distance. Their eyes rose to see Khysmet standing on a hill. Beside him was the black mare. Her saddle was empty and there was no sign of the Spirit Rider.

"Let's go, son," Safar said, suddenly realizing what they had to do next.

He whistled and the two magnificent animals raced down the hillside. A moment later they were both mounted—Safar on Khysmet, Palimak on the mare—and riding up the side of the volcano.

Soon they came to the ridge overlooking the Valley of the Two Kings. But it was the valley of the ancients, not the place they'd left a few hours before. And instead of being ravaged by storm, it had been destroyed by a great army. Farmhouses were still ablaze. The lake was filled with the charred corpses of men and animals.

And in the center was the fabulous golden Castle of the Two Kings, flames engulfing the domed palaces.

Only the great Keep remained unscathed, still standing defiant against what must have been a very long siege.

Surrounding the castle was a strange army consisting of thousands of soldiers. Half were human and half were demon. Some were mounted—horses for the human cavalry, big catlike beasts for the demons—while others were on foot or manning huge siege engines.

At the gate of the Castle Keep was a knot of soldiers, wielding a great battering ram. Flying over them was the Banner of Asper—the twin-headed snake with wings.

Palimak gaped at the scene. "Father!" he said. "Nothing's moving."

Safar nodded he too had noticed the strangeness. Not one soldier or beast moved. Even the flames licking at the buildings were still. In fact, the entire scene looked like a gigantic frieze of a long-ago battle from a war museum.

And the only sound was the thunder and grinding of the Hells Machine. And the only movement was the thick cloud of smoke issuing from the rumbling volcano.

"Come on, son," was all Safar said.

And the two rode down the broad avenue that led to the castle.

On either side of them lifelike statues of soldiers stared blankly at them as they passed.

The two moved through that eerie, frozen army for what seemed like an eternity.

Safar expected one of the demon or human soldiers suddenly to come alive at any minute and challenge them. But nothing and no one moved all the way to the gates.

The only change as they approached was the increasing loudness of the deadly machine.

Finally they were crossing the bridge and approaching the main gate where the soldiers with the battering ram were posed in mid-hammer. On one side of them was the planted banner of Asper. On the other was a huge, mounted demon.

Safar stared at the demon commander for a moment. Only mildly surprised that it was Asper, himself who was leading the attack.

Understanding dawned for Palimak and he said, "It's an illusion, isn't it, father? Just like in Caluz."

"Something like that," Safar replied. Then, "Are you ready, son?"

Palimak squared his young shoulders and grinned a brave demon smile. "Ready, father."

Safar drew his silver witch's-dagger and chanted this spell:

> *"If the world by Heaven's decree*
> *Should become a hell for thee and me;*
> *Where devils wear the gods' raiment*
> *And None dare answer our lament;*
> *Look for me by Asper's Gate,*
> *Knock on the doors and meet thy Fate."*

Then he returned the dagger to its sheath in his sleeve and drew his sword. Palimak followed suit.

Safar shouted, "Open!"

And that single word boomed across the valley, drowning out even the sound of the Hells Machine:

"OPEN!"

For a moment there was silence then came a grumbling and a groan, followed by a loud shriek of protesting hinges. And then the gate swung slowly inward, unleashing a blast of intense heat and foul air.

Safar sensed what was coming and shouted to Palimak, "Steady!"

A score of hellish creatures rushed out at them, each more terrible than the other. Some of them looked like the monsters Queen Charize had ruled—pale as death with enormous bat wings and long fangs. Others were like the tree creatures who had attacked them at sea, with dozens of limbs bearing snapping teeth.

But the warning to Palimak wasn't necessary, because Gundara and Gundaree had already armed their master.

"Ghosts!" they cried. "Nothing but ghosts. You've already killed them once, Little Master!"

So, like his father, Palimak held perfectly still, letting the creatures swirl all around him, threatening with fangs and teeth until they dissolved into nothingness.

Both Khysmet and the black mare seemed not to notice the spirit-world attack and only flicked their tails as if a few flies were troubling them.

Safar signaled and he and Palimak flicked their reins and entered the Castle Keep.

But now there was no royal grand palace entry to greet them. Even the magical wind rose was gone. Instead, they found themselves in the dim, steamy recesses of the Hells Machine. Iron grating beneath them, the horse's hooves clacking across the metal. Huge gears twice the size of a miller's grindstone turning this way and that with no apparent order or purpose. Wide chain belts, thick with old grease, thundering above them.

Flames and steam shot through the grates as they moved deeper into the interior, following the narrow avenue toward a dim light.

Palimak felt grimy—oily sweat gathering under his arms and streaming down his sides.

Gundara cried, "She's waiting, Little Master!"

To which Gundaree added, "Just at the light! Be ready!"

Palimak didn't need to ask who they meant. He *knew!*

Safar led them toward the light, which grew brighter with every step the horses took. Khysmet snorted at the steam and shook his head, great drops of sweat streaming from his mane.

Safar patted the stallion, comforting himself as much as the horse.

Then there was one more long blast of steam and they were through.

And he found himself in a vast chamber flooded with a strange red light that cast no shadows.

At the far end of the chamber was the Lady Lottyr. Her six hands waved gracefully, shooting out long sparks of magic. Driving the huge machine with their incredible power.

Her lush body moved rhythmically to music only she seemed to hear. The movements reminded Safar of the harvest dance he'd suffered through when he was spellbound.

And her six heads snaked in and out on long, slender necks that somehow made an eye-pleasing whole where they met her shoulders.

She was the size of a tall woman and backed by a miniature of the Demon Moon, which was symmetrically twice her length and breadth. Small black clouds swirled across the red face of the moon, making the goddess seem as if she were floating with them, although she always remained in the center.

A red gossamer gown, thin as spider's silk, draped her body—displaying all her substantial charms in an alluring light.

Despite himself, Safar felt heat stab at his loins. He heard Palimak's sharp intake of breath and knew that his son was also affected.

Khysmet snorted and moved closer to the mare who whinnied, then shied teasingly away. But not too far, Safar noticed. Not very far at all.

The whole atmosphere reeked of seduction.

And then, from a distance, Safar heard beautiful voices lifting in song: *"Surrender, oh, surrender."*

The goddess laughed, her tones silky and promising impossible things.

She said, "That's all I ask, Safar. Surrender and all I have shall be yours."

Then she turned to Palimak, saying, "You can have me, too, boy. I know that is your utmost desire, is it not?"

Palimak was shocked both by her offer and his body's unaccustomed reaction to the goddess. He didn't know what to say, or how to respond.

Safar felt like he was back in Coralean's harem, with one beauty after the other displayed to him. Especially the lovely courtesan, Astarias, who had so beguiled him in his youth.

And he kept hearing that spell song:

"Her hair is night,
Her lips the moon;
Surrender. Oh, surrender.
Her eyes are stars,
Her heart the sun;
Surrender. Oh, surrender.

Her breasts are honey,
Her sex a rose;
Surrender. Oh, surrender.
Night and moon. Stars and Sun.
Honey and rose;
Lady, oh Lady, surrender.
Surrender. Surrender . . ."

So powerful was her presence that for a moment he nearly succumbed. Nearly threw himself at her feet, begging her favor.

Then he fought back, thinking of Nerisa, his little thief of Walaria. And Methydia, a woman above all women who taught him all he truly knew about love, life and magic.

Ah, yes, and then there was Leiria. Lovely, lovely Leiria. Who would throw herself in front of a phalanx of charging chariots to save him.

Who needed this woman?

This goddess from the Hells?

All these thoughts—from seduction to hesitation to rejection—flashed through his mind in a split second. Although it seemed like an agonizing—and most tempting—eternity.

Safar formed a spell, a spell above all spells to cast her off. And these were the words he chanted to the unseen, far-away Leiria. It was song she'd taught him when they were lovers:

"Lovers when parted
From what they love,
Have no temptations
Or troubles to bear.
Outside might be temptation,

Inside only love.
There can be no wanting
For what is not there."

And suddenly the lust ran out of the atmosphere like a flood unleashed and the Lady Lottyr's spell was shattered.

Failure struck the goddess like a lightning bolt. The Demon Moon burst into flames and she rose from her throne, all six hands outstretched to blast Safar from the face of the world.

"How dare you?" she cried. "How dare you mock . . ."

But Safar didn't wait for her to finish. Instead, he hurled himself off Khysmet, straight into her waving arms.

His witch's-dagger was already out and as the Lady Lottyr cursed him and folded those killing arms around him he plunged the dagger into her heart. And kept stabbing, on and on.

Like a holy assassin from the temple of Walaria, killing whatever his mad soul and the imagined gods of murder drove him to kill.

Knife in.

Knife out.

Driving and gutting.

Although the goddess was caught by surprise, instead of fighting him off she wrapped all six arms around him and crushed him to her bosom.

Safar felt his ribs go in a ghastly series of cracks and his life's breath being crushed from his body.

But he kept driving the knife in without stop. On, and on, hoping and praying.

A frozen witness to his father's murder, Palimak hung back for a moment. Then he vaulted off the mare to the ground and charged forward.

The only thing he could think to do was to slash at the goddess with his sword and somehow free his father. But in the back of his brain he knew it was a hopeless effort. "

Lady Lottyr might die. But that was unlikely. More likely, it would be his father who would die and the goddess, although sorely wounded, would kill Palimak as well.

Then Palimak saw Asper's shell horn on the floor where Safar had dropped it during his mad attack.

He lifted it up, thinking to blow and raise any spirit he could to help.

But then the Favorites cried, "Smash it, Little Master! Smash it! It's the only chance we have!"

So he threw the horn to the floor and it shattered into hundreds of pieces.

And the last thing Palimak saw was his father driving his dagger once more into the breast of the Goddess Lottyr.

There might have been an explosion, but even years later, when telling the tale to friends, Palimak couldn't swear that was happened next.

If the truth were known, there was only a flash of golden light.

And the sound of angry voices.

Whose voices?

Palimak didn't know.

All he could say was that for a long, long time he seemed to exist in another world.

He saw farmers reaping harvests of plenty.

He saw forests rising unopposed to the sky.

He saw horses, fabulous horses, running wild across exotic plains.

And he saw seas, wild booming seas, full of flying fish and playing dolphins and sounding whales.

All eager for the promises of tomorrow.

But the sight that thrilled him the most was the sight of thousands of little turtles breaking free from their sandy nests and swimming out to sea.

Where no monsters—human or demon—waited to take them.

CHAPTER FIFTY SIX

THE RINGMASTER

It was Leiria's turn at the wheel.

All was peaceful on the airship as they sailed with summer winds to far Syrapis—and home.

Beneath her were the ships of the Kyranian fleet, every man happy at his survival.

Far off in the distance, she could see the destruction of Hadin. The volcano was still exploding, venting its wrath on all who had opposed it.

Hadin was gone, turned to molten earth and boiling seas just as Safar had seen in his boyhood dream.

But there was a difference, as Safar had explained to her after the airship had picked him up. The volcano had rent the very earth, to be sure. Except that now its effect was purely local. Both evil people and good people had died in its blast. But now there was no poison cloud to envelop the entire world.

Innocent or guilty, only the people of Hadin had been destroyed. After Safar's struggle with the Hells and the Lady Lottyr, the volcano's effect had been limited.

The rest of the world was safe. And might even return, Safar had said, to its previous bounty.

Leiria looked over the big wheel to see Safar tending Khysmet, giving the stallion sweet corn to eat. And there was Palimak standing next to his father, offering the black mare the same.

Palimak was now fully a demon—from his curled, dagger-armed toes to his green horned brow. And Leiria loved him just as much as the half-human, half-demon child she'd once carried on her back.

She wasn't sure how all the people she loved the most had come to be with her again. Eeda had directed the airship over the volcano, then she and Jooli had cast many powerful spells.

And then Safar and Palimak, together with Khysmet and the mare, had suddenly been with them. Both men had been exhausted and near death, but Jooli and Eeda had used all their skills to resurrect them.

Now Safar and Palimak—still wobbly in their legs—were feeding their charges and whispering words of comfort to them.

Leiria should have been bursting with happiness. Instead, she found herself glowering at the scene. Maddeningly, since his return Safar had kept her at an emotional distance. He was kind, his words gentle, but whenever they were alone together, he became uneasy and made some weak excuse to part company.

And now there he was, feeding that damned horse again! Talking so tenderly to

Khysmet that it drove her crazy. Suddenly, she realized she was jealous. Which was ridiculous. How could she feel jealous of a horse?

She gritted her teeth, not sure who she was angrier at, Safar or herself.

A booming voice came from behind her. "Avast, lass! Can't you see you're steering the wrong course!"

Confused, she turned and saw Biner standing there with a wide grin on his face.

"I don't understand," she said, pointing at the compass. "I'm steering just where you said I ought to."

Biner brushed her aside with a mighty hand and took the wheel. "Maybe you were and maybe you weren't," Biner said. "But the plain fact is, it sure as hells isn't the right course for *you.*"

He pointed at Safar. "There's your setting, lass," Biner said. "Can't you see that he's waitin' for you, but he just doesn't know it yet? Because after all that's happened he's not sure you'll have him."

Leiria need no further prodding. Immediately, she broke away and raced across the deck to Safar.

She grabbed him by the shoulder and spun him around.

"Come here, you!" she said.

Then she kissed the surprised look off his face.

And they embraced for a long, long time.

Biner watched, smiling. Then Arlain came up to stand beside him.

Looking at the scene, she said, "I'm glad to thee that Thafar finally know'th that thomebody lov'th him!"

Arlain sighed, breathing a little fire and smoke. And she added, sadly, "I only wi'th he knew it wath me."

Biner patted her, then spun the wheel, turning the airship about. "Never mind that, lass," he said. "I've set a course for the next landfall. And in one day's time we'll find kids and rubes aplenty and you'll forget all that."

Arlain brightened for a moment, then frowned, worried.

She cast down her dragon eyes, saying "But Thafar thaid the god'th might not be happy. What if they curth our performanthe and ruin everything?"

Biner slapped Arlain on her pretty back and bellowed, "Be damned to the Gods, Arlain! Be damned to them all.

"And be damned to everything but the circus!"

Arlain burst into laughter. And she laughed so long and so hard that she set the airship on fire.

AUTHOR'S NOTE

The character of Safar Timura is loosely based on Omar Khayyam, the ancient Persian poet and astronomer. The son of a tentmaker, Khayyam rose to become the chief astrologer of the sultan, his boyhood friend. Just as Safar, the son of a potter, rose to become the chief wazier of the king, his boyhood friend.

Khayyam (1044-1123 A.D) is best known to us today for his poetry, collected in the remarkable "Rubaiyat of Omar Khayyam." Of all the many English translations of this work, I prefer Edward Fitzgerald's.

Students of mathematical history also know him as a pioneer in algebra and geometry. Experts say his mathematical discoveries remained unmatched for centuries—to the time of Descartes (1596-1650).

I first came across "The Rubaiyat" in a bazaar when I was a boy living on the island of Cyprus. Battered and torn, I only paid a few pennies for it. But the first words I read tumbled out like upturned chests of gold:

> *"Awake! for the morning in the bowl of night*
> *Has flung the stone that puts the stars to flight.*
> *And lo! the hunter of the east has caught*
> *The sultan's turret in a noose of light."*

"The Tales of the Timuras" were inspired by that most fortuitous discovery.

Another major influence on these books—and those that may follow—are the hundreds of e-mails I have received from readers all over the world these past few years.

I'd particularly like to thank Julie Mitchell, who kindly contributed her own poem to "The Gods Awaken," which is printed here with her permission. You'll find the poem in the chapter titled, "Jooli's Song."

Ms. Mitchell, a Texas scientist, was the winner of my "Be A Hero Contest," which drew thousands of entries. The warrior woman character, Jooli, is named after her.

One of the main villains of this book—King Rhodes—was named for another contest winner, Bob Rhodes, a California engineer. Bob, a lovely fellow, is nothing like the barbarian king portrayed in this book. Another villain, Clayre—the Queen Witch—is named after my kind and gentle reader Clayre Kitchen, who lives in the United Kingdom.